Praise for *The Tale of Genji*

"An enormous achievement."
—*The New York Times Book Review*

"Both epic and intimate, [*Genji*] is a gorgeous evocation of a time and place that have long since disappeared. But it's also an exploration of feelings and relations between men and women, as fresh and beguiling to readers today as when it was first written. A new translation that makes *Genji* accessible to contemporary readers is a landmark event. [Tyler's translation] has clearly been a labor of love. In his beautifully written translation he tries to get as close to the original as possible, immersing us in eleventh-century Japan. Mr. Tyler's translation is richly embellished with footnotes that flag for us everything that Murasaki and her contemporaries would have taken for granted. All in all, Mr. Tyler's translation is likely to be the definitive edition of *The Tale of Genji* for many years to come."
—*The Wall Street Journal*

"*The Tale of Genji* set an insanely high standard for anything that came after it. This latest edition is reader friendly at every turn, with generous footnotes, character lists and lots of illustrations to show what robes looked like, or swords, or houses. You have to reach for comparisons to Tolstoy or Proust to convey just what a captivating experience this story can be."
—*Newsweek*

"Tyler's delicate ear for the language of the original helps breathe new life into the story of *Genji*."
—*The New Yorker*

"Though [Murasaki's] setting was the royal Japanese court of one thousand years ago, her characters managed to draw the reader into their passion and terrors in an uncannily modern way. [Tyler's translation is] beautifully readable . . . it sets a new standard. Not only is this new English edition the most scrupulously true to the original, it also is superbly written and genuinely engaging. We are blessed to have Tyler's help in reading it."
—*Los Angeles Times Book Review*

"The remarkable thing about *Genji* is . . . that it is a masterpiece, the oldest full-length novel in existence, and still very much alive. It is even livelier in the new translation by Royall Tyler. Tyler skillfully catches the erotic flavor, the vivid characterizations, and the allusive poetry of this classic. . . . Readers will quickly find themselves immersed in a strange and distant culture whose inhabitants' loves, rivalries, suffering and follies we can identify with our own."
—*The Philadelphia Inquirer*

"An astonishingly rich, absorbing drama that has stood, and will doubtless continue to stand, the severest tests of time and changing literary fashions. There is nothing else on earth quite like *The Tale of Genji*. Utterly irresistible."
—*Kirkus Reviews* (starred review)

"One of the undisputed monuments of world literature. Tyler offers a version that effectively captures the indirection and shades of Murasaki's court language. A major contribution to our understanding of world literature; highly recommended."
—*Library Journal* (starred review)

"Widely recognized as the world's first novel, as well as one of it's best . . . painstakingly and tenderly translated by Tyler. An epic narrative; it is also minutely attentive to particulars of character, setting, emotion—even costume. Tyler clearly intends his [translation] to be the definitive one. It is richer, fuller and more complicated than the others. Tyler's formality of tone offers readers a more graceful, convincing rendering of this one thousand-year-old masterpiece. Scholars and novices alike should be pleased."
—*Publishers Weekly* (starred review)

"Tyler has long shown himself to be one of the finest translators of Japanese in our era. In producing this new *Genji* translation, he has been able not only to draw upon his own skills as a writer, but also to build on the efforts and accomplishments of his predecessors . . . the Tyler version is by far the most helpful to the general reader."
—*The Washington Post Book World*

"[Tyler] has crafted an elegant translation that remarkably renders this eleventh-century tale in language so lively, vivid and transparent, one could easily believe that the book was written by some gifted postmodernist. Royall Tyler devoted space to explaining, through the introduction and footnotes, nuances of the time, helping help us place them into a modern context. This edition of *The Tale of Genji* is beautifully realized, both as a translation and as a seamless art object."
—*The Cleveland Plain Dealer*

THE
TALE OF
Genji

Murasaki
Shikibu

Translated by
Royall Tyler

PENGUIN BOOKS

For Susan

PENGUIN BOOKS

Published by the Penguin Group

Penguin Group (USA) Inc., 375 Hudson Street, New York, New York 10014, U.S.A.

Penguin Group (Canada), 90 Eglinton Avenue East, Suite 700, Toronto,
Ontario, Canada M4P 2Y3 (a division of Pearson Penguin Canada Inc.)

Penguin Books Ltd, 80 Strand, London WC2R 0RL, England

Penguin Ireland, 25 St Stephen's Green, Dublin 2, Ireland (a division of Penguin Books Ltd)

Penguin Group (Australia), 250 Camberwell Road, Camberwell,
Victoria 3124, Australia (a division of Pearson Australia Group Pty Ltd)

Penguin Books India Pvt Ltd, 11 Community Centre, Panchsheel Park, New Delhi – 110 017, India

Penguin Group (NZ), cnr Airborne and Rosedale Roads,
Albany, Auckland 1310, New Zealand (a division of Pearson New Zealand Ltd)

Penguin Books (South Africa) (Pty) Ltd, 24 Sturdee Avenue,
Rosebank, Johannesburg 2196, South Africa

Penguin Books Ltd, Registered Offices: 80 Strand, London WC2R 0RL, England

First published in the United States of America by Viking Penguin,
a member of Penguin Putnam Inc. 2001
Published in Penguin Books 2003

7   9   10   8

Translation, introduction, and notes copyright © Royall Tyler, 2001
All rights reserved

Illustrations on pp. 5–1107 reproduced by permission of the artist and original publisher.
Copyright Minoru Sugai and Shogakukan Publishing Company.

THE LIBRARY OF CONGRESS HAS CATALOGED THE HARDCOVER EDITION AS FOLLOWS:
Murasaki Shikibu, b. 978?
[Genji monogatari. English]
The tale of Genji / Murasaki Shikibu ; translated by Royall Tyler.
p.   cm.
ISBN 0-670-03020-1 (hc.)
ISBN 0 14 24.3714 X (pbk.)
I. Tyler, Royall. II. Title.
PL788.4.G4 E3 2001
895.6'314—dc21   2001017748

Printed in the United States of America
Set in Weiss
Designed by Jaye Zimet

Acknowledgments

I could not have completed this translation in any reasonable length of time without long-term assistance from the Australian Research Council. The International Research Center for Japanese Studies, too, provided extended support, as did the National Institute for Japanese Literature and the Japan Foundation. To all these institutions I am profoundly grateful.

I thank all those who commented on my initial drafts. They were kind about them, but they must have wondered whether there was any hope. Whatever merit this translation has took time to achieve, and glimpses of my work through others' eyes were very helpful. Tsvetana Kristeva, in particular, said exactly the right thing about my early translations of the poems, prompting me at last to mend my ways.

My indispensable collaborator throughout was my wife, Susan Tyler, whose knowledge, insight, and understanding of *The Tale of Genji* have contributed more to this book than I could ever describe. It is dedicated to her.

I am grateful to Machiko Midorikawa, the *Genji* scholar who volunteered to read my entire manuscript against the original and who scrupulously pointed out where I had gone astray. I cannot thank her enough. It is a pleasure also to thank Michael Watson, who has long been helpful in so many ways, and Tom Harper and Gaye Rowley for their good humor and encouragement.

I am grateful to Minoru Sugai, who did the line illustrations, for allowing their republication here, and the Shogakukan Publishing Company, which originally commissioned them, for making them available.

I wish to acknowledge, too, Mr. Yohei Izutsu, the owner and moving spirit of the Costume Museum in Kyoto, whose re-creations of Heian costumes and settings are an inspiration.

A final word of thanks is due to Wendy Wolf, Bruce Giffords, Peter Carson, Paul Buckley, Jaye Zimet, Clifford J. Corcoran, Maureen Sugden, and the entire team of people who worked on the project at Viking Penguin. Their enthusiasm and support were wonderfully heartening.

Contents

Maps and Diagrams

pecially the reader of a translation, there is no striking discrepancy between the *Kawachi-bon* and *Aobyōshi-bon* lines, but study of the *beppon* may yet yield insight into an earlier state of the text.

The World of the Tale

Something essential to remember while reading *The Tale of Genji* is that no one in it is ever alone. A lord or lady lived surrounded by a more or less large staff of women and, just outside, men. The notions of solitude and privacy did not exist. A lady slept within curtains, it is true, but they were only curtains, and any number of gentlewomen slept just outside them on the floor. When a lord went somewhere secretly at night, he might (at some risk to himself) take *only* two or three attendants with him. If he said something privately to a gentlewoman, he managed to do so in a room already containing a good many of them.

Still, a lord or lady with no one but attendants or household staff nearby was alone in a way, because in an important sense such people did not count. Relations between people of standing were what mattered, and these were not necessarily conducted face-to-face. Good manners maintained proper distance, which amounted to upholding the accepted social order. A messenger could not deliver even an oral message to a great lord in person. His words had to be relayed in, sometimes in more than one stage. He might not see even the first intermediary, let alone hear the lord's voice. Domestic space, divided by screens, curtains, blinds, and so on—objects hardly more substantial than ways of speaking—similarly upheld distance and inviolate dignity.

This is particularly striking in scenes of courtship. In many the man complains about having to talk to the woman through one of her gentlewomen. Of course, he cannot see her, and he may have no idea what she looks like. He will not normally see her even if she speaks to him in her own voice, since she will still be in another room, behind a blind and a curtain, and the curtain will remain even if she allows him into the room where she is. If he then takes it upon himself to brush her curtain aside and go straight to her, he will by that gesture alone have claimed something close to the final intimacy.

Such fastidious manners do not suggest the atmosphere of blithe permissiveness that moralistic readers down the centuries, and quite close to our own time, have found in the tale. On the contrary, they are meant to defeat erotic spontaneity. The language is similarly reticent. *Yume* ("dream"), for example, is the stock literary word for sexual intercourse between lovers. Some readers have wondered whether the men and women in the tale ever actually *do* anything, since they seem to spend their nights merely chatting; but *katarau*, which ostensibly means that, actually refers to other intimacies as well. (The same euphemism exists in medieval French and probably in many other languages.) The verb "see" can also be stronger than expected. A man who "sees" or "is seeing" a woman (a standard expression) is at least to some extent sharing his life with her, and Genji's having "seen" Utsusemi in a pitch-dark room (chapter 2) means bluntly that he has possessed her. With all the conventions of architecture, furnishings, and manners designed precisely to prevent a suitor or visitor from seeing a woman, the effect of an accidental glimpse (through a crack in a fence, a hole in a sliding panel, a gap in a curtain) could be devastating. In fiction, where the plot may hang on such a moment, *kaimami* ("seeing through a crack") is an understandably common motif. Of course, a man may also peer through a promising crack on purpose. Perhaps he should not, but at least in a tale the world might not go round so interestingly if he refrained.

In the language of the tale, *yo no naka* ("our world," "life," "*le monde*") also means the relationship between a particular man and woman. As often elsewhere, this aspect of life was especially absorbing for women because they so depended on men for their place in "the world." A woman had only one refuge outside a stable relationship with a man: she could become a nun. This did not mean that she joined a convent, an established monastic community. Instead, she took a certain level of religious vows, had her hair cut short, wore plain, discreet colors, and stayed at home. This radical step was not taken lightly.

A good many women in the tale become nuns this way. Among the men, Genji thinks constantly about leaving the world, and Kaoru after him, but neither one ever acts. The only man who becomes a monk roughly comparable to the kind of nun just described is the eccentric Akashi Novice, and the only one who has himself fully ordained is Retired Emperor Suzaku. Whatever their dreams of peace and piety, the men simply do not have the same incentive as the women.

The Pattern of Hierarchy

In an ideal image that Japan adopted from China, the Emperor faces south to survey his realm, flanked by his two Ministers: the Minister of the Left (the Emperor's left, the east) and the Minister of the Right. That is why in history, as in the world of the tale, the imperial palace compound is located in the north of the capital city, facing south, and why the residences of the nobility all face south as well. It also explains the government's bilateral symmetry. Many official organs had Left and Right components, and in the tale this division appears in the titles borne by their officers. The reader meets, for example, a Chief Left Equerry and an Aide of the Right Palace Guards. In the early chapters the same symmetry appears in the power struggle between the faction represented by the Minister of the Left and Genji, and that of the Minister of the Right and his daughter, the mother of the Heir Apparent. The City was also divided administratively into Left and Right. Court music and dance, too, were divided into Left and Right repertoires, and contests, from wrestling to poetry, were divided into "east" and "west" sides.

All offices were associated with a numbered rank, from one down to nine. These ranks were divided into full ("third rank") and junior ("junior third rank") levels, and at the fourth rank and below, the full and junior levels were further subdivided into upper and lower grades ("junior fourth rank, upper grade"; "junior sixth rank, lower grade"). Numbered ranks are not prominent in the text, but the characters are acutely aware of them.

The Emperor stood above this numbered system. The narrator may call him "without rank," or words to that effect, rather as something infinitely precious is "beyond price." However, significant imperial offspring, both male and female, also had their place on the ladder of rank. An example is the Princess whom Genji marries.

The degree to which Genji must honor her is soon a burden, and the burden becomes still heavier when she is promoted in rank.

The Emperor was not obliged to recognize all his children, particularly those from socially or politically insignificant mothers, but most of the imperial children prominent in the tale are recognized. Except for Genji himself, they are Princes and Princesses. In this book, a Prince (His Highness) is therefore an Emperor's son whom that Emperor has formally acknowledged and appointed to a suitable rank. The same can be said of a Princess (Her Highness). However, "Princess" also covers an imperial granddaughter in the male (*not* the female) line. For example, Suetsumuhana is a Princess because she is the daughter of the Hitachi Prince, whereas Aoi is not a Princess although her mother is one, because Aoi's father (the Minister of the Left) is a commoner. The personally daunting Aoi is of very high standing, and her father is exceptionally powerful. Her weight in her world is incomparably greater than that of the pathetic Suetsumuhana, whose father is in any case dead. Nevertheless, Suetsumuhana carries an aura of imperial quality that has not come down to Aoi. So do other Princesses in the tale, even ones as disadvantaged as Ōigimi and Naka no Kimi. Most of these Princesses, whether first or second generation, inhabit a twilight zone between imperial prestige and what seems to have been regarded as sturdy commoner banality. A Princess can seldom marry without marrying down (to a commoner), and that is reason enough that in principle she should not marry at all; but as Retired Emperor Suzaku observes in "Spring Shoots I," she may be dangerously vulnerable to scandal if she does not. Her position is often unhappy.

An Emperor who does not appoint a son as a Prince, but who nonetheless prefers not to consign him to oblivion, can give him a surname, which makes him a commoner. This is what Genji's father does for Genji. In English, Genji is often called "Prince Genji," but the usage of this translation forbids that. "Prince" is a title formally conferred by an Emperor on a son whom he wishes to recognize fully and to retain in the imperial family. Before Genji receives his surname he is an imperial son whose station in life remains to be determined, and afterward he is a commoner.

The Buddhist hierarchy glimpsed in the tale also deserves a word. A ranking cleric is likely to be the brother of a distinguished official, a Prince or Princess, or even an Emperor. Examples are Murasaki's great-uncle, Suetsumuhana's brother, and probably the cleric who exorcises Ukifune. The upper levels of the Buddhist hierarchy were often staffed by sons of the highest aristocracy.

Narration, Courtesy, and Names

The narrator of *Genji* is acutely aware of social rank and assumes the reader is, too. She seems to be a gentlewoman telling a tale to her mistress, and the way she refers to the characters is in most cases extremely discreet. The rare personal name she mentions is that of an intimate male subordinate to a great lord or an occasional page girl. Normally she refers to a character by official or customary title, if any. Those who have one include court officials, male or female, and Buddhist clerics. Officials move from title to title in the narration as their careers progress.

A gentlewoman is designated by her *meshina* ("service name"), which, as in the case of the author herself, alludes to a government organ or post associated with a male relative. Several gentlewomen in the tale therefore have the same *meshina*—for example, Chūjō (literally, "Captain") and Jijū (literally, "Adviser"). In this book these *meshina* are transliterated rather than translated, so that in practice they look like names. Princesses as well as several Princes are known by number—for example, First Princess (Onna Ichi no Miya), Second Princess (Onna Ni no Miya), Third Princess (Onna San no Miya), or Third Prince (San no Miya).

Women without a title or a *meshina* may have no personal appellation at all in the narration. Aoi, Genji's first wife, is an example. Readers call her Aoi only for convenience. "Murasaki," like "Aoi," resembles a name, but the word actually starts out as a common noun alluding to Fujitsubo, and it does not refer regularly to Murasaki until much later in the book. A great lady (like, in historical practice, a great lord) may also be designated by the place where she lives. Fujitsubo, for example, lives in the Fujitsubo ("Wisteria Pavilion"), a pavilion in the palace compound; Rokujō lives on Rokujō ("Sixth Avenue"); and the normal designation for Murasaki in a large section of the work is Tai no Ue (approximately, "the mistress [*ue*] of Genji's household, who lives in the wing [*tai*] of his residence"). Other female characters are identified as daughters. Ōigimi, the traditional appellation of the elder Uji sister, simply means "elder daughter"; Naka no Kimi means "younger daughter."

Keeping track of the characters easily in the original requires an almost instinctive grasp of its world, supported by memory and by the discreet, context-dependent clues that the narration provides. That is why readers long ago assigned the characters consistent designations after all. Most of the women's (Yūgao, Oborozukiyo, Hanachirusato, Tamakazura, Ukifune, and so on) are words from poems by them or addressed to them. An outstanding example among the men, with their changing titles, is Genji's oldest friend and colleague, Tō no Chūjō. Tō no Chūjō first appears in the tale (chapter 1) as a Chamberlain Lieutenant (Kurōdo no Shōshō), an initial appointment, and rises in time to the lofty office of Chancellor (Ōkiotodo). However, the title by which readers know him for convenience means Secretary Captain; it is the one he has in chapter 2. Genji, too, goes by his changing titles. The word "Genji" hardly appears in the text.

This translation follows the usage of the original in spirit, if not always in the letter. A character with an official or customary title (Captain, Commander, Minister, Mistress of Staff, and so on) keeps it, and all such titles are translated. A woman who lacks such a title appears as she does in the original, so that women distinguished only by the occasional "Princess" (Miya), "daughter" (*himegimi*), "his darling" (*onnagimi*), and so on remain unnamed. To assist the reader, each chapter begins with a list of characters (including designation in the translation, age, and customary appellation). Where necessary, a note provides a spot identification by customary appellation. Only these appellations appear in the notes.

For the most exalted personages the translation also adopts certain forms of address that acknowledge the social tie between the fictional narrator and the character, or among the characters themselves. Examples are "His Excellency" for a Minister or Chancellor, "Her Highness" for a Princess, "Her Majesty" for an Empress, and "His Eminence" for a Retired Emperor. Since this usage conveys recognition of community (only someone in a Minister's own social world would call him "His Excellency"), use of the title proper may be exploited in English to convey distance. In the early chapters "the Minister" designates preferentially the Minister of the Right, the political enemy of "our" (Genji's) side, whereas "His Excellency" is Genji's father-in-law, the Minister of the Left.

The only traditional name used throughout is that of Genji himself, although his current title appears in direct speech or interior monologue. The term of address reserved for him after his return from exile is "His Grace." Strictly speaking, "His Grace" might correspond better to the title of Honorary Retired Emperor, which he receives only much later, but the unique prestige he comes immediately to enjoy justifies this liberty, which identifies him consistently to the reader while also acknowledging his supreme distinction.

This feature of the original text has been retained to preserve the character and structure of the social world that the narrator brings to life. The fictional narrator speaks from within this structure, and for her, good manners require conventional discretion. As a gentlewoman to a great lady, she of course stands high in the overall population of her time, counting from peasants up, but peasants and so on do not belong to her world. Hers is that of the court, in which she has a modest place. Her language must acknowledge this place, and it must also convey the way her characters would think and talk about each other if they were real.

To put it another way, the absence of personal names from the narration is another distancing device that screens a lord or lady's person from the outsider's gaze. The holder of an official title, man or woman, could properly be identified by that title or, sometimes, by residence, but a personal name, even if recorded in a genealogy, was too private to use in speech. The way the narrator refers to people affirms less their individuality than their position in a complex of communally acknowledged relations that was of absorbing interest to all. To give the characters invariant designations (in effect, personal names) would therefore be to shift the narrator's courtly stance toward a modern egalitarian one. Sometimes it would also be to confuse a character (who could not possibly know the traditional nickname of someone else in the book) with the reader; to make one character privy to another's intimate secrets; or even to make a character, or the narrator herself, speak with offensive familiarity.

Poetry

Happily, the strictures of formality still left room for another mode of communication, one outside the domain of hierarchically marked language. This was poetry, then considered the noblest of all the arts. In poetry people could address each other from the heart. Many early anecdotes tell how an eloquent poem by someone of very low rank, addressed to a superior, gained the person recognition as a fellow human being. All of Japan's early literature includes poems (prose fiction may have first crystallized around them), and The Tale of Genji contains 795. Readers down the centuries have often valued them even above the prose.

In the world evoked by the tale it was possible to speak or write a poem for oneself, but poetry was first of all a matter of social necessity. Courting required an exchange of poems, as did many other moments in life, and someone distinctly inept at it was socially disadvantaged. People learned to write by copying poems, they acquired the language of poetry by memorizing a great many examples, and they confirmed what they knew by composing more themselves. Although many poems in the tale are spoken or written spontaneously, their spontaneity actually reflects a mastery of complex rules of diction, vocabulary, and form. Some poems achieved great heights of poignancy, passion, elegance, or wit. Among the characters in *The Tale of Genji*, the "best poet" is said to be the lady from Akashi.

The poems in question are called *tanka* ("short song"), *waka* ("Japanese song"), or simply *uta* ("song"). Each consists of five subunits of 5-7-5-7-7 syllables, for a total of thirty-one. *Tanka* are usually written in one unbroken line. They have no rhyme, which would be too easy and too low in variety to be interesting, and no meter, since the language does not lend itself to that either. Their character as poetry arises from a range of sophisticated devices, including wordplay, that make most of them extremely difficult to translate.

The poems in this book follow the *tanka*'s syllabic form and are divided into two centered lines, one of 5-7-5 syllables and the other of 7-7. Syllabic count is, of course, not natural as a form in English, but it sets the language of the poems off appropriately from that of the prose. Observing it often requires more words in translation than the polysyllabic original readily supplies, but the result suits poems integrated into a prose narrative. However, the poems quoted in the notes do not follow this form, being translated for basic meaning only. The ones without author attribution are anonymous.

Readers and Reading in the Author's Time

In Murasaki Shikibu's world, the men (apart from clerics) were all officials great or small. They studied philosophy, history, law, and so on in Chinese, learned to write the Chinese language, and also composed Chinese poetry—Chinese being the learned, written, formal language; its status was similar to that of Latin in medieval Europe. They of course composed poetry in Japanese as well, but fiction was in principle beneath their dignity, since it was classified as worthless fantasy—an idea hardly unique to early Japan. Still, some clearly knew about tales anyway, and once *Genji* came to be widely admired, it was men who most visibly championed its worth.

Women were not supposed to study Chinese, but some did. Murasaki Shikibu wrote in her diary that she taught the Empress to read Chinese poetry, although she had to do it in secret. Chinese was considered unladylike. The tale describes a scholar's daughter who taught her lover to write Chinese poetry and gentlewomen who liked to fill their letters with Chinese characters, but such things were plainly not encouraged. A lady who could read Chinese advertised her knowledge at her peril.

Prose fiction in phonetically written Japanese, with few Chinese characters, was therefore especially for women. In *Genji* only women openly read or listen to tales. In chapter 25 ("The Fireflies") Genji is talking to a young lady who has been copying out a tale for herself when he launches into what is taken to be the author's own defense of fiction. He seems to know a lot about tales, but he might claim, if asked, that he has only *overheard* them being read aloud to other people.

A woman caught in strange or painful circumstances might comb tales for examples like her own, just as an Emperor might review the formal histories of China and Japan in search of a precedent for his plight, but of course a tale's usual purpose was to entertain. A new tale in the possession of an imperial wife might even make her company more attractive to a young Emperor or Heir Apparent and so give her (hence her family) an advantage over her rivals. Paintings play just that role in chapter 17 ("The Picture Contest"). *The Tale of Genji* does not mention anyone writing a tale, but in "The Picture Contest" gentlewomen, as well as professional artists, paint illustrations for tales.

A great lady like an Empress would have owned copies of tales but seems not to have read any on her own. Instead she listened while a gentlewoman read the story aloud, exactly as in the case of *Genji* itself, and she herself looked at the pictures. This has led some to talk of "performance" merely supported by the written text. Seen this way, *Genji* might resemble a script intended to accommodate ad-libbing and improvisation, and no doubt some gentlewomen did that well. However, others believe the tale to be primarily a literary work. Certainly, it was read silently from the start by lesser people fortunate enough to have access to a copy. The Daughter of Takasue, for example, wrote that she shut herself up in her room to read it day and night. Over the centuries, countless readers have done the same.

Reading The Tale of Genji *Today*

The women of the world for which *Genji* was written had households to run or lords and ladies to serve, and they could be busy with many tasks, duties, or pastimes. Still, the pace of life was slow. The tale is for readers who have time. Not only is it long, but it invites a degree of reader participation—a kind of active absorption—that few contemporary novels demand.

The narration is never in a hurry, and it follows interweaving, indirect paths that may break off only to reappear later, like a stream that sometimes flows underground. This may even have been more or less the way the intended audience, especially the most exalted among them, properly expressed themselves, either in conversation or on paper. One young woman in the tale (the Ōmi Daughter) has decent looks and intelligence, but she talks at breakneck speed, and this alone makes her uncouth. Moreover, having just arrived from the country she does not understand the courtly world she has so suddenly joined, and she has no conception of the caution and decorum that should inform her every gesture. She assumes that if she wants the honor of serving the Emperor she need only ask, but she just makes a fool of herself instead. Occasional comments by the narrator suggest that the height of distinction in a great lady's speech could be for her voice to die away before the end of her sentence and that a letter written in "ink now dark, now vanishingly pale" could be particularly elegant. One not only spoke softly and at a measured pace, one also nurtured ambition with understatement and well-placed silence.

Moreover, the narration often juxtaposes elements and scenes rather than stating a connection between them, leaving it up to the reader to see and define the relationship between one thing and another. The moments or scenes juxtaposed this way are not necessarily adjacent to each other. They come together, if they do, only in the reader's mind, thanks to memory and association encouraged by repeated reading, and the connection is seldom demonstrably intended because the narrator says nothing about it. Overlooking such possible links does not make the tale difficult to understand, but it may make it appear more episodic or fragmented than it actually is. Is *Genji* a series of loosely related stories or does it have a larger narrative structure? The character of the narration makes it difficult to decide, and to some extent the tale is what the reader makes of it. Its reticences and silences solicit an informed and engaged imagination.

The Tale as Fiction and History

The Tale of Genji has often been taken, understandably, for a sort of documentary on court life in the author's time, but its hero is a plainly fictional character. Scattered touches also suggest that the tale was actually conceived as a historical novel and that Genji lived in the early tenth century, nearly a hundred years before the author's time. For example, he is a master of the *kin*, a Chinese musical instrument prominent in the tale. Historical sources, however, show that the *kin* dropped sharply in popularity after the mid-tenth century and that by the author's time it was no longer played. Sure enough, when the aging Genji finds himself obliged to teach someone the *kin* ("Spring Shoots II"), he complains that few people play it anymore.

What really betrays the tale as fiction, however, is simply that it is more beautiful than life. Not every moment or action in it is pleasing, and many are of course painful in one way or another. Rather, the narration gives grace and harmony to things that might otherwise be too tedious or distressing to sustain the reader's interest. It is as though the author had painted an immensely long and accomplished picture scroll. The scroll accurately conveys countless details of daily life, depicts troubling scenes, and generally hints at humanity's more or less deplorable failings. However, it selects and composes these things into engaging sequences. At the close of some upsetting passages the narrator actually observes that one would have wished to paint the scene.

The narrative displays many visually brilliant scenes, and its careful attention to matters of costume is famous. However, this interest in beautiful tableaux and in dress does not prove, as some have assumed, that these nobles really spent all their time organizing visually perfect moments, any more than the incense blending in chapter 32 ("The Plum Tree Branch") shows that they had little else to do but to enjoy incense. If they had, and if they had always succeeded as well when they tried as they do in the tale, such scenes would have been superfluous. *The Tale of Genji* evokes a world in which many things, much of the time, are really and truly done right for a change. Still, life's cruelties show clearly enough through the grace of color and form—the form of manners, words, and feelings as well as of things. The author saw life very clearly.

All this helps to make the tale more real than history. Its most celebrated characters live more vividly in the imagination than anyone known from historical documents, and their lives—their sufferings, their disappointments, their failings, and their grace—have remained a major legacy to the centuries that have passed since they were first conceived. Although invented, they are also immortal. Even Genji's Rokujō estate, lovingly reconstructed in drawings and models, is by far the most widely known example of the domestic architecture of its time. That it never existed makes no difference at all.

The Language of Genji

The words in *The Tale of Genji* are probably close to those spoken at the court ten centuries ago. The text consists of expository narration, direct speech, silent thought (interior monologue), occasional comments by the narrator, and poems, all in a harmonious style that accommodates variations of tone and mood, according to context and character. When two high-ranking gentlemen discuss a delicate subject, their language conveys the tension between them, and when scholars speak, their jargon resembles a local dialect.

The style of the tale is indisputably a great literary achievement, but it is also very difficult. Names are rare, and verbs seldom have a stated subject. After eight hundred years of *Genji* scholarship, it is still possible to argue that this or that speech or action should be attributed to someone else. Moreover, the vocabulary is relatively restricted and the available patterns of subordination relatively few. Neither the resources of the language itself nor the requirements of discretion encourage clarity of expression, and one feels sometimes as though the author is pressing against the received constraints of her medium. Still, the original was undoubtedly clearer then than it is now, and much of its famous elusiveness may be due to later readers' ignorance of reference, idiom, and telling turn of phrase.

Three linguistic features of the original deserve special comment. These are its evenness of flow, the integral role played in it by grammatical devices that indicate the speaker's social standing with respect to the person addressed or discussed, and certain modal inflections of the verbs in the narration.

The original has (with local exceptions) a lovely, smooth flow that cannot be conveyed in English, which resists such unstressed evenness word by word and sentence by sentence. However, one can still preserve the length of some of the tale's many long sentences and at least follow the original in avoiding blunt statement that might snag the reader's attention on a solid mental object. For example, the original will say that "Genji decided to act on his long-standing desire" rather than that "Genji finally decided to become a monk," and it will have a father "wish to see his daughter advantageously settled" rather than have him eager to find her a good husband. (The text has no stable term for either "marriage" or "husband.")

Polite and humble language may be the first issue mentioned when someone Japanese wonders how the tale can be translated into English at all. The modern Japanese language still makes it difficult to talk to or about someone without defining one's standing vis-à-vis that person, and other languages require similar linguistic acknowledgment of social relationship; but not so contemporary English, which offers relatively few means to achieve it. Appropriate diction and choice of vocabulary can make up the difference a little, and so can added interjections like "my lord" or "my lady," but an English translation cannot help sounding relatively informal.

Certain verbal inflections in *Genji* and other literature of its time have become an issue in recent years. The chief of these is *-keri*, which seems to indicate a verbal mode (rather than tense) that brings the events narrated into the present. Some scholars, for whom this quality of presence or immediacy is crucial to the sociopolitical significance of women's literature including *Genji*, hold that to translate such literature into the English past tense is to remove it from its audience in time and so to denature it completely. However, English lacks such a verbal mode of narrative immediacy, and translating into the present would not help, since the present is still a tense, not a mode, and is in any case difficult to sustain successfully throughout a long narration. In English, as in other related languages, a tale is normally told mainly in the past, and as a matter of naive reading experience it is untrue that events told in this tense lose their immediacy for the reader or listener. The basic tense of narration in this translation is therefore the past. However, most passages of interior monologue are in the first-person present.

Calculating Time

A final matter concerns the months of the year and the ages of the characters. The text often identifies the numbered month in which an event takes place, but these are lunar, not solar, months, and they differ from the months of the modern calendar. A lunar month is roughly six weeks later than the solar month with the same number. For example, the first day of the first lunar month is not the first of January, in the middle of winter, but the first day of spring (mid-February).

By the fifteenth century, scholars had worked out at least the approximate ages of most of the characters for each chapter, and these ages are given here according to the Japanese method of counting. In Japan, a child's first year is the calendar year of birth, and the child enters his or her "second year" with the New Year. For example, a child born in the twelfth month becomes "two" in the first month of the next year, so that age leaps ahead of the Western count. Genji's listed age of seventeen in chapter 2 means that he is in his seventeenth year and that his age in English would normally be counted as sixteen. In other words, all ages given are one year greater than in English usage.

The Illustrations

The illustrations in the text are details redrawn by a contemporary artist from a wide range of medieval material, mainly painted scrolls (*emaki*). Since nothing of the kind survives from the time of *The Tale of Genji* itself, these choices are as close as possible to authentic depictions of objects and scenes in the tale. A few—for example "Playing Go" in chapter 3—are from *Genji monogatari emaki* (twelfth century), the earliest known but unfortunately incomplete set of *Genji* illustrations. Those interested in identifying the source of each picture should refer to the Shogakukan edition of the original text, which includes the name of the source in the caption.

The figures on the slipcase are from full-book-page block prints included in one of the many editions of *Kojitsu sōsho* (*Compendium of Ancient Usages*), a collection of texts and illustrative material on ceremonies, properties, costumes, and so on associated with Japan's court and warrior aristocracies. This particular edition dates from the first years of the twentieth century. Two are from a section illustrating Heian court costume. The third, from a section on *bugaku* dances, shows a masked dancer performing "Ryōō" ("The Warrior King").

THE
TALE OF
Genji

1

The Paulownia Pavilion

Kiri means "paulownia tree" and *tsubo* "a small garden between palace buildings." Kiritsubo is therefore the name for the palace pavilion that has a paulownia in its garden. The Emperor installs Genji's mother there, so that readers have always called her Kiritsubo no Kōi (the Kiritsubo Intimate), although the text does not.

PERSONS

Genji, from birth through age 12

The Haven, Genji's mother (the Kiritsubo Intimate, Kiritsubo no Kōi)

His Majesty, the Emperor, Genji's father (Kiritsubo no Mikado)

The Haven's mother, Genji's grandmother

The Emperor's eldest son, appointed Heir Apparent at 7
when Genji is 4 (Suzaku)

The Kokiden Consort, mother of the Heir Apparent

Yugei no Myōbu, a gentlewoman in the Emperor's service

A physiognomist from Koma

The Right Grand Controller (Udaiben)

A Dame of Staff (Naishi no Suke)

Fujitsubo, daughter of an earlier Emperor,
enters the palace at 16 when Genji is 11

His Highness of War, Fujitsubo's elder brother
(Hyōbukyō no Miya)

His Excellency, the Minister of the Left, becomes Genji's
father-in-law at 46 (Sadaijin)

His daughter, Genji's wife, 16 at marriage when Genji is 12 (Aoi)

His son, the Chamberlain Lieutenant (Tō no Chūjō)

The Princess, the Emperor's sister, mother of Aoi and
Tō no Chūjō (Ōmiya)

The Minister of the Right, grandfather of the
Heir Apparent (Udaijin)

In a certain reign (whose can it have been?) someone of no very great rank, among all His Majesty's Consorts and Intimates, enjoyed exceptional favor. Those others who had always assumed that pride of place was properly theirs despised her as a dreadful woman, while the lesser Intimates were unhappier still. The way she waited on him day after day only stirred up feeling against her, and perhaps this growing burden of resentment was what affected her health and obliged her often to withdraw in misery to her home; but His Majesty, who could less and less do without her, ignored his critics until his behavior seemed bound to be the talk of all.

From this sad spectacle the senior nobles and privy gentlemen could only avert their eyes. Such things had led to disorder and ruin even in China, they said, and as discontent spread through the realm, the example of Yōkihi[1] came more and more to mind, with many a painful consequence for the lady herself; yet she trusted in his gracious and unexampled affection and remained at court.

The Grand Counselor, her father, was gone, and it was her mother, a lady from an old family, who saw to it that she should give no less to court events than others whose parents were both alive and who enjoyed general esteem; but lacking anyone influential to support her, she often had reason when the time came to lament the weakness of her position.[2]

His Majesty must have had a deep bond with her in past lives as well, for she gave him a wonderfully handsome son. He had the child brought in straightaway,[3] for he was desperate to see him, and he was astonished by his beauty. His elder son, born to his Consort the daughter of the Minister of the Right, enjoyed powerful backing and was feted by all as the undoubted future Heir Apparent, but he could not rival his brother in looks, and His Majesty, who still accorded him all due respect, therefore lavished his private affection on the new arrival.

1. The beauty Yōkihi (Chinese Yang Guifei) so infatuated the Chinese Emperor Xuanzong (685–762) that his neglect of the state provoked a rebellion, and his army forced him to have her executed. Bai Juyi (772–846) told the story in a long poem, "The Song of Unending Sorrow" (Chinese "Changhenge," Japanese "Chōgonka," *Hakushi monjū* 0596), which was extremely popular in Heian Japan.

2. She had no influential male relative on her mother's side and was often pushed aside when an event took place.

3. Such a birth took place not in the palace but at the mother's home.

Her rank had never permitted her to enter His Majesty's common service.[4] His insistence on keeping her with him despite her fine reputation and her noble bearing meant that whenever there was to be music or any other sort of occasion, his first thought was to send for her. Sometimes, after oversleeping a little, he would command her to stay on with him, and this refusal to let her go made her seem to deserve contempt;[5] but after the birth he was so attentive that the mother of his firstborn feared that he might appoint his new son Heir Apparent over her own. This Consort, for whom he had high regard, had been the first to come to him, and it was she whose reproaches most troubled him and whom he could least bear to hurt, for she had given him other children as well.

Despite her faith in His Majesty's sovereign protection, so many belittled her and sought to find fault with her that, far from flourishing, she began in her distress to waste away. She lived in the Kiritsubo. His Majesty had to pass many others on his constant visits to her, and no wonder they took offense. On the far too frequent occasions when she went to him, there might be a nasty surprise awaiting her along the crossbridges and bridgeways, one that horribly fouled the skirts of the gentlewomen who accompanied her or who came forward to receive her; or, the victim of a conspiracy between those on either side, she might find herself locked in a passageway between two doors that she could not avoid, and be unable to go either forward or back. Seeing how she suffered from such humiliations, endlessly multiplied as circumstances favored her enemies' designs, His Majesty had the Intimate long resident in the Kōrōden move elsewhere and gave it to her instead, for when he wanted to have her nearby.[6] The one evicted nursed a particularly implacable grudge.

In the child's third year his father gave him a donning of the trousers just as impressive as his firstborn's, marshaling for the purpose all the treasures in the Court Repository and the Imperial Stores. This only provoked more complaints, but as the boy grew, he revealed such marvels of beauty and character that no one could resent him. The discerning could hardly believe their eyes, and they wondered that such a child should have ever been born.

In the summer of that year His Majesty's Haven[7] became unwell, but he refused her leave to withdraw. He felt no alarm, since her health had long been fragile, and he only urged her to be patient a little longer. However, she worsened daily, until just five or six days later she was so weak that her mother's tearful entreaties at last persuaded him to release her. In fear of suffering some cruel humiliation even now, she left the child behind and stole away.

4. Her standing was too high to allow her to wait on the Emperor routinely, like a servant. She should have come to him only when summoned and for a limited time.

5. Because the Emperor himself seems to treat her like a servant.

6. The Kōrōden (den means approximately "hall") was very near the Emperor's residence. He gives it to her not to replace the Kiritsubo but as a nearby apartment (uetsubone) to stay in when he requires her company often.

7. Genji's mother. Her unofficial title (Haven, Miyasudokoro) seems to have designated a woman, especially one of Intimate or Consort rank, who had borne an Emperor or an Heir Apparent a child.

Bridgeway

His Majesty, who could no longer keep her by him, suffered acutely to think that he could not even see her off.[8] There she lay, lovely and ever so dear, but terribly thin now and unable to tell him of her deep trouble and sorrow because she lingered in a state of semiconsciousness—a sight that drove from his mind all notion of time past or to come and reduced him simply to assuring her tearfully, in every way he knew, how much he loved her.

When she still failed to respond but only lay limp and apparently fainting, with the light dying from her eyes, he had no idea what to do. Even after issuing a decree to allow her the privilege of a hand carriage, he went in to her again and could not bring himself to let her go. "You promised never to leave me, not even at the end," he said, "and you cannot abandon me now! I will not let you!"

She was so touched that she managed to breathe:

> "Now the end has come, and I am filled with sorrow that our ways must part:
> the path I would rather take is the one that leads to life.

If only I had known . . ."

She seemed to have more to say but to be too exhausted to go on, which only decided him, despite her condition, to see her through to whatever might follow. He consented only unwillingly to her departure when urgently reminded that excellent healers were to start prayers for her that evening at her own home.

With his heart too full for sleep, he anxiously awaited dawn. He expressed deep concern even before his messenger had time to come back from her house. Meanwhile, the messenger heard lamenting and learned that just past midnight she had breathed her last, and he therefore returned in sorrow. This news put His Majesty in such a state that he shut himself away, wholly lost to all around him.

He still longed to see his son, but the child was soon to withdraw, for no

8. She was too ill to stay in the palace, lest it be polluted by death, and imperial etiquette forbade the Emperor to see her off.

Hand carriage

precedent authorized one in mourning to wait upon the Emperor.[9] The boy did not understand what the matter was, and he gazed in wonder at the sobbing gentlewomen who had served his mother and at His Majesty's streaming tears. Such partings[10] are sad at the best of times, and his very innocence made this one moving beyond words.

Now it was time to proceed with the customary funeral. Her mother longed with many tears to rise with her daughter's smoke into the sky, and she insisted on joining the gentlewomen in their carriage in the funeral cortège. What grief she must have known on reaching Otagi, where the most imposing rite was under way!

"With her body plain to see before me," she said, "I feel that she is still alive even though she is not, and I will therefore watch her turn to ash to learn that she is really gone."

She spoke composedly enough, but a moment later she was racked by such a paroxysm of grief that she nearly fell from the carriage. "Oh, I knew it!" the gentlewomen cried to each other, not knowing how to console her.

A messenger came from the palace, followed by an imperial envoy who read a proclamation granting the deceased the third rank.[11] It was very sad. His Majesty had never even named her a Consort, but it pained him not to have done so, and he had wished at least to raise her a step in dignity. Even this made many resent her further, but the wiser ones at last understood that her loveliness in looks and bearing, and her sweet gentleness of temper, had made her impossible actually to dislike. It was His Majesty's unbecoming penchant for her, so his gentlewomen[12] now understood, that had made some treat her with cold disdain, and they remembered her fondly for the

9. After the year 905, children not yet in their seventh year no longer went into mourning for a parent, and the present of the story therefore seems to be earlier.

10. The death of a parent.

11. Appropriate to a Consort.

12. These gentlewomen, who rank below the ladies just referred to, would have known the deceased personally because they waited on the Emperor routinely.

warmth and kindness of her disposition. It was a perfect example of "Now she is gone."[13]

As the dreary days slipped by, His Majesty saw carefully to each succeeding memorial service.[14] The passage of time did so little to relieve his sorrow that he called none of his ladies to wait on him after dark but instead passed day and night in weeping, and even those who merely witnessed his state found the autumn very dewy indeed.

Carriage

"She meant so much to him that even dead she is a blight on one's existence" summed up the sentiments of the Kokiden Consort,[15] as merciless as ever, on the subject. The mere sight of his elder son would only remind His Majesty how much he preferred the younger, and he would then send a trusted gentlewoman or nurse[16] to find out how he was getting on.

At dusk one blustery and suddenly chilly autumn day,[17] His Majesty, assailed more than ever by memories, dispatched the gentlewoman dubbed Yugei no Myōbu[18] to his love's home; then, after she had left under a beautiful evening moon,[19] he lapsed again into reverie. He felt her there beside him, just as she had always been on evenings like this when he had called for music, and when her touch on her instrument, or her least word to him, had been so much her own; except that he would have preferred even to this vivid dream her simple reality in the dark.[20]

Myōbu had no sooner arrived and gone in through the gate than desolation touched her. The mother had kept the place up, despite being a widow, and she had lived nicely enough out of fond concern for her only daughter, but alas, now that grief had laid her low, the weeds grew tall and looked cruelly blown about by the winds, until only moonlight slipped smoothly through their tangles.

She had Myōbu alight on the south side of the house.[21] At first she could not speak. "I keep wishing that I had not lived so long," she said at last, "and I am so

13. *Genji monogatari kochūshakusho in'yō waka* 1: "When she was alive her presence was a trial, but now she is gone I miss her so!"

14. A rite was performed every seven days for the first forty-nine days after the death, in order to guide the spirit of the deceased toward peace. The Emperor probably sent a representative to each and provided for it generously.

15. The mother of the Emperor's first son, the future Heir Apparent. Kokiden (a Chinese-style name that means "Hall of Great Light") is the name of her residence within the palace compound. Many historical Consorts and Empresses lived there.

16. A woman who had nursed the Emperor in place of his natural mother. The relationship with a nurse was normally intimate and lasting.

17. A typhoon (*nowaki*) wind is blowing, and the season is early autumn by the lunar calendar.

18. A gentlewoman of middle rank (Myōbu) with a male relative in the Gate Watch (Yugei).

19. *Yūzukuyo*, the "evening moon" that lingers in the twilight sky up to the tenth day of the lunar month.

20. An ironic reference to *Kokinshū* 647: "Her reality in the dark of night is not worth more than a clear, bright dream."

21. Out of respect for the Emperor, who has sent Myōbu. The south side is the front.

ashamed now to see someone from His Majesty struggle all the way to me through these weeds!" She wept as though it were truly more than she could bear.

"The Dame of Staff told His Majesty how desperately sorry for you she felt after her visit here, and how heartbroken she was," Myōbu replied; "and even I, who pretend to no delicacy of feeling,[22] understand what she meant all too well." Then, after composing herself a little, she delivered His Majesty's message.[23]

" 'For a time I was sure that I must be dreaming, but now that the turmoil in my mind has subsided, what I still find acutely painful is to have no one with whom to talk over what needs to be done. Would you be kind enough to visit me privately? I am anxious about my son and disturbed that he should be surrounded every day by such grieving. Please come soon.'

"He kept breaking into tears and never really managed to finish, but he knew all too well, as I could see, that to another he might not be looking very brave, and I felt so much for him that I hurried off to you before I had actually heard all he had to say." Then Myōbu gave her His Majesty's letter.

"Though tears darken my eyes," the lady said, "by the light of his most wise and gracious words . . ." And she began to read.

"I had thought that time might bring consolations to begin lightening my sorrow, but as the passing days and months continue to disappoint me, I hardly know how to bear my grief. Again and again my thoughts go to the little boy, and it troubles me greatly that I cannot look after him with you. Do come and see me in memory of days now gone . . ." He had written with deep feeling and had added the poem:

> *"Hearing the wind sigh, burdening with drops of dew all Miyagi Moor,*
> *my heart helplessly goes out to the little hagi frond."*[24]

But she could not read it to the end.

"Now that I know how painful it is to live long," she said, "I am ashamed to imagine what that pine must think of me,[25] and for that reason especially I would not dare to frequent His Majesty's Seat.[26] It is very good indeed of him to favor me with these repeated invitations, but I am afraid that I could not possibly bring myself to go. His son, on the other hand, seems eager to do so, although I am not sure just how much he understands, and while it saddens me that he should feel that way, I cannot blame him. Please let His Majesty know these, my inmost thoughts. I fear

22. A conventionally modest statement. Myōbu ranks too low to claim finer feelings as a matter of course.

23. She speaks in the Emperor's own words, although she uses honorifics when the Emperor refers to himself.

24. "As the sad winds of change sweep through the palace, they bring tears to my eyes, and my heart goes out to my little boy." *Hagi*, an autumn-flowering plant, has long, graceful fronds that are easily tossed and tangled by the wind. Miyagino, east of present Sendai, is often associated with *hagi* in poetry, and here, the *miya* of Miyagino also suggests the palace (*miya*). The poem refers to *Kokinshū* 694.

25. *Kokin rokujō* 3057, in which the poet laments feeling even older than the pine of Takasago, a common poetic exemplar of longevity: "No, I shall let no one know that I live on: I am ashamed to imagine what the Takasago pine must think of me."

26. *Momoshiki*, a poetic term for the palace, particularly used by women.

that the child's dignity will suffer if he remains here, for I am a creature of misfortune, and it would be wrong for him to stay."

The little boy was asleep. "I had wanted to see him so that I could report on
him to His Majesty," Myōbu said as she prepared to hasten away, "but I am expected
back. It must be very late by now."

"I would so like to talk to you longer, to lift a little of the unbearable darkness
from my heart,"[27] she replied. "Please come to see me on your own, too, whenever
you wish. You always used to visit at happy, festive times, and seeing you here now
on so sad an errand reminds one how very painful life is. We had such hopes for her
from the time she was born, and my husband, the late Grand Counselor, kept urging me almost until his last breath to achieve his ambition for her and have her serve
His Majesty. 'Do not lose heart and give up,' he said, 'just because I am gone.' So I
did send her, although I felt that if she had to enter palace service without anyone
to support her properly, it might be wiser to refrain; because what mattered to me
was to honor his last wishes. Unfortunately, His Majesty became far more fond than
was right of someone who did not deserve that degree of favor, but she seems to
have borne the disgraceful treatment she received and to have continued serving
him until the growing burden of others' jealousy, and the increasing unpleasantness
to which she was subjected, led her to break down as she did; and that is why I wish
that His Majesty had not cared for her so much. I suppose I only say that, though,
because her loss has plunged me into such terrible shadows . . ." Her voice trailed
off and she wept.

By now it was very late. "His Majesty feels as you do," Myōbu assured her. " 'I
now understand,' he says, 'how damaging my love for her really was, because the
way I insisted despite my better judgment on favoring her to the point of scandal
meant that it could not have gone on very long. I had no wish to offend anyone,
and yet because of her I provoked resentment in those whom I should not have
hurt, only to lose her in the end and to linger on inconsolable, a sorrier spectacle
now than I ever made of myself before. I wish I knew what in my past lives could
have brought all this upon me.' This is what he says again and again, and as he does
so, he is never far from weeping."

Myōbu talked on and at last said tearfully, "It is now very late, and I must not
let the night go by without bringing His Majesty your answer." She hastily prepared
to return to the palace.

The moon was setting in a beautifully clear sky, the wind had turned distinctly
cold, and the crickets crying from among the grasses seemed to be calling her to
weep with them, until she could hardly bear to leave this house of humble misery.

> "Bell crickets may cry until they can cry no more, but not so for me,
> for all through the endless night my tears will fall on and on,"

she said. She could not get into her carriage.

27. *Gosenshū* 1102 (also *Kokin rokujō* 1412) by Murasaki Shikibu's ancestor Fujiwara no Kanesuke: "A parent's heart, although not in darkness, may yet wander, lost, for love of a child." The sentiment became almost proverbial, and the tale alludes to the poem so frequently that further occurrences will not be noted.

"Here where crickets cry more and more unhappily in thinning grasses
you who live above the clouds bring still heavier falls of dew.

I would soon have been blaming you," the answer came.[28]

This was no time for pretty parting gifts, and she gave Myōbu instead, in her daughter's memory, some things that she had saved for just such an occasion: a set of gowns and some accessories that her daughter had used to put up her hair.

The young gentlewomen who had served her daughter were of course saddened by the loss of their mistress, but they missed the palace now they were used to it, and memories of His Majesty moved them to urge that his son should move there as quickly as possible; but she felt sure that people would disapprove if one as ill-fated as herself were to accompany him, and since she also knew how much she worried whenever he was out of sight, she could not bring herself to let him go.

Myōbu felt a pang of sympathy when she found that His Majesty had not yet retired for the night. The garden court was in its autumn glory, and on the pretext of admiring it he had quietly called into attendance four or five of his most engaging gentlewomen, with whom he was now conversing. Lately he had been spending all his time examining illustrations of "The Song of Unending Sorrow" commissioned by Emperor Uda, with poems by Ise and Tsurayuki;[29] and other poems as well, in native speech or in Chinese, as long as they were on that theme, which was the constant topic of his conversation.

He questioned Myōbu carefully about her visit, and she told him in private how sad it had been. Then he read the lady's reply. She had written, "Your Majesty's words inspire such awe that I am unworthy to receive them; confusion overwhelms me in the presence of sentiments so gracious.

"Ever since that tree whose boughs took the cruel winds withered and was lost
my heart is sorely troubled for the little hagi *frond,"*

and so on—a rather distracted letter, although His Majesty understood how upset she still was and no doubt forgave her.[30] He struggled in vain to control himself, despite his resolve to betray no strong emotion. A rush of memories even brought back the days when he had first known his love, and he was shocked to realize how long he had already been without her, when once he had so disliked her briefest absence.

---

28. "Blaming you, instead of all that has happened, for my tears." These poems are carried by an intermediary, for the lady is still in the house. "You who live above the clouds" (*kumo no uebito*) is Myōbu, the Emperor's emissary, whose visit has started fresh tears.

29. The paintings were probably on screens, with poems set in cartouches as comments on each scene. Ise was a distinguished poet and gentlewoman in the entourage of Emperor Uda (reigned 887–97), while Ki no Tsurayuki (died 946) was the most influential poet at the early-tenth-century court.

30. Her poem neglects the Emperor's protection of the boy in favor of that provided by the boy's mother; it could even be taken to suggest that the Emperor cannot protect him.

"I had wanted her mother to feel it was worthwhile to have her enter my service," he said, "as the late Grand Counselor at his death had urged her to do. What a shame!" He felt very sorry. "At any rate, I should be able to do something for my son, as long as he grows up properly. She must take care that she lives to see it."

Myōbu showed him the gifts she had received. If only this were the hairpin that *she* sent back from beyond, he thought;[31] but, alas, it was not. He murmured,

> *"O that I might find a wizard to seek her out, that I might then know*
> *at least from distant report where her dear spirit has gone."*

A superb artist had done the paintings of Yōkihi, but the brush can convey only so much, and her picture lacked the breath of life. The face, so like the lotuses in the Taieki Lake or the willows by the Miō Palace,[32] was no doubt strikingly beautiful in its Chinese way, but when he remembered how sweet and dear his love had been, he found himself unable to compare her to flowers or birdsong. Morning and evening he had assured her that they would share a wing in flight as birds or their branches as trees,[33] but then she had died, and the resulting vanity of his promises filled him with unending sorrow.

The sound of the wind and the calling of crickets only deepened his melancholy, and meanwhile he heard the Kokiden Consort, who had not come for so long now to wait on him after dark, making the best of a beautiful moon by playing music far into the night. He did not like it and wished it would stop. Those gentlewomen and privy gentlemen who knew his mood found that it grated upon their ears. The offender, willful and abrasive, seemed determined to behave as though nothing had happened.

The moon set.

> *"When above the clouds tears in a veil of darkness hide the autumn moon,*
> *how could there be light below among the humble grasses?"*[34]

His Majesty murmured, his thoughts going to the lady whom Myōbu had recently left, and he stayed up until the lamp wicks had burned out.[35]

It must have been the hour of the Ox,[36] because he heard the Right Gate Watch

---

31. In "The Song of Unending Sorrow," the Emperor sends a wizard to find his beloved in the afterworld (the fabulous island of Hōrai [Chinese Penglai]), and the wizard brings back an ornamental hairpin from her.

32. These similes of the Taieki (Chinese Taiye) Lake and the Miō (Chinese Weiyang) Palace are from "The Song of Unending Sorrow."

33. In the "Song" the Emperor promises Yang Guifei that if reborn as birds they will share a wing as they fly and if reborn on earth they will share their branches as trees.

34. "When even I am weeping, how could a bereaved mother not weep, too?" "Above the clouds" (*kumo no ue*) refers to the palace, and the *asaji* grasses are those already mentioned by the lady in an earlier poem. The Emperor's poem also hints at the meaning "How can I go on living?"

35. Another touch from "The Song of Unending Sorrow."

36. Roughly 2:00 to 4:00 A.M.

reporting for duty. He then retired to his curtained bed, for he did not wish to make himself conspicuous, but still he could not sleep. He remembered when morning came, and it was time to rise, how once he had not even known that daybreak was upon him,[37] and again he seemed likely to miss his morning session in council.

He only went through the motions of breaking his fast and took no greater interest in his midday meal, until all who served him grieved to see his state. Those in close attendance upon him, ladies and gentlemen alike, murmured anxiously about how disturbing it all was. Perhaps he had been fated to love her, but for him to have ignored the reproofs and the anger of so many, to have flouted for her sake the standards of proper conduct, and even now to ignore public affairs as he was doing—this, they all whispered, was most unfortunate, and they cited in this connection events in the land beyond the sea.[38]

In time the little boy went to join his father in the palace. He was turning out to be so handsome that he hardly seemed of this world at all, and for His Majesty this aroused a certain dread.[39] The next spring, when His Majesty was to designate the Heir Apparent, he longed to pass over his elder son in favor of his younger, but since the younger lacked support,[40] and since in any case the world at large would never accept such a choice, he desisted for the boy's sake and kept his desire to himself. "He could hardly go that far," people assured one another, "no matter how devoted to him he may be." The Kokiden Consort was relieved.[41]

As for the grandmother, she remained inconsolable and wished only to join her daughter, which no doubt is why she, too, to His Majesty's boundless sorrow, at last passed away. The boy was then entering his sixth year. This time he understood what had happened, and he cried. Toward the end, she who had been close to him for so long spoke again and again of how sad she was to leave him.

Now the boy was permanently in attendance at the palace. When he reached his seventh year, His Majesty had him perform his first reading, which he carried off with such unheard-of brilliance that his father was frankly alarmed. "Surely none of you can dislike him now," he said; "after all, he no longer has a mother. Please be nice to him." When he took him to the Kokiden, the Consort there let him straight through her blinds and would not release him, for the sight of him would have brought smiles to the fiercest warrior, even an enemy one. She had given His Majesty two daughters, but by no stretch of the imagination could either be compared with him. Nor did any other imperial lady hide from him, because he was already so charmingly distinguished in manner that they found him a delightful and challenging playmate. Naturally he applied himself to formal scholarship,[42] but he also set the heavens

37. The Emperor had once slept through dawn in his love's arms. The expression is from *Ise shū* 55, by Ise, written to go on a screen illustrating "The Song of Unending Sorrow." The poem is based on two lines of Bai Juyi's original.

38. The catastrophe caused by Xuanzong's infatuation with Yang Guifei.

39. People believed that supernatural powers coveted unusually beautiful people and stole them. The tale often alludes to this fear.

40. He had no influential male relative on his mother's side to support him.

41. Her own son has now been formally appointed Heir Apparent.

42. Chinese studies, mainly in political philosophy, law, history, poetry, and court usage.

ringing with the music of strings
and flute. In fact, if I were to list all
the things at which he excelled, I
would only succeed in making
him sound absurd.

During this time His Maj-
esty learned that a delegation
from Koma[43] included an expert
physiognomist, and since it would
have contravened Emperor Uda's
solemn admonition to call him to
the palace, he instead sent his son
secretly to the Kōrokan.[44] The
Right Grand Controller, charged
with taking him there, presented
him as his own.

Blinds

The astonished physiognomist nodded his head again and again in perplexity.
"He has the signs of one destined to become the father of his people and to achieve
the Sovereign's supreme eminence," he said, "and yet when I see him so, I fear disorder and suffering. But when I see him as the future pillar of the court and the support of all the realm, there again appears to be a mismatch."

The Controller himself was a man of deep learning, and his conversation with
the visitor was most interesting. They exchanged poems, and when the physiognomist, who was soon to leave, made a very fine one expressing joy at having met so
extraordinary a boy, together with sorrow upon parting from him, the boy composed some moving lines of his own, which the visitor admired extravagantly before
presenting him with handsome gifts. The visitor, too, received many gifts, conveyed to him from His Majesty. News of this encounter got about, as such news
will, and although His Majesty never mentioned it, the Minister of the Right, the
Heir Apparent's grandfather, wondered suspiciously what it might mean.

His Majesty was greatly impressed to find that the visitor's reading tallied with
one that he had obtained in his wisdom through the art of physiognomy as practiced
in Japan, and on the strength of which he had refrained from naming his son a Prince.
He therefore decided that rather than set the boy adrift as an unranked Prince,[45] un-
supported by any maternal relative, he would assure him a more promising future
(since, after all, his own reign might be brief) by having him serve the realm as a
commoner; and in this spirit he had him apply himself more diligently than ever to

---

43. The ancient Korean kingdom of Koguryŏ.

44. When Uda abdicated, he wrote down articles of advice for his successor, Daigo (reigned 897–930),
and one of these advised against admitting any outsider to the palace. Judging from this passage, the Emperor in the tale corresponds to Daigo. The Kōrokan was the building where foreign ambassadors and
other visitors were received, near the crossing of Suzaku Avenue and Shichijō ("Seventh Avenue").

45. An imperial son was not a Prince until appointed by his father. The appointment was to one of four
ranks, and the appointee received a corresponding stipend. One not so appointed but still retained in the
imperial family was "unranked" (*muhon*).

his studies. It was a shame to make a subject of him, considering his gifts, but he was bound to draw suspicion as a Prince, and when consultation with an eminent astrologer only confirmed this prediction, His Majesty resolved to make him a Genji.[46]

Month after month, year after year, His Majesty never forgot his lost Haven. After summoning several likely prospects, he sorrowfully concluded that he would never find her like again in this world, but then he heard from a Dame of Staff about another possibility: the fourth child of a former Emperor, a girl known for her beauty and brought up by her mother, the Empress, with the greatest care. Owing that Emperor her office as she did, the Dame had served the young lady's mother intimately as well, and so she had known her, too, from infancy; in fact, she saw her from time to time even now. "In all my three reigns of service at court,[47] I have seen no one like Your Majesty's late Haven," she said, "but the Princess I refer to has grown to be very like her. She is a pleasure to look at."

His Majesty approached the mother with great circumspection, eager to discover the truth of this report. She received his proposal with alarm, because she knew how unpleasant the Heir Apparent's mother could be, and she shrank from exposing her daughter to the blatant contempt with which this Consort had treated her Kiritsubo rival. So it was that she passed away before she could bring herself to consent. Once the daughter was alone, His Majesty pressed his suit earnestly, assuring her that she would be to him as a daughter of his own.[48] Her gentlewomen, those properly concerned with her interests,[49] and her elder brother, His Highness of War, all agreed that she would be far better off at the palace than forlorn at home, and they therefore insisted that she should go.

She was called Fujitsubo. She resembled that other lady to a truly astonishing degree, but since she was of far higher standing, commanded willing respect, and could not possibly be treated lightly, she had no need to defer to anyone on any matter. His Majesty had clung all too fondly to his old love, despite universal disapproval, and he did not forget her now, but in a touching way his affection turned to this new arrival, who was a great consolation to him.

None of His Majesty's ladies could remain shy with the young Genji, especially the one he now saw so often, because he hardly ever left his father's side. All of them took pride in their looks, no doubt with good reason, but they were no longer in the first blush of youth, whereas the new Princess was both young and charming, and Genji naturally caught glimpses of her, although she did what she could to keep out of his sight. He had no memory of his mother, but his youthful interest was aroused when the Dame of Staff told him how much the Princess resembled her, and he wanted always to be with her so as to contemplate her to his heart's content.

46. Members of the imperial family had no surname, but after the early ninth century some excess imperial sons were made commoners (*tadabito*) with the surname Minamoto. "Genji" means simply "a Minamoto."

47. Since the present Emperor's reign is her third, she must have been appointed by his grandfather. The word *sendai* ("previous Emperor") means an Emperor who did not abdicate but died in office, and Kōkō (reigned 884–87), who preceded Uda (Daigo's predecessor), did just this.

48. That he would provide for her himself and not count on her mother's family.

49. The principal men in her mother's family.

His Majesty, who cared so deeply for both of them, asked her not to maintain her reserve. "I am not sure why," he said, "but it seems right to me that he should take you for his mother. Do not think him uncivil. Just be kind to him. His face and eyes are so like hers that your own resemblance to her makes it look quite natural." Genji therefore lost no chance offered by the least flower or autumn leaf to let her know in his

Coming-of-age ceremony

childish way how much he liked her. His Majesty's fondness for her prompted the Kokiden Consort to fall out with her as she had done with Genji's mother, until her old animosity returned and she took an aversion to Genji as well.

Genji's looks had an indescribably fresh sweetness, one beyond even Her Highness's celebrated and, to His Majesty, peerless beauty, and this moved people to call him the Shining Lord. Since Fujitsubo made a pair with him, and His Majesty loved them both, they called her the Sunlight Princess.

His Majesty was reluctant to spoil Genji's boyish charm, but in Genji's twelfth year he gave him his coming of age, busying himself personally with the preparations and adding new embellishments to the ceremony. Lest the event seem less imposing than the one for the Heir Apparent, done some years ago in the Shishinden, and lest anything go amiss, he issued minute instructions for the banquets to be offered by the various government offices and for the things normally provided by the Court Repository and Imperial Granary, eliciting from them perfection in all they supplied.

He had his throne face east from the outer, eastern chamber of his residence, with the seats for the young man and his sponsor, the Minister, before him.[50] Genji appeared at the hour of the Monkey. His Majesty appeared to regret that Genji would never look again as he did now, with his hair tied in twin tresses[51] and his face radiant with the freshness of youth. The Lord of the Treasury and the Chamberlain[52] did their duty. The Lord of the Treasury was plainly sorry to cut off such beautiful hair, and His Majesty, who wished desperately that his Haven might have been there to see it, needed the greatest self-mastery not to weep.

All present shed tears when, after donning the headdress and withdrawing to the anteroom, Genji then reappeared in the robes of a man and stepped down into the garden to salute his Sovereign. His Majesty, of course, was still more deeply

50. He sits on a chair in the aisle room (*hisashi*)—his day room (*hiru no omashi*)—on the east side of his residence, the Seiryōden; Genji and the Minister of the Left are a beam width below him in the second aisle (*magohisashi*), an open, floored space not found in ordinary dwellings.

51. *Mizura,* hair bunches that divided the hair evenly on either side of the head. Boys wore *mizura* until they came of age.

52. The Emperor's hair was normally cut by a Chamberlain.

Twin tresses

moved, and in his mind he sadly reviewed the past, when the boy's mother had been such a comfort to him. He had feared that Genji's looks might suffer once his hair was put up, at least while he remained so young, but not at all: he only looked more devastatingly handsome than ever.

By Her Highness[53] his wife the sponsoring Minister had a beloved only daughter in whom the Heir Apparent had expressed interest, but whom after long hesitation he felt more inclined to offer to Genji instead. When he had sounded out the Emperor's own feelings on the matter, His Majesty replied, "Very well, she may be just the companion for him,[54] now that he seems no longer to have anyone looking after him"; and this had encouraged His Excellency to proceed.

Genji withdrew to the anteroom and then took the very last seat among the Princes,[55] while the assembled company enjoyed their wine. His Excellency dropped hints to him about this marriage, but Genji was at a bashful age and gave him no real response. Then a lady from the Office of Staff sent His Excellency a message from His Majesty, requiring his presence, and His Excellency obeyed forthwith.[56]

One of His Majesty's gentlewomen took the gifts from his own hands to bestow them on His Excellency. They included, according to custom, a white, oversize woman's gown[57] and a set of women's robes. On handing him the wine cup, His Majesty gave pointed expression to his feelings:

> "Into that first knot to bind up his boyish hair did you tie the wish
> that enduring happiness be theirs through ages to come?"[58]

> "In that very mood I tied his hair with great prayers bound henceforth to last,
> just as long as the dark hue of the purple does not fade,"

His Excellency replied before stepping down from the long bridge[59] to perform his obeisance. There he received a horse from the Left Imperial Stables and a perched

---

53. Genji's aunt and the Emperor's sister. Genji is about to marry a first cousin.

54. After coming of age, Genji would normally receive material support from his wife's family. The wife to so young a man was called a "companion in bed" (*soibushi*).

55. The imperial sons, who were seated in order of rank. Genji sat next to his future father-in-law, for the Minister of the Left occupied the highest seat among the nonimperial nobles.

56. The woman (a Naishi no Jō, a third-level official in the Office of Staff) probably communicated the Emperor's message through a Chamberlain. The Minister is to receive the gifts customarily awarded to the "sponsor."

57. This *uchiki*, made for presentation, would have been reduced in size for actual use.

58. This poem, like the Minister's reply, plays on the verb *musubu*, "bind up" the hair and "make" a vow (of conjugal fidelity). The cord used was purple (*murasaki*), the color of close relationship.

59. *Nagahashi*, a plank bridge between the Seiryōden and the Shishinden.

falcon from the Chamberlains' Office. The Princes and senior nobles then lined up below the steps,[60] each to receive his gift.

The delicacies in cypress boxes and the fruit baskets had been prepared for the Emperor that day by the Right Grand Controller, at His Majesty's own command. There were so many rice dumplings and so many chests of cloth,[61] certainly more than when the Heir Apparent came of age, that there was hardly any room for them all. It was in fact Genji's ceremony that displayed truly magnificent liberality.

That evening His Majesty sent Genji to the Minister's residence, where His Excellency welcomed him and gave the ensuing rite[62] a dazzling brilliance. The family found Genji preternaturally attractive, despite his still being such a child, but His Excellency's daughter, somewhat older, thought him much too young and was ashamed that he should suit her so poorly.

His Excellency enjoyed His Majesty's highest regard, and the Princess who had borne him his daughter was moreover His Majesty's full sister. Both were therefore of supreme distinction, and the Minister of the Right cut a poor figure now that Genji had joined them, too, despite being destined one day to rule the realm as the grandfather of the Heir Apparent. His Excellency had many children by various ladies. By Her Highness he had, apart from his daughter, a very young and promising Chamberlain Lieutenant[63] whom the Minister of the Right had wished to secure as a son-in-law, even though he was hardly on good terms with the young man's father, and whom he had therefore matched with his beloved fourth daughter. He treated the young man just as well as Genji's father-in-law treated Genji, and the two sons-in-law got on perfectly together.

Genji was not free to live at home,[64] for His Majesty summoned him too often. In his heart he saw only Fujitsubo's peerless beauty. Ah, he thought, she is the kind of woman I want to marry; there is no one like her! His Excellency's daughter was no doubt very pretty and well brought up, but he felt little for her because he had lost his boyish heart to someone else; indeed, he had done so to the point of pain.

Now that Genji was an adult, His Majesty no longer allowed him through Fujitsubo's curtains to be with her as before. Whenever there was music, he would accompany her koto on his flute; this and the faint sound of her voice through the blinds[65] were his consolations, and he wanted never to live anywhere but in the palace. Only after waiting upon His Majesty for five or six days might he now and again put in two or three at His Excellency's, but he was so young that the Minister did not really mind, and he treated his son-in-law generously. His Excellency selected the least ordinary among the available gentlewomen for Genji's service. These entered with him into his favorite pastimes and looked after him very well.

His residence at the palace was the Kiritsubo, as before, and His Majesty kept his mother's gentlewomen together so as to have them serve him in turn. He also decreed that the Office of Upkeep and the Office of Artisans should rebuild his mother's home, which they did beautifully. The layout of the trees and garden hills was already very pleasant, but with much bustle and noise they handsomely enlarged the lake. Genji kept wishing with many sighs that he had a true love to come and live with him there.

They say that his nickname, the Shining Lord, was given him in praise by the man from Koma.

2

HAHAKIGI

The Broom Tree

Hahakigi ("broom tree") is a plant from which brooms were indeed made and that had the poetic reputation of being visible from afar and of disappearing as one approached. As the chapter title, it alludes to an exchange of poems between Genji and a woman who has frustrated him by making herself inaccessible. He writes:

"I who never knew what it was the broom tree meant now wonder to find the road to Sonohara led me so far from my way."

She answers:

"Stricken with regret to have it known she was born in a humble home, the broom tree you briefly glimpsed fades and is soon lost to view."

RELATIONSHIP TO PRECEDING CHAPTER

The last distinct event mentioned in "The Paulownia Pavilion," Genji's marriage to Aoi, takes place when he is twelve. At the beginning of "The Broom Tree" he is seventeen. The tale says nothing about the intervening years, save for an allusion in this chapter to at least an attempted affair with Asagao.

PERSONS

Genji, a Captain in the Palace Guards, age 17

The Secretary Captain, Genji's friend and brother-in-law
(Tō no Chūjō)

The Chief Left Equerry (Sama no Kami)

The Fujiwara Aide of Ceremonial (Tō Shikibu no Jō)

His Excellency, the Minister of the Left,
Genji's father-in-law, 51 (Sadaijin)

Genji's wife, 21 (Aoi)

Chūnagon, a gentlewoman in service at His Excellency's

Nakatsukasa, a gentlewoman in service at His Excellency's

The Governor of Kii, a retainer of the Minister of the Left (Ki no Kami)

The Iyo Deputy, father of the Governor of Kii and
husband of Utsusemi (Iyo no Suke)

The daughter of His Highness of Ceremonial (Asagao)

A young woman, the stepmother of the Governor of Kii (Utsusemi)

Utsusemi's younger brother, 12 or 13 (Kogimi)

Chūjō, Utsusemi's gentlewoman

Shining Genji: the name was imposing, but not so its bearer's many deplorable lapses; and considering how quiet he kept his wanton ways, lest in reaching the ears of posterity they earn him unwelcome fame, whoever broadcast his secrets to all the world was a terrible gossip. At any rate, opinion mattered to him, and he put on such a show of seriousness that he started not one racy rumor. The Katano Lieutenant[1] would have laughed at him!

While Genji was still a Captain, he felt at home nowhere but in the palace, and he went to His Excellency's only now and then. The household sometimes suspected his thoughts of being "all in a hopeless tangle"[2] over another woman, but actually he had no taste for frivolous, trite, or impromptu affairs. No, his way was the rare amour fraught with difficulty and heartache, for he did sometimes do things he ought not to have done.

The early summer rains were falling and falling, while at the palace seclusion[3] went on and on, so that he was there even longer than usual; but although at His Excellency's there was concern and annoyance, they still sent him clothing of every kind and in the height of fashion, and his brothers-in-law spent all their time at the palace in his rooms.

One,[4] Her Highness's son and like Genji a Captain, was a particularly close friend with whom he shared music and other amusements more willingly than with anyone else. The residence of the Minister of the Right,[5] where the young man was looked after so gladly, thoroughly depressed him, and he had a marked taste for romantic forays elsewhere. Even at home he had his room done up in style, and in Genji's comings and goings he kept him such constant company that the two were together day and night for both study and music, at which he was nearly as quick as

1. Katano no Shōshō, an amorous hero whose story has not survived.
2. From *Ise monogatari* 1 (*Tales of Ise*, tenth century), an episode in which the young hero is swept away by a glimpse of two pretty sisters: "Robe dye-patterned with young *murasaki* of the Kasuga meadows, all in a hopeless tangle is my heart as well."
3. *Monoimi*, a time of confinement indoors to avoid evil influences.
4. Tō no Chūjō, the Secretary (Tō) of the Chamberlains' Office and Captain (Chūjō) of the Palace Guards.
5. Tō no Chūjō's father-in-law.

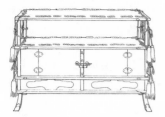

Cabinet

Genji himself, until he naturally dropped all reserve with Genji, told him whatever was on his mind, and treated him as a bosom friend.

It had been raining all the dull day long and on into an equally wet evening. There was hardly anyone in the privy chamber, and Genji's own room seemed unusually quiet as the two of them read beside the lamp. When the Secretary Captain took some letters on paper of various colors from a nearby cabinet shelf and betrayed curiosity about them, Genji demurred. "You may look at the ones that do not matter. Some could be embarrassing, though."

"But it is just the ones you think so personal and compromising that interest me," the Secretary Captain complained. "Even I get perfectly ordinary letters from ladies of one rank or another, in the course of my correspondence with them. The letters worth reading are those sent when the writer was angry, or when dusk was falling and she anxiously awaited her lover's coming."

Of course, as he well knew, Genji would hardly leave the important ones, the ones that must be kept secret, lying about on a shelf in plain view; he would have them put away somewhere, out of sight, which meant that these must be of only minor interest. "What a variety!" he exclaimed as he glanced over each, guessing at the sender and getting her now right, now quite wrong.[6] Genji was amused, but with laconic replies he managed in one way or another to put his friend off the track and to hide what he wished to hide.

"You are the one who must have a collection," Genji said. "I should like to see it. Then I would gladly open this whole cabinet to you."

"I cannot imagine that I have any you would wish to read." The Secretary Captain then took this occasion to observe, "I have finally realized how rarely you will find a flawless woman, one who is simply perfect. No doubt there are many who seem quite promising, write a flowing hand, give you back a perfectly acceptable poem, and all in all do credit enough to the rank they have to uphold, but you know, if you insist on any particular quality, you seldom find one who will do. Each one is all too pleased with her own accomplishments, runs others down, and so on. While a girl is under the eye of her adoring parents and living a sheltered life bright with future promise, it seems men have only to hear of some little talent of hers to be attracted. As long as she is pretty and innocent, and young enough to have nothing else on her mind, she may well put her heart into learning a pastime that she has seen others enjoy, and in fact she may become quite good at it. And when those who know her[7] disguise her weaknesses and advertise whatever passable qualities she may have so as to present them in the best light, how could anyone think ill of her, having no reason to suspect her of being other than she seems? But when you look further to see whether it is all true, I am sure you can only end up disappointed."

6. Letters like these were not signed.
7. Her gentlewomen.

He sighed portentously, whereupon Genji, who seemed to have reached on his own at least some of the same conclusions, asked with a smile, "But do you suppose any girl could have *nothing* to recommend her?"

"Who would be fool enough to be taken in by one as hopeless as that? I am sure that the utter failure with nothing to commend her and the one so superior as to be a wonder are equally rare. When a girl is highborn,[8] everyone[9] pampers her and a lot about her remains hidden, so that she naturally seems a paragon. Those of middle birth[10] are the ones among whom you can see what a girl really has to offer and find ways to distinguish one from another. As for the lowborn,[11] they hardly matter."

His apparent familiarity with his subject aroused Genji's curiosity. "I wonder about these levels of yours, though—the high, the middle, and the low. How can you tell who belongs to which? Some are born high and yet fall and sink to become nobodies, while common gentlemen[12] rise to become senior nobles, pride themselves on the way they do up their houses, and insist on conceding nothing to anyone. How can you draw the line between these two?"

Just then the Chief Left Equerry and the Fujiwara Aide of Ceremonial came in to join the seclusion. The Secretary Captain welcomed both as enterprising lovers as well as great talkers, and they went straight into a heated discussion of how to tell women of one level from those of another. They told some astonishing stories.

The Secretary Captain declared, "On the subject of those who rise high without being born to it, society does not actually feel quite the same about them, despite their rank, while as for those who once stood high but now lack means, times turn bad, and they decline until they have nothing left but their pride and suffer endless misfortune. Either group, I think, belongs to the middle grade.

"Even among those known as Governors, whose function it is to administer the provinces and whose grade is certainly fixed, there are actually different levels, and these days you can find considerable figures among them. What is a pleasure to see, more so than any mediocre senior noble, is a man of the fourth rank, qualified for Consultant,[13] with a solid reputation, from no unworthy stock, and with an easy and confident manner. His house boasts every luxury, and all those daughters of his, showered with love and dazzling wealth, grow up in grand style. Girls like that often do better in palace service than you might imagine."

"I suppose the thing is to keep an eye out for a father with means," Genji said, smiling, and the Secretary Captain grumbled, "I do not know how you can say that. It does not sound like you at all!"

---

8. *Shina takaku*, "born to a high standing in society." The notion of *shina* includes both formal rank and the family's general social distinction.

9. As before, the gentlewomen around her: talented gentlewomen devote themselves to developing whatever capacity she may have.

10. *Naka no shina*, including particularly the daughters of privy gentlemen or of provincial Governors, i.e., of gentlemen of the fourth or fifth rank.

11. *Shimo no kizami to iū kiwa*, presumably daughters of men in the lower ranks of the official bureaucracy. Such women were beneath the notice of young men like these.

12. *Naobito*, gentlemen of the fourth or fifth rank.

13. *Hisangi*, a man of the fourth rank, either a past Consultant (Sangi) or qualified for this office. Consultant (there were eight) was a distinguished appointment, below only Counselor and Minister.

"When a girl's rank at birth and her reputation agree," the Chief Equerry observed, "when she commands general respect but is still disappointing in her person and her behavior, you obviously cannot help wondering sadly why she turned out like that. Of course, when her personal qualities match her rank, you take them for granted and are not surprised. The highest of the high, though, are beyond my ken, and I had better say nothing about them.

"Anyway, the really fascinating girl is the one of whom no one has ever heard, the strangely appealing one who lives by herself, hidden away in some ruinous, overgrown old house; because, never having expected anyone like her, you wonder what she is doing there and cannot help wanting to know her better. Her father is a miserable, fat old man, her brother's face is none too prepossessing either, and there she is in the women's quarters, far at the back, where you expect nothing unusual: proud, spirited, and giving a touch of distinction to everything she does. Even if she has her limits after all, how could a surprise like that fail to delight anyone? Compared to someone truly flawless, she of course falls short, but for what she is, she is hard to let go." He glanced at the Aide of Ceremonial, who seemed to take this as a reference to his own well-regarded sisters, since he kept his peace.

Oh, come now, Genji thought, it is rare enough to find anyone like that among the highborn! Over soft, layered white gowns he had on only a dress cloak, unlaced at the neck,[14] and, lying there in the lamplight, against a pillar, he looked so beautiful that one could have wished him a woman. For him, the highest of the high seemed hardly good enough.

They talked on about one woman and another until the Chief Equerry remarked, "Many do very well for an affair, but when you are choosing your own for good, you may not easily find what you want. It is probably just as difficult to find a truly capable man to uphold the realm in His Majesty's service, but however demanding that sort of post may be, it takes more than one or two to govern, and that is why those above are assisted by those below and why inferiors obey their superiors and defer willingly to them. Think of the one and only who is to run your little household, and you realize how many important things there are to be done right. Even granting that having this she is bound to lack that, and that you have to take the good with the bad, very few can manage honorably, and so even if I do not recommend pursuing women forever in order to compare them all, I can hardly blame the man who is starting out to make his choice and who, to help himself make up his mind, looks around a little to find one he really likes—one who does not need him to tell her how to do every little thing. Things may not always work out perfectly, but the man who cannot bring himself to abandon a woman once he has made her his own deserves respect, and his constancy is also a credit to the woman with whom he keeps faith. It is true, though, that my own experience of couples has shown me no especially admirable or inspiring examples. And you young lords[15] who pick and choose among the most exalted, what height of perfection does it take to gain your approval?

14. His white, unstarched gowns are probably two, and his summer dress cloak (nōshi) is probably thin enough to be nearly transparent. He seems not to have on its normal complement, gathered trousers (sashinuki).

15. Genji and Tō no Chūjō (the Secretary Captain).

"As long as a girl has looks and youth enough, she avoids anything that might soil her name. Even when composing a letter, she takes her time to choose her words and writes in ink faint enough to leave you bemused and longing for something clearer; then, when at last you get near enough to catch her faint voice, she speaks under her breath, says next to nothing, and proves to be an expert at keeping herself hidden away. Take this for sweetly feminine wiles, and passion will lure you into playing up to her, at which point she turns coy. This, I think, is the worst flaw a girl can have.

Hair tucked behind the ears

"A wife's main duty is to look after her husband, so it seems to me that one can do quite well without her being too sensitive, ever so delicate about the least thing, and all too fond of being amused. On the other hand, with a dutiful, frumpish housewife who keeps her sidelocks tucked behind her ears and does nothing but housework, the husband who leaves in the morning and comes home at night, and who can hardly turn to strangers to chat about how so-and-so is getting on in public or private or about whatever, good or bad, may have happened to strike him and is entitled to expect some understanding from the woman who shares his life, finds instead, when he feels like discussing with her the things that have made him laugh or cry, or perhaps have inflamed him with righteous indignation and are now demanding an outlet, that all he can do is avert his eyes, and that when he then betrays private mirth or heaves a sad sigh, she just looks up at him blankly and asks, 'What is it, dear?' How could he not wish himself elsewhere? It is probably not a bad idea to take a wholly childlike, tractable wife and form her yourself as well as you can. She may not have your full confidence, but you will know your training has made a difference. Certainly, as long as you actually have her with you, you can let her pretty ways persuade you to overlook her lapses; but you will still regret her incompetence if, when you are away, you send her word about something practical or amusing that needs doing, and her response shows that she knows nothing about it and understands nothing either. Sometimes a wife who is not especially sweet or friendly does very well when you actually need her." The Chief Equerry's far-ranging discussion of his topic yielded no conclusion but a deep sigh.

"In the end, I suppose," he went on, "one should settle on someone wholly dependable, quiet, and steady, as long as there is nothing especially wrong with her, and never mind rank or looks. If beyond that she has any wit or accomplishment, simply be grateful, and if she lacks anything in particular, by no means seek to have her acquire it. Provided she is distinctly trustworthy and forgiving, you know, she will gain a more superficially feminine appeal all on her own.

"A woman may behave with comely modesty, put up with things that deserve reproof as though she did not even notice them and, in a word, affect prim detachment, until something is too much for her after all, and off she goes to hide herself away in a mountain village or on a deserted stretch of shore, leaving behind a shattering letter, a heartrending poem, and a token to remember her by. The gentlewomen used to read me stories like that when I was a boy. They upset me a lot—in fact, they seemed so tragic that I cried—but now that sort of thing strikes me as foolish and a bit of an act. Say our heroine *has* a legitimate grievance; she is still abandoning a husband who no doubt is very fond of her and running off as though she knew nothing of his feelings, and all she gains from upsetting him and testing his affection is lifelong regret. It is simply stupid.

"People keep telling her admiringly how right she was to act, until she is swept away, and all at once there she is, a nun. When she makes up her mind to do it, she is perfectly calm and cannot imagine looking back on her old life. 'Oh dear, I am so sorry,' all those who know her say when they come to call, 'I had no idea you felt so deeply about it.' Meanwhile, the husband she never really disliked bursts into tears when he learns of all this, prompting her staff and her old women to say, 'There, your husband cares for you after all, and now look what you have done!' She puts her hand to the hair at her forehead and despairs to find it so short. Self-control fails, she begins to cry, and she breaks down again and again each time she has reason to feel a new pang of regret, until the Buddha himself can only be disappointed with her. As far as I can see, halfhearted refuge in religion is more likely to get you lost in an evil rebirth than staying on in the mire of this world.

"Suppose this couple have strong enough karma between them that the husband finds and claims his wife before she has made herself into a nun: even so, once they are together again each is bound to worry about what the other may be up to next, despite the renewed affection that may come from their having lived through so much. Besides, it is silly for a wife to quarrel with a husband who is inclined to look elsewhere. Even if he is, she can always trust him to remain her husband as long as his first feeling for her still means anything to him, whereas an outburst like that may alienate him for good. She should always be tactful, hinting when she has cause to be angry with him that, yes, she knows, and bringing the issue up gently when she might well quarrel with him instead, because that will only make him like her better. Most of the time it is the wife's attitude that helps her husband's fancies to pass. It might seem endearingly sweet of her to be wholly permissive and to let him get away with everything, but that will only make her seem not to deserve his respect. It is too bad when, as they say, an unmoored boat just drifts away.[16] Do you not agree?"

The Secretary Captain nodded. "It is bound to be particularly difficult when one of a couple suspects the other, someone otherwise loved and cherished, of infidelity; but although the injured party, being blameless, may well then be quite prepared to overlook the matter, things may not go so easily. At any rate, the best remedy when something comes between a couple is surely patience." This remark, he felt, applied particularly well to his own sister,[17] and he was therefore both annoyed and disappointed that Genji was dozing and had nothing to add.

Having appointed himself the arbiter in these matters, the Chief Equerry con-

16. An image from a poem on marriage by Bai Juyi (*Hakushi monjū* 3564).
17. Aoi, Genji's wife.

tinued his exposition of them while the Secretary Captain, who was eager to hear him out, chimed in earnestly.

"Think of all this in terms of the arts," the Chief Equerry intoned. "Take, for example, the joiner who makes what he pleases from wood. He may turn out briefly amusing things, according to no set pattern and for only passing, minor uses—strikingly ingenious pieces that he keeps nicely attuned to fashion so that they pleasantly catch the eye; and yet one still distinguishes him easily from the true master who works with success in recognized forms, producing furnishings prized for being exactly right.

"Or take another example. By the time a skilled artist in the Office of Painting is deemed qualified to design a whole work, it is not easy to tell at a glance whether he is better or worse than another. Startling renderings of what no eye can see—things like Mount Hōrai, raging leviathans amid stormy seas, the fierce beasts of China, or the faces of invisible demons[18]—do indeed amaze the viewer, because they are convincing even though they resemble nothing real. Yet quite commonplace mountains and streams, the everyday shapes of houses, all looking just as one knows them to be and rendered as peaceful, welcoming forms mingling in harmony with gently sloping hills, thickly wooded, folded range upon wild range, and, in the foreground, a fenced garden: with such subjects as these, and there are many, the greater artist succeeds brilliantly in conception and technique, while the lesser one fails.

"In the same way, handwriting without depth may display a lengthened stroke here and there and generally claim one's attention until at first glance it appears impressively skilled, but although truly fine writing may lack superficial appeal, a second look at the two together will show how much closer it is to what writing should be. That is the way it is in every field of endeavor, however minor. So you see, I have no faith in the obvious show of affection that a woman may sometimes put on. And I shall tell you how I learned this, though I am afraid the story is a little risqué."

He moved closer to Genji, who woke up, while the Secretary Captain sat reverently facing him, chin in hand. The Chief Equerry might have been a preacher preparing to reveal the truth of existence, which was certainly amusing; but by now these young men were eager to share the most intimate moments of their lives.

"Long ago," he began, "when I was still very young, there was someone who meant a great deal to me. She was no great beauty, as I told you, and I, being young and inclined to explore, had no intention of staying with her forever, because although she was home to me, I felt I could do better, and so now and again I amused myself elsewhere. This drove her to a pitch of jealousy that I did not like at all, and I only wished she would stop and be more patient; but instead her violent suspicions became such a nuisance that I often found myself wondering why she was so intent on keeping me, since I was really no great prize. I felt sorry for her, though, and I began to mend my ways after all.

"It was like her to pour all her limited talent into accomplishing somehow for

18. Motifs from Chinese-style painting. Hōrai (Chinese Penglai) is a fabulous island inhabited by immortal beings.

her husband things that really were beyond her and to be so cautious about betraying her shortcomings to her own disadvantage that she looked after me very well indeed, so as to give me no reason for ever being dissatisfied with her. I had thought her headstrong, but she did as I asked and humored me quite well; and lest her lack of looks offend me, she made herself as presentable as she could and hid shyly from strangers for fear of embarrassing me, meanwhile remaining so attentive that, as we went on living together, I found myself well pleased, except for this one detestable failing of hers, which she could not control.

"Then I thought to myself, She seems desperately eager to please: well, I must teach her a lesson. I shall threaten her, cure her a little of this failing, and curb her tongue. I assumed that as long as she really was that devoted, she would mend her ways if I put on a show of being fed up and eager to let her go. I purposely acted cold and distant, and when she grew angry and accusing, as she always did, I said, 'If you must carry on this way, never mind the strength of the bond between us, I shall leave and never come back. If you want to get rid of me, by all means keep up these absurd suspicions of yours. If you want me to stay with you forever, you will have to be patient and put up with things that may offend you, and if you change your attitude, I will like you very well. Once I am properly established and carry some weight in the world, you will have no rival.'[19]

"I was pleased with my sermon, but when I boldly began to elaborate, she gave me a thin smile and had the effrontery to say, 'I do not in the least mind seeing you through these years when you have little credit or standing, or waiting until you matter. No, that does not bother me at all. But I do hate the thought of spending year after year putting up with your cruelty in the vain hope that you will reform, and so I suppose it is time for us to part.'

"Now I was really angry, and I began saying awful things that she could hardly accept. Instead, she pulled one of my fingers to her and bit it, at which I flew into a rage. 'I can't go out in society wounded like this!' I roared. 'My office, my rank of which you seem to think so little—just how, my fine lady, do you expect me now to hold my head up at all? As far as I can see, all that is left for me is to leave the world!' and so on.

" 'Very well,' I went on, 'as of today you and I are finished,' and I started to leave, hurt finger crooked. I said,

'Fingers crooked to count the many times you and I have been together
show that this outrage of yours is certainly not the first.[20]

You can hardly hold it against me!'

"Sure enough, she burst into tears and retorted,

'Talk of outrages: when in my most private thoughts I count up your own,
I believe this time at last I must take my hand from yours.'

19. "I shall acknowledge you as my wife."
20. In Japan one crooks the fingers to count. This poem and the reply rely on several wordplays.

"She and I had had a good fight, and although I still did not actually mean to leave her, I wandered here and there for several days without sending her a line. It was not until late one miserably sleety night, after the rehearsal for the Special Kamo Festival,[21] as we were all leaving the palace, that I realized I had no other home to go to than hers. The thought of spending the night at the palace did not appeal to me at all, and I knew how cold the company of some coy woman might be; so off I went, by way of just looking in on her to sound out her feelings, brushing away the snow and biting my nails with embarrassment, but still assuming that on a night like this she would welcome me after all.

"Her dimmed lamp was turned to the wall; a thick, comfortable robe was warming over a large censer frame; all the curtains you would expect to find raised were up; and everything looked as though this was the night when she was expecting me back. Well, well! I thought, very pleased, until I noticed that she herself was not there. I saw only her usual women, who answered that at dark she had moved to her parents' house. She had left no touching poem, no encouraging note, nor any evidence whatever of thoughtfulness or consideration. I felt betrayed, and although I could not really believe that her merciless complaining had been meant only to make me hate her, I was annoyed enough to entertain the idea. Still, what she had left for me to wear was even more beautifully made than before, and its colors were even more pleasing. Even after I stormed out of the house, she had still been looking out for my every need.

"Nonetheless, I could not imagine her to be serious about giving me up, and I did my best to mend things with her, but while she did not exactly reject me, did not pester me by going into hiding, and sent me tactfully worded answers, her attitude amounted to saying, 'I cannot go on with you as you have been. I will not have you back unless you reform.' I still did not believe she would let me go, though, and to teach her a lesson I said nothing about wanting to change. Instead, I put on a show of headstrong independence. She was so hurt that she died. That taught me that these things are no joke.

"I remember her as the model of a dependable wife. It was well worth discussing anything with her, whether a passing fancy or something important. At dyeing cloth she could have been called a Tatsuta Lady, at sewing she ranked with Tanabata,[22] and her skill at both made her a wonder." The Chief Equerry remembered her with feeling.

"I would have taken her faithfulness over her wonderful sewing," the Secretary Captain remarked to lighten the conversation. "I have no doubt her marvelous dyeing was a real prize, though. The simplest blossoms or autumn leaves are dull and dreary when their colors fail to suit the season. That is why choosing a wife is so very hard."

21. *Kamo no rinji matsuri*, on the last day of the Bird in the eleventh month. Music was performed for the deity by the palace musicians, and the rehearsal was held in the palace.

22. Tatsuta Hime, the "Tatsuta Lady," was associated with the beauty of colored autumn leaves and was therefore the patron goddess of dyeing. Tanabata, the Weaver Star who meets the Herdboy Star, her celestial lover, once a year on the night of the Tanabata Festival (the seventh day of the seventh month), was a patron of sewing, among other things.

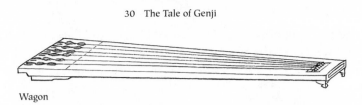

Wagon

"Anyway," the Chief Equerry went on, "I was visiting at the same time a very gifted woman who made poems with genuine wit and grace, wrote a beautiful running hand, had a lovely touch on the koto, and had a way with everything she did. And since there was nothing wrong with her looks either, I kept my scold to feel at home with and secretly went on seeing this other woman until I was quite attached to her. After the one I told you about had died, I was of course very sorry, but now that was behind me, and I saw the other one often until I noticed, as I had not before, that she was inclined to be vain and flirtatious, and so, to my mind, not to be trusted. After that I visited her less often, and meanwhile I discovered that secretly she had another lover.

"One beautifully moonlit night in the tenth month I was withdrawing from the palace when one of the privy gentlemen joined me in my carriage. I myself meant to spend the night at the Grand Counselor's,[23] but the fellow insisted he was concerned about a house where someone was expecting him that very evening, and the place was just on the way to where *she* lived. You could see the lake through a break in the garden wall, and it seemed a shame to go straight past a house favored even by the moon,[24] so I got out as well.

"He must have arranged it all with her beforehand, because he was excited when he sat down on the veranda, I suppose it was, of the gallery near the gate. For some time he watched the moon. The chrysanthemums had all turned very nicely,[25] and the autumn leaves flitting by on the wind were really very pretty. Taking a flute from the fold of his robe, he began to play and to sing snatches of 'You will have shade,'[26] and so on, while she accompanied him expertly on a fine-toned *wagon* that she had all ready and tuned. The two of them were not at all bad. The *richi* mode, softly played by a woman from behind blinds,[27] sounded like the height of style, and in the brilliant moonlight the effect was very pleasant indeed.

"The delighted fellow moved right up to her blinds. 'No footsteps seem to have disturbed the fallen leaves in your garden,' he teased her,[28] and then, picking a chrysanthemum,

> 'With all the beauty of a house filled with music and a lovely moon,
> have you yet successfully played to catch that cruel man?

---

23. Probably his father.
24. The moon is reflected in the garden lake.
25. Frost-withered chrysanthemums were prized.
26. A *saibara* folk song: "You must stop at the Asukai spring, for you will have shade, the water is cool, the grazing is of the best . . ." The singer hints that he hopes to spend the night.
27. The blinds hang between her room and the veranda. The *wagon* ("Japanese koto") has six strings, and the *richi* mode was rather "minor" in feeling.
28. "Dear me, you seem to be all alone this evening."

I would never have thought it of you! Do play on, though. You must not be bashful, now that you have an audience eager for more!'

"To all this shameless banter she replied archly,

> 'Why, I have no words to play to keep by my side music of a flute
> that joins in such harmonies with the wild and wandering wind.'[29]

"Little knowing how distasteful a show she was putting on, she next tuned a *sō no koto* to the *banshiki* mode and played away in the best modern style, and very nicely, too, but I was thoroughly put off. The come-hither ways of a gentlewoman you meet now and again may have their charm for as long as you continue to see her, but when you are calling on someone you do not mean to forget, even if you do not do so all that often, anything silly or loose about her can put you off, and that is why I made that night my excuse to end it.

"Looking back on those two experiences, I note that even then, young as I was, I found that sort of uncalled-for forwardness strange and upsetting. In the future I will no doubt feel that way even more. Perhaps your lordships take pleasure only in the tender, willing fragility of the dewdrop fated to fall from the plucked flower or in the hail that melts when gathered from the gleaming leaf,[30] but I know you will understand me once you have seen seven more years pass by.[31] Please take my humble advice and beware of the pliant, easy woman. Any slip of hers can make her husband look a fool."

The Secretary Captain nodded as usual, while Genji smiled wryly in seeming agreement. "From what you say, you made a fine spectacle of yourself both times!" he remarked. They all laughed.

"I will tell you a fool's tale," the Secretary Captain said.[32] "I had secretly begun seeing a woman who struck me as well worth the trouble, and although I assumed the affair would not last, the more I knew her, the more attached to her I became. Not that I necessarily visited her often, but I never forgot her, and things went on long enough that I saw she trusted me. There were of course times when even I supposed she might be jealous, but she seemed to notice nothing. She never complained about how seldom I came, even when it had been ages; instead she acted just as though I were setting out from her house every morning and coming home every evening. This touched me so much that I promised never to leave her. She had no parents, which made her life difficult, and it was quite endearing, the way she showed me now and again that for her I was indeed the one.

"Once, when I had not seen her for a long time (she was so quiet that I rather took her for granted), my wife, as I found out only later, managed to send her some

29. The wind refers with coquettish modesty to her own playing.

30. Both similes evoke a young woman ready at a touch to swoon into a suitor's arms. The "flower" is the poetic *hagi*, whose long, drooping fronds bloom deep pink, violet, or white in autumn; while the "gleaming leaf" is *tamazasa*, a species of "dwarf bamboo." The mention of *hagi* refers to *Kokinshū* 223.

31. He is apparently seven years older than Genji. Although he started out talking to Tō no Chūjō, he must have begun addressing the higher-ranking Genji when Genji woke up.

32. Commentators disagree over whether the "fool" (*shiremono*) is Tō no Chūjō or the woman.

veiled but extremely unpleasant threats. I had never imagined anything like that, and at heart I had not forgotten her, but she took it hard because she had had only silence from me so long; and what with her painful circumstances and, you see, the child she had as well, she finally resorted to sending me a pink—" He was almost in tears.

"But what did her letter say?" Genji asked.

"Oh, you know, nothing very much, really:

> 'Yes, ruin has come to the mountain rustic's hedge, but now and again
> O let your compassion touch this little pink with fresh dew!'[33]

"That reminder brought me straight to her. She was as open and trusting with me as ever, but her expression was very sad, and as she sat in her poor house, gazing out over the dewy garden and crying in concert with the crickets' lament, I felt as though I must be living in some old tale. I answered,

> 'I could never choose one from the many colors blooming so gaily,
> yet the gillyflower I feel is the fairest of them all.'[34]

I set aside the 'pink' for the time being, so as first to soothe her mother's feelings with 'No speck of dust' and so on. She replied mildly,

> 'To a gillyflower brushing a deserted bed with her dewy sleeves,
> autumn has come all too soon, and the sorrows of its storms.'[35]

"I saw no sign that she was seriously angry with me, because even when she cried, she shyly hid her tears from me as well as she could, and her keen reluctance to let me see she knew I had neglected her made me so sure all was well that I again stayed away for a long time, during which she vanished without a trace. Life can hardly be treating her kindly if she is still alive. If she had just clung to me in any obvious way, while I loved her, I would never have allowed her to disappear as she did. Instead of neglecting her, I would have looked after her well and gone on seeing her indefinitely. The "little pink" was very sweet, and I wish I could somehow find her, but so far I have not come across a single clue.

"This is a small illustration of just what you were talking about. She seemed so serene that I never knew she was hurt, and my lasting feeling for her went completely to waste. Even now, when I am beginning to forget her, she probably still

33. "Rustic boor that I am, I know that I hardly deserve your favor, but do at least sometimes remember our dear child." The "little pink" (*Yamato nadeshiko*) is the future Tamakazura. *Kokinshū* 695: "Ah, how I miss her, and how I long to see her, the Yamato pink blooming in the rustic hedge!"

34. "You are the only one I really care for." The *tokonatsu* ("gillyflower") and the *nadeshiko* ("pink") are the same flower, but the words have different associations. *Nadeshiko* refers to the child, *tokonatsu* to the mother. This is partly because of a play on *toko* (the "sleeping place" of lovers) in *Kokinshū* 167, by Ōshikōchi no Mitsune, to which Tō no Chūjō alludes a line or two later: "No speck of dust will I allow to soil this bed / gillyflower, abloom since you and I first lay down together."

35. The gillyflower's (lady's) sleeves are wet with tears; "brushing a deserted bed" refers to "No speck of dust will I allow . . ." in *Kokinshū* 167, Tō no Chūjō's source poem. The autumn storms are probably Tō no Chūjō's indifference and his wife's threats.

thinks of me and has evenings when she burns with regret, although she has no one but herself to blame. She is a perfect example of the woman you cannot keep long and cannot actually depend on.

"All in all, the scold, though not easily forgotten, was so demanding to live with that anyone would probably have tired of her; the ever-so-clever woman with her koto music was guilty of sheer wantonness; and there is every reason, too, to doubt the fragile one I just told you about.[36] And so, in the end, it is simply impossible to choose one woman over another. That is how it is with them: each is bound to be trying, one way or another. Where will you find the one who has all the qualities we have been talking about and none of the faults? Set your heart on Kichijōten[37] herself, and you will find her so pious and stuffy, you will still be sorry!" They all laughed.

"Come," the Secretary Captain urged the Aide of Ceremonial, "you must have a good story. Let us hear it!"

"How could your lordships take an interest in anything that a nobody like me might have to say?" But the Secretary Captain only muttered, "Come, come," and kept at him until after due thought he began. "I was still a student at the Academy[38] when I knew a brilliant woman. Like the one the Chief Equerry wanted, you could talk over public affairs with her, her grasp of how to live life was penetrating, and on any topic her daunting learning simply left nothing further to add.

"It all started when I was visiting a certain scholar's home to pursue my studies. Having gathered that he had several daughters, I seized a chance to make this one's acquaintance, which he had no sooner discovered than in he came, bearing wine cups and declaiming insinuatingly, 'Hark while I sing of two roads in life . . .'[39] I had no such wish, but I still managed somehow to go on seeing her, in order not to offend him.

"She was very good to me. Even while we lay awake at night, she would pursue my edification or instruct me in matters beneficial to a man in government service, and no note from her was ever marred by a single one of those *kana* letters, being couched in language of exemplary formality.[40] What with all this I could not have left her, because it was she who taught me how to piece together broken-backed Chinese poems and such,[41] and for that I remain eternally grateful. As to making her my dear wife, however, a dunce like me could only have been embarrassed to have her witness his bumbling efforts. Your lordships undoubtedly need that sort of conjugal tutelage even less than I did.[42] All this was foolish of me, I

36. He surmises that her disappearance might have involved another man.
37. A seductively ample goddess of good fortune, probably Indian in origin. Her image was common in Buddhist temples, where tales were told about monks falling in love with her.
38. *Daigaku*, largely a school for training lower-ranking officials. The students studied Chinese poetry, philosophy, and history.
39. A homily on marriage from a poem by Bai Juyi (*Hakushi monjū* 0075). The wine cups, too, are in the poem, which stresses the wisdom of taking a bride from a poor home.
40. Women wrote mainly in the phonetic *kana* script, men in more or less accomplished Chinese. This avoidance of *kana* (her letters are entirely in Chinese characters) creates a strangely formal, masculine effect.
41. "Broken-backed" (*koshi ore*) is a term of poetic criticism.
42. Genji and Tō no Chūjō rank so high that they need no accomplishment to get ahead.

agree, and I should have forgone my involvement with her, but sometimes destiny just draws you on. I suppose the men are really the foolish ones."

"But what an extraordinary woman!" The Secretary Captain wanted to get him to finish. The Aide of Ceremonial knew he would have to, but he still wrinkled up his nose before complying.

"Well, I had not been to see her for a long time when for some reason I went again. She was not in her usual room; instead she spoke to me through an absurd screen. Is she jealous, then? I wondered, at once amused by this nonsense and perfectly conscious that this might be just the chance I was looking for. But no, my paragon of learning was not one to indulge in frivolous complaints. She knew the world and its ways too well to be upset with me. Instead she briskly announced, 'Having lately been prostrate with a most vexing indisposition, I have for medicinal purposes been ingesting *Allium sativum*,[43] and my breath, I fear, is too noxious to allow me to entertain you in my normal fashion. However, while I cannot address you face-to-face, I hope that you will communicate to me any services you may wish me to perform on your behalf.'

"It was an imposing oration. What could I possibly answer? I just said, 'Very well,' got up, and started out. I suppose she had been hoping for something better, because she called after me, 'Do return when the odor has abated!' I hated to pretend I had not heard her, but this was no time to waver, and besides, the smell really was rather overpowering, so in desperation I glanced back at her and replied,

> 'When the spider's ways this evening gave fair warning I would soon arrive,
>   how strange of you to tell me, Come after my garlic days![44]

What kind of excuse is that?'

"I fled once the words were out, only to hear behind me,

> 'If I meant to you enough that you came to me each and every night,
>   Why should my garlic days so offend your daintiness?'

Oh, yes, she was very quick with her tongue," the Aide calmly concluded.

The appalled young gentlemen assumed that he must have made up his story, and they burst into laughter. "There cannot be any such woman!" cried the Secretary Captain. "You might as well have made friends with a demon. It is too weird!" He snapped his fingers[45] and glared at the Aide in mute outrage. "Come," he finally insisted, "you will have to do better!"

However, the Aide stood fast. "How do you expect me to improve on that?" he said.

"I cannot stand the way mediocrities, men or women, so long to show off all the tiny knowledge they may possess," the Chief Equerry put in. "There is nothing

43. Garlic.
44. His sally and her retort both play on *biru* ("garlic") and *biruma* ("daytime"). Poetic lore had it that a woman could tell whether her lover was coming by watching a spider's behavior.
45. A gesture of censure or irritation.

at all attractive about having absorbed weighty stuff like the Three Histories and the Five Classics, and besides, why should anyone, just because she is a woman, be completely ignorant of what matters in this world, public or private? A woman with any mind at all is bound to retain many things, even if she does not actually study. So she writes cursive Chinese characters after all and crams her letters more than half full of them, even ones to other women, where they are hopelessly out of place, and you think, Oh no! If only she could be more feminine! She may not have meant it that way, but the letter still ends up being read to her correspondent in a stiff, formal tone, and it sounds as though that was what she had meant all along. A lot of senior gentlewomen do that sort of thing, you know.

"The woman out to make poetry becomes so keen on it that she stuffs her very first line with allusions to great works from the past, until it is a real nuisance to get a poem from her when you have other things on your mind. You cannot very well not reply, and you look bad if circumstances at the moment prevent you from doing so.

"Take the festivals, for example. Say it is the morning of the Sweet Flag Festival. You are off to the palace in such a rush that everything is a blur, and she presents you with one of her efforts, quivering with incredible wordplays;[46] or it is time for the Chrysanthemum Festival, you are racking your brains to work out a tricky Chinese poem, and here comes a lament from her, full of 'chrysanthemum dew'[47] and, as usual, quite out of place. At other times, too, her way of sending you out of season a poem that afterward you might admit is not actually at all bad, without pausing to think that you may be unable even to give it a glance, can hardly be called very bright. She would do better to refrain from showing off her wit and taste whenever her failure to grasp your circumstances leaves you wondering why she had to do it, or cursing the fix she has put you in. A woman should feign ignorance of what she knows and, when she wants to speak on a subject, leave some things out."

Meanwhile Genji was absorbed in meditation on one lady alone.[48] By the standard of this evening's discussion she had neither too little nor too much of any quality at all, and this thought filled him with wonder and a desperate longing.

The debate reached no conclusion and lapsed at last into disjointed gossip that the young men kept up until dawn.

The weather today was clear at last. Genji went straight to His Excellency's, fearing that so long a seclusion at the palace might have displeased his father-in-law. The look of the place and the manner of the lady there were admirably distinguished, for neither could be faulted in any way, and it seemed to Genji that she should be the ideal wife singled out as a treasure by his friends the evening before, but in fact he found such perfection too oppressive and intimidating for comfort.

He amused himself chatting with such particularly worthwhile young gentlewomen as Chūnagon and Nakatsukasa, who were delighted to see him, loosely clothed as he was in the heat. His Excellency then appeared and talked with his

46. Poems for this occasion are full of plays on *ayame* ("sweet flag") and other words associated with the event, and so at this point is the Chief Equerry's own speech.

47. Ladies moistened a bit of chrysanthemum-patterned brocade with dew from chrysanthemum flowers, rubbed their cheeks with it to smooth the wrinkles of age (since chrysanthemum dew conferred immortal youth), and composed poems lamenting the sorrows of growing old.

48. Fujitsubo.

Standing curtain

son-in-law through a standing curtain, since Genji was not presentable, while Genji reclined on an armrest, making wry faces and muttering, "Isn't it hot enough for him?" "Hush!" he added when the women laughed. He was the picture of carefree ease.

At dark a woman remarked to him, "Tonight the Mid-God has closed this direction from the palace."

"That is right, my lord, this is a direction you would normally shun."[49]

"But Nijō[50] is in the same direction! How am I to avoid it? Besides, I am exhausted." Genji lay down to sleep.

"Oh, no, my lord, you must not!"

"The Governor of Kii, who is in His Excellency's service, lives in a house by the Nakagawa,[51] and the place is nice and cool—he recently diverted the stream through his property."

"That should do very well," Genji answered. "I am so tired, I do not care where it is, as long as they will let my ox in through the gate."[52]

There must have been many other houses where he could have gone discreetly to avoid that direction, but having only just arrived at his father-in-law's after a long absence, he did not wish to seek another lady's company in order to do so.

Kii bowed to Genji's command, but he groaned as he withdrew. "A difficulty at the Iyo Deputy's house has obliged all his women to move in with me," he said, "and my little place is so crowded that I am afraid he may suffer some affront to his dignity."

Genji heard him. "I shall be much happier to have them near me. I would be afraid to spend the night away from home without women. Just put me behind their standing curtains."

"That is right. I expect his house will do beautifully," a gentlewoman chimed in, and a runner was sent to announce Genji's arrival. Genji hurried off so secretly, to so purposely discreet a destination, that he kept his departure from his father-in-law and took with him only his closest companions.

---

49. The Mid-God (Nakagami), one of the deities of yin-yang lore, moved in a sixty-day cycle. Having spent the first sixteen days in the heavens, the deity descended to earth and circled the compass, spending five or six days in each of the eight directions. One shunned (*imu*) travel in a direction "blocked" (*futagaru*) by this deity. Genji's planned destination violates this taboo, and he must now "evade" (*tagau*) the "blocked" direction by taking refuge elsewhere, in another direction from his point of departure (the palace).

50. Genji's residence, on "Second Avenue."

51. A stream, now gone, in the northeastern part of the city.

52. Only a great lord could have had his ox carriage driven in through someone's gate.

"This is so sudden!" Kii's house-hold complained, but Genji's entourage ignored them. His men had the eastern aisle of the main house swept, aired, and made ready as well as they could.

The stream was very prettily done in its way.[53] There was a brushwood fence, as in the country, and the garden was carefully planted. The breeze was cool, insects were singing here and there, and fireflies

Lattice shutters

were flitting in all directions. The place was delightful. Genji's companions sat drinking wine and peering down at the stream that emerged from beneath the bridgeway.[54] While his host went darting about in search of refreshments,[55] Genji relaxed and gazed out into the night, remembering what he had heard the evening before about the middle class of women and reflecting that this must be the kind of place where such women lived.

He had noted a rumor that the young woman here[56] was proud, and he was sufficiently curious about her to listen until he detected telltale sounds to the west: the rustling of silks and the pleasant voices of young women. Yes, he caught stifled laughter that sounded somehow self-conscious.

Their lattice shutters had been up, but when Kii disapprovingly lowered them, Genji stole to where lamplight streamed through a crack over the sliding panel, to see what he could see. There was no gap to give him a view, but he went on listening and realized that they must be gathered nearby in the chamber, because he could hear them whispering to each other, apparently about him.

"He is still so young. It is a shame he is so serious and already so well settled."

"Still, I hear he often calls secretly on suitably promising ladies."

Genji, whose every thought was of *her*, was appalled to imagine them next discussing that in the same way, but he heard nothing more of interest and gave up his eavesdropping. They were talking about a poem that he had sent with some bluebells to the daughter of His Highness of Ceremonial,[57] although they had it slightly wrong. Well, he thought, she simply has time on her hands and a taste for poetry. I do not suppose she is worth looking at anyway.

53. It would have run north-south between the main dwelling and its east wing, hence next to where Genji was staying.

54. *Watadono*, between the main dwelling and the east wing.

55. A reference to a folk song in which a host leaves his guests the wine jar and "goes darting about" to fetch edible seaweed from the shore.

56. Utsusemi, the wife of the Iyo Deputy.

57. These bluebells (*asagao*) have supplied the traditional name of the lady (Asagao), who first appears in person in "Heart-to-Heart." She is Genji's first cousin, since her father is the Emperor's younger brother.

The Governor of Kii returned with more lanterns, raised the lamp wick, and offered him refreshments.[58]

"What about the curtains, then?" Genji asked. "It is a poor host who does not think of that!"[59]

"My lord, I have been told nothing about what might please you," Kii protested deferentially. Genji lay down as though for a nap near the veranda, and his companions settled down as well.

Genji's host had delightful children, one of whom Genji had already seen as a page in the privy chamber. The Iyo Deputy's children were there, too. One of the boys, a child of twelve or thirteen, had something special about him. While answering Genji's questions about which child was whose, Kii told him that this one was the youngest son of the late Intendant of the Gate Watch. "His father, who was very fond of him, passed away when he was small," Kii explained, "and he is here now under his elder sister's care. I hope to have him serve in the privy chamber, since he shows aptitude for scholarship and is generally bright, but things seem not to be going well."

"I am sorry to hear that. This sister of his—is she your stepmother?"

"Yes, my lord."

"Then you have a most unlikely one! Even His Majesty has heard of her. He was saying some time ago, 'Her father hinted that he was thinking of sending her into palace service—I wonder what became of her.' Ah," he sighed with grown-up gravity, "you never know what life will bring."

"It is a surprise to have her here. No, when it comes to love and marriage, it has always been impossible to divine the future, and unfortunately a woman's fate is especially hard to foresee."

"Does the Iyo Deputy pamper her? He must think the world of her."

"He certainly does, my lord. He seems to adore her, in fact, although, like the others,[60] I dislike his being so engrossed."

"He is not going to leave her to any of you, though, just because you are up on the latest fashions. There is nothing drab about the Iyo Deputy—he rather fancies a certain chic himself. Where is she anyway?"

"I sent them all off to the servants' hall, my lord, although perhaps not all of them managed actually to go."

Genji's companions, by now quite drunk, were asleep on the veranda. Genji, too, lay down, but in vain. Dislike for sleeping alone kept him awake, listening to the sounds from beyond the sliding panel to the north and fascinated that this must be where the lady they had talked about was now hiding. Silently he arose and stood by the panel to listen.

"Excuse me, where are you?" It was the appealingly husky voice of the boy who had caught his attention earlier.

"Lying over here. Is our guest asleep? I thought I would be next to him, but he

---

58. *Kudamono*, mainly fruit or nuts.

59. "It is a poor host who does not have a woman ready for his guest." Genji alludes to a *saibara* song: "In my house the curtains are all hung; come, my lord, come: my daughter shall be yours . . ." The song then mentions sea urchin (*kase*), a shell felt to resemble the female genitals.

60. The Iyo Deputy's other children.

is actually quite far away." The speaker's sleepy voice had a languid quality very like the boy's, and Genji realized that she must be his elder sister.

Chest

"He's gone to sleep in the aisle," the boy whispered. "Everyone is talking about how he looks, and I actually saw him! It's true, he is ever so handsome!"

"I'd have a peep at him myself if it were daytime," she answered drowsily, her voice sounding as though it came from under the covers.

Oh, come, he thought impatiently, do ask him a bit more about me than that!

"I'll sleep over here. It's so dark, though!" He seemed to be raising the lamp wick.

His sister must be lying diagonally across from Genji's door. "Where is Chūjō?"[61] he heard her say. "I am afraid when there is no one nearby."

"She went to the bath in the servants' hall—she said she would be back very soon." The answer came from the women lying a step below her.[62]

When all seemed quiet, he tried the latch. It was not locked from the other side. In the entrance stood a curtain, and by the lamp's dim glow he saw what seemed to be chests scattered about the room. Threading his way among them to where he guessed her to be, he came upon a slight figure lying all alone. The approaching footsteps startled her a little, but until he actually tugged at her bedclothes[63] she took him for the gentlewoman she had wanted.

"You called for a Chūjō, you see,[64] and I knew my secret yearning for you had inspired its reward."

Utterly confused, she thought she was having a nightmare and cried out, but the covers over her face stifled the sound.

"This is so sudden that you will surely take it for a mere whim of mine, which I quite understand, but actually I only want you to know that my thoughts have been with you for years. Please note how eagerly I have made the best of this chance, and so judge how far I am from failing to be in earnest."

He spoke so gently that she could not very well cry out rudely, "There is a man in here!" because not even a demon would have wished to resist him; but shock and dismay at his behavior drew from her, in an anguished whisper, "Surely you mean someone else!"

Nearly fainting, she roused him to pity and tenderness, and he decided that he liked her very much. "If only you would not doubt the unerring desire that has brought me to you!" he said. "I will take no liberties with you, I promise, but I must tell you something of my feelings."

He picked her up, since she was very small, and he had carried her to the sliding door when he came on someone else, presumably the Chūjō she had called

---

61. One of her women.

62. They are in the aisle room, diagonally across the chamber from Genji. The aisle was a beam-width lower.

63. People slept under robes.

64. He pretends to take the woman's name to mean himself. Chūjō means "Captain" (she may be the daughter or the wife of a Captain), and Genji is a Chūjō in the Palace Guards.

for. Chūjō, startled by his exclamation, was groping her way toward him when a breath of his pervasive fragrance enveloped her, and she understood. Although shocked and appalled, she found nothing to say. If he had been anyone ordinary, she would have wrested her mistress bodily from him, but even that would have been a risk, since everyone else would then have known what was going on; so she simply followed with beating heart while he proceeded, unruffled, into the inner room.[65]

"Come for your mistress at dawn." He slid the door shut.

The lady could have died to imagine what Chūjō might be thinking. Dripping with perspiration, she was so clearly miserable that Genji felt sorry for her, but he managed as always to draw from some hidden source a flood of tender eloquence to win her over.

"This is not to be believed!" She was indignant. "I may be insignificant, but even I could never mistake your contemptuous conduct toward me for anything more than a passing whim. You have your place in the world and I have mine, and we have nothing in common."

It upset him to find that his forwardness really did repel her, and he saw how justly she was outraged. "I know nothing of your place and mine in the world," he protested earnestly, "because I have never done anything like this before! It is cruel of you to take me for a common adventurer. You must have heard enough about me to know that I do not force my attentions on anyone. I myself am surprised by this madness, which has earned me your wholly understandable disapproval. I can only think that destiny has brought us together."

He gravely tried every approach, but his very peerlessness only stiffened her resistance, and she remained obdurate, resolved that no risk of seeming cold and cruel should discourage her from refusing to respond. Although pliant by nature, she had called up such strength of character that she resembled the supple bamboo, which does not break.

Her genuine horror and revulsion at Genji's willfulness shocked him, and her tears touched him. It pained him to be the culprit, but he knew that he would have been sorry not to have had her. "Why must you dislike me so?" he said accusingly when she refused to be placated. "Do see that the very strangeness of all this confirms the bond we share. I cannot bear your remaining so withdrawn, as though you knew nothing of the ways of the world!"

"If you had shown me such favor when I was as I used to be, before I settled into my present, unhappy condition, I might have entertained giddy hopes and consoled myself with visions of the day when you would think well of me after all, but the very idea of a night with you, when there can be no more, troubles me greatly. No, you must forget that this ever happened."[66]

No wonder she felt as she did. He undoubtedly did his best to comfort her and to convince her that her fears were misplaced.

---

65. It is not clear which room is meant, but the most plausible possibility is a divided-off section of the chamber itself—perhaps a fully walled-in "retreat" (*nurigome*).

66. "You must not imagine that the liberties you have taken constitute any kind of precedent for the future. What you have done has not established a relationship between you and me."

A cock crowed, and the household began to stir. "How long we have slept!" a voice exclaimed from among Genji's men, and another, "Advance his lordship's carriage!" The Governor appeared, too, and one of the women protested, "He is only here to avoid a taboo! There is no reason why he should hurry off again in the middle of the night!"[67] Genji suffered to think that such a chance might never come again, that he could hardly visit the house on purpose, and that even correspondence with her was probably out of the question.

She was so upset when Genji came in that he let her go, but then he drew her to him again. "How can I keep in touch with you? Both your unheard-of hostility and my feeling for you will leave vivid memories and be a wonder forever." His tears only gave him a new grace.

Cocks were crowing insistently. He said in despair,

"Dawn may well have come, but when I could still complain of your cruelty,
   must the cock crow me awake before I have all I wish?"[68]

Mortified by the gulf between them, since she was who she was, she remained unmoved by his attentions. Instead her thoughts went to the far province of Iyo and to the husband whom she usually dismissed with such loathing and contempt, and she trembled lest he glimpse this scene in a dream. She answered,

"Now that dawn at last has broken on the misery that I still bewail,
   the cock himself lifts his voice to spread my lament abroad."

It was quite light by now, and Genji saw her to the door of the room. He kept it shut as he said good-bye, because the house was alive with movement within and without, and he grieved that it should be about to part them, as he supposed, forever. Then he slipped on his dress cloak and gazed out south across the railing. To the west, shutters went up with a clatter: women must have been stealing a look at him. No doubt the more susceptible were thrilled by his dim form, visible over the low screen that divided their stretch of veranda from his. The moon still lingered on high, clear despite the pallor of its light, turning dull shadows to a lovely dawn. To one viewer the vacant sky intimated romance, while to the other it suggested aloof indifference. He was heartsick to think that he could not even get a note to her, and as he left, he looked back again and again.

At home once more he still could not sleep. What tormented him even more than being unable to see her again was the thought of her own feelings. Not that there was anything remarkable about her, but, as he knew, she nicely represented the middle grade they had discussed, with all its appeal, and he understood how truly the man of broad experience had spoken.

These days he spent all his time at His Excellency's. Forever anxious about her

---

67. As there would be if he had come for a secret rendezvous.
68. Genji's poem plays on *tori* ("cock") and *tori aenu* ("before I grasp [what I seek]"); hers similarly exploits *tori kasanete* ("again and again [I / the cock lament . . .]").

feelings in the absence of any message from him, he called the Governor of Kii and said, "Would you give me that boy I saw the other day—the late Intendant's son? He appealed to me, and I should like to take him into my personal service. I shall present him to His Majesty myself."

"You do him and us too great an honor, my lord. I shall convey your request to his elder sister."

"Has she given you any brothers or sisters?" Genji managed to ask with beating heart.

"No, my lord. It is two years now since she joined our family, but I gather that she regrets not having done as her father wished and that she dislikes her present condition."

"What a shame! People speak well of her. Is it true that she is pretty?"

"I expect so, my lord. She keeps me at such a distance that I am no closer to her than a stepson should be."

Five or six days later Kii brought Genji his young brother-in-law. The boy was not strikingly handsome, but he had grace, and his distinction was plain. Genji called him in for a very friendly talk. The boy was thoroughly pleased and impressed in his childish way. He answered pointed questions about his sister as well as he could, until his daunting composure made it difficult for Genji to go on. Still, Genji managed cleverly to convey his desire.[69]

The boy was surprised when Genji's point dawned on him at last, but he was too young to understand very well what it implied, and his arrival with Genji's letter brought tears of vexation to his sister's eyes. It horrified her to imagine what he might be thinking, and she opened the letter so that it hid her face. It was very long.

> *"Even as I mourn not knowing whether that dream[70] means another night,*
> *endless time seems to go by while my eyelids never close.*

At night I cannot sleep . . ."[71] His writing was so extraordinarily beautiful that her eyes misted over, and she lay down to ponder the strange destiny that had broken in upon her otherwise dreary life.

When Genji's summons reached her little brother the next day, he let her know he was going and asked for her answer.

"Tell him there was no one here to receive such a letter."

He only laughed. "How can I say that? He made himself perfectly clear."

She gathered that Genji had told him everything, and she recoiled. "I'll thank you not to be impertinent. Then just don't go."

He went anyway, though, saying, "He wants me—I cannot just ignore him."

Kii liked women too much not to think his stepmother's marriage a great shame, and he was always eager to please her, which is why he made much of her little brother and took him about everywhere.

---

69. That the boy should carry messages for him.
70. *Yume*, a lovers' meeting.
71. *Shūishū* 735, by Minamoto no Shitagō: "What comfort have I from my longing for you, when at night I cannot sleep and so never dream?"

Genji called the boy in. "I waited for you all day yesterday. Getting on with me seems to mean nothing to you." The boy reddened.

"Well, where is it?"

The boy explained what had happened. "It is really hopeless, isn't it," Genji said. "She is impossible." He handed him yet another letter.

"You may not realize this," he went on, "but I was seeing her long before that old man the Iyo Deputy. She probably thought me too spindly then to lean on, so she found herself a man of real substance to look after her, and now she is making a fool of me. Be a son to me, though. That fine husband of hers will not last much longer." It amused him to see the boy so gravely credulous and impressed.

He kept her brother with him all the time and took him even to the palace. He had those in charge of his wardrobe make clothes for him, and the boy really did treat him like a father. There was always a note for him to deliver. However, she worried that he was much too young, and that if unfortunately he lost one, she might find added to her present woes a light reputation unbecoming to someone in her position, and she therefore kept her answers formal, reflecting that what constitutes good fortune depends after all on where one stands in the world. Not that she failed to recall his figure and manner, extraordinary as these had been that one time when she had made him out through the gloom, but she concluded that nothing could come of her seeking to please him.

Genji thought of her endlessly, with mingled consternation and longing. He could not keep from dwelling on how much her distress had affected him. He might risk slipping in to see her, but with so many people in the house his misbehavior would be discovered, and that, he saw with alarm, would be disastrous for her.

While he was spending day after day at the palace, as always, a directional taboo favored him once more. Feigning an impromptu departure for His Excellency's, he turned off on the way there toward the house of the Governor of Kii. The surprised Kii took his visit for a gratifying tribute to the stream that he had diverted through his garden.

Genji had brought her little brother into the plot that afternoon. In the evening he immediately called for him again, since he had him at his beck and call day and night. The boy's sister had heard from him as well. She did not underestimate the interest that his scheme revealed, but she still had no wish recklessly to yield him her whole, modest person or to add new troubles to those already heaped upon her by their first, dreamlike encounter. No, decidedly, she would not fall in with his machinations and receive him; and so, as soon as Genji called her little brother away, she announced that she disliked being so near where he was staying and that anyway she was feeling unwell. "I shall move farther off for a quiet massage," she said, and she went to hide in Chūjō's room along the bridgeway.

Genji, whose plans were laid, had his entourage retire early and sent her a note, but her brother could not find her. Only after hunting high and low did he go down the bridgeway and come across her at last. "He'll think I'm no use at all!" the boy cried, nearly weeping with anger and frustration.

"I will not have you take this awful attitude!" she scolded him. "They say a child should never carry such messages. Tell him that I am not feeling well and that

I have kept my women with me for a massage. Everyone will be wondering what you are doing here."

In her heart of hearts, though, she felt that she might receive Genji gladly, however seldom, if only she were not now settled for life but were still at home, where the memory of her late parents and of their ambitions for her lived on. Despite her resolve, she suffered acutely to think that he must find her adamant rejection outrageously impertinent. However, it was too late now for such thoughts, and she made up her mind to remain stubbornly unresponsive to the end.

Genji lay waiting, eager to find out what her little brother might devise and at the same time nervous about his being so young. When he learned that there was no hope, her astonishing obduracy made him so detest his own existence that his distress was painfully obvious. For some time he was silent and only heaved great sighs. He was very hurt.

> *"I who never knew what it was the broom tree meant now wonder to find*
> *the road to Sonohara led me so far from my way.*[72]

I have nothing to say," he wrote at last.

She, too, was still awake, and she answered,

> *"Stricken with regret to have it known she was born in a humble home,*
> *the broom tree you briefly glimpsed fades and is soon lost to view."*[73]

She did not like to have her brother roaming about like this, too upset over Genji's annoyance to sleep, because she was afraid that he might arouse suspicion.

Genji's men slept soundly, as usual, while he alone gave himself over to vain, outraged ruminations. It infuriated him that her amazing resistance, far from disappearing, had instead risen to this pitch, and he was beside himself with outrage and injury, although he also knew perfectly well that strength of character was what had attracted him to her in the first place.

So be it, he told himself, but he remained so unconvinced that he was soon saying, "All right, then take me to where she is hiding."

"She has shut herself up in a little room and has several women with her—I wouldn't dare," her brother replied, desperately wishing he could do better.

"Very well, then you, at least, shall not leave me." Genji had the boy lie down with him. The boy so appreciated his master's youth and gentleness that they say Genji found him much nicer than his cruel sister.

---

72. Sonohara (in Shinano Province) is associated with a bush called *habakigi* ("broom tree"), similar to broom. *Kokin rokujō* 3019 (slightly modified as *Shinkokinshū* 997), by Sakanoue no Korenori, describes *habakigi* as visible from a distance and yet invisible as one comes nearer.
73. *Fuseya,* associated with the name Sonohara, may be a place name or a word for a low, humble dwelling.

3

The Cicada Shell

Utsusemi means "the cast-off shell of a cicada." In this chapter Genji continues pursuing the woman whom he sought vainly to tame in the last, and again she flees, shedding a gown as she does so. Genji picks it up and sends her the poem

"Underneath this tree, where the molting cicada shed her empty shell, my longing still goes to her, for all I know her to be."

She writes as a private comment on his letter:

"Just as drops of dew settle on cicada wings, concealed in this tree, secretly, O secretly, these sleeves are wet with my tears."

Genji could not sleep. "No woman has ever so rejected me," he said. "Tonight at last I have learned that to love means to suffer, and I doubt that I can survive the shame of it very long."

The boy lying beside him wept. Genji thought him very sweet. Small and slender to the touch, with quite short hair, he resembled his sister, which was probably why Genji found him so pleasing. Genji knew the spectacle he would make if he insisted on looking for her, so he spent the night instead heartily condemning her, asked less of her brother than usual, and left while it was still pitch-dark. The boy was very sorry and disappointed for him.

She, too, had her bitter regrets, but from him not a word. Perhaps he had learned his lesson, but still, it would be cruel of him to give up now, though there would be trouble unless he stopped his reprehensible behavior. Surely, she thought, it was time to put a stop to this when she could; but she often found herself lost in anxious musings.

The exasperated Genji did not see how he could break it off now, nor did he like to play the fool. "She is cruel and she is hateful," he kept saying to her little brother, "but I have lost every struggle to drive her from my mind. I cannot bear it. Find a good time and arrange somehow for me to talk to her." The boy hardly knew how to do this, but he was pleased to have Genji ask it of him.

He was on watch for an opening, in his childish way, when the Governor of Kii went down to his province; and so late one day, when dusk shrouded the lover's path[1] and the women of the household were relaxing alone, he took Genji to the house in his own carriage. Genji worried about what might come next, since the boy was so young, but he could not contain himself, and he rushed off, plainly dressed, to get there before they locked the gates.

The boy guided the carriage in through a deserted entrance and had Genji alight. Fortunately the watchmen almost ignored him, since he was a child, and they said nothing.

---

1. *Kokin rokujō* 371, by Ōyake no Iratsume: "Dusk shrouds the path: O love, await the moon to return, and I shall watch you as you go."

Playing Go

He posted Genji at the double doors to the east,[2] went south around the corner to knock and call at the lattice shutters, and then entered. "You can see straight in!" Genji heard the older women complain.

"It is so hot—why do you have the shutters down?" he asked.

"The lady from the west wing[3] came this afternoon. They are playing Go."

Ah, thought Genji, I want a look at her sitting across from her partner. He slipped in between the blinds.[4] They had not yet secured the shutter through which the boy had entered, and a gap remained. Genji went to it and peered in toward the west. The nearer end of a screen was folded, and the heat probably explained why a curtain that should have blocked his view had been draped over its stand, so that he could see quite well.

They had the lamp beside them. His first thought was that the one by the central pillar of the chamber,[5] facing away from him, must be she. She seemed to have on two layered, silk twill shifts of a deep red-violet, with some sort of garment over them. Her slender head and slight build left no marked impression, and she was keeping her partner from getting any view of her face. She was also doing her best to conceal her strikingly slim hands.[6]

Her opponent was facing east, toward Genji, and he could see all of her. She had on a pair of sheer white shifts and what seemed to be a violet outer gown, so casually worn that her front was bare all the way down to her scarlet trouser cord—a casual getup to say the least. Tall, very fair-skinned, and nicely rounded, striking in head and forehead and with a delicious mouth and eyes, she made an arresting sight. Her fine, thick hair was not long, but it flowed in handsome sidelocks to her shoulders, and there was in fact nothing about her to wish otherwise. She was a pleasure to look at. No wonder her father was so proud of her, although it occurred to Genji that her manner could do with a little restraint. She did not seem to be dull

2. The east end of the main house. There were *tsumado* (twin, hinged doors that opened outward) at each corner. This one leads toward the bridgeway to the east wing.

3. The Governor of Kii's sister, known to readers as Nokiba no Ogi ("reed at the eaves").

4. He follows the veranda around to where the boy went through; but the rest has been much discussed and resists convincing reconstruction. Some hold that the blinds hang outside shutters that open inward, so that Genji slips between them and a shutter panel (lowered again after the boy's entrance); but this, too, leaves unanswered questions. One also wonders why it was plausible for the boy to create a diversion by demanding admittance through a closed shutter when he could have simply entered through the doors.

5. Genji must be looking across the aisle, although in the dark (except for the oil lamp) this seems rather far for all he sees.

6. He sees her hands when she places a Go stone, but she keeps them otherwise in her sleeves.

either, because near the end of the game, when the contest was on for the last unclaimed territory, she seemed quite clever and keen.

"Just a moment," her opponent said calmly, "that spot is out of play. Let us finish by doing the exchange."

"Oh, dear, I have lost, haven't I! Now, how many do we have here in the corners? Dear me! Twenty, thirty, forty," she counted, crooking her fingers as though
taking a census of all the hot-spring tubs in Iyo.[7] She did lack a certain grace.

Her opponent kept her mouth so carefully covered that her face hardly
showed, but Genji's gaze never left her, and he glimpsed her profile. With her perhaps somewhat puffy eyes and a nose vague enough in form to age her, she had no
looks. Not to put too fine a point on it, she tended toward the plain, but her exquisite manners made up for it, and she obviously had more to her than her prettier
partner.

Her partner had liveliness and charm, though, and the growing abandon of
her gay laughter had a vivid appeal that made her delightful in her way. Yes, Genji
thought, I am a rascal; but with his roving eye he saw in her one more woman
whom he would not soon forget. The others he knew never let themselves go, all he
ever saw being an artful expression on an averted face, and he who had never before
spied on women going about their daily lives would have liked to watch these two
forever, despite his guilt at having them in plain view without their knowledge. But
her little brother was coming, and he stole away.

Genji was leaning against the door onto the bridgeway.[8] "She has a visitor, my
lord; I cannot approach her," the boy nervously explained.

"You mean she is going to turn me away again tonight? This is awful. I cannot
take it."

"Oh, no, my lord, I shall manage something once the visitor has gone."

Very well, he thought, perhaps he really can bring her round. He is only a boy,
but he has sense enough to see how things stand and to gauge someone's feelings.

The game of Go seemed to be over, for they heard a rustle of silks and the
sounds of people leaving. "Where's the young master, I wonder? I'll close this shutter." A clatter followed.

"She must have retired," Genji said. "Now, go and see what you can do."

The boy knew that his sister was too proper ever to be bent by persuasion, so
he planned to bring Genji to her once she was more or less alone.

"Is Kii's sister here, too? Let me have a look at her."

"But I cannot, my lord. There is a curtain in front of the shutter."

Ah yes; but nonetheless . . . Genji felt guilty, and despite his amusement he
had no wish to let the boy know what he had seen. Instead, he spoke of how much
he looked forward to later that night.

This time the boy knocked on the double doors. They were all lying down.

7. There was a song about the countless bathing tubs at Dōgo hot spring in Iyo, her father's province.
8. The door between the veranda and the bridgeway to the east wing. Across the veranda from Genji are
the double doors into the aisle of the main house.

"I'll sleep here by the sliding door," he announced, spreading a mat. "Come, wind, give me a breeze!" The older women must have crowded into the aisle on the east, and the little girl who had let him in went and lay down there, too.

For a while the boy pretended to be asleep. Then he stood a screen near the lamp and led the way in softly through the gloom; and Genji, fearing disaster, followed. He lifted the curtain at the edge of the room and stole very quietly in— except that in the silence the rustle of his robes, though faint, was hard to miss.

She had tried to be glad that he had forgotten her, but lately her mind lingered so much on that strange, dreamlike experience that she could hardly even sleep.[9] During the day she mused sadly, while at night she often lay awake; it was not spring, yet there she was, forever in tears.[10] Meanwhile her partner at Go, who had decided to stay the night, chattered on brightly until she lay down. She seemed to drop straight off into untroubled sleep.

The boy's sister looked up when the rustle and the rich fragrance reached her, and through the darkness she saw movement past the garment draped over the crossbar of the standing curtain.[11] Never pausing in her horror to think, she rose and silently slipped away, wearing only a gossamer silk shift.

In he came, and to his relief he found her lying alone. Two of her women were asleep outside on the level below.[12] When he drew the cover aside to join her, it seemed to him that there was rather more of her than he had expected, but even so the truth never dawned on him. What alerted him in the end was the strange soundness with which she slept, and despite his shocked recoil he understood that if this young woman ever guessed his mistake, she would be hurt and he would look a dunce. Never mind now pursuing the lady he had come for, because she would only evade him again and think him a fool for trying. But if this is that pretty girl in the lamplight, he decided, then so be it!—which was no tribute to his seriousness of character.

At last she awoke, in dismay and surprise, and she seemed frightened, too, but she gave no sign of deep or upsetting alarm. Her inexperience encouraged playful compliance, and she kept her head. Genji preferred not to say who he was, but he knew that once she began to wonder what he had been doing there, her conclusion, which to him would not matter, might damage that cruel woman who so fiercely protected her name, and he therefore gave her a smooth explanation of just why that taboo had brought him here again and again. Anyone with a little wit would have seen through him, but for all her forwardness she was too young to understand.

He did not dislike her, but he saw nothing in her to attract him either, and he remained preoccupied with his tormentor's maddening behavior. Where could she

---

9. *Shūishū* 727, a winter love poem (although it is now summer), which speaks of sleeplessness and frozen tears.

10. *Ichijō no Sesshō go-shū* 132 (Fujiwara no Koremasa): "At night I lie awake and spend the day dreaming, for these eyes of mine enjoy no spring." The poem plays on *konome*, "my eyes" and "buds on the trees."

11. Before the entrance to the two women's curtained bed (*michōdai*).

12. On the floor of the aisle to the north (*kitabisashi*), the thickness of the lintel beam below the level of the chamber.

be hiding? She must think him a perfect idiot. Few women were so intractable, and he wished that he could turn his thoughts elsewhere. Meanwhile, the young woman's youthful innocence so touched him that despite his reservations he pledged her his love with a great show of feeling.

"People used to say that it is more romantic to stay the way we are now than to make everything public," he intoned. "Love me then as I love you. After all, we have reason to be discreet, and, you know, I am in no position to do as I please. It also hurts me to imagine how some people might disapprove. Please be patient and do not forget me."

"It is so embarrassing to think how the others would feel if they knew!" she guilelessly replied to this string of platitudes. "I cannot write to you!"

"Of course it would be disastrous if anyone were to find out, but we can keep in touch through our little privy gentleman. Pretend that nothing has happened."

With this he left her, collecting on his way a sheer gown that *she* must have shed in her flight.[13]

The boy was asleep nearby, and he awoke easily when Genji roused him, having been anxious when he lay down about how things might go.

"Who's that?" an old woman's voice called as he softly opened the door. Bother! "It's me!"

"Where are you off to in the middle of the night?" She started for the door.

He hated her. "No, no, I'm just going out a little!" He thrust Genji before him. The moon, still bright in the dawn sky, suddenly revealed a second figure.

"Who's that with you?" the old woman said. "Ah, it must be Mimbu. You just go up and up, Mimbu, don't you!" The woman she thought he had with him was always being teased about her height. "And in no time you'll be just as tall as she is!" she muttered, emerging through the door.

He thought he was in for it, but he could not very well push her back in. Genji flattened himself against the door onto the bridgeway to hide.

"Were you waiting on her ladyship yesterday evening?" The old woman came straight up to him. "I've been down in my room[14] with a bad tummyache that started the day before yesterday, but she called me anyway because she wanted more of us with her, so last night I went after all, and it was too much for me." Without pausing for an answer, she groaned, "Oh, it hurts, it hurts! I'll talk to you later!" And off she went.

At last Genji managed to leave. The night must have taught him properly that gadding about like this was a perilous folly.

He returned to Nijō with her little brother riding in the back of his carriage and described what had happened, ruing his trust in one so young and snapping his fingers in irritation at her perverseness. The boy was crushed and said not a word.

"She seems to hate me so much that I, too, am disgusted with myself," Genji pursued his complaint. "Why, when I write, will she not at least give me a civil an-

---

13. The light *kouchiki* under which Utsusemi had been lying.
14. Not on a lower floor but in the servants' part of the house.

Writing box

swer? I cannot get from her even the courtesy she extends to the Iyo Deputy!" Still, he put her gown under his robe for the night. He had her brother lie beside him and talked on, now about the injury he had suffered, now about intimate concerns of their own. "You are very nice," he said gravely, "but that sister of yours is so hateful that I may not be able to go on liking you." The boy was miserable.

For a time Genji tried unsuccessfully to sleep. Then he called hastily for an inkstone and wrote on folding paper,[15] more in the manner of writing practice than of a proper letter,

> "Underneath this tree, where the molting cicada shed her empty shell,
> my longing still goes to her, for all I knew her to be."[16]

Her brother put it in the front fold of his robe and took it to her. Genji did not like to imagine that other young woman's feelings, but after considering the matter, he sent her nothing. He kept the gown, which was redolent of *her,* next to his body and sat contemplating it.

The boy's sister was waiting for him when he reached the house, and she gave him a piece of her mind. "Look what you did! I may have managed to cover it up somehow, but nothing can be done about people's suspicions. You have me in a fine fix! And what on earth can *he* be thinking of the childish way you botched this?"

Her brother, caught painfully in the middle, brought out Genji's letter nonetheless. She took it and read it after all. That cicada shell she had shed: she wondered anxiously whether it had been salty like the Ise fisherman's,[17] and she sank into confusion.

As for the young woman from the west wing, she had no one in whom to confide, so she went back there in shame and sank into secret gloom. She waited anxiously while the boy roamed about, but he brought her nothing. Although she could hardly know just how badly he had behaved, she must still have suffered a degree of wounded pride.

Meanwhile, despite her show of indifference, Genji's tormentor lingered in memory over his apparent devotion to her, and although the past was beyond recall, she so wished to be once more as she had been that she wrote along the edge of his letter,

> "Just as drops of dew settle on cicada wings, concealed in this tree,
> secretly, O secretly, these sleeves are wet with my tears."

15. *Tatōgami,* paper to be carried, folded, in the front fold of one's robe. Love notes were usually written on thin, colored paper (*usuyō*).

16. The cicada larva emerges from the earth, molts, and then climbs the tree as an adult, leaving behind its larval shell.

17. Fearing that her gown may smell of perspiration, she thinks of *Gosenshū* 718, by Fujiwara no Koremasa, "written when [the poet] sent for a robe that he had left at a lady's house." He worried that she might have "found the robe forgotten by the Ise fisherman a little salty."

4

YŪGAO

The Twilight Beauty

The *yūgao* ("twilight beauty";
more literally, "evening face") is a
vine that the chapter introduces
this way: "A bright green vine, its
white flowers smiling to themselves, was clambering merrily
over what looked like a board
fence." Near the start of the
chapter a mysterious woman
sends Genji a fan to go with
some *yūgao* flowers that he has
just had picked. Written on the
fan he finds a poem:

*"At a guess I see that you may indeed be he: the light silver dew
brings to clothe in loveliness a twilight beauty flower."*

He answers:

*"Let me then draw near and see whether you are she, whom glimmering dusk
gave me faintly to discern in twilight beauty flowers."*

The story in "The Twilight Beauty" begins in the summer when Genji is seventeen and continues up to the tenth month. Genji seems to have been inspired to pursue both Utsusemi and Yūgao by the "rating women on a rainy night" conversation in "The Broom Tree."

PERSONS

Genji, a Captain in the Palace Guards, age 17

Genji's nurse, the Dazaifu Deputy's wife, now a nun (Daini no Menoto)

Koremitsu, Genji's foster brother and confidant

The Adept, Koremitsu's elder brother

A young woman, about 19 (Yūgao)

The lady of the cicada shell (Utsusemi)

The daughter of the Iyo Deputy (Nokiba no Ogi)

The Iyo Deputy (Iyo no Suke)

The Rokujō Haven, widow of a former Heir Apparent
(Rokujō no Miyasudokoro)

Chūjō , a gentlewoman in the Rokujō Haven's service

Ukon, Yūgao's nurse

The steward

His son, a member of the Palace Guards

The Secretary Captain, Genji's friend and brother-in-law (Tō no Chūjō)

His wife, daughter of the Minister of the Right (Shi no Kimi)

His daughter with Yūgao, the "pink," 3 (Tamakazura)

A Doctor, Genji's former teacher

In the days when Genji was calling secretly at Rokujō, he decided to visit his old nurse, the Dazaifu Deputy's wife, on the way there, since she was seriously ill and had become a nun. Her house was on Gojō.[1]

When he found the gate that should have admitted his carriage locked, he sent for Koremitsu,[2] and while he waited he examined the unprepossessing spectacle of the avenue. Next door stood a house with new walls of woven cypress, surmounted by a line of half-panel shutters. Four or five of these were open, and through very pale, cool-looking blinds he saw the pretty foreheads of several young women who were peering out at him.[3] They seemed oddly tall, judging from where the floor they were standing on ought to be. He wondered who they were, to be gathered there like that.

Having kept his carriage very modest and sent no escort ahead, he was confident of remaining unrecognized, and he therefore peered out a little.[4] The gate, propped open like a shutter panel,[5] gave onto a very small space. It was a poor little place, really. Touched, he recalled "What home is ours forever?"[6] and saw that the house might just as well be a palace.[7]

A bright green vine, its white flowers smiling to themselves, was clambering merrily over what looked like a board fence. "A word I would have with you, O you

1. "Fifth Avenue," between the palace and Rokujō, "Sixth Avenue."
2. This use of his personal name suggests his intimate, subordinate relationship with Genji.
3. The house is an *itaya*, a modest dwelling roofed with boards rather than cypress bark thatch or tiles. To about chest height it has *higaki*—walls faced with thin, crisscrossed slats of cypress (*hinoki*) wood; these are then extended upward by half-panel shutters (*hajitomi*) that can be swung up and secured open in a horizontal position. Each panel covers the full space (*ken*) between two structural pillars. The "four or five" panels probably cover the full width of the house. The paleness of the blinds (*sudare*) shows them to be new.
4. Presumably through his carriage's side window (*monomi*) or past the edge of the blind that covered the carriage's rear entrance.
5. The gate was attached to a horizontal crosspiece and swung open vertically. It was propped open with a pole.
6. *Kokinshū* 987: "In all this world, what home is ours forever? Mine shall be the lodging I come upon tonight."
7. *Kokin rokujō* 3874: "What need have I for a palace? Rather to lie with you where the weeds grow thick."

from afar,"[8] he murmured absently, at which a man of his went down on one knee and declared, "My lord, they call that white flower 'twilight beauty.'[9] The name makes it sound like a lord or lady, but here it is blooming on this pitiful fence!"

The neighborhood houses were certainly cramped and shabby, leaning miserably in every direction and fringed with snaggle-toothed eaves, but the vine was climbing all over them. "Poor flowers!" Genji said. "Go and pick me some."

His man went in the open gate and did so, whereupon a pretty little servant girl in long trousers of sheer yellow raw silk stepped out through a plain but handsome sliding door and beckoned to him. "Here," she said, "give them to him on this—their stems are so hopeless." She handed him a white, intensely perfumed fan.

The other gate opened just then, and out came Lord Koremitsu. The man had him give Genji the flowers. "My lord," Koremitsu apologized, "we had unfortunately mislaid the key, and so we have caused you a great deal of trouble. No one in this neighborhood could possibly know you, but still, the way your carriage is standing out here in this grubby avenue . . ." He brought the carriage in, and Genji alighted.[10]

Koremitsu's elder brother the Adept, his brother-in-law the Governor of Mikawa, and his sister were all gathered in the house. Genji's arrival pleased them and made them very grateful.

The nun sat up. "For me it no longer matters," she said tearfully, "but what made it difficult to renounce the world was the thought that you would then have to see me in so strange a guise. I feel much better, though, now that I have received the Precepts and have had the joy of this visit from you, and I can look forward in peace to the light of Lord Amida."[11]

"It has worried and saddened me that your illness has continued so long unrelieved, but I deeply regret that you have now visibly renounced the world. Please live on to see me rise higher still. Once I have done so, you may achieve as swiftly as you wish the loftiest of the nine births in Paradise. They say one should retain no attachment to the world." Genji, too, spoke in tears.

The eyes of one as fond as a nurse will see implausible perfection even in the least gifted child; no wonder, then, that she felt honored to have been in his intimate service and wished to avoid causing him the pain of her loss. This was why she could not keep from weeping. Her acutely embarrassed children darted each other sidelong glances before so unbecoming a show of emotion in Genji's presence, as though their mother could not after all give up the world that she was supposed to have renounced.

---

8. *Kokinshū* 1007 (a *sedōka*): "A word I would have with you, O you from afar who gaze into the distance: that white flower blooming yonder—what is its name?"

9. *Yūgao* (more literally, "evening face"). Genji's attendant observes that this name makes the flower sound like a "person" (*hito*), meaning someone who "is someone," that is, socially distinguished. In this context *yūgao* refers either to Genji himself or to the woman for whom the chapter is named, and "beauty" is therefore meant as an allusion to both.

10. Genji enters this gate in his carriage, as he did at the Governor of Kii's, because the people are below him in rank.

11. She has vowed to uphold the Buddhist rules of conduct (the Precepts) and looks forward to going to the paradise of the Buddha Amida. There were nine possible grades of birth into this paradise. The lowest of these required a more or less long wait before the soul could fully witness Amida's glory.

He was very moved. "When I was little, everyone who should have loved me left me.[12] Of course I had people to look after me, but you were then the one to whom I felt especially close. Now that I am grown up and can no longer always be with you or visit you as I please, I still miss you when I have been away from you too long. How I wish that

Hand torch

there were no final parting!"[13] He talked on tenderly, and the scent of the sleeves with which he wiped his eyes meanwhile perfumed the whole room, until the children, who just now had deplored their mother's behavior, willingly granted that she had indeed enjoyed great good fortune in her life, and they all dissolved in tears.

After ordering further rites for her, he had Koremitsu bring in a hand torch in preparation for leaving. On inspecting the fan presented to him earlier, he found it to be deeply impregnated with the scent favored by its owner and delightfully inscribed with this poem:

> *"At a guess I see that you may indeed be he: the light silver dew*
> *brings to clothe in loveliness a twilight beauty flower."*[14]

The writing was disguised, but its grace and distinction pleasantly surprised him.

"Who lives in that house to the west?" he asked Koremitsu. "Have you inquired?"

Here he goes again! thought Koremitsu, but he kept his peace and only answered a little curtly, "My lord, I have been here five or six days, it is true, but I have been too occupied caring for my mother to learn anything about next door."

"You dislike my asking, don't you. Still, I believe I have reason to look further into this fan, and I want you to call in someone acquainted with the neighborhood and find out."

Koremitsu went inside and questioned the caretaker. "The place apparently belongs to an Honorary Deputy Governor," he eventually reported. "He says the husband has gone to the country and that the wife, who is young and likes pretty things, often has her sister visiting her, since the sister is in service elsewhere. That is probably all a servant like him can be expected to know."

I see, Genji thought, it must be the young woman in service. She certainly gave me that poem of hers as though she knew her way about! She cannot be anyone in particular, though.

---

12. Probably his mother, who died in his third year, and his grandmother, who died in his sixth.

13. *Kokinshū* 901 (also *Ise monogatari* 154, section 84), by Ariwara no Narihira: "Would that in this world there were no final parting, for a son who wishes his mother a thousand years!"

14. "You *are* Genji, are you not?" He is the dew, she the flower.

Still, he rather liked the way she had accosted him, and he had no wish to miss this chance, since in such matters it was clearly his way to be impulsive. On a piece of folding paper he wrote in a hand unlike his own,

"Let me then draw near and see whether you are she, whom glimmering dusk
gave me faintly to discern in twilight beauty flowers."

Folding paper

He had it delivered by the man who had received the fan.

She had known his profile instantly, despite never having seen him before, and she had not let pass this chance to approach him, but his prolonged silence upset her, and she was thrilled when his reply arrived. She then took so long discussing her answer with her women that Genji's messenger was offended and returned to his lord.

Genji set off very discreetly. His escort carried only weak torches. The house next door had its half-panel shutters down. The lamplight filtering through the cracks was more muted by far, and more moving, than the glow of fireflies.

There was nothing common about the groves or the garden at the residence where Genji was bound, and the lady there lived a life of supreme elegance and ease. Her distant manner, never more marked than now, obliterated for him all memory of the vine-covered fence he had just left. He slept quite late the next morning and left at sunrise, his looks in the early light making it clear why everyone sang his praises.

Today again he passed those shutters. No doubt he had come that way before, but now, with that little encounter lingering in his mind, he wondered whenever he went by just who it was who lived there.

Koremitsu appeared a few days later and came straight up to Genji. "My mother is weaker than ever, and I have been doing what I can for her. After you last spoke to me, I called in someone who knows the house next door and questioned him, but he told me nothing clear. Someone seems to have come in the fifth month to live there incognito, but he said the household has been told nothing about her. Now and again I have a look through the fence, and I have indeed seen young women wearing a sort of apron, which suggests they are serving a lady. Yesterday the late afternoon sun was shining into the house, and I clearly saw a pretty woman sitting down to write a letter. She looked sad, and the others around her were quietly weeping." Genji smiled and thought how much he would like to know who she was.

Koremitsu felt that despite the weight of Genji's exalted station it would be a shame if he did not take some liberties, considering his age and the admiring response he received from women; after all, those too low to be granted such freedom by the world at large fancied attractive women nonetheless. "I thought up a little pretext and sent over a note in case I might discover anything," he continued. "I got an answer straight back, written in a practiced hand. As far as I can tell, there are some quite nice young women there."

"Keep at it, then. It would be very disappointing not to find out who she is." This was the sort of house Genji had heard dismissed as inhabited by "the lowborn," but it excited him to imagine himself finding an unexpected treasure of a woman there.

Genji's astonishing rejection by the lady of the cicada shell had led him to think her hardly human, but if only she had given him a better hearing he might have contented himself with that one unfortunate misdeed, whereas under the circumstances he dwelled incessantly and with keen irritation on his dislike for giving up in defeat. He had never before set his heart on anyone so ordinary, but after that rainy night spent talking over the different levels of women, curiosity seemed to have inspired in him an inclusive interest in them all. He certainly felt sorry for that other girl, the one who was so innocently expecting him back, but it embarrassed him to imagine the first one listening quite coolly to what had passed between them, and he preferred to know *her* real intentions first.

Meanwhile the Iyo Deputy returned to the City and hastened to present Genji his respects. Naturally somewhat tanned from his sea voyage, he cut a thoroughly distasteful figure in Genji's eyes. Still, he was of quite good birth and handsome enough, though he looked his age, and he certainly carried himself well. Genji wanted to ask him when he spoke of his province how many hot-spring tubs he had found there, but he felt strangely awkward instead, and many memories came to him. It was odd and foolish of him to feel this way before a staid, mature man, and he remembered the Chief Equerry's warning, apt enough in his own case, about getting in too deep with a woman. Guilt toward the Iyo Deputy taught him that from her husband's standpoint her rejection of him had been admirable, however annoying it might have been to *him*.

On learning that the Iyo Deputy now meant to give his daughter to a suitable husband and then to go down again to his province, this time with his wife, Genji lost his head and enlisted her little brother in a plot against all odds to bring off one more meeting with her. Alas, considering who he was, he was unlikely even with her help to reach her undetected, and in reality she objected to the mismatch between them and found the very idea so demeaning as to be out of the question. Still, she knew how painfully disappointing it would be if he simply forgot her. She therefore answered him warmly whenever he wrote to her, adorning the poems she put in the least of her messages with ingeniously appealing expressions for him to remember her by and presenting herself to him as someone worthy of his love, until despite anger over her rejection he found her impossible to forget after all. As to the other girl, he took it for granted that she would welcome him even if she acquired a stalwart lord and master in the meantime, and various rumors on that topic therefore failed to upset him.

It was autumn now. Troubles for which he had only himself to blame weighed upon him and discouraged all but the most sporadic visits to His Excellency's, inviting further resentment from the lady there.

Meanwhile, after successfully overcoming the reserve of the great lady on Rokujō,[15] he had changed and taken most unfortunately to treating her like any

---

15. The way this lady, the Rojukō Haven, slips into the narrative as though the reader already knew her is intriguing enough to have prompted reflections on how these early chapters may have been composed.

other woman. One wonders why there lived on in him nothing of the reckless passion that had possessed him when he first began courting her. She herself, who suffered excessively from melancholy, feared at the same time that rumors of an affair already embarrassing because of their difference in age would soon be in circulation, and she spent many a bitter night, when he failed to come, despairing over her troubles.

One very misty morning when the still-sleepy Genji was at last taking his leave in response to insistent urging, though with many sighs, the gentlewoman Chūjō raised a lattice shutter and moved her mistress's curtain aside as though to say, "My lady, do see him off!" She lifted her head and looked out: there he was, standing before all the colors of the garden as though he did not wish to miss their beauty. No, there was no one like him.

Chūjō accompanied him toward the gallery.[16] Silk gauze train neatly tied at her waist, over an aster layering[17] perfect for the season, she carried herself with delicious grace. He glanced back and sat her down by the railing at the corner of the building. Her comely deference toward him, the length of her sidelocks[18]—all seemed to him a miracle.

> "I would not be known for flitting lightheartedly to every flower
> but this bluebell this morning I would be sad not to pick.

What do you suggest?" he said, taking her hand; but she replied with practiced wit,

> "Your haste to be off before morning mists are gone makes it all too plain,
> so I should say, that your heart cares little for your flower,"

so turning his poem to refer to her mistress. A pretty page boy, handsome in trousers that might have been made for this very moment and that now were wet with dew, wandered out among the flowers and brought him a bluebell. One would have liked to paint the scene.

Whoever chanced to lay eyes on Genji was smitten by him. After one glimpse of the radiance that attended him, men of every degree (for the crudest woodcutter may yet aspire to pause in his labors beneath a blossoming tree)[19] wished to offer him a beloved daughter, while the least menial with a sister he thought worthy entertained the ambition to place her in Genji's service. It was therefore all but impossible for a cultivated woman like Chūjō, one who had had occasion to receive poems from him and to bask in the warmth of his beauty, not to be drawn to him. She, too, must have regretted that he did not come more often.

Oh, yes, it must also be said that Koremitsu gave Genji a fine account of what

16. Probably the gallery leading to the middle gate where Genji will enter his carriage.
17. The aster (shion) layering presumably achieved the blue-violet of the simple shion color, close to that of the bluebell.
18. Kami no sagariba, locks cut short above the ears to frame the face.
19. The Japanese preface to the Kokinshū criticizes the "uncouthness" of Ōtomo no Kuronushi's poetry: "It is, so to speak, like a woodcutter pausing with his load of firewood beneath a blossoming tree."

he had learned from spying as ordered through the neighbors' fence. "I have no idea who she is," he reported. "As far as I can tell, she is hiding from everyone. Her women have little to keep them occupied. They seem now and again to cross over to the southern part of the house—the one with the half-panel shutters—and the younger ones go to look whenever they hear a carriage. The one I take to be their mistress is brave enough to do the same.[20] What I have seen of her face suggests that she is lovely. The other day a carriage passed with an escort, and a little page girl who was watching it cried, 'Look, Ukon, look! It's his lordship going by!' A rather older grownup then came out, calling 'Hush, hush' and motioning her to be quiet. 'How do you know?' she asked, and she added, 'Come, I'll look myself.' She was hurrying across what I suppose was the crossbridge when her skirts caught, and she stumbled and almost fell. 'Goodness,' she exclaimed, 'the God of Kazuraki certainly didn't make *that* one very well!'[21] I think they gave up watching after that. The girl said the gentleman in the carriage had been in a dress cloak, and to prove it had been the Secretary Captain[22] she named several of the attendants and pages she had seen with him."

"I wish I had seen his carriage myself." Genji wondered whether she might be the one the Secretary Captain could not forget.

"I am doing well at courting one of the women there," Koremitsu went on, smiling at Genji's obvious eagerness to learn more, "and I know the house by now, but the young women still talk to each other as though they were there by themselves, and I go about pretending to believe them. They think their secret is safe, and whenever a child threatens to blurt out something,[23] they talk their way past the difficulty and keep up their show of being alone."

"Give me a look through that fence next time I call on your mother." Judging from where she was living, at least for now, she must belong to that lower grade that his friend had so curtly dismissed. Yes, Genji thought, what if there really were a surprisingly pleasant discovery to be made there?

Koremitsu, who could not bear to disappoint his lord, marshaled his own wide experience of courtship to devise a way at last to introduce him into the house. All that makes a long story, though, so as usual I have left it out.

Having failed to discover who she was, Genji withheld his identity from her and pursued her in deep disguise,[24] with such patient ardor that Koremitsu let him have his own horse and walked beside his lord. "I should be sorry to have the great lover seen approaching the house on foot, like a menial," he complained; but Genji, who trusted no one else with his secret, had himself accompanied otherwise only by the man who had passed him the twilight beauty flowers and by a single page whose face no one in the house would know. He even avoided calling at the house next door, lest they guess after all who he was.

---

20. The bridge between the buildings seems to consist only of planks, and the word in the original, *hai-wataru* ("crawl across"), suggests that she crosses it in trepidation.

21. The god of the Kazuraki Mountains, ordered by a wizard to build a stone bridge from one mountain range to another, refused to work in daylight and so never quite finished.

22. Tō no Chūjō.

23. They talk to their mistress as equals, but the children sometimes begin to address her in honorific language.

24. Dressed so as to conceal his rank, and in this case apparently also his face.

In her bewilderment she had Genji's letter-bearer followed and tried to discover where Genji himself went after he left her at dawn, all in the hope of finding out where he lived, but he and his men always managed to evade hers, even as the thought of her so filled his mind that he could not be without her and was constantly appearing at her side, tormented by his unseemly folly.

An affair of this kind may lead the most staid man astray, but so far Genji had always managed to control himself, and he had done nothing to merit censure. It was extraordinary, though, how leaving her in the morning or being away from her only for the day made him miserable enough to wonder whether he had lost his senses, and to struggle to remind himself that nothing about her required this degree of passion. In manner she seemed very young, for she was remarkably sweet and yielding, and hardly given to deep reflection; yet she knew something of worldly ways, and she could not be of very high birth. Again and again he asked himself what it was that he saw in her.

He made a show of dressing modestly in a hunting cloak, of changing his costume, and of giving her no look at his face, and he never came to her until everyone in the house was asleep. He was so like a shape-changing creature of old[25] that he caused her acute anguish, although his manner with her, and her own sense of touch, made her wonder how great a lord he might be. It must be that great lover I have to thank for this, she reflected, her suspicion falling on Koremitsu; but Koremitsu only feigned ignorance and went on lightheartedly visiting the house as though he knew nothing, until confusion overcame her and she sank into a strange melancholy.

Genji assumed that she was in hiding only for the time being, and he wondered where he would seek her if she were to vanish after snaring him so artlessly. It worried him that he would never know on what day she might go, or where. She would have been just a passing distraction if he then failed to find her and accepted her loss, but he did not believe for a moment that he could forget her that easily. Every night when discretion kept him from her was such a trial that he thought of bringing her to Nijō, whoever she might be, and if the resulting gossip embarrassed him, so be it. Despite himself he wondered what bond from the past could have aroused a passion so consuming and so unfamiliar.

"Come," he said, "I want to talk quietly somewhere where we can be alone."

"But that would be so strange," she protested naively. "I understand your feeling, but that sort of thing is not done. The idea upsets me."

No doubt it does, Genji reflected with a smile. "Yes," he said gently, "one or the other of us must be a fox: so just let *me* bewitch *you*."

She let him have his way and yielded completely. Her utter submissiveness, however curious, was extremely engaging. She *must* be the "gillyflower" described, as he now remembered, by the Secretary Captain, but if she was in hiding she must have her reasons, and he refrained from pressing her. He saw no sign that she might suddenly flare up at him and vanish—he foresaw no such change unless he ne-

---

25. In the myth of Mount Miwa, for example, a young woman is visited every night by an invisible lover. At last she ties a thread to his clothing, follows it, and finds that he is the serpent deity of the mountain.

glected her badly—and he even fancied
despite himself that a little coolness from
him might add to her appeal.

On the fifteenth night of the eighth
month,[26] bright moonlight poured through
every crack into the board-roofed house,
to his astonishment, since he had never
seen a dwelling like this before. Dawn must
have been near, because he heard uncouth
men in the neighboring houses hailing one
another as they awoke.

"Goodness, it's cold!"

"Not much hope for business this
year—I'll never get out to the country![27]
What a life! Say, neighbor, you on the
north, d'you hear me?"

Fulling block

She was deeply embarrassed by this
chatter and clatter all around them of
people rising and preparing to go about their pitiful tasks. The place would have
made anyone with any pretensions want to sink through the floor, but she remained
serene and betrayed no response to any sound, however painful, offensive, or distressing, and her manner retained so naive a grace that the dismal commotion might
just as well have meant nothing to her at all. Genji therefore forgave her more readily than if she had been openly ashamed. Thud, thud, a treadle mortar thundered almost at their pillow,[28] until he understood at last what "detestable racket" means.
Having no idea what was making it, he only was aware that it was new and that it
was awful. The assortment of noises was no more than a jumble to him.

The sound of snowy robes being pounded on the fulling block reached him
faintly from all sides, and wild geese were crying in the heavens. These and many
other sounds roused him to painfully keen emotion.[29] He slid the nearby door open,
and together they looked outside. The tiny garden boasted a pretty clump of bamboo on which dew gleamed as brightly as elsewhere. Insects of all kinds were
singing, and to Genji, who seldom heard even a cricket in the wall, this concert of
cries almost in his ears was a bizarre novelty, although his love for her must have inclined him to be forgiving. She was engagingly frail in the modesty of her soft, pale
gray-violet gown over layers of white, and although she had nothing striking about
her, her slender grace and her manner of speaking moved him deeply. She could
perhaps do with a touch of pride, but he still wanted very much to be with her in
less constricting surroundings.

26. The great full moon night of the year. In the lunar calendar this date is in autumn.
27. Perhaps the speaker would normally be buying rice in the country to sell in town.
28. It is probably polishing rice.
29. These sounds, unlike the earlier noises, are poetically evocative. *Shirotae no* ("snowy") is a noble epithet for *koromo* ("robe"). The sound of a robe being beaten on a fulling block (*kinuta*), to clean it and restore
its luster, meant autumn and the waning of the year, and perhaps a woman under the moon calling to her
lost love; the motif is originally Chinese. The cries of migrating geese, too, told of autumn and farewell.

"Come, let us spend the rest of the night comfortably in a place nearby. It has been so difficult, meeting nowhere but here."

"But I do not see how . . . This is so sudden . . ." she protested innocently. Never mind his promises that their love would outlast this life; her meek trust was inexplicably gone, and he could hardly believe that she knew worldly ways. He therefore threw caution to the winds, had Ukon call his man, and got his carriage brought up. This demonstration of ardor gave her anxious gentlewomen faith in him after all.

It would soon be dawn. No cocks were crowing. All they heard was an old man's voice as he prostrated himself full-length, no doubt for a pilgrimage to the Holy Mountain.[30] The labor of throwing himself down and rising again sounded painful. Genji wondered what in this dewlike world he so desired that he insisted on such strenuous prayers.

"Hail to the Guide who is to come!"[31] the old man chanted. Genji was moved. "Listen to him: he, too, is thinking beyond just this life.

> *Let your own steps take the path this good man follows so devotedly*
> *and in that age yet to come still uphold the bond we share."*

He had avoided the old lines about the "Hall of Long Life" and turned "sharing a wing"[32] into a prayer that they should greet the Age of Miroku together. It was a grand leap into the future.

> *"Such are the sorrows that make plain what fate past lives require me to bear*
> *that I have no faith at all in better from times to come."*

Her reply, such as it was, was forlorn.

While he sought to persuade her, since she could not make up her mind to launch forth so boldly under the slowly sinking moon, the moon suddenly slid behind clouds and the dawn sky took on great beauty. He hurried out as always, lest day betray his doings to the world, and lifted her easily into the carriage. Ukon got in, too.

They soon reached a certain estate,[33] and while waiting for the steward they gazed at the ferns along the old gate's ruinous eaves. All was darkness under the trees. The fog hung wet and heavy, and Genji's sleeves were soaked merely because

---

30. He is "touching his forehead to the ground," that is, doing repeated, full-length prostrations. The pilgrimage to Mitake (now Sanjō-ga-take, 5,676 feet, in the Ōmine range) required strict purification and attracted both nobles and commoners. The mountain was then particularly sacred to Miroku, the future Buddha.

31. *Namo tōrai dōshi,* the invocation to Miroku, who will descend into a transfigured world many eons from now. The pilgrim prayed to be born into his age and to hear his teaching.

32. Excessively obvious allusions to "The Song of Unending Sorrow," where, in the Hall of Long Life, the lovers swear that in the hereafter they will be like trees with shared branches or birds that share a wing.

33. Reminiscent of Kawara no In ("Riverside"), built by Minamoto no Tōru (822–95) and later imperial property. Kawara no In was the scene of a famous ghost story, and its location matches the tale's description.

he had put up the carriage's blinds. "I have never done anything like this," he said. "It is nerve-racking, isn't it?

> *Once upon a time could it be that others, too, lost their way like this?*
> *I myself have never known such strange wanderings at dawn.*

Have you ever done this before?"
She answered shyly,

> *"The wayfaring moon uncertain what to expect from the mountains' rim,*
> *may easily fade away and disappear in mid-sky.*[34]

I am afraid."

It amused him to see her so tremulous and fearful. He assumed that she just missed the crowd always around her at home.

He had the carriage brought in and its shafts propped on the railing[35] while their room was made ready in the west wing. The excited Ukon thought back over the past, because the way the steward rushed officiously about showed what sort of man her mistress's lover was.

They left the carriage as day was beginning to restore shape and color to the world. The place was nicely arranged for them, despite their sudden arrival.

"I see you have no one else with you, my lord," said the steward, a close lower-level retainer in service also at His Excellency's. "This makes things rather difficult." He approached and asked through Ukon whether he should summon a suitable entourage.[36]

Genji quickly silenced him. "I came here purposely to hide. Say not a word about this to anyone." The man hastened to provide a morning meal, although he did indeed lack staff to serve it.

Genji had never slept away from home quite like this before, and he assured her over and over that he would love her even longer than the Okinaga River would flow.[37] The sun was high when they rose, and he lifted the shutters himself. The unkempt and deserted garden stretched into the distance, its ancient groves towering in massive gloom. The near garden and shrubbery lacked any charm, the wider expanse resembled an autumn moor, and the lake was choked with water weeds. The place was strangely disturbing and quite isolated, although there seemed to be an inhabited outbuilding some distance off.

"The place *is* eerie," he said, "but never mind: the demons will not trouble *me*."

---

34. The "mountains' rim" (where the moon sets) is Genji; the moon is the woman, who does not know how far Genji's intentions toward her go.

35. Around the veranda: a makeshift arrangement, since carriage shafts normally rested on a "shaft bench" (*shiji*).

36. The steward ranks too low to address Genji directly; his earlier speech, too, must be indirect.

37. In *Man'yōshū* 4482, by Umanofuhito Kunihito, the poet assures his lady that he will love her even if the Okinaga River stops flowing. This name, which can be taken to mean "long breath," is linked in the poem to the grebe (*nio*), which holds its breath to feed underwater.

She was thoroughly offended that he still had his face covered, and he agreed that this was unnatural by now.

> *"The flower you see disclosing now its secrets in the evening dew*
> *glimmered first before your eyes in a letter long ago,"*

he said. "Does the gleam of the dew please you?"

With a sidelong glance she murmured,

> *"The light I saw fill the dewdrops adorning then a twilight beauty*
> *was nothing more than a trick of the day's last fading gleam!"*

He was delighted. When at his ease he really was extraordinarily beautiful—in this setting, in fact, alarmingly so. "The way you kept your distance hurt me so much that I meant never to show you my face. Do tell me your name now. You frighten me, you know."[38]

"But you see, I am only a diver's daughter,"[39] she answered mildly, as always refusing to tell him more.

"All right, I suppose the fault is mine."[40] He spent the rest of the day now reproving her, now whispering sweet nothings in her ear.

Koremitsu managed to find them, and he brought refreshments. He avoided waiting on Genji in person because he did not want to hear what Ukon would say to him. It amused him that Genji had resorted to bringing her here, and, assuming that her looks deserved this much trouble, he congratulated himself rather bitterly (since he could quite well have had her himself) on his generosity in ceding her to his lord.

While gazing at the ineffably peaceful sunset sky, Genji remembered that she disliked the gloom inside the house. He raised the outer blinds[41] and lay down beside her. They looked at each other in the twilight glow, and despite her anxiety she forgot her cares and charmingly yielded to him a little. She had now lain by him all day, piercingly young and sweet in her shy terror.

He lowered the lattice shutters early and had the lamp lit. "Here we are," he complained, "as close as we could possibly be, but at heart you are still keeping yourself from me. I cannot bear it."

He knew how anxiously His Majesty now must be seeking him, though he could not imagine where his men might be looking. How strange a love this is! And on Rokujō, what a state she must be in! She above all stirred his guilt, and he understood her anger, however painful it might be. The more fondly he dwelled on the artless innocence before him, the more he longed to rid *her* a little of the pride that so unsettled him.

---

38. Genji plays at being afraid that she is a fox.
39. *Wakan rōei shū* 722 (also *Shinkokinshū* 1703), a reply to a gentleman's advances: "No home have I of my own, for I, a diver's daughter, live beside white-breaking waves upon the ocean shore."
40. Genji's reply acknowledges "I am a diver's daughter" with a wordplay on *warekara*: "my fault" but also the name of a creature alleged to live in seaweed.
41. Those between the aisle and the veranda.

Late in the evening he dozed off to see a beautiful woman seated by his pillow. She said, "You are a wonder to me, but you do not care to visit me: no, you bring a tedious creature here and lavish yourself upon her. It is hateful of you and very wrong." She began shaking the woman beside him awake.

He woke up, aware of a heavy, menacing presence. The lamp was out. In alarm he drew his sword and laid it beside her, then roused Ukon. She came to him, clearly frightened, too.

"Go," he commanded, "wake the guard on the bridgeway and have him bring a hand torch."

"But how can I, my lord, in the dark?"

"Don't be silly!" Genji laughed and clapped his hands. Eldritch echoes answered.

No one could hear him, no one was coming. She was shivering violently, helplessly. Soaked with perspiration, she seemed to be unconscious.

"She is always so timid anyway," Ukon said. "What she must be going through now!"

Genji pitied her, frail as she was and so given to spending her days gazing up at the sky. "I shall wake him myself. Tiresome echoes are all I get for my clapping. Wait here, stay with her."

He dragged Ukon to her, then went to the western double doors and pushed them open. The light on the bridgeway was out, too. A breeze had sprung up, and the few men at his service—just the steward's son (a young man he used on private errands), the privy chamber page,[42] and his usual man—were asleep. The steward's son answered his call.

"Bring a hand torch. Have my man twang his bowstring[43] and keep crying warnings. What do you mean by going to sleep in a lonely place like this? I thought Lord Koremitsu was here. Where is he?"

"He was at your service, my lord, but he left when you had no orders for him. He said he would be back for you at dawn." The young man disappeared toward the steward's quarters, expertly twanging his bowstring (he belonged to the Palace Guards) and crying over and over again, "Beware of fire!"[44]

Genji thought of the palace, where the privy gentlemen must have reported for duty and where the watch must even now be being announced.[45] It was not yet really so very late.

He went back in and felt his way to her. She still lay with Ukon prostrate beside her. "What is this? Fear like yours is folly!" he scolded Ukon. "In empty houses, foxes and whatnot shock people by giving them a good fright—yes, that is it. We will not have the likes of them threatening us as long as I am here." He made her sit up.

---

42. A youth described earlier as "a single page whose face those in the house could not know."
43. To repel the baleful spirit.
44. An all-purpose warning cry.
45. At the hour of the Boar (circa 9 P.M.), the privy gentlemen, reporting for duty in the privy chamber, announced their names to the official in charge. Then the guards reporting for the watch likewise announced their names.

"My lord, I was only lying that way because I feel so ill. My poor lady must be quite terrified."

"Yes, but why should she . . . ?" He felt her: she was not breathing. He shook her, but she was limp and obviously unconscious, and he saw helplessly that, childlike as she was, a spirit had taken her.

The hand torch came. Ukon was in no condition to move, and Genji drew up the curtain that stood nearby.[46]

"Bring it closer!" he ordered. Reluctant to approach his lord further in this crisis, the man had stopped short of entering the room. "Bring it here, I tell you! Have some sense!"

Now in the torchlight Genji saw at her pillow, before the apparition vanished, the woman in his dream. Despite surprise and terror, for he had heard of such things at least in old tales, he was frantic to know what had become of her, until he shed all dignity and lay down beside her, calling on her to wake up; but she was growing cold and was no longer breathing.

He was speechless. There was no one to tell him what to do. He should have recalled that at such times one particularly needs a monk,[47] but despite his wish to be strong he was too young, and seeing her lost completely undid him. "Oh, my love," he cried, throwing his arms around her, "come back to life! Don't do this terrible thing to me!" But she was quite cold by now and unpleasant to touch. Ukon's earlier terror yielded to a pathetic storm of weeping.

He gathered his courage, remembering how a demon had threatened a Minister in the Shishinden.[48] "No, no," he scolded Ukon, "she cannot really be gone! How loud a voice sounds at night! Quiet, quiet!" The sudden calamity had him completely confused.

He called for the steward's son. "Someone here has been strangely attacked by a spirit and appears to be gravely ill. Send my man straight for Lord Koremitsu and have him come immediately. If the Adept happens to be there, tell him privately to come, too. He is to be discreet and keep this from their mother. She disapproves of such escapades."

He got this out well enough, but he was in torment, and the awful thought that he might cause her death[49] gave the place terrors beyond words. Midnight must have passed, and the wind had picked up. The pines were roaring like a whole forest, and an eerie bird uttered raucous cries; he wondered whether it was an owl. The house was so dreary, so lonely, so silent. Oh, why, he bitterly asked himself in vain regret, why had he chosen to spend the night in this dreadful place? The frantic Ukon clung to him, shaking as though she would die. He held her and wondered miserably what was to become of her. He alone had remained lucid, and now he, too, was at his wits' end.

The lamp guttered, while from shadowy recesses over the screen between him

46. To conceal himself and the lady from the man with the light.
47. As an exorcist.
48. In legend the Chancellor Tadahira was passing the Emperor's seat in the Shishinden late one night when a demon seized the tip of his scabbard and threatened him. Tadahira drew his sword and cried, "How dare you interfere with His Majesty's emissary?" The demon fled.
49. He still seems to believe that she is somehow alive.

and the chamber[50] came the thump and scuff of *things* walking; he felt them coming up behind him. If only Koremitsu would come soon! But Koremitsu was hard to track down, and the eternities that passed while Genji's man hunted for him made that one night seem a thousand.

At last a distant cockcrow set thoughts whirling through his head. What could really have led him here to risk his life in such a catastrophe? His recklessness in these affairs now seemed to have made him an example forever. Never mind trying to hush this up—the truth will always out. His Majesty would hear of it, it would be on everyone's lips, and the riffraff of the town would be hawking it everywhere. All and sundry would know him only as a fool.

At last Koremitsu arrived. He had always been at Genji's service, midnight or dawn, yet tonight of all nights he had been delinquent and failed to answer his lord's call. Genji had him come in, despite his displeasure, and he had so much to tell that words failed him at first. Ukon gathered that Koremitsu was there, and she wept to remember all that had happened. Genji, too, broke down. While alone he had borne up as well as he could and held his love in his arms, but Koremitsu's arrival had brought him the respite to know his grief, and for some time he could only weep and weep.

At length his tears let up. "Something very, very strange has happened here, something horrible beyond words. In a moment so dire I believe one chants the scriptures, so I have sent for your brother to do that and to offer prayers."

"He returned to the Mountain[51] yesterday," Koremitsu replied. "But all this is quite extraordinary. Could it be that my lady was feeling unwell?"

"No, no, not at all."

Genji, weeping once more, looked so perfectly beautiful that Koremitsu, too, was overcome and dissolved in tears. After all, in this crisis their need was for someone mature, someone with rich experience of the world. They were too young really to know what to do.

"The steward here must not find out; that would be a disaster," Koremitsu said. "He can perhaps be trusted himself, but the retainers around him will spread the story. My lord, you must leave this house immediately."

"But how could anywhere else be less populated?"

"Yes, that is true. At her house the grieving women would weep and wail, and there are so many houses around that the neighbors would all notice. Everyone would soon know. At a mountain temple, though, this sort of thing is not unknown, and in a place like that it might be possible to evade attention."

Koremitsu then had an idea. "I will take her to the Eastern Hills, to where a gentlewoman I once knew is living as a nun. She was my father's nurse, and she is very old. The neighborhood looks crowded, but the place is actually very quiet and sheltered." He had Genji's carriage brought up, now that full day had returned the people on the estate to their occupations.

Genji did not have the strength to lift her in his arms, and it was Koremitsu

---

50. Genji, Ukon, and the lady seem to be in the aisle with a folding screen between them and the chamber.
51. Mount Hiei.

who wrapped her in a padded mat and laid her in the carriage. She was so slight that he was more drawn than repelled. He had not wrapped her securely, and her hair came tumbling out. The sight blinded Genji with tears and drove him to such a pitch of grief that he resolved to stay with her to the end.

However, Koremitsu would not have it. "My lord, you must ride back to Nijō before too many people are out." He had Ukon get in the carriage as well, then gave Genji his horse and set off on foot with his gathered trousers hitched up.[52] It was a strange cortège, but Genji's desperate condition had driven from Koremitsu's mind any thought of himself.[53] Genji reached home oblivious to his surroundings and barely conscious.

"Where have you been, my lord?" his women wanted to know. "You do not look at all well." But he went straight into his curtained bed, pressed his hand to his heart, and gave himself up to his anguish.

How can I not have gone in the carriage with her? he asked himself in agony. How will she feel if she revives? She will probably assume that I just took this chance to abscond, and she will hate me. He felt sick. His head ached, he seemed to have a fever, and all in all he felt so very ill that he thought he might soon be done for himself.

His gentlewomen wondered why he did not rise even though the sun was high. Despite their offer of a morning meal he just lay there, suffering and sick at heart. Meanwhile, messengers—the young gentlemen from His Excellency's[54]—came from His Majesty, whose failure to find Genji yesterday had worried him greatly. From within his blinds Genji invited the Secretary Captain alone to "Come in, but remain standing.[55]

"In the fifth month a former nurse of mine became so ill that she cut off her hair and took the Precepts," he explained, "and that seemed to make her better, but recently her illness flared up again, and in her weakened condition she asked to see me a last time. I went to her because, after all, she has been close to me since I was a baby, and I thought she would be hurt if I did not. Unfortunately, a servant of hers, one already unwell, died before they could remove her from the house. In fear of what this would mean for me, they let the day go by before they took her away, but I found out, and so now, in a month filled with holy rites, this tiresome difficulty means that I cannot in good conscience go to the palace.[56] I apologize for talking to you like this, but I have had a headache ever since daybreak. I must have a cold."

52. The legs of the gathered trousers were usually tied at the ankles with a cord, but for ease of movement Koremitsu brings the cord up to just below his knees.

53. He has accepted the inconvenience of contact with death and the embarrassment of being seen to walk when a man of his standing should ride.

54. Genji's brothers-in-law.

55. Genji is in the chamber, where the blinds are still down. Tō no Chūjō, if Genji had allowed him to sit, would have incurred the same pollution (from contact with death) as Genji, and he would have passed it on to his family, the palace, and so on.

56. This (fictitious) death means that both Genji and the household are defiled. Genji must stay at home in a sort of quarantine for thirty days until halfway through the ninth month, one particularly busy with Shinto rites. Moreover, the imperial envoy to an important rite at Ise (the Kanname-sai) left on the eleventh of the month, and for the occasion Buddhist priests and persons in mourning were banned from the palace.

"I shall report this to His Majesty," the Secretary Captain answered. "There was music last night, and he looked for you everywhere. He did not seem at all pleased."

He spoke now for himself. "What really is this defilement you have incurred? I am afraid I find your story difficult to believe."

Genji felt a twinge of alarm. "Spare His Majesty the details. Just tell him I have been affected by an unforeseen defilement. It is all very unpleasant." His reply sounded casual, but at heart he was desperate with grief. In his distress he refused to see anyone. Summoning the Chamberlain Controller,[57] he had him convey formally to His Majesty a report on his condition. To His Excellency's he wrote that, for the reason he mentioned, he could not present himself at court.

Koremitsu came at dark. There were few people about because all Genji's visitors had left without sitting down once he warned them that he was defiled. Genji called him in. "Tell me, did you make quite sure there was no hope?" He pressed his sleeves to his eyes and wept.

"Yes, my lord, I believe that it is all over." Koremitsu, too, was in tears. "I could not stay long. I have arranged with a saintly old monk I know to see tomorrow to what needs to be done, since that is a suitable day."[58]

"What about her gentlewoman?"

"I doubt she will survive this. This morning she looked ready to throw herself from a cliff in her longing to join her mistress. She wanted to let her mistress's household know, but I managed to persuade her to be patient and to think things over first."

Genji was overwhelmed. "I feel very ill myself, and I wonder what is to become of me."

"My lord, you need not brood this way. All things turn out as they must. I will not let anyone know, and I plan to look after everything myself."

"I suppose you are right. I have been trying to convince myself of that, too, but it is so painful to be guilty of having foolishly caused someone's death. Say nothing to Shōshō[59] or to anyone else," he went on, to make sure Koremitsu's lips were sealed. "Your mother, especially, disapproves strongly of this sort of thing, and I could never face her if she knew." Koremitsu assured him to his immense relief that he had told even the monks of the temple a quite different story.

"How strange! What can be going on?" the women murmured as they caught scraps of this conversation. "He says he is defiled and cannot go to the palace? But why are the two of them whispering and groaning that way?"

"Keep up the good work, then." Genji gave Koremitsu directions for the coming rite.

"But, my lord," Koremitsu answered, rising, "this is no time for ostentation."

Genji could not bear to see him go. "You will not like this, I know, but there will be no peace for me until I see her body again. I shall ride there myself."

---

57. Kurōdo no Ben, a younger brother of Tō no Chūjō. Genji may suspect Tō no Chūjō, who does not believe him, and want to make sure that his message gets through properly.
58. For a funeral, according to the almanac.
59. A gentlewoman, probably Koremitsu's sister.

Koremitsu thought this risky, but he replied, "So be it, my lord, if that is your wish. You must start immediately, then, and be back before the night is over."

Genji changed into the hunting cloak that he had worn lately on his secret outings and set forth. Oppressed as he was and burdened by sorrow, he wondered after that encounter with danger whether he really should undertake so perilous a journey, but the merciless torments of grief drove him to persevere, for if he did not see her body now, when in all eons to come would he look upon her again as she had once been?

As always he took his man and Koremitsu with him. The way seemed endless. The moon of the seventeenth night[60] shone so brightly that along the bank of the Kamo River his escort's lights [61] barely showed, and such was his despair that the view toward Toribeno troubled him not at all.[62] At last he arrived.

The neighborhood had something disturbing about it, and the nun's board-roofed house, beside the chapel where she did her devotions, was desolate. Lamplight glowed faintly through the cracks, and he heard a woman weeping within. Outside, two or three monks chatted between spells of silently calling Amida's Name.[63] The early night office in the nearby temples was over, and deep quiet reigned, while toward Kiyomizu there were lights and signs of dense habitation. A venerable monk, the nun's own son, was chanting scripture in such tones as to arouse holy awe. Genji felt as though he would weep until his tears ran dry.

He went in to find the lamp turned to the wall[64] and Ukon lying behind a screen, and he understood her piercing sorrow. No fear troubled him. *She* was as lovely as ever; as yet she betrayed no change. He took her hand. "Oh, let me hear your voice again!" he implored, sobbing. "What timeless bond between us can have made me love you so briefly with all my heart, only to have you cruelly abandon me to grief?" The monks, who did not know who he was, wondered at his tears and wept with him.

Genji invited Ukon to come to Nijō, but she only replied, "What home could I have, my lord, now that I have so suddenly lost the lady I have never left in all the years since she and I were children together? But I want to let the others know what has become of her. However dreadful this may be, I could not bear to have them accuse me of having failed to tell them." She went on amid bitter tears, "I only wish I could join her smoke and rise with her into the sky!"

"Of course you do," he said consolingly, "but that is life, you know. There has never been a parting without pain. The time comes for all of us, sooner or later. Cheer up and trust me. Even as I speak, though," he added disconcertingly, "I doubt that I myself have much longer to live."

"My lord," Koremitsu broke in, "it will soon be dawn. You should be starting home."

60. A moon two days past the full.
61. The runners who go before him with torches.
62. Genji is riding south down the Kamo River, bound for the southern end of the Eastern Hills. In the distance, to his left (eastward), he sees the burning ground of Toribeno, where Yūgao will be cremated.
63. The *nenbutsu*, the formula for calling the name of Amida, was usually voiced, but not for a funeral. The Buddha Amida welcomes souls into his paradise.
64. Away from the body, which has been laid out for the wake.

Sick at heart, Genji looked back again and again as he rode away.

The journey was a very dewy one,[65] and it seemed to him that he was wandering blindly through the dense morning fog. She had lain there looking as she did in life, under that scarlet robe of his, the one he had put over her the night before in exchange for one of her own. What had the tie between them really been? All along the way he

Monks calling on Amida

tried to work it out. Koremitsu was beside him once more to assist him, because in his present condition his seat was none too secure, but even so he slid to the ground as they reached the Kamo embankment.

"You may have to leave me here by the roadside," he said from the depths of his agony. "I do not see how I am to get home."

The worried Koremitsu realized that if he had had his wits about him he would never have let Genji insist on taking this journey. He washed his hands in the river and called in the extremity of his trouble on the Kannon of Kiyomizu,[66] but this left him no wiser about what to do. Genji took himself resolutely in hand, called in his heart on the buddhas,[67] and with whatever help Koremitsu could give him managed somehow to return to Nijō.

His gentlewomen deplored this mysterious gadding about in the depths of the night. "This sort of thing does not look well," they complained among themselves. "Lately he has been setting out more restlessly than ever on these secret errands, and yesterday he really looked very ill. Why do you suppose he goes roaming about like this?"

As he lay there, he did indeed seem extremely unwell, and two or three days later he was very weak. His Majesty was deeply disturbed to learn of his condition. Soon the clamor of healers was to be heard everywhere, while rites, litanies, and purifications went forward in numbers beyond counting. The entire realm lamented that Genji, whose perfection of beauty already aroused apprehension, now seemed unlikely to live.

Through his suffering he called Ukon to his side, granted her a nearby room, and took her into his service. Koremitsu managed to calm his fears, despite the anxiety that gripped him, and he helped Ukon to make herself useful, reflecting that

65. "Dew" means tears.

66. Koremitsu can probably still see Kiyomizudera to the east. The temple is dedicated to a form of Kannon, the bodhisattva of compassion and a savior from peril.

67. The buddhas (*hotoke*) invoked by Genji could be one or many. He, too, may have the Kannon of Kiyomizu in mind.

she had after all no other refuge. He called her whenever he felt a little better and gave her things to do, and she was soon acquainted with all his staff. Although no beauty, in her dark mourning[68] she made a perfectly presentable young woman.

"It is strange how the little time that she and I had together seems in the end to have shortened my life as well," he said to her privately. "If it had been given me to live long, I would have wanted to do all I could for you, so as to heal the pain of losing the mistress you trusted for all those years, but as it is, I shall soon be going to join her. How I wish it were not so!" The sight of his feeble tears made her forget her own woes and long only for him to live.

His household was distraught, while more messengers came from the palace than raindrops from the sky. He was very sorry to know that he was causing His Majesty such concern, and he did his best to rally his own strength. His Excellency visited him daily, and thanks perhaps to his attentive ministrations, Genji's indisposition all but vanished after twenty days and more of grave illness, and he seemed bound for recovery.

That night the seclusion imposed on Genji by his defilement came to an end, and he repaired to his apartment at the palace out of consideration for His Majesty, who had felt such anxiety on his behalf. His Excellency came for him there in his carriage and inquired solicitously about his period of seclusion. Genji felt for a time as though all this were unreal and he had returned to life in an unknown world.

By the twentieth of the ninth month he was quite well. He was extremely thin, it is true, but for that very reason his beauty had acquired a new and special grace. He was also prone to spells of vacant melancholy and of tears, which inspired curiosity and gave rise to the rumor that he must be possessed by a spirit.

Early one quiet evening he had Ukon come to him for a chat. "I still do not understand," he said. "Why did she keep me from knowing who she was? It would have been cruel even of 'a diver's daughter,' if she had really been one, to ignore my obvious love and to keep me so much at a distance."

"Why should she ever have wished to hide who she was from you, my lord? When might she have seen fit to tell you her own, wholly insignificant name? You came to her from the start in a guise so strange that, as she herself said, she could not quite believe you were real. Your very insistence on keeping your identity from her made it clear enough who you were, but it hurt her that you seemed so obviously to be seeking only your own amusement."

"What an unfortunate contest of wills! I had no wish to remain distant from her. But, you see, I still have very little experience of the kind of affair that others might criticize. In my position I must be cautious about a great many things, for fear above all of reproof from His Majesty, and I simply do not have the latitude to go courting any woman I please, because whatever I do could so easily open me to reproach. Still, I was so strangely drawn to her after that first evening's chance exchange that I risked visiting her after all, which I suppose was proof enough that the bond between us was foreordained. How sad it all is, and how bitter! Why did she

---

68. She would normally have worn light gray, but her intimacy with Yūgao called for a darker shade.

take such complete possession of my heart, if she and I really were destined to be with each other so briefly? Do tell me more about her. Why withhold anything now? I am having images made every seven days for her memorial services: to whom should I silently dedicate them?"[69]

"Very well, my lord, I see no reason not to give you the answers you seek. I had only wished to avoid gossiping after my lady's death about things that she herself had kept hidden while she lived. Her parents died when she was still young. Her father, known as the Third Rank Captain,[70] was devoted to her, but he seems to have suffered greatly from his failure to advance, and in the end he became too discouraged to live on. After his death it happened that his lordship the Secretary Captain, then a Lieutenant,[71] began coming to see her, and he continued to do so quite faithfully for three years. Last autumn, though, she received terrifying threats from the residence of the Minister of the Right,[72] and these so frightened her, for she was very timid, that she fled to hide at her nurse's house in the western part of the City. Life there was very trying, and she wanted to move to the hills, but this year that direction became closed for her,[73] and she avoided it by making do instead with the poor place where to her dismay, my lord, you at last came upon her. She was so exceptionally shy that she felt embarrassed to be seen looking unhappy, and she pretended to be untroubled whenever she was with you."

So that was it! Genji now understood, and her memory touched him more deeply than ever. "I have heard the Secretary Captain lament losing a child. Was there one?"

"Yes, my lord, born in the spring the year before last: a lovely little girl."

"Where is she? You must not tell anyone else about her—just give her to me. It would be such joy to have her in memory of her mother, who meant so much to me." And he continued, "I should really tell the Secretary Captain, but then I would only have to put up with his pointless reproaches. I see no reason why I should not bring her up. Please make up a story for the nurse who must have her now, and bring her here."

"I shall do so gladly, my lord. I do not like to think of her growing up so far out in the west of the City. My lady left her there only because she had no one else to look after her properly."

---

69. Rites to guide the soul toward a fortunate rebirth were held every seven days during the first forty-nine days after death and at widening intervals thereafter. New paintings of the Buddhist divinities involved were made for each service during the initial forty-nine-day period.

70. Sanmi no Chūjō. He had held the third court rank (sanmi) and the office of Captain in the Palace Guards. This combination was unusual because a Captain normally held only the fourth rank. Still, since a man of the third rank was a senior noble, Yūgao had in theory been born into the upper class discussed by the young men on that rainy night.

71. A Lieutenant in the Palace Guards. He appears briefly with this title in "The Paulownia Pavilion"

72. Tō no Chūjō explains in "The Broom Tree" that these were sent to her by his wife (Shi no Kimi), the fourth daughter of the Minister of the Right, who still lives in her father's residence.

73. Probably a "great obstacle" (ōfutagari) resulting from the movements of a deity known as Taishōgun Maō Tennō.

While peaceful twilight dimmed to evening beneath a lovely sky, a cricket sang falteringly from the fading garden, and here and there the autumn colors glowed. Surveying the pleasures of this scene, so like a painting, Ukon wondered to find herself in such delightful surroundings and blushed to recall the house of the twilight beauties.

A dove's throaty call from amid the bamboo brought back to Genji, with an affectionate pang, her look of terror when one had called that night at the old mansion. "How old was she? I suppose it was clear enough from her extraordinary frailty that she was not to live long."

"I believe my lady was nineteen. Her nurse's death left me an orphan, and when I remember now how kind my lady's father was, and how he brought me up with his own daughter, I hardly know how I shall go on living. By now I wish I had not been so close to her. I spent such long years depending on a mistress who was after all so very fragile!"

"It is frailty that gives a woman her charm, though. I do not care for a woman who insists on valuing her own wits. I prefer someone compliant, perhaps because I myself am none too quick or self-assured—someone easy for a man to take advantage of if she is not careful, but still circumspect and happy enough to do as her husband wishes. I know I would like such a woman more, the more I lived with her and formed her to my will."

"I am very, very sorry, my lord," said the weeping Ukon, "when I think how perfectly my mistress matched your ideal."

The sky had clouded over, and the breeze had turned cold. Genji murmured in blank despair,

> "When the clouds to me seem always to be the smoke that rose from her pyre,
>   how fondly I rest my gaze even on the evening sky!"

Ukon could give him no answer, and she thought with an aching heart, If only my lady were still alive!

In memory Genji treasured even the noise of the fulling blocks, which he had found so intolerable at the time. "The nights are very long now,"[74] he sang to himself as he lay down to sleep.

The young boy from the Iyo Deputy's household still went now and again to wait on him, but he no longer brought his sister the same sort of messages, and she decided unhappily that Genji had finally given her up. Still, she was sorry to learn that he was ill. Her impending departure on the long trip to her husband's province was causing her such misery that she tested Genji to find out whether he had really forgotten her.

"I gather that you are not well," she wrote, "yet I cannot properly express my wishes for you.

---

74. From a poem by Bai Juyi on the grief of a wife who beats a fulling block while longing for her absent husband (*Hakushi monjū* 1287).

You have failed so long to inquire why I have failed to ask about you,
perhaps you will understand all the turmoil of my thoughts.

'But *I* am the one' is perfectly true."[75]

Her letter was a surprise, but he had not forgotten his feeling for her. "Nothing now to live for? Are those your words or mine?

Once I learned from you how trying this world can be, this cicada shell,
and see how I again hang upon your every word!

Mine is a very slender hope!" The meandering writing from his trembling hand was extremely engaging. It both pleased and pained her that he had not forgotten the shell the cicada had left behind in her flight, but she had not meant to draw him closer, despite the warmth of this exchange; her only wish had been to remind him that she was not after all unworthy of his interest.

Genji heard that that other young woman had accepted the Chamberlain Lieutenant, and he wondered uncomfortably what the man could be thinking.[76] At the same time he wanted to know how she was getting on, and so he wrote to her via the boy: "Do you know how I pine for you?

Had I not at least tied that little knot around the reed by the eaves,
what excuse would I have now to voice my dewdrop complaint?"[77]

He tied the note to a tall reed and cautioned the boy to be careful. Still, as he assured himself with reprehensible self-satisfaction, the Lieutenant will probably be forgiving if the note unfortunately comes to his attention and he sees who sent it.

The Lieutenant was away when the boy gave it to her. Her hurt at Genji's neglect was tempered by pleasure that he had remembered her, and she gave the boy an answer for which her only excuse was that she had composed it in haste:

"Whispers on the wind murmuring of bygone ties leave the lowly reed
stricken with melancholy and half prisoner of frost."[78]

She made up for her poor handwriting with elaborate touches that lacked any quality at all. He recalled her face in the lamplight. Ah, that partner of hers, so primly seated across from her, was the one he could not dismiss! Still, this artless creature had carried on so brightly and confidently that she made a pleasant memory, too.

---

75. *Shūishū* 894, a reproach to a cruel lover: "Not you, who claim to be suffering so, but *I* am the one who now has nothing to live for."

76. He was presumably surprised to find that he was not his wife's first lover.

77. The "little knot around the reed" is the lovers' single night together, and it may also allude to the knot of the girl's trouser cord, seen in the lamplight. From this poem comes her traditional name of Nokiba no Ogi ("reed by the eaves").

78. "I was glad to receive your message after so long a silence, but it cannot relieve my sadness, especially now that I am married and no longer my own mistress."

No, he had not yet learned his lesson, and he seemed as susceptible as ever to the perils of temptation.

On the forty-ninth day[79] he secretly had the Sutra read for her in the Lotus Hall[80] on Mount Hiei, providing the vestments and every other accessory that a generous performance of the rite might require. Even the text and altar ornaments were of the finest quality, and Koremitsu's elder brother the Adept, a very saintly man, did it all beautifully.

Genji asked a Doctor, a former teacher he knew well, to come and compose the dedicatory prayer.[81] When he wrote out what he wished to have in it, not naming the deceased but stating that since one dear to him had passed away he now commended her to Amida's mercy, the Doctor said, "It is perfect as it is, my lord; I see nothing to add." Genji's tears flowed despite his effort to control himself, and sorrow overcame him.

"Who can she have been?" the Doctor asked. "Lacking any clue to who she was, I can only wonder at the loftiness of the destiny that led her to inspire such grief in so great a lord."

Genji called for the trousers that he had secretly had made as an offering,[82] and he murmured,

> "Amid streaming tears today a last time I knot this, her trouser cord—
> ah, in what age yet to come will I undo it again?"

He understood that until now she had been wandering restlessly, and as he called passionately for her on Amida, he wondered what path she might at last have taken.[83]

His heart beat fast whenever he saw the Secretary Captain, and he wanted to tell him that the "little pink" was growing up, but fear of his friend's reproaches kept him silent. At the house of the twilight beauties the women longed to know where their mistress had gone, but they could discover nothing; they could only lament the strangeness of what had happened, since no word reached them even from Ukon. Among themselves they whispered that judging from his deportment the gentleman must have been you-know-who, though of course no one could be sure, and so they presented their complaint to Koremitsu; but Koremitsu ignored them, claimed complete ignorance, and pursued his affair as before, leaving them more confused than ever. They decided that he had been the amorous son of a provincial Governor who had whisked her off to the provinces for fear of the Secretary Captain.

---

79. After Yūgao's death.

80. Hokkedō, dedicated to rites centered on the all-important Lotus Sutra.

81. *Ganmon*, a formal document in Chinese, normally composed by a specialist.

82. It was customary to offer clothing and other belongings of the deceased to the temple, but since at her death she had nothing but what she wore, Genji had had a new set of clothes made as an offering.

83. For the first forty-nine days the spirit wandered in a "transitional state" (*chū*), then went to rebirth according to its karma. "What path" means which of the six realms of transmigration: the realms of celestial beings, humans, warring demons, beasts, starving ghosts, or hell.

The house belonged to a daughter[84] of the nurse who lived in the west of the City. With vehement tears this nurse's three children all accused Ukon, to them an outsider, of not telling them what had become of their mistress because she did not care about them. Ukon herself well knew the scolding they would give her, and Genji's determination to keep the secret prevented her from even asking after the little girl, of whose fate she therefore remained painfully ignorant.

Cypress-wood fan

Genji always hoped to dream of his lost love, but instead, on the night after the forty-ninth-day rite, he glimpsed the woman who had appeared beside her in the deserted mansion, just as she had been then, and with a shiver of horror he realized that the tragedy must have occurred because she haunted the ruinous old place and had taken a fancy to him.

The Iyo Deputy started down to his province early in the tenth month. Genji sent particularly generous farewell presents, "since the ladies are traveling with you." He also had special gifts—unusually pretty combs, fans in abundance, and elaborate offering-wands[85]—conveyed privately to a certain lady in the party,[86] together with that gown of hers that he had been keeping.

> "This has been to me a mere token of yourself till we meet again,
> but my tears in all that time have crumbled the sleeves away,"

he wrote, together with many others things too tedious to record.

Genji's official messenger returned without a letter from her, but by her little brother she sent him a reply about the gown:

> "Now cicada wings are cast off and we have changed out of summer clothes,
> I cannot help shedding tears, seeing this gown back again."

Genji kept thinking that it was after all her own extraordinary stubbornness that had distanced him from her.

Today was the first of winter, and of course cold rain was falling from a mournful sky. He spent the day staring despondently before him, murmuring,

---

84. Earlier described as the wife of one Honorary Deputy Governor.

85. Variously colored cloth streamers (*nusa*) to offer the gods of the road (*sae no kami*), who protect travelers.

86. Utsusemi.

"One of them has died, and today yet another must go her own way,
bound I know not to what end, while an autumn twilight falls."

No doubt he understood by now how painful a secret love can be.

I had passed over Genji's trials and tribulations in silence, out of respect for his determined efforts to conceal them, and I have written of them now only because certain lords and ladies criticized my story for resembling fiction, wishing to know why even those who knew Genji best should have thought him perfect, just because he was an Emperor's son. No doubt I must now beg everyone's indulgence for my effrontery in painting so wicked a portrait of him.

5

Young Murasaki

Waka means "young," while *mura-saki*, a plant whose roots yield a purple dye, means also the dye and its color. In poetry *murasaki* purple stands for close relation-ship and lasting passion. In this chapter Genji comes across a lit-tle girl very like Fujitsubo (she is Fujitsubo's niece), who to him is *murasaki*, and whom he immedi-ately wants for himself.

"How glad I would be to pick and soon to make mine that little wild plant sprung up from the very root shared by the murasaki.*"*

Murasaki comes in time to refer to the girl herself and to work more or less as her name.

RELATIONSHIP TO EARLIER CHAPTERS

"Young Murasaki" begins in the spring when Genji is eighteen, while "The Twilight Beauty" ends late in the previous year, but there is little narrative link between them.

PERSONS

Genji, a Captain in the Palace Guards, age 18

A holy man

His Reverence, a distinguished Prelate (Kitayama no Sōzu)

The son of the Governor of Harima, a retainer of Genji's (Yoshikiyo)

A former Governor of Harima, around 50 (Akashi no Nyūdō)

His daughter, 9 (Akashi no Kimi)

Koremitsu, Genji's foster brother and confidant

A girl of about 10 (Murasaki)

A nun, the girl's grandmother and the Prelate's sister, past 40 (Kitayama no Amagimi)

Shōnagon, Murasaki's nurse

His Highness of War, Murasaki's father, 33 (Hyōbukyō no Miya)

The Secretary Captain, Genji's brother-in-law and great friend (Tō no Chūjō)

The Left Controller, a half brother of Tō no Chūjō (Sachūben)

His Majesty, the Emperor, Genji's father (Kiritsubo no Mikado)

His Excellency, the Minister of the Left, Genji's father-in-law, 52 (Sadaijin)

Genji's wife, 22 (Aoi)

Her Highness, Princess Fujitsubo, 23

Ōmyōbu, Fujitsubo's gentlewoman

Genji, who was suffering from a recurrent fever, had all sorts of spells cast and healing rites done,[1] but to no avail; the fever kept returning. Someone then said, "My lord, there is a remarkable ascetic at a Temple in the Northern Hills. Last summer, when the fever was widespread and spells failed to help, he healed many people immediately. Please try him soon. It would be dangerous to allow your fever to become any worse." Genji sent for him, but the ascetic answered that, being now old and bent, he never left his cave.

"Then I shall have to go very quietly to see him." He set off before daybreak with only four or five especially close retainers.

The place was a little way into the mountains. The blossoms in the City were gone now, since it was late in the third month,[2] but in the mountains the cherry trees were in full bloom, and the farther he went, the lovelier the veils of mist became, until for him, whose rank so restricted travel that all this was new, the landscape became a source of wonder.

The temple impressed him as well. The holy man lived near a high peak amid forbidding rocks. Genji climbed there without announcing who he was and quite plainly dressed, but there was no mistaking him.

"Ah, this is too great an honor!" the holy man exclaimed in great agitation. "You must be the gentleman who desired my presence the other day. I have lost all interest in this world by now, and I have given up my healing practices altogether. What has brought you all this way, my lord?" He smiled as his eyes rested upon Genji.

He proved to be a most saintly man. The sun rose high in the sky while he made the necessary talismans,[3] had Genji swallow them, and proceeded with the rite.

When Genji went outside a moment and examined his surroundings, he found himself on a height directly overlooking the monks' lodges. At the foot of a steeply twisting path and surrounded, like the lodges but more neatly, by a brushwood

1. "Spells" (*majinai*) are healing magic performed by specialists from the Office of Medicine; "healing rites" (*kaji*) are Buddhist rites done by monks.
2. Roughly early May in the solar calendar.
3. Slips of paper inscribed with the Sanskrit seed syllables of the appropriate deities.

Page girl

fence, there stood a pretty house, set with its galleries in a handsome grove.

"Who lives there?" he asked.

"That, my lord, is where I gather His Reverence ————[4] has been secluded these last two years."

"It certainly is the place for someone of a retiring nature. What a pity I am so inadequately dressed. He is certain to find out I am here."

Genji clearly saw several nice-looking page girls come out to offer holy water, gather flowers, and so on.[5]

"Why, there is a woman living there!" his companions exclaimed to one another.

"Surely His Reverence would not have one with him!"

"Who can she be?"

Some went down to peer at the house. They reported having seen some nice-looking little girls, young gentlewomen, and page girls.

Genji was wondering, as the sun rose toward noon and he continued the rite, how his fever would now behave, when one of his men remarked, "Instead of just worrying, my lord, you should somehow get your mind off the matter"; and so Genji went onto the mountain behind the temple and looked out toward the City.

Mist veiled the landscape into the distance, and the budding trees everywhere were as though swathed in smoke. "It all looks just like a painting," he said. "No one living here could wish for more!"

"But, my lord, this is nothing yet. How much more beautiful your painting would be if only you had before your eyes the mountains and seas of other provinces!" Someone else extolled Mount Fuji and another peak.[6] Then they went on to divert him further by describing the lovely seaside villages and rocky shores of the provinces to the west.

"Among places less far away, I think the coast at Akashi in Harima deserves special mention. Not that any single feature of it is so extraordinary, but the view over the sea there is somehow more peaceful than elsewhere. A former Governor of the province—a gentleman who has now taken up the religious life[7] and who is looking very carefully after his daughter—has an impressive establishment there. He ought to have done well in the world, because he is descended from a Minister, but being eccentric he never mixed with society, resigned his post as a Captain of the Palace

---

4. An ecclesiastic of high rank and a nobleman himself, hence not someone by whom Genji would wish to be seen improperly dressed. The text avoids naming him.

5. They seem to be placing holy water (*aka*) on a simple offering shelf (*akadana*), which would normally have stood just beyond the veranda of the house. The "flowers" are probably the customary star anise (*shikimi*).

6. Probably Mount Asama, also in central Honshu.

7. He is a Novice (Nyūdō): someone who has taken preliminary vows, wears Buddhist robes, and leads a life of religious devotion at home.

Guards, and requested his posting as Governor himself.[8] He became a bit of a laughingstock in his province even so, and he was too embarrassed to return to the City, so he shaved his head instead. Not that he retired to any sheltered spot in the hills, because he put himself right on the sea, which is rather strange. It is certainly true, though, that while the province offers many places suitable for retirement, a village deep in the mountains would have been miserably lonely for his wife and his young daughter; and besides, I expect he feels more comfortable there himself. When I was down in the province some time ago, I went for a look at his residence. He may never have made a place for himself in the City, but the sheer scale of the tract he has claimed makes it obvious that he has arranged things—he *was* the Governor, after all—so as to spend the rest of his life in luxury. He does all his devotions to prepare for the life to come,[9] and in fact he makes a better monk than he ever did a gentleman."

"Yes," said Genji, "but what about his daughter?"

"My lord, I gather she has her share both of looks and of character. I hear one Governor after another has respectfully shown interest in her, but her father rejects each one. 'It is all very well for me to have sunk this low,' he says, 'but she is all I have, and I have other things in mind for her.' 'If you outlive me,' he tells her, 'if my hopes for you fail and the future I want for you is not to be, then you are to drown yourself in the sea.' That, they say, is the solemn injunction he repeats to her."

Genji was indeed amused.

"She must be a rare treasure then," someone said, laughing, "if her father means the Dragon King of the Sea to have her as his Queen!"

"Spare me such high ambition!"

The young man who had been telling about her, a son of the present Governor, had risen this year to the rank above Chamberlain.[10] "You're enterprising enough in love," one of them said. "You'd like to break her father's solemn injunction yourself, wouldn't you!"

"Oh, yes, I'm sure he's always lurking around her house!"

"Get on with you! She must be a country girl, whatever you say. Look at where she grew up, after all, and with no one but her ancient parents to teach her anything!"

"No, no, her mother seems to be of excellent birth. Thanks to her relations she manages to get pretty young gentlewomen and page girls from the best families in the City, and she is bringing up her daughter in grand style.

"He would not feel so safe about having her there if the Governor assigned to the province happened to be unscrupulous."

"I wonder what it means that his ambitions for her reach all the way to the bottom of the sea," Genji mused. "It cannot be much fun down there, with all that seaweed."[11] He was keenly intrigued. His marked taste for the unusual ensured that he would remember her story, as his companions clearly noted.

---

8. He had resigned a lower-fourth-rank post to take up one rated at upper fifth.
9. For rebirth in the paradise of the Buddha Amida.
10. The fifth rank, lower grade. In the "Suma" chapter he appears as Yoshikiyo.
11. Genji's remark plays, as do many poems, on the syllables *mirume*, which refer both to seaweed and to a lovers' meeting. The girl's fate will be gloomy if she ends up drowned among the seaweed, and she must be gloomy if that is what she thinks about.

"Your fever seems not to have flared up today, my lord, even though the sun will soon be setting. You should start back."

But the venerable monk demurred. "My lord, you seem also to have come under the influence of a spirit, and I prefer that we quietly continue our rites tonight before you return."

All approved. Genji was pleased, too, since he had never spent the night away like this before. "Very well, I shall start at dawn."

For want of better to do during what remained of the long day, he melted into the heavy twilight mists toward the brushwood fence that had caught his eye. He then sent the others back and peered through the fence with Lord Koremitsu.

There she was, straight before him on the west side of the house, engaged in practice before her personal buddha:[12] a nun. The blinds were a little way up, and she seemed to be making a flower offering. She was leaning against a pillar, with her scripture text on an armrest[13] before her and chanting with obvious difficulty, and she was plainly of no common distinction. Past forty and very thin, with elegantly white skin, she nonetheless still had a roundness to her cheeks, fine eyes, and hair so neatly cut[14] that to Genji it seemed much more pleasingly modern in style than if it had been long.

Two handsome, grown-up women and some page girls were wandering in and out of the room. In among them came running a girl of ten or so, wearing a softly rumpled kerria rose layering[15] over a white gown and, unlike the other children, an obvious future beauty. Her hair cascaded like a spread fan behind her as she stood there, her face all red from crying.

"What is the matter?" The nun glanced up at her. "Have you quarreled with one of the girls?" They looked so alike that Genji took them for mother and daughter.

"Inuki let my baby sparrow go! And I had him in his cage[16] and everything!" declared the indignant little girl.

"So that silly creature has managed to earn herself another scolding! She is hopeless!" a grown-up said. "And where did he go? He had grown to be such a dear little thing. Oh," she went on, rising to leave, "I hope the crows do not get him!" She was a fine-looking woman with very nice long hair. Apparently she was in charge of the girl, since the others seemed to call her Nurse Shōnagon.

"Oh, come, you are such a baby!" the nun protested. "You understand nothing, do you! Here I am, wondering whether I will last out this day or the next, but that means nothing to you, does it! All you do is chase sparrows. Oh, dear, and I keep telling you it is a sin![17] Come here!"

The little girl sat down. She had a very dear face, and the faint arc of her eye-

---

12. *Jibutsu*, a buddha image that is the focus of a person's private devotions.

13. *Kyōsoku*, a common item of furniture used here as a reading desk.

14. Her hair is probably cut not far below her shoulders (*ama-sogi*), as was the custom for a nun who remained at home.

15. *Yamabuki*, of which the top layer is ocher (*usu kuchiba*) and the lining yellow.

16. A makeshift cage, since it is actually a *fusego*, a sort of frame that went over an incense burner and on which a robe could then be laid to be perfumed.

17. The Buddhist sin of capturing and imprisoning a living being.

brows, the forehead from which she had childishly swept back her hair, and the hairline itself were extremely pretty. *She* is one I would like to see when she grows up! Genji thought, fascinated. Indeed, he wept when he realized that it was her close resemblance to the lady who claimed all his heart that made it impossible for him to take his eyes off her.

"You hate even to have it combed," the nun said, stroking the girl's hair, "but what beautiful hair it is! Your childishness really worries me, you know. Not everyone is like this at your age, I assure you. Your late mother was ten when she lost her father, and she perfectly understood what had happened. How would you manage if I were suddenly to leave you?" She wept so bitterly that the watching Genji felt a wave of sorrow, too. Child though she was, the little girl observed the nun gravely, then looked down and hung her head. Her hair spilled forward as she did so, glinting with the loveliest sheen.

> *"When no one can say where it is the little plant will grow up at last,*
> *the dewdrop soon to leave her does not see how she can go,"*

the nun said. With tears and a cry of sympathy, a woman replied,

> *"Alas, does the dew really mean to melt away before she can know*
> *where her tender little plant will at last grow to be tall?"*[18]

His Reverence appeared from elsewhere in the house. "This side seems to be open for anyone to look in. Today is not the day for you to be sitting so near the veranda. I have just learned that Captain Genji is now with the holy man higher up the mountain, seeking a cure for a recurrent fever. He came so quietly that I knew nothing about it, and despite being here I have not even been to call on him yet."

"How dreadful! Here we all are in disarray, and someone may actually have seen us!" Down came the blinds.

"This is a chance, if you like, to see the Shining Genji whose praises all the world is singing. His looks are enough to make even a renunciate monk forget his cares and feel young again. Well, I shall go and greet him." Genji heard him and returned to where he was staying.

What an enchanting girl he had found! Those companions of his, so keen on women and always exploring, might indeed come across their rare finds, but he had found a treasure just on a chance outing! He was delighted. What a dear child! Who could she be? He now longed for the pleasure of having her with him day and night, to make up for the absence of the lady he loved.

He was lying down when a disciple of His Reverence came inquiring for Koremitsu. The place was so small that he heard everything.

The disciple said on behalf of his master, "I have just learned that his lordship is favoring us with a visit, and despite the suddenness of the news I should be wait-

---

18. "How could you die before you know what will become of your granddaughter?" The "little plant" (*wakakusa*) image recalls *Ise monogatari* 90, section 49.

ing upon his pleasure, but, you see, it pains me that his lordship, who knows I am on retreat at the temple here, should have chosen nonetheless to keep his arrival a secret. I should really have offered him a poor mat in my own lodging. It is all quite upsetting."

Genji replied,[19] "A little before the middle of this month I began to suffer from a recurrent fever, and the severity of its repeated attacks prompted me to accept advice to come here in all haste. I have kept my visit quiet, however, because it seemed to me that it would be a shame if the intervention of so saintly a man were to fail, and that consideration for him enjoined special caution on someone like myself. I shall gladly accept, if that is your wish."

To Genji's embarrassment His Reverence quickly appeared. Monk though he was, his birth entitled him to society's highest esteem, and Genji's present casual dress made its wearer uncomfortable.

His Reverence first told Genji about his life on retreat and then pressed his invitation. "It is only a common brushwood hut,[20] my lord, but I would gladly show you its pleasantly cool stream." Genji blushed to think of the extravagant terms in which his host had described him to those of the household who had not yet seen him themselves, but interest in the little girl who had so caught his fancy encouraged him to go.

The place, which really was very well done, boasted the usual plants and trees. Cressets were lit along the brook, and there were lights in the lanterns,[21] too, because at this time of the month there was no moon. The room on the south side[22] had been nicely prepared for him. A delicious fragrance of rare incense filled the air, and Genji's own scent as he passed by was so unlike any other that those in the house must have been overawed.

His Reverence talked of mutability and of the life to come while Genji pondered the fearfulness of his own transgression,[23] the way in which this sinful preoccupation had driven all else from his mind, the likelihood that it would torment him all his days, and, worse still, the agonies that awaited him in the hereafter. How he wished that he himself might live as did his host! But the figure he had seen by daylight still called out to him.

"May I ask Your Reverence what lady lives here? I had a dream on which I wished to consult you, you see, and I have only just remembered it."

His host smiled. "How unexpectedly your dream has entered our conversation, my lord! I am afraid that my answer will disappoint you. You probably do not know about the late Inspector Grand Counselor, because it is a long time now since he died. His widow is my sister, you see. She renounced the world after he was gone, and when recently her health began to fail, she sought refuge with me, since I myself no longer visit the City. She has secluded herself here."

19. Through Koremitsu.
20. A stock description of a humble dwelling, hence a stock expression of modesty.
21. A cresset (*kagaribi*) is a wood fire contained in an iron cage, used for illuminating a garden at night; a lantern (*tōrō*), containing an oil lamp, was made of wood, bamboo, or metal and hung from the eaves.
22. The "front" of the house, normally used for guests.
23. His love for Fujitsubo.

"I had heard that the Grand Counselor's daughter was still living, though," Genji ventured. "Of course I mean nothing frivolous; my inquiry is quite serious."

"Yes, he had a daughter. It must be ten years and more since she died. The late Grand Counselor brought her up very carefully in the hope of offering her to His Majesty, but he passed away before he could do so, leaving the present nun to look after her as well as she could, all alone. Meanwhile, someone[24] allowed His Highness of the Bureau of War[25] to take up with her in secret. However, His Highness's wife is a very great lady, and the resulting unpleasantness made her so continually miserable that in the end she died. Oh, yes, I have seen with my own eyes how someone can sicken from sheer disappointment and sorrow."

Ah, Genji thought, then the girl is her daughter. I suppose it is being His Highness's, too, that makes her look so much like her.[26] He was now more eager than ever to have her for his own. She was of distinguished parentage, she was delightful, and she showed no distressing tendency to talk back. How he would love to have her with him and bring her up as he pleased!

"All this is sad news," he said, still keen to be certain who she was. "Did the daughter leave no child to preserve her memory?"

"Yes, she did, not long before she died—another girl. I am afraid she is a great worry to her grandmother, who seems extremely anxious about her as her own life draws to a close."

So I was right! Genji said to himself.

"Please forgive me for being so forward, but would you be good enough to advise the child's grandmother to entrust her granddaughter's future to me? I have certain ideas of my own, and although there are of course ladies upon whom I call, they seem not to suit me as well as they might, since I live alone. You may attribute the most common intentions to me and therefore feel that she is hardly yet of a suitable age, but if so, you do me an injustice."

"My lord, your proposal should be very welcome, but she is still so young and innocent that I do not see how you could propose even in jest to favor her that way. At any rate, I myself can make no decision, since it is not for me to rear a girl into adulthood. I shall give you an answer after discussing the matter with her grandmother." He spoke curtly, and his young guest found the formality of his manner so forbidding that he was at a loss to reply. "It is time for me to busy myself in the hall where Amida dwells," His Reverence continued. "I have not yet done the evening service.[27] I shall be at your disposal once more when it is over." He went up to the hall.

Genji felt quite unwell, and besides, it was now raining a little, a cold mountain wind had set in to blow, and the pool beneath the waterfall had risen until the roar was louder than before. The eerie swelling and dying of somnolent voices chanting the scriptures could hardly fail in such a setting to move the most casual visitor. No wonder Genji, who had so much to ponder, could not sleep.

24. Probably a gentlewoman in the service of the girl and her mother.
25. Fujitsubo's older brother.
26. Fujitsubo.
27. *Soya*, a regular service that lasted from about 6:00 to 10:00 P.M.

His Reverence had mentioned the evening service, but the night was in fact well advanced. Obviously the nun and her gentlewomen in the chamber[28] were not asleep yet, because despite their efforts to be quiet he could hear the click of rosary beads against an armrest, as well as a rustling of silks most pleasing to his ears. Since they were so close, he opened a gap in the line of screens that bounded his room and rapped his fan on his palm. Though surprised, they seemed to see no point in pretending not to have heard him, for he caught the sound of a gentlewoman slipping toward him. "How odd!" she murmured, flustered, after retreating a little. "I must be hearing things!"

"I have heard it said that even in darkness the Lord Buddha is an unerring guide," Genji began, overwhelming her with the youthful grace of his voice.

"A guide to what? I do not understand."

"So sudden an approach on my part naturally perplexes you, but I hope that you will convey this message for me:

> Ever since that time I first spied the tender leaves of the little plant,
>   the traveler's sleeves I wear are endlessly wet with dew."

"But, my lord, no one here could possibly make anything of such a message, as you must surely know. To whom, then, do you wish me . . . ?"

"Please grant me reasons of my own for expressing myself this way."

The gentlewoman went back to speak to her mistress, the nun, who was both puzzled and shocked. Oh, dear, she thought, he certainly is modern in his ways! He must have got it into his head that our girl is old enough for this sort of thing! But how did he manage to hear what we were saying about the "little plant"? In her confusion she failed to answer him for so long that she feared she was being uncivil.

> "O never compare dews that gather for a night on your own pillow
>   to those that in these mountains wet many a mossy robe![29]

Here, the dew never dries."

"I am afraid I am a novice at conversing this way, through somebody else," Genji replied. "I have something to discuss with you seriously, if you will forgive my presumption."

"Surely he has been misled," the nun said to her women. "It is so intimidating to have him here that I do not know how to answer."

"But, my lady, you are making him uncomfortable."

"Well, yes, I suppose it would be one thing if I were a young woman myself, but as it is, I really cannot ignore him when he is so much in earnest." She came to Genji herself.

---

28. They seem to be on the west side of the house, while Genji (in the aisle) is on the south. They seem to be separated only by folding screens.

29. "Do not compare the tears of a brief visitor to these mountains with those shed by one whose whole life is spent among them." She ignores the romantic connotations of the dew (the pining lovers' tears) in Genji's own poem.

"You may imagine after my abrupt approach that I am only seeking my own amusement," he began, "but as the Lord Buddha surely knows, I find no such feelings in my heart." Restrained by the quiet circumspection in her manner, he could not at first get out what he had to say.

"Why, no, my lord, how could you assume that I make light of your feelings, now that you and I are so unexpectedly conversing with each other?"

"I have been pained to learn of the difficulties that your granddaughter faces, and I hope that you will kindly allow me to take the place of the mother whom I believe she has lost. I myself was very young when those who would have brought me up were taken from me, and the life I have led ever since has been a strangely rootless one. Her situation and mine are so alike that I have longed to beg you to recognize how much she and I share, and so I have seized this rare opportunity, even at the risk of offending you, to address you frankly."

"Your words should make me glad, my lord, but caution restrains me, for I fear that in some things you may be misinformed. There is indeed here one for whom only I am responsible, however little I may deserve it, but she is still extremely young, and since I cannot imagine how you could overlook this difficulty, I see no way to take your proposition seriously."

"I understand you perfectly, but I still urge you to take no narrow view of what I ask. Please consider instead the exceptional nature of my most sincere desire."

However, she remained convinced that he simply did not understand the incongruity of his proposal, and her answers conceded nothing. Meanwhile, His Reverence had returned. Very well, Genji reflected as he once more closed the gap between the screens, it is a relief at least to have broached the subject.

Dawn was near, and the awesome voices chanting the Confession in the Lotus Meditation Hall came to them on the wind down the mountain, mingled with the noise of the waterfall.

> "The wandering wind blowing down the mountain slopes sweeps away the dream,[30]
> and then tears begin to flow at the clamor of the falls,"

Genji said, and His Reverence,

> "The swift mountain stream that so much to your surprise has moistened your sleeves
> stirs no trouble in a heart its waters have long washed clean.

I am just so used to it, I suppose."

The lightening sky was thick with mist, and mountain birds were singing everywhere. Flowers Genji could not even name carpeted the ground with a many-colored brocade of petals, on which deer now stood or wandered past—a sight so wonderful that all thought of his fever melted away. The holy man managed to per-

---

30. "The dream of the passions that obscures insight into the truth." Genji is paying a compliment to his host.

form a protective rite for him, despite his difficulty in moving about. His hoarse voice was quite indistinct, but his chanting of the *darani*[31] conveyed an impressive sanctity.

Those who had come from the City to escort Genji home now presented themselves before him, expressed their pleasure that his fever had abated, and conveyed as well His Majesty's wishes for Genji's health. His Reverence scoured the depths of the valley to entertain Genji with all sorts of fruits and nuts unknown to the world at large.

"Alas, my lord," he remarked, offering Genji wine, "my solemn vow to remain on the mountain through this year prevents me from accompanying you as I should otherwise wish to do."

Single-pointed vajra

"While my heart remains in these mountains, His Majesty's kind expressions of concern leave me no choice but to return," Genji replied. "This year's blossoms shall not pass before I come again.

> *I shall go forth now and describe to all at court these mountain cherries,*
> *that before the winds arrive they themselves should come and see."*

His manner of speaking and the sound of his voice were both utterly captivating.

> *"At last I have seen the* udumbara *flower: that is how I feel,*
> *till I have no eyes at all for mountain cherry blossoms,"*[32]

His Reverence courteously replied.

Genji smiled. "What you have before you cannot be the flower of which you speak, for surely that one blooms only once, and at its proper time."

The holy man took up the wine cup in his turn.

> *"Having just for once opened deep in these mountains my lowly pine door,*
> *I see the face of a flower I have never seen before!"*[33]

he said, contemplating Genji with tears in his eyes. He gave Genji a single-pointed *vajra*[34] to protect him.

His Reverence then gave Genji his own most appropriately selected gifts: a rosary of embellished bo tree seeds, obtained by Prince Shōtoku from Kudara, still in its original Chinese-style box and presented in a gauze bag attached to a branch

---

31. The protective rite was centered, like many others, on the chanting of a *darani*, a mystically powerful utterance voiced in the Japanese pronunciation of a Chinese transliteration from Sanskrit.

32. The *udumbara* flower blooms once in three thousand years, when a perfected ruler appears and unites all the world in the Buddha's truth.

33. The modest "pine" door contrasts evergreen constancy with the flower's passing beauty.

34. *Toko*, an esoteric Buddhist ritual implement and a symbol of supreme insight. Other variants of it have three, five, or more points or prongs.

of five-needled pine; and dark blue lapis lazuli jars containing diverse medicines and tied to sprays of wisteria or cherry blossoms.[35] Genji had already sent for the varied gifts, formal and informal, with which to reward the holy man and the other monks who had chanted the scriptures for him, and he now distributed suitable presents to all, even the local woodcutters. At last he took his leave, after providing for further chanting of the scriptures.

His Reverence went into the house and repeated to the nun all that Genji had told him, but her only comment was "At any rate, we cannot answer him now. If in four or five years his wish remains unchanged, then perhaps . . ."

The reply Genji received therefore only confirmed the nun's opposition. Through a small boy in His Reverence's service, he sent,

> *"Now that I have seen faintly the flower's color through the gathering dusk,*
> *I can hardly bear to leave while morning mists still rise"*;[36]

to which the nun answered in a casual hand remarkable for its character and distinction,

> *"Whether it is true you would never wish to leave the flower you prize,*
> *that we shall look to discern in the mists of future skies."*

Genji was entering his carriage when a crowd of young gentlemen from His Excellency's arrived to see him home, complaining that he had simply vanished from among them. The Secretary Captain, the Left Controller, and his other brothers-in-law had insisted on coming after him.

"We would have gladly accompanied you on a trip like this," the Captain said reproachfully, "and it really was not very nice of you to leave us behind. Anyway, it would be a great shame if we were to turn round and start back again without a moment to rest beneath these magnificent blossoms."

They all sat together on the moss, in the lee of a rock, and the wine cup went round. The tumbling stream beside them made a beautiful cascade. The Captain took a flute from the fold of his robe and played, while the Left Controller sang, "Westward from the Toyora Temple . . . ,"[37] lightly tapping out the rhythm with his fan. These young gentlemen were all certainly splendid, but Genji's peerless, indeed disturbing beauty as he sat leaning against a rock, quite unwell, made it impossible to have eyes for anyone else.

One of the Secretary Captain's company was as usual a *hichiriki* player, while

---

35. The Buddha reached enlightenment under a bo tree, the seeds of which were valued as rosary beads. Prince Shōtoku (574–622) established Buddhism in Japan after its official introduction from Kudara (an ancient Korean kingdom). The medicine jars (associated with Yakushi, the Buddha of Healing) are made of *ruri*, in theory lapis lazuli (a blue stone) but in practice, at least in Japan, more often glass.

36. "Now that I have seen the little girl, I do not wish to be parted from her by her guardians' objections."

37. From a felicitous *saibara* song entitled "Kazuraki."

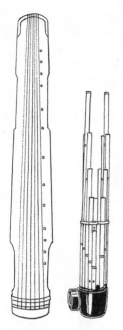

Kin, shō, *and* hichiriki

another young man of taste had been entrusted with a *shō*.[38] His Reverence brought Genji his own *kin*.[39] "Do play a little, my lord," he said. "If it please you, I should like to give the birds of these mountains a pleasant surprise." Genji protested that he was not feeling himself, but he played enough not to be disobliging. Everyone then set out.

The very least of the monks and young servants wept to see him go, while of course the old nuns in the house, who had never seen his like before, assured each other that he could not possibly be of this world at all. His Reverence himself exclaimed, wiping tears from his eyes, "Ah, it is sad to think what karma can have got him born with such looks into these latter days, and into this poor land of ours!"[40]

To the little girl's childish eye, Genji was so splendid that she declared, "He is much better-looking than Father!"

"Then why not be his little girl instead?" a gentlewoman suggested. She nodded and seemed very pleased with the idea. Whenever she played with a doll or painted a picture, she pretended that the figure was Lord Genji, dressed it up nicely, and made a great fuss over it.

Genji first went to the palace and gave His Majesty an account of all that had happened. His Majesty was dismayed to see him so thin. He inquired about the quality of the holy man and was sufficiently impressed by Genji's long description to remark, "I believe he deserves elevation to Adept. How strange that he should have lived a life of practice for all these years without ever coming to his Sovereign's attention!"

Just then His Excellency arrived. "I had thought I should at least come out to meet you, but then I reflected that since you had gone so discreetly, I might do better to refrain. Do come and spend a few quiet days with us. I shall accompany you there straightaway." Genji had little enthusiasm for this, but he let himself be dragged off. His Excellency invited him into his own carriage and modestly got in behind him. Genji was touched after all by his attentions.

The household was eagerly awaiting his arrival. His Excellency had had all sorts of things done since Genji's last visit, some time ago, to make the place grander than ever. His daughter slipped off as always to hide and refused to appear until her father persuaded her at last to come forth; and there she sat, precisely where her gentlewomen placed her, as still and as perfect as a lady in a painting.

38. Tō no Chūjō, known for his mastery of the transverse flute (*fue*), presumably made sure that he traveled with suitable accompanists. The *hichiriki* is a small reed instrument made of bamboo; the *shō* is a cluster of fine bamboo pipes rising from a single air chest into which the player blows.

39. A seven-stringed instrument of the koto family. Highly respected in China, it was prized in Japan, too, in the early tenth century, and Genji's taste for it figures prominently in such chapters as "Suma" and "Akashi." However, it seems not to have been played much in the author's own time.

40. The "latter days" of the Buddhist teaching and *mutsukashiki hi no moto*, "miserable little Japan."

I could try talking to her about whatever I have on my mind, or tell her about my trip to the mountains, and it would be so nice if only she would then give me some sort of decent response! Genji reflected; but no, she would not unbend, and she remained cold and forbidding. The gulf between them had widened over the years, until he felt provoked to say, "I do wish I might occasionally see you treat me in a normal way. For example, there I was, deathly ill, and you did not even ask after my health—not that this is anything new, I know, but I cannot help feeling hurt."

At last she spoke. "Was it really 'so painful to be ignored'?"[41] She threw him sidelong a chilly glance that accented the stern character of her beauty.

"You so seldom speak, but when you do, you say the most extraordinary things! That is hardly our relationship to each other. What a way to talk! I keep trying this and that in the hope that you may change your mind and give up rejecting me all the time, but as far as I can tell, you only dislike me the more! Well, one day perhaps . . ."

He went into their curtained bed, but she did not immediately follow. At a loss for what else to say, he lay down unhappily and proceeded—for he was no doubt feeling thoroughly out of humor—to feign drowsiness, the better to turn over in his mind all the troubles that love had brought him.

He was still keen to watch the "little plant" grow up, but there was a good deal to be said for the nun's opinion that she was far too young. This is such a tricky business on which to approach anyone! he said to himself. What will I have to do to be able to take her home and enjoy her company always? His Highness of War is a decent enough gentleman, but he has nothing in particular to recommend him, so why is she so like *her*? Because they were both born to the same Empress, I suppose.[42] This intimate tie to her made up his mind that he must have her for his own.

The next day he sent off letters to the Northern Hills. The one to His Reverence no doubt hinted at his wish. He wrote to the nun, "I felt constrained by your distant manner and unfortunately never managed to say all I wished. I should be glad if a note such as this were to convince you that there is nothing mild about my hopes . . . ," and so on. Inside the letter he placed a little knotted one:[43]

> *"That vision of you never, never leaves me now, O mountain cherry,*
> *even though I left behind in your care all of my heart.*

I worry so about you when the night winds blow!"[44] His writing, of course, but even the casual way he had done up the letter dazzled the eyes of the aging nuns.[45]

41. The poem Aoi quotes has not been identified. Perhaps Genji responds with disapproval because the poem had to do with illicit lovers, not a married couple.

42. "Why does the girl look so much like Fujitsubo? Probably because His Highness of War and Fujitsubo are the children of the same Empress." The girl is Fujitsubo's niece.

43. A playful courting note for the girl. This sort of letter (*musubi bumi*) was written on a piece of paper, then folded up very thin and knotted.

44. *Shūishū* 29, by Prince Motoyoshi: "Before dawn I rose to see my plum blossoms, worried about what the night winds might have done." Genji fears that "night winds" may scatter the blossoms' petals, that is, take the girl away somewhere beyond his reach.

45. There seem to be several older nuns, presumably former gentlewomen, around the little girl's grandmother.

How very difficult all this is! What reply can I possibly give him? She wrote, "I confess that I gave little weight to the kind words that I was privileged to have from you, and now that it has pleased you to return to the matter, I find it difficult to frame a reply. Surely there is no point in pursuing it, since she cannot even write her *kana* letters[46] properly yet. After all,

> *Just that little while the blossoms cling to the bough on a windswept hill:*
> *so long you have left your heart, and such times are quickly gone.*

I worry about her more and more." His Reverence answered in the same vein.

The disappointed Genji sent Koremitsu there two or three days later. "The woman they call Nurse Shōnagon should be in the house," he said. "Find her and have a good talk with her."

He never misses a single one, does he! Koremitsu remembered with amusement his own inadequate glimpse of the girl, and how very young she had been.

His Reverence professed deep gratification upon receiving yet another letter. Koremitsu asked to see Shōnagon and spent some time with her, telling her what Genji had to say and describing something of Genji's life. He was a great talker, and he made it all sound very convincing, but the little girl was so impossibly young that her guardians remained troubled about what Genji might have in mind.

Genji's letter itself was sincerely felt, and as before it contained a little note: "I should still like to see this broken writing[47] of yours.

> *Ah, Mount Asaka! Shallow all my love for you cannot ever be—*
> *but why does the face in the spring melt away when I draw near?*"[48]

The nun replied,

> *"They tell of a spring such that one who draws from it knows only regret;*
> *shallow as your waters are, how could they reveal her face?"*[49]

Koremitsu conveyed the same message to Genji.

Nurse Shōnagon wrote in her own reply, "We are soon to move back to my lady's residence in the City, as long as her condition improves, and I expect that she will wish to communicate with you further from there." Genji did not find this encouraging.

Princess Fujitsubo was not well and had withdrawn from the palace. Genji felt

---

46. The letters of the phonetic syllabary, with which writing lessons began.

47. She is still writing the *kana* letters separately instead of running them together.

48. The little girl must know the poem to which Genji's alludes, since any child learning to write had to copy it out. Both play on the place-name Asaka-yama ("Mount Asaka") and on *asashi* ("shallow"). The original poem (*Man'yōshū* 3829), also cited in the Japanese preface to the *Kokinshū*) was spoken in ancient times by a pretty court lady to an ill-humored lord from the north: "Mount Asaka, shallow the spring that now mirrors your face, but not this heart of mine in desire." Her declaration brightened the visitor's mood.

49. "I cannot believe you are serious, and I cannot give you my granddaughter." *Kokin rokujō* 987: "Alas that I should have begun to draw water from a mountain spring so shallow that it only wets my sleeves."

deep sympathy for His Majesty, whose anxious distress was evident, but he also anticipated feverishly now, at last, a chance for himself, and he no longer went out at all. At the palace or at home he spent the daylight hours daydreaming and those after dark hounding Ōmyōbu.[50] How Ōmyōbu brought off their meeting is impossible to say, but to poor Genji even these stolen moments[51] with her seemed quite unreal. To Her Highness the memory of that last, most unfortunate incident was a source of enduring suffering, and she had resolved that nothing of the kind should ever happen again; yet despite her obvious consternation she remained thoughtful and kind, even while she continued to resist him with a profound dignity so far beyond the reach of any other woman that Genji could not help wondering in anguish why it was never possible to find in her the slightest flaw.

How could he have told her all he had to say? He must have wished himself where darkness never ends,[52] but alas, the nights were short now, and their time together had yielded after all nothing but pain.

> "This much we have shared, but nights when we meet again will be very rare,
> and now that we live this dream, O that it might swallow me!"

he said, sobbing; to which Her Highness compassionately replied,

> "People soon enough will be passing on our tale, though I let our dream
> sweep me on till I forget what misfortune now is mine."

Genji could not blame her for being in such torment, and he deeply regretted having caused it. Ōmyōbu gathered up his dress cloak and so on and brought it to him.

At home again, he lay down and wept all day. He gathered that she was refusing as usual to read any letter from him, and although this was indeed her normal practice, the pain of it now all but destroyed him. For two or three days he remained shut up without even calling at the palace, until His Majesty was moved yet again to a concern about what might be wrong that only filled Genji with terror.

Her Highness continued to lament the misery of her lot, and meanwhile she began feeling more and more unwell, so that she could not make up her mind to go straight back to the palace, despite a stream of messengers from there urging her to do so. No, she really did not feel herself, and her silent guesses at what this might mean reduced her to despair over what was to become of her.

She rose less and less during the summer heat. By the third month her condition was obvious enough that her women noticed it, and the horror of her fate overwhelmed her. Not knowing what had actually happened, they expressed surprise

---

50. The regular intermediary between Genji and Fujitsubo. The initial Ō element shows that she was of imperial blood. *Myōbu* was a title borne by middle-ranking women in palace service.

51. The original expression contains the verb *miru* ("see"), which implies sexual intimacy. The passage is studiously understated because of Fujitsubo's exalted position. The "last, most unfortunate incident" mentioned just below does not otherwise appear in the tale.

52. The original speaks of Kurabu no Yama, a place-name that sounds as though it means "Dark Mountain" and that appears in poetry for that reason.

that she had not yet told His Majesty. She alone understood just what the matter was. Women like Ōmyōbu or her own foster sister, Ben, who attended her intimately when she bathed and therefore had before their eyes every clue to her condition, did not doubt that something was seriously wrong, but they could not very well discuss the matter, and Ōmyōbu was left to reflect in anguish that her mistress's fate had struck after all. To His Majesty, Ōmyōbu presumably reported that a malevolent spirit had obscured Her Highness's condition,[53] so that at first it had gone unnoticed. This was at any rate what Her Highness's own women believed. His Majesty was deeply concerned about her, and the unbroken procession of messengers from him inspired mingled dread and despair.

Genji himself had a dream so strange that he summoned a dream reader. In answer to his questions he received an interpretation beyond the bounds of all plausibility.

"I see, too, my lord, that you are to suffer a reverse and that something will require the most urgent caution."

Genji was troubled. "It is not my own dream. I have only described someone else's. Say not a word about it until it comes true."

He was wondering what it all meant when he heard about Her Highness and realized that he probably knew what the matter was. But despite his pleas, now more passionate than ever, Ōmyōbu was too cowed by fear and guilt to contrive anything for him. His love's rare, one-line replies to his letters now stopped altogether.

She did not return to the palace until the seventh month. His Majesty, whose love was extraordinary, showed her renewed affection. A new roundness of figure and a face wasted by suffering gave her now a truly peerless beauty. As usual His Majesty spent all his time in her rooms, and since it was the season for music, he was always summoning Genji to attend him and perform on the *kin* or the flute. Genji struggled to conceal his feelings, but whenever he failed and betrayed a hint of his torment, Her Highness was overcome, despite her best efforts, by a host of disturbing thoughts.

The nun at the mountain temple had recovered well enough to come down to the City. Genji discovered where she lived and sent her frequent messages. Not unnaturally, her position remained unchanged, and what with the more absorbing sorrows that had overtaken him during the last few months, he had no latitude to think of anything else.

Late that autumn he was feeling very reduced and disheartened. One beautifully moonlit night he had at last made up his mind to visit a lady he had been seeing in secret when the weather turned and a cold rain began to fall. He was bound for the vicinity of Rokujō and Kyōgoku[54]—rather far, to his mind, since he was coming from the palace—when he caught sight of an unkempt house amid the darkness of ancient trees.

---

53. By causing an illness that diverted attention from the symptoms of pregnancy. In the roughly contemporary historical work *Eiga monogatari* (*A Tale of Flowering Fortunes*), a gentlewoman may watch her mistress's periods, count days, and report to the man concerned. The Emperor would normally have had a clear idea of when Fujitsubo got pregnant and of when to expect the child.

54. These are streets. Locations in the City were designated in terms of the nearest intersection.

"That is the house of the late Inspector Grand Counselor," explained Koremitsu, who was with him as always. "I happened to call there the other day, and they told me that my lady the nun is very weak now, and they hardly know what to do."

"What sad news! I should really have called on her before. Why did they not let me know? Do go in and convey my greetings."

Koremitsu sent a man to tell the household of Genji's arrival, instructing him to say that Genji had come purposely to call. The man therefore announced when he entered that His Lordship had been pleased to pay them a visit.

"This is most unfortunate!" The women were startled. "For days now my lady's health has been a great worry, and she is in no condition to receive him." They could not just send him away, though, so they tidied up the south aisle room and invited him in. "This is most unworthy accommodation, my lord, but my lady wishes at least to thank you. It is unfortunately a very dreary room in which to receive you on so unexpected a visit."[55] Genji agreed that the room was indeed unusual for such an occasion.

"I have often thought of calling on you," he began, "but you have always given me so little hope that in the end I refrained. Your illness, of which I had not heard, troubles me very much."

The nun replied, "It is very good indeed of you to look in upon me now that I, who have never been a stranger to failing health, am at last nearing my end, and I apologize for not speaking to you myself. Do by all means approach her once she is no longer a child, if it happens that you remain disposed as you are now. I am afraid that leaving her this way without a protector may well hinder my progress on the path I so long to take."[56]

She was so near that Genji now and then caught her feeble voice. "There is every reason to be grateful for his interest, you know," she was saying. "If only our little girl were just old enough to thank him properly!"[57]

He was moved to answer, "But why would I exhibit my immodesty this way if I had taken only a passing fancy to her? There is an unfathomable bond between her and me, and my heart went out to her the moment I saw her—indeed, with such uncanny speed that I cannot believe this tie to be from this life alone." And he continued, "I understand that any further pleading would be wasted, but if I might possibly just hear the sound of her voice . . ."

"But, my lord, she does not know you are here, and she is in bed!"

Just then footsteps approached from the depths of the house, and a little girl's voice called, "Grandma, they say Lord Genji is here, the gentleman at the mountain temple! Why are you not looking at him?"[58]

"Hush!" said the shocked women.

"But she said seeing him made her feel so much better!"

This was welcome news, but in consideration for the women's embarrassment

---

55. Genji seems to have been received not in the main house but in one of the wings, but the precise meaning of the passage is uncertain.
56. The path to rebirth in paradise.
57. She is speaking to her women, including the one through whom she is talking to Genji.
58. If she had received him in person, she could have seen him through her curtains.

Genji pretended despite his pleasure not to have heard, and he brought his visit to a correct conclusion before leaving. Yes, he thought, she really is just a little girl, but I will teach her properly.

The next day he sent the nun a courteous note with as usual a smaller one, tightly folded, inside it:

> "Ever since these ears listened to that single cry from the little crane,
>   I have despaired that my boat should be caught among the reeds.

'And ever to that same love . . .' "[59] He had purposely written in a youthful hand so appealing that all the gentlewomen urged the little girl to put it straight into her copybook.

Shōnagon composed the reply: "The lady you visited seems unlikely to live many days longer, and she will therefore move presently to the temple in the mountains. She will wish to thank you for your kind letter even if she can no longer do so in this life." Genji was deeply moved.

His thoughts would turn of an autumn evening to the one who so constantly stirred his heart, and he surely thirsted more than ever for any relation of hers. He remembered that evening when the nun spoke of being unable to let the little plant go, and he yearned for her, although he also felt a pang of apprehension that if he did have her she might disappoint him; and he murmured,

> "How glad I would be to pick and soon to make mine that little wild plant
>   sprung up from the very root shared by the murasaki."[60]

In the tenth month His Majesty was to make a progress to the Suzaku Palace.[61] He had chosen as dancers those sons of the greatest houses, senior nobles or privy gentlemen, who showed any aptitude for such things, and everyone from the Princes and Ministers on down was busy rehearsing his part.

Genji remembered how long it had been since his last correspondence with the lady in the mountains, and he sent a messenger there. The only answer he received was from His Reverence, who wrote, "She breathed her last on the twentieth of last month, in my presence, and although death comes to us all, hers is a very great loss," and so on. Genji felt the frailty of life sharply as he read it, and he wondered anxiously how the little girl whose future had so worried her was now getting on. Young as she was, did she miss her grandmother? He remembered losing his own mother, if only dimly, and he took care to keep in touch with her. The replies he had from Shōnagon were not unsympathetic.

---

59. Genji's progress is impeded by the nun's resistance. In *Kokinshū* 732 the lover protests that his "little boat" will always return to the same love.

60. *Murasaki*, later the girl's name, refers to Fujitsubo. A common meadow plant, *murasaki* was associated with love because of the purple dye extracted from its roots. The *fuji* ("wisteria") in Fujitsubo's name links her to the same color. *Kokinshū* 867: "Because of a single stem of *murasaki*, I love all the plants and grasses on Musashi Plain."

61. A residence built by Emperor Saga (reigned 809–23) and occupied by Retired Emperors.

Once he heard that the mourning confinement[62] was over and the household was back in the City, he let some time go by and then went in person one quiet night to call. It was a depressing, ruinous place, all but deserted, and he could easily imagine how it might frighten a child. He was shown into the same room as before, and there the weeping Shōnagon described to him how the end had come for her mistress, until his own sleeves were wet with tears.

"I gather that she is to go to His Highness's," Shōnagon went on, "but her mother always hated the cruelty she suffered there, and my mistress herself believed that although the child is certainly not a baby, at her awkward age, among all her father's other children, she might well be treated more as a nuisance than anything else, since she does not yet understand very well what is expected of her. There is good reason, in fact, to believe that my mistress was right, and at a time like this we should therefore welcome the interest you have been kind enough to express, however casual it may be, and not insist too much on gauging your future feelings toward her. Even so, my lord, we are perplexed about what to do, because she is hopelessly unsuited to you and is actually even more of a child than she should be at her age."

"But why must you be so reluctant to accept the assurances that I have already given you repeatedly? That her very childishness should so attract me suggests—for I can make no other sense of it—that the tie between her and me really is unusual. I should like to tell her so, not indirectly but in person.

Perhaps the young reed, where she grows on Waka Shore, is for no one yet,
but, say, now the wave is high, can it slip back to the sea?

That would not do at all."[63]

"Nor would I presume to ask it of you, my lord.

Should the gleaming reed on Waka Shore lean to meet the approaching wave,
never knowing what he means, hers no doubt would be light ways.

How difficult this is!"

Genji partly forgave her for thwarting him, since she spoke with a thoughtfulness born of experience. "Why does that day never come?"[64] he sang to himself, dazzling the younger gentlewomen.

The little girl was lying down, crying for her grandmother, when her playmates exclaimed, "A gentleman is here in a dress cloak! It must be His Highness!"

She got up and called, "Shōnagon! Where is the gentleman in the dress cloak? Is Father here?" Her voice as she approached was very sweet.

---

62. *Imi*, probably thirty days, though perhaps twenty (starting in this case on the twentieth of the ninth month), during which the mourner remained at home. Mourning gray was worn much longer.

63. "You may not wish me [the wave] to see her, but I do not mean to make it easy for you by giving up." The main motif of this and the next poem, with all their wordplay, is that of an impetuous wave surging in toward an object of desire on the shore.

64. From *Gosenshū* 731, by Koremasa: "Secretly I am impatient, but why, for years and years, does that day never come when I meet her at last?"

"No," Genji said, "I am not His Highness, but that does not mean you should not like me, too. Come here!"[65]

She recognized the voice of the gentleman who had overawed her, and she regretted having spoken. Instead, she went straight to her nurse. "Come," she said, "I am sleepy!"

"Why are you still hiding from me? Sleep on my lap, then! Do come a little closer!"

"You see how little she understands yet at her age, my lord." Shōnagon propelled her toward him.

The little girl sat down innocently, and he reached under the blind to touch her. He felt a delicious abundance when his hand came to the end of her tresses, which spilled richly over her soft clothing, and he imagined the beauty of her hair. Next he took her hand, at which she bridled to have a stranger so close and drew back, complaining to Shōnagon, "But I want to go to sleep!"

He slipped straight in after her. "But I am the one who is going to love you now. Be nice to me!"

"My lord, what are you doing?" Shōnagon was appalled. "Oh, dear me! I assure you, it does not matter how you talk to her, you will get nothing from her at all!"

"What do I care if she is still only a little girl? Just wait and see how much I love her: more than anyone, ever!"

Hail was coming down hard, and it promised to be a bad night. "How can you live all by yourselves like this, when there are so few of you?" Genji began to weep. He could not possibly leave them. "Lower the lattice shutters! This looks to be an unpleasant night, and I mean to protect you. Gather near me, all of you!"

With this he strode into the little girl's curtained bed as though it were the most natural thing in the world,[66] leaving the shocked and astonished gentlewomen rooted to the spot. Shōnagon could not very well intervene with a sharp reproof, despite her anxiety, and she only sat there, sighing. The girl began to shiver with fright, and Genji, his heart melting to find her lovely skin so chilly, wrapped her in another shift.

He knew perfectly well how outrageously he was behaving, but he began nonetheless to talk to her gently about things he thought might catch her fancy. "Come with me, and I will take you to where there are lots of pretty pictures and you can play with dolls!" He spoke so kindly that in her childish way she stopped being quite so afraid, but she never relaxed enough to sink into a sound sleep, and she continued to toss and turn.

The wind roared all night long, while the gentlewomen whispered among themselves, "It's true, you know, we would have been miserable without him. Oh, if only she were old enough for him!" The anxious Shōnagon stayed very close to her charge.

Genji left before daybreak, once the wind had dropped a little, looking quite

65. Genji seems to be seated in the aisle, with a blind between him and the women in the chamber. The only light, an oil lamp, is on the women's side.
66. He seems to carry her in with him, though the text does not say so.

pleased with himself. "She was already constantly on my mind," he said, "and now I shall worry more than ever. I want to take her to where I myself spend my dreary nights and days. She cannot go on this way. It is a wonder she was not frightened half to death!"

"His Highness seems to be talking about having her come to live with him as well," Shōnagon answered. "I suppose he means to do it after my lady's forty-nine days are over."

"I am sure he will look after her, but he must be as much of a stranger to her as I am. She has never lived with him, after all. I myself have only just come to know her, but even so, I have no doubt that I am more attached to her than he." He stroked her hair, and he looked back at her many times as he left the house.

The sky, thick with fog, was unusually lovely, and all was white with frost: a scene to please the replete lover, but for Genji not quite enough. He remembered that someone he had been visiting secretly lived on his way, and he had a man of his knock at her gate. No one heard. He was reduced to having an attendant with a good voice sing twice over,

"By the dawn's first light, while rising mists shroud the skies and confuse the gaze,
I just cannot bring myself to pass by my darling's gate!"[67]

At this, a nice-looking servant woman came out and replied,[68]

"If it is so hard to pass straight on by a gate just glimpsed through the mist,
surely its flimsy portal need not really bar your way!"[69]

Then she went back in. No one came out again. He had no wish to retreat, but he felt exposed under the lightening sky, and he went his way.

He lay smiling to himself in fond recollection of that delightful little girl. The sun was high by the time he arose to write the customary letter,[70] and what he had to say was so unusual that he often laid down his brush and simply dreamed. With the letter he sent some pretty pictures.

As it happened, this was the day when His Highness came to see his daughter. The house had deteriorated remarkably in recent years, and its being so big and old made it even more forbiddingly lonely. "How could a child spend a moment living in a place like this?" He contemplated the scene before him. "I *must* bring her home with me.[71] There is no reason why you should be uncomfortable there. You will have your nurse, who will have a room of her own, and there are children for you to play with. You should be perfectly happy."

He had her come to him, and he caught the delicious scent her clothing had

67. Genji's poem weaves in expressions from a *saibara* song known as "My Darling's Gate" ("Imo ga yado").
68. For her mistress.
69. The shut "flimsy portal" (*kusa no tozashi*) is from *Gosenshū* 899 and 900, an analogous exchange between Fujiwara no Kanesuke and an unnamed woman.
70. The letter (*kinuginu no fumi*) that a lover sent his mistress after returning home from her house in the early morning.
71. Spoken to the gentlewomen. Hereafter he addresses his daughter directly.

picked up from Genji's. "What a lovely smell!" he exclaimed, only to add ruefully, "Your clothes are all limp, though!"[72] He went on, "What a pity she spent all those years with an old and ailing lady! I have urged her to come and get to know my household, but for some reason she has resisted the idea, and actually there has been some reluctance at my house as well.[73] I am sorry she must move there at a time like this."

"But must she really, Your Highness? This house is certainly lonely for her, but she ought to stay a while longer. Surely it would be better for her to move after she has grown up a little more. She always misses her grandmother, and she will not eat." It was true, too: the little girl was painfully thin, although this only gave her looks a more enchanting grace.

"But why are you so upset?" His Highness hoped to make her feel better. "Your grandmother is gone, and no mourning will bring her back. You have me, after all."

When evening came and His Highness prepared to leave, the little girl was so unhappy that she cried. Tears sprang to his eyes as well. "Now, now, you must not be so sad," he said comfortingly, over and over again. "I shall have you come to me very soon."

When he was gone, she wept inconsolably. What life might hold in store for her concerned her not at all; she knew only that the lady she had been with every moment through the years was now no more, and, child though she was, the pain of her loss consumed her. She no longer played as she used to, and if she forgot during the day, night returned her to her misery. Her women wondered how she could go on living this way, and they did all they could to comfort her, only to fail and burst into tears themselves.

Toward evening Genji sent Koremitsu to the house with the message "I should come myself, but unfortunately His Majesty has summoned me. I was distressed to see her situation, and now it worries me very much." Koremitsu was to guard the house.

"This is too awful of him!" Shōnagon said. "It is a game to him, I am sure, but what a thing to do at the very start![74] If His Highness were to hear of it, he would accuse us in her service of sheer folly. Do not forget, you must never be foolish enough to give him any hint of what has happened!" Alas, to the little girl none of this meant anything at all.

Shōnagon remarked while recounting their woes to Koremitsu, "When she is older, I doubt that she will escape the destiny he intends for her, but for the moment his proposition seems to me hopelessly unsuitable; in fact, I cannot even imagine what he means by all the extraordinary things he says. I do not know what to do. Just today His Highness was here, warning us to make sure that he need not worry about her and to keep a proper eye on her at all times. I hardly know which way to turn, and now I worry far more than before about the liberties someone might take with her." Shōnagon refrained from complaining too pointedly, because

---

72. They lack the starched look of new ones, which the household presumably cannot afford.

73. His wife did not want to see his mistress's daughter.

74. She is incensed that Genji, having slept once (though chastely) with the girl, will not do so again on the two following nights so as to seal their relationship in the manner of a marriage. Genji recognizes this obligation, but the girl is so young that, despite his future intentions, he seems not to take it very seriously for the present.

she did not wish to give Koremitsu ideas. Koremitsu himself could not make out what she was
talking about.

Genji felt Shōnagon's predicament keenly
when Koremitsu returned and told him what he
had heard, but the thought of visiting her regularly still upset him, because if people learned
what he was up to, they would certainly condemn
his dubious eccentricity, and that idea did not appeal to him at all. No, he decided, he would take
her home. He sent repeated notes and dispatched

Sewing

Koremitsu there after sundown, as before, to say that he hoped they would not take
it amiss if certain difficulties prevented him from coming in person.

"We are very busy now because we have just heard from His Highness that he
suddenly plans to take her to his residence tomorrow," Shōnagon explained. "I hate
after all to leave this tumbledown old place where I have lived so long, and the others are upset, too." She had little more to say and seemed preoccupied only with her
sewing.[75] Koremitsu returned to Genji.

Genji was at His Excellency's, but the lady there refused as usual to receive
him. He toyed in frustration with a *wagon*[76] and sang to himself in a pleasant voice,
"In Hitachi here I've my field to hoe . . ."[77] Then Koremitsu arrived. Genji called
him in and asked for his news.

Koremitsu's report alarmed him. If she went to her father's, any attempt to remove her from there would appear indecent, and he would be accused of having ab-
ducted an innocent child. No, he would have to silence her women for the time
being and take her before that could happen.

"I shall go there before daybreak," he announced. "The carriage will do very
well as it is, and I shall want you to bring one or two men." Koremitsu left to do as
he asked.

Genji now wavered, reflecting anxiously that if anyone found out, he would
be considered debauched; that a man would look normal in comparison if people
assumed that the woman involved had been old enough to know what was what and
had acted in concert with him; and that he would have no excuse for himself when
His Highness discovered the truth. But despite this whirl of misgivings he could not
let the opportunity pass, and he therefore prepared to leave while the night was still
dark. His lady was displeased as always, and she had no forgiveness for him.

"You see, I just remembered something urgent I must go back and look after.
I shall not be gone long." Not even her women knew it when he left. In his own
room he donned a dress cloak, and then he drove off with only Koremitsu riding
beside him.

He had a man of his knock at the gate, and a servant who knew nothing

75. She is probably making new clothes for the girl to wear at her father's.
76. *Azuma* (*goto*), that is, the *wagon*, the six-stringed "Japanese koto."
77. A folk song in which a peasant woman rejects her lover: "In Hitachi here I've my field to hoe—who
have you come for this rainy night, all the way over moor and mountain?" He is thinking of Aoi.

opened it. He ordered his carriage quietly brought inside. Koremitsu then rapped at the double doors and cleared his throat. Shōnagon came out when she recognized his voice. "His lordship is here," he announced.

"But she is asleep! He seems to be out very late." She took it for granted that Genji was on his way home from elsewhere.

"I hear she is to move to her father's, and I have something to tell her before she goes," Genji explained.

"What in the world could it be?" Shōnagon smiled. "And how could she possibly give you a proper answer?"

To her dismay he came straight in. "But there are unsightly old women just lying about in here!"

"I suppose she is still asleep. Come, I shall get her up. There is no excuse for sleeping through such a beautifully misty dawn." He went in through her curtains. There was no time even for them to cry out.

The little girl was lying there, oblivious to everything. Genji put his arms around her to wake her, and when she woke up she was still so sleepy that she took him for her father, come to fetch her. She did not realize her mistake until Genji tidied her hair and said, "Come! Up! I am here from His Highness!" and in her surprise she took fright. "Now, now, I might just as well be your father," he said, reemerging with her in his arms.

"My lord, what are you doing?" Taifu, Shōnagon, and the others cried.

"I have already told her I want to take her where I can be more comfortable with her, because I do not like being unable to come here often; and now, you see, I learn to my consternation that she is to move to her father's, which will make it even harder for me to keep in touch with her. I want one of you to come with me."

"My lord," the distraught Shōnagon answered, "today is just not the day for this! What would you have us tell His Highness when he comes? Everything will surely work in the fullness of time, if you are to have what you wish, but as it is, you have not left us a moment to think, and you are putting us all in an impossible position."

"Very well, someone may come and join her later." With this, to their utter amazement, he had his carriage brought up. She was alarmed and crying. Shōnagon, who could do nothing to stop him, changed into better clothes and got into the carriage, carrying the things she had been sewing the evening before.

Nijō was not far away, and the carriage reached it before daylight. Genji had it drawn up to the west wing and alighted. He easily lifted her down in his arms.

Shōnagon hesitated. "I still feel as though I am dreaming. What would you like me to do?"

"Whatever you please. Now I have brought your young mistress here, I will see you home again if you want."

With a wry smile Shōnagon stepped out of the carriage, too. The suddenness of it all had dazed her, and her heart was pounding. She wept to think of His Highness's displeasure, of her charge's perilous future, and, above all, of the child's pathetic plight now that she had lost all those who could claim her trust; but she mastered her feelings as well as she could, despite her tears, so as not to blight this moment[78] with ill-omened grief.

The wing lacked a curtained bed and other such furnishings, since Genji did not live in it. He summoned Koremitsu and had him put one up, together with screens and so on. Apart from that, there was no need to do more than let down the standing curtains and tidy the place up a little. He sent to the east wing for night-clothes and lay down.

The little girl wondered fearfully what he might have in mind for her, but she managed to keep from sobbing aloud. "I want to sleep with Shōnagon!" she declared in a childish tone.

"No." Genji was firm. "That is not the way you are to sleep anymore." She lay down, weeping with unhappiness. Her nurse, who could not sleep at all, sat up in a daze.

Looking around as day came on, Shōnagon was overwhelmed not only by the opulence of the building and its furnishings but even by the sand in the garden, which resembled a bed of jewels and seemed to give off light; and she began to feel like an intruder, even though no other women were actually present. Only house-hold guards were stationed outside the blinds, since Genji lodged no more than the occasional guest here. One of them had heard that Genji had just brought a lady home. "Who can she be?" he whispered. "He must be extremely keen on her!"

Washing water and breakfast[79] were brought in. The sun was high when Genji arose. "She will need her gentlewomen," he said to Shōnagon. "This evening she must call for the ones she prefers." He sent off to the east wing for some children. "I especially want little ones," he added. So it was that four very pretty little girls appeared.

She was lying wrapped in a shift, and he insisted that she get up. "You must not be so unfriendly," he said. "Would I be looking after you this way if you did not mean a great deal to me? A woman should be sweet and obedient." And so began her education.

She looked prettier than ever here. Genji chatted disarmingly with her, showing her all sorts of nice paintings and toys that he had had brought from the east wing and doing all he could to please her. At last she got up and looked properly at what he was showing her. She made such an engaging picture in her layering of soft, dark gray,[80] wreathed in innocent smiles, that Genji found himself smiling, too, as he watched her.

With Genji off to the east wing, she went for a look[81] at the park's lake and trees. The near garden, now touched by frost, was as pretty as a painting, and the unfamiliar whirl of fourth- and fifth-rank gentlemen, bustling in and out,[82] convinced her that she had come to a very nice place. In no time she was happily distracted by the fascinating pictures on the screens.

78. The moment when her charge begins a new life with Genji.
79. Ōnkayu, cooked rice.
80. Mourning for her grandmother. The mourning period in this case was three months.
81. Through blinds.
82. The fourth rank wore black, the fifth red.

Genji did not go to court for two or three days; he devoted himself instead to making her feel at home. He wrote or painted all sorts of things to show her, no doubt with the thought of making them up for her straightaway into a book,[83] and he turned them into an extremely attractive collection.

She took out an exceptionally beautiful "Talk of Musashi Plain arouses my complaint . . ."[84] that he had written on *murasaki*-colored paper; and he had added in smaller writing,

> *"Her root is unseen, and yet I do love her so, the kin to that plant*
> *the dews of Musashi Plain put so far beyond my reach!"*[85]

"Come now," he said, "you write one."

"But I do not know how to write very well yet." She looked up at him with the most engaging artlessness.

He smiled. "Still, you cannot write nothing at all. I shall teach you." Her manner of turning away to write and the childish way she held her brush so entranced him that he wondered at himself.

"Oh, I made a mistake!" She tried in embarrassment to hide what she had written, but he insisted on having a look.

> *"Why you should complain I have not the least idea, and that troubles me:*
> *who, then, is the kin you mean, and what plant have you in mind?"*

The generous lines of her letters were certainly immature, but they showed great promise.[86] Her hand closely resembled the late nun's. It seemed to him that she would soon write beautifully, as long as she had an up-to-date copybook. As far as dolls went, he made her one dollhouse after another, and he found his games with her the perfect distraction from his cares.

For the women who had not come with her, it was acutely embarrassing to have nothing to say when His Highness arrived and wanted to know what had become of his daughter. Genji had warned them to keep the secret for the time being, and Shōnagon, who agreed, had insisted that they remain silent. They told His Highness only that Shōnagon had taken his daughter off to hide her; they did not know where. He was obliged to assume that since the late nun had never approved of sending him her granddaughter, the girl's nurse had taken it upon herself in an ex-

---

83. As calligraphy models.

84. *Kokin rokujō* 3507, which Genji had written out: "I have never been there, but speak of Musashi Plain, and I will complain; yet ah, there is no remedy—the fault is the *murasaki's.*" The poem alludes to *Kokinshū* 867 and many others about *murasaki* on the great plain of Musashi. The *murasaki* refers to the woman whom the poet desires: in Genji's case, Fujitsubo, whose name (because *fuji* means "wisteria") also recalls the color of the *murasaki* dye.

85. The start of the poem can also be read to suggest "She is too young to sleep with." It comments on the poem just mentioned and alludes to another, earlier in this chapter: "How glad I would be to pick and soon to make mine that little wild plant sprung up from the very root shared by the *murasaki.*" The inaccessible plant is Fujitsubo.

86. Her lines are broad (*fukuyoka ni*), in a manner said in old commentaries to be characteristic of a child's writing.

cess of zeal to jeopardize her charge's whole future by spiriting her away instead of objecting openly, and he returned to his residence in tears. "Please let me know if you ever have any news of her!" he said, to their intense discomfort. He also made fruitless inquiries at the residence of His Reverence. He was sorry to have lost so remarkably attractive a daughter, and he continued to miss her. Even his wife was disappointed, since her antipathy toward the girl's mother had faded by now, and she had been looking forward to making the most of her authority.

By and by the gentlewomen gathered around their young mistress. Her playmates—young girls in service as pages or even smaller ones[87]—gladly lost themselves in games with so striking and stylish a pair. The young lady might still cry for her grandmother on evenings when her friend was away and she was lonely,[88] but she retained no special memory of her father. Never having been used to living with him anyway, she now cared only for this second father, to whom she became deeply attached. She would always go straight to greet him when he came home, chatting prettily and snuggling into his arms, and she was never in the least reserved or bashful with him. As far as that sort of thing went, she was as sweet with him as she could possibly be.

A woman may be so querulous and so quick to make an issue of the smallest lapse that the man takes a dislike to her, fearing that whatever he does may unleash bitter reproaches, until an estrangement that neither had wished for becomes a reality; but not so for Genji with his delightful companion. No daughter by the time she reaches this age can be as free with her father, sleep so intimately beside him, or rise so blithely with him in the morning as this young lady did with Genji, until Genji himself must have wondered at being able to lavish his affection on so rare a treasure.

87. Her playmates are *warawabe* (page girls of her age or older) and *chigo* (smaller girls who perform no services yet).

88. She is called *kimi* ("the young lady") for the first time, rather than *wakagimi* ("the little miss"); while Genji is called *otokogimi* ("the young gentleman"). This pairing of *kimi* and *otokogimi* acknowledges the two as a couple.

6

SUETSUMUHANA
The Safflower

Suetsumuhana ("safflower") is a yellow or orange flower that yields a scarlet dye, and this chapter, in which scarlet is a recurrent motif, features a woman known to readers as Suetsumuhana. Her name comes from a poem by Genji:

"This is not at all a color to which I warm; what then did I mean by letting myself brush sleeves with a safflower in full blush?"

The chapter makes Genji's hidden meaning plain.

RELATIONSHIP TO EARLIER CHAPTERS

"The Safflower" covers about the same period, the year when Genji is eighteen, as "Young Murasaki," but no narrative connection between the two appears until the end of the chapter. It extends into the first month of the following year.

PERSONS

Genji, a Captain in the Palace Guards, age 18 to 19

Taifu, a young gentlewoman

Her Highness, the daughter of the Hitachi Prince (Suetsumuhana)

The Secretary Captain, Genji's brother-in-law and great friend
(Tō no Chūjō)

His Excellency, the Minister of the Left, 52 to 53 (Sadaijin)

Nakatsukasa, a gentlewoman in service at His Excellency's

Jijū, Suetsumuhana's gentlewoman

Murasaki, roughly 10 to 11

No, despite the passing months he could not forget how someone he still loved had gone like dew from a twilight beauty, and those proud, fastidious ladies who always withheld themselves from him[1] were so demanding that he yearned particularly for the one who had touched his heart by yielding to him utterly.

How he longed, incorrigible as ever, to find someone dear and sweet, with no great name to uphold and with whom he need never feel required to be on his best behavior! He missed no news of any likely prospect, and one may assume that if he detected any further sign of promise, he sent her at least an encouraging line. Who by now can doubt that very few rebuffed him or received him with indifference? Those who remained willfully cool simply failed, in the prim and proper heartlessness of their ways, to know their place; nor did they often persist long in their pride, for they would then collapse ignominiously into marriage with one nobody or another. He dropped many for that reason.

Now and again he recalled that woman of the cicada shell with irritation. She of the reed,[2] too, must have been surprised sometimes by a note from him, whenever a favorable breeze blew her way. He would gladly have seen her again at her ease in the lamplight. On the whole, he was not one to forget any woman he had once known.

The daughter of Nurse Saemon, his favorite after Nurse Daini,[3] was now serving at court, where she was known as Taifu, the Commissioner's Myōbu.[4] Her father, the Commissioner of War, was of imperial descent. Genji himself sometimes called on her for one errand or another, since she was a young person much given to gallantry. When not at the palace she lived at her father's, now that her mother had gone down to the provinces as the wife of the Governor of Chikuzen.

Taifu once happened to tell Genji how the last and best-loved daughter born to

1. Particularly Aoi and Rokujō.
2. Utsusemi ("cicada shell") and Nokiba no Ogi ("reed"). "Reed" (ogi) and "breeze" (kaze) were conventionally linked; a breeze stirring the reeds might announce a lover's visit.
3. The old lady, now a nun, whom Genji visited at the beginning of "The Twilight Beauty."
4. Taifu no Myōbu, "the Myōbu who is a Taifu's (Commissioner's) daughter."

His Highness of Hitachi[5] was living in sad circumstances now that her father was gone.

"What a shame!" Genji, intrigued, asked to hear more.

"I know little about her character or looks. She is so shy and reticent that when I visit her of an evening, I speak to her through curtains and so on. Her one real friend seems to be her *kin*."

"That is one of the 'three friends,' though I can think of another that would ill become her.[6] Please let me hear her. His Highness her father played so well that I cannot imagine she is no better than anyone else."

"I wonder whether her music would really interest you," she answered, although she spoke in a manner designed to pique his interest.

"You are trying to tempt me, aren't you! I shall go there secretly one of these nights when the moon is veiled.[7] You must come with me."

Taifu had not wanted to get in this deep, but she still went there one fine spring evening when all was quiet at the palace. Her father had taken up residence elsewhere and visited the place only now and again, but Taifu, who had never felt comfortable at her stepmother's, had become a familiar presence there.[8]

Genji arrived, as he had said he would, at the prettiest hour for the moon of the sixteenth night.[9] "What a pity!" Taifu exclaimed. "This is not at all the kind of night to bring out an instrument's tone."

"Do go to her, though, and get her to play a little. I would hate to leave again without hearing her at all."

Taifu installed him in her own comfortably casual room and set off, guilty and nervous, for the main house. The lattice shutters were still up, and Her Highness was gazing out at a deliciously fragrant plum tree. Taifu judged the moment to be propitious. "I could not resist the promise of so beautiful a night, my lady, when I realized how lovely your *kin* would sound. I so regret that in the rush of all my comings and goings I am never able to hear you play."

"I gather that some people really do appreciate the *kin*," Her Highness answered, "but how could my playing possibly interest anyone who frequents His Majesty's Seat?" She sent for her instrument, and Taifu trembled to think how she might sound to Genji.

She played very softly. It was quite nice. Not that she was any sort of master, but her instrument was so superb in tone that Genji was not displeased by what he had heard. That so great a lord should have brought up his daughter so tenderly, to manners strict and now long abandoned, in a house so sad and neglected, and all for nothing! Ah, what regrets she must have! Why, in the old tales this is just the kind

5. A Prince who had held the title of Governor of the province of Hitachi. As in the case of Kazusa and Shimōsa, the titular Governor of Hitachi was a Prince, but the post was a sinecure, and only the Deputy Governor actually went to the province.

6. Bai Juyi celebrated in one of his poems (*Hakushi monjū* 2565) his "three friends": the *kin*, wine, and poetry. Friendship with wine would not suit a lady.

7. A poetically perfect spring night with a mist-veiled moon.

8. Taifu's father apparently used to live at Suetsumuhana's, which suggests that he may be an elder brother.

9. A moon one night past the full.

of place that provides the setting for all sorts of moving
scenes! Such musings encouraged him to want to approach
her, but fear that she might
think him forward made him
hesitate after all.

Taifu, whose wits were
always about her, had no wish
to give him his fill of the
Princess's music. "The sky
seems to be clouding over, my
lady," she said. "A guest of
mine said he would be coming, and he might suspect me
of having no use for him.
Soon, though, when I have

Screening fence

the time . . . Do let me put the shutters down!" And off Taifu went without encouraging her further.

"She stopped almost before she began!" Genji complained. "I had no time
even to decide whether or not she was worth listening to! What a bore!" Her Highness's music had been well received.

"Let me stand nearer to listen, if you don't mind," he went on, and Taifu saw
he was intrigued.

"I think I would rather not, though," she replied. "The dismal life she has to
lead is so depressing for her, and her whole existence is really so sad, I do not see
how I could take it upon myself . . ."

He agreed that she was probably right. One could get on perfectly easily with
some lesser women right from the start, but her very rank aroused his sympathy, and
so he urged Taifu to "convey something of my feelings to her nevertheless." He then
prepared quietly to leave, having no doubt a rendezvous elsewhere.

"My lord, I often think how amusing it is that His Majesty worries so much
about your being too serious. He will never see you in this disguise."[10]

Genji turned back toward her, smiling. "You had better not bring up my failings as though they were none of yours!" he said. "If mine is what you call wanton
behavior, then I know a young woman who would be hard pressed to defend herself!" He often teased Taifu for being rather loose in her ways, and she was too
abashed to say more.

He stole off toward the main house, hoping for a sound from the lady within.
When he reached a sheltered spot where only the tattered fragments of a screening
fence remained, he discovered that another man had been standing there all the
time. Who could he be? No doubt some gallant with his eye on the lady, he
thought, melting into the shadows; but no, it was the Secretary Captain. Earlier that

10. Genji is dressed below his station so as to pass unrecognized.

evening they had both left the palace together, and when, after they parted, Genji made for neither His Excellency's nor Nijō, the Captain so longed to know where he was going that he followed him despite having a rendezvous of his own. Genji had failed to recognize him on the nag he was riding, casually dressed in a hunting cloak. The Captain was intrigued to see Genji enter an establishment quite new to him. He stood there listening to the music and then lay in wait on the assumption that Genji would soon be leaving. Genji, who still did not know who he was and who had no wish to be recognized, was slipping quietly away when the Captain came straight up to him.

"My lord, I was so put out when you just left me that I decided to keep you company.

> *We were together when we turned our steps away from Palace Mountain,*
> *but I see, this sixteenth night, the moon hides where he will set."*

Genji was at once amused and annoyed when he grasped who the speaker was. "What a thing to do to me!" he complained bitterly.

> *"One certainly may gaze upon a radiance that illumines all,*
> *but who would wish to hunt out Mount Irusa, where it sets?"*[11]

"What would you do if someone else were to follow you this way? When you are gadding about like this, you would be much safer with an attendant. You should not leave me behind. There could be an embarrassing incident when you are out at night in disguise."

Genji hated to be found out this way, and he gave himself full credit for the Secretary Captain's failure so far to locate his "little pink."[12]

Now in high good humor, the two did not set off again each to his promised assignation. Instead, they rode together in one carriage to His Excellency's, under a moon pleasingly veiled by clouds, blowing away in concert on their flutes.

They stole in silently, since they had sent no men ahead to clear their path, and they changed to dress cloaks in a deserted gallery. Then they launched into playing their flutes, looking the picture of innocence as though they had just arrived. His Excellency, who could never pass up a concert, brought out his own Koma flute[13] and played it beautifully, for he was an expert musician. Then he called for instruments that he had various gentlewomen skilled at music play behind the blinds. Nakatsukasa[14] was very good on the *biwa*, but she who had spurned the Secretary Captain had not refused Genji's kind attentions on his sporadic visits, and she had then inevitably seen her involvement with him become common knowledge,

---

11. The *irusa* of the place-name Irusa Yama can be read to mean "moment of setting" and also plays on "enter" (a house).

12. His daughter by Yūgao.

13. *Komabue*, a flute shorter and thinner than the *yokobue* being played by the two young men.

14. A gentlewoman.

which had in turn earned her the displeasure of Genji's mother-in-law.[15] Now she was reclining against a pillar, obviously unhappy and ill at ease. She was miserable at the thought of going away where she would never see him again.

Biwa

The young gentlemen remembered the music they had heard on the *kin* and dwelled with pleasure on how different that sad house had been; and the Captain dreamed of the lady sweet and fair whom he would begin courting there after all her long years alone and with whom he would then fall so recklessly in love that all the world would be talking about it and he himself would teeter on the brink of folly. He recalled with mingled annoyance and apprehension the self-assured way Genji went roaming about—would *he* let slip a chance like this?

Both were soon apparently writing to Her Highness. Neither got an answer, which baffled and irritated them. It was really too awful of her! Any lady living in a place like that should sometimes give poignant voice to her feelings by conveying the sorrows she knew so well in terms of the fleeting moods of plants, trees, or the sky. The Captain fretted even more than Genji that it was dull of her, and rude as well, to remain so shut up in herself, however ponderously serious she might be.

"Have you had any reply from her?" he plaintively inquired of Genji, from whom he could keep nothing. "I sent her a line to see what would happen and got back only a strange silence."

Sure enough, Genji thought, he *has* been courting her; and he replied with a smile, "Perhaps I have had no answer from her because I for one am not really that keen." The Captain was very annoyed to be put off.

Faced with such indifference, Genji had lost interest in an adventure that mattered little enough to him anyway, but he supposed that if the Captain was now showering Her Highness with notes, she would yield to the one who sent her the most. The thought of how pleased with herself she would be after casting aside her first suitor was more than he could bear, and he therefore called Taifu into solemn conclave.

"It is extremely irritating of her to turn me away like this without even hearing me out," he said. "She must suspect me of wanting only to amuse myself, whereas in reality I am not frivolous at all. Things cannot help going wrong when the other person assumes the worst, and it always ends up being one's own fault. I should have

---

15. Ōmiya, the Minister of the Left's wife, the mother of Aoi and Tō no Chūjō. She is also Genji's aunt (his father's sister).

thought someone well disposed, someone living in peace without parents or brothers and sisters to bother her, would be far more attractive."

"Oh, no, my lord, I doubt she would suit you. I cannot imagine her being the 'sweet shelter from the rain'[16] that you have in mind. Few people are so desperately shy and withdrawn." She told him what she knew of the lady.

"Apparently she is neither witty nor clever. After all, though, it is the childlike, innocent ones who are the most apt to catch one's fancy." He had not forgotten.

Spring and summer passed while he suffered from his recurrent fever and remained absorbed in his secret grief.

That autumn, as quiet, persistent recollection led him to remember with longing even the sound of the fulling blocks and that other noise that had so offended his ears, he wrote often to the residence of the Hitachi Prince; and when he still got no response, he waxed indignant with the lady for her boorish inexperience, vowed to reject defeat, and began pressing Taifu vigorously. "What is going on?" he fumed. "I have never seen anything like it!"

She sympathized. "Not once have I suggested to her that you do not deserve her. As I see it, her crippling shyness is the reason why she cannot bring herself to answer you."

"Exactly! That is just what I mean by inexperience! A girl may well be shy as long as she still knows little of life or is too young to do as she pleases, but I should think that this lady would give all things due consideration. I myself for some reason am feeling listless and low, and I would be quite satisfied to get an answer from her in the same vein. I am not out for hanky-panky; all I want to do is sit for a while on her creaky veranda. I just cannot understand her, and that is why I want you to arrange it for me, if necessary without her leave. I will not lose my head or do anything foolish."

Taifu had mentioned Her Highness to him, that night when they were almost alone, only because it had then still been his habit to gather with feigned indifference news of any lady at all, and she did not like having him press her now in such deadly earnest. Her Highness lacked both experience and accomplishment, and in the end she might suffer (so Taifu feared) from Taifu's indiscretion. Still, it might be perverse just to turn a deaf ear to his pleas.

The old place had been so antiquated even in her father's time that nobody went there, and now visitors struggled even less often through the garden's weeds, so that when, wonder of wonders, Genji's resplendent notes began to arrive, her pathetic gentlewomen broke into eager smiles and urged her, "Oh, my lady, do answer him, do!"

Alas, their hopelessly timid mistress would not even read them. Well, then, thought the careless, fun-loving Taifu, when the time comes and he talks to her through her blinds, if she doesn't like him, fine, that will be the end of it, but if things go well and he begins calling, there is no one to stop him. She breathed not a word of this even to her father.

After the twentieth of the eighth month, on a night when the moon would rise so late that the wait for it seemed endless, when the only light was from the

---

16. An expression from a *saibara* love song.

stars and the wind moaned in the pines, the lady, weeping, began to talk of the past. Taifu saw that the moment was at hand, and she must then have sent Genji a note, because he soon arrived, as always in great secrecy.

Cushion

At last the moon rose, only to illumine gloomily for him the stretch of ragged fence at which he was gazing when, at Taifu's urging, Her Highness began softly to play her *kin.* No, she was not bad. The giddy Taifu anxiously wished her music might have something more accessibly modern about it. Genji slipped inside without further ado, since there was no one to see him, and he had Taifu called.

"This is very awkward!" She feigned surprise at the news of his arrival. "I gather he is here to speak to you, my lady. He is always displeased with you, you see, and because I keep reminding him that I can do nothing for him, he has been saying that he means to come and explain himself to you in person. How am I to answer him? He is not as free as other people to do as he likes, and he surely deserves some consideration for that. Do listen to what he has to say, with something between you if you wish!"

Her Highness was stricken with embarrassment. "But I do not know how to talk to people!" she cried, slipping off in naive terror toward the farthest recesses of the house.

Taifu smiled. "It pains me to see you behaving so much like a child, my lady. It is quite acceptable for the most exalted lady to retain a girlish innocence as long as she has her parents to look after her, but it simply is not right for you in your present unfortunate situation to remain shut up forever in yourself."

"Very well," said Her Highness, who could never bring herself to say no to anything, "if you mean me only to listen and not answer, we must have the lattice shutters and so on properly locked."[17]

"But it would be rude to leave him on the veranda," Taifu tactfully reminded her. "As for anything forward or tasteless, why, he would never . . ." With her own hands she fastened the sliding panel between the chamber and the little aisle room[18] securely shut and arranged a cushion in the aisle for Genji to sit on.

Having not the slightest idea how to talk to anyone like Genji, Her Highness resigned herself despite grave misgivings to faith that Taifu knew best. An old woman, probably her nurse, had by then gone off sleepily to her room to lie down. There remained two or three younger gentlewomen, who in their eagerness for a glimpse of Genji's widely celebrated looks were nervously preparing themselves for

17. The shutters between the aisle and the veranda.
18. *Futama,* a smaller space divided off from the aisle.

the great moment. Once changed into decent clothes and suitably tidied up, the lady herself went to meet her visitor with no flicker of any such anticipation.

The visitor lent such enthralling grace to the discretion with which he had clothed his own peerless beauty that Taifu longed to show him off to someone able to appreciate him. Poor man, she thought, there is nothing here for him. At least, though, she could feel relieved that Her Highness was behaving with dignity and would probably do nothing eccentric in his presence. She worried that what she had done to evade Genji's constant reproaches might now bring sorrow to the one whose plight so affected her.

Genji assumed from Her Highness's rank that she would flaunt no modish charms but instead exhibit a supremely distinguished manner; and once she had moved a little closer, at Taifu's insistence, the delicious scent that then reached him, and her quiet composure, convinced him that he was right. With great eloquence he confided to her the yearning she had inspired in him for so long, only to meet more resoundingly than ever with dead silence.

I give up! he groaned to himself, and he said aloud,

> *"Ah, how many times have I found myself undone by such silences,*
> *and sustained by just one thought: you never say, Do not speak!*

Tell me to go away, if you must. This uncertainty is very painful."[19]

A lively young person named Jijū, a daughter of Her Highness's nurse, was in such an agony of embarrassment by now that she moved beside her mistress and answered,

> *"Why, I would never ring the bell[20] as though to say, The debate is closed;*
> *but at a loss to reply?—there I find myself surprised."*

So young a voice, and one so lacking in gravity (for Jijū had spoken not as an intermediary but as her mistress in person), seemed rather familiar in tone, considering who Her Highness was. "Now it is I who am silenced," the astonished Genji replied.

> *"That you do not speak means far more than any words—that I know full well;*
> *yet your taciturnity has been a hard trial to bear."*

He kept up a stream of pleasantries, bantering or serious, but nothing worked. In frustration before this evidence that she must be odd in some way or her feelings engaged elsewhere, he gently slid the panel open and entered.

How awful of him! And he promised he wouldn't! Taifu felt such pain for Her Highness that she averted her eyes and went off to her room. The young gentlewomen

---

19. A paraphrase for narrative meaning of *tamadasuki kurushi*, a highly ornamental expression from *Kokinshū* 1037: "Will you not just tell me that you do not love me? Why should love be so vacillating?"
20. Rung to close a doctrinal debate during the Rite of the Eight Discourses (Mi-hakō).

forgave his behavior, so famous were his supreme good looks, and they could not bring themselves to raise any serious outcry, even though it certainly was all very sudden and their mistress was pitifully unprepared. Her Highness herself was numb with shame and wounded modesty, for which Genji did not blame her, since the moment was one in which her state easily touched his tenderest feelings and since she still led so sheltered and so virtuous a life; yet he also found her comportment peculiar and somehow pathetic. What about her could possibly have attracted him? Groaning, he took his leave late in the night. Taifu was lying awake, listening for clues to how things were going, but she did not rouse anyone to see him off because she did not wish to betray her involvement. He stole away very quietly indeed.

He returned to Nijō and lay down to brood on and on over life's endless frustrations and to lament that anyone of this Princess's not inconsiderable standing should have so little to offer.

These miseries were still whirling through his head when the Secretary Captain arrived. "You are certainly sleeping late!" he said. "I am sure there must be a reason."

Genji arose. "I was overindulging in the luxury of sleeping alone. You have come from the palace?"

"Yes, I was there just now," his friend answered breathlessly. "Today is the day when the musicians and dancers are to be chosen for His Majesty's progress to the Suzaku Palace. I heard about it last night, and I am on my way now to inform His Excellency. I shall have to go straight back."

"Well, then, I shall go with you." Genji had them both served a morning meal, after which they got into the same carriage, though the other one followed it.

"You still look rather sleepy," the Captain observed reprovingly, and he added with some rancor, "You have a good deal to hide."

This was a day when many things were to be decided, and Genji spent the rest of it in attendance at court.

Remembering with a pang of guilt that he owed her at least a letter,[21] he finally sent one that evening. What with the weather having turned wet and his not really being free to leave, he may well have wanted nothing to do with any "sweet shelter from the rain."

At Her Highness's, Taifu felt very sorry indeed once the time to expect a letter had passed. She herself remained deeply ashamed, and it never occurred to her to blame Genji even when his morning letter turned up in the evening.

He had written,

> "I have never seen any sign the evening mist proposes to clear,
> but to make things even worse, tonight it must rain and rain!

How anxiously time passes while I await a break in the clouds!" The gentlewomen urged their mistress to answer him anyway, despite their bitter disappointment at this evidence that he would not be coming.

21. Required after a man had spent the night with a woman, although in this case to send a mere letter was to treat the relationship wrongly as an affair. Her rank was such that Genji should have returned for another two nights, to confirm a marriage.

It was at last Jijū who invoked the lateness of the hour to give her the words as before:

> *"Kindly give a thought to one who awaits the moon*[22] *in the dark of night,*
> *though your own melancholy have another cause than hers."*

With the encouragement of all present, Her Highness wrote this poem out on *murasaki* paper so old that it had reverted to ash gray, in startlingly definite letters, antique in style and evenly balanced top and bottom.[23] It did not deserve a glance, and Genji put it down. He did not like to speculate about what she thought of him. Her Highness meanwhile lamented her misfortune, never knowing that although he did indeed by now regret having won her, he understood his duty and had every intention of upholding it to the end.

His Excellency insisted on bringing Genji home with him when he withdrew from the palace late that night. His sons, who were looking forward to this imperial excursion, gathered to talk it over and busied themselves every day rehearsing each his own dance. The clamor of instruments was never so loud, for each was keen to excel, nor were theirs the usual ones, for the voice of the greater *hichiriki* and the *sakuhachi* now rent the air, and they even rolled a great drum up to the railing and beat it themselves.[24] Genji was so absorbed that he managed to steal time only for those ladies who meant the most to him, and he allowed all communication with the Hitachi Prince's residence to lapse. Autumn drew to a close while Her Highness's hopes dwindled away.

Taifu came to see Genji when the imperial excursion was near and the air rang with music under rehearsal.

"How is she?" he asked guiltily.

Taifu told him. "Your complete indifference to her is extremely painful for those who are with her daily." She was almost in tears.

He understood how he had betrayed Taifu's trust that he would never treat Her Highness with less than the highest consideration, and he shuddered to imagine Taifu's opinion of him. For Her Highness herself he felt only commiseration when he imagined how silent and withdrawn she must be. "I haven't a moment these days," he said, sighing. "I really cannot help it." He added with a smile, "She knows so little of the sorrows of love, you see; I want only to make her wiser." His smiles and his youthful charm made Taifu smile, too. It is hopeless, she thought. He is of just the age to make women suffer, and no wonder he is often thoughtless and does as he pleases.

At any rate, he occasionally renewed his visits once this busy time was over.

He became so caught up in pampering his *murasaki*'s little kinswoman,[25] now that he had taken her for his own, that he called even less often at Rokujō; and as for that ruinous mansion, he could not despite his sympathy find the will to go there

---

22. Genji.
23. The paper has reverted to the color of the ashes (lye) used as a mordant. The definiteness of the characters is unfeminine, and their even balance lacks personality.
24. This huge drum was normally kept outside and beaten by servants.
25. Murasaki, Fujitsubo's niece.

or, as the days went by, feel any great wish to see more deeply into the extraordinary reticence of its inhabitant. But then his mood changed, and he came to suppose that she might still have virtues to recommend her, that touching her in the dark might have left certain of her mysteries unrevealed, and that he did want to see her properly. However, it would have been rude to throw direct light on her,[26] and one evening when he was not expected he therefore stole in and peered through the gap between two lattice shutters.

Alas, he had no view of her at all. The standing curtains, though dismally worn, had remained in place for all these years and had never been moved aside, and to his regret he therefore saw before him only four or five gentlewomen. They had withdrawn from their mistress's presence and were now eating a heartrendingly insipid meal from stands laden with Chinese bowls of more or less the reserved, celadon color,[27] but in pathetic condition. Farther off in the corner room[28] shivering women sat in unspeakably grubby white, wearing filthy aprons at their waists and looking impossibly ancient. Still, he was amused to note that with those combs in their hair over their foreheads—they were nearly falling out—they had their like elsewhere, after all, in the Women's Music Pavilion or the Hall of the Sacred Mirror.[29] To him they bore no resemblance to women charged with waiting on a lady.

"Oh, dear, it is so cold this year!" one cried with tears in her eyes. "This is what you get for living so long!"

"Why did I ever think life was hard when His Late Highness was alive?" This one was shivering so hard that she nearly leaped from the floor. "Look at the miserable way we live now!"

Their pitiful complaints were too painful. Genji drew back and knocked at the shutter as though he had just arrived. With "Good gracious!" and similar cries they trimmed the lamp, swung open the shutter, and admitted him to the room.

Jijū had not been there lately, for she was among the young women who served the Kamo Priestess. This time they all seemed so much stranger, so much more uncouth, that he felt as though he hardly knew the place. The snow that had provoked their sharp complaints was falling more thickly than ever. The sky looked grim, a hard wind was blowing, and no one moved to relight the lamp when it went out. He recalled his moment of danger from a spirit, and he found relief from the equal desolation here in reflecting that the place was at least smaller and somewhat better populated; but he knew that during this eerie night he would get little sleep. The scene had its charm, its pathos, and a strange appeal, but he felt cheated when she remained so inaccessible and so unresponsive that he had no pleasure from her at all.

26. By turning the lamp full on her.
27. Celadon (a light gray-green glaze) was called the "reserved color" (*bisoku*) in accordance with Chinese custom and was used by the highest nobility.
28. A corner of the aisle.
29. By the author's time, and perhaps earlier, gentlewomen no longer put their hair up with a comb. The Women's Music Pavilion (Naikyōbō) was for training the women musicians and dancers of the palace, while the Hall of the Sacred Mirror (Naishidokoro), in the Unmeiden, was where the sacred mirror (one of the three imperial regalia) was kept. Both were inhabited by ancient gentlewomen whose ways belonged more or less to the past.

Dawn seemed to have come at last. He raised the shutters himself and looked out over the snow-covered garden. No footprint broke the vast, empty, and chillingly lonely expanse.

"Look at how beautiful the sky is now!" he said, feeling that a prompt departure would be too cruel, and he added with some rancor, "The distance you keep between us is very painful."

It was not yet quite light, and he looked so wondrously young and handsome by the glimmer of the snow that the sight brought grins to the aged women's faces. "Do go out to him, my lady,"[30] they encouraged her, "you *must*! It makes such a difference to be nice!" She tidied herself up more or less, since despite her timidity she could never say no when told what to do, and slipped out toward him. He pretended not to look at her and gazed into the garden, but he gave her many a sidelong glance. What was she like? How glad he would be (ah, foolish hope!) if their present intimacy had brought out anything at all attractive!

First, her seated height was unusual; she was obviously very long in the back. I knew it! he thought in despair. Next came the real disaster: her nose. He noted it instantly. She resembled the mount of the Bodhisattva Fugen.[31] Long and lofty that nose was, slightly drooping toward the end, and with at the tip a blush of red—a real horror. In color she was whiter than snow, in fact slightly bluish, and her forehead was strikingly broad,[32] although below it her face seemed to go on and on for an extraordinarily long way. She was thin to the point of being pitifully bony, and even through her gown he could see the excruciating angularity of her shoulders. Why had he insisted on finding out what all of her looked like? At the same time, though, she made a sight so outlandish that he could not keep his eyes off her. The shape of her head and the sweep of her hair all but equaled those he admired in the greatest ladies he knew, and he noted how her hair trailed a foot or so beyond the hem of her dress gown.

It may be cruel to go through her costume, but the old romances always start out by describing a character's clothes. Over a deplorably faded layering of sanctioned rose[33] she wore a dress gown dark with grime and, over that, a richly glossy, scented coat of sable pelts[34]—no doubt distinguished attire in ages past but a shockingly eccentric getup for a lady who after all was still young. Her face showed how cold she would be without the furs, though, and he felt sorry for her.

He, too, felt bereft of speech when he got nothing in reply, but he tried conversing with her to test her silence. Even the way she put her hand to her mouth in acute embarrassment was so rustic and antiquated that it reminded him of the way officials in procession on ceremonial occasions held their arms, and her accompany-

---

30. Out of the curtained bed.
31. Who rides a white elephant.
32. Or "bulged." The two verbs are homophones.
33. *Usu* ("light") *kurenai*, a light, cool reddish pink in the *kurenai* range, the darker end of which was "forbidden" (*kinjiki*) to all but the Emperor and the imperial family. *Kurenai* comes from the safflower (*suetsumuhana*) dye.
34. Sable from Siberia was favored by noblemen early in the Heian period but had gone out of fashion by the time of the tale.

ing smile was thoroughly disconcerting. At once pained and sympathetic, he hastily made ready to depart.

"I would be much better pleased if you who have no one to care for you were to welcome the man you now have," he said by way of excuse.[35] "Your refusal to yield is too disappointing . . .

> *When the morning sun has melted the icicles all along the eaves,*
> *why are the waters within even now frozen so hard?"*

But she gave him only an "Mmm" and a smile, and her abject failure to find a reply was so pathetic that he left.

It had been obvious even by night, when darkness hid a thousand other flaws, that the middle gate where his carriage waited was perilously warped and tottery, and now, in this mournful solitude where nothing looked warm but the pines in their thick coats of snow, the house felt remarkably like a mountain village. No doubt this was what those fellows had meant by an "overgrown old house." Ah, he thought, how I would love to have someone very dear come here to live, and then miss her and worry about her. She might take my mind off this forbidden longing. What a shame that the one who does live here must spoil a perfect place by having nothing to offer. Who else would ever put up with her? If she and I are now a couple, it must be because her late and doting father remained with her in spirit and led me to her.

Genji had a man of his brush off a heavily burdened orange tree, at which a pine broke free, too, as though in defiance, and with a swish shed tumbling billows of snow.[36] How he longed for someone, even if not wholly enthralling, with whom he could at least enjoy the normal give-and-take!

The gate his carriage had to pass through was not yet open, and he sent for the caretaker with the key. Out came a strikingly ancient man, accompanied by a woman who might have been his daughter or his granddaughter—one could not tell which—and whose soiled clothes stood out against the snow. Visibly half frozen, she was clutching, wrapped in her sleeves, a horrid sort of box containing a few live coals. When the old man failed to get the gate open, she went to give him ineffectual help. Genji's men opened it in the end.

> *"He who sees these snows so cruelly heaped upon so ancient a head*
> *moistens with no fewer tears this morning his own cold sleeves.*

'And the younger one's body is bare,' " he hummed, smiling as the memory of that cold, cold figure with her blushing nose suddenly came to mind.[37] What simile

---

35. "The man who has begun seeing you": "your man" or "your husband."

36. More literally, "the spilling snow looked like the famous Sue." *Gosenshū* 683, by Tosa: "Are my sleeves the famous pine mountain of Sue, that waves should come down on them from the sky every day?"

37. Genji derives his poem from one by Bai Juyi (*Hakushi monjū* 0076) on the sufferings of the peasants, then hums a line of the original, in which "the younger one" is a boy rather than the woman before him. The nose comes to mind because the succeeding lines in Bai Juyi's work speak of how the peasants' noses smart in the cold.

The middle gate

would the Secretary Captain find for that nose if he showed it to him? He hated to imagine his friend, who was always after him, actually coming across him here.

He might have dropped Her Highness then and there if she had been quite ordinary and had had nothing remarkable about her one way or the other,[38] but now that he had actually seen her, his sympathy for her was keener than ever, and he sent her constant messages together with thoroughly practical gifts: not sable furs but silks and silk twills, cotton wadding, or clothes for the old gentlewomen and even (since his thoughtfulness embraced all, high or low) for the old gatekeeper. He was relieved when all this practicality seemed not to offend her, and he decided to look after her in this manner from now on. His most unusual presents included things that no one would normally have dared to give her.

She of the cicada shell, as he had seen her at her ease in profile that evening, had no looks at all, but her deportment had more than made up for it, and she had not displeased him. Could a Prince's daughter be worth less? It was true, these things had nothing to do with rank. Such had been her maddening strength of character that he was the one who had lost in the end. Memories like these ran through his head whenever chance recalled them.

The year came to a close. Genji was in his room at the palace when Taifu turned up. He liked having her dress his hair because she never flirted with him, but he often teased her or asked her for personal favors, and she came without being called whenever she had something to tell him.

"I have something odd to tell you about, but I am afraid I do not quite know how," she said, lapsing with a grin into silence.

"What kind of thing do you mean? Surely you have nothing to hide from me."

"Oh, no, my lord, as far as any trouble of my own might be concerned, you would of course in your kindness be the very first . . . But this matter is so difficult to bring up, you see." Words failed her.

---

38. Since another man would turn up to look after her.

"You are leading me on again, aren't you," he said testily.

"You have a letter from Her Highness!" she announced and produced it.

"Then what was the mystery about?"

Taifu's heart sank merely to have him take it. It was on thick Michinokuni paper,[39] heavily perfumed. Her Highness's writing had certainly improved. Her poem read,

> "*Robe from far Cathay! Your heart turns so cruelly, O love, against me:*
> *look upon my sleeves and see how wet they are now with tears!*"[40]

While he pored uncomprehendingly over these words, Taifu placed before him a heavy, old-fashioned clothing box and undid its cloth wrapping. "My lord, it is impossible to view the contents of this box without a shudder, but Her Highness insisted that you must have it to wear on New Year's Day, and I could not very well make her take it back. Perhaps I should simply have put it away, but that would have meant ignoring her express wish, and so after you have had a look . . ."

"You would have been quite wrong to put it away. Such thoughtfulness brings great joy to one upon whose moistened sleeves no love pillows her dear head."[41] He said no more.

Good heavens, he groaned to himself, what an awful poem! This must be the best she can do on her own—I suppose Jijū is the scholar who usually retouches her poems and guides her brush. He contemplated it with a smile, reflecting that this might well be the time to speak of "awestruck gratitude," considering the effort it must have cost her. The watching Taifu reddened.

In the box there offered itself most tediously to the gaze a plum red dress cloak, insufferably old and drab, and of the same color inside and out.[42] Impossible! he thought, then spread out the letter and casually wrote along one edge these words, which Taifu read from beside him:

> "*This is not at all a color to which I warm; what then did I mean*
> *by letting myself brush sleeves with a safflower in full blush?*[43]

Yet I had so admired the flower's depth of hue."[44]

Taifu pitied the lady when she understood that various moonlit glimpses of

---

39. A white paper made especially in northern Japan (Michinokuni, or Michinoku) from tree bark—and an odd choice for a love letter.

40. "Robe from far Cathay" (*karakoromo*) is a decorative "pillow word" unrelated in meaning to the rest of the poem. It should have a conventional association with the syllable that follows it, but her effort to bring this off did not work. The rest of the poem is extremely trite. The rest of the poem refers to Suetsumuhana's poem as well.

41. His ironically elaborate speech quotes from *Man'yōshū* 2325 and refers to Suetsumuhana's poem as well.

42. The underlayer and the outside of a dress cloak were supposed to be different.

43. *Suetsumuhana* ("safflower") means, literally, "flower picked by the tip," referring to the way the flowers are harvested; and *hana* ("flower") is a homophone of "nose."

44. *Genji monogatari kochūshakusho in'yō waka* 448: "I had thought the safflower a flower deep of hue, yet it has faded so much that it is very dreary!" Depth of hue may refer to the lady's imperial lineage, from which one might expect better; and the dye color from the safflower soon fades.

her must have given Genji good reason to complain about the safflower, but she enjoyed his poem anyway.

> "The robe may be pale, dipped as it has been just once in the scarlet dye,
>   but oh, do take care at least never to damage her name!"[45]

she murmured with seasoned wit, and she added, "All this is such a worry!"

Her verse was no masterpiece, but if only (he thought bitterly) Her Highness could manage that much! It hurt to receive such nonsense from anyone so well born, and he trembled lest it disgrace her.

Several gentlewomen arrived. "We had better hide this. Who ever heard of such a thing?"[46]

Why did I ever show it to him? Taifu lamented. He probably takes me, too, now, for a perfect bore! She stole away, mortified.

The next day he peered into the gentlewomen's sitting room while Taifu was in waiting on His Majesty. "Here!" he called. "Here is my answer from yesterday. What a time it gave me!" He tossed it to her. The others longed to know what it was. "Farewell to the maiden of Mount Mikasa, so like the blushing red of the plum,"[47] he sang as he left.

This struck Taifu as very funny, and those not in on the joke demanded to know what she was laughing to herself about. "Oh, nothing!" she answered. "One frosty morning he probably happened to see someone in scarlet silk with a matching nose. I didn't much like that snatch of song."

"You'll have to do better than that!" they answered, uncomprehending. "None of *us* has a red nose! He must have caught sight of Sakon no Taifu or Higo no Uneme."[48]

The gentlewomen at Her Highness's all gathered around to admire Genji's reply when Taifu delivered it.

> "To the lonely nights when a robe comes between us, would you then, you say,
>   have me add more layers yet to keep us farther apart?"[49]

It was on white paper and all the more delightful for having been written so casually.

---

45. "Though you care little for her, make sure never to soil the reputation of one so highborn by abandoning her." A robe dipped just once in the safflower dye (*hitohana goromo*) is therefore very pale, like Genji's tenuous affection. The poem plays on *hana*, "flower" and "nose."

46. Of a woman sending the man who supports her formal clothing.

47. This snatch of song (apparently taken from two different songs) may possibly be read in the following way: *Tada ume no hana* ("the blushing red of the plum") is a copyist's error for *tadarame no hana*, which could mean not only "the [red] *tadarame* flower" but "the red nose of the [sacred] maiden who protects the forge." This "red nose" could then suggest the maiden's *hoto* ("hearth" but also "sex"). A "maiden of Mount Mikasa" would serve the Kasuga Shrine, and since this shrine's main deity came originally from Hitachi province, this expression, too, may allude to the daughter of the Hitachi Prince. In fact, since the Kasuga deity may have been associated in the eleventh century, as later, with the work of the forge, both expressions may allude to the red nose—i.e., sex—of the maiden of the forge: Suetsumuhana.

48. Presumably fellow gentlewomen.

49. "When so many nights go by without our meeting, are you asking me to stay away for still more nights?"

On the evening of the last day of the year Taifu delivered that same clothing box to Her Highness, now filled with a set of gowns originally given to Genji, a grape-colored gown, and a layering in kerria rose or something like that. He obviously disapproved of the color Her Highness had sent him, but the old women declared nonetheless, "Well, the scarlet one was a lot more dignified. It was just as good as these. Furthermore, our mistress's poem was nicely done and made perfect sense, while his is just clever." As for their mistress, that poem had taken her so much trouble that she wrote it down for safekeeping.

The gentlemen were to go mumming this year,[50] after the first days of the New Year, and as always the air everywhere rang with the songs they were rehearsing, but despite the commotion Genji's sympathy went to the lonely Princess. After the festival on the seventh[51] he withdrew from His Majesty's presence, made as though to settle into his room at the palace, and then appeared late that night at her residence. The place had more life to it now, and she herself seemed a little less stiff. He kept wondering whether even she could possibly have turned over a new leaf.

He purposely lingered until the sun rose in the sky. When he opened the double doors to the east, its rays streamed in unimpeded, since the roof of the gallery opposite had fallen in, and the light glancing off a powdering of snow allowed him to see easily into the room. She had come forward a little and was now lying watching him put on his dress cloak. The tilt of her head and the way her hair spilled away from her were lovely. He lifted a lattice shutter, thinking how glad he would be if the turn of the year had brought her out a bit, but he did not put it up all the way, for he had learned his lesson. Instead, he brought over an armrest to prop it on and then set about smoothing his disordered sidelocks. A woman brought him the Chinese comb box and hairdressing chest that went with an impossibly ancient mirror stand. Yes, she even had a few man's accessories, so ornate as to be comical. Today she was dressed more like other ladies, having dressed precisely according to the contents of that box. That he did not register, though; he noted only the oddness of her jauntily patterned dress gown.

"Do let me hear your voice sometimes, at least this year. Never mind the long-awaited warbler;[52] what I really look forward to is a change in you."

"Spring carolings . . . ,"[53] she at last replied tremulously.

"There, you see?" He laughed. "I am sure it is the New Year that has done it!"

---

50. *Otoko tōka.* On the fourteenth, a song leader, dancers, and musicians chosen from among the privy gentlemen and the lower courtier ranks (*jige*) went round the palace grounds, dancing and singing *saibara* songs. Women did this every year (*onna dōka*), but to have men doing it was exceptional. The practice lapsed in 983.

51. The Festival of the Blue Roans (Aouma no Sechie), originally a Chinese event. Twenty-one horses, the sight of which brought good luck, were paraded before the Emperor and the court. Up to the reign of Murakami (reigned 946–67), who corresponds in the tale to the present Emperor's successor, the horses really were blue roans, but after that they were white.

52. The *uguisu*, whose return from the mountains in spring was awaited by such poets as Sosei, in *Shūishū* 5: "After the dawn of the new year, what one waits to hear is the warbler's voice."

53. *Kokinshū* 28: "Though all things are renewed amid the birds' spring carolings, I only grow old." She is making a trite complaint that Genji neglects her.

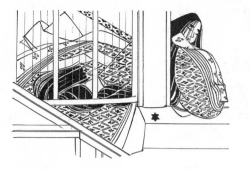

Young woman in a "long dress"

He then took his leave, humming "I must be dreaming"[54] while she, leaning against a pillar, watched him go. She had her hand over her mouth, but he still glimpsed the rich bloom of that blushing flower, and his mind was invaded by the thought, It makes her look such a fright!

His young Murasaki[55] looked deliciously pretty to him when he returned to Nijō, and he was delighted to enjoy the color scarlet so much after all. The plain, pleasantly rumpled cherry blossom[56] long dress she had on, coupled with the artlessness of her ways, made her simply enchanting. In deference to her grandmother's old-fashioned manners her teeth had not yet received any blacking,[57] but he had had her made up, and the sharp line of her eyebrows[58] was very attractive. He wondered with all his heart why he spent so much time on his foolish adventures instead of staying at home with this dear companion. Meanwhile, the two of them began as usual to play with dolls.

She drew pictures and colored them, scattering them about happily in her excitement. Genji made a picture of his own. He drew a lady with very long hair, and at the tip of her nose he put a dab of rouge:[59] yes, she was still ugly, even in a painting. Noting in a nearby mirror how handsome he was,[60] he gave himself a bright red nose and looked again: no, no beauty of his could survive having *that* in the middle of his face. His young lady laughed merrily at the sight.

"How would you feel if I were disfigured this way?"

"I would hate it!" She began to worry that the red might stick.

He pretended to wipe it off and gravely announced, "It won't come off! What a horrible trick I have played on myself! What will His Majesty say?"

She came and wiped it off tenderly for him. "Now, now," he teased her, "don't go daubing me up like Heichū![61] With red I can still manage!" They made a delightful couple.

The sun was bright and warm, and the plums, among all the budding trees swathed in spring haze, were most visibly promising to burst into bloom. The red

54. *Kokinshū* 970, in which the poet expresses surprise and delight at an unexpected visit.

55. *Murasaki no kimi:* the first use of *murasaki* as a quasi name for the girl herself rather than as an allusion to Fujitsubo.

56. White over *kurenai* red (yielding a pale pink effect).

57. In principle, a young woman's teeth were blackened only at marriage with a mixture of substances known as *hagurome*.

58. By this time her natural eyebrows would have been plucked out and new ones drawn on higher up.

59. *Beni*, the makeup color from the safflower dye.

60. A bronze mirror on a stand.

61. Heichū, the comic lover of Heian folklore, took a bottle of water with him when he went courting so that he could feign sensitive tears as needed, until his wife found the bottle and put ink in it. When Heichū came home the next morning, he saw a black-faced monster in the mirror.

plum tree by the steps down to the garden flowered especially early, and it was already tinged with color.

> *"Why I do not know, but I cannot say I like any scarlet flower,*
> *though I have great affection for the tall sprays of the plum.*

Ah, me!" The perplexed Genji sighed.

I wonder what happened to all these ladies in the end.

7

MOMIJI NO GA

Beneath the Autumn Leaves

Ga means a celebration (a jubilee) for a great personage on
the occasion of his attaining a felicitously advanced age. The personage here is a former Emperor
(the father or perhaps the elder
brother of Genji's father); the occasion is probably his entering
his fortieth or fiftieth year; and
the celebration takes place under
bright autumn leaves (*momiji*).

RELATIONSHIP TO EARLIER CHAPTERS

"Beneath the Autumn Leaves" begins in the autumn of the year in which Genji is eighteen and overlaps with the later part of "The Safflower" and, somewhat less, with the later part of "Young Murasaki." It continues to the autumn of the following year, when Genji is nineteen.

PERSONS

Genji, a Captain in the Palace Guards, then a Consultant, age 18 to 19

His Majesty, the Emperor, Genji's father (Kiritsubo no Mikado)

Her Highness, then Her Majesty, the Empress, Fujitsubo, 23 to 24

The Secretary Captain (Tō no Chūjō)

The Heir Apparent's mother, the Kokiden Consort

The Heir Apparent, 21 to 22 (Suzaku)

Genji's wife, 22 to 23 (Aoi)

Genji's young lady, 10 to 11 (Murasaki)

His Highness of War, Murasaki's father and Fujitsubo's brother,
33 to 34 (Hyōbukyō no Miya)

Ōmyōbu, Fujitsubo's intimate gentlewoman

Shōnagon, Murasaki's nurse

His Excellency, the Minister of the Left, 52 to 53 (Sadaijin)

Fujitsubo's newborn son (Reizei)

A Dame of Staff, 57 or 58 when Genji is 19 (Gen no Naishi)

His Majesty's progress to the Suzaku Palace took place after the tenth of the tenth month. The excursion was to be exceptionally brilliant, and his ladies were disappointed that they would not see it. Since he did not want Fujitsubo to miss it, he arranged a full rehearsal in her presence.

Captain Genji danced "Blue Sea Waves." His partner the Secretary Captain, His Excellency of the Left's son, certainly stood out in looks and skill, but beside Genji he was only a common mountain tree next to a blossoming cherry. As the music swelled and the piece reached its climax in the clear light of the late-afternoon sun, the cast of Genji's features and his dancing gave the familiar steps an unearthly quality. His singing of the verse could have been the Lord Buddha's kalavinka voice in paradise.[1] His Majesty was sufficiently transported with delight to wipe his eyes, and all the senior nobles and Princes wept. When the verse was over, when Genji tossed his sleeves again to straighten them[2] and the music rose once more in response, his face glowed with a still-greater beauty.

Even in his moment of triumph the Heir Apparent's mother remarked bitterly, "With those looks of his, the gods above must covet him. How unpleasant!" The young gentlewomen listening thought her hateful.

Fujitsubo knew that she would have liked his dance still better if he were not so importunate in his desires, and she felt as though she had dreamed this vision of him. She went straight to attend His Majesty for the night.

" 'Blue Sea Waves' made the rehearsal today, did it not?" he remarked. "How did it strike you?"

"It was very nice." She was too flustered to answer him better.

"His partner did not do at all badly either. In dancing and gesture, breeding will tell. One admires the renowned professional dancers,[3] but they lack that easy grace.

---

1. The "verse" (ei) of the dance is a poem in Chinese attributed to Ono no Takamura (802–52); the music stopped while the lead dancer sang it. The Buddha's voice was often compared to that of the kalavinka, the bird that sings in paradise.

2. The dancer had marked the climactic moment of the "verse" by flipping his sleeves so they wrapped themselves around his arms.

3. Dancers from hereditary lineages specialized in bugaku dancing.

The performance under the autumn trees may be an anticlimax now that the rehearsal day has gone so well, but I had them do their best so that you should see it all."

Genji wrote to her the next morning, "How did you find it? All the time I was more troubled than one could ever imagine.

> My unhappiness made of me hardly the man to stand up and dance;
> did you divine what I meant when I waved those sleeves of mine?

But I must say no more."

She replied, for no doubt she could not banish that beauty and that dazzling grace from her mind,

> "That man of Cathay who waved his sleeves long ago did so far away,[4]
> but every measure you danced to my eyes seemed wonderful.

Oh, yes, very much."

Overjoyed by the miracle of an answer from her, he smiled to see that with her knowledge even of dance, and with her way of then bringing in the realm across the sea, she already wrote like an Empress. He spread the letter out and contemplated it as though it were holy writ.

Kalavinka

The entire court accompanied His Majesty on the progress itself, as did the Heir Apparent. The musicians' barges rowed around the lake, as always, and there were all sorts of dances from Koma and Cathay.[5] The music of the instruments and the beat of the drums set the heavens ringing. His Majesty had been disturbed enough by the magic of Genji's figure at sundown that other day to have scriptures read for him at temples here and there, and everyone who heard of it wholly sympathized, save the mother of the Heir Apparent, who thought the gesture absurdly overdone.

His Majesty had pressed into the circle of musicians[6] every officeholder of recognized talent from among the privy gentlemen or the lesser ranks. Two Consultants—one the Intendant of the Left Gate Watch, the other that of the Right—were put in charge of the music of Left and Right.[7] Every gentleman had chosen a first-rate teacher and practiced assiduously at home.

---

4. "Blue Sea Waves" came from Tang China. The poem alludes to a story about a magic moment in a Chinese dancer's performance.
5. Ancient Korea and China. There was an elaborately decorated barge for the "Korean" music and another for the "Chinese."
6. *Kaishiro.* The dancers emerged after donning their costumes inside the circle.
7. Chinese music was "music of the Left"; Korean, of the "Right." Such high-ranking officials seldom assumed responsibility for the music.

Under the tall autumn trees breath from a circle forty strong roused from the instruments an indescribable music that mingled with the wind's roaring and sighing as it swept, galelike, down the mountain, while through the flutter of bright falling leaves "Blue Sea Waves" shone forth with an awesome beauty. When most of the leaves were gone from Genji's headdress, leaving it shamed by the brilliance of his face, the Intendant of the Left Gate Watch picked chrysanthemums to replace them from among those before His Majesty. In the waning light the very sky seemed inclined to weep, shedding a hint of rain while Genji in his glory, decked with chrysanthemums now faded to the loveliest of shades, again displayed the marvels of his skill. His closing steps sent a shiver through the gathering, who could not imagine what they saw to be of this world. Among the undiscerning multitude sheltered beneath the trees, hidden among the rocks, or buried among fallen leaves on the mountainside, those with eyes to see shed tears.

The greatest treat after "Blue Sea Waves" was "Autumn Wind," danced by the Fourth Prince (then still a boy), the Shōkyōden Consort's son.[8] Attention wandered now that the best of the dances was over, and what followed may even have spoiled things a little.

That evening Captain Genji assumed the third rank, upper grade, while the Secretary Captain rose to the fourth rank, lower grade.[9] If every senior noble had reason to rejoice,[10] each in the measure due him, it was because Genji's own ascent had drawn him upward. How gladly one would know what merit from lives past allowed him to dazzle all eyes and bring such joy to every heart!

Her Highness had withdrawn from court, and Genji gave himself up as always to watching for a chance to see her, subjecting himself to further complaints from His Excellency's. Nor was this all, for a gentlewoman there reported his abduction of the "young plant" as his having taken a woman to live with him at Nijō, and her mistress was not at all pleased. He quite understood that she should feel as she did, since she knew nothing of the circumstances; but if only she had unburdened herself frankly to him like any ordinary woman, he might have explained things to her and calmed her fears, whereas in fact she was so intent on misinterpreting all he did that he could hardly be blamed for seeking refuge in dubious diversions. In her person he found nothing lacking or amiss. She was the first woman he had known, and he trusted that even if she failed for the present to appreciate his high regard, she would change her mind in time. He displayed his exceptional quality in the unswerving steadfastness of this faith.

The more Genji's young lady grew accustomed to him, the more she improved in manner and looks, and she snuggled up to him now as though it were the most natural thing in the world. He still kept her in the same distant wing, because he did not wish his household staff to know yet who she was; and there he had her room done up beautifully, visited her day and night, and gave her all sorts of lessons. He wrote out calligraphy models for her and had her practice, he felt, just as

8. The Shōkyōden Consort to Genji's father is mentioned nowhere else.
9. Tō no Chūjō's new rank is high for a Captain in the Palace Guards, and Genji's is very unusual.
10. Over his promotion.

though he had taken in a daughter from elsewhere. He assigned her a household office and a staff of her own so as to have her properly looked after.

No one but Koremitsu could make out what he was up to. His Highness her father still knew nothing. When she remembered the past, as she often did, her grandmother was usually the one she missed. Genji's company took her mind off her sorrows, but although he sometimes stayed with her at night, he was more often taken up with calls here and there and would leave at dark, and then she would arouse all his tenderness by making it quite clear how much she wished he would not go. It so upset him to see her in low spirits, after he had spent two or three days at the palace or His Excellency's, that he felt as though he were responsible for a motherless child and hesitated to go out at all. Reports of all this greatly pleased His Reverence, despite the irregularity of the girl's situation. Whenever His Reverence performed a memorial service for her grandmother, Genji provided the finest offerings.

Genji was anxious for news of Fujitsubo and called at her Sanjō residence, to which she had withdrawn. He was entertained by such gentlewomen as Ōmyōbu, Chūnagon, and Nakatsukasa. It vexed him to be treated so obviously as a guest, but he swallowed his feelings and was chatting idly with them when His Highness of War[11] arrived.

His Highness received Genji when he learned that he was there. Elegant and romantically languorous as His Highness was, Genji speculated privately about the pleasures of his company if he were a woman and, having a double reason to feel close to him, engaged him in intent conversation. His Highness for his part noted how much more open and easy Genji was than usual, liked his looks a great deal, and, being unaware that Genji was his son-in-law, indulged his roving fancy in the pleasure of imagining him, too, as a woman.

Genji was envious when at dark His Highness went in to his sister through her blinds. Long ago Genji's father had allowed him to talk with her in person rather than through go-betweens, and now he could only feel hurt that she kept him at such a distance.

"I have been remiss in failing to call upon you more often," he said with stiff formality, "but unfortunately I am inclined to be neglectful in the absence of any pressing errand. Should you need me for any reason, I shall be pleased to place myself at your service." He then left. Ōmyōbu could devise nothing better for him, since plainly Her Highness was far less warmly disposed toward him than in the past, and her evident displeasure so shamed and distressed Ōmyōbu that all Genji's subsequent entreaties to her went for naught. How soon it was over! each lover cried silently, in an anguish that had no end.

Shōnagon, on the other hand, was astonished to see so happy a pair before her, and for this she felt that she must thank the blessings of the buddha to whom her late mistress had addressed so many prayers of concern for her granddaughter. The lady at His Excellency's was no doubt very grand indeed, and the many others whom Genji favored might easily cause trouble when the child was grown, but his

---

11. Fujitsubo's elder brother and the father of Murasaki.

special consideration for her charge was deeply reassuring.

On the last day of the month[12] Genji had his young lady doff her mourning ("Now, now," he said, "for your mother's mother three months will do"); but she had grown up without any other parent, and after that she wore not bright, showy colors but dress gowns of unfigured scarlet, purple, or golden yellow; and very smart she looked in them, too.

Genji came around on his way to the morning salutation.[13] "You are looking ever so grown-up this morning!"[14] he said, with the most winning smile.

Chasing devils

She was already busy setting up her dolls, laying out her collection of accessories on a pair of three-foot cabinets, and filling the room with an assemblage of little houses that Genji had made her. "Inuki broke this chasing out devils,[15] and I am mending it," she announced solemnly.

"How careless of her! I shall have it repaired for you straightaway. We are not supposed to say anything sad today,[16] so you must not cry."

As he left, his imposing presence amid his large retinue brought her and her gentlewomen out near the veranda to watch him go, after which she dressed up her "Genji" doll and had him set off for the palace.

"Do grow up a bit this year, at least." Shōnagon wanted to chasten her for thinking only of her games. "A girl over ten should not be playing with dolls. Now you have a husband, you must be sweet and gentle with him, like a proper wife. You do not even like having me do your hair!"

So I have a husband, do I! The men all these women call their husbands are nothing to look at, but *mine* is a handsome young man! The idea was a revelation. Still, the addition of one more to the count of her years did seem to have made a difference. The household staff were taken aback whenever she turned out still to be a child, but they never imagined how innocently the two were sleeping together.

Genji as usual found the lady at His Excellency's dauntingly perfect when he withdrew there from the palace, and her lack of warmth prompted him to remark, "How happy I would be if this year you were at last to consent to engage with me a little!" But now that she knew he had brought a woman to live with him, she was convinced that he had lofty plans for the newcomer and undoubtedly thought him a sorrier embarrassment than ever.

With an effort she feigned ignorance and responded to his joviality after all in

12. Also the last of the year. Mourning for a maternal grandparent lasted three months, for a paternal one five. Murasaki's grandmother had died about the twentieth of the ninth month.

13. *Chōbai,* when the assembled courtiers saluted the Emperor on the morning of the first day of the year. Genji looks in on Murasaki the day after he has stopped wearing mourning.

14. Because she is a year older than she was yesterday.

15. During the devil-expelling rite (*tsuina no gi*) held on the last night of the year.

16. "Today we must practice *kotoimi*": abstention from ill-omened language, including the sound of weeping.

her own distinctive way. Four years older than he, she had a more composed dignity and a mature beauty that put his youth to shame. How could *she* be wanting? Obviously, Genji reflected, it is my own, dissolute behavior that has earned me her rejection. Her lofty pride at being the only daughter not just of any Minister but of the greatest of them all, and of no less than a Princess, moved her to condemn his every lapse, while he on his side kept wondering why he must defer to her so

Gentleman wearing a stone belt

and keep trying to bring her round. Such were the distances that kept them apart.

His Excellency meanwhile deplored Genji's misconduct, but he still forgot his displeasure every time he saw his son-in-law and did all he could to please him. Early the next morning he looked in as Genji was preparing to leave, and when he found him dressed, he personally brought him a famous stone belt,[17] went round behind him to straighten his robe, and all but held his shoes for him to step into. It was very touching.

"I look forward to wearing this at the privy banquet[18] and other such occasions," Genji said.

"Oh, I have better. I just thought this one a little unusual." He insisted that Genji put it on. In fact, looking after Genji in every way was his pleasure in life, and he asked only to welcome such a man and see him off, no matter how rarely.

Genji set out on his round of New Year's calls, although it was not really long: His Majesty, the Heir Apparent, His Eminence, and then, of course, Fujitsubo at her Sanjō residence.

"Today again he is a wonder to behold," Fujitsubo's gentlewomen observed to their mistress. "The more he matures, the more frighteningly beautiful he becomes!" Just a glimpse of him through her curtains threw her feelings into turmoil.

It was worrying that the twelfth month had passed without any sign of the anticipated event.[19] Her Highness's women all looked forward to it this month, at least, and His Majesty pursued his preparations on the same assumption. However, the month went by uneventfully. The rumor went round that a spirit was to blame, and meanwhile Her Highness despaired, because she knew that this might ruin her

17. *Sekitai,* worn with the full-dress cloak (*hō*): a black leather belt with a double row of squares or circles made of stone, jade, or horn set in it so as to show at the wearer's back. (A fold of the *hō* covered the front.) The color and material varied with rank. Genji's new rank required white jade.

18. *Naien,* a banquet given by the Emperor on the day of the Rat that fell on the twenty-first, twenty-second, or twenty-third of the first month. The guests composed poetry in Chinese.

19. The birth of Fujitsubo's child.

forever.[20] She also felt very unwell. Genji, who had less and less doubt what the matter was, had rites done in several temples[21] without saying why. Life being uncertain at best, he was tormented by the prospect that their love might end in tragedy, until a little past the tenth of the second month she gave birth to a boy, and for His Majesty as well as for her own women anxiety gave way to happiness. She personally dreaded the life that lay

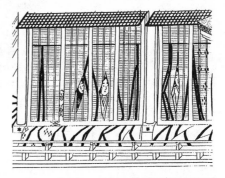

Peering out through standing curtains

before her, but reports that the Kokiden Consort was muttering imprecations against her reminded her that news of her death might only provoke laughter, and this gave her the strength gradually to recover. His Majesty was impatient to see the child.

Genji, who had his own private reasons for apprehension, called on the new mother at a moment when no other visitor claimed her. "His Majesty is very keen to see him," he said, "and I thought I might do so and report"; but she understandably pleaded that it would be awkward just now and would not allow it. Actually, the boy was astonishingly, frighteningly like Genji himself. The resemblance was impossible to miss. Her Highness, conscience-stricken, wondered how anyone could fail after a single look at him to perceive and to censure a misdeed that she herself found repellent. What would they call her when the truth dawned on a world eager to spy out the slightest flaw? Pondering these things led her to despair.

When Genji managed to talk to Ōmyōbu, he filled her ears with passionate entreaties,[22] but without any prospect of success. He pleaded so desperately to see the little boy that Ōmyōbu protested, "Why must you insist against all reason, my lord? You will naturally do so in due course"; but her own manner betrayed equal distress.

On so grave a matter Genji could hardly speak plainly. "Will I never be allowed to talk to her in person?" He wept piteously.

> *"What can be the tie that bound us two together a long time ago,*
> *that in this life she and I should be kept so far apart?*

I just do not understand."

Knowing her mistress's suffering as she did, Ōmyōbu could not dismiss him without a reply.

> *"Heartsick thoughts for her when beside him and, for you, sorrow not to be;*
> *ah, this, then, is what they mean by the darkness of the heart!"* [23]

she whispered. "It is such a shame that neither of you should ever be happy!"

---

20. Or perhaps "that she might die [in childbirth]."
21. To ensure safe childbirth.
22. Entreaties addressed through her to Fujitsubo.
23. "Beside him" means beside the newborn child. Ōmyōbu alludes to *Gosenshū* 1102, by Fujiwara no Kanesuke, about the darkness in the heart of a parent troubled about a child.

Thus barred from communication, Genji went away again, but Her Highness, who feared the perils of gossip and warned against them, retreated from her once affectionate familiarity with Ōmyōbu. She continued to treat her equably, so as not to arouse comment, but to Ōmyōbu's sorrow and surprise she must sometimes have betrayed her displeasure.

In the fourth month the young Prince went to the palace. He had developed faster than most children and by now could sit up on his own. His Majesty completely missed the extraordinary, indeed unmistakable likeness between him and his father and assumed instead that it was only natural for supremely beautiful people to resemble one another. He was completely devoted to the child. He had felt the same way about Genji, but in the end, when it became clear that those around him would not tolerate such a move, he had refrained from appointing Genji Heir Apparent, and this had been an enduring disappointment, for it pained him to see all the beauty and distinction of the maturing Genji wasted on a commoner. His new son, on the other hand, had a mother of the highest rank and shone with a light equal to Genji's, and so he loved him as a flawless gem—which for Her Highness only made one more reason for continual sorrow and anguish.

When Genji visited Her Highness's residence as usual, to join in music making, His Majesty appeared with the child in his arms. "I have many children," he said, "but you are the only one I have seen day and night since you were this small. I expect it is the way he reminds me of those days that makes him look so very like you. Perhaps all babies are like that." He simply doted on his little son.

Genji felt himself go pale. Terror, humility, joy, and pity coursed through him until he nearly wept. So eerily adorable was the burbling, smiling child that there came to Genji, despite himself, the immodest thought that if *this* was what he looked like, he must indeed be a treasure. Her Highness was perspiring in torment, and Genji's own pleasure in the boy turned to such anguish that he withdrew.

At home again he lay down, and after allowing the worst of his agitation to pass, he decided to go on to His Excellency's. Gillyflowers stood out brightly there in the garden's green expanse. He had one picked and sent it to Ōmyōbu with what must have been a long letter, in which he said,

> "I see him in this, and yet even so at heart I am not consoled;
> on the lovely little pink there settles only heavier dew.[24]

I had so wished the flower to bloom, but everything in this world is hopeless."[25] It must have come at just the right time, because when Ōmyōbu showed it to her mistress, urging her to give him back "just a word or two, my lady, here on the petals,"[26]

---

24. *Shinkokinshū* 1494, by Keishi Joō: "I see the resemblance yet am not a whit consoled—what am I to do with this little pink?"

25. "Gillyflower" (*tokonatsu*) and "pink" (*nadeshiko*) are the same flower, but the two words have different associations. "I had so wished the flower to bloom" is from *Gosenshū* 199, which Genji quotes also in his own verse. The poem is about planting *nadeshiko* so as to have them stand consolingly for someone much loved—in this case, the little boy.

26. *Kokinshū* 167, a romantic poem about *nadeshiko* by Ōshikōchi no Mitsune: "I shall let no speck of dust [translated here as "a word or two"] settle on these pinks where my love and I have lain."

Her Highness herself was very deeply moved. In faint ink, as though her writing had given out in midline, she simply wrote,

> *"Oh, I know full well he only calls forth further dews that moisten my sleeves,*
> *yet I have no heart to scorn so lovely a little pink."*

Ōmyōbu happily conveyed this to Genji, who was lying gazing disconsolately into space, convinced that as always his letter would go unanswered. His heart pounded, and a rush of joy started tears from his eyes.

When it gave him no relief to lie there in gloom, he went for comfort as so often to the west wing. He peeped in with a robe thrown casually over his shoulders, his sidelocks rumpled and wispy, and blowing a sweet air on his flute. There was his young lady, leaning on an armrest, as sweet and pretty as could be and, he felt, moist with the same dew as that other flower.[27] Irresistible or not, she still had a mind to make him smart for not having come straight to see her when he got home, and so for once she was pouting.

"Come here!" He sat down near the veranda.

Sō no koto

She hummed "when the tide is high" and put her sleeve bewitchingly to her mouth.[28]

"Dear me, when did you start quoting poems like that? It is not good for people to see each other *all* the time."[29]

He had a koto brought in for her to play. "The *sō no koto* is awkward because the highest treble string breaks so easily," he remarked, tuning the instrument down to the *hyōjō* mode. She could not maintain her ill humor once he had tested the tuning with a few notes and pushed the instrument from him, and she played very nicely indeed. She was still quite small, and the way she had to lean over to put in a vibrato[30] was extremely engaging.

Entranced, he taught her more music by playing his flute. She was very quick and knew the most difficult pieces after a single hearing. He was satisfied that the

---

27. The "gillyflower" or "little pink" of his exchange with Fujitsubo.

28. *Shūishū* 967 (also *Man'yōshū* 1398), by Sakanoue no Iratsume: "Is he seaweed on the shore, covered when the tide is high? I see him so little and miss him so much!" Murasaki's gesture is one of embarrassment.

29. Thanks to double meanings from *Kokinshū* 683, Genji's words prolong the seashore imagery of the poem quoted by Murasaki: "Would that I might have enough of the seaweed [*mirume*, also "meeting" with a lover] for which the seafolk dive, they say, morning and evening at Ise."

30. The left hand depresses and relaxes the string plucked by the right, to make the pitch undulate.

liveliness of her intelligence met all his hopes. When he amused himself by giving a very nice performance of "Hosoroguseri," despite the piece's peculiar name, she accompanied him in a manner still youthful but very pretty and true to the rhythm.

The lamps were lit, and the two had started to look at pictures when Genji's men, who had been told he would be going out, began clearing their throats to remind him, and someone observed that it looked like rain. Then as always she became sad and dejected. She stopped looking at pictures and only lay facedown, which to Genji was so enchanting that he stroked the rich cascade of her hair and said, "Do you miss me when I am gone?"

She nodded.

"I miss you, too. I hate to spend a whole day without seeing you. As long as you are still a child, though, I must trust in your patience and try not to offend other people who are easily hurt. It is all very awkward, you see, and that is why for the time being I keep going off on these visits. Once you are grown, I will never go anywhere. The reason why I do not want them angry with me is that I hope to live a long and happy life with *you!*"

His earnest reassurances only embarrassed her, and instead of answering, she just put her head in his lap and went to sleep. His heart melted, and he announced that he would not go out after all. The women rose and brought him his evening meal in place.

"I am not going out anymore," he said after he roused her. She felt better then and sat up, and they ate together.

"Then sleep here," she said, hardly touching her food, since she still suspected that he might go away. He did not see how he could ever leave such a companion, even on the last and most solemn journey of all.

He ended up being detained this way time after time, until word of it reached His Excellency's. "Who is she?" the gentlewomen asked each other.

"How can he treat my lady this way?"

"So far no one has suggested who she could be."

"No one at all nice or well brought up would keep the pleasure of his company all to herself this way."

"She must be someone he happened to meet at the palace, and now he is so keen on her, he is keeping her out of sight for fear of criticism."

"They say she is childish and immature."

His Majesty, too, had heard there was such a woman. "It has pained me very much to learn that His Excellency is so displeased," he said to Genji, "and I entirely sympathize, because he is the one who did everything to turn the mere boy you once were into the man you are now, and I hardly think that you are too young to appreciate his kindness. Why, then, are you treating him so thoughtlessly?"

Genji assumed an attitude of contrite deference and did not reply.

I suppose he does not like her,[31] His Majesty reflected commiseratingly.

"Still," as he remarked later, "he shows no sign of tossing caution to the winds

31. Aoi.

and losing his head over any gentlewoman of mine, or indeed over anyone else. What nooks and crannies can he have been poking about in, to have earned himself this degree of resentment?"

Despite the passing years His Majesty himself had not managed so far to give up his interest in the same sort of thing, and he had a particular taste for pretty and clever waiting women,[32] hence the presence of many on his staff. Genji's most casual approach to any of them was seldom rebuffed, but perhaps he found them simply too easy, because he seemed strangely uninterested, and even when now and then one did try her wiles on him, he would answer her tactfully but never really misbehave, with the result that some thought him a perfect bore.

There was an aging Dame of Staff, a lady of impeccable birth, witty, distinguished, and well respected by all, who nevertheless was intensely coquettish; and Genji was curious to know why, when a woman might of course be light in her ways, she should be so thoroughly dissolute even in her declining years. On jokingly testing the waters he was shocked to find that she did not think his proposition at all incongruous, but the adventure still amused him enough to pursue it, although to her great chagrin he kept his distance for fear of starting gossip about his liaison with an old woman.

Once, when she had finished combing His Majesty's hair, he called for a maid of the wardrobe and went out, leaving her and Genji alone in the room. She was more prettily got up than usual, with a graceful bearing and lovely hair, and her costume was assertively brilliant—all of which to Genji's distaste betrayed her refusal to show her age; but he could not resist tugging at the end of her train to see how she would respond. From behind a heavily decorated fan she shot back a languid glance from dark-rimmed, sunken eyes set amid nests of wrinkles.

Fan

No one her age should carry that fan, he thought. Offering his in exchange,[33] he took the fan and examined it. On paper red enough to set his face aglow he saw painted in gold a picture of tall trees. On one side, in a style now passé but not undistinguished, were casually written the words "Old is the grass beneath the trees."[34]

This is all very well, but what a horrid idea! "What we have here, I see, is 'the wood in summer,'"[35] he remarked with a smile. He felt strange enough just talking to her to fear being seen, but no such worry crossed her mind.

32. *Unebe* and *nyokurōdo*, two types of junior servants on the Emperor's staff. *Unebe* (or *uneme*) assisted with his meals, *nyokurōdo* with his wardrobe.

33. So that she could still hide her face from him, as manners required.

34. *Kokinshū* 892: "Old is the grass beneath the trees at Ōaraki; no steed grazes there, no one comes to mow it." Genji recognizes the poem as a declaration that she is hungry for a man.

35. *Saneakira shū* 28, by Fujiwara no Saneakira: "I hear the cuckoo calling, for the wood of Ōaraki must be its summer lodging."

> *"Whenever you come, I shall cut for your fine steed a feast of fresh grass,*
> *be it only lower leaves, now the best season is past,"*

she said with shameless archness.

He answered,

> *"If I made my way through the brush I might be seen, for it seems to me*
> *many steeds must like it there, underneath the forest trees.*

It is a bit risky." He rose to go.

She caught his sleeve and cried out through dramatic tears, "Never in my life have I been made to feel so wretched! Oh, the shame of it, after all these years!"

"I shall be in touch later. There are other things, you see . . ." He broke free and continued on, but she clung to him, angrily bewailing the treachery of time.[36]

Meanwhile His Majesty had finished changing and was now watching this scene through the doorway. What a very odd pair! he thought, greatly amused, and he remarked with a chuckle, "I hear constant complaints about your lack of interest in women, but you did not let this one escape you, did you!" She made no real effort to defend herself, despite a degree of embarrassment, perhaps because she was one of those who are glad enough to have a liaison known as long as the lover is worth it.

Well, the Secretary Captain said to himself when he heard how all were agog over this incident, I pride myself on leaving no cranny unexplored, but I certainly had never thought of *her!* He then struck up an affair, wishing to taste her undying randiness himself. He was a promising catch who might (she thought) make up for Genji's unkindness, but apparently it was only Genji she wanted—an extravagant choice! The Secretary Captain kept his doings so quiet that Genji never found out about them.

The Dame of Staff would start straight in on her grievance whenever she came across Genji, and her age so aroused his pity that he wished to console her, but the idea was too depressing in practice, and for a long time he did nothing. Then once, when he was roaming around the Unmeiden under cover of dusk, after a cooling shower of rain, there she was, playing her *biwa* very nicely. No one was better at it than she, for she joined the men in concerts before His Majesty, and her wounded feelings now made her music especially poignant. "Shall I cast my lot with the melon grower?" she was singing in a voice of great quality. Genji was not entirely pleased.[37] He wondered as he listened whether his feelings might resemble that other's, long ago at Gakushū.[38] Then she stopped, apparently in the grip of emotion.

---

36. "There are other things, you see" (*omoinagara zo ya*) contains syllables that form the name of the Nagara (Bridge), often mentioned in poems that lament old age. Her answer, *hashibashira* ("bridge pillar"), here rendered for narrative meaning as "bewail[ing] the treachery of time," is taken from such a poem, probably *Shūishū* 864.

37. In her *saibara* song a girl, courted by a melon grower, wonders whether to say yes. Genji takes her to mean, "Shall I give up that man [Genji] who rejects me and make do with someone else?"

38. In "On Hearing a Girl Sing at Night," Bai Juyi (*Hakushi monjū* 0498) described being on a journey at Ezhou (Gakushū) and hearing a woman on a nearby boat sing a heartbreaking song that turned to piteous weeping.

He approached her, softly singing "The Eastern Cottage," and in song she supplied him the line "Open the door and come in."[39] He thought her a most extraordinary woman. Next came, with a sigh,

"Nobody is there, surely, standing all wet through—ah, how cruelly
my humble eastern cottage suffers in the soaking rain!"

He objected to taking all the blame for her troubles and wondered what he had done to deserve this.

"Someone else's wife is more trouble than she's worth; what with this and that,
in her poor eastern cottage I give up making her mine."

He meant to pass on by, but it felt so unkind to do so that he changed his mind and humored her by engaging in a bantering exchange from which he did derive a certain enjoyment.

Considering that Genji seemed to be calling secretly on all sorts of women, despite his innocent airs, the Secretary Captain resented his show of sober seriousness and his constant sermons, and he was forever plotting to catch him in the act. Now he was delighted to have found his chance. He bided his time in the hope of frightening and upsetting Genji just enough to teach him a lesson.

A chilly wind was blowing rather late one night when the Secretary Captain gathered that the two must have dropped off to sleep, and he stole into the room. Genji heard him, since he had not meant to sleep soundly, but he did not recognize him, and he assumed that the intruder was a certain Director of Upkeep who apparently had never been able to forget her.

"Well, I do not like this at all. I am leaving," he declared, humiliated to be found by a man of mature years in so incongruously compromising a situation. "You undoubtedly knew quite well that this gentleman was coming,[40] and I will not put up with being made out to be a fool." With this he gathered up his dress cloak and retired behind a screen.

Smothering his mirth, the Secretary Captain strode up to the screen that Genji had just opened and with a great clatter folded it up again, producing a spectacularly menacing din. Meanwhile the lady, who played the proud beauty despite her age and who knew something of crises like this one, having been through several before, was not too panic-stricken to restrain the intruder firmly, trembling with apprehension over what he might do to Genji. Genji would gladly have escaped unrecognized, but a vision of himself from the rear in full flight, clothing flapping around him and headdress askew, gave him pause, for he saw how silly he would look.

39. In the *saibara* song "Azumaya" ("The Eastern Cottage"), a man arrives at the woman's door in the pouring rain and demands to be admitted. The woman, inside, answers that the door is unlocked and urges him to come in. An *azumaya* was a form of thatched house characteristic of eastern Japan. This song inspired the poem that gave the "Azumaya" chapter its title.

40. Literally, "I am sure the spider's behavior was perfectly clear." In the proverbial *Kokinshū* 1110, by Princess Sotōri, "the spider's behavior" clearly foretells a lover's visit.

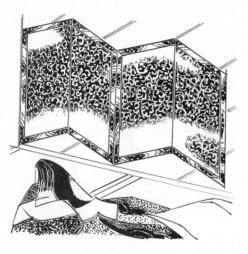

Screen

To keep Genji from recognizing him, the Captain next put on a dumb show of maddened rage and drew his sword, at which the lady cried out, "Oh, no, my darling, no!" and wrung her hands entreatingly before him. It was all he could do not to burst out laughing. Her veneer of comely youthfulness was all very well, but the spectacle of a distraught woman of fifty-seven or -eight, caught in the throes of terror between two superb youths of twenty, was absolutely absurd.

The Secretary Captain's ostentatious disguise and the very fierceness of his pantomime now betrayed him to Genji, who felt an utter idiot when he understood that the entire performance had been for his own benefit. Highly amused, now that he knew his opponent, he seized the Captain's sword arm and gave it a hard pinch. The Captain got angry, but he nevertheless broke down and laughed.

"Seriously, though," Genji said, "are you sure you are in your right mind? What a joke to play on me! Anyway, I shall put on my cloak"; but the Secretary Captain got a grip on it and refused to let go.

"All right, you, too, then!" Genji undid the Captain's sash to strip the cloak off him. They wrestled back and forth while the Captain struggled to keep him from succeeding, until a seam gave way and Genji's cloak came apart.

> *"The misdeeds you hide may well soon be known to all, now our tug-of-war*
> *has torn a rent in the cloak that covered so many sins!"*

the Captain said. "Wear it now, and everyone will know!"[41]

> *"Such a summer cloak may hardly hide anything, that I know full well,*
> *but what a poor friend you are to uncover me that way!"*[42]

Genji retorted; and the two of them went off together, their garments trailing about them, the best of friends.

Genji lay down to nurse his vexation at having been found out. As for the out-

---

41. This exchange of poems bristles with wordplays. Tō no Chūjō's remark after his poem alludes to *Kokin rokujō* 3261, which evokes a red robe that when worn on the outside displays the wearer's amorous preoccupation to all.

42. "If you did not want everyone to know about *your* affair with this lady, you should have thought twice before barging in on me like this."

raged Dame of Staff, the following morning she sent back a pair of trousers and a sash they had left behind, with the message

> *"No complaint of mine could relieve my misery, now the double wave*
> *that dashed itself on my shore has again slipped out to sea.*[43]

The river is dry . . ."[44]

She has no shame! Genji's thought was unkind, but he was still sorry to have upset her, and he therefore answered simply,

> *"Never mind that wave and its boisterous assault—that I can let pass;*
> *but I would lodge a complaint against the welcoming shore."*

The sash was the Secretary Captain's. He observed that it was darker than his own dress cloak, and he noted also that his cloak was missing the outer band of one sleeve.[45] What a ridiculous business! he said to himself. He was beginning to feel better. I suppose you are bound to play the fool when you let yourself in for this sort of thing.

From his room at the palace the Secretary Captain now sent Genji the missing piece of sleeve, wrapped in paper, with the advice to have it sewn back on. How did he manage to make off with that? Genji grumbled to himself. If I had not got his sash . . . He wrapped the sash in matching paper and sent it to him with the verse,

> *"In fear of your blame, lest the sash should tear in two, and so you and she,*
> *I have not once looked upon the bright color of its blue."*[46]

> *"Now that none but you has made off as you have done with that sash of mine,*
> *I shall not spare you my blame for having torn us two apart.*

My wrath will strike you in the end!" the Captain retorted.

Both set off when the sun was high to wait upon His Majesty. Genji cultivated a bland innocence that greatly amused his friend, but the day was crowded with memorials and decrees, and the sight of each other behaving with such punctilious gravity allowed them no more than an exchange of grins.

The Secretary Captain came up to Genji during a lull in the proceedings and said with a detestable leer, "I trust you have now learned not to keep secrets."

"Why should I have? The fellow I pity is the one who got nothing for all his

---

43. "It is no use my complaining (although I would like to), now that the two of you have gone, never to return." The image of waves breaking on a beach suggests erotic desire.

44. The river of my tears.

45. *Hatasode*, an extra width of cloth that further lengthened the sleeve.

46. "Lest you blame me if that woman wants no more of you, I have not even touched this blue sash of yours." The poem plays on "tearing" the sash (the liaison) and borrows twice (for example, *hanada no obi*, "blue sash") from the *saibara* song that Tō no Chūjō, too, quotes in his reply.

long wait. Seriously, though, rumor is rife!" The two of them swore each other to silence.[47]

Thereafter the Secretary Captain brought up the incident whenever he had a chance, thus impressing Genji ever more vividly with what he owed to that tiresome woman. Meanwhile Genji stayed out of her way, lest she subject him again to her tragic complaint that he had done her a grievous wrong.

The Secretary Captain kept all this from his sister, but he reserved the idea of telling her as a threat to hold over Genji when the occasion might warrant it. Even Genji's half brothers, born to the greatest of their father's ladies, held Genji in awe and deferred to him as His Majesty's favorite, but not so the Secretary Captain, who rose bravely to Genji's every challenge and clearly remained determined never to be outdone. Only the Secretary Captain was his sister's full brother. Yes, Genji was an Emperor's son, but he himself was the preferred son of His Majesty's foremost Minister and of a Princess, and for that reason he did not feel at all Genji's inferior. His person combined all desirable qualities, and there was no attribute of excellence that he lacked.

The rivalry between these two took some peculiar turns, though it would be a bore to describe them all.

It appears that in the seventh month Fujitsubo was elevated to Empress.[48] Genji became a Consultant. Soon His Majesty would act on his desire to step down from the throne, and he had the little Prince in mind for the next Heir Apparent. However, there was no one suitably placed to look after him when that time came. The Prince's maternal relatives were all imperial, hence excluded from governing, and His Majesty had therefore wished at least to make his mother's standing unassailable in order to strengthen his position.

All this compounded the Kokiden Consort's agitation, as well it might, but His Majesty assured her, "The Heir Apparent's reign is coming soon, and you will then be the Empress Mother. You need not worry." People had indeed been complaining, as one would expect, that His Majesty could not just set aside the lady who was the Heir Apparent's mother and who had been his Consort for twenty years in order to appoint someone else Empress over her.

Genji, the new Consultant, was in Her Majesty's escort on the night when she entered the palace in state. She whose own mother had been Empress glowed with the beauty of a jewel, even among the exalted company of past Empresses, and she enjoyed such unexampled esteem from His Majesty that everyone else, too, held her in the highest regard. No wonder, then, if the despairing Genji thought of her in her palanquin and knew that she had now well and truly passed beyond his reach. It was almost too much for him.

---

47. "Rumor is rife!" is from *Kokin rokujō* 2108 ("Though rumor be as rife as seaweed the seafolk gather, as long as we love each other, let the world talk as it will!"); and "swore each other to silence" (a paraphrase for narrative meaning) is from *Kokinshū* 1108.

48. The brevity and indirection of this announcement has to do with the solemnity of the event.

"There can be no end to a darkness in my heart that blots out all things,
now that I must watch her go off to live among the clouds,"[49]

he murmured to himself. For him it was a tragedy.

The more the little Prince grew, the less one could tell him apart from Genji, but although this tormented Her Majesty, no one else seems to have noticed. In truth, one wonders how anyone could be born as handsome as Genji and yet at the same time look unlike him. They were to all as the light of sun and moon coursing through the sky.

49. Into the "cloud dwelling" (*kumoi*), a noble expression for the palace.

8

HANA NO EN
Under the Cherry Blossoms

This chapter begins with a party (*en*) to honor a blossoming cherry tree (*hana*).

RELATIONSHIP TO EARLIER CHAPTERS

The events in "Under the Cherry Blossoms" take place in the spring following those narrated in "Beneath the Autumn Leaves."

PERSONS

Genji, a Consultant, age 20

His Majesty, the Emperor, Genji's father (Kiritsubo no Mikado)

Her Majesty, the Empress, 25 (Fujitsubo)

The Heir Apparent, 23 (Suzaku)

The Kokiden Consort, mother of the Heir Apparent

The Secretary Captain (Tō no Chūjō)

His Excellency, the Minister of the Left, 54 (Sadaijin)

A young woman, sixth daughter of the Minister of the Right (Oborozukiyo)

Koremitsu, Genji's foster brother and confidant

Yoshikiyo, son of the Governor of Harima and Genji's close retainer

Genji's young lady, 12 (Murasaki)

His Excellency, the Minister of the Right, grandfather of the Heir Apparent (Udaijin)

A little past the twentieth of the second month, His Majesty held a party to honor the cherry tree before the Shishinden.[1] To his left and right were enclosures[2] for the Empress and the Heir Apparent, whose pleasure it was to be present according to his wishes. The Kokiden Consort took offense whenever Her Majesty received such respect, but she came, for she would not have missed the event.

It was a lovely day, with a bright sky and birdsong to gladden the heart, when those who prided themselves on their skill—Princes, senior nobles, and all—drew their rhymes and began composing Chinese verses.[3] As usual, Genji's very voice announcing, "I have received the character 'spring,'" resembled no other. The Secretary Captain came next. He was nervous about how he might look, after Genji, but he maintained a pleasing composure, and his voice rang out with impressive dignity. Most of the rest appeared tense and self-conscious. Naturally, those belonging to the lesser ranks were even more in awe of the genius of His Majesty and the Heir Apparent, which stood out even then, when so many others excelled at that sort of thing. They advanced in dread across the immaculate expanse of the broad court, only to make a painful labor of their simple task. His Majesty was touched by seasoned performances from the shabby old Doctors, and he derived great pleasure from them, too.

He had of course arranged the dances perfectly. The one about the warbler in spring[4] was charming as sunset approached, and after it the Heir Apparent, who remembered Genji under the autumn leaves, gave him his own blossom headdress and urged him to dance again. Genji, who could not refuse, rose and with casual ease went through the part where the dancer tosses his sleeves. The effect was incomparable. The Minister of the Left forgot all his displeasure and wept.

"Come, where is the Secretary Captain?" His Majesty said. And so beautifully

1. *Sakon no sakura*, a cherry tree by the steps at the front (south) side of the Shishinden. This kind of party, like the one beneath the autumn leaves, was especially favored about a century before the author's time.
2. *Tsubone*, made by setting up curtains and screens around their places.
3. The gentlemen advanced in order of rank, each to draw a single rhyme character (as in a lottery) from those set out on a table; then, before retiring, each announced his clan name, his office, and his rhyme character. His poem developed this rhyme.
4. "Song of the Spring Warbler" (Shun'ōden), a "Chinese" *bugaku* piece.

did the Secretary Captain then dance "Garden of Flowers and Willows," rather more intently than Genji and evidently well rehearsed in case of need, that to everyone's wonder he received His Majesty's gift of a robe. The senior nobles then danced on into the evening, in no particular order, but none stood out for better or worse. When the time came to declaim the poems, the Reader could not get on with Genji's because the gathering repeated and commented admiringly on every line. Even the Doctors were impressed. His Majesty was undoubtedly pleased, since to him Genji was the glory of every such occasion.

The Empress wondered while she contemplated Genji's figure how the Heir Apparent's mother could dislike him so, and she lamented that she herself liked him all too well.

> "If with common gaze I could look upon that flower just as others do,
>   why should it occur to me to find in him any flaw?"

she murmured. One wonders how anyone could have passed on words meant only for herself.

The festival ended late that night. Once the senior nobles had withdrawn, once the Empress and the Heir Apparent were gone and all lay quiet in the beauty of brilliant moonlight, Genji remained drunkenly unwilling to grant that the night was over. His Majesty's gentlewomen all being asleep, he stole off toward the Fujitsubo, in case fortune should favor him at this odd hour, but the door through which he might have approached her[5] was locked, and so he went on, sighing but undeterred, to the long aisle of the Kokiden, where he found the third door open.[6] Hardly anyone seemed to be about, since the Consort had gone straight to wait on His Majesty. The door to the inner rooms was open, too. There was no sound.

This is how people get themselves into trouble,[7] he thought, stepping silently up into the hall. Everyone must be asleep. But could it be? He heard a young and pretty voice, surely no common gentlewoman's, coming his way and singing, "Peerless the night with a misty moon . . ."[8] He happily caught her sleeve.

"Oh, don't! Who are you?" She was obviously frightened.

"You need not be afraid.

> That you know so well the beauty of the deep night leads me to assume
>   you have with the setting moon nothing like a casual bond!"

With this he put his arms around her, lay her down, and closed the door. Her outrage and dismay gave her delicious appeal.

---

5. More precisely, the door to where he might have found Ōmyōbu and persuaded her to take him to her mistress.

6. The Kokiden is opposite the Fujitsubo, to the east.

7. Genji's criticism, appropriate for himself, is probably aimed at the laxness of the Kokiden Consort's household. He has a low opinion of the household's mores.

8. *Shinkokinshū* 55, by Ōe no Chisato: "Nothing compares with the misty moon of a spring night, neither brilliant nor clouded." Oborozukiyo ("Night with a Misty Moon") is the name by which she has been known ever since.

"A man—there is a man here!" she cried, trembling.

"I may do as I please, and calling for help will not save you. Just be still!"

She knew his voice and felt a little better. She did not want to seem cold or standoffish, despite her shock. He must have been quite drunk, because he felt he must have her, and she was young and pliant enough that she probably never thought seriously of resisting him.

She pleased him very much, and he was upset to find daybreak soon upon them. She herself seemed torn. "Do tell me your name!" he pleaded. "How can I keep in touch with you? Surely you do not want this to be all!"

With sweet grace she replied,

> *"If with my sad fate I were just now to vanish, would you really come—
> ah, I wonder!—seeking me over grassy wastes of moor?"*[9]

"I understand. Please forgive me.

> *While I strove to learn in what quarter I should seek my dewdrop's dwelling,
> wind, I fear, would be blowing out across the rustling moors.*[10]

We might be frank with each other. Or would you prefer to evade me?"

He had no sooner spoken than gentlewomen began rising noisily, and there was much coming and going between the Kokiden and His Majesty's apartments.[11] They were both in peril. He merely gave her his fan as a token, took hers, and went away.

Some of the many women at the Kiritsubo[12] were awake. "He certainly keeps up his secret exploring, doesn't he!" they whispered, poking each other and pretending all the while to be asleep.

He came in and lay down, but he stayed awake. What a lovely girl! She must be one of the Consort's younger sisters—the fifth or sixth, I suppose, since she had not known a man before. He had heard that the wife of the Viceroy Prince[13] and the fourth sister, who meant so little to the Secretary Captain, were both beauties, and it certainly would have been rather more of a lark if she had been either of them. As for the sixth, her father intended her for the Heir Apparent—yes, that *would* be unfortunate. It was all very difficult, and he was unlikely to find out which one she was even if he tried. She did not seem eager to break it off, though—so why did she not leave me any way to correspond with her? These ruminations of his no doubt confirmed his interest in her, but still, when he thought of *her*, he could not help admiring how superbly inaccessible she was in comparison.

9. "If I were to vanish [die], would you fail to seek me only because I had not told you my name?"

10. "[I asked you to tell me who you are only because] if I come looking for you, people may notice and condemn us."

11. The Kokiden Consort is about to return; some gentlewomen precede her, while others go out from her own apartments to meet her.

12. Genji's own rooms at the palace.

13. Genji's younger brother, a Prince who is Viceroy of Kyushu (Dazai no Sochi).

The second party[14] was to be today, and he was busy from morning to night. He played the *sō no koto*. The event was more elegant and amusing than the one the day before. Dawn was near when Fujitsubo went to wait on His Majesty.

Desperate to know whether she of the moon at dawn[15] would now be leaving the palace, he set the boundlessly vigilant Yoshikiyo[16] and Koremitsu to keep watch. When he withdrew from His Majesty's presence, they gave him their report. "Several carriages have just left from the north gate,[17] where they were waiting discreetly," they said. "Relatives of His Majesty's ladies were there, and when the Fourth Rank Lieutenant and the Right Controller[18] rushed out to see the party off, we gathered that it must have been the Kokiden Consort who was leaving. Several other quite distinguished ladies were obviously in the party, too. There were three carriages in all."

Genji's heart beat fast. How was he to learn which one she was? What if His Excellency her father found out and made a great fuss over him?[19] That would be highly unwelcome, as long as he still knew so little about her. At any rate, he could not endure his present ignorance, and he lay in an agony of frustration about what to do. He thought fondly of his young lady. How bored she must be, and probably dejected as well, since he had not seen her for days!

The keepsake fan was a triple cherry blossom layered one[20] with a misty moon reflected in water painted on its colored side—not an original piece of work but welcome because so clearly favored by its owner. Her talk of "grassy wastes of moor" troubled him, and he wrote on the fan, which he then kept with him,

> *"All that I now feel, I have never felt before, as the moon at dawn*
> *melts away before my eyes into the boundless heavens."*

It had been too long since his last visit to His Excellency's, as he well knew, but anxiety over his young lady won out, and he went to Nijō to cheer her up. The more he saw of her, the lovelier she became, and she also had exceptional intelligence and charm. Her unblemished perfection certainly made her the right girl for him to bring up on his own, as he so longed to do. The only worry was that having a male teacher might make her a little too familiar with men. Genji spent the day telling her what he had been up to lately and giving her a koto lesson, and although she was as sad as ever when he went out again, she was used to it now and did not cling to him as before.

14. *Goen*, a "follow-up party" held for a smaller circle of the highest rank. The absence of the lower ranks made it less formal and more elegant than the earlier one.
15. Oborozukiyo. Genji calls her *ariake* ("moon at dawn") by association with "misty moon," and also because this is the time of the lunar month (the twentieth and after) for the *ariake* moon, to which he refers again in a poem below.
16. Yoshikiyo, the son of the Governor of Harima and the man who, in "Young Murasaki," told Genji about the old man and his daughter at Akashi.
17. Kita no jin (also called Sakuheimon), the north gate to the palace compound.
18. Brothers of the Kokiden Consort, not mentioned elsewhere.
19. As a son-in-law.
20. "Triple" because the fan, with its eight cypress ribs, folds into three panels together. The fan is white on one side and scarlet on the other.

At His Excellency's the lady refused as usual to see him straightaway. Caught up in his idleness by a swarm of thoughts, he toyed a while with a *sō no koto* and sang, "I never sleep at ease . . ."[21]

His Excellency joined him and told him how much he had enjoyed the other day. "At my advanced age I have witnessed the reigns of four enlightened Sovereigns," he said, "and yet what with the quality of the verse and the harmony of the music and dances, the years never lay so lightly upon me. We have so many now who are expert in all the arts, and I am sure it was you who selected and guided them. Even I, an old man, felt like stepping out and stumbling through a dance."

"I did nothing at all to prepare them. It was simply my duty to find them the best instructors, whoever that might be. To my eye, 'Garden of Flowers and Willows' so far outshone the rest that the performance must stand for all time; and if you yourself had ventured to show off your skill, Your Excellency, in defiance of the years, the glory of His Majesty's reign would have shone more brightly still."

The Left Controller, the Secretary Captain, and the others arrived. With their backs against the railing they tuned their instruments together and played away in concert very nicely indeed.

The lady of the misty moon remembered that fragile dream with great sadness. Her father had decided that her presentation to the Heir Apparent was to take place in the fourth month, and the prospect filled her with despair. Meanwhile her lover, who thought he knew how to pursue her if he wished, had not yet actually found out which sister she was, and besides, he hesitated to associate himself with a family from which he had nothing but censure. Then, a little after the twentieth of the third month, the Minister of the Right held an archery contest attended by many senior nobles and Princes and followed immediately by a party for the wisteria blossoms.

The cherry blossom season was over, but two of His Excellency's trees must have consented to wait,[22] for they were in late and glorious bloom. He had had his recently rebuilt residence specially decorated for the Princesses' donning of the train.[23] Everything was in the latest style, in consonance with His Excellency's own florid taste.

His Excellency had extended an invitation to Genji as well, one day when they met at court, and Genji's failure to appear disappointed him greatly, for to his mind this absence cast a pall over the gathering. He therefore sent the Fourth Rank Lieutenant to fetch him, with the message,

> "If in their gay hues the flowers that grace my home were like all others,
> why should I so eagerly be waiting to welcome you?"

Genji, at the palace, told His Majesty. "He certainly is pleased with himself!" His Majesty remarked with a smile. "Go then, since he seems so eager to have you. After all, he is bringing the Princesses up there, so you are hardly a stranger to

21. From a *saibara* song; the singer is a young woman in love (quite unlike Aoi).
22. *Kokinshū* 68, by Ise: "O cherry tree in a mountain village with no one to admire you, wait to bloom until the flowers elsewhere are gone."
23. Two imperial daughters of the Kokiden Consort, hence the Minister's granddaughters.

him."[24] Genji dressed with great care, and the sun had set by the time he arrived to claim his welcome.

He wore a grape-colored train-robe under a cherry blossom dress cloak of sheer figured silk.[25] Among the formal cloaks worn by everyone else, his costume displayed the extravagant elegance of a Prince, and his grand entry was a sensation. The very blossoms were abashed, and the gathering took some time to regain its animation.

He played beautifully, and it was quite late by the time he left again, on the pretext of having drunk so much that he was not well. The First and Third Princesses were in the main house, and he went to sit by the door that opened from there toward the east. The lattice shutters were up, and all the women were near the veranda, since this was the corner where the wisteria was blooming. Their sleeves spilled showily under the blinds as though for the New Year's mumming, but Genji disapproved and only found his thoughts going to Fujitsubo.

"I felt unwell to begin with," he said, "and then I was obliged to drink until now I am quite ill. May I be allowed to hide in Their Highnesses' company, if it is not too forward of me to ask?" He thrust himself halfway through the blind in the double doorway.

"Oh, no, please!" one cried. "Surely it is for little people like us to claim protection from the great!"

Genji saw that these ladies, although not of commanding rank, were not ordinary young gentlewomen either. Their stylish distinction was clear. The fragrance of incense hung thickly in the air, and the rustling of silks conveyed ostentatious wealth, for this was a household that preferred modish display to the deeper appeal of discreet good taste. The younger sisters had no doubt taken possession of the doorway because Their Highnesses wished to look out from there.

He should not have accepted the challenge, but it pleased him, and he wondered with beating heart which one she was. "Alas," he sang as innocently as could be, still leaning against a pillar, "my fan is mine no more, for I have met with woe . . ."[26]

"What a very odd man from Koma!" The one who answered seemed not to understand him.

Another said nothing but only sighed and sighed. He leaned toward her, took her hand through her standing curtain, and said at a guess,

"How sadly I haunt the slopes of Mount Irusa, where the crescent sets,
yearning just to see again the faint moon that I saw then!

---

24. They are Genji's half sisters as well as the Minister's granddaughters.

25. His dress cloak (nōshi) is of a "cherry blossom" (sakura) layering, suitable for a young man in spring. Under that he has on an ebi dyed shita-gasane, which normally went under the formal cloak (hō) for a solemn court occasion. A dress cloak is relatively informal, and its color does not convey rank. Genji is flaunting his exalted station.

26. He intentionally misquotes a saibara song ("A man from Koma stole my sash, oh, bitter regret is mine . . ."), substituting "fan" for "sash."

Why should that be?"

This must have been too much for her, because she replied,

*"Were it really so that your heart goes straight and true, would you lose your way
even in the dark of night, when no moon is in the sky?"*

Yes, it was her voice. He was delighted, though at the same time . . . [27]

27. Oborozukiyo, the daughter of a political enemy, is promised to the Heir Apparent. Besides, Genji already dislikes her family's shallow ostentation, and he may be disappointed by how easily she gave herself to him.

9

A O I

Heart-to-Heart

The plant *aoi* (more precisely, *futaba aoi*), sacred to the Kamo Shrine, grows on the forest floor and consists of a pair of broad, heart-shaped leaves that spring from a single stem. At the Kamo Festival people decorated their headdresses and carriages with it, as well as with laurel (*katsura*). In its Heian spelling (*afuhi*), the word can also be read to mean "day of (lovers') meeting." This wordplay and the plant's configuration suggest the translation "heart-to-heart."

As the chapter title, *Aoi* refers particularly to an exchange of poems at the Festival between Genji and the amorous Dame of Staff. Seeing Genji with someone else (Murasaki) in his carriage, she writes,

> "*Ah, it is too hard! Today when our heart-to-heart told me that the god blessed our meeting, I perceive that another sports those leaves.*"

He replies,

> "*Yours, so I would say, was a very naughty wish to sport heart-to-heart, when this meeting place today gathers men from countless clans.*"

Aoi must have been accepted as the chapter title because of the incident that takes place at Kamo the day before; and since the person responsible for the incident is above all Genji's wife, she is known to readers as Aoi.

There is a gap of two years or so between "Under the Cherry Blossoms" and "Heart-to-Heart." In the interval Genji's father has abdicated; Suzaku, his son by the Kokiden Consort, has become Emperor; and Fujitsubo's son by Genji has become Heir Apparent.

PERSONS

Genji, the Commander of the Right, age 22 to 23

Her Majesty, the Empress, 27 to 28 (Fujitsubo)

His Eminence, the Retired Emperor, Genji's father (Kiritsubo In)

The Empress Mother, the Kokiden Consort

The Heir Apparent, Fujitsubo's son, 3 to 4 (Reizei)

The Rokujō Haven, 29 to 30 (Rokujō no Miyasudokoro)

The High Priestess of Ise, her daughter, 13 to 14 (Akikonomu)

The lady of the bluebells, Her Highness (Asagao)

Genji's wife, 26 (Aoi)

The High Priestess of Kamo, third daughter of Kokiden (Saiin)

Her Highness, mother of Aoi and Tō no Chūjō (Ōmiya)

His Highness of Ceremonial, Asagao's father (Shikibukyō no Miya)

Genji's young lady, 14 to 15 (Murasaki)

Shōnagon, Murasaki's nurse

A Dame of Staff, Genji's aged admirer, early sixties (Gen no Naishi)

His Excellency, the Minister of the Left,
father of Aoi and Tō no Chūjō, 56 to 57 (Sadaijin)

The Third Rank Captain, Aoi's brother (Tō no Chūjō)

The son of Genji and Aoi, birth to 2 (Yūgiri)

Chūnagon, a gentlewoman at His Excellency's

Ateki, a page girl of Aoi

Koremitsu, Genji's foster brother and confidant

Ben, Shōnagon's daughter, in the service of Murasaki

The Mistress of the Wardrobe (Oborozukiyo)

The Minister of the Right, her father, grandfather of the Emperor (Udaijin)

The change of reign made all things a burden for Genji, and perhaps his rise in rank[1] explains why he now renounced his lighter affairs, so that for many he multiplied the sorrows of neglect even while he himself, as though in retribution, continually lamented his own love's cruelty.[2] She was so constantly at His Eminence's side that she might as well have been a commoner, and this seemed to displease the Empress Mother, who kept to the palace and left her in peace. Now and again His Eminence might hold a beautiful concert or something of the sort, one that set the whole court talking, so that he shone more brightly than ever; but he sadly missed the Heir Apparent, whose lack of effective support worried him, and his request that Genji look after him moved the new Commander to mingled joy and dismay.

Oh, yes, the late Heir Apparent's daughter by the Rokujō Haven had been named High Priestess of Ise, and her mother, who doubted Genji's devotion, had quickly invoked concern over her daughter's youth as a reason for considering going down to Ise herself.

His Eminence remarked to Genji on learning of her plan, "His Late Highness thought very highly of her and showed her every attention, and I find it intolerable that you should treat her as casually as you might any other woman. I consider the High Priestess my own daughter, and I should therefore appreciate it if you were to avoid offending her mother, both for her father's sake and for mine. Such wanton self-indulgence risks widespread censure." The displeasure on his countenance obliged Genji to agree, and he kept a humble silence.

"Never cause a woman to suffer humiliation," His Eminence continued. "Treat each with tact and avoid provoking her anger."

Genji withdrew contritely from his presence, terrified to imagine his rebuke were he to learn the full impudence of his own inadmissible passion.

1. Suzaku, the son of the Kokiden Consort, has succeeded Genji's father as Emperor. This has brought the faction represented by the Kokiden Consort and her father, the Minister of the Right, to power. Moreover, Genji's father seems as a last gesture to have appointed Genji Commander of the Right, so that he must now travel with an escort of eight guards.

2. Fujitsubo's. *Kokinshū* 1041: "As though in retribution for my not loving the one who loves me, the one I do love does not love me."

That even His Eminence should know of his misconduct and express himself on the subject showed how painfully the lady's name as well as his own had been compromised in the affair, and he guiltily redoubled his attentions toward her, but he still showed no sign of acknowledging their tie openly. She herself remained constantly constrained by shame over the discrepancy between their ages, and he countered with matching formality. The affair had reached His Eminence's ears by now and was well known to one and all, but she still suffered acutely from his relative indifference toward her.

News of all this confirmed the lady of the bluebells[3] in her resolve that nothing of the kind should happen to her, and she rarely gave him the simplest reply. Still, he often thought how unusual it was of her, and how like her, too, not to dismiss him outright.

At His Excellency's there was no praise for Genji's obviously roving fancy, but the lady there did not hold it deeply against him, perhaps because the way he almost flaunted it was beneath comment. For a very touching reason she was sadly unwell.[4] Genji felt wonder and sympathy for her. Everyone was pleased, but her parents had penances done for fear of rejoicing too soon.[5] These things kept him fully occupied, and while he never forgot the lady at Rokujō, he must have failed more often than not to visit her.

The High Priestess of the Kamo Shrine resigned at this time, and her successor was His Eminence's third daughter by the Empress Mother. This Princess's parents were sorry to see her life take this odd turn, since she was a great favorite of theirs, but no other would do. The attendant rites, although not unusual, were done with great pomp and animation. When the time for the Festival came,[6] the customary events received many embellishments, and there were all sorts of sights to see. Her Highness's personal distinction seemed to explain it all.

On the day of the Purification[7] the senior nobles took part in the requisite numbers,[8] but only the best-looking and most highly regarded among them. They were all perfect in the color of their train-robes, in the pattern of their outer trousers,[9] and even in their choice of saddle and mount. Genji took part as well, by His Eminence's special decree. The sightseeing carriages had been made ready well in advance. Ichijō Avenue was packed and terribly noisy. The viewing stands put up here and there were elaborately adorned, each according to its owner's taste, and even the sleeves spilling from under their blinds were a wonder to behold.

The lady at His Excellency's rarely went out for such events, and she had not

---

3. Asagao.
4. With morning sickness.
5. Ritual abstinences, performed by others on her behalf, to ensure safe childbirth.
6. The Kamo Festival, on the middle Bird (*tori*) day in the fourth month, one of the major annual events in the City.
7. Strictly speaking, the second Purification, held on the day of the Horse (*uma*) or Sheep (*hitsuji*) preceding the day of the Festival proper.
8. According to the *Engi shiki*, the first Purification required a single Consultant as imperial envoy, while the second required one Grand Counselor, one Counselor, and two Consultants.
9. They had on full civil dress, with a formal cloak of a color to match their rank, contrasting train-robes, and two pairs of open-legged trousers (the inner pair of plain red silk, the outer of brocade).

even thought of going this time, since she was indisposed, but her younger gentlewomen protested, "Oh, come, my lady, we would not enjoy stealing off there on our own! All the world longs for a glimpse of his lordship the Commander[10] at the Festival today, and they say even the poorest woodcutters will be there to see him. Some people are even bringing their families from far-off provinces! My lady, you simply cannot miss it!"

Carriage and shaft bench

"You really are feeling better lately," Her Highness remarked to her daughter when she heard, "and your women seem so disappointed." The household therefore suddenly learned that she would see the Festival after all.

The sun was already high when she set out with as little fuss as possible. Her imposing train of carriages halted, since by now every place was taken and it had nowhere to go. Her grooms fixed on a spot occupied by many fine ladies' carriages but free of any press of attendants, and they began having them cleared away. Among them were two basketwork carriages, a little worn but with elegant blinds through which spilled a hint of sleeves, trains, and jackets in the loveliest colors worn by those seated deep within. The occupant clearly wished to go unrecognized. "These carriages are *not* ones you can push aside this way!" her grooms insisted loudly, and they would not let them be touched, but by now the young men on both sides were drunk and rowdy and out of control. The more sober personal escort from His Excellency's warned them in vain.

The Rokujō Haven, the mother of the High Priestess of Ise (for it was she), had come secretly for relief from her troubles. Her people said nothing about who she was, but the other side of course knew her. "Take no such nonsense from the likes of them! They must be counting on protection from his lordship the Commander!" shouted the men from His Excellency's. Some of them, Genji's own men, were disturbed to see what was happening, but they feigned indifference because it would have been too difficult to intervene.

By the time all the carriages were in place, the Rokujō Haven's had been pushed behind the least of the gentlewomen's, and she had no view at all. She was not only outraged but extremely put out that she had been recognized after all. With her shaft benches broken and her carriage shafts now resting willy-nilly on the wheel hubs of other carriages, she looked so ridiculous that she rued her folly and wondered helplessly why she had ever come. She would gladly have left without seeing the procession, but there was no room for her to get out, and her resolve must have faltered after all when she heard cries of "Here they come!" and under-

10. Genji.

stood that her own cruel lover would be passing by. And pass on by he did, to her bitter chagrin, without so much as a glance her way.[11]

Beneath the blinds of carriages far more elaborately done up than usual, many eager ladies had indeed put forth a bright display that Genji affected to ignore, but on some he bestowed a sidelong glance and a smile. The carriages from His Excellency's stood out, and he rode gravely past them. The profound deference and respect shown by his own retinue brought home to the Rokujō Haven the sting of her ignominious defeat.

> "One fugitive glimpse as of a face reflected in a hallowed stream
> tells me with new cruelty that I matter not at all!"

She did not like being seen to weep, but she knew how much she would have regretted missing the dazzling beauty and presence that on this great occasion shone more brilliantly than ever.

The gentlemen of Genji's escort were perfect in dress and deportment, each as his station warranted, and the senior nobles among them especially so, but the brightness of that single light seemed to eclipse them all. It was unusual for a Commander to be specially guarded by a privy gentleman from the Palace Guards, but this procession was so exceptional that that office was filled for once by someone from the Right Palace Guards. The rest of Genji's retinue was equally brilliant in looks and finery, until it seemed as though the very trees and grasses must bow down before a beauty so universally admired. The way quite respectable women in deep hats[12] or nuns to whom the world was dross came lurching and stumbling along to see him would ordinarily have merited cries of horrified disapproval, except that today no one could blame them. Women with puckered mouths and gowns over their hair[13] gaped up at him, palms joined or pressed to their foreheads in idiot adoration, while peasant simpletons grinned beatifically, innocent of any thought of how they looked themselves. Even miserable Governors' daughters, girls beneath his notice, were there in cleverly tricked-out carriages, preening and congratulating themselves. Yes, there were many amusing sights to see. Of course, there were also many whom Genji had secretly favored and who now could only sigh that they meant so little to him.

His Highness of Ceremonial was watching from a stand. The older he grows, the more devastatingly handsome he becomes, he said to himself with a feeling of vague dread; surely he must catch the eye even of the gods! To his daughter,[14] who well knew from the letters she had had from him all these years how little his sentiments resembled those of other men, Genji would no doubt have been pleasing enough even if

---

11. More literally, "And perhaps because this was not even Sasanokuma, he passed by with no sign of recognition . . ." *Kokinshū* 1080, attributed to the goddess at Ise: "At Sasanokuma, by the Hinokuma River, stop, let your horse drink, that I may look upon you!"

12. *Tsubo sōzoku*, the attire for a respectable woman outdoors. She draped a shift over her head and hair, then put on a deep, broad-brimmed hat. She also hitched up her skirts a little for walking.

13. Women too modest in standing to wear *tsubo sōzoku* would still tuck their hair under their outer robe when outdoors.

14. Asagao.

quite ordinary in looks, and she wondered as she felt his attraction how he could possibly be so dazzlingly beautiful as well. Still, she desired no greater intimacy with him. Her young gentlewomen praised him until she wished they would stop.

There were no sightseers from His Excellency's on the day of the Festival proper.[15] With shock and dismay Genji received from his men a full account of the quarrel the previous day over the placement of the carriages. Alas, he thought, despite her dignity she lacks kindness and tact. She cannot really have meant this to happen, but I suppose she sees so little reason why the two of them should think warmly of each other that those men of hers then took it on themselves to act as they did. The Haven is so fastidious and reserved by nature—it must have been a terrible experience for her.

He anxiously went straight to call on her, but her daughter, the Ise Priestess, was still at home, and she invoked respect for the sacred *sakaki* tree to turn him away.[16] He quite understood, yet he could not help whispering to himself, "But why? I do wish they would both be less prickly with one another!"

On the day, he sought refuge at Nijō, from where he went to watch the Festival. He crossed to the west wing[17] and had Koremitsu order the carriage. "Are you gentlewomen going, too?"[18] he asked and watched, all smiles, while the young lady got herself ready very prettily indeed. "Come along, then," he said, "let us see it together."

Her hair was lovelier than ever. "You seem not to have had it trimmed for ages," he observed while he stroked it. "I imagine today is a good day for that."[19] He called for a Doctor of the Almanac and had him questioned about the proper hour. "Out you come now, gentlewomen!" he said and surveyed the delightful picture the children presented. The line of their bewitching hair, boldly cut straight across, stood out sharply against their damask-patterned outer trousers.

"I shall trim your hair myself. But oh, dear, how thick it is! I wonder how long it will grow!" He hardly knew what to do next. "People with very long hair still seem to have it shorter at the sides, but you have no stray locks at all! I am afraid you are not going to look very nice!"[20] When he was done, he made the "thousand fathom" wish, while Shōnagon looked on with pleasure and deep gratitude.

He said,

> "Rich seaweed tresses of the unplumbed ocean depths, a thousand fathoms long,
> you are mine and mine alone to watch daily as you grow."[21]

15. On this day the High Priestess actually went to the Kamo Shrine.

16. Once appointed, the High Priestess moved to special quarters in the palace and there underwent purification until the seventh month of the following year, when at last she went on to Ise. In this case, however, her move seems to have been delayed. Meanwhile, her house has been purified, and branches of the sacred *sakaki* tree, hung with cloth or paper streamers, have been set up at the four corners and at the gate to mark the place as ritually pure.

17. Where Murasaki lives.

18. Genji playfully addresses Murasaki's playmates as adults.

19. An auspicious day according to the almanac.

20. Ladies with long hair, Genji says, still have shorter sidelocks (*bitai gami*, the hair that falls from the temples over the cheeks); but Murasaki's *bitai gami* seems as long as the rest of her hair. His lament that she "will not look very nice" is not serious.

21. It was apparently customary to wish that a girl's hair should grow "a thousand fathoms" long. Genji's poem compares the little girl's hair to seaweed in praise, and it plays on *miru* (a kind of seaweed) and *miru* ("see," i.e., "possess" [a wife]).

Riding ground pavilion

> *"How am I to know whether a thousand fathoms measure your love, too,*
> *when the ever shifting tides so restlessly ebb and flow?"*

she wrote on a bit of paper, looking so grown-up yet at the same time so fresh and young that she was a joy to behold.

Today again there was no room for one carriage more. Genji's found nowhere to go, and it waited by the riding ground pavilion.[22] "It is awfully crowded here, with all these senior nobles' carriages," he remarked, and he was wondering whether to pass on when from a very fine one overflowing with a bright profusion of sleeves there emerged a fan that beckoned to one of his men.

"Would you not like to put your carriage here?" the occupant inquired. "I cede you my place."

Genji wondered what sort of coquette she could be, but since the spot was indeed a good one, he had his carriage brought up to it. "I envy you having managed to find it," he replied.

At this she broke a bit off a prettily decorated fan[23] and wrote upon it,

> *"Ah, it is too hard! Today when our heart-to-heart told me that the god*
> *blessed our meeting, I perceive that another sports those leaves.*

I should not presume . . ."[24]

22. The riding ground ([*sakon no*] *baba*) was near the intersection of Ichijō and Nishi no Tōin; the pavilion (*otodo*) there was where the Captains and Lieutenants sat during the *yabusame* riding events that took place on the third and fifth days of the fifth month. For the Festival the High Priestess was to come down from her temporary residence north of the city and proceed eastward along Ichijō to the Kamo Shrine.

23. Presumably a *hiōgi*, made of thin slips of cypress (*hinoki*) wood. She would have written on a piece of one of these.

24. Continuing the mood of the poem, "I should not presume" relies on vocabulary special to a sacred festival.

He knew the handwriting: it was the Dame of Staff's. How she will play the gay young thing, despite her years! He was sufficiently irritated to retort,

> *"Yours, so I would say, was a very naughty wish to sport heart-to-heart,*
> *when this meeting place today gathers men from countless clans!"*

She answered, deeply wounded,

> *"How I rue the day I wished to sport heart-to-heart, those perfidious leaves*
> *that with no more than a name stir such foolish pangs of hope!"*

Many ladies were disappointed to see that he had someone with him and did not even raise his blinds. The other day he was so correct, they said to themselves, but he certainly is making a casual outing of it today. Who can she be? She must be worth looking at, if she is with him.

What a dismal skirmish that was, over heart-to-heart! Genji was annoyed. Certainly, anyone less shameless than that woman would have deferred to the lady beside him and refrained from tossing off rash repartee.

The Rokujō Haven had never through all the years known such misery and turmoil. As to her cruel lover, she had given him up, but she knew how badly she would miss him if she were actually to break with him and go down to Ise, and she also feared ridicule for doing so; yet the thought of staying after all left her afraid of encountering once more the hideous contempt that she had already suffered. "Am I the float on the fisherman's line?"[25] she asked herself in anguish day and night, and perhaps this was why she lived like an invalid, her mind seeming to her to have come adrift.

Genji never insisted that it would be madness for her to go; he only argued, "I quite understand that you should wish to see the last of me, worthless as I am, but even if you are fed up with me by now, it would still be much kinder of you to continue receiving me." This made the storm of that day of Purification,[26] which she had attended only for relief from her indecision, more hateful to her than before.

At His Excellency's a spirit, it seemed, was making the lady extremely unwell, and her family was alarmed. This was therefore no time for Genji to pursue adventures elsewhere, and it was only at odd moments that he managed even to visit Nijō. It pained him deeply that someone who so commanded his consideration should suffer this way, especially in her already delicate condition, and he had many prayers and rites done for her in his own apartment within the residence.

Many spirits and living phantoms[27] came forth and identified themselves in one way or another, but one refused to move into the medium and clung instead to

---

25. *Kokinshū* 509: "Am I the float on the line of the fisherman, fishing in Ise Bay, that I should be unable to make up my mind?"

26. Literally, "the violent rapids of the lustration stream" (*misogigawa*, the stream that runs before the Kamo Shrine).

27. "Spirits" (*mononoke*) are the spirits of the dead or other supernatural, generally troublesome entities. "Living phantoms" (*ikisudama*) are the malevolent spirits of living persons.

the lady herself; and although it did her no great violence, it never left her. Its resistance even to the most potent healers was extraordinarily stubborn.

After considering all the ladies with whom Genji had a liaison, people began to whisper that only the Rokujō Haven and the lady at Nijō engaged his deeper feelings, so that either might be intensely jealous; but divination performed at His Excellency's insistence still yielded nothing clear. None of the other spirits was especially hostile. One appeared to be a deceased nurse, while others were entities that had haunted her parents' families for generations, but these were not serious, and they were manifesting themselves only at random because of her weakened condition. She herself just cried and cried, and sometimes retched, suffering such unbearable agony that her parents wondered in fear and sorrow what was to become of her.

There were constant inquiries from His Eminence, whose most gracious solicitude, expressed in the prayers that he was kindly having offered on her behalf, made it seem still more urgent that she be saved. The Haven was shaken to learn that all the world feared for the lady's life. No one at His Excellency's guessed that that little quarrel over placement of the carriages had inflamed in her heart a rivalry hitherto dormant for many years.

Her troubled mood convinced her that she was simply not herself, and she moved elsewhere to have healing rites done. The news made Genji wonder with uneasy sympathy what state of mind had prompted her to do this, and he resolved to go and see her. He went very discreetly, since for once she was not at her own home. He begged forgiveness at length for his recent, quite unintentional neglect, and he appealed to her with an account of the afflicted lady's condition.

"I myself am not all that worried," he earnestly explained, "but I feel for her parents, who are desperately anxious, and so, you see, I thought I should stay with her for the time being. I would be grateful if you were to view my behavior more indulgently." He understood that she was suffering more than usual, and was pained to see it.

His departing figure, at dawn after a night of distances, was so enchanting that again she could not bear to leave him, but now that he had reason to devote himself more than ever to the one who commanded his first allegiance, he would doubtless settle his affections upon her, and this endless waiting would mean nothing but misery; his occasional visit would arouse only fresh despair. These thoughts were running through her mind when she had a letter from him—only a letter, and toward sunset: "She had seemed a little better lately, but all at once she took such a turn for the worse that I could not get away."

To her this was just another of his excuses, and she replied,

> "I knew all too well that no sleeve goes unmoistened by the mire of love,
> yet in the slough of that field I labor in helpless pain.

How true it is, that line about the mountain spring!"[28]

To Genji her writing stood out easily in any company. Ah, he thought, why

28. Rokujō's poem develops a play on *koiji* ("mud-filled [flooded] rice field" and "path of love"), and her final remark means, "It is true that you care little for me." *Kokin rokujō* 987: "How bitterly I regret dipping water from the mountain spring, so shallow that I only wetted my sleeves."

must it be like this? He was caught agonizingly between his reluctance to give up both her spirit and her looks and his incapacity to commit himself to her. His reply reached her well after dark: "Only your sleeves are wet? So your feelings have no depth . . .

> It is shallow, then, the field of your hard labors, not at all like mine,
> for I am wholly immersed in the deep slough of love's mire.

Have I failed to answer you in person only because you mean so little to me?"

At His Excellency's the spirit was very active, and the lady was in agony. The Haven heard that some were calling it her own living phantom or the ghost of His Late Excellency her father, but on reflection she found in herself only her own misery and no desire at all to see the lady harmed, though she conceded that a soul wandering in distress, as souls were said to do, might well act in this manner. Despite years plumbing the depths of despair, she had never before felt, as now, utterly destroyed, and after the Purification, when in that foolish incident she had been as though singled out for contempt and treated as naught, she knew that her mind, which had then drifted briefly from her, was now indeed beyond her control; and perhaps this was why she dreamed repeatedly, on dozing off, that she went to where that lady (as she supposed) lay in her finery, pushed and tugged her about, and flailed at her with a baneful violence strange to her waking self. Time after time she felt that she was not herself and that to her horror she had wandered away from her own body, until she saw that even if she were wrong, the world so unwillingly speaks well of anyone that the rumor of it would be embroidered upon everywhere with glee. She would, she knew, be talked of far and wide. No doubt it was common enough to leave a still-active malevolence behind after death, and this alone, when told of another, would arouse repulsion and fear; but that it should be her tragic destiny to have anything so horrible said of herself while she was still alive! No, she could not remain attached to so cruel a lover. Such were her thoughts, but hers was a case of "trying too hard to forget."[29]

The High Priestess was to have gone to the palace the year before,[30] but various difficulties had prevented her from doing so until this autumn. She was then to move in the ninth month directly to the Shrine on the Moor,[31] which meant that preparations for the Second Purification had to go forward urgently at the same time; but the Haven was overcome by a strange lassitude and spent her time in despondent brooding, to the intense anxiety of the High Priestess's staff, who offered prayers of every kind.[32] Still, her condition was not actually dire, and she got

---

29. From a riddling poem (Genji monogatari kochūshakusho in'yō waka 76) built on the multiple implications of the verb omou: "Trying too hard to forget, I only remember; why, when one tries to forget, does one not forget?"

30. An Ise Priestess was appointed by divination at the start of a new reign. She first purified herself on the bank of the Kamo River (first purification), then entered the Shosai-in ("Hall of First Abstinence") within the palace compound. In the autumn of the next year she underwent the second purification and then entered the Shrine on the Moor; she went to Ise in the ninth month of the following year, after further purification in the Katsura River.

31. Nonomiya, a temporary shrine built for the purpose on Saga Moor (Sagano), just west of the City.

32. If she became unambiguously ill, her presence would pollute the sacred space inhabited by her daughter.

through the days and months without displaying any clear symptoms. Genji called on her often, but the lady to whom he owed his allegiance was so ill that he remained deeply preoccupied.

It was still early, and the family were unprepared, when all at once she began to show obvious signs and to suffer pain. Ever more potent prayers were commissioned in great numbers, but that single most obstinate spirit refused to move, until the mightiest healers were surprised to find their efforts frustrated. Their assault was nonetheless fierce enough that the spirit wept in misery and cried, "Oh, please be a little more gentle with me! I have something to say to the Commander!"

"What did I tell you?" the women whispered among themselves. "Now we shall know!"

They led Genji in to the curtain that stood near where she lay. She was so clearly dying that His Excellency and Her Highness withdrew a little, understanding that she might have some last word for him. The priests chanting the Lotus Sutra lowered their voices, to awesome effect. He lifted the curtain and looked in. Anyone, not only her husband, would have been moved to see her lying there, so beautiful and with so vast a belly, and since she was indeed his wife, he was of course overcome by pity and regret. Her long, abundant hair, bound at the end, lay beside her, contrasting vividly with her white gown. He thought her dearer and more beautiful than ever before.

He took her hand. "This is dreadful! What a thing to do to me!" When weeping silenced him, she lifted to his face her expiring gaze, so filled in the past with reproach and disapproval, and tears spilled from her eyes. How could he not have been profoundly moved?

She wept so piteously that he assumed her thoughts were on her sorrowing parents, as well as on the pain of leaving him. "You must not make too much of all this," he said soothingly. "You are going to be well after all. At any rate, whatever happens, you and I will meet again. People do. Remember what a strong bond you have with His Excellency and Her Highness, because it will remain unbroken in lives to come, and you will be with them again."

"No, no, you do not understand," a gentle voice answered. "I only wished you to have them release me a little because I am in such pain. I did not want to come at all, but you see, it really is true that the soul of someone in anguish may wander away.

> *This spirit of mine that, sighing and suffering, wanders the heavens,*
> *oh, stop it now, tie a knot where in front the two hems meet.*"[33]

The voice, the manner, were not hers but those of someone else. After a moment of shock he understood that he was in the presence of the Rokujō Haven. Alas, what he had dismissed so far as malicious rumor put about by the ignorant now proved to be patently true, and he saw with revulsion that such things really did happen. "I hear your voice, but I do not know you. Please make it clear to me who you are." To his under-

---

33. An old poem-spell, to be repeated by one who has seen a ghost, enjoins the speaker to knot the overlapping hems at the front of his or her robe.

standable horror, the answer was not in doubt. He shuddered to imagine the gentlewomen coming to their mistress now.

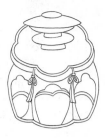

When her cries died down a little, her mother brought the hot medicinal water in case she might be in reprieve; then she was lifted upright and quickly gave birth.[34] Her parents' joy knew no bounds, but the spirits expelled by the healers[35] now raised a wild clamor of jealous rage, and what remained to come[36] was still a great worry. When all finally ended well, no doubt thanks to urgent prayers renewed in numbers beyond counting, the Abbot of the Mountain and

Bowl of water for the toilette, on a stand

the other most holy prelates wiped away their perspiration in triumph and hurried away.

Days of acute and widespread anxiety now gave way to a welcome lull, and at last her parents breathed easily. His Excellency commissioned a new round of protective rites, but happiness reigned, and exceptional delight in the child put everyone off guard. His Eminence, Their Highnesses the Princes, and the senior nobles all attended the splendid birth celebrations that enlivened the succeeding evenings.[37] These events were especially bright and gay because in the bargain the child was a boy.

This news shook the Rokujō Haven. She was supposed to be near death, she silently exclaimed, and now she has actually given birth without a hitch! Curiously, she still felt unlike herself, and her clothing reeked of poppy seeds.[38] To allay her misgivings she tried washing her hair and changing, but the smell lingered until she came to look on herself with horror and of course to mourn inwardly (for the matter was hardly one she could discuss) what others must be saying about her. As she did so, she sank into ever more disturbed states of mind.

Genji, who was now a little less anxious than before, shuddered to recall that dreadful moment when the spirit had so startlingly addressed him. He knew he had been wrong to neglect her for so long, but he had grave doubts about how he would feel in her presence, and after careful reflection (for he did not wish to be unkind) he only sent her a letter.

Her parents were still apprehensive, since they feared the effects of so serious an illness, and Genji tactfully abstained from his private excursions. She was not yet well enough to receive him as she usually did. The little boy was so handsome, in fact disturbingly so, that Genji was soon captivated, while His Excellency rejoiced that things had turned out well after all, if it were not for the worry that his daughter had yet to recover; but this he attributed to the difficulty of getting over everything she had suffered, and in truth he had little reason to fear.

Seeing how closely the little boy's engaging looks resembled the Heir Appar-

34. Her gentlewoman lifted her to the then-normal squatting position. Hot medicinal water was provided for a birth.
35. Driven by the healers (male Buddhist clerics) into the attendant (female) mediums, through whom the healers interrogated and dismissed them.
36. The afterbirth.
37. Parties (*ubuyashinai*) were given on the third, fifth, seventh, and ninth evenings after a birth. The guests brought gifts of food and clothing for the child.
38. Poppy seeds were thrown on the sacred *goma* fire during the rite to quell a spirit.

ent's, Genji gave in to fond memories and went to call at the palace. "I feel guilty not to have seen His Majesty for so long," he said reproachfully, "and now I am going at last, I hope that I may come a little nearer to talk to you. It is too unkind of you to keep yourself from me as you do."[39]

"Indeed, my lord," a gentlewoman replied, "you and my lady need no longer present yourselves flatteringly to each other, and although my lady is very reduced, there is no reason why a curtain should stand between you."

They arranged a seat for him near where she lay, and he went in to talk to her. She was very weak even now, as her few answers showed. Still, the memory of thinking her well and truly lost seemed a dream, and as he told her of his fears for her then, he was assailed by the grim recollection of how, while she lay all but lifeless, that flood of speech had suddenly burst from her. "Ah," he said, "I have so much more to tell you, but they tell me you are not up to it, you see. Do take your medicine," he went on, and in other ways, too, he made himself so useful that her gentlewomen were touched and wondered when he could have learned all this. The sight of her lying there, so beautiful yet so thin and weak that she hardly seemed among the living, aroused his love and his keenest sympathy. The hair streaming across her pillow, not a strand out of place, struck him as a wonder, and as he gazed at her, he found himself unable to understand how for all these years he could have seen any flaw in her.

"I shall call upon His Eminence, too, and then I shall be back very soon. I would gladly stay with you like this all the time, but Her Highness is always beside you, and I am afraid that I have held back so far for fear of being indiscreet. In your usual room, though, once you have gradually recovered your strength . . . One reason why you do not get better is that you treat yourself too much like a child." When he had finished, he set out in his magnificent robes, while she lay there and watched him go for longer than ever before.

His Excellency, too, left for court, since the autumn appointments were to be announced,[40] and all his sons, who had ambitions of their own and kept him close company, set off with him.

The residence was quiet, for there was hardly anyone about, when she was suddenly racked by a violent fit of retching. Before word could reach the palace, she was gone. All present there withdrew in shock. Appointments list evening or not, this disaster had clearly put an end to the proceedings. His Excellency could not call on the Abbot of the Mountain or on any other great monk because it was already night when the cry went up. The people of the household, who had thought the danger past, went stumbling about blindly in their horror. The messengers who crowded in from far and near found no one to talk to because all was turmoil, and the parents' desperate grief was truly frightening to see. The spirit had possessed her so often in the past that they watched for two or three days, leaving her pillow and so on undisturbed,[41] until signs of change convinced them at last, in their misery, to give up hope.

---

39. He speaks to Aoi through a gentlewoman.

40. Appointments were announced each spring and autumn, and the Minister of the Left, the court's senior nonimperial official, presided over the event.

41. The pillow was the soul's resting place. If it was moved, the soul might fail to find the body again if life returned.

Cremation

Genji had now suffered blow on blow, and life was intolerable to him. Condolences from those closest to him aroused only irritated impatience. The expressions of sorrow and sympathy from His Eminence were still a great honor, and His Excellency, who had also reason to rejoice, wept without end. At the urging of those around him he commissioned solemn rites of every kind, in case his daughter should revive, and in his anguish he persisted even when the workings of change had become all too plain, but after the vain passage of several days he resigned himself at last, and they took her to Toribeno amid scenes of heartrending grief.

The ground, though very broad, was still crowded with mourners from far and near, as well as with priests from temple after temple, who were there to chant the Name of Amida. Envoys from Her Majesty and the Heir Apparent, to say nothing of His Eminence, came and went among those from elsewhere, and all brought expressions of the deepest sorrow.

His Excellency could not rise. "Now that at my age I have lost a daughter in the flower of her youth," he said, weeping in shame before many sympathetic mourners, "I can only writhe upon the ground." All night the clamorous rites went on, but when he returned home, just before dawn, he took away with him only a few poor remains.[42]

Such losses strike often enough, but no doubt because Genji had known so few—perhaps only one[43]—he was consumed in his bereavement by the fires of longing.[44] The moon still hung aloft in the dawn, since the twentieth of the eighth month was past, lending no little pathos to the lightening sky, when in keen agreement with the feelings of His Excellency, whom he saw wandering in the darkness of a father's grief, Genji gazed sorrowfully upward and murmured,

42. When the family returned home, a retainer carried the ashes in an urn.
43. Presumably his grandmother or Yūgao.
44. An intentional allusion also to the fire that has consumed the body of Aoi.

"No, I cannot tell where my eyes should seek aloft the smoke I saw rise,
but now all the skies above move me to sad thoughts of loss."

When he returned to His Excellency's residence, sleep eluded him. Images of her as he had known her down the years ran through his mind, and he wondered in vain regret why she had taken such offense at each of his casual diversions, undertaken while he complacently assumed that she would eventually change her mind about him, and why she had persisted to the end in disliking him so. It seemed like a dream now to be wearing gray, and the thought that her gray would have been still darker if she had outlived him[45] prompted,

"I may do no more, and the mourning I now wear is a shallow gray,
but my tears upon my sleeves have gathered in deep pools."

He went on to call the Buddha's Name, looking more beautiful than ever, and his discreet chanting of the scripture passage, "O Lord Fugen who seest all the manifest universe,"[46] outdid the most practiced monk's. The sight of his little son would start fresh tears for "the grasses of remembering"[47] and yet without this reminder of her . . . The thought gave him some comfort.

Her Highness had been brought so low that she no longer rose at all, until she, too, seemed near death, and in great agitation His Excellency commissioned prayers for her as well. He ordered the memorial services,[48] for the days were slipping by, and he made them very grand because it had all been so sudden. No wonder he mourned his daughter so, considering how a parent loves even the least favored child! He and his wife had been sorry to have no other daughter, and for them this tragedy surpassed the loss of the most priceless gem.

Genji went nowhere, not even to Nijō, but from the depth of his heartfelt grief he spent days and nights in earnest prayer. To his secret destinations he sent only letters. As to the Rokujō Haven, the Ise High Priestess had now taken up residence in the Headquarters of the Left Gate Watch,[49] and he invoked the strict purity prevailing there to avoid corresponding with her at all. He now held the world and its ways, so distasteful already, in unqualified aversion, and he thought that without this fresh tie he would certainly assume the guise to which he aspired,[50] except that every time his mind took this turn, he would straightaway start thinking

45. A wife mourning her husband wore darker gray than a husband mourning his wife, and she mourned him a year in contrast to his three months.

46. A Chinese phrase in praise of the Bodhisattva Fugen, closely associated with the Lotus Sutra. It refers to enlightened insight into the nature of existence.

47. *Gosenshū* 1187, by Kanetada no Haha no Menoto: "Were it not for the child conceived between you and me, how should I now pluck the grasses of remembering?" These "grasses" are *shinobu*, a plant the name of which is homophonous with the verb that means "remember fondly."

48. The services held every seven days for the first forty-nine days after a death.

49. The building that was converted when necessary into the Shosai-in, where the priestess spent a period of purification.

50. The guise of a monk; the "fresh tie" is his new son.

how much his young lady in the west wing must miss him. He still felt a void beside him, however closely his women might gather around him while he lay at night alone in his curtained bed. Often he lay wakeful, murmuring, "Is autumn the time to lose one's love?"[51] and listening, sick at heart, to the priests, whom he had chosen for their voices,

Curtained bed

calling the Name of the Buddha Amida.

Oh, how sadly the wind moans as autumn passes! he thought as for once he lay alone and sleepless into a foggy dawn; but then a letter arrived on deep blue-gray paper, tied to chrysanthemums just now beginning to open and placed beside him by a messenger who left without a word.[52] The delightful effect pleased him, and he noted that the writing was the Haven's.

"Have you understood my silence?

> *The sad news I hear, that a life can pass so soon, brings tears to my eyes,*
> *but my thoughts go first of all to the sleeves of the bereaved.*

My heart is so full, you know, beneath this sky."

Her writing is more beautiful than ever! He could hardly put it down, but her pretense of innocence repelled him. Still, he had not the heart to withhold an answer, and he hated to imagine the damage to her name if he should do so. Perhaps the lady he had lost had indeed been destined somehow to meet this end, but why should he have seen and heard the cause so clearly? Yes, he was bitter, and despite himself he did not think that he could ever feel the same about the Haven again.

After long hesitation, since the Ise Priestess's purification might well present another difficulty,[53] he decided that it would be cruel not to answer a letter so pointedly sent, and he wrote on mauve-gray paper, "My own silence has indeed lasted too long, but although I have thought of you, I knew that in this time of mourning you would understand.

51. *Kokinshū* 839, by Mibu no Tadamine, laments the special cruelty of losing a loved one in autumn, which was a sad season of separation even for the living.

52. The messenger did not say from whom the letter came perhaps because the sender's present ritually pure situation prevents her from corresponding openly with someone in mourning.

53. A message from someone in mourning (hence polluted by death) might not be admissible into the priestess's dwelling.

Those who linger on and those all too swiftly gone live as dewdrops, all,
and it is a foolish thing to set one's heart on their world.

You simply must let these things go. I will close, since for all I know you may not read this."

She happened to be at home, and she read his letter in private. By the pricking of her conscience she understood his cautious hints and saw with anguish that he was quite right. Hers was the greatest of misfortunes. How would His Eminence take it, when the rumor spread? He and the late Heir Apparent,[54] among all the brothers, had been especially close, and he had gladly agreed when the Heir Apparent begged him to look after the present Ise Priestess. He had also pressed the Priestess's mother often to stay on at court, although she had rejected even that for fear of the consequences; and now to her astonishment she found herself caught in love's toils like any girl and certain in the end to have her name bandied about invidiously. Such were the thoughts that whirled through her mind, leaving her as unwell as ever.

Renowned as she was for deep charm and rare taste, her fame had grown and grown until even after she moved to the Shrine on the Moor her wonderfully original ways inspired the most discriminating privy gentlemen to devote themselves morning and night to following the dewy path to her gate. News of this did not surprise Genji at all, considering her undoubted genius. He readily agreed that she would be sorely missed if she tired of the world and went down to Ise.

The memorial rites passed by one by one, but Genji remained secluded at His Excellency's until the last day. The Third Rank Captain[55] visited Genji often, pained by the unfamiliar tedium of his existence, to discuss recent events or to distract him with the usual mischievous gossip; and then the notorious Dame of Staff generally provided the occasion for their mirth. "Why, the poor thing!" Genji cried reprovingly. "You must not make such fun of the Honorable Granny!"[56] Still, he enjoyed every word. Tales of their romantic adventures, including the story of that cloudy sixteenth night in autumn, passed freely between them, until their rambling review of this world and its sad ways often ended in tears.

A cold rain[57] was falling late one dreary afternoon when the Captain came in, looking jauntily splendid enough to put anyone to shame. He had changed to a dress cloak and gathered trousers of a gray lighter than the one he had worn in the season just past.[58]

Genji was leaning on the railing by the west door to his room, gazing out over the frost-withered garden. The wild wind blew, the rain poured down, and his tears,

---

54. Her husband.

55. Tō no Chūjō, who has apparently been promoted to the third rank. Captain was a fourth-rank office, but an exceptionally wellborn young man could be promoted higher. He is probably no longer Secretary.

56. *Oba otodo*, a nickname for the old lady featured in "Beneath the Autumn Leaves." Genji's father gave it to her, according to a passage in "The Bluebell."

57. The *shigure* rain of late autumn and early winter.

58. On the first day of the tenth month (the first of winter), courtiers changed into new clothes. Although still in mourning, Tō no Chūjō had lightened the mood of his costume.

it seemed to him, vied with the rain as he murmured, chin in hand,
"Did she turn to rain, to cloud? I shall never know . . .";[59] and the
Captain, gazing at him with his mind as always on pleasure, knew
that if he were a woman his soul would stay with Genji instead
of setting off for the hereafter. Genji was in a very
casual state of dress, and he simply rethreaded
the cords of his dress cloak when the Captain
sat down beside him. It was a summer cloak,
a little darker than his visitor's, worn over a
perfectly plain scarlet gown.[60] The Captain
could hardly keep his eyes off him. He, too,
gazed sorrowfully into space.

Summer dress cloak

> *"Among all these clouds that drift across the sodden skies, turning into rain,*
> *which am I to look upon with the gaze of one who mourns?*

No one will ever know where she has gone," he went on, as though to himself.

> *"The very heavens where she who so long was mine turned to cloud and rain*
> *darken, and winter showers deepen the skies' heavy gloom."*

Genji was obviously deeply afflicted.

The Captain did not quite understand, since Genji had never shown such devotion to his sister before. His Eminence had had to speak to him, and it was surely
His Excellency's attentiveness, as well as the restraining influence of the exalted
family connection with Her Highness,[61] that had kept Genji in the end from simply
leaving her, although the Captain had often had occasion to note his unhappiness
with sympathy. He regretted her loss more than ever when he saw now that Genji
must actually have held her in the highest regard. He felt in his great sorrow as
though the light had gone from the world.

Gentians and pinks were blooming among the withered grasses. Genji had
some picked, and after the Captain had gone, he sent Saishō (his little son's nurse)
with one to Her Highness, with the poem,

> *"This dear little pink, lingering on after all in my wintry hedge,*
> *shall be to me a token of the autumn that is gone.[62]*

To you it can hardly be as pretty as the one you have lost." The little boy was certainly very sweet, with all his innocent smiles.

---

59. From a poem by the ninth-century Chinese poet Liu Mengde, included in the anthology *Wenxuan*
(Japanese *Monzen*). Tō no Chūjō's poem, below, picks up the same reference.

60. Scarlet (*kurenai*) could easily be worn under the gray of relatively light mourning.

61. Aoi and Tō no Chūjō's mother was a sister of Genji's father.

62. The "little pink" (or pinks, *nadeshiko*) stands for Genji's son; "the autumn that is gone," for his wife and
her death.

Her Highness's tears fell more easily than leaves from gale-swept trees, and she could only weep to read it.

> "I need only see that most lovely little pink in his wasted hedge
> for these sleeves of mine again to melt in a rain of tears."

It seemed to Genji, at loose ends, that Her Highness of the bluebells would understand how sad this day had been, and although it was dark by now, he sent her a note. The last one had come a long time ago, but his messages were like that now, and she had no qualms about reading it. On Chinese paper the color of today's sky he had written,

> "Never have such dews as this evening come to fall on my moistened sleeves,
> though I have known in my time many a somber autumn.

Cold rains always fall . . ."[63]

He had taken great care with his handwriting, which was finer than ever, and the Princess agreed with her gentlewomen that she could not fail to answer him. "My thoughts have often gone out to you," she wrote, "but I could not very well . . . [64]

> Ever since I heard that even as autumn mists rose you were left forlorn,
> my sorrowing thoughts have gone to the rains from wintry skies."

That was all, and to him the faint handwriting had a profound appeal. It was rare for a woman to improve in all ways on long acquaintance, and he was struck by how truly in her case "distance is the secret of lasting charm."[65] Distant she might be, but she never failed to respond just as she should, and this, he believed, was why their feeling for each other would endure, for surely the pretensions and affectations that put a woman on show for everyone only display her worst shortcomings. No, he said to himself, that was not how he meant to bring up the young lady in his west wing. He never forgot how much she must miss him, but he felt as though he had taken in a motherless child, and he was pleased that while away he at least did not need to wonder what doubts and misgivings she might have about him.

After dark he ordered the lamp brought up and called the best of the gentlewomen to come and talk to him. For years he had had a weakness for the one called Chūnagon, but he had made no approaches to her during this time of sorrow. Chūnagon admired his tact. "Day after day now," he began with blameless warmth, "I have been seeing more of you all than I ever used to, and you can be sure that I will miss you when we are no longer together. Quite apart from our loss, I find the thought of the future painful in many ways."

---

63. *Genji monogatari kochūshakusho in'yō waka* 514: "The cold rains of the tenth month always fall, but never have my sleeves been as wet as now."

64. "I could not very well write to you."

65. Apparently a quotation from a poem now lost.

"To say nothing of the darkness we feel since my poor lady's passing," one answered with renewed tears, "the very idea that you, too, my lord, are now to leave us forever . . ." She could not finish.

He looked at them fondly. "Leave you forever? How cruel you must think me! If you can only be patient, you will soon see how wrong you are. Ah, life flees so quickly!" His tear-filled eyes as he gazed into the lamp were very beautiful.

A little girl, an orphan of whom their late mistress had been especially fond, was looking very sad. "Ateki," he said, weeping bitterly in sympathy, "I must be the one you will have to love now." She looked very sweet in a girlish gown dyed a darker gray than the others, a black overgown, and trousers of leaf gold.[66]

Page girl in a kazami *dress gown*

"I hope that those of you who wish to honor the past will stay on with our little son," he went on, "even if that means putting up with a rather quiet life. I will feel even less like returning if you all leave and nothing remains of the household I once knew." None doubted, though, that he would come only rarely, despite his talk of the future, and they were sadder than before.

His Excellency had given each gentlewoman very simply, as her rank and station deserved, the accessories that his daughter had favored in daily use, and to some, more substantial mementos.

Genji, who knew that he could not stay shut up like this forever, set off to call on His Eminence. A cold rain fell while they brought out his carriage and gathered his men, as though the very heavens were weeping, and the wind rustled the leaves so noisily on the trees that his gentlewomen were disconsolate. Even those whose sleeves sometimes dried lately now moistened them again. His people presumably went to Nijō to await his arrival, since that was where he was to spend the night, and although this would surely not be his last time at His Excellency's, those who stayed behind were very downcast. To His Excellency and Her Highness his departure only meant fresh sorrow.

Genji addressed Her Highness in a letter. "I mean to wait upon His Eminence today, since he has graciously expressed anxiety about me. Dismayed as I am to have survived her all this time, I am shaken to have to go out at all, and conversation would be beyond me. For that reason I have refrained from saying good-bye to you in person."

Tears blinded Her Highness when she read it, and she could not reply. It was His Excellency who came straight to him, too overcome to take his sleeve from his eyes. The gentlewomen present shared their grief. The sight of Genji weeping over his sorrows was extremely touching, but he also looked very beautiful as he did so.

66. She has on an *akome* (often worn by little girls) under a *kazami* (a girl's formal dress gown). The darker gray conveys deeper mourning.

Standing curtains

For a time His Excellency struggled to master his feelings. "At my great age anything may bring tears to my eyes, and so of course it is more than I can do to calm the feelings that never leave my sleeves dry; that is why I cannot very well present myself before His Eminence, for I know how likely I am to make a spectacle of myself. Please explain this to him, if you find a moment to do so. It is very hard to lose a child this way, when one has so few years left." The effort that it cost him to master himself was painfully obvious.

"Indeed," Genji answered, repeatedly blowing his nose, "one never knows who will go first and who last, but to experience such a loss is a trial unlike any other. I shall describe your condition to His Eminence, and I am sure that he will understand."

"Then go before dark, because I see no sign that the rain will let up."

Genji looked about him and saw through open sliding panels or behind standing curtains a crowd of some thirty gentlewomen dressed in varying shades of gray, light or dark, and with deep sorrow plain to see on their tearful faces. He was very moved.

"It is a comfort that you will be calling here sometimes," His Excellency said, "since one whom you will not wish to neglect remains behind; but these women who understand so little are grieving, and who could blame them? They imagine that you are now leaving your home forever, and the prospect of losing the occasional pleasure of your presence, to which these years have accustomed them, troubles them more than the sorrow of our common loss. You were never at ease with her," he went on, weeping, "but alas, I always kept up hope. Yes, this is a sad evening, it is indeed."

"Their sorrow shows how little they know me. There may indeed have been times when I deprived her of my company, even as I took it for granted that somehow all would be well, but now I have, if anything, less reason to neglect this house than before. You will see, I promise."

He then took his leave. His Excellency went to Genji's room after seeing him off. It was as it had always been, to the last detail of its furnishings, but to His Excellency it was as empty as a cicada's cast-off shell.

An inkstone lay abandoned before the curtained bed. The young gentlewomen must have smiled through their sadness to watch him examine the pieces of practice calligraphy left nearby, wiping his eyes as he did so. Genji had jotted down moving old poems, Chinese and Japanese, in a rapid cursive, in characters square and formal, and in various other unusual styles. How beautifully he writes! His Excellency exclaimed to himself, lifting his gaze skyward. He must have been very sorry indeed to have lost Genji as a son-in-law.

Where Genji had written the line "Who will now share with me our old pillow, our covers . . ."[67] he had added,

> "Her departed soul must feel yet deeper sorrow for this bed we shared,
> when it is beyond me still to leave it and go away."

And beside "The frost flowers are white,"

> "Now that you are gone, I have lain so many nights, brushing off the dew,
> on our gillyflower bed covered now only with dust!"[68]

He must have had in mind the pinks of the other day, because among the papers there were withered ones.

"Far be it from me to understate our loss," His Excellency said when he showed them to Her Highness, "but I take comfort from the thought that sorrows like this one visit us all and that the old tie[69] that briefly brought her to us, apparently only to cause us pain, may have been more cruel than kind. As the days go by, though, and I miss her more, it seems just too hard that the Commander should be soon to become a stranger. Whenever he stayed away and failed to come for a day or two, I looked forward to his return, and once his light is gone from my life, I do not know how I will be able to go on!" He sobbed so openly that the more mature of Her Highness's women were overcome, and on this dismally chilly evening they, too, burst into tears.

The younger ones meanwhile clustered together here and there in sad conversation. "Just as His Excellency says," they observed, "I do not doubt that having the young master to look after is a great comfort, but even he can hardly make up for the lady who left him behind." Others were saying, "I plan to go home for a while; I will be back later on." There were many touching scenes as one and all said goodbye to one another.

"You are awfully thin," His Eminence observed sympathetically when Genji called on him—"all those days spent fasting, I suppose."[70] He had Genji dine in his own presence and showered him with the most touching attentions.

When Genji called on Her Majesty, the gentlewomen there looked on him with wonder. Through Ōmyōbu she asked, "How have you been all this time, which for me, too, has been so filled with sorrow?"

"I knew in a general way how precarious life is, but seeing it with my own eyes has upset and repelled me, and until today only your kind messages have sustained me." His manner was even more sadly subdued than in the past. In mourning, wear-

---

67. A line (like "The frost flowers are white," below) from Bai Juyi's "Song of Unending Sorrow."

68. Here as elsewhere, *tokonatsu* ("gillyflower") plays on *toko* ("bed"). The dew is Genji's tears.

69. From past lives.

70. During the first forty-nine days a mourner kept to the plainest food and especially avoided meat and spices.

ing an unpatterned formal cloak over a gray train-robe and with the pendant tails of his headdress rolled, he was more beautiful than in his most brilliant finery. He spoke of how concerned he was at not having seen the Heir Apparent for so long, and the night was well advanced when at last he withdrew.

Every room at Nijō was spic-and-span, and the whole staff, men and women alike, awaited his arrival. The senior gentlewomen were all back, and seeing each of them dressed and made up to her best advantage recalled to him with a pang the sorrowing company that he had just left. He changed and went straight to the west wing. The curtains and furnishings for the new season were bright and gay,[71] the handsome young gentlewomen and page girls, with their graceful airs and ways, made a most agreeable sight, and Shōnagon's warm welcome pleased him greatly.

His young lady was dressed extremely prettily. "See what a big girl you are, now I have been away so long!" He lifted her little standing curtain to see her, and her looks as she bashfully turned away were beyond reproach. Her profile in the lamplight, her hair—everything told him that she would exactly resemble that other lady for whom he pined, and he was overjoyed.

He sat beside her and described what had happened while he was gone.[72] "I so look forward to telling you all about it," he said, "but all that would be too much now. I shall go and rest a little first and then be back. I shall be seeing so much of you now that you may grow tired of me!"

Shōnagon was pleased to hear all this, but she still worried about him. That may not have been very nice of her, but he kept up with so many great ladies that she was afraid a new one might now appear and ruin everything.

Genji returned to his own apartments, where he had the gentlewoman Chūjō rub his legs before he fell asleep. The next morning he sent off a letter for his little son. The sorrowful reply filled him with melancholy.

With so little to occupy him now he remained very pensive, but he could not yet muster the ambition to set out on casual evening calls. It was a pleasure to see that his young lady had turned out to be all he could wish, and since he judged that the time had now more or less come, he began to drop suggestive hints; but she showed no sign of understanding.

He spent whole days with her, whiling away the time at Go or at character-guessing games,[73] and such were her wit and grace, so enthralling in quality her every gesture, that after those years of forbearance while her charm had offered nothing more, he could endure it no longer; and so despite his compunction it came to pass one morning, when there was nothing otherwise about their ways with each other to betray the change, that he rose early while she rose not at all.

"What can be the matter?" her women asked each other anxiously. "She must not be feeling herself."

71. Curtains and other furnishings had been changed for winter, which began on the first of the tenth lunar month.

72. He addresses her very politely, despite his intimate tone.

73. The guessing game (hen-tsugi) involved guessing partly hidden characters or making up new ones by adding elements to given parts.

Before leaving he put a writing box beside her, inside her curtains.[74] At last, when there was no one nearby, she lifted her head and found a knotted letter at her pillow. Opening it uncomprehendingly, she read,

> *"Ah, what distances kept us so strangely apart, when night after night*
> *we two yet lay side by side in our overlapping clothes."*

He seemed to have dashed it off with the greatest of ease. She had never suspected him of such intentions, and she could only wonder bitterly why in her innocence she had ever trusted anyone with such horrid ideas.

Toward midday he returned. "You seem to be ill. What is wrong, then? Today will be no fun if we cannot play Go." He peeped in: she was still lying with the bedclothes over her head. The gentlewomen drew back as he went to her. "Why will you not talk to me? You do not like me after all, do you. Your gentlewomen must be wondering about all this." He pulled the covers off her and found her drenched in perspiration. Even the hair at her forehead was soaking wet. "Oh, dear, we cannot have this! What a fuss you are making!" She was still furious with him, though, despite his attempts to console her, and she refused him a single word in reply. "Very well, then," he said reproachfully, "I will not come anymore. I feel quite unwanted." He opened the writing box and peered inside, but there was nothing in it. What a little girl she still is! He contemplated her fondly. He spent the whole day trying to make her feel better, and her refusal to yield only made her more precious.

That evening they were brought baby boar cakes.[75] The event was nothing elaborate, since Genji was in mourning, and the cakes were served only there in the west wing. When he saw them in all their colors, presented in pretty, cypress boxes, he went out to the front of the house and called Koremitsu. "Bring me cakes like these tomorrow evening, although not nearly so many. Today was not lucky."[76]

Koremitsu, always so quick, noted his smiles and caught his meaning instantly. He asked no questions but only said with a perfectly straight face, "Certainly, my lord, a new couple should of course choose the right day to have them. How many baby rat cakes should I provide?"[77]

"About a third as many should do." Koremitsu, who understood him perfectly, withdrew. He certainly knows his way about! Genji thought. Koremitsu said nothing to anyone, and he all but made the cakes himself, at home.

---

74. So that she can answer the poem he has left by her pillow. After a couple's first night together the man was supposed to leave the woman a poem, and she to respond. Being "knotted," Genji's note has visibly to do with love.

75. Glutinous rice cakes, each shaped like a baby boar (*inoko mochii*), eaten for good luck at the hour of the Boar (about 9:00 to 11:00 P.M.) on the first day of the Boar in the tenth lunar month. The rice was mixed with ingredients like sesame, chestnut, or persimmon, so that the cakes came in seven different flavors and colors.

76. Newlyweds were served white rice cakes on their third night together, the one when their marriage was sealed. However, the day of the Boar (only the second night in this case) was unlucky for the start of anything as important as marriage.

77. The day of the Rat followed that of the Boar, but "baby rat cakes" (*nenoko [no mochii]*) did not exist; the term is Koremitsu's invention.

Genji, at his wits' end to placate his darling, was highly amused to feel as though he had just stolen a bride. *What she used to mean to me is nothing compared to what she means to me now!* he reflected. *How unruly the heart is! I could not bear one night away from her!*

Discreetly, very late at night, Koremitsu brought the cakes that Genji had ordered. He was acutely aware that Shōnagon, who was older, might embarrass Genji's young lady, so he called for her daughter, Ben. "Take them these, quietly." He handed her the cakes in an incense jar box.[78] "They are to celebrate a happy event, and you are to put them beside the pillow. Be careful, now, do not do anything wrong."

"But I have never done anything wrong like that," Ben said in surprise as she took them.[79]

"Actually, avoid that word for now. Just don't use it."[80]

Ben was too young to grasp what he meant, but she delivered the cakes, slipping them in through the standing curtain by their pillows. No doubt it was as always Genji who explained them.

The gentlewomen knew nothing of all this, but when Genji had the box removed early the next morning, those closest to their mistress understood what had happened. Where could those dishes have come from? The little carved stands were so delicate and the cakes themselves so beautifully made—it was all as pretty as could be.[81] Shōnagon, who had never dreamed Genji would go this far,[82] dissolved in tears of gratitude before such evidence of his unstinting devotion.

"I do wish he had quietly told *us*, though," the women whispered to each other. "What can that man of his have thought?"

Thereafter Genji missed her and worried about her whenever he called a moment at the palace or at His Eminence's, so much so that his feelings surprised even him. He was not insensitive to the bitter complaints addressed to him by the ladies he was visiting, but he was so reluctant to hurt his new wife by being away a single night that he arranged things to look as though he were ill. "I shall begin going out once I am again ready to face the world" was the only kind of answer he gave them.

The Mistress of the Wardrobe still had her heart set only on Genji, and the Empress Mother[83] did not at all like the feelings that His Excellency their father expressed on the subject. "After all," he would say, "I see nothing wrong with her having what she wants, now that I gather that proud wife of his is no more." The Empress Mother, to whom there was nothing dishonorable about her sister's entering palace service as long as she did so with dignity, was determined to offer her to His Majesty.

Genji, who was so fond of her, found this prospect thoroughly disappointing,

---

78. Ben must be behind a curtain. The box serves to disguise its contents.
79. She mistakes Koremitsu's meaning. *Ada* ("wrong") can mean specifically something wanton.
80. *Ada* is too ill-omened to use at the time of a marriage.
81. "Third-night cakes" were served on silver dishes, with silver chopsticks, silver chopstick rests in the shape of cranes, etc.
82. As to marry Murasaki relatively formally.
83. Oborozukiyo and Kokiden (Ima Kisaki, "the new Empress"), Oborozukiyo's elder sister and Genji's implacable foe.

but he was in no mood just now to divide his affections. Why do that? He
had learned, to his cost, the value of caution. Life is short enough as it is, he reflected, and besides, I have made my choice.
I should never have provoked jealousy.

As to the Rokujō Haven, her plight
affected him very much, but things
would never go well if he acknowledged
her formally, whereas she was just the
woman to discuss things with now and
again, if she would only let him go on
seeing her as in the past. He could not
bring himself to give her up even now.

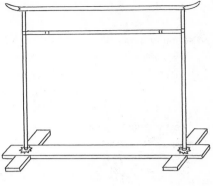

Clothing frame

It occurred to him that society still did not know who his new love was, and
that that reflected poorly on her; and he decided accordingly to inform His Highness her father. He invited a chosen few to a donning of the train that he planned to
bring off more amply than usual—which was all very well, except that she had now
taken a keen dislike to him. She so bitterly rued giving him all those years of trust
and affection that she would not even look him properly in the eye, and she displayed only aversion for his lightest remark. The change that had come over her
both amused and pained him. "Those years when I was so fond of you have all gone
to waste," he would complain, "and the way you keep yourself from me hurts me
very much!" On this note the New Year came.

On the first day of the year he called first, as usual, on His Eminence, then on
His Majesty and the Heir Apparent. After withdrawing from the palace he went on
to His Excellency's. New Year or not, His Excellency was deep in forlorn reminis-
cences, and Genji's arrival just then overwhelmed every effort of his to master his
emotions. The passing years seemed to have conferred on Genji still greater dignity
of presence and looks even more dazzling than before.

When he left His Excellency to visit the rooms of the lady he had lost, the
gentlewomen there were overcome by the joy of his rare visit. He found that his little son had grown a great deal, and the boy's ready smiles were very touching. He
shared the Heir Apparent's eyes and mouth, which gave Genji a twinge of alarm
that others might wonder at the resemblance. Everything was as it had been, and
there were robes hanging as ever on their frames, but the absence of anything belonging to a woman cast a pall over it all.

He received a note from Her Highness. "Today I have been striving to contain
my sorrow," she wrote, "but I can no longer do so now that you have been good
enough to call." She continued, "My eyes have been so dim all these months with
weeping that the clothing I have made you, as I always used to do, may look very
dull, but I hope that at least today you will condescend to wear it."

The exquisite items that accompanied this message joined the others already
on the frames. In color and workmanship the train-robe she wished him to have was
so exceptional that he knew he could not let it go unappreciated, and he put it on.

He understood with a rush of sympathy how disappointed she would have been if he had failed to come. He wrote in reply, "I came to remind you that spring is here, but so many memories crowd through me now that I hardly know what to say.

> *For so many years you have renewed on this day the bright hues I wear,*
> *and now I don them again, I feel my tears fall like rain.*

My heart is overflowing."
  She answered,

> *"There is nothing new in the coming of the year, only an old rain:*
> *the tears an aging mother sheds for all that she has lost."*

And they did indeed have reason to mourn.

10

The Green Branch

Sakaki, a broadleaf evergreen tree, figures in Shinto ritual, hence in this chapter's best-remembered scene: Genji's visit to the Rokujō Haven at the Shrine on the Moor. She reproaches him when he arrives and slips a branch of *sakaki* under her blinds:

"When no cedar trees stand as though to draw the eye by the sacred fence, what strange misapprehension led you to pick sakaki?"

He replies,

"This was where she was, the shrine maiden, that I knew, and fond memories made the scent of sakaki *my reason to pick a branch."*

His *sakaki* branch gave the chapter its title.

"The Green Branch" follows "Heart-to-Heart" in unbroken narrative sequence, from the ninth month of that year, when Genji is twenty-three, to the summer a year and a half later, when he is twenty-five.

PERSONS

Genji, the Commander of the Right, age 23 to 25

The Rokujō Haven, 30 to 32 (Rokujō no Miyasudokoro)

The High Priestess of Ise, daughter of the Rokujō Haven,
14 to 16 (Akikonomu)

His (Late) Eminence, the Retired Emperor, dies when Genji is 23 (Kiritsubo In)

Her Majesty, the Empress, then Her Cloistered Eminence, 28 to 30 (Fujitsubo)

The Heir Apparent, her son, 5 to 7 (Reizei)

His Majesty, the Emperor, 27 to 29 (Suzaku)

The Empress Mother, daughter of the Minister of the Right (Kokiden)

His Excellency, the Minister of the Right,
grandfather of the Emperor (Udaijin)

His Highness of War, brother of Fujitsubo and father of Murasaki, 38 to 40
(Hyōbukyō no Miya)

Ōmyōbu, a gentlewoman in the service of Fujitsubo

The Mistress of the Wardrobe, then Mistress of Staff,
daughter of the Minister of the Right (Oborozukiyo)

His Excellency, the Minister of the Left,
resigns when he is 59 and Genji is 25 (Sadaijin)

The mistress of Genji's west wing, 15 to 17 (Murasaki)

Shōnagon, Murasaki's nurse

The lady of the bluebells, the High Priestess of the Kamo Shrine (Asagao)

Chūjō, a gentlewoman in the service of Asagao

Chūnagon, a gentlewoman in the service of Oborozukiyo

The Fujiwara Lieutenant, brother of the Shōkyōden Consort

Ben, a gentlewoman in the service of Fujitsubo

A Master of Discipline, Genji's maternal uncle

A Secretary Controller, nephew of the Empress Mother

The Abbot of the Mountain, Fujitsubo's uncle

The Captain, brother of Genji's late wife, Aoi (Tō no Chūjō)

The Captain's second son, 8 or 9 when Genji is 25 (Kōbai)

As the High Priestess's journey to Ise approached, her mother the Rokujō Haven felt increasingly miserable. Now that His Excellency's daughter, whose commanding rank she had so resented, was no more, people told one another that her time had come, and her own gentlewomen looked forward eagerly to the future; but when she considered Genji's subsequent silence and his shabby treatment of her, she recognized that something must really have happened to distress him, and she therefore put her feelings aside to prepare for a resolute departure.

No Priestess had ever gone down to Ise with her mother before, but the Haven invoked anxiety over her daughter's welfare and held firm in her wish to put her troubled life behind her, even as Genji, disappointed that she really did mean to leave, now began at least sending her sympathetic letters. She felt unable to receive him in person. No doubt she sternly reminded herself that although he might think this decision unkind, seeing him would make things so much more difficult for her that she was not obliged to do so.

Now and again she went home for a time, but so quietly that Genji never knew when to find her there. He was not free to call on her where she was living at present, and days and months therefore went by without a visit from him. Meanwhile His Eminence began often to feel unwell, although he was not alarmingly ill, and this burdened Genji with yet another care.

Concern that she might condemn his cruelty and fear that others might actually agree decided him after all to set out for the Shrine on the Moor. He knew that she would be leaving soon, for it was the seventh of the ninth month, and she did indeed have a great deal to occupy her, but his repeated appeals to give him a moment whether or not he even sat down, coupled with her wish to avoid appearing too distant, overcame her misgivings and persuaded her that yes, she might converse with him as long as she kept something between them; and in this mood she began privately to look forward to his coming.

Melancholy overwhelmed him as soon as he set out across the moor's vast expanse. The autumn flowers were dying; among the brakes of withering sedge, insect cries were faint and few; and through the wind's sad sighing among the pines there

Brushwood fence

reached him at times the sound of instruments, although so faintly that he could not say what the music was. The scene had an intensely eloquent beauty. The ten or more close retainers in his escort were modestly outfitted, but he had dressed elaborately, despite the private character of his journey, and he looked handsome enough to give the setting a new charm for the young gallants with him. He asked himself why he had not come before, and regretted having failed to do so.

Within a low, frail, brushwood fence stood a scattering of board-roofed buildings, very lightly built.[1] The unbarked *torii*[2] evoked a holy awe that reproved his own concerns, and the priests clearing their throats[3] here and there or conversing with their fellows gave the precincts an air all their own. The fire lodge[4] glowed dimly. With so few people about, a deep quiet reigned, and the thought that she had spent days and months here alone with her cares moved him to keen sympathy.

He hid at a suitable spot by the north wing[5] and announced his visit, at which the music ceased and he heard promising sounds of movement within. She showed no sign of receiving him in person, and he was not at all pleased to exchange mere commonplaces with her through a go-between. "You would not persist in keeping the sacred rope between us if only you knew how hard it is for me now to get away on so personal a quest," he said earnestly. "A good deal is clear to me by now, you know."

His appeal moved her women to intercede for him with their mistress. "Yes, my lady," they said, "it is a shame to leave him just standing there; one must feel sorry for him."

Oh, dear, she thought, I do not like the spectacle I am making—he can hardly think well of me for it; I would much rather not go out to him at all. She did not have the courage to treat him coldly, though, and at last she emerged amid reluctant sighs, delighting him with the grace of her form.[6]

"I wonder whether, here,[7] I might be allowed up on the veranda," he said and promptly installed himself there. In the brilliant moonlight his movements had a charm unlike anyone else's. Too abashed now to make fluent excuses for his long silence, he slipped in to her under the blind a *sakaki* branch that he had picked, and he said, "This is the constant color[8] that led me to penetrate the sacred paling, yet now you cruelly . . ."

1. They were temporary, for the shrine was rebuilt as needed at a new spot.
2. The gateway to a Shinto shrine, normally made of finished wood; this one emphasizes the shrine's temporary character.
3. Probably as a warning at Genji's approach.
4. Perhaps where the food offerings were prepared.
5. Where Rokujō lives. Her daughter occupies the main house.
6. A blind still separates them, but Genji sees her silhouette through it.
7. At the house rather than at the sanctuary proper.
8. That of the evergreen *sakaki* and of Genji's own constant heart.

She answered,

> *"When no cedar trees stand as though to draw the eye by the sacred fence,*
> *what strange misapprehension led you to pick sakaki?"*[9]

> *"This was where she was, the shrine maiden, that I knew, and fond memories*
> *made the scent of sakaki my reason to pick a branch,"*[10]

he replied. Despite the daunting character of the surroundings he came in halfway under the blind, and there he remained, leaning on the lintel that bounded the room.

For years, while he could see her whenever he wished and she herself thought of him with longing, a proud complacency had made him somewhat indifferent to her; and then that shocking discovery of her flaw had cooled the last of his ardor and turned him away. Now, however, he was undone by all that this rare meeting brought back to him from the past, and he wept helplessly over what lay behind them and what might yet be to come. Her own failure to control emotions that she had seemed resolved never to betray affected him more and more, and he begged her to give up her plan after all.

As he laid his whole complaint before her, his eyes on a sky perhaps lovelier still now that the moon had set, all the bitterness pent up in his heart melted away, and she, who had given up clinging to him, was not surprised to find her feelings in turmoil nonetheless. Meanwhile young scions of the great houses passed the time with one another while they wandered the grounds, presenting as they did so a scene of incomparable elegance.

No one could ever convey all that passed between those two, who together had known such uncounted sorrows. The quality of a sky at last touched by dawn seemed meant for them alone.

> *"Many dews attend any reluctant parting at the break of day*
> *but no one has ever seen the like of this autumn sky,"*

Genji said. Wavering and unwilling to leave, he very tenderly took her hand. An icy wind was blowing, and the pine crickets' faltering song so truly caught the mood of the moment that not even someone free of care could have heard it without a pang; no wonder, then, if in their deep anguish neither could find words of farewell.

> *"There has never been a parting in the autumn untouched by sorrow,*
> *but oh, do not cry with me, pine crickets upon the moor!"*

she replied.

---

9. "Why have you come and why are you giving me this *sakaki* branch when I have no wish to respond?" From *Kokinshū* 982, attributed to the Miwa deity, to whom the cedar (*sugi*) is sacred: "My humble dwelling is below Miwa Mountain: come, if you love me, to the gate where the cedars stand."

10. "Shrine maiden" (*otomego*) seems to mean Rokujō herself, though it would better suit her daughter. It is an *engo* ("associated word") of *sakaki*. The poem draws on *Shūishū* 1210, by Kakinomoto Hitomaro, and *Shūishū* 577.

Genji, who knew the vanity of all his regrets, heeded the coming dawn and left at last. The path he followed home was a very dewy one, while she, no longer resolute, mourned his going. His figure so recently glimpsed in the moonlight, that fragrance of his lingering nearby—her intoxicated young women threw discretion to the winds to sing his praises. "Oh, how can my lady set out on this journey," they tearfully asked each other, "when to do so means leaving such a gentleman behind?"

Genji's unusually expansive letter bent her wishes well enough to his own, but alas, she could not again reconsider her plans. He was capable of such eloquence in the service of romantic ambition, even when the affair did not interest him greatly, that regret and compassion must have truly inspired him when he reflected that someone who meant so much to him was now to leave and go her way.

He gave clothing for the journey to her and even to her gentlewomen, as well as other furnishings of the finest, most ingenious design, but these things meant nothing to her. The nearer the day came, the more continually she lamented, as though the thought were ever new, the cruel reputation she would leave behind and the sad fate that now awaited her. The High Priestess herself was young enough simply to be pleased that this often delayed departure should be settled at last. Some people in the world no doubt criticized the unprecedented step her mother was taking, even as others sympathized. Those whose standing spares them reproach in all they do are fortunate indeed. Alas, one singled out above the rest can act so seldom on her desires!

On the sixteenth the High Priestess of Ise underwent purification in the Katsura River.[11] His Majesty chose gentlemen of loftier ancestry and higher renown than usual for the imperial escort[12] and the party of senior nobles. His Eminence's wishes, too, must have played their part in the matter.

A letter came from Genji as the Priestess was setting out, one filled with the usual endless entreaties. It was attached to a mulberry-cloth streamer[13] and addressed "To the High Priestess, in reverence and awe."[14] "The Thunder God himself would refrain, you know,"[15] Genji had written.

> *"Ye great gods of earth, who guard this Land of Eight Isles, if you can be kind,*
> *judge in favor of a pair to whom parting means such pain!*

I cannot think of you without wishing that you would not go."

He had answers, too, despite all there was to do. The Priestess had hers written by her Mistress of the Household:

> *"If the gods of earth from aloft in the heavens issued their decree,*
> *they might hasten to denounce the lightness with which you speak."*

11. West of Kyoto.

12. A party of four nobles, headed by a Counselor or a Consultant, that accompanied the Priestess to Ise on the Emperor's behalf.

13. A streamer cut in zigzag pattern from mulberry-bark cloth, used in Shinto rites.

14. *Kakemakumo*, a formula of respect used in Shinto prayers.

15. *Kokinshū* 701 protests that even the fearsome thunder god refrains from severing the relations between lovers.

Genji would have gladly gone on to the palace to witness what was to follow,[16] but he thought that it might look odd of him to see off someone who was leaving him, and he therefore gave up the idea and lost himself in his musings. The High Priestess's reply, so grown-up in tone, made him smile. His interest aroused, he imagined her attractive beyond her years. Seduced as he always was by strange complications, he now rued his failure to see her for himself while she was young enough for that to be easily possible, and he assured himself that the vicissitudes of life might in time allow him to meet her after all.

The personal distinction of mother and daughter had attracted many sightseeing carriages. The two arrived at the hour of the Monkey.[17] For the Haven in her palanquin it was sad to see the palace again after so many years, and under circumstances so different from what her father, with his high ambition for her, had fondly brought her up to expect.[18] She had married the late Heir Apparent at sixteen and been widowed at twenty. Now, as she again beheld His Majesty's dwelling, she was thirty,[19] and this poem came to her:

> "No, I do not wish today to lament again a life I once knew,
>   but deep in my heart I feel a vague, pervasive sorrow."

The High Priestess was fourteen. She was very pretty already, and her mother's careful grooming had given her a beauty so troubling that His Majesty's heart was stirred. He shed tears of keen emotion when he set the comb of parting in her hair.[20]

A line of display carriages[21] stood before the Eight Bureaus, waiting for the Priestess to come forth, and the sleeves spilling from them made a brilliant show that for many a privy gentleman evoked a painful parting of his own.[22] She set out by night, and when the turn from Nijō onto Tōin brought her before Genji's Nijō residence, he was moved to send her mother this poem, caught in a *sakaki* branch:

> "Go then if you will, and abandon me today, but those sleeves of yours—
>   will the Suzuka River not leave them wet with its spray?"[23]

16. The priestess's farewell to the Emperor and her formal departure.

17. Roughly 3:00 to 5:00 P.M.

18. She had last come to the palace in a palanquin as a future Empress.

19. This age disagrees with the chronology for the other characters in the tale. If with her history she is now thirty, Genji is only fourteen.

20. When a Priestess set out, the Emperor put the "comb of parting" in her hair with the words "Set not your face toward the City again." She will remain at Ise until the Emperor abdicates.

21. *Idashiguruma*, carriages under the blinds of which gentlewomen allowed their sleeves to hang in a brilliant display of color.

22. These ladies will accompany the Priestess to Ise, and some have lovers who will not see them again for a long time. The Eight Bureaus (*Hasshō*), a compound housing the offices of the eight major government bureaus, was continuous with the Great Hall of State, the major ceremonial building in the palace precincts.

23. "You will soon be weeping with regret at having left me." The Suzuka River had to be crossed on the way to Ise.

It was so dark then, and the commotion around the Haven so great, that Genji had no answer until the next day, from beyond the Barrier:[24]

> *"Whether leaping spray from the Suzuka River wet my sleeves or not,*
> *whose thoughts will still follow me all the long way to Ise?"*

Her writing in this hasty note still conveyed great distinction and grace, but Genji wished that she might have shown a little more sympathy for his feelings. A thick fog shrouded all things this unhappy dawn as he stared before him, murmuring to himself,

> *"I shall let my gaze rest upon where she has gone: this autumn at least,*
> *O mists, do not hide from me the summit of Ōsaka!"*

He did not go to the west wing but chose instead to spend the day in lonely brooding. What torments she must have known on her journey!

Display carriage

By the tenth month His Eminence's illness was serious, and all the world longed only to see him recover. His Majesty was acutely worried and called on him in person. His Eminence in his weakened condition spoke again and again of the Heir Apparent and then turned to the subject of Genji. "Keep nothing from him, great or small," he said, "but seek his support in all things, as I have done while I lived. Despite his youth I believe that you need not fear to entrust him with government. He has the mark of one born to rule. That is why, considering the complexity of his situation, I did not make him a Prince but decided instead to have him serve the realm as a commoner. I beg you not to disregard my intention."

His last touching injunctions were many, but a woman has no business passing them on, and the little said of them here is more than enough. His Majesty was deeply saddened and promised repeatedly never to contravene his father's wishes. He was so handsome and so agreeably mature that His Eminence looked on him with happy confidence. The visit then had to end, and His Majesty hastened homeward more than ever burdened with sad forebodings.

The Heir Apparent had wished to accompany His Majesty, but his doing so would have caused such a stir that he changed his visit to another day. He was very grown-up and attractive for his age,[25] and he loved his father so much that his innocent happiness when he saw him again made a touching sight. His Eminence was greatly troubled to see his Empress dissolved in tears. He instructed the

---

24. The Ōsaka Barrier, a low pass with a tollgate at the summit, just outside the City on the main road toward the east. Its name suggests *au saka*, "hill of meeting."

25. He is now five.

Heir Apparent on a wide range of matters, but the future of so young a boy still worried him greatly. On Genji, too, he urged repeated advice on how to serve the realm, as well as admonitions to look after the Heir Apparent. The Heir Apparent withdrew only late in the evening, his visit having caused no less of a commotion than His Majesty's own. Even then His Eminence could hardly bear to let his little son go.

The Empress Mother had meant to call on His Eminence, too, but Her Majesty's presence beside him gave her pause, and while she vacillated, he quietly passed away. The court was distraught. Despite having renounced the throne he had continued to wield the powers of government just as he had during his reign, and now, with His Majesty so young and His Majesty's grandfather, His Excellency of the Right, so testy and impatient, the senior nobles and privy gentlemen all groaned to imagine what might await them when His Excellency came into his own.

Her Majesty and Genji were even more stricken with grief. It goes without saying that everyone was profoundly moved to see Genji, the most brilliant presence among all his father's Princes, so devotedly perform the memorial rites. His beauty was perfect even in drab mourning. Last year the spectacle of mortality had convinced him that this world is dross, and this year he learned the same lesson, but although this loss confirmed him in his resolve,[26] many ties yet restrained him.

His Eminence's Consorts and others remained at his residence until the forty-ninth day, but they dispersed once it was past. On the twentieth of the twelfth month, under a lowering sky that threatened to seal off the world, Her Majesty found herself beset by stubbornly gathering gloom. Knowing the Empress Mother's mind as she did, she understood how painful it would be to inhabit a palace subject to this lady's will, and she saw that she could not remain forever as she was, absorbed in the memory of that noble presence whose intimate she had been for all those years. Now, when the others were going home, her sorrow knew no bounds.

She was to move to her Sanjō residence, and His Highness of War came to accompany her there. Snow was blowing on a stiff wind, and by the time Genji arrived, His Late Eminence's residence was all but deserted. He began to speak of the past. His Highness observed that the five-needled pine before Her Majesty's rooms was weighed down by snow and that its lower branches had died. He said,

> "Alas, that great pine whose broad shade inspired such trust seems to live no more,
> for the year's last days are here, and the lower needles fall."[27]

The poem was no masterpiece, but it caught their feelings so well that Genji's tears moistened his sleeves.

Seeing the lake frozen from shore to shore, Genji added,

---

26. To leave the world.
27. The "lower needles" are the members of Genji's father's household, who are dispersing.

> *"That face I once saw, clear in the spotless mirror of this frozen lake,*
> *I shall never see again, and I am filled with sorrow."*

His quite artless words merely gave voice to his heart.

Ōmyōbu offered,

> *"The year soon will end, the spring there among the rocks is caught fast in ice,*
> *and the forms we knew so well vanish from before our eyes."*

Many others put in poems of their own, but one could hardly record them all.

The protocol for Her Majesty's return followed custom; perhaps it was her own state of mind that made the move unusually sad. She felt when she arrived that, far from having come home, she must have set out on a journey, because it came to her that she had hardly been back in all these years.

The New Year had come, but without any festive display. All was quiet. Genji had heart only for solitude at home. When the time came for the appointments list,[28] the horses and carriages that had of course thronged to his gate during his father's reign, and even more so in recent years, were few and far between, and few, too, the sets of bedding put out for his retainers on duty; instead, the sight of no one but trusted household officials, obviously with little urgent to do, reminded Genji unpleasantly that this was what things were to be like henceforth.

In the second month the Mistress of the Wardrobe was named Mistress of Staff,[29] her predecessor having been moved by mourning for His Late Eminence to become a nun. Distinguished of manner and imposing in rank, she among all His Majesty's ladies enjoyed his greatest regard. The Empress Mother, who spent more and more time at home, adopted the Umetsubo as her palace residence, while the new Mistress of Staff occupied the Kokiden. She who had once languished in the gloom of the Tōkaden[30] now lived gaily amid countless gentlewomen, and yet in her heart she grieved, for she could not forget what had begun so unexpectedly. Her secret correspondence with Genji must have continued. He dreaded the consequences if their affair should become known, but that familiar quirk of his probably made him more eager than ever. The Empress Mother, with her sharp temper, had restrained herself while His Late Eminence lived, but now she seemed bent on revenge for every grudge she nursed against him. He met nothing but disappointment, and although this was no surprise, being so strangely at odds with the world robbed him of any wish to appear among people.

His Excellency of the Left was similarly disheartened and made no effort to appear at the palace. The Empress Mother resented it that he had withheld his late daughter from the then–Heir Apparent and reserved her for Genji instead, and she had no use for him. His relations with His Excellency of the Right, too, had always

---

28. *Jimoku*, the list of appointments (generally to regional posts) and promotions announced in the first month. Candidates once flocked to Genji for his favor.

29. Oborozukiyo rose to Naishi no Kami. In principle, the incumbent supervised female palace staff, palace ceremonies, and the transmission of petitions and decrees. In practice, she was a somewhat junior consort.

30. The pavilion north of the Kokiden, hence farther from the Emperor and less advantageous.

been prickly, and whereas fortune had smiled on him in His Late Eminence's reign, times had changed, and it was he of the Right who now lorded it as he pleased. No wonder Genji's former father-in-law felt bitter.

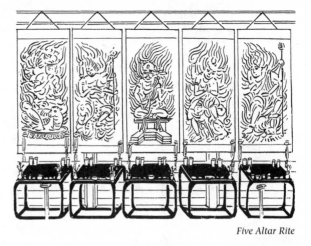

Five Altar Rite

Genji called upon him as always. He was if anything more attentive to the women who had once served him there, and he showed great devotion to his little son; and all this so pleased and surprised the old gentleman that he still did for Genji whatever lay in his power. Once Genji's exalted standing had put far too many demands on his time, but now he lost touch with several ladies he had been visiting, and he also gave up as unbecoming the more lighthearted of his secret adventures, so that for once his leisured life suited him perfectly.

All the world admired the good fortune enjoyed by the lady in Genji's west wing. Privately, Shōnagon attributed it entirely to the prayers of her mistress, the late nun. His Highness corresponded with his daughter as he pleased, no doubt to her stepmother's chagrin, since the daughters this lady had thought destined to rise high had failed instead and were only a disappointment. The happy fate of Genji's darling was just like a fiction in a tale.

Mourning had obliged the High Priestess of the Kamo Shrine to resign, and she was succeeded by the lady of the bluebells. Few precedents authorized an imperial granddaughter to serve as Kamo Priestess, but presumably there was no qualified daughter. Genji had not given her up, despite the passage of time, and he was sorry to see her life take so unusual a course. He was presumably still writing to her, his letters reaching her as before through Chūjō. A change of fortune had failed to impress him, but he now wavered painfully between two capricious affairs that gave him little consolation.

His Majesty thought well of Genji, as his father on his deathbed had enjoined him to do, but his youth made him still too weak and pliable successfully to oppose anything undertaken by the Empress Mother or by His Excellency his grandfather, and the ways of the court therefore seemed greatly to displease him.

Life brought Genji trouble upon trouble, but thanks to his secret understanding with the Mistress of Staff, the two were not wholly parted, despite the risk. Genji saw His Majesty enter seclusion at the start of a Five Altar Rite and immediately met her in what, as always, seemed a dream. Chūnagon managed to lead them undetected into the hall they remembered so well. There were many people about at the time, and they were frightened to be so near the veranda. She cannot have been indifferent to him, for he never wearied even those who saw him day in and day out. She herself was in full womanly bloom, and despite perhaps a certain want of gravity, the delightful youth and grace of her looks made her thoroughly desirable.

It must have been nearly dawn when a man cleared his throat directly beside them and cried, "Present at your service, my lord!" Genji gathered that another Palace Guards officer was concealed nearby and that some wag among his colleagues had sent the fellow to report.[31] He was amused but also upset. They heard the fellow hunting his superior high and low and calling, "Hour of the Tiger, first quarter!"[32]

> *"My own heart alone explains the many reasons why I wet my sleeves,*
> *when cockcrow warns me of dawn and of your drifting away,"*[33]

she said, lovely in her frail distress.

Genji replied,

> *"Do you mean to say I must live my life this way amid endless sighs?*
> *There will never come a dawn when you do not have my heart."*

He hastened away. With everything so beautifully misty under a dawn moon, the very thoroughness of his disguise made him incomparable as he passed—alas, without realizing it—the Fujiwara Lieutenant, the Shōkyōden Consort's elder brother,[34] who had just emerged from the Fujitsubo and was standing by a shutter, a little out of the moonlight. Genji could easily have become a figure of fun.

This sort of thing sometimes led him to admire the one who kept herself at such a distance from him, but as far as his own wishes went, he often was more inclined to hold her discretion against her. She herself now felt too constrained and out of place to go to the palace, and she was upset that she could no longer see the Heir Apparent. Lacking anyone else to trust, she looked only to Genji in all things, and his failure to give up his unfortunate obsession often reduced her to despair. Meanwhile the mere idea that His Late Eminence had noticed nothing terrified her, and in fear that some hint of the truth might spread at any moment, with grave consequences for the Heir Apparent (since she hardly cared what it might mean for herself), she commissioned prayers and used every device to stay out of Genji's way, in the hope that he would give up. In time, though, to her horror, he found his way to her after all, after plotting so deep a stratagem that nobody knew. It was like a dream.

---

31. During the first half of the night the Left Palace Guards were on duty, to be followed in the second half by those of the Right. This guardsman, jokingly sent to report to his superior officer (apparently occupied like Genji), would have announced his name as well. Genji, who commands the Right Palace Guards, knows him and for a moment fears that the man has been sent to *him*.

32. Roughly 3:00 A.M.

33. Her poem, like Genji's reply, plays on *aku*, "[day] dawns" and "be weary of."

34. The identities of this Consort and her brother are unclear. However, she may conceivably be the mother of the Emperor who marries Genji's daughter, and he may be Higekuro.

He talked for so long that no one could ever repeat all he said, but she steadfastly withheld any response until sharp chest pains alarmed Ōmyōbu and
Ben, her intimate gentlewomen, into giving her urgent
care. Bitterness and despair so blinded him to all
thought of past or future that he lost his head and
failed to leave even when dawn was upon him.

In the confusion while anxious gentlewomen
clustered around their stricken mistress, a distraught
Genji found himself thrust hastily into the retreat.[35]
Frantic women rushed to get his clothes out of sight.
Her Majesty was faint with anguish and in fact quite ill.

Screen

His Highness of War and her Commissioner of the Household arrived, and Genji
was aghast to hear them calling loudly for a priest. Not until the day was almost over
did she revive. She had no idea that Genji was still shut up nearby, and her women
were too afraid of upsetting her again to tell her.

She had moved to her day sitting room. His Highness had gone, believing her
now to be well, and she was nearly alone. Most of her women were discreetly out of
sight behind curtains and screens, for she usually kept only a few beside her.

"How can we get his lordship away from here?" Ōmyōbu and Ben whispered
to each other. "It would be too awful if my lady were to feel faint again tonight."

Meanwhile, Genji silently opened the door of the retreat, which was already
slightly ajar, and came in upon Her Majesty through the gap between two screens.
The joy of so rare a sight started tears from his eyes.[36] She was gazing outside,
thinking how unwell she still felt and how little time she might yet have to live, offering him as she did so a profile of inexpressible beauty. Fruit lay beside her in case
she should wish to eat. The way it was arranged in a box lid[37] made it look tempting
enough, but she had never even glanced at it. Absorbed as she was in anxiety over
the course her life was taking, she struck him as touchingly frail. Her hairline, the
shape of her head, the sweep of her hair—all in their lovely way recalled precisely
the lady in his own west wing.

After so many years he had begun to forget how extraordinarily the two resembled each other, and this fresh reminder helped to console him. In noble dignity, too, they were indistinguishable, but perhaps because he had loved the one
before him so deeply and so long, he saw her now matured to the greater perfection, and the conviction that she really was peerless troubled him until he stole in
beneath her curtains and rustled his robe. It was he, his fragrance told her so. In
fright and surprise she sank facedown to the floor. "At least look at me, won't you?"
he cried, thwarted and angry, and drew her to him. She slipped off her dress robe to

35. *Nurigome*, a completely walled room, continuous with the chamber, with hinged, double doors. It
could serve as a sleeping room or for storage.
36. He has probably not seen her in daylight since before coming of age.
37. Fruit and nuts were often served in a writing box lid.

escape, only to discover with horror that he had accidentally caught her hair as well, and with a sinking heart she knew the force of her fate.

The self-control that Genji had so fought to maintain now broke down. Lost to reason, he poured forth a thousand miseries and complaints, in a flood of tears, but she was repelled and did not even deign to reply. "I am not feeling at all well, and I prefer to answer you at another time," she said, but he pressed on with his endless recital of woe. Some of his words undoubtedly struck home. Not that all this had not happened before, but she so shrank from having it repeated that despite her tender feelings for him she managed to talk him past anything worse, until dawn broke at last.

Genji was ashamed to have willfully disobeyed her and sufficiently daunted by her dignity to seek to placate her. "I would do nothing I might regret," he pleaded, "if only I could sometimes tell you like this all I suffer." Love like theirs must be fraught with pain, and their feelings were beyond any comparison.

Both gentlewomen desperately urged him to go now that it was light. In dismay at seeing her half expiring, he said, "I would gladly die of shame to have you hear I am still alive, if it were not that this sin of mine will last beyond this life." He spoke from a disturbing reverie.

"If there is no end, today and forevermore, to what severs us,
    I wonder how many lives I shall spend in misery,"

he went on, "and my clinging will shackle you as well."

She answered with a sigh,

"Leave me, if you will, burdened with your bitterness through all lives to come,
    but know your real enemy is your heart, and yours alone."

The simplicity of her words was beyond all praise, but respect for her feelings and fear for his own situation now led him, dazed, to take his leave.

How could he have the face ever to appear before her again? To let her know how sorry he was, he did not even send her a letter. Calling on neither His Majesty nor the Heir Apparent, he shut himself up at home, where the thought of her cruelty kept him prisoner to the sad torments of longing until he fell ill, for the spirit was indeed gone from his body. He asked himself in misery why in life woe should only pile upon woe, and he resolved to accept these trials no more—only to remember how dear his own young lady was, how sweetly she depended upon him, and how impossible she would be for him to leave.

The aftermath still left Her Majesty unwell. She gathered from the grieving Ōmyōbu that Genji had shut himself up at home and had sent no note. For the Heir Apparent's sake she feared that he might now have turned alarmingly against her, and that if he had had enough of worldly life, he might even act to renounce it. She at last decided that unless this sort of thing ceased, her name would soon be bandied about to her dishonor in a world that in any case brought her nothing but misery, and she preferred to give up a title that the Empress Mother (so she was told) felt should never have been hers in the first place. The memory of His Late Eminence's exceptional regard brought home to her how profoundly all things had changed. She might be spared the fate of Lady Seki,[38] but she was nonetheless sure to suffer widespread ridicule.

These bitter musings on the hatefulness of worldly life decided her to reject it, but it so pained her to go through this change without seeing the Heir Apparent that she first went quietly to the palace. Genji always waited thoughtfully on her on the least occasion, but this time he pleaded indisposition to absent himself from her cortège. He saw to her needs as correctly as ever,[39] but those who understood felt very sorry for him.

The Heir Apparent had grown into a beautiful little boy, and the joy of seeing his mother again made him very affectionate, but although love for him shook her resolve, she perceived well enough that shifting fortunes had taken their toll and that little now remained of the court she had once known. The constant threat of displeasing the Empress Mother made it perilous even to visit the palace this way, and there were indeed moments sufficiently awkward that fear for her son came to trouble her deeply.[40]

"How would you feel, Your Highness, if you did not see me for a long time, and then afterward I looked different and not very nice?"[41]

He studied her face. "Like Shikibu?[42] But how could you look like that?" he answered, smiling.

Alas, he was too young to understand. "Shikibu is ugly because she is old." She was weeping. "No, no, the thing is that I am going to cut my hair even shorter than hers and wear a gray robe like the priests on night watch,[43] and I shall not be able to see you nearly as often as I do now."

"But I shall miss you if you are gone that long!" His tears caused him to turn bashfully away from her with a sweep of his lovely hair. The older he grew, the kinder his eyes became, as though Genji's face had slipped over his own. Mild decay affected his teeth, darkening the inside of his mouth and giving him a smile so winsome that she would gladly have seen such beauty in a girl.[44] This distressing resemblance to his father, which was his single flaw, put her in fear of the world and its censorious gaze.

Genji missed him badly, but the wish to make his mother regret her cruelty led him to restrain himself, until concern that such idleness ill became him prompted him to set out on a trip through the autumn fields and, by the way, to visit Urin'in.[45] He spent two or three days in the hall of a certain Master of Disci-

38. Lady Qi (Japanese Seki) was loved by the Han dynastic founder, Emperor Gaozu. She and her son were killed by Gaozu's jealous Empress after his death.

39. By sending retainers and members of his household to help Fujitsubo.

40. In the palace she is treated with disdain, and she fears plots to depose her son. An early commentary cites the Han dynasty story of an Empress who poisoned the Heir Apparent while the Emperor was out hunting.

41. In a nun's short hair and sober habit.

42. Presumably an aged gentlewoman.

43. *Yoi no sō:* priests who performed rites during the night for the Emperor's health.

44. His mouth looks as though his teeth have been blackened like a girl's.

45. A temple north of the City. Originally an imperial villa, it was favored by devout residents of the City.

pline,[46] his maternal uncle, reading the scriptures and performing rites of devotion, and while he was there he often felt very moved. All the leaves had turned by now, and he nearly forgot the City before the beauty of the autumn fields.

He summoned the most gifted of the temple monks and set them to debating before him.[47] In such a place he spent the night absorbed in the vanity of all things, but toward dawn he again remembered her who to him meant suffering. Meanwhile the monks clattered about offering holy water beneath a lingering moon, scattering chrysanthemums and red leaves dull or bright—modest occupations, no doubt, but, he felt, sufficient to relieve the tedium of this life and of course to assure a happy prospect for the life to come. He kept thinking how dismally he was squandering his own existence. "All who call his Name, he will gather to himself, nor once cast them aside,"[48] his host slowly chanted in lofty tones while Genji asked himself in intense envy, Why not make this life my own?—only to be most ignominiously caught up in troubled thoughts of his darling at home.

He was rarely away from her for so many days, and he was worried enough to send her a flurry of letters. "I thought I might see whether I really could give it all up," he wrote, for example, "but time drags by all too slowly, and I am gloomier than ever. I still have more questions, and I am uncertain what to do. What about you?"

Even this from him, casually set down on Michinokuni paper,[49] was a pleasure to look at.

> "Having left you there, frailly lodged as a dewdrop trembling on a leaf,
>   I am prey to many fears whenever the four winds blow,"

he had added with deep feeling, and his reader wept. On thin white paper she replied,

> "Ah, when the winds blow, how the spider's thread that hangs on that fading leaf
>   quickly tangles, and my heart trembles lest it be betrayed!"[50]

That was all.

Her writing is prettier all the time, he said to himself, smiling with pleasure at how lovely she was. They corresponded so often that her writing looked very like his, though with an added touch of feminine grace. I seem to have brought her up quite nicely in every way.

He wrote also to the Kamo Priestess, since the breeze had so short a way to blow between them.[51] "Your mistress will never know how I have longed for her be-

---

46. *Risshi*, the first rung on the ladder of ranks held by the highest class of Buddhist priests. The title means "Master of the Vinaya," the body of monastic discipline.
47. Formal debates were common in monastic life.
48. A passage in Chinese from the Kanmuryōju-kyō (Sutra on the Contemplation of Eternal Life), referring to Amida's vow to save all who call his Name.
49. A thick white paper of fiber from spindle-tree (*mayumi*) bark. Genji probably found this rustic paper more in keeping with his setting than the thinner, colored *torinoko* paper commonly used for such letters.
50. "I who have only you, with all your shifting moods and loves, cannot feel secure."
51. Asagao. The wind figuratively carries messages, and Urin'in was near Kamo.

neath these unfamiliar skies," he observed rather bitterly to Chūjō;[52] and to the Priestess herself:

> *"Far be it from me to offend the mighty gods, but your raiment now*
> *cannot help reminding me of that autumn long ago.*[53]

All I want to do, and foolishly, I know, is 'to turn the past to now';[54] yet I feel as though it should be possible . . ." He had written his letter, so familiar in tone, on green Chinese paper and attached it solemnly to a *sakaki* branch.

Chūjō replied, "Having so little to do I let my mind dwell on memories, and then, my lord, my thoughts often turn to you; but it really is no use." Her letter was long and thoughtful.

The Priestess had written along the edge of a sacred streamer,

> *"Long ago, you say—what is it that happened then, that my raiment now*
> *should arouse such memories and once more detain your heart?*

More recently . . ." Her writing, which had no great character, nevertheless showed practiced skill, and her cursive letters[55] were nicely done. He was sacrilegiously stirred to imagine the bluebell now more richly beautiful than ever.[56]

The season, he remembered, was just the same as that sad time at the Shrine on the Moor, and in his deplorable way he reproached the gods for the strange coincidence. It was odd of him to have these regrets now, considering the years he had allowed to go by while he could have won her if he had really wished to. She herself recognized his special interest in her and seems in her sporadic replies to have made little effort to discourage him, which was not entirely admirable of her.

All the monks of the mountain temple, down to the least of them, were pleased, because Genji's stay while he read the Sixty Scrolls[57] and sought help with perplexing passages seemed a bright reward for their prayers and a signal honor for their buddha.[58] Quiet reflection on the world and its ways should have discouraged him from turning home again, but the thought of one lady bound him, and he did not linger. Before leaving he generously commissioned scripture readings at the temple, bestowed gifts on all who deserved them—monks high and low and local mountain folk—and exhausted the sum of holy works. Ragged woodcutters gathered here and there, weeping, to see him on his way. Within his black-draped carriage he wore mourning,[59] so that one saw little of him, but the least glimpse showed that there was no one like him in the world.

---

52. The gentlewoman through whom Genji corresponds with Asagao.
53. Genji seems to refer to a moment between himself and Asagao that the reader does not otherwise know about. "Raiment" conveys *yūdasuki*: cords of mulberry-bark fiber with which those in shrine service tied back their sleeves so as to busy themselves with the rites.
54. *Ise monogatari* 65, which expresses the wish to "spin" (as one spins thread) the past into the present.
55. *Sō*, cursive Chinese characters used for phonetic value in the *man'yōgana* writing style.
56. "Bluebell" (*asagao*) refers to the flowers that he once sent her and suggests, in context, that he then saw her plainly, hence that they were lovers.
57. The canon of doctrinal writings favored by the Tendai school of Buddhism.
58. The main image of Urin'in.
59. For his father.

His darling seemed to have grown still more beautiful during his absence, and on finding her so subdued and apprehensive about the state of his affections (for the undignified confusion of his feelings had no doubt been obvious to her), he was touched by her "fading leaf" poem and gave her more than his usual attention.

The autumn leaves he had sent her from the mountains were brighter in color than those from his own garden, and since he could not ignore the message of the dews that had stained them,[60] and deplored in any case his own prolonged silence, he sent some to Her Majesty, ostensibly as a gesture of civility.

To Ōmyōbu he wrote, "I have been surprised to learn that Her Majesty is at the palace, but while I would not have her neglect the Heir Apparent, I have preferred not to cut short the days I had set aside for practice and prayer, and that is why you have had nothing from me for so long. Viewing autumn leaves alone reminds me of admiring brocade in the dark.[61] Please show Her Majesty these when you find the moment to do so."

They were indeed fine branches, and while examining them Her Majesty noticed the usual tiny note. She paled, because her gentlewomen were watching, and she thought how hateful he was still to be pursuing her this way; surely they would wonder why so thoroughly tactful a man should suddenly take to doing this sort of thing. She was sufficiently annoyed to have the branches put in a vase and placed beside an outer pillar, and she gave him no more than a correct reply, confining herself to generalities and expressing her confidence in all that he had to say about the Heir Apparent. Her message conveyed her unrelenting vigilance, and he read it with bitter disappointment, but since he had always done so much for her, he feared to arouse suspicion now, and he went to the palace on the day when she was to withdraw.

He called first on His Majesty, who was enjoying an idle moment, and they talked over old times. His Majesty looked very like their father, although he had an even sweeter grace, and his face was gentle and kind. They were extremely glad to see each other. His Majesty had heard of Genji's relations with his Mistress of Staff, and he had noted signs of it himself, but he felt that the affair was after all not new and that since it had lasted so long already, they might as well continue to indulge their feeling for one another. He spoke never a word of reproach. After he had questioned Genji on a wide range of subjects, including passages of the classics that eluded him, the two began explaining to each other their love poems,[62] and His Majesty took this opportunity to observe how beautiful the High Priestess had been on the day when she set out for Ise. Genji then confided to him the story of that extraordinary dawn at the Shrine on the Moor.

The moon of the twentieth night rose at last,[63] inspiring His Majesty to observe that the moment called for music. Genji answered that he preferred to go and assist Her Majesty, who was, he gathered, to leave that evening. "His Late Eminence

---

60. Autumn leaves are reddened by cold dews and rains (tears), so that especially bright leaves evoke intense, unhappy love. Genji thinks of Fujitsubo.

61. *Kokinshū* 297, by Ki no Tsurayuki: "Autumn leaves that fall in the mountains, with no one to see them, are like brocade in the dark of night."

62. That is, talking about their love affairs.

63. On this night in the ninth lunar month the moon rises at about 10:00 P.M.

charged me with looking after her, you see, and since she appears to have no other support, her welfare concerns me for the sake of the Heir Apparent."

"His Late Eminence urged me to accept him as my own son," His Majesty said, "and I try to keep an eye on him, but I do not see what more I can do. His handwriting and so on seem accomplished beyond his years; in fact, it is he who is a credit to me, for I do nothing well."

"On the whole he is very clever and behaves in a grown-up manner, but he still has far to go." Genji gave him an account of the young Prince.

As he withdrew, a certain Secretary Controller, the son of the Fujiwara Grand Counselor, the Empress Mother's elder brother, met the advance members of his escort, who were discreetly clearing his path. The Controller, a brilliant young man in high favor, was on his way to his sister's in the Reikeiden.[64] He stopped for a moment and solemnly intoned, "A white rainbow curved across the sun; the Heir Apparent trembled."[65]

The shocked Genji could not very well reprove him. He often heard about the Empress Mother's alarming hostility, and he pretended to notice nothing, despite irritation that a close relative of hers should have such gall. He apologized to Her Majesty for the lateness of the hour, having been in waiting on the Emperor until just a moment ago.

There was a brilliant moon, and Her Majesty remembered how at such times His Late Eminence had called for music and shown a lively feeling for beauty. She grieved to see how much had changed, even if the palace remained the same. Through Ōmyōbu she sent her visitor,

> "Perhaps ninefold mists cut me off from all the world, for my longing goes
> to the moon so far away, riding high above the clouds."[66]

She was near enough that a glimpse of her, however faint, called up Genji's old feeling for her, and he wept, forgetting all the hurt that he had suffered.

> "The bright moon still shines as in autumns we once knew, all those years ago,
> but the mists that hide its light are a cruel trial to bear,"

he replied. " 'The mists, like the heart,' they say[67]—it must have been the same long ago." Her Majesty did not wish to leave the Heir Apparent, and she gave him

64. An imperial consort, a niece of Kokiden and Oborozukiyo, and a granddaughter of the Minister of the Right.

65. This *Shiji* passage insinuates that Genji, the Heir Apparent's protector, is plotting rebellion but will fail. A certain loyal subject plotted to assassinate the First Emperor of Qin on behalf of the Crown Prince of Yen, but Heaven revealed his plan by displaying a white rainbow that crossed the sun. (The sun stands for the Emperor, the white rainbow for weapons or warriors.) The Prince of Yen then feared that the plot would fail, as it did.

66. "Ninefold mists" are those of ill will who come between the speaker and the Emperor (the moon).

67. In an otherwise unknown poem cited by an early commentary (*Genji monogatari kochūshakusho in'yō waka* 464), the speaker compares the mists that hide a distant cherry tree to the cruel heart of one who keeps lover from beloved.

lengthy advice about what to do and what not, but she was disappointed to find that he did not take it all in very well. Usually he retired early, but he seemed to want to stay up until she left. She was especially touched to see that he refrained from begging her to stay, despite being indignant that she meant to go away again.

Genji reflected on the Controller's pointed allusion and was moved by the prick of conscience to feel the world's censure keenly. For a long time he did not correspond with the Mistress of Staff. The skies were promising the first early-winter rains when it was she who sent him word, for reasons of her own.

> "While autumn wore on, bitter winds set in to blow, and I languished still,
> your silence, and nothing else, pervaded day after day,"

she had written. He was not displeased that she should feel deeply enough in this saddest of seasons to contrive a secret note, so he had the messenger wait, opened the cabinet where he kept his Chinese paper, chose a particularly fine sheet, and prepared his brush with great care. The gentlewomen present nudged each other and wondered who the lady could be, for his every gesture was a lover's.

"I gave up once I understood that no correspondence with you could lead further," he wrote. "And while I suffered on,[68]

> Are my tears to you, wept in longing memory while we do not meet,
> no more than the common rain shed by early-winter skies?

If only we were really in touch, how easily we might forget this dreary rain!" It had become quite a passionate letter. A good many ladies must have claimed his attention this way, and he made sure that his replies were not discouraging, although he felt deep attachment for none.

Her Majesty was variously occupied with preparations for her Rite of the Eight Discourses,[69] which was to follow the anniversary observances for His Late Eminence. A heavy snow fell on the anniversary day, early in the eleventh month. From Genji she had this:

> "That unhappy day when he was taken from us has come round once more,
> but when shall we see again the man we once knew so well?"

Today was so sad for her, too, that he had a reply:

> "Living on this way is a burden while it lasts, but to meet again
> this day among all others makes him seem present once more."

She had made no effort to dress up her writing, but to him it certainly conveyed supreme distinction. Although not strikingly unusual or fashionable, it resembled

---

68. *Gosenshū* 1260: "While I who hardly count only suffer on, it has been so long that even I am missed."
69. Mi-hakō, a four-day rite celebrating the Lotus Sutra. Each day a formal debate, held in morning and afternoon sessions, developed the content of two of the sutra's eight scrolls.

no one else's. He quelled his thoughts of her today and gave himself up to offices of prayer, wet with drops from the evocative snow.

The Eight Discourses were held a little past the tenth of the twelfth month. It was an imposing event. By Her Majesty's order the scripture scrolls dedicated each day, with their jade rollers, their silk gauze covers, and their beautifully decorated wrapping, were more splendid than any ever seen before. Since even as a matter of common practice she made it a point to do things exceptionally well, her arrangements this time were obviously a marvel. The altar furnishings and the

Nun's short hair

very cloths on the altar tables brought to mind thoughts of paradise.

The first day was dedicated to the former Emperor, the donor's father, the second to the Empress her mother, and the third to His Late Eminence. On the day for the Fifth Scroll[70] the senior nobles overcame their fear of giving offense[71] and attended the rite in great numbers. Her Majesty had chosen the day's Lecturer so well that the familiar passages, beginning with the one about gathering firewood and so on, were profoundly inspiring.[72] The Princes in the procession bore offerings of many kinds,[73] but those prepared by Genji far surpassed the others. Perhaps I seem only to repeat the same praises about him, but I cannot help it, because he was a wonder to behold whenever one had the good fortune to do so.

Her Majesty reserved the last day's merit for herself, and everyone was astonished when she had it announced to the Buddha that she would renounce the world. His Highness of War and Genji were both aghast. His Highness went in to her halfway through. After insisting that her mind was made up, she summoned the Abbot of the Mountain, and when the rite was over, she had him informed that she wished to receive the appropriate Precepts.

A commotion spread when the Abbot, her uncle, approached and cut off her hair,[74] and her residence filled with loud weeping. It is strangely moving whenever anyone, however insignificant and however obviously old, takes the great step of leaving the world, and that so great a lady should do so without having ever hinted at her plan gave her brother still more reason for ceaseless tears. Those present had found the rite itself sufficiently stirring, and they all left with wet sleeves.

His Late Eminence's sons felt even sorrier for her when they recalled her bet-

---

70. A key scroll, expounded during the morning session on the third day.

71. Offense to the Kokiden Consort and to the Minister of the Right.

72. The Lecturer (Kōji) was central to each day's debate. The sutra's "Devadatta" chapter describes how the Buddha served his teacher by picking fruit, drawing water, and gathering firewood, until he received the Lotus Sutra teaching.

73. The assembly probably moved in procession around the garden lake (assimilating it to the lake in paradise) while bearing bundles of firewood, buckets of water, and offerings attached to artificial gold or silver branches.

74. To just past shoulder length.

ter days, and each gave her a message of sympathy. Genji stayed behind, at a loss for what to say and in a state of dark confusion, but he went to her after the Princes had left, since people were sure to wonder otherwise what had come over him.

The household was quiet at last, and the women were clustered here and there, sniffling and blowing their noses. Brilliant moonlight on the snowy garden brought back unbearably scenes from days gone by, but he mastered himself sufficiently to ask, "What was it that decided you and made you so suddenly . . . ?"

She replied through Ōmyōbu, as always, "There was nothing abrupt about my decision, but I knew that it would cause a stir, and I was afraid I might falter."

Genji divined her presence behind the blinds, caught a rustling of silks from the women waiting on her as they moved quietly about, and was touched, although not surprised, to gather from certain other sounds that their grief had not yet abated. Outside, the wild wind blew, but within her blinds the air was fragrant with her intense, "deep black" scent[75] and with a trace of her altar incense. Genji's own fragrance mingled so beautifully with both that one could think only of paradise.

A messenger came from the Heir Apparent. The memory of talking with her son so shook her fortitude that she could not answer, and it was Genji who provided her reply.

The household was too agitated for him to be able to tell her all he wished.

> *"Though I, too, aspire to give my heart to those skies where a clear moon shines,*
> *I should only wander still in the darkness of this world,"*[76]

he said; "I so wish it were possible, but alas . . . I envy you your decision!" That was the best he could do, while she, with her women nearby, could convey nothing to him of her own suffering.

Her heart was very full.

> *"What I have renounced covers the common troubles that beset us all,*
> *but, ah, when will even I truly give up all the world?*

Its worries are still mine," she answered, some of what she said having no doubt been tidied up by her messenger. Genji withdrew sick at heart, in thrall to boundless sorrow.

At home again he lay down alone in his own room, but his eyes would not close, and each time disgust with the world invaded him, he was assailed by anxiety for the Heir Apparent. It had been his father's wish to have the young Prince's mother, at least, uphold her son's dignity before all, but now that her unhappiness had led her so far, she could never reclaim her former rank; and what if he, too, were to abandon him? So ran the thoughts that kept him wakeful hour after hour.

He wanted her to have the furnishings for her new life from him, and he

---

75. *Kurobō,* a blend of six incenses used to scent clothing, especially in winter.
76. Both Genji and Fujitsubo (below) allude by a discreet wordplay to their child, the Heir Apparent.

Privy banquet

therefore hastened to have them ready before the end of the year. His generosity included Ōmyōbu as well, since she had taken vows with her mistress. A full account of all this seems not to have reached me; there would have been just too much to tell. That is a shame, though, because this is just the sort of occasion that may yield fine poetry.

Genji could now call on Her Cloistered Eminence more openly than before, and at times he even spoke to her in person. Not that that secret yearning had left him, but what he desired was even less possible now.

The New Year had come, and with it new life to the court, but news of the privy banquet and the mumming only confirmed Fujitsubo in her present solitude, and while she went quietly about her litanies and prayers, keeping her thoughts on the life to come, she felt as though she was putting behind her at last all that had so troubled her before. Apart from the chapel that had always been hers she had built another specially, south of her west wing, and she now moved to this rather isolated retreat in order to pursue her intent devotions.

It was there that Genji visited her. The breath of the New Year had not touched her silent, all but deserted dwelling, where one now encountered no more than a few faithful members of the Empress's household,[77] their heads bowed and to all appearances sadly downcast. Only the Blue Roans came round as usual,[78] and her women went to see them. No wonder the senior nobles, who once had flocked to her, now took another path to gather at the residence across the avenue.[79] This did

77. *Miyazukasa:* members of the Empress's household staff (*chūgū shiki*) with a personal tie to Fujitsubo or her family.

78. On the seventh of the first month, twenty-one horses, the sight of which was held to ward off misfortune, were led before the Emperor, then before the Retired Emperor, the senior imperial ladies, and the Heir Apparent. The custom was originally Chinese. They were blue roans up to Murakami's reign (946–67), which corresponds to the present in the tale, but after that they were white. This was the only New Year observance retained when an Emperor was in mourning, which is probably why the horses went to Fujitsubo's residence, too, even though she was now a nun.

79. That of the Minister of the Right, across Nijō (Second Avenue).

not surprise her, but it was very sad, and the vision of Genji, who had come all the way to find her—a sight splendid enough to be worth a thousand callers—somehow brought tears to many an eye.

Her visitor himself seemed deeply affected, and after glancing about he sank into silence. In this new life of hers the borders of her blinds and the standing curtains around her were blue-gray, and through the gaps between them he glimpsed sleeves of gray or yellow:[80] a prospect that for him evoked only greater depths of grace and beauty. "Indeed, a most discerning . . . ," he murmured,[81] pensively noting how the outdoor scene alone—the thin ice now gone from the lake, the willows on the bank—kept faith with the seasons. He looked incomparably elegant as he did so.

> *"Now that I perceive a nun lives here, gathering sea-tangle sorrows,*
> *briny drops spill from my eyes upon this, the Isle of Pines,"*[82]

he said; and since her rather small room was given over to the altar, her low answer sounded quite near:

> *"Of the world I knew there remains no trace at all on this Isle of Pines,*
> *and it is a miracle any wave should come to call."*[83]

He could not stop his tears, and he said little else before he left, for the gaze of nuns who had renounced worldly ways embarrassed him.

"What an absolute marvel he has turned out to be!" the old nuns cried to their mistress in tearful praise. "When all the world was his and he had not a care in it, one wondered how anyone that fortunate could know much of life; but he is very thoughtful now, and almost anything makes him look so sad that one's heart goes out to him." Memories flooded through their mistress, too.

Her Eminence's retainers failed to receive their due when the appointments list was announced, and to the bitter disappointment of many, promotions that should have come to them as a matter of course or as their patron's normal prerogative[84] were withheld. There was no reason why in her new condition she should lose her former dignity or be deprived of her established emoluments,[85] but that condition was nonetheless the pretext for the many changes that now came upon her.

---

80. Blue-gray (*aonibi*) was normal for a nun; other possibilities were gray (*usunibi*) or yellow (*kuchinashi*), worn here by gentlewomen who had taken vows with their mistress.

81. "Indeed, she shows the same discerning taste as that imperial nun of old." *Gosenshū* 1093, by Sosei: "Today I see with my own eyes the celebrated Isle of Pines and, indeed, find dwelling here a most discerning *ama*." *Ama* in this poem and the next means both "shore-dweller" and "nun." The Isle of Pines (Matsu no Urashima) was in Shiogama Bay in northern Honshu. Sosei wrote his poem on pine bark from the artificial island in the garden lake of an Empress who had just become a nun.

82. "Sea-tangle sorrows" are *nagame*, "sorrow" and also a kind of seaweed.

83. The "wave" is her visitor, Genji.

84. A prerogative involving benefices that accrued to persons of Fujitsubo's standing through provincial sinecures awarded to their retainers.

85. An Empress normally enjoyed production and labor imposts from fifteen hundred households.

Despite having given up just such concerns, she was often pained to see her retainers in distress, as though cast adrift, but her one heartfelt wish was to have the Heir Apparent's accession proceed smoothly, even at the cost of her own ruin, and to this end she dedicated her unflagging devotions. Having a secret reason to dread the worst, she calmed her fears by begging the Buddha to lift her burden of sin from her and grant her forgiveness. Genji saw her feelings and understood them well. His own people often encountered similar disappointments, and he therefore shut himself up at home in disgust with the world.

His Excellency of the Left was sufficiently upset by the change that now pervaded his own world, public or private, to tender his resignation, but His Majesty remembered how greatly His Late Eminence had trusted this adviser, and how at the last he had commended him to his successor as an enduring pillar of the realm, and accordingly he considered him too valuable to release. Although he repeatedly declined to accept the resignation, His Excellency stubbornly resubmitted it again and again, until at last he was able to withdraw to his residence. Now that single faction flourished as never before. His Majesty was left forlorn once the Minister whose weight steadied the realm had removed himself from its affairs, and the wise everywhere groaned.

All His Excellency's sons had enjoyed the world's esteem and lived free of care, but now they were brought low, and the future promised the Captain[86] only gloom. Now and again he still visited the Minister of the Right's fourth daughter, but his poor treatment of her led her father to exclude him from among his favored sons-in-law. His omission from the recent promotions list, perhaps in warning, did not upset him unduly. With Genji himself idle and life so obviously treacherous in any case, his situation hardly surprised him; and in this spirit he visited Genji often, sharing with him both study and the pleasures of music.

Remembering how madly he had once set himself to challenge Genji, he now vied again with his friend in all things, however small. Genji commissioned the most imposing rites for the spring and autumn scripture readings, of course, but also for lesser, irregular occasions of a similar kind,[87] and he convened those Doctors who seemed otherwise to be idle, so as to pass the time composing Chinese poems, guessing rhymes, and so on.[88] In short, he took his ease, and instead of presenting himself for service at court, he amused himself exactly as he pleased, so much so that some must have begun talking very unpleasantly about him.

One lazy day of quiet summer rain, the Captain turned up with a bearer carrying a suitable choice of poetry collections. Genji, too, had his library opened. After ordering a few rare and curious old volumes from cases never examined before, he discreetly called together those whose interests inclined them that way. The many present from the Academy and from among the privy gentlemen were divided at

---

86. Tō no Chūjō.

87. In the palace and the great houses, solemn readings of the Daihannya-kyō were a regular spring and autumn event, but Genji seems to have added other, similar events of his own.

88. "Doctors" are the scholars of the Academy for young men of the aristocracy. "Guessing rhymes" (*in futagi*) involved guessing the rhyme words in a Chinese poem unknown to the contestant.

Playing the shō

Genji's order into a company of the Left and one of the Right.[89] The superb prizes on offer aroused intense competition. Difficult rhymes predominated as the guessing went on, and Genji's way now and again of proposing the right one when even renowned scholars were stumped made his exceptional learning plain. "How is it possible that he should have every talent?" everyone murmured in praise. "It must simply have been his destiny to be far better at everything than anyone else!" In the end the Right lost.

Two days later the Captain gave the loser's banquet. It was modest enough, but the cypress boxes were handsome and the prizes varied, and he invited the same gathering as before to compose Chinese verses and so on. The roses below the steps were then just coming into bloom,[90] and in so mild a season, more peaceful than those of the spring and autumn flowers, all joined happily in music making.

One of the Captain's sons, a boy of eight or nine who had only this year begun to frequent the privy chamber, sang and played the *shō* prettily enough to attract Genji's delighted attention. He was the second son born to the Minister of the Right's fourth daughter. All the world had high hopes for him and treated him fondly, since he had his wits about him and was also pleasing in looks. When the music picked up a little, he gave full voice to a very fine rendition of "Takasago."[91] Genji took a layer from his costume and placed the garment over the boy's shoulders.[92] His face, flushed with unaccustomed excitement, gave forth a beauty beyond any in the world, and his skin glowed wondrously through the silk gauze dress cloak and shift, until the ancient scholars watching him from their distance wept.

"How I long for you, my lily flower!" the boy's song ended, and the Captain gave Genji a cup of wine.

"All have longed to see those first blossoms this morning burst into full bloom,
　　yet I contemplate in you beauty just as great as theirs!"[93]

he said.

---

89. The procedure for contests of all kinds (poetry, paintings, incense, and so on).

90. This phrase recalls two poems by Bai Juyi (*Hakushi monjū* 0850, 1055) and evokes the mood of Chinese poetry. The steps led down to the garden from the main building of the Minister of the Left's residence.

91. A *saibara* folk song in which a lover addresses a passionate appeal to his beloved.

92. A gesture of special appreciation. Genji has given the boy a gown, worn under the dress cloak.

93. Tō no Chūjō's poem quotes the song that his son has sung and even alludes to the roses described as "then just coming into bloom."

Genji took it, smiling.

"Those flowers in bloom this morning out of season, in the summer rain
seem to have drooped and wilted before their beauty could show.

I am not what I used to be, you know," he bantered, resolutely taking this tribute for tipsy civility, but the Captain only reproved him and urged more wine upon him. As Tsurayuki warns,[94] there is no point in recording all the faulty poems spoken at such times, and I have therefore obediently and conveniently left them out.

In both Chinese and Japanese verse the guests pursued no theme but Genji's praise, and Genji, swept up in visions of his own glory, went so far as to declaim on his own behalf the line "The son of King Bun I am, King Bu's younger brother." It was a great moment, but what might he have said about King Sei? Perhaps that still gave him pause.[95]

His Highness of War, too, often called on Genji, and he played so beautifully that he made Genji a perfect partner in music.

The Mistress of Staff now withdrew from court. Having long suffered from a recurrent fever, she wanted the freedom to commission healing rites. Her whole family rejoiced to find her better once the rites had begun, and meanwhile, in concert with Genji, she managed by hook or crook to receive him every night.

A stylishly engaging young woman in full flower, she was slimmer now because of her slight illness, and extremely attractive. Genji feared discovery because the Empress Mother was then at home as well, but as usual, danger only spurred him to pursue his visits in deep secrecy. Some gentlewomen must have noticed these goings-on, but they neglected to inform the Empress Mother lest they cause trouble.

His Excellency of course knew nothing about all this when one night, just before dawn, rain suddenly came pelting down and thunder roared, alarming his sons and the Empress Mother's staff. People were everywhere, the gentlewomen gathered nearby in terror, and the desperate Genji found no escape before daylight was upon him. There were enough women even around their mistress's curtained bed to set his heart pounding. The two who knew were frantic.

When the thunder stopped and the rain let up, His Excellency went first to call on the Empress Mother. Then, while a sudden shower drowned out the sound of his arrival, he stepped abruptly up to his younger daughter's room and lifted the blinds.[96]

"Are you all right? It was an awful night, and I kept thinking of you—I should

94. No such injunction survives in the works of the early-tenth-century man of letters Ki no Tsurayuki.
95. The Duke of Zhou declares in the *Shiji*, "The son of King Wen [Japanese, Bun] I am, King Wu's [Japanese, Bu] younger brother, and uncle to King Cheng [Japanese, Sei]. In this realm I am not to be despised." These figures are all sage rulers of Chinese antiquity. King Wen apparently corresponds to the Kiritsubo Emperor, King Wu to his son Suzaku, and the Duke of Zhou to Genji. If so, King Cheng matches the Heir Apparent, who is actually Genji's own son.
96. The Empress Mother is in the main house and Oborozukiyo in the chamber of one of the wings. The Minister comes straight across the aisle room to the blinds hanging between it and the chamber.

really have come round before. Has the Captain or the Empress Mother's Deputy[97] looked in on you?" he rattled on breathlessly, and even in this crisis Genji could only smile at the difference when the image of His Excellency of the Left sprang to mind. At least the man could have saved his remarks until he was all the way into the room!

In panic the Mistress of Staff slipped out through her curtains, blushing so profusely that her father assumed she was still ill.

"What is wrong with you? These spirits are a menace! We should have kept those rites going longer," he went on, until he was surprised to see a violet sash, which had emerged with her, entangled in her skirts. There was also a piece of folding paper with some sort of writing on it lying by her standing curtain. "Whose are these?" he said, startled to contemplate what they suggested. "What are they doing here? Give me that. Here, pick it up, and I'll see whose it is."

Only then did she glance behind her and see the paper, too. What could she answer, when there was no hiding the truth? A man of his standing should have seen her embarrassment and restrained himself in consideration of her acute discomfort, even if she was his own daughter; but no, he was too hotheaded and irascible for that. Paper in hand, he peered past the curtain and saw, sprawled shamelessly within it, a young man who only now stealthily covered his face and moved to hide. For all his shock and outrage he could not very well bluntly require the young man to identify himself. In a blind fury he strode off with the paper toward the main house. The Mistress of Staff, all but fainting, thought she would die. Genji regretted a series of pointless escapades that now was certain to burden him with widespread condemnation, but he did what he could to console her in her all too obvious distress.

Ever a willful man, incapable of discretion, her father had gained nothing from the passing years but the testiness of age, and he was not one to waver now. He laid his whole complaint before the Empress Mother.

"This is what has been going on, you see. The writing on this paper belongs to the Commander of the Right. All this began long ago and without my leave, but I forgave him, considering who he was, and told him I would accept him after all,[98] but he turned up his nose at the proposal and behaved so badly that I was extremely displeased. Still, I dismissed it as fate and offered her to His Majesty after all, trusting him not to consider her tainted. In the end, however, the cloud she is under has kept her from being appointed a Consort, which is a very great shame, and this latest incident disgusts me more thoroughly than ever. This is what men are like, I know, but it just shows how despicable the Commander really is. They say he has the audacity even now to pursue the Kamo Priestess, and that he corresponds secretly with her and encourages certain suspicions, which is so obviously a risk not only for the realm[99] but for himself that no one can believe such lunacy of him; he seems to have the world in awe as though he were the paragon of our time."

---

97. The Captain is one of the Minister's sons; the Deputy (Miya no Suke) is the second-ranking officer in charge of the Empress Mother's personal staff.

98. As a son-in-law.

99. In pursuing Asagao, Genji violated a religious prohibition and so perhaps endangered the realm, for the Kamo Shrine protected the City, and the deity's displeasure might cause disaster.

The Empress Mother was even more vehement on the subject than he. "My son may be the Emperor," she said, "but no one has ever granted him any respect. That Minister of the Left did not offer his precious only daughter to *him*, the elder brother and the Heir Apparent; no, he gave her to the younger, a commoner and a stripling not yet even of age. And when we were so hoping to send our girl into palace service, did anyone object to the ridiculous position this Genji had left her in? It seems everyone admired him so much that she is in service there anyway, even though our first plan for her failed, but I have still felt obliged to ensure that the poor thing could hold up her head properly, if only to show that miserable man who is who; except that now she has taken it on herself to follow her own secret inclination. What they say about the Kamo Priestess is undoubtedly quite true. Yes, there is every reason to fear for His Majesty, considering the way this man counts on the Heir Apparent reigning!"

Her father found this merciless tirade so painful that he wondered why he had brought up the matter at all. "At any rate," he said in an effort to calm the waters, "for the time being I would like knowledge of this to go no further. Do not tell His Majesty. Yes, she is guilty, but I suppose she is counting on his indulgence to escape rejection. Warn her in private, and I shall have to take the blame myself if she will not listen."

The Empress Mother's countenance nevertheless failed to lighten. She could not have Genji pointedly mocking and belittling her by brazenly invading her house while she herself was at home, so nearby, and this gave her a fine reason to set in train the measures to accomplish his downfall.

11

HANACHIRUSATO
Falling Flowers

Hanachirusato means "village where flowers fall." Genji visits a lady there and gives her this poem:

*"Many fond yearnings for an orange tree's sweet scent draw the cuckoo on
to come seeking the village where such fragrant flowers fall."*

"Falling Flowers" takes place late in the period covered by "The Green Branch," in the fifth month of the year after Fujitsubo's entry into religion.

PERSONS

Genji, age 25

Koremitsu, Genji's confidant

A woman, in a house near Nakagawa

The Reikeiden Consort

Her younger sister (Hanachirusato)

Genji's secret consuming sorrow seems always to have been with him, but now that the world itself meant only a gathering host of griefs and disappointments, he rejected it all in despair, even though in fact so much still called to him.

The lady known as Reikeiden[1] had given His Late Eminence no children, and after his death she had sunk into an increasingly straitened existence, from which Genji's thoughtful generosity seemed to provide her only relief. At the palace Genji had briefly known her younger sister, and being who he was, he had not forgotten her, although he had never much cultivated her either; so that now, when troubles beset him on all sides, he remembered what misery her own life must be, and during a rare break in the summer rains he could not resist calling on her.

He set out very modestly, with no escort to clear his path, and as he passed the Nakagawa, he heard from a little house set among handsome trees a full-voiced koto played brightly in the *azuma* mode. The sound pleased him, and since the house was quite close to its gate, he leaned out a little to look. From a great laurel tree the wind brought him a fragrance reminiscent of the Kamo Festival,[2] and with a rush of feeling he recognized in this strangely engaging place one where he had called once before.

He stopped himself, for it had been so long that she might not recognize him, but he was nonetheless reluctant to leave. Just then a passing cuckoo called. This was encouragement enough; he had his carriage turned round and sent in Koremitsu, as always, with,

> "He has come again in thrall to unquenched longing, the cuckoo of yore,
>   to the fence where once he sang a moment of passing song."[3]

The women were on the west side of what Genji took to be the main house.

---

1. She was named after the palace pavilion where she lived, one suitable for a Consort.
2. Participants in the festival wore heart-to-heart (*aoi*) and laurel (*katsura*) leaves in their headdresses; the leaves of both are heart-shaped.
3. *Kataraishi* ("he sang . . .") applies more often to people and means "speak together"; it commonly refers to what lovers do together in private.

Koremitsu, who already knew their voices, cleared his throat in warning and spoke his message. They seemed young, and they must have wondered who had sent it.

> *"Cuckoo, I know well the song that your visit brings, yet that memory*
> *leaves as clouded as before the will of these rainy skies,"*

the lady replied, purposely (in Koremitsu's opinion) feigning uncertainty.

"Very well, then," he said, " 'One mistakes the hedge' ";[4] and off he went again, to the lady's secret pique and disappointment. Still, she may have had reason enough to be cautious,[5] and so Genji did not insist; instead, he thought how attractive, among ladies of this degree, the Gosechi Dancer from Tsukushi had been.[6] He seems to have cared forever for each one of his loves. The passing years never effaced his feeling for any lady he had known, although this only aroused in many the sorrows of the lovelorn.

He felt a pang of sympathy when he found his destination as silent and deserted as he had expected. He called first on the Reikeiden Consort and kept her company until late in the evening, talking over old times. Moonrise on this twentieth night further darkened the shadows beneath the looming trees, and the scent of orange blossoms nearby called up many a fond memory. The Consort's manner betrayed her years, but she retained all her great kindness and the dignity of her charm. He thought of how His Late Eminence, for whom she had never been the greatest of favorites, had nonetheless esteemed her gentle sweetness, and visions of those days passed before him till he wept.

A cuckoo, perhaps the one he had heard earlier, gave the same call. He supposed it rather charmingly to have followed him. "How did it know?"[7] he murmured to himself; and to the lady,

> *"Many fond yearnings for an orange tree's sweet scent draw the cuckoo on*
> *to come to find the village where such fragrant flowers fall",*[8]

and he went on, "I should have come long ago in search of comfort for all the memories that are still with me. It would have been consoling in many ways to do so, although it might have saddened me, too. People change so with the times that by now there are very few with whom I can share the past, and you must have even less to distract you from your daily cares."

She showed every sign of having long resigned herself to melancholy, as well

4. "I must have the wrong house." An early commentary cites this poem (*Genji monogatari kochūshakusho in'yō waka* 639): "So thick the leaves, in the garden where all the cherry petals have fallen, that one mistakes the hedge planted long ago."

5. She may have taken another lover since Genji's visit.

6. This daughter of an official assigned to Tsukushi (Kyushu) appears briefly in the next chapter. She had been a dancer for the Gosechi Festival.

7. *Kokin rokujō* 2804: "While we talked of the past, a cuckoo (how did it know?) called in the voice that we heard long ago."

8. This poem draws on *Kokinshū* 139 ("The perfume of orange blossoms awaiting the fifth month recalls the sleeves of someone long ago") and *Man'yōshū* 1477 (also *Kokin rokujō* 4417): "The cuckoo in the village where the orange blossoms fall sings and sings on many and many a day.

she might, and perhaps it was the very quality of her person that for Genji gave her plight a particular sadness. She replied only,

> *"No one ever visits this shabby home of mine, and the flowers alone*
> *that grace the tree at my eaves inspire your longing to come."*

Even so she remained to him unlike anyone else.

Casually and most discreetly Genji looked in at the western room,[9] where the wonder of his visit and his still-rarer beauty must have made her forget anything she may have had against him. He spoke as always so kindly that he must have meant it.

No lady Genji had known, however briefly, lacked a distinction of her own, nor did any give him reason to regret courting her; and perhaps that is why nothing came between them and him, and why they always got on so well. That those who wished for more should lose interest in him was something he accepted as the way of the world. She to whose house the cuckoo had called him was one who for just that reason had turned elsewhere.

---

9. On the west side of the main house. The lady there seems to have been the ultimate object of Genji's visit.

12

SUMA

Suma

Suma, a stretch of shore backed by hills, is now within the city limits of Kobe. *Ama* ("seafolk") lived there, and in poetry the typical *ama* was a young woman, a saltmaker, whose burning love was betrayed by the smoke from her salt fire. Suma was also famous as the place where Ariwara no Yukihira (818–93) was sent into exile. It comes to Genji's mind for this reason when he thinks of leaving the City.

The chapter is exceptionally rich in allusions to literature in Chinese, especially the poetry of two other famous literary exiles: Bai Juyi and the Japanese scholar-statesman Sugawara no Michizane (846–903).

RELATIONSHIP TO EARLIER CHAPTERS

There is a gap between the summer with which "The Green Branch" and "Falling Flowers" end and the beginning of "Suma" in the third month of the following year. "Suma" ends a year later, when Genji is twenty-seven.

PERSONS

Genji, age 26 to 27
The mistress of Genji's west wing, 18 to 19 (Murasaki)
The lady of the falling flowers (Hanachirusato)
Her Cloistered Eminence, 31 to 32 (Fujitsubo)
Genji's son, 5 to 6 (Yūgiri)
His Excellency, formerly the Minister of the Left, 60 to 61 (Sadaijin)
The Captain, also appointed a Consultant (Tō no Chūjō)
Chūnagon, a gentlewoman at His Excellency's
Her Highness, the mother of Aoi and Tō no Chūjō (Ōmiya)
Saishō, Yūgiri's nurse
His Late Eminence, Genji's father, after his death (Kiritsubo In)
His Highness, the Viceroy Prince, Genji's brother (Hotaru or Sochi no Miya)
The former Reikeiden Consort
Shōnagon, Murasaki's nurse
The Mistress of Staff (Oborozukiyo)
An Aide of the Right Palace Guards, brother of the Governor of Kii
Ōmyōbu, one of Fujitsubo's gentlewomen
His Highness, the Heir Apparent, Fujitsubo's son, 8 to 9 (Reizei)
Yoshikiyo, a son of the Governor of Harima and Genji's retainer
The Governor of Settsu, one of Genji's retainers
His Reverence, Murasaki's great-uncle (Kitayama no Sōzu)
The Rokujō Haven, 33 to 34 (Rokujō no Miyasudokoro)
His Excellency, the Minister of the Right (Udaijin)
His Majesty, the Emperor, 28 to 29 (Suzaku)
The Commissioner of Civil Affairs (probably Koremitsu)
The Dazaifu Deputy
The Gosechi Dancer, his daughter
The Governor of Chikuzen, a Chamberlain, son of the Dazaifu Deputy
The Novice, around 59 to 60 (Akashi no Nyūdō)
His daughter, 17 to 18 (Akashi no Kimi)
His daughter's mother, early 50s (Akashi no Amagimi)

He faced mounting unpleasantness in a hostile world, and he knew that to ignore it might well provoke still worse. There was Suma, yes, but while someone had lived there long ago, he gathered that the place was now extremely isolated and that there was hardly a fisherman's hut to be seen there—not that he can have wished to live among milling crowds. On the other hand, merely being away from the City would make him worry about home. His mind was in undignified confusion.

He reflected at length on what was past and what was yet to come, and the effort brought many sorrows to mind. Now that he was considering actually removing himself from the world he rejected, a great deal of it seemed impossible to give up, especially his darling, who suffered more with each passing night and day. A day or two away made him anxious about her, even when he had faith that "time once more would join them,"[1] and she herself was forlorn; and now they despaired that he would be gone for years and years and that despite their longing to be reunited, life might play them false and he might be setting out for good. He therefore wondered sometimes whether he should quietly take her with him; but it would be wrong of him to bring anyone so lovely to so dreary a seaside, where she would have no company but the wind and the waves, and he knew that he, too, would only worry if he did. "Never mind the terrors of the journey," she would hint, clearly hurt, "if only I could be with you!"

He rarely called on the lady of the falling flowers, but of course she grieved as well, since only his generosity sustained her depressing life. Many of the ladies he had known even in passing suffered secret heartbreak at the prospect of his departure.

He had constant private messages from Her Cloistered Eminence as well, despite her desire to avoid damaging rumors. He wished that she had shown him such fond consideration long ago; but no, he reflected bitterly, his love for her had been meant only to acquaint him with every variant of pain.

---

1. *Kokinshū* 405, by Ki no Tomonori: "As the undersash goes two ways to come round and join again, so I long for time again to join us."

It was just after the twentieth of the third month when he set out from the City. He told no one the hour of his departure but left almost invisibly, with a mere seven or eight intimate retainers. To those due something from him he merely sent discreet letters, some of which, in the moving fullness of their eloquence, must have been well worth reading; but it was all so upsetting that I never inquired about them properly.

Two or three days before, Genji had called at His Excellency's under cover of darkness. His furtive entrance in a common basketwork carriage that looked like a woman's[2] was sad and might have been a dream. In *her* rooms he felt only loneliness and desolation. His son's nurses and the women who had stayed on to serve him gathered to see him, wondering at his visit, and the younger, giddier ones wept at this evidence of fortune's fickle ways. The little boy ran about very prettily. "How dear of him not to have forgotten me after all this time!" Genji said, taking him on his lap and struggling visibly to control his feelings.

His Excellency came to receive him. "I had hoped to come and rattle on to you about this and that while you were idle at home," he said, "but my poor health now keeps me from serving at court and has obliged me to resign my office, so I thought it might not be well received if I were to go about on business of my own— I need no longer defer to the world, but I do fear the evil temper of the times. Seeing you this way reminds how much I wish I had never lived to see so corrupt an age. My wildest fancies could not have led me to imagine this. I am appalled." He wept bitterly.

"They say that whatever happens to us is our reward from past lives, which means in short that all this springs from my own failings," Genji answered. "I gather that in the other realm,[3] too, it is considered quite wrong for anyone whom a small lapse has earned his Sovereign's displeasure to live as do the just, even if he has not been stripped like me of rank and office. The decision to send me into distant exile—for I hear one has been taken—only shows how exceptional an offense is imputed to me. I dare not ignore such censure merely because my heart is pure, and I have therefore resolved to remove myself from the world before I face still greater dishonor." He went on at some length in this vein.

His Excellency then spoke of the past, and of His Late Eminence and his express wishes concerning Genji; and he never took the sleeve of his dress cloak from his eyes. Genji did not manage to be any braver himself. It tore at his heart to see his little boy tripping innocently in and out, snuggling up now to one grown-up, now to another.

"She is gone, I know, but I never, never forget her," His Excellency said. "Yes, I still mourn her, but I take comfort from considering how your present circumstances would upset her if she had lived, and I am relieved that her passing spared her this nightmare. The saddest thing of all, for me, is to reflect on how her son, who is so young, is left with an old couple, and on how long it will be until he has his father

2. With fully lowered inner blinds (*shita sudare,* lengths of silk that hung down inside the carriage blinds proper).
3. China.

again. In the old days even a man who *had* misbehaved was spared this. Yes, it is all destiny, and many in other lands have suffered like you. They, however, were victims of slander. No, to me, all this is simply inconceivable." He spoke for a long time.

The Captain[4] then joined them, and they drank together so late that Genji stayed on, gathered the gentlewomen around

Veranda, railing, double doors

him, and engaged them in conversation. Chūnagon, whom he secretly favored, was mute with sorrow, and he silently commiserated with her. When all was quiet at last, he devoted himself solely to her. That must be why he had stayed on in the first place.

He left very late indeed, with dawn coming on and a lovely moon lingering in the sky. The cherries' great flowering was over; mist trailed through a garden pale beneath thinning branches, to merge here and there with the blossoms and yield a scene more beautiful than any autumn night. He watched it for a time, leaning on the railing. Chūnagon, who no doubt wanted to see him go, opened the double doors and sat looking out.

"We may never meet again, you know," he said. "I did not know what the world was like, and I never tried hard enough to see you, when all this time it would have been so easy." She wept in silence.

A message came from Her Highness through his son's nurse, Saishō: "I had wished to speak to you in person, but in my trouble and sorrow I wavered; and I hear that you are now leaving late in the night and, it seems to me, in a manner quite unlike your old ways.[5] You do not even stay your departure while one dear to you still sleeps."

Genji wept and murmured as though not meaning an answer,

"Now I go to see whether yonder on that shore where seafolk burn salt
their fires send such smoke aloft as rose at Toribeno."

And he went on, "Is *this* then the pain of parting at dawn?[6] Oh, to have beside me one who knew it, too!"

Saishō replied with tears in her voice, "The word 'parting' is always cruel, but, my

---

4. Tō no Chūjō.

5. Genji did not have to leave before dawn when Aoi was alive.

6. *Gosenshū* 719, by Ki no Tsurayuki: "I would gladly ask her: what is it like, the pain of an unwilling parting at dawn?

Serving table

lord, this morning it is surely unlike any other." There was no mistaking her genuine depth of feeling.

Genji said in answer to Her Highness, "I had many things to tell you, and I beg you to understand what anguish has silenced me. To see the little sleeper would only make this world more difficult for me to leave, and I have therefore resolved to go quickly."

Ladies peeped at him as he left. The renewed beauty and grace of his sorrowing form, seen by the light of the sinking moon, would have moved a wolf or tiger to weep; no wonder those privileged to have known him since his boyhood were shocked to see him so changed.

Oh, yes, Her Highness had answered,

"Between you and her there will spread as time goes by wider distances,
for you will no longer see the skies that received her smoke."

After a departure that added new woes to old, the gentlewomen abandoned all dignity and wept.

At home again he found his own gentlewomen, who seemed not to have slept, clustered here and there in acute distress. There was no one in his household office; the men in his intimate service were no doubt busy with their own farewells, in preparation for accompanying him. It amounted to grave misconduct for anyone to visit him, and to do so more and more to risk reprisal, so that where once horses and carriages had crowded to him, a barren silence now reigned, and he felt the treachery of life. Dust had gathered here and there on the serving tables, some of the mats had been rolled up, and he was not even gone yet. He could imagine the coming desolation.

He crossed to the west wing. Her page girls had dropped off to sleep on the veranda and elsewhere, for she had spent a sad, sleepless night with the lattice shutters open, and they were only now bustling about getting up. He watched them sadly, so pretty in their night service wear, when otherwise he might not have given them a glance, and he reflected that with the years they would all drift away.

"I stayed very late, you see, what with one thing and another," he said. "You must be imagining strange things as usual. I would much prefer not to leave you at all at a time like this, but now that I am going so far away I naturally have many urgent concerns, and I cannot be here all the time. The world is cruel enough as it is, and I could not bear to have anyone think me unkind."

"Strange things? Could anything be stranger than what is happening already?" She said no more.

No wonder she grieved more than anyone else. His Highness her father was so distant that she had long loved Genji instead, and now fear of rumor discouraged him from ever writing
or visiting, which shamed her before her women and made her
sorry that he had ever found out where she was. She happened to
know that her stepmother had remarked, "Her luck did not last, did
it! She is accursed! She loses anyone who loves her, every time."
This hurt her so badly that she then gave up all communication
with her father. She really was in a sad plight, since Genji was
all she had.

"If years from now there is still no pardon for me, I
will bring you to join me, yes, even 'among the rocks,' "[7]
Genji went on. "It would start unwelcome gossip, though, if
I were to do so now. A man suffering his Sovereign's displeasure shuns the light of sun and moon, and it would be a
serious offense for him to live as he pleases. I am blame-

Mirror on its stand

less, but I know that this is the sort of trial destiny brings, and no precedent allows
me to take someone I love with me; no, in a world evermore gone mad that would
only make things worse."[8] After he had spoken, they slept until the sun was high in
the sky.

The Viceroy Prince[9] and the Captain came. Genji put on a dress cloak to receive them: an unpatterned one, since he had no rank, but which by its very plain-
ness showed him off to still better advantage. Approaching the mirror stand to
comb his sidelocks, he noted despite himself the noble beauty of the wasted face he
saw. "I am so much thinner now!" he said. "Just look at my reflection! It really is too
hard!" She turned on him eyes brimming with tears. He could not bear it.

> "I may have to go and wander far, far away; yet, forever near,
>   this your mirror will retain the presence I leave with you."

> "Were it only true that the image may linger when the person goes,
>   then a glance in this mirror would be comforting indeed."

She was sitting behind a pillar to hide her weeping. The sight reminded him afresh
that she alone, among all the women he had known, was beyond compare.

His Highness pursued their melancholy conversation until he left at dusk.

The village of falling flowers was desolate. The former Consort there understandably wrote to him often, and he knew that her sister would be hurt if he failed

7. From *Kokinshū* 952: "Where could I live, among the rocks, that I should hear no more of the world and
its troubles?"
8. Heian law allowed a man to take his wife into exile, but Genji seems to mean that no one had ever actually done so.
9. Prince Hotaru, Genji's younger brother and later on His Highness of War.

to call on her a last time; and so that night he reluctantly set out again. It was very late by the time he arrived.

The Consort was extremely pleased. "It is too kind of you to honor us with your visit," she said; however, it would be tedious to convey her remarks at length. She owed the sad succession of her days to him alone, and he foresaw the greater ruin that might now await her. The house was very still. The lake's broad expanse in muted moonlight, the trees' shadowy depths on the garden hill, all spoke to him of forlorn despair, and his thoughts went to his own future existence far away among the rocks.

The lady on the west side of the house was wondering sadly whether he really would come, when through the poignant flood of moonlight she caught the singular fragrance that wafted before him, and he stole in to her. She slipped out toward him and lifted her gaze to the moon. Dawn came on while they still talked.

"What a short night it has been!" Genji exclaimed. "And when I think that we may never be together like this again! What a waste these years have been, with nothing passing between us! My story, past and future, will be on everyone's lips, and meanwhile I seem in the end never to have found a quiet time . . ." He spoke of days gone by until cockcrows came often; then he prepared to leave for fear of being seen.

Alas, the setting moon meant as always that he was going. "A face wet with tears"[10] shone indeed from her deep purple sleeves, and she said,

> "Narrow they may be, these sleeves of mine that welcome the face of the moon,
>   yet I so long to detain the light I shall always love!"[11]

The strength of her feelings moved Genji to compassion. Troubled as well, he tried to console her.

> "There will come a time when as this life turns and turns the moon will shine forth:
>   for a while avert your eyes from an all too cloudy sky.

I am sad, too, though, because 'tears of ignorance',[12] darken my heart as well." He left as day began to break.

He put his affairs in order. Among the close retainers who resisted the trend of the times he established degrees of responsibility for looking after his residence. He also chose those who would follow him. The things for his house in the mountain village,[13] items he could not do without, he kept purposely simple

---

10. The moon reflected in her tears: an image from *Kokinshū* 756, by Ise.

11. Her sleeves are "too narrow" (unworthy) because she believes her personal and social worth insufficient to retain Genji's affection.

12. *Gosenshū* 1333, by Minamoto no Wataru: "Tears of ignorance, alas, as to what lies ahead fall here, straight before my eyes."

13. Although most obviously by the sea, Suma is referred to as a *yamazato*, a "mountain village." Hills rise behind the shore.

and plain, and he added to his baggage a box of suitable books, including the *Collected Poems*,[14] as well as a *kin*. He took no imposing furnishings with him and no brilliant robes, for he would be living as a mountain rustic. To the mistress of his west wing he entrusted his staff of gentlewomen and everything else as well, and he also gave her the deeds to all his significant properties—estates, pastures, and so forth. As to his storehouses and repositories, Shōnagon struck him as reliable, and he therefore instructed her on their care, assigning her for the purpose a staff of close retainers.

He had never been attentive to Nakatsukasa, Chūjō, or other such gentlewomen of his own, but it was comfort enough for them to see him, and they wondered where they would turn for solace now. "I will certainly be back, if only I live long enough," he said, "and those of you who wish to wait must serve your mistress." He had them all, high or low, go to join her.

He naturally sent pretty gifts to his little son's nurses and to the village of falling flowers, but he did not fail to be generous with welcome necessities as well.

He managed to get a message to the Mistress of Staff.[15] "I am not surprised to have heard nothing from you," he wrote, "but I am sorrier and more disappointed than words can say now that I am leaving all my world behind.

> *Did the way I drowned in a sad river of tears that we could not meet*
> *set running the mighty flood that has now swept me away?*

I know when I look back that I must take the consequences." He wrote little, for the letter would have a perilous journey.

She was very upset, and the tears overflowed her sleeves despite her attempt at self-control.

> *"Ah, river of tears! The froth floating on that stream will vanish quite soon,*
> *long before the current runs laughing over happier shoals."*[16]

What she had written through her tears was very beautiful. He wondered whether he might not try to see her again after all, but then he thought better of the idea, and since she was surrounded by relatives who detested him and was herself keeping very quiet, he renounced any heroic attempt to correspond with her further.

The evening before he was to leave he went to the Northern Hills to salute His Late Eminence's tomb, but first he visited Her Cloistered Eminence, since at this time of the month the moon would still be up at dawn. She seated him directly before her blinds and spoke to him in person. The Heir Apparent worried her acutely. The conversation of a pair so deeply engaged with one another must have been extremely moving.

---

14. Of Bai Juyi. Bai Juyi, too, took a *kin* with him into exile.
15. Oborozukiyo.
16. "Shoal" (*se*) suggests also "change of fortune" and "lovers' meeting."

Blinds

The sweet promise of her presence was what it had always been, and he felt a wish to chide her for her cruelty, but she would only have disliked him for it. He calmed the renewed clamor in his heart and said only, "There is one thing that comes to mind, now that a punishment so unforeseen has come upon me—one thing for which I still fear the heavens above. I would gladly give my life to assure the Heir Apparent's smooth accession." One could hardly blame him. Her Eminence, who fully shared his feelings, was too moved to reply. He wept as he thought back over the past, making as he did so a vision of infinite beauty.

"I am going to His Eminence's tomb," he said. "Have you any message for him?" But she could not immediately speak, and she seemed to be struggling to master her emotions.

> "The man I once knew is gone now, and he who lives bears many sorrows:
>   all in vain I left this world to live out my life in tears,"

she said. Their hearts were too troubled to allow their teeming thoughts to find voice.

> "When he went away, I discovered just how far grief and pain may go,
>   yet the sorrows of this life only rise and rise anew,"

Genji replied.

He left once the moon had risen, with a mere half dozen companions and only the closest servants. He rode.[17] Needless to say, everything was so different from his excursions in happier days that those beside him were very downcast.

One of them, a Chamberlain Aide of the Right Palace Guards, had been assigned to his escort that Purification Day; he had been denied due promotion, barred from the privy chamber, and stripped of his functions, and that was why he was with Genji now. The sight of the Lower Kamo Shrine in the distance brought that moment back to him. He dismounted, took the bridle of his lord's mount, and said,

> "I recall the days when we all in procession sported heart-to-heart,
>   and the Kamo palisade calls forth a great bitterness."[18]

Genji could imagine the young man's feelings, and he grieved for him, since he had once shone brighter than the rest. He, too, dismounted and turned to salute the shrine. Then he said in valediction,

17. In acknowledgment of his disgrace, rather than travel in a carriage.
18. The "palisade" (*mizugaki*) is the sacred fence around the shrine. The syllables *sono kami* ("then") mean also "(remember) that divinity (with bitterness)."

"Now I bid farewell to the world and its sorrows, may that most wise god
of Tadasu judge the truth in the name I leave behind."[19]

Watching him, these young men so enamored of beauty were filled with the wonder of his stirring grace.

He reached the tomb, and there came into his mind the image of his father as he had once been. Only ineffable sorrow remained now that even he, who had been beyond rank, was gone. Genji reported in tears what had befallen him, but his father's judgment remained inaccessible. Alas, what had become of all his parting injunctions?

Wayside grasses grew thickly by the tomb, which Genji had approached through gathering dews, and meanwhile clouds had covered the moon and the darkness of the forest weighed upon him. He felt as though he might never find his way back again. While he prayed, he shivered to behold a vision of his father as he had seen him in life.

"What is it his shade beholds when he looks on me—I, before whose eyes
the moon on high, his dear face, hides from sight behind the clouds?"

Once full day had come, he left again for home, and there he also wrote to the Heir Apparent. The letter was to go to Ōmyōbu in her room, since he had charged her with representing him. "I leave the City today, and the greatest of all my regrets is that I am now unable to call upon His Highness.[20] Please understand my feelings and convey them to him.

When will I again set my eyes on the City blossoming in spring,
now that I am of the hills, a peasant whose time is past?"

He tied the letter to a cherry branch bare of flowers.

His Highness grew boyishly serious when it was shown to him. "What reply do you wish me to give him?" Ōmyōbu asked.

"Tell him how very quickly I begin to miss him, and how with him far away I really wonder . . ." Ōmyōbu was touched by his sad little answer. Looking back on the past, when Genji had suffered so much for his impossible desires, and on all his encounters with her mistress, she grieved to think that he had brought these torments on them both, when they should have lived free of care, and she felt that the blame rested on her alone.

She wrote in reply, "My lord, there is nothing I can say. I have spoken to His Highness. It is a shame to see him so unhappy." The scattered character of her remarks must have reflected her troubled state of mind.

"It is very sad that the flowers quickly fall; yet, O passing spring,
come again to smile upon the City your blossoms grace!"

19. The Lower Kamo Shrine is in Tadasu Grove, a name homophonous with the verb for "ascertain the truth."
20. Being under imperial ban, he cannot enter the palace.

There will surely come a time . . ." In this somber mood
His Highness's household talked on through their tears.
No one who had laid eyes on Genji could see his affliction without grieving for him, and of course those in his
personal daily service, even maids and latrine clean-
ers[21] he would never know but who had been touched
by his kindness, particularly lamented every moment
of his absence.

Man in hunting costume

Who could have remained indifferent to him,
even in the world at large? He had waited day and night
on His Majesty since he was seven, he had told him no
wish that remained unfulfilled, and all had therefore come
under his protection and enjoyed his generosity. Many great
senior nobles or court officials were among them, and
lesser examples were beyond counting. Although they did
not fail to acknowledge their debt, they did not call on him, for they were cowed by
the evil temper of the times. People everywhere lamented his fate and privately deplored the court's ways, but apparently they saw no point in risking their own careers
to express their sympathy, for many of them disappointed or angered him, and all
things reminded him how cruel the world can be.

On the day, he talked quietly with his darling until dark and then set out
late at night, as people do. He had kept his traveling costume—hunting cloak and
so on—very plain. "The moon is up," he said. "Do come out a little farther and see
me off. There will be so much I will wish I could tell you! Somehow, you know, I
have no peace when I am away from you only a day or two." He rolled up the
blinds and beckoned her out to the edge of the aisle. Dissolved in tears, she
paused before she slipped out to sit like a lovely vision in the moonlight. What
would become of her once he was gone from the dreary world around them? The
matter desperately worried him, but in her present state he only feared to upset
her more.

> "Even while alive, people may yet be parted: that I never knew,
> even as I swore to you to stay by you till the end.

So much for promises . . ." he said, striving to take it lightly.

> "I would soon give up this unhappy life of mine if that might just stay
> a little while the farewell now suddenly upon us."

He did not doubt that she had spoken truly, and he could hardly bear to leave
her, but he did not wish dawn to find him there, and he hastened away.

Her image was with him throughout the journey, and he boarded his ship

21. Men used outside latrines and women chamber pots.

with a stricken heart.[22] The days were long then, and with a following wind he reached his destination at the hour of the Monkey.[23]

Having never traveled this way before, even for pleasure, he experienced mingled desolation and delight. The place called Ōe Hall was sadly ravaged, for only its pine trees showed where the building had stood.[24]

> *"Is it then my lot even more than his, who left his name in Cathay,*
> *to roam on and never know anywhere to call my home?"*[25]

Seeing the waves washing the shore and slipping back to the sea, he murmured, " 'With what envy . . . ' ";[26] and on his lips the old poem sounded so fresh and true that sorrow overwhelmed his companions. Looking back, he saw the mountains behind them melting into the mists and truly felt "three thousand leagues from home."[27] He could not bear the drops from the boatman's oar.

> *"Mist over the hills may conceal my home from me, yet perhaps that sky*
> *my eyes turn to in longing is hers, too, beyond the clouds."*

All things weighed upon him.

He was to live near where Counselor Yukihira had lived before him, with the "salt, sea-tangle drops falling as he grieved."[28] The place stood a little back from the sea, among lonely hills. Everything about it, even the surrounding fence, aroused his wonder. The miscanthus-thatched pavilions and what seemed to be galleries thatched with rushes were nicely done. At any other time a dwelling so novel and so in keeping with the setting would have delighted him, and his thoughts returned to pleasures past.

He summoned officials from his nearby estates, and it was sad to see Lord Yoshikiyo, now his closest retainer, issuing orders for all there was to be done.[29] In no time the work was handsomely finished. The streambed had been deepened, trees had been planted, and Genji felt to his surprise that he could actually live

---

22. He would have ridden to Fushimi and then taken a boat down the Yodo River to Naniwa (now Osaka), a day's journey. He probably "boarded his ship" the next morning at Naniwa, to sail the thirty miles westward to Suma.

23. Roughly 4:00 P.M.

24. It is unclear what this building was or had been.

25. An allusion to a Chinese poet (Qu Yuan, 340–278 B.C.) who also wandered in exile.

26. *Ise monogatari* 8 (section 7): "My heart so longs to cross the distance I have come: with what envy I watch the waves as they return!"

27. From a poem by Bai Juyi (*Hakushi monjū* 0695).

28. From *Kokinshū* 962, by Ariwara no Yukihira, the poem that provides the poetic authority for Genji's exile at Suma: "Should one perchance ask after me, say that, on Suma Shore, salt, sea-tangle drops are falling as I grieve." The "salt, sea-tangle drops" are Yukihira's tears and the brine that drips from those who gather seaweed along the Suma coast. Suma was known for its saltmakers, and seaweed was used in the salt-making process.

29. Sad presumably because in the capital Yoshikiyo never had to speak to anyone as lowly as an estate official. One of Genji's men, he is the son of the Governor of the neighboring province of Harima, in which Akashi was located.

there. The Governor of the province[30] was another of Genji's familiar retainers, and he quietly did all he could to help. The place was lively with visitors even though Genji had just arrived, but he still felt lost in a strange land, for he had no one with whom to discuss things properly, and he wondered how he would get through the years ahead.

The rainy season came as life began at last to take on a normal rhythm, and Genji's thoughts turned to the City: to the many there whom he loved, to his dear lady in her sorrow, to the Heir Apparent, and to his little son at innocent play. He sent off messengers. It was beyond him to complete the letters to his Nijō residence and to Her Cloistered Eminence, for tears blinded him. To Her Cloistered Eminence he wrote,

> "How, then, fares the nun in her seafolk's but of rushes at Matsushima,
> these days when brine is dripping from the man of Suma Shore?[31]

Amid my prevailing sorrows, the past and the future lie in darkness, and alas, the floodwaters are rising . . ."[32]

To the Mistress of Staff he wrote, as always, as though addressing himself privately to Chūnagon, but he enclosed, "Now that I have such leisure to dwell on the past, I wonder,

> While, all unchastened, I on Suma Shore still miss sea-tangle pleasures,
> what of you, O seafolk maid, whose salt fire never burns low?"[33]

One easily imagines his passionate eloquence.

To His Excellency's and to Nurse Saishō as well he sent instructions for his son's upbringing.

In the City his letters aroused strong feelings in most of those who read them. The mistress of Nijō lay down at once, grieving and yearning, and she would not rise again, until the women in her service were at their wits' end to console her. An accessory he had favored in daily use, a koto he had played, the scent of a robe he had worn: these only recalled him to her now, as though he had passed beyond her world, with consequences so ominous that Shōnagon asked His Reverence to pray for her. His Reverence did a protective rite for her and Genji, and he begged, "Oh, let her cease to mourn as she is doing and enjoy a life free from care!"

She made him nightclothes to wear while he was away. A dress cloak and gathered trousers of plain, stiff silk were so different and strange that the face of

---

30. Settsu, where Suma was.

31. *Ama* ("nun") also means someone who lives from the sea; and Matsushima, like Suma, is poetically famous for its saltmakers. This wordplay therefore assimilates Fujitsubo's condition to Genji's own as a "man of Suma Shore."

32. The flood of my tears. *Kokin rokujō* 2345: "Because you are gone, my tears fall and fall, and the river will soon overflow its banks."

33. "I should have learned my lesson, even now I want to see you—would you want that, too?" The marine wordplays in the poem include even the hidden name of Suma. The chief play is on *mirume*, a kind of seaweed, but also "lovers' meeting." Genji likens Oborozukiyo, too, to a saltmaker.

which he had spoken, the one "forever near in your mirror" (and indeed it was) was no comfort at all. It broke her heart to see a doorway he had come through, a pillar he had leaned on. She would still have been unhappy even if she had been old enough to have thought things over better and known more of life, and no wonder she missed him keenly, considering how close she was to him and how he had been both father and mother to her while she grew up. If he really had no longer been among the living, that would have been that, and she might have begun to forget, but although she knew that Suma was not far away, she could not know how long they would be parted, so that she had no relief from her sorrow.

Needless to say, Her Cloistered Eminence grieved, too, because of the Heir Apparent.[34] How could it leave her indifferent to ponder her karma from past lives? Fear of rumor had kept her wary all these years, for if she had shown Genji affection, the result might have been censure, and she had often ignored his own to remain impassively formal; but despite the world's cruel love of gossip he had so managed things in the end that nothing was said; he had resisted his unreasoning passion and kept the affair decorously concealed. Could she then fail to remember him with love? Her answer was unusually warm. "More and more, lately,

> *Her every labor goes to firing dripping brine: at Matsushima,*
> *while her years go by, the nun heaps up the sad fuel of sighs."*

The Mistress of Staff replied,

> *"She whose love this is, the saltmaker with her fire, dares not have it seen,*
> *and for all her smoldering the smoke has nowhere to go.*

I shall not repeat things that need not be said . . ." Her short note was enclosed in the one from Chūnagon, who vividly conveyed her mistress's sorrow. Some passages were so affecting that Genji wept.

The letter from his darling, her reply to a long and passionate one from him, was often very moving. She had written,

> *"Hold up to your sleeves ever wet from dipping brine, O man of the shore,*
> *the clothes I wear every night that watery road parts us."*

The things she had sent were lovely in both color and finish. She was so skilled at every task that he could not have wished for more, and he bitterly regretted not having her with him now that other absorbing affairs no longer claimed him and he should have been living in peace. Her image was before him day and night, and her memory haunted him unbearably until he quietly considered bringing her down after all, only to dismiss the idea again as hopeless and to aspire instead to erase his sins at least in this blighted lifetime. He went straight into continual practice of purifying fasting.

From His Excellency he had news of his little son, too, and although he

---

34. She fears that the Heir Apparent's position may suffer in Genji's absence.

missed him very much, he did not worry unduly, because he knew that he would see him again and that he was in good hands. Perhaps he was not completely absorbed in a father's grief.

Oh, yes, in all the confusion I left something out. Genji had also sent a messenger to the Ise Shrine, and he had had one from there as well. She[35] had written with great warmth. Her turn of phrase and the movement of her brush showed exceptional mastery and grace. "News of the conditions under which you are living, and which I can scarcely believe, leaves me, so to speak, caught in the night without a dawn,[36] yet I take it that you will not be away long, whereas I, deep in sin,[37] will speak to you again only in the far future.[38]

> *Give thought when you can to the Ise saltmaker gathering sorrows,*
>   *you who are of Suma Shore, where I hear the brine drips down.[39]*

Oh, where will it lead, this life that is so painful in every way?" It was a long letter.

> *"Though I scour the strand at low tide on Ise Bay, there is not a shell*
>   *nor anything such as I can do in my affliction."[40]*

She had joined four or five sheets of white Chinese paper into a scroll, on which she had written fitfully, as her sorrows moved her, and there was a lovely quality to the strokes of her brush.

The thought that he had turned against her in an unkind moment, when she meant so much to him, that he had hurt her and driven her away, made her timely letter especially moving. He felt so grateful and so sympathetic that her very messenger was welcome, and he detained him for several days to learn all about her life. The messenger was a young and most accomplished member of his mistress's household. In his present reduced circumstances Genji did not keep even a man like him too far away, and the dazzled messenger wept at his glimpses of Genji's beauty.

Genji framed a reply. His words are easily imagined: "If I had known that I was to leave the City in any case, I would have done better to follow you after all," and so on. Bored and lonely, he wrote,

> *"If only I, too, had boarded the little boat she of Ise rows*
>   *lightly out over the waves, and gathered in no sorrows!*[41]

> *How long, languishing here at Suma on the shore, must I dream and mourn*
>   *while the briny drops rain down on the seafolk's fuel of care?*

35. The Rokujō Haven.
36. The (Buddhist) night of subjection to the passions.
37. The sin of doing no Buddhist devotions. At Ise, as at the Shrine on the Moor, contact with Buddhism was taboo.
38. When a change of reign occurs and the Ise Priestess returns to the City.
39. *Ukime* ("gathering sorrows") also means "harvesting seaweed."
40. The poem plays on *kai*, "shellfish" and "reward."
41. A partial variation on a folk song: "The people of Ise are odd ones, and why? In little boats they row over the waves, row over the waves."

I cannot get over not knowing when I shall speak to you again."

In this way he kept consolingly in touch with all his ladies.

He was at once pleased and disconcerted to see how the ladies of the village of falling flowers had conveyed each her own mood in an artless message of grief;[42] but although both messages were comforting, they also deepened his sorrow.

Collapsed earthen wall

"On and on I gaze at the ferns fringing the eaves of my dreary home while the dew in ceaseless drops moistens my forsaken sleeves,"[43]

she had written, and Genji understood that in truth they had no protection but their garden weeds. Upon learning that their earthen wall had collapsed in several places during the long rains, he had his retainers in the City bring men from his nearby provincial estates to repair the damage.

The Mistress of Staff was extremely unhappy to be laughed at, and His Excellency her father, who was very fond of her, made such strenuous representations to the Empress Mother and His Majesty that His Majesty reconsidered; after all, she was neither a Consort nor a Haven but merely a palace official, and besides, that lapse of hers had already caused her trouble enough. She gained His Majesty's pardon and could once more go to court, though even now her sole desire was the one who had claimed her heart.

She went to the palace in the seventh month. His Majesty, who still thought highly of her, ignored the vicious gossip and kept her constantly with him as before, now chiding her for this or that, now asserting his love, and he did so with great beauty and grace; but alas, her heart had room only for memories of Genji.

Once when there was music, His Majesty remarked, "His absence leaves a void. I expect many others feel it even more than I do. It is as though all things had lost their light"; and he went on, "I have not done as my father wished. The sin of it will be upon me." Tears came to his eyes and, helplessly, to hers as well. "I have no wish to live long, now that I know life only becomes more cruel as one ages. How would you feel if something were to happen to me? I cannot bear it that such a parting would trouble you less than another, more benign, does already. No, I cannot think well of him who wrote, " 'While I am still alive . . .' "[44]

---

42. "Disconcerted" because of the strangeness of reading such letters in a place like Suma.

43. The "ferns" are *shinobu*, a fernlike plant the name of which is also the verb for "remember fondly." *Shinobu* grows easily in the thatch of a neglected roof. *Nagame* ("gaze") means also "long rain" (of the rainy season).

44. *Shūishū* 685, by Ōtomo no Momoyo: "What do I care for the future once I have died for love? My longing to see you is for while I am still alive."

His manner was so kind, and he spoke from such depth of feeling, that her tears began to fall. "Ah, yes," he said, "for which of us do you weep?" He continued, "I am sorry that you have not yet given me any children. I should like to do for the Heir Apparent as my father asked, but that, I am afraid, would only have unpleasant consequences." Those whose manner of governing offended him gave him many reasons to regret being still too young to have any strength of will.

At Suma the sea was some way off under the increasingly mournful autumn wind, but night after night the waves on the shore, sung by Counselor Yukihira in his poem about the wind blowing over the pass,[45] sounded very close indeed, until autumn in such a place yielded the sum of melancholy. Everyone was asleep now, and Genji had hardly anybody with him; he lay awake all alone, listening with raised[46] pillow to the wind that raged abroad, and the waves seemed to be washing right up to him. Hardly even knowing that he did so, he wept until his pillow might well have floated away.[47] The brief music he plucked from his *kin* dampened his spirits until he gave up playing and sang,

> "Waves break on the shore, and their voices rise to join my sighs of yearning:
> can the wind be blowing then from all those who long for me?"

His voice awoke his companions, who sat up unthinkingly here and there, overcome by its beauty, and quietly blew their noses. What indeed could their feelings be, now that for his sake alone they had left the parents, the brothers and sisters, the families that they cherished and surely often missed, to lose themselves this way in the wilderness? The thought pained him, and once he had seen how dispiriting they must find his own gloom, he purposely diverted them with banter during the day and enlivened the hours by joining pieces of colored paper to write poems on, or immersed himself in painting on fine Chinese silk, which yielded very handsome panels for screens. He had once heard a description of this sea and these mountains and had imagined them from afar; and now that they were before him, he painted a set of incomparable views of an exceptionally lovely shore.

"How nice it would be to call in Chieda and Tsunenori, who they say are the best artists of our time, and have them make these up into finished paintings!" his impatient companions remarked.[48] He was so kind and such a delight to the eye that the four or five of them forgot their cares and found his intimate service a pleasure.

One lovely twilight, with the near garden in riotous bloom, Genji stepped

---

45. A somewhat confused reference to *Kokinshū* 184 ("mournful autumn wind"), *Shoku Kokinshū* 868, by Ariwara no Yukihira ("wind blowing on the pass") and *Shin Kokinshū* 1599, by Mibu no Tadami (the waves along the shore joining the sighing of the wind).

46. A wooden or ceramic pillow that Genji has turned so that it keeps his head higher than normal.

47. *Kokin rokujō* 3241: "With all the tears that fall upon the bed of one who sleeps alone, even a pillow of stone might well float away."

48. A painter named Tsunenori lived in the time of Emperor Murakami (reigned 946–67), and perhaps a Chieda did, too. Genji's paintings (in ink only) would serve these artists as *shitagaki* (design sketches) for finished paintings in color.

onto a gallery that gave him a view of the sea, and such was the supernal grace of his motionless figure that he seemed in that setting not to be of this world at all. Over soft white silk twill and aster[49] he wore a dress cloak of deep blue, its sash only very casually tied; and his voice slowly chanting "I, a disciple of the Buddha Shakyamuni . . ."[50] was more beautiful than any they had ever heard before. From

The near garden

boats rowing by at sea came a chorus of singing voices. With a pang he watched them, dim in the offing, like little birds borne on the waters, and sank into a reverie as cries from lines of geese on high mingled with the creaking of oars, until tears welled forth, and he brushed them away with a hand so gracefully pale against the black of his rosary that the young gentlemen pining for their sweethearts at home were all consoled.

> *"Are these first wild geese fellows of all those I love, that their cries aloft*
> *on their flight across the sky should stir in me such sorrow?"*

Genji said.

Then Yoshikiyo:

> *"How all in a line one memory on the next streams across the mind,*
> *though the wild geese never were friends of mine in that far world."*

The Commissioner of Civil Affairs:[51]

> *"The wild geese that cry, abandoning of their own will their eternal home,*
> *must find their thoughts returning to that world beyond the clouds."*

The Aide of the Right Palace Guards:

> *"The wild geese that leave their eternal home to fly high across the sky*
> *surely find it comforting at least not to lag behind.*

---

49. He seems to have on a shift of white silk twill (*aya*) and gathered trousers of *shion* color.
50. Words likely to begin a Buddhist prayer or the chanting of a sacred text.
51. Apparently Koremitsu.

What would happen to one that lost its companions?" His father[52] had gone down to Hitachi as Deputy Governor, but he had come with Genji instead. At heart he was probably in despair, but he put up a brave show of unconcern.

Genji remembered when a brilliant moon rose that tonight was the fifteenth of the month.[53] He longed for the music at the palace, and the thought of all his ladies with their eyes to the heavens moved him to gaze up at the face of the moon. "Two thousand leagues away, the heart of a friend . . ."[54] he sang, and as before his companions could not contain their tears. There came back to him with unspeakable yearning the occasion of Her Cloistered Eminence's poem, "Perhaps ninefold mists," and he wept bitterly to remember his times with her. "It is very late," they said, but he still would not go in.

> *"That vision alone comforts me a little while, though it will be long*
> *till time brings me round again to the city of the moon."*[55]

Genji recalled fondly how intimately that night His Majesty had spoken of the past and how much he had then resembled His Late Eminence, and he went in, singing, "Here is the robe he so graciously gave me . . ."[56] It was true, he really was never parted from His Late Eminence's robe but kept it constantly with him.[57]

> *"Bitterness alone: no, that is by no means all I feel in my heart,*
> *for the left sleeve and the right, both, are wet at once with tears."*[58]

The Dazaifu Deputy was then on his way back up to the City. Traveling in grand style, with a vast entourage, he could not accommodate his many daughters, and his wife was therefore going by sea. They came along the coast from harbor to harbor and were pleased by Suma, for it was prettier than elsewhere; and the news of the Commander's[59] presence there in such a plight made the younger, more romantic daughters blush most fancifully to be aboard ship, until they began in their hearts to primp and preen. The Gosechi Dancer was hoping desperately, and no wonder, that they would not be towed straight past, when there reached them from afar, down the wind, the notes of a *kin*; and such were the place, the man, and the poignancy of the music that all those alive to finer feelings wept.

The Deputy sent his respects. "I had meant to wait on you as soon as I had returned from so far away and to talk over events in the City, and it is for me a matter

---

52. The Iyo Deputy.
53. The fifteenth of the eighth lunar month, the great full moon night of the year.
54. A line from a poem by Bai Juyi (*Hakushi monjū* 0724), also written on the fifteenth night of the eighth month.
55. The imperial city was poetically associated with the moon.
56. A line from a poem in Chinese by Sugawara no Michizane, written in exile. Michizane had received the gift of a robe from Emperor Daigo.
57. The robe is probably his father's, although it could also be his brother's.
58. "I am angry with the Emperor, but I also miss him: hence bitter tears on one side, tears of love on the other."
59. Genji's former title.

of deep sorrow and regret to find myself, to my great surprise, passing the spot where you now reside. Alas, I must excuse myself for the present, for many people I know have come forward to greet me, including some members of my family, and considering the possible awkwardness involved, I think it preferable to refrain. I shall call upon you at an appropriate time."

The message came through his son, the Governor of Chikuzen. The young man, who owed Genji his appointment as a Chamberlain, was shocked and saddened, but many eyes were on him, and he bore rumor in mind and left quickly. Genji replied, "Now that I am absent from the City, I no longer see those to whom I was formerly close, and it is very good of you to have come so far . . ." He said the same thing in his answering letter. The Governor wept as he left, and his account of Genji's circumstances drew from the Deputy and all those who had come to meet him an undignified flood of tears.

The Gosechi Dancer managed somehow to send him,

> "Have you eyes to see in the towrope's tug and slack my own swaying heart
> helplessly drawn toward you by the music of your kin?

Oh, do not reproach me!"[60]

The devastatingly handsome Genji read this with a smile.

> "If such were your wish that your heart goes taut and slack as the towrope does,
> would you then pass straight on by, O wave along Suma Shore?"

he wrote back. "I never thought to take fish from the sea!"[61] There was once a man who spoke a verse to a stablemaster;[62] and her only wish then was of course to disembark and stay.

As the days and months slipped by, many in the City, not least the Emperor himself, had frequent occasion to regret Genji's absence. The Heir Apparent, who naturally thought of him constantly, quietly wept—a sight that aroused sharp pangs of sympathy in his nurses and even more in Ōmyōbu herself.

Her Cloistered Eminence had always trembled for the Heir Apparent, and her alarm was very great now that Genji himself had been banished. His brothers the Princes and the senior nobles closest to him had all at first inquired after his health, but their affectionate correspondence with him, and the resulting evidence that he still enjoyed the world's esteem, drew strong words from the Empress Mother when she heard of it. "It is my understanding that one under imperial ban does not properly enjoy even the taste of food," she said, "and for him to inhabit a fine house, to

60. *Kokinshū* 508: "Oh, do not reproach me, for I am these days like the towrope of a ship, now slack, now taut."

61. *Kokinshū* 961, by Ono no Takamura: "I never thought to fall so low, banished to the wilds, as to haul a fisherman's line and take fish from the sea!"

62. When Sugawara no Michizane stopped at Akashi, on his way into exile in Kyushu, he consoled the stablemaster there with a Chinese verse.

mock and slander the court, and to have his flatterers spouting the same nonsense as those who, they say, called a deer a horse . . ."[63] Word of trouble spread, and for fear of the consequences Genji's correspondents lapsed into silence.

The passage of time brought the mistress of Nijō less and less comfort. When his gentlewomen from the east wing first went to serve her, they wondered what all the fuss could be about, but the more they knew her, the more they were drawn to her kindness, her pleasant manner, her steadiness of character, and her profound tact, and not one of them left. Now and again she saw the more senior ones in person, and they were not surprised that he loved her more than he did anyone else.

The longer Genji spent at Suma, the less he felt that he could bear it, but he kept reminding himself that since life there was hard penance even for him, it would be quite wrong to bring her there as well. Everything at Suma was different, and the very presence of the mountain folk, who were a mystery to him, constituted an affront and an offense. There was always smoke drifting past. He had assumed it was from their salt fires, but now he found that it was what people called "brush" burning on the slope behind his house. He said in wonder,

> *"Ever and again, as the mountain folk burn brush on their humble hearths*
> *day after day, how I long for news of my love at home."*[64]

Winter came, and blowing snow. Eyes on the forbidding skies, he made music on the *kin* while Yoshikiyo sang for him and the Commissioner of Civil Affairs played the flute. Whenever he put his heart into a beautiful passage, the others stopped to dry their tears. His thoughts went to that lady long ago, sent off to the land of the Huns,[65] and he wondered what *that* was like, to send away one's only love; the thought was so chillingly real that he sang "A dream after frost."[66] Bright moonlight shone in, illumining every corner of his poor refuge. The floor afforded a view of the night sky,[67] and the sinking moon evoked such solitude that he repeated to himself, "I merely travel westward";[68] and he said,

> *"Where am I to go, wandering what unknown lands down what cloudy ways?*
> *Coming under the moon's gaze, I find myself filled with shame."*

While as so often he lay sleepless beneath the dawn sky, he was moved by the plovers' piping:

63. The *Shiji* tells of an evil official who tested his men's loyalty by seeing whether they would agree with him in public that a deer was a horse.

64. The poem is built on a play on *shiba* ("brush") and *shibashiba* ("often").

65. A Han Emperor was persuaded by a ruse to present the concubine he loved to a Hun ruler.

66. From *Wakan rōei shū* 703, a Chinese poem on the same theme by Ōe no Asatsuna. According to an early gloss, "a dream after frost" means the lady's dream of home, from which she wakes after a night of frost.

67. Probably because from there one could look up past the eaves. From *Wakan rōei shū* 536, a Chinese poem by Miyoshi no Kiyoyuki.

68. A line of Chinese verse written by Sugawara no Michizane as he went into exile (the speaker is the moon): "I merely travel westward: no banishment is this." The sentiment in Genji's poem also echoes Michizane.

"While into the dawn plovers flocking on the shore lift their many cries,
all alone I lie awake, knowing just a moment's peace."

No one else was up, and he said it to himself over and over again as he lay there. In the depths of the night he would rinse his hands and call the Buddha's Name, which to his companions was so wonderful and so inspiring that they never left him. They did not make even short visits to their homes.

The Akashi coast was close enough[69] that Lord Yoshikiyo remembered the Novice's[70] daughter and wrote to her, but he got back only a message from her father: "I have something to discuss with you, and I would be grateful for a moment of your time." He will never consent, though, Yoshikiyo reflected gloomily, and going to talk to him would only mean leaving empty-handed, looking foolish. He did not go.

The Novice aspired to unheard-of heights, and although in his province an alliance with him was apparently thought a great prize, his eccentric mind had never in all the years considered a single such proposal; but when he learned of Genji's presence nearby, he said to his daughter's mother,[71] "I hear that Genji the Shining, who was born to the Kiritsubo Intimate, is living in disgrace at Suma. Our girl's destiny has brought us this windfall. We must seize this chance to offer her to him."

"What an idea!" her mother replied. "According to people from the City, he already has a large number of distinguished women and he has in fact secretly violated one of His Majesty's. Would anyone who can start a scandal like that take any interest in a miserable country girl?"

The Novice was angry. "You do not know what you are talking about," he retorted with unrepentant and all too visible obstinacy. "I disagree. You must understand that. I will have to find a chance to bring him here."

The way he looked after both his house and his daughter yielded dazzling results.

"But why must we start out with our hopes on a man, however magnificent, who has apparently been banished for his crimes?" her mother objected. "Besides, even if he does take a liking to her, nothing can possibly come of it."

The Novice's only reply was angry muttering. "In our realm or in China, people who stand out or who differ at all from the rest always end up under a cloud. What sort of man do you take this Genji for? His late mother was the daughter of my uncle the Inspector Grand Counselor. When she became known as an extraordinary beauty, they sent her to the palace, where His Majesty singled her out for favor until she died under the burden of others' jealousy. Fortunately, however, her son survived her. A woman must aim high. He will not spurn her just because I live in the country."

His daughter had no remarkable looks, but she was attractively elegant and

---

69. About five miles away, across the border between Settsu and Harima Provinces.
70. A "Novice" (Nyūdō) has taken preliminary vows and pursues a life of Buddhist devotion at home. He is not fully ordained and is not subject to collective monastic discipline.
71. Not "his wife" because he is now a monk.

had wit enough to rival any great lady. Knowing full well that her station left much to be desired, she took it for granted that no great lord would deign to notice her and that no worthy match would ever be hers; if in the end she outlived her parents, she would become a nun or drown herself in the sea. Her father overwhelmed her with fond attentions and sent her to Sumiyoshi[72] twice a year. What he secretly expected was a boon from the gods.

At Suma the New Year brought lengthening, empty days, and the little cherry trees that Genji had planted came into first faint bloom. Such memories assailed him under those mild skies that he often wept. The twentieth of the second month was past, and he desperately missed those who had aroused his sympathy last year when he left the City. Yes, the cherry tree before the Shishinden would now be in its glory. Everything now came back to him: His Eminence that other year at the party under the cherry blossoms, and the then–Heir Apparent's[73] beauty and grace, and the way he had chanted Genji's own poem.

> "Never do I fail to call to mind with longing those of the palace,
>   yet today more than any, when I wore cherry blossoms."[74]

Life was very dull. His Excellency's son the Captain,[75] now also a Consultant, was a sufficiently fine young man to enjoy great esteem,[76] but he still found the world a dreary place and missed Genji constantly, until he made up his mind that he did not care if he were discovered and charges were laid against him; suddenly he appeared at Genji's door. The sight of his friend aroused such joy and sorrow that tears of both spilled from his eyes.

Genji's house looked indescribably Chinese. Not only was its setting just like a painting, but despite their modesty the woven bamboo fence around it and its stone steps and pine pillars were pleasingly novel.[77] One could only smile before Genji's beauty, for he dazzled the eye in his purposely rustic blue-gray hunting cloak and gathered trousers, worn over a sanctioned rose[78] veering toward yellow, and all in the simple manner of a mountain peasant. He had kept his furnishings unpretentious, and his room lay open to view. Boards for Go and backgammon, assorted accessories, the wherewithal for tagi:[79] he had chosen everything to remain in keeping with country life, and Buddhist implements showed that he called the Name.

Genji made sure that their meal offered the delicacies proper to the place. The seafolk had brought a harvest of shellfish, and he invited them to come and show it

72. On the coast near Naniwa; the present shrine is surrounded by the city of Osaka.
73. Suzaku's.
74. In "Under the Cherry Blossoms," when the Heir Apparent "gave [Genji] his own blossom headdress." The language of Genji's poem alludes to *Wakan roei shū* 25: "The denizens of His Majesty's palace must be at leisure, for all day long they have worn cherry blossoms in their hair."
75. Tō no Chūjō.
76. His father, the former Minister of the Left, is out of power, but he is also a son-in-law of the Minister of the Right.
77. This description is derived from the poetry of Bai Juyi (*Hakushi monjū* 0975).
78. *Yurushi-iro no ki-gachi:* a color in the range of light pink.
79. Go and backgammon (*sugoroku*) are board games. *Tagi* seems to have involved skipping stones, rather as in tiddlywinks.

off. When he had them questioned about their life on the shore, they told him of their perils and sorrows. Despite their impenetrable jargon[80] he grasped sympathetically that their hearts moved as did his own, and that it must be so. He had them given robes, and in their joy they felt as though they had not lived in vain.[81]

Genji's horses were then led to a spot nearby and fed unthreshed rice from a structure, visible some way off, vaguely re-

Playing backgammon

sembling a granary. His fascinated friend sang a bit of "Asukai,"[82] and they talked on amid tears and laughter about the life they had been leading. "His Excellency finds your little boy's utter innocence so sad that he sighs about it day and night," he said, and Genji was overcome. To repeat their whole conversation or even a part of it would be impossible. They spent the night not sleeping but making Chinese poems. Still, the Captain was sensitive to rumor after all, and he made haste to leave, which only added to Genji's pain. Wine cup in hand, they sang together, "Tears of drunken sorrow fill the wine cup of spring."[83] Their companions wept. Each seemed saddened by so brief a reunion.

In the first light of dawn a line of geese crossed the sky. Genji said,

> "O when will I go, in what spring, to look upon the place I was born?
> What envy consumes me now, watching the geese flying home!"[84]

The Captain still had no wish to go.

> "With lasting regret the wild goose knows he must leave his eternal home,
> although he may lose the way to the City of blossoms."[85]

The presents he had brought Genji from the City were superb. When they parted, Genji gave him a black horse in thanks. "This may be an awkward gift,"[86] he

---

80. *Saezuru*, used for the song of the spring warbler, refers also to incomprehensibly foreign speech.

81. The robes are a reward for the shellfish. This sentence plays on the word for shellfish (*kai*) and the business of diving for them (*kazuku*).

82. A *saibara* song: "You must stop at the Asukai spring, for you will have shade, the water is cool, the grazing is of the best . . ."

83. A line from a poem by Bai Juyi (*Hakushi monjū* 1107), written when a friend came to visit him in exile.

84. The motif of the departing geese (the departing friend) is from a poem in Chinese by Sugawara no Michizane.

85. The wild goose is Tō no Chūjō, who likens Genji to the "eternal home" of the geese.

86. Since it is from someone in disgrace.

said, "but you see, he neighs whenever the wind blows."[87] The horse was a very good one.

"Keep this to remember me by," his visitor said, and he gave him among other things a fine flute of considerable renown, although that was all, for they exchanged nothing that might stir criticism.[88] By and by the sun rose, and Genji's friend set out in haste, with many a backward glance. Genji only looked sadder than before as he watched him go.

"When will I see you again?" his friend asked. "Surely this is not to be your fate forever."

> *"You who soar aloft so very close to the clouds, O high-flying crane,*
> *look down on me from the sky, blameless as the sun in spring,"*[89]

Genji replied. "Yes, I keep up hope, but men like me, even the wisest in the past, have never really managed to rejoin the world, and I remain doubtful; in truth, I have little ambition to see the City again."

> *"Forlorn in the clouds, I lift in my solitude cries of loneliness,*
> *longing for that old, old friend I once flew with wing to wing,"*

the Captain answered. "I now so often regret, after all, having enjoyed the undeserved privilege of your friendship!" His departure was not easy, and it left Genji blank with sorrow the rest of the day.

On the day of the Serpent that fell on the first of the third month, an officious companion observed, "My lord, this is the day for someone with troubles like yours to seek purification"; so Genji did, since he also wanted a look at the sea. After having a space roughly curtained off, he summoned the yin-yang master who came regularly to the province, and had him begin the ritual. He felt a sense of kinship as he watched a large doll being put into a boat and sent floating away:[90]

> *"I, sent running down to the vastness of a sea I had never known,*
> *as a doll runs, can but know an overwhelming sorrow."*[91]

Seated there in the brilliance of the day, he displayed a beauty beyond words.

The ocean stretched unruffled into the distance, and his thoughts wandered over what had been and what might be.

---

87. Genji's present of a black horse alludes to a story told in the *Han shu*, and the horse's neighing (whenever the wind blows from the direction of the capital) to a poem in the Chinese anthology *Wenxuan*. The customary gift to a departing visitor was called *uma no hanamuke*, a gift to "turn the horse's nose toward home."

88. Because too lavish for someone in exile to give or to receive.

89. "You who have the privilege of frequenting the palace . . ." The "clouds" allude to the palace (*kumoi*, the "cloud dwelling").

90. This kind of purification (*harae*) involved transferring disruptive influences into a doll that was then sent floating down a river or out to sea.

91. The poem plays on *hitokata* ("doll") and *hitokata naku* ("completely").

"Myriads of gods must feel pity in their hearts when they look on me:
there is nothing I have done anyone could call a crime,"

he said. Suddenly the wind began to blow, and the sky darkened. The purification broke off in the ensuing confusion. Such a downpour followed that in the commotion the departing gentlemen could not even put up their umbrellas. Without warning a howling gale sent everything flying. Mighty waves rose up, to the terror of them all. The sea gleamed like a silken quilt beneath the play of lightning, and thunder crashed. They barely managed to struggle back, feeling as though a bolt might strike them at any moment.

"I have never seen anything like this!"

"A storm gives warning before it starts to blow! This is terrible and strange!"

Through their exclamations the thunder roared on, and the rain drove down hard enough to pierce what it struck. While they wondered in dismay whether the world was coming to an end, Genji calmly chanted a scripture. At dark the thunder fell silent for a time, but the wind blew on through the night.

"All those prayers of mine must be working."

"The waves would have drowned us if that had gone on any longer!"

"I have heard of people being lost to what they call a tidal wave, but never of a storm like this!"

Toward dawn they finally rested. When Genji, too, briefly dropped off to sleep, a being he did not recognize came to him, saying, "You have been summoned to the palace. Why do you not come?" He woke up and understood that the Dragon King of the sea, a great lover of beauty, must have his eye on him.[92] So eerie a menace made the place where he was now living intolerable.

---

92. Early commentaries observe that the Dragon King, whose daughter is famous in myth, desires a beautiful son-in-law.

13

Akashi

Akashi, like Suma, is a stretch of
shore backed by hills. It was then
in Harima Province, while Suma,
only five miles to the east, was
in Settsu. The border between
them divided Harima from the
"home provinces" that were at
least nominally under direct imperial rule.

"Akashi" continues "Suma" without a break. It begins in the third month, when Genji is twenty-seven.

PERSONS

Genji, first stripped of rank, then promoted to Acting Grand Counselor, age 27 to 28

A retainer from Nijō

Genji's lady at Nijō, 19 to 20 (Murasaki)

His Late Eminence, Genji's father, after his death (Kiritsubo In)

The Akashi Novice, around 60 to 61 (Akashi no Nyūdō)

Yoshikiyo, the Minamoto Junior Counselor, Genji's retainer

The daughter of the Akashi Novice, 18 to 19 (Akashi no Kimi)

Her mother, early 50s (Akashi no Amagimi)

His Majesty, the Emperor, 29 to 30 (Suzaku)

The Empress Mother (Kokiden)

The Chancellor, her father, formerly Minister of the Right (dies) (Udaijin)

The Heir Apparent, 9 to 10 (Reizei)

Her Cloistered Eminence, Fujitsubo, 32 to 33

The Gosechi Dancer

The lady of the village of falling flowers (Hanachirusato)

It rained and thundered for days on end. Genji's miseries multiplied endlessly until his unhappy history and prospects made it too hard for him to be brave, and he wondered in despair, What am I to do? I will be more of a laughingstock than ever if this weather drives me back to the City before I have my pardon. No, let me rather disappear far into the mountains—although if they then start saying I could not take a little wind and a few waves, future generations will know me only as a fool.

The same being kept haunting his dreams. Day followed day without a break in the clouds, and he worried more and more about the City, meanwhile fearing miserably that he himself might well be lost; but no one came to find him, for the weather was too fierce to put one's head outdoors.

Someone from Nijō struggled through, though, barely recognizable and soaking wet. Genji's rush of warm feeling for the man, whom he might have swept from his path if he had met him on the road, wondering whether he was really human, struck even him as demeaning and brought home to him how low his spirits had sunk.

She had written, "There is never a lull in this terrifying storm, and the very heavens seem sealed against me, for I cannot even gaze off toward where you are.

> How the wind must blow, where you are, across the shore, when the thought of you
> sends such never-ending waves to break on my moistened sleeves."

Her letter was full of sadly distressing matters. Darkness seemed to engulf him as soon as he opened it, and the floodwaters threatened to overflow their banks.

"The City, too, takes this wind and rain for a dire, supernatural warning," the man said haltingly, "and I gather that there is to be a Rite of the Benevolent King.[1] For senior nobles on their way to the palace the streets are all impassable, and government has come to a halt." His none too clear account disturbed Genji, who summoned him and had him questioned further.

"It is strange and frightening enough that for days now there has been no

---

1. Ninnō-e, a solemn Buddhist rite performed in the palace for the protection of the realm.

letup in the rain, and that the wind has kept blowing a gale," the man said, "but we have not had hail like this, such as to pierce the earth, or this incessant thunder." His face as he sat there betrayed sheer terror, and their gloom only deepened.

At dawn the next day Genji wondered whether the world was coming to an end; a mighty tempest howled, the tide surged in, and it seemed amid the waves' furious roar as though neither rocks nor hills would be spared. Thunder boomed, lightning flashed with such awesome violence that they feared a strike at any time, and none of them remained calm. "What have I done to deserve such a fate?" they groaned. "To think I must die without ever seeing my father or mother, without setting eyes on my dear wife and children!"

With his companions in such panic Genji collected himself. Despite his conviction that no misdeed of his required him to end his life on this shore, he had many-colored streamers[2] offered to the gods and made plentiful vows, praying as he did so, "O God of Sumiyoshi,[3] your dominion embraces all these lands nearby. If you are a god truly present here below, I beg you, lend me your aid!"

His companions forgot their own troubles to grieve bitterly that such a gentleman should face so unexampled a doom. Those still somewhat in possession of their senses roused their courage and called out to the buddhas and gods that they would give their lives to save their lord's. "Reared in the fastness of our Sovereign's palace and indulged with every pleasure, he has nonetheless extended his profound compassion throughout our Land of Eight Isles,[4] and he has raised up many who were foundering! For what crime is this prodigy of wind and wave now to swallow him? O Heaven and Earth, discern where justice lies! Unjustly accused, stripped of rank and office, torn from his home to wander afar and to lament his lot dawn and dusk beneath cheerless skies, does he meet this dire fate and now face his end to atone for lives past or for crimes in this one? O gods, O buddhas, if you are wise, we beg you to grant this, our anguished prayer!"

Genji turned toward the shrine[5] and made many vows. He had vows made also to the Dragon King of the sea and to countless other divinities, whereupon the heavens redoubled their thunder and a bolt struck a gallery off his own rooms. Flames leaped up and the gallery burned. Everyone was struck witless with terror. They moved him to a structure in the back, one that he took to be the kitchen, where they all huddled, high and low together, weeping and crying out to rival the thunder. The day ended beneath a sky as black as well-ground ink.

At last the wind fell, the rain let up, and stars appeared. Mortified to see Genji so strangely lodged, they considered moving him back to the main house. "The remains of the fire are horribly ugly, there are all sorts of people still tramping aimlessly about, and besides, all the blinds have been blown away," one objected; and another, "We should wait until morning."

While they wavered, Genji pondered what had happened and meanwhile

2. Strips (*mitegura*) of paper or cloth in the five colors (green, yellow, red, white, black).
3. The Sumiyoshi cult was strong all along this coast. A patron of seafaring and of poetry, Sumiyoshi had a strong link with the imperial house.
4. A noble name for Japan.
5. Of Sumiyoshi.

called in great agitation on the buddhas. The moon came out, and the high-tide mark showed just how close the tide had come. He opened his brushwood door and contemplated the still-violently lunging and receding surf. In all the surrounding region there was no one wise, no one familiar with past and future and able to make sense of these things.

The humble seafolk now gathered where the gentleman lived, and despite the strangeness of the jargon they spoke among themselves, one he found impenetrable, no one drove them away. "If the wind had gone on much longer, the tide would have swallowed up everything," they were saying. "The gods were kind."

"Despair" is a pale word for the listening Genji's feelings.

> *"Had I not enjoyed divine aid from those great gods who live in the sea,*
> *I would now be wandering the vastness of the ocean."*

He was so exhausted after the endless turmoil of the storm that without meaning to he dropped off to sleep. While he sat there propped upright, for the room was unworthy of him, His Late Eminence stood before him as he had been in life, took his hand, and drew him up, saying, "What are you doing in this terrible place? Hasten to sail away from this coast, as the God of Sumiyoshi would have you do."

Genji was overjoyed. "Since you and I parted, Your Majesty, I have known so many sorrows that I would gladly cast my life away here on this shore."

"No, you must not do that. All this is simply a little karmic retribution. I myself committed no offense during my reign, but of course I erred nevertheless, and expiation of those sins now so absorbs me that I had given no thought to the world;[6] but it was too painful to see you in such distress. I dove into the sea, emerged on the strand, and despite my fatigue I am now hurrying to the palace to have a word with His Majesty on the matter." Then he was gone.

Genji, who could not bear him to leave, wept bitterly and cried out that he would go with him; but when he looked up, no one was there, only the shining face of the moon. He did not feel as though it had been a dream, because that gracious presence seemed still to be with him; and meanwhile, lovely clouds trailed aloft across the sky. He had seen clearly and all too briefly the sight he had longed for through the years but always missed, even in his dreams; and with that dear image now vivid in his mind he reflected wonderingly how his father had sped to save him from dire affliction and impending death, until he was actually grateful for the storm, for in that lingering presence he felt boundless trust and joy. With his heart full to bursting, he forgot in this fresh turmoil every grief of his present life, and dream or not, he so regretted not answering his father better that he disposed himself to sleep again, in case he should return; but day dawned before his eyelids would close.

Two or three men had brought a little boat up on the beach and were now ap-

---

6. Emperor Daigo (to whom Genji's father corresponds) was reputed to have suffered in hell for his misdeeds, which included exiling Sugawara no Michizane in 901. The monk Nichizō saw him there, "squatting on glowing coals," in a famous vision that Nichizō recorded in 941.

proaching the exile's refuge. His companions asked them who they were. "The Novice and former Governor is here from Akashi," they said. "He would be grateful to see the Minamoto Junior Counselor,[7] if he is present, and explain."

Yoshikiyo could not get over it. "I knew the Novice well when I was in his province, and I talked to him often over the years, but then he and I fell out a little and have not corresponded for ages. What can have brought him here through such seas?"

Genji remembered his dream. "Go and meet him," he said; and so Yoshikiyo went to see the Novice in his boat. He could not imagine how the man had set sail so quickly through so violent a storm.

"In a dream early this month a strange being gave me a solemn message that I found difficult to believe," the Novice began, "but then I heard 'On the thirteenth I will give you another sign. Prepare a boat and, when the wind and rain have stopped, sail to Suma.' I got a boat ready just in case, and then I waited until fierce wind, rain, and lightning made me fear sufficiently for his lordship that I have now kept the appointed day and brought him my message, though he may not heed it, because in other realms, too, faith in a dream has often saved the land. An eerie wind followed my boat when I set out, and my arrival shows how truly the god spoke. I wonder whether here as well his lordship might have had a sign. I venture to hope that you will be good enough to tell him."

Yoshikiyo quietly informed Genji, who considered the matter. Neither his dreams nor his waking life encouraged complacency, and in the light of these apparent warnings he contemplated what was past and what yet to come. I do not want to risk calumny from those who will eventually pass my story on, he reflected, but if I ignore what may really be divine assistance, I may, worse yet, become a mere laughingstock. One avoids crossing even mortals. I should certainly have been more cautious in small things, too, and heeded those older than I am or higher in rank and more generally respected. There is no blame in yielding, as a wise man once observed.[8] Just now I was in mortal danger and witnessed disasters of all kinds. No, it hardly matters, even if my name suffers in the end. After all, my father and my Sovereign admonished me even in my dreams. Can I doubt any longer?

He replied in this spirit. "In this wilderness where I am a stranger I have suffered every outlandish affliction, and yet no one brings me words of comfort from the City. Your fishing boat is a welcome refuge,[9] when my only old friends here are the sun and the moon in their course across the sky! Could your shore offer me a quiet place to hide?"

The Novice was very pleased and expressed his thanks. "At any rate, my lord, do go aboard before it is day," Genji's men said to him; and so he did, with the usual four or five close companions. The same wind blew, and the boat fairly flew all the way to Akashi. So short a journey took hardly any time, but one could only marvel at the will of the wind.

---

7. Yoshikiyo.
8. The source of this Chinese sentiment is unclear.
9. *Gosenshū* 1224, by Ki no Tsurayuki: "To one ever wet from the waves, a fishing boat offers a welcome refuge."

The coast there was indeed exceptional, its only flaw being the presence of so many people. By the sea or among the hills, there stood on the Novice's land here a thatched seaside cottage for the pleasures of the seasons; there, by a stream that invited pure thoughts of the next life, an imposing chapel for his meditation practice; for the needs of this life rows of rice granaries replete with

Reed-thatched cottage on the shore

sufficient bounty from the autumn fields to last him through the fullness of his age; and, elsewhere, whatever pleasant feature the setting and the season might suggest. He had lately moved his daughter to the house below the hill, in fear of the monstrous tides and also so that Genji might freely occupy the mansion on the shore.

The sun slowly rose as Genji stepped from the boat into a carriage, and at this first faint glimpse of him the Novice felt age dissolve and the years stretch out before him; he bowed at once to the God of Sumiyoshi, wreathed in smiles. The light of sun and moon seemed to him now to lie in his hand. No wonder he danced attendance on his guest.

The setting of the house, of course, but also its style, the look of the groves, the standing stones and nearby garden, the lovely inlet—all would have required exceptional genius to do them justice in painting. This was a brighter and more welcoming place by far than the one where Genji had spent the recent months. The furnishings were superb, and the Novice did indeed live among them like the mightiest grandees in the City. In fact, in grace and brilliance his mode of life rather outdid theirs.

Genji rested and then wrote to the City. The messenger from home was still at Suma, bewailing the miseries he had had to endure on his hard journey. Genji summoned him and sent him back loaded with gifts beyond his station. He probably addressed a detailed account of recent events to favored monks adept at intercession, and to many others as well. It was only to Her Cloistered Eminence that he described his miraculous escape from death.

The deeply moving letter from Nijō was too much for him to answer, and the way he put down his brush again and again to wipe his eyes betrayed intense feeling. "After surviving so long a catalog of horrors I want now more than ever to put this world behind me, but the face you spoke of seeing in the mirror is always present to me, and fear that this anxiety may be all I ever have of you is driving every other trouble from my mind.

How my longing flies, over what new distances, now that I have moved
far along that other shore to a shore I never knew!

All this makes me feel I am in a dream, and as long as I have not woken up from it, I wonder what nonsense I may talk." The lengthy, troubled wanderings indeed obvious in his writing were just what made them deserve a stolen glance, and his companions took it as proof of his supreme devotion. No doubt each had his own unhappy message to send home.

The sky that had rained and rained was now one perfect blue, and the seafolk seemed to be fishing in high spirits. Suma, where there was hardly a fisherman's shelter anywhere against the rocks, had been extremely dreary, and while Genji disliked finding so many people here, the spot offered such beauty that he felt a great deal better.

To all appearances the Akashi Novice was fiercely devoted to his practice, but he had one serious worry: his only daughter, who entered his talk with distressing regularity whenever he was with Genji. Genji had already noted her existence with interest, and he saw that his unlikely presence here might indicate a bond of destiny between them, but he intended only piety while still in disgrace, and he was so ashamed to imagine his love in the City charging him with broken promises that he betrayed no such thought to his host. Not that on occasion he did not avidly imagine the excellence of her person and her looks.

The Novice, who was afraid of intruding, seldom visited Genji and confined himself to an outbuilding some distance off. Still, his only wish was to be with Genji from morning to night, and he redoubled his prayers to the buddhas and gods that he might somehow have his desire. Although sixty, he was still a fine-looking man, pleasingly lean from his practice and distinguished in temper, and perhaps for that reason his considerable qualities, as well as his knowledge of the ways of the past, sufficiently outweighed his vagueness and his eccentricities that his conversation helped to relieve Genji's tedium.

Little by little he treated Genji to tales of bygone days, ones that Genji had never really heard, having been taken up by his own affairs or those of the court; until Genji was sufficiently intrigued to feel at times as though it might have been a shame never to have come and met the man. For all the Novice's ready talk, however, Genji's courtliness daunted him, and despite his earlier tirades he was too abashed to bring up, as he longed to do, what he really had in mind. With many sighs he told his daughter's mother about his worry and disappointment.

As for the young lady, the sight of Genji in this desert where no one, however ordinary, seemed in the least presentable taught her at last that such a man could exist and made it all too plain where she stood herself; for she thought of him as far, far beyond her. When she learned about her parents' plans for her, they struck her as preposterous, and she felt more forlorn than ever before.

The fourth month came, and Genji got fine clothes and bed curtains for the new season. These ceaseless attentions oppressed and embarrassed him, but his host was so unfailingly noble and courteous that he let the matter pass.

A constant stream of letters arrived from the City. One quiet evening, with the moon still in the sky and the whole vast sea before him, he saw, as it were, the lake in his own garden, where he had always been at home, and with the island of

Awaji looming in the distance an ineffable yearning seemed to fill all the world. "Alas, how far away . . ." he murmured.[10]

> *"Ah, how grand a sight! The island of Awaji calls forth every shade*
> *of beauty and of sorrow tonight under this bright moon."*[11]

He took from its bag the *kin* he had not touched for so long and drew a little music from its strings, while emotion surged through those sadly watching him. His full, masterly rendering of "Kōryō" reached that house below the hill through the murmuring of the pines and the sound of waves, no doubt thrilling the bright young women there. Here and there mumbling old people who could not tell one note from another found themselves wandering the beach in defiance of the wind. The Novice helplessly gave up his prayers and hastened to Genji's side.

"I think the world I left will claim me after all," he said, weeping with delight. "I cannot help seeing tonight the land where I pray to be reborn." Genji found his mind going back to the music on this or that occasion—the koto of one, the flute of another, a voice raised in song; to the praise he had received so often and to the way he had been preferred and feted by one and all, not least His Majesty himself; and to people he remembered and his own fortunes then. The present seemed so dreamlike that the strings as he touched them rang strangely loud.

The Novice could not stop the tears of age, and after sending to the house below the hill for a *biwa* and a *sō no koto* he became a *biwa* minstrel,[12] playing one or two rare and lovely pieces. Genji, when pressed, played the *sō no koto* a little, leaving his host in awe of his accomplishments. Even a fairly dull instrument may sound splendid in its time, and these notes rang out across the sea while depths of leafy shadow here and there surpassed in loveliness spring blossoms or autumn colors, and a moorhen's tap-tap-tap called up stirring fancies of "the gate favored tonight."[13]

The Novice's sweet music on instruments so superb in tone delighted Genji. "It is on this instrument[14] that a charming woman's casual music is most pleasing," he remarked conversationally, to which his host replied with a curious smile, "Where would one find playing more charming than your own? For myself, I have my skill in the third generation from His Engi Majesty,[15] and being so hopeless, you see, and unable ever really to forget the world, I turn to it often when I am deeply troubled—so much so that to my surprise someone else here has picked up what I play. Her style recalls His Highness who taught me, unless my poor ears have simply

---

10. *Shinkokinshū* 1515, by Ōshikōchi no Mitsune: "The moon that on Awaji seemed, alas, so far away, tonight—it must be the setting—seems very near." The "setting" is the City, which was associated with the moon.

11. Genji's poem alludes to Mitsune's (above) and repeats three times the syllables *awa* of "Awaji."

12. *Biwa bōshi*: a strolling musician in Buddhist robes, who sang to his own *biwa* accompaniment.

13. The cry of the *kuina* (a kind of moorhen or water rail) sounds like someone knocking lightly on a gate, and the hearer may think of a young man secretly visiting his love. For this phrase early commentaries cite an otherwise unknown poem (*Genji monogatari kochūshakusho in'yō waka* 120).

14. A *sō no koto*, the one the Novice has just been playing.

15. Emperor Daigo, whose reign (897–930) included the Engi era (901–23). The Novice would therefore have learned from one of Daigo's sons.

misheard the wind's sighing among the pines. I wish I could discreetly arrange for you to hear her!" He was trembling and seemed on the verge of tears.

"For you, then, to whom my koto can be nothing . . . [16] I have made a great mistake," Genji said, pushing the instrument from him. "Somehow the *sō no koto* seems always to have been a woman's instrument. In Emperor Saga's[17] tradition it was his own Fifth Princess who stood out in her time, although no one has really continued her line. People who enjoy some renown nowadays play only desultorily, for their own amusement, and I am delighted that someone hidden away here should have kept it alive. But how could I possibly hear her?"

Biwa *minstrel*

"I see no reason why you should not. You might even call her to play for you. After all, even among merchants someone once heard the old music with pleasure.[18] Speaking of the *biwa*, few in the old days either managed to elicit its true sound, but she plays it very beautifully and makes no mistakes. I wonder how she does it. I am sorry to hear her music through the crash of great waves, but what with all the sorrows one has to bear, it is often a great consolation." His discernment delighted Genji, who gave him the *sō no koto* and took back the *biwa*.

The Novice did indeed play the *biwa* exceedingly well. His style was one no longer heard, his fingering was thoroughly exotic,[19] and the quaver he gave the strings yielded deep, clear tones. Though the sea off Ise was far away, Genji had a man of his with a good voice sing, "Come now, all to gather shells on the pristine strand!"[20] He often picked up the clappers and joined in the song himself, while the Novice took his fingers from the strings to speak his praise. The Novice called for most unusually presented refreshments and pressed wine upon his guests until the night soon became one to banish every care.

It was late. The sea breeze had cooled, and the sinking moon shone with a pure light. When all was quiet, the Novice poured forth his tale to Genji, little by little describing his plans when he first moved to this shore, his practice for the life to come, and, all unasked, his daughter herself. Although amused, Genji was often touched as well.

"If I may allow myself to say so, my lord," his host went on, "I believe that your

---

16. With "unless my poor ears have simply misheard . . ." the Novice apparently alludes to a poem cited in an early commentary (not included in *Genji monogatari kochūshakusho in'yō waka*): "He whose ears, because he lives in the mountains, are accustomed to hearing the wind in the pines, does not even recognize [the music of] a koto as [the music of] a koto." The Novice is modestly calling himself a hopeless rustic. Genji, with equally ceremonious modesty, takes him to have said that the sound of a koto means nothing to him because he is accustomed to the higher music of nature.

17. Reigned 809–23.

18. The exiled Bai Juyi described in a poem (*Hakushi monjū* 0603) hearing a woman play the *biwa* one night on a boat moored along a river. A former courtesan of the capital, she had then married a provincial merchant.

19. Reminiscent of the continent. The *biwa* came ultimately from Persia.

20. From "Sea of Ise" ("Ise no umi"), a *saibara* song.

brief stay in a land so strange to you may be a trial devised by the gods and buddhas in compassionate response to an old monk's years of prayer. I say this because for eighteen years now I have placed my trust in the God of Sumiyoshi. I have entertained certain ambitions for my daughter ever since she was small, and twice a year, in spring and autumn, we go on pilgrimage to his shrine. Quite apart from my own prayers for birth on the lotus,[21] in all my devotions through the hours of day and night I beg only to be granted my high aims on her behalf. It must be for my sins in lives past that I have become, as you see, a hopeless mountain rustic, but my father held the office of Minister. Yes, I myself now belong to the country, and I sadly wonder what life awaits those who will come after me if we remain this low; but I have had hope ever since she was born. I want a great lord from the City to have her, and that desire runs so deep that I have incurred the enmity of many and suffered much unpleasantness because of my pretensions. None of that matters to me, however. I tell her, 'As long as I live, I will do my poor best to look after you. If I go while you are still as you are now, then drown yourself among the waves.'" Between frequent spells of weeping he told Genji this and much else that defies a full account.

This was a troubled time for Genji, too, and he listened with tears in his eyes. "I had been wondering for what crime I was falsely accused and condemned to wander an alien land, but all that you have said tonight leaves me certain and, I may say, moved that this is indeed a bond of some strength from past lives. Why did you not tell me of what you have seen so clearly? I have been sickened by the treachery of life ever since I put the City behind me, and with only my devotions to occupy my months and days my spirits have sunk very low. Distant rumor had told me of such a lady, but I had sadly assumed that she would recoil from a ne'er-do-well. Now, however, I gather that you wish to take me to her. Her solace will see me through these lonely nights."

The Novice was transported with delight.

> *"Do you know as well what it is to sleep alone? Think, then, how she feels,*
> *wakeful through the long, long nights by herself upon this shore!"*[22]

he said. "And please imagine my own anxiety all these years!" Despite his trembling he did not lack dignity.

"But surely, someone accustomed to the shore . . .

> *How traveling wears through the long melancholy of the wakeful nights*
> *that keep a pillow of grass from gathering even dreams!"*[23]

Genji's casual demeanor gave him intense allure and a beauty beyond all words.

The Novice talked on and on about all sorts of things, but never mind. Having got wrong everything I have written, I must have made him seem even odder

21. In paradise.
22. The poem plays on *akashi*, the place name and "be awake through the night."
23. This poem plays on *akashi* and also on words associated with clothing. The "pillow of grass" is a stock image for travel, while "dream" hints at sexual union.

and more foolish than he was. He was enormously relieved to see his hopes on the way to fruition.

Meanwhile, near noon the next day, Genji sent off a letter to the house below the hill. He was acutely aware that with her reputedly daunting standards the lady might be a startling rarity in these benighted wilds, and he did it very beautifully on tan Korean paper:

> *"Gazing in sorrow at skies so wholly unknown that near and far merge,*
> *through the mists I seek the trees above your whispered refuge.*

My longing heart . . ."[24] That may well have been all. The Novice was of course there already, eagerly waiting, and he plied Genji's envoy with astonishing quantities of wine.

When his daughter took a very long time to reply, he went in to her to urge her on, but she refused to heed him. Genji's dazzling missive so awed her that she shrank from revealing herself to him, and agonized thoughts of his station and hers made her sufficiently unwell that she had to lie down. Her father, at his wits' end, wrote it himself.

"Alas, your most gracious letter has proven overwhelming to someone so much of the country. She is too awestruck even to read it. Still, I believe,

> *That your gaze like hers rests upon these very skies she has always seen*
> *surely means that you and she are one also in your hearts.*

But perhaps I am too forward . . ." He had written it on Michinokuni paper, in a style old-fashioned but not without its airs and graces. Forward? Yes, thought Genji, mildly shocked. His envoy enjoyed the gift of a splendid woman's robe.

"I know nothing of decrees issued through a secretary,"[25] he wrote the next day.

> *"Ah, how cruelly I am required to suffer in my secret heart,*
> *for there is no one at all to ask me, How do you feel?*

The words will not come . . ."[26] He had made his writing very beautiful. If it did not impress her, she must, young as she was, simply have been too shy; and if it did, she no doubt still despaired when she measured herself against him, so much so that the mere thought of his noticing her enough to court her only made her want to cry. She therefore remained unmoved, until at her father's desperate urging she at last wrote on heavily perfumed purple paper, in ink now black, now vanishingly pale,

---

24. *Kokinshū* 503: "My longing heart at last has bested me, though I had sworn never to show my love."
25. Decrees composed by a secretary at the Emperor's direction, hence answers written by someone else.
26. From a poem cited in an early commentary, attributed to Emperor Ichijō: "I am sick at heart, for the words will not come, to tell one whom I have never seen that I am in love."

"Your heart's true desire: hear me ask you its degree and just how you feel.
Can you suffer as you say for someone you do not know?"

The hand, the diction, were worthy of the greatest lady in the land.

All this reminded him pleasantly of life in the City, but it did not become him to write too often, and every two or three days he would therefore seize the pretext of a languid evening or a lovely dawn (moments likely to appeal to her as well) and soon decided—since she was far from an unworthy correspondent—that he did not wish to miss knowing someone so deeply proud; and yet Yoshikiyo's possessive talk about her offended him, and he did not like to ruin years of hope before the man's very eyes. After some thought he decided to go further only when someone came forward toward him. Alas, she whose pride surpassed the greatest lady's remained so maddeningly reticent that they spent their days in a contest of wills.

Now that the pass[27] stood between him and the distant City, he worried more and more about his love there and wondered what he really should do. Not having her was indeed no joke.[28] Should he have her come to him in secret? His resolve wavered now and then, but he told himself that he would not be there forever and that in any case it would not look well if he did.

That year there were frequent omens and repeated disturbances at the palace. On the thirteenth of the third month, the night when lightning flashed and the wind roared, His Majesty dreamed that His Late Eminence stood below the palace steps, glaring balefully at him while he himself cowered before him in awe. His Eminence had much to say, and no doubt he spoke of Genji. His Majesty described his dream in fear and sorrow to the Empress Mother. "One imagines all sorts of things on a night when it is pouring and the skies are in tumult," she said. "You must not allow it to disturb you unduly."

Something now went wrong with His Majesty's eyes, perhaps because he had met his father's furious gaze, and he suffered unbearably. Penances of all kinds were ordered, both at the palace and at the Empress Mother's home.

The Chancellor[29] passed away, which was natural enough at his age, but to add to this series of crises the Empress Mother herself became vaguely indisposed, and she grew weaker with time. Thus varied sorrows afflicted the court.

"I do think there will be retribution, though, if Genji really is in disgrace when actually he is blameless," His Majesty would often remark. "I have a mind to restore him to his offices."

"You would gain no respect by doing so," the Empress Mother would strenuously insist. "What will people say if before even three years are out you pardon a man whose offenses have driven him into banishment?"

---

27. The *seki* ("pass," "barrier") mentioned in Yukihira's poem on the wind, hence poetically associated with Suma and its region. Nothing is known about it.

28. *Kokinshū* 1025: "When I do not go to see her, just to find out whether it is true, I so long for her that it is no joke."

29. The previous Minister of the Right, the Emperor's grandfather.

Days and months passed while His Majesty wavered, and meanwhile both his condition and the Empress Mother's grew worse.

At Akashi there was as always something new in the autumn wind, and Genji found sleeping by himself so horribly lonely that he now and then approached his host. "Do find one reason or another to bring her here," he would say; for he did not feel that he could go to her, and she herself showed no sign of encouraging him. She had heard that miserable country girls were the ones who foolishly surrendered that way to the flattering talk of a gentleman briefly down from the City. He could not possibly have any respect for me, she said to herself, and I would only burden myself with grief. I suppose that as long as I remain unmarried, my parents, with their impossible ambitions for me, entertain affectionately fanciful visions of my future, but I myself will only suffer for them. No, it is quite enough for me to correspond with him like this while he remains here on this shore. After years of listening to rumors about him she had never expected to catch the least glimpse of anyone like him where she actually lived, but she had nonetheless had a glimpse of him, she had heard on the wind the music of his koto, which was said to be superb, and she knew a good deal about how he spent his time; and the very idea that he should deign to notice her sufficiently to court her was simply too much for one whose life had been wasted among seafolk like these. Such were her thoughts, and the more embarrassed she felt, the less she could even contemplate allowing him nearer.

Her parents, who saw their long-standing prayer close to fulfillment, began anxiously imagining the grief that would follow, now that they had rashly given him their daughter, if he were to scorn her, for however great a lord he might be, that would be a bitter blow. Yes, they constantly fretted, we trusted the invisible buddhas and gods in ignorance of his feelings and of our daughter's karma.[30]

"I so long to hear her music against the sound of the waves we have had lately," Genji would often say. "It will be a great shame if I cannot."

The Novice quietly chose a propitious day, ignored her mother's varied objections, all on his own and without a word to his acolytes did up her room until it shone, and once the almost full moon[31] had risen in glory lightly remarked to his guest, "On so lovely a night . . ."[32]

You're a rascal, aren't you! thought Genji; but he put on a dress cloak, tidied himself up, and set out at a very late hour. His carriage was splendidly ready, but that seemed a little too much, and he rode instead. He took only Koremitsu and one or two others with him. It was quite a long way. From the path he looked out over distant stretches of shore, and the moon shining from waters dear to lovers of beauty[33] only recalled the lady he missed, until he felt as though he would ride on by and go straight to her.

---

30. Karma that would in principle determine her marriage partner.
31. The moon of the twelfth or thirteenth night, two or three nights before the full.
32. *Gosenshū* 103, by Minamoto no Saneakira: "On so lovely a night, how gladly I would share the moon and the flowers with one who knows their beauty as I do."
33. *Genji monogatari kochūshakusho in'yō waka* 126: "Come, then, O lovers of beauty, to see the moon in the depths of the waters at Tamatsushima!"

"On this autumn night, O steed with coat of moonlight, soar on through the skies,
that for just a little while I may be there with my love!"[34]

he murmured to himself.

The house, a fine one, was magnificently situated deep among the trees. The mansion by the sea was curious and imposing, but here, he felt with a pang, life would be lonely and one would know every shade of melancholy. The bell of the nearby meditation hall rang mournfully while the wind sighed among the pines, and the pines' roots gripping the rocks had a dignity all their own. Insects of many kinds were singing in the near garden. He looked carefully about him. The part where his host's daughter lived was done up with special care. The handsome door had let in the moonlight and still stood a little ajar.[35]

Her reluctance to expose her person to any liberties from him ran so deep that his hesitant tries at conversation met only mournful resistance. What airs she puts on! he thought. The most inaccessibly grand lady would have yielded with good grace after all this courting, but no, not she. Does she despise me, then, for being out of favor? He was annoyed and pondered varied misgivings. Heartlessly to force her would confound good sense, but he would gain no credit from losing a contest of wills. One would have wished to show him off in his trouble and anger to someone who really did know something of beauty. A ribbon on a nearby standing curtain brushed the strings of a *sō no koto*, which called up a pleasant picture of her playing alone for her own pleasure. "Will you not at least allow me to hear your famous koto?" he asked, multiplying his attempts to draw her out.

Standing curtain

"O for a dear friend to join me in the pleasure of sharing sweet talk,
that I might perhaps awake from the dream of this sad life."

She answered,

"How could I who roam the long darkness of a night unbroken by dawn
even know what is a dream, that I should join in your talk?"

Her shadowy form was very like the Haven's at Ise. Having been comfortably alone, thinking no harm, she now found the surprise too great a shock; entering the

---

34. A "moon-colored horse" (*tsukige no koma*) was rose gray roan.

35. This partly opened door that has already admitted the moonlight and that will in a moment admit Genji himself was praised as sublime by Fujiwara no Teika (1162–1241), the great poet and scholar who edited the Genji text fundamental to most later editions.

neighboring room, she somehow fastened the sliding panel so securely that he made no move to force it open. Yet that could not very well be all.

Elegantly tall, she had daunting dignity. It greatly saddened him to consider the contrived character of their union.[36] Now that he knew her, he surely felt still more deeply about her. The always tediously long night seemed to pass in an instant into dawn. Anxious to be gone before anyone should notice him, he left her with heartfelt assurances of love.

His letter came that day, very privately. Could he have been suffering, alas, from pangs of conscience? She did not wish anyone to know, and she gave his messenger no festive welcome. Her father could hardly bear it.

After that, Genji sometimes called on her in secret. Since her house was some way off, he restrained himself, lest gossiping seafolk turn up on his way, and this so sadly confirmed her fears that the Novice, too, in sympathy, forgot to long for paradise and waited only for signs of Genji's visits. It was a shame that his thoughts should be so troubled even now.

Genji suffered and smarted that his lady at Nijō might somehow catch wind of all this and be hurt to imagine his heart straying, even in a flight of folly; which no doubt gave the measure of his extravagant love. Whenever she had occasion to note and, in a manner quite unlike her, to protest goings-on of this kind, he would wonder why he had let a silly amusement provoke her, and want to undo it all. The thought of the lady at issue this time therefore only aroused a longing that nothing could slake, until he wrote to Nijō more expansively than usual and appended this note: "I should add that although it is agony to remember how my foolishness has sometimes earned me your displeasure, when it disappoints even me, I have again strangely enough dreamed a little dream. Please understand from this unprompted confession how wholly I am yours. 'If my promise . . .'"[37] And he continued, "At each thought of you,

> Salty streams of brine spring to his eyes and he weeps: the man of the shore
> harvesting seaweed pleasures followed just a passing whim."

Her answer, written with engaging artlessness, had at the end, "The dream that you felt obliged to mention brings many thoughts to mind:

> How innocently I let you have all my trust that once we were joined,
> waves would never sweep across any height covered with pines."[38]

This hint, piercing through the mildness of her tone, so affected him that he could not put her letter down. The mood lasted, and he renounced the traveler's secret nights.

---

36. Contrived because he and she were brought together only by a highly unusual set of influences. Normally they would never have met.

37. *Genji monogatari kochūshakusho in'yō waka* 475: "If my promise never to forget you should lapse, may the judgment of the God of Mount Mikasa be upon me."

38. "That you would never be unfaithful." *Kokinshū* 1093: "Should I ever prove fickle and leave you, may waves wash over the pine-clad hill of Sue."

The lady, who was not surprised, now really did feel like throwing herself into the sea. Lacking anyone but her aging parents, she had never expected to command the respect others enjoyed, but during the months and years that had drifted by, nothing after all had happened to cause her anguish. Now that she knew what cares life can bring, they seemed far worse than anything she had imagined, but she retained her composure and received Genji gracefully enough. She meant more to him as time went by, but he felt very sorry that a far greater lady should spend years of anxious waiting, tenderly thinking of him, and more often than not he slept alone.

He painted a varied collection of pictures and wrote his thoughts on them so that she could add her replies.[39] No one who saw them could have failed to be moved. Across the heavens their hearts must somehow have touched, for at Nijō she, too, when excessively burdened by her sorrows, began to paint pictures of her own and to set straight down on them, as though in a diary, the telling moments of her life. What future did they have in store?

The New Year had come, and to the court's loud distress His Majesty required treatment. One of his children was a son born to the Shōkyōden Consort, a daughter of the current Minister of the Right; but the boy was now in his second year and still too young.[40] His proper course was to abdicate in favor of the Heir Apparent, and when he pondered who might then govern in the service of the realm, Genji's disgrace so shocked and offended him that at last he ignored his mother's remonstrances and decreed that Genji was to be pardoned. The previous year the Empress Mother had begun to suffer from an afflicting spirit, and frequent oracles had disturbed the court, while recently the eye trouble that strict penances seemed to have relieved had worsened again, causing His Majesty such misery that after the twentieth of the seventh month he issued another decree recalling Genji to the City.

Genji had counted on this happening in time, although this treacherous world did not encourage him to look forward to what might follow, but the moment came so suddenly that his joy was mixed with sorrow at having now to give up this shore. The Novice, who wholly approved, still found his heart full at the news. He soon thought better of that, though, since the fulfillment of Genji's ambitions also meant success for what he himself desired.

By now Genji was with her every night. In the sixth month she began to look and to feel sadly unwell.[41] Now that he was to leave her, he seemed unfortunately to value her more than before, and he was troubled to see her destined inexplicably for sorrow. Needless to say, she herself despaired, and for that no one could blame her. After undertaking this strangely melancholy journey Genji had always found comfort in the belief that he would return one day, but with that happy prospect now before him he reflected unhappily that he might never see the place again.

The men in his service rejoiced, each as his circumstances moved him to do. A party came from the City to greet him, which was pleasant, but the Novice wept

---

39. He wrote poems on the paintings, leaving room for Murasaki to add poems of her own.
40. To displace the Heir Apparent.
41. With morning sickness.

Saltmaking: raking up seaweed, salt-fire smoke

and wept; and meanwhile the eighth month arrived. Under these autumn skies, sad enough in themselves, Genji wondered wretchedly why now as in the past he still gave himself up to these reckless adventures, until those who knew what the matter was grumbled, "Look at that! There he goes again!" Nudging each other, they went on, "All these months, without a word to anyone, he has been stealing off to see her, and now he has just made her unhappy after all." To Yoshikiyo's great discomfort they whispered that he was the one who had first told Genji about her.

Genji went to her earlier than usual in the evening, since he was to leave the day after tomorrow. This was the first time he had seen her properly, and her poised dignity so impressed him that he found it very painful to leave her behind. He wished she would come and join him in some suitable manner and sought to console her with assurances to this effect. His looks and bearing needed no description, but his devotions had given him a fine leanness of feature that lent him inexpressible grace, and while he poured forth in tears the tenderest promises, she may even have wondered whether this was not happiness enough, and whether she should not now renounce the thought of more. His very beauty made her own insignificance painfully obvious.

The noise of the waves had changed in the autumn wind. Smoke from the salt fires drifted thinly by, and all that gave the place its character was present in the scene.

> "Our parting has come, and for now I must leave you, but I pray the smoke
> rising from your salt fires here may still lean the way I go."

She replied,

> "Sea-tangle sorrows the saltmaker gathers in to heap on her fires
> are no more than what life brings; she has no wish to complain."

Although hardly able to speak through her tears, she could still give him an eloquent reply when one was needed.

Genji, who had always longed to hear her play for him, was very disappointed that she had not done so. "Just a little, then," he said, "to remember you by." He sent for the *kin* he had brought from the City and softly plucked its strings in a lovely tune that ineffably filled the clear depths of the night. This was too much for the

Novice, who took the *sō no koto* and slid it through the curtains to his daughter. His invitation must have elicited as well tears that flowed freely while her quiet playing revealed what she could do. Her Cloistered Eminence's touch struck him as peerless in his time, for her brilliance, which often gave the listener a thrill of pleasure, also conveyed an image of herself, and that made her music truly supreme. In contrast, this lady excelled thanks to unfailing mastery and an enviably absorbing tone. Her music, too, called up deep, fond feelings, and while she played pieces he had never heard before, pausing so often that he could hardly bear it, he longed for more and wondered bitterly why for months he had failed to insist on her giving him this pleasure.

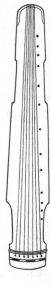

Kin

He poured forth promises about the future. "You must have this *kin* until we can play together again," he said.

> *"That casual gift you give to make me believe you will remain true*
> *I shall honor in my thoughts with a long music of tears,"*[42]

she replied, so low that he could hardly hear her; and he, nettled,

> *"This koto is yours, that you may remember me till we meet again,*
> *and I hope you will not change the pitch of the middle string.*[43]

We will see each other before it loses its tuning," he went on, to encourage her trust; but she was understandably lost in tears of anguish at the prospect of his going.

On the day, he left her in the darkness before dawn. Even when caught up among those who had come to escort him, he still found a lull to send her,

> *"Alas that the wave is to rise now and withdraw, leaving you behind*
> *to what sorrows of your own I imagine all too well."*

She answered,

> *"This house of rushes, where I have lived all these years, will be desolate—*
> *ah, how I long to follow after the withdrawing wave!"*[44]

The words said what she meant, and tears spilled from his eyes, though he tried to stop them. Those who did not know the circumstances thought this natural enough, despite the sort of place it was, considering that he had lived there a long time by now and that he was leaving forever. Such evidence of serious attachment did not at

---

42. The poem plays on *hitokoto* ("one word" and "a koto" [Genji's *kin*]) and *ne* ("music" and "sound of weeping").

43. It is unclear what the "middle string [or strings]" of the instrument is, but metaphorically it both links the lovers and confirms their separation.

44. "I would willingly drown myself in the sea" or "I would willingly follow you to the City." The common people on the shore lived in *tomaya*, houses thatched with rushes.

all please Yoshikiyo. The others were happy but also sad, for today really was to be their last by the sea, and their talk among themselves suggested that they, too, had their reasons to weep—not that one need go on about them, though.

The Novice's preparations for the day were grand indeed. Everyone, down to the least of Genji's men, had clothes of the best for the journey.[45] One wondered when he could possibly have had them made. Genji's own costume was finer than words can describe, and uncounted chests of clothing joined his train. Each gift was worthy of presentation in the City, and each had its own merit, for the donor had neglected nothing.

On the hunting cloak given him to wear, Genji found,

> "Perhaps you will spurn this travel cloak after all for its saltiness,
> washed as it has often been by the brine of wave on wave."

Despite his agitation he still managed to reply,

> "Yes, let us exchange something to give each of us the other's presence:
> a robe to be between us till the day we meet again";[46]

and he put it on in acknowledgment of her kindness. He sent her the things he had been wearing, and they did indeed make a keepsake for her to remember him by just that much better. How could the fragrance suffusing his exquisite cloak not permeate her own thoughts as well?

"Having at last put this world behind me, I still regret that I cannot go with you today," the Novice said. He made a sad sight, with his mouth turned down at the corners, but the younger people must have laughed.

> "Weary of the world, I have lived by the salt sea many, many years,
> yet it is true even now that I cannot leave this shore,"[47]

he said to Genji. "Perhaps to the border, at least, since the heart's darkness is certain to claim me . . ."[48] And he went on ingratiatingly, "Please forgive my presumption, but if you ever chance to think of her . . ."[49]

Genji was very deeply moved, and the flush here and there on his face gave his looks an inexpressible charm. "I have good reason not to forget her, you know. You will very soon know me better than that. But it is so difficult for me to leave your house! What am I to do?" he said, and, wiping his eyes,

> "Was that sorrow worse, setting out to go that spring far from the City,
> than this one, when in autumn I leave a familiar shore?"

45. Each must have got a hunting cloak and gathered trousers.
46. The "robe to be between us" (*naka no koromo*) parallels the "middle string" (*naka no o*) of an earlier exchange.
47. The "shore" is both Akashi and "this shore" (i.e., "this world") as opposed to "the other shore," paradise.
48. The darkness that engulfs the heart of a father worried about his child. The border is the one between Harima Province and Settsu.
49. "I hope that she may expect a letter from you."

The Novice was beside himself and only wept the more. He could hardly even stand.

His daughter's state was beyond words. She calmed herself to keep it from showing, but fairly or unfairly, her plight drove her to helplessly bitter resent-

Garden stream

ment at his leaving, and with his image always before her she could only collapse in tears after all.

Her mother did not know how to comfort her. "Why did we ever think of causing you this misery?" she said. "It is all my fault for having listened to anyone so mad."

"Stop it!" her father said. "He has every reason not to neglect her, and I am sure he still has something in mind for her"; and, to his daughter, "Take hold of yourself and drink your medicine. What a way to behave!" However, he himself was slumped in a corner.

Her nurses and her mother all condemned his delusions. "He has been so eager for years to see her as he wants her to be," they said, "and we thought he *had* managed it this time, but no, it is a disaster already!" Their distress and hers upset him so much that he became more and more confused, sleeping through the day and rising briskly at night to sit there, praying and rubbing his hands together, muttering, "My rosary has just vanished!" One moonlit night, after the servants had mocked him, he went outside to do his circumambulations, fell into the garden brook, bumped his backside on a picturesque rock, and went to bed to recover, which at last gave him something else to think about.

Genji traveled to Naniwa, where he underwent purification, and through a messenger he also announced to Sumiyoshi that he would give thanks for his safe journey and for the blessings received in response to his vows.[50] His entourage had suddenly grown too large to allow him for now to go in person, and he hastened to enter the City without pausing for any further excursions.

When he reached his Nijō residence, the people of his household and those traveling with him met in what felt to them like a dream, and there arose an alarming tumult of tears and laughter. His darling must have valued after all the life that had meant so little to her. She had grown up to be absolutely lovely, and to her great advantage the weight of her sorrows had slightly thinned her once overabundant hair. He was now deeply content to see that she would always be his this way,

50. At the time of the storm.

but at the thought his heart went out with a pang to the one whom he had so unwillingly left. Yes, such things would clearly never give him any rest.

He began talking about her, and the memories so heightened his looks that the lady before him must have been troubled, for with "I care not for myself"[51] she dropped a light hint that delighted and charmed him. When merely to see her was to love her, he wondered in amazement how he had managed to spend all these months and years without her, and bitterness against the world rose in him anew.

Very soon he was awarded a new office, that of Acting Grand Counselor. All his followers for whom it was proper to do so were restored to their former functions and privileges, until in both mood and manner they resembled wintry trees at last touched by spring.

An invitation came from His Majesty, and Genji called on him. The gentlewomen wondered while he was in the presence how a man of his now mature dignity could have endured all those years in so strange a place. The ancient women in service there since His Late Eminence's reign mourned again with tears and cries, and they sang Genji's praises. Even His Majesty felt called upon to mind himself, and he came forth attired with special care. Although greatly reduced because of his long illness, he had lately been feeling a little better. They talked quietly on into the night. The moon of the fifteenth night[52] hung aloft, lovely and tranquil, while fragments of the past drifted through His Majesty's mind, and perhaps in dread of the future he wept. He said, "How long I have gone without music and missed the sound of instruments once so familiar!"

> "Feebly languishing in disgrace beside the sea, the forlorn Leech Child
> for year after endless year could not stand on his own feet,"[53]

Genji replied.

Deeply moved, and also ashamed, His Majesty replied,

> "Now that we at last have circled to meet again around the sacred pole,
> O forget the bitterness that spring when we were parted!"[54]

He spoke with the most engaging kindness.

Genji hastened to arrange a Rite of the Eight Discourses for His Late Eminence. He was extremely pleased to find that the Heir Apparent had grown up very nicely indeed, and he looked upon him with great emotion. The Heir Apparent's

51. *Shūishū* 870, by Ukon: "I care not for myself, who am forgotten, but I grieve for the life of him who made me those vows."

52. Of the eighth month. Genji saw this moon at Suma just two years ago.

53. Genji likens himself to the first, defective offspring of Izanagi and Izanami, the primordial pair in the Japanese creation myth. The Leech Child had no bones and was therefore sent drifting out to sea. *Nihon shoki* 66, by Ōe no Asatsuna: "Do his parents not pity him? The Leech Child has reached his third year and still cannot stand."

54. The Leech Child was defective because after Izanagi and Izanami circled in opposite directions around a sacred pole, Izanami (the female) spoke first to invite Izanagi to intercourse. When they repeated the circling and Izanagi (the male) spoke first, the resulting children were sound.

brilliant success in his studies made him obviously able to assume with confidence the duties of the Sovereign. Once Genji had composed himself a little, he called on Her Cloistered Eminence, too, and their conversation must have touched on many a moving theme.

Oh, yes, on the retreating waves he sent a letter down to Akashi.[55] It seems to have been a long one, stealthily written. "How are you getting on, when waves night after night . . . ?

> *My thoughts go to you, imagining morning mists rising down the shore*
> *while you at Akashi spend sleepless nights lost in sorrow."*

The Gosechi Dancer, the daughter of the Dazaifu Deputy, felt that she was now over her secret, hopeless misery, and she had her messenger give Genji this, with a wink:

> *"I would have you see how swiftly the mariner found her sleeves undone*
> *once she had given her heart to longing for Suma Shore."*

She writes so much better now! he thought, divining the sender, and he replied,

> *"No, it should be mine to present you my complaint, for after your note*
> *there has hardly been a time when my sleeves have ever dried."*

Her unexpected message brought her vividly to mind, for he still remembered how very much he had liked her, but he seems in those days to have abstained from that sort of thing.

He only wrote to the village of falling flowers, so that the lady there doubted him and was more hurt than ever.

---

55. With the Akashi men who had escorted him to the City and were now returning.

14

MIOTSUKUSHI
The Pilgrimage to Sumiyoshi

The syllables *mi-o-tsu-ku-shi* occur in the poetic exchange by which this chapter has often been remembered. Their primary meaning is "channel marker" (a pole set in an estuary bottom to mark the channel), but they also convey "give my all" (for love).

Genji has gone to the Sumiyoshi Shrine, near Naniwa, to thank the god for his blessings. By chance the Akashi lady arrives on the same day, on her own pilgrimage to Sumiyoshi; but the beach is so crowded with Genji's vast entourage that she, feeling very small, passes straight on to the harbor of Naniwa.

Discovering what has happened, Genji goes sightseeing in Naniwa, where he notices the Horie Channel (a name famous in poetry), marked by its rows of *miotsukushi*. He then sends her,

> *"I who give my all for your love have my reward, for to find you here,*
> *where so deep a channel runs, proves the power of our bond."*

She replies,

> *"Lacking any worth, I have no title to claim any happiness;*
> *what can have possessed me, then, so to give my all for love?"*

"The Pilgrimage to Sumiyoshi" continues "Akashi," beginning in the tenth month when Genji is twenty-eight and extending to the eleventh month of the following year.

PERSONS

His Grace, Genji, rises from Grand Counselor to Palace Minister, age 28 to 29

The Empress Mother (Kokiden)

His Majesty, the Emperor, then His Eminence, 30 to 31 (Suzaku)

His Late Eminence, Genji's father, after his death (Kiritsubo In)

The Mistress of Staff (Oborozukiyo)

Genji's lady at Nijō, 20 to 21 (Murasaki)

His Highness, the Heir Apparent, then His Majesty,
the Emperor, 10 to 11 (Reizei)

Her Cloistered Eminence, his mother, 33 to 34 (Fujitsubo)

The Shōkyōden Prince, named Heir Apparent, 2 to 3

His mother, the Shōkyōden Consort

His Excellency, the Chancellor, formerly Minister of the Left, 62 to 63 (Sadaijin)

The Consultant Captain, then the Acting Counselor (Tō no Chūjō)

His daughter, the Kokiden Consort, 11 to 12

His son (Kōbai)

Genji's son, 7 to 8 (Yūgiri)

The lady at Akashi, 19 to 20 (Akashi no Kimi)

Her daughter, born (Akashi no Himegimi)

The daughter's nurse

The Novice, around 61 to 62 (Akashi no Nyūdō)

The former Reikeiden Consort

The lady of the falling flowers (Hanachirusato)

The Gosechi Dancer

His Highness of War, brother of Fujitsubo and father of Murasaki
(Hyōbukyō no Miya)

The Aide of the (Right) Palace Guards, then in the Gate Watch

Yoshikiyo, Genji's retainer

Koremitsu, Genji's confidant

The Governor of Settsu, one of Genji's retainers

The Rokujō Haven, 35 to 36 (Rokujō no Miyasudokoro)

The High Priestess of Ise, her daughter, 19 to 20 (Akikonomu)

Genji thought of His Late Eminence often after that clear dream, and he sorrowfully wished somehow to save him from the sins that had brought him so low. Once he was back in the City, he quickly prepared to do so, and in the tenth month he held a Rite of the Eight Discourses. All the world bowed to his wishes, as it had done before.

The Empress Mother, even gravely ill, took it hard that she must fail to suppress this Genji, but His Majesty, who recalled his father's last wishes and foresaw certain retribution, was greatly relieved to have raised him up again. The eye trouble that had so often afflicted him was now gone, but his doubt that he would live much longer weighed heavily on him, and the knowledge that he had little time left prompted him to call Genji constantly to his side. He derived such obvious satisfaction from discussing all things openly with him that his pleasure brought happiness in turn to the whole court.

With his planned abdication rapidly approaching, his sympathy went to the Mistress of Staff, whose experience of life had been so painful. "His Excellency the Chancellor is no more," he said to her, "the Empress Mother's health gives every cause for concern, and now that I feel my own time is coming, I am afraid of leaving you sadly on your own in a very different world. You have never thought as well of me as of a certain other, but my greater affection has always moved me to care for you above all. The one you prefer may take pleasure in you, too, but I do not think that his feeling for you approaches mine, which is far stronger, and this alone is very painful." He began to weep.

She blushed scarlet, in all the full, fresh ripeness of her beauty, and her tears spilled forth until he forgot her transgressions and looked on her only with pity and love. "I wonder why you would not even give me a child," he said. "That is a very great regret. I know you will have one for him, with whom your tie is so much stronger, and the thought makes me very sad indeed. After all, he is what he is and no more, and your child will have a commoner father."

This and other remarks from him about the future overwhelmed her with sorrow and shame. His face gave off such a lovely sweetness, and his behavior so clearly proved a boundless devotion that had seemed to grow with the passage of the years, that despite Genji's merits she could only acknowledge what suffering his lukewarm attentions had brought her, until she no longer knew why she had followed her youthful leanings and caused that dreadful scandal—one damaging not only to her name but to his. Such memories led her to rue the life that she had led.

The Heir Apparent's coming of age took place in the second month of the following year. His Highness, now eleven, was tall and dignified for his age, and his face appeared to be traced from Genji's own. Both shone so dazzlingly that everyone sang their praises, but His Highness's mother was appalled and only wished fervently that it were not so. His Majesty looked on the boy with pleasure and gently let him know, among other things, that he meant soon to cede him the realm.

The abdication took place after the twentieth of the same month, suddenly enough to upset the Empress Mother. His Majesty sought to calm her, saying, "I shall no longer have any importance, but I look forward to seeing you more at my ease." The Shōkyōden Prince was named Heir Apparent. The new reign began, for a change, amid many moments of novel brilliance. Genji rose from Grand Counselor to Palace Minister. His post had been added to the others, since no regular one of the kind was vacant.[1] Although expected now to take up the reins of government, he ceded the role of Regent to His Excellency, the former Minister of the Left, on the grounds that he was not up to its many responsibilities.

"Illness obliged me to resign my office," His Excellency said, declining to accept, "and now that I am also so much older, I doubt that I could actually manage." In the other realm,[2] too, though, the very men who vanished into the mountains in unstable, troubled times came forth, white hair and all, to serve in time of peace, which brought them acknowledgment as true sages;[3] and so all agreed in both public and private that there could be no objection to His Excellency taking up again, under the new reign, a post he had given up for reasons of poor health. It had been done before. For that reason he broke off his retirement and became Chancellor. He was then sixty-three.

He had shut himself away in part because he felt the world against him, but now he flourished as before, and all his sons who had languished in disfavor rose high. The Consultant Captain, in particular, became an Acting Counselor. The girl he had had by the late Chancellor's fourth daughter was twelve, and he was bringing her up with care in order to present her to His Majesty. The son[4] who had sung "Takasago" was now of age. Genji envied his old friend all the children he kept having by one mother or another, and the resulting liveliness of his household.

His own little son by His Excellency's daughter was exceptionally handsome, and he frequented both His Majesty's and the Heir Apparent's privy chambers. His

---

1. The posts provided for by the law codes were those of Minister of the Left and of the Right. The posts of Palace Minister (Naidaijin, Uchi no Otodo), and Chancellor (Daijōdaijin, Ōkiotodo) were therefore in a sense unofficial, although they were recognized by custom and normally filled. Genji is now expected to act as Regent for the young Emperor.
2. China.
3. The *Shiji* provides the example of four wise and ancient men who returned from retirement to serve Empress Lu of Han in her effort to secure her son's succession to the throne.
4. The future Kōbai.

grandparents still felt their grief for their late daughter keenly, although even now, when she was gone, Genji's light alone so lifted His Excellency that his years of despair vanished into glory. Genji came to call on every occasion, for his goodwill had not changed, and his tactful kindness to his son's nurses, as well as to the other gentlewomen who had stayed on through the years, undoubtedly brought happiness to many.

His sympathy went to those who similarly awaited him at Nijō. Wishing to raise the long-despondent spirits of women like Chūjō and Nakatsukasa, he showed them such attentions, each according to her station, that he had no leisure even to call elsewhere. He ordered a magnificent rebuilding of the mansion—a legacy from His Late Eminence—to the east of his Nijō residence, and he had its rooms done up with the idea of bringing the lady of the falling flowers there, as well as others whose plight concerned him.

Oh, yes—he never forgot his anxiety about the lady he had left in so delicate a condition at Akashi, and despite a press of affairs, both public and private, that kept him from giving her the attention he desired, he realized when the third month came that the day might soon be at hand, and in a rush of secret feeling sent off a messenger.

The messenger quickly returned. "The birth took place on the sixteenth," he reported. "The child is a girl, and all is well."

Genji was especially happy to gather that he had a daughter. He wondered bitterly why he had not brought her mother to have her child in the City.

An astrologer had foretold to Genji that he would have three children, of whom one would be Emperor and another Empress, while the third and least among them would reach the highest civil rank of Chancellor. To all appearances he had been right. Expert physiognomists had all agreed that Genji would rise to the highest rank and govern the realm, but years of unpleasantness had so dampened his hopes that the new Emperor's successful accession brought him pleasure and satisfaction. He agreed that his father had been right to remove him from the line of succession. His father had taken greater pleasure in him than in any other of his many sons, but on due consideration that decision to make him a commoner now confirmed that it was not he who had any such calling; no, it could never be told who His Majesty really was, but the physiognomist had not been wrong. Looking to the future, Genji saw in all this the guiding influence of the God of Sumiyoshi. Yes, *hers*, too, was an extraordinary destiny, and her eccentric father had certainly entertained ambitions properly beyond him. What a shame it was, though, and what a waste, that one destined for such heights should have come into the world in a place so remote! He would have to bring her here, once everything was quiet again. He gave orders to hasten the rebuilding of his mansion to the east.

He could not imagine finding anyone worthy[5] in a place like Akashi, but meanwhile he heard of the daughter of a senior gentlewoman under His Late Eminence, whose father at his death had been Lord of the Palace Bureau and a Consul-

5. To be his daughter's wet nurse.

tant and who, blighted by the loss of her mother, had in these discouraging circumstances given birth to a child. Through the person who had told him about her he managed satisfactorily to obtain her consent. Still young and artless, and sadly depressed by a life spent grieving in a ruined house, she hardly paused to think; she liked the thought of being near him so well that she declared herself at his disposal. Genji, who felt quite sorry for her, sent her straight down to Akashi.

He had stolen off to see her himself when he had the opportunity to do so. Despite her initial assent she was worrying about what she should really do, but his gratifying visit soothed her fears, and she agreed to satisfy his wish.

It was an auspicious day, and he urged her to set off immediately. "You will think it strangely unkind of me," he said, "but I have a particular reason.[6] Be patient a little while and remember that I, too, have languished where I never thought to go"; and he went on to tell her all about her destination. He had seen her before because she had often waited on his father, although her fortunes had declined sadly since then. Her house, too, though large, was indescribably run-down, and the trees looming over it were so forbidding that he wondered how she could possibly live there. Still, she was young and pretty, and he could not take his eyes off her.

"I feel like keeping you here after all—and you?" he said banteringly, and it seemed to her that yes, all things being equal she would just as soon seek comfort from her sorrows in his intimate service.

> "It is not as though we have been for years and years the closest of friends,
> but our parting, even so, is a painful one to bear!"

he said. "Perhaps I should come after you."

She smiled.

> "This complaint of yours, that we are obliged to part all too suddenly,
> can mean only that you yearn to go where your longing goes,"

she answered. Her deft repartee caught his fancy.

She left the City by carriage. Genji had her escorted by a close retainer whom he sent off with injunctions to strict secrecy. The baggage was bursting with the dagger[7] and other similarly suitable gifts, for he had left nothing undone. He showed exceptionally kind generosity to the nurse as well. The thought of the Novice doting on his granddaughter often made Genji smile, and the depth of his fond concern for her left no doubt about the strength of that karmic bond. He begged her mother in his letter never to neglect their daughter.

---

6. He knows that his daughter is a future Empress, and he is anxious to have the nurse start out on a day auspicious enough to be worthy of the baby's future.

7. A girl of high rank received a dagger (mihakashi) at birth.

"O that soon these sleeves might touch her with their caress, that she long endure
like the rock the angel's wing brushes age after long age."[8]

The party traveled by boat as far as the province of Settsu, and from there they rode on quickly to their goal.

The Novice greeted the nurse with raptures of delighted respect. When he turned to bow in the direction of the City, the thought of Genji's most august concern made the little girl still more precious and prompted him even to feelings of dread.

She was so sweetly and so perfectly lovely that it was disconcerting: no wonder Genji in his wisdom intended to give her every advantage. The nurse had felt as though she were dreaming when she set out on her strange journey, but at this thought her distress melted away. She looked after her with the tenderest care.

The little girl's mother, for months now sunk in gloom, had felt herself weaken steadily until she doubted that she had much longer to live, but this new step by Genji made her feel a little better. She raised her eyes once more and gave Genji's messenger a very warm welcome. Since the messenger was eager to start back, she wrote down for Genji some of her thoughts:

"These poor sleeves of mine are too narrow: I cannot caress her alone,
and I look to the tall pine for his overspreading shade."[9]

Genji felt extraordinarily drawn and simply could not wait to see his daughter.

So far he had said little to his lady at home, but he did not want her to hear things from other people. "So that seems to be that," he remarked. "What a strange and awkward business it is! All my concern is for someone else, whom I would gladly see similarly favored,[10] and the whole thing is a sad surprise, and a bore, too, since I hear the child is a girl. I really suppose I should ignore her, but I cannot very well do that. I shall send for her and let you see her. You must not feel resentful."

She reddened. "Don't, please!" she said, offended. "You are always making up feelings like that for me, when I myself detest them. And when do you suppose that I learned to have them?"

"Ah, yes," said Genji with a bright smile, "who can have taught you? I have never seen you like this! Here you are, angry with me over fantasies of yours that have never occurred to me. It is too hard!" By now he was nearly in tears.

Memories of their endless love for each other down the years, and of the letters they had so often exchanged, told her that all his affairs were simple amusements, and the matter passed from her mind.

"If I am this anxious about her," Genji said, "it is because I have my reasons. You

8. Buddhist lore defines a "minor kalpa" (an aeon) as the time it takes a rock brushed once every three years by an angel's wing to wear away.

9. *Gosenshū* 64: "O for sleeves wide enough to cover the whole sky, that I might keep from the winds the blossoms of spring!" The poem also plays on *matsu*, "pine" and "wait."

10. "I wish *you* had a child."

Sō no koto

would only go imagining things again if I were to tell you too soon what they are." He was silent a moment. "It must have been the place itself that made her appeal to me so. She was something new, I suppose." He went on to describe the smoke that sad evening, the words they had spoken, a hint of what he had seen in her face that night, the magic of her koto; and all this poured forth with such obvious feeling that his lady took it ill.

There I was, she thought, completely miserable, and he, simple pastime or not, was sharing his heart with another! Well, I am I! She turned away and sighed, as though to herself, "And we were once so happy together!

> *Not as fond lovers' languid plumes follow the wind toward reunion,*
> *no, but as smoke myself I wish I were long since gone!"*[11]

"What? Why, what a thing to say!

> *Just who is it, then, for whom I suffered so much, roaming hills and seas,*
> *often enough near drowning in an endless stream of tears?*

Oh, I wish I could show you how I really feel! I suppose that demands a lifetime, though, and one never knows . . . It is all for you, you see, that I so want to avoid having other women condemn me over nothing." He drew her *sō no koto* to him and went through the modal prelude idly, to tempt her, but she would not touch it, since she was perhaps piqued by what she gathered of that other's skill. For all her quiet innocence, sweetness, and grace, she still had a stubborn side to her, and, when she was offended, as now, her wrath had a quality so delicious that he only enjoyed her the more.

Genji calculated privately that the fifth of the fifth month would be his daughter's fiftieth day, and he thought of her with eager, affectionate curiosity. How much more satisfyingly he could have celebrated her birth here, and how much happier the occasion would have been! What a shame that she had entered the world in a place that hopeless! She would not have preoccupied him nearly so much if she had been a boy, but he regretted for her sake the affront of her birth, and he reflected that his own flawed destiny had all been for her.

---

11. "I wish I were dead."

He sent a messenger with urgent instructions to get there on the day, and the man did indeed arrive on the fifth. Genji's thoughtful gifts were magnificently generous, and he had included more practical items as well. He had written,

> *"How is she to know, the little sea pine whose life is all in shadow,*
> *today's Sweet Flag Festival from her own fiftieth day?"*[12]

My heart has flown to her, you know. Do make up your mind to come, because I cannot go on living this way. I promise that you need not worry." As usual the Novice wept for joy. It will come as no surprise that at a time like this happiness all but drowned him in tears.

He, too, at Akashi had seen to everything magnificently, but without Genji's ambassador all would have seemed as though swallowed by darkness. Meanwhile the nurse was happy in the company of this most perfect and attractive of ladies, and she forgot her sorrows. Other gentlewomen, hardly less worthy, had been brought in as family connections allowed, but they, sadly fallen from service in the great houses of the City, had meant only to settle here quietly "among the rocks," while the nurse retained all her poise and pride. The tales she told were well worth hearing, and on the subject of His Grace[13] she enlarged with a woman's enthusiasm on his looks and on the warm regard in which he was universally held, until her new mistress, who meant so much to him and to whom he had actually given a child, came to think more highly of herself. They read his letter together. Ah, the nurse said to herself, some have all the luck, while I have none! But Genji's thoughtful inquiry about her pleased her greatly, and she felt much better.

> *"Yet again today, the fiftieth for the crane crying in the lea*
> *of this islet, all unseen, no one has asked after her,"*[14]

the lady gravely replied. "My fragile existence, you understand, hangs on the rare comfort of a letter from you, for everything draws me downward toward despair. I would indeed be glad of a reason to look forward to the future."

Genji read her letter again and again, and he sighed to himself loud and long. His lady gave him a sidelong look, then stared sorrowfully before her, murmuring under her breath, "The boat that rows seaward from the shore . . ."[15]

"You really mean to make an issue of it, don't you," Genji said irritably. "I feel sorry for her just now, that is all. Those days come back to me when I think what the place is like, and I talk to myself a bit; and you do not miss it, do you!" He showed her only the letter's outer cover.[16] The writing had such character as to put

---

12. With wordplays made explicit here, Genji's poem laments his daughter's remote birth. "Sea pine" (*umimatsu*) is actually a kind of seaweed more often called *miru*.

13. Genji. This will be his designation hereafter in this translation.

14. The "crane" is the little girl, the "islet" her mother.

15. *Kokin rokujō* 1888: "The boat that rows seaward from the shore at Kumano is leaving me and drawing ever farther away."

16. This sort of letter would have been wrapped, first, in a formal envelope (*raishi*) and then in an outer cover (*uwazutsumi*) that bore the name of the person addressed.

the greatest lady to shame, and she understood why Genji felt about the sender as
he did.

Alas, while placating his lady he completely neglected another in the village
of falling flowers. Public affairs now absorbed him, the constraints of his rank encouraged discretion, and one gathers that nothing came from her to rouse him from
his complacency.

He pulled himself together and went to call on her during the tedium of the
long rains, when little else claimed him at home or abroad. He felt no apprehension, for the household lived only from his generosity on the many occasions when,
from his distance, his thoughts turned to them, and she was unlikely to indulge in
modishly self-important complaints.

The house had deteriorated alarmingly since his last visit, years ago. The former Consort received him, and it was late at night when he went to the west double
doors. A pale moon shone in, revealing all of Genji's enchanting beauty. More
abashed than ever, she still sat gazing out from near the veranda, and her quiet figure was very pleasing to the eye. A moorhen called nearby.

> *"If no moorhen cried as though knocking at my gate, what would startle me*
> *into admitting the moon to my sadly ruined home?"*

she said with an engaging reticence that only reminded Genji how dear each of his
ladies was to him and how difficult a position her very mildness put him in.

> *"The moorhen, you know, tries his knock at every gate; if that startles you,*
> *you may find that you let in an all too light-minded moon.*

It is rather a worry," he parried, although he did not for a moment actually suspect
her of any such wantonness. He did not fail to appreciate her patient waiting for
him over the years.

She spoke of the time when he had enjoined her to "avert your eyes from an
all too cloudy sky."[17] "Why did I ever imagine that to be the worst misery I could
suffer?" she said. "My misfortune now is just the same." Her manner conveyed quiet
charm. As always, Genji called from somewhere a flood of eloquence to console her.

Not even this sort of thing could make him forget the Gosechi Dancer, but it
was not easy to see her again, though he looked forward eagerly to doing so, and he
could not manage to get away. She still pined for him after all, and despite her parents' fond attempts to change her mind she had given up the thought of a normal
life.[18] Genji meant his expansive building plan, even once he had gathered ladies
like her together, to allow him to look after anyone else who deserved his attention,
should such a one appear. The mansion was to be still richer in pleasant features and
more modern in style than his present one. He had picked men of taste from among
the provincial Governors and given each his task so as to hasten the construction.

17. During his farewell visit to her in "Suma."
18. Of marrying.

Even now the Mistress of Staff could not give him up. Incorrigible as ever, he returned her feeling, but she had learned her lesson from bitter experience and no longer encouraged him as before. Despite his happy return he felt uncomfortably constrained, and he missed their affair.

His Eminence,[19] who now looked tolerantly on life, from time to time held very pleasant musical gatherings and so on. His Consorts and Intimates all continued to serve him; only the Heir Apparent's mother failed to enjoy any great favor, being eclipsed in his affections by the Mistress of Staff. She therefore turned to reliance on her inalienable good fortune and moved away to attend His Highness.

Genji's lodging at the palace was the Kiritsubo, as of old. The Heir Apparent, who lived in the Nashitsubo,[20] conferred with him on every occasion, in a spirit of neighborly intimacy, and Genji lent him his assistance.

Since Her Cloistered Eminence could not properly assume a new rank, she was granted the emoluments of a Retired Emperor.[21] The officers of her household were correspondingly redesignated, and she lived in imposing style. Her constant occupation remained her religious devotions and the performance of acts of merit. Fear of appearing at court had prevented her from seeing her son during those years of intense worry and chagrin, but happily she could now come and go to him as she pleased, and it was the Empress Mother[22] who found life very bitter. On occasion Genji would treat her with embarrassing courtesy, and this only brought her new distress that would in its turn set off a buzz of gossip.

His Highness of War had maintained an unfortunate attitude over the years, and Genji, who condemned his surrender to court opinion, no longer kept up with him the old close ties. Although generally well disposed toward everyone, he sometimes displayed toward His Highness an antipathy that Her Cloistered Eminence noted with sorrow and disappointment.

The Chancellor and Genji shared government evenly between them and wielded its powers as they thought best.

In the eighth month of that year the Acting Counselor[23] sent his daughter to serve His Majesty. Her grandfather put himself into it, and the ceremony was all anyone could have wished. His Highness of War had carefully reared his well-regarded second daughter with the same ambition in mind, but Genji failed to see why she should be preferred over anyone else. What can he have been thinking of?

That autumn he went on a pilgrimage to Sumiyoshi. His retinue was grand, since he was to give thanks for many answered prayers, and the whole court, senior nobles and privy gentlemen alike, offered him their services on the journey.

It happened that the lady from Akashi, who made the pilgrimage every year, had decided to go, too, partly to atone for having failed to do so last year or so far

---

19. Suzaku, who recently ceded the throne to Reizei.
20. Immediately south of the Kiritsubo.
21. Being a nun, Fujitsubo cannot assume the rank and title of Empress Mother. She had previously enjoyed income from the produce and labor of fifteen hundred households; this number has now risen to two thousand.
22. The former Kokiden Consort, the mother of the present Retired Emperor.
23. Tō no Chūjō.

this year because of her condition.[24] She traveled by sea. On reaching the shore she found the beach covered with a vast and noisy throng of pilgrims, while a procession bore magnificent treasures for the god. Ten musicians, plainly selected for their good looks, were dancing all in a single color. Her men must have asked what pilgrim had arrived, for a hopelessly low menial burst into laughter and cried, "Look! Here are people who don't even know that His Grace is here to give thanks!"

Ah, she thought, considering all the days there are, in all the months of the year, this really is too cruel! To see his glory this way from a distance only makes me sorry to be who I am. Yes, I have a fated tie to him, but what dire karma is mine, when even so miserable an underling can blithely pride himself on being in his service, that I who yearn for him should have set out in utter ignorance of this great day? This train of reflections overwhelmed her with sorrow, and she secretly wept.

Formal cloaks light and dark drifted in untold numbers beneath the pines' deep green, as though the ground were strewn with flowers or autumn leaves. The Chamberlains in leaf green stood out among the young gentlemen of the sixth rank, and that Aide of the Palace Guards who had spoken so bitterly of the Kamo palisade now belonged to the Gate Watch and was also a Chamberlain, with his own imposing corps of attendants. Yoshikiyo, likewise a Gate Watch officer, wore a particularly carefree air, and in his red cloak[25] he looked very fine indeed. Those whom she had seen at Akashi were all scattered about here and there, transformed, brilliant and apparently without a care, while young senior nobles and privy gentlemen vied eagerly with one another, their very horses and saddles glitteringly adorned, and making a dazzling spectacle for the watchers from the country.

It only upset her to notice Genji's carriage in the distance, and she could not make out the figure she so longed to see. He had been given an escort of young pages, following the example of the Riverside Minister:[26] ten of them, handsome and of even height, delightfully dressed, and with their hair in twin tresses bound by white cords shading to deep purple ends. They had all together an especially fresh appeal. Genji's son by His Excellency's daughter, a young man whose father gave him every advantage, had his grooms and pages all dressed alike, so that there was no mistaking them. The heaven of His Majesty's City[27] seemed so distant and so glorious that she lamented her daughter's insignificance. She could only turn toward the shrine and pray.

The Governor of the province[28] arrived, and he no doubt prepared a magnificent reception for Genji, one far beyond any given an ordinary Minister. She felt agonizingly out of place. The god himself would neither notice her nor listen if she mixed with the throng to go through her own tedious little rite, and to start straight

24. Not only had her pregnancy made the journey too taxing for her, but in that state she was polluted and so unfit to approach the shrine.

25. The color of the fifth rank, one higher than sixth-rank green.

26. The Riverside Minister (Kawara no Otodo), Minamoto no Tōru (822–95), was the first imperial son to receive the Minamoto (or Genji) surname.

27. An explanatory rendering of kumoi ("the cloud realm," "the sky"), which frequently alludes to the lofty realm of the Emperor and the court.

28. Of Settsu, where the Sumiyoshi Shrine (and Suma) was located.

Dance from the "Eastern Dances"

home again would be too disappointing. No, she would put in today at Naniwa, where she would at least undergo purification. With this in mind she rowed away.

Genji, who knew nothing of this, spent the night variously entertaining the god. He left out no touch that might give the god true pleasure and, quite beyond his thanks for blessings in the past, he kept the heavens ringing until dawn with beautiful music and dancing. Men of his like Koremitsu felt sincere gratitude for the divine aid they had received. When Genji emerged briefly,[29] Koremitsu presented himself and said,

> "This great grove of pines here at Sumiyoshi brings many woes to mind
> when in thought I dwell upon those days under the god's care."[30]

Indeed it does, thought Genji, who remembered, too.

> "No such pounding waves as dashed themselves on that shore could shake me enough
> to drive from my memory Sumiyoshi and his boons.

His blessings are very great," he justly replied.

Genji was very sorry to learn that all the commotion had driven a boat from Akashi away, and he wished he had known. He who knew the god's blessing so well thought of comforting her at least with a note, for she must be hurt. He set out from the shrine and went roaming far and wide to see the sights. At Naniwa he underwent the most solemn purification. A view of the Horie Channel[31] started him humming, "I have nothing left now but to try to meet her, at Naniwa . . ."[32] Koremitsu, who was near his carriage, must have heard him, because the next time the

29. From the pavilion where he sat to watch the dancing.
30. "Those days under the god's care" (*kamiyo*, literally, "the age of the gods") refers to Suma and Akashi and acknowledges the divine protection Genji enjoyed there.
31. A channel or canal, well known in poetry, said to have been dug in the reign of Emperor Tenmu (reigned 673–86).
32. From *Gosenshū* 960, by Prince Motoyoshi: "Being so unhappy, nothing is left me now but to seek to meet her, at Naniwa, though it means giving my all." The poem plays on the syllables *mi-o-tsu-ku-shi* ("giving my all"), which also form the word for "channel marker" (a pole set in an estuary bottom to mark the channel). In poetry, *miotsukushi* was associated with the Horie Channel.

carriage stopped, he gave him a short-handled brush—one he kept in the front fold of his robe in case Genji should call for it. Genji was pleased, and he wrote on folding paper,

> "I who give my all for your love have my reward, for to find you here,
> where so deep a channel runs, proves the power of our bond."[33]

He gave it to Koremitsu, who sent it on with a well-informed servant.

Her heart beat when she saw his retinue ride by all abreast, but his message, however brief, touched her deeply, and in her gratitude she wept.

> "Lacking any worth, I have no title to claim any happiness;
> what can have possessed me, then, so to give my all for love?"[34]

She sent it tied to a sacred streamer from her purification on the Isle of Tamino.[35] Soon the sun would set. The scene's stirring mood, with the evening tide flooding in and the cranes along the inlet crying in full voice, must have been what made Genji long to be with her in defiance of prying eyes.

> "As wet now with dew as in those days we once knew, my traveling clothes
> find no shelter in the name of the Isle of Tamino."[36]

All along the way he enjoyed the pleasures of the journey, to ringing music, but his heart was still with her after all. Singing girls crowded to his procession, and all the young gallants with him, even senior nobles, seemed to look favorably on them; but not Genji, for he thought, Come now, all delight, all true feeling spring from the quality of one's partner, and a little frivolity, even playfully meant, is quite enough to put one off. Their airs and graces served only to turn him away.

She who filled his thoughts let his procession pass, and she made her offerings the following day,[37] since it was propitious. She had managed after all, as well as she was able, to put before the god prayers proper to her station. Then melancholy claimed her again, and she spent day and night lamenting the misery of her lot. A messenger from him reached her even before she imagined him reaching the City. I shall bring you here very soon, Genji had said, and yet she wavered, for although his words conveyed reassuring respect, she feared that troubling experiences might await her once she had rowed far away from the island.[38] She knew that her father must be very apprehensive about letting her go, although it was also true that the

---

33. The poem's key play on *miotsukushi* is lost in translation. The "channel markers" of the Horie Channel have reminded Genji of "give my all."

34. The play on *miotsukushi* is repeated, and there is another on the syllables of the name Naniwa.

35. The Isle of Tamino that once stood near the mouth of the Yodo River vanished long ago.

36. "I weep with longing for you as I did at Akashi." The syllables *mino*, in the name Tamino, make the word for "(straw) raincoat"; hence, "Tamino Isle gives me no protection from the dew of my tears."

37. At the Sumiyoshi Shrine.

38. The "island" is Awaji, opposite Akashi; the phrase refers to a complex of poems involving departure from Akashi.

thought of wasting her life here now distressed her
more than it had ever done in years past. She
gave Genji a cautious, irresolute answer.

Oh, yes! After the Rokujō Haven
returned to the City, the time having come for a new Ise Priestess,[39]
Genji provided for her as generously as before and showed her
such kindness that she was indeed
grateful, although she did not encourage him; for she had no wish to test a
devotion that had once proven doubtful and that, such
as it might be by now, would only upset her again. For
that reason he seldom actually called on her. He would

Leaning on an armrest

never know how his own feelings might change, even if he were to go about winning her back, and besides, it seemed to him that clandestine expeditions no longer
became him. What he longed to know was what the grown-up Ise Priestess was like.

The Haven led an elegant life once more in her old residence, for Genji still
saw to having it done up and maintained. Her taste and flair had not deserted her,
many distinguished gentlewomen and cultivated gentlemen gathered around her,
and despite her apparent loneliness she was living very pleasantly when, all at once,
she fell gravely ill and sank into such despair that alarm over her years in so sinful a
place[40] decided her to become a nun.

This news brought the astonished Genji to her, for even if they were no
longer lovers, she was still to him someone to talk to, and he wished that she had
not done it. His expressions of sympathy and concern were extremely moving. She
gave him a seat near her pillow and answered him leaning on an armrest, but even
this much made it clear how weak she was, and Genji wept bitterly, fearing that it
might be too late for him to assure her of his enduring devotion.

Deeply affected to find that he cared so much, she began to speak of the Ise
Priestess. "Please think of her whenever she may need you," she said, "because she
will now be left all alone. Hers is a perilous position, you see—she has no one else
to turn to. I myself am no help, but I hope still to keep an eye on her, as long as I am
able, until she can more or less look after herself." Her breath all but failed her, and
she wept.

"I would never abandon her, even if I had not heard you talk this way, and
now I am resolved to do for her all I possibly can. On that score please set your
mind at rest."

"It is so very difficult," she went on. "Even if she had someone like a father to
trust perfectly naturally, the loss of her mother might well prove a great misfortune.
And if her guardian were then to look on her with a lover's eyes, the consequences
for her could sometimes be cruel, and for some she could become an object of dis-

---

39. The Rokujō Haven had been at Ise for about six years. The accession of the new Emperor had
brought her daughter's term as Ise Priestess to an end.
40. The Ise Shrine, where taboo had cut her off from any contact with Buddhist teaching or practice.

Chin in hand

like. I know it is unkind of me to imagine such things, but please, never allow yourself to think of her that way. My own life has taught me that a woman is born to endure many sorrows, and I should like somehow to spare her as many as I can."

Genji failed to see why she spoke as she did, but he replied, "Recent years have made me much wiser, and I am sorry to gather that you still believe I am given to the wanton ways of my past. Very well, all in good time . . ."

It was dark outside her curtains, but through them he caught the dim light of a lamp. I wonder . . . , he thought and peered stealthily in through a gap where the cloth failed to meet.[41] There she was, her short hair very handsome and striking, leaning on an armrest and looking piercingly beautiful, just like a painting; and yes, the girl lying beside her along the curtains to the east must be the Priestess. With the standing curtain swept casually aside this way, he could see straight through to her. Chin in hand, she seemed very sad. By this faint light she looked extremely attractive. The way her hair fell across her shoulders and the shape of her head had great distinction, but she was still charmingly slight, and Genji felt a sharp surge of interest, although after her mother's speech he thought better of it.

"I am not feeling at all well," the Haven said. "I hope that you will forgive me if I ask you to leave." She lay down with a gentlewoman's help.

"I am so sorry," Genji replied; "I would have been very glad if you had felt better with me near you. How *are* you feeling?"

She could tell he was watching. "I shudder to think what I must look like," she said. "It has been extremely good of you to call on me now when, as you will have gathered, my illness is unlikely to trouble me much longer. Now that I have told you a little of what has been on my mind, I can, I think, go in peace."

"I am moved and grateful that you should include me among those worthy to receive your last wishes. His Late Eminence had many other sons as well, but I have seldom felt close to them, and since he was pleased to count her as a daughter of his own, I shall look on her in the same spirit. Now that I am rather more grown-up, I am disappointed to have no one to look after."

Their conversation was soon over, and Genji left. His generous attentions now increased somewhat, and he wrote to her often.

Seven or eight days later she was gone. The blow left him acutely aware of life's uncertainty and so grief-stricken that instead of going to the palace he busied

41. She seems to be lying in a curtained bed, at the entrance to which stands the curtain through which Genji is peering.

himself only with the inevitable arrangements. There was not really anyone else to do it. The trusted members of the Ise Priestess's former staff were left with few decisions to make.

Genji went there himself and sent in greetings to Her Highness.

"I am afraid that I am in no condition . . ." she sent back through her Mistress of the Household.

"It would please me if you were to think of me as a friend," he replied, "because your mother and I reached an agreement." He called in her gentlewomen and instructed them on all there was to be done. His manner inspired complete confidence, and he seemed to have changed the attitude that had been his so long. He had the rite performed with the utmost solemnity, assisted by countless members of his own household.

He mourned, fasted, and practiced devotions behind lowered blinds; and he wrote often to Her Highness. Little by little she recovered her composure and began to answer him herself. Doing so made her shy, but her gentlewomen encouraged her with reminders that she must not disappoint him.

On a day of blowing snow and sleet he found himself imagining how sad and dispirited she must be, and he sent her a messenger. "How does our sky look to you just now, I wonder," he had written on paper the dull color of the sky.

> *"Now the skies are filled with such swirling flakes of snow, I mourn to imagine*
> *the departed roaming still the heavens above your home."*

He had done up his letter with particular care, so as to catch a young woman's eye, and it was dazzling. The Ise Priestess could not think what to answer, but her women insisted that it would be rude of her to give the task to anyone else, and so she wrote on gray, intensely perfumed paper, in strokes light or dark as the ground required,

> *"Like unmelted snow I linger reluctantly, and in my darkness*
> *find that I cannot be sure who I am or where I go."*

Her cautious hand, innocent of pretense, was unremarkable, but he saw charm and dignity in it. Ever since she went down to Ise, he had felt that that was not to be all, and now it seemed to him that he might well decide to court her, although tact led him to restrain himself as before, since her mother the late Haven had anxiously given him her last wishes on the subject, and people at large—understandably, alas—might entertain similar suspicions; no, he thought, he would on the contrary see chastely to her needs, and when His Majesty was old enough to understand a little more, he would install her in the palace, for this sort of thing was otherwise missing from his life, and he would enjoy having her under his care.

He sent her long, impeccably earnest messages and called on her whenever the opportunity arose. "If I may be permitted to say so, it would give me great pleasure if you were to allow me into your confidence, in memory of your mother," he would say; but she, by nature extremely reserved and shy, shrank from the thought of allowing him to hear her voice at all, however faintly, until her gentlewomen despaired of persuading her and could only deplore her disposition. Genji reflected, Some of them, for instance her Mistress of the Household, her Chief Lady in Waiting, and so on, are close relatives of hers in the imperial family, and most have a good deal of talent. If I do successfully place her as I hope, I see no reason why she should please him[42] less well than any other. But if only I had had a better look at her face! His attitude may not have been wholly a devoted father's. Unable in the end to make up his mind, he told no one what future he planned for her. His special attentiveness to the funeral rites greatly surprised and pleased her staff.

Her loneliness increased as the months and days slipped by, a growing succession of miseries led those in her service to go their ways, and living near Kyōgoku in the lower district of the City meant deserted surroundings and a life often spent in tears amid the booming of the mountain temples' evening bells.[43] Not every mother, however devoted, would have remained so completely inseparable from her daughter or have gone down with her against all precedent to Ise, and her bitter regret that after so insisting on her mother's company she had not after all taken that last journey with her left her inconsolable.

Her large household staff included people of ranks both high and low, but once Genji, like a dutiful father, had forbidden even her nurses to take it on themselves to convey approaches to her, his daunting authority assured general assent that nothing improper must be brought to Her Highness's attention, and no breath of courtship ever reached her.

His Eminence had never forgotten the Ise Priestess's almost disturbing beauty at that solemn farewell ceremony in the Great Hall of State. "Do enter my service, and join the Kamo Priestess and my other sisters," he had urged her, and he had mentioned the subject to her mother as well. The idea had not appealed to her mother, however, because while he was indeed surrounded by very great ladies, she doubted that her daughter had adequate support, and moreover she feared that his exceedingly fragile health might burden her in the end with added cares. Now, when her gentlewomen could not imagine who might be willing to assist her, His Eminence was still pressing her to come.

Genji shrank, when he learned this, from the thought of brazenly crossing His Eminence and making off with her himself, but she *was* very attractive, and he was so reluctant to let her go that he broached the subject to Her Cloistered Eminence.

"I hardly know what to do about it, you see," he said. "Her mother was a lady of great dignity and intelligence, and I deeply regret the way my self-indulgence earned me both an unfortunate name and her own rejection. While she lived, she never set aside her anger toward me, but since at the very end she talked about the Ise Priestess, she must have heard good things about me and decided she could be frank with me after all; and that is extremely sad. One could not ignore so distressing a matter even in the most commonplace circumstances, and I want to ensure

42. Emperor Reizei.

43. The lower district of the City (she lives near the intersection of Rokujō [east-west] and Kyōgoku [north-south]) was sparsely inhabited, and Kyōgoku was near the many temples built along the Eastern Hills.

that at least in death she can forget her bitterness; I wonder whether it might not be a good idea for His Majesty, who is still young although of course quite grown-up, to have in his service someone a little more mature. It is all up to you, you see."

"That is an excellent idea. His Eminence's interest in her of course makes one hesitate to disappoint him, but you might simply invoke her mother's last wishes to bring her to the palace as though you knew nothing about it. By now this sort of thing preoccupies him less than his devotions, and I doubt that he really will be seriously put out when you tell him."

"Very well," Genji replied, "if you agree and are prepared to lend her your support, I shall have a few words with her and let her know. I have thought all this over very carefully, and I have been quite frank with you about my conclusion, but I am uneasy about what others may have to say."

He thereupon decided that he would indeed feign ignorance and move her to Nijō.[44] To his lady there he explained, "That, at any rate, is what I have planned. She is just the age to make you a good companion." She was pleased and began preparing to receive her.

His Highness of War seemed to be grooming his daughter carefully in the hope of quickly achieving the same success, but Her Cloistered Eminence wondered unhappily how Genji would greet his ambition, in view of the rift between them. The Acting Counselor's daughter was now known as the Kokiden Consort. His Excellency had adopted her as his own daughter, and he maintained her in dazzling style.[45] She made a fine playmate for His Majesty.[46] Her Cloistered Eminence said to herself and others that His Highness of War's middle daughter would only be joining a game of dolls, as it were, since she was the same age, whereas having someone older to look after him would be extremely welcome; and she told His Majesty what he had to anticipate. Meanwhile Genji, needless to say, missed nothing in the service of the realm, and he showed her such complete and tactful devotion at all times that she came to trust him implicitly. Her Cloistered Eminence could not easily attend His Majesty even when she went to the palace, since her health was poor, so that he urgently needed beside him a guardian somewhat older than himself.

44. In order to introduce her into the palace as his adopted daughter.
45. The former Minister of the Left has adopted his own granddaughter in order to lend her the weight of his supreme eminence as Chancellor.
46. Reizei is eleven, she twelve.

15

YOMOGIU
A Waste of Weeds

Yomogiu means a ruined house with grounds overgrown by plants like *yomogi* (*Artemisia vulgaris*)—weeds.

The time of "A Waste of Weeds" matches roughly "Suma" through "The Pilgrimage to Sumiyoshi"; the principal matter of the chapter overlaps with "The Pilgrimage to Sumiyoshi."

PERSONS

Genji, the Commander, then the Acting Grand Counselor, age 28 to 29

The daughter of His Highness of Hitachi (Suetsumuhana)

Her brother, a monk

Jijū, her foster sister

Suetsumuhana's aunt, wife of the Dazaifu Deputy

Shōshō, Jijū's aunt and Suetsumuhana's gentlewoman

Koremitsu, Genji's confidant

In the days when salt, sea-tangle drops were falling,[1] many in the City grieved as well, and the securely settled ones[2] certainly seemed to miss him badly; but the mistress of Nijō could be at peace, because corresponding with him kept her abreast of his life, and the sad round of the seasons often brought her the comfort

Water basin

of making him such garments, stripped of any mark of rank, as he now wore. Others, though, unknown by anyone to count among his loves and who had witnessed his departure only in imagination, suffered invisibly the most cruel of torments.

His Highness of Hitachi's daughter had languished sadly after his death, having no one else to look after her, until Genji appeared from nowhere to see loyally to her needs; and although to him in his grandeur such attentions were no more than the least he could do, she, whose sleeves were really too narrow to receive them, had felt as though all the stars above now shone up from her water basin. Then came the upheaval at court, one that upset and embittered Genji until he seemed to forget all about her, having never in any case felt any deep attachment; and once he was far away, she never heard from him again. What remained of his largesse sustained her for a time, amid frequent tears, but the passing months and years consigned her to an ever more desperately lonely plight.

"Look at my lady's miserable luck!" the women long in her service whispered in despair. "His lordship's interest made it seem as though a god or buddha had suddenly come for her, till one happily believed in such alliances, and even if all this is

---

1. While Genji was in exile at Suma.
2. Who (unlike Hanachirusato or Suetsumuhana) had a secure source of material support.

only to be expected, it hurts to see her left with no one to provide for her!" Years of life very like this had once led their mistress to take desperate isolation for granted, but the better times that had followed must have made the present unbearably painful. Then, women with any quality to commend them had come naturally to join the household; but now, one by one, they drifted away. Some, too, simply died, and the number of women high and low dwindled with time until hardly any remained.

Her ever-ruinous house became more and more the lair of foxes; owls hooted day and night from the grimly forbidding groves,[3] and horrid creatures—tree spirits and so on—once driven into hiding by human presence stalked abroad in full view, with many a distressing consequence, until the rare few who still served her exclaimed, "No, my lady, it is really too much! This provincial Governor, the one so keen on putting up a stylish house, is very taken with your groves, and he keeps approaching your staff to find out whether you might part with them; and we wish you would, my lady, and make up your mind to move somewhere less frightening! We who are still with you can bear no more!"

Their mistress wept and refused to hear of it. "What a horrible idea! Besides, other people would draw their own conclusions. How, for as long I live, could I ever betray my father's memory? The place is in frighteningly poor repair, I know, but it is such a comfort to think that this house, where I still feel his presence, was his home!"

Some of her domestic furnishings, all antique in style and well used, remained as handsome as ever, and persons with tedious pretensions to elegance, eager to acquire them, made condescending approaches on the assumption that poverty left her no choice, invoking as they did so the special interest that attached to them because His Late Highness had commissioned them from so-and-so or so-and-so; and her gentlewomen tried now and again to bring her round in the hope of relieving the misery that faced them day after day. "What else is one to do?" they would say. "That is life, after all." But her only response was sharp reproof. "My father left them to me on the understanding that I would look after them," she would say. "How could I allow them to adorn the house of a nobody? It would be too sad to disobey his wishes." She would not allow it.

It was her fortune never to receive a single visit, however casual. Only her most reverend brother looked in on her, on the rare occasions when he came to the City, but he, too, was so impossibly old-fashioned that even for a monk he made a strikingly impoverished, unworldly sort of hermit, and he hardly noticed having to struggle to her through dense grasses and weeds. The grounds had in truth vanished beneath scrubby reeds, thick wormwood towered to the eaves, and humulus blocked both gates, east and west, although horses and oxen had trodden paths over the crumbling earthen wall. Even the herd boys who freely grazed them there in spring and autumn allowed themselves outrageous behavior.

The galleries collapsed in the eighth month of the year of the great storm. The servants' halls, once pathetically roofed with boards, were stripped to bare frames, and

---

3. This description harks back to a passage of a poem by Bai Juyi (*Hakushi monjū* 0004).

of the servants themselves not a single one stayed
on. Smoke rose no more from the cooking
hearth, and one misery followed another.
Those who live from thievery must lack
imagination, because even they ignored the
Hitachi residence, walking straight past it on
the assumption that it had nothing to offer.
The main house therefore remained, inside,
just as it had always been, despite its thickets of weeds. Dust there was aplenty, since
no one swept or cleaned, but here His
Highness's daughter lived out her cheerless,
perfectly appointed days.

Nun with rosary

Little amusements like tales or old
poems are what help to pass the time
in a house like that, and to take one's
mind off life, but these things failed to interest her. No young woman need affect
refinement in order to enjoy the consolation of conveying her feelings in terms
of plants and trees,[4] in correspondence with like-minded friends or when otherwise at leisure; but this lady was so afraid of the world, as her father had brought
her up to be, that she made no gesture toward anyone with whom she might at
least have exchanged the occasional note. Now and then she would only open an
ancient cabinet to toy with pictures from tales like *Karamori*, *Hakoya no toji*, or
Kaguya-hime.[5]

The pleasure of old poems has to do with enjoying picking ones with appealing topics[6] and authors, ones simple to understand. Trite ones everyone already
knows, written on solemn utility paper or puffy Michinokuni, are a perfect bore, but
these are what she spread before her on the rare occasions when she looked at any
at all. She shrank in embarrassment from chanting scriptures or performing devotions, as so many people do these days, and she never touched a rosary, even
though no one would have seen her anyway.[7] Such was her prim mode of life.

Her foster sister, known as Jijū, was the only one who in all these years had
never actually left her service, but the passing of the Kamo Priestess, whom Jijū
often visited, had left Jijū in such dire straits that she now called sometimes on a sister of her mistress's mother, a lady who had stooped to marry a provincial Governor.
This lady was bringing up cherished daughters, and it occurred to Jijū that, among
presentable young women, she might prefer to a perfect stranger one who had actually known her parents.

Jijū's mistress, as distant as ever, made her aunt no welcoming overtures. "I feel

---

4. In terms of the sights and sounds of nature.
5. Antique tales favored by earlier generations. The first two have been lost, and the third is now known
as *The Old Bamboo Cutter* (*Taketori monogatari*).
6. *Dai*, the assigned topics on which a great many poems were written.
7. She thought it unladylike to betray any active interest in Buddhism, which in her father's time was
judged too serious for a woman.

sorry for my niece," the aunt would remark sourly to Jijū, "but I really cannot do anything for her, considering that her mother despised me and thought me an embarrassment." Now and again, however, she would send her a note.

Most people born to this aunt's standing in life strive at heart to cultivate the attitudes of their betters, but falling that far from so lofty a station must really have been her destiny, for she had quite a common streak. She who had once been despised as inferior wanted her niece for her daughters' maid of all work. Yes, she reflected, my niece's manners are dated, but what a wonderful nanny she would make! "Do come and see me sometimes," she wrote. "Some of us here long to hear your koto." Jijū, too, kept trying to interest her mistress in going, but her mistress had no wish to confront anyone, and since she was impossibly shy, she refused to respond, which her aunt thought horrid.

Meanwhile the aunt's husband had been appointed Dazaifu Deputy, and she meant to see her daughters properly provided for before she went down there with him. "I am afraid I have done less for you than I should have," she wrote ingratiatingly, still eager to have her niece with her, "but it was always a comfort to know you were nearby, and I worry about you so much, you know, now we are going far away." She got no answer. "How revolting of her! What airs she puts on!" she railed malevolently. "Well, she can be as stuck-up as she likes; the Commander[8] will hardly be impressed by someone who spends year after year living in a wilderness like that!"

Soon enough all the world was loudly rejoicing that Genji had indeed received his pardon and was coming back to the City. Ladies and gentlemen vied to convince him of their lasting devotion, and this evidence of everyone's regard, high or low, touched him in a great many ways. Amid all the excitement the days and months passed with no sign from him that he remembered His Highness of Hitachi's daughter.

This is the end, then, she told herself in black despair. I was shocked and saddened by the unforgivable treatment he received, and I always prayed that spring might come for him again, but in the end—when, I gather, the very tiles and pebbles were celebrating his promotion—I was to hear of it only as though it were no concern of mine. Now I know that my sorrow over his suffering was really for no one but myself.[9] What a waste it has all been! She secretly spent her days in tears.

Sure enough! the Deputy's wife said to herself. Who on earth would give a thought to such a miserable pauper? Those whose sins are light, they say, are the ones the saints and buddhas lead to salvation, but in her present state it is too pathetic of her to look down on everyone else and to uphold a pride acquired in her father and mother's time! She felt more and more certain her niece was a fool.

"Do make up your mind to it, though," she still sweetly insisted. "When life turns against you, it is time to seek a refuge in the mountains.[10] I am sure you think the countryside unworthy of you, but I promise that no one there will treat you improperly."

"Oh, I wish my lady would!" her niece's women muttered to each other in de-

---

8. Genji, appointed Commander of the Right between "Under the Cherry Blossoms" and "Heart-to-Heart."

9. Kokinshū 948: "Can life have always been this hateful, or has it become like this only for me?"

10. In Kokinshū 951 the speaker, weighed down by care, resolves to "tread the steep mountain trails of Yoshino."

spair. "How can she keep up these standards of hers when nothing about her situation encourages hope of anything much better?"

Jijū herself was involved by now with a young man who seemed to be the Deputy's nephew, and since he was unwilling to leave her behind, she prepared reluctantly to go. "I so hate to leave you, my lady," she said, urging her mistress to join her; but even now her mistress pinned all her hopes on a man who had stopped coming long ago, and she said to herself, as she had all these years, One day, though, however distant, something *will* remind him of me. Despite all his dear and tender promises I am a creature of misfortune and yes, I have slipped his mind, but he will come forward to help me, I know he will, if a breath of wind brings him news of my desperate need. This was why, when her whole house was nearer than ever to falling down, she would not part with the least utensil and bravely persisted in living exactly as before. Given to frequent tears and increasingly to despair, she looked in profile as though a mountain rustic had stuck a red berry on her face—so much so that no casual suitor could have borne the sight. I will say no more, though, because that would be too unkind and too evil-tongued.

Winter came on, her destitution grew, and her mood gave way to blank despondency. All the world gathered eagerly to Genji's residence, to attend his Eight Discourses for His Late Eminence. Genji pointedly called in no ordinary monks, having chosen only the most learned and, by their long practice, the most saintly; and that meant that her brother was there, too.

He came to see her on his way home. "I have come from the Eight Discourses held by the Acting Grand Counselor," he explained. "He did it all very nobly, with many touches as flawlessly beautiful as any in paradise. He himself seems to be a manifest buddha or bodhisattva. One wonders why he was ever born into a world so marred by the five defilements."[11] Straight after that he left. He was a man of few words, and he did not behave with his sister as anyone else might have done, for he never spoke to her about anything foolish or profane.

She took the news hard. Well, then, she thought, he is a most unkind buddha or bodhisattva, because here I am, condemned to misery while he cruelly ignores me; I suppose, then, that he really is gone for good. She was absorbed in such thoughts when the Dazaifu Deputy's wife arrived.

This lady was not normally given to such familiarity, but she had rushed off, all pride and high spirits, in a fine carriage and equipped with gifts of clothing and so on, to persuade her niece to come along after all. Ordering the gate opened, she saw before her at a glance boundless desolation. The doors of the gate, left and right, had tottered and slumped to such a degree that it took several of her men and much noise and commotion to help to move them. And where, she wondered when she entered, were the three trodden paths that she had heard should lead even to so wretched a dwelling?[12]

11. The five defilements (*gojoku*) that according to the Lotus Sutra characterize the world into which a buddha is born.

12. A Chinese allusion. Two sources available to the author describe a poor dwelling with "three paths" through its garden. One is a poem by the Tang poet Tao Yuanming; the other is a note in *Mōgyū*, a Japanese primer of Chinese literature.

Lattice shutters

At last she managed to have her carriage drawn up at the raised lattice shutters on the south side, where to her niece's mounting horror[13] Jijū came forth, thrusting an utterly filthy standing curtain ahead of her. Jijū's looks were not what they had once been, but despite the ravages of the years she retained genuine grace and distinction, and the visitor would have much preferred, alas, to see her in her mistress's place.

"I plan to leave soon," she began, "but I simply cannot bear to abandon you in this dreadful condition! I have come for Jijū, you see. You have been too coldly reserved ever to come to see me, and I think you must at least allow me to have her. But what is the point of your staying behind in these pathetic surroundings?" At this point she should have burst into tears, but with her mind all on her journey she was actually quite cheerful. "We began drifting apart because your mother rejected me while His Late Highness was alive as a blot on the family, but I myself could not feel that way for long. I was awed to witness the good fortune that sanctioned your pride and allowed you to enjoy the Commander's attentions, and there was many a time over the years when I did not even dare to address you; but one never knows what life will bring, and now it is I, the nobody, who am comfortably off. It is very painful to see you suffering this way, when you used to seem so far beyond me, and although it gave me some peace of mind to live near you, even when I failed actually to keep in touch, I am sorry now that I am to go so far away, and I am worried about you, too." Her speeches got her nowhere at all.

"This is very kind of you, but I am not like other people, and I do not see how . . . No, I just want to fade away as I am." Her Highness said no more.

"*You* may feel that way, but I doubt that anyone else could give up all of life to stay on in this ghastly place. You would obviously have a proper palace instead if the Commander did it up for you, but I gather that for the time being he thinks of no one but the daughter of His Highness of War. They say he has given up all the ladies with whom his wandering fancy once got him involved in casual affairs. Surely you do not expect him to come calling on you just because here in this hopeless wilderness of yours you are chastely trusting him to do just that!"

---

13. Suetsumuhana is horrified not merely to have a visitor but to see her aunt (whose low rank does not permit her this liberty) drive straight up to the south side of the house.

She is quite right, her niece conceded before this barrage, and she quietly wept in bitter grief. However, she showed no sign of changing her mind, and after spending the day going over every argument, her aunt prepared to hurry off as the sun went down, saying, "Well, then, I shall at least take Jijū."

Jijū, weeping with distress, said privately to her mistress, "Very well, I shall go just for today, since she wants me to, to see her safely on her way. There is some truth in what she says. But, my lady, I do not blame you for being so unwilling to leave, and it is very painful to be caught this way between you."

So even she is to abandon me! her mistress thought, sad and angry; but she could say nothing to stop her, and she therefore only wept more loudly still.

The favorite robe that she might have given Jijū as a memento was too salt-stained[14] to do. Lacking anything else to acknowledge Jijū's years of service, she took a pretty box and placed in it a fall that she had made of hair from her own head, over nine feet long and very beautiful, adding as well a jar of old and especially fragrant clothing incense.

> *"They would never break—so I once fondly believed—these long, shining strands
> that now to my sad surprise fail me and will soon be gone,"*[15]

she said. "I had thought you would always stay with me, however hopeless I may be, since after all Mama[16] left you her last wishes. Not that I blame you for going, but who, I ask you, will take your place?" Her words gave way to a storm of tears.

Jijū could not speak. "Never mind Mama's last words, my lady, because I have lived with you through years of life's worst trials, and that I should now be drawn into a journey I never meant to take and leave you to go far, far away . . .

> *Though these shining strands fail you now, they will not break: that I swear to you
> by the gods who deign to guard the road that lies before me.*

What I cannot promise is that I myself will live."

"Come along, it is getting dark," the aunt whispered. Jijū boarded the carriage that was brought forward, hardly knowing what she was doing, and she looked back again and again as it drove away.

His Late Highness's daughter was heartsick at losing someone who had never left her in all these years, not even in the most desperate times. Meanwhile, her last, useless old women were saying "Well, she is quite right. How *could* she have stayed? Why, we ourselves can hardly bear it!" Each was considering the possibilities and planning to leave. Their mistress listened to them in despair.

In the eleventh month the weather turned to snow and sleet that sometimes

---

14. Too dirty.

15. This poem equates Suetsumuhana's gift (the fall of hair) with the bond between Suetsumuhana and Jijū, then with Jijū herself. "Strands in shining coils" loosely renders *tamakazura*, a word that generally means "vine" but that is here divided into the poetically noble prefix *tama* ("jewel," "jewel-like," "shining") and *kazura*, a homophone (or perhaps just a related meaning) of the word for "wig" or "fall."

16. Suetsumuhana's nurse, Jijū's mother. *Mama* is the original word.

melted elsewhere; but the Hitachi residence, buried in weeds that blocked the morning and afternoon sun, remained as deep in snow as White Mountain yonder in Etchū,[17] until not even servants were seen abroad, and the mistress of the place languished in vacant apathy. She had no one even to comfort her with a light remark or to divert her with tears or laughter, and at night, in the grubby confines of her curtained bed, she tasted all the misery of sleeping alone.

Genji, at his residence, was more and more openly caught up in the rare pleasure of his darling's company, and he made no effort to call elsewhere unless he had the most pressing of reasons; still less was he moved to visit His Highness of Hitachi's daughter, although he sometimes thought of her enough to wonder whether she was still alive. Meanwhile the New Year came.

In the fourth month he remembered the village of falling flowers and set out quietly, bidding his love a brief farewell. The last light rain was falling after several wet days, and the moon came out at the perfect moment. His journey to her long ago returned to mind, and he was dwelling in memory on all of that deliciously moonlit night when he passed a shapeless ruin of a dwelling set amid a veritable forest of trees.

Rich clusters of wisteria blossoms billowed in the moonlight from a giant pine, their poignant, wind-borne fragrance filling all the air around him. It did so well for the scent of orange blossoms[18] that he leaned out and saw a weeping willow's copious fronds trailing unhindered across a collapsed earthen wall. I have seen this grove before, he thought; and he recognized His Late Highness's. Thoroughly moved now, he stopped his carriage. Koremitsu was with him on this as on all his secret expeditions, and he presented himself. Genji called him closer.

"This is His Highness of Hitachi's residence, is it not?"

"Yes, my lord."

"I wonder whether the lady who once lived here is still lost in her sorrows. I ought to have visited her, but that sort of thing is such a bother. Go and make sure, though. I would look silly calling on the wrong person."

His Late Highness's daughter, increasingly despondent, was nonetheless bearing up as well as she could. One day she dozed off and dreamed of her father, and such sadness lingered on after she awoke that she had the outer edge of the aisle cleaned, where water had come in through the eaves, had her rooms tidied, and murmured as anyone else might have done, though most unusually for her,

> "*When these sleeves of mine are forever wet with tears shed over my loss,*
> *new drops from these ruined eaves must now flood them yet again!*"

The moment was indeed heartrending in the extreme.

Koremitsu entered and roamed about in search of human sounds, but he found no sign that the place was inhabited. Sure enough, he thought, it is all very well to look

---

17. Hakusan ("White Mountain," 8,917 feet), a peak toward the Japan Sea side of Honshu, in the old province of Etchū, now Toyama Prefecture.

18. It recalled the past vividly, as *tachibana* blossoms do.

in that way from the road, but no one seems to be living here. He was on his way back to Genji when by a burst of moonlight he saw two raised lattice shutters with the blinds behind them moving. The idea of having found the inhabitants after all actually gave him a shiver of fear, but he approached and coughed politely, to which an ancient voice replied after a preliminary clearing of the throat, "Who is it? Who is there?"

Koremitsu gave his name. "May I speak with the woman known as Jijū?" he asked.

"I am afraid she is away, but someone else should be able to answer you just as well." The voice was weaker and more tremulous now, but he recognized in it an old woman he had heard before.

The stealthy arrival of a graceful man dressed in a hunting cloak caused such astonishment within that eyes unaccustomed to such sights might have seen in him a fox or some other magic creature. Koremitsu came nearer. "I should be grateful to learn whether Her Highness is still as she was when my lord last knew her. I believe that my lord is still eager to call on her. He was passing by this evening when he stopped here. What answer shall I give him? You need not be afraid."

The women broke into smiles. "Would my lady still be living here in this wilderness of weeds if she were different in any way from what she used to be? Use your own head and tell him whatever you please. For us, who are old, the times we have seen here have been a trial cruel and strange beyond anything you could imagine." They seemed all too willing to talk.

"Very well." Koremitsu wished to silence any unwelcome garrulousness. "I shall inform my lord." He returned to Genji.

"What took you so long? Well, what did you find? Is it only a wormwood waste, and is nothing left from the past?"

"My lord, I made my way up to the house as best I could. Jijū's aunt, the old woman they used to call Shōshō, is the one who answered me. Her voice was the same." Koremitsu described all that he had found.

Genji was quite upset and wondered what it could have been like for her all this time amid such thickets. He regretted the cruelty of having failed so far to visit her. "What am I to do?" he said. "A secret outing like this is always so tricky. This is the only sort of time when I could actually come. If she *is* just the same, this is exactly what one would expect of her." However, he hesitated to go straight in. He badly wanted to send her a dazzling note, but he gave up the idea out of pity for his messenger, who, unless her old slowness of wit had changed, would have waited interminably for an answer. Besides, Koremitsu assured him that he would never get through the dew on all those weeds. "You must not go in until I have brushed it off a little," he said.

Genji murmured to himself,

> "Now that I am here, I myself shall seek her out through her trackless waste,
>   to see whether all these weeds have left her as she was then";

and he alighted after all, whereupon Koremitsu led him in, brushing the dew from before him with his riding whip. "I have an umbrella, my lord," he said, because the drops from on high recalled cold autumn showers; "the dew beneath these trees

Umbrella

really is wetter than rain."[19] The legs of Genji's gathered trousers got soaking wet. Of the middle gate, which had been shaky enough even in those days, there was nothing left at all, and the further he penetrated the grounds, the more self-conscious he felt, though it helped that no one was there to see him.

His Late Highness's daughter shrank from his presence, despite her joy at being right that he really would come again one day, and she could hardly bring herself to receive him. She had never even glanced at the robes from the Dazaifu Deputy's wife, whom she disliked, but when her women brought them, evocatively perfumed from being stored in a fragrant chest, she resigned herself to changing after all; and she had that filthy standing curtain of hers placed nearby.

Genji entered. "My heart, at least, has been constant toward you through all these years of silence," he began, "yet my disappointment over the absence of any word from you made me wish hitherto to try you a little further. I could not pass a grove so striking, though, whether or not your trees are cedars,[20] and so, as you see, I have lost after all." He drew the curtain a little aside, but she, desperately shy as always, remained mute. Still, the way he had come to her proved that he was serious, and at last she summoned the courage to give him a faint reply.

"The distress of knowing how long you have spent hidden among these thickets, added to my unchanging devotion, has led me to you, wet with dew. I know nothing of your own wishes in the matter, however, and in this regard I wonder what your feelings are. Perhaps I may hope that you will forgive me, as you would another, my neglect over the years. If after this I fail to please you, I will indeed confess to the sin of having broken my word." He seems to have made her many such speeches, tender if not entirely heartfelt, to draw her out.

He might have stayed, but the state of the place, and her own shocking condition, drew many fluent excuses from him, and instead he prepared to go. The pine on her grounds had not been intentionally planted, but it touched him by the height it had reached over the years,[21] and his musings on life's dreamlike quality moved him to say,

> "What so caught my eye, when the rich wisteria tempted me to stop,
> was your pine that seemed to speak of someone pining nearby.[22]

19. Koremitsu has caught the resemblance between their situation and that evoked in "The Eastern Cottage" ("Azumaya"), a romantic *saibara* folk song; the sentence alludes to "The Eastern Cottage" twice. His language also recalls *Kokinshū* 1091 on the same theme: "My good man, tell your lord he must have an umbrella: the dew beneath the trees at Miyagino is wetter than rain."

20. *Kokinshū* 982: "My humble dwelling is below Miwa Mountain: come, if you love me, to the gate where the cedars stand." The speaker is the Miwa deity, to whom the cedar (*sugi*) is sacred.

21. The sentence to this point alludes to *Gosenshū* 1107, by Ōshikōchi no Mitsune: "Of course the one who planted the pine has aged, and yet how tall, meanwhile, the tree has grown!" The pine (*matsu*) that has grown tall hints at Genji's recognition of how patiently Suetsumuhana has awaited (*matsu*) his return.

22. The poem plays on *matsu*, "pine tree" and "wait." It also alludes to *Kokinshū* 982.

So many years have passed, when one counts them, and alas, so much in the City has changed. Soon, when there is time, I must tell you all about how I, too, languished far off in the wilds.[23] I gather that you have no one but me to hear you complain of the suffering you have borne, season by season, through the years. It is so strange, you know."

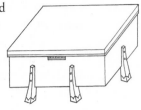

Fragrant chest

> *"Year after long year I have pined, always in vain—are those flowers, then,*
> *all that made you look this way and at last notice my home?"*

she replied, and a glimpse of her in discreet movement, added to the fragrance of her sleeves, suggested that she had matured since those days.

The moon, which was setting now, shone in brilliantly, for nothing like a bridgeway remained beyond the double doors to the west, and the projecting eaves were gone as well. He looked about by its light and saw a room appointed just as it had been long ago, and far more elegant than anything suggested by the outside of a house so deep in the "grasses of remembering."[24] Pictures from old tales came to mind, and he wondered sadly at her years here without a breath of change. Her resolutely prim deportment impressed him as admirably worthy of her rank, and he greatly regretted that after compassionately seizing on that very reason not to forget her, he should have lost touch with her for so long, having been absorbed by troubles of his own, until she no doubt thought him extremely unkind. His lady of falling flowers was likewise little given to stylish brilliance, and a mental comparison of the two now excused in his eyes a multitude of sins.

The season of the Festival and the Purification had come, bringing Genji all sorts of gifts "to assist him with his preparations," but he gave them all away to his deserving ladies. He was especially attentive toward His Highness of Hitachi's daughter, directing his closest retainers to see to her needs, sending servants to clear the weeds from her grounds, and ordering the unsightly gaps in the garden wall mended with stretches of board fence. He did not visit her, because that would not redound to his credit if the world at large were to learn how he had found her. Instead he wrote to her at length to say (since he was building close to Nijō), "That is where I mean to move you. Please find some nice little girls and so on to look after you." His solicitude embraced even providing her with servants, and he was so generous otherwise that her wilderness of weeds hardly had room for it all. Her rejoicing women turned toward where he lived with their eyes lifted to the heavens.

As far as anyone knew, Genji had not even a casual interest in the sort of women in whom the world abounds, but sought only those who appeared to offer something a little unusual, something that caught his fancy; and yet there he was,

---

23. *Kokinshū* 961, by Ono no Takamura: "I never thought to fall so low, banished to the wilds, as to haul a fisherman's line and take fish from the sea!"

24. *Kokinshū* 200: "Here at my old home, encumbered as it is with the grasses of remembering, a pine cricket's singing fills me with sorrow." The "grasses of remembering" are *shinobu*, a kind of fern that grows in a thatched roof, and the name of which suggests "remember [you] fondly."

and one can only wonder why, making much of a lady whose appeal failed in all ways to attain even the mediocre. He must have had a bond with her from the distant past.

Some former members of her staff, high and low, who had once contemptuously dismissed their poverty-stricken mistress and left her as quickly as they possibly could, now came rushing back to offer their services. Others had become so accustomed to her manner, correct as it was to the point of painful reticence, that they found themselves completely at sea in such households as those of vague provincial Governors, and now all of them at once were inspired to return.

Genji had only grown more thoughtful as he rose to new heights of glory, and he ordered things so well that he wrought a wondrous change, for her residence was soon amply populated. Where once rank foliage had cast a dismal and pervasive pall there now ran a newly diverted stream, while shrubbery near the house yielded cooling shade, and junior household staff, barely noticed so far but zealous to serve him, so clearly discerned his deep interest that they danced most assiduous attendance upon her.

She languished two years in her father's house, and then Genji brought her to live in his east pavilion.[25] It was rare for him actually to call on her there, but she was so close that he looked in on her whenever he came her way at all, and his treatment of her was not really demeaning.

I would happily rattle on a bit about how surprised the Dazaifu Deputy's wife was when she came back up to the City and about how Jijū, though very pleased, smarted with shame at her own faintheartedness for having failed to wait a little longer; but for now my head is aching so badly that I am not up to it, and I am afraid I shall have to go on another time, when I remember more.[26]

25. That he had just built near his Nijō residence.
26. This paragraph is written as though spoken directly to someone far higher in rank.

16

SEKIYA

At the Pass

Sekiya means "barrier post" (staffed by a barrier guard) and alludes to the Ōsaka Barrier, between Kyoto and the provinces to the east. The spot is the scene of this short chapter.

RELATIONSHIP TO EARLIER CHAPTERS

"At the Pass" takes place toward the end of the period covered by "The Pilgrimage to Sumiyoshi," from the ninth into the tenth or eleventh month.

PERSONS

Genji, the Palace Minister, age 29

The Deputy Governor of Hitachi, formerly of Iyo (Iyo no Suke)

His wife, the lady of the cicada shell (Utsusemi)

The Governor of Kawachi (formerly of Kii), Utsusemi's stepson (Ki no Kami)

His younger brother, an Aide of the Right Palace Guards

The Second of the Right Gate Watch, Utsusemi's younger brother (Kogimi)

The year after His Late Eminence's passing, the Iyo Deputy was appointed to Hitachi,[1] and he invited his wife, the lady of the cicada shell, to come with him down to his province. Her own secret thoughts went often enough to Genji, for she had distantly heard that he was going to Suma, but she had no way even to get a letter to him, and since she was wary of the winds over Mount Tsukuba,[2] the months and years passed by without a word between them. No term limited his exile, but at last he returned to life in the City, and in the autumn of the following year Hitachi came back up himself.

Genji went on pilgrimage to Ishiyama to fulfill a vow on the very day when Hitachi was to reach the barrier.[3] The former Governor of Kii, as well as Hitachi's other sons, had come out from the City to greet their father, and their warning that the road would be filled because his lordship would take it prompted the party to set off at dawn in a dense, swaying train of women's carriages. The sun rose high. At Uchide Beach,[4] Genji's arriving outrunners crowded the road before they could even move aside, announcing that their lord had passed Awata,[5] and so higher up, near the barrier, they all alighted, unyoked the oxen, put the carriages here and there under the cedars, and withdrew respectfully beneath the trees to let him by. Some carriages had been allowed to trail behind and others sent on in front, but even so Hitachi's company was obviously large. Sleeves and skirts in tasteful colors spilled from ten of the carriages. Their elegance, not in the least provincial, reminded Genji of the sightseeing carriages on occasions like a High Priestess's depar-

1. As Deputy Governor (Suke), since the Governor of Hitachi was a Prince who held the post as a sinecure.
2. *Kokinshū* 1098: "O how I long to send her word on the wind blowing over the hills and mountains, the mighty mountains of Kai." Mount Tsukuba, which is in Hitachi rather than Kai, acknowledges that Utsusemi lives in Hitachi. Distrust of the wind means distrust of any possible messenger.
3. The Ōsaka barrier between the City and Lake Biwa, on a low pass crossed by the road to the eastern provinces. Ishiyamadera was a Buddhist temple near the southern end of Lake Biwa and a favorite destination for pilgrims from the City.
4. Along the southern shore of Lake Biwa, within the present city of Ōtsu.
5. The gateway, as it were, to the City, at the western end of the road over Ōsaka pass.

ture for Ise. Every man in the vast entourage that accompanied this most rare and imposing excursion noticed them as he passed.

It was the last day of the ninth month.[6] Autumn leaves glowed in many colors, and expanses of frost-withered grasses drew the eye, while a brilliant procession in hunting cloaks embroidered or tie-dyed to splendid advantage strode on past the barrier lodge. Genji lowered his carriage blind and summoned the little brother of long ago; he was now the Second of the Right Gate Watch. "I am sure you will not soon forget how I came to the barrier to meet you," he said in words meant for the young man's sister. Touching memories of all kinds swept through his mind, but he was obliged to keep his remarks innocuous.

She, too, had kept old memories in her heart, and now their sadness rose in her again.

> *"Coming and going, I found here no barrier to these tears of mine—*
> *perhaps they may seem to you the slope's ever-welling spring."*[7]

He would never understand, she knew, and she was overcome by helpless sorrow.

The Second of the Watch came out to meet Genji on Genji's way back from Ishiyama. He apologized for having passed on by the other day.[8] Years ago, as a boy, he had been so close and so dear to Genji that until he first wore the cap of office, he had enjoyed Genji's unstinting protection; but then, when the world lapsed strangely into turmoil, fear of rumor moved him to go down to Hitachi, and this had put Genji off him a little, though he kept his feelings to himself. Although no longer so warmly disposed, Genji still counted him among his intimate retainers. It was the younger brother of the former Governor of Kii (now of Kawachi), the one who had lost his Palace Guards post and gone down with Genji to Suma, whom Genji singled out for particular favor. The lesson was lost on none of the others, who wondered when they thought over the past why they had ever considered bowing to worldly opinion.

Genji summoned the Second of the Watch and gave him a letter to deliver. What a long memory he has, the young man thought, for things he should have forgotten long ago!

"The other day I understood how strong a tie binds us to each other," Genji had written. "Did you, too?

> *I had little doubt that we would meet after all on the Ōmi road,*
> *yet those waters were too fresh not to betray my fond hope.*[9]

---

6. The last day of autumn.

7. The "spring" of Ōsaka Barrier (*seki no shimizu*) was known in poetry. *Gosenshū* 1089, by Semimaru (a legendary figure associated with the barrier) is the source for "coming and going": "See, O see! Coming and going they follow their ways, while friends and strangers meet at Ōsaka Barrier." "Ōsaka" is written with characters that mean "slope of meeting."

8. For having failed to accompany Genji to Ishiyama.

9. This tissue of double meanings begins with a play on *ō* (or *au*, "meet," "come together") and *Ōmiji* (the "Ōmi road"). The mention of Ōmi (Province) evokes *Ōmi no umi*, the "lake of Ōmi" (Lake Biwa); and the lake, which is fresh, has no *kai* ("shellfish," but also "desired benefit").

He was hateful, that wretch of a watchman!"[10]

"I feel ill at ease after being out of touch with her for so long," Genji said, "but I think of her often, you know, and it might all have been just yesterday. I suppose this romantic leaning of mine will only turn her against me more."

He gave the letter to the young man, who took it to his sister. "Do answer him," the young man said. "I have always assumed that he cares less for me than he used to, and it is wonderful that he treats me as kindly as though nothing had changed. I understand that such diversions may not appeal to you, but you cannot just ignore him. A woman may be forgiven for yielding to a gentleman."

Although more deeply embarrassed than ever, and less confident in all ways, she must have given in to the surprise, for she replied,

"O what can it be, the Ōsaka Barrier, that in just this place
one must make one's mournful way through a forest of sorrows?"[11]

I think I must be dreaming."

Genji had found her unforgettable both for her touching plight and for her maddening ways, but now and again he further shook her resolve by sending her new messages. Meanwhile, Hitachi suffered so much from ill health, no doubt under the burden of advancing age, that his only instructions to his sons concerned his well-born wife. "Follow her wishes in everything," he urged them morning and night, "and serve her exactly as I did while I lived." Seeing her distress over the dismal prospect of losing even her husband, to add to her already sad fate, he longed (for life has its term, and no regret can stay its passing) to be able to leave his spirit with her, and he thought and spoke often of his sorrow and worry, since he did not know his sons' intentions toward her; but his concern availed him nothing, and he died.

For some time his sons made as though to respect his wishes, but their good-will was all on the surface, and there were many painful moments. Such is the way of the world, after all, and she spent her life lamenting her solitary misfortune.

Only the Governor of Kawachi, who had always had an eye for her, showed her any consideration. "My father spoke to us feelingly about you," he said. "I understand how inadequate I am, but please do not hesitate to let me know if I can do anything for you." His flattering advances blatantly revealed what he had in mind, and she told herself that any unfortunate like herself who went on living this way would only have to hear more and more of these horrors; and so without a word to anyone she became a nun. This drastic step left her gentlewomen aghast.

The Governor was very angry. "All right," he railed at her, "you may have no use for me, but you still have many years before you, and I just wonder how you are going to manage!"

"What a meddlesome bore!" seems to have been one comment on the subject.

10. The "watchman" is the "watchman of the barrier" (sekimori), a stock figure in love poetry, where he stands for anyone who keep lovers apart. Here he refers at once to Utsusemi's husband and to the Ōsaka Barrier, where Genji passed Utsusemi's carriage.

11. The poem again plays on ō (or au, "meet") and Ōsaka; and on nageki ("sorrows"), which suggests the idea of many "trees" (ki).

17

EAWASE

The Picture Contest

The word *eawase* means a "picture
contest," in which two competing
sides submit paintings in pairs for
judgment. No such contest is
known to have taken place in the
period before the tale was written,
but the one in this chapter follows
the established pattern for poetry
contests (*utaawase*), and in particular for a fully documented example held at the palace in the third
lunar month of 960.

RELATIONSHIP TO EARLIER CHAPTERS

"The Picture Contest" takes place from spring to autumn, a year or so after the time covered by "The Pilgrimage to Sumiyoshi."

PERSONS

Genji, the Palace Minister, age 31

Her Highness, the former Ise Priestess, the Ise Consort, 22 (Akikonomu)

Her Cloistered Eminence, 36 (Fujitsubo)

His Eminence, the Retired Emperor, 33 (Suzaku In)

The Mistress of the Household, of Akikonomu

His Majesty, the Emperor, 13 (Reizei)

The Kokiden Consort, Tō no Chūjō's daughter, 14

The Acting Counselor (Tō no Chūjō)

His Highness of War (Hyōbukyō no Miya)

Genji's love, 23 (Murasaki)

Hei, Jijū, and Shōshō, gentlewomen on the Left,
the Umetsubo side in the contest

Daini, Chūjō, and Hyōe, gentlewomen on the Right,
the Kokiden side in the contest

The Viceroy Prince, Genji's brother (Hotaru or Sochi no Miya)

The former Ise Priestess's entry into palace service had Her Cloistered Eminence's willing support, but Genji worried that she had no one in particular to do for her all she would need to have done, and he therefore refrained from taking up the matter with His Eminence; and since he had decided to bring her for the time being to Nijō, he pretended instead to know nothing about it. However, he generally honored his parental responsibility toward her.

Incense jar

His Eminence was thoroughly disappointed, but for the sake of appearances he gave up writing to her. When the day came at last, however, he had her specially presented with the most beautiful sets of robes; with a comb box, a toiletry box, and a box for incense jars, all extraordinary in their way; and with such incenses and clothing perfumes as to fill the air far beyond a hundred paces.[1] The idea that Genji might be watching had no doubt put him on his mettle.

Genji was there at the time, and the Mistress of the Household showed him everything. He knew at first glance from the comb box just how marvelous they were in the exquisite refinement of their beauty.

On the gift knot that graced the box of ornamental combs he saw written,

> "*Did the gods decree, when the time of parting came and I, in your hair,*
> *set the comb of last farewell,[2] that we should not meet again?*"

This gave him pause. He was very sorry, and his own heart's wayward fancies made it clear enough that His Eminence must have been smitten by her on that occasion when she left for Ise. How might he feel about having his hopes thwarted this way, now that she was back after all those years, and just when he could look forward to

---

1. The "hundred paces" are a proverbial measure of a perfume's excellence.
2. The comb of parting that Suzaku gave Akikonomu when she left for Ise ("The Green Branch").

their being fulfilled? Was he bitter in retirement, after resigning the throne? I would be upset if I were he, Genji reflected. What can have moved me to force this through and make him so unhappy? He felt very bad. Yes, he had once been angry with His Eminence,[3] but he could only think fondly, too, of his gentle nature, and in his confusion he fell for a time into abstracted gloom.

"What sort of answer does she have in mind? And what about His Eminence's letter itself?" However, the Mistress of the Household was too nervously discreet to produce it. Genji heard the gentlewomen protesting vainly to their mistress, who was then unwell and in no mood to reply, that it would be rude and unkind of her not to, and he chimed in, "You really must, you know, if only for appearances"; and despite her confusion she remembered so vividly being touched as a girl by his graceful beauty and his many tears, and the memory brought with it such sad thoughts of her mother, that she managed after all,

"When I went away, you gave me that last command never to return,
and now I am back again, the memory makes me sad."[4]

That was probably all. The messenger received various gifts. Genji, who wanted desperately to know what she had said, could hardly ask.

His Eminence's looks were such that one would have gladly seen him as a woman, but Her Highness[5] did not seem unworthy of him, and they would have made a handsome pair. It even occurred to Genji to wonder indiscreetly whether she might not privately regret his having been disappointed, since after all His Majesty was still very young. The thought was torment, but there was no turning back. He explained what needed to be done,[6] told the Upkeep Consultant,[7] whom he favored, to see to his orders, and set off for the palace.

Out of deference to His Eminence, Genji refrained from any ostentatiously paternal gesture and only assured her well-being. Her residence had long boasted many worthy gentlewomen, and even the ones who were often at home gathered around her now, so that she lived there in admirable style. Genji's old feeling for her mother returned, and he thought, Ah, if only she were still alive, how pleased she would be to have brought her daughter this far herself! By any standard she was a wonder and a very great loss. No, there will never be anyone like her! Such had been her rare distinction that many things recalled her memory.

Her Cloistered Eminence was at the palace, too. The news that someone special was coming caught His Majesty's interest in a charming way. He was quite grown-up for his age. "Yes," his mother told him, "she is a very fine lady, and you must mind your manners with her."

He was secretly worried that a grown-up might make forbidding company.

---

3. Because Suzaku (under his mother's influence) had forced Genji into exile.
4. Suzaku gave Akikonomu the comb together with the ritual injunction "Set not your face toward the City again."
5. Akikonomu.
6. For Akikonomu's formal entry into the palace.
7. Does not appear elsewhere. The man is Director of Upkeep for the palace and also a Consultant on the Council of State.

She arrived very late that night. She was very discreet and quiet, and so small and slight that he thought her very pretty indeed. By now he was used to his Kokiden lady, whose company he enjoyed and with whom he felt quite at ease, but this new one was so dauntingly self-possessed, and Genji treated her with such respectful formality, that he found it difficult to think ill of her, and he therefore divided his nights equally between them, although when he set off by day in search of youthful amusement, he usually went to the Kokiden. The Acting Counselor had nursed a particular ambition when he presented his daughter to His Majesty, and it did not please him to find her now in competition with the new arrival.

His Eminence at the Suzaku Palace considered the reply to his poem on the comb box and realized how difficult it was to give her up. Then Genji appeared, and the two began a conversation during which he happened to mention the High Priestess's departure for Ise, since he had touched on it before; though he concealed his interest in her. Genji pursued the matter so as to learn more about his feelings, without letting on that he already knew, and he felt sorry when he gathered how strong they were. He longed to know what feature of her beauty had so smitten him, and he chafed that he could not see her for himself. She was too profoundly deliberate in manner to allow any youthful liberty into her deportment, or he would have glimpsed her by now, and what hints he caught of her appearance were so un-failingly encouraging that he imagined her to be flawless.

His Highness of War could not bring himself to make any move of his own, now that His Majesty was fully taken up by this pair of ladies, and he bided his time instead, confident that His Majesty would surely not turn his daughter away once he was older.

His Majesty loved painting above all, and perhaps because he liked it so much, he was also extremely good at it. The Ise Consort painted very prettily, too, and so his interest shifted to her. The way they did paintings for each other meant that he went to see her often. He had been taking a pleased interest in the younger privy gentlemen who favored the same art, and he was charmed even more by this lovely lady whose paintings were not copybook exercises but en-tirely her own and who, reclining sweetly beside him, would pause gravely to consider the next stroke of her brush. He therefore visited her frequently and liked her far better than before.

This news spurred the Acting Counselor, always so forward and quick to rise to a challenge, to gather his wits (Why, am I to be bested?), call in expert painters, swear them to silence, and have them turn out the most beautiful work on the finest papers. "Pictures of scenes from tales have the most charm and give the greatest pleasure," he said; and he chose the prettiest and most amusing tales and set the painters to work illustrating them. He also had his daughter show His Majesty paintings of the round of monthly festivals, done in a novel format with accompa-nying text. When His Majesty wanted to look at them with the Ise Consort, the Kokiden side would not bring them out at all; instead they hid them and would not let His Majesty take them to the rival. "The Acting Counselor is such a boy at heart!" Genji laughed when he heard. "He will never learn!"

"It is quite wrong of the Acting Counselor to upset you this way by deliberately hiding them and keeping them from you," he said. "Some of mine, though, are from early times, and you shall have them." At his residence he had cabinets full of paintings old and new thrown open, and with his darling he thoughtfully selected those most pleasing to modern taste. The ones on subjects like "The Song of Unending Sorrow" or the story of Ōshōkun were attractive and moving, but they were also ill omened, and he decided for now to leave them out.[8]

He removed the record of his travels from its box and took the opportunity to show it to his love. It would have drawn willing tears from anyone in the least familiar with life's sorrows, even if the viewer was only barely acquainted with the circumstances, and for these two it brought back still more vividly the unforgettable nightmare that had engulfed them both. She let him know how unhappy she was that he had not shown it to her before.

> "Rather than lament all alone, as I did then, I, too, should have gone
>   to see for myself this place where the seafolk spend their lives,"

she said. "I would have worried a great deal less."

Touched, Genji replied,

> "Still more vividly than in those sad days now past, when I suffered them,
>   those ordeals return to mind, bringing with them many tears."

He must at least show these pictures to Her Cloistered Eminence. Choosing the scrolls least likely to be flawed and the most apt at the same time to convey a clear picture of "those shores,"[9] he dwelled in thought on the house at Akashi.

The Acting Counselor redoubled his efforts when he learned that Genji was assembling his own paintings, and he was more attentive than ever to the excellence of rollers, covers, and cords. It was the tenth or so of the third month, a delicious time of mild skies and expansive moods, and since no festival was under way now at the palace, both ladies spent their days absorbed in nothing else, until Genji saw that he, too, might as well do what he could to catch His Majesty's eye. He began marshaling paintings in earnest. Both sides had a great many. Since illustrations of tales were the most attractive and engaging, the Ise Consort's Umetsubo[10] party had theirs done for all the great classics of the past, while the Kokiden side favored tales that were the wonder and delight of their own time, so that theirs were by far the more brilliantly modern. Those of His Majesty's own gentlewomen who had anything to say for themselves spent their time, too, rating this painting or that.

Her Cloistered Eminence, too, was then at the palace, and she neglected her devotions to look through each side's paintings, since she could not resist the desire to see them. When she heard His Majesty's women discussing them that way, she

---

8. Both stories concern tragically separated lovers and are therefore ill omened for any felicitously matched couple.

9. Suma and Akashi. The expression *uraura* ("those shores") is from *Shūishū* 477, which names both.

10. "Plum court," Akikonomu's residence at the palace. Red and white blossoming plum trees grew beside it.

divided the contestants into two sides, Left and Right. On the Umetsubo side there were Hei, Jijū, and Shōshō, while on the Right were Daini, Chūjō, and Hyōe—in other words the quickest and most astute gentlewomen of their time. Their lively debates delighted her. In the first round *The Old Bamboo Cutter*, the ancestor of all tales, was pitted against the "Toshikage" chapter of *The Hollow Tree*.[11]

"This tale about the bamboo is certainly hoary enough, and it lacks lively touches, but Princess Kaguya remains forever unsullied by this world, and she aspires to such noble heights that her story belongs to the age of the gods. It is far beyond any woman with a shallow mind!"[12] those of the Left declared.

The Right retorted that the heavens to which Princess Kaguya returned were really too lofty to be within anyone's ken, and that since her tie with earth involved bamboo, one gathered that she was in fact of contemptible birth. She lit up her own house, yes, but her light never shone beside the imperial radiance![13] Abe no Ōshi threw away thousands and thousands in gold, and all he wanted from the fire rat's pelt vanished in a silly puff of smoke;[14] Prince Kuramochi, who knew all about Hōrai, ruined his own counterfeit jeweled branch.[15] These things, they claimed, marred the tale.

The paintings were by Kose no Ōmi and the calligraphy by Ki no Tsurayuki.[16] The whole was on utility paper backed by Chinese brocade, with a red-violet cover and a rosewood roller—a quite common mounting.[17]

"Now, Toshikage," the Right proclaimed, "was overwhelmed by mighty winds and waves that swept him off to unknown realms, but he still got where he wanted to go, spread knowledge of his wonderful mastery through foreign lands as well as our own, and achieved the fame to which he had so long aspired: that is the story the tale tells, and the way the paintings include both China and Japan, and all sorts of fascinating incidents, too, makes them incomparable."[18] The work was on white paper with a green cover and a yellow jade roller. It fairly sparkled with stylishness, since the paintings were by Tsunenori and the calligraphy by Michikaze.[19] The Left had no reply.

---

11. *The Old Bamboo Cutter* (*Taketori monogatari*) is a short, fairy-tale-like work of uncertain date. Toshikage is the hero of the first chapter of the long tenth-century romance known as *The Hollow Tree* (*Utsubo monogatari*).

12. Kaguya-hime ("Princess Brightly Shining," the heroine) is found by the old bamboo cutter as a tiny baby, inside a joint of bamboo. She has been born onto earth from the palace in the moon, and at the end of the tale she returns to the heavens after refusing many suitors, including the Emperor. The original passage starts with a line filled with familiar puns on *yo* ("age" and "joint of bamboo") and *fushi* ("passage" and, again, "joint of bamboo").

13. She never married the Emperor and shed her light over all the land.

14. An incident in the tale. Kaguya is courted by five suitors, to all of whom she gives such impossible tasks that they fail comically. From Abe she requires the pelt of the "fire rat," which no fire can burn. At vast expense Abe buys an alleged fire-rat pelt that goes up in smoke when she tests it.

15. Kuramochi's task was to bring back from Hōrai, a paradise mountain far out in the sea, a branch from the jewel trees that grow there. He had craftsmen make one instead, and they turned up to demand their fee just as he was presenting it to Kaguya-hime.

16. Kose no Ōmi, a painter active in the first two decades of the tenth century, was the son of the famous Kose no Kanaoka. Ki no Tsurayuki (died 946) was the most influential poet at the early-tenth-century court.

17. The mountings of the Left are in the red range, those of the Right in the range of green or blue. The same pattern appears in the poetry contest of 960 (see the chapter introduction) as well as in the colors of the two divisions (Left for "Chinese" pieces, Right for "Korean") of the *bugaku* dance repertoire.

18. During his wanderings, which took him as far as Persia, Toshikage gained ultimate mastery of the koto.

19. Both figures belong roughly to the present of this scene. The painter Tsunenori lived from 946 to 967 and the great calligrapher Ono no Michikaze from 894 to 966.

Next, *Tales of Ise* was matched against *Jōsanmi*,[20] and again the decision was hard to reach. This time, too, the Right's work was bright and amusing, and its scenes of a world familiar to them all, starting with pictures of the palace itself, made it the more pleasingly attractive.

> *"In rank ignorance of the great Sea of Ise's magnificent depths*
> *must the waves now wash away words thought merely old and dull?"*[21]

Hei objected lamely. "Is Narihira's name to be demeaned by tales of common licentiousness tricked out in pretty colors?"

Daini replied,

> *"To the noble heart that aspires to soar aloft, high above the clouds,*
> *depths of a thousand fathoms appear very far below."*[22]

"Whatever splendid ambitions the Guardsman's Daughter[23] may have entertained," Her Cloistered Eminence declared, "the name of Narihira is not to be despised.

> *At first glance, indeed, all that may seem very old, but despite the years*
> *are we to heap scorn upon the fisherman of Ise?"*[24]

The ladies' passionate arguments sustained an interminable debate over every scroll. Meanwhile the younger ones, who really had no idea what it was all about, were dying just for a look at them, but none of them, either Her Cloistered Eminence's or Her Highness's,[25] saw anything at all, because Her Cloistered Eminence kept them well hidden.

Genji joined them. "We may as well decide victory and defeat before His Majesty himself," he said, pleased by the spirit with which each speaker put her case. That had in fact been his idea all along, which is why he had kept some exceptional works in reserve; and among these, for reasons of his own, he had placed his two scrolls of Suma and Akashi.

The Acting Counselor was no less keen. It was all the rage in those days to make up amusing paintings on paper,[26] and despite Genji's warning that it would not

---

20. *Tales of Ise* (*Ise monogatari*) is a tenth-century classic, the influence of which is visible in *Genji* itself. *Jōsanmi* has been lost.

21. "Must those who champion the modern, and who know nothing of the excellence of *Tales of Ise* [Ise is by the sea], now consign the work to oblivion?" Narihira (below) is the central figure of the work.

22. "*Jōsanmi* is far superior in theme to *Tales of Ise*." The hero of *Jōsanmi* is apparently summoned to high station ("high above the clouds") by the Emperor, making Narihira's adventures seem contemptible in comparison.

23. Apparently the heroine of *Jōsanmi*.

24. On Narihira. Fujitsubo's poem plays on words associated with love and with the sea, and its defense of the exiled Narihira implies a defense of the recently exiled Genji.

25. Akikonomu's.

26. *Kamie*, paintings to go into handscrolls, as opposed to paintings for screens or sliding partitions. "Make up" refers to mounting as well as to painting the work.

be in the spirit of things to do new ones now, and that they should keep to the ones they already had, the Acting Counselor went to great lengths to prepare a secret room where he put his painters to work.

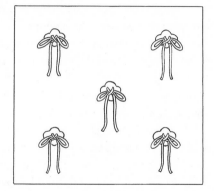

When His Eminence heard of this, he gave paintings to the Ise Consort. To scrolls by several old masters, showing delightful scenes from the round of annual festivals, on which His Engi Majesty had left comments in his own hand, and to others that he himself had had done of signal events of his own reign, he added one painted under his own close supervision by Kinmochi,[27] depicting

Gift knots on an incense box

the rite in the Great Hall of State that had so captivated him on the day when she went down to Ise as Priestess. They were dazzling works. Their lovely openwork aloeswood box, with its equally pretty gift knots, was in the height of fashion. The message with it was delivered orally by the Captain of the Left Palace Guards,[28] who was in service at His Eminence's palace. On the awesomely solemn scene that showed the High Priestess's palanquin beside the Great Hall of State, he had written simply,

> "Yes, as I am now, the sacred rope keeps me out, but that does not mean
> I could one instant forget all I felt then in my heart."[29]

It would have been unforgivable of her not to reply, and so she overcame her reluctance to do so. She broke off a bit of the comb she had had from him then, wrapped it in light blue Chinese paper, and sent with it:

> "It now seems to me here within the sacred rope that all things have changed,
> and I think back longingly to the presence of the gods."[30]

She rewarded the messenger very handsomely.

His Eminence was greatly moved to receive this, and he wished that he really could bring back the old days. He surely held a grudge against Genji in the matter—one he no doubt owed to what he himself had done. His paintings had come to him from his mother, and the Kokiden Consort must have received many of hers in the same way.[31] The Mistress of Staff[32] was extremely fond of pictures, too, and she had had a great many made for her own collection.

27. Kose no Kinmochi, a contemporary of Tsunenori.

28. Sakon no Chūjō. He does not appear again.

29. The "sacred rope" (*shimenawa*) alludes first to Akikonomu's priestly duty at the Ise Shrine, which removed her from him, and second to the holy precincts of the imperial palace, where she is again inaccessible.

30. "To the days when I served the gods at Ise."

31. His mother, the Kokiden Consort of the early chapters, was the daughter of the Minister of the Right and the elder sister of the present Kokiden Consort's mother.

32. Oborozukiyo, one of the Kokiden Consort's younger sisters.

The day was set, and with the arrangements prettily but still lightly made, impromptu as they were, the paintings of Left and Right were presented to His Majesty. His seat was prepared in the gentlewomen's sitting room, with the two sides before him to the north and the south. The privy gentlemen sat on the Kōrōden[33] veranda, each one across from the gentlewoman he favored. On the Left, the scrolls' rosewood boxes, covered by grape-colored Chinese silk, rested on sappanwood stands placed on purple Chinese brocade. Six page girls wore cherry blossom dress gowns over red, and wisteria layerings over scarlet. They looked marvelous and seemed beautifully trained. The Right's scrolls, in aloeswood boxes, rested on stands of fragrant wood set out on green Koma brocade; the design of the stands as well as the cords with which the brocade was secured to their legs was wonderfully stylish. The page girls were in dress gowns of willow and of kerria rose over green. They all went to place their stands and boxes before His Majesty. His Majesty's gentlewomen were divided into two sets, front and rear, each dressed accordingly.[34]

His Grace and the Acting Counselor were present at His Majesty's invitation. The Viceroy Prince, too, was there that day.[35] Genji must have urged him privately to come, fond as he was of painting, because no general invitation had gone out, and he was at the palace when a word from His Majesty brought him to the gathering. He served as judge. Some of the paintings were truly magnificent, and he found it impossible to decide among them. Those scenes of the four seasons, painted by the old masters so fluently and with so keen an eye, were incomparable, but their scope was limited after all, and it could not convey the full richness of mountains and waters; so that the more ephemeral modern ones, works of human understanding and of the wiles of the brush, proved just as lively and entertaining as the legacy of the past and stood out in their way. What with the debate that raged around them, Left and Right today both gave great pleasure to all.

Her Cloistered Eminence sat within the doors of the breakfast room.[36] Genji was very pleased, considering how deeply versed she must be in such things, and when the judge wavered, she often put in a word or two of her own, exactly as it was proper for her to do. The contest remained undecided on into the night.

The Left had one more turn, and when the Suma scrolls appeared, the Acting Counselor's heart beat fast. His side, too, had saved something special for last, but this, done at undisturbed leisure by a genius at the art, was beyond anything. Everyone wept, His Highness[37] the first among them. Genji's paintings revealed with perfect immediacy, far more vividly than anything they had imagined during those years when they pitied and grieved for him, all that had passed through his mind, all that he had witnessed, and every detail of those shores that they themselves had never seen. He had added here and there lines in running script, Chinese or Japa-

---

33. The building immediately west of the Seiryōden, across a narrow strip of garden.

34. The front women are dressed in red tones, the rear ones tones more in the range of green. "Left" (red, Akikonomu) is senior to "Right" (green, Kokiden).

35. Genji's younger brother, traditionally known as Prince Hotaru because of his role in the "Fireflies" chapter.

36. The *asagarei* adjoined the gentlewomen's sitting room to the north. There were sliding panels between the two rooms.

37. Prince Hotaru.

nese, and although these did not yet make it a true diary, there were such moving poems among them that one wanted very much to see more. No one thought of anything else. Emotion and delight prevailed, now that all interest in the other paintings had shifted to these. The question answered itself: the Left had won.

Dawn was coming on, and the wine cups were going round, when in a rush of feeling Genji began to talk of the past. "From my earliest youth I put my heart into my studies, and perhaps His Late Eminence believed that I might really acquire some knowledge, because he gave me a warning. He said, 'What is recognized as learning commands weighty respect, and

Holding a wine cup

I expect that that is why those who pursue it to excess so rarely enjoy both good fortune and long life. One born to high station, or at least to an honorable position among his peers, ought not to carry it too far.' He instructed me in the extra-academic arts, but there I was neither particularly inept nor endowed with any special gift. Painting, though, was different, because I often longed to paint to my heart's content, however odd and idle a pastime it may be, and when all at once I found that I was now a mountain rustic and saw into the truth of the mighty oceans, I rose to heights I had not dreamed of before. However, I remained dissatisfied, since there is a limit to what the brush can convey, and I could not very well have shown you these at all without a suitable occasion. I suppose I may be called conceited for doing so."

"No art or learning is to be pursued halfheartedly," His Highness replied, "but each has its professional teachers, and any art worth learning will certainly reward more or less generously the effort made to study it. It is the art of the brush and the game of Go that most startlingly reveal natural talent, because there are otherwise quite tedious people who paint or play very well, almost without training. Still, among the wellborn there are some exceptionally gifted people who seem to love every art and to do wonderfully well at them all. Who among His Late Eminence's Princes and Princesses did not learn several directly from him? And he used to speak of one who most truly repaid his special attention and who mastered every art, one after the other—letters, needless to say, but the *kin* as well, for which he had a magnificent gift, and the flute, the *biwa*, and the *sō no koto*, too. No one would disagree with this appraisal, and I had therefore assumed that you toyed also with the brush, as the spirit moved you, but it is extraordinary to find that you so utterly put to shame the finest artists of the past!" His words tripped over themselves, and perhaps it was the wine that now, at this mention of His Late Eminence, brought tears to every eye.

The moon rose. It was now past its twentieth day,[38] and while the room re-

---

38. At this time of the lunar month the moon rises just before dawn.

mained in shadow, the sky was so pretty that His Majesty sent for instruments from the Library. The Acting Counselor received the *wagon* and played almost as well as Genji himself. His Highness played the *sō no koto*, Genji the *kin*, and Shōshō the *biwa*. His Majesty also called on the best of the privy gentlemen to mark the rhythm.[39] It was perfectly lovely. As dawn came on, to the caroling of birds, the colors of flowers and faces emerged from darkness into the light of a beautiful new day. Her Cloistered Eminence provided the gifts for the musicians. His Highness again received a robe.[40]

Genji was absorbed then in deciding what to do with these paintings of his. He asked that the scrolls of the shores be presented to Her Cloistered Eminence, and when she asked to see those that came before and after them, he let her know that she would have them later, one by one. He was delighted to see His Majesty, too, so pleased with them.

With Genji tending the Ise Consort this way, the Acting Counselor must have trembled lest his own daughter's standing suffer. However, he did not really despair, because privately he could see quite well that His Majesty, who had always been fond of her, remained devoted to her even now.

This was an extraordinarily brilliant reign, for Genji aspired to add new touches to the festivals of the court—ones that would then pass on down the generations—and he carried off in grand style even little amusements of his own. Life still seemed treacherous to him, though, and his deepest wish was surely to renounce the world after all, once he had seen His Majesty mature a little more. All the past examples he knew suggested that those who rise to dizzying heights when young do not endure. In this reign his rank and fame had risen beyond his merit. Yes, he had outlived the annihilation of his painful fall, but he still doubted that his glory would last. His desire to shut himself away in peace, so as to prepare for the life to come and perhaps to prolong this one, moved him (one gathers) to secure a quiet plot in the hills and to have a temple built there and holy texts and icons consecrated; and yet his longing to bring his children up to be what he wished them to be dissuaded him from acting promptly. It is not easy to fathom what he really meant to do.

39. Probably with their batons (*shaku*) or with their folded fans.
40. Having received one already for serving as judge.

18

MATSUKAZE

Wind in the Pines

Matsukaze means "wind in the pines." The "Akashi" chapter associates the lady from Akashi, her house, and her music with this sound, and the motif reappears when she moves to Ōi, near the City, and plays music there. Her mother says,

*"Here at my old home, where I have returned alone and in a changed guise,
I hear blowing through the pines a familiar-sounding wind."*

"Wind in the Pines" takes place during the same year as "The Picture Contest" and during roughly the same time, in the autumn.

PERSONS

His Grace, the Palace Minister, Genji, age 31

The lady of Falling Flowers (Hanachirusato)

The lady from Akashi, 22 (Akashi no Kimi)

The Novice, her father, around 64 (Akashi no Nyūdō)

The caretaker at Ōi

Koremitsu

The Nun, the mother of the Akashi lady, 55 or 56 (Akashi no Amagimi)

Genji's daughter, 3 (Akashi no Himegimi)

Her nurse

An Aide in the Gate Watch

His Majesty, the Emperor, 13 (Reizei)

The Controller Chamberlain

The Secretary Captain

The Left Grand Controller

The Intendant of the Watch

Genji's lady, 23 (Murasaki)

Genji's east pavilion was now finished, and he brought the lady called Falling Flowers to live there. All along the bridgeway from its west wing[1] to the main house he provided suitable accommodation for his household office and retainers. Its east wing he reserved for the lady from Akashi. He had the north wing made especially large and partitioned it into separate lodgings so that he could gather there all the ladies whom his attentions, however fleeting, had encouraged to trust in a lasting tie with him, and each apartment was done up with exquisite charm. He left the main house unoccupied and made sure it was suitably appointed for a residence that he visited often.

He corresponded constantly with Akashi, and he still urged the lady there to come up to the City, but she remained too acutely aware of where she stood. Having heard how the very greatest ladies could suffer from neglect, even when not yet wholly abandoned, she asked herself what consideration *she* enjoyed that she should go out into such company, and she feared to make an embarrassing spectacle of her daughter's insignificance. What misery it would be, she thought, to have them all laughing at me for being reduced merely to awaiting the odd visit from him! Still, it would be a great shame if growing up in a place like this were to prevent her daughter from ever being counted among them, and she could never reject Genji's invitation out of hand. Her parents sympathized, and Genji's very eagerness therefore only caused them sharper distress.

They remembered that long ago her mother's grandfather, Prince Nakatsu-kasa,[2] had owned a property beside the river Ōi,[3] one that had fallen to ruin after his time in the absence of any real successor; and they accordingly summoned the care-taker of a sort who had always lived there. "After I decided it was time to give up the world, I grew accustomed to the obscurity I find here," the Novice told him, "but now, in my old age, an unexpected event requires me again to seek a house in the

1. Where Hanachirusato lives. The fact that she is close to the household office and retainers suggests that she is in charge of Genji's east pavilion.
2. An early commentary speculatively identifies this person as Kaneakira (914–87), a son of Emperor Daigo.
3. A stretch of the Katsura River in northwestern Kyoto, near Arashiyama.

City, and since sudden exposure to the glare of society would be awkward, and also upsetting for country people, it occurred to me to go to that old house of His Highness's. I shall send up everything required. I should like you please to look after the repairs and to make the place more or less livable."

"It has been many years now since any owner has lived there, and the house is so impossibly overgrown that I myself have moved into the servants' hall; besides, the temple His Grace is building nearby has made the place awfully noisy. There are several impressive halls going up, and a large number of men are working on them. If quiet is what you have in mind, I doubt that that is where you will find it."[4]

"No, no, not at all. You see, there is a matter for which I count on His Grace's goodwill. I will of course look after everything connected with doing up the house. I would like you now to lose no time seeing to the preliminary work."

"Perhaps I do not own the house," the caretaker answered with a defiant look and a reddening nose, "but in the absence of any successor I have lived secluded and at peace there for many years. The wet and dry fields of the estate had deteriorated so badly that the late Commissioner of Civil Affairs granted them to me, at my request, and they are mine now, subject to suitable repayment of his kindness." He feared that his enjoyment of the yield was under threat.

"I have absolutely no interest in the fields and all that. Consider them yours as before. The deeds and so on are here, but I have given up the world and its ways and have not even tried to find them for years. Now, though, I shall put all this in good order." His mention of Genji had given the caretaker pause. A great quantity of materials then arrived, and the man began the work promptly.

Genji knew nothing of all this, and he could not fathom why she was so reluctant to come up to the City. He worried that if his little girl went on living down there that way, all by herself, talk of it later on might easily blight her reputation even more. Only when the work at Ōi was finished did the Novice let Genji know that the place had come to mind. Genji understood then that this business had to do with her unwillingness to mingle with society, and he was impressed by her thoughtful discretion.

Genji sent Lord Koremitsu there to make sure everything was in good order, since it was Koremitsu who always attended him on his secret outings.

"The setting is very pretty," Koremitsu reported, "and it is just as though one looked out from there over the sea." It struck Genji that the place would not be at all unsuitable for her. The temple he was building was south of Daikakuji,[5] and its halls, for example the one beside the waterfall, rivaled in grace those of Daikakuji itself. Meanwhile, in a lovely grove of pines down by the river, a very simple, unpretentious house presented all the charm of a mountain village. Genji saw even to its interior furnishings.

4. Legal ownership of the property presumably passed on to Prince Nakatsukasa's descendants, including the Akashi Nun, but since the place has remained unclaimed for so long, the caretaker feels that the right to dispose of it belongs to him.
5. A still-extant temple in the Saga district of western Kyoto. Originally a villa belonging to Emperor Saga, it became a temple in 876 and remained under imperial patronage.

With great discretion he sent his most intimate retainers down to Akashi. The thought that the time had come, that she could put it off no longer, made her sad to leave this familiar shore, and she felt desperately sorry for her father, who would remain forlornly behind all alone. Sorrow consumed her. She wondered why she seemed destined only to suffer hereafter in so many ways, until she envied those whom Genji's favor had never touched. For her parents the good fortune of this journey, made with such an escort, meant the happy fulfillment of their oldest, fondest prayers, and yet their coming separation still affected her father so unbearably that he spent vacant days and nights saying over and over again, "Will I then never see this little girl again?"

Her mother, too, was very sad. Who was there to detain her, since it had been many years since she and the Novice last lived under one roof? Still, it was troubling to part from someone she had been with for so long, even if they seldom actually had much to do with each other, and despite that odd head of his and the vagaries of his moods, this was after all where she had meant to live out what remained of her days. The sudden departure was therefore painful. The young gentlewomen who had been so dejected here were happy, of course, but even so, many wet their sleeves with each breaking wave at the thought that they would never return to this beautiful shore.

It was autumn, and all things seemed to weigh upon the heart. The day came, and the autumn wind blew chill in the dawn, while busy insects cried and the lady sat gazing out to sea. Her father had risen long before the hour for his customary late-night devotions and was now blowing his nose while he did them. They all tried their best to shun ill-omened words, but it really was more than they could bear. To the old man the quite enchanting little girl was like a jewel that illumines the night. He had never allowed her far from him, and she had clung to him fondly; and now his own strange guise repelled him as he wondered, amid unfortunate tears that he could not control, how he would manage to get through a single moment without her.

> "I can hardly bear that for her bright future's sake she must go away,
> and it is beyond my strength to stop these tears of old age!

Oh, I mustn't, I mustn't!" he said, wiping them away to hide them.
The Nun replied,

> "You were with me once, when we came from the City—am I then this time
> to make my way all alone along pathways through the moors?"

No wonder she was weeping. When she thought over all their years together, all their pledges to each other, it seemed so foolish to turn back to the world she had left, just because of someone's casual promises!

> "What have I to hope from a world that keeps from me when I may expect
> in this life, once I have gone, ever to see you again?

Please at least keep us company there!" his daughter begged, but he explained that one thing and another made that impossible, even as his face revealed how greatly their journey upset him.

"When I first thought of renouncing the world, it was for you that I came down to this alien land, for I hoped that here I could bring you up day by day exactly as I pleased; but many things then brought home to me how poor my prospects were—not that returning to the City to join the obscure company of former Governors would have cleared any weeds from my pitiful door. No, I shrank from having all and sundry know me merely as a fool and from bringing only shame on my late father. It soon became clear that my departure had meant my giving up everything for good, and I myself believed that I really had done that, until you began to grow up and understand what was going on around you, because the more you did so, the more I asked myself in the endless darkness of a parent's heart how I could have hidden such a treasure here in this miserable wilderness. Yes, I prayed to the buddhas and the gods, and all I ever asked of them was that you, at least, should not be dragged down by your hopeless father to spend your life in a peasant's hut. I still lamented my condition in many, many ways even when wonders began happening out of a blue sky, but then our little girl came into the world with a sound destiny after all,[6] and it would be so wrong for a child of such high promise to spend her months and days here like this, by the sea, that it does not matter that I will miss her desperately—after all, I have given up profane life forever. You two, however, are undoubtedly meant to light up the world. Never mind, then, if fate brought her to trouble the heart of a peasant like me: I think of her as one who, born in the heavens, fell back to suffer only briefly the horrors of the Three Paths;[7] and in that spirit today I take leave of her forever. Do not trouble yourselves to mourn me even if you hear that I am no more. Do not be shaken by the parting that none can evade!" And his words tumbled on, "Weak as I am, I shall pray for our little girl in all my devotions, day and night, until the very night when I turn to smoke!" His face became contorted with grief.

A great train of carriages would have attracted too much attention, and smaller parties would have been tricky to manage. For this reason the lady's escort, who preferred to pass unnoticed, decided that she should go quietly by sea. The ships were launched at the hour of the Dragon.[8] While the shore's morning mists that so moved the old poet slowly veiled them from the Novice's eyes,[9] he thought in sorrow and longing that his heart would never have peace again.

After all these years the Nun found her return overwhelming, and she wept.

> "When this nun at heart longed only for the journey to that distant shore,
> now her boat rows back again to all that she had renounced!"[10]

6. The Novice speaks of her far more politely than he does of his wife or daughter.
7. The three lower realms of transmigration: beasts, hungry ghosts, and hell.
8. Roughly 8:00 A.M.
9. *Kokinshū* 409: "My heart is with the boat that draws away, dim through the mists off Akashi, and disappears behind the island."
10. "That distant shore" is the shore of paradise, and perhaps Akashi, where she had led a life of religious devotion. The poem plays on *ama* ("nun" and "woman [or man] of the sea").

And her daughter:

> *"Ah, how many times am I to live through autumn, as it comes and goes,*
> *before upon buoyant wood I make my way home again?"*[11]

A favorable wind blew, and they arrived on the intended day. They had traveled modestly, for they did not wish to be noticed. The house was pretty, and the view there so nearly resembled her familiar one of the sea that she felt as though she had not moved at all.[12] Times long past returned to mind,[13] with many touching memories. The galleries built onto the house looked very nice, and the stream in the garden was pleasant to see. The house did not feel lived in yet, but it would do very well once they had settled in. Genji charged his intimate retainers with giving them a proper welcome. As for his calling there himself, days passed while he pondered how to free himself to do so. This did nothing to relieve her melancholy. She felt listless and missed home so much that she turned to playing the *kin* he had left her, and since she could no longer conceal her sorrow, she went to play a little in a place apart; at which the wind in the pines indiscreetly enough joined in her music. The Nun, who was reclining sadly, sat up.

> *"Here at my old home, where I have returned alone and in a changed guise,*
> *I hear blowing through the pines a familiar-sounding wind,"*[14]

she said, and the lady:

> *"In lonely longing for the friends I used to know at the home I loved,*
> *I stammer a country tune that no one can understand."*

So it was that she spent her joyless days. Genji worried more about her now than ever, but he feared that going to her openly would only result in his darling, whom he had not yet really informed, learning the truth from somebody else. He therefore said to her, "I have an errand to look after at Katsura,[15] and I am afraid more days have gone by than I would like. Someone near there is expecting me, too, and I feel a little bad about it. I also need to see to adorning the Buddha at the temple on Saga Moor.[16] All that should take me two or three days."

She knew that he was suddenly building a Katsura villa, and she suspected him of keeping the woman from Akashi there. She did not like that at all. "You will

---

11. Apart from being simply a boat, "buoyant wood" (*ukiki*) also alludes to a Chinese legend about a man who rode a piece of wood up a great river to its source in the fabulous Kunlun Mountains.

12. The river is wide and shallow at this point, and her house, like the one at Akashi, is surrounded by pines.

13. When her great-grandfather had lived there.

14. Not only the wind itself (as at Akashi) but her daughter's music. Her "changed guise" is that of a nun.

15. Katsura was along the Ōi River. Genji seems to be building a villa there, although this is the tale's first allusion to it.

16. Sagano, the general location also of the Shrine on the Moor ("The Green Branch"). Genji's temple is presumably at the edge of the moor, against the hills that bound it.

no doubt be gone long enough to need a new handle for your ax,"[17] she said with visible annoyance. "I shall have a wait!"

"How prickly you always are! And I hear everyone is saying that I am quite unlike what I used to be!" The sun rose high while he strove to placate her.

He went to the new arrival in secret, very cautiously, and with only trusted men among his escort. It was twilight by the time he arrived. Even in a plain hunting cloak he conveyed unearthly beauty, and now, in a carefully chosen dress cloak, he looked so dazzlingly lovely that light shone through the lady's dark forebodings for her child. The moment was profoundly moving—how could he take lightly this first sight of his daughter? How bitterly he regretted all the time they had spent apart! The son given him by His Excellency's daughter looked very sweet, everyone said, but that was because the times inclined them to see him that way. At this age one could tell a child of bright promise at a glance, and his little girl, with all her innocence and her winning smiles, was absolutely enchanting. The nurse had not been at her best when she went down to Akashi, but she was now handsomer than ever. She told Genji everything that had happened since he left, and he sadly marveled that his daughter should have lived so long beside those saltmakers' huts.

"This place, too, is very cut off, and it is difficult for me to get here. Please move after all to where I would like to have you!"

"I prefer to accustom myself to life here first," the lady answered, reasonably enough.

They spent all night assuring each other in all ways of their love.

Genji directed the caretaker and some of his new retainers to look after what needed doing. The men from his nearby estates all came calling, since he was to visit his Katsura villa next. He had the garden near the house put right, where the plants had been crushed or broken. "All the standing stones here and there have fallen over or disappeared," he remarked, "but what a lovely place it would be if it were thoughtfully looked after! It would be a shame to take too much trouble with it, though. You will not be here forever, and leaving would only be painful—it was for *me*."[18] Amid tears and laughter he talked on intimately of the past, and he was very beautiful as he did so. The Nun stole glances at him and forgot her years; she felt her sorrows melt away and broke into smiles.

The lady, entranced and delighted, watched him sauntering about gracefully in his gown,[19] ordering improvements to the stream that emerged from beneath the eastern bridgeway. Then Genji noticed the holy-water shelf and remembered. "Is my lady the Nun here, too? My costume is disgraceful!" He called for his dress cloak and went to her standing curtain.

"I take it as an impressive tribute to your practice that you should have brought up your daughter so free of all offense.[20] Great devotion was required to

17. A Chinese story tells how a woodcutter deep in the mountains came upon two immortals playing Go. His ax handle rotted away while he watched, and he found on returning home that seven generations had gone by.

18. To leave Akashi.

19. Genji has taken off his dress cloak. The gown (*uchiki*) is the next layer down.

20. That is, of poor karma due to offenses committed in past lives.

leave the home where you had such peace and return to this fickle world, and I can well imagine how
the Novice, who remains behind, must be thinking
of you." He spoke very kindly.

"It is a great consolation to me in my old age
that you have divined how greatly this return to
the world I once left troubles me, but while I rejoice that the seedling pine[21] I cherished on that
stony shore should now have her future assured, I
cannot help worrying that the soil where she took
root is very thin."[22] She was weeping. What Genji
gathered of her person was by no means unworthy,
and he therefore encouraged her to continue talking about the past and about the Prince's mode of
life. The murmur of the mended stream meanwhile
reached them like a complaint.[23]

Holy-water shelf

> *"She whose home this was actually by now forgets many, many things,*
> *but the clear stream babbles on like the mistress of the house,"*

she said, and Genji admired the elegance with which her voice unaffectedly died
away.

> *"No such limpid brook could retain a memory of the distant past:*
> *perhaps it feels after all that the mistress has not changed—*

Ah me!" Standing there so pensively, Genji seemed to her lovelier than anyone in
the world.

He went on to his temple, where he ordered not only the regular litanies to
Fugen or the invocations to Amida or Shaka that are done on the fourteenth, fifteenth, and last days of the month but many other services that he wanted performed. He also gave out instructions for adorning the halls and providing
furnishings for the buddhas there. He returned under a bright moon.

That night then came back to her from the past, and she did not fail to mark it,
for she offered him his *kin*. He could not help playing it a little, caught up as he was
in warm emotions. The tuning had not changed, and he felt now as he had then.

> *"You who faithfully left the tuning of this* kin *just as it was then,*
> *did you hear in its music all that you still mean to me?"*

---

21. A common literary figure for a child. The evergreen pine promises everlasting vigor.
22. "That my own undistinguished standing should compromise her future."
23. Because the stream was here in the Prince's time and knew him well, yet Genji and the Nun are ignoring it.

She replied,

"Resting in my trust that as you had promised me your heart would not change,
I joined my weeping music to the sounding of the pines."

It showed how far she surpassed all one could have expected of her that her side of the exchange was not unworthy. Genji was captivated by her looks and manner, which had matured magnificently, and he could hardly keep his eyes off his daughter. What am I to do? he wondered. It would be a terrible shame to let her grow up like this in obscurity, and her reputation may easily suffer later on[24] unless I bring her to Nijō and provide for her there as I hope to do. He said nothing of all this, though, because he feared her mother's likely feelings too much, and tears came to his eyes. The girl was a little shy with him at first, being so small, but she soon came round, and the more she snuggled up to him, chattering and laughing, the more exquisitely lovely she became. It was well worth seeing him with her in his arms, and the picture clearly conveyed their exceptional fortunes.

He was to return to the City the next day, and he ought to have gone straight back from there, since he slept a little late, but many people had gathered at his Katsura villa, and a crowd of privy gentlemen appeared at Ōi, too. "What a bore!" he exclaimed as he dressed. "They should not be coming for me here." The press of business required him to leave, which he was sorry to do, and as he stood by the door with an air of detached innocence, the nurse came out with the child in her arms. He caressed his daughter tenderly. "I know it is selfish of me," he said, "but it will be very painful not to be with you. What can I do, though? You are so far away!"

"Not knowing how you may be disposed toward me in the future, my lord," the nurse replied, "I am more anxious now than I ever was in those years when I knew I could not see you at all!"

The little girl reached out affectionately to him as he started away, and he knelt on one knee beside her. "It is strange how many sorrows I have. I so hate to be gone at all. Where is your mother? Why has she not come out with you to say good-bye? That is what would make me feel better!" The nurse smiled and passed his words on to her mistress, who was in truth prostrate with sorrow and could barely move. Genji felt she rather overplayed the great lady. It was too much for her women as well, and so very reluctantly she came out after all. Her profile, half hidden behind her curtain, had a wonderfully fine distinction, and the grace of her manner would have put a Princess to shame. Genji turned back to draw her curtain aside and talk to her privately, and despite her efforts to contain herself, this time she did watch him go. He was at the ineffable peak of his beauty. Always tall, he had now filled out somewhat, in harmony with his height, and she thought he had acquired a weightier dignity than before; but perhaps it was only her own predilec-

---

24. Because it might be said of her that her mother was a country woman of low rank.

tion that gave him such enchanting grace, right down to the ends of his gathered trousers.

The Chamberlain once stripped of his post[25] had been reinstated. Now an Aide in the Gate Watch, he had this year received his cap of office and was a jolly fellow, quite unlike his former self. He approached to bear Genji's sword.

"Those days are not forgotten," he hinted upon glimpsing a certain gentlewoman within, "but I hesitated to take the liberty. I lay awake at dawn, in a wind that reminded me so much of the one there on the shore, but I had no hope of getting any word to you."

"When 'the mountains, fold on fold,' do as well as 'gone behind the isle,' and when I was just thinking, 'long ago even the pine,' it is a real pleasure to come across someone who has *not* forgotten me!" she retorted.[26]

He was amazed. Well, I certainly got it! he said to himself. And I was actually quite fond of her, too! "Another time, then," he answered curtly and went to wait upon Genji.

Genji's escort cleared the way with loud cries when he set out in grand style. The Secretary Captain and the Intendant of the Watch rode in the rear of his carriage.

"I dislike the way you have tracked me down when, here, I would have much preferred to pass unnoticed." Genji was extremely put out.

"There was such a beautiful moon last night that we regretted not coming with you, and this morning we made our way here through the mists. The colors in the fields were lovely, though it is still too early for brocade on the hills."[27]

"Some of us were busy hawking and fell behind. I wonder what has happened to them."

Genji set off toward his Katsura villa, where he was to spend time again today. The sudden need to receive him had thrown the place into a great commotion, and the jargon of the cormorant fishermen, when they were summoned, reminded him of the seafolk. The young gentlemen who had stayed out in the fields now arrived and presented their token gift of small birds attached to a *hagi* frond.

The wine went round and round until the riverbank became such a threat that in their drunkenness they all spent the day at the villa instead. Each contributed his share of Chinese verses, and the music began when a brilliant moon rose. It was very lively. The *biwa* and the *wagon* were the only stringed instruments, but there were several expert flutists whose music nicely caught the mood of the moment,

25. Together with Genji, when Genji went into exile at Suma.

26. "You seem to find me as inaccessible at Ōi as I ever was at Akashi, and I was just thinking that there is no one left who cares about me." (1) "The mountains, fold on fold," is from *Gosenshū* 1173: "The longer one lives where the mountains, fold on fold, are crowned by white clouds, the more willingly one stays." ("Ōi is as remote as Akashi, and we are so comfortable here, no wonder you didn't write!") (2) "Gone behind the isle" is from *Kokinshū* 409: "How this heart of mine goes to the boat that fades into the morning mists and is gone behind the isle." (3) "Long ago even the pine" is from *Kokinshū* 909: "Whom have I to call a friend, when long ago even the pine of Takasago did not know me?"

27. The colors of the autumn leaves.

while the wind sang with them along the river and the moon soared high into a carefree night.

Rather late, four or five privy gentlemen arrived. They had been on duty in the privy chamber, and when there was music His Majesty had remarked, "It is the sixth today, and the seclusion at the palace is supposed to be over. I was sure that he would be here. What is he doing?" When he learned where Genji was, he had a message taken to him by the Controller Chamberlain:

"Since that place of yours lies far across the river and boasts a bright moon,
no doubt the katsura tree feels there perfectly at home.[28]

I envy you." Genji expressed his apology. The company rose to new heights of intoxication, inspired by music that in this setting surpassed in majesty the concert at the palace.

Wagon

Having no reward for the messenger, Genji sent to Ōi for something not too ostentatious. He was brought what had come to hand. It arrived in two clothing chests, and he placed a woman's robe across the shoulders of the Chamberlain, who was obliged to go straight back. He also entrusted him with his reply:

"It is just the name that suggests proximity to that glorious light,
for in this mountain village mists hang heavy, dawn and dusk."

He probably meant that he hoped for an imperial visit.

He no doubt shed tears of drunken elation as he hummed "grows in the heavens,"[29] remembering the island of Awaji and how Mitsune suggested that "it must be the setting."[30]

"So the months have turned, and there, aloft in the sky, close enough to touch,
shines the moon that I saw then, veiled, above Awaji Isle!"[31]

The Secretary Captain added,

"The moon's brilliant light that misfortune veiled awhile with such dreary clouds
now at last shines forth again, and the world can be at peace."[32]

28. In East Asian lore a *katsura* tree (resembling a laurel) grows in the moon; and the word plays on the name of the place (Katsura) where Genji is. The poem also hints that the *katsura* tree is Genji.

29. From the source poem for Genji's message to the Emperor, *Kokinshū* 968 by Ise, also written at Katsura: "Since this village [Katsura, see note above] grows in the heavens, all my trust here is in their light [i.e., in the imperial favor]."

30. Genji remembers his view of Awaji across a moonlit sea and goes on to recall the same poem that he thought of then (*Shinkokinshū* 1515, by Ōshikōchi no Mitsune): "The moon that on Awaji seemed so sadly distant, tonight—it must be the setting—seems very near." He weeps with joy at the contrast between then, when he was in exile, and now, when the Emperor is "very near" and regards him highly.

31. Genji is thinking of his poem in "Akashi," "Ah, how grand a sight . . ."

32. The moon this time is Genji.

The Left Grand Controller, a little older than the rest, had served His Late Eminence intimately:

"The full midnight moon has forsaken his proud dwelling far above the clouds,
in what dark, distant valley forever to hide his light?"[33]

There were many others, in varied moods, but all that is too much of a bother. One would have liked to spend a thousand years watching Genji and listening to his quiet, informal, and somewhat rambling conversation—one's ax handle might well have rotted away—but Genji had promised himself not to do it again today, and he hurried home. He laid a robe across the shoulders of each in consonance with his rank, and their colors amid the flowers of the garden made a very pretty picture indeed. Some well-known members of the Gate Watch, men adept at dancing and music, felt the need to add a further touch by performing a lively "That Horse of Mine,"[34] and to reward them the gentlemen slipped off robes that lay on their shoulders like autumn brocade spread by the wind. Such was the uproar of Genji's departure that news of it traveled all the way to Ōi,[35] where the lady was silently overcome by sorrow. Genji regretted not being able to send her a word.

He rested a little on returning home and then told his lady there about Ōi. "I regret having stayed so much longer than I said I would. Those dashing young men of mine came after me and made it impossible for me to leave. I do not feel at all well this morning either." He went to bed. He could tell she was angry with him as usual, but he paid no attention. "This will not do, you know," he admonished her. "In rank there is simply no comparison between the two of you. You are you, after all—remember that." One easily imagines to whom he was writing at nightfall, turned aside from her that way, just before setting off for the palace. Furtive glances told her that his letter was long. Her gentlewomen did not like the way he whispered when he sent it off.

He remained in attendance at the palace through the evening, too, but to appease her he withdrew late in the night.

The answer to his letter came, and he read it without any attempt to hide it. "Destroy this, please," he said, since there was nothing in it to upset her. "How difficult it all is! This is not the sort of thing I can afford to leave lying about anymore." As he leaned on his armrest, his inmost heart went out longingly to the sender, and he gazed at the lamp in silence.

There the letter lay, open, but his lady paid it no heed. "Those poor eyes of yours! They must be burning for a look!" He smiled, and his charm carried all before it. He moved toward her and went on, "Actually, now that I have seen the dear little thing, I understand how strong a tie I have with her, and I only wish there were less need for caution if she is to succeed. Please consider the matter yourself in that light and make up your mind. What are we to do? Do you think you could look after her

---

33. This moon is the Kiritsubo Emperor (His Late Eminence).
34. A *saibara* song suitable for a gentleman's departure on horseback: "That horse of mine wants his feed, yes, wants his feed. I'll bring him his grass, yes, I'll fetch him his water, I'll bring him his grass."
35. Ōi and Katsura were about 2.5 miles apart.

here? She is just the Leech Child's age by now.[36] Her very innocence makes her difficult simply to forget. I would like to put trousers on her, and I hope you will tie them for her, if you do not mind."[37]

"It is just that I can hardly pretend not to notice, you know, when you become impatient with me over feelings I really do not have. I am sure that I will do very well by such a little girl. What a pretty age she must be now!" She gave him a faint smile. She did love children, and she wanted very much to have this one to cuddle and look after.

Genji still wondered what to do. *Should* he bring her to Nijō? It was so difficult for him to go there. He seems to have promised her just twice a month, when he went for the rites at his temple on Saga Moor. That was better than the Tanabata stars' once a year, but despite being resigned to this arrangement she could only grieve.

---

36. In her third year. He may also mean here that his daughter needs special support to "stand on her own feet."

37. Genji wants to give her a "donning of the trousers" (*hakama gi*), a rite of passage in which a child was first dressed in *hakama* trousers. The tying on of the trousers was central to the ceremony, and to perform it was to act as a sort of formal sponsor.

19

USUGUMO

Wisps of Cloud

The chapter title comes from a
poem spoken by Genji in mourning for Fujitsubo:

*"Those thin wisps of cloud trailing there over mountains caught in sunset light
seem to wish to match their hue to the sleeves of the bereaved."*

RELATIONSHIP TO EARLIER CHAPTERS

"Wisps of Cloud" begins in the winter of the year covered (spring and fall) by "Wind in the Pines" and ends the following autumn.

PERSONS

His Grace, the Palace Minister, Genji, age 31 to 32

The lady at Ōi, 22 to 23 (Akashi no Kimi)

The Nun, her mother, mid-50s (Akashi no Amagimi)

Genji's daughter's nurse

Genji's daughter, 3 to 4 (Akashi no Himegimi)

The lady in Genji's west wing, 23 to 24 (Murasaki)

The lady in Genji's east pavilion (Hanachirusato)

Chūjō one of Genji's, now Murasaki's, gentlewomen

The father of the lady at Ōi, around 64 to 65 (Akashi no Nyūdō)

His Excellency, the Chancellor, the former Minister of the Left, 65 to 66 (dies) (Sadaijin)

Her Cloistered Eminence, mother of the Emperor, 36 to 37 (dies) (Fujitsubo)

His Majesty, the Emperor, 13 to 14 (Reizei)

A certain Prelate

His Highness of Ceremonial, Asagao's father (dies) (Shikibukyō no Miya)

The Acting Counselor, then Grand Counselor and Commander of the Right (Tō no Chūjō)

Her Highness, the Ise Consort, daughter of the Rokujō Haven, 22 to 23 (Akikonomu)

Ōi became drearier still with winter, and the lady there spent her days feeling completely lost. "You cannot go on like this," Genji told her. "You must make up your mind to move near me"; but she was in turmoil, because if going only brought her more such misery, she would sink into the pit of despair, and what would tears avail her then?[1]

"Very well, our little girl, then. It is a shame that this should be the only life she knows, and an affront as well, considering what I intend for her. The lady in my west wing has heard of her and often asks about her, and once they have made friends, I mean to hold a donning of the trousers that does not go completely unnoticed." He broached the topic gravely.

That she had long suspected it only made it worse. Whatever treatment she may receive there, he surely does not expect to be able to hide the truth forever, she quite naturally reflected; but Genji reassured her.

"Have no fear," he said. "There is no need for you to worry." That lady still has no children, you know, after all these years, and she is so disappointed that she insists on looking after the former Ise Priestess[2] even now, when she is quite grown-up. You can be sure that she will not lightly neglect any child as impossible to dislike as this one." He went on to tell her more about how admirable the lady was.

Yes, she thought, the power of destiny must have brought them together, and she must be a marvel among women if those old ways of his—ways rumored long ago, ways such that one wondered who could ever induce him to settle down—are really over and done with now. She might well take offense if I, who could not possibly stand beside her, tried to put myself forward nonetheless. But never mind what happens to me, because it is certainly her wishes that could make or break my daughter's future, and if that is so, then I should give my daughter up while she is

---

1. From *Gosenshū* 705, the complaint of a woman whose fate was what the lady from Akashi fears. When her lover, who hardly ever came anymore, told her that she simply lived too far away, she moved closer: "Though I moved and I waited, he still failed to come—ah, how many miseries there are to suffer!" Also *Shūishū* 985: "If, even after I am wronged, he wrongs me again, what will tears avail me to give voice to my pain?"

2. Akikonomu, a year younger than Murasaki.

still too little to understand. I shall worry so much, though, if I do! Only she relieves the dullness of my days, and I do not know how I shall live without her! And what will bring him here then? Her confusion made her very unhappy indeed.

Her mother the Nun spoke to her from her profound understanding. "This is foolishness," she said. "Yes, it will be painful not to have her anymore, but remember that it is for her own good. It is not indifference that makes him talk this way. Just trust him and let him take her. An imperial son's rank seems to come from his mother, and I expect the reason why His Grace is a mere official, despite his extraordinary qualities, is that the late Grand Counselor was one step too low,[3] so that he was called an Intimate's son. It is obviously not for the likes of us to measure ourselves against such people. In fact, a child's mother, even if a Princess or a Minister's daughter, had better be the father's formal wife;[4] otherwise, people will think less of her child, and not even the father will be able to treat it equally. As for your daughter, it is all too obvious that in such exalted company a girl like her would simply be ignored. The girl whose father has given her just that extra degree of care, in the manner proper to his station, is the one who need never fear other people's contempt. And as far as this donning of the trousers goes, no trouble you could take, lost as you are in these hills, could give it any luster whatever. Just let him do as he thinks best and watch how well he acquits himself."

Sensible people she consulted always gave the same answer, that her daughter should go to Nijō, and she therefore began to yield. Genji shared their opinion, but he felt for her so much that he could not bring himself to press the matter.

"What will you do about her donning of the trousers?" he inquired; and she answered, "As far as I can see, I am so insignificant that I may jeopardize her future if I keep her with me, and yet I still cannot help feeling that in your world she may only be mocked." Genji sympathized with her more than ever. He had a day selected[5] and quietly ordered the necessary preparations for receiving his daughter. Her mother was still in despair over letting her go, but she bore up for her daughter's sake.

"Are you leaving me, too, nurse?" she asked, weeping. "Your conversation has been such a comfort through all these times when I have been sad or bored, and I shall feel your absence as well very much!"

"It can only be fate that brought me to you so unexpectedly, and I shall not forget all your kindness; nor shall I ever lose touch with you, my lady, since you will be good enough to miss me. One day soon you will come, too, I know, but for now I must leave you, and I wonder what life will be like there, where I never imagined I would ever go!" The nurse was in tears herself.

The last month of the year had come. The weather turned to snow and sleet, and her affliction grew. How strangely I was born to bear many sorrows! she lamented, and more than ever she caressed and fussed over her daughter. One morning when falling snow darkened the skies and she was absorbed in pondering all that had been and

---

3. Not quite a Minister, so that his daughter was never appointed Consort.

4. Not one of the other women by whom he may have had children, and with whom his relationship commands less social recognition.

5. By a diviner, according to the almanac.

would be, she who so seldom approached the veranda sat dressed in many layers of soft white, gazing at the ice along the edge of the water; and it seemed to her women that her pensive figure, the lines of her hair, and her figure from behind made her the very picture of the greatest lady in the land. "I shall miss you so much more on days like this!" she sighed charmingly, brushing away a tear.

> *"The snow may be deep and the paths across the hills lost in banks of cloud,*
> *but please still keep coming here; never fail to keep in touch."*

The nurse wept and said comfortingly,

> *"Even if my goal were the Yoshino Mountains and their constant snows,*
> *how could I lose touch with you, when my heart goes to you so?"*

He came once the snow had melted a little. She usually awaited him eagerly, but this time she knew what to expect, and she felt an anguish for which she had no one but herself to blame. It is all up to me, she thought—he would not insist if I were to refuse. Oh, I should never have agreed! She checked these capricious impulses, though. The sight of her daughter, sitting so sweetly before her, reminded her that this little girl was not to be taken lightly. Her hair had grown since spring to the length of a nun's, and it now swayed very prettily; and of course her face and eyes were lovely, too. Genji felt such pain, imagining her mother's despair once she knew that her daughter belonged to someone else, that he spent the night explaining himself all over again.

"No, no, all I ask is that you treat her better than her worthless mother deserves!" Her self-control collapsed, and she burst into pathetic tears.

The little girl was innocently eager to board the carriage. Her mother carried her to it herself. Her lisping speech was very dear, and when she tugged at her mother's sleeve, crying, "Come, get in!" her mother was overcome.

> *"Now that I am torn from my little seedling pine and her years ahead,*
> *when shall I with my own eyes see her as a mighty tree?"*

Tears prevented her from saying more.

Of course, poor thing! Genji thought, and he answered soothingly,

> *"Since she first struck root in such deep, nurturing soil, let her add henceforth*
> *her own thousand years to those of the Takekuma pine."*[6]

She hoped he was right, but it was more than she could bear.

6. "Her bright future is ours as well." The seedling pine is the little girl. The Takekuma pine, which grew near the government outpost in the far northern province of Mutsu, was (according to *Goshūishū* 1041, by Tachibana no Suemichi) a single pine with twin trunks (*aioi no matsu*), a happy emblem of conjugal felicity. Genji refers to himself and the lady from Akashi as a couple.

Godchild

The nurse and an elegant gentlewoman known as Shōshō were the only ones to get in, and they brought the dagger, the godchild,[7] and so on with them. Various nice, younger gentlewomen and page girls rode in the accompanying carriages. They were to see the party to their destination. Genji felt guilty all the way there for having so hurt the lady who remained behind.

They arrived after dark, and the carriage was no sooner drawn up than the magnificence of the place, so unlike what they knew in the country, made them wonder how they could live here without making fools of themselves, but the aisle room on the west side had been made ready just for their little mistress and equipped with small, very pretty furnishings. The nurse had her room on the north side of the western bridgeway.

The little girl, who had fallen asleep on the way, did not cry when she was lifted down from the carriage. In her room she ate some nuts and sweets, but when by and by she looked around and missed her mother, it was charmingly clear from her face that there would soon be tears, and her nurse was called in to comfort and distract her. Genji could hardly bear to imagine the monotony her mother faced, there among her hills, but it was surely also a great satisfaction to him that he could now look after his daughter as he pleased, day in and day out. He wondered bitterly why no such dear and perfect little girl had been born in his own house.

His daughter cried for a time, missing people she knew, but on the whole her nature was sweet and happy, and she made friends so nicely with the lady who reigned over Genji's household that this lady was delighted to have so dear a child. She was always taking her in her arms and playing with her, and naturally the nurse was soon waiting on her intimately as well. Genji brought in another nurse, too, a lady of high rank with lots of milk.

Genji made no great show of preparing for the donning of the trousers, but he nonetheless gave it special thought. All the furnishings were done beautifully, as though for dolls. The guests attracted no particular attention, since there were always so many people coming and going, day or night. All noted how perfectly charming she looked with the cords of her trousers crossed that way over her chest to tie back her sleeves.

The lady at Ōi missed her acutely, and she lamented her error. Her mother was more than ever prone to tears, despite her persuasive speeches, but she rejoiced at the way Genji looked after her granddaughter. What gifts could they possibly send? They could only prepare gowns in the loveliest colors and send them off to her nurse and her women. Genji knew how the lady longed for his visits, and he wished to spare her seeing her fears confirmed. He therefore went there quietly be-

---

7. A girl received a dagger (*mihakashi*) at birth, as a protective talisman. Another protective device was the godchild (*amagatsu*), a doll that served the same purpose as the purification doll described near the end of "Suma." The child was supposed to transfer into the doll any evil influence that could harm her. A child retained the godchild until roughly her third year.

fore the year was over. The house was lonelier than ever, and it so upset him to imagine her feelings after losing the child whose care had absorbed her that he sent her constant letters. His darling had given up any real jealousy by now, having forgiven him for the sake of the dear little girl.

The New Year came. Genji, more carefree than ever, flourished beneath balmy skies, and among those who gathered to the spotless magnificence of his establishment, a procession of older gentlemen presented themselves on the seventh to thank him,[8] while younger ones called happily for no particular reason at all. Other, lesser visitors may have had their private sorrows, but this was a time for all to show a proud and pleased face to the world.

The lady in Genji's east pavilion[9] lived handsomely, too. No gentlewoman or page girl of hers ever misbehaved, and she watched herself vigilantly. A wonderful benefit of having Genji so close was that he might come and see her at any time, when he was at leisure, although nothing suggests that he ever tried to spend the night. In the tranquil innocence of her nature she was simply thankful for her good fortune, and she maintained such wonderfully reassuring serenity that Genji provided for her, season by season, hardly less well than he did for his own love. People came to her and served her equally, because it was impossible to think poorly of her. The women under her Mistress of the Household were so exquisitely attentive that she upheld the most impeccable standard in all things.

Genji always remained aware that life was very dreary in the hills, and he made up his mind to go there once the press of his public and private engagements had passed. For this visit he prepared himself with exceptional care, donning a cherry blossom dress cloak over an indescribably lovely gown, both sweetly perfumed, and the clear light of the setting sun made his figure even more entrancing. His darling saw him off with a troubled heart. The little girl clung childishly to his gathered trousers, wanting to go with him, and he stopped, deeply moved, just before stepping out through the blinds. "I'll be back tomorrow,"[10] he sang to soothe her as he left, and his love, waiting by the bridgeway door, had Chūjō take him:

> "If there were no one over there on that island to detain his boat,
> then indeed I would expect my husband back tomorrow!"

The message was delivered with knowing ease, and he gave a charming smile.

> "I shall go and see and yes, be back tomorrow; and I shall not care
> if yonder on the island she is not especially pleased!"

The little girl, running merrily about and understanding nothing, had so captivated his lady that all her feeling against "that other woman" was gone. How her

8. For promotions and appointments that they owed to his patronage.
9. Hanachirusato, the lady of Falling Flowers.
10. From a *saibara* song: "[The husband] Stay your boat, O cherry blossom man, I've to see to my fields on the island, and I'll be back tomorrow, yes, I'll be back tomorrow! [The wife] Tomorrow, you say, but he who has a woman there won't really be back tomorrow, no, not really back tomorrow."

mother must long for her! I would miss her so much if I were she! she would reflect as she gazed at the child, and then she would playfully cuddle her and give her her own pretty breast to suck. The sight was well worth seeing. The women around her whispered to each other, "Why, when it could just as well have been *she* . . . ?" and "Oh, what a shame!"

The lady at Ōi led a life at once quiet and distinguished. Her house was unusual, but as for herself, Genji admired whenever he saw her the looks and the mature dignity of demeanor that placed her very little below the greatest in the land. If only it were possible to pass her off as simply another provincial Governor's daughter, people would be glad enough to remember that this was not the first time such a thing had happened. Her father's fame as an egregious crank was a problem, but he had quite enough to make him acceptable. Genji did not at all want to rush home again, since this visit had no doubt been too short for him as well. "Is it a tossing bridge crossed in dreams?"[11] he sighed, then drew a nearby *sō no koto* to him and insisted until she took up her *biwa* and accompanied him a little; for he remembered as so often the sound of her music that night at Akashi. Her playing made him wonder how she could have mastered so many instruments. He took the time to tell her all about their little girl.

He stayed at Ōi quite often, despite what the place was like, and there were also times when he took a light meal of fruit and steamed rice there. He would come under cover of a trip to his nearby temple or to his Katsura villa, and even if his behavior toward her suggested no headlong passion, he did not by any means treat her dismissively, as he might have any other woman, for he clearly thought a great deal of her. She herself understood his regard for her, and she never took what he might construe as a liberty or betrayed the slightest vulgar touch; she never failed his standards in any way, and her company was always a pleasure. She had heard that he was less at ease with the greatest ladies than he was with her and that he stood on his dignity with them, and perhaps she therefore felt that if she moved any closer, those around him might just dismiss her as being of no interest, and that the preservation of her own self-respect lay precisely in attracting these rare visits from him.

Despite what her father had said at Akashi, he longed to know how Genji was disposed toward her and how she herself was getting on, and since his messengers kept him informed on these matters, he knew now and again a moment of anguish, but also, often enough, of pride and joy.

At about this time His Excellency the Chancellor[12] passed away. Even His Majesty mourned him, for he had carried great weight in the world. Many others regretted his loss especially, because even during his short retirement, troubles had come upon the realm. Genji grieved, and he was very sorry also because he owed his leisure to having ceded His Excellency so many of his own responsibilities, and

---

11. *Genji monogatari kochūshakusho in'yō waka* 148: "Is this world of ours a tossing bridge crossed in dreams, that crossing it should call up such sorrows?" "Dreams" suggests erotic liaisons, and *yo no naka* ("this world of ours") alludes to matters of love. The *uki* of *ukihashi* ("tossing bridge") means both "floating" and "sad."

12. Genji's former father-in-law, previously the Minister of the Left.

he feared a tedious press of duties henceforth.[13] He felt no anxiety concerning affairs of state, because His Majesty was by now mature far beyond his years, but there was no one else at all obvious to assist him, and he could not see who might assume these duties and leave him the peace he craved above all. This troubled him very much. He contributed more thoughtfully and more generously to the funeral rites than did any of the children or grandchildren.

That year the world was in turmoil. A flurry of oracles on matters of state had shaken it from its complacency, and in the heavens the light of sun, moon, and stars shone strangely, while patterns in the clouds gave frequent alarm. Memorials from experts in many lines of knowledge mentioned strange and disturbing events. His Grace alone suffered at heart from having some idea why.[14]

Her Cloistered Eminence had been ill since early spring, and by the third month her condition was so grave that His Majesty made a progress to call upon her. He had been too young to mourn His Late Eminence's[15] loss deeply, but this time he betrayed such distress that his mother felt keen sympathy. "I did not expect to escape this year," she said, "but then, I did not really feel so very unwell, and since I did not wish to seem to advertise any miraculous presentiment of my own passing, I made no effort to pray more than before for my own happiness in the life to come. I had thought I might call and quietly talk over the past with you, but I seldom felt well enough to do so, and alas, I have not in the end managed to dispel my misgivings." She spoke very weakly. This was her thirty-seventh year.[16] His Majesty looked on her with regret and sorrow, for she was nevertheless in the full flower of youthful beauty. Her months of poor health had already worried him, in a year that required such vigilance, and he was appalled to learn that she had taken no unusual precautions at all.[17] He had only recently grasped her condition, and he commissioned relief of every kind. Genji, too, worried greatly that for months she should have complacently assumed nothing more to be wrong than her usual complaint. His Majesty was then obliged to end his visit and return, amid many sad farewells.

Pain had kept Her Cloistered Eminence from expressing herself well, but she understood on silent, sustained reflection that whereas she had stood above all others in high destiny and worldly glory, she had also suffered more in her heart. Despite everything it seemed to her a tragedy that His Majesty should never have any inkling of the truth,[18] and she felt that this one thing would burden her unhappy spirit forever.

Merely from the standpoint of the interests of His Majesty's court, Genji grieved that its greatest figures should soon follow one another in death. Privately, his sorrow was beyond measure, and there was no prayer or rite that he neglected to commission. The torture of no longer being able to tell her, a last time, all that he

---

13. Genji is currently Palace Minister and Regent (Sesshō), and he had entrusted the duties of the Regent to his late father-in-law.

14. The natural disasters are a warning of grave disorder in government: the present Emperor's (Reizei's) reign is illegitimate, since he is actually Genji's son.

15. The Kiritsubo Emperor, his purported father.

16. A particularly dangerous "year of trouble" (yakudoshi) for a woman, according to a still-current belief.

17. Measures to promote long life, such as fasting, purification, and prayer.

18. Of his paternity.

had set aside himself these many years, brought him to the standing curtain near where she lay, and there he questioned her women about her condition. Those closest to her were all there, and they informed him fully.

"My lady never once relaxed her devotions during all these last months of poor health," they said, "until she entered a decline so serious that by now she will not even touch a bit of fruit. There is no hope for her, no hope at all." Many of them were weeping.

Her Eminence spoke, so faintly that Genji caught only a few of her words.[19] "I have often had occasion to appreciate all you have done for His Majesty, as His Late Eminence asked you to do, but I put off saying so for a long time because I did not know when I would be able to thank you as warmly as I would have liked, and now I am afraid it is too late."

Genji was beyond answering her, and he made a pathetic figure as he wept. He wondered why he betrayed such weakness while others' eyes were on him, but in truth he had succumbed to the abyss of his sorrow, helpless as he was—since wishes are unavailing—to stay the loss of a lady he had known so long, a lady whom all would miss so sorely in their way. "I am of very little use," he said, "but I have always tried my best to do what needed to be done for him, and it is a great blow now to find you like this, when His Excellency's passing has already taught me that all is vanity; I do not think I shall survive it long." She expired as he spoke, like a dying flame, and he was left alone to mourn.

Among those acknowledged truly to matter, it was she whose kindness had embraced the whole world, and although to accept the protection of the mighty often means to court trouble as well, she never committed the smallest lapse of that kind, for she would allow no one in her service to do anything that might cause others distress. With respect to good works, under the wise reigns of the past there were those who, when urged to do so, performed them with grandeur and magnificence, but Her Majesty was not like that. She simply gave all she could spare from her own resources, or from the revenue due her from sinecures, benefices, and emoluments,[20] and since her generosity always proceeded from the heart, she was mourned by the most churlish mountain ascetic.[21] At her funeral the world rang with cries of universal grief. All the privy gentlemen wore black, and spring ended in gloom.

For Genji, the sight of the cherry tree before his Nijō residence brought back times like the party in honor of the blossoms.[22] "Just for this year, I beg,"[23] he murmured and withdrew to his private chapel lest someone notice him, there to weep all day. The setting sun shone bright, each bough at the mountains' rim stood out

---

19. She is speaking to a gentlewoman who will relay her words to Genji.

20. *Tsukasa, kōburi,* and *mifu. Tsukasa* means income to the court derived from fees paid by persons appointed to sinecures; this income was redistributed to high-ranking officeholders, including women. *Kōburi* had a similar source. *Mifu* means income attached to court rank and derived from the labor of a set number of households.

21. *Yamabushi,* a low-ranking Buddhist practitioner, often a healer, who might not be fully ordained and whose practice was centered on sacred mountains.

22. Twelve years before, in "Under the Cherry Blossoms."

23. From *Kokinshū* 832, by Kamutsuke no Mineo, lamenting the death of Fujiwara no Mototsune: "O cherry trees upon Fukakusa Moor, if you are kind, just for this year, I beg, blossom in gray!"

sharply, and gray wisps of cloud trailed across the sky.[24] He who no longer had eyes for anything was still deeply moved.

> *"Those thin wisps of cloud trailing there over mountains caught in sunset light*
> *seem to wish to match their hue to the sleeves of the bereaved,"*

he said; but alas, there was no one to hear him.

Once the rites were over and quiet had returned, His Majesty remained disconsolate. A certain Prelate who had served both Her Cloistered Eminence and her exalted mother as Chaplain, and whom Her Eminence had greatly trusted and revered, enjoyed His Majesty's devout esteem as well, for he was a most holy man and had fulfilled many an imperial vow.[25] At seventy he had gone into retreat to prepare for his end, but he emerged from it again to pray for Her Cloistered Eminence and then answered His Majesty's call to stay on in his service. When Genji, too, urged him to remain in service as before, he consented. "Night attendance[26] is very hard for me now," he said, "but I shall put my heart into it for her sake, in accordance with your most august wishes."

Monk

One quiet night, just before dawn, no one else was in waiting nearby, and some attendants were already on their way home. He was talking to His Majesty about this and that, clearing his throat now and then the way old people do, when he began, "Your Majesty, I have things to say that are very difficult to place before you, and I believe that I might only call down punishment upon myself if I were to do so, and yet it would be a grave offense for me not to, and I would remain in terror of the eye of Heaven;[27] moreover, it would profit you nothing if I were to end my life with these things still locked up painfully in my heart." He stopped and could not bring himself to proceed.

His Majesty wondered what he meant. Is he then prey to a regret so consuming that its bitterness may live on after his death?[28] Alas, a monk may be saintly and still harbor an abyss of jealous evil. "I have felt close to you ever since I was a

---

24. Gray is the main color of mourning. The sun setting behind the mountains reminds Genji of Amida's paradise.

25. He had performed rites and practices that the Emperor had vowed to have done.

26. An important duty of the Chaplain was to remain in attendance through the night, in a room close to where his patron slept, so that the patron should enjoy while sleeping the beneficent influence of his prayers. In the palace, priests performed this function in a small space (*futama*) separated by a partition from the Emperor's pillow.

27. Because the Emperor would then continue to honor the wrong man as his father, thus disturbing the proper order of the human realm and inviting consequent perturbations in the realms of heaven and earth.

28. The Prelate might retain a grudge because of never having been sufficiently promoted. There were two ranks above Prelate, although in the tenth century promotion to them was still rare.

child," he said, "and it pains me that you should have been concealing such profound rancor."

"I beg your pardon, Your Majesty, but my way is to spread rather than conceal even the profundities of the Esoteric path, which the Buddha himself would have us keep secret.[29] How could my heart harbor such dark recesses? No, this is a crucial matter affecting past and future, and the evil rumor of it, damaging both to Their Late Eminences[30] and to His Grace who now governs the realm, might easily get out in the end. An old monk like me has no use for regret, whatever trouble he may bring upon himself. I speak of this to you only because the Protectors[31] wish me to do so. My dear lord, Her Late Eminence was in despair after you were conceived, and she felt the need to order prayers from me, although it was not for me to judge just what the matter was. She grew increasingly fearful when everything went wrong and His Grace was unjustly accused, and she entrusted me with more prayers; and when His Grace heard that, he added even more on his own. I continued to perform them until Your Majesty's accession. This is what I know."

His careful account threw His Majesty into an agony of horror, amazement, sorrow, and dread. When he remained speechless, the Prelate feared that he had angered him by speaking, and he had begun to steal away when His Majesty called him back. "If I had never known this, I would have carried the offense with me into the hereafter, and it actually disturbs me a little that you have never told me before. Does anyone else know?"

"No, Your Majesty. Ōmyōbu and I are the only ones who have any inkling of the truth. That is what frightens me.[32] This is why Heaven is now issuing so many disastrous warnings and why there is such unrest in the world. It was one thing when you were too young to understand, but now that you are at last of age and competent to comprehend all matters, great or small, Heaven is proclaiming your offense. Everything seems to begin with one's parents. I was afraid that you might never know what the transgression was, and that is why I have told you what I myself had resolved to forget." Day came while he spoke, weeping, and he withdrew.

His Majesty's mind reeled at the nightmarish truth he had just learned. He trembled for His Late Eminence and was overcome by pity and dismay that His Grace should serve the realm as a mere commoner; and both these preoccupations caused him such anguish that he did not come forth until the sun was high in the sky. He now found the sight of Genji, who arrived in alarm when told he was unwell, extremely difficult to bear, and upon noting his tears Genji assumed that they were for Her Late Eminence, since he was mourning her so deeply at the time.

That same day His Highness of Ceremonial passed away, and the news only added to His Majesty's lament that such troubles should have come upon the world.

---

29. In Esoteric Buddhism (*mikkyō*), most teachings are to pass from a master only to a properly prepared disciple, and Esoteric texts warn against giving them to the uninitiated.

30. The Kiritsubo Emperor and Fujitsubo.

31. The deities who guard the enlightened buddhas.

32. "Because the responsibility for telling you falls on me alone." Ōmyōbu, formerly Fujitsubo's gentlewoman, is the person through whom Genji gained access to Fujitsubo. As a woman, she would never speak and cannot be considered responsible in the same way.

Under the circumstances Genji remained in close attendance and was not even able to go home. His Majesty remarked during a quiet conversation, "My reign seems to be coming to an end. I myself feel strange and fearful, and these disturbances have affected the whole realm. I have so far refrained from taking any decisive step, in deference to Her Late Eminence's feelings, but, you know, I would much prefer a quieter life."

"You cannot consider it," Genji replied. "The current disturbances do not necessarily have anything to do with whether government is ordered well or ill. Misfortune may occur under the wisest reign. Even in Cathay troubles have broken out wrongfully under a sage Emperor. It has happened in our land, too.[33] Besides, at their age it was perfectly natural,[34] and there is really no reason for concern."

Genji marshaled all the arguments he could, but I should not have repeated any of them.[35] In a sober costume that inclined unusually toward black, he looked exactly like His Majesty. His Majesty had long ago noted the resemblance in his mirror, but after what he had heard, and after scrutinizing his face more closely, he wanted very much to broach the subject with him; and yet it would so obviously upset him to do so that he timidly retreated from touching on it at all, passing instead to more commonplace topics that he discussed with unusually personal warmth. To Genji's sharp eye his deferential manner appeared strangely new, but it never occurred to him that he had actually been told the truth.

His Majesty was eager to question Ōmyōbu, but he did not wish her to find out that he now knew his mother's secret. No, he thought, he would somehow hint to His Grace at what the matter was and ask him whether history offered any similar examples; but when no appropriate occasion arose, he plunged into his studies more ardently than ever in order to peruse all sorts of works. These taught him that while in Cathay there had been many such irregularities, some open and some concealed, no example of the kind was to be found in Japan. And even if something like that happened, how, if it was kept that well hidden, could knowledge of it have been passed on? Yes, there were several instances in which a first-generation Genji[36] had been appointed Grand Counselor or Minister, had gone on to be appointed a Prince, and then had at last acceded to the imperial dignity.[37] His Majesty considered invoking His Grace's superior ability to abdicate in his favor.

He privately decided that Genji would be named Chancellor at the autumn appointments, but when he mentioned in that connection what he planned for himself, the shocked and terrified Genji let him know that anything of the kind was out of the question. "His Late Eminence was pleased to prefer me to his other sons," he said, "but it certainly never occurred to him to abdicate in my favor. How could I now ignore his wishes and rise to a dignity so far beyond me? No, my only desire is

33. Perhaps a reference to the exile of Sugawara no Michizane, which occurred in the Engi era (901–22), in the sage reign of Emperor Daigo.

34. The deaths of the Chancellor and of His Highness of Ceremonial.

35. Because matters of history and government are not for a woman to discuss.

36. An imperial son who, like the Genji of the tale, had been made a commoner and excluded from the line of succession.

37. An early commentary (*Kakaishō*, fourteenth century) cites Emperors Kōnin (709–81, reigned 770–81), Kanmu (737–806, reigned 781–806), Kōkō (830–87, reigned 884–87), and Uda (867–931, reigned 887–97).

to serve the realm as he intended and, when I am a little older, to give myself to my devotions in quiet retirement." To His Majesty's intense disappointment, he spoke on this subject as he had done before.

Genji preferred to put off accepting his appointment as Chancellor, despite confirmation of it, and he therefore received only a promotion in rank and a decree permitting him to come and go from the palace in an ox-drawn carriage.[38] This by no means satisfied His Majesty, who made it clear that he thought Genji should become a Prince, but Genji doubted that anyone at court would support such a move. Besides, the Acting Counselor had just become Grand Counselor and Commander of the Right, and once he had risen a step further, Genji would be able to leave everything to him and one way or another to live in peace.

Genji thought the matter over further. He felt very sorry for Her Late Eminence, and after seeing His Majesty so troubled, he wondered who could have revealed her secret to him. Ōmyōbu had moved away to serve the new Mistress of the Wardrobe, and she now had a room in the palace.[39] He talked to her and asked her whether her late mistress could have by chance given His Majesty any hint. "No, my lord, certainly not," Ōmyōbu replied. "My lady was terrified to think that any breath of it might reach His Majesty, even as she feared for him in case he should suffer for the offense." Once more Genji felt boundless longing for so extraordinarily prudent a lady.

Genji's support for the Ise Consort had succeeded brilliantly, and she enjoyed His Majesty's highest favor. In wit and looks she left nothing to be desired, and he watched over her as though over a treasure. In the autumn she withdrew to Nijō. He did up the main house there magnificently, and this time he treated her as a father should.

An autumn rain was quietly falling when Genji made his way to where the Consort lived, moved by the garden's profusion of dew-laden colors to wet his sleeves in memory of all that had once been. Carefully groomed and utterly beguiling in dark gray, and with his prayer beads well hidden—for these upsetting events had meant a succession of fasts—he went straight in through her blinds. She spoke to him herself, with only a standing curtain between them.

"All the petals are gone from the garden," he began. "This year has been so sad, but it is touching that the flowers still enjoyed their season's display." It was a pleasure to see him leaning that way against a pillar in the light of the setting sun. He talked to her about the past and about that dawn when he had found it so hard to leave the Shrine on the Moor.

Her Highness noted how deeply moved he was. She, too, perhaps in sympathy, showed signs of the most appealing tears, and her slightest movement seemed

---

38. It was common to refuse appointment to extremely high office (Chancellor or Regent) once or twice before accepting it. Genji is instead promoted from second rank (suitable for his post as Palace Minister) to first rank, junior grade, the normal rank for a Chancellor. Permission to enter the palace grounds in an ox-drawn carriage was granted to a Prince, a Regent, a very senior Minister, or a very high member of the Buddhist ecclesiastical hierarchy.

39. This sentence has also been read as meaning that Ōmyōbu herself has been appointed Mistress of the Wardrobe. Either way it is curious to find her in service at the palace when she became a nun long ago, at the same time as Fujitsubo.

dazzlingly soft and graceful. What a shame I never really saw her! His heart beat wickedly.

"In the old days, when I should have been free of care, I still managed to suffer constantly from my own wanton ways, and among those whom I hurt by doing things I should not have done, there are especially two who never surrendered to me and who died in pain. One of them, you see, was your mother. She was in a very dark mood at the end, for which I will always be extremely sorry, and I had hoped that I might afford her some comfort by serving you as I have done and by gaining your goodwill, but I am afraid the smoke that rose from her pyre may linger on blackly even now." He said nothing of the second.

"Everything I wanted to do in those years when I was no one has turned out little by little," he went on. "The lady in the east pavilion, whose circumstances once worried me so, is now secure. Pleasant as she is, she and I understand each other, and we give each other no trouble at all. Now that I am back, the pleasure of serving the realm as I do means little enough to me. Will you please be good enough to understand, though, that while I find my waywardness difficult to master, I have in all I have done for you kept myself under strict control. I shall be very sorry if you can offer me no word of sympathy!"

The Consort was too embarrassed to reply.

"I see. Ah, you are too cruel!" He shifted the topic elsewhere. "What I want now is to spend the rest of my life free of sorrow and to devote myself in seclusion to prayers for the life to come; but actually, I regret not having anything yet to re-member this one by.[40] I have a daughter, after all, and despite her failings I long to see how she will grow up. Forgive me, but I hope that you will wish to promote the greatness of this house by assisting her after I am gone."

The way she gave him her reply—the merest hint delivered in a single, artless word—appealed to him keenly, and he stayed on talking to her quietly until evening.

"Quite apart from these weighty hopes of mine, I should like to indulge in the pleasures of the seasons—the blossoms, the autumn leaves, the changing skies. Peo-ple have long weighed the flowering woods in spring against the lovely hues of the autumn moors, and no one seems ever to have shown which one clearly deserves to be preferred. I hear that in China they say nothing equals the brocade of spring flowers, while in Yamato speech[41] we prefer the poignancy of autumn, but my eyes are seduced by each in turn, and I cannot distinguish favorites among the colors of their blossoms or the songs of their birds. I have in mind to fill a garden, however small, with enough flowering spring trees to convey the mood of the season, or to transplant autumn grasses there and, with them, the crickets whose song is so wasted in the fields, and then to give all this to a lady for her pleasure. Which would you choose?"

The Consort did not know what to say, but she could hardly not answer him at all. "How could I pronounce myself either way? But between them, equal though they

40. He may mean his ambition to see his daughter (now four) become Empress and bear an imperial heir.

41. Japanese poetry, especially *Shūishū* 511.

are, I will take the evening when the poet felt 'strangely more,' because then I feel close to the dew that vanished all too soon."[42]

Genji found her casual reticence so thoroughly charming that he could not keep himself from answering,

"Why, then, let us share all our most tender feelings, for here in my heart
I, too, know all the sadness of an autumn evening's wind.

There really are times when I can hardly bear it!"

Where was she to find a reply? She pretended not to understand, which no doubt started him on a stream of helpless reproaches. He very nearly went on to do something rather worse, but she was naturally horrified, and he himself thought better of his own detestably juvenile intentions. By now she abhorred even the profound grace of his sighs. He gathered that she was softly, little by little, retreating from him toward the inner room. "You have taken a cruel aversion to me, have you

Hanging lantern

not. I doubt that anyone of genuinely deep sympathy would do so. Very well, but please do not hate me after this. That would be too painful," he said and went away. She loathed even the tender fragrance that lingered after him.

"It is simply indescribable, the perfume that still clings to his cushion!" her gentlewomen exclaimed as they closed the shutters. "How *does* he manage to be as though in him blossoms opened on spring willow fronds?[43] Frightening, that is what it is!"

Genji went to the west wing, but rather than go straight in he stared moodily before him and then lay down near the veranda. He had lanterns hung a good distance off and called in the gentlewomen to chat. Despite himself he could not help seeing that that old habit of his, to suffer agonies for impossible desires, was with him still. This was beneath him. Not that he had not done far worse, but he reminded himself on the subject of his early escapades that the gods and buddhas must have forgiven errors committed in his thoughtless youth, and that thought reminded him how much better he now understood the perils of this path.

The Consort, covered with shame, rued ever having answered him as though she knew the moving quality of autumn, and she accused herself so bitterly that she even began to feel unwell. Meanwhile, Genji remained perfectly composed and acted more fatherly than ever. He said to his darling, "The Consort's heart touchingly favors autumn, while you, understandably enough, have given your heart to dawn in spring. I would like to give you for your pleasure concerts attuned to the plants and flowers of each season." He said again, "It does not suit me to be so busy with affairs, whether the government's or my own. I must manage to live more as I please." And also, "I worry about you—I imagine that you must be so lonely."

---

42. To her mother. *Kokinshū* 546: "All times are equal for I love you in them all, yet, on an autumn evening, O how strangely more!"

43. *Goshūishū* 82: "How gladly I would have cherry blossoms that smell like plum blossoms open on spring willow fronds!"

He constantly wondered, too, how she was getting on in that mountain village, but he found it extremely difficult to get there because he was less and less free to move about.[44] She seems resigned to the idea that I have no use for her, he said to himself. Why must she be so gloomy? If she is refusing to move here because she fears being humiliated, she just does not understand her situation. He still felt sorry for her, though, and he went to see her under cover of his monthly invocations to Amida.

Life in so lonely a place would in time turn anything into one more dreary burden, and so naturally it was torment for her to see him, because it reminded her how strong the painful bond between them really was. Genji, who saw this well enough, found her impossible to console. The fishermen's cressets,[45] seen through the dense trees, mingled beautifully with the fireflies along the garden stream. "You would appreciate this sort of setting a great deal more if you were not already so accustomed to it," he said.

She replied,

> *Cressets that recall scenes I can never forget, of lights out at sea,*
> *perhaps only mean my cares have come sailing after me.*

My sorrows, at least, are just the same."

> *"You do not yet know what flames of true devotion burn deep in my heart:*
> *that may be why your cressets shed so unsteady a light.*

Who told you life is so sad?"[46] he chided her back. He was feeling at peace these days, so he enjoyed his holy pastimes and stayed on at Ōi longer than usual. That probably made her feel a little better.

---

44. His recent promotion has once more limited his freedom of movement.

45. *Kagaribi,* wood fires contained in iron cages that the cormorant fishermen on the river held aloft to attract fish.

46. From *Kokin rokujō* 1726.

20

ASAGAO

The Bluebell

Asagao ("bluebell") is the flower associated since "The Broom Tree" with Genji's courtship of the Princess who figures in this chapter. As the chapter title it refers particularly to an exchange of poems between her and Genji, after Genji fails to win her.

RELATIONSHIP TO EARLIER CHAPTERS

"The Bluebell" continues "Wisps of Cloud," covering the autumn and winter of the same year.

PERSONS

His Grace, the Palace Minister, Genji, age 32

Her Highness, the former Kamo Priestess (Asagao)

Her Highness, the Fifth Princess, Asagao's aunt

Senji, Asagao's gentlewoman

The former Dame of Staff, in the household of the Fifth Princess, 70 or 71 (Gen no Naishi)

The lady in Genji's west wing, 24 (Murasaki)

The Kamo Priestess had resigned, because she was in mourning.[1] Genji, whose peculiarity it was as usual never to break off a courtship he had once started, sent her frequent notes, but she remembered the trouble she had had with him before, and she kept her answers strictly correct. He was keenly disappointed.

In the ninth month he heard that she had returned to her father's Momozono residence, and since that was where the Fifth Princess lived, he went there under the pretext of calling on her.[2] His Late Eminence had thought a great deal of both Their Highnesses, and Genji seems still to have been in touch with several such ladies. They shared the main house, east and west. The place was very quiet and seemed to Genji already to have declined sadly.

The Fifth Princess received him and spoke to him. Thoroughly old-fashioned in manner, she was prone to clearing her throat. His Late Excellency's wife,[3] the elder of the two sisters, had always managed admirably to avoid betraying her age, but not so this one, with her thick, gravelly voice; and so each was what her life had made her.

"His Late Eminence's passing was a great blow," she said, "and now that His Highness, too, has left me, when the years incline me anyway more and more to tears, I linger on, hardly knowing whether or not I am alive; but this kind visit from you may allow me to forget."

She has aged so! Genji said to himself, maintaining nonetheless a deferential manner. "After His Late Eminence passed away and the world came in so many ways no longer to seem the same, unjust accusations were brought against me, and I wandered unfamiliar lands until by rare good fortune His Majesty was pleased to acknowledge me again, which then left me so little time to myself that I always regretted being prevented from calling on you and talking over the past."

"Oh, it was dreadful, dreadful, and for many reasons I detest living on and on

1. Asagao's father, His Highness of Ceremonial, died in the previous chapter.
2. Momozono is thought to have been a spot north of Ichijō ("First Avenue") and west of Ōmiya avenue. The Fifth Princess is her aunt (her father's younger sister).
3. Aoi's mother (Ōmiya). Asagao, Genji, and Aoi are cousins, but Asagao is a Princess because she is the recognized daughter of a Prince, while Aoi, the daughter of a Princess, was a commoner because her father was one.

this way, ever the same, when either misfortune[4] shows how little this world is to be trusted; and yet I know very well from the joy of seeing you come into your own again how sorry I would have been to know no more of you after those years." She began to tremble. "What a splendid-looking man you are now! When I first knew you, as a boy, I wondered that so bright a light should have come into the world, and I feared for you after that whenever I saw you. People tell me His Majesty is very like you, but I cannot believe he really compares with you!"

She talked and talked, and Genji thought with amusement that one really did *not* praise someone to his face that way. "I am not at all what I used to be, though, after those miserable years as a mountain rustic. No one can ever have been as handsome as His Majesty, and to my eye he is a wonder. No, no, I am afraid you are quite wrong!"

"This interminable life of mine might last even longer if only I could see you now and again. I feel today as though old age were forgotten and all the cares of this sad world were gone!" She wept once more. "The Third Princess[5] was extremely fortunate to gain so worthy a new tie[6] with you, and I envy her being so close to you. His Late Highness often felt a similar regret."[7]

This last caught Genji's attention. "How happy I would be now if I had been able to serve him in that manner! But neither of them would have me, you see," he said with a frown.

Glancing at the garden along the other side of the house, Genji noted especially how handsome the withered plantings were, and he longed sympathetically to know how *she* got on, and how she looked during the quiet melancholy of her days. He could resist no longer. "I should really call there, too," he said. "It would be unkind to let the opportunity pass when I am already here to wait upon you." He went straight to her along the veranda. It was dark by now, but what he glimpsed through gaps between gray blinds and black curtains was thoroughly pleasing, as was the suave fragrance that wafted out toward him from within. He was admitted to the southern aisle, since he could not be left on the veranda. Senji spoke to him and conveyed his messages.

"It makes me feel young again to be outside the blinds," he said ruefully. "I thought you might give me license to come through, considering my loyalty through all your years of sacred service."

"That past is all a dream," she replied, "and now that it is over, I wonder after all whether I can agree. I hope that I may quietly give your loyalty further consideration."

Yes, Genji reflected, it is a treacherous world indeed![8]

> "While I silently waited till at last the god sanction my desire,
> how many bitter moments your coldness made me endure!

4. The Kiritsubo Emperor's death or Genji's exile.
5. Aoi's mother, Ōmiya.
6. Yūgiri, the son of Genji and Aoi.
7. That Genji had never married his daughter, Asagao.
8. Asagao has just spoken of it being, literally, "difficult to decide" (*sadamegataku haberu ni*) whether or not to give Genji the freedom he feels is his due; now Genji picks up the same word, but in a fixed expression (*sadamegataki yo*) quite different in implication and tone.

I wonder what divine prohibition you mean to invoke *this* time. All sorts of troubles have afflicted me ever since I had to suffer that misfortune. I can hardly begin to tell you . . ." He was pressing her. His attitude was somewhat kinder and more tactful than in the past, but despite all his years of life since then, it remained unworthy of a man of his rank.

> *"Had I asked of you in the simplest way a word about your sorrows,*
> *the god might well have charged me with breaking my solemn vow,"*

she answered.

"Ah, you are cruel! The winds of heaven have carried off all my misdeeds from those years," he protested with bewitching charm.

"My lord, how do you think the gods look on your purification?"[9] This comment from her gentlewoman greatly upset Her Highness. The passing years had only confirmed her profound reticence, and her incapacity to respond made her women very uncomfortable.

"I am afraid our talk has turned to gallantry." He arose, sighing deeply. "It is embarrassing at my age. I believe your treatment entitles me to ask that you now

Inkstone

see what has become of me."[10] With that he went away, leaving behind as usual a buzz of praise. This was a season of lovely skies. To the rustling of the leaves Her Highness pondered absorbing passages from her past, and she remembered how thoroughly amusing he had been at times, and at others how profoundly moving.

Having left in such ill humor, Genji naturally lay awake, deep in thought. He had the shutters raised early and gazed at the morning mist. Bluebells bloomed forlornly here and there among the dying flowers, and he picked a particularly pretty one and sent it to her. "Your summary treatment of me was humiliating," he wrote, "and I shudder to imagine with what eyes you watched me leave. And yet,

> *Could it really be that the bluebell I once knew and cannot forget*
> *no longer displays the bloom that was hers in days gone by?*

I believed you would look kindly on my many years, you know . . ."

It was a judicious letter, well meant, and she saw that failure to answer it might amount to cutting him dead. Meanwhile, her gentlewomen brought her an inkstone.

> *"Yes, autumn is past, and entangled in a fence swathed by many mists*
> *the bluebell pales and withers as though hardly there at all.*

9. *Kokinshū* 501 (or *Ise monogatari* 119, section 65): "So as to love no more, I sought in the Mitarashi River purification that the gods at last did not accept."

10. *Genji monogatari kochūshakusho in'yō waka* 157: "As I pass your gate now, come forth and see what has become of the man who loves you."

I have tears in my eyes, your image fits me so well," she wrote. That was all, and there was nothing remarkable about it, but for some reason he found it difficult to put down. Perhaps it was the soft lines of her brush on the blue-gray paper that so pleased him. One matches one's words to the writer's quality and style, and remarks that are innocuous at the time may turn out to be troublesome when one seeks plausibly to convey them, which is why there are many things here that I have patched together and that may easily be wrong.

Genji felt that by now it would ill become him to turn again to writing her youthful letters, but the thought of having wasted so many years while she went on never quite rejecting him decided him not to give up, and he reverted to ardent courtship.

He went off to his east wing and had Senji there for a talk. Some of Her Highness's women—those apparently disposed to give any man his way, even one of no great rank—praised Genji beyond all reason, but their mistress had cooled toward him long ago, and her age and station, like his own, now discouraged liaisons. If she still responded in kind to notes from him on a foolish flower, she nonetheless feared anything that might start gossip, and she gave no sign of yielding. Her long-standing constancy of resolve thus made her seem to Genji unlike anyone else in the world, and at once admirable and maddening.

Word got out anyway. "He is courting the former Kamo Priestess," people said, "and the Fifth Princess has no objection. Those two would not go at all badly together." This talk reached the lady in his west wing. No, she told herself at first, he would not conceal that sort of thing from me; but then she began to keep an eye on him and was troubled to find him unusually restless. So, she thought, he has been simply laughing off something about which he is quite serious! I am her equal by birth,[11] but she has an outstanding reputation and has always enjoyed the highest esteem. I shall be lost if his feelings shift to her. Am I to be cast aside, then, when I have never had any serious rival? She was secretly in great distress. Perhaps he will not really cut me off entirely, but even so, all these years of keeping me so close to him, when nothing about me required him to do so, could turn only to slights and condescension! It was things she could tolerate that had provoked her tactful reproaches, whereas now, when she was seriously hurt, she showed nothing at all. Genji so often sat daydreaming near the veranda, stayed away at the palace, or spent his time writing letters, that there appeared to be a good deal to the gossip. If only he would say something! she thought, detesting him.

The rites to honor the gods had been canceled.[12] One evening, overcome by the empty hours, Genji decided on one of his so-called visits to the Fifth Princess. It was a lovely dusk with lightly falling snow, and he had spent the day dressing with special care in charmingly soft robes, expressly perfumed; one wondered more than ever how any susceptible woman could resist him.

He did say good-bye, though. "I gather that the Fifth Princess is unwell, and I thought I might pay her a call," he said, going down on one knee, but she did not even

11. Each is a Prince's daughter.
12. Because the court was in mourning for Fujitsubo.

look at him. Her profile as she played instead with her little girl suggested that something was wrong. "You are looking strangely unlike yourself these days," he said. "I have not done anything. I have been staying away a bit because I thought you might find the same old salt-burner's robe rather dull by now.[13] Now, what can you possibly have been making of that?"

"Familiarity often breeds contempt." She lay down with her back to him. He did not like to leave her this way, but he set out nonetheless, since he had already let Her Highness know that he was coming.

She lay there thinking how naive she had always been. Even in gray, Genji just looked lovelier than ever in his layering of its shades, and as she watched him go, his exquisitely graceful figure illuminated by the snow, she ached unbearably to think that he might really be leaving her.

Broken garden fence

His escort consisted only of trusted retainers. "I no longer care to go anywhere except to the palace," he told them, "but the Fifth Princess is in a sad plight, and although I could trust His Highness of Ceremonial to look after her while he was alive, now, alas, she understandably wishes to turn to me." He said the same thing to his women.

"Oh, come now!" they whispered among themselves. "He is as much of a lover as ever—it seems to be his great flaw. He will be getting himself into trouble."

It would have been undignified for Genji to enter through the busy north gate, and he therefore sent a man in through the formal west one to announce his arrival. Her Highness, taken by surprise since she no longer expected him that day, ordered it opened. The shivering gatekeeper who rushed out could not immediately move it, and there seemed to be no one to help him. "The lock is all rusted," he grumbled, rattling away at it, "that's why it won't open."[14] Genji felt sorry for him. It feels like yesterday, he thought, and it was thirty or more years ago. Ah, life! And still I cling to this passing lodging and give my heart to the beauty of plants and trees![15] He hummed to himself,

> *"All too soon, I see, the house has nearly vanished among wastes of weeds,*
> *and the snows of many years weigh upon the garden fence."*

The gate came open after a good deal of pushing and tugging, and he entered.

13. "I thought you might be a bit tired of seeing me all the time." Genji alludes to the poetic lore of the lovelorn saltmaker girl, whose "salt-burner's robe" (*shioyaki-goromo*) is also, by a play of words, her erotic longing.

14. The gatekeeper's words recall a line in a poem by Bai Juyi (*Hakushi monjū* 2392).

15. "This passing lodging" is the spirit's temporary fleshly abode in this life, but it is unclear what "thirty or more years ago" refers to. Perhaps the original expression was proverbial for the swiftness with which a death recedes into the past ("His Highness died this summer, and already his gate is rusted shut").

He talked over the past with Her Highness, as usual, on her side of the house, and she rambled on and on interminably about the old days, but he became sleepy when nothing he heard caught his interest, and she herself began to yawn. "I am so drowsy this evening, I can hardly speak!" she said, and the curious sound that soon followed might well have been snoring. Pleased, he rose and was on his way out when someone else came in, clearing her throat in a thoroughly antique manner. "I beg your pardon," she said, "I thought you might have been told I was here, but I see it makes no difference to you. His Late Eminence used to laugh at me and call me Honorable Granny."

The nickname jogged Genji's memory. Yes, he had heard that the lady once known as the Dame of Staff had since then become a nun and was practicing her devotions under Her Highness, but he was amazed, for it had never occurred to him even to wonder whether she was still alive. "I am very glad to hear your voice," he said, "since his reign now belongs to the past, and those distant memories of it make one so sad! Please look after me as you would the orphan fallen beside the road!"[16]

His dim approaching form took her back to those days. She put on those old coy airs again and set mumblingly about her banter, in a voice that plainly issued from a toothless, puckered mouth. "I always complained . . ."[17] she simpered—what nerve! He could not suppress a smile at being suddenly now an old man, but her fate stirred him at the same time to pity. Some of the Consorts and Intimates who had been such rivals in her prime were no doubt dead and gone and others cast helplessly adrift in a cruel world. Why, look what age Her Late Eminence was when she died! No, life was too hard, he himself had so little time left, and there *she* was, a frivolous old woman, still alive, quietly pursuing her devotions. Ah, the perfidy of this world! To Granny, however, his thoughtful looks spoke of tender emotion, and she felt young again.

> "*After all these years I can still never forget what you and I shared,*
> *or that name, 'mother's mother,' he was pleased to give to me,*"

she said; and he, in disgust,

> "*Once you are reborn, bide your time to wait and see whether in this life*
> *anyone has gone so far as to forget his mother!*

Oh, the bond is a lasting one, certainly! We must have a quiet talk another time."[18] With that he left.

---

16. *Shūishū* 1350, attributed to Prince Shōtoku: "Alas for the traveler, a poor orphan, who lies there starving on Kataoka Mountain!"

17. "Although I am old, you are older, too [and so we are both now in the same boat]." *Genji monogatari kochūshakusho in'yō waka* 160: "I always complained of my sad lot, yet now I must groan for yours."

18. Both poems play on "Honorable Granny" by alluding to *Shūishū* 545, which contains the words *oya no oya* ("mother's mother"). While a certain lady was in Ōmi, just east of the capital, her grandson passed by, on his way back to the capital from the eastern provinces. When he did not even stop to see her, claiming to be in too much of a hurry, she sent him, "You would have called on me, if you thought of me as your mother's mother; perhaps you are not really my child's child."

The shutters on the west side of the house were down, although the gentle-women had left one or two open so as not to risk appearing unfriendly. The moon was out, illumining a thin fall of snow, and it was actually a lovely night.[19] He recalled with amusement having heard those same simperings of old age cited as a bane.

That evening he addressed the former Kamo Priestess very earnestly. "I shall trouble you no more if only you will master your repugnance and speak to me this once yourself," he said, going straight to the point; but she who even long ago, when the world gladly overlooked their youthful indiscretions, had still shrunk bashfully from her late father's ambition[20] could not all these years later, at her age, countenance giving him a single word in her own voice, and she maintained this resolve so staunchly that Genji became extremely impatient. Not that she was in the least curt with him, but it infuriated him to receive her answers through somebody else.

It was very late by now, a high wind was blowing, and he felt wretched enough decorously to wipe away his tears.

> "You are too cruel, when I learned no lesson then from your cruelty,
>   to afflict me even now with those old and cruel ways.

The fault is mine, I know . . ."[21] he insisted, and her gentlewomen murmured as always that it was such a shame.

> "What could make me now wish to give myself to you—though it may be true,
>   as I hear, that some others find their feelings quickly change.

It is not my way to do otherwise than I have always done."

The desperate Genji gave voice to a stream of the bitterest reproaches, feeling all the while like a callow youth. "Please tell no one how I have behaved," he whispered urgently, "not a word—I would be a joke before all the world. I could speak of the Isara River, but that might be to take too great a liberty."[22]

The gentlewomen wondered what the matter could be. "What a thing to do to him!"

"Why does my lady insist on treating him so unkindly?"

"Nothing about him suggests that he would thoughtlessly force himself on her."

"Poor man!"

She herself had never missed Genji's great quality or compelling appeal, but she felt that to show him sympathy would be to range herself in his eyes beside those other women who made so much of him and to betray her own lack of char-

19. "Actually" (*nakanaka*) because the season for beautiful nights is supposed conventionally to be spring or autumn.

20. To marry her to Genji. She did not wish to suffer the fate of Rokujō, and for a Princess the ideal was to remain unmarried.

21. *Nakatsukasa shū* 249: "If I love, the fault is mine, I know, and so I suffer and know not what to do."

22. *Kokinshū* 1108 plays on the syllables of this name (that of a river in Ōmi Province) to seal a lover's lips *after* a stolen night together.

acter as well. Besides, his magnificence was too daunting, and it would not become her to act tenderly toward him. No, she would correspond with him sufficiently to keep in touch, giving him prudent replies; she would still converse respectably with him; and otherwise she would pursue her devotions so as to erase the sin of all those years away.[23] It would only look capricious of her suddenly to acquiesce or to seem to want no more to do with him, and people would not fail to make much of it, being as evil-tongued as she knew them to be; and so she was formal even with her gentlewomen, cultivated strict discretion, and, meanwhile, gave herself increasingly to her devotions.

She hardly knew her many brothers and sisters because they did not have the same mother, and her residence was therefore more and more deserted. This drew her staff together in unanimous support of the great and glorious gentleman who showered her with such attentions.

Genji did not exactly burn for her, but her coolness maddened him, and he hated to admit defeat. In bearing and reputation he was of course all anyone could wish, and he had pondered many things and acquired by now a far wider, more discriminating knowledge of people. Long and varied experience reminded him that any renewed misbehavior on his part would certainly earn him criticism, but he worried that failure might provoke still louder laughter. What shall I do? he fretted, meanwhile absenting himself night after night from Nijō, which to his lady there was no joke at all.[24] She tried and tried, but naturally there were times when her tears flowed.

"You are looking curiously unlike yourself—I cannot imagine why," he said to her, stroking her hair, and his expression of tender concern made one want to paint them both. "It pained me to see how much His Majesty missed Her Late Eminence when she was gone, and without the Chancellor, you know, I have been kept very busy by things I have no one else to do for me. You are probably wondering why I have been here so strangely little lately, and I sympathize, but please set your mind at rest. You are quite grown-up now, but you still seldom consider others, and it is just that way you have of getting their feelings wrong that makes you so dear." He tidied a wet lock of hair at her forehead, but she turned farther away from him and said not a word.

"Who can have brought you up to be such a baby?" It was such a pity, when life was short anyway, to have her so upset with him! But then daydreams swept him off again.

"Perhaps you have misunderstood my little messages to the former Kamo Priestess. If so, you are quite wrong, as you will see. I may tease her at odd moments with an enticing note, because she has always been very distant, and she sometimes answers me, since she herself has little to fill her time, but there is nothing serious to any of this, and I see no reason I should come crying to you and tell you all about it. Please understand that you have no need to worry." He spent the whole day trying to make her feel better.

23. Away from contact with Buddhist teaching or practice. The Kamo Priestess, like the Ise Priestess, could have nothing to do with Buddhist things.
24. In *Kokinshū* 1025 the poet discovers that an experimental separation from his beloved (to see how it might feel) is "no joke at all."

The snow was very deep by now, and more was falling. The waning light set off pine and bamboo prettily from one another, and Genji's face took on a clearer glow. "More than the glory of flowers and fall leaves that season by season capture everyone's heart, it is the night sky in winter, with snow aglitter beneath a brilliant moon, that in the absence of all color speaks to me strangely and carries my thoughts beyond this world; there is no higher wonder or delight. Whoever called it dreary understood nothing."

Rolling snowballs

He had the blinds rolled up. The moon illumined all before them in its single color, while the garden shivered under the weight of snow, the brook uttered pathetic sobs, and desolate ice lay across the lake. Genji had the page girls go down and roll a snowball. Their charming figures and hair gleamed in the moon-light, while the bigger, more knowing ones were lovely in their varied, loosely worn gowns[25] and their night ser-vice wear with the sashes half undone; meanwhile their hair, far longer than their gowns, stood out strikingly against the white of the snow. The lit-tle ones were a pleasure to watch running about happily, dropping their fans and show-ing their excited faces.[26] They wanted to roll their snowball even bigger, but for all their struggles it would not budge. Some of them sat on the east end of the veranda, laughing nervously.

"One year they made a snow mountain in Her Late Eminence's garden—not that that is remarkable in itself, but the smallest thing she did always seemed mirac-ulous. How one misses her on every occasion! I never came to know very well what she was like, because she kept herself so far from me, but I believe she thought well of me while she was at the palace. I relied on her and kept in touch with her about all sorts of things, and although she never put herself forward, talking to her was al-ways worthwhile, and she did the smallest thing precisely right. We shall never see her like again. For all her serenity, she had a profound distinction that no other could attain, whereas you, who despite everything have so much of the noble murasaki,[27] have a difficult side to you as well, and I am afraid you may be a little

---

25. *Akome*, a robe worn by adult men between the shift (*hitoe*) and the train-robe (*shitagasane*), but by chil-dren on top.

26. Even a little girl was supposed to keep her face hidden behind her fan.

27. "You have so much of her, despite not having grown up with your father [her brother]." In "Young Murasaki" the dye plant and color (purple) known as *murasaki* was first associated by Genji with Fujitsubo because of its use in poetry; then the association passed to the little girl, who became Murasaki.

headstrong. The former Kamo Priestess's temperament seems to me very different. When I am lonely, I need no particular reason to converse with her, and by now she is really the only one left who requires the best of me."

"But the Mistress of Staff[28] is outstanding in intelligence and character! What happened is very strange, considering that she shuns any hint of indiscretion."

"That is true. She does indeed deserve mention as a beautiful and attractive woman. Now that I think of her, there is a great deal I have to regret and to be forgiven. Imagine, then, how many regrets a rake must have as he ages! After all, I see myself as having led a much quieter life than most." Talking about the Mistress of Staff moved him to shed a few tears.

"That woman in her mountain village, the one of whom you think so little, understands more than one would expect of someone like her, but she is not in the same class with the others, and I overlook her pretensions.[29] I have never known anyone completely worthless. So few in this world are really exceptional, though! The lady languishing in the east pavilion is still as appealing in manner as ever, but it takes more than that. I took up with her because I liked her so much for what she was, and with great discretion she has remained like that with me ever since. I am sure she and I will never part, and I am very fond of her."

Girls in akome *gowns*

Genji talked on this way late into the night about the present and the past. The moon shone more and more brightly through the marvelous stillness. She said,

"Frozen into ice, water caught among the rocks can no longer flow,
and it is the brilliant moon that soars freely through the sky."[30]

Leaning forward a little that way to look out, she was lovelier than any woman in the world. The sweep of her hair, her face, suddenly brought back to him most wonderfully the figure of the lady he had loved, and his heart, which had been somewhat divided, turned again to her alone. A mandarin duck cried,[31] and he said,

"Amid all this snow that brings back fond memories of times now gone by,
ah, what fresh melancholy in a mandarin duck's cry!"

When he went in again and lay down, his mind still on Her Late Eminence, he saw her dimly—it was not a dream—and perceived her to be extremely angry. "You promised never to tell, and yet what I did is now known to all. I am ashamed, and

28. Oborozukiyo. What happened is the scandal over her and Genji.
29. Genji's strikingly dismissive discussion of the lady from Akashi contains no polite language at all.
30. The water is Murasaki, the moon Genji.
31. The beautiful mandarin duck, which adorned many gardens like Genji's, mates for life, and in East Asia it is therefore the emblem of conjugal fidelity.

my present suffering makes you hateful to me!" It seemed to him that he was answering her when he felt set upon and awoke to hear his darling crying, "What is it? What is the matter?" Bitter disappointment overwhelmed him, and his heart pounded furiously. When he sought to calm himself, he found that he had been weeping, and he moistened his sleeves all over again.

Lying stock-still, with his love beside him wondering what had come over him, he murmured,

> "Ah, how brief it was, the vision that came to me while, bereft of sleep,
> on a lonely winter's night I was caught up in a dream!"

He yearned for her so sharply that he arose early and commissioned rites at temples here and there, though he never said for whom they were. It was torture to him at last to understand, after a process of deep reflection, that her anger at what he had put her through was well and truly meant, and despite her devotions, despite all the things she had done to lessen her fault, she had still failed because of that one lapse to cleanse herself of the foulness of this world; and he longed again and again to go to her in that alien realm where she must be now, to bring her comfort there, and to make her sin his own. He remained cautious, however, because people would wonder if he were too pointedly to have services done for her, and His Majesty, too, might feel the prick of conscience. Meanwhile he gave himself devoutly to calling the Name of Amida. If only I might share her lotus![32] he prayed; and yet,

> "Should I let my heart follow this longing to seek the love I have lost,
> I might, if she is not there, wander myself the Three Fords"[33]

—which, some say, was a detestable thought.

---

32. In Amida's paradise. The soul was reborn there enthroned on a lotus flower that rose from the lake before Amida and his palace, and it became a commonplace for lovers to wish to be reborn there on the same lotus throne.

33. The River of Three Fords (*mitsu no se*, usually *sanzu no kawa*), which encircles the afterworld. Those who crossed it did so via one of three fords—shallow, middling, or deep, according to the gravity of their sins.

21

OTOME

The Maidens

Otome ("maiden") refers particularly to a girl chosen as a Gosechi dancer. In this chapter Genji sends a poem containing the word *otome* to the Gosechi Dancer already mentioned in "Falling Flowers" and "Suma." Meanwhile, Yūgiri, his son, notices a younger Gosechi dancer and sends her a poem containing the same word.

RELATIONSHIP TO EARLIER CHAPTERS

"The Bluebell" ended in the winter. "The Maidens" begins the next spring and continues on into the autumn of the following year.

PERSONS

His Grace, the Chancellor, Genji, age 33 to 35

The former Kamo Priestess (Asagao)

Senji, Asagao's gentlewoman

Her Highness, the Fifth Princess, Asagao's aunt

Her Highness, the Third Princess, Yūgiri's grandmother (Ōmiya)

The Commander, then His Excellency, the Palace Minister (Tō no Chūjō)

His daughter, 14 to 16 (Kumoi no Kari)

Her stepfather, the Inspector Grand Counselor (Azechi no Dainagon)

The Adviser, Genji's son, 12 to 14 (Yūgiri)

The Doctors of the Academy

The Left Grand Controller

Yūgiri's tutor, a Chief Clerk

The Ise Consort, Her Majesty the Empress, 24 to 26 (Akikonomu)

The Kokiden Consort, daughter of Tō no Chūjō, 16 to 18

The Lord of Ceremonial, formerly His Highness of War,
brother of Fujitsubo, 48 to 50 (Shikibukyō no Miya)

The daughter of the Lord of Ceremonial, a Consort

Ōmiya's gentlewomen

His Majesty, the Emperor, 15 to 17 (Reizei)

The Intendant of the Left Gate Watch, a half brother of Tō no Chūjō

Saishō, Yūgiri's nurse

Kumoi no Kari's nurse

Yoshikiyo, Governor of Ōmi

Koremitsu, Governor of Tsu and Left City Commissioner

His daughter, a Gosechi dancer, then Dame of Staff

Her brother, a privy page

His Eminence, the Retired Emperor, 35 to 37 (Suzaku In)

The former Viceroy Prince, now His Highness of War
(Hotaru Hyōbukyō no Miya)

Her Majesty, the Empress Mother (Kokiden)

The Mistress of Staff (Oborozukiyo)

The Mistress of Genji's west wing, 25 to 27 (Murasaki)

The New Year came, and with it the end of mourning for Her Late Eminence. The world put on new colors, the change of clothes for the new season[1] went off brilliantly, and of course by Kamo Festival time the skies above gladdened every heart; yet the former Kamo Priestess only gazed sadly before her, and the breeze through the laurel tree nearby in the garden brought her younger gentlewomen many memories. Then there came a note from Genji, surmising that she must be particularly enjoying the peace of this Purification Day. "Today," he wrote,

> "Can you have believed that the Kamo River waves would wash this day back
> while you purify yourself only from your mourning gray?"[2]

It was a formal, straight-folded letter on purple paper, tied to a cluster of wisteria blossoms.

Touched by its timeliness, she replied,

> "It seems yesterday that the only robes I wore were of mourning gray,
> and for me such purity today means that all things pass.

Life is so frail." That was all, but Genji gazed at it as always. When she actually changed out of mourning, he had sent her a wealth of thoughtful gifts in care of Senji, which greatly embarrassed her; but the absence of any accompanying arch, enticing letter silenced any objection, since he had long been accustomed to making her such earnest gifts on public occasions, and she seems not to have known how to refuse them.

1. The change to summer clothes on the first day of the fourth month.
2. "Can you have imagined that when the Day of Purification came round again you would play no part in it as Kamo Priestess, and that your only purification would be that associated with coming out of mourning?" The death of her father had obliged Asagao to step down as Priestess and wear mourning, and the change back from mourning to ordinary colors involved its own purification ritual. "Mourning gray" translates *fujigoromo* ("wisteria clothing"); in early times, mourning presumably involved wearing rough clothing woven of wisteria-bark fiber. The *fuji* ("wisteria") of *fujigoromo* is connected to the wisteria blossoms to which the note is tied.

He did not let pass this chance to do something for the Fifth Princess as well, and she, too, was moved. "It was only yesterday, or so I thought, that this young man was just a boy, and now he looks after me like such a grown-up! He is so handsome, and at heart he has turned out so much nicer than other people!" Her young gentlewomen smiled at the way she praised him.

"I gather that His Grace has been keen on you for ages," she observed to her niece when they met; "it is not as though this were anything new for him. His Late Highness regretted His Grace's life taking another course, so that he could not welcome him; he often said how sorry he was that you ignored his own preference, and there were many times when he regretted what you had done.[3] Still, out of respect for the Third Princess's feelings I said nothing as long as His Late Excellency's daughter was alive. Now, though, even she, who commanded great consideration, is gone, and it is true, I simply do not see what could be wrong with your being what he wished, especially when His Grace is again so eager that this seems to me almost to be your destiny." To her niece's distaste she went on at some length in this antiquated fashion.

"I certainly do not intend to give in to him now, you know, when even His Late Highness found me so intractable." She spoke sternly enough to discourage the Fifth Princess from insisting further. Genji's next move worried her because all the women were on his side, but he was biding his time until his devoted attentions and manifest affection should soften her attitude toward him, and he seems never to have considered forcibly breaking her resistance that way.

He was preparing for the coming of age of his son by His Late Excellency's daughter, which he meant to hold at Nijō, but Her Highness[4] wanted very much to be there, and out of consideration for her he had it at her residence after all. The Commander of the Right and the boy's other uncles[5] were all senior nobles high in His Majesty's esteem, and everyone on that side, too, eagerly contributed whatever the event might require. The whole world buzzed and bustled with lavish preparations.

At first he planned to have his son assume the fourth rank,[6] as everyone expected, but then he changed his mind. The boy was very young, and in any case he felt that when he could now do whatever he pleased, the gesture would be all too obvious. Her Highness was aghast, and, poor lady, one can hardly blame her, when her grandson returned to the privy chamber in light blue.[7] She brought the matter up the next time Genji called on her.

"For the moment I prefer not to make too much of a grown-up of him too soon," he replied. "For various reasons I would rather have him spend some time at

---

3. Regretted your becoming the Kamo Priestess so that he could not have Genji as a son-in-law.
4. Ōmiya (the Third Princess), Aoi's mother, Yūgiri's grandmother, and the sister of the Fifth Princess.
5. Tō no Chūjō and his half brothers.
6. The rank conventionally given to the son of a Prince or to a first-generation Genji (Minamoto) after his coming of age. Yūgiri is a second-generation Genji, but his father's exceptional power and prestige make the fourth rank (lower grade) obvious for him, too.
7. *Asagi*, a bright but quite light blue worn by the sixth rank. Yūgiri has apparently been serving as a privy page.

the Academy. With two or three more years before he begins his career[8] he will come naturally to be capable of serving His Majesty, and by then, you see, he will be a man. I myself grew up in the palace and knew nothing of the world; instead, I spent day and night in waiting on my father and barely learned what was in a few books. I never caught the larger meaning even of what he so graciously taught me himself, and meanwhile, my knowledge of the classics and my mastery of koto or flute left a great deal to be desired. It is very rare for a clever son to outdo a duller father, and what then passes down the generations only wanders more and more perilously astray. This, you understand, is what prompted my decision. The son of a noble house, one who is promoted at his pleasure and who swells with his own glory, is unlikely to feel that it is any business of his to put himself out studying. He prefers to amuse himself, and those who bend to the times fawn on him since he rises in rank as he wishes, although they deride him meanwhile in secret; they curry his favor and do his bidding until by and by he resembles a great man, but once change intervenes and the one to whom he owes it all is gone, his fortunes decline, leaving him scorned and without a friend in the world. After all, learning is what provides a firm foundation for the exercise of Japanese wit.[9] He may be impatient now, but if he aspires in the end to become a pillar of the state, he will do well even after I am gone. Never mind if he is none too secure for the present, because as long as this is *my* way of looking after him, I cannot imagine anyone sneering at him for being one of those poverty-stricken Academy students."

Her Highness responded to speeches like this with a sigh. "I understand how thoroughly you have thought it over, but I gather that the Commander, for example, is shaking his head over this extraordinary idea of yours, and the young man himself is miserable, because even the Commander's sons and those of the Intendant of the Left Gate Watch,[10] on whom he used to look down as his juniors, have all gone up in rank and seniority.[11] This makes his light blue hateful to him, and I for one pity him."

Genji smiled. "He has a very grown-up complaint against me, I see. Ah, foolish youth! It is his age." He found it thoroughly appealing. "His disappointment will soon be gone once he acquires some learning and understands a little more."

The young man received his academic style in the east pavilion, where the east wing was prepared for the event. Senior nobles and privy gentlemen all rushed to be there, agog with wonder and curiosity, but the Doctors must have been terrified.

"Do it right," Genji commanded them. "Stint on nothing and do not relax whatever precedent may require."

With desperately affected composure they shamelessly wore odd, ill-fitting clothes that they had had to borrow elsewhere, and everything about them presented

8. A young man at the Academy was not on the ladder of official promotion.
9. "Learning" (*zae*) means study of the Chinese classics (literature, philosophy, law). *Yamato-damashii* ("Japanese wit") centuries later became the more exalted "Japanese spirit." This is its earliest occurrence in surviving Japanese literature.
10. Saemon no Kami, presumably a younger half brother of Tō no Chūjō. The incumbent normally held the junior fourth rank.
11. These cousins of Yūgiri would have been appointed to the fifth rank on coming of age.

a novel spectacle, including their manner of taking their seats with grave voices and pompous looks. The younger nobles could not stifle their grins. Genji had chosen only quiet, collected men to pour their wine, men unlikely ever to give in to mirth, but even so the Commander of the Right, the Lord of Civil Affairs, and the others who so earnestly kept their cups filled got a fine tongue-lashing.

The corner of a fishing pavilion

"Fie upon your manners, sirs! You presume to serve His Majesty, yet you fail to know a man of my renown? You are fools, sirs!"

The company broke into laughter.

"Silence! I will have silence! Your conduct is disgraceful! Sirs, I must require you to leave!"[12]

Such magisterial censure was great fun. Those who had never heard anything like it before thought it a rare treat, and the senior nobles who had come through the Academy beamed with satisfaction. Everyone felt it was a wonderful thing that His Excellency should have chosen this course for his son. Was there a buzz of talk? They put a stop to it. A cheeky remark? They issued their rebuke. But as the night wore on and their stridently disapproving expressions stood forth a little in the lamplight, they took on instead a pathetically comical sadness, and this among other things made the occasion a strange and curious one indeed.

"It is a great oaf and dullard like me who merits your reproof," Genji said, watching them from behind his blinds. Hearing that some Academy students were leaving because there had been no room for them, he detained them in the fishing pavilion[13] and had them given special gifts.

When it was over and everyone was going, Genji called on the Doctors and other like-minded gentlemen to make more Chinese verses. To this end he detained all the most likely senior nobles and privy gentlemen. The Doctors composed poems in four rhyming couplets, and Genji and the other amateurs four-line stanzas.[14] The Doctor of Letters chose the wording of a splendid topic.[15] The nights

12. The speaker's language, strikingly different from that of the courtiers, includes words and locutions that must have been peculiar to the Academy.

13. *Tsuridono*, a pavilion built on stilts over the garden lake of a Heian dwelling and joined to the rest of the house by an open walkway. It was used for relaxing pastimes.

14. The poetic form assigned to the professionals consists of four rhyming couplets of five characters each; the form given the amateurs consists of four lines of either five or seven characters.

15. The assigned topic (*dai*) was normally worded as a five-character line of poetry.

were short then, and it was day by the time the poems were read out. The Reader was the Left Grand Controller,[16] a fine-looking man whose voice as he read was marvelously awesome and impressive. He enjoyed especially high esteem as a scholar. The poems praised variously, with many elevated references, how nobly a young man whom lofty birth entitled to pursue only glory and its pleasures had befriended the fireflies at the window and the snow upon the bough.[17] Every line had such quality, as all in those days wonderingly agreed, that one would have wished to have them known in Cathay as well. Needless to say, His Grace's was especially accomplished, but it also conveyed a father's love so movingly that all present wept while they hummed it. However, a woman has no business repeating what she cannot know, and since I do not wish to give offense, I have omitted it.

Genji next saw his son through his admission to the Academy,[18] and he promptly gave him a room in his residence; after which he gravely entrusted him to a learned tutor and set about putting him to his studies. The young man seldom even called on Her Highness.[19] Genji doubted that he would ever learn anything there, since she spoiled him day in and day out and still treated him like a child, and he confined him instead to a quiet place by himself. He allowed him just three visits to her a month.

The young man chafed at being shut up this way all the time, and the more he did so, the more he detested his father; for were there not others who rose high and held distinguished office without ever having to suffer this way? On the whole, though, he was serious, and there was nothing frivolous about him. He buckled down and decided somehow to get through these classics as quickly as possible and on with a successful career, so that in four or five months he had read all the way through the work entitled *The Records of the Historian*.

Genji, who proposed to have him take the foundation examination, first had him tested in his own presence. The Commander attended as before, as well as the Left Grand Controller, the Commissioner of Ceremonial, and the Left Controller. Genji summoned the Chief Clerk and had him select difficult passages from the *Records*, ones that the Doctors were likely to dwell on at the examination, and he required the young man to read them out, which he did with such perfect fluency and manifest understanding as to dispel all doubt. All present were wholly convinced by his brilliant performance, and they were moved to tears. "If only His Late Excellency were here!" the Commander exclaimed, weeping more than anyone.

Genji, too, failed to keep his composure. "I know I have thought other people old fools, but the father fails as the son matures, and I do not have that many years left—well, such is life," he said, wiping his eyes.

The tutor was glad and proud at the sight. His face in his drunken daze—for the Commander kept his cup filled—was awfully thin. He was too great an eccen-

16. The incumbent in this office, which required an education in Chinese literature, held the fifth rank, upper grade.

17. Two hallowed Chinese examples of devotion to study. One young man who cannot afford oil for his lamp reads at night in summer by the light of fireflies caught in a gauze bag, and the other reads in winter by light reflected off snow.

18. *Nyūgaku*, a formal event in which the new student presented gifts to his teacher.

19. His grandmother.

tric to have found employment commensurate with his learning, and he lived in poverty and neglect, but Genji had singled him out that way because he saw something in him. The man seemed destined for even greater things in the future, considering that he now enjoyed Genji's favor far beyond his station and that he therefore owed to his young charge this sudden renewal of his life.

Countless carriages belonging to senior nobles gathered at the Academy gate on the day when Genji's son went there to be examined. It seemed impossible that there should be any others left elsewhere. The magnificently cosseted and appareled young man did indeed look far too distinguished for the company in which he now found himself. No wonder it offended him to take so low a seat among the same rabble as before.[20] Once again there were shockingly loud, scolding voices, but he read straight through without a tremor. The Academy still flourished then, as it did in its early days, and people of all ranks flocked eagerly to the instruction it offered, so that the number of learned, well-prepared scholars was constantly growing. Genji's son easily passed his examinations at every level, from Provisional Candidate to Candidate and on, and he applied himself so well to his studies that he inspired his teachers and their other students to ever greater efforts. At his father's residence there were many occasions to compose Chinese verses, and Doctors and other men of learning were always at home there. That was a reign when talent, whatever its nature, always came into its own.

Meanwhile, it was time to have an Empress. "The Ise Consort is the one Her Late Eminence was pleased to charge with seeing to his needs, you know," Genji insinuated. People objected to yet another non-Fujiwara Empress,[21] and Kokiden had after all gone to him first, had she not? Anyone secretly sympathetic to either side was anxious. The present Lord of Ceremonial, once known as His Highness of War,[22] enjoyed even higher esteem in this reign than before, and his daughter had already come to His Majesty with hopes of her own. She herself was a Consort of imperial lineage and certain to be close to His Majesty, since she was a relative on his mother's side, and so she seemed—his partisans insisted—a thoroughly plausible choice to tend His Majesty now that his mother was no more. Each side therefore had its claims, but the title still went to the Ise Consort. People at large were astonished that fortune should have favored her so much more than her mother.

His Grace rose to Chancellor and the Commander[23] to Palace Minister. Genji ceded all the affairs of government to him. In his person this gentleman was resolute and imposing, and in judgment he was wise. He had worked particularly hard at his studies and showed great discernment in all matters, public or private, although he still lost to Genji at guessing rhymes. He had ten or more sons from various mothers, and his house boasted all the glory of Genji's own, since each one was growing up to enjoy a successful career. In the way of daughters he had the Consort and one

20. When he received his academic style.
21. Literally, "another Genji"; but since both Fujitsubo and Akikonomu are of imperial descent, "Genji" refers here, as later in "Spring Shoots I," to any non-Fujiwara.
22. Murasaki's father and Fujitsubo's elder brother.
23. Tō no Chūjō.

other,[24] a girl of imperial blood whose lineage was no less distinguished than his other children's. Her mother, however, had married the Inspector Grand Counselor, by whom she had had many more, and he had therefore taken her away and entrusted her to Her Highness; he felt that it would be wrong to let her stepfather have her with all the rest. She was charming in both personality and looks, although he thought a great deal less of her than he did of the Consort.

His Grace's son had grown up with her, but they had lived separately[25] ever since they were ten, when her father told her, "You may be good friends, the two of you, but you are not to yield your intimacy to any man." However, the boy still thought of her in his youthful way, despite this new distance between them, and he was always eager to play dolls with her or to take whatever chance passing blossoms or autumn leaves might offer him to send her a word. She responded warmly to his open affection and was not markedly shy with him even now. The women looking after them were reluctant to intervene. "It is all very well, but they are still children," they said. "How could anyone be so cruel as to keep them apart, when they have been together all these years?" But while the young lady may still have been girlish and innocent, the young man, perhaps because of whatever naughty moments they might have shared, seemed despite his obviously tender age to have taken their separation hard. Being so young, they of course sometimes lost their letters to each other, done in writing still immature but attractively promising, and so the women on either side had some idea what was going on. They undoubtedly looked the other way, though, because after all, why announce it?

The celebratory banquets[26] were over, there were no court festivals to prepare for, and things were quiet at last. Early one evening, while the season's cold rain fell and a mournful wind sighed through the *hagi* fronds, His Excellency the Palace Minister went to call at his mother's. There he summoned his daughter and had her play the koto. Her Highness, who played every instrument well, had taught her them all.

"One would prefer not to watch a woman play the *biwa*,"[27] His Excellency observed, "but what a beautiful sound it has! Few in our time have received any genuine transmission of its music—Prince So-and-So, perhaps, or Genji This-and-That . . ." He counted some off. "Among the women, I hear the one His Grace keeps out there in that mountain village is superb. She learned it from an expert, of course, but even so, one wonders how anyone that remote from her source,[28] and who has lived that long as a mountain rustic, could possibly be so good. His Grace seems to think highly of her, and he often talks about her. In music, unlike the other arts, the best way forward is to play a great deal with others and to attempt many styles. It is rare indeed to become accomplished on one's own."

He urged Her Highness to play. "I hardly know how even to adjust the bridge

24. Kumoi no Kari.
25. In separate rooms.
26. To celebrate the recent promotions.
27. Because of the posture the instrument requires.
28. From the source of her musical lineage, Emperor Daigo.

anymore," she replied, but she nonetheless played very nicely. "That woman is certainly fortunate," she observed, "but beyond that, she seems to have extraordinary personal quality. To have given him the daughter he did not yet have at his age, and then to decide to give her up to a great lady rather than keep her and condemn her to obscurity—that, they say, shows her exceptional quality." Her Highness talked on for some time as she played.

"What gains a woman respect is her character," His Excellency remarked, and he went on to discuss one example and another. "The Consort, now—there is nothing wrong with her looks, as far as I can see, and she got as good an upbringing as anyone else, but it was her luck to be eclipsed by someone completely unforeseen, which I can only take as a lesson that nothing in this world ever goes as it should. I mean to have *this* girl at least turn out the way I want, though. The Heir Apparent will soon be of age, and I am privately laying my plans, even if this fortunate mother's future Empress is breathing down her neck. Once she has gone to His Highness, I am afraid there will be no stopping her." He sighed.

"But why? His Late Excellency was convinced that in the end this house would produce a girl with her future,[29] and he was keen to make sure that the Consort had the best possible chance. This injustice would never have occurred if he were still alive." On this issue she was quite angry with Genji. Contemplating the graceful sweep of her granddaughter's hair and the lovely way it fell as she sweetly and innocently played the *sō no koto*, it seemed to her that this charming face, these shy, sidelong glances, and the way her left hand pressed the strings, all had a doll-like perfection. The girl seemed to her infinitely dear. Her granddaughter pushed the instrument away after accompanying her grandmother a little.

His Excellency drew the *wagon* to him, and the freedom of his playing, in the latest style for a change and in the *richi* mode, was a great pleasure. The leaves dropped from the trees in the garden until there were no more,[30] while the old women leaned on one another here and there behind the standing curtains. "And yet how light the breeze!"[31] His Excellency sang; and he remarked, "It has not the depth of the *kin*,[32] but what a strangely moving evening this is! Will you not play again?" They did "Autumn Wind" together, and when His Excellency sang as well, in superb voice, Her Highness thought him, too, very dear. Just then the new young gentleman arrived, as though to add to their pleasure.

"Do come in." His Excellency sat the young man down beyond a standing curtain. "I see so little of you these days! What keeps you so hard at your books? It will do you no good to know more than your birth requires, as His Grace must know, and I am very sorry that you should be shut up this way, though I grant he must

29. Tō no Chūjō plans to marry Kumoi no Kari to Suzaku's son (now nine), despite the threat posed by the daughter of the lady from Akashi ("this fortunate mother").
30. As though moved by the music.
31. From the preface to a poem in the *Wenxuan*, a Chinese anthology that every courtier knew: "The leaves await a breeze to fall, and yet how light the breeze!"
32. An anecdote that follows the *Wenxuan* passage just quoted tells how a gentleman wept on hearing another play the *kin*, although the emotional depth of the *kin* was not really that great. Presumably tears, like autumn leaves, simply fall of themselves, when the moment comes.

have his reasons." He went on, "Do take up something else now and again! After all, the flute gives us the words of the ancients, too."[33] He handed the young man a flute.

His charmingly stylish playing was so delightful that the two other instruments stopped, and instead His Excellency discreetly beat the rhythm, singing, "Dyed with *hagi* flowers,"[34] and so on. "Your father, who loves this sort of music making, too, has escaped the troublesome burden of his duties, has he not? Yes, in this cruel world one may well hope to live as one pleases." He had some wine. Meanwhile, it grew dark, the lamps were lit,

Flute and rhythm clappers

and all partook of fruit and hot watered rice.[35] Then he sent the young lady off to another room.

"Those two are in for a great disappointment," whispered the older women who served Her Highness intimately. His Excellency was now keeping them so strictly apart that he would not even let the young man hear the sound of his daughter's koto.

His Excellency had got up as though he were leaving, in order to have a private word with one of the women; and while he was stealing away again, he caught the sound of these whisperings. He listened, intrigued. They were about him.

"He thinks he knows best, but that's a father for you."

"Something or other is going to happen one of these days."

"It's the parent who knows the child, they say, but I don't believe it." They were nudging each other.

How awful! he thought. I knew it! No, I am not surprised, but they are children, and I have not been on my guard. Ah, life is nothing but trouble! He saw the whole picture, but he went away in silence nonetheless.

His escort's warning cries were imposingly loud. "My lord has only just left, then!" the gentlewomen said to each other. "What cranny can he have been hiding in? To be playing about that way, at his age!"

"When that strong scent came wafting through, I thought it was the young gentleman!" The whisperers regretted their talk.

"I am afraid! What if he heard some of what we were saying? He has such a temper!"

On the way back His Excellency reflected that everyone would be thinking and saying that the match, even if no disaster, still offered nothing brilliant. Ah, he

33. A scholar may play music, since Confucius attributed great value to it.

34. A line from a *saibara* song.

35. The "fruit" (*kudamono*) may include also nuts and prepared confections; the "watered rice" (*yuzuke*) consists of steamed brown rice in hot water.

said to himself, this really makes me angry, when His Grace disposed of the Consort so ruthlessly, and I had hoped perhaps just this once to get ahead of him! On the whole he had always got along very well with Genji, and he still did, but he remembered their long rivalry over such things bitterly, and he slept little that night. "Her Highness *must* have noticed what is going on, you know; she must simply be allowing her beloved grandchildren to do as they please." That was what the women had been saying, and it infuriated him. He was so angry that he could not suppress the somewhat impetuous impulse to have the matter out.

Nun

He called on Her Highness two days later. She was very pleased when he came often, so this for her was a happy occasion. She tidied up her nun's sidelocks, put on a formal dress gown, and took care not to receive him completely face-to-face, since despite his being her son she held him in awe.[36]

His Excellency seemed to be in a bad humor. "It is awkward for me, calling on you like this," he began, "and I do not like to imagine what your women must think of me. I am not all I should be, I know, but I did hope to go on seeing you as long as I live and always to remain in close touch. Now, however, thanks to that hopeless daughter of mine, something has happened to make me angry with you, and although I should much prefer not to be, I am afraid that I simply cannot help it." He wiped his eyes.

Her Highness paled under her makeup, and her eyes widened. "In what have I so displeased you, at my age?" she asked, and he felt for her after all.

"I confidently entrusted this young person to you, and I myself have never had that much to do with her, but what with the disappointment of seeing the daughter I kept lose out at court, I had counted on making something of this one at least, and this latest surprise is a considerable blow. He may indeed be the most erudite young man under the sun, for all I know, but they *are* relatives, and people will find all that a bit tedious and dull, which will be a pity for him, too. It would look better for him to be given a warm welcome somewhere strikingly desirable and quite unrelated. His Grace will have a thing or two to say as well when he hears about this curious match between cousins. And even if it *were* all right, you might at least have let him know, and put on a visible welcome, and done something to make it a bit of an occasion. I can only deplore the way you allowed these young people to do as they pleased."

Her Highness had known nothing about it, and she was shocked. "I quite understand that you should speak this way, but I had absolutely no idea what those two were up to. It is indeed deplorable, and especially so for me. I resent your accusing me as well. I have given her special attention ever since I took her on, and I have hoped privately to make her superior even in things that you would never notice. Not once has affection so blinded me that I have wished to allow any

36. She kept a curtain at least partially between them.

such thing before they are even grown-up. But who told you this? You should be ashamed of yourself, scolding me this way over a rumor put about by malicious gossips, because there is nothing to it, and you are only risking soiling the poor girl's name."

"There is nothing to it, is there? Why, all your women seem secretly to be laughing about it, which is both infuriating and extremely disturbing!" With these words he left. Those who knew what the matter was felt very sorry indeed. The ones who had been whispering among themselves the other evening were even more upset and wondered miserably why they had ever done it.

His Excellency looked in on his innocently unsuspecting daughter and was touched by the spectacle of her sweetness and charm. "She is young, yes," he reproached her nurses, "but I am a great simpleton, because I who knew nothing of her youthful folly entertained high ambition for her." They had no reply.

"In this sort of thing, my lord, the old tales suggest that even a Sovereign's cherished daughter may go astray, but then someone privy to the affair is generally the one to arrange it for her. In this case, though, they have been together day in and day out for years, and we took it for granted that since they are so young, we could not very well go beyond what Her Highness herself thought best and separate them ourselves. Then it seems to have been decided the year before last to keep them apart, and although some young people seem to manage one way or another to be precocious in secret, these two showed so little sign of straying that nothing like that ever occurred to us." They all sighed.

"Very well, keep this quiet for the time being. It will get out in the end, but for now take care to deny that it ever happened. I will move her to my house. Her Highness's attitude is extremely disappointing. Still, I cannot imagine that you ever condoned this."

The gentlewomen welcomed his words, despite their distress on the young lady's behalf. "Oh, no, my lord, never! Just think how the Grand Counselor[37] would take this! The young gentleman is thoroughly worthy, of course, but what appeal would he see in a match to a commoner?"

His Excellency spoke to his daughter, but she was still too much a girl, and nothing he said got through to her. This reduced him to tears, and he took up secret consultations with the appropriate women to find some way to keep her from going to waste, meanwhile saving all his anger for Her Highness.

Her Highness grieved deeply for them both, but she may have especially favored the young man, whose sentiments she found endearing, because she could not understand why her son should be so heartlessly outraged. He had never given the girl much thought before, and it was the way she herself had taken charge of her that encouraged him to consider the Heir Apparent in the first place. Besides, if it was her destiny to marry a commoner, could any other compare with him? Why, he might aspire to heights far beyond the likes of her! Yes, her penchant for him must be what made her so angry with His Excellency. How much angrier *he* would have been if she had allowed him to divine her thoughts!

37. Kumoi no Kari's stepfather.

The young gentleman now arrived, never expecting a scolding. There had been too many people about the other evening to let him express all he had in his heart, and so he came toward nightfall, more than usually eager. Her Highness, who normally greeted him with pleasure, wreathed in smiles, embarked on a serious conversation that gave her an opening to say, "I am painfully caught, you know, because His Excellency is angry with me over you. You have given your heart all too tamely, and that, I am sorry to say, is causing trouble for other people. I would rather not have told you, but I thought you should know."

He understood instantly, since the matter was so much on his mind, and he blushed. "What can you possibly mean? I have been among people so little since I retired into quiet study that I can hardly have done anything to make anyone angry."

His shamefaced looks aroused her pity. "Very well, but be careful henceforth." She turned the conversation elsewhere.

He saw with anguish that corresponding with his friend would be more difficult than ever. He ate none of the food that he was offered and put up a pretense of going to bed, but he was desperate, and once everyone had retired, he tried the intervening sliding panel.[38] It had never normally been locked, but it was this time, quite firmly, and there was no sound within. He lingered there miserably, leaning against it. Meanwhile the young lady awoke to hear bamboo rustling in welcome to the wind and a passing wild goose utter a faint cry, and in the turmoil of her girlish feelings she murmured to herself, "Is the goose on high sad as I am sad?"[39]

He was profoundly troubled when he divined a sweetly youthful presence on the other side. "Do open the door! Is Kojijū with you?" But there was not a sound. Kojijū was her nurse's daughter. Embarrassed to have let him hear her talking to herself, she had unthinkingly drawn her head in under the covers—not that the naughty little thing mistook what he had in mind. With her nurses and others lying nearby she dared not move, and both remained silent.

"When deep in the night wild geese pass by aloft, calling to their mates,
    how cruelly the wind, too, then comes rustling through the reeds!"

And what a chill it brings![40] Sighing, he returned to Her Highness, lay down, and kept very still lest she hear him and wake up.

The next morning he went straight off to his own room, feeling vaguely ashamed, and wrote her a letter; but he despaired because he could neither find Kojijū nor go to her himself. As for the young lady, she was ashamed only because she had had a scolding, and she remained otherwise as bright and sweet as ever, giving little thought either to what might lie ahead for her or to what others might

38. The one into Kumoi no Kari's room. He is probably in one subdivision of the chamber and she in another.

39. *Kumoi no kari,* an expression from *Genji monogatari kochūshakusho in'yō waka* 165: "Is the goose on high in the fog-filled heavens sad as I am sad? Why does my melancholy never clear?" This is the source of the name by which the speaker is conventionally known.

40. This sentiment echoes *Kokin rokujō* 423 on the autumn wind.

feel. She did not even object when her gentlewomen discussed the matter among themselves. To her mind it hardly deserved all this fuss, but those most concerned with her welfare reproved her thoughtlessness so thoroughly that she could not get a word to him either. An adult might still have devised a way to do so, but her young man was still less grown-up than she, and he could only mourn.

His Excellency, who was furious with Her Highness, had not been back since. He breathed not a word of his discovery to his wife; he only made it clear that he was in a thoroughly bad humor. "The Empress made a particularly impressive entry,"[41] he conceded, "and the Consort is so pessimistic about her prospects that it hurts me to see it. I am going to have her withdraw for some quiet and a rest. Her women never have a moment's peace, what with His Majesty still calling her constantly to attend him and visiting her day and night, and I gather they are under great strain."

So it was that he suddenly brought his daughter home. His Majesty resisted granting her leave to go, but His Excellency grumbled until he unwillingly gave in, and at last he managed to extract her from the palace. "You may find yourself rather at loose ends," he told her. "Do bring your sister here, so that you can amuse yourself with her. I have her at Her Highness's, where she is quite all right, except that I am afraid she has not been able to help becoming involved with some tiresomely precocious company, company wholly unsuitable for her at her age." He abruptly brought her to his own residence.

Her Highness was extremely disappointed. "I was very sad and lonely after I lost my only daughter, and taking this girl on was such a joy. I thought I would be looking after her the rest of my life, and I hoped to have the comfort of her presence every day in my old age. Alas, your sudden decision to exclude me is a bitter blow."

"I have only given natural expression to a discontent I cannot help but feel," he answered respectfully. "How could there possibly be any question of my excluding you? The daughter I have in His Majesty's service is hurt over her own prospects, and lately she withdrew to my house, where I have been sorry to see her so listless and downcast. I just thought I would have the young lady come to me for a while so that the two of them can amuse themselves together and make my visitor feel better. I have no wish to make light of all you have done to look after her and bring her up."

He had made his decision, and he was not one to change it for anything she might say. She could only feel deep and painful regret. "How very cruel the heart can be," she said, weeping. "Even those two young people hatefully kept things from me. Never mind, though, because you yourself, with all your fine understanding, have turned against me, and now you are taking her away. I tell you, she will be no safer there than she has been with me."

Just then the young gentleman arrived. He had been looking in often lately, hoping for any opportunity, however remote. The presence of His Excellency's carriage pricked his conscience, and he stole away to hide in his room. His Excellency's

41. Her ceremonial entry into the palace at her new rank.

sons—the Left Lieutenant, the Junior Counselor, the Second of the Watch, the Adviser, the Commissioner—were all there, but none of *them* was allowed through Her Highness's blinds. The Intendant of the Left Gate Watch and the Acting Counselor, although born of another mother, waited assiduously on Her Highness even now, and all their own sons were present, too, but apparently none had anything like this young gentleman's charm. Her Highness favored him far beyond the others, and this granddaughter of hers had become her only darling, to cherish and to keep with her always. She felt very, very lonely now that the girl was going away.

"I am off to the palace now, and I shall be back for her toward evening," His Excellency announced as he left.

I suppose I might make the best of a bad job and just let things take their course, he said to himself, but he still bridled at the idea. No, once that young man has risen a bit and seems worthy, then perhaps I may weigh the seriousness of his intentions and approve the match after all, but only if it is done properly. Anyway, no reproof from me could prevent those two from making a childish spectacle of themselves as long as they were there together, and it is not Her Highness who would put a stop to it. So it was that the Consort's listlessness provided him with the excuse to move her, after tactful representations to both sides.[42]

"I suppose His Excellency is angry with me, but I know that you, dear, still understand how much you mean to me. Please come and see me," Her Highness wrote; and so she came, all dressed up and looking very pretty. She was fourteen. Although obviously not quite grown-up yet, she had a charming and thoroughly childish poise.

"You have been my special pet day and night, and I have never let you go far away. I shall miss you terribly. It has already been such a disappointment that I have too little time left to see how you will turn out. And how sad it is, too, now you are leaving me, to think where you are going!" She wept. For shame the young lady never lifted her head but only stood there, crying.

The young man's nurse, Saishō, came in and whispered, "My lady, I looked as much to you as I ever did to my young lord, and I so wish you were not going! Stand firm, even if His Excellency decides to marry you to someone else!" The girl was more ashamed than ever and said nothing.

"Come now, do not put ideas in her head. We all have our own destiny, and no one knows where it will lead."

"No, Your Highness, His Excellency seems to hold my lord in contempt. But just ask anyone whether my lord really is less worthy than anyone else!" Anger made her quite blunt.

The young gentleman was looking on from behind a screen. Normally he would have worried about being caught, but now he was simply wiping away tears of misery when, with a sharp pang of pity, his nurse noticed him and put a plan to Her Highness. In the confusion that reigned as darkness fell, she brought the two together.

They were shy in each other's presence, their hearts beat fast, and at first they

---

42. To move Kumoi no Kari after representations to his wife and to his mother.

only wept in silence. "I feel as though I might as well give up, now that His Excellency is acting so cruelly," he said, "but I know how badly you would miss me if I did. Why did you keep me away, when these last few days might have offered us a chance to meet?" He looked very young and charming.

"I am sure I feel as you do," she replied.

"Do you love me?"

She nodded slightly, with girlish artlessness.

The lamps were lit, and signs of His Excellency's arrival from the palace, especially his escort's ostentatious cries, now sent the women rushing about with exclamations of surprise. The young lady shivered with fear, but her obstinate young gentleman dismissed whatever reprimand he might receive and refused to let her go.

Lamp on a stand

Her nurse came looking for her. "Oh, no," she said when she saw what was going on, "they *can't*! Why, it is true, Her Highness *must* know!" She continued in an angry whisper, "This is awful, it really is! How will my lord the Grand Counselor take it, not to mention what His Excellency will have to say! He is all very well, but to think it was her fate to start out with someone of the sixth rank!" They could just hear her, since her complaint came from right behind their screen.

What she means, he said to himself, is that my rank does not even count. He so raged against the world that his ardor cooled somewhat. It was too much. "Listen to that!" he said.

> *"How can she dismiss as a light and worthless blue these sleeves I must wear,*
> *dyed a far deeper color by the scarlet of my tears?*[43]

I feel so ashamed!"

> *"From my many woes I have, alas, learned to know the hues of sorrow:*
> *how did the robe between us come to be so deeply dyed?"*[44]

She had hardly spoken when His Excellency came in. Like it or not, off she went.

The young man went to lie down in his room, suffocating with bitter resentment at having, as it were, been left behind. He was so upset to hear the three carriages discreetly hurrying away that he pretended to be asleep when Her Highness sent for him, and he did not move. It was his tears that flowed on. He spent the night sighing and hurried home while the frost still lay white on the ground. He did not want anyone to see his swollen eyes, and since Her Highness was bound to call him to her again, he quickly escaped to where he could feel more at ease. All the

---

43. The tears of blood shed (so convention had it) by someone in particularly intense grief.

44. "How did we become so attached to each other?" *Nakagoromo* ("the robe between us") is a literary expression for a love relationship.

way there he wallowed in this misery of his own creation. The sky, still dark above him, remained densely clouded.

> *"How the skies above, in a dawn that ice and frost bind so cruelly,*
> *close in, and darkness gathers in a steady shower of tears!"*

Gosechi dancer

This year His Grace was to present a Gosechi dancer. He made no extraordinary preparations for doing so, but as the time approached, his household busied itself with the costumes for the page girls and so on.[45] He had the costumes for the women who would accompany the dancer to the palace[46] made in the east pavilion, and he looked after everything else at his own residence. Her Majesty[47] offered him the most beautiful things for the attendants and page girls. The disappointment left by the cancellation of last year's event meant that this year the privy gentlemen seemed unusually eager to do things brilliantly, and people were talking about how each dancer's household was bent in a thousand ways on outdoing every other. Dancers came from the Inspector Grand Counselor, the Intendant of the Left Gate Watch, and, among the privy gentlemen, from Yoshikiyo, now Governor of Ōmi, and from the Left Grand Controller. They all had their dancer stay on at the palace, since His Majesty had decreed that this year the dancers should wait upon him: that was why every gentleman had been so eager to have his daughter chosen.

For his own dancer Genji summoned the daughter of Lord Koremitsu, then Governor of Tsu and Left City Commissioner, since rumor made her out to be a beauty. Koremitsu disliked the idea,[48] but others insisted. "The Grand Counselor is apparently presenting *his* daughter by an outside mother,"[49] they said, "so why should you be ashamed to put forward your own?" In the end he decided reluctantly

45. The Gosechi Festival accompanied the Daijōsai rite in the year of a new Emperor's accession, or the Niinamesai rite, as on this occasion. It took place on the middle days of the Ox (*ushi*), Tiger (*tora*), Rabbit (*u*), and Dragon (*tatsu*) in the eleventh month. In the former case there were five dancers and in the latter four; of these, two in a Niinamesai year came from among the senior nobles and two (three in a Daijōsai year) from among the privy gentlemen or provincial Governors. On the day of the Ox the dancers and their escort of gentlewomen entered the Gosechi chamber in the Jōneiden. On the last day (that of the Dragon) there was the great court banquet known as Toyo no Akari, and on this occasion the Gosechi dancers danced the dance of the heavenly maidens.
46. The entry into the Jōneiden on the day of the Ox.
47. Akikonomu.
48. He did not want his daughter put on display that way.
49. *Sotobara*, a woman other than the formal wife.

that he might as well have her go straight to the palace. He had her learn her dance very nicely at home, gave careful thought to choosing the best gentlewomen to tend her, and on the day sent her off toward evening. Genji, at home, looked over all his ladies' page girls and attendants and picked the prettiest of them. Each, according to her station, therefore took it as a great honor to be selected. He decided to have them pass before him in order to rehearse them for their presentation to His Majesty. All were worthy, and their looks and faces left him at a loss to discriminate between them. "I wish I could offer His Majesty one more!" he said, laughing. He based his final choice on quickness and deportment.

The young scholar lay brokenhearted and in blank despair, never glancing at his food or even reading, until he quietly set out to explore in the hope of lightening his mood. With his marvelous looks and bearing and his quiet dignity and grace, the younger gentlewomen were very pleased to see him. For reasons best known to his conscience Genji did not allow him anywhere near the mistress of Nijō, not even up to her blinds, but instead kept him so far away that he hardly knew even her chief gentlewomen. Today, though, he seems somehow to have slipped in[50] amid all the confusion. They had ushered the dancer out of her carriage and into a screened-off space prepared specially for her in the aisle near the double doors. He stole up to the screens and peeked through: there she was, lying there exhausted. She seemed to be just his friend's age but a little taller and, if anything, rather more striking. It was too dark to see her clearly, but on the whole she reminded him a great deal of his friend, and although he did not exactly lose his heart to her, he was sufficiently stirred to rustle his robes. She was wondering innocently what the sound could mean when he said,

> "You whose privilege it is to serve the Goddess of Toyo-oka,
> never forget how I long soon to claim you as my own.[51]

Within the sacred fence . . ."[52] His was indeed an abrupt approach. The voice was youthful and pleasing, but she could not imagine whose it was, and she was feeling a little alarmed when her women came bustling up to put her makeup right. All the commotion induced him unwillingly to leave.

He had been staying away from the palace because he so detested his light blue, but he went now because novel dress-cloak colors were allowed in honor of the Gosechi Festival. Youthful good looks or not, he was grown-up for his age, and he went about in high good humor. Everyone made much of him, from His Majesty on down, and he was prized by all.

---

50. Into the west wing, where Murasaki lived.

51. *Shūishū* 579 mentions a sacred *"Toyo-oka-hime,"* whose identity remains uncertain. Yūgiri seems to mean that as a Gosechi dancer the girl is now in the service of the gods. His "claim" is *shime*, the word not only for roping off (claiming possession of) a plot of ground but for the sacred rope (*shimenawa*) that marks off a sacred space.

52. "I have always loved you." "Within the sacred fence" (*mizugaki no*) is from *Shūishū* 1210, by Hitomaro: "O maiden who toss your sleeves within the sacred fence on the hill of Furu, since I first loved you long ages have passed." The "maiden" of the poem serves the Isonokami deity, whose shrine is on the "hill of Furu."

The Gosechi dancers were all exquisitely groomed for their entry into the palace, but Genji's and the Grand Counselor's were the ones whose looks caused a sensation. Both were undoubtedly a pleasure, but it was Genji's whose fresh charm truly set her apart. She was such a wonder of stylish beauty that one could hardly believe her really to be what she actually was,[53] and that is probably why everyone praised her so. The dancers were all somewhat older than usual, which made the festival this year a little different.

Genji came for a look, too, and he remembered the maiden who had caught his eye long ago. He wrote to her at dusk on the day of the Dragon.[54] You can imagine what his letter was like.

> *"That fair dancing girl must have grown wise in her time, for the friend she knew*
> *when she tossed her angel sleeves is himself much older now."*[55]

The poor thing was very touched that after all these years he should still feel moved to express such feelings.

> *"Since you mention it, all that is present to me as though it were new:*
> *how beneath my sunshade band I melted like frost on your sleeves."*[56]

Her answer came back, fittingly enough, on green patterned paper[57] and written in a disguised hand in ink now dark, now light, and leaning here and there toward the cursive. For someone like her, Genji thought, it was a delight.

The young man went roaming about in secret, now that a certain someone had caught his fancy, but he was not allowed anywhere near her. He was curtly sent away instead, and being at a bashful age, he gave up with many an inward sigh.

His Majesty had seemed to wish the dancers to attend him immediately, but for the moment they were dismissed; Ōmi's daughter went to the purification at Karasaki, and Tsu's to Naniwa.[58] The Grand Counselor submitted a plea to have his daughter formally admitted to the palace.[59] The Intendant of the Left Gate Watch was reprimanded for having presented an ineligible dancer, but she, too, was kept on in His Majesty's service. When Tsu observed that a Dame of Staff post lay vacant, His Grace, to his son's keen regret, was glad enough to honor his retainer's loyal service. If my rank were not what it is, the young man reflected, I should have

---

53. The daughter of a mere privy gentleman.

54. The day when the dancers performed, on the occasion of the *Toyo no akari* banquet.

55. "Grown wise" more or less translates *kamisabinu*, "grown [in age and dignity] to be like a god." The expression alludes to the sacred character of the Gosechi dance.

56. The vocabulary of the original hints in various ways at the Gosechi dance that the writer once performed. The "sunshade band" (*hikage*) is something a Gosechi dancer wore.

57. *Aozuri no kami*, paper that may have been patterned by a wax-resist method. The robes worn by the Gosechi dancers were also described as *aozuri*.

58. Yoshikiyo's daughter and Koremitsu's. Karasaki is a promontory at the southern end of Lake Biwa, while Naniwa corresponds roughly to the site of Osaka. Purification rites associated with the Gosechi Festival took place at both locations.

59. Presumably as a Consort.

liked at my age to ask for her myself. She did not mean that much to him, but the prospect of renouncing her without even having told her his feelings only multiplied his tears.

A brother of hers, a privy page, came often to wait on him, and he now spoke to the young fellow with unusual warmth. "When does your Gosechi dancer go to the palace?"

"This year, my lord, or so I hear."

"She is so pretty that I am a little in love with her. I envy you being with her so much. Will you make it possible for me to see her again?"

"How could I, my lord? Even I cannot see her as I please. How could I give a young gentleman a look, when none of her brothers is allowed anywhere near her?"

"Then a letter, at least." The young gentleman in question gave him one.

This was a blow, since the page had already been warned against such things, but his master was in dead earnest, and pity won out. He took the letter away with him.

His sister was very pleased with it—she may have been clever for her age. It was on thin, deep green paper,[60] prettily layered, and the still-youthful writing showed happy promise.

> "Was it clear enough, in the fullness of bright day, how my heart is set
> on that fair dancing maiden and her angel's feather sleeves?"[61]

They were reading it when their father came in, and they failed in their terror to hide it. "What is that letter?" he demanded to know, seizing it. The two children flushed scarlet. "You are up to no good, are you!" he grumbled. He called back his son, who had moved to flee.

"Who wrote this?"

"His Grace's young gentleman gave it to me. He insisted."

His father grinned broadly. "What a delightfully forward young man!" he exclaimed. "You are his age, but you are not worth much, are you!"

After praising the writer he showed the letter to his son's mother as well. "As long as the young gentleman deigns to notice her, I would rather let him have her than send her into palace service. He can be trusted, I think, considering the man His Grace is and how he never forgets any woman he has known. I would not mind playing Akashi Novice!" Still, the preparations went on as before.

Once deprived even of writing, the young man only set his heart the more resolutely on the nobler of his two loves, and as time heightened his desperate longing, he could not help wondering whether he would ever see her again. He had no wish even to call on Her Highness. Memories of where she had lived and of where they had played together all these years flooded through him until he lost any desire to visit the house at all. Instead he shut himself up again in his room.

---

60. The color alludes to that of the "sunshade band" (*hikage*).

61. "Bright day" is *hikage*, a homophone for the "sunshade band." The "feather sleeves" (*ama no hasode*) are, in the imagination, those of a Gosechi dancer, whose dance was that of a celestial being.

Genji decided to entrust him to the lady in the west wing of his east pavilion.[62] "I doubt that Her Highness has long to live," he said, "and considering that you have known him ever since he was small, I hope that you will look after him once she is gone." She willingly agreed, and she set warmly and kindly about doing just that.

She certainly is no beauty! the young man would say to himself after the fleeting glimpses he had of her, and even so my father has never abandoned her! How I wish I were less helplessly drawn to a face that brings me so much suffering! And how I would prefer someone as kind and gentle as she! Still, I pity a woman there is no point in actually seeing. No wonder His Grace, who knows her heart and her looks, keeps many veils[63] between them even after all these years, though to make up for it he still provides her with everything she requires. (How clever of him to think of things like that!) Her Highness dressed unusually,[64] of course, but she was still very handsome, as he had long assumed any woman to be, whereas the lady in the west wing had actually never had any looks, and now she seemed to be losing what little she could offer to age; she was so thin and her hair was so sparse that, alas, one felt like saying so.

As the year came to an end, Her Highness busied herself with New Year's clothes for her grandson alone. She made many lovely sets, but the sight of them only oppressed him. "Why are you doing so much," he asked, "when I may not even go to court on New Year's Day?"

"Why not? You are talking like a decrepit old man."

"I may not be old, but I do feel decrepit," he murmured with tears in his eyes.

Her Highness heard him with sorrow, well knowing what the matter must be, and she, too, seemed on the verge of tears. "A man carries himself with pride even when of humble rank," she said. "You should not mope this way. What is your excuse for being moody and dejected? You are only putting yourself at risk."[65]

"What do you mean? People dismiss me contemptuously as a mere sixth-ranker. I know I will not be one forever, but it is a trial, you know, just to go to the palace. No one would even dream of scorning me this way if His Late Excellency were still alive. I have my father, of course, but he keeps me so distinctly at a distance that I cannot easily go to him. I can only approach him at all in the east pavilion. The lady in the west wing there is very kind to me. I would not have any of these troubles, though, if only I had a mother, too."

His tears were streaming down now, and the sight of him trying to hide them touched Her Highness so deeply that she wept even more. "Anyone, high or low, who loses his mother is affected as you are, but you, like anyone else, have your destiny in life, and I am sure there will come a time when people leave off dismissing you; no, you must not be downhearted. I do wish, though, that His Late Excel-

---

62. Hanachirusato.

63. The original expression, *hamayū*, is from *Shūishū* 668, attributed to Hitomaro. *Hamayū* is a perennial plant (a crinum) that grows on seaside dunes. Its leaves lap over one another, layer on layer, hence its use here to suggest "many veils" (curtains, blinds, etc.). The poem reads, approximately, "*Hamayū*, manifold on the Kumano shore, manifold my thoughts of you, and yet we do not meet."

64. Because she was a nun.

65. Because by allowing himself to mope he invites the malevolent attentions of roving spirits.

lency had lived a little longer! Your father's vast influence shelters us just as well, I know, but there are many things I wish were otherwise. I hear everyone praises the Palace Minister for his exceptional character, but he is less and less like what he used to be, and I regret having lived to see it, because it angers me to see someone like you, with all your future before you, caught up in these difficulties, however trifling they may be." She was weeping.

Genji stayed quiet on the first day of the New Year and did not go out. The Blue Roans were led to his residence, according to the precedent established by the Minister Yoshifusa,[66] and on the festival days[67] past practice was given a new magnificence.

After the twentieth of the second month His Majesty made a progress to the Suzaku Palace.[68] It was too soon for the best of the cherry blossoms, but the third month would be one of remembrance for Her Late Eminence.[69] The early blossoms were so lovely that His Eminence had had his residence done up especially nicely, and all who escorted the progress, even the senior nobles and Princes, took care to be at their best. They all wore leaf green over a cherry blossom layering, and His Majesty wore red. The Chancellor was there by imperial command, and since he, too, wore red, they shone more than ever as one and were hard to tell apart. All present stood out in costume and bearing. His Eminence, too, had matured very handsomely and grown in grace of bearing and deportment. No academicians were summoned today, just ten students known for their talent at Chinese poetry. The topic was announced as though for the Ceremonial Bureau examination,[70] probably because His Grace's son was to take the examination in earnest. The more fainthearted of the students, numb and helpless, set themselves adrift in boats on the garden lake. Soon the orchestra barges[71] were rowing about under a westering sun, playing modal preludes to which the wind off the hills nicely added a music of its own, while the young gentleman nursed his grudge against the world, groaning that if his path were not such a hard one, he would be amusing himself with the rest.

When they danced "Song of the Spring Warbler," His Eminence remembered that party under the cherry blossoms long ago. "I wonder whether we shall ever see the like again," he said, setting Genji off on a train of fond memories of that reign.

When the dance ended, Genji offered him a cup of wine.

> "The warbler still sings as sweetly as ever then in those bygone days,
> but the blossoms he once loved do not look at all the same."

---

66. Fujiwara no Yoshifusa (804–72), the first official to hold the offices both of Regent (Sesshō, Regent for a minor Emperor) and of Chancellor (Daijōdaijin).

67. *Sechie no hibi*, the days of the year on which the Emperor feasted his courtiers. During the first month these included the first, the seventh (the day of the Blue Roans), and the fourteenth and sixteenth (the mumming).

68. The palace of the Retired Emperor Suzaku. He is in principle Reizei's older half brother, but the difference in age makes him more like a father.

69. Fujitsubo. Mourning for her would have prevented the visit.

70. This examination allowed the student to pass from *gimonjō* ("provisional candidate") status, Yūgiri's present one, to *monjōshō* ("regular candidate").

71. There were two, elaborately decorated and each with a tall prow in the form of a fabulous beast.

And His Eminence:

> *"Even at a home veiled from the Ninefold Palace by thick banks of mist*
> *I still hear the warbler's voice proclaiming that it is spring."*

The former Viceroy Prince, now His Highness of War, offered His Majesty the cup and added with keen wit,

> *"The hollow bamboo that calls such sweet music forth out of the old days*
> *now rouses the spring warbler to carolings ever new."*

> *"When the bird of spring carols on and on so long fondly for the past,*
> *does he mean that blossoms now lack the beauty they had then?"*[72]

His Majesty spoke with superlative grace.

All this went on in private, among a select company, so that some poems may not have reached me, or perhaps they were never written down.

His Majesty called for stringed instruments, since the musicians were too far off to hear very well. His Highness of War took the *biwa*, His Excellency the Palace Minister the *wagon*, and His Eminence the *sō no koto*, while His Grace as usual received the *kin*. No words can convey the quality of their music, for they were superb masters, and they played with all the art at their command. Many privy gentlemen were there to sing the solfège.[73] They first performed "Ah, Wondrous Day!" and then "Cherry Blossom Man." Cressets were lit here and there on the island, under the charming light of a misty moon, and His Majesty's music came to an end.

The dance "Song of the Spring Warbler"

On his way back His Majesty called upon the Empress Mother, though the night was well advanced, for he felt that it would be unkind to pass by on this occasion without doing so. His Grace courteously accompanied him. Her Majesty received them with pleasure. Noting the all too obvious signs of her great age, Genji thought of Her Late Eminence and lamented to himself that some people did indeed live very long lives.

---

72. A modest suggestion, in response to the praise expressed in the previous poem, that the speaker's reign is less brilliant than his predecessor's.

73. They sang *sōga*, which should mean that they sang strings of wordless syllables (such as *taririra*), each syllable being the name of the corresponding note. Judging from what follows, however, they seem to have been singing songs.

"Someone as old as I am, forgets everything," she said, "and yet, you know, your most gracious visit has brought back to me after all that reign of long ago." She began to weep.

"I no longer recognized the coming of spring now that I have lost those dear, fostering presences,"[74] His Majesty replied, "but today has consoled me greatly. We simply must sometimes . . ."

"I shall not neglect to wait upon you," His Grace added.

Her heart beat fast, sure enough, at the noisy commotion of His Majesty's departure. She rued what Genji must think of her and lamented that his destiny to govern should have proven so impossible to thwart.

The Mistress of Staff,[75] in her quiet meditations, came across many absorbing memories of her own. Genji probably still allowed the wind to take her word from him. Whenever the Empress Mother had something to say to His Majesty, whenever she felt dissatisfied with the sinecures and benefices granted her or with anything else at all, she longed to turn back the sad decline that her long life obliged her to witness, and she condemned it all bitterly. The older she grew, the more ill-tempered she became, until even His Eminence found her company unbearable.

The young scholar submitted a fine composition that day, and he became a regular candidate. Only three of his fellows passed, even though His Majesty had chosen learned aspirants with years of study behind them. When the autumn appointments were announced, he received his cap of office and was named an Adviser. He never for a moment forgot his love, but his uncle the Minister kept such a hateful eye on him that no trick succeeded in bringing him to her. He found a way to pass her letters, but their plight remained a sad one.

Genji wanted a quiet place to live—it might as well be large and handsome enough to accommodate any ladies who lived in uncomfortably far-flung mountain villages—and he therefore set aside four *chō* of land[76] at Rokujō and Kyōgoku, where Her Majesty's old residence had been, and had the work begun. The following year would be His Highness of Ceremonial's fiftieth, and the mistress of Genji's west wing was therefore planning a celebration[77] that Genji quite agreed could not be omitted. He urged the construction on for this reason, because it seemed to him that the preparations could go forward very nicely on his splendid new estate. Once the New Year had begun, he devoted himself further to the preparations, to the banquet,[78] and to the choice of musicians and dancers. The mistress of his west wing looked after the adornments for the sacred scrolls and images, the vestments, the rewards,[79] and so on. He assigned tasks also to the lady in his east pavilion. The relations between them grew in warmth and frequency.

74. The Kiritsubo Emperor and Fujitsubo.
75. Oborozukiyo.
76. About 14 acres. Akikonomu's mother, the Rokujō Haven, apparently left this property to Genji when she entrusted her daughter to his care.
77. He is her father.
78. *Toshimi*, a celebratory banquet held after a solemn Buddhist service to pray for the long life and happiness of the gentleman being honored.
79. *Roku*, the gifts to compensate the priests for their efforts. Murasaki is taking care of everything to do with the Buddhist service that preceded the banquet.

The world was abuzz over all this, and His Highness of Ceremonial heard about it, too. His Grace is always so good to everyone, His Highness reflected with mingled bitterness and guilt, yet he has acted callously toward me and mine. He has embarrassed me on occasion, slighted members of my household, and made me smart many a time—yes, he must have a reason for disliking me. Still (and here his thoughts turned to joy), this mark of his consideration, and this way of setting all the world ringing while he prepares it, comes as a most unexpected honor so late in my life, even if the good fortune of my daughter, whom he prizes before the world and loves beyond all his other ladies, has not passed to my own house. His Highness's wife, however, objected and thought it all a great bore. She probably detested Genji even more now because of the way he had failed to help her daughter when she went to serve His Majesty.

Genji's Rokujō estate was finished in the eighth month. Her Majesty had the southwest quarter, no doubt because that was where her residence had once stood. The southeast quarter was for himself. He gave the northeast to the lady from his east pavilion and the northwest to the lady from Akashi. He had the existing hills and lake shifted about as necessary, changing the shapes of mountains and waters to suit each resident's wishes.

The southeast quarter boasted high hills, every tree that blossoms in spring, and a particularly lovely lake; and in the near garden, before the house, he took care to plant not only five-needled pines, red plums, cherry trees, wisteria, kerria roses, and rock azaleas, all of which are at their best in spring, but also, here and there, discreet touches of autumn. In Her Majesty's quarter he planted the hill already there with trees certain to glow in rich autumn colors, turned springs into clear streams, added rocks to the brook to deepen its voice, and contrived a waterfall, while on the broad expanse of his new-laid meadow, flowers bloomed in all the profusion of the season. The result was an autumn to put to shame the moors and mountains of Saga and Ōi. The northeast quarter, with its cool spring, favored summer shade. Chinese bamboo grew in the near garden, to freshen the breeze; tall groves offered welcoming depths of shade, as in a mountain village; the hedge was of flowering deutzia; and among the plantings of orange, fragrant with the past, of pinks and roses and peonies, there also grew spring and autumn flowers. The east edge of this quarter was divided off into a riding ground with a pavilion and surrounded by a woven fence. Sweet flag had been induced to grow thickly beside the water, for the games of the fifth month,[80] and the nearby stables housed the most superb horses. The northwest quarter's northern sector was given over to rows of storehouses. Along the dividing fence grew a dense stand of pines intended to show off the beauty of snow. There was a fence entwined with chrysanthemums to gather the morning frosts of early winter, a grove of deep-hued oaks,[81] and a scattering of nameless trees transplanted from the fastnesses of the mountains.

---

80. The Sweet Flag Festival of the fifth month involved riding events.
81. *Hahaso* (probably the *nara* oak), a tree honored in poetry for the deep red of its late-autumn leaves.

Genji and his lady moved during the equinox.[82] He had wanted them all to move in then, but Her Majesty thought the idea ostentatious and waited a little. The lady of Falling Flowers, as docile and undemanding as ever, arrived the same night. Everything done for spring was out of season now, but it was still lovely. They

Arched bridge

came in fifteen carriages, their escort made up largely of gentlemen of the fourth and fifth ranks, but including Genji's pick of the best from the sixth and also from among the privy gentlemen. It was not excessive. He had kept his train modest, lest he incur the world's disapproval, and nothing about it was showy or self-important. Nor did he at all neglect that other lady, because he placed the Adviser[83] at her service, and the Adviser attended her so well that one would have thought the two of them did indeed belong together. The rooms in the gentlewomen's part were much more nicely laid out than usual.

Her Majesty came from the palace five or six days later, but her arrival was nonetheless grand. It goes without saying that great good fortune was hers, but her own elegance and dignity, too, had earned her the world's highest approbation. Between the quarters of the estate ran walls and galleries that Genji had designed so as to encourage friendly commerce between them all.

In the ninth month splashes of autumn color appeared, and Her Majesty's garden became indescribably lovely. One windy autumn evening she sprinkled many-colored flowers and leaves into a box lid and sent them to the residence of His Grace. The tall page girl, in deep purple under a patterned aster layering and a light russet dress gown, came tripping with easy grace along the galleries and over the arched bridges. Despite the formality of the occasion Her Majesty had not been able to resist sending this delightful girl, whose long service in such company gave her an air and manner far more distinguished than any other's.

Her Majesty had written,

> *"You whose garden waits by your wish to welcome spring, at least look upon
> these autumn leaves from my home, carried to you on the wind."*

---

82. The autumn equinox was celebrated for seven days, centered on the tenth day of the eighth lunar month.
83. Hanachirusato and Yūgiri.

The younger gentlewomen gave her emissary a lovely welcome. In answer their mistress spread a bed of moss in a box lid, dotted the moss with mighty boulder pebbles, and planted in it a five-needled pine[84] to which she tied,

> *"They are trifling things, fall leaves scattered on the wind: I would have you see*
> *in the pine gripping the rock the truest color of spring."*

Close inspection of the pine among its rocks revealed exceedingly fine workmanship. Her Majesty was delighted by this evidence of the sender's quick and searching wit, and her gentlewomen praised it, too.

"She has you, you know," Genji remarked, "with this message of autumn leaves. You must answer her properly in the season of spring flowers. I wonder whether the way you spoke ill of autumn leaves just now may not offend the Tatsuta Lady—your answering poem would have greater force if you had retreated and sought refuge under the blossoms." Giving forth as he did a youthful charm that unfailingly captivated those dear to him, he brought his home ever closer to his ideal. Back and forth the messages flew.

The lady at Ōi decided that she who mattered so little might slip in unnoticed once the mighty were settled, and she arrived in the tenth month.[85] Genji saw to it that both her furnishings and her arrival itself should be a credit to her. For her daughter's sake he made little distinction in protocol between her and the others, and he gave her a thoroughly dignified welcome.

---

84. Apparently artificial.
85. The tenth lunar month is the first of winter, her season.

22

TAMAKAZURA

The Tendril Wreath

Tamakazura resists translation, but the choice made here is "tendril wreath." The word became the chapter title and Tamakazura's traditional name because Genji uses it to refer to her in a poem late in the chapter:

"Yes, my love lives on, just as it did long ago; yet, O tendril wreath, say what long and winding stem led you all the way to me!"

RELATIONSHIP TO EARLIER CHAPTERS

"The Tendril Wreath" overlaps with the later part of "The Maidens." It begins early in the year when Genji is thirty-five and continues, past the end of "The Maidens," to the end of that year.

PERSONS

His Grace, the Chancellor, Genji, age 35

Ukon, Murasaki's gentlewoman, formerly Yūgao's

Yūgao's nurse

The young lady, Yūgao's daughter, called Fujiwara Ruri-gimi by Ukon, 21 (Tamakazura)

The nurse's husband, the Dazaifu Assistant (Dazai no Shōni)

The Audit Commissioner, Tamakazura's suitor, about 30 (Taifu no Gen)

Hyōtōda, the Bungo Deputy, eldest son of the Dazaifu Assistant

The second son

Ateki, now Hyōbu, younger daughter of the Dazaifu Assistant

Her elder sister

The innkeeper at Tsubaichi

Sanjō, Tamakazura's gentlewoman

The priest at Hasedera

Genji's lady, 27 (Murasaki)

Genji's daughter, 7 (Akashi no Himegimi)

The lady of the northeast quarter of Rokujō, the lady of summer (Hanachirusato)

The Captain, 14 (Yūgiri)

The safflower (Suetsumuhana)

Despite the passing months and years he had not forgotten someone he loved even now, though she was gone like dew from off a twilight beauty, and after his wide experience of many ladies' hearts and ways he only wished that she were still alive. He remained fond of Ukon, who although unremarkable in herself reminded him of her and who counted now among his most long-serving and familiar gentlewomen. She had waited on the mistress of his west wing ever since his move to Suma, when he had sent his women there, and she had been valued there for her quickness and discretion. At heart, though, she knew that her mistress would have equaled the lady from Akashi in Genji's esteem, if she had lived, and that considering how long he went on tactfully caring even for women who meant little to him, she, too, although hardly among the great, would certainly have moved by now to his Rokujō estate; and this caused her sorrow and regret.

Ukon had kept Genji's secret. She had never discovered the fate of the little girl left in the western district of the City and, in deference to his warning to protect his name, since it was all over now anyway, she had not even undertaken to make inquiries. Meanwhile, the nurse's husband had been named Dazaifu Assistant, and his household had gone down with him to his post. So it was that in her fourth year the girl went off to Tsukushi.

Her nurse wept day and night with longing to know where her mistress had gone. She addressed all the buddhas and gods in prayer and hunted in every likely place, but she learned nothing at all. Very well, then, she thought, there is no help for it; at least I have her daughter to preserve her memory. What a shame it is for this little girl to have to come so far with us on so unworthy a journey! She wanted to get word to the girl's father, but the right moment never seemed to come.

"We don't know where her mother has gone, and what we would say if he were to ask?" she and her women reminded each other in the meantime.

"She has had hardly anything to do with him, after all, and anyway, he would only worry if he kept her."

"I am afraid he would never let us take her away if he knew."

So the decision was made. Still, the little girl was already proud and hand-

Ship

some, and her nurse felt very sorry when she took her aboard a ship wholly unequipped to receive her, and the ship rowed away. The girl in her childish way still
remembered her mother, and her nurse's tears flowed on and on whenever she asked
whether they were going to Mummy now. Her own daughters missed the lady, too,
and she had to keep admonishing them, and herself as well, that they were endan-
gering the voyage.[1]

"My lady was so young at heart—I wish we could have shown her all this!"
one daughter said while they passed endless beautiful scenes; but the other was
thinking longingly of the City, and she replied, "If my lady were alive now, we
would not be going away!" Heads together in sad envy of the returning waves,[2] they
wept to hear the boatmen sing in their rough voices, "How far we have come, and
with what heavy hearts!"

> *"What loves do they mourn, that our stalwart boatmen, too, should with sad voices*
> *sing their way along the shore of yonder Ōshima Isle?"*

> *"On the trackless seas that stretch behind and ahead into the unknown,*
> *where, alas, are we to seek the lady for whom we long?"*

So each, "banished to the wilds,"[3] gave voice to what was in her heart.

"I shall not forget," the nurse repeated at every breath as they rounded Cape
Kane,[4] and once they were there, she only wept the more to think how very far
they had come. Night and day her mistress's little daughter was her darling. At rare
intervals she even dreamed of her mistress, and she would see that same woman[5] be-

1. Because tears aboard ship invite misfortune.
2. *Ise monogatari* 8 (section 7): "My heart so longs to cross the distance I have come: with what envy I
watch the waves as they return!"
3. *Kokinshū* 961, by Ono no Takamura: "I never thought to fall so low, banished to the wilds, as to draw a
fisherman's line and take fish from the sea!"
4. Kane no Misaki, on the north coast of Kyushu. "I shall not forget" is from *Man'yōshū* 1234, a poem of
thanks to a sea deity on safely passing this perilous cape: "Though I have passed the mighty Kane no Misaki, I shall not forget the august Shiga Deity."
5. The woman Genji had seen beside Yūgao on the night of Yūgao's death.

side her and feel so oppressed and ill afterward that she knew with anguish that her mistress was no longer alive.

The Dazaifu Assistant was due to go back up again, now that his term of office was over, but it was a long voyage, and he was too worried about his lack of men and means to leave right away. Then he fell gravely ill, and when he felt death approaching, he considered his little charge, who was ten by now and frighteningly pretty. "What will become of her if I am to leave her, too? It seemed to me very wrong for her to grow up in this unfortunate place, but I meant to take her to the City in time, to inform those who would wish to know about her, and to see her worthily settled, since all the possibilities the City offers encouraged high hopes; and now I am to end my life here after all!" He left his three sons this injunction: "Think of nothing else but taking this young lady back to the City. Never mind your obligations to me."[6]

None of his household staff knew whose child she was, for he had described her as a granddaughter whose upbringing had fallen to him. He had never let anyone see her and had looked after her with great care. His sudden death was so cruel a blow that his wife wanted only to leave, but he had many local enemies whose machinations she feared,[7] and while strangely unreal years went by, her charge grew up into a young lady, one not only more beautiful than her mother but, perhaps because of what she owed to her father, of exquisite distinction. In her person she was perfectly sweet and poised. A great many country gallants set about courting her when the rumor of her quality spread, but no one in the family took any notice, since the very notion was an offense.

"Yes," her nurse explained to all and sundry, "she has looks enough, but there is something too wrong with her for me to give her away in marriage; I mean to make a nun of her instead, and to keep her with me the rest of my life."

"They say the late Assistant's granddaughter is defective," the rumor went round. "What a shame!"

This was unnerving talk. "We *must* get her to the City somehow and let His Excellency her father know about her," her nurse said. "I doubt that he will ignore her, considering how sweet he thought her when she was little." In desperation the nurse addressed many prayers to the buddhas and gods.

Her sons and daughters had formed their own ties to the place and settled down, and although she herself at heart was as eager to go as ever, the City had indeed begun to seem very far away. The better she came to know the world, the more disappointing she found it, and she began to do the three yearly retreats.[8] By twenty the young lady was fully mature and strikingly lovely.

The province where they lived was Hizen. Everyone there with any preten-

---

6. The memorial services to be performed at regular intervals after a person's death.

7. Perhaps her husband's scrupulousness (in matters of taxation, for example) angered the local powers and ensured that he derived no personal profit from his tour of duty. His enemies could easily make travel impossible for his widow.

8. Fasting and purification, and prayers for a happier rebirth, during the first fifteen days of the first, fifth, and ninth months.

sion to quality had heard about the Assistant's granddaughter and was nonetheless pursuing her, even now, to the point of being a complete nuisance. One of them, a man known as the Audit Commissioner, had relations throughout Higo, where he enjoyed a high reputation. He was a powerful warrior, but his fierceness included a streak of gallantry as well, and he liked to collect pretty women. "Never mind what is wrong with her," he said when he heard about the young lady. "I do not care how bad it is. I shall look after her and ignore it."

His insistent suit alarmed her nurse. "No, no," she had him told, "it is impossible. She cannot listen to any such talk; she is about to become a nun." This only aroused him further, however, and it brought him straight to their province. There he called her sons together.

"If things go my way, my power is yours to command," he told them, and two of them were inclined to yield.

"At first we agreed that this would be sadly beneath her," they said, "but he is someone we all could trust to do right by us. Do you think we could go on living here if he were to turn against us? She is of high lineage, yes, but she means nothing to her father, and what good does it do her if no one knows? By now she is lucky to have him so keen. This is what she must have come for, all the way down to these wilds. What is the point of her running off to hide? There is no telling what he may do if he gets his back up, and he will not take no for an answer."

Their warnings shocked the Bungo Deputy, the eldest of the three. "That is wrong, and it is a very great shame. Remember what our father told us. We must find some way to take her up to the City after all."

The daughters wept with dismay. "Her mother wandered off and disappeared without a trace," they cried, "and when the least we can do for her is to make sure she has the life she deserves, why, the very idea that she should spend it with someone like that!" But the suitor in question knew nothing of this. He fancied himself a fine gentleman and blithely plied her with letters. His writing was not all that bad, and he was very pleased with them, despite his marked country accent, what with the colored Chinese paper he used[9] and the penetrating incense with which he perfumed it.

He prevailed on the second son to bring him to the house. A tall and imposingly massive man of about thirty, he was not unsightly, but his attitudes were repellent and his brusque manners painful to watch. His color made him the picture of health, but his voice was remarkably gruff, and his jargon was hard to follow. This was all in all a most unusual spring evening, considering that the "night gallant"[10] properly comes in secret, under cover of darkness. Although perhaps not autumn, the moment certainly qualified as "strange."[11] The young lady's "grandmother" received him in the hope of avoiding wounding his feelings.

---

9. A rare commodity in the City, although perhaps slightly easier to get in Kyushu, where the trading ships from China docked.

10. *Yobai,* a custom by no means confined to the amorous adventures of gentlemen like Genji. It seems to have been common in the countryside as well.

11. A joking allusion to *Kokinshū* 546: "All times are equal for I love you in them all, yet, on an autumn evening, O how strangely more!"

"The late Assistant was such a kind and dignified gentleman that I looked forward to getting on with him," he began, "and I was very sorry indeed when he passed away before I could bring up with him the matter I have at heart. I have let nothing today prevent me from rushing to your side, determined as I am to place myself, in his stead, entirely at your service. I understand that the young lady who resides here belongs to an exceptional lineage, and that therefore I hardly deserve her. Your humble servant will always look up to her in his heart, and he will forever hold her above him. Madam, your manifest reluctance no doubt springs from disapproval of what you have heard concerning my involvement with many unworthy women, but I ask you, would I ever wish to honor the likes of *them*? No indeed, and my darling will never be less to me than the Empress herself!" It was a vigorous speech.

"Oh, no, not at all! Your words are most gratifying, but you see, she must have the very worst of karma, because she privately grieves that a delicate reason forbids her ever to marry at all, and her unhappiness, I assure you, is painful to witness."

"Think nothing of it! Be she blind or broken-legged, I myself shall see to it that she is healed, for I have the gods and buddhas of this province at my beck and call." After this proud declaration he insisted on deciding the day.

"This month is the last of the season, though," she countered, in a successful appeal to country ways.[12]

On leaving the house he paused a while in thought, for he wished to deliver himself of a poem:

> "*If to my darling I should ever prove untrue, I solemnly swear*
> *by the god of the mirror of the shrine of Matsura.*[13]

Now, *that* is a poem,[14] if I say so myself," he declared, grinning, with what colossally naive innocence!

The nurse, whose head was spinning, was not up to a reply, but her daughters said when she asked them for one that they were even dizzier than she; and so, after blank ages, this, in a trembling voice, was the best she could do:

> "*If my heartfelt prayers offered up year after year should now come to naught,*
> *I might easily condemn the god and the mirror, too.*"

"Just a moment! What was that you said?" All at once he loomed before her, and she paled with fear.

---

12. The present month is the third, the last of spring. Perhaps it was thought unlucky to marry in the last month of a season.

13. The poem does not follow; something like "I will accept the punishment of the gods" is missing between its two halves. Its great virtue, for the speaker, seems to be that it gets in a wordplay (on *kakete*), according to accepted poetic practice. This divine mirror is enshrined in the Kagami Jinja ("Mirror Shrine") in Matsura, now Karatsu, on the north coast of Kyushu.

14. Instead of *uta* (the light Japanese word) he uses the hard Chinese-style *waka*, which here reeks of schoolbookish effort.

Her daughters nonetheless beamed at him gamely through their daze. "The young lady is simply not like other people, you see," they earnestly explained.

"Of *course* it would be a great disappointment if things were not to turn out as you wish, but I am afraid my poor mother is very muddled in her old age and got it all wrong."

"Oh. I see, I see!" He nodded. "No, no, the turn of phrase was delightful! Here in the provinces we are all supposed to be bumpkins, but we have a lot more to us than that! What is so wonderful about people from the City? I know all about this. Don't you go looking down on me!" He had a good mind to give them another, but perhaps that was too much for him, because he went away.

The nurse had it out with her eldest son, in fear and despair at seeing the second won over. He remained at a loss, protesting that no, they could *not* let the fellow have her, but the only two brothers he had were against him because he would not fall in with the man, insisting that they would be caught if they made an enemy of him and that anything they tried might only make things worse. Meanwhile, the young lady herself was in a pathetic state and quite naturally sure that she would rather die. All this decided her nurse to take drastic action after all. Her two daughters left their husbands of many years and set off with her. The one once called Ateki, now known as Hyōbu, slipped out with her by night to board their ship.[15] They made good their escape while the Audit Commissioner was back in Higo, from where he planned to return on the appointed day, the twentieth of the fourth month.

The elder sister had so many relations there by now that she could not go with them. When the time came for sad farewells, and the younger one knew that she might never see her sister again, she realized how little it troubled her to leave what had been her home so long. The only regret that turned her gaze backward was for the coast before the Matsura shrine and for the elder sister she was leaving.

> *"On and on we row, in our wake Ukishima[16] and our troubles past,*
> *yet we are still sick at heart, for we know not where we go,"*

she said, and the young lady:

> *"Down endless wave lanes our ship speeds on to a goal still invisible,*
> *while I drift at the wind's will through a broad sea of sorrows."*

She lay facedown, overcome by a mood of helplessness.

They were afraid he might come after them, determined to have his way, when news of their flight got about, as it was certain to do, and so they had asked

---

15. Both sisters accompany their mother and Tamakazura to the port of Matsura, but only Hyōbu, the younger, sails with the party. Her "name" is apparently derived from a title once borne by her eldest brother, who (as a later passage makes clear) was then a minor functionary in the Bureau of War and known as Hyōtōda ("the Bureau of War official who is a Fujiwara eldest son").

16. The location of Ukishima is uncertain, but its overtones suit the context, since *uki* means both "float" and "sad." Tamakazura's poem, below, incorporates the same wordplay.

pointedly for a fast ship that a following wind now sped on with perilous swiftness. They safely passed the Thundering Coast.[17] "Is that pirates, that little ship speeding this way?" a voice cried; but they could not help fearing, more than swashbuckling pirates, the idea of that terrible man in hot pursuit.

> *"With our misfortunes stirring a thunderous storm here within my breast,*
> *there is nothing frightening about the Thundering Coast!"*[18]

The news that they had reached Kawajiri let them breathe a little more easily. As before, the sailors' uncouth voices were very moving as they sang, "Driving on to Kawajiri from Karatomari."[19] The Bungo Deputy sang pensively with them. "We have forgotten our dear wives, our children," the song went on, and he thought, Yes, I have left them all behind, and what will become of them? The men who might have stood by them have come with us, every one. What might he still do in his hatred of me, even after he has hounded them from their homes? Ah, he reflected now that he felt some degree of relief, what a fool I was to pick up and go without giving them a thought. He shed weakling tears as he continued to dwell on their sad plight, and he hummed, "In vain I abandoned wife and children in a barbarian land."[20]

Hyōbu heard him, and her thoughts ran in the same vein. Yes, she said to herself, I have done a strange thing. What can I have meant by suddenly betraying the man who has been my support all those years and running away? Call it "going home," perhaps, but I really have no home to go to, no friends or relations to turn to. All for just one young lady I have left the land where I lived so long to drift at the mercy of wind and wave, and I can do nothing to help myself—what, then, could I ever do to help *her*? Blank despair overwhelmed her, but it was too late. All they could do was to hasten on into the City.

They looked up old acquaintances of theirs who still lived on Kujō[21] and secured lodgings with them, but even if this was indeed the City, it was not an area where the best people lived, and they fretted among shabby shopwives and peddlers until autumn came on. They were soon despairing often over what they had done and what lay before them. Even their trusted Bungo Deputy felt like a waterbird caught on dry land. Lost and at loose ends in these unfamiliar surroundings, he could not face going back, and yet he rued the folly of leaving; and meanwhile, the men who had followed them were all fleeing to relations elsewhere or returning to their province.

It saddened him to hear his mother lamenting day in and day out that they

---

17. Hibiki no Nada: the Harima coast, which included Akashi. It was apparently considered especially dangerous. They are approaching the site of modern Osaka.

18. Presumably spoken by the nurse.

19. Apparently from a folk song. Karatomari ("Korea port" or "China port") was probably along the Harima (Hyōgo Prefecture) coast. Kawajiri is the mouth of the Yodo River, which empties into Osaka Bay.

20. A line from a poem by Bai Juyi (*Hakushi monjū* 0144). The speaker, taken captive by the Tibetans, escaped at last only to be mistaken by the Chinese for a Tibetan and sent off to a penal colony.

21. "Ninth Avenue," one of the major, numbered east-west avenues of the City, in its distant southern, or "lower," sector.

Market women

would never manage to settle down. "But why?" he said. "I am quite comfortable here. Surely there is nothing wrong with vanishing hither or yon in our young lady's service. How would we feel if we had just abandoned her to the likes of *him,* no matter how well off we might have been?" He wanted to console her. "It is for the gods and buddhas to lead her where she should properly go. The Yawata Shrine, not far from here, is the same as the ones down there at Matsura and Hakozaki,[22] where you prayed before. You addressed many appeals to them when we were leaving. Now that we are back in the City, you must go straight there and give thanks for the aid we have received." So he started her off on a journey to Yawata, where he found someone familiar with the place; and he located a saintly monk his father had once known as a temple secretary,[23] and who was still there. Thus he brought their pilgrimage to a successful close.

"Next there are the buddhas, among whom Hatsuse is famous even in Cathay for vouchsafing the mightiest boons in all Japan.[24] Hatsuse will certainly be quick to confer blessings on our lady, since she has always lived in our own land, however far away." He had her set out again.

He had purposely decided that they should walk.[25] The unfamiliar experience was very distressing and painful to her, but she did as she was told and walked on in a daze, calling out to the buddha,[26] What sins burden me, that I should wander this way through the world? If you have pity on me, take me to where my mother is, even if she is no longer on earth, and if she still lives, show me her face! She did not remember her mother at all, and she had spent her life merely sighing for her sadly, but her desperate state now redoubled her misery. In this condition she stumbled

---

22. The Yawata Shrine is Iwashimizu Hachiman on Otoko Yama, immediately southwest of the City. The speaker believes that the same deity is honored in all three places. (The language makes no distinction between a deity and the structure in which the deity is honored.) However, while the shrine at Hakozaki, on the north coast of Kyushu, is dedicated to Hachiman, the shrine at Matsura is not.

23. A *goshi* (a second-level temple administrator) at Iwashimizu Gokurakuji, the Buddhist temple associated with the Iwashimizu Hachiman Shrine.

24. Hatsuse is the place-name associated with Hasedera, a temple in the mountains roughly east of Nara. Hasedera is dedicated to Eleven-Headed Kannon (Jūichimen Kannon). In Japan as in the Catholic world, particular sacred images could be revered as having special powers, and the Kannon of Hasedera made the temple a major pilgrimage center.

25. The forty-five miles from Kyoto to Hasedera could be covered in two days on foot and in three by ox carriage. Since a noble lady seldom walked any distance, this pilgrimage must indeed have tested Tamakazura's endurance. However, walking conveyed greater piety than going by carriage.

26. The Kannon of Hasedera.

into Tsubaichi[27] more dead than alive, at the hour of the Serpent on their fourth day.

What she had done could be barely called walking, and they had helped her as well as they could, but her feet hurt so much that she could not move, and they had no choice but to rest. The party consisted of their trusty Deputy, with two archers and three or four pages, and the three ladies in deep hats, accompanied by some sort of chamber-pot cleaner and two old women. There were very few of them, and they kept to themselves. They took this opportunity to provide themselves with altar lights and so on, and meanwhile the sun began to sink lower in the sky.

Meal on a tray

"I have other people coming. What are *you* doing here?" their host, a cleric,[28] grumbled to their dismay. "These maids do whatever they please!" Another party did indeed arrive.

They, too, seemed to be on foot. There were two noble ladies and apparently a large number of servants, both men and women. Some fine-looking gentlemen, too, were supervising the leading of four or five horses, and they were taking care to pass unnoticed. The cleric, who was determined to put them up, went about scratching his head. The party already there could not change inns, whatever sympathy they might feel, so they tried to help by moving to the back or to other rooms, or to one side. A cloth panel[29] screened off the young lady. The new arrivals seemed to feel quite at home. Both parties were discreet and did what they could not to disturb each other.

In point of fact the party was that of Ukon, who for ages had been longing in tears for her first mistress. She felt more and more awkward and out of place as the years went by, and she had been making this pilgrimage regularly.[30] After setting out readily enough, since she was quite used to it, she was tired after all from walking and was half lying down when the Bungo Deputy came up to the cloth panel beside her, personally carrying a tray—food, presumably. "Please give this to my lady," he said. "I am extremely sorry, but there is no meal stand for her."

She must be above us, whoever she is, Ukon thought, and she peered through a gap. It seemed to her that she had seen the man before, but she could not place him. She had known him when he was very young, and by now he was so much darker and heavier that after all the intervening years she did not recognize him.

"Sanjō," he called, "my lady wants you"; and she knew the woman who answered him, too. She had served Ukon's own mistress, in fact so long and so inti-

27. At the foot of Mount Miwa, about two and a half miles short of Hasedera and a customary stopping place for pilgrims. She arrives about midmorning.
28. The place is probably a temple as well as an inn.
29. *Zejō*, a long curtain suitable for partitioning a room.
30. In the hope of coming across Tamakazura.

mately that, as Ukon now realized with a strong impression of dreaming, she was one of those who had gone with their mistress to the house where she went into hiding. Ukon was extremely eager to know who her present mistress was, but the arrangements did not allow her to see. Very well, she thought, I shall simply have to ask her. That man must be the one I used to know as Hyōtōda. I wonder whether my lady's daughter is there. She called excitedly across the panel to Sanjō, but Sanjō, too busy eating to come, was impatient enough to be quite annoyed.

"I do not remember *you,*" Sanjō finally said. "How strange that someone from the City should recognize a servant who has spent the last twenty years in Tsukushi! Are you sure you are not thinking of someone else?" She came closer. She wore her gown over countrified softened silk, and she had put on a great deal of weight.

Ukon felt more and more acutely conscious of her own age. "Look at me again." She thrust her face past the cloth. "Do you know me now?"

Sanjō clapped her hands together. "Why, it's *you!* Oh, how wonderful, how wonderful! Where have you come from? Is my lady with you?" She burst into dramatic sobs.

The memory of knowing her as a girl made Ukon painfully aware of all the years that had passed since they had last met. "First, though, is Nurse with you? What happened to my lady's little girl? And Ateki?" She said nothing about their mistress herself.

"They are all here! My lady's daughter is grown up now. But I must tell Nurse!"

They were all astonished. "I must be dreaming!" the nurse exclaimed. "How extraordinary to find again someone I had thought was so utterly hateful!" She came up to the cloth panel.

They cleared away the cloth and everything else, such as screens and so on, that separated the two parties, but at first they could only weep speechlessly. "What happened to my lady? All these years I have been praying and praying just to dream of where she is, but we were much too far away to get any news at all, and that made me so sad, I wished I had never grown old. The little girl she left behind was very sweet and dear, though, so I lingered on, because I was afraid she would hold me back on the path to the afterlife."

Ukon knew even less how to answer her now than she had long ago, when it happened. "Come, come," she replied, "there is no point in my telling it all to you now. Our mistress is dead." As soon as she spoke, the three of them[31] dissolved in tears.

The Bungo Deputy now roused his party to pack up their altar lights and be on their way, since the sun was going down, and they parted in greater agitation than ever. Ukon suggested going together, but both felt that that would only arouse their attendants' curiosity, so they set off without even telling the Deputy what was going on and quite content to dispense with any formality on either side. Ukon secretly noted a fine-looking young lady in the other party, very discreetly dressed and wearing something like an early-summer shift over her hair, which

31. Ukon, the nurse, and presumably Sanjō.

looked dazzlingly beautiful through the thin silk. The sight struck her as touching and sad.

It was the more seasoned walker who reached the temple first. The others arrived during the evening service, nursing their lady along as best they could. The place was crowded with noisy pilgrims. Ukon's space was near the altar, to Kannon's right.[32] The priest[33] looking after the others had put them a good way off toward the west, perhaps because he hardly knew them yet, and this prompted Ukon to consult those around her and to invite the young lady to join her after all. She explained things to the Deputy, left the men where they were, and brought the young lady back with her.

"I myself am of no importance," she said, "but since I serve the present Chancellor, I can be sure of escaping any unpleasantness even when I travel this discreetly. The miserable fools in places like this look down quite shamelessly on country people." She would have liked very much to go on talking, but what with the din from the service itself, the noise inspired her to salute Kannon instead. She said in her heart, "I have always told you I longed to find her, and now that I have caught a glimpse of her, my prayer is answered. His Grace seems very anxious to find her. Please let him know, and please grant her happiness."

Country people had gathered there from everywhere, and likewise the provincial Governor's wife.[34] Sanjō was jealous of her magnificence, and she prayed in dead earnest, her palms pressed to her forehead, "Most Merciful One, I ask of you only this: if my lady is not to marry the Dazaifu Deputy, then let her be the wife of the Governor of this province! That will benefit all of us, too, and we will not be ungrateful!"

Ukon thought this a very ill-omened prayer. "What a country girl you are! What consideration do you think the Captain[35] enjoyed all those years ago? Why, now that he is a Minister, with the realm at his beck and call and certain to think the world of our mistress, do you imagine she will end up as a provincial Governor's wife?"

"Hold your tongue!" Sanjō retorted. "Spare me your Ministers! Do you mean to say when her ladyship from the Dazaifu Deputy's mansion went on pilgrimage to Kanzeonji,[36] her train was less imposing than an Emperor's? What are you talking about?" She went on praying, her palms to her forehead as before.

The party from Tsukushi planned to remain on retreat for three days. Ukon, who had not meant to stay that long, called a priest to let him know that she would do so. She looked forward to a quiet talk with the young lady. Since the priest was likely to know all about what she had been putting in her petitions,[37] she told him

---

32. Assuming that the Kannon image of Hasedera faced south then as now, both parties are to its right, but Tamakazura's is much farther away.

33. *Oshi*, a priest whose profession included assisting pilgrims to a sacred site. The two parties seem to have different *oshi*.

34. Yamato Province, where Hasedera is located.

35. Tō no Chūjō's title when Tamakazura was conceived.

36. The most important temple in Kyushu, and often paired in popular faith with Hasedera. Both are dedicated to Kannon.

37. *Miakashi-bumi*, a written prayer formally offered up by suitably commissioned priests.

as a matter of course, "This is for Fujiwara Ruri-gimi,[38] as usual. Mind you pray carefully. I recently found her, you see. I shall offer my thanks later on." Those who heard her were moved.

"That is very good," the priest replied. "It must be a boon in response to our unceasing prayers."

The services seem to have gone on loudly all through the night.

At dawn the party went down to the lodge of Ukon's priest. They probably meant to have an undisturbed talk. The young lady was admirably embarrassed to be seen so poorly dressed.

"I have seen a great many ladies," Ukon began, "keeping the surprisingly exalted company I do, but I have taken it for granted for years that not one of them could equal my present mistress[39] in looks. The little girl she has now is of course extremely pretty, though, and His Grace looks after her beautifully, too, which makes it a special pleasure to see that my lady here, even so plainly dressed, is every bit as lovely. His Grace has been acquainted with every Consort, Empress, or lesser lady you can imagine ever since his father's reign, and as he tells my mistress, His Majesty's mother and that little girl I mentioned are the ones who remind him what 'a beauty' really means. As to comparing them, I never knew Her Late Eminence, and his daughter is only half grown, so he is imagining what she will be like later on. I still want to know who could stand beside my mistress, though. His Grace, too, clearly feels she is exceptional, though he could not very well include her out loud in his list. 'You are a bold one, staying with *me*!' he teases her. Just the sight of those two adds years to one's life, and I never imagined that looking at anyone else could do the same, but what about our young lady here makes her less worthy? There is a limit, after all—I do think she is remarkable, even if she can hardly give off light from the crown of her head to announce that she is a wonder!"[40] To the old nurse's delight, she contemplated the young lady wreathed in smiles.

"I almost let her beauty go to waste in those thankless surroundings," the nurse replied, "but that seemed too great a shame. I gave up house and hearth, left the sons and daughters who were my hope for the future, set out toward what for me might as well be the unknown, and came up to the City. My dear, do take her straight to where she belongs. You who serve in so great a house surely have opportunities to meet His Excellency her father. Please speak to him and see to it that he acknowledges her."

The embarrassed young lady remained turned away from them.

"Goodness no, I am nobody myself, but when my lord calls me for one reason or another, I often wonder aloud to him what can have become of her, and he listens. He says, 'I *do* want to find her, you know. If you happen to hear anything . . .' "

"His Grace is of course a fine gentleman, but I gather he has some very distinguished ladies, and I wish you would get in touch with her actual father first."

---

38. Tamakazura, a Fujiwara because her father is one. Ruri-gimi ("Miss Ruri") is either Tamakazura's childhood name or a pseudonym invented by Ukon.
39. Murasaki.
40. Unlike a buddha, whose enlightenment, according to the Ryōgon-kyō, is revealed in this way.

In reply Ukon told her what had happened. "My lord mourned her too much to get over it, you know, and he has said ever since, 'I should so love to have *her* instead! I regret having so few children, and I could put it about that I had found one of my own.' My poor judgment made me overly cautious, and I let too much time go by without undertaking to look for her. Then I heard your husband's name mentioned in connection with an appointment as Dazaifu Assistant, and I actually caught a glimpse of him on the day when he went to take leave of His Grace, but I could not speak to him. I assumed, though, that you must have left her at the house on Gojō, the one with the twilight beauties. But how awful! To think she might have been condemned in the end to stay in the country!"

They talked on through the day, now reminiscing, now calling the Name or chanting the sutras.

They looked down from where they were on the throng of pilgrims. Before them ran the Hatsuse River.

> *"If I had not come all this way to find the place where twin cedars stand,*
> *here by the Furu River, would I ever have met you?*[41]

How happy this has made me!" Ukon told the young lady, who replied through most becoming tears,

> *"What in the old days the Hatsuse River was, that I hardly know,*
> *but my tears of joy flow on, meeting you this way today."*

She really is quite lovely, but how blemished she would still be if she were boorishly inept! How *did* she manage to grow up this way? Ukon felt joy and gratitude toward the nurse. Her mother was all youth and innocence, ever pliant, ever yielding, but *her* manner shows daunting distinction and pride. She certainly gives one a high opinion of Tsukushi, although everyone else I know from there seems to be straight from the country. No, I just do not understand it!

At dark they all went up to the temple, and they spent the next day there at their devotions. The autumn wind sweeping up from the valley below was chill against the skin, but their elated hearts teemed with many thoughts. They had feared they might never hold their heads high again, but now that they had heard from Ukon about their young lady's father, and about the way he assured success even for the least of his children, by any mother, they and especially the young lady herself had come to believe that even the lowliest need not be afraid.

Before leaving they exchanged news about where they lived, since it would have been too awful to lose touch again. There was no great distance between them, since Ukon's house was close to the Rokujō estate, and they felt that this favored their keeping in touch.

---

41. *Kokinshū* 1009 (not a *tanka* but a slightly longer *sedōka*): "By the Hatsuse River, the Furu River through the years the twin cedars stand, and may we meet again, where the twin cedars are." "Furu" seems to be another name for the Hatsuse River.

Ukon hurried to Rokujō in the hope of finding a moment to drop a hint of all this to His Grace. The vastness of the place struck her as soon as she drove in through the gate, and she saw a throng of carriages coming or going. This was a jade palace to daunt and dazzle a humble visitor. That night she did not go to her mistress but lay instead lost in thought.

The next day she was flattered to be summoned specially, by name, from among all the women young or old who had returned from home the previous day. His Grace saw her as well. "What kept you away so long? It is not like you. Proper people sometimes turn about and kick up their heels, I suppose.[42] You must have been having a good time." He was teasing her mercilessly, as usual.

"It has been seven days since I left, my lord, but I do not know very well how I could have been doing *that*. I came across someone I was glad to see, though, off in the mountains."

"And who was that?"

Ukon hesitated to tell him straightaway, because she had not yet said anything to her mistress, and if she were to tell him in private and her mistress to hear of it later on, she might assume that Ukon no longer cared about her. "I shall tell you presently, my lord," she replied, and new arrivals allowed her to break off their conversation.

The lamps were lit. Genji and her mistress were well worth seeing this way, quietly together at home. She must have been twenty-seven or twenty-eight, and she had matured into all the fullness of her beauty. Ukon thought that she had acquired a new bloom even during this short absence. Having found this new young lady so pretty, she had not expected her to suffer from the comparison, and yet—or was she imagining it?—she seemed to see the difference between someone who had been blessed by fortune and another who had not.

Genji was going to bed, and he called her to massage his legs. "I hear the young ones don't like doing this—it's too much work," he remarked. "No, it takes a couple of old people really to get on together."

Everyone laughed discreetly. "That is right! Who could complain about His Grace asking a favor?"

"I wish he were not such a tease, though!"

"My lady might not like the old people getting too cozy with each other!" he joked to Ukon. "This could be trouble—if you ask me, it is not like her to let such a thing pass!" He was so charming and so amusing. His service to His Majesty did not occupy him unduly, and he therefore took life as easily as he pleased, joked a great deal, and so loved baiting the gentlewomen that he teased even his old intimates, like Ukon.

"Who have you come across, then? Have you brought yourself back some sort of holy man?"

"What a thing to say, my lord! No, the person I found is kin to the dew gone so soon from the twilight beauties."

42. Literally, "turn back into colts" (*komagaeru*).

"I see. Yes, you must have been very glad indeed. Where has she been all these years?"

Ukon hesitated to tell him the whole truth. "In a poor mountain village, my lord.[43] Her people are still more or less the same, so we were able to talk over those times. I could hardly bear it."

"Wait, not here in front of somebody who knows nothing about any of this." He was being discreet.

"Oh, do not bother!" Ukon's mistress broke in. "I am much too sleepy to listen!" She put her sleeves over her ears.

"Her looks now: surely she is not as pretty as her mother, is she?"

"I had hardly thought that possible, my lord, but actually, to my eye she has grown to be much prettier."

"How wonderful! *How* pretty, do you think? As pretty as this one?"

"Dear me, no, my lord, not *that* pretty!"

"You seem remarkably pleased with her, though. Well," he added paternally, "I shall not worry about her if she looks like *me*!"

After receiving these first tidings Genji called Ukon back again and again. "Very well, then I shall bring her here. Through the years I have had occasion bitterly to regret losing track of her, and since your news pleases me so much, it would be awfully sad not to, considering that I have been out of touch with her all this time. Why tell His Excellency her father? He has quite enough children to keep him busy as it is, and it might easily turn out to be a mistake for her to join them now, as the least among them. I, on the other hand, have very few, and I can quite well say that I have unexpectedly discovered another. I shall make a great fuss over her and drive the gallants wild."

This sort of talk from him pleased Ukon very much. "As you wish, my lord. If His Excellency were to hear of her, who else but you would be the one to tell him? Your assisting her in one way and another can help redeem the fault of her mother's death."

"You still accuse me, don't you." He smiled, but he was close to tears. "I have thought all these years what a terribly short time she and I had together. I have not loved one of the ladies gathered here as I did her, and I have so regretted that among the many who can still testify to my steadfastness, you were the only one left to remind me of her once she was gone. I never, never forget her, and I would be so happy if she were still alive!"

He sent her daughter a letter. The memory of the hopeless safflower[44] was not reassuring, considering how the young woman had grown up in the country, and he wanted first to see what a letter from her would be like. He adopted a serious, correct tone and wrote along the edge, "The one who so addresses you

---

43. Ukon implies by omission that Tamakazura was at least not too far from the City.
44. Suetsumuhana.

you do not yet know, but you need only ask and will quickly learn
what lasting bond, stem by stem, the Mishima reeds proclaim."[45]

Ukon delivered it herself, and she also passed on what Genji had said. Clothing for the young lady and for all her people came with it.

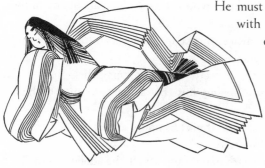

He must have discussed the whole thing with Ukon's mistress, because he had collected these gifts from his main wardrobe and had chosen items distinguished by their color and finish. To country people they were nothing short of astonishing.

The least message from her father, even a simple excuse, would have made the young lady very happy, but she seemed distressed and let it be known that she could not possibly join the company of a man she did not even know. However, Ukon explained to her what her moving there would mean, and the others joined in, too, to encourage her.

Woman in a kouchiki dress gown

"His Excellency will hear about you, my lady, of course he will, once you are established there."

"The tie between parent and child is not so easily broken."

"Why, Ukon is no one, and she could not imagine how she would ever find you, and yet the buddhas and gods led her to you, did they not? Obviously, then, in your own case, as long as you and your father remain in good health . . ."

The young lady was also reminded that she must lose no time composing an answer. The idea was mortifying, because she knew how countrified she must seem. Her nurse took out some highly perfumed Chinese paper and made sure she wrote:

"Whence does her stem spring, this unhappy reed whose worth is so very small,
that she has struck such deep root into the sorrows life brings?"

That was all, in faint lines. Her hand was wandering and uncertain, but it had distinction. No, it was not contemptible. Genji felt reassured.

He realized when he considered where she might live that there was no vacant wing in the southeast quarter, and besides, the particularly large staff there meant that she would be far too exposed. Her Majesty's quarter was certainly quiet enough, but there, it occurred to him, she might easily look as though she were in

45. This poem is grammatically continuous with the prose that precedes it. It affirms the lasting tie between Genji and Tamakazura. It is quite difficult; perhaps Genji means it as a sort of test. Mishima Cove (Mishima-e), a spot along the Yodo River between Kyoto and Naniwa, was associated in poetry with densely growing *mikuri* reeds, the many *suji* ("lines") of which introduce, or ornament, the idea of *suji* as "connection" between one person and another.

Her Majesty's service. No, the place was a little out of the way, but he decided to move the library in the west wing of the northeast quarter elsewhere. The lady there[46] would then be sharing her house, but she was so kind and discreet that the two of them would certainly get on. Well, that was decided.

At last Genji told the lady who reigned over his household the whole story of what had happened all those years ago. She reproached him for having kept it locked up in his heart so long.

"You are unjust," he replied. "Could I have simply volunteered a story like that, even about someone still alive? It is only because you are so special to me that I have been candid with you now." The memory had visibly called up great sorrow.

"I had often noted in the case of others, too, how deeply a woman may care, even when the sentiments involved are not that strong, and I had resolved never to indulge in gallantry; but of all the many women I came to know after all, when I ought not to have done so, she is the one I still remember as incomparable for her unfailing sweetness. If she were alive today I would certainly rank her with the lady in the northwest quarter.[47] People are all so different. She lacked spirit and wit, it is true, but how noble and gentle she was!"

"Still, I doubt that she would have held her own with Akashi." She still felt a twinge of jealousy toward that lady; but then, the little girl listening with sweet innocence to their talk was so dear that she changed her mind again, and she decided that he was quite right.

All this was in the ninth month, but the young lady could not possibly move that readily. Her nurse began looking for suitable page girls and young gentlewomen. In Tsukushi she had been able to bring into her charge's service, as the opportunity arose, whatever acceptable women drifted down there from the City, but in the haste and confusion of her departure she had left them all behind, and she did not know any others. In the end the City was so large that she had women from the market find them and bring them to her. She did not tell them anything about whose daughter the young lady was.

Ukon first moved her quietly to her own house on Gojō, where she selected her staff and prepared her wardrobe and so on. She moved to Rokujō in the tenth month.

Genji entrusted her to the lady of the northeast. "Someone I was fond of lost faith in me and hid herself away in a poor mountain village," he explained. "There was a little girl, too, though, and I spent years secretly looking for her, always in vain, until she grew into a woman and at last I had news of her from an unexpected source. I am moving her here, you see. Better late than never, after all.

"Her mother is dead," he continued earnestly. "I know that I asked you to look after the Captain,[48] but surely it was not too great an inconvenience. Please treat her just as you do him. I assume that she shows her country upbringing in many ways. Do teach her what she should know, as the need arises."

---

46. Hanachirusato.
47. Akashi.
48. Yūgiri. This is the first reference to his most recent promotion.

"I see," she answered mildly. "I had no idea that there was anyone like that. How nice! It has been so disappointing for you to have only one daughter."

"Her mother had an extraordinarily gentle character. I have great faith in yours, too, you see."

"It will be a pleasure. The young gentleman I quite properly look after gives me little enough to do."

The women had no idea the new arrival was Genji's daughter. "Who has he gone and rediscovered this time?" they asked each other. "What an impossible collector he is!"

Her party came in three carriages, and having Ukon with them ensured that they did not look like rustics. Genji had provided them with variously patterned silks.

He went straight to see her that evening. Long ago her women had heard often enough of the Shining Genji, but after all their years away from the world they expected nothing special, and the elusive glimpses they had of him through gaps in the curtains, by dim lamplight, left them all but terrified by the vision they saw.

"I see this door is for special visitors only!" he joked to Ukon when she opened it for him. Then he sat down in the aisle room. "What a romantic light! They say a daughter likes to see her father's face—do you not agree?" He slid the standing curtain a little to one side. The young lady was extremely embarrassed and turned away, looking so lovely as she did so that he was very pleased.

"Do give us a bit more light! This is all too genteel."

Ukon turned up the lamp and moved it closer. "You have no modesty!" he chuckled.

Ah, yes, those eyes! How they put all else to shame!

"I mourned you every moment of all the ages you were lost to me," he began in a thoroughly fatherly way, showing no sign of keeping distance between them, "and I feel as though I am dreaming now that I actually have you before my eyes. The past comes flooding back so painfully that I find I do not know what to say." He wiped his eyes. The memories really did affect him. He counted up the years. "Surely no parent and child have ever been parted for so long! What grief that bond brought me! You are no longer of an age to be girlishly shy, and I want to tell you everything that happened! Why are you so silent?" He spoke reproachfully.

Too bashful to speak, she murmured in a youthful voice that reminded him vividly of her mother, "I vanished 'before I could yet stand,'[49] and since then I have never felt more than half alive."

Genji smiled. "Then who else but me will pity your sad fate?" he said. Her reply struck him as not at all unworthy.

He went away after giving Ukon a series of instructions.

Genji was delighted to be so pleased with her, and he told the lady who reigned over his household all about her. "I was all ready to deplore her sad state, considering the way she grew up among mountain rustics, but not at all—she actually impressed me. I must let people know I have a girl like this here and confound

---

49. *Nihon shoki* 66, by Ōe no Asatsuna: "Do his parents not pity him? The Leech Child has reached his third year and cannot yet stand."

those gentlemen—His Highness of War, for example—who are so fond of coming to call. The gallants are all very prim and proper when they turn up, but that is only because there has been no one like that here to set them off. I shall make a great fuss over her. We shall see how gallant they really are."

"You make a strange father. Your very first thought is to get people all worked up. You should be ashamed of yourself."

"Why, yes, I should have fussed over *you* and tested them the same way, if only I had had a mind for it then. What a fool I was! I missed my great opportunity!" He laughed, and she blushed most youthfully and beautifully. Drawing an inkstone near, he jotted down,

> "Yes, my love lives on, just as it did long ago; yet, O tendril wreath,
>   say what long and winding stem led you all the way to me!⁵⁰

Dear me!" he sighed to himself, and he really did strike her as deeply affected by this reminder of someone whom he had once loved very much.

He described the young lady he had discovered to the Captain, too, and he commended her to his affection. The Captain accordingly went to visit her. "You should have called on me, although I am hardly worthy, because I am at your service," he gravely declared. "I can only apologize for having failed to present myself on the occasion of your move." It was a painful speech for those who knew the truth.⁵¹

Her room in Tsukushi had been beautifully done up, but now they saw as plain as day how thoroughly the place belonged to the country. The rooms here were so perfectly appointed, all in the height of fashion, and in dress and looks the gentlemen who now accepted their mistress as family were so dazzling that even Sanjō now despised the Dazaifu Deputy.⁵² The mere memory of the Audit Commissioner's attitude and manner was of course unspeakable. The young lady fully acknowledged all that the Bungo Deputy's devotion meant to her, as did Ukon, who often mentioned it, too. Genji himself selected and trained her household staff, fearing that any laxness might cause trouble. The Bungo Deputy joined them. He who had spent so long in rustic obscurity, and to whom a great lord's residence was normally inaccessible, now all at once was going in and out day and night, doing things and giving orders, and this pleased him very much. His Grace's most kind attention to every detail was greater than one could ever have been entitled to expect.

As the year came to a close, Genji pondered his new arrival's New Year furnishings and the clothing for her gentlewomen, as he did for the greatest of his ladies, although he assumed disparagingly that her upbringing would have given her somewhat rustic tastes. He was meaning to give her these things, but when he saw all the stuffs that the weavers had so eagerly and magnificently supplied, all the long dresses and dress gowns in every color and style, he remarked to the lady of his

---

50. In the original, *tamakazura* ("tendril wreath") functions mainly as an ornament to the *suji* ("stem") that appeared, with its implications of "connection," in Genji and Tamakazura's exchange of poems.
51. Because he speaks as to a sister.
52. Whom she had found so overwhelmingly impressive when she was in Tsukushi (Kyushu).

house, "What a lot there are! We must let everyone have some, so that there are no hurt feelings." He had brought out everything that his wardrobe staff or she herself had made. She was a great expert at this sort of thing, and her dyeing yielded such superb colors and shadings that he viewed her work with wonder. Looking over the beaten silks from both sources, he chose dark purple ones, red ones, and so on, put them in clothing chests or boxes, and with the help of experienced gentlewomen made them up into sets for each recipient.

She looked on. "There is really very little to choose among them. When you make such a gift you have to consider the person's looks. It is all wrong when the costume fails to suit the wearer."

Genji smiled. "You are trying to find out what they all look like, aren't you, without letting on! Well, which would you like for yourself?"

"But I know only what the mirror tells me,"[53] she replied as bashfully as always.

She got a grape-colored dress gown with a nice clear pattern in plum pink, over beautiful plum red; while a cherry blossom long dress over a glossy, softened gown went to her little girl. A sky blue "seaside" dress gown, beautifully woven but discreet in quality of color, over a softened, deep red-violet were for the lady of summer,[54] and he allotted a kerria rose long dress over clear red to the new resident in her west wing.[55] His companion imagined the young lady's appearance, all the while pretending not to watch. As far as she could make out (for Genji had been quite right), she was probably like her father, the Palace Minister: arrestingly handsome but lacking in grace.

Her expression betrayed nothing, but it still upset Genji to see her so intent. "Oh, come," he said, "your assimilation of their clothes to their looks might very well annoy them. These are fine garments, certainly, but their colors go only so far, while looks, even when less than perfect, can sink only so low." With a secret smile he chose for the safflower a willow silk woven with a Chinese tendril pattern,[56] and a very pretty one at that. With disapproval for the personal distinction they suggested she watched him set aside for Akashi a white dress gown, Chinese in flavor, with birds and butterflies flitting among plum branches, over glossy gowns in a deep purple. For the nun of the cicada shell[57] he picked out a very handsome blue-gray dress gown and, from what he had chosen for himself, gowns of yellow and sanctioned rose; and he sent each a letter asking her to wear her gift on the day.[58] Yes, His Grace meant to see how each of them looked.

They replied with great care and rewarded Genji's messenger thoughtfully, but the safflower, who lived in Genji's east pavilion[59] and so should have responded more coyly,[60] being somewhat farther away, instead stuck precisely to convention,

---

53. "I leave it to you."
54. Hanachirusato.
55. Tamakazura. The nature of these garments remains unspecified, except for the first "dress gown" (kouchiki) and the two "long dresses" (hosonaga). Commentators suggest uchiki or kouchiki for all.
56. The "Chinese" probably alludes to Suetsumuhana's antique taste and manners.
57. Utsusemi.
58. The first day of the New Year.
59. The recently built east pavilion of his Nijō residence.
60. More like a mistress than a wife.

like the prim and proper person she was, and laid across the messenger's shoulders an orphan[61] kerria rose gown with horribly grimy sleeves.

Her letter was on thick, heavily perfumed Michinokuni paper, yellowed with age: "Forgive me, but this gift is not necessarily what I would prefer.

> *When I have you on, bitterness is my reward: robe from far Cathay,*
> *I would gladly turn you back, now your sleeves are wet with tears."*[62]

The writing was strikingly out of date. Genji, his face set in a grim smile, simply could not put it down, and she wondered what had got into him. Shock and distress at what his messenger had received gave him so black an expression that the messenger stole away. The gentlewomen were all busily whispering and laughing. Considering how impossible she was, with her hopelessly ancient ways, he wished despairingly that she had given the man nothing at all. His glance was forbidding.

"Those old poets could never give up their 'robe from far Cathay' or their 'sleeves wet with tears,' could they," he said. "Oh, I suppose I am one of them, too. No doubt there is something admirable about keeping to that single rut and never allowing oneself to stray into any freshness of language. Mention being among friends, for instance, and in a formal assembly of poets before His Majesty you must be sure to talk of 'gathering in a ring.'[63] And in those wonderful old contests of love, you could rest assured that your words went trippingly if only you got 'O cruel tormentor!' in at the break."[64] He laughed.

"One can hardly sound very different from them if one absorbs all the manuals and lists of hallowed place-names[65] and never deviates in one's own poems from the words they supply. She once gave me a book that His Highness of Hitachi,[66] no less, had written on utility paper, and it was crammed with bits about 'the essence of poetry' or 'defects to avoid'—so many that I was afraid it might paralyze a simpleton like me forever, so I gave it back. It was just too much trouble. For someone who knows all about poetry, hers is decidedly trite." His amusement at the poor lady's expense was so unkind!

"But why did you return the book?" she asked gravely. "You should have copied it and shown it to our little girl. I had some like that, but the bugs ate them all. People who miss out on them really do not know what they are doing."

"I cannot imagine what good it would have done her. It is never becoming for a woman to identify herself too closely with something she especially likes. Not that one can approve her being wholly ignorant either. To please, a woman need only be poised, calm, and self-assured."

---

61. The garment is *utsuo* ("empty") because it has no shift with it, as it should.
62. Suetsumuhana's poem, a merciless string of trite wordplays, resembles the poem that accompanied her gift of a robe to Genji in "The Safflower." "Turn you back" is meant to convey at once "send back" (to the giver) and "turn inside out," an accepted method of encouraging a dream visit from one's lover.
63. Literally, "the syllables *ma-to-i* are mandatory." *Matoi*, a poetically noble expression, means "sitting in a circle."
64. The "break" (*yasumedokoro*) is the third syllabic unit of the standard, five-unit poetic form.
65. *Utamakura*, place names admissible in poetry.
66. Her father.

He showed no sign of composing a reply.

" 'I would gladly turn you back,' she wrote—it would be quite wrong of you not to return her favor yourself."

He therefore wrote something after all, as kindly as ever. There was no need to try very hard.

"You would, so you say, turn that gift robe inside out—ah, how my thoughts go
to the sleeves you spread alone through night after endless night!

How well I understand!"

23

HATSUNE
The Warbler's First Song

The chapter title, which means "first song [of the year]," is from a poem that the lady from Akashi sends with a New Year's gift to the daughter whom she has not seen since Murasaki adopted her:

"One who through the years has clung to a single hope, O let her today pine no more and hear at least the little warbler's first song!"

RELATIONSHIP TO EARLIER CHAPTERS

"The Warbler's First Song" follows "The Tendril Wreath." "The Tendril Wreath" ends at the close of the year when Genji is thirty-five, and "The Warbler's First Song" takes place in the first month of the following year.

PERSONS

His Grace, the Chancellor, Genji, age 36

Genji's lady, 28 (Murasaki)

Chūjō, Murasaki's gentlewoman

Genji's daughter, 8 (Akashi no Himegimi)

The lady in the summer quarter (Hanachirusato)

The young lady in the west wing, 22 (Tamakazura)

Akashi, 27 (Akashi no Kimi)

Her Highness of Hitachi (Suetsumuhana)

The cicada shell (Utsusemi)

The Captain, 15 (Yūgiri)

The Controller Lieutenant (Kōbai)

The sky on New Year's Day was bright and perfectly cloudless. Within the lowliest hedge fresh green now glimmered amid the snow, a promising haze of buds swathed the trees, and people's hearts, too, naturally seemed to swell with gladness. What delights there were to be seen, then, in the jewel-strewn garden before Genji's residence, and how poorly mere words convey the exquisite beauty of the gardens of his ladies! The one before the spring quarter, where the scent of plum blossoms mingled with the fragrance within the blinds, especially recalled the land of a living buddha, although actually the mistress of the place lived there in peace and quite at her ease. She had given her little girl the pick of the younger women in her service, and the ones who were somewhat older, hence all the more pleasingly dignified in manner and dress, were now clustered here and there, amusing themselves celebrating long life. They had even brought in mirror cakes[1] to praise a year rich with the promise of a thousand more.[2] Just then Genji peered in. "Oh, no, we are caught!" they cried, snatching their hands from the breast fold of their robes.[3]

"How nicely you are all assuring your own good fortune! I expect each of you has her wishes. Tell me some of them. I shall look after praying for them." To their eyes his smiling figure summed up all the felicity of the New Year.

"We were talking about 'even now I see,'[4] my lord, and about what the mirror shows. Why, what could we possibly wish for ourselves?" the outspoken Chūjō[5] replied.

1. Large, round cakes made of glutinous rice (mochii), commonly offered to the gods on festive occasions. There may also be only one.
2. They seem to be singing the congratulatory Kokinshū 356, which is partly quoted in the text: "I have celebrated your living the pine tree's myriad years, for I wish to make my home beneath your millennial shade." "Celebrating length of days" (ha-gatame) was done during the first three days of the New Year; for the occasion one ate a set range of foods that included boar or pheasant, venison or snipe, and sweetfish (ayu).
3. Keeping a hand in the front fold of one's robe (futokorode) seems to have been as casual as a man keeping his hands in his pockets.
4. Kokinshū 1086, which was sung during ha-gatame: "There stands in Ōmi the Mirror Mountain, and even now I see in it my lord's thousand years." Kagami-yama, "Mirror Mountain," is a hill in Ōmi Province, near Lake Biwa.
5. Chūjō was mentioned briefly in "Heart-to Heart" as one of Genji's gentlewomen, and she now serves Murasaki. Her ostensibly irreproachable remark seems to hint secretly at disappointment that Genji is neglecting her and at dismay over her own aging looks in the mirror. The mirror motif is also connected with the "mirror cakes."

Crowds of visitors kept Genji busy all morning long, but toward sunset he prepared to call on his various ladies, for which purpose he dressed and groomed himself so beautifully that he certainly was well worth seeing. "I envied the women this morning, amusing themselves together that way, and I must show my lady one of those cakes," he said and proceeded to sing the celebratory poems for her, sprinkling in a few risqué remarks as well.[6]

> "A thin sheet of ice has melted from the mirror of the garden lake,
> and I see reflected there two incomparable forms,"

he said. They made a truly beautiful couple.

> "Plain as plain can be, I see there in the mirror of the pristine lake
> two forms destined to endure, spotless for ten thousand years."

So they exchanged as sweetly as you please promises to be each other's forever. Today was the day of the Rat[7]—indeed the day on which to look forward to a thousand springs.

When Genji reached his daughter's, the page girls and maids were playing about on the garden hill, uprooting seedling pines, and the young gentlewomen were clearly impatient to join them. They were presenting their mistress with fringed baskets and partitioned boxes apparently sent specially from the northwest quarter.[8] The warbler intriguingly perched on a magnificent branch of five-needled pine must have looked especially significant.[9]

> "One who through the years has clung to a single hope, O let her today
> pine no more and hear at least the little warbler's first song!

The village where none sings . . . ' "[10] the lady had written, and Genji, who understood, was very sorry. He looked as though the ban on ill-omened words would be too difficult for him.[11]

"You must answer her yourself. You cannot keep your 'first song' from her." He provided her with an inkstone and made sure that she wrote. Her engaging looks

---

6. Perhaps having to do with the hope that Murasaki might conceive a child of her own.

7. A rare coincidence of the year's first day and of the first day of the Rat in the first month. On this first day of the Rat, people uprooted seedling pines, a gesture that encouraged longevity, and picked the first spring shoots.

8. Akashi's.

9. Warbler and branch are both artificial; the branch would have been attached to the baskets and boxes. In poetry a warbler (*uguisu*) normally perches on flowering plum, so that its presence on the pine makes a statement: it is the little girl, who has forsaken her natural mother for a new home.

10. "Please let me hear directly from my daughter." The poem plays on *matsu* ("pine" and "wait"), *furu* ("pass [speaking of time]" and "old"), *hatsune* ("first song [of the year]" and "first [day of the] Rat"), and *hikarete*, which alludes to the New Year custom of pulling up seedling pines. "The village where none sings" is from (*Genji monogatari kochūshakusho in'yō waka* 177): "Today at least, O let me hear your first song, for what good is the village where no warbler sings?"

11. He looked as though he would weep. Ill-omened speech and action were taboo in the early days of the New Year.

never wearied even those who saw her day in and day out, and he felt guilty and sad for having kept her mother from her all this time.

"Many years have passed since she was taken from you, yet the warbler still knows that she will not forget the pine whence she first took flight."

Child that she was, she naively did her assignment.[12]

The summer quarter seemed extremely quiet, perhaps because it was out of season, and it nicely conveyed its occupant's[13] unassuming yet dignified mode of life. The passage of time had only brought the two closer together and made them fonder of each other. Genji no longer insisted on intimacy between them. They confined themselves to exchanging unusually affectionate assurances of mutual regard. A curtain separated them, but she was still there when Genji moved it a little to one side. The sky blue was discreet, as he had foreseen, and her hair had known better days. She was quite acceptable as she was, but, he thought, she really ought to wear a wig—anyone else would be put off by looks like hers, though I myself am happy to stay by her this way. What if she had been less faithful and rejected me? Whenever he was with her, he took pleasure above all in his loyalty to her, as well as in her own steadiness of heart. He conversed with her at length about the year just past and then went on to her west wing.

The young lady there had hardly settled in yet, but even so her style of life was pleasant to see. Her pretty page girls made a graceful picture, her gentlewomen were many, and while her furnishings no more than met her needs, handsome accessories, though still incomplete, still added distinction to her surroundings. She herself was dazzling in her perfectly chosen kerria rose. Her brilliance banished every shadow until all was light and loveliness, and one wished only to gaze at her. Her hair thinned out somewhat toward the ends, perhaps because of the trials she had suffered, and it fell with a beautiful, clean grace. She was in all ways so striking that Genji keenly appreciated what he would have missed if he had not known her, and he also understood how little he would be able to let her go. Although accustomed to being with him this way, face-to-face, she felt on reflection that many matters still came between them, matters sufficiently awkward to give her manner a delightful reticence.

"I feel as though I have known you for ages," he said. "It is a pleasure to be with you, because, you see, my wish has been fulfilled. Please make yourself quite comfortable here, and come visiting over there, too, if you like. A certain young person there is taking her first koto lessons, and I hope that you will join her. No one there will look askance at you or show you any disrespect."

"I shall do as you suggest," she replied. It was just the right answer.

As darkness fell, he went on to visit Akashi. When he opened the door from the nearby bridgeway, the breeze from within her blinds wafted him a sweet fragrance, and it seemed to him that *this* was where true distinction was to be found.

---

12. She dutifully played back the vocabulary and wordplays used by her correspondent.
13. Hanachirusato's.

Brazier

She herself was not to be seen. He looked about him, wondering where she might be, and noticed papers and notebooks scattered beside the inkstone. He picked them up and glanced at them. A *kin* rested on a sitting cushion impressively bordered with Chinese brocade, while *jijū* incense smoldered in a strikingly fine brazier, perfuming all around it, and mingled deliciously with *ebi* fragrance.[14] The scattered practice sheets displayed a writing of great interest and originality. Not that she had pretentiously shown off her learning by mixing in a lot of cursive characters;[15] no, she had simply written naturally and pleasingly. The answering poem about the pine had been such a precious treat for her that among various touching old poems he found,

> *"Ah, how rare a joy! From the blossoms where she lives, the little warbler,*
> *tree to tree, has come again to the valley she first knew!*

I had waited so long to hear her song!" There were also lines, like "My house is by the blossoming hill,"[16] which she had written out for her own consolation. Genji's figure as he held the papers, smiling, was enough to put anyone to shame.

He had just wetted a brush and begun to write when she slipped in, and he thought how very discreet she still was in her deportment, indeed how pleasantly so, and how unlike anyone else. She was wearing the white, and the sharp sweep of her hair, thinning modestly as it did toward the ends, so heightened her fondly remembered grace that he spent the night there, despite some apprehension about the trouble he might let himself in for at home. Others, elsewhere, deplored the favor she enjoyed. Some in the southeast quarter objected to her even more strongly.

He returned home long before it was full day. He really did not have to leave while it was still dark, she thought, and her distress lingered on well after he had gone.

She was waiting for him, with what disapproval he could well imagine. "I cannot understand it," he began in a comical effort to placate her, "I simply dropped off and slept on and on like a boy, and you see, you never did anything about waking me up!" When this got no particular answer from her, he lay down, not knowing what else to do, and pretended to sleep, until he rose at last with the sun high in the sky.

---

14. Both the incense types mentioned are blends of various substances, especially fragrant woods.

15. Chinese characters written cursively to represent phonetic sounds.

16. *Kokin rokujō* 4385: "Since my house is by the hill where the plum trees are in bloom, I shall not seldom hear the warbler sing." The warbler among plum blossoms is a frequent motif in spring poetry.

He spent the day hiding from her behind everything that had to be done for the special guests.[17] As usual every last one of the Princes and senior nobles came. There was music, and the gifts and rewards were second to none. Every visitor made it clear that he would not be outdone, but no, not one of them could compare in any way with his host! Many in those days, taken by themselves, made thoroughly worthy gentlemen, but alas, his presence eclipsed them all. Even underlings beneath notice looked carefully to themselves when they visited his estate; no wonder, then, that the young senior nobles, with their particular preoccupation,[18] were somehow keener and more animated than in ordinary years. While the blossom-scented evening breeze at last coaxed the plums in Genji's garden into bloom, instruments rang out nobly in the gathering dusk, and when they struck up "This Lord of Ours,"[19] the clapping of the rhythm sounded simply magnificent. Now and again His Grace joined in, and from "*sakigusa*" on to the end his voice was utterly entrancing. His participation, as anyone could tell, brought color and sound to new heights on any occasion.

Overhearing the noise of horses and carriages, the ladies here and there felt as though they now knew what it must be like inside the still-unopened lotus flower.[20] This was truer yet for those far away in Genji's east pavilion, since less and less claimed their attention over the years; but in thought they likened their home to the mountain retreat untouched by worldly sorrows,[21] for how could they really blame him for neglecting them? In truth they had no other cares. The one who had chosen her devotions pursued them untroubled, while the one whose taste ran to studying *kana* books of every kind had her wish as well, since the provisions Genji had kindly made allowed each to live as she pleased.

He came to see them once the busy days were over. Compassionate regard for Her Highness of Hitachi's rank prompted him to treat her for form's sake as well as he could. The marvelous hair of her youth had suffered through the years, until he was obliged to avert his eyes in sorrow before a profile whiter than any pool below a waterfall. He now saw that the willow robe was indeed a disaster, presumably because of its wearer. She had it on over a dark and lusterless layering, cracklingly starched,[22] and she looked pathetically cold. What could she possibly have done with the layered gowns that had come with it? Only the color of her nose shone undimmed through the mists. Despite himself he sighed and adjusted her standing curtain so as to put it safely between them. She seemed to have no idea why,

17. *Rinji kyaku*, Princes and senior nobles who came to call, generally on the second day of the New Year. They had to be formally entertained.

18. Courting Tamakazura.

19. A simple *saibara* song that begins, "This lord of ours, well deserved are his riches!" The word *sakigusa* (just below, an unidentified plant) occurs toward the middle of the song and recurs as a sort of refrain thereafter.

20. Most souls that went to Amida's paradise were born not onto open lotus flowers but into closed lotus buds, and they had to wait a longer or shorter time for their flowers to open. Meanwhile, they could only distantly hear the music before Amida's throne.

21. *Kokinshū* 955, by Mononobe no Yoshina: "Should one long for a mountain retreat untouched by worldly sorrows, the beloved is a tie that binds one still."

22. Under Genji's gift she should normally have worn three compatible gowns (*uchiki*) instead of this starched monstrosity.

though, and her meekly trusting faith in his loyalty was certainly touching. Poor thing, he said to himself in this rare moment of concern for her, even in things like this she is eccentric. Well, at least she has me! Her voice, too, seemed to tremble with cold as she conversed.

"Do you have anyone to help you dress?" He could not bear it. "In a nice house like this you should make yourself perfectly at home and wear comfortably soft clothes. It is not right to mind only your dress gown."

Dull or not, she replied with a smile, "I am so busy looking after the Daigo Adept,[23] you know, that I have not managed to sew anything for myself. He even took my fur coat, and I have been cold ever since." A fine pair they made, that red-nosed brother and sister!

This is all very well, Genji thought, but she *is* carrying it a bit far. He always ended up being solicitously stern with her. "You did the right thing with the coat—there is nothing wrong with letting a mountain ascetic have something to keep the weather off him. But why not wear seven layers of those white shifts? There is no need to stint on them. If I happen to forget something you need, please let me know. I am not very quick on the uptake, and sometimes I simply miss things. I suppose that is natural enough, what with all the competing demands on my attention."

He had the storehouse opposite[24] opened and made sure that she received silks and damasks. There was nothing neglected about the place, but his absence made it very quiet; the only real pleasure was the trees in the near garden. Genji saw that there was no one to enjoy either them or the scent of the blossoming red plum.

> "Having come again to visit the springtime tree where I lived of old,
>   I observe before my eyes a flower like none seen before!"[25]

He murmured it for himself, and she can hardly have caught his meaning.

He looked in on the cicada shell, too, in her nun's robes. She lived without ostentation in a modest room where she devoted space only to the Buddha, and he was moved to see the evidence of her piety, for the sutra scrolls, the altar ornaments, and even the simple provisions for holy water[26] were intriguingly pretty and showed her even now to be someone of taste. She hid herself so thoroughly behind her charming blue-gray standing curtain that only the ends of her sleeves, with their varied colors,[27] invited him to respond to her presence. His eyes filled with tears.

"I should only have imagined the Isle of Pines," he said, "from a distance."[28]

---

23. Her brother, a monk of Daigoji, a great temple southeast of the City.

24. The one belonging to the main Nijō house.

25. *Hana* ("flower") also means "nose." Genji likens himself to the warbler who visits the flowering plum in spring.

26. A holy-water offering shelf (*akadana*), like a little shrine on stilts, that stood just outside the veranda, with a tub of water, also on a stand, beside it.

27. Under Genji's main gift to her, the same blue-gray as the curtain, she is also wearing the colored gowns that he gave her.

28. "I should only have imagined you and not really come." *Gosenshū* 1093, by Sosei: "Today I see with my own eyes the celebrated Isle of Pines and, indeed, find dwelling here a most discerning *ama*." *Ama* means both "shore-dweller" and "nun." Genji alluded to the same poem in "The Green Branch," the first time he visited Fujitsubo after she had become a nun.

"What a difficult time we have always had with each other! Still, we have at least managed to remain this close, after all."

The nun he addressed seemed moved as well. "It shows how strong a tie we really share, that I should be so wholly in your hands."

"I am sorry that you are now atoning before the Buddha for all those times when you made me suffer so. Do you realize what I went through? Not everyone is as mild as I am, as I am sure you know."

She gathered with acute embarrassment that he must have heard of that miserable business years before.[29] "What atonement could hurt more than your simply seeing what has become of me?" She wept in earnest. By now she was even more profoundly modest than she had been long ago, and the very gulf that yawned between them made it impossible to imagine ever giving her up; yet he could hardly banter with her. Instead he only chatted innocuously about past and present, glancing meanwhile toward where he had just been and wishing that *she* could at least manage this much of a conversation.

Many ladies lived this way under his protection. He looked in on them all, fondly assuring each that despite his long silence he was always thinking of her. "My only care is the parting that no one evades. 'I know not what life remains . . . ' "[30] he would say, and so on. He loved them all, each according to her station. At his rank he might deservedly have swelled with pride, and yet he seldom advertised himself, treating all instead with tact and kindness as place or degree required, so that just this much from him sustained many through the years.

This was a year for the men's mumming. After performing before His Majesty the mummers went to the Suzaku Palace, then on to Rokujō. It was a long way, and they did not get there till daybreak. A perfectly clear moon illumined the garden's thin fall of snow, and there were so many fine musicians among the privy gentlemen in those days that their flutes rang out very beautifully, especially when they played before Genji himself. It had been arranged beforehand that the other ladies should all come and watch, too, and each now occupied a curtained-off space in the east or west wing, or along a bridgeway. The young lady from the west wing[31] came to the south side of the main house, where she met Genji's little girl, and since the mistress of the house was with her, the two conversed with only a standing curtain between them.

Dawn was near by the time the mummers got round to the Empress Mother[32] at the Suzaku Palace, and although Rokujō should have been only a water stop,[33] they received there a lavish welcome that added a great deal to what precedent required. The snow deepened slowly, beneath the wan light of an early-morning moon. What charm could they offer, in their white layerings over soft leaf green,

29. When her stepson forced his attentions on her, after her husband's death, and obliged her to take refuge in religion.

30. *Saneakira shū* 50, by the daughter of Prince Atsuyoshi: "I know not what life remains for me, and yet this heart of mine still believes that I never will forget you."

31. Tamakazura.

32. The Kokiden Consort (Genji's nemesis) of the early chapters.

33. *Mizumumaya*, literally "water, and stabling for the horses" but actually wine and hot rice gruel. Other places along the route were designated as *iimumaya*, where the men got a meal.

when a cold wind from the sighing pine-tree tops threatened only desolation? Nor did the cotton flowers in their headdresses charm the eye—and yet somehow, in that setting perhaps, the effect was so lovely that one felt the years melt away. His Grace's son, the Captain, and the sons of His Excellency the Palace Minister, stood out most agreeably among the rest. Under a gradually lightening sky, amid a scattering of snowflakes in the insistent cold, they swayed as one, singing "Bamboo River" in sweet voices; and what a shame it is that no painting could ever have done them justice! The sleeves, each lovelier than the last, spilling out from where each lady sat, recalled by the brilliance and the beauty of their colors spring brocade glowing through the mists of dawn. It all made a remarkably satisfying spectacle, despite the oddness of the dome caps[34] and the clamor and portentously delivered nonsense of the blessings,[35] none of which could possibly flatter the ear. They all withdrew at last after receiving their gifts of cotton cloth.[36]

Once full day had come, the ladies went home again. Genji slept a little and rose when the sun was high. "The Captain's voice was hardly less good than the Controller Lieutenant's,"[37] he observed. "What an extraordinary number of worthy gentlemen we have nowadays! Those of the past may have excelled in the pursuit of learning, but in the expressive arts they can hardly have outdone the ones we have now. As for the Captain, the reason why I decided to make him a proper official is that I wanted to steer him away from my own foolishness and frivolity, although actually I think he could do with a little more of a roving eye. His outward gravity and composure just make him harder to deal with." He thought very affectionately of his son. "I should so like to have these ladies play together, now that they are all here," he went on, humming "Ten thousand springs."[38] "I must have my own concluding banquet."[39] He took all the instruments out of the bags in which they had been carefully stored, wiped them, and tuned the strings that had gone slack. No doubt his several ladies were attentive to his wishes and disposed themselves in every way so as not to disappoint him.

34. *Kōkoji*, especially high caps worn by the dancers (generally two men of the sixth rank, wearing cloth masks).
35. *Kotobuki*, raucously delivered blessings to invite good crops, increase, and so on in the coming year.
36. Traditional gifts that the mummers received especially at the palace; Genji's magnificence is imperial in character.
37. The Captain is Yūgiri, and the Controller Lieutenant is Tō no Chūjō's son, later known as Kōbai.
38. *Bansuraku*, the refrain of a song always sung by the mummers.
39. *Goen*, the banquet given by the Emperor to the mummers, normally in the second or third month.

24

KOCHŌ

Butterflies

The chapter title, which means
"butterfly" or "butterflies," comes
from an exchange of poems between Murasaki and Akikonomu:

*"Will you look askance, O pine cricket in the grass, longing for autumn,
even at these butterflies from my own flower garden?"*

and

*"Come, they seemed to say, and your butterflies might well have lured me away,
if between us did not grow bank on bank of kerria rose."*

RELATIONSHIP TO EARLIER CHAPTERS

"Butterflies" begins late in the third month, about two months after the end of "The Warbler's First Song," and takes the story of Tamakazura into the fourth month.

PERSONS

His Grace, the Chancellor, Genji, age 36

The mistress of the southeast quarter, 28 (Murasaki)

Her Majesty, the Empress, 27 (Akikonomu)

The lady in the west wing, Yūgao's daughter, 22 (Tamakazura)

His Highness of War, Genji's brother (Hotaru Hyōbukyō no Miya)

The Captain, son of Tō no Chūjō, 20 or 21 (Kashiwagi)

The Captain, Genji's son, 15 (Yūgiri)

The Commander of the Right, 31 or 32 (Higekuro)

Miruko, Tamakazura's gentlewoman

Hyōbu, the daughter of Tamakazura's nurse

The twentieth of the third month had passed, and the spring garden's flowers and birdsong were lovelier than ever, until people began to wonder how they could possibly have lasted so long. The groves on the hills, the view of the island,[1] the expanses of richly glowing moss—when all these seemed to make the younger women a little restless, Genji had Chinese-style barges made and outfitted, and on the very day they were launched, he summoned people from the Office of Music to perform aboard them. A great many Princes and senior nobles came.

Her Majesty was then at home. The mistress of the southeast quarter thought it time to answer Her Majesty's challenge to one "whose garden waits to welcome spring,"[2] and he himself had spoken of wishing he could show her all their flowers, but since she could not visit without sufficient reason, merely for the pleasure of the blossoms, he had young gentlewomen of hers—ones apt to enjoy the adventure—board a boat and row toward them along the southern lake. The boundary knoll he had put between the gardens did not keep them from coming right round its little promontory and up to the east fishing pavilion, where he had assembled other women from his side.

The dragon-prow and roc-prow barges[3] were adorned magnificently in continental style, and the boys wielding the steering oars wore twin tresses as in China. The astonished women were thrilled and delighted to see them launched on so broad a lake, and they felt as though transported to an unknown land. When they came under the great rocks of the island's little cove, they marveled to find the least stone standing as though in a painting. The trees near and far, their branches merging in veils of brocade into the mist, drew their gaze toward their distant goal, where willows trailed bright green fronds and blossoms cast ineffable perfumes upon the air. The cherries that were gone elsewhere smiled here in all their beauty, and the wisteria twined about the galleries opened into deep-hued clusters, flower

---

1. The hills are artificial, and the island is the one that belonged in any such garden lake.
2. Akikonomu's poem to Murasaki, near the end of "The Maidens."
3. *Ryūtō gekishu*, (two) barges with a "dragon head" and a "roc head." Dragons were associated with water. The *geki* ("roc") was a fabulous bird able to survive great storms at sea and to fly very high.

Dragon- and roc-prow barges

by flower. How marvelously the kerria roses were mirrored in the water and spilled in superb profusion from the bank! Waterbirds, sporting in loyal pairs, flitted about with twigs in their bills, while mandarin ducks made a brilliant pattern on the ground weave of the waves, until one longed only to turn it all into a painted design.[4] That day one's ax handle could well have rotted away.

> *"When the breezes blow, the very waves seem to bloom in lovely colors:*
> *could this then be the far-famed Cape of Kerria Roses?"[5]*

> *"Why, the lake in spring must recall the glinting stream of Ide River,*
> *for the kerria roses blossom also in its depths!"[6]*

> *"No, I shall not seek the mountain the tortoise bears! It shall be my fame*
> *I chose immortality here aboard this very boat!"[7]*

> *"As our boat glides on through the sweetly mild sunshine of a fine spring day,*
> *every drop the oars let fall blossoms into a flower!"*

Such were the trifles with which they amused each other, almost forgetting as they did so where they were going and whence they had come, because they had of course lost their hearts to the mirroring water.

4. The waterbird pairs and the mandarin ducks are Chinese textile motifs. The passage also contains echoes from the poetry of Bai Juyi.

5. These four poems are spoken by the gentlewomen aboard the boat. "Cape of Kerria Roses" (Yamabuki no Misaki) is a poetic place-name associated with the province of Ōmi.

6. Ide, too, a locality between Kyoto and Nara, was known for its *yamabuki.*

7. Hōrai, the island-mountain of the immortals, rested on the back of a great tortoise.

"The Royal Deer" rang out nobly as dusk fell, and it was only then that they reluctantly put in to the fishing pavilion and disembarked. The place was done up very plainly, but gracefully so, and the young women from each side, all dressed to uphold their pride, and very pretty, too, presented the beauty of a floral brocade. The dances performed were novel and rare.[8] Genji had chosen the dancers with particular attention, and he made sure that they devoted all their art to pleasing the watching ladies.

After dark he was still eager for more. He ordered cressets lit in the near garden, called the musicians onto the moss below the steps,[9] and had each of the Princes and senior nobles take up his own favorite instrument, stringed or wind. After the pick of the professionals had played in the sō mode,[10] those above them took up the music brilliantly on the koto and so on. Their playing of "Ah, Wondrous Day!" brought the most ignorant menservants in to listen among the horses and carriages crowded by the gate, smiling broadly as though life was at last worth living. The beauty of the sky, the tone of the instruments, the spring mood and mode, had surely made plain to all by now that season's higher worth. The music went on through the night. When the mode shift[11] led into "Joy of Spring," His Highness of War sang "Green Willow" twice, very nicely. His Grace, their host, joined in as well. Dawn came, and at daybreak Her Majesty beyond the knoll was sorry to hear the singing of birds.

Despite the spring light that forever shone in the southeast quarter, some regretted that the lady there had no one to receive her deepest love;[12] meanwhile, talk of Genji's visibly pleased attentions to the flawless lady in that west wing of the northeast spread far and wide until, as he had foreseen, many gentlemen found themselves under her sway. Those who had reason to esteem themselves worthy seized every opportunity to signify their interest and to pass her word of it as well, but no doubt there were other young and noble sons who burned with the inner pent-up fires of love. Smitten, too, was the Captain, the Palace Minister's son, for he did not know.

His Highness of War made no secret of his intentions, having lost his wife of many years and struggled through three years alone. He made a very amusing spectacle this morning as he pranced about with wisteria in his headdress, under cover of gloriously feigned drunkenness. Genji, secretly pleased, did his best to take no notice of him.

"Now would be the time for me to make my escape, if I had no reason to stay!" His Highness said in great distress when the cup came round again. "This is all too much for me!" He declined to accept more.

---

8. The *bugaku* dancers are performing in a sort of tent (*hirabari*) between the house and the lake.

9. The steps down into the garden from the south side of the main house.

10. One of the six *gagaku* modes, associated with spring. The professional musicians start off by playing *netori* (a short, tuning piece) on their wind instruments (in the order *shō*, *hichiriki*, flute); and the gentlemen seated above the steps (the professionals are below them) take up the piece on their stringed instruments.

11. *Kaerigoe*, the passage from a "major" mode to a "minor" one, or vice versa.

12. No daughter of Murasaki's own.

"I have dyed my heart so deeply in the charming hue of murasaki,
why care if all think me lost to these flowers' sweet abyss?"[13]

He offered Genji wisteria for his headdress, too.
Genji smiled warmly.

*"Then, while this spring lasts, take good care never to stray far from these flowers,
and see whether you in truth will leap into the abyss,"*

he replied. He detained His Highness so pressingly that His Highness renounced his departure and so added further charm to the pleasures of the morning.

Today was the first of Her Majesty's scripture reading. Many of those present for the music did not withdraw to attend it just as they were, but rather found a discreet corner to change into full civil dress. Some who had engagements elsewhere actually left. Everyone who planned to attend went there at the hour of the Horse,[14] led by Genji himself. All the privy gentlemen came. Most of them joined Genji's entourage, and the event went forward with imposing splendor.

The lady of spring graciously sent an offering of flowers. Eight page girls dressed as birds or butterflies appeared (she had made sure they were especially pretty ones), the birds bearing cherry blossoms in silver vases, the butterflies kerria roses in vases of gold; and the flowers were the most glowingly perfect of their kind. They rowed out from beside the knoll. A breeze sprang up as they came before Her Majesty, scattering a few cherry petals. The day was clear and calm, and the way they came forth from the mists was charmingly moving.

The dancers' tent had been left purposely where it was, and the gallery between the two pavilions had been done up for the musicians and provided for the time being with folding chairs. The girls came up to the steps and presented their flowers. The incense bearers[15] received the flowers and stood them beside the holy-water vessels. It was the Captain, Genji's son, who read out the donor's message:

Dancer dressed as a bird

---

13. Thanks to an allusion to *Kokinshū* 867, *murasaki* (the color of wisteria flowers) suggests that Tamakazura is a blood relation (the speaker being Genji's brother). The poem also plays on *fuchi / fuji,* "wisteria" and "abyss."

14. Roughly noon.

15. Privy gentlemen entrusted with distributing incense to the participating priests.

"Will you look askance, O pine cricket in the grass, longing for autumn,
even at these butterflies from my own flower garden?"[16]

Her Majesty smiled, recognizing the reply to her poem about autumn leaves. "My lady," the gentlewomen of the day before insisted, still intoxicated by the flowers, "you could have found no fault there with the beauty of spring!" "The Birds"[17] resounded bravely amid warblers' sweet carolings, while here and there upon the lake waterbirds sang their own songs, and the effect of the rapid conclusion was endlessly delightful. How lightly, then, the butterflies flitted about, to flutter into the hedge at last among cascading kerria roses!

Her Majesty's Household Deputy and the other privy gentlemen so entitled passed their rewards on one to the other[18] and gave the page girls theirs. The birds got cherry blossom long dresses and the butterflies ones in kerria rose. It was just as though these had been prepared beforehand. The musicians, according to rank, got a white layering or a roll of silk.[19] The Captain had laid across his shoulders a wisteria long dress as well as a full set of women's robes.

This was Her Majesty's reply: "Yesterday, you know, I could have cried aloud.[20]

Come, they seemed to say, and your butterflies might well have lured me away,
if between us did not grow bank on bank of kerria rose."[21]

It may be that despite their distinction and accomplishment they both found the effort too great, because their poems are hardly what one would wish to have from them.

Oh, I had forgotten: Her Majesty's gentlewomen, the ones who had been on the excursion, all received token gifts, too.[22] There were too many to describe. Little amusements like these went on day and night, since these ladies had no one to please but themselves, and those who served them therefore also lived untroubled lives. Both sides wrote back and forth to each other.

The lady in the west wing and the mistress of the southeast had kept in touch ever since they met at the time of the mumming. No doubt the former lacked in some ways the fullest depth of character, but she had a quality born of wide experience, she seemed kind, and since there was nothing about her to dislike, all the ladies enjoyed friendly relations with her. A great many gentlemen were courting her, but Genji avoided any hasty decision, and for himself it was perhaps a certain reluctance always to behave paternally toward her that prompted him at times to

16. The "pine cricket" (*matsumushi*), an autumn insect, is Akikonomu. Murasaki's poem amounts to a declaration of victory in the spring and autumn wars.

17. A *bugaku* piece properly entitled "Karyōbinga" (Sanskrit "Kalavinka") after the bird that sings in paradise.

18. They receive gifts of clothing, which they pass on to each other down the line.

19. *Koshisashi* ("inserted in the belt"), a roll of silk that the recipient stuck in his sash before withdrawing.

20. At not being able to be present. *Kokinshū* 498: "On my plum tree's highest branch a warbler sings, and I, too, could cry aloud, so sorrowful is my love."

21. Akikonomu's poem plays on the *ko* ("Come!") of *kochō* ("butterfly").

22. From Murasaki.

consider informing His Excellency her father. It made her feel rather shy that Genji's son, the Captain, should come so close, right up to her blinds, and answer her remarks in person, but the women around her knew of no reason why he should not, and he himself was too serious ever to think of taking advantage of her.

The Palace Minister's sons felt sufficiently encouraged by his example to let their interest in her be known, and they went about putting on tragic airs, which privately stirred her feelings, though not in *that* way,[23] but because at heart she longed to come to her real father's attention. She gave no hint of this to Genji, though, instead behaving toward him with engagingly youthful familiarity and trust. He saw her mother in her quite clearly, despite the lack of obvious resemblance, but it was certainly she who displayed the greater wit.

When the time came for the change to stylish new clothes for the new season,[24] the very sky somehow acquired a curious charm. Genji was at leisure, and he spent his time at music making of all kinds. Meanwhile letters arrived in increasing numbers for the young lady in the west wing. This pleased him, since he had expected no less, but his habit of visiting her at odd moments for a look at them, and of then advising her on which ones she should answer, made life difficult for her, since it meant that she could never feel comfortably at home. She soon had a fine collection of ardently reproachful letters from His Highness of War, and Genji laughed heartily when he read them.

"I have always been very close to him," he said, "and among all the Princes it is he who most deserves my affection, but when it comes to things like this, he has kept his distance, which is why I find it at once so amusing and so touching at last to see these romantic outpourings of his. You simply must answer him. I can think of no more worthy correspondent for any moderately cultivated woman. Oh, yes, he has a great deal to recommend him!" He enlarged on the subject of his brother so as to make him seem desirable to a young woman, but he managed only to make her uncomfortable.

The travails of the thoroughly stalwart and dignified Commander of the Right[25] appeared to repeat the fall suffered by Confucius in the mountains of love,[26] which struck Genji as comical in its way. Then, while examining the letters further, he came across one on blue Chinese paper, deliciously perfumed and folded very thin and small. "Why is this one so tied up in knots?"[27] he asked, opening it. The hand was delightful.

> "You can hardly know that my thoughts are all of you, for the stealthy spring
> welling from among the rocks leaves no color to be seen."

The writing was fresh and exuberant.

---

23. Not in a romantic way.
24. On the first day of the fourth month, the first day of summer.
25. Higekuro no Taishō, "Commander Blackbeard." A brother of the Shōkyōden Consort and an uncle of the Heir Apparent, he is married to an elder half sister of Murasaki.
26. Confucius's fall seems to have been proverbial, but no *locus classicus* for it is known.
27. Genji's question plays on *musubu* ("be knotted," as love letters were) and *musubōru* ("be dejected").

"Whose is this?" Genji asked, but she gave him no clear reply.[28]

He summoned Ukon. "I want you to vet the authors of all these letters before they get an answer. A giddy young thing these days can make a great mistake, and it may not be all the man's fault. I, too, have often thought, How awful of her! I won't have it! and then called her obtuse or, if she happened to be a bit beneath me, simply rude; but when a man is not that keen anyway, and she still hatefully ignores a simple note on the theme of flowers and butterflies, it may only serve to spur him on; or else he may forget all about her, and who could blame him? It is no good either, making a glibly clever reply to what was merely a casual and quite functional note: that can lead to trouble later on. In general a woman is bound to suffer for it in the end if she is careless enough to indulge in showing off her delicate sensibility and her sparkling wit. His Highness and the Commander, though, are too passionate ever to express themselves casually, and it would ill become your mistress to treat them as though she accorded them less than their due. As for the others, who come below them, by all means be kind in proportion to what you gather of their own seriousness."

The lady sat turned away from him, revealing a striking profile. Over a long dress in a pink layering[29] she wore a dress gown stylishly in harmony with the season's flower.[30] Her deportment, once marked after all by a sort of natural guilelessness—the only visible trace of her provincial upbringing—was by now impeccably pliant, as she came more and more to know how people really behaved, and her judicious use of makeup so heightened her already splendid looks that she was a dazzling pleasure to behold. What a terrible shame it would be, he thought, to let anyone else have her!

Meanwhile, Ukon looked on, smiling and thinking to herself, No, really, he is much too young for her to call him her father! What a beautiful pair they make like that, side by side! "My lord," she said, "you may rest assured that I give my lady no letters from *any* gentlemen. I suppose we let in the three or four you were looking at a moment ago—just the letters—because we hesitated to offend the senders by returning them, but my lady would never . . . At least, not without your express permission, and even then only most unwillingly."

"What about this one, then, tied up in these boyish knots? It certainly is very nicely written." Genji gazed at it, smiling.

"The messenger absolutely insisted on leaving that one, my lord. You see, His Excellency the Palace Minister's son, the Captain, already knows our Miruko,[31] who is in service here, and she is the one who accepted it. No one else has seen it, I promise."

"How sweet of him! They are still junior, those young gentlemen, but one would certainly not wish to offend them that way. I doubt that there are many even among the senior nobles who can match the esteem he enjoys. None of his peers

28. It is from Kashiwagi, actually her half brother.
29. A plum pink *hosonaga* lined with leaf green (the "pink" layering).
30. A *kouchiki* in a deutzia (*unohana*) layering (white lined with grass green [*moegi*]). The deutzia flowers in the fourth lunar month, in long clusters of small white blossoms.
31. A page girl, apparently.

has as much sense as he does. Well, he is bound to find out in time. You must put him off, but of course not abruptly. What a beautiful letter it is, though!" For some time he could not put it down.

"I am afraid you may have your own thoughts about my talking to you this way," he said to the young lady, "but you are still too young and too poorly established to come to His Excellency's attention, and moreover, in my estimation it would be risky for you to go and join his family now, after all these years. I am sure there will be a suitable occasion for you to meet him in a dignified manner, once you have settled down as others do.

"His Highness in principle lives alone, but he is very fond of the ladies; he frequents a good many different houses, or so I hear, and he keeps a large number of women unpleasantly called 'concubines'[32] or something. A wife able to cure him of that sort of thing without getting his back up would certainly do very well. Of course, a woman with a little quirk of her own[33] can easily drive her husband to tire of her, and that is something for which you will need to look out.

"The Commander is courting you because his wife of all these years is old now, and he is tired of her, but her family naturally objects. Nothing much can be done about that, so I have been quietly considering the matter myself, although I have not reached any conclusion. On this sort of subject it is not easy for a girl to tell her father frankly what she prefers to do, but you are past that age now, and I see no reason why you should not make up your own mind. You must think of me as you would have done of your late mother. I would hate to see you unhappy."

His grave speeches so confounded her that she could think of no reply. Still, she felt that it would be too girlishly silly of her to say nothing at all. "I have had no parents for as long as I can remember," she ventured in all innocence, "and I am afraid that I can hardly have an opinion."

Genji sympathized. "Well, then, will you not accept your guardian as your father, as the saying enjoins, and acknowledge the very great depth of my concern for you?"[34] The real nature of his interest in her was too shocking to confess. Now and again he admitted suggestive expressions into his speech, but she appeared not to notice, and he was sighing when at last he went away.

Chinese bamboo grew in her garden, youthfully strong and green, and Genji, who missed its yielding pliancy, stopped to contemplate it.

> "Must that dear bamboo, so young when I planted her deep in my garden,
>   grow up with the passing years to a life apart from mine?"[35]

he said, lifting her blinds. "I believe that I will take that badly."
   She slipped out toward him.[36]

32. *Meshiudo*, a term for a gentlewoman taken by her master as a sort of minor mistress.
33. A tendency to jealousy.
34. The "saying" appears to be something like "Honor the parent who reared you over the one who bore you" (*umi no oya yori sodate no oya*).
35. The poem plays on *yo*, "passage of time" or "period of years" and "joint [of bamboo]"; and in this context *yo* also suggests "love relationship."
36. He lifts the blinds between the veranda and the aisle, and she slips from the chamber out into the aisle.

*"Which of all those years will bring with it the right time for the young bamboo
to seek out at last the root whence she first began to grow?*

No doubt it might not really work very well to try," she replied, and his heart went
out to her. Perhaps she did not really believe it, though. Oh, when, she wondered,
worried and sad, will he ever bring up the subject with my father? And yet she certainly valued Genji's kindness, and she supposed that although she called that gentleman father, she could hardly be as close to him as to Genji himself, since she had
never spent any time with him; in fact, the more her reading of old tales taught her
what people are like and what the ways of the world are, the more timid she became, and the more she doubted that she could ever of her own will bring herself to
her father's notice.

Increasingly smitten, Genji even talked about her to the mistress of his house.
"What an extraordinarily attractive person she is! Her mother all those years ago
lacked a certain liveliness, but *she*, as far as I can tell, is quick, warm, and approach-
able, and there is no need whatever to worry about her."

To his lady, who knew him well, this sort of praise betrayed a heightened interest, and she understood. "She may be quick to grasp many things, but I pity her if
in her innocence she ever trusts you too far."

"And what about me should encourage her not to?"

"Oh, come now! Do I not remember the misery your ways have so often
caused me?" She smiled.

She misses nothing, does she! "But you have it all wrong!" he continued aloud.
"She herself could hardly fail to notice!" He said no more, since he knew that he was
in trouble, and now that she had seen through him, he struggled in vain to make up
his mind what to do, meanwhile reflecting ruefully on his own warped and deplorable disposition.

He thought constantly of the young lady and often went to fuss over her. One
very damp evening after a spell of rain he looked out at the richly interlacing green of
the oaks and young maples against a somehow encouraging sky, hummed ". . . pure
and in harmony,"[37] found his thoughts wandering to her deliciously fresh beauty, and
stole off to her as usual.

She was relaxing, practicing writing, and embarrassment lent delightful color
to her face when she arose. His glimpse of her gentle grace suddenly swept him
back to the past, and in an excess of emotion he began, "I am sure you yourself have
never realized it, but ever since I first saw you, I have been strangely convinced,
time after time, that I see *her* before me.[38] It is very troubling. To my eye the Captain[39] has none of the beauty I once knew, and I assumed that you would not resemble your mother that closely either, but now I know that such things happen after
all!" His eyes filled with tears. Toying with an orange that happened to be among
the fruit in a nearby box lid, he went on,

37. From a description of a spring landscape in a poem by Bai Juyi (*Hakushi monjū* 1280).
38. Yūgao, Tamakazura's mother.
39. Yūgiri.

"Now that this perfume calls to mind those sleeves of hers, fragrant with orange,
I simply cannot believe that you are other than she!

I could never, never forget her, and after remaining unconsoled for all these years, I cannot help asking myself when I see you this way whether I am dreaming. It is too much for me. Please do not turn me away."

She kept her composure when he took her hand, despite the revulsion that her inexperience naturally prompted her to feel.

"If this present fruit so recalls the scent of sleeves you knew long ago,
no doubt it, too, soon enough, will meet an untimely end,"

she replied.

With her eyes downcast in dread, she looked infinitely appealing. The delicious plumpness of her hands, the entrancing fineness of her skin, and her whole figure only stirred yet more troubled yearnings in him,[40] and this time he spoke a little to her about his feelings. She wondered, aghast, what she was to do and began all too obviously to tremble, but he pressed on nevertheless. "Why must you dislike me so? I assure you that I have every intention of keeping all this so well hidden that no one will ever find out. You need only betray nothing in your behavior. I am so deeply fond of you already that I know my renewed devotion will then rise beyond any in the world! Am I to be less to you than all these others from whom you have letters? I worry about you, you know, because there can hardly be anyone else, anywhere, as profoundly concerned with your welfare as I." He had a very strange way of being a father.

The rain had stopped, there was wind in the bamboo, and the bright moonlight on this lovely night encouraged the gentlest of moods; meanwhile, her women had withdrawn a certain distance, shy of intruding on an intimate conversation. He was always this way with her, but so rare an opportunity, and perhaps also the passion aroused by his own declarations, now moved him skillfully to disguise the rustling of his meltingly soft robe[41] and to lie down beside her. Heartsick and appalled by what her women might imagine, she felt dreadful. She knew that no such a disaster could have overtaken her if she had been with her real father, whether he thought highly of her or not, and her tears spilled over despite her effort to hide them, until she made an extremely unhappy sight.

"It is very unkind of you to feel this way. Any woman should properly yield, it seems to me, even a complete stranger, because that is the way of the world; and considering the long and close relationship between us, I cannot see why this degree of familiarity on my part should provoke such hostility. I will not trouble you again with my unwelcome attentions. All I desire is solace from the flood of memories that over-

---

40. Since it is summer, she is probably wearing above her waist only a single layer of dark, nearly transparent silk gauze.

41. His outer robe, as he took it off; he had probably made sure that he wore a comfortably unstarched one.

whelms me." He said much more to her besides, kindly and tenderly—the more so since it was extraordinary how thoroughly he felt now as he had then. Despite himself he could not help remorsefully acknowledging his own wantonly foolish behavior, and he left before too much of the night had passed, since her women, too, would soon be wondering what he was doing there. "I will be very sorry indeed if henceforth you dislike me. Other people are not as easily swept away as I am! My boundless consideration for you would dissuade me from ever doing anything that might merit blame. I should like only to talk to you about this and that, to soothe my longing for what once was. I hope that you will answer me in the same spirit." But despite his earnest entreaties she remained profoundly upset and disgusted with him. "I had no idea you felt so strongly about me. You really do seem to hate me," he sighed. "Please make sure that no one suspects anything." He went away.

At her age she had a certain number of years behind her, but quite apart from her own ignorance of men's ways, she knew no one with the smallest experience of the world, and greater intimacy than this was therefore still beyond her ken. She was so visibly devastated by this shocking turn in her fortunes that her gentlewomen thought she was ill and could not imagine how to make her feel better.

"My lord is so extraordinarily attentive and kind!"

"Surely not even your real father would be so unfailingly devoted to your welfare, my lady!" Hyōbu[42] and the others whispered, but Genji's astonishing behavior had by now made him so hateful that she could only lament her unhappy lot.

A letter came from him early the next morning. She still lay as though ill, but she read it reluctantly when her women brought her an inkstone and so on and urged a quick reply. Its seemingly innocent white paper conveyed detachment, but it was very beautifully written.

"What an extraordinary way to treat me! Your cruelty will not be easy to forget. I wonder what it all looked like to your women.

> Not once have we lain in a lovers' full embrace—why, then, little plant,
> are you so sadly downcast, as though something had happened?

What a child you are!"

This last, paternal remark particularly repelled her, and since it certainly would have looked strange for her not to answer at all, she only wrote on thick Michinokuni paper, "Thank you for your note. I am unwell, and I hope that you will therefore forgive my failure to reply." Genji could only smile to see how her modesty betrayed the promise of her beauty, and it seemed to him, as deplorably as ever, that she was well worth a lover's bitter complaint.

Once he had shown his colors, he did not stop at "pine of Ōta"[43] intimations but wrote to her instead so often and so insistently that she felt more and more hedged about until, trapped and at her wits' end, she fell frankly ill. Very few people

---

42. Tamakazura's foster sister (the daughter of her nurse).

43. *Genji monogatari kochūshakusho in'yō waka* 186: "Such are the pangs of love that I would fain show my colors, like the pine of Ōta, and ask her plainly to meet."

knew what the matter was, and considering that everyone else, near or far, was lost in admiration of Genji's fatherly ways, it seemed to her that if any rumor of this got out, she would be a laughingstock and her name would be ruined forever. Why (she said to herself in a frenzy of anxiety), even if my father did find out about me, he would probably make no great effort, and if he heard news like this, it would probably mean the end!

His Highness and the Commander, who had gathered indirectly that Genji did not look unfavorably on them, pursued their courtships intently. The Captain, he of "welling from among the rocks," knew only through Miruko that Genji sanctioned his suit, which gave him great joy, since he did not know the truth, and he seems to have devoted himself entirely to voicing distraught expressions of bitter complaint.

25

The Fireflies

Hotaru means "fireflies." In this
chapter Genji gives one of Tamakazura's suitors, His Highness of
War, a glimpse of her by the light
of fireflies.

"Butterflies" ends in the fourth month, and "The Fireflies" goes on to cover the fifth.

PERSONS

His Grace, the Chancellor, Genji, age 36

The lady in the west wing, 22 (Tamakazura)

His Highness of War, Genji's brother (Hotaru Hyōbukyō no Miya)

Saishō, Tamakazura's gentlewoman

The lady in the northeast quarter (Hanachirusato)

The lady from Akashi, 27 (Akashi no Kimi)

Murasaki, 28

The young lady, Genji's daughter, 8 (Akashi no Himegimi)

The Captain, Genji's son, 15 (Yūgiri)

The Right Captain, Tō no Chūjō's eldest son, 20 or 21 (Kashiwagi)

His Excellency, the Palace Minister (Tō no Chūjō)

An expert in interpreting dreams

Genji's weighty dignity now relieved him of all care and left him so entirely at peace that those who depended on him were satisfied and lived secure, fortunate lives. Sad to say, the lady in the west wing was the one assailed by unforeseen troubles and the one who suffered anguish and perplexity. Not that these troubles could compare to the threat posed by the dreadful Audit Commissioner, but this sort of thing was so unlike what anyone could imagine of Genji that she kept it to herself and disliked him intensely for it. Being old enough by now to understand many things, she pondered it in all sorts of ways, grieved afresh for her mother, and bitterly regretted her loss.

Now that Genji had declared himself, he, too, only suffered from the consequences. Fear of being caught discouraged him from sending her the most trivial word, which was such a torment to him that he was constantly calling on her. Whenever her women had left her quietly to herself, and he yet again betrayed his ardor, she merely pretended with a stricken heart to notice nothing, since she could not openly shame him. Smiling and friendly as she naturally was, her resolute attempts at grave caution still failed to conceal her delightful appeal.

His Highness of War, like the others, kept up his earnest campaign. He had not yet been at it that long when, after complaining to her about the fifth-month rains, he went on, "If only you would allow me a bit closer! I so long to unburden myself to you a little!"

Genji saw his letter. "Why not? I am sure it is worth seeing these gentlemen courting. Do not be distant when you address him, and please sometimes give him an answer." He told her what to write, but she was only more repelled than ever and pleaded indisposition not to do so. Very few among her gentlewomen had any great rank or backing. The only one who did was Saishō, the daughter of a Consultant, an uncle of her mother's, and a woman of quite acceptable taste whom Genji had rescued from declining fortunes. She wrote a good hand and was generally sensible, and Genji had her write suitable replies as needed. He therefore summoned her to do this now. No doubt he was curious in any case about all His Highness's letters.

After the wretchedness of Genji's indiscretions, she herself began now and then at least to glance over His Highness's heartrending missives. Not that he particularly interested her, but by now even she had the finesse to wish to find a way out of seeing a man she could no longer abide.

His Highness, astonished to receive a passable reply from her, came very discreetly to call without ever guessing that Genji in his disgraceful way was lying in wait for him. He was offered a cushion inside the double doors, and she sat nearby with only a standing curtain between them. Genji had seen to it that a seductive incense floated on the air, and despite his hateful and unfatherly perverseness his elaborately groomed figure looked marvelous. When poor Saishō just sat there, hardly knowing how to convey her mistress's answers, he compounded her confusion by pinching her to reprove her for being so dull. The dark evenings[1] were over now, and by the dim light from a cloudy sky His Highness's subdued dignity had a marked allure. The air wafting faintly from within, mingled with the more distinctive fragrance from Genji's own person, enveloped him in exquisite odors, and what he gathered of the lady's presence suggested that she was even lovelier than he had imagined. He poured forth his declaration with great dignity, avoiding any suggestiveness of tone and cutting meanwhile an unusual figure. Genji caught some of what he said and thought it all great fun.

She had retired to lie down in the eastern aisle, and Genji added his own reproaches when Saishō slipped in to convey His Highness's words. "You are making it very difficult for His Highness. Tact is always to be preferred. This is no time for you to insist on behaving like a mere girl. You simply cannot have someone running back and forth this far when you are talking to a Prince. You could at least stay a little closer to him, even if you prefer him not to hear your voice."

Desperate, and unwilling either to go or to stay, since staying might give Genji the excuse to invade at any moment, she slipped out to lie on her side behind the standing curtain at the edge of the chamber. She was hesitating over how to answer a particularly long speech from His Highness when Genji approached and tossed a curtain panel over the crosspiece. At that moment, to her horror, there was a burst of light; she thought someone had held up a hand torch.

Earlier that evening Genji had put a swarm of fireflies in thin silk and covered them up, and just now, as innocently as though merely adjusting his costume, he had removed the cover. The sudden illumination made her hide in dismay behind her fan, revealing an enchanting profile as she did so. A bright light will give him a good look at her, Genji had reasoned. I am sure it is only her being my daughter that makes him so eager—he can hardly assume that she has such grace and beauty on her own. I shall sow turmoil in that heart no doubt so tried in love. Genji would never have made all this fuss if she had really been his daughter. No, he was not very nice. Once the deed was done, he stole out by another way and went home.

His Highness had been gauging where the young lady might be, and his heart beat when he gathered that she was after all a little closer than he had thought. He was just peering through the gap in an impossibly delicate silk gauze curtain when,

---

1. In the last part of the lunar month when there is no moon; the moon is therefore in its first quarter.

not ten feet off[2] and in full view, there came a marvelous and completely unexpected flash of light. It was smothered in a moment, but not before its glow had shown him the pleasures that she promised. Never mind that it had been only a glimpse, because now he dwelled eagerly on the beauty of a slender reclining form that had indeed left a lasting impression.

> "Labor as you please, those fires that the ardent fly nurtures in longing,
>   though its cry is never heard, burn too brightly to be quenched.[3]

Do you follow me?"

Too much thought about the reply to a poem like that would only yield something clever, and she spoke what came first to mind:

> "Rather, the firefly, who burns with an inner flame and utters no cry,
>   is the one whose devotion passes all that words can say."[4]

After this offhand reply she withdrew, leaving him to rage at her cruelly distant treatment. He did not stay until dawn, since that would have been excessively forward of him; instead he left late at night, wet with rain, amid many painful drops from the dripping eaves. A cuckoo must have called, too, but I did not take the trouble to listen.[5] Her women praised his elegant appearance and his close resemblance to His Grace. Being ignorant of the truth, they all expressed gratitude and admiration for the motherly care His Grace had given their mistress that evening.

It seemed to her that her own misfortune accounted for Genji's deceitful zeal. If I had already come to my father's notice and had gained my own place in the world, she reflected, and His Grace still felt this way toward me, there would be nothing especially wrong with what he desires; no, it is the strange position I am caught in that may in the end make me the talk of all. Her anguished thoughts dwelled on the subject day and night. Nonetheless, Genji remained determined never to make a tedious spectacle of her. What with that quirk of his, one of course need not imagine that his thoughts of Her Majesty, for example, were entirely pure, and at times he would address her quite provocatively, although her impossibly exalted rank kept him from making his words or his approaches to her too clear. As for this young lady, her warmth and freshness made her so nearly irresistible that he often indulged in behaving with her in ways that would have aroused suspicion if anyone had seen them together; but, wonder of wonders, he refrained from going further and so kept their relationship in perilous balance.

---

2. Literally "the distance between two pillars" (*hitoma*), about ten feet.

3. The central device of this poem is a play on *omohi* (thoughts of love or longing) and the final *hi* in the same word, which means "fire." Because of this double meaning, fireflies figure in many summer love poems.

4. *Shigeyuki shū* 264 (also *Goshūishū* 216), by Minamoto no Shigeyuki: "The firefly who silently burns with inner fires deserves greater pity than the one who cries."

5. *Kokinshū* 153, by Ki no Tomonori: "While I languish sadly amid the fifth-month rains, late in the night a cuckoo calls—whither can it be bound?"

On the fifth,[6] a visit to the riding ground pavilion gave him an occasion to call on her as well. "How was it?" he asked. "Did His Highness stay late? We must not allow him *too* close. He has his unfortunate peculiarities, you know. After all, few people have never hurt anyone or been guilty of any serious lapse." He looked endlessly young and handsome while he praised and damned His Highness in turn. Over a gown exquisite in gloss and hue he casually wore a dress cloak so perfectly right that one wondered how it was possible, for the dyeing appeared beyond the craft of anyone in this world; even its color, the same as always, seemed a miracle to her on this Sweet Flag Festival day, and a miracle, too, his fragrance, which would have completed the pleasure of his presence, if it were not for all the sorrows that he brought her.

A letter came from His Highness. It certainly looked very nice, since it was written with great distinction on thin white paper,[7] but when read aloud it turned out to have little to it.

> *"Has a sweet flag root spurned by all even today, where it grows unseen,*
> *hidden beneath the water, no solace but cries of grief?"*[8]

He had tied the poem to a memorably splendid root. Before Genji left, he urged her to reply. "You really ought to," others reminded her, and for some reason she actually wrote,

> *"But when seen at last, how shallow that sweet flag root then appears to be,*
> *lifting its pathetic cries in defiance of all sense—*

and childish, too." That was all, in faint ink. Fastidious as he was, His Highness probably thought her hand could do with a bit more style and felt somewhat disappointed.

The herbal balls, all indescribably pretty, poured in from everywhere. Gone now were her years of trial, and with so much to be thankful for that she naturally wished if at all possible to avoid giving offense.

Genji looked in on the lady in the northeast.[9] "The Captain[10] said he would bring his men around—his Palace Guards' archery contest is today.[11] I hope that you will be ready to receive them. I gather they will be here before dark. I had wanted to keep our event quiet and informal, but the whole thing is turning out to be quite elaborate, since Their Highnesses have heard about it and will be coming, too. Please be prepared."

---

6. The day of the Sweet Flag Festival.

7. White because it came tied to a white sweet flag root.

8. "Must you spurn me?" For the Sweet Flag Festival people pulled up sweet flag (*ayame*) roots in search of especially long ones. The poem's sentiments and wordplays (*ne* ["root" or "cry"] and *nakare* ["weep" or "flow"]) follow convention.

9. Hanachirusato.

10. Yūgiri.

11. Presumably the mounted archery contest (*yabusame*) held on the palace riding ground, on the fifth of the fifth month by the Left Palace Guards and on the sixth by those of the Right.

From his position in the gallery he could see the riding ground pavilion, a short distance away. "The young
women should look on through the open bridgeway
doors," he said. "There are a lot of fine young officers in
the Left Palace Guards these days. They easily equal the
minor privy gentlemen." The women were pleased to be
able to watch, and the page girls from the west wing
came to join them. Fresh green blinds were hung in the
gallery entrance, and curtains in the latest style, darkening toward the hem,[12] stood across it; the page girls,
servants, and so on wandered about
behind them. The page girls in sweet
flag layered gowns and violet silk
gauze dress gowns seemed to be the
ones from the west wing; and the four
pleasantly practiced servants in bead-

The dance "Strike the Ball"

tree trains darkening toward the hem and Chinese jackets the color of young pink
leaves were especially well dressed for the day's festival. The ones from the east
wing, in deep scarlet layerings artlessly worn under pink dress gowns, made an attractive sight as each side vied to be seen. The bright-eyed young privy gentlemen
were showing off, too. At the hour of the Sheep,[13] Genji went out to the riding
ground pavilion and, sure enough, found Their Highnesses gathered there. This
contest, unlike the one at the palace, brought in the Captains and Lieutenants as
well, and Genji enjoyed these novel amusements until darkness fell. The ladies understood little of what was happening, but even the rank-and-file guardsmen were
most attractively dressed, and it was a pleasure to watch their dashing display of the
archer's magic. The southeast quarter, too, offered a clear though distant view of the
riding ground, and young women watched from there as well. The dancing of
"Strike the Ball" and "Twin Dragons," as well as the victory music, went on till it was
too dark to see anything at all. The guardsmen received gifts according to their
rank. Those present did not leave until it was very late indeed.

Genji stayed where he was for the night. "What a very fine gentleman His
Highness of War is!" he exclaimed in the course of his conversation with the lady
there. "His looks do not stand out, but his wit and presence make him attractive.
Have you managed to steal a look at him? One can do better, though, despite the
praise he gets."

"I know that he is your younger brother," she replied, "but to me he looked
older than you. I gather that he comes faithfully to keep you company on these occasions, but I had not seen him since my last glimpse of him at the palace. He is
very handsome and dignified now. One could say that His Highness the Viceroy
has a degree of looks, but he lacks presence and hardly resembles a proper Prince."[14]

12. *Susogo,* cloth dyed so as to be light at the top and dark at the bottom.
13. About 2:00 P.M.
14. Literally, he looks like an *ōkimi:* an imperial child who has not been appointed a Prince or Princess or
even given a surname. This is the only mention of him.

She misses nothing, does she, Genji thought. He smiled and skirted discussing the others who had been present. Disapproving as he did of those who criticize or belittle others, he said nothing of the Right Commander,[15] although despite that gentleman's fine reputation he found himself for some reason shying from the idea of a close alliance with him.

His relationship with her was perfunctory now, and they slept apart. He wondered unhappily why this distance had come between them. Nothing ever piqued her to look at him askance. So far she had only heard of such entertainments from other people, and she was pleased to see today's rare event confer luster on her quarter, too.

> "Have you then today chosen to pluck after all at the water's edge
> the sweet flag that everyone knows full well a steed disdains?"[16]

she said quietly.

It was no masterpiece, but he was touched.

> When would the young steed who aspires to company with the faithful grebe
> ever let himself be drawn to abandon the sweet flag?"[17]

he said. They certainly were blunt enough with each other. "We seem to be apart day in and day out, but I still feel quite at home with you like this!" he joked, though the peaceful quality of her presence kept his voice low. She ceded the curtained bed to him and went to sleep beyond a standing curtain. Genji agreed that it would ill become her to sleep beside him and made no effort to invite her to do so.

The long rains were worse this year than most, and to get through the endless wet the ladies amused themselves day and night with illustrated tales. The lady from Akashi made up some very nicely and sent them to her daughter. This sort of thing particularly intrigued the young lady in the west wing, who therefore gave herself all day long to copying and reading. She had several young gentlewomen suitably gifted to satisfy this interest.[18] Among her assemblage of tales she found accounts, whether fact or fiction, of many extraordinary fates, but none, alas, of any like her own. The trials faced by the young lady in *Sumiyoshi*[19] were remarkable, of course, and so, too, was her fame still in the present world, and her narrow escape from the Director of Reckoning certainly had a good deal in common with the terrors of that Audit Commissioner.

15. Higekuro.
16. The "sweet flag" (*ayame*) is herself. "Chosen" translates the verb *hiku*, which plays on "pull up" (a sweet flag root) and "lead" (a horse). The poem alludes to the distinctly erotic *Kokinshū* 892: "Old is the grass beneath the trees at Ōaraki; no steed grazes there, no one comes to mow it."
17. The steed (Genji) wants to be like the grebe (*niodori*), which pairs for life; he will never abandon the sweet flag (Hanachirusato). The "bluntness" of the exchange (below) has to do with its frankly conjugal sentiments, untempered either by indirection or by a tone of artful courtship.
18. Presumably, women good at collecting tales, copying them, or painting pictures to illustrate them.
19. A classic already in the author's time, it survives only in a rewritten version that dates roughly from the thirteenth century.

Finding her enthralled by works like these, which lay scattered about every-where, Genji exclaimed, "Oh, no, this will never do! Women are obviously born to be duped without a murmur of protest. There is hardly a word of truth in all this, as you know perfectly well, but there you are caught up in fables, taking them quite se-riously and writing away without a thought for your tangled hair in this stiflingly warm rain!" He laughed but then went on, "Without stories like these about the old days, though, how would we ever pass the time when there is nothing else to do? Besides, among these lies there certainly are some plausibly touching scenes, con-vincingly told; and yes, we know they are fictions, but even so we are moved and half drawn for no real reason to the pretty, suffering heroine. We may disbelieve the blatantly impossible but still be amazed by magnificently contrived wonders, and although these pall on quiet, second hearing, some are still fascinating. Lately, when my little girl has someone read to her and I stand there listening, I think to myself what good talkers there are in this world, and how this story, too, must come straight from someone's persuasively glib imagination—but perhaps not."

"Yes, of course, for various reasons someone accustomed to telling lies will no doubt take tales that way, but it seems impossible to me that they should be any-thing other than simply true." She pushed her inkstone away.

"I have been very rude to speak so ill to you of tales! They record what has gone on ever since the Age of the Gods. The Chronicles of Japan[20] and so on give only a part of the story. It is tales that contain the truly rewarding particulars!" He laughed. "Not that tales accurately describe any particular person; rather, the telling begins when all those things the teller longs to have pass on to future generations—whatever there is about the way people live their lives, for better or worse, that is a sight to see or a wonder to hear—overflow the teller's heart. To put someone in a good light one brings out the good only, and to please other people one favors the oddly wicked, but none of this, good or bad, is removed from life as we know it. Tales are not told the same way in the other realm,[21] and even in our own the old and new ways are of course not the same; but although one may distinguish be-tween the deep and the shallow, it is wrong always to dismiss what one finds in tales as false. There is talk of 'expedient means'[22] also in the teaching that the Buddha in his great goodness left us, and many passages of the scriptures are all too likely to seem inconsistent and so to raise doubts in the minds of those who lack understand-ing, but in the end they have only a single message, and the gap between enlighten-ment and the passions[23] is, after all, no wider than the gap that in tales sets off the good from the bad. To put it nicely, there is nothing that does not have its own value." He mounted a very fine defense of tales.

20. *Nihongi*, an official history of Japan written in Chinese and completed in 720. It begins with an ac-count of *kamiyo*, the divine age that preceded that of humans proper.

21. China. The original for this whole sentence is confusing and suspect, and it varies especially widely in different manuscripts.

22. *Hōben*, a device adopted by an enlightened being in order to lead one unequipped to accept more di-rect guidance to enlightenment. The term may cover what could be called in conventional terms a lie. The issue is treated at length in the Lotus Sutra.

23. A paradox of Japanese Mahāyana Buddhism is that "the passions are enlightenment," the passions due to desire and the senses being precisely that which is furthest from enlightenment as commonly con-ceived.

"But do any of these old tales tell of an earnest fool like me?" He moved closer. "No, no cruelly aloof heroine in any of them could possibly pretend to notice nothing as heartlessly as you do. Come, let us make our story one like no other and give it to all the world!"

She hid her face. "Even if we do not, I doubt that one so strange could help feeding everyone's talk."

"Strange? Is that what it is, for you? No, there can be no one like you!

> Though excess of care turns me to seek far and wide old stories like ours,
> I find none of any child so set against her father!

Even the Buddha's teaching has much to say about those who offend filial piety!"

When she failed to look up, he stroked her hair, so upset that at last she replied,

> "Yes, search as you please through the tales told of the past: you will never find
> in all the world a father with feelings resembling yours!"

Her response shamed him, and he took no further liberties. As she was, though, what was to become of her?

Lady Murasaki,[24] too, invoked her young lady's wishes and found it hard to put down her tales. "What a beautifully done picture!" she said, examining one from *The Tale of Kumano*.[25] The little girl, napping there so sweetly, reminded her of herself all those years ago.

"How knowing they are, even such little children! I myself was so impossibly slow—I should have been famous for it!" Genji remarked.[26] Famous, yes, he certainly should have been, for his rare collection of wanton adventures.

"Please do not read our young lady naughty tales like that," he said. "Not that a heroine secretly in love is likely to catch her interest, but she must not come to take it for granted that things like that really happen." The lady in the west wing would have been outraged to hear him talk that way.

"It is painful to see anyone mindlessly mimic this sort of thing," she replied, "but then, look at the young Fujiwara lady in *The Hollow Tree*. Grave and sober as she is, she never goes astray, but her stiff speech and behavior are so unladylike that she might as well."

"That can happen in real life, too. People insist on having their own way and lose all sense of proportion. When a girl's perfectly respectable parents have carefully brought her up to nothing better than childish innocence, and she has little to offer otherwise, one unfortunately wonders what their idea of an upbringing can have been; but when a girl turns out just as she should, the effort is well worth it, and her parents then deserve every credit. It is very disappointing when nothing

---

24. The first occurrence of "Murasaki no Ue," henceforth translated this way wherever it occurs.
25. Now lost.
26. He seems to be joking that, unlike the children (presumably a boy and a girl) in the picture, he was a dull, slow boy to whom romantic preoccupations meant nothing.

about a girl's words or deeds suggests that she merits the lavish praise she gets.[27] One must manage never to let tedious people praise a girl." His sole care was that no one should find fault with his daughter. He wanted to avoid putting ideas about evil stepmothers into her head, since the old tales are full of them, and so he was strict in his choice of the ones he had copied and illustrated for her.

He kept the Captain well away from his own residence, but he did not forbid him his daughter's to anything like the same degree; in fact, he encouraged him to visit her.[28] It does not matter so much while I am alive, he reflected, but an old closeness between those two might make a great difference once I am gone. He therefore allowed him inside her southern blinds,[29] although he forbade him access to the gentlewomen's sitting room.[30] Having so few children, he could afford to pay close attention to him. On the whole the young man was thoroughly dignified and serious, and Genji felt safe giving him this much latitude. When the young man saw how innocently preoccupied the little girl still was with her dolls, he remembered all the months and years he had spent playing with *her*,[31] and he therefore gave yeoman service at the dolls' palace[32] and sometimes even shed a tear as well. He kept up a casual correspondence with a good many ladies, as long as there was nothing about them to discourage him from doing so, but he was careful not to encourage false hopes. When he liked one well enough to think of courting her seriously, he made a joke of it to himself, since all that really absorbed him was still the wish that he had never worn those light blue sleeves.[33] He suspected that His Excellency might well yield and grant his permission, if only he were to insist stubbornly enough, but whenever he thought over the wrong he had suffered, he found that he could not renounce his desire to have his tormentor acknowledge it, and the only one to whom he showed devoted attention, maintaining outward composure all the while, was that lady herself. Her brothers often felt fed up with him.[34] The Right Captain[35] was profoundly under the spell of the lady in the west wing, but since his access to her was quite unreliable, he appealed instead to Genji's son, who coolly replied that in someone else this sort of preoccupation seemed to him no more than foolishness. The relationship between these two resembled the old one between their fathers.

His Excellency the Palace Minister, who had many children by different mothers,[36] brought them all up to the wealth and success that their quality and condition[37] encouraged them to desire. Having had few girls, he greatly regretted both the Consort's failure to fulfill his hopes and the reverse that now affected his other

27. Above all from her nurses and gentlewomen.

28. The main house in Murasaki's southeast quarter of Rokujō is divided between the part that she shares with Genji and the part occupied by Genji's daughter.

29. Into the aisle room, but not as far as the chamber.

30. *Daibandokoro*, on the north side of the house, used also by Murasaki's women. He is making sure that Yūgiri cannot gain access to Murasaki through one of her women.

31. Kumoi no Kari.

32. An expression particularly suited to an officer of the Palace Guards.

33. The color of the sixth rank, at which he had started his career. He now holds the fourth rank.

34. They assume that he is not courting Kumoi no Kari more actively because he thinks she is not good enough for him. (His correspondence with her is a secret.)

35. Tō no Chūjō's son, Kashiwagi.

36. As far as one can tell, ten sons and four daughters.

37. As determined above all by the standing of their mothers.

daughter.[38] Nor did he forget his little pink,[39] and after having once had occasion to talk about her,[40] he continued to wonder what had become of her. To think my little girl was caught up in her mother's unwarranted fears and simply vanished! No, when it comes to girls, you can never, never let them out of your sight. Why, she may be living in squalor and still calling herself *my* daughter! Well, he fondly decided, never mind what condition any girl who presents herself as mine may be in! He was always saying to his sons, "If any young woman turns up calling herself my daughter, listen to her! Of all the reprehensible things I did for mere amusement, this was one: a woman who meant much more to me than anyone else took offense at something or other, and suddenly I, who have so few daughters, actually lost one of them! I wish it had never happened!" Recently he had tended more often to forget about her, but what with other people looking so happily after their own daughters, he still bitterly lamented the collapse of his hopes.

He had a dream and called in an expert at such things to divine its meaning. "My lord," the man asked, "could you have heard of a child of yours, one lost to you years ago, who has now become someone else's daughter?"

But people so seldom adopt a girl, he thought. What can this mean? This was when he began pondering the matter again in earnest and talking about it.

38. Kumoi no Kari's involvement with Yūgiri.
39. Yūgao's daughter.
40. During the "rainy night" conversation in "The Broom Tree."

26

TOKONATSU

The Pink

Tokonatsu ("gillyflower") is the same flower as *nadeshiko* ("pink"). Because of Tō no Chūjō's account of Yūgao and her daughter in "The Broom Tree," *nadeshiko* refers particularly to Tamakazura, and *tokonatsu* to Yūgao. (The reason is explained in the glossary "gillyflower.") This is not always obvious in "The Pink," but it is clear in the poem by Genji that gives the chapter its title:

"If he were to see all the inviting beauty of the little pink,
he might wish to know as well more of the gillyflower."

RELATIONSHIP TO EARLIER CHAPTERS

"The Pink" directly follows "The Fireflies," covering the sixth month.

PERSONS

His Grace, the Chancellor, Genji, age 36

His son, the Captain, 15 (Yūgiri)

His Excellency, the Palace Minister (Tō no Chūjō)

The Controller Lieutenant, his second son (Kōbai)

The Right Captain, his eldest son, 20 to 21 (Kashiwagi)

The Fujiwara Adviser, his third son

The young lady in the west wing, his daughter, 22 (Tamakazura)

His daughter, 17 (Kumoi no Kari)

His eldest daughter, the Consort, 19 (Kokiden no Nyōgo)

Gosechi, a gentlewoman attached to Ōmi no Kimi

Chūnagon, the Kokiden Consort's gentlewoman

Tō no Chūjō's newly discovered daughter (Ōmi no Kimi)

One very hot day Genji went to enjoy the cool of the east fishing pavilion. His son the Captain was with him. Intimates of his from among the privy gentlemen attended him as well, preparing for him such delicacies as sweetfish sent from the western river and bullheads from the river nearby.[1] His Excellency's sons arrived as usual to seek the Captain's company. "I was bored and sleepy," Genji declared. "You have come just in time!" They all had some wine and called for iced water to make chilled rice,[2] which they then ate noisily.

There was a fine breeze, but when the sun began sinking toward the west in a bright and cloudless sky, the cicadas' singing became thoroughly oppressive. "A lot of good it does one in this heat to be on the water! I hope you will excuse me." Genji stretched out on his side. "Music is not much fun in weather like this, but one wonders how else to get through the day. It must be almost unbearable for you young people when you are on duty. You cannot even loosen your sashes! At least make yourselves comfortable here, then, and if you have any good stories about what has been going on lately, stories that might wake me up a little, I want to hear them! I am so out of touch, I feel like an old man."

Somewhat shamefaced at having nothing worth telling, they sat there with their backs against the cool railing.

"Someone, I forget who, told me His Excellency has found a daughter of his by an outside mother and is now looking after her. Is that true?" Genji's question was directed to the Controller Lieutenant.

"My lord, there is really nothing very extraordinary about it. This spring His Excellency spoke of having had a dream, and a woman who distantly heard of it came forward to claim that she had something to say on the matter. When this came to the Captain's[3] attention, he inquired to find out whether she had any proof. I myself hardly know what the upshot was. You are right, though, that people lately

---

1. The sweetfish (*ayu*), still a delicacy in Kyoto, are from the Katsura River, and the bullheads (*ishibushi*, modern Japanese *kajika*) are from the Kamo.
2. *Himizu* (water cooled with ice preserved through the summer in an ice house [*himuro*]) to make *suihan* (boiled rice chilled in cold water).
3. Kashiwagi, the speaker's older brother.

Veranda and railing

have been making quite a thing of it. This sort of business does my father no good, nor of course his house either."

Genji agreed. "He has so many geese already on the wing with him, it is greedy of him to insist on searching for one that may have strayed. I have so few that I would love to come across one like that, but I have never heard of any—I suppose they see no point in making themselves known. Anyway, she must have some sort of connection with him. He used to flit about so busily here and there, no wonder the moon deep in unclean water is not entirely spotless."[4] He smiled. His son the Captain,[5] who knew the whole story, could not keep a straight face. The Lieutenant and the Fujiwara Adviser were extremely put out.

"*You* might pick up that fallen leaf, my friend," Genji teased his son. "Rather than leave a dubious name, why not embellish it after all with the same ornament?"[6] On this sort of matter, and despite their superficially cordial relationship, Genji and his old friend had actually long been at odds with each other. In this case particularly, Genji could not accept the way His Excellency had slighted the Captain and hurt him, and he did not at all mind if His Excellency found out how displeased he was.

This news started Genji thinking that whenever he did show the young lady in the west wing to His Excellency, she would no doubt be received in a worthy manner. Her father is a perfect gentleman, he reflected, with much to be said in his favor, someone who discriminates sharply between what he approves of and what he does not and who metes out praise or condemnation accordingly, and he would not despise her if I were suddenly to give her to him out of nowhere, however annoyed he might be. He would treat her with the greatest consideration.

The breeze turned very cool as evening came on, and the young men did not

---

4. "Noble though he may be himself, no wonder a child of his, born to a lowly mother, is somewhat inferior."

5. Yūgiri.

6. "You might take her yourself. Rather than leave your name soiled by Tō no Chūjō's refusal to let you marry Kumoi no Kari, why not do just as well and marry her sister?"

wish to leave. "I might just go and enjoy the cool at my ease. I am a bit old now for such company!" Genji returned to the west wing, and the young gentlemen all went with him. They were hard to tell one from another in the twilight because their dress cloaks were all the same color,[7] so he asked the young lady to come forward a little and whispered to her in private, "I have brought the Lieutenant and the Adviser. They seemed eager to come—it was thoughtless of that solemn Captain not to bring them himself. I expect each has his own hopes. The most common woman is bound to attract whatever attention her condition encourages, as long as she remains sheltered at home, and the less my house does to feed gossip, the more people seem to entertain grand ideas about it. There *are* several ladies here, but they are not for anyone to court. Now that you are here, too, though, I thought I might pass the time testing the depth of their interest, and I seem to be succeeding."

He had planted no elaborate garden before her wing, because here Chinese and Japanese pinks bloomed in harmonious colors, weaving their way charmingly through the low fence and catching the glow of the last light of day in the profusion of their flowers.[8] The young gentlemen went to them and paused, disappointed not to be able to pick as many as they pleased.

"There are our learned young men," Genji went on. "Both are very pleasantly able. The Right Captain[9] is a little quieter and more dignified than either of them. Is he writing to you already? I wonder. Do be careful not to embarrass him by just turning him away."

His son's grace and beauty stood out in such fine company. "I cannot understand what His Excellency dislikes about him. Perhaps someone of imperial descent hardly deserves notice amid the unadulterated brilliance that surrounds him."[10]

"Someone did say, though, 'My lord, if you come.' "[11]

"Now, now, I do not ask for any great welcoming feast.[12] But the two of them have been fond of each other since they were children, and I resent the way he has kept them apart for years. If he feels the Captain is still too junior and too little considered, then I wonder—could it mean that something troubling did happen and that he has just left it all to me instead?" He sighed.

Then they really do not get on well, she thought. The idea that in the end she might never come to her father's knowledge made her miserable.

The lanterns were lit, since at this time of the month there was no moon. "It feels too hot to have them that close," he said. "A cresset would be nicer." He called someone over to order, "I want a cresset, just here." There was a pretty *wagon* nearby. He drew it to him, touched the strings, and found it beautifully tuned in

---

7. They are all wearing violet (*futaai*) dress cloaks, and that color merges easily into the twilight. Yūgiri ("that solemn Captain," below) appears to be with Tō no Chūjō's two younger sons.

8. The pinks allude to Tamakazura.

9. Kashiwagi.

10. Tō no Chūjō is the son of a Princess, who is also Yūgiri's maternal grandmother. However, Yūgiri's imperial descent on his father's side should lift him above Tō no Chūjō.

11. "He would be welcome if he came forward on his own to press his suit." Tamakazura alludes to (rather than quotes from) a *saibara* song: "In my house, the curtains are all hung; come, my lord, come: my daughter shall be yours . . ." She is prompted to do so by Genji's use of *ōkimi* ("someone of imperial lineage"), which is the "my lord" of the archaic song.

12. The song goes on, "What will do for the feast? Will abalone, turbo, and sea urchin do?"

the *richi* mode. Its tone was lovely, too, and he played a little. "All this time I had been thinking less well of you because I assumed you had no interest in this sort of thing! It has a sweet, fresh sound when the moonlight is cool on an autumn night and you sit not too far from the veranda to play it while the crickets sing. Perhaps the instrument in full concert lacks character, but on the other hand it has the marvelous property of conveying the timbre and rhythm of all the others. What people dismiss as merely "the Japanese koto" is actually extremely cleverly made. They think it is just for women who know nothing of China. You should really apply yourself to practicing it in company with other instruments. It has no deep secrets, but I doubt that it is easy to play genuinely well. At the moment no one compares with His Excellency the Palace Minister. One hears the sound of every instrument in his slightest toying with the strings,[13] and from there comes the most wonderful music."

She understood him well enough, and she wanted so much to play nicely that she longed to hear more music. "Might I listen, too, whenever there is that sort of concert here? So many people, even mountain rustics, seem to learn it, and I always assumed it was easy. I suppose someone really good must be quite different, though." She seemed curious and completely in earnest.

"Yes, people have come to associate it with the East,[14] but it is the first instrument ordered from the Library even for music performed before His Majesty. I cannot vouch for China, of course, but here it seems to be considered the father of all instruments. I am sure you will do extremely well if you learn how to play it properly from your father. He will probably come here when a suitable occasion arises, but I doubt that he will be likely then to display all his skill. The best practitioners of any art are reluctant to do that sort of thing. Still, I expect you will be able to hear him in the end."

He played a little. It was absolutely lovely and delightfully fresh in style. She did not see how any playing could be better, and she only longed the more to hear her father himself. Even so, she could only wonder when she would ever hear him play at ease.

Genji sang very prettily, "Soft beyond the Nuki River's leaping waves, her pillowing arm . . ." He smiled a little when he got to "the lover her parents banish,"[15] and the unaffected quaver[16] he put in just there was simply enchanting.

"Come, *you* play. A performer should never feel too embarrassed. Well, I hear someone once kept 'I Love Him So' to herself,[17] but it is far better to play boldly with whomever you can." However, she had learned to play only in her distant province, from an ancient woman who claimed a vague connection with the City

---

13. *Sugagaki,* apparently the name of a particular technique.

14. The *wagon* was also called *azumagoto* ("koto of the East"). The East (typically, the Kanto Plain) was a wild area with uncouth inhabitants.

15. Genji last sang this *saibara* song ("Nuki River") in "Under the Cherry Blossoms," when Aoi refused to welcome him. It is the complaint of a lover who is barred by his girl's parents from seeing her. This time, Genji is consoling himself for not being able to make love to Tamakazura. He smiles because *he* is the parent who will not allow the lover (himself) to do so.

16. "Quaver" is a mere guess for the *sugagaki* discussed above.

17. *Sōfuren,* a "Chinese" *gagaku* piece. The anecdote in question has not survived.

and with the imperial house, and despite his insistence she was too afraid of making mistakes to touch it.

I wish he would play a bit more, she thought; I might get it after all. She was eager enough just this once to slip closer to him. "What wind can be blowing, then, to make it sound so beautifully?"[18] she said, head tipped to one side and quite enchanting in the lamplight.

Genji smiled. "You have sharp ears after all, and for me the autumn wind blows more cuttingly than ever."[19] He pushed the instrument away. She was extremely put out.

He could not joke with her as usual because her women were attending her closely. "Those young gentlemen are gone, and they never got enough of the pinks. Yes, I should like His Excellency to see this flower garden, too, and you never know when it may be too late. He talked about you once, long ago—it might have been just now, I remember it so well." The mere mention moved him deeply.

> *"If he were to see all the inviting beauty of the little pink,*
> *he might wish to know as well more of the gillyflower.*

This is why I have kept such a cocoon around you, for which I am very sorry."

She wept.

> *"Who would wish to know where it was the little pink first of all took root,*
> *when she came into the world in a mountain rustic's hedge?"*

The way she veiled her feelings made her seem very young and sweet. "If he did not come,"[20] Genji hummed, and his feelings rose to a pitch so painful that he did not think he could contain himself much longer.

His intuition prompted him to desist when his many visits to her began to risk attracting attention, and instead he wrote to her on every possible occasion. She was all he thought of, day or night. Why am I so caught up in a venture in which I should not be engaged at all, and only making myself miserable at it? If I told myself that that was enough and had my way, it would be a disaster for her, quite apart from the widespread and humiliating denunciations to which I would be subjected. Whatever she may mean to me, even I know perfectly well that she could never challenge all I feel for my lady of spring; and what good would it do her just to join the others? Yes, I stand alone above the rest, but what sort of renown would *she* have, once she ended up merely as one of my women? No, she would be far better off marrying some perfectly innocuous Counselor, whose affection she need not share. The more he lectured himself, the more he felt for her. At other times he said to himself, Shall I let His Highness have her, then, or the Commander? Will I stop wanting her just be-

---

18. The sounds of the wind and of strings are often linked in poetry, as in *Shūishū* 451, by Saigū no Nyōgo: "The sound of the pines on the mountain wind mingles with the music of the *kin*; and, for this concert, which string was tuned to which?"

19. "You hear music perfectly, yet you pretend not to hear my pleas." The "cutting wind" (*mi ni shimu kaze*), a poetic expression easily associated with such music, evokes the sorrows of autumn and of solitary longing.

20. An obvious quotation, but the source is unknown.

cause she is not here anymore and someone has taken her away? No, it is hopeless. I might as well do it. He continued his visits, though, and seeing her now inspired him to invoke teaching her music so as to spend time with her. At first she was nervous and apprehensive, but by and by, when she found him mild and not in the least disposed to alarm her, she gave in and no longer recoiled from him, conversing with him instead as necessary while still avoiding excessive intimacy. Meanwhile, she seemed to grow in charm and beauty before his very eyes, until he doubted that he could long resist her after all. Should I then insist on keeping her here[21] and steal off to her whenever I can for a consoling word? I hate to think of pressing her further while she remains unfamiliar with men's ways, but of course if I put my heart into it once she understands things better, then nothing will keep me from her, no matter how often I go, and never mind the stern gatekeeper![22] That was his idea, and a thoroughly disgraceful one it was, too. It would be misery to go on more and more desperately wanting her. There is nothing for it; I just cannot give her up. Such was the improbable tangle in which both of them were caught.

The Palace Minister had no sooner learned that his household staff were ignoring his new daughter and that all the world was treating her as a joke when the Lieutenant remarked in conversation that His Grace the Chancellor had been asking about her. "No doubt he has," His Excellency replied. "Look at him: *he* has taken in a peasant girl of whom no one has ever heard and is doing everything for her. His Grace rarely speaks ill of anyone, but he never misses a chance to run *us* down. He does us too much honor."

"They say the lady he has there in that west wing is a raving beauty. His Highness of War and so on are extremely keen on her, but I hear they are not getting very far. People seem to assume she must be quite remarkable."

"Oh, come, they only carry on that way because she is supposed to be His Grace's daughter. People are like that. She cannot possibly deserve her reputation. If there really were anything to her, one would have heard of her long ago. There he is, spotless above all the rest in affluence and glory, but the lady who really matters to him has given him no daughter to bring up, no one to treasure as a genuinely perfect jewel. By and large it is a worry to have few children. The girl that woman from Akashi gave him is destined for great things, despite her mother's low birth—it seems to me there must be somewhere a reason for that. It would not surprise me if this new one of his is not really his daughter at all. He has his idiosyncrasies, that man, and I would not put it past him." His Excellency had nothing kind to say about Genji.

"And what is he going to do with her anyway? I imagine His Highness will get her. They have always been especially close, and with the qualities they have, they should get on perfectly together." He was still bitter about his own daughter. He, too, would have liked to show her off and sow turmoil in the hearts of her suitors, and being unable to do so was sufficiently annoying that he had no intention of allowing the mar-

---

21. Marry her off but insist on an uxorilocal marriage, so that she remains at home.

22. "Never mind how well her husband [*sekimori*, the "gatekeeper"] guards her." *Kokinshū* 632 (also *Ise monogatari* 6, section 5), by Ariwara no Narihira: "May the barrier guard stationed on the path I take secretly fall asleep night after night!" The guard has been placed there by the father of the young woman Narihira has been visiting.

riage as long as that young man's rank remained so impossibly low. He thought he might perhaps give in after all if only Genji would earnestly plead his son's cause, but it was very irritating, the way the young man himself betrayed no impatience whatever.

He was still pondering such matters as these when he casually and quite unexpectedly dropped over to see his daughter. The Lieutenant went with him. She was taking a nap at the time. She looked very slight and sweet, lying there in her gauze shift and not hot in the least. Her skin showed through very prettily, her head lay pillowed on her arm, and it was charming, too, the way her hand still held a fan, while

Wearing a silk gauze shift

her hair streamed out around her, not exceptionally long, it is true, but handsomely even at the ends. Her gentlewomen were resting, propped half upright behind screens and so on, and they did not immediately wake up. He rapped his fan, and the innocent way she looked up at him was lovely. To a father's eye the flush in her cheeks was pure enchantment.

"Why are you lying heedlessly asleep this way, when I have warned you against taking naps? There is no one anywhere near you. No, this will not do. A woman must always be alert and watchful. It does not become her just to let herself go this way. Not that she need remain fiercely prim and spend her time chanting the Fudō *darani* and making mudras.[23] That would be disagreeable, too. It may seem ever so ladylike to keep people too far off and to overdo talking from behind screens and blinds, but it is neither engaging nor kind. What I gather His Grace the Chancellor has taught that future Empress of his is not demanding, because he holds that a woman should be generally familiar with many things and yet single herself out as an expert at none, while at the same time remaining neither ignorant nor vague. No doubt he is right, but people have certain leanings in what they feel or do, and I am sure that her own will become clear as she grows up. I look forward to seeing what she is like when she is grown and he sends her into palace service.

"As you are now, I am afraid that what I first wanted for you is no longer within reach, but whenever I hear what life has held in store for other people, I give careful thought to ensuring at least that you are never laughed at. For the time being, please do not respond to anyone's entreaties or offers of service. I have an idea of my own." As he talked he dwelled fondly on how pretty she was.

Remembering now how her thoughtlessness had had such painful consequences and how she had brazened it out with her father even then, she felt a sharp pang and was overcome by shame. Even Her Highness held it against her that she did not see her anymore, but she could not bring herself to go because she feared to encounter there the sort of advances of which her father had just spoken.

---

23. The fiercely energetic deity Fudō ("The Unmoving") sits or stands on a rock, surrounded by flames, and quells the demons of craving. Chanting his *darani* ("spell," "invocation") summons up his presence and power, as does forming the mudras (hand gestures) associated with his rites.

What am I to do with this girl I have now in my north wing? His Excellency asked himself. I am the one who brought her here, and it would be both mad and unworthy of me simply to send her back on the grounds that people are speaking ill of her. I wish they would not assume that I mean seriously to do everything for her, just because I have her here. No, I shall send her off to the Consort's and make her the Consort's jester. After all, she is not such a fright that people can despise her as a monster.

He put it this way, with a smile, to his daughter the Consort. "She is yours. You can have your dotty old women and so on correct her manners, and mind they give her no quarter. And please do not talk about her and encourage the younger ones to laugh at her. She has an unfortunate taste for misplaced levity."

"I do not see how she could very well be *that* odd," the Consort replied. "Surely it is just that she does not come up to the Captain's[24] glowing advance reports of her. She must hardly know what to do with herself, with people talking about her this way, and for one thing she must be feeling terribly self-conscious."

Her father was impressed. She had more noble simplicity than absorbing beauty, and with it a warmth of manner that recalled plum blossoms just opening at dawn; and he felt that her smile, which seemed to leave so much unsaid, distinguished her from anyone else. "I know what the Captain said," he replied, "but he is young and he knows so little." The poor girl they were discussing had a sad reputation.

He went straight to look in on her, since he was in that part of the house anyway. There she was, fairly bursting through her blinds,[25] playing backgammon[26] with a lively young woman called Gosechi. "Keep it low, keep it low!" she prayed at breakneck speed, rubbing her hands briskly together.[27]

Oh, no! His Excellency groaned. Motioning to suppress his escort's warning cries,[28] he stood at the gap between the double doors and peered into the room through an open sliding panel. Gosechi was all worked up, too. "Do her in, do her in!" she cried, brandishing the cup and taking her time to release the dice. Perhaps the cup was hiding its own secret sorrows;[29] at any rate, they both made a foolish spectacle. His daughter's lively presence, appealing manner, and well-groomed hair atoned for her failings, but her narrow forehead and giddy mode of speech accused her. Although she was not exactly a beauty, he could not deny his share in her traits. He remembered what he saw in his mirror and deplored the workings of karma.

"Do you not feel awkward and uncomfortable here?" he asked. "I have so much to do that I am hardly ever able to visit you."

Her answer came at her usual, breakneck speed. "Why should I mind anything here? But it makes me feel the dice have let me down that I can't always see you, after all those years wondering about you and longing to see your face."

---

24. Kashiwagi's.

25. The blinds are down, but she is pressed up so close to them that they are bellying outward. Her posture is far from ladylike.

26. *Sugoroku*, a board game long popular in Japan.

27. She is rubbing her hands together in prayer that her opponent will get a low number from her roll of the dice.

28. A great lord's escort uttered warning cries to clear his path even in the house.

29. A joking reference to a poem (*Genji monogatari kochūshakusho in'yō waka* 745 or 754) on the sorrows that lurk at the heart of stones, sorrows that "cannot get out."

"I see. I have so few people in my intimate service that I had hoped originally to have you join them, but unfortunately that seems not really to be possible. An ordinary attendant mingles easily with the others, whoever she may be, and most of the time neither her words nor her looks attract much attention. That would have been safe enough for you, except that even then she is all too likely to embarrass her family when people are certain to know she is so-and-so's daughter, and so you see . . ." He said no more, and the confusion on his face meant nothing to her.

"Why worry, though? I know there might be a problem if you put me on show that way, but I'd gladly just empty chamber pots!"

This was too much, and he burst into laughter. "That duty would not become you. Please speak a little more slowly, if it means so much to you to serve the father you have been fortunate enough to find. It might help me to live longer."

To this taunt she responded, with a smile, "My tongue just works that way, I think. My late mother was always scolding me for it even when I was small. She complained I got it from His Reverence the Abbot of Myōhōji,[30] when he came to the birthing room. How am I supposed to stop?"

Despite her rush of words he was touched to see how anxious she was to serve him. "Well, then, we shall just have to blame that worthy cleric who, as you say, got a little too close. He himself must have owed it to misdeeds in former lives. They say being born deaf or mute comes from having slandered the Buddha's teaching, and I suppose this is the same sort of thing." The Consort awed him, even though she was his own daughter, and the very idea of presenting this girl to her was embarrassing. She will wonder how I could possibly have failed to find out how odd she was before I decided to take her in, he reflected, and her women will spread their talk in all directions. He was reconsidering his plan.

"The Consort is at home now," he said. "You might visit her from time to time and learn from her. Someone who has nothing particularly wrong with her can still improve herself in one way or another by cultivating other's company."

"What a lovely idea! All I've ever dreamed of day and night for years and years has been to manage to have my sisters recognize me as one of them! I'll happily draw her water, if you want, and bring it to her on my own head!" In her happiness she rattled off her words faster than ever. It was obviously no use.

"Never mind slaving away collecting firewood.[31] You need only go to her. Just make sure you stay away from that priest you seem to have caught it from."

She never knew he was making fun of her; it never entered her head that he of all the Ministers was the one whose looks, dignity, brilliant ways, and mighty presence overshadowed the rest. "Well," she said, "when would it be a good time for me to get myself on over there?"[32]

---

30. A temple in Ōmi Province (now Shiga Prefecture), which is why the girl is known as Ōmi no Kimi, the Ōmi Daughter. The priest would have been called to the birth to pray for a safe delivery.

31. Drawing water and collecting firewood, essential activities sanctioned in the scriptures as the basic work to perform in the service of a buddha.

32. The turn of phrase she uses (*mairi-haberan-zuru*) is condemned as low class by Sei Shōnagon in *The Pillow Book*.

"It is only a matter of choosing a favorable day. No, why make a great thing of it? Today, if you want," he concluded and left.

His daughter watched him go, majestic in his slightest movement and eagerly escorted by fine representatives of the fourth and fifth ranks. "Just look at my father! To think I'm his daughter and I was *still* born into such a miserable little family!"

"He's really *too* grand and intimidating. You should have found yourself a middling one who would have just loved you and looked after you," Gosechi said in vain.

"There you go again, spoiling everything I say! You're awful! Now, I don't want to hear another word out of you! I'm on my way to better things!"

Her angry expression was engaging after all, and she had despite her outrageous prattle a charm that redeemed her misdeeds; it was just that she did not know how to speak, being so horribly countrified and having grown up among distressingly humble folk. Even quite uninteresting remarks sound worthy when delivered with gravity and composure, and a discussion of poems[33] that are nothing in themselves may leave the heart of the matter veiled and yet at first hearing sound fascinating when done in the right sort of voice, leaving room for the imagination and seeming to withhold the beginnings and the endings. The most profound and absorbing remarks will find no audience when indifferently spoken. What with her accent as well, her giddy way of talking made her speech rough and hard to follow, and all that her nurse had proudly taught her had given her such peculiar manners that it did her a very great disservice. No, she was by no means hopeless, and she could string thirty-one syllables together into a disjointed poem at breathless speed.

"Now," she went on to Gosechi, "he told me to take myself on over to the Consort, and he won't like it if I don't seem eager. I'll go tonight. Oh, His Excellency my daddy thinks the world of me, just the world, but what will I look like here if these ladies want nothing to do with me?" Her reputation was indeed in peril. She sent the Consort a letter immediately.[34]

"So near and yet so far from your reed fence,[35] I lament not yet having enjoyed the privilege of walking in your shadow, and I fear that you may have preferred to erect a Come-Not-Hither Barrier.[36] I know you not, and I therefore dare hardly presume to speak of Musashi Plain . . .[37] Your very, very, very humble servant."

There were lots of repetition dots[38] and, on the back, "Oh, I forgot! I have de-

---

33. *Utagatari*, "talk about poems": probably an account of an exchange of love poems, with the poems themselves sung in the customary manner.

34. The letter is a dense mosaic of tedious and unrelated allusions to stock poems, hence a caricature of a reasonable letter.

35. *Kokinshū* 506 laments that although the speaker is very near his beloved, he cannot meet her. The "fence of reeds" (*ashigaki*) in the poem is "closely woven" (*ma chikakereba*) as the lovers should be, yet it keeps them apart.

36. *Gosenshū* 682, by Kohachijō no Miyasudokoro: "Although I am close enough to you to tread upon your shadow, who is it who erected the Nakoso [Come-Not-Hither] Barrier?" Nakoso, a place in northern Japan, was favored in poetry for this play on its name.

37. *Kokin rokujō* 3507: "Although I have not been there, talk of Musashi Plain arouses my complaint; but ah, there is no remedy—the fault is the *murasaki's.*" "To speak of Musashi Plain" means to claim, via the poem's mention of *murasaki*, a blood relationship with the recipient.

38. The letter ends *ana kashiko, ana kashiko,* and the second *ana kashiko* (a closing phrase in the range of "your humble servant") is indicated simply with a series of dots that show repetition of the preceding phrase. One *ana kashiko* would have done.

Reed fence

cided to come to see you this evening—I am afraid that otherwise I may grow more fond of you the more you dislike me.[39] Oh, dear, oh, dear, if only you would be kind enough to look on my writing as upon the Minase River!"[40] And along the edge was this:

> "Tender as she is, the plant from Hitachi Shore longs on Query Point
> to see as soon as she can the billows on Tago Beach.[41]

The great river's waters . . ."[42] It was on double-layered green paper, in an assertive hand crammed with cursive characters, wandering, unrecognizable, and with long tails everywhere, and it conveyed insufferable self-importance. The lines drifted off toward the edge and looked as though they might topple over at any moment. She contemplated her work with a smile of pleasure, at least rolled it up small,[43] knotted it tight, and tied it to a pink in bloom.

A very pretty and self-assured chamber-pot girl,[44] a new arrival, now turned up at the gentlewomen's sitting room in the Consort's residence. "Please give this to her ladyship," she said. The servant she spoke to recognized her. "Why, you're a girl from the north wing, aren't you!" she exclaimed as she took it. The gentlewoman known as Taifu brought it to her mistress and opened it for her to look at. When her mistress smiled

---

39. *Gosenshū* 608: "How strangely I grow fonder of you the more you dislike me! What could I ever do to make myself stop?"

40. "If only you would forgive my poor handwriting." *Genji monogatari kochūshakusho in'yō waka* 199 begs the recipient to look (*mi*) indulgently on the writer's poor handwriting, making the point with a wordplay on the name of the Minase River.

41. "I long to meet you." The places have nothing to do with each other, Hitachi being in eastern Japan, Ikaga Saki ("Query Point"; the word *ikaga* means "how?") on the Inland Sea, and Tago below Mount Fuji.

42. "I long to meet you": a dubious allusion to *Kokinshū* 699 about the "great river" at Yoshino.

43. "At least" (*sasuga ni*) because however unladylike the letter itself may be, at least her treatment of it in this sentence is acceptable.

44. A highly unsuitable messenger, even if in looks and manner she is in better harmony with her surroundings than the Ōmi Daughter.

and put it down, Chūnagon, in close attendance nearby, got a look at it, too. "That is a stylish-looking letter if ever there was one, my lady," she said, plainly curious.

"I can make neither head nor tail of it. I suppose I am simply no good at reading cursive characters." The Consort gave it to her. "She will be disappointed in me if my answer is less grandiose. Draft something immediately."

It was all so funny that the younger women laughed, though they could not do so openly.[45]

"And her ladyship's answer?" the messenger inquired.

"The letter has so many wonderful touches that we hardly know how to reply. It would be a shame if it appeared to be written by someone else," Chūnagon answered. She made sure it seemed to come from her mistress herself.

She wrote, "It is a great pity that your being so nearby has brought us no closer together.

> *Then, O wave, arise, yonder along Suma Shore in far Suruga*
> *on the sea of Hitachi: the Hakozaki Pine waits!"*[46]

"Oh, no! What if people really think I wrote it?" the Consort protested when Chūnagon read it out to her.

"Those who hear it will know, my lady." Chūnagon wrapped it up and sent it off.

"Beautifully put! And she says she's expecting me!" The young lady steeped her clothing again and again in the sweetest incense,[47] put on the most brilliant rouge, combed her hair, primped and preened, and made herself quite attractive in her way. No doubt she did all sorts of extraordinary things when they were together.

---

45. Because the Ōmi Daughter is the Consort's sister.
46. These places, too, are outrageously unrelated to each other.
47. Incense was sweetened with honey, but excessively sweet perfume was considered vulgar.

27

KAGARIBI

The Cressets

Kagaribi means "cresset," a fire held aloft in an iron cage and used for outdoor illumination. The word owes its function as the chapter title to its role in an exchange of poems between Genji and Tamakazura.

"The Cressets" directly follows "The Pink." It takes place in the seventh month, which in the lunar calendar is the first of autumn.

PERSONS

His Grace, the Chancellor, Genji, age 36

The lady in the west wing, 22 (Tamakazura)

The Captain, 15 (Yūgiri)

The Secretary Captain, Tō no Chūjō's eldest son, 20 or 21 (Kashiwagi)

The Controller Lieutenant, Tō no Chūjō's second son, 19 or 20 (Kōbai)

The whole world was talking in those days, whenever the occasion arose, about His Excellency the Palace Minister's new daughter. "No," Genji remarked, "I fail to understand how anyone, under any circumstances, could draw this much attention to a girl who presumably has so far been hidden away, and make such a spectacle of her just because she happened to come forward to put her claim. He is always so hasty—I suppose he took her in without finding out much about her, and this is what he did to her when she disappointed him. Remaining discreet is never more than a matter of how one goes about doing things." He felt quite sorry for her.

Cresset

"I *was* lucky, then!" the young lady in the west wing said to herself when these goings-on made it clear what humiliation she might have suffered if she had sought out His Excellency, even if he *was* her father, without knowing what he was really like. Ukon had turned all her eloquence to encouraging this conclusion. Genji had that one unpleasant failing, but he did not actually seek to force himself on her as he might in fact have wished to do, and since otherwise his devotion to her continued to grow, she began little by little to respond.

It was autumn now. When that first, cool wind began to blow, he desperately missed "my true love's" tossing clothes,[1] and he went constantly to see her and spend the day giving her music lessons and so forth. The evening moon of the fifth

1. *Kokinshū* 171: "How it tosses and blows my true love's clothes about him, ah, so fresh and strong, the first wind of fall!"

or sixth night[2] had set very early. Clouds lightly covered the sky, reeds were rustling,[3] and the moment was one for tender feelings. The two of them lay together, their heads pillowed on her koto. He knew that someone might notice them if he spent the night, and he sighed that such things should be possible. He was therefore preparing to leave when he summoned one of his escort, the Right Guards Commissioner, to light the cressets that by then were all but out.

The man placed the split pine fuel discreetly beneath the handsome, spreading branches of a spindle tree[4] that grew beside the deliciously refreshing brook. Then he drew back to light the cressets, leaving the garden beside the house cool and filled with a lovely light that showed her off to wonderful advantage. Her hair was elegantly cold to the touch, and her manifestly thoughtful reserve gave her great appeal. Genji did not wish to leave.

"You should always have your staff keep cressets lit. A summer garden on a moonless night is disturbingly mysterious and foreboding.

> *With these cressets' smoke another rises, of desire, from such inner flames*
> *as I know now will burn on for as long as this world lasts.*

Ah, how long indeed![5] You do not see me smoking, perhaps, but I smolder so painfully underneath!"

This is all so strange! she thought.

> *"Let it then dissolve in the vastness of the sky, if the cressets' smoke*
> *sets your own to smoldering from such other, unseen fires.*

People will be wondering what we are up to!"

"Just look, though!"[6] he said and started off. A flute rang out prettily from the east wing,[7] accompanied by a *sō no koto*. "The Captain must be playing music with one of those inseparable friends of his—the Secretary Captain, I suppose.[8] What a lovely sound!" He stood to listen.

"I am over here, detained by the cressets' beautifully cool light," his message said.[9] All three came immediately.

"That flute was too much for me; it sounded so much as though the song of the wind had turned to autumn." Genji took out the koto to play some lovely music. The Captain played his flute very nicely in the *banshiki* mode, but the Secretary

---

2. Of the seventh lunar month, the first of autumn.
3. In poetry, wind rustling the reeds (*ogi*) may announce the coming of a lover.
4. *Mayumi no ki*, a deciduous tree that bears small blue-green flowers and reddens nicely in autumn.
5. *Kokinshū* 500: "Now that it is summer, a mosquito coil burns in my home, and ah, how long am I likewise to smolder underneath?" In Genji's poem, "smoke" is connected to "desire" by a play on *kohi* ("desire"), because the syllable *hi* by itself means "fire." The motif of smoke rising from the lover's burning heart, to vanish (or not) into the vastness of the sky, is a common one.
6. "Look! I have behaved myself after all!"
7. Yūgiri's.
8. Kashiwagi, who now holds the same office his father held in "The Broom Tree."
9. One delivered orally by messenger.

Captain was too nervous to sing. "Well?" Genji said. The Controller Lieutenant sang low, beating time and sounding just like a bell cricket.[10] Genji put him through his song twice, then passed the koto to the Secretary Captain, whose brilliantly attractive touch was, sure enough, hardly less good than his father's.

"Someone else is behind these blinds, I believe, someone who knows music, too. I must mind myself with the wine tonight. An old man weeping in his cups can be indiscreet."

True enough, she thought, and she was touched. She secretly paid close attention to all she saw and heard of the young gentlemen, no doubt because her lasting tie with them was destined to be strong, but they themselves suspected nothing, and the Secretary Captain, who felt this time as though he would not be able to refrain from pouring out his heart, actually behaved extremely well and never even let himself go to play a piece straight through.

10. His voice was sweet and pure.

28

The Typhoon

Nowaki ("tempest") means the typhoon winds of early autumn. The chapter's key event is a typhoon.

"The Typhoon" takes place in the eighth month, immediately after the time of "The Cressets."

PERSONS

His Grace, the Chancellor, Genji, age 36

Her Majesty, the Empress, 27 (Akikonomu)

The lady of the southeast quarter, 28 (Murasaki)

The Captain, 15 (Yūgiri)

Her Highness, Yūgiri's grandmother, about 70 (Ōmiya)

The lady of the northeast quarter (Hanachirusato)

The lady from Akashi, 27

The lady in the west wing, 22 (Tamakazura)

Genji's daughter, 8 (Akashi no Himegimi)

His Excellency, the Palace Minister (Tō no Chūjō)

His daughter, Yūgiri's love, 17 (Kumoi no Kari)

The flowers Genji had had planted in Her Majesty's garden flattered the eye this year as never before, for they were of every hue and kind, and they twined about low, handsome fences of barked or unbarked wood looking more perfect than the same ones elsewhere, even to the way dew gleamed on them morning and evening and made them shine like jewels. One forgot the spring hills before the skillful prospect of their many colors, and one's heart wandered forth among their cool delights. Autumn had always had more partisans than spring in the debate over which is to be preferred, and those who once favored that celebrated spring garden now turned, as people do, to look elsewhere.

Her Majesty stayed on at home in order to enjoy it all, and she would have liked meanwhile to call for music, but the eighth month was that of her father's death;[1] and while she watched the flowers continue to grow more beautiful, rather than fade as she feared they soon might, the wind set in to blow, and changed skies threatened a worse tempest than any normally known. Those who did not much care that the flowers should suffer cried disaster nonetheless, and Her Majesty almost despaired as dewy pearls were swept, unstrung, from petal and leaf. She seemed to crave sleeves wide enough to cover the *autumn* sky.[2] She lowered her shutters as night fell and the storm raged on unseen, since it was so frightening, but she continued even then to tremble for her flowers.

In the southeast quarter it had begun to blow just when work was being done on the garden, and this wind cruelly surprised the languishing *hagi* fronds.[3] From near the veranda she watched the wind again and again sweep away every last drop of dew. Genji was with their daughter when his son, the Captain, came round. The Captain glanced absently over the standing panel[4] on the eastern bridgeway and in

1. Rokujō's husband, the Heir Apparent, who died long ago.
2. *Gosenshū* 64: "O that I had sleeve enough to cover the wide sky! No wind should then take the flowers that blossom in spring."
3. *Kokinshū* 694 evokes the languishing lover in terms of *hagi* fronds awaiting the wind. The *hagi* fronds are *motoara* ("bare toward the base of the stems," hence "languishing") because autumn (the season of separation) is advancing.
4. *Kosōji*, a rigid, low panel (made of wood or the same material as sliding panels [*shōji*]) and mounted on a stand so that it could be moved about.

The near garden

through the open double doors, and he stood still to watch in silence when he noticed a crowd of gentlewomen. The screens had been folded up and moved aside because of the wind, and he could see straight through to a lady seated in the aisle room. There was no mistaking her nobly warm and generous beauty: she looked like a lovely mountain cherry tree in perfect bloom, emerging from the mists of a spring dawn. The breath of her enchantment seemed irresistibly to perfume his face even as he watched. She was nothing less than extraordinary. For some reason she smiled to devastating effect when the wind blew the blinds in and her women held them down; she was too worried about her flowers to leave them and come in. He could not take his eyes off her, despite also the varied charms of her women, and he knew now how right his father had been, in case precisely this should happen, to keep him well away from a lady who could not fail to trouble anyone who saw her.

He was making off again for fear of being noticed when Genji, returning from his daughter's, opened the inner sliding panel and entered the room. "What a horrible, maddening wind! Get your shutters down. There must be men about, and anyone could see you."

The Captain approached again and watched as she said something to Genji, who looked at her and smiled. He could not imagine that Genji was his father; he looked too glowingly young and graceful and handsome. She was in full flower, too, and he was deeply impressed by how perfect they both were; nonetheless, the shutter onto his bridgeway had blown open as well, and he, too, was in plain view. He retreated in terror and came forward toward the veranda, clearing his throat as though he had just arrived. I knew it! Genji said to himself. She must have been there to see: those double doors were wide open. He instantly realized what this must mean.

Nothing like this has ever happened before! the Captain exulted. The wind really can toss boulders into the sky! They are both extremely upset, despite their precautions, and I have seen a rare and wonderful sight!

Household retainers appeared. "The wind will be appalling, my lord," they said. "It is mild here because it is blowing from the northeast. The riding ground pavilion and the southern fishing pavilion may go at any moment." They noisily set about looking after one thing and another.

"Where have you come from?" Genji inquired.

"I was at Sanjō," the Captain replied, "but people said it is going to blow such a storm that I came here—I was worried. It is Her Highness who is really afraid, though. The sound of the wind frightens her at her age as though she were a child, and I feel so sorry for her that I am going back there now."

"That is a good idea. Age should not turn people into children again, but I am afraid that is what happens." Genji expressed his sympathy for the lady in various other ways, and he had the Captain tell her, "I am confident that despite the commotion you are in good hands with this young lord to look after you."

There was never a day when the always proper young man failed to present himself both at Sanjō and at Rokujō, even when buffeted all the way by the wind, and apart from those times when seclusion inevitably confined him to the palace, no press of official business, no lengthy or complex ceremonial duties could keep him from Rokujō first, then Her Highness, then on, and it was touching to see how today, in this weather, he went flying about even more swiftly than the wind.

Her Highness was very pleased to receive him and greatly reassured. "I have never in all my years seen such a terrible storm," she said, trembling helplessly. "To think that you have come here through the crash of breaking tree limbs, while the wind seems to be stripping every tile from the roof!" Gone was that once brave and splendid show,[5] and now the Captain was all she had in this shifting world. Not that on the whole she enjoyed less consideration now than then, but the Palace Minister remained quite distant.

The Captain lay all night amid the howling of the wind, under the spell of an indefinable sadness. Quite apart from the lady for whom he always longed, he could not forget the sight he had just seen, and such startlingly forbidden thoughts accompanied the vision that he roused himself in fright to turn his mind elsewhere; but they kept returning. There could never have been many like her, nor would there ever be. When his father had *her*, how could the lady of the northeast quarter[6] possibly still stand beside her? Poor thing, he thought, there is just no comparison between them; and he wondered admiringly at his father's kindness. Serious as he was, it never occurred to him to entertain any culpable ambition, but he did want if he possibly could to spend his life with someone just like her, and he could not help feeling that doing so would help a little to prolong what years he had allotted to him.

The wind dropped somewhat toward dawn, and rain began falling in heavy bursts. He had word that outbuildings had collapsed at Rokujō. While the wind raged, many people on that vast and proud estate gathered around the great lord and his lady, but he realized with a start that in the northeast quarter she must be very lonely, and he set out under a still barely lightening sky. A freezing, almost horizontal rain blew in[7] all the way there. Under these troubled skies he felt strangely foreign to himself. What is this? Have I yet another sorrow to bear? No, it is unthinkable! I must be completely mad! He went straight to the northeast and found her terrified. Having done what he could to reassure her, he summoned people to put things right as needed and then went on to the southeast, where the shut-

5. The press of retainers, visitors, petitioners, and so on when her husband was alive.
6. Hanachirusato.
7. Into his carriage.

ters were still down. He leaned against the railing at the point where he judged them both to be and looked out over the garden. The trees on the hill were leaning with the wind, and many broken branches lay on the ground. Needless to say, the plants were in wild disorder, but so, too, were the bark shingles, the tiles, the standing shutters, the screening fences, and so on. A weak sun rose, and dew sparkled in the garden as on a grieving face, while the sky remained densely shrouded in fog. He wiped away his own unreasoning tears and cleared his throat.

"That sounds like the Captain," Genji said. "I doubt that it is even dawn yet." There were sounds of him getting up. Whatever she said was inaudible, but he laughed. "This is the famous 'parting at dawn' that I never put you through even in our early days.[8] I wish I were not doing it to you now!" They chatted on very nicely together. Her replies did not reach the Captain, but he could tell how close they were from their playful tone of voice.

Genji raised the shutters himself. Alarmed to be so near, the Captain withdrew to a respectful distance. "Well?" Genji said. "Was Her Highness glad to see you yesterday evening?"

"Yes, she was. I felt awfully sorry for her—anything can put her in tears."

Genji smiled. "I doubt that she will be with us much longer. Do what you can to make her happy. She must wish His Excellency were more attentive. He is lively and manly in character, and he has made a great show of being scrupulously filial, but there is very little depth to him, you know. Still, he is also remarkably clever and complex, and so much more learned than this degenerate age deserves that despite his testiness there can hardly be anyone as far beyond reproach as he.

"I wonder whether Her Majesty has anyone reliable attending her in this awful wind," he went on, and he gave his son this message for her: "What did you think of the noise the wind made last night? A wind has caught me, too,[9] with a storm like this going on, and I have been very low. I am afraid I am obliged for the time being simply to look after myself."

The Captain stepped down from the veranda and started toward Her Majesty's through the door onto the connecting gallery. He looked very splendid in the breaking dawn. Standing to the south of Her Majesty's east wing, he saw that her main house had two shutters raised and the blinds rolled up, and that there were women sitting there in the faint early-morning light. There were a lot of them, young ones, leaning on the railing. The freedom of their behavior left some doubt about how they might be dressed, but their varied colors made them a pretty picture in the half-light. Her Majesty was having her page girls go down into the garden to feed dew to the crickets in their cages. Four or five of them in aster and pink, with light or dark gowns and maidenflower dress gowns perfect for the season, were wandering here and there with variously colored cages, picking such charming flowers as pinks and bringing them to their mistress. They all looked quite lovely as

---

8. A lover normally left at daybreak (*akebono no wakare*, a stock expression), but Genji and Murasaki were never normal lovers and lived together from the start.

9. Various indispositions were attributed to a "wind" having entered the body. Genji is excusing himself for failing to visit Akikonomu in person.

their colors blurred into the mists. The wind brought him a scent as of asters, and such a fragrance of incense that he thought that it must have caressed Her Majesty's own sleeves.[10] Such exquisite elegance overwhelmed him, and he hesitated to go farther, but after discreetly clearing his throat he stepped forward nonetheless. The women slipped back inside without visible dismay or haste. As a page, when Her Majesty first went to the palace, he had been allowed in to see her, so that her gentlewomen were not that shy of him. After delivering his message he took the opportunity to give Naishi and Saishō messages of his own,[11] since he had divined their presence there. Even so, the lofty dignity of their surroundings brought to mind other, sad preoccupations.

All the shutters were up in the southeast quarter, where she was gazing at the flowers she had found so hard to leave the evening before—flowers that now lay ravaged as though they had never been. The Captain delivered Her Majesty's reply from the steps: "I had hoped like a fearful child that you might keep me from the storm, but I feel better now."

"How strangely timid Her Majesty is!" Genji said. "I must have disappointed her—a night like that could have frightened any woman." He went to her straightaway.

Genji rolled up the blinds and went in to put on a dress cloak, and the Captain just glimpsed a sleeve moving a low standing curtain closer. It must be she! The thought set his heart pounding all too loudly, or so it seemed to him, and he looked away.

"The Captain is very handsome this morning," Genji remarked quietly, contemplating the mirror. "He should properly still be a mere boy; perhaps it takes a father's eye to see such a worthy young man." He appeared pleased with the lasting youthfulness of his own face. "Meeting Her Majesty always makes me nervous. There is nothing obviously intimidating about her, but I cannot help it; she has such subtle depths. However gently feminine she may be, there is more to her than meets the eye."

On his way out he noticed how abstracted the Captain was, to the point of hardly noticing his father, and whatever it was his sharp eye had caught, he turned back to his darling and said, "I wonder whether the Captain might have seen you yesterday in that wind. The doors were open, you know."

She blushed. "How could he? I never heard anyone on the bridgeway."

There is something odd about him even so, Genji reflected as he set off.

The Captain detected the presence of Her Majesty's women at the door onto the bridgeway once his father had gone in through her blinds, and he went up to them to exchange a few bantering remarks. However, his cares made him more subdued than usual.

Genji went straight north from there to the lady from Akashi's, where instead of proper household staff he saw only experienced servant women moving about in

10. The meaning of this passage is contested. One puzzle is that asters have no smell.
11. Gentlewomen attached to Akikonomu.

the garden. The low fences entwined with her specially planted bluebells and gentians were scattered far and wide, and the simply dressed page girls in their pretty gowns seemed to be looking for them and putting them back up as well as they could. She was sitting near the veranda, sadly toying with her *sō no koto*, when she heard the warning cries from his escort, and the way she then dropped a dress gown over her soft, casual attire[12] to mark the deference she owed him was deeply impressive. To her disappointment he abruptly left again after sitting with her a moment to ask how she had got on during the storm.

> *"The sound of the wind passing as the wind will do, rustling the reeds,*
> *seems, unhappy as I am, to bring a new touch of chill,"*[13]

she murmured to herself.

The lady in the west wing had slept late, after a terrified and sleepless night, and she was only now looking into her mirror. Genji told his escort not to cry warnings, and he purposely entered in silence. There she sat, picked out in dazzling beauty by a brilliant shaft of sun, with her folded screens leaning in a corner and the room around her in complete disarray. He sat beside her and turned even the storm into one more occasion to embarrass her with his usual banter, which upset her so much that she burst out at last, "This awful obsession of yours is exactly why I wished last night that the wind would just take me away!"

Genji smiled with delight. "You want to go with the wind? You cannot be serious. Still, I suppose you have somewhere else in mind. So this is how you have come gradually to feel about me. Well, I can hardly blame you."

She, too, smiled when she realized how frankly she had spoken, giving lovely color and expression to the face that peeped out, full as a Chinese lantern pod,[14] from between the strands of her beautiful hair. So broad a smile lacked a certain dignity, but nothing else about her could possibly be faulted.

The Captain longed to see her himself, now that his father was talking to her so intently. A standing curtain was in place behind the corner blind, but a little untidily, and he found when he gently lifted a panel that every barrier was gone and he had a perfect view. It took him aback to see Genji clearly flirting with her, and he was fascinated. He is supposed to be her father, he thought, but she is much too old for him to take in his arms! The startling strangeness of the scene kept him watching despite his fear of discovery. She was hidden behind a pillar and looking a little away from Genji, but he drew her toward him, and her hair spilled forward like a wave. The yielding way she leaned on him suggested complete familiarity, despite her obvious trouble and distress. No! This is impossible! What does it mean? He did not bring her up himself— that must explain why he feels that way about her now. He has never left any corner unexplored. Who can blame him? I do not like it, though! The Captain was ashamed

---

12. The "dress gown" (*kouchiki*) was semiformal. An early commentary explains "dropped" by suggesting that one was hanging on a clothing rack nearby and that she simply pulled it down over her.

13. The wind rustling the reeds is Genji's perfunctory visit.

14. The paper-thin, orange fruit envelope of *Physalis alkekengi*, the Chinese lantern plant or Japanese bladder cherry.

of his own thoughts. She was his sister, yes, but considering her looks he could easily imagine himself stepping back a little, deciding that, after all, they had different mothers, and straying in exactly the same way himself. Although not up to the lady he had glimpsed the day before, she certainly was of the same order; to see her was to smile with pleasure. There came to his mind all at once a picture of richly blooming kerria roses, laden with dew in the light of the setting sun. The image did not match the pres-

Making a robe

ent season, but still, it felt right. Flowers do not last, though, and their stamens all too soon begin to droop. Her beauty was really beyond such comparisons. No one came to disturb their intent whisperings, but for some reason he could not catch, Genji presently stood up with a grave look on his face.

She said,

> "Caught up in the wind's wandering and willful ways, a maidenflower
> feels she has no other hope than at last to wilt and die."

He could not actually hear her, but Genji repeated the poem. Mingled pleasure and revulsion urged him to go on watching, but he drew back nonetheless, since he did not wish Genji to see how close he had been.

Genji replied,

> "If she would just yield to the hidden dew's appeal, the maidenflower
> at the touch of the wild wind need not ever wilt or die.[15]

Just reflect on the pliant bamboo."

The Captain must have misheard him. No one should overhear such things.

From there Genji went on to the northeast. For one reason or another, perhaps the early-morning chill, several older gentlewomen were busy sewing before their mistress, while younger ones stretched cloth on what looked like narrow chests. All about her the lady had scattered some very pretty ocher silk gauze and some plum-red stuff beaten to a most beautiful luster.

"Is this a train-robe for the Captain?" Genji asked. "I expect His Majesty's garden-court[16] party will be canceled. What would be the point, after what this wind has done? I think we are in for a sad autumn." What *could* it be? he wondered. All the colors were exquisitely lovely, and he realized that she was just as good at this sort of thing as the lady to the south.

---

15. "If you would only give in to my secret desires . . ."

16. *Tsubo senzai*, the garden space confined between the Emperor's residence (Seiryōden) and the Kōrōden, immediately to the west.

A dress cloak for him, in a pattern of floral circles, had been lightly dyed to an absolutely perfect hue with freshly picked dayflower blossoms. "It is for the Captain to wear this sort of thing," he said. "It looks better on a young man." After various other remarks of this nature he continued on his way.

The Captain was beginning to tire of accompanying his father on this tedious series of visits; besides, he had a letter to write, and it worried him to see the sun already so high. Meanwhile, they came to the residence of Genji's daughter.

"My lord, she is still with my lady," her nurse said. "The wind frightened her, and she could not get up this morning."

"The uproar of the storm made me hope that I could be of assistance here," the Captain put in, "but Her Highness was too distressed. How is her doll's house?"

The gentlewomen smiled. "The mere breeze from a fan makes her fear disaster, and this wind nearly destroyed it. We are not quite sure how to mend it."

"Do you have some modest paper? I need that, and your inkstone."

One went to a cabinet and took out a roll of paper that she gave him in the inkstone box lid. "Oh, no," he said, "I would not presume."[17] Still, he felt a little better when he considered where the lady in the northwest stood,[18] and he proceeded with his letter. It was on thin purple paper. He ground the ink carefully and wrote intently, pausing now and again to inspect the tip of the brush. He made a very nice picture. Still, his poem was awfully trite, and it certainly deserved no praise:

> "Let the wild winds blow this evening, and lowering clouds wander the heavens,
> there is no forgetting you, no, not even when I try!"

He tied it to some storm-tossed beardgrass.[19]

"The Katano Lieutenant made sure his plant or flower matched his paper," they objected.

"Oh, I never thought of considering the color! What would you recommend instead?"[20] He seemed to have little to say to women like these, and he did not play up to them, treating them instead with haughty pride. Next, he wrote another letter and gave both to the Second Equerry, who, amid much whispering, passed one each to a pretty page and to a thoroughly reliable-looking retainer. The young women were desperate to know whom they were for.

They sprang to life at the news that their mistress was returning, and they began straightening the standing curtains and so on. The Captain, who never normally showed such interest, was eager to pursue comparing the flowerlike faces he had seen, and he went to some lengths to conceal most of himself behind the blind near the double doors and to peer through a gap in the standing curtain; and all at once there she was, just coming in from behind a screen. There were too many

17. He asked for the woman's own paper and inkstone, but what she gives him belongs instead to his half sister.
18. He need not feel too awestruck, considering who the Akashi lady is.
19. *Karukaya*, a type of tall grass with long awns, distantly related to rice. *Kokin rokujō* 3785: "Being so serious does me no good at all; ah, I would toss about with you like windblown beardgrass, in wild abandon."
20. He is being ironic. The women have not recognized the sexual significance of the beardgrass.

women in the way, and he was thoroughly annoyed to find that he could make out very little. Her hair, which did not yet reach the floor, fanned out over her pale gray-violet gown, and she looked so engagingly slender and small that he liked her very much. He had not had a glimpse of her for two years, and he thought how nicely she seemed to have grown out since then. What will she be like when she is grown-up? Beside the cherry blossoms and kerria roses he had seen, she might be called wisteria—yes, he decided, hers was the rich beauty of wisteria blooming on some mighty tree and swaying in the breeze. If only I could be with such women as these all I like, day and night! And it should be possible, too, if it were not for this hateful barrier between us! The stalwart young man could hardly contain himself.

He found Her Highness his grandmother quietly occupied with her devotions. Many fine young women attended her, but none yet resembled in bearing, grace, or dress the ladies he had just seen in their glory. It was the handsome nuns, in the modesty of their inky habits,[21] who really gave the scene its moving quality. His Excellency was there as well. The lamps were lit, and the two were talking quietly.

"It has been so long since I last saw my girl!" Her Highness said, openly weeping. "It is so hard!"

"Oh, yes, I shall have her come to you soon. She seems to be pining in some way and looks decidedly reduced. To tell the truth, I think one can do without daughters. They are nothing but trouble." He spoke with the same obstinate disapproval as ever, hurting her so much that she did not press him further. "And now that I have one who is completely hopeless, I have no idea what to do with her," he continued with a bitter smile.

"Oh, no, surely not! No daughter of yours could be as bad as that!"

"That is just it," they say he replied. "She is a disaster! I must manage to let you see her."

---

21. Yūgiri's grandmother's senior gentlewomen would have taken vows with her.

29

MIYUKI

The Imperial Progress

Miyuki means "imperial progress."
In this chapter Emperor Reizei
goes on a winter outing to Ōharano, just southwest of the city.
The word appears (as a wordplay
on *miyuki*, "snow") in a poem that
Genji sends in reply to one by
the Emperor:

*"Never as today can the slopes of Oshio, where repeated snows
weigh upon the forest pines, have seen true magnificence."*

RELATIONSHIP TO EARLIER CHAPTERS

"The Imperial Progress" begins in the twelfth month of the year covered in the previous six chapters and goes through the second month of the following year (Genji's thirty-seventh).

PERSONS

His Grace, the Chancellor, Genji, age 36 to 37

The lady in the west wing, 22 to 23 (Tamakazura)

Genji's lady, the lady of the southeast quarter, 28 to 29 (Murasaki)

His Majesty, the Emperor, 18 to 19 (Reizei)

His Excellency, the Palace Minister (Tō no Chūjō)

His Highness of War, Genji's brother (Hotaru Hyōbukyō no Miya)

The Commander of the Right, early 30s (Higekuro)

The Captain, Genji's son, 15 to 16 (Yūgiri)

Her Highness, Tō no Chūjō's mother (Ōmiya)

The Captain, Tō no Chūjō's eldest son, early 20s (Kashiwagi)

The Controller Lieutenant, around 20 (Kōbai)

The Kokiden Consort, Tō no Chūjō's daughter, 19 to 20

The girl from Ōmi, Tō no Chūjō's daughter (Ōmi no Kimi)

Thus Genji examined every possibility in the hope of having things turn out well, but that "silent waterfall" of his[1] made a sad and troubling burden for the young person in the west wing, and his fair name was in grave peril, just as the mistress of the southeast quarter[2] surmised. No doubt His Excellency, who always reacted so sharply and could not tolerate the smallest slip, would give him a welcome for all the world to see, but Genji knew that that might only make him look foolish, and he thought better of the idea.

In the twelfth month His Majesty was to make a progress to Ōharano,[3] and everyone in the world longed to be there. All the ladies from Rokujō went to watch. His Majesty set off at the hour of the Hare[4] and turned west from Suzaku along Gojō.[5] The sightseeing carriages stood in an unbroken row all the way to the Katsura River. Not every imperial progress achieved *this*, by any means. On the day, the Princes and senior nobles all gave special attention to preparing their mounts and saddles and chose tall, handsome retainers and grooms whom they dressed lavishly, so that they presented a spectacle of rare magnificence. Naturally their Excellencies of the Left and Right, His Excellency the Palace Minister, the Counselors, and all those below them attended without exception. The privy gentlemen down even to the fifth and sixth ranks wore leaf-green formal cloaks over grape trainrobes. The lightest of snows was falling, so that the very sky along the way lent the occasion its own grace. The Princes and senior nobles who were to join the hawking each had brought a striking hunting costume. The falconers from the Palace Guards wore a riot of unusual rubbed patterns[6] that gave the scene a special touch.

1. His secret pursuit of Tamakazura. Otonashi no Taki ("Otonashi Waterfall") is properly a name, but *oto nashi* also means "no sound," and this double meaning is exploited in poetry. Early commentaries cite two otherwise unknown poems to which this passage may allude (*Genji monogatari kochūshakusho in'yō waka* 205, 1481).
2. Murasaki.
3. Ōharano, just west of the City, is the sloping area (*no*) below Mount Oshio and the site of the Ōharano Shrine, the Kyoto counterpart of the Kasuga Shrine in Nara, the tutelary shrine of the Fujiwara clan. Early commentaries suggest that this account was inspired by Emperor Daigo's visit to Ōharano on the fifth day of the twelfth month of 928.
4. Between 5:00 and 7:00 A.M.
5. Suzaku was the City's central north-south thoroughfare. Gojō ("Fifth Avenue") ran east-west.
6. *Surigoromo*, clothes on which patterns had been imprinted by rubbing on the juices of various dye plants.

Everyone had rushed out to witness the spectacle, and some pitifully humble carriages that belonged to people one did not know made a sad sight with their broken wheels. Many fine carriages were driving imposingly about near the very start of the floating bridge.[7]

The young lady from the west wing was there, too. Among all the gentlemen before her in their finery, she still found none to compare with His Majesty seen in profile, stock-still in his red robes. She secretly paid particular attention to His Excellency her father, but despite his dazzling looks and weighty presence there was only so much and no more to be said for him. He was by far the most impressive figure among the commoners, but she could not keep her eyes off that One in the palanquin. Captain, Lieutenant, or Privy Gentleman So-and-so, for whom other young women were swooning and sighing, Isn't he handsome! or I love his style! naturally meant nothing to her, for His Majesty eclipsed them all. Genji so resembled him that they could have been the same man, but to her mind His Majesty somewhat surpassed Genji in dignity, and it was he whose looks and bearing were truly a marvel to behold. Surely there had never been anyone like him. She had assumed that all noble gentlemen were comely, accustomed as she was to the grace of Genji and the Captain, but such company as this cast a shadow over them, for they seemed not even to have the same eyes or noses, and they hardly deserved a glance. His Highness of War was there, too. The Commander of the Right, ever weighty and imposing, served His Majesty in great style today with a quiver on his back, but his heavy black beard was thoroughly unprepossessing.[8] What could such a face ever have had in common with a prettily made-up woman's? She had grave doubts about what Genji had in mind for her, because palace service might turn out to be hideously demeaning,[9] but apart from the intimacies involved, the mere prospect of serving him and being with him seemed to her very pleasant indeed.

His Majesty's palanquin halted once the procession reached Ōharano. The senior nobles ate under a tent and changed from court dress into hunting costume. From Rokujō, Genji provided wine and refreshments. He had meant to attend himself and had let it be known that he would come, but he had had to inform His Majesty that seclusion required him to be absent after all. His Majesty sent the Chamberlain Aide of the Left Gate Watch to him with a brace of pheasants on a branch. Whatever his message, it would be a bore to repeat here the particulars of any such occasion.[10]

> "O do come today and favor again a haunt where pheasants once rose
> that time on Mount Oshio, over the slopes deep in snow,"[11]

---

7. Ukihashi, a sort of temporary bridge (boards laid across boats or rafts) over the Katsura River.

8. He is therefore known as Higekuro, "Blackbeard." Perhaps he really has a beard, or perhaps heavy facial hair just gives him dark jowls.

9. Since the Emperor was already surrounded by women (Akikonomu, the Kokiden Consort) who outranked her.

10. It would be out of place for a woman to repeat what the Emperor said on a formal occasion.

11. "A haunt where pheasants once rose" (tatsu kiji no furuki ato) alludes to a previous visit to Ōharano by a Chancellor, on the occasion of an imperial progress.

his poem went. A Chancellor must have joined a progress to Ōharano before.

Genji gave His Majesty's messenger a warm and respectful welcome. He replied,

> *"Never as today can the slopes of Oshio, where repeated snows*
> *weigh upon the forest pines, have seen true magnificence."*[12]

I remember only bits and pieces of what I heard then, and all this may be wrong.

The next day Genji sent a note to the west wing: "Did you see His Majesty yesterday? Perhaps you feel more like it now." It was on plain white paper, quite casually written and not at all suggestive.

She read it with pleasure. "What is he talking about?" she asked, smiling, astonished that he should understand her so well; and she answered,

> *"With that veil of mist and the hazy morning clouds sprinkling down snow,*
> *how could I, do you suppose, have seen all the heavens' light?*[13]

I hardly know what to think of any of this."

Genji showed her note to his darling. "I urged her to consider it, as you know, but there is Her Majesty, and as long as she stays here, that might make things difficult; and once His Excellency finds out about her, there is then the Consort. That is what seems to worry her. A girl who has glimpsed His Majesty can hardly fail to be pleased with the idea of entering his intimate service, as long as she is not too shy."

"You are awful! Even if His Majesty impressed her favorably, she could hardly put herself forward to choose palace service on her own!" She smiled.

"Oh, come now, I am sure you are the one he has impressed!"

To her in the west wing he replied as encouragingly as ever,

Warrior with bow and quiver

> *"When that brilliant light shines in unhindered glory throughout the heavens,*
> *how could just a little snow have come so to cloud your gaze?*

Do make up your mind and go!"

At any rate, he first had to look after her donning of the train, for which he conscientiously provided the most beautiful furnishings. With him any ceremony tended to be grandly perfect, even one that hardly concerned him, and this one, which might give him a chance to tell the Palace Minister the truth, promised to be imposing indeed.

---

12. Genji's poem, like the two that come after it, plays on *miyuki*, "imperial progress" and "snow."
13. "How could I have seen the Emperor properly?"

He decided on the second month of the New Year. Even a woman highly regarded and old enough no longer to hide her name[14] may still dispense for a while with openly honoring her ancestral deity, as long as she remains among her family, and so leave things vague for years; but (he reflected) if this one makes the choice I propose, the God of Kasuga will be displeased,[15] and the truth will come out in the end anyway, leaving me a lasting and unfortunate reputation as a master of devious plots. No, the way people do things now, it would be easy enough for her to take a new name[16] if she were merely common, but as it is . . . Besides, the bond between parent and child survives every attempt to sever it—I might as well come forward myself to let him know.

He therefore wrote to His Excellency to invite him to tie the cord,[17] to which His Excellency pleaded in answer that he could not very well accept because Her Highness his mother had been continually ill ever since winter set in. This was hardly the moment for the Captain either, since he was spending day and night in attendance at Sanjō, too absorbed even to think of anything else. Genji wondered what to do. Life is fleeting, he said to himself; Her Highness's passing would mean a time of mourning that *she*[18] could not possibly ignore either. No, I shall speak while Her Highness is still alive. He therefore set out for Her Highness's Sanjō residence, ostensibly to inquire after her health.

By now his slightest journey, however private in nature, assumed the grandeur of an imperial progress, and the increasing radiance of his presence moved Her Highness to wonder as she watched him that such a man should be seen in this world at all, until her mounting suffering seemed to drop away and she sat up to receive him. She talked to him very well, despite the evident weakness with which she leaned on her armrest.

"Your condition has not been that serious, I know, but it has greatly upset our young gentleman, who seems so distressed for you that he has made me worry a great deal about how you are. Anything at all can astonish and overwhelm me, since I no longer even go to court save on special occasions, and I live quietly by myself, quite unlike someone who serves His Majesty. Past and present supply many examples of older men, painfully bent by age, who have served the realm nonetheless, but quite apart from my native dullness I seem to have acquired sloth as well."

"It has been months now since I began to know the sufferings of age, and this year, when I feel as though I have only little longer to live, I have lamented that I might never see you or talk with you again; but today it seems to me that I have a

---

14. Her surname. A very young woman remained so entirely within her family that she had no social identity at all. Being the daughter of Tō no Chūjō, Tamakazura is really a Fujiwara, not the Minamoto (Genji) that she appears to be.

15. The Kasuga Shrine is the ancestral shrine of the Fujiwara, and the deity will be displeased if Tamakazura goes out into the world as a Minamoto. "Openly honoring her ancestral deity" refers to pilgrimage or to rites performed by the woman herself.

16. To be adopted by someone of a different surname.

17. To act as the *koshiyui*, the sponsor who tied the waist cord of the girl's train. Genji apparently means to tell Tō no Chūjō who the girl is *after* this event.

18. Tamakazura. Mourning for a grandmother normally lasted five months.

while yet. At my age I need have no regrets. Those who live on after everyone who meant anything to them is gone make a distressing sight, in my opinion, and I have wished my own departure to be swift, if it were not for our Captain, whose extraordinary kindness has made me sufficiently anxious about him to remain alive." Her prolonged weeping and her quavering voice had a degree of foolishness about them, but Genji well understood why she should feel as she did, and he sympathized with her.

Genji and Her Highness were discussing this and that from past or present when Genji remarked, "His Excellency the Palace Minister no doubt comes to see you daily. I should be pleased if his visit were to allow me to speak with him. There is something that I must tell him, but so far, you see, I have been prevented from doing so by the absence of a suitable occasion to meet him."

"He does not come that often, whether the reason be the press of his official duties or his own lack of will. What sort of thing do you wish to say? The Captain certainly has cause to be put out with him, and as I often tell him myself, 'I do not know how all this began, but as far as your present, quite unkind treatment of him is concerned, there is no retracting a rumor once it has begun to spread, and the way people are talking about it now makes it all sound rather silly.' He is not one to go back on anything he has ever said, though, and as far as I can tell, he does not understand what I am talking about."

Genji smiled at her assumption that he was thinking of the Captain. "I heard that he might give it up as a mistake and grant his permission after all, so I actually broached the subject myself, but when I saw how severely he then reprimanded the young man, I regretted having ever taken it upon myself to intervene. As they say, anything can be purified one way or another, and I fail to understand why he will not wash this away, although our world does make it difficult for the stream to run clear again after so unfortunately prolonged a turbid spell. My impression is that the longer something takes, the more likely it is to go wrong. I am very sorry to have heard about all this."

He continued in this vein for some time and then went on, "By the way, I confess to a mistake regarding a young lady who should properly be under his care, because strangely enough I came across her myself, and since she failed at the time to correct my error, I made no effort to discover more but decided instead to take her story at face value, since I have so few children of my own. I have not done a great deal for her since then, however, and now His Majesty has somehow heard about her and is expressing interest. He complains privately that he lacks a Mistress of Staff, and without one the office is poorly governed, the women assigned to it give inadequate service, and all sorts of things seem to go wrong. 'At present,' he says, 'the two experienced Dames of Staff and other qualified women, too, are letting it be known that they are available, but none of them will do. The one appointed has always been of high birth and good reputation, and unencumbered by concern for her own house. If the choice is to go to competence and intelligence, there are some whose long service has gained them promotion even when they lacked other things, but if no one like that is to be found, one can go only on general repute.' That is what His Majesty says, and I do not see how His Excellency could very well object. Palace service is always an honor, and it is therefore a worthy ambition for anyone, high or low. People feel that the official duties involved—directing the office concerned and taking responsibility for certain matters of government—are tedious and of no interest, but I see no reason why that need be so.[19] I can only agree with him that what really matters after all is the lady's own disposition, and when in that connection he inquired about her age, I realized that she must be the daughter His Excellency was seeking. I wanted to discuss with you how to proceed. I cannot very well meet him, except when the occasion properly warrants it. I thought of a way to tell him sooner, and I wrote to him, but he seemed reluctant and pleaded your illness to decline. He was right, I decided, it was not the moment, and I thought I might speak to you now that your health is a little better than it might otherwise have been. Please let him know."

"What? What can you possibly mean? When he has evenhandedly taken into his residence several young women who make this sort of claim, what can have possessed this one to approach somebody else? Could she have felt she had reason to believe she was yours?"

"It is a long story," Genji replied. "I am sure His Excellency will wish to hear it, too. Any revelation of it could provoke tiresome gossip, since it might be construed as involving relations with someone tediously common, and for this reason I have not yet told even the Captain. Please do not let it go any further," he added to seal her silence.

His Excellency at his residence learned of His Grace's arrival at Sanjō. "How poorly so forlorn an establishment must welcome so great a lord!" he exclaimed in surprise. "I doubt that anyone there really knows how to entertain his escort or prepare a room to receive him. I suppose the Captain must have accompanied him." He sent over his sons and other suitable young gentlemen from among their friends. "Take them refreshments and wine as needed," he added. "I ought to go myself, but that would only complicate things."

Meanwhile, Her Highness's letter arrived: "His Grace is visiting from Rokujō, and with the house so deserted I am at once embarrassed for myself and concerned about him. Could you come, too, discreetly and without making it obvious that I asked you to do so? Besides, there seems to be something that he wants to tell you when you are together."

What could it be? The Captain's complaint about this business of my daughter, I suppose. I could hardly argue if Her Highness were to insist, since she has so little time left, and His Grace were then to put in a well-turned, impassioned plea of his own. I dislike that young man's show of indifference, but if a suitable occasion turns up, I might as well allow myself to be persuaded and agree. He knew that he would have even less room to refuse if the two of them had actually planned a joint appeal, and since he was of an irredeemably contrary nature, this only made him waver again, asking himself why after all he should not. However, Her Highness

---

19. "Palace service" refers particularly to intimate relations with the Emperor, with all that such relations may mean to the woman and her family. The duties nominally attached to the office carry little weight in comparison.

had written, His Grace was probably expecting him, and he did not wish to offend either. He decided to go and see what they had to say.

In this spirit he dressed carefully and set out with no more than a modest escort. His arrival in the company of so many gentlemen was majestic and imposing. His weight became him, for he was tall, and his great dignity of gait and countenance made him a worthy Minister indeed. Over grape-colored gathered trousers he wore a cherry blossom train-robe, very long behind, and the easy poise of his bearing left a brilliant impression. Meanwhile, His Grace of Rokujō, in a cherry blossom dress cloak of light Chinese twill[20] over a plum-red gown, displayed a casually imperial grace more indescribable than ever. But although he shone more brightly, he did not otherwise match the magnificently attired lord beside him.

His gentlemen gathered around him one after another, in splendid array. The Fujiwara Grand Counselor and the Heir Apparent's Commissioner, both highly esteemed sons of His Late Excellency,[21] were enjoying great success. Present, too, in the natural course of things were such promising and well-regarded privy gentlemen as the Head Chamberlains, Fifth Rank Chamberlains, Palace Guards Lieutenants and Captains, and Controllers as well: ten or more very fine gentlemen indeed, all perfectly turned out, and many lesser colleagues below them. The wine cups went round until all were merry, and the topic on everyone's lips was Her Highness's great merit and admirable ways.

For His Excellency this rare meeting recalled the past, and although his estrangement from Genji might only have heightened his impulse to vie with him on every point, however minor, talking face-to-face this way brought up so many memories moving to both that they renewed their friendship and spent the day catching up on countless things, old or new, that had struck them over the years.

His Excellency offered Genji more wine. "It would have been wrong of me not to wait on you at all," he said, "but without an invitation from you I feared to impose. If I had simply ignored your presence here, you would have had one more reason to declare our friendship at an end."

"That declaration is yours to make. I have done much to deserve it," Genji hinted in reply.

This must be it, His Excellency thought apprehensively, assuming an attitude of deferential respect.

"You and I used to be at one on every matter, public or private," Genji began, "and I consulted you on all things, great or small. I looked forward to our sustaining the realm as though we shared a wing while we flew. More recently, there have been things that failed to turn out as I had hoped, but all that is merely between the two of us. Speaking more broadly, my disposition remains quite unchanged. I miss those old days more and more as the years go by, considering how rarely we meet now, and while I recognize that you have the dignity of your

---

20. The garment is made of *kara no ki*, a light silk twill or patterned weave.
21. Tō no Chūjō's father and Genji's former father-in-law; they are Tō no Chūjō's half brothers—probably the "Intendant of the Left Gate Guards" and the "Acting Middle Counselor" mentioned in "The Maidens."

rank to uphold, that does not prevent me from wishing rather bitterly at times that as long as we *are* friends, you might temper your grandeur somewhat and visit me after all."

"We did indeed see a lot of each other then," His Excellency replied circumspectly, "so much so that I am afraid my manner toward you became all too familiar, for there was indeed no distance between us. It never occurred to me that we shared a wing, though, once we began serving His Majesty; rather, I never ceased to be grateful for your most welcome favor, even when I came at last, unworthy as I am, to serve the realm in the office I now hold. It is true, however, that we seem in many ways somehow to have drifted apart as we have grown older."

Genji then touched on the matter at hand. "How moving and how extraordinary!" His Excellency immediately wept. "I believe that on one occasion, in an excess of grief, I mentioned something about how I had been trying ever since to find out what happened to her. Now that I can hold my head up a little in the world, I have disreputable children of mine roaming about everywhere, and one of them is a hopeless embarrassment, but at times I still think fondly of them all, and then my first thought is always of *her*." His words brought back the way they had told their most intimate secrets on that rainy night, until both gave themselves up to tears and laughter.

They parted very late that night. "Seeing you like this calls up such memories of old times, and such nostalgic feelings, that I have no wish to leave you at all," Genji said, and he who so seldom betrayed any weakness now began, perhaps from drunkenness, to weep. As to Her Highness, she remembered her daughter even more longingly, and the spectacle of Genji's now far greater glory stirred such bitter sadness that she could not stop her tears. The way she moistened her robe as saltily as any woman of the sea[22] made her quite a sight.

Genji did not seize this excellent opportunity to bring up the matter of the Captain. He decided to spare himself the awkwardness of pressing His Excellency, for he judged that His Excellency had no intention of yielding, while His Excellency for his part felt that it would be excessively forward of him to broach it without some encouraging sign from Genji. On this they therefore remained wary of each other after all.

"It would be proper tonight for me to see you home," His Excellency said, "but it might only be a burden to you if I were to do so too abruptly. I shall call on you on another occasion to thank you properly for today."

In reply Genji exacted from him the promise that he would not fail to come on the day Genji had mentioned before,[23] since Her Highness's health gave no cause for alarm. Both left in excellent spirits, amid an imposing clatter and commotion.

---

22. This somewhat jocular description, in the language of poetry, relies on the expression *amagoromo*, "ama's robe." *Ama* ("nun") also means someone who lives from the sea, hence associated with brine-drenched (tear-drenched) clothing. This use of *amagoromo* therefore yields the incongruous image of a nun weeping over a past that, as a nun, she is supposed to have renounced.

23. The day for Tamakazura's donning of the train.

"Something must have happened," someone remarked in the escort for His Excellency's sons.

"They hardly ever meet, and now there they are in a merry mood—perhaps His Excellency got something he wanted." But their wild guesses never hit on what the two had actually discussed.

The suddenness of all this aroused His Excellency's suspicions, and he began to worry, but he doubted that he should

Comb box

take the girl on immediately himself and act the part of her father. He considered the circumstances under which Genji must originally have found her and said to himself, No, he cannot be letting her go untouched. Respect for his other, greater ladies has no doubt kept him from flaunting her openly, and the difficulty of pursuing the affair, together with the risk of discovery, must be what has led him to tell me about her. This was hardly a reassuring train of thought. Would anyone ever hold it against her, though? Why should her reputation suffer for it, even if I were the one who encouraged it in the first place? I do not like to imagine the Consort's feelings if he sends her into palace service. So his mind ran on, to arrive nonetheless at the conclusion that at any rate it was not his business to thwart Genji's decision, whatever it might be.

The sixteenth, early in the period of the equinox, was a wholly favorable day. There was no other like it nearby, or so Genji was informed, and since Her Highness was reasonably well, he hastened to begin the preparations. He continued his visits to the young lady, but he told her everything he had disclosed to His Excellency, and he taught her otherwise everything that she would need to know. She was grateful enough to reflect that no father could have done more for her than he had, and she was very happy indeed.

Genji then told the story privately to the Captain as well. How strange all this is! *Now* I understand! the Captain thought. Now that everything made better sense, he found his treacherous memory supplying him with far more images of her than of the young lady who was his torment. And I never thought of it! he groaned, feeling like a complete fool. However, the way he nonetheless thought better of his impulse and dismissed it as impossible no doubt testified to his rare seriousness of character.

So the day came, and with it a discreet messenger from Sanjō. With very little time Her Highness had still put together a very pretty set of comb boxes and so on. A letter accompanied them. "It would not be right for me to speak to you as I am now, and I have therefore remained at home, but I entertain the hope that you will still be inspired to live as long as I. Perhaps I should forbear to speak of my emotion upon hearing all about you, but if you will allow me,

Whether from one line or again from that other, O lovely comb box,
     you will always be to me a treasure I gladly keep."[24]

The hand was tremulous and extremely old-fashioned. Genji was there over-
seeing the arrangements. "This is a letter from out of the past, but, oh, dear," he said
when he saw it, "just look at her writing! Once upon a time she was very good, but
the passing years have not treated her kindly. It is painful to see the way her hand
trembles!" He looked at the letter again. "She kept very successfully to her 'pretty
comb box,'" he observed with secret mirth. "Very few of the poem's thirty-one letters are unrelated to it, and that is not easy to manage."

Her Majesty sent the white train, the Chinese jacket, the gowns, the
wherewithal for putting up the hair, and so on,[25] all of it unusually beautiful, as
well as especially deep and rich Chinese incenses in the usual jars. The other
ladies sent what clothing they pleased, and even combs and fans for the
gentlewomen; and not one of their gifts was unworthy of the rest, for each had
been so eager to display her good taste that the results were very pleasing
indeed.

The ladies in Genji's eastern pavilion[26] heard of these preparations, too, but
they were ignoring the news, being of insufficient standing to contribute themselves, when the daughter of His Highness of Hitachi, whose ancient and strangely
fastidious ways forbade her to let such an occasion pass, presented exactly what formality required: a long dress in a blue-gray layering, a set of trousers in fallen chestnut or the like, such as people prized in days of yore, and a dress gown in a hail
pattern with purple checks, all most decorously wrapped and presented in a handsome clothing chest.[27] She had written, "I am reluctant to put myself forward, since
I am no one whom you will ever know, but I cannot keep myself from thinking of
you on this occasion. These are wholly unworthy, but you might perhaps give them
to your women." She sounded artlessly kind.

Genji read her letter with horror and thought, There she goes again! He
blushed. "She is such an impossible relic! Anyone as shy as she is should keep completely to herself, but no, she must embarrass even me!" He went on, "You must answer her—she will be hurt otherwise. I cannot bear the thought of slighting her
when I think how much His Highness her father used to love her."

A sleeve of the dress gown had on it a poem in a familiar vein:

"Alas and alack, such cause have I to complain, robe from far Cathay,
     when despair tells me your sleeves will never lie next to mine."[28]

24. "Whether you are Genji's daughter or my son's . . ." This warm, grandmotherly poem is a tissue of
wordplays associated with boxes, lids, and so on.
25. Things to be used in the ceremony itself. The gowns mentioned are worn with the train (*mo*) and
Chinese jacket (*karaginu*).
26. Utsusemi and Suetsumuhana, at Nijō.
27. Suetsumuhana's colors suggest mourning or some similarly sad occasion. "Fallen chestnut" (*ochiguri*)
may be a deep reddish brown. The "hail" pattern (*arare-ji*) consisted of rows of little squares in alternating
colors ("with purple checks").
28. A tissue of trite wordplays associated with *karakoromo* ("robe from far Cathay"), Suetsumuhana's favorite motif. Its complaining tone ill suits a happy occasion.

As in the past her writing was hopelessly cramped, emphatic, solid, and stiff. Despite his annoyance Genji could not repress his mirth. "Think what this poem must have cost her, especially now, when she has less help than ever!" he exclaimed in sympathy. "No, no, I may be busy, but I am not *too* busy to answer her myself! Something escapes me, though. Where on earth did she get this idea? She should not have done it!" He wrote in exasperation,

> *"Robe from far Cathay, robe from far Cathay once more, robe from far Cathay,*
> *over and over again, I hear robe from far Cathay!"*

"Seriously, though, I did it only because this is her own favorite ploy." He showed it to the young lady, who broke into a dazzling smile. "The poor thing!" she said reproachfully. "Why, I believe you are making fun of her!"

But I talk far too much nonsense.

His Excellency had at first taken little interest in the event, but Genji's extraordinary revelation made him look forward to it after all, and he soon arrived. The ceremony went beyond anything one would commonly expect. Genji had made it a wonder. His Excellency was overwhelmed by this evidence of Genji's particular consideration, and he acknowledged the extraordinary quality of what he had done.

He was admitted at the hour of the Boar.[29] Genji had had the room itself done up magnificently, quite apart from the usual accessories, and he offered his guest refreshments there. The lamps shone a little more brightly than usual, for he had provided a particularly considerate welcome. His Excellency was extremely anxious to see her, but it was really too soon for that, and when he tied on the train, he seemed only barely to have himself under control.[30]

"I undertake not to allude to the past this evening," his host announced, "and I hope that you will not betray any knowledge of it either. Put up a good front for those who do not know, and confine yourself to custom."

"I hardly know what else to talk about, though!" His Excellency replied. He put the wine cup to his lips and went on, "I readily confess the gratitude I owe you for all your extraordinary kindness, and yet I do not see how I could fail to resent your having hidden her all this time.

> *She has been unkind, the seagirl who on her shore remained long concealed,*
> *until the time came at last when she was to don her train!"*[31]

He could not stem the flow of his salt tears.

Overwhelmed by these commanding presences, the young lady could find no reply. Genji answered in her stead,

---

29. Admitted to the room where the ceremony would take place at roughly 10:00 P.M.

30. Tamakazura has her fan before her face, as propriety requires, and there is no prospect of her lowering it.

31. A web of wordplays on seashore imagery. One of these is on *mo* ("train" or "seaweed") and *kazuku* ("dive" or "don"), so that the other meaning of "until the time came at last when she was to don her train" (*oki tsu tamamo o kazuku made*) is "until the time came at last when she was to dive for seaweed."

"The waves cast her up, defenseless and all alone, here upon this shore,
like a plaything of the sea that no fisherman would want.

You are being quite unjust."

"I understand perfectly," His Excellency answered as he withdrew. It was really all he could say.

The Princes and the rest were all there. Many suitors were among them, and they had begun to wonder at how long it had been since His Excellency went in. Among his sons, only the Captain and the Controller[32] had some inkling of the truth. Both were at once pleased and chagrined to have set their hearts on her.

"I am glad I never said anything," the Controller whispered.

"His Grace seems to have unusual tastes."

"I suppose he wants to turn her into someone like Her Majesty."

Genji overheard them. "Do still be careful a while," he said to his visitor, "and avoid giving anyone reason to be critical. People in a position to please themselves can always muddle on through their own mistakes, but you and I may suffer for what people have to say about us. It might be preferable to let people become accustomed to the idea slowly, since we have more to lose than others."

"I leave the handling of all this to you," His Excellency replied. "The way she came to your attention and found shelter under your superb care suggests a powerful bond between you from lives past."

The presents for His Excellency, and also the gifts and largesse dispensed to others, naturally had each their customary measure, according to the recipient's rank, but Genji surpassed it to treat everyone magnificently. He dispensed with any extravagant music out of respect for His Excellency's past appeal to Her Highness's illness.

"Now you have nothing further to put in my way," His Highness of War observed earnestly.

"His Majesty has dropped certain hints," Genji replied, "and I have declined, but I shall have to decide other claims according to whether or not he returns to the subject."

His Excellency her father had only glimpsed her, and he longed to see her plainly. The idea that Genji would never have made so much of her if he had noted any flaw only moved him to think of her with impatient affection. He now understood how right that dream of his had been. The Consort was the only one to whom he explained the whole truth.

Genji did his best to ensure that the matter should not be discussed abroad for some time yet, but people love to gossip. The news naturally got out anyway, and it spread little by little until that peculiar young woman heard it as well; whereupon she sallied forth to the Consort at a time when the Captain[33] and the Controller Lieutenant were in attendance upon her. "I gather my lord has found himself a daughter," she brashly declared. "How nice! What can she be like, if both these gen-

32. Kashiwagi and Kōbai.
33. Kashiwagi.

tlemen are making such a fuss over her? They say *she* did not have much of a mother either." The Consort maintained an outraged silence.

"I am sure there must be some reason she is so well looked after," the Captain answered. "But who told you this, that you should so heedlessly bring it up here? Just imagine if some gossiping gentlewoman should hear you!"

"Nonsense! Why, everyone knows! She is supposed to be the next Mistress of Staff. That is just the sort of consideration I had in mind when I eagerly entered my lady's service, and that is why I gladly took on jobs no ordinary woman would do! My lady, you are perfectly horrid!"

Her tirade brought smiles to the faces of everyone there.

"I have my eye on that post, if it comes vacant! What nerve, coveting it for yourself!" The speaker was the Captain.

"Oh, no," she retorted, "a nobody like me has no business among grand lords and ladies like you! Yes, my fine Captain, I have a quarrel with you. You are the busybody who brought me here, and now you are laughing at me! A mere mortal does not belong here! You are awful, just awful!" She slipped backward in retreat, glaring at him, her eyes narrowed in fury, but it was hard really to dislike her. Her speech convinced the Captain that he had indeed made a mistake, and he maintained a serious expression.

"As far as that goes"—the Controller smiled—"I cannot imagine that my lady fails to recognize your great merit. Please calm down. You seem ready to reduce great boulders to powder,[34] but I am sure that you will have your wish in due time.

"Would you please confine yourself to the Celestial Rock Cave, though?[35] It might be safer." The Captain rose.

She burst into tears. "Even my brothers turn up their noses at me! My lady, it is only your kindness that keeps me in your service! Put me up for Mistress of Staff! You must, you must!" she insisted—she who ran about so willingly, so conscientiously everywhere, doing tasks no servant or page girl would touch. The Consort, who could not imagine what possessed her to say such things, found not a word to reply.

His Excellency laughed aloud when told of her ambition. "Where are you? Come here, you girl from Ōmi!" he once called when he was at the Consort's.

"Present!" Her voice rang out, and she appeared.

"The way you work, I am sure you would do well in any office," he said gravely. "Why did you not tell me right off that you want to be Mistress of Staff?"

"I *had* wanted to talk to you about it, but I allowed myself to trust that her ladyship would naturally do so herself, and now I hear the office is to go to someone else, I feel as though I only dreamed of riches—all I can do is put my hand to my heart."[36] The pace of her tongue was very lively indeed.

His Excellency suppressed a smile. "I do not understand what makes you so reticent. If only you had told me what you wanted, I would have spoken up for you

---

34. As the Sun Goddess (Amaterasu) did when she confronted her brother, Susanoo, in a rage.

35. In another episode of her quarrel with Susanoo, Amaterasu shut herself up in the Celestial Rock Cave (Ama no Iwato), thus plunging the world into darkness.

36. To calm her own unhappy emotions.

before anyone else. Never mind what claims His Grace's daughter may have, I cannot imagine His Majesty refusing me if I plead a good case. You must immediately
compose a loftily worded petition. His Majesty will not disappoint you when he
sees how well your long poem[37] conveys your desire. He is particularly sensitive to
things like that, you know." His clever joke at her expense was not at all fatherly.

"A poem in Yamato speech, yes, I can put one together, more or less." She was
rubbing her hands. "If you will be kind enough to ask him properly for me, I will add
a few words of my own, so to speak, and anticipate his gracious favor." The gentlewomen listening from behind their standing curtains thought they would die. Some
were laughing so hard they had to slip out for relief. The Consort blushed profusely
and felt utterly mortified.

"When things go wrong, I have only to spend time with that Ōmi girl to feel
all is well again," His Excellency declared. His only use for her was to make him
laugh.

"He only torments her because he is so ashamed of her" is the sort of thing
other people had to say on the subject.

---

37. *Nagauta* (or *chōka*), a poem of indeterminate length, in the same meter as the short poems common in
the tale. A petition of the kind mentioned by Tō no Chūjō would normally be written in Chinese and include a Chinese poem. He is recommending the "long poem" as a substitute, since women did not write
Chinese.

30

FUJIBAKAMA

Thoroughwort Flowers

Fujibakama (Eupatorium fortunei), here translated "thoroughwort," is a wildflower closely related to the North American boneset (*E. perfoliatum*). It puts forth clusters of tiny, light mauve flowers in autumn. The chapter derives its title from the *fujibakama* mentioned by Yūgiri in a poem addressed to Tamakazura (and tied to a spray of *fujibakama* in bloom):

"Here is thoroughwort laden with the very dews that soak your own field—
O have pity on me, then, if only just to be kind!"

"The Imperial Progress" went up to the second month of Genji's thirty-seventh year. "Thoroughwort Flowers" covers the eighth and ninth months of the same year.

PERSONS

His Grace, the Chancellor, Genji, age 37

The lady, 23 (Tamakazura)

The Consultant Captain, Genji's son, 16 (Yūgiri)

His Excellency, the Palace Minister (Tō no Chūjō)

The Secretary Captain, Tō no Chūjō's eldest son, 21 or 22 (Kashiwagi)

Saishō, Tamakazura's gentlewoman

The Commander, uncle of the Heir Apparent, 32 or 33 (Higekuro)

His wife, Murasaki's elder half sister, 35 or 36 (Higekuro no Kita no Kata)

His Highness of War, Genji's brother (Hotaru Hyōbukyō no Miya)

The Intendant of the Left Watch, Murasaki's half brother

Both gentlemen urged the lady in question[1] to accept appointment as Mistress of Staff, but she remained uneasy. There was no telling what she might risk in such company, considering that she had had to remain on guard even against the man she thought of as a father, and if something unfortunate did happen, and Her Majesty and the Consort both held it against her, where would she be then? I am not in a position to claim any real liking from either, she reflected, and my uncertain reputation gives many people reason to doubt me and to be all prepared to hold me up to ridicule. Yes, I have many troubles in store for me, one way or another. Being quite old enough to understand where she stood, she was disturbed and secretly saddened. I am perfectly all right after all as I am now, but His Grace's attentions are unwelcome and distasteful, and I wonder how I will ever escape them and clear up all the conjectures that people must be making about me. My real father defers to his every wish, and he is so unlikely to take a position of his own that I seem certain in any event to suffer from compromising appearances and to start a scandal.

Now that her father knew about her, Genji only dealt with her more shamelessly than ever, and this caused her silent anguish. She had no woman relative to whom to disclose even a few of her worries, let alone all of them, and how could she possibly have brought up any hint of her anxiety to either of the two gentlemen whose splendor she found so forbidding? She looked utterly enchanting as she gazed out from near the veranda at the beautiful twilight sky, contemplating meanwhile all that made her different from those around her.

The unusual color of her attractively plain, light gray costume set off her looks perfectly, and the women waiting on her were smiling at the sight when the Consultant Captain arrived, likewise more graceful and handsome than ever in a dress cloak of the same color, though a slightly darker shade, and a formal cap with its tail rolled.[2] He was always so kindly attentive that she had made it her practice

1. Genji and Tō no Chūjō urge Tamakazura, now no longer a "young" lady after her donning of the train.
2. Yūgiri and Tamakazura are in mourning for Ōmiya, who died between chapters. Yūgiri's gray is a little darker because he was closer to her. The fact that the tail (*ei*, a long, narrow, springy appendage made of lacquered cloth) on his cap is rolled rather than straight is also a sign of mourning. This is the first reference to him as "the Consultant Captain" (Saishō no Chūjō).

Man's court cap with rolled tail

not to keep him at any unnecessary distance, and since it would have been too cruel greatly to change that custom now that he knew the truth, she still conversed with him directly, with only a standing curtain between her and her blinds.[3]

He first delivered a message from Genji about His Majesty's remarks and then passed to what he himself had gathered on the subject. Her reply was quietly composed, but its skill and warmth, and the wonderful quality in what he gleaned of her presence as she spoke, recalled to him the face he had seen the morning after the storm—a face that had aroused his longing, although he had then dismissed his feelings as wrong, and that now, when at last he knew who she was, disturbed him even more. No, he thought, it is not her entering palace service that will decide my father to give her up; considering what fascinating women he already has, those looks of hers are certain to mean trouble.

He managed to say coolly enough, despite the rush of feeling that oppressed him, "I must convey to you something that I am told is for no one's ears but your own. May I do so?" At this hint her women retreated a little and averted their faces from him behind their standing curtains. With great feeling he poured forth a long and thoroughly plausible but invented message from Genji concerning His Majesty's exceptional eagerness and the dispositions that she should take in consequence.

She had no words with which to answer him but only sighed, secretly and so sweetly, so touchingly that he could bear no more. "You are to doff your mourning this month," he said, "and today was not the day for a speech like that. According to His Grace you are to go out to the riverbank on the thirteenth.[4] I look forward to escorting you there."

"That might turn the trip into rather a procession, might it not? One ought really to keep it discreet." It was wise of her to hint that she preferred not to have everyone know she had been in mourning.[5]

"I am sorry to hear that you wish to keep it a secret. This mourning is for me a reminder of an unbearable loss, and removing it will be another sorrow. But I do not understand the tie that continues to bind us. The color you wear is the only sign of it, as far as I can see."

"I who understand so little can make nothing at all of such things, but I know that this color is strangely sad to wear." She did indeed seem more than usually subdued, and she was only the more delightfully lovely for it.

Perhaps the Captain had foreseen such a moment, because he had brought some very pretty thoroughwort flowers that he now slipped in to her past the edge of a blind. "You should look at these—there is a reason why,"[6] he said but retained

3. Yūgiri sits outside the blinds.
4. For the purification to end her mourning, probably in the Kamo River. The month is the eighth.
5. Because everyone would then know she was Tō no Chūjō's daughter and not Genji's.
6. Because *fujibakama* flowers are light *murasaki* (purple) in color, and *murasaki* is the color of relatedness.

his hold, which she failed to notice; and when she moved to take them, he tugged at her sleeve.

> *"Here is thoroughwort laden with the very dews that soak your own field—*
> *O have pity on me, then, if only just to be kind!"*[7]

"At the road's end," I suppose he means,[8] she said to herself, shocked and angry, but she pretended not to notice and only slipped quietly away from him to reply,

> *"Ah, if, after all, the dew you have brought me here came from a far field,*
> *then these flowers' light purple might earn you kindness at least.*[9]

Talking together this way does not mean that we share anything very deep."

The Captain gave a little smile. "Shallow or deep, I am sure that you follow me well enough," he said. "Seriously, though, I well know the lofty state to which you are called, but I wonder whether you can possibly understand the stubborn turmoil in my heart. I have endured it in bitter silence for fear of your displeasure, but you see, 'Nothing is left me now' describes my own misery.[10] Do you really know how the Secretary Captain feels? For that matter, I wonder why I ever imagined that I spoke for someone else.[11] When it comes to my own interests, I am a fool, as I know all too well. I feel jealous and disappointed when I see how he can actually enjoy the solace of being near you, now that he knows the truth. Do at least grant me some sympathy for that!" He said much more in this vein, with great feeling, but it was all too unpleasant to write down.

Repelled, she[12] had slowly withdrawn farther and farther from him. "You are very cruel!" he protested. "I am certain you know quite well that I would never commit any offense." He wanted to go on to pour out a little more of his heart, but she now withdrew completely, claiming that she felt strangely unwell, and so he left, too, amid pathetic sighs.

Why did I have to go and say all that? he asked himself ruefully, wondering at the same time when he would ever see again, even through curtains and blinds, a figure now more than ever sharply graven in his mind, or hear that voice however faintly. He reached Genji's residence preoccupied by these unhappy thoughts. Genji came forth, and he gave him her reply.

---

7. "Have pity on me, you who suffer from the same grief [the loss of Ōmiya] as I . . ."

8. "He must be making advances to me." Tamakazura associates "if only just to be kind" (*kagoto bakari ni*) with the same expression in a riddling poem of amorous entreaty (*Shinkokinshū* 1052): "Sash-buckle of Hitachi at the road's end in the far-off East, if only out of kindness, please let me be with you!" The poem plays on *kagoto*, which also means the metal fastener for a belt or sash.

9. "There is no such tie between you and me. If there were, the light *murasaki* of these flowers might promise you at least kindness, but it does not."

10. From *Gosenshū* 960, by Prince Motoyoshi: "I am so unhappy, nothing is left me now but to seek to meet her, at Naniwa, although it means giving my all."

11. In "The Fireflies" he acted as an intermediary between Kashiwagi (the Secretary Captain) and Tamakazura.

12. The text here calls her "the Mistress of Staff," which suggests that she may have already been appointed, but the matter is far from clear.

"She does not much like the prospect of palace service, does she," Genji remarked. "It is sad to think that with His Highness and those other tried-and-true gentlemen turning all their charm on her and pursuing her with their entreaties, she may actually have taken a fancy to them. Still, she was greatly attracted to His Majesty when she saw him during his progress to Ōharanō. No young woman could catch a glimpse of him and still dismiss the idea of serving him. That is why I decided to do things this way."

"But how could she ever really find her place there?" The Captain spoke in his most grown-up manner. "Her Majesty is a very, very great lady, and the Kokiden Consort enjoys such consideration that it would be difficult for her to compete with them, whatever His Majesty's personal feeling for her might be. His Highness is extremely keen on her, and he might well take it amiss, even though her service to His Majesty will not earn her a proper title.[13] That could in turn have unfortunate consequences for your own relationship with him."

"It is difficult, yes. Her fate is not entirely in my hands, but I gather that even the Commander has it in for me. I suppose it is foolish of me only to invite people's resentment, when I have no need to do so, but I simply cannot ignore her unfortunate situation. I have never forgotten her mother's touching words to me about her, and how she complained that His Excellency would want to know nothing further about someone from a miserable mountain village. That is why I brought her here in the first place, for her own good. The only reason why His Excellency takes her at all seriously is that I make so much of her myself." He sounded thoroughly plausible. "I think she should do very well for His Highness, considering the sort of person she is," he went on. "She is stylish and graceful but also bright and unlikely to stray—yes, she would make him a good match. She is perfect for palace service, though. She has looks and intelligence, she is reliable and well up to her duties, and she would never fail to satisfy His Majesty's desires."

The Captain decided to press him further. "I gather that some people speculate unflatteringly on your motive for having kept her here all this time. His Excellency hinted at the same thing in his answer to the Commander, when the Commander approached him about her."

Genji smiled. "They are all talking nonsense. As to palace service and so on, I still mean to do whatever His Excellency prefers. A woman owes obedience to three men in her life,[14] but it would be quite wrong to confuse things and have her obey *me*."

"In private, or so I have it on good authority, His Excellency thanks you for your brilliant scheme more or less to leave her to him—since your distinguished ladies have been with you so long that she could not very well join their company now—and then, while she goes through the motions of palace service, to have her for yourself." He spoke with exquisite correctness.

Yes, I suspect that *is* what he thinks. Genji pitied him. "What extraordinary ideas he has!" he said aloud. "I suppose it is just like him to think too hard." He

13. A Mistress of Staff's real function as a quasi wife was unofficial, and she therefore ranked well below a Consort.
14. Her father before marriage, her husband, and then her son.

laughed. "Anyway, everything will soon be perfectly open and aboveboard. How tactless of him!" His manner was completely convincing, but the Captain still had his doubts.

So that is what people are inferring! Genji reflected. It would be a disaster if they ever turned out to be right. I *must* convince His Excellency that I have only good intentions. It frightened him to think that His Excellency was acute enough actually to have divined what might lurk behind the ambiguity of this proposed palace service.

The lady doffed her mourning, and Genji announced, "You will still have to abstain from going next month, too.[15] In the tenth, then." The news disappointed His Majesty, and meanwhile, her thwarted suitors all tearfully implored whatever gentlewoman of hers they happened to favor to do something while there was still time; but they might as well have been asking them to dam the Yoshino Waterfall,[16] and they all got back the same answer, to wit, "There is nothing I can do."

Ever since blurting out his feelings the Captain had been rushing about in misery over what she must think of him, and it was in a spirit of simple kindness that he busied himself doing everything he possibly could for her. He no longer rashly indulged in bringing up the subject, and he behaved instead with exemplary discretion. Her real brothers, who now felt unable to approach her, impatiently awaited the opportunity to serve her once she was at the palace.

The Secretary Captain's tragic ardor had vanished so swiftly that his agility of sentiment amused her women, and he now arrived with messages from His Excellency. He did not come forward, since in the past he had presented his messages to her only in secret; instead, on this brightly moonlit night he remained hidden beneath the laurel tree in the garden. She who had ignored his every word now willingly had him seated before the blinds on her south side. She had Saishō convey her remarks to him, for she was reluctant even now to address him directly.

He was annoyed. "That His Excellency my father chose me to represent him suggests that he preferred not to address you through an intermediary. I myself do not matter, but they say there is a lasting tie between people like you and me. I thought that I might be able count on your trust, if I may resort to so old-fashioned an expression."

"I should indeed like to talk over with you all that has happened in recent years," she replied gravely, "but lately I have been feeling so strangely unwell that I have hardly even been able to get up. Your reproach only serves to persuade me that you have little regard for me after all."

"Will you not allow me in up to your standing curtain, if you are feeling unwell? Ah, never mind. I should not have spoken as I did." He quietly gave her His Excellency's messages. His thoroughly agreeable manner could not have been more tactful. "My father was unable to learn the particulars surrounding your forthcoming entry into His Majesty's service," he went on, "but on matters of that nature you

---

15. The ninth month (like the first and fifth) was ill omened for a marriage, which her "palace service" amounts to.

16. *Kokin rokujō* 2233 proposes damming the Yoshino Waterfall as a simile for the impossible.

might consult him personally. He regrets very much that the fear of being indiscreet should always prevent him from coming to talk to you himself."

"No, you will hear no more foolishness from me," he felt obliged to add, "but it upsets me more and more that you should manage to ignore my affection for you in *both* roles. Look at the way you have treated me tonight, for example. I should have been glad to be admitted on the north[17] and to have spoken at least to some of the servants, even at the risk of offending you. When has anyone ever been received like this? Ah, our relationship is so strange in so many ways!"

Saishō was amused by the way he nodded while pouring forth his complaint, and she conveyed his remarks to her mistress, who replied forthrightly, "Yes, of course, but I prefer not to risk being thought too quickly accessible. For that reason I can give voice to none of the feelings that have burdened me in recent years, and I find that still more oppressive."

The Secretary Captain was abashed and kept his peace. He only answered,

> *"We who never found in the Hills of Man and Maid those most hidden depths,*
> *like our letters went astray on the Bridge of Odae!"*[18]

His bitterness was no one's fault but his own.

> *"Ah, but it is you in the Hills of Man and Maid who strayed from the path,*
> *and I, ever wondering, who read those letters from you,"*[19]

she replied.

"My lady seemed not to know how to take your letters," Saishō added. "It is her excessive caution before the world that prevents her from speaking to you in her own voice. She will certainly not keep this up forever."

"Very well." He rose. "I must not stay too long. I shall claim the reward for all my services in due time." The brilliant moon aloft in a lovely sky gave his figure great beauty and distinction, and he carried himself in his dress cloak with a pleasingly attractive flair. Although not comparable to the Consultant Captain in looks or grace, he had his own appeal. The younger women wondered that two such men should be cousins, and as usual they gave loud praise even to things about him that hardly deserved it.

The Commander[20] was always summoning the Secretary Captain, his deputy

---

17. The "back" of the house.
18. "We who never knew each other as brother and sister instead lost touch with each other because of a courtship pursued only through letters." The "Hills of Man and Maid" (Imoseyama) face each other across the Yoshino River and often stand for lovers, but here they clearly refer to brother and sister. The "Bridge of Odae," the name of which (*odae*) suggests "rupture," is in northern Japan, a long way from Yoshino; presumably this disjunction emphasizes the vast distance between the two kinds of relationship. A final wordplay in the poem involves *fumi-madoikeru* ("lose the way"), the *fumi* of which also means "letter."
19. "It is you who were confused. I, who knew all the time that we were brother and sister, was upset to receive courting letters from you."
20. Higekuro.

in the Right Palace Guards, and passionately urging him to press his suit with
His Excellency. His Excellency could see
nothing wrong with him, since he was a
fine man who promised to become a pillar of the realm, but he could hardly object to Genji's own plans for her, granting
as he did that Genji might after all have
his reasons, and he therefore left Genji
free to do as he pleased.

This Commander was a brother of
the Consort who had borne the Heir
Apparent,[21] and after His Grace and His
Excellency it was he who enjoyed the
highest reputation at court. He was thirty-
two or thirty-three. His wife was Lady
Murasaki's elder half sister, I believe—

Knotted letter

that is to say, His Highness of Ceremonial's elder daughter. The elder of the couple
by three or four years, she had nothing particularly wrong with her, but something
about her personality seemed to have put him off her, because he referred to her as
"the old woman" and wanted very much to be rid of her. Perhaps that is why His
Grace of Rokujō felt that he would make an improper and perhaps troublesome
match. Nothing in the gentleman inclined him to amorous adventures, but in this
case he was an extremely eager suitor. He knew quite well from an inside source that
the Palace Minister did not reject him outright and that the lady disliked the
prospect of palace service, and he therefore gave the gentlewoman Ben no quarter.[22]
"His Grace of Rokujō is alone in disagreeing," he said, "and as long as it is not against
her real father's wishes . . ."

The ninth month came. On the lovely morning of the first frost, each of the
women in league with a suitor stealthily brought their mistress her letter, as usual,
but their mistress looked at none of them; she just had them read to her instead.
The Commander had written, "I had still thought of this month with hope, but the
passing skies only leave me desolate.

> *Alas, I could hate, if anyone cared at all, this fatal Long Month,*
> *when my very life depends on the slenderest of hopes."*[23]

He seems to have known all about the decision to send her off the following month.

His Highness of War had written, "Now all hope is lost, I do not know what
to say.

---

21. Emperor Suzaku's Shōkyōden Consort, mentioned in "The Pilgrimage to Sumiyoshi."
22. One of Tamakazura's senior women.
23. The Long Month (*nagatsuki*) is the ninth.

Though you gaze upon the light of the morning sun, O still bear in mind
the frost consigned to shadow on the gleaming sasa *leaves!*[24]

It would be such a comfort, you know, if only you understood." Even the messenger who brought it—tied to pathetically withered and still frost-covered leaves from low on the *sasa* plant—was just right.

The Intendant of the Left Watch,[25] His Highness's son, was a half brother of His Grace's dearest lady. A frequent visitor to her residence, he naturally knew well enough what the future held in store, and he suffered accordingly. A bitter letter from him included this:

"I want nothing more than to forget you at last, yet in my distress
I know neither what to do nor even how to begin."

The colors of the paper, the tones of the ink, the letters' varied fragrances—all these moved her gentlewomen to say, "It will be so sad when all these gentlemen give up at last!" For some reason His Highness was the only one to whom she gave a trifling reply:

"Of its own accord a sunflower may indeed turn toward the light,
yet for that must it forget every thought of morning frost?"

The faint writing struck him as a true wonder, and her suggestion that she might indeed feel for him brought him at least a touch of happiness. In this way she received many a bitter complaint from one gentleman or another, although without notable incident.

They say that His Grace and His Excellency both hoped to make her a model for all women.

---

24. "Though you enjoy the Emperor's favor, do not forget miserable me!" *Sasa*, a ground-cover plant related to bamboo, is ubiquitous in the Japanese mountains.

25. Sahyōe no Kami, a suitor not mentioned before.

31

MAKIBASHIRA
The Handsome Pillar

Makibashira means, roughly, "pillar of fine wood" or "handsome pillar": here, a house pillar probably of Japanese cypress (*hinoki*). The word forms the chapter title because of its role in the poem that Higekuro's daughter leaves attached to a pillar when she and her mother move out of Higekuro's house:

"I am leaving now a home that has long been mine: O handsome pillar, you whom I have loved so well, please do not forget me yet!"

It is also the traditional name for Higekuro's daughter herself.

"The Handsome Pillar" begins soon after "Thoroughwort Flowers" ends, in the tenth month, and covers roughly the twelve succeeding months.

PERSONS

His Grace, the Chancellor, Genji, age 37 to 38

The Mistress of Staff, 23 to 24 (Tamakazura)

The Commander of the Right, early 30s (Higekuro)

His Excellency, the Palace Minister (Tō no Chūjō)

His Majesty, the Emperor, 19 to 20 (Reizei)

His Highness of War, Genji's brother (Hotaru Hyōbukyō no Miya)

The Intendant of the Watch, Murasaki's half brother

His sister, Higekuro's first wife, mid-30s (Higekuro no Kita no Kata)

His Highness of Ceremonial, the father of Higekuro's first wife, 52 to 53 (Shikibukyō no Miya)

Chūjō, a gentlewoman of Higekuro's first wife

Moku, in the service of Higekuro

Higekuro's daughter, early teens (Makibashira)

His Highness of Ceremonial's wife

The lady of spring, Lady Murasaki, 29 to 30

The Consultant Captain, Genji's son, 16 to 17 (Yūgiri)

The Secretary Captain, Tō no Chūjō's eldest son, early 20s (Kashiwagi)

The girl from Ōmi, Tō no Chūjō's daughter (Ōmi no Kimi)

I should not like His Majesty to hear of this. You had better keep it to yourself for the time being," Genji warned, but the gentleman[1] was beyond self-restraint. There was no sign that the passage of time had at all inclined her to accept him, for she remained as disheartened as ever by such evidence of her disastrous karma, which certainly made him very angry, but he was also moved and happy to find his bond with her so strong. The more he saw of her, the more marvelous he found her, and his heart almost failed him at the very idea that he might have lost her to someone else, until he felt like worshipping both the Kannon of Ishiyama and the gentlewoman Ben, to whom her mistress had meanwhile taken a dislike so profound that she was barred from her mistress's presence and remained confined at home. After all those agonies suffered by so many suitors, it was one without interest who had received the boon.

Genji, too, was annoyed and disappointed, but it was too late now, and he held the ceremony[2] in grand style, judging that with both parties[3] otherwise in agreement it would be out of place, and unhelpful to her, for him to show signs of withholding consent.

The Commander could hardly wait to bring her to his residence, but Genji appealed to consideration for the feelings of another lady who, he gathered, might not necessarily be pleased to receive her there if she were to move abruptly and without adequate deliberation. "Please," he urged him, "maintain your composure and behave with sufficiently calm discretion to avoid incurring anyone's condemnation or hatred."

His Excellency her father observed privately, "She is much better off this way. I was especially worried that anyone who went into mildly amorous palace service without full backing[4] might regret it. I want the best for her, but quite apart from the matter of the Consort, what could I really have done?" It was perfectly true that serving even His Majesty would have been a mistake if she had been scorned, or if

---

1. The Commander (Higekuro), who has just married Tamakazura.
2. To confirm the marriage.
3. Presumably Tō no Chūjō and Genji.
4. Without both parents to look after her interests.

Going to a shrine festival

he had seldom had time for her or had shown her no regard. Reports of the poems exchanged by Genji and the new husband on the third night aroused in His Excellency the warmest and most admiring gratitude for Genji's kindness.

Despite the secret character of the marriage people naturally loved to talk about it, and as the news got about, it set everyone whispering happily. His Majesty heard it, too. "It is disappointing that her destiny lay elsewhere," he said, "but I had my hopes. As to her service here, though, surely she would wish to renounce it only if it were to be somewhat personal in nature."

The eleventh month came, and with it many rites in honor of the gods.[5] Those who served in the Hall of the Sacred Mirror had a great deal to do, but to her disgust the Commander remained surreptitiously closeted with her even during the day, through all the busy commotion, while women officials came constantly to see the Mistress of Staff. His Highness[6] and the others were still more put out. The Intendant of the Watch objected to his sister, the Commander's wife, being exposed to public ridicule, and he repeatedly considered doing something about it, but he thought better of the idea in the end because by now no foolish maneuver of his could have helped. The Commander, once widely known for his stalwart ways, was no longer the man who never erred, for now, to everyone's great amusement, his infatuation drove him to steal gallantly in and out every night and every dawn, like any lover, in a manner quite foreign to what he had once been.

His new wife lost her normally lively cheerfulness and sank into profound

5. Between these two paragraphs Tamakazura has indeed taken up the duties of Mistress of Staff. The Hall of the Sacred Mirror was staffed by the members of the Office of Staff.
6. Hotaru.

gloom, and although what had happened was obviously not her doing, she felt such shame and regret whenever she wondered what Genji might be thinking of her, or when she remembered all His Highness's tact and kindness, that her manner never failed to betray her unhappiness.

Now that Genji had cleared himself of suspicions injurious to her, he looked back over his past and assured himself that he had really never cared for anything sudden or strange. "You doubted me, didn't you!" he said to Lady Murasaki. Still, he had known full well where that quirk of his might lead him, and when sorely tempted he had still decided just to act. He was thinking of her even now.

He called on her near midday, in the Commander's absence. Her strangely prolonged indisposition had left her continually listless and depressed, but she rose after all when he arrived and took shelter behind a standing curtain. He himself was sober and somewhat formal in manner, and he confined his conversation to banalities. Accustomed by now to commonplace, genteel company, she felt more keenly than ever both the ineffable quality of his presence and the surprise of her own embarrassing situation, and she wept. By and by the topic shifted to more personal matters, and Genji, leaning on a nearby armrest, peeped at her a little, while he continued their talk. She was very pretty indeed, and what with the new dignity and charm of her somewhat more slender features, he rued the folly of having let her go to anyone else.

> *"I who never drank all I craved of your waters withheld the promise*
> *to let you with another cross the River of the Fords.*[7]*

I can hardly believe it!" He blew his nose with touching grace.
     She hid her face to reply,

> *"If only somehow, before my time comes to cross the River of Three Fords,*
> *I might melt away like foam on a flowing stream of tears!"*

"A child's wish! They say that crossing is one we must all make, and I so want at least to hold your hand to help you!" He smiled and went on, "Seriously, though, there is something you yourself must recognize. Surely you will grant me that foolishness like mine and security like yours have never been known in this world before."

His words distressed her so much that he took pity on her and turned the conversation elsewhere. "What His Majesty has had to say about all this makes me very sorry, and I should like to see you go at least for a time to the palace. I expect that it will be difficult for you to be with His Majesty once *he* has made you entirely his own. This is not what I first had in mind, but since His Excellency is pleased, I feel all is well." He spoke intently and at length. Much of what he had to say moved and embarrassed her, but she only wept. Her evident misery so troubled him that he

---

7. "I never actually made love with you, but I still never meant that anyone else should carry you across the River of Death." A woman's first man carried her across the river (Watari no Kawa, "River of the Fords," or Sanzu no Kawa, "River of Three Fords") between this world and the land of the dead.

never took the liberties he had been contemplating; instead he just instructed her on how to feel and behave. He gave no sign of being willing to let her move directly to the Commander's.

The Commander did not at all like the idea of her going to the palace, but he agreed nonetheless that she might do so briefly, because it occurred to him that from there he could bring her straight home. Being ill at ease with this unfamiliar business of stealthy visits, he did up his house and set about renewing in all sorts of ways a place that for years now had been going to rack and ruin. He gave never a thought to his wife's likely distress, never a glance to the children he had loved, because while a kinder, more sensitive man would have understood what might cover another with shame, his inflexible single-mindedness all too often gave offense.

His wife could certainly not properly be placed below anyone else. As the much-loved daughter of His Most Esteemed Highness her father, she enjoyed in principle no light consideration in the world at large, and she had looks as well; but she was afflicted by a spirit so strangely persistent that for years now she had ceased to be like other people, and the frequency of those times when she was not herself had long estranged him from her, although he still gave her the supreme regard that was her due. Meanwhile, he was naturally more and more impressed and delighted not only by the extraordinary beauty of the lady to whom his heart had now so strikingly shifted, but by the way she had even managed to dispel the suspicions that people had been entertaining about her.

His Highness of Ceremonial heard of these goings-on. "The gossip will be intolerable if he brings this bright young thing of his home and then relegates my daughter ignominiously to a corner," he said. "As long as I am still alive, she can at least escape the ridicule with which he threatens her." He had the east wing of his residence done up and announced his intention to move her, but although she would then be with him, the proper course of her life was already set, and it troubled him to think of taking her back again. In the meantime her wits wandered ever further, and illness confined her to her bed. By nature she was sweet, quiet, and childishly meek, but at times, when in one of her states, she would blurt out very unpleasant things indeed.

The miserably run-down condition of the Commander's residence and his wife's unlovely, painfully sequestered mode of life compared distressingly with this new lady's splendor, but the Commander's long devotion to his wife had not really changed, and in his heart he felt affectionate pity for her. "They say a touch of forbearance is what sees a wellborn lady through any affair of her husband's, fleeting though it may be," he observed. "It has been difficult, you see, to bring up what I have to tell you when you have been so ill. Have I not always promised to keep faith with you? I made up my mind ages ago to stand by you through your infirmity, so please do not turn against me out of unwillingness to respond in kind. There are the children, too, and I keep telling you that for their sake as well I have no intention of neglecting you; yet in the confusion of a woman's mind you persist in being angry with me. I can understand that you should feel this way as long as you have not yet seen how truly I mean what I say, but I hope that you will give me the benefit of the doubt and be patient a little longer. His Highness has heard about all this, and he has taken a dislike to me because of it, and now he is saying all at once, just like that, that he wants to take you back. That is really a very foolish idea, though. Is he serious, I wonder, or does he just want to give me a warning?" To her intense annoyance and disgust, he smiled.

Even Chūjō, and also Moku[8] whose intimate service made her more or less a concubine, were as shocked and angry as any such women could be, and since the lady herself was then in her right mind, she sat and shed pathetic tears. "I do not wonder that you should shame me by calling me odd or perverse, but it is painful to think that my father may hear of it and that my misfortune should, as I gather, discredit my family as well. For myself, I am used to it by now, and I hardly think about it anymore." There was something sweet about her, with her back to him like that. Slight as she was already, her relentless illness had made her pinched and frail, while her beautifully long hair, which she seldom combed, had fallen out as though thinned. Her huddled, weeping figure made a pathetic sight. Lacking any notable beauty of her own, she nonetheless preserved her father's grace, but in so pitifully changed a condition how could she have had any real appeal?

"I certainly am *not* suggesting any reflection on His Highness! You must not say such terrible things!" The Commander tried to calm her. "The place where I am going now, though, is overpoweringly splendid, and my solemn visits there make me feel so awkward that I am certain all eyes are on me; I prefer the comfort of bringing her here. I need hardly remind you of the supreme honor that His Grace the Chancellor enjoys. It would be extremely unfortunate if any unpleasant rumor were to reach a gentleman of such penetrating understanding. Please get on well with her and see that things go smoothly between you. I shall never forget you, even if you move to His Highness's, and whatever happens, my devotion to you will not fail, but it would be damaging to me as well if people began laughing at us, and I hope that you will see your way to joining me in our continuing support for each other."

"Your cruelty does not concern me," she replied. "I believe it is my strange misfortune that troubles His Highness and that inflicts upon him the misery of now seeing me become a laughingstock, and I am so sorry that I wonder how I shall ever face him. It is hardly as though His Grace's wife were a complete stranger either. That she, who grew up outside the family, should now play the mother's part this way, at this late date, is so unkind that His Highness dwells on the matter in thought and word, although for myself the matter hardly interests me either way. I watch only to see what you will do."

"I grant all you say, but these episodes of yours make it likely that there are more painful incidents to come. His Grace's wife has nothing to do with this—she lives the life of a sheltered daughter, and I doubt that she knows anything about anyone so little regarded. She does not at all play the mother as far as I know; on the contrary. I should be very sorry if talk like that were to reach her." He spent the day in conversation with her.

Once the sun had set, his mood lightened and he longed to get away, but

8. Neither of these women has appeared before.

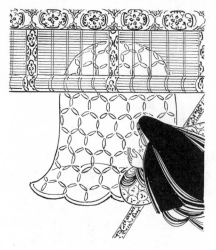

Censer frame

thick snow was falling. He would make a painful spectacle if he were to insist on leaving in such weather. An angry flare-up from her would only give him a chance to blaze back; but no, her calm, unruffled manner drove him to such distraction that he hardly knew what to do, and he just sat near the veranda with the shutters still up, gazing out.

His wife noted his looks. "How will you get through this awful snow? It is very late, I believe," she said encouragingly. She was thinking, This is the end, it is no use my trying to keep him; and her face showed the great sorrow of this knowledge.

"How could I go, in this?" But then, "Just for a little while, though . . . I do not like to stay away, you know, because I worry about what His Grace and His Excellency may think when they hear tales told them by people who fail to understand my feelings. Please remain calm and bear with me. Everything will be much easier once I have brought her here. When you are yourself like this, I lose any wish to divide my affections, and I think of you fondly."

"Even if you did stay, you would do so against your wishes," she answered quietly, "and that would make things all the more painful. I know the ice will melt from my sleeves if only you will remember me when you are away."[9]

She called for a censer and had his clothes given a further touch of perfume. Casually dressed in worn, limp robes, she looked weaker and more wasted than ever. It was agony to witness her despair. Her eyes, sadly swollen from weeping, put him off a little, but as he considered her with his present sympathy, he had no wish to blame her. At least I held out this long! I *am* fickle, though, to have completely lost my heart to someone else! he said to himself over and over again. Meanwhile, keen and eager amid his feigned sighs, he continued dressing. Then he drew a little censer near to put it in his sleeves and scent them. Genji's incomparable radiance certainly overshadowed him, but his looks in these pleasantly soft robes had a superb manliness that placed him visibly above the common run of courtiers and that could daunt anyone looking on.

"The snow has let up a bit!"

"It must be late!" Voices from the household office encouraged him discreetly to be on his way. His men were clearing their throats.

"My poor lady!" Chūjō and Moku sighed as they lay chatting together. Their mistress herself was reclining very sweetly and with perfect composure on an armrest when suddenly she arose, took the censer from beneath a large frame, came up be-

9. *Gosenshū* 481: "When lost in love I lie awake through a winter's night, the ice [frozen tears] does not even melt from my sleeves."

hind her husband, and emptied it over him. No one even had time to cry out. He froze in horror. The fine ash in his eyes and nose confused and blinded him. He brushed and slapped at it, but it was everywhere, and he had to take off all his clothes. Her women would have had enough and would never have even looked at her again if they had thought she

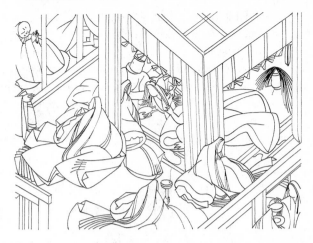

Subduing an evil spirit

was in her right mind when she did it, but instead they pityingly took this as one more attempt by that spirit to turn her husband against her. They rushed to provide him with fresh clothes, but the copious ash had floated up into his sidelocks, too, and it seemed to have got into everything so thoroughly that he could not possibly have called in this state on someone whose dwelling was always immaculate. Deranged or not, she had never behaved so outlandishly before. He snapped his fingers and felt all his sympathy for her vanish. Instead revulsion overcame him, but he controlled himself because a scandal now might be disastrous. Although it was the middle of the night, he summoned monks to offer up noisy prayers. One can hardly blame him for finding her cries and babble repellent.

All night long, until dawn came at last, she was smacked and tugged about, weeping meanwhile with wild abandon, and during a brief lull he dispatched a note. "Yesterday evening someone here was very close to death," he wrote primly, "and what with the added difficulty of going out into all that snow, I hesitated to venture forth. I was cold through and through.[10] Quite apart from you, I wonder what other people will make of all this.

> *My poor heart as well whirled aloft into the sky's confusion of snow,*[11]
> *while below I slept forlorn, all alone on frozen sleeves.*

It was too hard!" His note was on thin white paper and imposingly written, but nothing about it particularly caught the eye. The hand was very fine. He actually had a great deal of learning. The Mistress of Staff, to whom his absence for a night meant nothing, ignored his earnest concern and did not even answer. He was crushed and spent the day in gloom.

Since his wife seemed still to be suffering, he commissioned a solemn Great Rite and prayed in his heart that at least for now she should remain safely in her

10. A reference to the misery of sleeping alone on a winter's night.
11. A literal reading (required by the snow in the poem) of a usually figurative idiom that means "be out of oneself" or "beside oneself."

right mind. He thought that he would never have survived the horror of this night if he had not known how deserving she really was.

After sunset he hurried off as always. Not having been handsomely dressed, he had resented his ill-assorted costume; and now, without even a proper dress cloak, he was a sight. His outer garments from the evening before, burned through here and there, smelled curiously and most unpleasantly scorched. His gowns had picked up the odor, too. That he had got it from his wife was all too obvious, and he changed and took a thorough bath, since otherwise even his darling might want no more to do with him.

> *"That fire to my mind flamed up from the agony of a heart that burns*
> *with the ceaseless, searing pain of one left always alone,"*

Moku said, perfuming a robe. "How could the simplest onlooker not be shocked by the way you have put my lady out of your life?" She covered her mouth as she spoke, but her glance accused him, and all he could think (and how cruelly!) was What did I ever see in a woman like *her?*

> *"Ah, when that outrage confounds my serenity, then tendrils of smoke*
> *rise indeed, and more and more, from all my burning regret!"*

As he left, he sighed, "I would be in a proper fix if word of these extraordinary goings-on ever got out."

A single night apart from his love only disclosed to him new visions of her beauty, until he could hardly imagine portioning out his affections to anyone else, and all this had been so frustrating that he shut himself up with her for a very long time. The news that the spirit had persisted in its violent ravings, despite the rite of intercession and so on, terrified him, and he stayed well away lest some unspeakable blot or shame disgrace him. When he did go home, he stayed elsewhere in the house and summoned only his children. These were a daughter of twelve or thirteen and two younger sons. He had always treated his wife with the highest regard, despite the distance that had come between them in recent years, and now that she knew the end had come, her gentlewomen grieved bitterly as well.

His Highness her father heard what had happened. "It would earn you nothing but shame and ridicule if you were still to forbear, now that he is about to leave you openly. Why should you gamely put up with him further, as long as I am alive?" he said;[12] and suddenly he brought her home. She herself was sufficiently in her right mind to lament this calamitous break. I might insist on staying on to see this through to the very end, she thought, but I would only make myself look a little more foolish for it. She made up her mind to go.

One of her brothers, the Intendant of the Watch, was a senior noble, and his presence would have made too much of the move. The Captain, the Adviser, and the Commissioner of Civil Affairs therefore came for her in three carriages. Her

---

12. Probably in an orally transmitted message.

gentlewomen had long assumed that this day would come, but even so, the thought that it had actually arrived reduced them all to abundant tears. "How can we all stay with our lady, when she is setting out on her first journey in many years and will be living under such awkwardly restricted circumstances?" they asked each other. "Some of us should go home instead and wait until she is better settled." They therefore sent off their meager belongings and dispersed each to her own home.

All, high or low, wept loudly while they packed the furnishings that their mistress would require, presenting as they did so a thoroughly ill-omened scene.[13] She summoned her children, who were wandering about through it all, uncomprehending. "Now that I have no doubt about my unhappy destiny, I have no further wish to cling to the world, and I accept whatever lies ahead. It will be so sad for you all to part while you are still so young! You," she told her daughter, "must stay with me whatever happens. I am afraid that you boys will have to see your father often, although he is unlikely to pay much attention to you and you may feel quite lost. You may do well enough as long as His Highness is still with us, but in a world subject to the will of His Grace and His Excellency you will bear the burden of their disapproval, and you will not easily succeed. How terrible it will be for me, even in the life to come, if you then follow me into the mountains and forests!"[14] She was weeping, and they, who did not understand very well what all this was about, wrinkled up their faces and wept with her.

She gathered the children's nurses about her, and they grieved together. "In the old tales, too, there are fathers who mean as well as any and who still turn out to be callous after all, as they change with the times and follow shifting favor," a nurse observed.

"Then just look at *him!*" her mistress cried. "He is a father in name only—he no longer thinks of his children at all, and despite appearances he will do nothing for them."

The sun set, and the sky this dreary evening promised more snow. Her brothers had come to fetch her, and while they urged her to make haste because, they said, the weather looked threatening, she sat staring vacantly before her, wiping her eyes. Her daughter, always the Commander's great favorite, lay facedown nearby, wondering how she would live without seeing her father. What if I were to go away forever and not even say good-bye? she thought. She seemed quite unwilling to move.

"It is not at all nice of you to feel this way," her mother protested. The girl just wanted her father to come home *now*, but what was the chance of that, with night approaching? It upset her to think of leaving the pillar on the east side, against which herself she had leaned so often, to someone else, and she therefore pasted together some bits of paper the color of cypress bark, wrote on them in tiny letters, and with a hairpin pushed the paper into a crack in the pillar:

> "*I am leaving now a home that has long been mine: O handsome pillar,*
> *you whom I have loved so well, please do not forget me yet!*"

Tears almost prevented her from finishing.

---

13. Because the scene resembles the aftermath of a death.
14. She means to become a nun.

"Come along!" her mother said.

> *"That handsome pillar may still recall your love, but what then? I ask:*
> *what is it I leave behind that could ever make me stay?"*

Her women were sad, too, each in her own way. They all were blowing their noses and resting their gaze fondly on some little plant or tree that they had never noticed much before.

Moku, who served her lord, was to stay on, which moved Chūjō to say,

> *"Shallow it may be, but the stream among the rocks still runs sweet and clear—*
> *yet the mistress of the house is obliged to go away!*[15]

I never thought to see the like! Oh, to think that I must leave you!"

Moku replied,

> *"No, among these rocks the stream is choked and silent, for I have no words,*
> *and this is no life for me, that I should now wish to stay!*

Dear me, no!"

Chūjō looked back as the carriage drove away and mourned that she might never see the place again. Her mistress gazed at every branch and turned back again and again until the house was lost to view, not because her love lived there[16] but because this was where she had spent so many years and amassed so many memories.

His Highness received her with anguish, and her mother wept aloud. "You thought the Chancellor made such a superb alliance," she cried, "but all I see is what an enemy he has always been. He has never missed a chance to embarrass our Consort, but you, like everyone else, claim he only meant to teach us a lesson as long as you and he remained on bad terms. Is that right, I ask you? It never made much sense anyway, because if he was to be so keen on that girl, past example suggests that his feelings should have extended to those around her—but no, far from it, he takes in some sort of vague stepdaughter and then, out of pity when he is finished with her himself, he snares her the very thing, a completely reliable gentleman unlikely ever to misbehave! Is that not unforgivable?"

"That will be enough!" His Highness replied. "You may not abuse His Grace as you please, when he receives not a breath of public criticism. He is a far-seeing man, and I imagine that he laid his plans and has been looking forward to getting back at me this way for a long time. It is my own misfortune that he feels this way about me. He always manages very skillfully, without betraying himself, to help or harm people according to how they behaved when he was in disgrace. It is only because he

---

15. "You, whose bond with our lord is slight, are staying, while our lady . . ." The "stream" is at once Moku and the garden brook. The poem plays on *sumi*, "run clear" and "live," and on other words associated with water.

16. *Shūishū* 351, by the exiled Sugawara no Michizane: "On and on I go, looking back again and again until the branches above the house where my love lives are lost to view."

after all considers me a close relative that a year or two ago he gave me a celebration far more brilliant than anything my house deserved. That should do me enough honor for this lifetime."

His wife, however, only became still angrier and spouted all sorts of imprecations. She had an evil temper, that woman.

The Commander heard that his wife had left. How extraordinary! he thought. She has gone off in a fit of jealousy, just as though we were newlyweds! *She* is not that prickly or hotheaded, though—no, His Highness is the one who goes in for that sort of nonsense. There were the children, too. All this was extremely embarrassing for them, and that troubled him.

"That is what has happened. It is astonishing!" he explained to the Mistress of Staff. "I actually think it makes things easier in a way, but I had been counting on someone as mild as she staying quietly in her corner. This sudden move must be His Highness's doing. I must go and give him some idea of how bad this makes me look as well. I shall be back." He went imposingly dressed in a superb outer garment,[17] a willow train-robe, and blue-gray gathered trousers of light silk twill. The gentlewomen could see nothing unworthy about him, but his news had only impressed their mistress with the reality of her own misfortune, and she gave him not so much as a glance.

Having set off to give His Highness a piece of his mind, he went first to his own residence, where Moku came out and told him everything that had occurred. Touchingly enough, her description of his daughter's departure moved him to tears, despite his manly efforts at self-control. "Then in the end she has ignored the loyalty with which I have for years overlooked all sorts of strangeness on her part, as no one else would have done!" he said. "Would any man who only pleased himself have stayed with her that long? Never mind, though. It hardly matters anymore, now that she seems to be lost either way. I wonder what she means to do with the children." He sighed. He had a look at the "handsome pillar" and was moved to such tender feelings by the spirit it conveyed, despite the childishness of the writing, that he wiped his tears away all the way to His Highness's, where he had no chance of seeing his wife.

"And why *should* you see him?" His Highness naturally insisted. "This is not the first time his mind has changed with the times. I have been hearing for ages how infatuated he is, and I would just like to know how long we might have to wait for him to come to his senses. It would only mean your making a further spectacle of your unfortunate condition."

"All this makes me feel like such a child," the Commander began. "I cannot apologize enough for the foolishly complacent way I assumed that she would never leave the children. For the present, though, I can only beg your indulgence and hope that you will not go through with this until it is plain to everyone that my offense is irretrievable." He hardly knew what else to say. "I should so like at least to see my daughter," he went on; but she was not to be allowed out. His ten-year-old

---

17. Clearly provided by Tamakazura, that is, by Genji. It is probably a *bō* (a formal cloak), and it would have been black, the color of Higekuro's third rank.

son was a privy page and extremely attractive. People liked him, for although he had little in the way of looks, he was extremely clever and quick. The younger son, now eight, was very sweet, and he was so like his sister that the weeping Commander caressed him and said to him fondly, "You are the one I have now to remind me of the child I miss!" He hoped that His Highness would consent to meet him in person, but all he got back was "Unfortunately, I am unwell, and I doubt that I am up to it." He went away nursing this rebuff.

He put his sons into his carriage and talked to them on the way. Since he could hardly take them to Rokujō, he stopped instead at his own residence. "I want you to stay here, where I can come and see you easily," he said. Their sad looks as they watched him leave deeply affected him, and he felt still more burdened by care, but it was a great comfort to see his new wife, who was so beautiful—dazzlingly so, in fact, compared to that other, pathetic figure. He soon felt much, much better. No more was heard from him at His Highness's. His excuse seemed to be the slight he had suffered there, but His Highness found his behavior reprehensible.

"I am extremely sorry that even I have caused resentment in this affair," the lady of spring[18] said, sighing, when she heard the news.

Genji felt for her. "It is difficult," he said. "Her marriage was not entirely up to me, and His Majesty is displeased as well. I heard that His Highness of War, among others, was angry with me, too, but being the thoughtful man he is, he seems to have informed himself and to have given up any animosity. People find out all about these things in the end, whatever one may do to keep them quiet, and in this case I do *not* believe there is anything for which I need blame myself."

Amid this uproar the Mistress of Staff sank further and further into melancholy that the sympathetic Commander did his best to dispel. The plan that she should go to the palace has come to nothing, he reflected, and in fact I stopped it, which for His Majesty must make me a jealous boor, while those two gentlemen no doubt have their own ideas on the subject. Can no husband ever have trusted a wife in His Majesty's service? He changed his mind and sent her to the palace in the New Year.

There was to be the men's mumming, which made just the moment for her to go amid great pomp and splendor. His Grace, His Excellency, and the Commander actually joined forces for the occasion, and the Consultant Captain[19] lent her his tireless assistance. Her brothers gathered to place themselves at her disposal and looked after her very gallantly indeed.

She was lodged on the east side of the Shōkyōden.[20] Since the Consort from His Highness's[21] occupied the west side, only a corridor separated them, but their hearts must have remained far apart. This was a particularly brilliant time at court, and all His Majesty's ladies vied with one another. He had few mischievous Inti-

18. Murasaki.
19. Yūgiri.
20. A relatively long and narrow (east-west) pavilion near the center of the inner palace compound, north of the Shishinden. A passageway (*medō*, north-south) divided it into two apartments, each of which consisted of a chamber and of aisle spaces on three sides.
21. The daughter of Higekuro's irate father-in-law.

mates in his service at the time,[22] being attended by Her Majesty, the Kokiden Consort, His Highness's Consort, and His Excellency of the Left's Consort. The only ones were the Counselor's and the Consultant's daughters.[23]

All these ladies' relatives then came from home for the mumming, and they wore their very best because it was to be a particularly unusual treat. Their richly cascading sleeves[24] were a wonder to behold. The Consort and mother of the Heir Apparent[25] put on a magnificent display, and everything was done in the height of style, although the Prince himself was still very young.

The mummers went first to His Majesty, then to Her Majesty, and then to His Eminence Suzaku, by which time the night was so well advanced that Genji, at Rokujō, decided not to overdo it this time and excused them. They had returned from the Suzaku Palace and were performing for the Heir Apparent's ladies when day broke; and there, among the terribly drunk young men singing "Bamboo River" by the lovely light of early dawn, were four or five of the Palace Minister's sons, a handsome and splendidly gallant band whose voices soared above those of the other privy gentlemen. The eighth of them, His Excellency's son by his wife and still a charming privy page, was his father's great favorite. The Mistress of Staff noted his presence beside the Commander's eldest and allowed her eye to rest on him, since he was kin. The colors of the sleeves that spilled from her rooms made a fresher and more stylish spectacle than any seen before His Majesty's greatest ladies, and even their most familiar color combinations stood out with exceptional brilliance. Both she and her gentlewomen longed to live awhile yet amid such happy splendor. Even the cotton wadding[26] that she had distributed equally to all the mummers was especially handsome and nicely done, and although this was only a water stop, all present were eager to look their best in so lively a scene. By the Commander's order the customary reception offered them had been arranged with special care.

The Commander remained in his palace quarters[27] and spent the whole day reminding his darling, over and over again, "I shall require you to leave tonight. I do not like the idea of your now being tempted to remain here in service." She did not reply.

"My lord," her women objected, "His Grace told you that there is no hurry and that since my lady comes so rarely, she should stay until His Majesty is pleased to release her. This evening is really much too soon!" However, this only annoyed him. I have been telling her and telling her, he thought, sighing. Are things really so difficult between us?

His Highness of War, who was waiting on His Majesty for the mumming, was

---

22. "Mischievous" (*midarigawashi*) because of their intense rivalry, consequent upon their relatively low rank, for the Emperor's favor.

23. The last three gentlemen mentioned do not figure otherwise in the tale.

24. Spilling forth from beneath the blinds through which they watched the mumming.

25. Higekuro's sister, who had been a Consort of Emperor Suzaku (Genji's brother).

26. The traditional gift on this occasion.

27. *Tonoi-dokoro*, the lodging assigned to him for use when on duty in the palace. As Commander of the Right, Higekuro would have had quarters near the Inmei Gate, on the west side of the inner palace compound.

troubled to find himself thinking of her there in her palace rooms, and he could not resist sending her a note. The Commander was then in the Guards' Office, and since His Highness had it brought to her as though from there, it was only with great reluctance that she read it at all.

> *"You who waste your wings on a common mountain tree, O bird, with your song*
>   *you now usher in for me a most aggravating spring!"[28]*

It is a song I cannot help heeding." She blushed in sympathy for him, and she was wondering what to answer when His Majesty arrived.

His Majesty's face was ineffably beautiful in the bright moonlight, and everything about him recalled His Grace the Chancellor. Can there really be two such men? she wondered as she watched him. Genji's peculiarly keen interest in her had added cruelly to her cares; and His Majesty—why did *he* feel so strongly about her? She just wanted to disappear when he spoke, ever so kindly, of his unhappiness that what he had hoped had not come to pass. He said when she remained mute, her face hidden behind her fan, "How strangely silent you are! I assumed that you would know from your recent good fortune[29] what my feelings for you are, but I suppose it is your way to continue pretending not to notice." He continued,

> *"Why is it my heart thirstily welcomes the hue of* murasaki
>   *when the dye takes so poorly, and we really cannot meet?[30]*

Could the color not have darkened?"[31] He spoke with dauntingly youthful grace, but she managed to reply by reminding herself that he *was* just like Genji. Perhaps she meant to thank him for her recent promotion, since she had not yet served him at all.

> *"It was by design that the dyer stained me then with* murasaki,
>   *though I never understood just what the color might mean!*

After this I shall know,"[32] she said.

He smiled. "Perhaps so, but if the color has only just taken on you, then alas, it is too late.[33] I should be glad to beg someone else's judgment in the matter, if anyone would hear my complaint." The profound displeasure visible on his countenance was clearly genuine, and she was troubled. How awful! I must not do

---

28. The tree is an unflattering image for Higekuro.
29. The Emperor has recently promoted Tamakazura to the third rank.
30. "Why have I become so fond of you . . . ?" Light *murasaki* (purple) is associated with the third rank, and the color in general is associated with the affections of the heart. Since the dye is difficult to manage, the poem plays on *hai aigataki* ("does not take the ash" [the mordant, lye]) and *aigataki* ("difficult to meet").
31. "Could we not have become closer?"
32. "From now on I shall know it is you I have to thank for my promotion, and I shall serve you as well as I may."
33. "That you understand now will do me no good, since you still will not give yourself to me."

anything more to encourage him. How difficult they always end up making things! She behaved so properly that he never managed to strike up a suggestive conversation with her, as he had meant to do, but he decided that time would bring her round.

The news that His Majesty had gone to see her put the Commander in a frenzy of anxiety, and she, too, was sufficiently alarmed by the peril of her position to contrive some plausible reasons why he should release her. At last her father's skillful pleading obtained leave for her to go. "Very well," His Majesty said, "I know someone who has learned his lesson and will not allow you here again. It is very hard. I who came forward for you first have now fallen behind and can only seek others' indulgence! I feel as though that man's plight long ago matches mine all too well."[34] He was extremely disappointed. She was far more beautiful in person than report had led him to imagine, and he would not have wished to lose her now even if she had not interested him from the start. For that reason he felt all the more thwarted and angry, but he still did not wish to appear hatefully shallow of heart, and he therefore assured her of his devotion with such depth of feeling that she was abashed and said to herself, But I am afraid I am what I am!

He called for a hand carriage, to the envy of all the gentlewomen whom His Grace and His Excellency had both sent for her, and he did not leave her until the Commander came to fuss and fret officiously beside her. "It is extremely irritating to find you so closely guarded," he complained.

> "Now that ninefold mists must keep you and me apart, lovely plum blossom,
> shall I never have from you the least breath of your perfume?"

The verse was unremarkable, but it may well have pleased her, since she had the speaker before her. "I so love these meadows that I hoped to spend the night,[35] but there is someone else whom that might offend, and you know, when I take his part, I feel guilty after all. How am I to keep in touch?"

His trouble once more made her feel very small.

> "Send me on the breeze just a breath of scent, I pray, though my own perfume
> be unworthy there among the flowers on other boughs."[36]

No, she seemed not to be keeping herself from him, and as he left, he looked back at her tenderly, again and again.

The Commander had wanted to bring her straight home that evening, but he had said nothing to anyone about it because he was highly unlikely to receive advance leave to do so. Now he blandly announced that all of a sudden he felt quite unwell and wanted to rest somewhere comfortable, but that he would worry about

34. Taira no Sadafun (also known as Heichū, died 923) had a woman he was visiting stolen from him by the leading courtier of the time, Fujiwara no Tokihira (871–909).

35. *Man'yōshū* 1428, by Akahito: "I who came to pick violets in the fields of spring love these meadows so much that I lay here through the night."

36. "Do keep at least in touch with me, although I am nothing compared to your other, greater ladies."

Delivering a letter

her if she were not with him. With that he took her directly home. His Excellency her father feared that so abrupt a move might violate protocol,[37] but he decided that an unsolicited objection from him might only earn him the Commander's hostility. "As you please, then," he said. "What she does has never really been up to me anyway."

At Rokujō, Genji found the brusque change offensive and arbitrary, but what could he do? She, too, was dismayed by the direction the salt fire's smoke was taking,[38] but the Commander was so pleased and satisfied that he might as well have made off with stolen treasure. His furious jealousy over the way His Majesty had come to her struck her as crudely obnoxious, and she granted him nothing of herself, which made him angrier still.

His Highness hardly knew what to do or say, despite his brave speeches, and from the Commander he had not a word. Now that the Commander had what he wanted, he was busy day and night.

The second month came. Genji thought what a callous business it was. He felt constantly embarrassed by his own anger at having been caught out that way, since nothing so bluntly possessive had ever occurred to him, and he remembered her with longing. No doubt destiny has played its part in all this, he reflected, but my own carelessness is what has brought this misery on me. Meanwhile, her image haunted him day and night. It seemed to him that as long as she was with that dull and dreary fellow, that Commander, he would have to renounce even the lightest banter with her, and he therefore restrained himself; but there came days of empty calm and ceaseless rain when he desperately missed the way he used to go to her to talk and pass the time, and he wrote her a letter. He sent it secretly to Ukon, although in deference to what Ukon's feelings might be, he kept it short and left his real meaning to the lady's imagination.

> "All through these long days, quiet as they are and empty in endless spring rain,
>   say, what are your memories of that man at your old home?

The monotony stirs many bitter recollections, but how can I spell them out to you now?"

She wept when Ukon found a private moment to show it to her, because her memory dwelled on him, too, ever more fondly as time went by, and she only

---

37. Tamakazura should have returned to Rokujō before moving to Higekuro's.
38. "By the direction her marriage was taking." From *Kokinshū* 708: "The smoke from the sea girl's salt fire at Suma, in this high wind, has taken a direction she had never imagined."

wished she could see again the father to whom she could never say that she missed him or wished to be with him. Never having told even Ukon how much she disliked his occasionally trying behavior, she could reflect on it only inwardly. Ukon had glimpsed something of the truth, but she still could not quite make out how much had happened between them.

She wrote in reply, "It is an embarrassing confession, but I thought you might want to know:

Wet as my sleeves are with drops falling from the eaves in these long, long rains,
how could not my fondest thoughts dwell on someone I miss so?

The more time passes, it is true, the drearier I feel; but I shall say no more." Her letter was thoroughly restrained.

Genji felt his own gleaming drops poised to fall when he spread it out and read it, but he feigned detachment lest he betray himself to any onlooker. Still, his heart was very full, and despite memories of how the Empress Mother had kept another Mistress of Staff[39] shut away from him in Emperor Suzaku's reign, this was the one who, in her innocence, claimed his greater sympathy. How the roving lover brings his own troubles on himself! he thought. What requires me to now suffer? No, she is not for me! When he failed to dispel his delusions, he turned to playing his koto and dwelled fondly in mind on the dear music that her fingers had once drawn from the strings. "Cut not the gleaming waterweed!"[40] he sang as he toyed with the *azuma* mode, and she who longed for him would not have missed the magic of the sight, if only one could have allowed her to see it.

His Majesty, too, lingered on the face and figure that he had seen so briefly. "The one I saw leave me, red skirts asweep"[41]—the old poem was crude perhaps, but he kept repeating it as he sat daydreaming. She had secret letters from him. Convinced by now that she was destined for misfortune, she shrank from such unbecoming diversions and did not encourage him in her replies. All things considered, it was Genji's rare kindness that stayed with her after all, and she could never forget it.

By the third month the spectacle of wisteria and kerria rose in her Rokujō garden, beautifully picked out in the light of the setting sun, recalled so vividly the way she had looked when she sat enjoying that same view that Genji abandoned his own spring garden to go and contemplate it. The glow of the kerria roses artlessly blooming on the woven Chinese bamboo fence was very pleasing. "The color shall I wear . . ."[42] he murmured.

"Would it were not so, but the road down through Ide parts us two as well;
yet in silence I still love blossoming kerria rose.

39. Oborozukiyo, in "The Green Branch."
40. A passage from a folk song (*fūzoku uta*) known as "Mandarin Ducks" ("Oshidori").
41. *Kokin rokujō* 3333: "Standing I yearn, and sitting, too, for the one I saw leave me, red skirts asweep."
42. *Kokin rokujō* 3508: "Of love and longing I shall never speak, but the color I shall wear remains always mute." The color is the yellow dye from gardenia (*kuchinashi*, which also means "mouthless") seeds—the same color as kerria rose (*yamabuki*) flowers. Genji is trying to put Tamakazura out of his mind.

'My face betrays . . .' "[43] he went on, but there was no one to hear him. Only now did he truly grasp that she was gone. His heart really did play strange tricks on him. When his eye fell on a large number of duck eggs, he did them up like tangerines and oranges to send her casually,[44] and he wrote blandly, lest his words catch anyone's interest, "I have not seen you for a long, long time, and I might protest that you treat me strangely, except that I gather these things are not entirely up to you. I regret that it may be difficult for us to meet except under particular circumstances," and so on in a fatherly vein.

> "One duckling, alas, though hatched in this very nest, nonetheless is gone!
> Tell me, then, what sort of man has claimed it now for his own?[45]

But why does it have to be like this? I do not like it at all!"

The Commander read it and smiled. "A wife may not visit even her parents without sufficient reason," he muttered. "What business has His Grace, then, to cling to you constantly and to complain this way?" His words grated on her ears.

She had no idea what to write. "I cannot really answer him," she said.

"Leave it to me." It was maddening, the way he volunteered.

> "Who is it you say should return a worthless duckling, once lost in the nest,
> and where would you have it go, to regain what rightful place?

Your apparent displeasure is surprising, and I may have resorted to somewhat vivid language."

"This Commander has never to my knowledge expressed himself with such imagination—I can hardly believe it!" Genji laughed, but at heart he was furious at the way the man had appropriated her.

This outcome brought the Commander's first wife worsening torment as time went by, and her mental state deteriorated. The Commander provided for her well, and he still looked attentively after his sons, so that he could not detach himself from her completely; in the domain of her basic needs he remained as reliable as before. Although desperate to see his daughter, he was refused all access to her. In her youthful innocence she suffered acutely from everyone's merciless condemnation of her father and from the mounting insistence on keeping her away from him. Meanwhile, her brothers, who were often at his residence, would naturally tell her from time to time about the Mistress of Staff. "She is nice, and she is kind to us," they said. "She spends all her time doing pretty things." Their sister envied them and sighed that she had not been born to any such freedom as theirs. It is extraordinary, the way the Mistress of Staff upset everyone, men and women alike!

In the eleventh month of that year she had a very pretty little son of her own,

---

43. Ide, a place-name established in poetry, was associated with *yamabuki* flowers. *Kokin rokujō* 4488: "At evening in the fields, they say, the cuckoo ["face bird"] calls, and my face betrays that I will not forget you."

44. All three items mentioned were standard gifts.

45. The poem also contains the meaning, "There is no point [*kai*, a homophone of the poetic word for "egg"], then, in my having looked after you here."

and the Commander, who could not have asked for more, pampered him endlessly. All this is easily imagined, though, and there is no need to insist. Her father, too, was of course gratified by her good fortune. In looks and so on she was fully worthy of the other children whom he had always cherished. The Secretary Captain[46] was very fond of this sister of his and treated her warmly, but at times he still betrayed a certain disappointment, and the charm of the new arrival only made him wish that her palace service had borne fruit. He even took the liberty of remarking, "Whenever I hear His Majesty sigh that he has no sons, I think of the honor it would have been." She still carried out her official duties conscientiously, but there seemed no longer to be any chance of her actually going to the palace. Such, no doubt, was her destiny.

Oh, yes, there was that other daughter of His Excellency's, the one so eager to be Mistress of Staff. She was a bit of a flirt as well, like so many of her kind, and that made things difficult for her father. The Consort, too, lived forever in fear of her provoking some sort of incident. Her father had even forbidden her to appear in the Consort's presence, but she ignored him and went anyway.

On one occasion the pick of the privy gentlemen had gathered at the Consort's and were playing music to a languorous sort of rhythm. It was a delicious autumn evening, and the Consultant Captain,[47] who was there, too, was surprising her women with his unaccustomed gaiety. They were exclaiming how remarkable he was when the girl from Ōmi came barging past them.

"Oh, no! What are you doing?" She glared balefully at them when they pulled her back.

"Here comes something outrageous, I know it!" They nudged each other in acute embarrassment.

"He's the one, he's the one!" she whispered enthusiastically, loud and clear, on the subject of that most exceptionally stalwart young gentleman. It was very painful.

> "Boat upon the sea, if you know not where to go, lost among the waves,
>   let me then row out to you; but tell me what port is yours!"

her voice rang out. "You always row your little boat back to the same girl![48] It isn't fair!"

The shocked Captain was wondering who on earth at the Consort's would ever express herself so crudely when he realized with amusement that this must be the young lady of whom he had heard.

> "The boatman you see, though uncertain where to go, plaything of the winds,
>   disdains to approach a shore where he has no wish to go,"

he replied. That, they say, silenced her.

---

46. Kashiwagi.
47. Yūgiri.
48. Kumoi no Kari. *Kokinshū* 732: "The little boat that rows across Hori Inlet rows back and back, and, it seems, always to the same person."

32

UMEGAE
The Plum Tree Branch

"Umegae" ("The Plum Tree Branch") is the title of a *saibara* song sung at a festive gathering by one of Tō no Chūjō's sons.

"The Plum Tree Branch" follows "The Handsome Pillar" in chronological sequence.

PERSONS

His Grace, the Chancellor, Genji, age 39

The lady of the southeast quarter, 31 (Murasaki)

His Highness of War, Genji's brother (Hotaru Hyōbukyō no Miya)

The former Kamo Priestess (Asagao)

The Consultant Captain, Genji's son, 18 (Yūgiri)

The Secretary Captain, Tō no Chūjō's eldest son, 23 or 24 (Kashiwagi)

The Controller Lieutenant, 22 or 23 (Kōbai)

Her Majesty, the Empress, 30 (Akikonomu)

The young lady, Genji's daughter, 11 (Akashi no Himegimi)

The Heir Apparent, 13

His Excellency, the Palace Minister (Tō no Chūjō)

His daughter, 20 (Kumoi no Kari)

G enji planned something exceptional for his daughter's donning of the train. The Heir Apparent was to come of age in the same second month, and her presentation to him would presumably follow.

It was the last day of the first month, and Genji passed the lull at home and at court blending incense.[1] He felt when he examined the incense wood presented to him by the Dazaifu Deputy that wood from an earlier age might perhaps be superior, and he therefore had the storehouses at Nijō opened and Chinese things of all kinds brought to him. "When it comes to brocades, twills, and so on," he said as he compared them, "the old ones are still the finest and the best." To cover her personal accessories or for them to rest on, or to make the borders of her cushions and so on, he chose from among a wealth of twills and madder red and gold brocades,[2] ones of a quality beyond any seen nowadays, left over from those presented to the court by the Koma embassy in His Late Eminence's reign; and he bestowed the twills and gauzes he had just received on her gentlewomen. He had his incense woods old and new arranged before him and then passed out to his ladies with the request that they make two blends each. Everyone at Rokujō and elsewhere was caught up in preparing superb gifts for the guests, rewards for the senior nobles, and so on; but now each had choices to make as well, and iron mortars[3] rang loudly everywhere.

Genji sequestered himself in the main house and blended away according to the two methods (how had he ever learned them?) covered in the Sōwa Instructions.[4] His lady had had herself specially installed in the deepest recess of her eastern extension to master the method taught by the Hachijō Lord of Ceremonial.[5] So the two vied with each other, and her strict secrecy moved Genji to remark, "After all, a fragrance wins or loses according to whether it is shallow or deep!" He was so eager that he hardly seemed to be the father. Few gentlewomen waited on either of

1. For his daughter to take to the palace. The process involved mixing powdered incense wood and a binder like honey or the sweet, boiled-down sap of the *amachazuru* vine into incense balls.
2. *Higonki*, red brocade with gold thread.
3. Incense wood was pounded to powder with an iron mortar and pestle.
4. The two recipes (for types of *kurobō* and *jijū* incense) taught by Emperor Ninmyō in the Sōwa (also Shōwa or Jōwa) period (834–48). In principle they were to be passed on only to women.
5. Prince Motoyasu, the seventh son of Emperor Ninmyō.

them. The ladies had made the accessories as pretty as they could possibly be, and among them the design of the incense jars and boxes, and the style of the censer, were so fresh, novel, and intriguing that Genji looked forward to filling them with the very best once he had sampled the scents they were now all so busy making.

On the tenth of the second month a light rain was falling, and the red plum before Genji's residence was in magnificent and incomparably fragrant bloom, when His Highness of War came to present his greetings, for everything was to be ready that day or the next. He and Genji had always been especially close, and they were talking happily of this and that, praising the flowers and so on, when a messenger arrived with a letter attached to a plum branch from which most of the flowers were gone.[6] The messenger reported that it was from the former Kamo Priestess.

Censer

His Highness had heard about that. "What kind of letter has she sent you?" he asked with amused interest.

Genji smiled. "I took the liberty of making a request, and she seems to have met it bravely." He hid it.

In an aloeswood[7] box she had placed two glass jars filled with generously large incense balls. The gift knots on the dark blue one represented five-needled pine and those on the white one plum blossoms,[8] and she had made even the cords that tied them both charmingly pretty. "What lovely things!" His Highness said. Then he noticed a poem in faint ink:

> "The scent of flowers lingers not upon the bough whence they have scattered,
> but may this deeply perfume the sleeves it will soon infuse."[9]

After reading it he made rather a show of humming it again.

The Consultant Captain found the messenger, detained him, and got him thoroughly drunk. Genji had a set of women's robes laid across his shoulders, together with a long dress of Chinese material in a red plum blossom layering. His reply was on paper of the same color, and he picked a spray of flowers from his tree to tie it to.

"I wonder what can be in that letter," His Highness said with some spirit. "What secret requires you to conceal it?" He was extremely curious.

6. *Shūishū* 1063, by Nyokaku Hōshi: "Spring is past and they are gone, the flowers of the plum; this is all that is left of them."

7. *Jin*, incense wood from the particularly fragrant heartwood of the tree; it was called *jin* ("sinking") because it sank in water.

8. The blue presumably contains *kurobō* incense (based on aloeswood, musk, sandalwood, cloves, and other ingredients, and particularly associated with winter) and the white one *baika* (cloves, sandalwood, plum blossoms, associated with spring).

9. "The flower fragrance of this incense is no use to me, for my time is past, but I hope that it will suit the young lady."

"Yes, what can it be? I am sorry that you should imagine me to have secrets from you." Genji allowed his brush to answer something like,

"Your blossoming bough suffuses my heart still more with its sweet perfume,
though you would suppress a scent others might note on the air."

"I admit that all this may seem rather frivolous," he said, "but she *is* my only daughter, and I believe it is the right thing to do. It would be awkward to ask anyone but a relative,[10] since she is nothing to look at, and I thought that I might invite Her Majesty here from the palace. I am very close to her, but her dignity is so thoroughly daunting that I would not dare expose her to anything common."

"Yes, of course," His Highness agreed, "and you must consider, too, that she is someone whose good fortune deserves to be emulated."

Genji took the occasion to send to each of his ladies for the incenses they had been blending, saying that he meant to try them all in the dampness of the evening.[11] They complied and presented them in many delightful ways. "Please rank these. To whom else would I show them?"[12] Genji said. He sent for a censer and insisted that His Highness test them.

"It is not *I* who know!" His Highness modestly replied, but he established fine distinctions of quality between them, even ones of the same kind, and so managed after all to decide which was better than which. At last Genji had the two he had blended himself brought forth. Just as at the palace incense is buried by the stream that runs past the Right Guards' quarters, he had buried his beside the one that flowed from beneath his west bridgeway. The Aide of the Watch, a son of the Consultant Koremitsu, dug it up, and the Consultant Captain took it and conveyed it to Genji.

"What a task you set your unhappy judge! My mind is all smoke!" One would have expected the same blending method to have passed on to them all, but no, each had gone about it as she pleased, and it was a thoroughly delightful business to rank the depth or shallowness of the achievement.

Among the many that resisted ranking, the former Kamo Priestess's *kurobō* nonetheless[13] had a wonderfully soothing quality that made it special. As to the *jijū*,[14] His Highness decided that Genji's own had a fragrance of particular sweetness and grace. She who reigned over Genji's southeast quarter had provided three incenses, of which the *baika* was novel and brilliant, with a keen, personal touch that gave it rare quality. "There could be no finer fragrances than these to send off on the season's breezes," His Highness remarked in praise. The lady of the summer quarter had not wished to put herself forward among the others in the competition, and she quailed even to think of smoke from incense of hers rising in such company. She had therefore compounded only one, a *kayō*.[15] It was unusual, and the fragrance was

10. To be the sponsor who "ties on" (*koshiyui*) the train.
11. Damp air (it has been raining) enhances the fragrance of incense.
12. *Kokinshū* 38, by Ki no Tomonori, which the Prince half quotes also in his reply: "If not to you, to whom else would I show them, these plum blossoms with their scent, for only he who knows them knows."
13. Despite Asagao's self-deprecating poem.
14. The *jijū* range, associated with autumn, included fine aloeswood and cloves among other ingredients.
15. A summer incense felt to resemble the scent of a lotus flower.

tranquil and touchingly gentle. The lady in the winter quarter, who had disliked the idea of being bested in the seasonal fragrances, had hit upon a wonderful blend of clothing incense passed on by His Late Eminence Suzaku[16] to His Majesty and made according to the "hundred paces" method specially selected by Lord Kintada.[17] The superlative grace gathered into it bore witness to superior conception. His Highness acknowledged merit in them all, which prompted Genji to remark, "You do not seem to be much of a judge, do you!"

When the moon came out, they drank wine and discussed the old days. The misty moonlight was enchanting, a little breeze blew after the recent rain, and with the blossoms' delicious scent ineffably filling the air around them, they fell into a very tender mood.

In the staff office, people were stringing instruments to rehearse tomorrow's music, and with so many privy gentlemen about, flutes could be heard playing prettily here and there. His Excellency's sons, the Secretary Captain and the Controller Lieutenant, had come from the palace to look in, just for form's sake, but Genji detained them and called for several stringed instruments. His Highness got a *biwa*, Genji a *sō no koto*, and the Secretary Captain a *wagon*, on which they played spirited music to delightful effect. The Consultant Captain's flute sent the mode, one perfect for the season, resounding throughout the heavens. The Controller Lieutenant beat the rhythm, and "The Plum Tree Branch"[18] as he sang it was quite lovely. He was the one who had sung "Takasago" as a page, that time when the gentlemen assembled to guess rhymes. His Highness and Genji both joined in, and the very informality of the occasion gave the evening's music a special charm.

His Highness offered Genji the cup and said,

> "Ah, this heart of mine could rise forever higher on the warbler's song,
>   now these delicious blossoms so pervade it with their charm—

and for a thousand years, I am sure."[19]

Genji replied,

> "I would have you come this spring to this home of mine where such flowers bloom,
>   till their color and their scent make themselves wholly your own!"

He passed the cup to the Secretary Captain, who then offered it to the Consultant Captain.

> "Play on, O play on many a sweet melody night-long on your flute,
>   till the sleeping warbler sways where he perches on the bough!"

---

16. The historical Emperor Uda (lived 867–931).

17. Minamoto no Kintada, a distinguished courtier and poet (889–948).

18. A *saibara* song: "To the plum tree branch the warbler comes, to sing all spring long, all spring long, yet snow is still falling. Look, how lovely! snow is falling."

19. *Kokinshū* 44, by Sosei: "How long will my heart wander the meadows? Perhaps a thousand years, as long as the blossoms do not fall."

The Consultant Captain answered,

> "When the very breeze seems resolved with tactful stealth to avoid this tree,
> would you really have me play till the bird must simply leave?

You are too unkind!"

Everyone laughed. The Controller Lieutenant:

> "As long as no mist drifts between the moon aloft and the blossoms here,
> surely the bird on his perch will still lift his voice in song."[20]

His Highness did not leave until it was really dawn. By way of gifts, Genji had him board his carriage with a dress cloak and a full set of robes of his own, and two jars of incense that he had left unopened.

> "With such sweet perfume wafting from such lovely sleeves, my darling at home
> may well have a word to say to reprove my sinful ways!"

His Highness said.

"What a timid husband!" Genji laughed and followed him while the ox was being yoked.

> "Your darling at home will look on you when you come with astonishment,
> to see you superbly dressed in a brocade of blossoms!

You will make quite a spectacle!" he said, and His Highness grudgingly conceded defeat. Without further ado Genji laid long dresses or gowns across the other young gentlemen's shoulders.

He reached the southwest quarter at the hour of the Dog.[21] The west wing, where Her Majesty lived, had been done up for the event, and a senior gentlewoman from Her Majesty's staff, charged with putting up the young lady's hair, was already there. On this occasion the lady of Genji's southeast quarter came, too, to meet Her Majesty. The crowd of gentlewomen from the several quarters of Rokujō seemed beyond counting.

The young lady donned her train at the hour of the Rat.[22] The lamps were low, but Her Majesty found what she gathered of her presence extremely pleasing.

"My confidence that you would not abandon her encouraged me to bring her before you in this impertinent guise,"[23] Genji said. "A fond father's private hope is that this may set an example for generations to come."[24]

20. Because he will mistake the light of the moon for dawn.
21. Roughly 8:00 P.M.
22. Roughly 1:00 A.M.
23. The Akashi Daughter came dressed as the child she remains until she has actually put on her train, and in this guise is still, in principle, unworthy to be seen by so great a lady.
24. No Empress has ever before played this role at a donning of the train, and Genji hopes that Empresses will now continue at times to confer this honor on such distinguished fathers as himself.

"The grandeur you gave the event was actually quite intimidating, since I had no idea how to do it properly," Her Majesty answered modestly, exuding youthful charm. With these perfectly delightful presences thus gathered around him, Genji took great pleasure in the harmony that reigned between them. The young lady's mother grieved bitterly that she was not to see her daughter even then, and Genji had compassionately considered inviting her after all, but fear of what people might then have to say had discouraged him from doing so.

Ceremonies like this involve a great deal of troublesome detail, even when done in the ordinary way, and I have recorded none of it because a rambling account of only one part might do more harm than good.

The Heir Apparent's donning of the trousers came after the twentieth of the month. His Highness was very grown-up, and people were all set to rush to offer him their daughters, but Genji's intentions were so obvious that the Minister of the Left and so on refrained on the grounds that they might only regret it if they did.

"That is extremely unfortunate. Surely the very essence of palace service is striving to rise a little above the rest. Life will be very dull if all these excellent girls are to remain shut up at home," Genji remarked when he heard about it, and he put off his daughter's move. The other interested parties had not wished simply to troop in after her, and when they heard of his decision, the Minister of the Left's third daughter did go. She was known as Reikeiden.

Genji redid the Kiritsubo, once his own palace apartment, for his daughter, and he decided on the fourth month because His Highness did not like the idea of having her arrival postponed. He improved the furnishings, gave the designs for the accessories and the sketches for the paintings his personal attention, gathered the very finest craftsmen to execute them, and had everything brought to a high degree of polish. To fill her book chest he chose books[25] that could serve her straight off as calligraphy models. They contained a great many examples that had made the best masters of the past famous in later generations.

"Everything is on the decline, compared to the old days," Genji confided to his love, "and this latter age of ours has lost all depth, but at least *kana* writing is superb now. The old writing certainly looks consistent, but it conveys no breadth or generosity and seems always to follow the same pattern. It is only later on that people began writing a truly fascinating hand, but among the many simple models that I collected when I myself was so keen on cultivating the 'woman's style,'[26] a line quickly dashed off by the Haven, Her Majesty's mother—one she meant nothing by and that I acquired—struck me as particularly remarkable. Yes, in the end I am afraid I brought her name unfairly into disrepute. I really did not mean it, but it hurt her very deeply. She understood many things, and perhaps now that she is gone, her spirit has considered all I have done for Her Majesty and pardoned me. Her Majesty's own writing has accomplished charm, but," he whispered, "it may lack a certain spark. Her Late Eminence's[27] writing showed great depth and grace,

---

25. *Sōshi*, bound volumes as distinguished from scrolls (*makimono*).
26. *Onnade*, so called because it was in principle women who wrote in *kana*.
27. Fujitsubo's.

but there was something weak about it, too, and it had little flair. His Eminence's Mistress of Staff[28] is the one who stands out in our time, although hers has too many tricks and flourishes. Still," he concluded generously, "she, the former Kamo Priestess, and you yourself are the ones who really and truly write."

"Surely I do not belong in such company!"

"Do not be too mo-

Reed writing

dest! For warmth and sweetness, you know, there is no one like you. The better one is at characters, the more likely it is that inept *kana* will creep into one's writing." He also made up some blank books with exquisite covers and cords. "I must have His Highness of War and the Intendant of the Left Gate Guards[29] do some, too, and I shall do a pair myself. Those two may fancy themselves, but I am sure I can keep up with them." He thought highly of himself as well.

He selected the finest brushes and ink and sent urgent requests to the usual ladies, disconcerting them so greatly that some declined more than once, at which he only redoubled his entreaties. He had some extremely pretty Koma paper, very thin, and to test "our young gallants" he sent some to the Consultant Captain, to the Intendant of the Watch, His Highness of Ceremonial's son, and to the Palace Minister's son, the Secretary Captain, with the order to do whatever reed writing[30] or poem pictures[31] they pleased.

He went off to the main house as before to do his writing. The cherry blossoms were over, the sky was a tranquil blue, and he wrote out the old poems as he pleased, just as they came to him, in astonishing numbers, some in running script, some in plain, and some in the woman's style.[32] He had few gentlewomen with him, just two or three to grind his ink—women worth talking to when weighing one poem or another from some old and noble collection. All the blinds were up, and lost in thought that way near the veranda, with the book on an armrest before him and the tip of the brush in his mouth, he made a sight too marvelous for one ever to tire of watching. For anyone with a discerning eye it was a wonder simply to see the

28. Oborozukiyo.
29. A half brother of Tō no Chūjō.
30. *Ashide*, which involved painting a waterside scene (with reeds, water swirls, rocks, and so on) in such a way that the lines of the painting formed the *kana* letters of a poem.
31. *Utae*, in which a poem inspired by a painting was written over the painting in fainter ink.
32. The "running script" (*sō*) consists of cursively written Chinese characters used for their phonetic value, and the "plain" (*tada*) script is ordinary *kana*, that is to say, purely phonetic signs without ideographic value. The difference between "plain" and "woman's style" (*onnade*) is unclear.

way he addressed himself to the sharply contrasting red or white of the paper, adjusted his hold on the brush, and applied himself to the task.

When His Highness of War was announced, the startled Genji straightened his dress cloak, ordered another cushion set out for his visitor, and had him brought straight in. His Highness grandly mounted the steps, looking splendid himself, while the women peeped at him from within. The grave formality with which they greeted each other was also admirable. "I have been shut up here with little to do," Genji began cheerfully, "and the quiet was beginning to weary me. You have come at just the right time!"

His Highness had brought his own finished book, and Genji immediately looked through it. His visitor's hand was not inspiring, but it was his little accomplishment, and he had written very cleanly indeed. The poems he had chosen from the old anthologies were distinctly unusual ones, and he had given them just three lines each, with pleasantly few Chinese characters. Genji was surprised. "I never imagined such wonders from you!" he exclaimed ruefully. "I shall have to throw all my brushes away!"

"I thought I might as well do my best, as long as I was shamelessly to introduce my writing into such company," His Highness lightly replied.

Genji could not very well hide the books he had been filling, so he took them out. They examined them together. His running script on stiff Chinese paper struck His Highness as a miracle, while his quiet, perfectly self-possessed woman's style on soft, fine-grained Koma paper, lovely yet unassertive in color, was beyond anything. His Highness felt his tears gathering to join the flow of these supple lines that he knew would never pall, and the poems in expansively free running script, on magnificently colored papers from Japan's own court workshop, gave endless pleasure. The rich and varied charm of these things so captivated His Highness that he never even glanced at anyone else's.

In what he had done the Intendant of the Left Gate Guards had consistently sought the ostentatiously clever line, but one felt something murky in the movement of his brush, and one detected, too, an attempt on his part to hide it. His choice of poems was somewhat arch.

Genji gave his visitor no real look at the ladies' work; in fact, he did not take out the Kamo Priestess's at all.

The books of reed writing, each different in its way, were sheer delight. In the Consultant Captain's the water was powerfully drawn, the reeds' lively growth recalled the shore at Naniwa, and the intermingling of the two showed great poise. There were also pages on which with fresh inventiveness he had tried a quite different style and done full justice to the letters, the placing of the rocks, and so on. "It is dazzling," His Highness said with keen appreciation. "It must have taken him ages to do." He who so loved fine things and cultivated such elegance was extremely impressed.

They spent the rest of the day talking about calligraphy, and when Genji brought out a selection of poetry scrolls pieced together from different papers,[33]

33. *Tsugigami:* papers of different colors torn along irregular lines and pasted together into a scroll.

His Highness sent his son, the Adviser, back to his residence for some of his own. There were four scrolls of the *Man'yōshū*, chosen and written by Emperor Saga,[34] and a *Kokin wakashū* by His Engi Majesty[35] on lengths of light blue Chinese paper pasted together, with a mounting paper strongly patterned in darker blue, rollers of dark green jade, and flat cords woven in a Chinese ripple pattern, all to lovely effect. His Engi Majesty had wielded marvelous skill to change his hand for each *Kokin wakashū* scroll, and they brought a lamp close to examine them. "They never disappoint one, do they," Genji remarked in praise. "People now can manage only a contrived approximation."

His Highness presented them to Genji on the spot. "Even if I had a daughter, I would not want them to go to someone who hardly knew what to see in them, and as it is, they would just go to waste," he said.

Genji put some Chinese calligraphy scrolls in a very nice aloeswood box for the Adviser, and he added a beautiful Koma flute.

Genji also immersed himself then in connoisseurship of *kana* writing, and he sought out everyone at all known for that skill—high, middle, or low—so as to have each write out whatever might be most congenial. He placed nothing of base origin in his daughter's book box, and he carefully distinguished the rank of each writer when he asked for a book or a scroll. Among all her wondrous treasures, some unknown even in the realm across the sea, it was these books that most aroused young people's interest. He also prepared a collection of paintings for her. He wanted to see his Suma diary go to her and her descendants, but he did not take it out now, having decided not to do so until she knew a little more of the world.

News of these preparations reached His Excellency the Palace Minister from afar and left him at once intensely worried and bitterly disappointed. His daughter was now in full flower and too pretty to waste. He hated to see her bored and dispirited, but that young man of hers remained as serene as ever, and he would look silly if he meekly approached him himself. No, he groaned, if only I had let myself be persuaded when he was so obviously keen on her! He could not blame just the young man. The Consultant Captain heard that he had softened his attitude somewhat, but he was still so angry about the rude way he had once been treated that he pretended not to care, and although he often felt in no mood for laughter, since in fact he had no interest in anyone else, her nurse's gibes about that light blue of his only confirmed his resolve to have them see him rise to Counselor first.

Genji deplored the strangely rootless life that his son was leading. "If you have given up your ambition in that direction," he said, "the Minister of the Right and Prince Nakatsukasa both seem to be interested in you, and I hope that you will decide one way or the other." However, his son only maintained an attitude of silent deference. "I did not much feel like obeying His Late Eminence's lessons on this sort of subject either, so I hesitate to put you through the same thing," Genji went on. "Still, experience suggests that what he said is as true now as ever. As long as you remain unattached, people will suspect you of doing so for a particular reason, and

---

34. Reigned 809–23.
35. Emperor Daigo (reigned 897–930). The *Kokin wakashū Kokinshū*) has twenty scrolls.

they will be sadly disappointed if you merely allow your destiny to lead you to settle for someone tediously dull. To aim too high is to court failure, because all things have their proper measure, but that is no reason to give yourself too much license. From my earliest youth I grew up in the palace, where I could never do as I pleased and where I lived in fear that any slip might make me a reprobate, and even so the world condemned me for my profligacy. Do not allow yourself to do as you please while your rank is low and you have little importance. The heart goes its own way sometimes, and you can easily come to grief over a woman when you have no one to make you wish to control yourself, as the examples even of past sages show. If you overreach yourself and hold someone up to scandal, you yourself will bear the burden of her hatred, which will then continue to bind you to this life. Once you have married the wrong woman, it may be extremely difficult to endure her in violation of your feelings, but you must still cultivate a willingness to reconsider and to yield to the wishes of her parents or, even if she unfortunately has none, to try always to keep in mind whatever about her may be most attractive. Confidence that all will be well in the end is what matters most, both for your sake and for hers." He passed the time giving out this sort of advice whenever he happened to be at leisure.

The young man needed no prompting to recoil on his young lady's behalf, just as Genji's sermons enjoined him to do, from the most casual preoccupation with anyone else. She, meanwhile, was ashamed to see her father more than usually troubled, and she sorrowfully blamed her own misfortune for it; but on the surface she lived out all her dreary days with unruffled calm.

He wrote her touchingly impassioned letters whenever his feelings demanded release. She might wonder "whom else to believe,"[36] but it takes someone more experienced seriously to doubt a lover's heart, and many passages affected her deeply. People were saying that Prince Nakatsukasa had been sounding out His Grace and that the two of them had decided to proceed, which to her father must have been yet another blow. "That is what I hear," he told her privately with tears in his eyes. "How cruel he is! I suppose he is getting back at me for being stubborn when he approached me about it. What a fool I would look if I were just to give in!" Desperately ashamed, she found herself weeping as well and turned away in embarrassment, looking infinitely dear as she did so. What am I to do? he kept wondering. Shall I step forward even now to see how he feels? These and other questions ran through his mind.

She lingered there near the veranda even after he had gone, abstracted and disconsolate. How strange it is, the way my tears came all by themselves! What can he have thought of me? As she sat there pondering these things, a letter came from him, and yes, she read it. It was long and earnest. He had written,

> "Cruel ways like yours are no more than one expects in this world of ours,
>   but for not forgetting you am I then so very strange?"

---

36. *Kokinshū* 713: "Though I believe you lie, by now, whom else have I to believe?"

She could not get over the coldness with which he had failed even to hint at what she had just learned, but she replied despite her anger,

"That this should be all, and that you should now forget one whom you could not: surely that is what it means to give in to worldly ways!"

This so puzzled him that he could not put it down. He just sat staring at it, shaking his head.

33

FUJI NO URABA
New Wisteria Leaves

Fuji no uraba ("new wisteria leaves") appears in an old poem quoted by Tō no Chūjō when in this chapter he approves Yūgiri's marriage to his daughter Kumoi no Kari.

"New Wisteria Leaves" follows "The Plum Tree Branch" in chronological sequence.

PERSONS

His Grace, the Chancellor, then Honorary Retired Emperor, Genji, age 39

The Consultant Captain, then Counselor, Genji's son, 18 (Yūgiri)

His Excellency, the Palace Minister, then Chancellor (Tō no Chūjō)

The Secretary Captain, Tō no Chūjō's eldest son, 23 or 24 (Kashiwagi)

The Controller Lieutenant, 22 or 23 (Kōbai)

The young lady, Tō no Chūjō's daughter, 20 (Kumoi no Kari)

The mistress of Genji's east wing, 31 (Murasaki)

The Fujiwara Dame of Staff, Koremitsu's daughter

The young lady, Genji's daughter, Consort of the Heir Apparent, 11 (Akashi no Himegimi)

Her mother, Akashi, 30 (Akashi no Kimi)

Taifu, Kumoi no Kari's nurse

Saishō, Yūgiri's nurse

His Majesty, the Emperor, 21 (Reizei)

His Eminence, Retired Emperor Suzaku, 42

A mid all these preparations[1] the Consultant Captain still felt melancholy and abstracted; in fact, even he was surprised by the depth of his attachment. If my heart is that set on her,[2] then I hear the barrier guard has relented enough to show himself disposed to sleep,[3] he reflected, but I might as well see the thing through more creditably than that. Still, his restraint cost him much turmoil and pain. Meanwhile his young lady gathered from what her father had told her, if it was true, that she must no longer mean anything to him, and so each turned surprisingly away from the other; which only showed how much they were in love. Despite his past obduracy, His Excellency hardly knew what to do next, since he would have to start looking all over again if Prince Nakatsukasa decided to proceed. I pity any new prospect I might find, he thought, and as for myself, I have no doubt people would be laughing and joking at my expense. There is no point in trying to hide that furtive misbehavior of theirs[4]—it, too, must be common knowledge by now. I suppose I shall have to put the best face I can on it and yield after all.

He hesitated to approach Genji abruptly on the subject, since beneath their superficial cordiality they were still at odds with each other, and he would look foolish if he raised it too formally. He wondered when he would ever find the right moment to drop him a word about it.

On the twentieth of the third month he made a pilgrimage to Gokurakuji,[5] for it was the anniversary of the death of Her Highness his mother. All his sons accompanied him in fine array, and with them came a great number of senior nobles who by no means eclipsed the Consultant Captain, whose looks were just now reaching their manly glory and whose figure was the sum of every grace. Ever since becoming so angry with His Excellency he had felt nervous in his presence, and his consequently judicious manner and quiet dignity of bearing now caught His Excellency's particular attention. Genji,

1. For Genji's daughter to enter the palace.
2. Kumoi no Kari.
3. "I hear her father is by now willing to permit the marriage." *Kokinshū* 632 (also *Ise monogatari* 6, section 5), by Ariwara no Narihira: "May the barrier guard stationed on the path I take secretly fall asleep night after night!" The guard has been placed there by the father of the young woman Narihira has been visiting.
4. The precocious sexual intimacy, years ago, between Yūgiri and Kumoi no Kari.
5. A funerary temple for the senior Fujiwara nobility.

too, had commissioned scripture readings. The Consultant Captain came forward to take all the arrangements in hand, and he displayed affecting devotion.

That evening, when everyone was leaving, cherry petals lay thick on the ground and mist veiled all things while His Excellency gracefully hummed old poems and dreamed of the past. The Consultant Captain, too, more and more caught up in the evening's melancholy mood, remained pensive and absorbed despite the voices crying, "It looks like rain!"

His Excellency imagined him lost in thoughts of *her* and tugged at his sleeve. "Why are you so angry with me? Surely you can forgive me if you will only think what today's services mean for us both. I do not have many years left, you know, and I must tell you that your rejection has hurt me."

The young gentleman assumed a deferential attitude. "Although Her Late Highness kindly gave me reason to hope, you yourself seemed not to concur, and you will therefore understand that I have not wished to presume." Everyone rushed home as quickly as he could amid a flurry of wind and rain. The subject was of such abiding interest that the Consultant Captain spent the night turning over and over in his mind what His Excellency might have meant by his unusual overture.

His Excellency now found his resistance gone, thanks perhaps to the Captain's constancy over the long years, and he gave thought to some slight occasion on which lightly, yet still properly, to further the matter. Meanwhile, the fourth month came, bringing his residence so magnificent a profusion of wisteria blossoms that he could not let their glory pass, and he arranged music for the occasion. Toward evening the blossoms were more beautiful than ever, and he had his own son, the Secretary Captain, take the young man a note: "Our talk that day under the blossoms left me eager for more. Please come, if you are not otherwise engaged." The note included a poem:

> *"In the dim twilight, wisteria round my home glows in vivid hues:*
> *will you then not come to see this, the last bounty of spring?"*[6]

He had tied it to an especially lovely branch.

The Captain had expected this, and with beating heart he composed a polite reply:

> *"My faltering hand yet might hesitate to pluck such wisteria,*
> *when amid twilight shadows my gesture might go astray."*

"My courage fails me, I am afraid. Please make whatever changes it needs."

"I shall accompany you," His Excellency's envoy declared.

"That is more of an escort than I require!" After sending him back,[7] the Captain told his father what had happened and showed him His Excellency's note.

---

6. Tō no Chūjō hints at giving Yūgiri his daughter, Kumoi no Kari. His poem may allude to lines by Bai Juyi (*Wakan rōei shū* 52, *Hakushi monjū* 0631).

7. Kashiwagi is a Guards officer, and the sort of escort in question would have been provided by the Guards to someone of very high rank; hence Yūgiri's mild joke.

"He certainly has something particular in mind. If he really has come forward this far, he must have forgiven you your past unfilial conduct."[8] Genji spoke with a maddening look of triumph.

"It cannot be *that* serious. I gather that his wisteria is blooming more beautifully than usual, and with things so quiet now, I suppose he just wants some music."

"You got quite a messenger, though. You must go immediately." He gave his approval, and the Captain remained apprehensive about what might be in store for him.

"That dress cloak you have on is too dark, and to my eye it lacks dignity. Violet suits someone merely qualified for Consultant, or a young man with no rank worth mentioning. Here, let me dress you properly."[9] Genji sent him off with a bearer carrying a marvelous dress cloak of his own, together with a full set of exquisitely beautiful gowns.

Back in his own room the Consultant Captain prepared his appearance with extreme care, allowed twilight to pass, and then arrived just when his host would be wondering anxiously whether he was coming at all. Seven or eight of His Excellency's sons, the Secretary Captain among them, turned out to welcome him. All were fine-looking young gentlemen, but he still surpassed them, since quite apart from his distinctive looks he had a noble grace that put everyone to shame.

His Excellency took care to receive him in a room done up for the occasion, but before going forth to greet him, formal cap and all, he spoke to his wife and her young gentlewomen. "Have a look at him!" he said. "He is turning into a remarkably handsome man, and he has a composed, quiet dignity as well. Considering how clearly he rises above his peers, I should say he outdoes even his father. His Grace has the most extraordinarily engaging charm, and merely to look at him is to smile and forget the world's cares, but in the service of the realm he is a little soft and inclined to please himself, which I suppose is natural enough. This young gentleman, though, has greater learning than his father, and everyone seems to credit him with admirably manly steadiness and soundness."

They devoted a moment to suitable pleasantries and then went on to admire the blossoms. "All the flowers of spring are a wonder when they bloom, but they are gone so cruelly soon that one reproaches them for it; these are the only ones that linger on into summer, and that is why I am so especially fond of them. Even their color, you know, speaks of loving ties." His Excellency's smiles conveyed a welcoming warmth.

The blossoms remained indistinct even after the moon had risen, but they had their music and wine in a spirit of praise. His Excellency soon began pretending to be tipsy and boisterously pressed drink on his guest, who had ideas of his own and insistently declined. "You may well be the most gifted official in all the realm, too good, in fact, for this degenerate age, but I reproach you for having abandoned an old man. Surely even the Classics mention respect for one's elders. I take it that you are familiar with that fellow's teaching[10] as well. I tell you, it makes me angry to

---

8. His violation of Kumoi no Kari, which was unfilial toward Ōmiya, his grandmother and hers.

9. Yūgiri is wearing *futaai*, that is, a dress cloak dyed with both indigo (blue) and safflower (scarlet). Perhaps Genji gives him instead a blue one more suited to a young man with a bright future.

10. That of Confucius.

think of all the suffering you have caused me!" Drunken tears or not, he did very well at telling the young man a thing or two.

"Oh, no, my lord!" the Captain protested politely. "I would gladly give everything for the sake of those in whom the past lives on for me, and I do not know how you could imagine such a thing! It must be my foolish heart's own dullness that has made it seem that way."

This was the moment for His Excellency to launch into singing "new wisteria leaves,"[11] at which the Secretary Captain picked a particularly long, dark cluster of blossoms and laid it beside the guest's cup. The young gentleman struggled for a reply, and meanwhile His Excellency said,

> *"I shall then complain to the wisteria blossoms' comely purple hue,*
> *though I am not pleased at all that they have outreached the pine."*[12]

Cup in hand, the Consultant Captain acknowledged him with a slight and thoroughly graceful bow.

> *"Ah, how many times have I had to suffer through all too dewy springs,*
> *to come at last on this day when flowers burst into bloom?"*

he replied and passed the cup to the Secretary Captain.

> *"The wisteria that in tender bloom recalls a fair maiden's sleeves*
> *no doubt looks lovelier still to a ravished watcher's eyes."*

The cup went on round, but the poems tottered drunkenly, and no one managed to do better.

The lake spread its tranquil mirror beneath the pale evening moon of the seventh night. Yes, the leaves aloft in the trees were slender and new, but the pine, although not tall, reclined suggestively, and there hung from it such blossoms as the world seldom sees. The Controller Lieutenant, as always, sang "Fence of Rushes" in his lovely voice.[13]

"What an odd song to choose!" His Excellency teased, and he joined in to sing ". . . this ancient, noble house" in his own fine voice.[14] Their evening was pleasantly relaxed, and all constraint between them vanished.

It was growing late at last when the Consultant Captain turned to the Secre-

---

11. *Gosenshū* 100, the speaker being a woman who has just received assurances of devotion from her lover: "Illumined by the springtime sun, the new wisteria leaves yield, and if you love me, I will trust in you." Tō no Chūjō is offering Yūgiri his daughter.

12. "I shall then blame my daughter after all, though I deplore that it should have taken you so long to declare yourself that I had to come forward further toward you than I wished."

13. A *saibara* song about a lover who comes to steal his bride from her father's house and gets caught. The singer, Kōbai, apparently alludes—rather wickedly—to the old sexual intimacy between Yūgiri and Kumoi no Kari.

14. *Toshi henikeru kono ie* instead of the song's original phrase, *todorokeru kono ie* ("this celebrated house")— the house of the bride's father.

tary Captain with a great show of being ill.[15] "I really am not feeling at all well, and by now I doubt that I should try to get home. May I beg a room for the night?"

"Find him somewhere to sleep!" His Excellency cried. "This old man is too drunk to do it himself. Please excuse me!" He staggered from the room.

"Well, a traveler's night beneath the blossoms, I see," the Secretary Captain remarked. "Oh, dear. That makes things a little difficult for your guide!"

"You think the flower a wanton, wedded to the pine?" the Consultant retorted. "You might have chosen another expression!"[16]

Although personally put out, the Secretary Captain had desired this match himself, since the Consultant's quality left nothing to be desired, and he showed him the way willingly.

The young man thought that he was dreaming, and he must have felt extremely proud of himself as well. His young lady was very bashful, but her new, more womanly beauty pleased him better than ever. "I might well have gone down in song and story,"[17] he complained, "but my constancy seems to have persuaded His Excellency after all. *Your* blindness to my feelings is extraordinary, though! And did you notice what that 'Fence of Rushes' the Lieutenant sang is about? The nerve of him! I wanted to give him back 'At Kawaguchi'!"[18]

She took this badly.

> *"Yes, Kawaguchi, it is you who made our shame familiar to all,*
> *and what did you do it for, letting all our secrets through?*[19]

You are horrid!" she cried, like a little girl.

> *"Please at least refrain from blaming Kawaguchi for his carelessness*
> *when Kukida Barrier is where the whole thing came out!"*[20]

he replied with a little smile. "After all those years of waiting I feel absolutely awful, and I hardly know what I am doing." Pleading drunkenness and certainly acting ill, he ignored the coming of dawn.[21] When her gentlewomen failed to rouse him, His Excellency remarked with some irritation that he must be very pleased with himself

---

15. From drink.

16. Yūgiri reacts sharply to Kashiwagi's teasing. "A traveler's night beneath the blossoms" (*hana no kage no tabine*) suggests a passing encounter with a woman of pleasure, and Kashiwagi jokingly feigns embarrassment. Yūgiri is not amused.

17. *Gosenshū* 1036, by Mibu no Tadamine: "No one has ever yet died of the pain of love, but I might well have gone down for that in song and story!" *Kokin rokujō* 1986, by Ise, is very similar.

18. Another *saibara* song in the voice of a girl who boasts of having escaped through "the rough fence of the Kawaguchi Barrier," despite her father's watchful eye, to lie with her lover.

19. Kumoi no Kari's poem continues the Kawaguchi Barrier motif with a wordplay on the barrier's "crude fence" (*aragaki*) that let the truth escape.

20. "Do not blame me: your father is the one who spread it about." The Kawaguchi Barrier (in present Mie Prefecture) and the Kukida Barrier appear to be one and the same, but the Kawaguchi Barrier is rare in poetry, and the Kukida Barrier appears nowhere else.

21. At this stage he should have left Kumoi no Kari well before dawn, to return the following night. Instead, he behaves as though they have already been married for years.

to be lying asleep so long. He left before full day, however, and his still-sleepy face as he left was well worth seeing.

His letter reached her as before with the usual precautions, but a reply today was really more than she could manage. She found it exceedingly trying when His Excellency turned up and read it, and her evil-tongued old gentlewomen poked each other in glee. The letter said, "The airs you still put on taught me my place more clearly than ever, but while that hurt may yet be the end of me,

> *Spare me your reproach, when my hands have lost the strength to wring secret tears,*
> *if I come to you today with too plainly dripping sleeves."*

The tone was strikingly familiar.

His Excellency smiled. "How beautifully he writes now!" he remarked, among other things, with never a trace of his old wariness. When he saw her unprepared to reply, he reminded her of what appearances required and then went away again, since her reluctance was natural enough. He had the Consultant's messenger rewarded especially generously, and the Secretary Captain entertained him warmly. This gentleman had so far been obliged to go about in secret, keeping the letters well hidden, but today at last he could hold his head high. He was an Aide of the Right Palace Guards in whom the Consultant Captain had the greatest confidence.

Genji, who heard about all this, watched the Captain carefully when he turned up looking more radiant than ever. "How did you get on this morning? Did you do your letter? Even the wise may err over a woman, as many examples show, and to my mind the way you managed to avoid unseemly insistence or impatience shows that you are a little ahead of the others. His Excellency's position was really too unbending, and I suppose people will be talking about him now that he has given in so thoroughly. Still, you must not take liberties or gloat as though you had won. I know he seems liberal and openhearted, but underneath he has some unmanly quirks and certain traits that make him difficult." Genji was holding forth as usual. It had gone well, he felt, and they made a lovely couple.

Genji much more resembled the young gentleman's older brother than his father, and even then not by much. When apart their faces seemed to be copied from each other, but when together each had a beauty of his own. Genji wore a light-colored dress cloak[22] over a white, sharply patterned gown, rather Chinese in style and glossily translucent. Even now he made a figure of supreme distinction and grace. His lordship the Captain's dress cloak was somewhat darker,[23] and he conveyed a nicely cultivated elegance in the deeply clove-dyed[24] gown and shift of soft white silk twill that he wore with it.

The Lustration Buddha[25] was brought in, and since the officiant had been late arriving, it was after sunset when the ladies sent page girls to him with whatever of-

---

22. Presumably *hanada* (medium blue) in color.
23. A darker *hanada* than his father's, because he is younger.
24. *Chōjizome*, generally a light brown, but here, apparently, somewhat darker.
25. A statue of the Buddha as a baby for the Buddha Lustration Rite (Kanbutsu-e) on the eighth day of the fourth month, to honor the Buddha's birthday. The rite involved lustrating (pouring water over) the statue.

ferings it pleased them to make, and all as generous as any from the palace. The rite went forward exactly as in His Majesty's presence. Young gentlemen gathered from everywhere to attend it, and strangely enough they felt more flustered and timid there than they ever did in the formal setting of the palace.

The Lustration Rite

Some of the young gentlewomen the Captain had casually favored hated him when he restlessly set forth, more eager and more elaborately dressed than ever. After all those years of patience he and his wife seemed so perfectly pleased with each other that no one else could possibly have come between them. His Excellency, who found that he only improved on closer acquaintance, gladly showered him with attentions. He was still disappointed to have lost, but he willingly and wholeheartedly forgave a son-in-law whose single-minded constancy of purpose had never wavered. Some people, such as his wife and her gentlewomen, found reason to complain now that his younger daughter's situation was happier and more thoroughly gratifying than the Consort's, but that hardly mattered. The outcome thoroughly satisfied the Inspector's wife.[26]

The preparations at Rokujō[27] now aimed at a day just past the twentieth of the fourth month. The mistress of Genji's east wing planned to go to the Divine Birth at Kamo,[28] and as usual she invited the other ladies to come, too, but they preferred to avoid merely following her, and all stayed home. No officiously large escort accompanied her quite modest train of twenty carriages, to which this simplicity gave a charm all its own.

On the day of the Festival she set off before dawn, and on her way back she took her place in a viewing stand to see the procession. The other ladies' women all followed in their carriages, which occupied so vast a space before her that their imposing number made it plain from afar exactly who she was.

Genji remembered the time when the carriage of the Empress's mother, the Rokujō Haven, had been pushed back into the crowd. "It was cruel of her[29] to let the

26. Kumoi no Kari's mother. Tō no Chūjō's wife is unhappy that as a Consort her own daughter has not done as well.

27. For the Akashi Daughter's entry into the palace.

28. Miare, a nighttime rite that reenacted the appearance on earth of Wakeikazuchi, the deity of the Upper Kamo Shrine. It took place on the middle *saru* ("Monkey") day in the fourth month and was followed the next day by the Kamo Festival, or Aoi Festival.

29. Aoi.

Imperial envoy

arrogance of passing favor encourage such a thing," he said. "She who so despised another died herself under a burden of great suffering." He passed over many things in silence. "Among those who remain, the Captain,[30] a simple commoner, barely manages to rise, while Her Majesty stands supreme. I find this extremely moving. Life is treacherous, and that is exactly why I hope to spend the rest of mine doing as I please, but you know, I cannot help worrying that hardship may overtake you in the end, once I am gone." The senior nobles then gathered in the viewing stands, and he went to join them.

The Palace Guards' envoy was the Secretary Captain. These gentlemen had gathered first at His Excellency's residence and then come from there to wait upon His Grace. Another envoy was the Fujiwara Dame of Staff.[31] Highly regarded, she enjoyed such happy esteem that gifts in great numbers poured in to her from everywhere, including His Majesty, the Heir Apparent, and Rokujō itself. The Consultant Captain even sent her a congratulatory message as she set out. In private they had shared their intimacy, and the way he had settled down to such great advantage had upset her. He had written,

> *"What is it they call the leaf we all sport today? There it is, I see,*
> *yet such ages have gone by, I no longer know its name.*[32]

What a pity!"

30. Yūgiri.

31. The daughter of Koremitsu, Genji's old confidant. The organs of government that sent a formal representative to the Kamo Festival included the Office of Staff.

32. "We have not been together for so long that I have even forgotten what this leaf is called." The leaf is *aoi*, "heart-to-heart."

He had not let the moment slip past him, no, and for one reason or another she managed even in the confusion of boarding her carriage to reply,

"As to that green leaf you sport merrily enough, ignorant or not,
surely he who won laurel could manage to know its name![33]

It takes a Doctor, I suppose." It was a slight reply, but it stung him. Yes, she certainly was the one he kept stealing off to after all.

A man's wife properly accompanied his daughter to the palace, but Genji reflected that his could not possibly stay there long and that the time might then be right to provide *her* assistance instead.[34]

The mistress of his east wing, too, had come to feel that this long separation, which was certain to end one day, must be very sad and trying for the young lady's mother and that by now it must be troubling the young lady herself. No, she did not like the thought of turning them both against her. "Do let her have her mother this time," she said. "It worries me that she is still at a tender age and that many around her are also very young. Her nurses can only see to so much, and as long as I am not to stay with her myself, I should like to leave her in good hands."

Genji was pleased that her thoughts matched his own so well, and he broached the subject with his daughter's mother. This was what she had hoped for, and she was very happy. She set about making sure that her daughter's gentlewomen were as well dressed and every detail as perfect as for that other, far greater lady. Her ladyship the Nun, to whom it meant so much to live to see her granddaughter settled, had clung stubbornly to life in the hope one day of meeting her again, but now she wondered sadly how that could ever be.

When the mistress of his east wing accompanied the young lady to the palace that night, the girl's mother walked humbly behind her hand carriage. This would have been humiliating if she had had any thought for herself, but she only regretted that she, the flaw in the gem Genji had polished, had nonetheless lived this long.

Genji had wanted to avoid turning his daughter's ceremonial arrival into a dazzling spectacle, but of course the event was extraordinary. The mistress of his east wing, who had looked after her with selfless devotion, really loved her, and she just wished that she had a little girl of her own, one she need never send away. Both Genji and the Consultant Captain actually saw this as her only flaw. She withdrew from the palace three days later.

The two ladies met on the night when they changed places. "Seeing her suddenly so grown-up reminds one how many years it has been, and I hope that we need no longer remain distant from each other," Genji's began cordially, and they talked.

---

33. Laurel, (*katsura*), too, was worn at the Kamo Festival, and to "pluck the laurel" meant to pass the official examinations, as Yūgiri had done.

34. Genji reflects that, strictly speaking, Murasaki does not quite qualify as his wife (*kita no kata*); she is merely his closest equivalent to one. She will take her adopted daughter to the palace and stay with her there briefly, but she will then have to return to Rokujō. Genji will replace her with the lady from Akashi, the girl's natural mother.

This was the start of their friendship. No wonder he took up with her, Genji's reflected, astonished by the elegance with which she spoke. Akashi, for her part, met this superbly distinguished lady with pleasure and saw how rightly His Grace loved her best and set her above all others. Is it not an honor, she thought, to address her as an equal this way? The ceremony surrounding the departure of Genji's lady was particularly splendid, and her license to board a hand carriage conferred on her nothing less than the dignity of a Consort, by which Akashi knew her own place after all.

She gazed as though in a dream at the dear, sweet, doll-like girl before her, and the tears streaming from her eyes by no means looked all the same.[35] The life that had so tried and burdened her through the years, that had only moved her in a thousand ways to lament her lot, seemed precious, and in the glory of the moment she knew how much she owed to the God of Sumiyoshi. Her daughter was now hers to cherish as she wished, and while the young lady's quickness and rare intelligence naturally won her general esteem, her exceptional grace and looks appealed keenly to the Heir Apparent's boyish feelings. There were gentlewomen in her rivals' service who called it a blemish that her mother was looking after her, but no such talk could possibly do her any harm. That she had supreme nobility of presence goes without saying, and since her mother nurtured her charming distinction with attentions perfectly gauged to the finest detail, the privy gentlemen and so on centered on her the prodigies of their rivalry,[36] while her mother lavished exquisite care even on the looks and deportment of those of her women whom they favored.

The mistress of Genji's east wing came visiting on appropriate occasions. The friendship between the two progressed wonderfully, but Akashi never presumed upon it, nor did her conduct ever invite the slightest disparaging comment, for in person and disposition she was very nearly ideal.

Genji had never expected to live long, and now that he had at last seen his daughter in grand style to the palace and that his son the Captain, whose purposely rootless life had so little become him, was admirably settled, he felt sufficiently at peace to decide to act at last on his cherished desire.[37] He would find it hard to give up his dearest lady, but in Her Majesty she had no contemptible ally. In the eyes of the world she was also the mother of his daughter, to whom she undoubtedly came first; no, she would be well looked after. The lady of summer would miss the occasional brilliance of his visits, but *she* had the Captain. It seemed to him that he need not really worry about any of them.

The following year would be his fortieth, and people everywhere, His Majesty first of all, were preparing for the jubilee. That autumn he was granted a rank equivalent to Retired Emperor. His emoluments rose, and he enjoyed new sinecures and benefices. Life already offered him all he could wish, but a rare precedent from the past was invoked, a Retired Emperor's staff was appointed for his use, and he acquired such awesome dignity that to his chagrin he could hardly call at the palace anymore. Even so, His Majesty longed as always to do still-greater things for

---

35. *Gosenshū* 1188 suggests that tears, whether of joy or of sorrow, are all one and the same.

36. Rivalry in matters of dashing elegance and romantic success—one addressed not directly to the little girl but to her court, so to speak.

37. To enter religion.

him, and he lamented day and night that in deference to the world's wishes he could not abdicate in Genji's favor.

The Palace Minister was promoted,[38] while the Consultant Captain became a Counselor and set out on his round of thanks. Everything about him, not least the growing radiance of his face and person, was so far beyond reproach that his father-in-law was grateful after all not to have sent his daughter into a palace service in which she might only have lost out to someone else.

The new Counselor had occasion from time to time to remember the evening when Taifu, his wife's nurse, had whispered, "To think her fate was to start out with someone of the sixth rank!" He therefore tied this note to a very prettily turned chrysanthemum:[39]

> *"Did you ever dream before the chrysanthemum's young leaves of pale green*
> *to see it put forth blossoms so richly purple in hue?"*[40]

That was a sad time, and there is one thing I heard then that I cannot forget." He gave it to her with a dazzling smile.

She found him very attractive, despite her embarrassment and pain on his behalf.

> *"No chrysanthemum nurtured in such a garden from its seedling days*
> *could long languish, that I knew, very long a mere pale green.*

Where can you have got such an idea, my lord?" she protested smoothly.

So great a rise in dignity made the young couple's present mode of life rather cramped, and they therefore moved to Sanjō.[41] The place had rather suffered from neglect, but the Counselor had it beautifully repaired and took up residence there after having the rooms that had been Her Highness's redone. The residence was filled with moving memories of the past. The garden trees along the house, so small then, now cast dense shade, and a clump of pampas grass had run wild. He put all this to rights. He also had the waterweeds cleared from the brook so that it ran gaily again.

One lovely dusk the two of them were gazing out over it all, talking about how young they had been and what sad times they had had, and his darling fondly recalled many things, although with twinges of shame at what her women may have thought. The ones who had always served Her Highness were still there, each in her own room, and they now came to gather happily before their new lord and lady.

> *"It is you, I know, whose rocks these are to protect, but, O limpid brook,*
> *only tell me, if you can: where is she whom we once loved?"*

---

38. To Chancellor.
39. A chrysanthemum that has turned dark when touched by frost.
40. A Counselor wore purple. For the leaves the poem specifies *asamidori,* the color both of chrysanthemum leaves and of the sixth rank. However, while the rank color was light blue, chrysanthemum leaves are green; *asamidori* covers both.
41. Yūgiri and Kumoi no Kari have been living in the residence of Kumoi no Kari's father, Tō no Chūjō. Now that Yūgiri and Tō no Chūjō have both been promoted, this arrangement (one perfectly normal for a young couple) is no longer adequate. Sanjō is the former residence of Yūgiri's grandmother.

he said, and she,

> *"I can see no sign of that figure we have lost, slender, flowing stream;*
> *yet you still, and cruelly, babble on just as you please!"*

The colors of the autumn leaves meanwhile captivated His Excellency on his way home from the palace, and he came to join them. The place had hardly changed since his parents lived there, and it was extremely moving to see the young couple now happily installed amid these peaceful surroundings. The Counselor's face was a little flushed; he looked unusually serious, and his manner was quite subdued. They made a delightfully handsome pair, but it seemed to His Excellency that her pretty face was of an order that might turn up anywhere, whereas his looks were exceptional. The old gentlewomen placed themselves at his disposal and entertained him with their antique remarks. The poems that his daughter and son-in-law had noted down a moment ago lay scattered about, and he wept to see them. "I, too, would gladly question the stream," he said, "but an old man like me must refrain.[42]

> *It is no surprise that most venerable pine should at last have died,*
> *but the seedling she planted gathers now a coat of moss."*[43]

The young gentleman's nurse, Saishō, had not forgotten how angry His Excellency had made her, and she added with obvious satisfaction,

> *"I shall look to both for the kindliest of shade: to these seedling pines*
> *one at root long since and bound for long years of happiness."*

The old women then went on to offer similar verses of their own, which the Counselor found amusing. Their blushing young mistress listened in intense embarrassment.

After the twentieth of the tenth month there was to be an imperial progress to Genji's Rokujō estate. It promised to be delightful, since the autumn colors would be at their height, and His Majesty therefore invited Retired Emperor Suzaku to join him on the journey. The result was a rare and wondrous event that astonished everyone. Genji, their host, prepared such a welcome that one could hardly believe one's eyes.

When Their Majesties arrived, at the hour of the Serpent,[44] the horses from the Left and Right Imperial Stables were immediately lined up before the riding ground pavilion, and the Left and Right Palace Guards assembled in ranks beside them exactly as for the Sweet Flag Festival in the fifth month. As the hour of the Sheep[45] drew to a close, the company moved to the main house of the southeast quarter. Genji had prepared the way magnificently, for the arched bridges

---

42. Must refrain from pursuing the subject for fear of shedding more tears. It was ill omened to weep in the presence of a newly married couple.

43. The ancient pine is presumably Ōmiya and the tree grown from its seed Tō no Chūjō.

44. About 10:00 A.M.

45. After 2:00 P.M. or so.

and bridgeways along their path were spread with brocade, and cloth panels hung wherever Their Majesties might be exposed to view. He had invited the chief cormorant fisher attached to the Imperial Kitchen, as well as those from his own staff, to release their birds from boats on the eastern lake. The cormorants took little carp.[46] Genji had not meant this as a specta-

Cloth panels

cle in itself, however; he had only wanted to provide something of interest to see along the way. The autumn leaves were lovely on every hill, but particularly so the ones before the southwest quarter,[47] and for this reason he had removed the walls of the intervening gallery and left its gate open, so as to give Their Majesties a perfectly clear view. A seat for each was prepared somewhat above Genji's own, but by His Majesty's decree this arrangement was rectified. This was an honor indeed, but His Majesty still regretted that he could not give His Grace all the formal respect that he longed to show him. A Left Lieutenant bore the fish from the lake, a Right Deputy carried a brace of birds taken at Kitano by the falconers of the Chamberlains' Office, and both came forward from the east to go down on one knee on either side of the steps[48] and offer Their Majesties their bounty. The Chancellor ordered all this prepared and served to Their Majesties. There were intriguing refreshments, done in unusual ways, for the Princes and the senior nobles, too. Everyone became quite drunk. Toward sunset they called for the palace musicians, who played no grand ceremonial music; instead, the privy pages danced very nicely. As usual Genji could not help thinking back to the celebration beneath the autumn leaves at the Suzaku Palace. When the musicians struck up "Our Sovereign's Grace,"[49] it was the Chancellor's youngest son, a boy in his tenth year, who danced it very prettily indeed. His Majesty doffed a robe and presented it to him, and the Chancellor descended the steps to perform his obeisance of thanks.

Meanwhile Genji had chrysanthemums picked in memory of "Blue Sea Waves."

---

46. *Funa*, a small fish related to carp.
47. Akikonomu's, with its autumn garden.
48. Those leading down to the garden, on the south side of the main house.
49. "Gaōn," a *bugaku* piece associated with "Tang music" (*tōgaku*).

"These chrysanthemums blooming in still-deeper hues look as though they yearn
for autumns of long ago, when we gaily tossed our sleeves."[50]

His Excellency, who had indeed danced beside him then, saw that whatever superiority his gifts may have given him, Genji's own lifted him incomparably higher. The early-winter rain seemed to catch the moment's mood.

"These chrysanthemums that mingle in company with the purple clouds
glitter to my eyes like stars pristine in a spotless reign.

They have their own time,"[51] he replied.

In the garden, autumn leaves in colors dark or pale lay wind-blown like brocade along the bridgeways, and handsome pages, the sons of noble families, in leaf green, red, sappanwood, or grape, their hair as usual in twin tresses and their foreheads just peeping past their crowns, gently danced a set of short pieces, to withdraw again beneath the brilliant trees as though they wished the sun would never set. The musicians kept their music low, until at last the noble lords called for instruments from the Library and began their own.

At the height of the concert, instruments were laid before the greatest of them all. His Eminence Suzaku was both moved and astonished once more to hear, unchanged, the voice of "Priest Uda."[52]

"As the autumns pass, I in my humble village have known many rains,
and yet I have never seen such brilliance given the leaves."

He sounded perhaps a little piqued.[53]

His Majesty replied,

"Are these, would you say, no more than mere autumn leaves? Why, they are brocade
spread across the garden here in memory of old times."

His features, which displayed a growing maturity, were hard to distinguish from Genji's own. It was moreover simply astounding that the Counselor, in waiting nearby, looked just like him as well. In true nobility of presence one caught (or was it just imagination?) a difference of quality between them, but he had perhaps the freshest charm. His performance on the flute was simply delightful. The Controller Lieutenant's voice stood out among those of the privy gentlemen gathered below the steps to sing the songs. Yes, such success was apparently the destiny of both houses.

---

50. The darker color of the flowers alludes also to the darker robes now worn by Tō no Chūjō in his new and more exalted office.

51. *Kokinshū* 279, by Taira no Sadafun: "Beyond autumn they have their own time, chrysanthemums that gather color even as they pass." The "purple clouds" praise the happy character of this imperial reign, and the rest of the poem congratulates Genji in particular for his extraordinary rise.

52. Uda no Hōshi, the name of a *wagon* favored by Emperor Uda.

53. Suzaku's "village" (*sato*) is the residence (the Suzaku Palace) to which he moved after abdicating. He seems to be complaining that nothing as wonderful as this took place during *his* reign.

34

WAKANA 1

Spring Shoots I

Wakana means "new shoots" or, if they are to eat, perhaps something like "spring greens." In this chapter Tamakazura arranges a *wakana* banquet in honor of Genji's fortieth year, and in the course of it Genji uses the word in a poem:

"Those seedlings may yet, plucked from such happy meadows, draw a new shoot up toward a still-longer span of endlessly happy years."

Although *wakana* recurs as the title of "Spring Shoots II," the allusion in that case is to a different event.

"Spring Shoots I" follows "The Plum Tree Branch" in chronological sequence, beginning late in the year in which Genji is thirty-nine.

PERSONS

His Grace, the Honorary Retired Emperor, Genji, age 39 to 41

His Eminence, Retired Emperor Suzaku, 42 to 44

His daughter, Her Highness, the Third Princess, midteens
(Onna San no Miya)

His Highness, the Heir Apparent, Suzaku's son, 13 to 15

The Consort, mother of the Heir Apparent (Shōkyōden no Nyōgo)

The Counselor, then Right Commander, Genji's son, 18 to 20 (Yūgiri)

The Left Controller, retainer of Onna San no Miya, also in Genji's service

The senior nurse of Onna San no Miya

The Intendant of the Right Gate Watch, Tō no Chūjō 's eldest son,
mid-20s (Kashiwagi)

His Excellency, the Chancellor (Tō no Chūjō)

His Highness of War, Genji's brother (Hotaru Hyōbukyō no Miya)

The Grand Counselor, Suzaku's Master of the Household

His Majesty, the Emperor, son of Genji and Fujitsubo, 21 to 23 (Reizei)

Her Majesty, the Empress, 30 to 32 (Akikonomu)

The Mistress of Staff (Oborozukiyo)

The mistress of the east wing, 31 to 33 (Murasaki)

The Mistress of Staff, Higekuro's wife, 25 to 27 (Tamakazura)

His Highness of Ceremonial, Murasaki's father, 54 to 56 (Shikibukyō no Miya)

Chūnagon, Oborozukiyo's gentlewoman

The former Governor of Izumi, Chūnagon's brother

The Heir Apparent's Kiritsubo Consort, then Haven, Genji's daughter,
11 to 13 (Akashi no Nyōgo)

Her mother, 30 to 32 (Akashi no Kimi)

Her grandmother, the Nun, mid-60s (Akashi no Amagimi)

Her son, His Highness, the First Prince, born

Her grandfather, the Novice, around 75 (Akashi no Nyūdō)

His messenger

Chūnagon, Onna San no Miya's gentlewoman

Kojijū, a foster sister and gentlewoman of Onna San no Miya

His Eminence Suzaku began feeling unwell soon after His Majesty's visit to Rokujō. His health had never been strong, but this time he felt a distinct foreboding. Despite an old longing to devote himself to practice, he had refrained from that as from many other things while the Empress Mother[1] still lived, and hitherto he had therefore renounced the idea. Perhaps it was to restore his courage for it that he now talked of feeling as though he had little time left and began his preparations.

Apart from the Heir Apparent he had four daughters, of whom one, his Third Princess, was dearer to him than any of the others. Her mother, known as Fujitsubo,[2] had been named a Genji by the former Emperor[3] and had come to him while he was Heir Apparent. She might have looked forward to still-higher honor, but she lacked any effective support, and she found her presence among such company a great trial, since her mother was a mere Intimate of no particular lineage; meanwhile, the Empress Mother gave him the Mistress of Staff, beside whom all others paled. This was a crushing blow. After his abdication, bitterness and disappointment in life seemed to overwhelm her, despite the commiseration he personally felt for her, because she died. Her daughter was thirteen or fourteen. Now that he was soon to turn his back on the world and retire into the mountains, his sole and consuming anxiety was the question of who would provide for her once he was gone.

The temple he had had built in the Western Hills[4] was finished, and while the preparations for his move went forward, he also made ready for her donning of the train. To her alone he gave not only his favorites among the precious things and furnishings in his palace but the least trinket of any interest at all. The remainder went to his other children.

The Heir Apparent went to see his father when he heard that he was not

1. His mother, the Kokiden Consort of the early chapters.
2. Does not figure otherwise in the tale; she had lived in the same pavilion as Genji's Fujitsubo.
3. *Sendai*, who preceded the Kiritsubo Emperor (His Late Eminence), Genji's father.
4. Traditionally identified with Ninnaji, built in 888 by Emperor Uda in the hills just west of the City as it was then.

merely ill but meant actually to leave the world. His mother the Consort[5] accompanied him. Although no great favorite of His Eminence's, she had had the extraordinary good fortune to bear him a son, and they talked at length of times gone by. He advised his son on every aspect of governing the realm. The Heir Apparent was remarkably grown-up for his age, and the weighty patronage that he enjoyed on either hand[6] gave His Eminence great confidence in his future. "For myself I shall leave this world without regret," he said, "were it not that the thought of what is to become of all my daughters after I am gone seems likely now to keep me from that final parting. I gather from all I have seen and heard that it is a woman's destiny, like it or not, to be dismissed as light-minded, and that is something that I deeply deplore. When the realm is at your command, be sure to give thought to how they are all getting on. Those who are in good hands already I leave where they belong, but the third is still very young, and she has no one but me. I worry that she may be quite lost once I have left her." He wiped away tears as he spoke.

He tactfully made the same request of the Consort, but the rivalry that had prevailed in the days when the young Princess's mother enjoyed particular favor had ruined any friendly feeling between them, and the Consort could hardly have been eager to lend Her Highness genuine support, even if she no longer particularly disliked her.

His Eminence fretted about this day and night. As the year drew to a close, his condition worsened, until he no longer went outside his blinds. At times he suffered from the workings of a spirit, but he was not in fact continuously unwell; still, he believed this illness to be his last. He had of course abdicated, but those who had first looked to him during his reign, and whose pleasure it was still to serve so kind and noble a lord, grieved for him from the bottom of their hearts. There were constant messengers from Rokujō as well. His Eminence was extremely happy to learn that Genji himself would soon come to see him.

When Genji's son the Counselor arrived, His Eminence called him in through his blinds and addressed him earnestly. "His Late Eminence on his deathbed gave me many last instructions," he said, "among which he spoke particularly of your father and our present Sovereign. As Emperor myself, however, I discovered limits to what I could do, and while your father still meant a great deal to me personally, a little slip of his came to earn me his displeasure, or at least so I assume, since nothing in the years since then has led him to reveal any trace of such a feeling. The wisest of men will rage, when some misstep affects his own fortunes, and then exact vengeance by an act of folly, as many examples from ancient times confirm. People have been expecting him to betray that same desire at one time or another, but in the end he has refrained, and he even treats the Heir Apparent warmly. That the two of them should now be on the best of terms is something I greatly appreciate, but I am not very clever, and besides, the darkness in a parent's heart could easily tempt me to disgrace

---

5. The Shōkyōden Consort, a sister of Higekuro.
6. From Higekuro and from Genji.

myself,[7] and for that reason I prefer to stay out of it after all. As far as our present Sovereign is concerned, I have done all that His Late Eminence asked of me, and I am therefore delighted to see a lord whose light shines as his does in this latter age so fully uphold the honor of our line. The past has been coming back to me ever since the progress last autumn, and with it a great longing to see your father. He simply must come himself. Do tell him so." While he spoke, he now and again shed tears.

The Counselor replied, "I myself know nothing of what may have happened long ago. Ever since I became old enough to serve the realm, I have noted what goes on in the world around me, and not once, with regard to any matter great or small or in the most intimate conversation, have I heard him allude to any unfortunate incident from the past. What he does do is to lament that after withdrawing entirely from court service in order to satisfy his own taste for peace and quiet, he has been so little able to uphold His Late Eminence's last wishes that it is as though they did not even concern him. He says, 'I was too young to be of any use while His Eminence reigned; there were many officials older and wiser than I, and I could never place myself at his disposal as fully as I wished. I should like to visit him, now that he has laid down the burden of governing to lead a quieter life, so that we might open our hearts to one another; but even now my position hardly leaves me free, and meanwhile, the months and days keep passing by.' "

Although not yet even twenty, the Counselor was thoroughly presentable, striking to look at, and extremely handsome. His Eminence considered him attentively and began privately to wonder whether he might not entrust *him* with this daughter whose future worried him so. "I hear that your home is now at the Chancellor's," he said. "I could never quite make out what the matter was all that time, and you had my sympathy; the news was welcome. At the same time, though, I wished for another reason that I had not heard it."

The astonished Counselor wondered what he could possibly mean. Naturally, he had heard how much His Eminence worried about his daughter and how he made no secret of hoping to find her a suitable protector so that he might renounce the world at peace. *That* must be it, I suppose, he said to himself; but he could hardly show by his answer that he had understood instantly. "I have little to offer, and not that many people would have me." He said no more.

Once he was gone, the gentlewomen who had been peeping in at him gathered to talk about how splendid he looked and how sensible he was. "He is such a pleasure!" they exclaimed; but the foolish old women among them protested, "Oh, come now! Say all you like, but you can hardly compare him to His Grace at that age!"

His Eminence heard them. "Yes," he said, "it is true, he was exceptional; and now, in his full maturity, he has a charm that reminds one still more of just what it means to say that someone shines. When grave and dignified, he has so superbly commanding a presence that one hardly dares to approach him, and when relaxed

---

7. The love that clouds a parent's judgment could tempt Suzaku to make some such inappropriate gesture as explicitly thanking Genji.

and in a playful mood, he is sweeter and more engagingly amusing than anyone in the world. No, there is no one like him. He is a wonder, and everything about him speaks of what he must have brought to this life from his earlier ones. He grew up in the palace, and the Emperor loved him above all; in fact, he pampered him and thought more of him than he did of himself. Even so, though, he never indulged in any display of arrogance; instead, he remained so modest that he did not even become a Counselor until he was in his twenties.[8] He was twenty-one, if I am not mistaken, when he became at once Consultant and Commander. Look what advancement his son has had in comparison! His children seem destined for greater heights even than he. In truly sound learning and judgment his son comes very little below him, and even if I exaggerate, the young man certainly has grown to enjoy a remarkable reputation."

Her Highness was very sweet, and the sight of her youthful innocence would prompt him to say, "I so long to give you to someone worthy—someone who would make much of you, and who would overlook what you still lack and teach you." He called together her more experienced nurses to discuss her donning of the train and so on, and while they talked, he remarked, "How I wish there were someone who would take this Princess in hand and bring her up as His Grace of Rokujō did His Highness of Ceremonial's daughter. There cannot be any such man among the commoners, and our present Sovereign has his Empress. All the other Consorts are very exalted indeed, and without proper patronage her presence in such company would only work against her. I should have dropped a hint to that Counselor[9] while he was still single. He is very able despite his youth, and he has a bright future ahead of him."

"The Counselor is extremely serious," they replied, "and for all those years he had his heart set on that young lady. He never gave any real sign of looking elsewhere, and now that he has her, he will be even less likely to waver. His Grace, judging from what they say about him, is the one who remains as susceptible as ever to what any woman may seem to offer. Moreover, one gathers that he deeply desires a lofty alliance and that he has so little forgotten the former Kamo Priestess[10] that he still corresponds with her."

"Yes, but it is precisely his ever-wandering fancy that so worries me." Still, His Eminence must have felt that he might as well give her to Genji after all, even if certain people[11] failed to respect her, as long as Genji agreed to be a father to her. "Really," he said, "anyone with a daughter he wanted to see turned into a proper lady might well hope to have her spend her life with him. No one has long in this world, and *that* is the life one would wish a daughter to lead. I would want to be close to him if I were a woman, even a sister. That is the way I felt when we were young. No wonder women cannot resist him!" He must have been thinking of the Mistress of Staff.

---

8. The tale does not mention this appointment
9. "Acting Counselor" (Gon Chūnagon) in the original and sporadically hereafter. The number of Chūnagon was fixed, but a young man of high birth like Yūgiri could be given the office even when there was no regular vacancy.
10. Asagao.
11. Genji's women.

One of his daughter's retainers, a Left Controller and a brother of her senior nurse, had long been in Genji's intimate service. The gentleman was devoted to Her Highness as well, and the nurse therefore talked to him the next time he came round. She described the terms in which His Eminence had discussed his daughter and asked him to inform His Grace when he had a chance to do so. "An Emperor's daughter often remains unmarried," she said, "but she is certainly more secure with someone to care for her in various ways and to give her the support she requires. No one except His Eminence really thinks a great deal about her, and we cannot do that much for her ourselves, however we try. Not that it is all up to me, but what a shame it would be for her to find herself caught in an unforeseen situation and become the subject of compromising rumor! I could serve her better if only her future were somehow to be settled while His Eminence is still alive. A girl of even the highest birth is the plaything of destiny and has many sorrows to bear. As long as His Eminence singles her out this way from her sisters, there will be their jealousy to expect as well. I hope that I can manage to get her through it all unscathed."

"I wonder what is to be done," the Controller replied. "His Grace is extraordinarily loyal. He gathers to himself anyone he has known at all or who has pleased him, even when he does not feel that deeply about her, until by now he has many ladies, but there seems really to be only one in the end, who means everything to him while the others often appear to live more or less empty lives. However remarkable that one lady may be, I do not see how she could very well insist on standing beside Her Highness, if it is Her Highness's destiny to join him as you suggest; but even so, it seems to me that there is still reason for caution. Actually, though, I gather he often jokes privately about feeling that while his glory in this life honors this latter age beyond what it deserves, when it comes to women, he has escaped neither censure nor personal disappointment. Someone like me, looking on, can only agree. None of the ladies he has taken under his wing is distinctly unworthy of him, but they rise only so high, and I doubt that any brings with her such rank as to be his true equal. And so, all things considered, I expect that if Her Highness does go to His Grace, he and she will be very well matched."

The nurse reported this to His Eminence when circumstances allowed her to do so. "When I touched on the matter to his lordship the Controller," she explained, "he replied that His Grace would undoubtedly welcome the idea, since it would mean the fulfillment of his own enduring hopes, and he added that if Your Eminence approves, he will transmit your proposal. How does Your Eminence wish to proceed? His Grace is sensitive to the gradations of rank among his ladies and is unusually scrupulous about observing them, but even a commoner woman[12] may object when a new arrival comes to share the favors she enjoys, and something distressing *could* happen. There appear to be others who aspire to serve her. Your Eminence should consider the matter carefully. Her Highness is beyond rank, it is true, but while as the world is now there certainly seem to be some who cheerfully have their way and live as they please, she gives the impression of being extremely vulnerable and unaware, and there is only so much that we in her service can do for

12. All Genji's women are commoners (*tadabito*) compared to Onna San no Miya.

her. Things seem to work best when competent people lower down follow broad instructions from above. Her Highness is likely to feel lost as long as she lacks a particular patron."

"Those are more or less my own thoughts, you see," His Eminence replied. "Imperial daughters like mine are not always settled at all happily in life, and besides, once a woman has given herself to a man, no lofty rank can shield her from one thing or another that she may regret or quite understandably find offensive, and that is why I have been hesitating so painfully. On the other hand, when someone in her position has lost the person who mattered most to her,[13] so that she must get on without him and then sets out to manage on her own, well, once upon a time people were obedient and never dreamed of doing anything that custom forbade, but I gather that nowadays one never knows what wanton outrage to expect next. A daughter who only yesterday was at home with her noble parents and enjoyed all their affection and esteem, today, they say, may well have her name bandied about by the most tedious gallants, sully her late father's honor, and cover his memory with shame. In short, one choice is as bad as the other. What they call good fortune in life is unpredictable for anyone, of any degree, and that is what makes me so uneasy. For better or worse, a woman will have her destiny, whatever it may be, as long as she lives in obedience to the one responsible for her, and if later there comes a time of decline, at least it will not have been her fault. There may seem to have been nothing wrong with a woman making her own choice in the first place, when it turns out to be successful after all and the outcome honors her, but actually, everything I hear suggests that the worst mistake a girl can make is to act as she pleases in secret, merely because of something someone happens to have told her, without a word to her parents or the permission of those from whom she should seek it. Even for an utterly tedious commoner that is a foolish and heinous thing to do. Not that her wishes are entirely to be ignored in the matter either, since it is folly, too, for her to find herself irrevocably committed[14] to someone she has never wished to accept; her mood and conduct then are all too easy to imagine. As for my daughter, who seems to me disconcertingly childish, it would be extremely unfortunate if any of you were to take matters into your own hands and the thing then become known." His desperate anxiety over what might become of her after he was gone made her women increasingly uncomfortable.

"I had been biding my time until she should understand things a little better," His Eminence went on, "but you see, I can no longer be patient now that I fear I may never be able to do what I want to do. Say what you will, His Grace of Rokujō knows what matters, and since no one could be more responsible than he, I see no need to take the number of women around him into account. Everything depends after all on the character of the man himself. In dignity and composure he is an example for all the world, and he deserves the highest confidence. Who else is there in any case? His Highness of War is a fine man, certainly. He and she share the same

13. Her father above all.
14. Because of action taken by one of her gentlewomen, acting on behalf of the suitor.

lineage,[15] and he would never ignore her or slight her, but he is too languid and dandyish to have much substance, and he seems perhaps to be somewhat lightly regarded. No, I do not hold such a man to be wholly reliable. Then there is the Grand Counselor, who, I gather, aspires to administer her household.[16] As far as that goes, I am sure he would do very well by her, but I still cannot help wondering. A man of such mediocre rank could only be a disappointment. In the past as well it was outstanding merit that decided this sort of choice. I believe that it would be a great pity to be too impressed merely by the prospect of loyal and devoted service. The Intendant of the Right Gate Watch[17] is quietly languishing for her, or so the Mistress of Staff[18] tells me, and at a slightly more presentable rank he might well deserve consideration, but he is still very young and hopelessly junior. His high ambition has led him to remain unmarried, and meanwhile he has acquired an exceptionally proud and deliberate manner. His learning is irreproachable, and in the end he will certainly make a pillar of the realm, but although his future looks bright, I cannot consider him worthy." He hardly knew which way to turn.

No one at all was pursuing His Eminence about the elder daughters in whom he himself had little interest, but strangely enough, his wholly private conversations on the subject of Her Highness had spread far and wide, and many gentlemen were now eager to win her.

The Chancellor told the Mistress of Staff through his wife, her elder sister, "The Intendant of the Gate Watch has remained single, and he is resolved to marry no one but a Princess. I should therefore be honored and delighted if you were to convey that to His Eminence when he brings up the subject, and if he were then to summon the young man." He had her pass on all he had to say to His Eminence and sound him out.

His Highness of War, who had unsuccessfully courted the Left Commander's wife,[19] knew that she would hear of where he turned next, and he therefore looked very carefully first, lest an unfortunate choice make a fool of him. The news of Her Highness could hardly have failed to arouse intensely covetous feelings.

The Grand Counselor dreaded losing His Eminence when His Eminence withdrew to the mountains, for he had long served him intimately as his Master of the Household, and he must therefore have done all he could on the subject of Her Highness to persuade His Eminence to look on him with favor.

Whenever news like this reached the Counselor, whom His Retired Majesty had approached in person and who had watched His Eminence's face as he did so, he swelled with pride to think that if he did show interest, he would certainly not be dismissed, but his darling had now yielded to him for good, and through all those years he had never once turned elsewhere, even when he might have sought his excuse in hardship. How could he now suddenly go back on himself and make her so

15. He is a half brother of both Suzaku and Genji.
16. Not otherwise mentioned in the tale. His wish to administer her household (*iezukasa*) amounts to wishing to marry her.
17. Kashiwagi. He has not been referred to by this title before.
18. Oborozukiyo.
19. Tamakazura, married to Higekuro.

unhappy? No, he thought, if I were to attach anyone that exalted to myself, nothing would go as I wished, I would never feel at ease, and I would know only grief. He had never been given to gallantry in any case, so he suppressed his excitement and kept silent, but the thought of her going to someone else still troubled him, and his ears took in every rumor about her.

The Heir Apparent heard about all this, too. He observed, "Rather than favor what is immediately attractive, Your Eminence should consider above all what will set a fortunate example for ages to come. A commoner, however worthy, is of limited rank, and if you mean to choose one, then it is His Grace of Rokujō who is to be preferred as a father to her."

This was no more than a casual remark in a letter about other matters, but it had a serious ring, and His Eminence was hardly surprised. "That is quite true," he answered, "and you have expressed yourself very well." Being now more and more of the same opinion, he at last sent the Left Controller to sound Genji out.

Genji already knew all about His Eminence's concern over his daughter. "I feel sorry for him," he said. "Still, if *he* has little time left in this world, can *I* count on surviving him long enough to agree to look after her? Assuming that I outlive him, as I may do in the natural course of things, I will never look on any of his daughters with indifference, and since he has been pleased to approach me about one in particular, I shall gladly give her special attention, but life's vagaries permit no certainty even then.

"In any case," he continued, "if I were to become the one familiar and intimate object of her trust, I would feel all the sorrier when it came to be time for me to leave this world, and she would constitute a tie that would be painful for me to break. The Counselor, for example, appears to be young and to lack substance, but he has a long life ahead of him, and as far as ability goes, he promises to lend great strength to the realm; His Eminence could not be far wrong if he were to agree. His Eminence has no doubt preferred discretion, however, since the young man is extremely serious and seems already to have settled his affections elsewhere."

He appeared not to entertain the idea himself, for which the Controller was sorry, considering how seriously His Eminence had pondered his decision; and he therefore went on to evoke more personally what had moved His Eminence to reach it. "He loves Her Highness very much," Genji answered, smiling, "and I expect that that is why he has gone to such lengths to study everything that bears on her future. But the matter is simple: let him present her to His Majesty. No doubt she will find there earlier arrivals to be reckoned with, but no matter. They do not constitute an objection. The latecomer need not lose out. In His Late Eminence's case the Empress Mother went to him first, while he was still Heir Apparent, but then Her Cloistered Eminence, who came to him only long afterward, won his favor from her. As I understand it, the Consort who bore the Princess in question was Her Cloistered Eminence's sister,[20] and they say that she was nearly as beautiful. Her Highness must have more than most people to recommend her, considering whose daughter she is on both sides." He must have been curious about her after all.

The New Year was coming. At the Suzaku Palace, His Eminence detected no

---

20. Her half sister, by an Intimate.

sign that he would recover, and he decided in haste on a donning of the train that would be the wonder of the ages. He had the west side of the Kaedono[21] done up, and he would have none of *our* twills or brocades for the curtained bed, standing curtains, and so on; no, he aspired to the furnishings of a Chinese Empress, and he had everything made to glitter with formal grandeur. He had long since invited His Excellency the Chancellor to tie on the train, and despite this gentleman's usual fussy reluctance he came after all, since he had never refused His Eminence anything. Their Excellencies of the Left and Right[22] and the other senior nobles all managed somehow to be there, even those with pressing reasons to decline. The eight Princes, and of course all the Emperor's and the Heir Apparent's privy gentlemen, assembled as well, since these magnificent preparations had become quite famous. His Majesty and the Heir Apparent were particularly sad, because they assumed that this would be His Eminence's last such event, and they made available many Chinese things from the Chamberlains' Office and the Imperial Stores. There were dazzling contributions from Rokujō, too. It was, moreover, Genji who provided the gifts, the rewards, and the present for the presiding Chancellor.

From Her Majesty as well there came gowns and comb boxes, all fondly prepared, and that set of hair accessories from all those years ago,[23] now prettily refashioned, although not to such a point that it had lost its original character. She presented them on the evening of the day, and she made it clear from whom they came. Her messenger not only was her own Household Deputy, but he had served His Eminence as well, and she told him to place it before Her Highness. This poem, however, was in the box:[24]

> "This exquisite comb, always welcome in my hair to bring back the past,
> has since those days long ago taken on the grace of age."[25]

For His Eminence this called up vivid memories. Her Majesty had hoped that the gift might carry her own good fortune, and since the comb was indeed worthy, he, too, left old feelings out of his congratulatory reply:

> "May she, after you, succeed to happy fortune those ten thousand years
> this exquisite comb foretells, till it has the gods' own grace."

Bearing up under great suffering, His Eminence summoned his courage and three days after the event took the tonsure at last. It is always sad when that change comes for anyone, and so naturally his ladies grieved deeply that it had come for him. The Mistress of Staff did not leave his side and was so disconsolate that he hardly knew how to comfort her. "There is an end to the path of a parent's love after

21. "Oak Pavilion," a separate residence at the northeast corner of the historical Suzaku Palace.
22. Of whom the reader knows nothing.
23. The comb box set that Suzaku had given her when she joined Emperor Reizei ("The Picture Contest").
24. The poem addresses Suzaku, not his daughter, since Suzaku is sure to see it.
25. A comb in poetry has magical associations, and its many teeth connote many years (longevity). The language of the poem, as of Suzaku's reply, is distinctly felicitous.

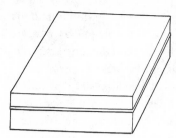

Comb box

all," he said, "but this parting that so distresses you is very painful indeed." He resolutely raised himself onto an armrest, although he was in imminent danger of losing his self-control. The Abbot of the Mountain and two attendant monks then administered the Precepts. The ceremony confirming his renunciation, the one at which he put on his religious robes, was extremely sad. Not even monks to whom the world was dross could restrain their tears on that day, and of course his daughters, his Consorts and Intimates, and ladies and gentlemen of all degrees gave themselves up to loud weeping, which greatly pained him, since it was all so unlike the peace and quiet to which he longed to retire—except that the young Princess still tugged at his heart. There was a constant stream of messengers from the palace and elsewhere to inquire after his health.

His Grace of Rokujō came, too, when he learned that His Eminence was feeling a little better. Although he enjoyed the same emoluments and so on as a Retired Emperor, he did not insist on the degree of ceremony proper to one, and he kept his train discreet despite the high regard in which he was universally held. He rode there in as modest a carriage as usual, accompanied only by those senior nobles whose presence beside him was to be expected.

His Eminence was very pleased that he had come at last, and forgot his suffering to receive him. Abandoning all formality, he had Genji brought in and seated beside him. The sad change that had come upon him overwhelmed Genji, who wept in sorrow and took some time to recover himself. "Ever since His Late Eminence was taken from me, I have understood that nothing lasts, and I have longed to do as you have just done," he said; "yet I have instead only wavered feebly time after time, until I am ashamed of my faintheartedness when I see you before me like this. How often have I made up my mind that for someone like me nothing seriously stands in my way; and yet there are always so many things that make it unbearable after all actually to take that step." He was inconsolable.

His Eminence was too downhearted to be any braver, and it was with frequent tears that he began in a very weak voice to speak of things old and new. "For years now I have been expecting my time to come any day," he said, "but you know, I took that step myself only because I was afraid that if I hesitated, I might never take it at all. Even so, I have too little time left to practice as I would like. No, I shall simply quiet my mind a while and call the Holy Name. Having so little to offer, I know all too well that I have lasted this long only because that desire has detained me, and it disturbs me to reflect that to this day I have done no practice at all."

He described his feelings over the years, and as he did so, he chanced to remark, "I hate to leave all my daughters, and the one for whom I have found no one yet worries me particularly. I simply do not know what to do."

His roundabout approach elicited Genji's compassion. Genji could not let the moment pass, for despite everything he was curious about her. "Yes," he replied, "it is true, a Princess without personal sponsorship of some kind may find herself in an awkward position. The Heir Apparent, being what he is, inspires everywhere devout confidence that he is the wisest of imperial successors in this latter age, and if you were to explain her situation to him, he of course would never neglect her or treat her with disrespect; you would never need to worry about her future. However, he could do only so much and no more, and he could not then single her out for favor once he came to reign on his own, no matter how thoroughly the state of government accorded with his own wishes. The man chosen to provide for a woman in every way will merit far greater confidence when he and she commit themselves fully to each other and he undertakes to cherish and protect her in every circumstance that life imposes. If you cannot give up your concern for her future, you should select suitable prospects and very discreetly decide to whom you wish to entrust her."

"I quite agree, but that is not at all easy to do. I gather from past example that a Sovereign, even one at the height of his powers, has usually preferred to select a gentleman with just that sort of arrangement in mind. I, on the other hand, am now soon to depart this life, and even if this is no time for me to set demanding requirements, she is the one among all those I will leave behind to whom I am most particularly attached. I therefore worry a great deal about her in all sorts of ways, and meanwhile my condition grows steadily worse, and days and months that will never return keep slipping by. That, you understand, is why I am so desperate. I know that my request can hardly be welcome, but I should like to ask you to take this young Princess under your special care and to work out on your own who would make a good match for her. The Counselor would have been well worth approaching when he was on his own, and I am disappointed that the Chancellor got to him first."

"My young lord the Counselor can be relied upon for loyal service, but he lacks experience, and I believe there are many things that he does not yet understand. Please forgive my presumption, but if I were to devote myself to her welfare, she would find her life unchanged from what you have made it. Alas, my only anxiety is that since I, too, have little time left, I may conceivably fail her." With these words Genji accepted.

At nightfall all His Eminence's gentlemen and the senior nobles with Genji were entertained in these two great lords' presence with a meal—a fasting one less formal than gracefully plain. They wiped the tears from their eyes to see His Eminence eating in so unfamiliar a manner from the bowl placed on the aloeswood meal stand before him.[26] Many touching moments followed, but it would be tedious to write them all down. Genji withdrew late that night. Each gentleman received a reward appropriate to his station. The Counselor and the Master of the Household saw Genji home. The day's snow had made His Eminence's condition worse, and he felt very ill, but his mind was at peace now that the matter of his daughter was settled.

26. A bowl is the only eating vessel permitted to one who has taken holy vows.

Meal stand

At Rokujō, Genji felt somewhat oppressed and torn. Lady Murasaki[27] had already heard talk of the decision, but she had difficulty believing it. She told herself that he had also seemed in earnest when he was courting the former Kamo Priestess but that he had avoided taking courtship to its extreme conclusion. She did not even bother to ask him about it.

Her unquestioning trust disturbed him. What will she make of this? he wondered. My own feeling for her will not change in the least; in fact, I will only love her more if it really happens. What doubts will she have toward me, though, until experience at last proves them wrong? He was worried. Nothing divided them by now, after all these years. They were remarkably close, and he did not for a moment like keeping things from her, yet that night he lay down to rest without a word.

The next day it snowed, and there was a deeply moving quality to the sky. They talked together of things past and things yet to come. "His Eminence is not at all well, and I called on him yesterday," he remarked. "It was all very touching, you know. The thought of leaving Her Highness his third daughter has been a great worry to him, and he told me all about it. I felt so sorry for him that I simply could not refuse. I suppose people will make quite a thing of it. It is all rather embarrassing by now, and unbecoming as well; and when he first approached me through someone else, I managed somehow to get out of it. Face-to-face, though, he spoke so long and so earnestly that I just could not find any decent argument against it. He means to live far away in the hills,[28] and when he does, it will be time for me to bring her here. Will you be very upset? Nothing will change for you in any way, no matter what happens. Please do not dislike me. She is the one for whom I feel sorry. I mean to look after her properly, though. Just as long as everyone involved gets on together . . ."

He wondered how she would feel, she who with her quick temper objected to the least of his little amusements; but her answer revealed nothing. "What an extraordinary thing for him to ask of you!" she said. "As for myself, why should I wish to dislike her? I shall be perfectly happy as long as she does not find *my* presence here offensive. Anyway, it may encourage her to look kindly on me that I am related to the Consort her mother."

Her modesty took Genji by surprise. "Such exceedingly mild acquiescence

27. The way the original names her here (Murasaki no Ue) contrasts her pointedly with Onna San no Miya. She is Genji's "true love" (*murasaki*), while his relationship with Onna San no Miya is perfunctory, and her personal quality gives her standing after all vis-à-vis Onna San no Miya's overwhelmingly high rank. From here on, her real stature will continue slowly to rise, and the text will call her Murasaki no Ue more and more often.

28. Omuro is by no means "far away" for any present inhabitant of Kyoto, nor is it at all far into the hills; but it seemed much more remote then, and in any case the religious world that Suzaku is about to join felt very far away indeed.

worries me. I wonder what lies behind it. Really, though, you know, if you mean it, and if you and she can manage sensibly with each other, then I shall love you better than ever. Pay no attention to the nonsense people talk. No one ever knows where gossip starts, but it can badly misconstrue the relationship between people and have the strangest consequences. You would be wiser to keep your own counsel and take things the way they really are. Please do not be alarmed without good reason or entertain pointless jealousy." He gave her a very fine sermon.

This came on him out of the blue, and he could hardly avoid it, she told herself; I refuse to say an unkind word in protest. It is not as though they hatched any sort of romantic plot together, or as though despite reluctance he was still amenable to persuasion. There was nothing he could do about it, and I will not have people gather that I am sulking. His Highness of Ceremonial's[29] wife is forever calling down disaster on me—she is even madly jealous and bitter over that miserable business of the Commander.[30] How she will gloat when she hears about this!

Hers was no doubt a heart without guile, but of course it still harbored a dark recess or two. In secret she never ceased grieving that her very innocence—the way she had proudly assumed for so long that his vagaries need not concern her—would now cause amusement, but in her behavior she remained the picture of unquestioning trust.

The New Year came. At the Suzaku Palace, His Eminence's daughter was preparing to move to Rokujō, and her other suitors were extremely disappointed. His Majesty had hoped for his part that she might come to the palace, but he gave up the thought now that the matter was settled.

Actually, this was Genji's fortieth year, and His Majesty for one did not mean to neglect the jubilee. The event promised to involve the entire court and was already causing a great stir, although Genji, who had never liked tiresomely solemn occasions, wanted no part of it.

On the twenty-third of the first month, the day of the Rat, her ladyship the Left Commander's wife offered Genji a repast of spring shoots.[31] She had told him nothing about it beforehand and made all her arrangements in secret, so that he found himself caught and could not refuse. Despite her modesty she was too great a lady for her arrival not to cause a great stir.

The setting was the west extension in the main house of the southeast quarter. The screens, the lintel curtains, and all the other furnishings were new. Instead of a pompous throne,[32] there were forty mats, cushions, and armrests, all by her wish especially handsome. There was also a pair of mother-of-pearl inlaid cabinets that supported four chests of summer and winter clothing, and besides these, incense jars, medicine boxes, inkstones, water vessels[33] for dressing the sidelocks, and a

29. Her father's.
30. Tamakazura's marriage to Higekuro.
31. Tamakazura holds this event on the day (the first day of the Rat in the first month) on which courtiers went out into the fields to pick the green shoots of the plants that sprout first in spring, traditionally seven in number.
32. A very solemnly "Chinese" item of furniture for the honored, quasi-imperial guest. The "forty mats" and so on are for Genji's forty years.
33. *Yusurutsuki,* lidded cups on tall stands.

chest of hairdressing implements. She had quietly made sure that everything was as pretty as it could be. The stands bearing headdress flowers were of aloes heartwood and red sandal carved with marvelously novel designs and in the height of fashion, even to their gold trim and colors; for she who was so clever and so profoundly elegant had given all these things a touch not seen before. She had stopped everywhere carefully short of ostentation.

The guests gathered, and Genji had a moment with her on his way to join them. All sorts of memories must have come back to him. He looked so young and handsome that one refused to believe the count of his years, and such was his grace that he hardly seemed a father. Although thoroughly abashed to find herself in his presence again after all this time, she marked no great distance between them, and they conversed. She had her pretty little sons with her. She herself had not wanted to show him two boys born so close together,[34] but the Commander had insisted on taking advantage of this opportunity, so there they were, both innocently alike in dress cloaks and evenly parted hair.

"I myself hardly notice that I am getting older," Genji said, "because I feel as young as ever, but it brings my age home to me to be entertained now and again this way by my children. The Counselor had a baby some time ago, but he is being very independent and has not yet allowed me to see it. I deplore this day of the Rat, though—you were the first to count up my years for it. I should have preferred to forget old age a little longer!"

The Mistress of Staff had matured very handsomely and acquired as well a new weightiness of presence. It was a pleasure to see her.

> *"I have brought today seedling pines plucked from meadows where such new shoots grow*
> *to pray that eternity bless the great rock whence I sprang,"*[35]

she said in her most motherly manner.

Genji partook ceremonially of spring shoots served in four aloeswood trays. Then he took up his wine cup.

> *"Those seedlings may yet, plucked from such happy meadows, draw a new shoot up*
> *toward a still-longer span of endlessly happy years,"*[36]

he said, and other such things besides, and meanwhile, the senior nobles arrived in the south aisle.

His Highness of Ceremonial had been reluctant to come, but he turned up after all later that morning, since he had been invited and since he was close to

34. She seems to feel that it is immodest of her to have two sons so close in age by Higekuro, especially considering the old feeling between herself and Genji.

35. On the year's first day of the Rat, people went into the fields not only to pick new greens but to pull up little pines, tokens of long life, and the poetry associated with the day alludes to both activities. Here the "seedling pines" are her sons, whom she has "brought today" (*hiki-tsurete*) as people pull up (*hiki*) the pines. The great rock is Genji.

36. "Your little boys make me feel young again." Genji's poem plays again (although in a different way) on *hiki*, and also on *tsumu* ("pick" [greens] and "pile up" [years]).

Genji;[37] besides, he might do well to avoid giving the impression that he was somehow displeased. The way the Commander, smug looks and all, so visibly prided himself on his connection with His Grace was indeed very irritating, but His Highness of Ceremonial's grandsons made themselves admirably useful on both sides.[38] The Counselor, and after him all those for whom it was proper to do so, offered Genji his forty fruit baskets and forty cypresswood boxes of delicacies. The wine cup went round, and everyone partook of spring shoots in clear broth. Four meal stands of aloes heartwood stood before Genji, and all the cups and utensils on them were as gracefully fresh in style as they could be.

No musicians were summoned, since His Eminence was still indisposed. His Excellency the Chancellor had seen to providing the wind instruments. "Never in all the world could a celebration be prettier or more intriguing than this one," he said, and a discreet concert followed. He had chosen only instruments with a superb tone. Among the ones presented for Genji's pleasure, the *wagon* was His Excellency's great favorite, and the music it yielded when played intently by so great a master was magnificent. When no one else would take it up, he overrode a strenuous refusal by the Intendant of the Watch,[39] who indeed played it very nicely—in fact, hardly less well than his father. Everyone was deeply impressed, because although a son may indeed inherit his father's skill, it hardly seemed possible to do so to that degree. The set patterns associated with each mode, and the written transmission from China, actually make it relatively easy to master the pieces involved,[40] whereas a wonderfully stirring and resonant music arises from successful improvisation among other instruments, in harmony with them all. His Excellency slackened the strings and tuned his instrument low to accompany the others, while his son played high and sweetly, with results that astonished Their Highnesses, who had heard nothing like it before. The *kin* went to His Highness of War. It was from the Imperial Stores and had been treasured by generations of Emperors; near the end His Late Eminence had bestowed it on his first daughter, who also loved music, and His Excellency had persuaded her to lend it in order to give the occasion a last touch of grace. Moved, Genji fondly remembered many scenes from the past. His Highness, who could not restrain drunken tears, found the right moment to cede the instrument to Genji himself, and Genji, too caught up in his feelings to decline, played just one rare piece. No, although not solemnly grand, the concert that evening was as beautiful as it could possibly be. The singers were called to the top of the steps, where they sang in magnificent voice until the mode change came.[41] The later the night, the sweeter the music, until by the time they reached "Green Willow,"[42] the

---

37. He is Murasaki's father but also Higekuro's ex-father-in-law.

38. Tamakazura is the stepmother and Murasaki the aunt of Higekuro's sons by his former wife, His Highness of Ceremonial's daughter.

39. Kashiwagi.

40. "Secret pieces" (*hikyoku*) associated with the various modes and Chinese pieces, for which the notes were all written down.

41. The singers (who sang solfège, *sōga*) were privy gentlemen, and they sang in this case from the top of the steps leading from the south side of the building down into the garden. The "mode change," from *ryo* to *ritsu*, presumably involved a marked change in mood.

42. A *saibara* song about warblers weaving a *kasa* hat from weeping willow fronds.

very warbler on its perch might have wondered at such enchanting harmonies. The rewards and so on were particularly beautiful, since the event was private in character.[43]

Genji had gifts for the Mistress of Staff when she went home at daybreak. "Living as far out of touch as I do, as though I had abandoned the world, I hardly know that the months and years are passing, and it is a shock when you make it so plain how many have gone by. Do come sometimes to see how much older I look. I am very sorry, you know, that at my age I am so seldom at liberty to meet you." She brought him many memories, both happy and sad, and it was a great sorrow and disappointment that she had to hurry away again after just that glimpse of her. She herself felt no more for her real father than any daughter might, but now that she had settled into her present life, her gratitude for all the kind attentions Genji had shown her only grew with the passage of time.

So it was that after the tenth of the second month Her Highness, His Eminence's daughter, moved to Rokujō. Here, too, she was splendidly accommodated. Her curtained bed was placed in the west extension, where Genji had partaken of the spring shoots, and the rooms for her gentlewomen were thoughtfully and prettily laid out in the two wings on that side and along the bridgeways. Furnishings were brought from the Suzaku Palace, too, just as when a woman goes to join His Majesty. One need hardly describe the ceremony attending her move, which was accompanied by a large number of senior nobles. The Grand Counselor, who had aspired to administer her household, waited upon her as well, although without pleasure. His Grace went to meet her when her carriage was brought up and helped her to alight, which differed from established protocol. He was a commoner after all, and she did *not* go to him as a Consort does when she enters the palace; nor were things done after all quite as they are when the bridegroom is a Prince. Their relationship to each other was highly unusual.

Both Genji and His Eminence saw to it that all things were done with the utmost pomp for three days thereafter. At times the mistress of Genji's east wing hardly knew where she stood. In truth, none of this meant that the new arrival now seriously overshadowed her, but she was not accustomed to seeing her position challenged, and she could not help feeling uneasy, since Her Highness had so many brilliant years before her and was so impossible to take lightly. She betrayed nothing of these feelings, however, and when Her Highness arrived, she even assisted Genji in all sorts of little ways, until he wondered more than ever at how dear she was.

Her Highness was indeed still very small and poorly grown, and she was also extremely girlish and immature. He remembered his kin to the noble *murasaki*,[44] when he had first found her and made her his own, but *she* had been bright and attractive, whereas this girl was merely childish. Well, no doubt it is all for the best, he thought; at least she will not insist unpleasantly on her prerogatives. Still, he found her too dismally dull.

---

43. Rewards and gifts for the guests were limited by regulation in the case of a "public" (government, imperial) function, but they could be more generous at a private one.
44. An allusion to the way Genji thought of Murasaki when he first discovered her ("Young Murasaki"): as kin to his great love then, Fujitsubo.

He went to Her Highness faithfully every night for the first three nights, and his Murasaki bore it, but she suffered, for she was unaccustomed to anything of the kind. She saw more faithfully than ever to the perfuming of his robes, but she often lapsed into melancholy daydreams, looking very dear and lovely as she did so. Why, Genji asked himself, why had he let *anything* persuade him to try setting another beside her? He had imprudently allowed a wanton weakness to get the better of him: that was why it had happened. His Eminence had not chosen the Counselor in the end, no, despite his youth. These bitter thoughts helplessly preoccupied him, and tears came to his eyes. "Please understand and forgive me for being away again tonight," he said. "If I neglect you after this, I will really hate myself. Even then, though, there are His Eminence's feelings to consider."

She pitied his confusion and replied with a little smile, "It appears that you yourself cannot decide what to do. How, then, can I advise you? I wonder what course you will choose in the end." She would not discuss it, and he lay back ashamed, chin in hand. Drawing an inkstone to her, she wrote,

> "Ah, how trustingly I believed that what we had would last on and on,
> when your feelings in this world shift and change before my eyes."

She had written it down among some old poems, and he picked it up and read it. It was slight enough, but he knew what she meant.

> "Life, it is too true, must end when that moment comes, but this shifting world
> never has known such a bond as the one between us two,"

he replied.

He could not bring himself to go. "No, no, I will not let you do this to me!" she insisted; and so off he went in his lovely, soft, deliciously perfumed robes.

She must have felt thoroughly uneasy as she watched him leave. There had been times over the years when she feared just this, but he seemed to have put all that behind him, and she had come at last to believe that that was the way things would always be; and then *this* had happened, to set the tongues of all the world wagging. I was wrong after all to be so sure of him, she thought, and I shall never be able to trust him again.

"This will not do!" her women sighed to each other despite her brave show of calm. "He has many ladies, it is true, but all cede pride of place to our mistress, and that is why things go so well. This one, though, values herself too much ever to put up with that! There could well be some sort of unpleasantness if any little incident happens to cause trouble." Their mistress pretended not to notice anything wrong, and she went on conversing with them very nicely until late in the night.

She was not pleased to hear them speaking so apprehensively. "My lord does have a good many women," she said, "but really, none of them has the fashionable brilliance he wants, and he felt that he had seen rather too much of all of us. It is just as well Her Highness has come. I must still be a girl at heart, because I should like to be close to her, but people seem to be talking instead as though there were a gulf between us. I wish they would not. Yes, one can imagine some sort of incident if she were my equal in the eyes of the world, or perhaps below me, but instead she commands the highest respect and very great sympathy as well, and I do not see how anyone could disapprove of her."

Nakatsukasa, Chūjō, and the others exchanged glances and murmured that she was being much too nice. Long ago they had served Genji particularly intimately, but for years now they had been in their mistress's service instead, and they were very fond of her. Messages came from his other ladies, wondering how she was taking it and hinting that it might be their turn now to feel like the lucky ones, since they saw so little of him anyway. But it is *they* who are making me miserable with these conjectures of theirs! she said to herself. Why should I be unhappy, when this world is so uncertain already?

Realizing guiltily that her women would wonder why she was staying up so long, she went to bed, and they drew the covers over her. It was true, though, these nights were lonely, and she *was* upset. She remembered when he was away at Suma. Yes, she thought, he was gone then, too, perhaps forever, and all that mattered was being sure that he was alive; never mind what happened to me—I only loved him and grieved for him. And if in all that turmoil he and I had just disappeared, that would have been the end of that. It was a windy, chilly night, and sleep eluded her, but she made not the smallest movement lest her women nearby hear her and wonder, and this, too, was a very great trial. A cock crowed forlornly in the depths of the night.

She had no wish to accuse him, but perhaps her distress explains why he dreamed of her only to waken in alarm, his heart pounding. He waited until cockcrow and then left, pretending not to notice that it was still night. Her Highness was still such a girl that her nurses were in attendance nearby. She watched him open the double doors and go. Only the snow glimmered in the first light of dawn. His scent lingered behind him, and a nurse murmured, "Darkness covers all."[45]

Here and there snow lay in patches that still merged with the whiteness of the garden.[46] "Snow still lies against the wall,"[47] he hummed to himself, tapping at a shutter. Nothing like this had happened for a long time, though; the women pretended to be asleep and made him wait before they raised it.

"It took them so long!" he said. "I am frozen! I suppose that is what comes of being afraid of you. I have done nothing, though!" He pulled her covers aside, and she drew her damp sleeves away to hide them. Her simple warmth stopped well short of an open welcome, which daunted and delighted him all at once. Talk about the greatest lady in the land, he thought, remembering the one he had just left—*she* could never do that!

He spent a day filled with memories reproaching her for refusing to forgive him, and after that he could not go there again. Instead he sent a note to the main house: "The snow this morning left me feeling too unwell, and I am lazily enjoying the comforts of home."

---

45. *Kokinshū* 41, by Ōshikōchi no Mitsune: "On a night in spring, darkness covers all; plum blossoms remain unseen, but their scent cannot be hidden."

46. Because much of the garden is strewn with white sand.

47. A line from a poem by Bai Juyi (*Hakushi monjū* 0911).

"I have informed my lady." The nurse's reply came by word of mouth.

What an answer! I should hate to have His Eminence hear of this. I *must* put a brave face on it for the time being. He could not, though. I knew it! he went on to himself. *Now* what am I to do? His thoughtlessness troubled even his darling.

In the morning he rose as usual and sent Her Highness a letter. Though not particularly in awe of her, he still wrote it carefully, on white paper:[48]

> *"It is no great way that lies between where you are and I am myself,*
> *yet I suffer this morning from this sprinkling of snow!"*[49]

He attached it to a branch of blossoming plum and summoned a messenger. "Present this from the west bridgeway,"[50] he said; then he sat in his white gowns looking out from near the veranda, toying with white blossoms and meanwhile gazing up at a sky from which snowflakes drifted down to join the lonely few that still lingered below.[51] When a warbler sang its earliest song from the tip of a red plum bough, he hid his blossoms and murmured, "My very sleeves are perfumed!"[52] Gazing out into the distance that way, past the raised blinds, he looked nothing at all like a father or like someone who held a weighty title. One saw only youth and grace.

When her answer seemed a little long in coming, he went back in and showed off his flowers. "This is how blossoms should smell," he said. "If only one could give cherry blossoms this perfume, I doubt that people would care any longer for any other kind."[53] And he went on, "I suppose these catch the eye because there is little else now to look at. I should like to put them beside cherry blossoms at their best." He was going on like this when an answer arrived, gaudily wrapped in thin scarlet paper. His heart sank. Her writing is so much a little girl's, he thought; I had better not show it off just yet. Not that I mean to keep her letters to myself, but really, considering who she is, I may harm her if I am not careful. He left it just slightly open, since his darling would only be hurt if he hid it, and she caught a sidelong look at it from where she lay propped on an armrest:

> *"Wandering the wind in a swift flurry of flakes, so light a spring snow,*
> *pitifully frail, must soon melt away into the sky."*[54]

The hand was indeed thoroughly childish. No one Her Highness's age should write like that, she thought, and she pretended not to have seen it.

---

48. In keeping with the snow and with the white plum blossoms to which the letter is tied.

49. *Gosenshū* 479, by Fujiwara no Kagemoto: "This sprinkling of snow that melts away into the sky is the heart of one tormented by love." Genji's poem is an excuse for not coming and a reassurance that he would if he could.

50. Where Onna San no Miya's women have their rooms.

51. "Lonely" snow longing for more to fall is from *Yakamochi shū* 284, by Ōtomo no Yakamochi.

52. From *Kokinshū* 32: "Now that I have plucked them, my very sleeves are perfumed; ah, plum blossoms—perhaps their presence has brought the warbler here to sing!" For Genji (poetically speaking) the early warbler's song betrays his wayward preoccupation with Onna San no Miya.

53. Genji may be explaining his attraction to Onna San no Miya: despite Murasaki's cherry blossom beauty she lacks Onna San no Miya's perfume (rank).

54. Presumably by one of Onna San no Miya's nurses or gentlewomen, reproaching Genji for his failure to come.

Just look at that! Genji would have remarked if it had been anyone else, but he could not bear to do so; he only said, "You need not fear."

Today he went to Her Highness in daylight. He had dressed with special care, and he must have impressed her women, since they had not actually seen him before. Some of the older and more experienced ones, her nurses and so on, thought to themselves, Come, *he* at least is a pleasure to look at; but there is going to be trouble!

Charmingly girlish, Her Highness lived amid the proudest and most imposing magnificence, but at her tender age she had hardly a thought in her head, and she was so slight that she all but disappeared under her layers of gowns. She was not especially shy with him; she merely failed to be put off by a new face, as so many children are, and her manner remained sweetly serene. People have often felt that His Eminence unfortunately lacks manly gravity and learning, Genji reflected, although he excels in lighter matters of taste and sensibility. What *can* he have meant by bringing her up to this degree of ingenuousness? Nonetheless, I gather that she is his favorite daughter. It was all very disappointing, but he looked on her kindly enough. She would meekly do whatever he asked, and in the way of an answer she would simply blurt out whatever came into her head. No, he could not abandon her. As a young man I would have felt betrayed, he reflected, but wider experience has made me more tolerant; women can be this or that, I know, but they are only what they are and no more. There are simply all kinds. I suppose any outsider would assume she is ideal. Yes, the mistress of my east wing continues to astonish me after all our years together—I certainly brought *her* up properly, if I say so myself. After a night or just a morning away he worried about her and missed her, and the longer he lived, the more he loved her, though it was almost with dread that he wondered why.

His Eminence moved to his temple that same month. Many affecting letters from him reached Rokujō. He spoke of his daughter, of course, and he repeatedly urged Genji to do whatever he thought best for her, without regard to his own opinion on the matter. In reality, though, she was so young that she continued to weigh on his mind.

There was a letter for Lady Murasaki as well. "Please look indulgently on the young girl who has gone in all innocence to join you, and give her the assistance she needs," he had written. "I believe that you may have a particular reason to call upon her.[55]

> This fond heart of mine, lingering still in a world that I had renounced,
> detains me yet, when I would now enter on the mountain path.

You may think me very foolish for so failing to dispel a father's darkness."

Genji read it, too. "What a touching letter!" he said. "You must respect his wishes." Through the gentlewomen he plied the messenger with wine. He did not feel that he could very well tell her how to reply, and since this was no time for anything clever, she simply confined herself to what she felt:

55. Because Murasaki and Onna San no Miya are first cousins.

*"If the world you left burdens you with such concern and the tie you feel
is so difficult to break, do not try too hard to go."*

She presented the messenger with a long dress and a set of women's gowns. When
His Eminence saw her beautiful writing, he deeply regretted that his all too childish
daughter should have come into the company of anyone so impressive.

His Eminence's Consorts and Intimates now all received leave to go, and there
were many moving scenes. His Mistress of Staff, who meant more to him than anyone except his daughter, occupied the Nijō residence once inhabited by the Empress Mother. She had considered becoming a nun, but he reminded her that so
hasty a gesture would suggest that she had nothing more in mind than following
him, and in the end she only commissioned the making of holy images.

Losing her had been a painful wrench for Genji, who had not forgotten her
and who had long wanted to find a way to see her again and talk over the past they
shared. Unfortunately, both were obliged by their circumstances to wish to avoid
causing gossip, and the memory of that tragic scandal still made him extremely cautious. Still, he longed to know how she was, now that she was her own mistress
again and that life was no doubt much quieter for her, and accordingly, he began
despite his misgivings to write to her warmly under the pretext merely of civil inquiries after her health. She replied, since they could no longer be to each other
what they were when they were young. It was always more than he could bear to
see her writing, expansively full and generous as it was, and he would then send off
an imploring letter to the Chūnagon of old.

He summoned Chūnagon's brother, formerly the Governor of Izumi, and
talked over the past with youthful fervor. "I have something to tell her," he said, "but
in person, just through a curtain. You must persuade her to allow that, and then I
will pay her a very secret visit. I shall have to be extremely careful, since in my position I cannot really do this sort of thing anymore, and I know that you will not
speak of it to anyone. I am certain we can trust each other."

Oh, dear me, no! the Mistress of Staff sighed to herself; I know a bit more
about life now, and after all the misery those ways of his have caused me over the
years, I cannot imagine what of the past we would find to talk about, apart from
commiserating with each other over His Eminence. I would still have my own conscience to answer to, even if his visit remained a secret forever. She replied that she
could not consider it.

It is hardly as though we were not in it together back then when we took
those risks, Genji reflected. Yes, I can see she might be anxious about His Eminence,
now that he has renounced the world, but all that did happen, and no modesty of
hers now will save her good name from the scandal that touched it then. His mind
was made up, and he would follow the path through Shinoda Forest.[56]

He said to his darling, "Her Highness of Hitachi in the east pavilion[57] has

---

56. The former Governor of Izumi, since Shinoda Forest was in Izumi Province. *Kokin rokujō* 1049 speaks
of the lover whose heart is torn in a thousand ways, like the thousand leaves "in Shinoda Forest in Izumi."
57. Suetsumuhana, who lives in the east pavilion of his Nijō residence.

been ill for a long time now, and you know, I feel rather guilty for having let all the recent commotion prevent me from going to see her. It would be tactless of me to go too obviously, though, during the day; I think I shall go more discreetly instead, at night. I do not want anyone to know." She was surprised to note his intense excitement, since this was not a visit that would normally have affected him this way, and she guessed something of what was going on; but things were no longer as they had been since Her Highness appeared, and a certain distance had come between them. She let the matter pass.

He did not go to the main house[58] that day but only exchanged notes. Until nightfall he spent the time perfuming his clothes, and then, once the early evening was past, he set off in a basketwork carriage that recalled his surreptitious expeditions of long ago, accompanied by four or five of his closest retainers. The Governor of Izumi announced his arrival.

The whispered news astonished the Mistress of Staff. "I do not understand!" she said reproachfully. "What on earth did the Governor tell him?" Chūnagon insisted, however. "It would be most unfortunate to mistake the spirit of my lord's visit and to send him away," she said, and by hook or crook she got him admitted.

Genji inquired politely after the lady's health. "Do come *here*," he pressed her. "The panel can stay. Those wicked old ways of mine are all gone now." With sighs of bitter reluctance she slipped out toward him. I knew it! he thought. She still cannot resist! Each was acutely aware of the other's movements, and the level of feeling rose.

The setting was the east wing.[59] He was seated where she had placed him, in the southeast corner of the aisle, and the bottom of the sliding panel was firmly fixed in place. "I feel like a callow youth!" he complained. "Oh, I could tell you exactly how many months and years it has been, and it is awful of you, you know, to pretend you could not!"

The night grew late. Mandarin ducks sported with suggestive cries among the waterweeds, and the silent, all but deserted dwelling set him to pondering the world's endless changes; not that he meant to mimic Heichū, but he felt inclined to weep.[60] He spoke to her reasonably, as he had not done then, but he tugged at the panel nonetheless, as though to say, Do you really mean to leave it like this?

> "With such months and years already lost between us, and our meeting now
> an Ōsaka Barrier, no rampart can stop my tears!"[61]

She replied,

"Tears, yes, they may well flow as imperiously as any clear spring,
but the path we took to meet vanished a long time ago."[62]

She tried with this sort of talk to keep her distance, but when she looked back over the past and asked herself just whose fault that dreadful scandal had really been, it seemed to her that yes, she had always known that they would meet again, and she faltered; gravity of deportment had never been her strength anyway, and while all that life had taught her over the years, all her regrets and her wide experience at home or at court, had encouraged her to live beyond reproach, this meeting so reminiscent of the old days brought their times together very close again, and she found it impossible to sustain her resistance. She still had youth and warmth and her lively wit, and the conflict between prudent restraint and passionate feeling drew from her such sighs as to enchant Genji even more than at a first encounter. The coming of dawn was misery to him, and he did not want to leave.

At daybreak the air beneath an entrancing sky rang with the sweet singing of birds. The cherry blossoms were all gone, and in their place a pale green haze swathed the trees. That party of his[63] under the wisteria—it must have been at about this time! he reflected. Many years had passed since then, but what had happened still stirred him. Chūnagon opened the double doors to watch him go, and he turned back toward her. "Ah, this wisteria!" he said. "Where can it have got its color? Such beauty surely suggests a rare grace of spirit! How can I possibly leave it?" He simply could not bring himself to go.

The light of the sun just then rising over the hills gave him a dazzling beauty, and after all this time it was still such a wonder to see him in his full magnificence that she could hardly believe he belonged to this world. Why, oh why, had her mistress not been married to a man like *him*? Chūnagon remembered how certain constraints had kept her mistress from rising particularly high in His Eminence's service, for the late Empress Mother had made much too much of what had happened, and the ensuing scandal had tarnished her name forever. Oh, I hope that this will not be all, she thought, when they must have so much more to tell each other! But Genji feared watching eyes too much merely to please himself, and his anxiety grew as the sun rose. His men had brought his carriage up to the gallery door, and he could hear them discreetly clearing their throats.

He called one and had him pick a cluster of those blossoms.

"Not that I forget the disgrace I suffered then, but I have not learned
and feel poised to cast myself into your blossoms' abyss."[64]

---

62. This poem acknowledges the "Ōsaka" in Genji's. "Clear spring" (*shimizu*) is a word associated with Ōsaka in poetry, and "the road to meeting" (*ō michi*) is identical in phonetic writing with Ōmi ji, "the road to (the province of) Ōmi"; Ōmi is on the other side of the Ōsaka Barrier from Kyoto.
63. The Minister of the Right (Oborozukiyo's father) in "Under the Cherry Blossoms," twenty years earlier.
64. Genji ties this poem to the blossoms and gives it to Chūnagon to take to her mistress. It plays on *korizuma ni* ("I have not learned [my lesson]"), which contains the syllables "Suma"; and on *fujinami* ("wisteria waves"), in which *fuji* is written with the same phonetic signs as *fuchi*, "abyss."

Sorrowfully she watched him lean on the railing in an anguish of indecision. Despite the troubled modesty that overcame her, she longed for those blossoms, too.

> *"That fatal abyss, yawning to swallow you, is not one at all,*
> *for I would not wet my sleeves in such unrepentant waves."*[65]

Genji could not condone his own boyish behavior, but perhaps the gatekeeper's laxness had set his mind at rest,[66] because before leaving he secured her consent to meet again. She had meant a great deal to him in the old days, too, but after all they had had little time together, and he could hardly fail now to be deeply stirred.

He made his way home again very stealthily indeed and all too clearly just out of bed, and his darling was there to greet him. She had a good idea what he had been up to, but she did not allow herself to show it, and this actually bothered him more than the fit of jealousy he had expected. Wondering why his doings concerned her so little reduced him to promising her eternal love and devotion more earnestly than ever before. He could not very well talk about the Mistress of Staff elsewhere, but she knew what had once happened, and he therefore told her just a little. "She and I were screened from each other, you know, and there was not much to our meeting. It was disappointing, really. I should like to go again if I can keep from being seen."

She gave him a little smile. "Why, you are quite the young gallant again! There you are, reliving your past, only to leave *me* wondering what is to become of me." Tears came to her eyes after all, and she looked very dear indeed.

"This pettishness of yours makes things very difficult. I would rather you just came straight at me and pinched me to let me know how you feel. I never taught you to keep things to yourself, and I cannot imagine where this attitude comes from." He did all he could to bring her round, and in the end he apparently had to confess everything.

He did not immediately go to Her Highness but instead remained where he was, consoling his beloved. To Her Highness this meant nothing, but those entrusted with her care let him know that they considered him delinquent. He would have felt even worse if Her Highness had expressed displeasure herself, but as it was, she was nothing more to him than a fetching, obedient toy.

For ages the Kiritsubo Consort[67] could not withdraw from the palace. Never having leave to go was hard for someone so young and hitherto always able to please herself. That summer she began to feel unwell, and she was outraged when the Heir Apparent would not allow her to go straight home. Her condition was delicate, and

---

65. Her poem exploits the same wordplays as Genji's. "Unrepentent waves" (*korizuma no nami*) contains the meaning "the waves of Suma"; and *nami* ("waves") is a word also conventionally associated with *fuji* ("wisteria").

66. A pointedly romantic allusion to an episode (number 5) in *Ise monogatari*; the "gatekeeper" (*sekimori*) is the stern father or husband who keeps the lovers apart. Oborozukiyo now lives alone.

67. The Akashi Daughter, who now lives in the Kiritsubo as the Consort to the Heir Apparent.

those most concerned must have been apprehensive, since she was still very small and frail. At last she withdrew, and space was prepared for her at the front of the main house, on the east side, where Her Highness lived. To be so much with her daughter now was a fate that represented the sum of the Akashi lady's wishes.

The mistress of Genji's east wing intended to visit the Consort. "I should like to open the door in between and call on Her Highness, too," she said with a smile. "For some time I have been thinking of doing so, but I felt that I should wait for the proper moment. Things will be easier after this, if she and I can make friends now."

"That would be just the thing. She is so young. Do see that she learns what she needs to know."

It was the prospect of meeting less Her Highness than Akashi that she found daunting, and she washed her hair and dressed so beautifully that Genji thought her clearly beyond compare.

He went to talk to Her Highness beforehand. "The lady from the east wing is coming to see the Kiritsubo Consort this evening," he explained, "and I gather that she would like to become acquainted with you at the same time. Please be good enough to receive her. She is very nice. She is still young, too, and you might enjoy amusing yourself with her."

"But I shall be so embarrassed! What shall I say to her?" Her Highness replied artlessly.

"You must answer people according to what they say to you. Please do not be shy!" He carefully told her what to do. Oh, I hope they get on together! he said to himself. He knew that it would be embarrassing to reveal Her Highness's blank innocence, but it would also be wrong of him to discourage their meeting.

Here I am soon to call on Her Highness, Murasaki reflected pensively in her east wing, but is she really above me? Yes, he kindly took me under his care at a time when my future was uncertain, but even so . . . The old poems she found herself writing out for practice would evoke whatever weighed on her mind, and she would then read her own preoccupation in them.

Genji came in, and he who found Her Highness and his daughter the Consort each charming in her own way saw that he would not feel anything like what he did for his familiar companion if hers were any common beauty: no, she really was peerless. Pride and dignity were hers to just the right degree, and vivid freshness, and all the loveliest touches of delicious grace, for she was in her richest and most glorious flower. How, he wondered, was it possible that year to year and day to day she always had about her something marvelous, something new?

She slipped her casually written sheets under the inkstone, but he found them, took them back out, and had a look. There was nothing self-conscious about her skill; her writing simply had a sweet elegance. His eye fell particularly on the lines,

> "Is autumn for me coming nearer every day? Here before my eyes
> all the green leaves on the hills have turned the colors of fall";

and beside them, as though playfully, he added,

"Why, the waterbird in the color of his wings sports the same old green;
but the hagi's lower leaves look indeed not quite the same."[68]

This distressing mood of hers betrayed itself on occasion, but he loved and admired her for keeping it so well under control.

He would not be needed that evening either in the east wing or in the main house, and he therefore managed somehow or other to set off for his secret assignation. He knew quite well that he should not and tried hard to reconsider, but he failed.

The Kiritsubo Consort loved and trusted the mistress of the east wing more than she did her own mother, and that lady felt great affection for her when she saw how exquisitely pretty she had grown up to be. Once they had chatted happily together, she opened the intervening door and went in to meet Her Highness. It was reassuring to find Her Highness so obviously still a child, and in a quiet, motherly way she took up with her the question of how they were related. Then she summoned Chūnagon, Her Highness's nurse. "I have spoken to Her Highness about the ancestry she and I share, and I regret that despite our being closely related,[69] if I may presume so to express myself, I should have felt unable to call on her except when a suitable occasion arose. I hope that from now on she will feel free to visit me and to bring any thoughtlessness of mine to my attention."

"My lady seems to feel quite abandoned after losing the protection of those whom she trusted most," Chūnagon answered, "and I am extremely grateful for your kind indulgence toward her. I am certain that His Eminence hopes you will both be close in just that way, now that he has renounced the world, and that you will be good enough also to look after my lady while she is young."

"Ever since receiving his most gracious communication I have longed to do just that, but alas, I often have occasion to regret my own lack of capacity." She spoke with a fine, quiet poise. Then she went on in a youthful tone to please Her Highness by talking about pictures and about how she herself had never been able to give up her dolls. How young she is, and how very nice! Her Highness thought, and she liked her a great deal. After that they wrote to each other often and took pleasure in each other's company whenever some charming entertainment gave them the opportunity to do so.

People gossip impudently about anyone that exalted, and they had wondered at first what thoughts the mistress of Genji's east wing might be having. "Surely His Grace no longer favors her as he used to," they said. "He must think less of her than before." When it turned out that all this had if anything heightened his devotion to her, some made much of that as well, but such pleasant relations between the two ladies then put an end to all these rumors and restored a happy harmony.

In the tenth month the mistress of the east wing dedicated an image of the

---

68. "I have not changed at all, nor ever will. It is your feelings that have changed." The "waterbird" (*mizu-tori*) is the male mandarin duck, which has a bar of deep green on its wings.

69. More literally, Murasaki says figuratively that she and Onna San no Miya sport the same headdress (*kazashi*), referring to *Gosenshū* 809, by Ise: "If you come to Yoshino, which to me is home, I shall be wearing the same headdress as you."

Buddha Yakushi at Genji's temple on Saga Moor, to honor his fortieth year. She had planned a discreet event, since he had forbidden anything too grand. The style of the image, the scripture boxes, and the wrappings[70] suggested paradise itself. The prayers offered were ample indeed, for they included the Sutra of the Victorious King, the Diamond Wisdom Sutra, and the Sutra of Eternal Life.[71] A great many of the senior nobles were present. The temple was extremely handsome, and the many sights along the way, including the path there through the fields and beneath trees in their autumn colors, no doubt helped also to encourage them to attend. There was a great clatter of horses and carriages passing each other on their way across meadows withered by frost. Each lady from Rokujō had commissioned her own solemn scripture reading.

The fast[72] was over on the twenty-third, and Rokujō was already so full that the sponsor held the banquet at Nijō, which she considered her home. She made there the robes and everything else required, and the other ladies contributed whatever else they could, each as she pleased. The wings, which had been given over to gentlewomen's rooms, were cleared to provide space for entertaining the privy gentlemen, the Commissioners,[73] the Rokujō household officers, and even the servants in grand style. The extension in the main house was done up as usual for such an occasion and furnished with a mother-of-pearl throne. In the west room there were twelve costume tables, each bearing the customary summer and winter clothing and nightclothes, and decorously covered with purple figured silk so that one could not tell what was underneath. The two accessory tables before the seat of honor were covered with Chinese silk that darkened in color toward the bottom. The blossom-foot aloeswood stand for headdress flowers, with its golden birds perched on silver branches, was from the Kiritsubo Consort; Akashi had had it made according to her own profoundly ingenious design.[74] It was His Highness of Ceremonial[75] who had seen to the four folding screens behind the seat of honor. Their paintings showed the four seasons, as one would expect, but they were extremely ingenious, and their mountains, valleys, and waters had a pleasing freshness of invention. Two pairs of cabinets supporting chests full of things stood against the north wall. The other furnishings were the usual ones. The senior nobles, the Ministers of the Left and Right, His Highness of Ceremonial, and so on were seated in the south aisle, and of course every gentleman of lesser rank was present as well. To the left and right of the stage there were curtained-off spaces for the musicians, while to the east and west there stood in rows eighty sets of rice dumplings and forty chests of gift cloth.

70. *Chisu*, the cloth wrappings for the sutra scrolls.
71. In Japanese the Konkōmyō saishōō-kyō, which promotes the peace and stability of the realm; the Kongō hannya haramitta-kyō, which teaches enlightenment as achieved by practice of the Buddha's teaching; and the Issai nyorai kongō jumyō darani-kyō, which promises to those who read it long life and eternal freedom from the three evil realms of transmigration. These sutras serve to pray for peace in the realm and for Genji's felicity in this life and the afterlife.
72. The days of fasting associated with observances at the temple.
73. *Taifu*, the privy gentlemen who ran the households of the highest nobles.
74. An early commentary suggests that the stand bore a "mountain," also of aloes heartwood, from which the silver "branches" grew; and that the golden birds held the headdress flowers in their beaks. The stand's "blossom feet" are *kesoku*, legs that end in a flowerlike form.
75. Murasaki's father.

Rice dumpling

The dancers and musicians arrived at the hour of the Sheep.[76] They performed "Ten Thousand Years" and "The Royal Deer," and then toward sundown danced the Koma prelude,[77] followed by the rarely seen "Twin Dragons." When it was over, the Counselor and the Intendant of the Gate Watch went down into the garden and danced a little encore,[78] after which they disappeared among the autumn trees. The delighted gentlemen were sorry to see them go. Those who remembered "Blue Sea Waves" on that marvelous evening of Emperor Suzaku's excursion found them both worthy of their fathers, whom they equaled in reputation, looks, and wit and slightly surpassed in rank and office—which in view of their ages suggested that their birth had long destined them to such heights. Genji was moved nearly to tears, and many memories returned to him.

When night came, the musicians withdrew. The senior officers of the household led them to the chests, and each received his gift. Seen against the garden hill as they passed along the lake, the white garments across their shoulders looked like the feather raiment of cranes enjoying their thousand years of life. The gentlemen's music then began, and it, too, was delightful. Genji had the stringed instruments from the Heir Apparent; the *biwa* and *kin* came from His Cloistered Eminence's palace and the *sō no koto* from His Majesty. All had a tone that recalled times gone by, and Genji, joining in the concert as he rarely did anymore, found himself remembering how His Late Eminence had looked at one time or another, and his own life at court, and he reflected with bitter sorrow and regret: *If only Her Cloistered Eminence had lived, I would have given her a celebration like this one myself! How could I have shown her otherwise how much she meant to me?*

Her Cloistered Eminence's absence cast a pall over life for His Majesty, too, and the passing years only made him feel more troubled that he could not, as he should, show Genji all the respect that was a father's due. He had decided that the present celebration would give him an opportunity to visit Genji this year, but Genji repeatedly advised him against any course of action that people might find disturbing, and he had been disappointed to have to give up the idea.

After the twentieth of the twelfth month Her Majesty withdrew from the palace, and as her last act of devotion on his behalf for the year she commissioned scripture chanting at the seven great temples of Nara,[79] to which she had distributed four thousand bolts of cloth; and she gave out four hundred bolts of silk to forty temples closer to the City. She recognized her debt to him and had looked forward to showing him her gratitude whenever circumstances might allow her to do so, for she knew that she would have done no less for her mother and father if they had still been alive; but Genji's severe remarks even to His Majesty had obliged her to give up most of her plans. "What I gather from past example is that after celebrating

---

76. About 2:00 P.M.
77. A "Korean" musical piece that served as a prelude to "Twin Dragons."
78. *Iriaya*, a sort of encore normally done by the dancers themselves after finishing a programmed piece.
79. These included the famous Tōdaiji, Kōfukuji, and Hōryūji.

one's fortieth year one can seldom expect to live much longer, and I should therefore prefer you on this occasion to curtail all ostentatious display and to save yourself for celebrations yet to come." Those had been his words, but His Majesty still
meant to mark the occasion with due solemnity.

The main house of Her Majesty's quarter was decorated for an event that had
all the grandeur of the earlier ones.[80] The rewards for the senior nobles and so on
emulated those specified for major court festivals; Their Highnesses received
women's gowns, while gentlemen of the fourth rank qualified for Consultant, as well
as privy gentlemen in His Majesty's service, got a white, layered long dress and also
a roll of silk. The costumes were extremely beautiful, and famous sashes and swords
inherited from the Late Heir Apparent[81] also gave the occasion a moving touch.
The event seems to have brought together every celebrated property from earlier
reigns. The old tales make a great thing of the gifts presented on such occasions,
but such lists are a bore, and I could not possibly go through all the people to whom
Genji was obliged to make them.

His Majesty could not accept giving up the plan he had formed, and he entrusted the Counselor with executing it. The incumbent in the post of Right Commander had recently resigned because of illness, and His Majesty had intended to
award the office to the Counselor in conjunction with his own event for Genji, but
he now made the appointment immediately. Genji thanked him, but with modest
circumspection. "I cannot help feeling that this sudden honor is premature," he said,
"since it far exceeds what he deserves."

The new Commander oversaw the preparations in the northeast quarter.[82] He
tried to keep them discreet, but this was no ordinary ceremony, and he brought in
for it and the others taking place in the other quarters whatever was needed from
the Court Repository and the Imperial Granary.[83] The Secretary Captain[84] received
His Majesty's order to provide the rice dumplings and so on, just as for an event at
the palace. Present were five Princes, the Ministers of the Left and Right, two Grand
Counselors, three Counselors, five Consultants, and almost all the privy gentlemen
who served His Majesty, the Heir Apparent, and His Eminence. The Chancellor
had seen to the room's decoration and furnishings, under His Majesty's detailed
guidance, and he joined the company today at His Majesty's express command.
Gratified and astonished, His Grace took his seat as well. They faced each other in
the chamber of the main house. His Excellency, by now a handsome and imposingly weighty figure, visibly enjoyed the fullness of prosperity and success, while
His Grace was still the young Genji of old. The four folding screens behind him
bore inscriptions in His Majesty's own hand, on grass green Chinese figured silk,
written over paintings that were also of exceptional interest. In ink and line the
writing had a dazzling quality that the identity of the writer only enhanced. The
stringed and wind instruments, and the cabinets upon which they rested, all came

80. Tamakazura's in the first month and Murasaki's in the tenth.
81. The Empress's (Akikonomu's) father.
82. Hanachirusato's.
83. Kokusōin, the storehouse for rice and cash collected from the Inner Provinces (Kinai).
84. Does not otherwise figure in the tale.

from the Chamberlains' Office. The day's events were particularly impressive because the Commander's personal authority was now much greater than before. The sun set while men from the Left and Right Imperial Stables and the officers of the Six Guards Headquarters[85] ranged forty horses before the guests, in order of the guests' precedence.

Dances like "Ten Thousand Years" and "Our Sovereign's Grace" were done as usual, although only in token form, because His Excellency's presence inspired them all to put their hearts instead into the music that he so much enjoyed. His Highness of War as always took the *biwa*, for he was a rare and peerless master. Genji received the *kin*, and His Excellency the *wagon*. Genji found His Excellency's music very fine and moving indeed, perhaps because they had been playing so long together, and he therefore kept back nothing of his own mastery of the *kin*, which at his touch gave forth the most marvelous sound. Then they talked over old times and drank often, since the ties between them at last encouraged the friendliest intimacy, until the pleasures of the occasion moved them to drunken tears that they could not withhold.

The dance "Ten Thousand Years"

As parting gifts Genji sent out to His Excellency's carriage a superb *wagon*, together with a Koma flute of which he was fond, and a pair of red sandalwood boxes, one containing admirable examples of calligraphy from China and the other similarly fine pieces of running script from Japan. The men from the Right Imperial Stables, there to fetch the horses, boisterously danced a Koma piece. The officers from the Six Guards Headquarters received their rewards from the Commander. Genji had discouraged any pomp or display, for he wished to keep everything simple, but his close ties with the Emperor, the Heir Apparent, the Retired Emperor, and the Empress as well gave him such overwhelming prestige that a magnificent tribute to him had seemed inevitable. It was disappointing that the Commander should be his only son, but the young man enjoyed particularly high regard among his peers and stood alone in ability, although the destiny consequent upon the fiercely jealous rivalry between his mother and the Rokujō Haven had nonetheless declared itself in the end in various ways.[86]

The Commander was dressed that day by the lady of the northeast quarter, while one gathers that his wife at Sanjō prepared the rewards. Seen from the northeast quarter, these occasional festive events, even the prettiest and most intimate of them, seemed very far off indeed, and the lady there had wondered whether she

---

85. Hyōefu (the Watch), Emonfu (the Gate Watch), and Konoefu (the Palace Guards), each of which was divided into separate units of Left and Right.

86. In particular, Akikonomu, the daughter of the Rokujō Haven (who spent many years at Ise), is now Empress, while Yūgiri is a mere commoner.

would ever be admitted to such grand company; but her tie to the Commander accomplished this for her very well.

The New Year came. The Kiritsubo Consort's time was approaching, and from the first of the first month Genji accordingly commissioned continuous performance of the Great Rite. Prayers beyond counting were made at temples and shrines everywhere. That appalling experience[87] had instilled in him a terror of these things, and despite regret and disappointment he was glad that neither the mistress of his east wing nor the others had been through anything similar. The Consort was so slight that he was already thoroughly apprehensive about how she would get on, when to general consternation a striking change came over her in the second month, and she became quite unwell. The diviners recommended penance for her elsewhere,[88] but he knew that he would worry if she were to go anywhere else, and he therefore moved her to the middle wing of Akashi's quarter. The residence consisted of two large wings surrounded by several galleries[89] along which rows of earthen altars were now erected, and powerful ascetics were summoned to work their rites loudly before them.[90] The Consort's mother knew that her own fate hung in the balance, and she was very anxious indeed.

The venerable Nun must have been *very* old and odd by now, because for her it was like a dream to see her granddaughter this way, and she went straight to be with her in the hope that the event would be soon. The Consort's mother had never really told her daughter about the past, despite her long attendance on her, and the Nun, bursting with happiness, therefore approached her now and described in a trembling voice, amid frequent tears, what their life had once been. The Consort at first thought her strange and horrid and only stared, but she *had* heard talk of such an old woman and was nice to her after all. The Nun went on about the circumstances surrounding her birth and about how His Grace had lived there on the shore. "We were very upset when the time came for him to go back to the City, because we thought that that was the end and that it was all over between them, but then *you* came along with your marvelous destiny and changed everything!" She was weeping.

Yes, the Consort said to herself, I would never have known the sad story of my past if she had not told it to me! She began to cry. I really have been in no position to flaunt myself—it is the mistress of His Grace's east wing who brought me up to be more or less what people expect. I think myself superior, and even in service at the palace I have looked down on everyone else. How excessively proud I have been! I suppose that that is just what people have been secretly saying about me. At last she knew who she was. She had always known that her mother was not as highly considered as she might be, but as far as her own birth was concerned, she had never associated it

---

87. Witnessing Aoi's death after giving birth.

88. They fear that she is subject to a baneful influence of the kind that Genji avoided in "The Broom Tree" by going to spend the night at Utsusemi's house.

89. This description is hard to picture. Granted that the dwelling lacks a main house (*shinden*) and consists of two "wings" (*tai*), it is hard to know what the "middle wing" (*naka no tai*) might be. It is also hard to be sure what "surrounded by several galleries" means.

90. The earthen altars are for the burning of *goma* ritual fires before paintings of the five deities of the Great Rite.

with anywhere so remote. Perhaps she had simply given the matter too little thought. It distressed her to learn that the Novice was living beyond the world, like an immortal, and this and everything else she had heard troubled her greatly.

She was lost in melancholy musings when her mother arrived and the ascetics gathered from here and there to pursue their clamorous midday rites. She had none of her women with her, and the Nun had seized this chance to come very close to her indeed.

"This will not do!" her mother chided the Nun. "You are not to wait on my lady without a low curtain of your own before you!⁹¹ With this wind a gap could blow open. Behave like a physician, for example. It is too long since you were young." She was quite annoyed.

The Nun, who in her own estimation was behaving perfectly well and who could hardly hear, only nodded and answered, "Beg pardon?" Actually, at sixty-five or sixty-six she was not as old as all that, and she wore her habit with sprightly distinction. Her swollen eyes, glistening with tears, made it plain that she had unfortunately been dwelling on the past.

The Consort's mother's heart sank. "She must have been onto some sort of nonsense about years ago. I suppose she has been telling you tall tales about the past, fed by preposterous fantasies of her own. She makes me wonder whether I am dreaming!" She smiled ruefully as she watched the Consort, so graceful and pretty, and now so unusually preoccupied and subdued. She could hardly believe that a young lady this exalted was her daughter. It must have upset her to hear about that sad business, she reflected. I was meaning to tell her myself once she rose to the very heights. Fortunately, this will not convince her that she cannot do so, but the poor thing must be feeling very downcast.

Once the prayer rites were over, she had refreshments set before the Consort and pressed her sympathetically to take some. The helplessly weeping Nun gazed at her granddaughter in wonder and delight. Face smiling and mouth hideously agape, she was all damp and puckery about the eyes. She ignored her daughter's glances of sharp disapproval.

> *"Ripples of old age come wrinkling upon a shore generously blessed:*
> *who could blame such an old nun for constantly dripping brine?*⁹²

Once upon a time," she said, "they used to put up with old people like me!"
  The Consort wrote on a piece of paper that lay beside her inkstone,

> *"I would have that nun dripping brine still be my guide to far Awaji,*
> *that I might see for myself that reed hut upon the shore."*⁹³

---

91. The Consort is sitting behind a curtain, and the Nun has seated herself directly in front of it. The Nun cannot see the Consort, but the Consort might see the Nun, who is unsightly because of her age.

92. "Who could blame an old woman for weeping with joy, now that she at last has reason to be glad she has lived this long?"

93. "Reed hut" (*tomaya*) is a poetic convention for any dwelling on the shore; this one is the house where the Consort was born.

This was too much for her mother, who wept.

> *"He who left this world to remain forevermore on Akashi Shore,*
> *even he, cannot have cleared all the darkness from his heart!"*

With words like these she sought to disguise her tears.

What a shame I remember nothing of that dawn when we left him there! the Consort said to herself.

She gave birth easily, a day or two after the tenth of the third month, and despite all the earlier anxiety she suffered no great pain. Her mother was utterly delighted, since to crown it all the baby was a boy, and Genji felt relief at last.

A glittering series of birth celebrations would certainly have enlivened the Nun's old age, but otherwise they would have been wasted in that cramped, secluded house, and the Consort therefore prepared to move back to the southeast quarter. The lady from the east wing there had come for the birth, and she looked lovely all in white,[94] holding the young prince in her arms as though she were his grandmother. Everything moved and fascinated her, since she had never been through this herself or even been present on such an occasion. She continued holding the little boy, although he was still difficult to manage, and his real grandmother allowed her to do so and busied herself meanwhile with looking after his baths.[95] A Dame of Staff—the one who had brought the Heir Apparent notice of his appointment[96]—oversaw them, and she was moved to see the Consort's mother act so scrupulously as Bath Nurse,[97] since she knew something of her background and was ready to deplore any lapse. Instead, however, the lady showed such surprising distinction that she seemed obviously born to her good fortune after all.

There would be no point in recounting every ceremony that took place during this time.

On the sixth day the Consort returned to her proper home. His Majesty sponsored the birth celebration on the night of the seventh day. Perhaps it was on His Eminence's behalf, since he had now renounced the world, that an imperial order appointed the Chamberlain Controller from the Chamberlains' Office to arrange the event in grand style. Her Majesty provided the gowns that the guests received as rewards, and she had them made even more beautifully than for an occasion at court. The Princes and the Ministers of State, too, all hastened to do their part magnificently.

Genji never tried to keep these festivities simple; on the contrary, they displayed such unheard-of grandeur that the finer, quieter touches of elegance, ones that should have been noted and passed on to generations to come, drew no atten-

94. The new mother and others assisting at the birth dressed in white for the first nine days of the child's life, and all the curtains and so on in the room were also white.

95. A newborn imperial son was bathed morning and evening for the first seven days after the birth.

96. An explanatory translation of the woman's title, Senji ("decree [of appointment as Heir Apparent]"). Her chief role in the ritualized bathing is normal.

97. Mukaeyu, the "assistant" role in the bathing. The fact that this part was normally taken by one of the mother's senior gentlewomen underscores both the Akashi lady's prudent modesty and her still-ambiguous standing.

tion at all. Soon enough he, too, held the young Prince in his arms. "The Commander has several by now," he remarked, "but he still prefers me not to see them, and I must say I hold that against him. Look what a dear little boy I have anyway, though!" No wonder he was so taken with him!

Day by day the young prince grew as though being stretched. Genji called no untried nurses and so on, and he chose from among the women in his service only the quickest and most distinguished. Wise and dignified though she was, the Consort's mother effaced herself whenever necessary and never indulged in any show of pride, for which everyone praised her. The mistress of the east wing already knew her informally, and the young Prince's charm now turned her old reproachful feelings to full warmth and respect. She who so loved children busied herself making godchild dolls and whatnot with her own hands, like a girl. Day and night she spent her time looking after the baby. The Nun with her old-fashioned ways was extremely put out that she might not see the young Prince as she pleased, and alas, now that she *had* seen him, she missed him so much that her very life seemed to hang in the balance.

When the news reached Akashi, no aspiration to sage detachment could quell the old man's joy. "Now I can leave this world behind with a light heart," he told his disciples. He turned his house into a temple, to which he assigned all the surrounding rice fields and similar wealth. He meant next to shut himself away at a place where no one would find him again, one he had long ago made his own, too far into the province's mountains ever to be frequented. One little concern remained, but after all his years at Akashi he simply left that to the buddhas and gods and moved away. In recent years he had sent a messenger to the City only when one was specially needed, although he had had the messengers from there take back at least a line of advice on one thing or another for the Nun. Now, as a last gesture to the world he was leaving, he addressed a letter to his daughter.

"For some years now I have inhabited the same world as you and yet felt somehow quite different from before, which is why I have neither written, except as necessary, nor sought to learn your news. Letters in *kana* take me time to read,[98] and moments spent otherwise than calling the Name are moments lost. That is why I have sent you nothing. I gather that your daughter is now with the Heir Apparent and that she has borne him a son. That is a very great joy. I say that because although I am only a mountain ascetic and desire no worldly glory, I must confess that I have for many years thought of nothing but you, even during my day and night devotions, and that my prayers have been for you, to the neglect of any longing of mine for the dew on the lotus.

"My dear, one night in the second month of the year when you were born, I had a dream. My right hand held up Mount Sumeru,[99] and to the mountain's right and left the sun and moon shed their brightness on the world. I myself stood below,

---

98. His wife or daughter would write in *kana*, the purely phonetic script, while he now reads nothing but the Chinese of the Buddhist scriptures.
99. The central mountain of the Buddhist cosmos.

in the shadows under the mountain, and their light did not reach me. I then set the mountain afloat on a vast ocean, boarded a little boat, and rowed away toward the west. That was my dream. I then woke up, and that very morning I, even I, began to hope, although I also wondered at heart why I should look forward to anything so grand. Then you were conceived. After that, both secular writings and the scriptures gave me so many reasons to believe in dreams that although unworthy I was awed, and I sought to rear you fittingly. The task seemed far beyond my poor means, however, and that is why I undertook the journey here, where I stooped to absorb myself in the affairs of this province and gave up any hope that old age might return me to the City. During my time on this shore I said a great many prayers in my heart, for you were all my hope. Happily, the time has now come for you to give thanks in return for their fulfillment. Please do so above all at the Sumiyoshi Shrine, as soon as our young lady has become Mother of the Realm and all that I have prayed for is accomplished. Doubt is no longer possible. Now that my consuming desire is all but satisfied, and I may trust in rebirth at the highest of the nine degrees in paradise, westward beyond the one hundred thousand buddha-lands, I shall pursue my practice among the pure trees and waters of the most distant mountains while I await my call to the lotus throne.[100]

> "That dawn is coming, when the long-awaited light will shine forth at last,
>   and I would now have you know all I dreamed so long ago."

Here he had written the month and day.

"Do not seek to know the month and day of my death," he had added. "Why should you wear mourning as people always do? Reflect that you are a transformed presence[101] and simply work for an old monk's benefit.[102] Whatever pleasures this life offers, do not forget the life to come. We shall meet again, as long as I can reach the place where I long to go. Have faith that we shall be together when you reach the shore beyond this world."

With his letter came a large, sealed aloeswood box containing the texts of all the prayers that he had addressed to the Sumiyoshi Shrine.

To the Nun he had sent only a few words. "On the fourteenth day of this month I shall leave my humble dwelling and go on into the depths of the mountains, where I shall leave my worthless body to feed the bears and the wolves. You must remain patiently as you are until the time I anticipate has come.[103] We shall meet again in the light." That was all.

---

100. The paradise of the Buddha Amida is scripturally defined as lying westward beyond one hundred thousand intervening worlds, each with its own buddha. At the highest of nine different levels of birth into paradise, the soul rests immediately upon a fully open lotus flower and directly witnesses the presence of Amida and the glories of his land. At the lower levels the soul is born into a more or less tightly closed lotus bud and must wait a greater or lesser time before the bud opens.

101. *Henge*, the temporary, limited, "transformed" manifestation of a divine being.

102. "Do things to encourage my birth into paradise: chanting the name of Amida, copying sacred texts, commissioning prayer rites, and so on."

103. When his granddaughter becomes Empress and her son is appointed Heir Apparent.

Document box

The Nun read the letter and then questioned the holy monk who had brought it. "He went off into the trackless mountains three days after he wrote it," the monk replied. "We went to the foot of them with him, but there he turned us all back and continued on with only one monk and two acolytes. I had thought after he renounced the world that we would never grieve again, but there was more sorrow to come. He put his *kin* and *biwa* beside him—the ones he played so often, sitting against a pillar between spells of practice—and drew music from each once more; then he bade farewell to the Buddha[104] and left them as offerings in the chapel. He left most of his other possessions, too, as offerings, and what he did not he gave out to the more than sixty disciples[105] who were so close to him through the years, each according to his station. Finally, he sent me with what remained to you in the City. Then at last he withdrew into the clouds and mists of a certain distant mountain, leaving us who remained in the house to our grief." The worthy speaker had gone down there from the City as a boy and would now stay on as an old man, and he was desolate. Even the Buddha's wise disciples, so deeply versed in his teaching upon Vulture Peak, were stricken with grief when his flame expired, and the Nun's sorrow naturally exceeded all measure.

The Consort's mother was in the southeast quarter, and she came quietly when word of the letter reached her. She could not very well do so without adequate reason, for she now upheld the utmost gravity of deportment, but she gathered that this was something disturbing, and she was sufficiently concerned to make a discreet visit. She found her mother overcome, and she could not withhold her tears either when she drew up the lamp and read the letter. Memories—things that could have meant nothing to anyone else—came to her out of the past, and she who had always missed her father so much realized with a bitter pang that she would never see him again. She could not stop weeping. Her father's account of his dream gave her faith in the future, and yet she also thought, Why, then, all my misery, when he sent me off in that strange way of his to a place where I should never have gone, came from his trust in a little dream and his hopes for the heights it promised! At last she had understood.

The Nun spoke after a long silence. "Thanks to you, he and I were able to pride ourselves on good fortune far beyond what we deserved; and great griefs and worries, yes, we had those as well. I know that he had not distinguished himself, but

104. The main sacred image in his chapel.
105. His household staff, who all took Buddhist vows with their master. The speaker is one of them.

it still seemed a strange, strange fate to leave our home in the City for obscurity far away, and even then I never imagined that he and I might be separated, since I believed all those years that after this life we would share the same lotus. Then, suddenly, that extraordinary thing happened. My reward for returning to the world I left has made me happy, but at the same time I have always missed him and worried about him, and it is very hard to have in the end to leave this life without seeing him again. His peculiarities led him to rail against the world even when he was in it, but still, we were young and trusting, and no couple could have been more devoted. We shared a very deep faith in each other. Why must I be parted from him, when he is still so close that his letters come quickly?" She wept bitterly.

"It means nothing to me to have risen above others in the end," the Consort's mother said. "No glory I enjoy can make any difference, when I matter so little anyway, but what is cruel is that now I shall never know what became of him. I suppose his destiny explains everything that has happened, yet it seems such a waste that he has vanished forever into the mountains and that since life is always so fragile, he will soon be no more!"

They continued their sad conversation through the night. "His Grace saw me there yesterday," she said, "and I will seem delinquent for suddenly slipping away. For me that hardly matters, but for the sake of His Highness's mother I cannot simply do as I please." She went back at daybreak.

"How is His Highness?" the Nun asked, shedding fresh tears. "I so long to see him!"

"And you shall, I am sure, very soon. My lady the Consort seems to remember you fondly. His Grace has apparently remarked that although he does not wish to peer into the future, he hopes that, assuming all goes well, you will live to see the day. I wonder what he means."

The Nun smiled. "There!" she said happily. "I knew it! My destiny is so unlike anyone else's!"

The Consort's mother set off to join her daughter and had the box of prayers brought with her.

The Heir Apparent often begged his Consort to return to the palace. "I can hardly blame him," Lady Murasaki said. "He must be very concerned about her, especially after this remarkable event." She prepared to have the young Prince quietly visit his father.

The Heir Apparent's Haven[106] preferred to stay where she was for the time being, having learned her lesson about the difficulty of obtaining leave to withdraw. What she had just been through, a frightening experience for someone so young, had slimmed her features a little and given her a marvelous elegance. "She has not yet recovered, and she should not go until she is able to look after herself properly," her mother declared, but Genji disagreed. "With her new fineness of feature," he said, "he will only be better pleased with her than ever."

---

106. The Akashi Daughter, who, as the new mother of an imperial child, is first referred to here by the title Miyasudokoro.

One quiet evening, after the mistress of the east wing and her women had gone home, the Consort's mother went to her daughter to tell her about the box of prayers. "My lady, I ought not to show you these until thanks to you they have been fully answered, but life is too uncertain for that. There are certain little things that I believe I should tell you now, you see, while I still have my wits about me, because if anything were to happen to me before you are fully able to make up your mind on your own, it might not be possible for me, considering who I am, to have you beside me at the end. I know that the writing is strange and forbidding,[107] but please read it anyway. Keep the prayer sheets in a nearby cabinet and go through them when you can, and please do as they say.[108] Do not discuss them with anyone. Now that I have seen you come this far, I, too, would prefer to renounce the world, for I am by no means at peace. You must never take lightly the goodwill of the lady of the east wing. When I see what a rare wonder she is, I only hope that she will enjoy a life far longer than mine. As to my staying with you or not, my condition is too humble to allow me to do so, and that is why I ceded you to her in the first place. I never imagined, though, that she would do as much for you as she has; I always assumed that in that respect she would be like anyone else. As things are, I have no anxiety about you, your upbringing, or your future." She went on this way at length.

The Haven listened with tears in her eyes. Her mother, who should have been entirely at ease with her, was always correct and extremely deferential. The letter was written in a horribly forbidding hand on five or six sheets of thick Michinokuni paper, yellowed with age but still beautifully scented. She was deeply moved, and her profile, with her by now quite damp sidelocks, had a sweetly noble grace.

Genji had been with Her Highness,[109] and he now entered so suddenly through the panel between them that she could not hide the papers; she only drew up a standing curtain to conceal at least her person. "Is your little Prince awake?" he asked. "I cannot be away for a moment without missing him."

The Haven failed to answer him. "My lady has sent him to the east wing," her mother replied.

"What a strange thing to do! Why, she has almost appropriated him, and the way she hardly ever allows him out of her arms, she is practically asking constantly to have to change her wet clothes! What could have induced you to let her have him so casually? She should come here if she wants to see him!"

"You are too unkind! How *can* you talk that way? Why, there would be nothing wrong with her looking after him even if he were a girl, and a boy, however exalted, is perfectly all right![110] Please do not put any such cruel ideas into my lady's head!"

Genji smiled. "I see I need only leave the two of you to sort things out on your own. What nonsense to imagine I go around putting ideas in people's heads! *You* seem to be the ones who creep off to hide and say awful things about me!" He swept

107. The Akashi Novice's letter, accompanying the prayer texts, contains a lot of Chinese characters.
108. They enjoin acts of thanks, especially pilgrimages, for the fulfillment of the Novice's prayers.
109. Onna San no Miya.
110. A girl would normally be kept more protected and sheltered, but Murasaki is after all the child's adoptive grandmother.

the curtain aside, and there she was, leaning against a pillar of the chamber, looking very handsome and dauntingly composed. There, too, was the box, which she had felt it would be undignified to conceal in haste.

"What is that box? It must mean something. You must have a long, long poem from some lover of yours in there."

"You are dreadful! You seem to be a boy again, and sometimes you say the most impossible things!" She was smiling, but she and her daughter were clearly upset as well. Genji cocked his head quizzically. "These are records of prayer offerings made and of vows not yet acknowledged.[111] They came up quietly from the cave[112] at Akashi," she said, embarrassed. "I thought that I might ask you to look at them if I found the moment to bring them to your attention, but this is not the time, and I should be obliged if you were to leave the box unopened."

He understood that she might well feel deeply about the matter. "What practices he must have done! Having lived a long life, he must over all those years have amassed a great deal of merit. Some people in this world may have taste and learning, but however clever they may be, they turn out on closer acquaintance to go after all only so far, being perhaps too deeply mired in the profane world, and they certainly come nowhere near *him*. What an extraordinarily discerning, far-seeing man! He never put on holy airs or made himself out to be otherworldly, but underneath he seemed to live fully in the realm beyond our senses, and by now, with all the ties that bound him gone, he has certainly renounced this world for good. I would like very much to go quietly to see him, if only I were at liberty to do so."

"It appears that he has left his home and withdrawn to a mountain so remote that no birds sing there."[113]

"Then this is his last testament! Have you been in touch with him? I wonder how your mother feels. Her tie with him must be even stronger than a daughter's to her father." There were tears in his eyes. "The more I learn of him over the years, the more I feel strangely fond of him, and I can imagine how deeply you must be affected, since you were so much closer to him."

It occurred to the Consort's mother that her father's account of his dream might explain many things for Genji. "I have a letter from him, so eccentrically written that it might as well be in Siddham,[114] and I think that some of it might interest you. I knew when I left that I would not see him again, but it is true that he still means a great deal to me." She wept decorously.

Genji took the letter. "Why, the writing has great authority! I see nothing vague or decrepit about it. In calligraphy as in so many other things he could have been called a master; all he lacked, really, were some of the practical skills of life. I gather that something happened during the period of wholly wise and valuable

---

111. *Inori no kanju*, records of what scriptures were read when, and how many times, to pray for the fulfillment of the Novice's hopes; and *madashiki gan*, prayers the fulfillment of which has not yet been acknowledged by a pilgrimage of thanks.

112. A humbly figurative expression for her father's house.

113. *Kokinshū* 535: "Would that she understood the depth of my love, deep as a mountain fastness where one hears no song from the birds of the air."

114. Bonji, the Indian script known to educated Buddhist priests, who used it for ritual purposes.

service that the Minister his ancestor devoted to the realm, and that that is why his line died out, although one can hardly say that he had no successor on the female side. All that, I suppose, is thanks to his prayers."

He wiped the tears from his eyes and considered the part about the dream. People criticized him for his strangely overweening ambition, he thought, and I myself could not help feeling that I should never, never have done it. It was not until our little girl was born that I knew how powerful the bond between us was, and even then I had no idea what lay behind it in the unseen past. So this was what claimed his faith and fed his improbable hope! It is for *him* that I unjustly suffered such trials and wandered in exile! What can those prayers of his possibly have been? He took up the papers with great curiosity and also with reverence.

"I myself have something to add to these for you,"[115] he said to the Consort. "I shall let you know about it soon." He went on, "Now that you have some idea what lies in your past, do not for a moment take lightly the goodwill of the lady in my east wing. A stranger's passing kindness, or a thoughtful word or two, may make more difference than any natural or inevitable tie, and I can assure you that she is no less devoted to you than your mother, even though your mother is now always beside you. It might seem wise to conclude from well-known examples[116] that the goodwill of someone like that is all on the surface, but even if that were so, and her intentions were in fact not kind, you could easily make her feel guilty about her treatment of you and so change her mind by ignoring it and being quite open with her. The nicest people in the world have always had their fallings-out, but example suggests that they always manage to get on when one or the other is truly blameless. Someone who is always touchy, someone who makes no effort to please and who spurns other people, is difficult to like and also thoroughly inconsiderate. Not that my experience is that wide, but it seems to me when I consider the way different people are, that they all have *something* to say for themselves in taste or accomplishment. Everyone has some sort of merit—no one has nothing to offer at all—but you know, when you go seriously about looking for just the right companion in life, it is still not easy to make the choice. When it comes simply to being nice through and through, I think the lady of my east wing here can be described as genuinely good and kind. Some people, though wellborn, are still all too heedless and capricious, and that is a very great shame." The Consort's mother could easily imagine who *that* meant.

Genji lowered his voice to continue, "Now, *you* seem to understand certain things, and that is excellent. The two of you must be friends and look after our Consort together."

"You need hardly say that, because the more I see of her rare quality, the more often I talk about it. She would never have acknowledged me as she has done if she objected to me or was offended by my existence. On the contrary, she is so kind that I am actually embarrassed. It pains me a great deal anyway, when I think what

---

115. A written prayer or prayers of his own.
116. "Evil stepmother" stories.

people must be saying, that I who matter so little should still live on, but you know, she always protects me as though there were nothing wrong with me at all."

"I doubt that she really does it for you. I expect she is just concerned about our Consort, since she cannot always be with her herself, so that she leaves her to you. At the same time, though, the way you refrain from putting yourself forward or making any claims of your own does a great deal to make things go smoothly, and that pleases me very much. When someone who lacks proper sense becomes involved with someone else, the result can be unpleasant for the other person as well. It is reassuring that you are both beyond reproach in that regard." He returned to the east wing.

Yes, she thought, it is a good thing that I have tried to efface myself. Why, he seems only to think more and more highly of her! There certainly is far more to her than to most people, and it is a pleasure to see how thoroughly she deserves it. As for Her Highness, the honor he pays her is all on the surface; he can hardly be said to visit her often, and that is an affront to her pride. The two are close relatives, but she, poor thing, is after all a step higher. Such musings brought to mind the extent of her own good fortune. Things did not always go well even for them, exalted though they were, while she who could not claim to stand beside them now had nothing in life to regret. The only thing that troubled her was the thought of her father, who had gone into the mountains forever. Meanwhile her mother the Nun put her faith in the line about "sowing seeds in the garden of happiness"[117] and absorbed herself entirely in thoughts of the life to come.

The Commander could easily have aspired to Her Highness himself, and her presence so close at hand thoroughly roused him; he frequented her residence whenever the occasion allowed it, on the pretext of simple civility, and therefore came naturally to know a good deal about her. She was at all times girlishly and obliviously serene, and although His Grace's scrupulously correct treatment of her might have set an example for the ages, there was no sign that she actually meant much to him. Few of her women were really grown-up, most of them being young things with pretty faces who did little but primp and preen, and she had such a crowd of them[118] that gaiety reigned all around her; the quiet ones would not have wished to betray themselves, and if any had secret cares, such company swept them up into the same untroubled merriment as the rest. They were like children caught up day and night in youthful games, and Genji, whose nature it was to grant that there are all kinds of people in this world, allowed them their way since they so enjoyed it, but it by no means pleased him. He never tried to stop them, but he did very well at teaching Her Highness herself, and he managed to get a little sense into her.

The Commander gathered from all this that in Murasaki his father really did have someone rare. Her manner and disposition were such that in all these years she had not once started any rumor or drawn attention to herself, for she was prudent through and through; and yet she was kind as well, never stooping to belittle anyone

117. The source of the line has not been identified.
118. Probably several dozen. According to *Eiga monogatari*, Empress Akiko (Shōshi) first came to the palace with forty gentlewomen.

and behaving with enchanting grace. He would never forget that glimpse he had had of her. His wife had no great merit or any particular wit, despite his deep affection for her. Familiarity had dulled his enthusiasm now that all was settled between them, and at heart he still found it hard to turn his thoughts from the varied charms of the ladies his father had brought together—especially Her Highness, of course, since, considering her birth, his father showed no sign of any great interest in her, and he could tell that his father was only keeping up appearances. Not that he had anything untoward in mind, but he did not want to miss any chance to see her.

The Intendant of the Gate Watch, who often went to wait on His Cloistered Eminence, had seen for himself at length just how highly he valued his daughter. As soon

A man with a short bow

as those deliberations began, he had let his hopes be known, and he had gathered, too, that His Eminence did not find them impertinent. When she went to someone else, he was too bitterly disappointed to have given her up yet, and it brought him a sad sort of comfort still to have news of her through the gentlewoman whose good offices had served him then. He heard that people often said she was overshadowed even now by the mistress of Genji's east wing, and he protested frequently to Kojijū, whose mother's breast Her Highness had shared, "I may presume too greatly, but *I* would never have caused her that sort of unhappiness! Of course, I realize that I am hardly the man to aspire so high." Life being ever changing, his enduring hope was that His Grace one day might actually take the step he had planned so long.[119]

One mild day in the third month His Highness of War, the Intendant of the Gate Watch, and the rest gathered at Rokujō. Genji came out to converse with them. "Life here is so quiet that I have extremely little to occupy me lately," he said. "There is simply nothing happening, either at home or at court. How am I ever to get through these days?

"The Commander was here this morning," he added. "Where can he have disappeared to? Things are so dull that I had hoped at least to enjoy the usual smallbow archery contest.[120] The young men who are keen on that sort of thing were all here—I wish he had not gone." He was told that the Commander was off in the northeast quarter, watching a kickball game that he was having them play. "It is perhaps rather a rough game," Genji observed, "but it is lively and requires skill. Well, then, have him come here."

119. That of taking Buddhist vows.
120. The small bow (*koyumi*), used only for contests, was used in a half-kneeling position.

The Commander arrived with a crowd of young gentlemen. "Did you have them bring the ball?" Genji asked. "Are so-and-so and so-and-so with you?"

The Commander said they were.

"Why not play here?"

The east front of the main house made a discreet area for the purpose, since the Kiritsubo Consort was at the palace with the young Prince.[121] They set off to find a promising spot where the two garden streams came together. His Excellency the Chancellor's sons—the Chamberlain Consultant, the Second of the Watch, the Commissioner, and the others not yet fully grown—stood out among the rest.

The sun was beginning to sink when the perfect, windless day proved to be too much for the Chamberlain Consultant, who could no longer resist joining the game.[122] "You see?" Genji said. "The Consultant could not contain himself. Senior nobles or not, why should you young guards officers not have a bit of fun, too? At your age I hated just to sit by. It *is* undignified, though. Just look at them!"

The Commander and the Intendant went down into the garden, where they, too, looked very fine, roaming about in late-afternoon sunlight beneath the gloriously blossoming trees. Kickball is hardly a stately sport, being quite boisterous and rough, but much depends after all on where it is played and who plays it. Mists shrouded the park's lovely groves, while beneath trees abloom in many colors or just putting forth new green, young men vied for the chance to excel, forgetting that it was only a game. Each face shone with the resolve not to be bested. The Intendant of the Gate Watch stood head and shoulders above the others in skill, even though he joined them only briefly. He was a very handsome, graceful man, polished in manner and therefore all the more amusing to see when animated. Both Genji and His Highness came out to watch from the corner of the railing. There beside the cherry tree at the foot of the steps they were so intent on their sport that they had forgotten all about the flowers.

Skill told more and more, and as round followed round,[123] the ranking gentlemen became very lively, and their headdresses slipped back a little from their foreheads. The Commander well knew that for a man of his standing he was letting himself go, but to the onlookers he seemed younger and more delightful than the rest in his rather soft, cherry blossom dress cloak and with his trousers, somewhat full at the bottom, hitched up just a trifle. When cherry petals fell like snowflakes on his comely figure, spirited but not in the least unkempt, he looked up, picked off a broken branch, and sat down with it on the middle step.

The Intendant followed him. "The blossoms are scattering fast, aren't they," he said. "Like the wind, we should keep our distance."[124] He darted a sidelong glance toward where Her Highness lived, and detected presences bustling about there as

121. The Akashi Daughter, when at home, occupies the east side of the main house, while Onna San no Miya occupies the west.

122. The higher the young gentleman's rank, the less likely he is to be able to play this "somewhat rough" game without compromising his dignity.

123. A new "round" began each time the ball hit the ground.

124. *Genji monogatari kochūshakusho in'yō waka* 244: "If the blowing wind is kind, may it keep its distance from the cherry this spring, that the blossoms may not fall."

usual; the many colors visible through the blinds, or peeping out beneath them, reminded him of the gods' bright offerings in spring.[125]

He noted that they had casually moved the standing curtains aside and were indecently close to the veranda. Just then a very small and pretty Chinese cat darted out from under a blind, pursued by a somewhat larger one and followed by a practically deafening rustle of silks as the women inside rushed about in alarm and confusion. The cat must not have been quite tame yet, because it was on a long cord in which it became entangled, and its struggle to escape lifted the blind to reveal the space immediately beyond. No one moved quickly to mend the gap. The women who had just been near the pillar seemed flustered and a little frightened.

There was a curtain against the blind, and a step back from it stood a young woman in a gown.[126] In that position, on the east side of the second bay[127] west of the steps, she was in perfectly plain view. Her many layers of darker to lighter color—red plum blossom, perhaps—like the pages of a book set her off sharply, and she seemed also to have on a cherry blossom long dress in figured silk. Her hair, rich all the way down and nicely trimmed, swept cleanly and most beautifully to the floor seven or eight inches behind her. Slender and slight as she was, her skirts were quite long, and her hair and figure seen from the side had an inexpressibly elegant appeal. However, the light was failing, and the Intendant was deeply disappointed not to see more clearly into the shadows of the room. Her women must have been intent on watching the young men absorbed in their game, oblivious of the falling petals, because they did not immediately notice that they were exposed. Her look and movement when she turned to glance at the loudly mewing cat conveyed charming and utterly guileless youth.

The shocked Commander could not possibly take the liberty of going to help, and he therefore confined himself to clearing his throat in warning, at which the lady slipped back out of sight. He, too, would actually have been glad to see more of her, and he found himself sighing once the cat had been freed. The Intendant's heart, which was hers anyway, naturally all but stood still: for who else could it have been? Dressed as she was, there was no mistaking her among the others, and the sight remained graven in his heart. His expression betrayed nothing, but the Commander could not believe that he had failed to notice, and he felt sorry for her. To relieve his powerful feelings the Intendant called the cat and cuddled it, and with its delicious smell and its dear little mew it felt to him naughtily enough like its mistress herself.

Genji looked over at them. "That is no place for senior nobles to be sitting. Come with me," he said, and he went in at the front of the east wing. Everyone fol-

---

125. More literally, "the bags of [multicolored] cloth offerings to the gods in spring." These gods may have been Saohime, the goddess of spring, or the wayside gods (*saenokami*) often associated with fruitful increase.

126. There is a standing curtain up against the blind, and Onna San no Miya should at least be *sitting* behind it. However, she has stood up in an unladylike manner to see the game better. In her gown (*uchiki*) she is dressed more casually than her gentlewomen, who are probably wearing outer gowns (*uwagi*).

127. *Ma*, the space between two pillars. The "first" bay is the one occupied by the steps on which the two young men are sitting.

lowed. His Highness remained with him, and they continued their conversation. The privy gentlemen had round mats put out for them on the veranda. Camellia cakes, *nashi*,[128] tangerines, and other such things then appeared, quite informally, mixed together in box lids, and the young men ate them merrily. Then there was wine, accompanied by the appropriate dried seafood.

The thoroughly pensive Intendant gazed vacantly for the most part at the blossoming cherry tree. The Commander, who knew him, had no doubt that he was remembering the figure they had so unfortunately glimpsed beyond the blinds. He must be thinking that it was silly of her to be so near the veranda, he told himself. Why, the lady *here* would never do a thing like that! That is why she really interests my father less than her worldly standing suggests she should. This girlish oblivious-ness of hers, toward herself as well as others, is certainly charming in its way, but it is obviously worrying, too.

However, her shortcomings meant nothing to the Intendant, because through that chance gap he had actually seen her, however indistinctly, and this was a joyous omen that what he had so long desired was really to be. All he wanted was more.

Genji brought up old memories. "His Excellency the Chancellor was always trying to outdo me," he said, "but it was only at kickball that I could not keep up with him. It is just a game after all, and I doubt that there is any tradition about it to pass on, but even so, skill at it seems to run in a family. Yours is certainly far beyond mine."

"For those of us who lack real ability in office, this is hardly the sort of fame that will impress our descendants," the Intendant replied with a smile.

"Oh, come now. Outstanding achievement of any kind deserves to be passed on. Surely there is a great deal to be said for keeping it all written down in the fam-ily records." His playfulness had such charm that the Intendant wondered what could ever move any woman, once she knew him, to shift her allegiance elsewhere. What could *he* possibly do to win her respect and affection? He left with despair in his heart at the thought of being so far below her.

He and the Commander rode in the same carriage and talked all the way. "His Grace's is certainly the place to go to pass the time these days, when there is so lit-tle else to do," the Intendant began.

"He said we should come whenever we can, on a nice day like today, so as not to let the blossoms go to waste. Come there with your small bow before the month is over, if we are to enjoy what is left of spring." And so it was agreed.

Their conversation continued until they actually separated, and the Intendant then felt like pursuing the subject of Her Highness. "His Grace seems to spend all his time in his east wing," he said. "I suppose he thinks especially highly of her. I wonder how Her Highness feels. His Eminence treated her as his pride and joy, and she must miss that now. I feel sorry for her."

---

128. Camellia cakes (*tsubaimochii*) were normally served after a kickball game. Cakes of powdered gluti-nous rice and powdered cloves, sweetened with syrup from the *amachazuru* vine, were wrapped each in two camellia leaves. The fruit known as *nashi* is round and crisp like an apple but in color and taste more like a pear.

This uncalled-for remark moved the Commander to reply, "You do not understand. It is not like that at all. What makes him so particularly close to her must be the unusual manner in which he brought her up. He is extremely attentive to Her Highness in every way."

"Oh, come, stop that. I know all about it. Why, I hear that her life is a succession of humiliations. And to think that she was once so favored! I have never heard of such a thing!

> *Why should the warbler who flits so from tree to tree among the flowers*
> *each time avoid the cherry and never perch there at all?*

Imagine a bird of spring who singles out the blossoming cherry for neglect! To me it seems very, very strange!"

Oh, no! the Commander thought in response to this lyrical outburst. What a nuisance! I just knew it! And he said,

> *"How could that bright bird who has chosen for his perch a mountainside tree*
> *tire of the cherry blossoms' delicate beauty of hue?*[129]

This is absurd. Is he simply to give up all the rest?" He did not care to pursue the topic and changed the subject to make sure that it did not recur. Soon each went his way.

The Intendant was still living alone in His Excellency's east wing. Having long done so for reasons of his own, he had only himself to blame if at times he felt lost and lonely, but he was proud enough to see no reason why such a man as himself should not have what he desired. However, after that evening he became excessively gloomy and morose. When will I ever again have the glimpse of her that I had then? he wondered. A woman of one perfectly ordinary rank or another, yes, what with the vagaries of seclusions, directional taboos, and so on, I could easily find a moment at least to visit her. But there was nothing he could do. Sheltered as she was, how could he even manage to let her know of his deep devotion?

The question so tormented him that he wrote to Kojijū as before. "How little Her Highness must have thought of me when by the wind's will I made my way the other day to that noble garden! Ever since then I have been sorely troubled and have given my days to melancholy dreaming," he said, and so on.[130]

> *"From afar I spied but could never pluck that branch, source of all my sighs,*
> *so that I long for it still, blooming in the evening light."*

129. The "bright bird" (*hakodori*) is Genji, the "mountainside [dull, ordinary] tree" is Murasaki, and the "cherry blossoms" are as before Onna San no Miya.

130. His letter as reported here is self-consciously "literary" in diction, and "melancholy dreaming" alludes pointedly to *Kokinshū* 476 (also *Ise monogatari* 174, section 99), by Ariwara no Narihira. After barely glimpsing a woman through the blinds of her carriage, Narihira sent her, "For love of one I never saw yet did not fail to see, I may well give my days to melancholy dreaming."

However, Kojijū did not know what had happened the other day, and she could therefore make nothing of this except a suitor's common complaint. She took the letter to her mistress, since just then there was hardly anyone else with her. "My lady, I am sorry to say that this gentleman is appealing to something or other that he cannot forget," she said, smiling. "He seems to be in a pitiful state, and I am not quite sure myself that I shall be able to resist the urge to help him."

"What an awful thing to say!" Her Highness exclaimed, looking over the open letter. The "melancholy dreaming" brought straight to mind that shocking business of the blind, and she blushed. His Grace was always reminding her when they were together, "Please make sure that you never allow the Commander to see you. You are so young in some ways that a moment of inattention on your part might easily give him a chance to do so." It never even occurred to her when she remembered these warnings that someone *else* might have seen her, because she could think of nothing but how angry Genji would be if the Commander ever told him that such a thing had occurred. Her instant fear of Genji made it plain just what a girl she really was.

Her Highness took so much longer than usual to reply that the disappointed Kojijū, who could not very well press her further, wrote back in secret, as so often, "You were a cool one the other day. What do you mean by that 'melancholy dreaming' of yours, when I have always objected to your addressing my lady in the first place?" From there she tripped on into,

"I will have no more appeals and pathetic sighs telling me your heart
yearns for a mountain cherry so high up beyond your reach!

It is no use, I tell you!"

35

WAKANA 2

Spring Shoots II

As in "Spring Shoots I" *wakana* means "new shoots." Here, however, the word refers to a later occasion: the celebration of Retired Emperor Suzaku's fiftieth year. Genji offers him a banquet centered upon the new shoots of the traditional plants of early spring.

RELATIONSHIP TO EARLIER CHAPTERS

There is no break between "Spring Shoots I" and "Spring Shoots II," which begins in the third month of Genji's forty-first year and extends to the end of his forty-seventh.

PERSONS

His Grace, the Honorary Retired Emperor, Genji, age 41 to 47

The Intendant of the Right Gate Watch, then also Counselor,
Tō no Chūjō's eldest son, mid-20s to early 30s (Kashiwagi)

The Left Commander, then Minister of the Right,
mid-30s to early 40s (Higekuro)

The Right Commander, then also Grand Counselor,
Genji's son, 20 to 27 (Yūgiri)

His Highness, the Heir Apparent, then His Majesty, the Emperor, 15 to 21

The Mistress of Staff, Higekuro's wife, 27 to 33 (Tamakazura)

The daughter of the Left Commander, midteens to early 20s (Makibashira)

His Highness of Ceremonial, Makibashira's grandfather, 56 to 62
(Shikibukyō no Miya)

His wife (Shikibukyō no Miya no Kita no Kata)

His Highness of War, Genji's brother (Hotaru Hyōbukyō no Miya)

His Majesty, the Emperor, then His Eminence,
Retired Emperor Reizei, 23 to 29

His Excellency, the Chancellor, then His Retired Excellency (Tō no Chūjō)

The Kiritsubo Consort, Genji's daughter, 13 to 19 (Akashi no Nyōgo)

Her son, becomes the Heir Apparent

Her Majesty, the Empress, 32 to 38 (Akikonomu)

Her Highness, the Third Princess, midteens to early 20s (Onna San no Miya)

The mistress of the east wing, 33 to 39 (Murasaki)

The lady from Akashi, 32 to 38 (Akashi no Kimi)

Her mother, the Nun, mid-60s to early 70s (Akashi no Amagimi)

Nakatsukasa, Murasaki's gentlewoman

His Cloistered Eminence, Retired Emperor Suzaku, 44 to 50 (Suzaku In)

The lady of summer, mistress of the northeast quarter (Hanachirusato)

Kojijū, Onna San no Miya's gentlewoman

Her Highness, the Second Princess (Ochiba no Miya)

The Haven, Her Majesty's mother, deceased (Rokujō no Miyasudokoro)

The Nijō Mistress of Staff (Oborozukiyo)

The Haven, Ochiba no Miya's mother (Ichijō no Miyasudokoro)

His Retired Excellency's wife, Kashiwagi's mother (Shi no Kimi)

The Intendant saw what she meant. Still, he thought, what an awful thing to say! And how, I should like to know, am I to find comfort enough in mere pleasantries? Oh, for the time when I might hear a single word in her own voice without this intervening presence, and speak to her as well! On the whole he loved and admired Genji, but such ruminations as these gave an odd twist to his feelings.

On the last day of the month the young men gathered at Rokujō. The Intendant was hardly in the mood for it, but he went anyway in the hope that seeing the flowers there might make him feel better. The privy gentlemen's archery contest[1] at the palace, planned for the second month, had to general disappointment been put off because the third month was one of mourning,[2] so that they all came when Genji announced a contest of his own. The fact that the Left and Right Commanders were related[3] put their subordinate officers on their mettle, and although the occasion was to be devoted to the small bow, so many experts at standing archery[4] were present that they, too, were invited to show off their skill.

The privy gentlemen so disposed divided into two staggered lines, front and back.[5] The last of the spring mists seemed doubly precious today with sunset coming on, and the mischievous ways of the late-afternoon breeze made it more difficult than ever to leave the shelter of the blossoms. Everyone was quite drunk.

"Such beautiful prizes no doubt say a good deal about the ladies they are from, and it would be too bad to have guardsmen who can hit a willow leaf every

1. *Noriyumi*, held regularly on the eighteenth of the first month; the privy gentlemen held a similar contest a month or two later.
2. For Fujitsubo, the reigning Emperor's mother.
3. Higekuro and Yūgiri are related through Tō no Chūjō, Higekuro's father-in-law and Yūgiri's uncle.
4. *Kachiyumi*, archery with the longbow, done on foot; longbow archery from horseback was called *umayumi*.
5. They divided into two lines, Left (the odd-numbered men) and Right (even numbered). They then shot their arrows pair by pair, each pair consisting of one man from the Left and one from the Right. Since the man from the Left always stepped forward to shoot first, the Left team was called "front" (*mae*) and the Right "back" (*shirie*).

time at a hundred paces gleefully make off with them all,"[6] the Commanders remarked to each other. "I prefer a contest between men a little less expert."

They and the others stepped down into the garden. The Intendant was more pensive than the rest, and the Right Commander, who had an idea what the matter was, kept an eye on him. He is just not the man I know, he thought with a pang; this may end in disaster. They both got on extremely well, being so close that they understood one another perfectly and had only sympathy for each other's least sorrow or fancy. The Intendant, who looked on His Grace with dazzled awe, shrank from his own thoughts, since he would never have wished to give the least offense and this one was beyond the pale, but he longed in his trouble at least to have the cat—not that I could pour out my heart to it, he thought, but it would be a comfort when I am feeling lonely—and he schemed frantically to steal it for himself. That alone would be tricky enough, though.

He tried going to the Kokiden Consort's[7] to pass the time in conversation. Her admirably formal reception, and the way she kept him from actually seeing her, brought it home to him after all that if even she, despite what they were to each other, kept this sort of distance between them, why then, what just happened *was* careless and strange! However, he was too infatuated to think less well of Her Highness for it.

He next called on the Heir Apparent and examined him in the conviction that he must resemble her. His looks lacked any charm, although so great a lord of course had a grace and distinction all his own. His Majesty's cat had had a large litter of kittens that had gone off to one household and another, and His Highness had one, too. The sight of it scampering fetchingly about immediately reminded him of that other one. "I have never seen a cat with a prettier face than the one Her Highness has at Rokujō," the Intendant remarked. "I caught a little glimpse of it, you know."

His Highness, who was particularly fond of cats, pressed his visitor to tell him more. "It is a Chinese cat," the Intendant said; "it does not look at all like this one. A cat is a cat, of course, but it is so tame and friendly that it really is remarkably attractive." He hoped to make him feel like seeing it himself.

His Highness was inspired to get in touch with the Kiritsubo Consort,[8] and the cat arrived. The gentlewomen liked the dear little kitty very much, and the Intendant noted that His Highness wanted to keep it. A few days later he was back. His Eminence Suzaku had favored him and given him errands already when he was a page, and now that he was off in the mountains, the Intendant had become a familiar visitor at the Heir Apparent's.

"What a lot of cats!" the Intendant remarked, preparing to give His Highness a koto lesson. "But where is the darling I saw?" He found it and petted it affectionately.

"Yes, it *is* pretty," His Highness said. "It is not very friendly yet, but I suppose

---

6. The *Shiji* describes a warrior who could do just this. A simple guardsman would rank too low to deserve such prizes, and his triumph (that of the professional over the gentleman amateur) would be tedious.
7. His younger sister.
8. His Consort, Genji's daughter.

that is because of the new people. It does not seem that much better than the others here."

"Most cats hardly recognize anyone, but I am sure that a clever cat actually has a soul," the Intendant replied; and he went on, "You seem to have some even nicer cats here, Your Highness. May I keep this one for a while?" He felt secretly like a complete idiot for asking.

So he had the cat at last, and he got it to sleep with him at night. By day he caressed it and fussed over it. Soon it was no longer shy, and it curled up in his skirts or cuddled with him so nicely that he really did become very fond of it. He was lying against a pillar near the veranda, lost in thought, when it came to him going Meow! Meow! ever so sweetly.

My, we *are* eager, aren't we![9] He smiled and stroked it, then gazed into its eyes:

> *"You I make my pet, that in you I may have her, my unhappy love:*
> *what can you be telling me, when you come crying this way?*

This is destiny, too, I suppose." It meowed more endearingly still, and he clasped it to him.

"How odd of him all at once to take such a liking to a cat!" the old women muttered. "He never cared about such creatures before!"

The Heir Apparent sent for the cat, but the Intendant never returned it; instead he kept it to whisper sweet nothings to all by himself.

The Left Commander's wife still felt closer to the Right Commander than to the sons of His Excellency the Chancellor.[10] She was quick and easy to like, and she welcomed the Right Commander so warmly whenever he called that the company of the all too distant and formal Kiritsubo Consort[11] paled in comparison, and an unusual affection grew up between them.

She was the pride and joy of her husband, who by now had lost all interest in his first wife. It was disappointing to have had nothing but sons from her, and he wanted also to take charge of his daughter, the one of the "handsome pillar,"[12] but her grandfather would not allow it. "I can make sure no one laughs at *her*, at least," His Highness of Ceremonial would often say.

His Highness enjoyed the highest esteem, and His Majesty himself held him in exceptional favor, denying him nothing he asked for and liking him very much indeed. Always sensitive to the prevailing winds, he was the most popular and respected gentleman of his day after Genji and the Chancellor. The Commander, too, was destined to be a leading figure at court, and his daughter could hardly be taken lightly. A good many gentlemen had declared an interest in her at one time or another, but His Highness had not made up his mind. He wished the Intendant would drop some sort of hint, but unfortunately the gentleman had never even thought of

9. The cat's meow (in Heian pronunciation something like *nyon nyon*) apparently sounds to Kashiwagi like *nen nen*, "Let's go to bed, let's!"

10. Higekuro's wife, Tamakazura, feels closer to Yūgiri than to her half brothers, the sons of Tō no Chūjō.

11. Yūgiri's half sister, whose exalted station forbids the slightest informality.

12. Makibashira. "Handsome pillar" is from the poem that gave "The Handsome Pillar" its title.

it, perhaps because she interested him less than his cat. She herself regretted that her mother was odd and eccentric enough hardly to exist for other people, and she felt drawn to her stepmother instead, since she shared the lively tastes of the time.

His Highness of War[13] still lived alone. The failure of every courtship he tried had blighted his life and given him the feeling that people were laughing at him. He did not see how he could very well allow himself to go on this way, though, and accordingly he intimated his own interest in the young lady.

"Why not?" said His Highness of Ceremonial. "After giving a daughter to His Majesty, the next best thing to do for her is to marry her to a Prince. No one these days values anyone but proper, tedious commoners; it is quite demeaning." He accepted His Highness of War's proposal and kept him in no further suspense. Although disappointed to be left without a complaint, His Highness of War could hardly withdraw, since the alliance was not one to be despised, and he therefore began visiting her. Her father made him feel entirely welcome.

His Highness of Ceremonial, who had had several daughters himself, knew that he should have learned his lesson by now, since they had given him a good many regrets, but it was hard to desert this granddaughter of his. Her mother is quite odd, he reflected, and more so with every passing year, and as for the Commander, his refusal to listen to me seems to have led him merely to abandon her. It is very painful. In this spirit he saw personally to doing up her rooms and looked after everything with great care.

His Highness of War always missed the wife he had lost, and he only wanted another like her. There was nothing wrong with his new one, but he did not find in her the resemblance he sought, and perhaps that explains why he was so visibly reluctant to visit her. His Highness of Ceremonial was highly displeased, and her mother lamented this deplorable failure whenever a lucid moment broke in upon her strangeness. I knew it! the Commander said to himself. That Prince was always too much the lover. He had never approved of the match in the first place, and he detested the man.

The news of such inconstancy, so near at hand, prompted the Mistress of Staff to wonder with mingled sadness and amusement what His Grace and His Excellency would have thought if the same thing had happened to her. I never wanted to see any more of him even then, though, she reflected. He never failed to address me warmly and sincerely, but I expect he decided in the end that I was tiresomely dull. The idea had always embarrassed her a great deal, and she saw that she needed to be careful now that his wife might be hearing stories from him.

She offered to help in whatever way she could. Through the young lady's brothers she kept in touch with her very nicely, ignoring what she heard of the situation, and the young lady's father by no means abandoned his sympathy and concern, but that evil woman, His Highness of Ceremonial's wife, remained angrily unforgiving. "I know a Prince has little enough to offer," she grumbled, "but at least he could be loyal to the girl and cause no trouble!"

Her complaints reached His Highness of War. I have never heard of such a

13. Hotaru.

thing! he said to himself. Then, too, I sought solace at times from women other than the one I really loved, but I never had to put up with accusations like these! He was thoroughly offended and only felt his loss the more, and he often shut himself up moodily at home. Still, the second year of the marriage came after all, and both made their peace with it, such as it was.

The months and years sped by all too swiftly,[14] and soon it was eighteen years since His Majesty had acceded to the imperial dignity. "It is sad not to have a son to follow me, and life is a disappointment," he often said. "I would so much rather spend my time talking to people I like and doing as I please!" At last he fell gravely ill, and suddenly he abdicated. People were very sorry indeed to see him do so when still in his prime, but the Heir Apparent was sufficiently grown-up by now to succeed to the throne, and the way the realm was governed hardly changed.

His Excellency the Chancellor announced his resignation and entered retirement. "What could be wrong with my hanging up my hat,"[15] he said, "life being as treacherous as it is, when our most gracious Sovereign has renounced his high office?" The Left Commander became the Minister of the Right and took government in hand.[16] His sister the Shōkyōden Consort, who had not lived to see her son's reign, was appointed to the highest rank,[17] but alas, she had always been overshadowed, and the gesture seemed rather empty. The Consort's[18] eldest son was named Heir Apparent. This was no surprise, but the reality was gratifying nonetheless, and the ceremony was a wonder to behold. The Right Commander became a Grand Counselor. He and the new Minister of the Right got on better than ever.

Genji, at Rokujō, nursed his disappointment that Retired Emperor Reizei had no successor of his own. The Heir Apparent was his direct descendant, too, it was true, but while no trouble had ever arisen to disturb His Eminence's reign, so that Genji's transgression had not come to light and now would never be known, as fate would have it, that line was not to continue. Genji regretted this very much, and since he could hardly discuss the matter with anyone else, it continued to weigh on his mind.

The Consort, who had several children, enjoyed His Majesty's highest regard. People objected to the prospect of yet another non-Fujiwara Empress,[19] but Her Majesty[20] reflected on the kindness with which His Eminence Reizei had appointed her when she lacked any particular claim to the honor,[21] and as the months and years passed, she felt more keenly how much she owed to support from Rokujō. It was easier now for His Eminence to call there, as he had hoped it would be, and this made his life much more pleasant than before.

The Third Princess[22] still preoccupied His Majesty particularly. She had never

14. This phrase covers the passage of four years.
15. A literal translation of *kōburi o kaku*.
16. Higekuro became Regent as well as Minister of the Right.
17. Higekuro's sister was promoted posthumously, a common practice.
18. Genji's daughter. She probably no longer occupies the Kiritsubo.
19. Literally, "another Genji," that is, "another Minamoto." However, Fujitsubo was of imperial descent, as is Akikonomu. The expression must therefore refer to any non-Fujiwara.
20. Akikonomu.
21. She had not given the Emperor a son.
22. Onna San no Miya, the Emperor's younger sister.

surpassed the mistress of Genji's east wing, despite the widespread esteem that she enjoyed. The passing months and years had only brought those two more perfectly together, until nothing whatever seemed to come between them.

"I would now much rather give up my present commonplace existence and devote myself instead to quiet practice," that lady quite seriously said to Genji again and again. "At my age I feel as though I have learned all I wish to know of life. Please give me leave to do so."

"You are too cruel!" he would reply. "I could not consider it! That is exactly what I long to do myself, and if I am still here, it is only because I cannot bear to imagine how you would feel once I had left you behind, and what your life would be then. Once I have taken that step, you may do as you please." He would not have it.

The Consort saw her as her real mother, and it was the way her natural mother modestly helped from the shadows that so splendidly assured her future. Meanwhile the Nun shed tears of excessive joy at every excuse, presenting as she wiped her reddened eyes the very picture of a happy old age.

Genji opened that box[23] in preparation for the Consort's pilgrimage to pray at Sumiyoshi, and he found in it many demanding vows. To his offerings of *kagura*[24] each year in spring and autumn the old man had joined such promised inducements to everlasting good fortune that he had clearly never imagined anyone less wealthy than Genji seeking to provide them. His rapid, fluent writing showed masterly learning, and the buddhas and gods could hardly have failed to heed his words. How had a mere mountain ascetic managed even to conceive of such things? Genji was at once moved and shocked. Perhaps the old man had been a holy man from ages past, called by destiny to enter this world again in humble guise for a little while. Genji thought of him with growing awe.

For the present he said nothing of what these documents contained and set out on the pilgrimage as though it were his own. He had long since fulfilled all the vows he had made in those tumultuous days when he moved on down the shore,[25] but his continued enjoyment of life and great good fortune made the deity's assistance difficult to forget. The news that he would take the mistress of his east wing with him caused a great stir. He kept it all as simple as he could and omitted a great deal so as not to put anyone out, but his position imposed certain requirements, and the event went forward with striking brilliance.

All the senior nobles except the two Ministers joined him.[26] He had chosen the Seconds of the Watch and so on as dancers[27]—fine-looking men all, and equal in height. Certain young gallants felt doleful and ashamed not to have been included. By his order the musicians were drawn from the best of those normally called to the special festivals at Iwashimizu, Kamo, and elsewhere, and to these were added two celebrated musicians from the Palace Guards. A large number of men turned out to

---

23. The box of written prayers to Sumiyoshi, sent by the Akashi Novice to his daughter in "Spring Shoots I."
24. Music and dance offered at a shrine to a Shinto divinity.
25. From Suma to Akashi.
26. The absence of the Ministers of Left and Right was normal on such an occasion.
27. Ten men to perform the Azuma Asobi dances at Sumiyoshi.

perform the *kagura*. The three bands of privy gentlemen—His Majesty's, His Highness the Heir Apparent's, and His Eminence's—were all in attendance. The senior nobles' horses, saddles, grooms, retainers, footmen, and various servants were matched to one another, and they made an endlessly rich and colorful spectacle.

The Consort and the mistress of Genji's east wing rode in the same carriage, followed by another bearing the lady from Akashi and, discreetly, her mother the Nun. The Consort's nurse rode with them, since she knew their story. The lady from the east wing was accompanied by five carriages of gentlewomen, the Consort likewise, and Akashi by three. Needless to say, all the carriages were dazzlingly adorned.

"As long as your mother is to make this pilgrimage at all," Genji had said, "I should like her to do so with sufficient honor to smooth away the wrinkles of old age."

"It would not be a good idea to have her join so public an event," the lady replied discouragingly. "Perhaps she might wait until things have really gone as one hopes they will." Still, it was impossible to know how long the Nun might yet have to live, and she was so eager to see everything for herself that she went, too. One plainly saw in her, far more than in those always meant for glory, the workings of an exceptional destiny.

It was the middle of the tenth month; the kudzu vines clambering along the sacred fence had turned, and the reddened leaves beneath the pines announced not only in sound the waning of autumn.[28] The familiar Eastern Dances,[29] so much more appealing than the solemn pieces from Koma or Cathay, merged with wind and wave; the music of the flutes soared on the breeze through the tall pines, conveying a shiver of awe not to be felt elsewhere; the rhythm, marked on strings rather than on drums, was less majestic than gracefully stirring; and the place lent its own magic to the whole. The musicians in their bamboo pattern dyed with wild indigo[30] mingled with the deep green of the pines, and the many-colored flowers in their headdresses so resembled the flowers of autumn that one hardly knew one from the other. When "Motomego" ended, the senior nobles each bared a shoulder and stepped out to dance.[31] From dull, black formal cloaks burst sappan or grape layered sleeves, while the deep scarlet sleeves of gowns moistened by a touch of winter rain eclipsed the pines and recalled a carpet of autumn leaves. All these lovely figures then decked themselves with tall white reeds to dance just once more and bring the music to a close. One would have wished to watch them forever.

---

28. The middle of the tenth lunar month is already early winter, well into the season of red leaves. (a) The vines along the shrine fence at Sumiyoshi recall *Kokinshū* 262, by Ki no Tsurayuki: "The kudzu vines on the sacred fence of the god, so swift and mighty, could not withstand autumn and have turned." (b) The "reddened leaves beneath the pines" contrast with the pines' lofty constancy of color and suggest a love poem, *Shūishū* 844: "My trust is in the lofty green of the pine, which knows nothing of the leaves turning color below." (c) "Announced not only in sound" alludes to *Kokinshū* 251, by Ki no Yoshimochi: "On the mountain where leaves never turn, perhaps it is blowing wind that announces autumn."

29. Azuma Asobi, a set of dances based on folk songs from Azuma ("the East"), the region now called the Kanto and centered on Tokyo.

30. *Yamaai*, a wild indigo plant that yields a green dye.

31. "Motomego," one of the Eastern Dances, was danced with the outer robe off one shoulder. After it, the senior nobles join the regular dancers to bring the sequence of dances to an end.

The past returned to Genji, who seemed to see before his eyes all that he had known in his disgrace those short years before, and he fondly recalled His Retired Excellency,[32] having no one else with whom to share such memories. He went back in and privately sent this to the second carriage:[33]

> "Who else but we two knows all that has brought us here and so may address
> the pines of Sumiyoshi, witness to the gods' own time?"

It was on folding paper. The Nun began to weep. Her present life brought back to her how His Grace had left them on that shore when the Consort was already on the way, and she reflected again on their unmerited fortune. She also missed the man who had renounced the world, but she turned from that and other ill-omened sorrows to answer in purposely felicitous language,

> "Today an old nun is to learn a great lesson: that Sumiyoshi
> is a most generous coast rich in many, many boons!"

The words were whatever had come into her head, for she feared more than anything else being slow to reply. To herself she murmured,

> "I cannot forget all that I know from the past when before my eyes
> I behold these witnesses to the Sumiyoshi God."

The dances and music went on until dawn. A twentieth-night moon shone on high, the ocean stretched magnificently into the distance, and one shivered to see the pines whitened by a heavy frost that lent the scene a still more moving beauty. The mistress of the east wing had of course seen and heard something of the dances of each season at home within her own garden fence, but she had hardly been beyond her gate before, and this novel trip outside the confines of the City filled her with wonder and delight.

> "In the depths of night, frost upon the noble pines of Sumiyoshi
> gathers like a sacred wreath[34] conferred by the deity!"

She thought of the morning snow in Lord Takamura's poem "Mount Hira, too,"[35] and she felt more than ever confident that the honor rendered the divine presence had been accepted.

The Consort:

---

32. Tō no Chūjō.

33. Akashi's. He has gone back into his own carriage.

34. A wreathlike headdress of mulberry-bark fiber threads, worn by the officiant at a shrine ritual.

35. *Fukuro no sōshi* 140, where the poem is attributed to Sugawara no Fumitoki: "The god appears to have accepted our offerings: Mount Hira, too, wears a sacred wreath." Mount Hira rises above the western shore of Lake Biwa, north of Mount Hiei.

> *"To sakaki leaves priestly hands reverently offer to the god,*
> *frost in the depths of the night adds sacred streamers of white!"*

Nakatsukasa:[36]

> *"Yes, the pure white frost that might be sacred streamers in such priestly hands*
> *shows off visibly to all that the god accepts our prayers."*

A great many more followed, but there was no point in noting them all. The poems composed on such occasions generally fall flat, even those by men who greatly fancy their skill, and these were just not worth the trouble—there is simply no stylish way around "the pine's thousand years"[37] and whatnot.

Dawn broke slowly, and the frost lay thicker still. While the cressets burned low, *kagura* musicians too drunk by now to know what they were singing gave themselves to merrymaking, oblivious to the spectacle they made, yet still waving their *sakaki* wands and crying "Ten thousand years! Ten thousand years!" until one imagined endless years of happy fortune. These pleasures had lasted all too briefly, and a night of which one would have gladly had a thousand passed blandly into day. The young gentlemen regretted having to leave again, like the returning waves.

The line of carriages stretched away among the pines, and one glimpsed through their blinds, tossing in the breeze, something like a brocade of flowers beneath the everlasting green, while the delighted servants watched gentlemen in formal cloaks of many colors take pretty meal stands to each in turn.[38] "Destiny has certainly done well by *her*!" they muttered as they brought the Nun a tasting meal on an aloeswood tray spread with blue-gray paper.

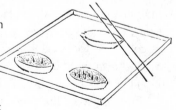

The journey to Sumiyoshi had been a solemn one, burdened with a great profusion of sacred treasures, but on the way back they wandered about to see the sights. Going through them would be a bore, though. Only the Novice, alas, was not there to see it all, having sequestered himself bravely in a world none of them knew—not that his presence

A meal on a tray

might not have been awkward, too. It appears that by now the Nun's success gave others as well greater pride in themselves. Her happiness aroused wonder and admiration at every turn, and everyone cited her as a model of great good fortune. Whenever His Retired Excellency's Ōmi daughter demanded that the dice favor her at backgammon, she would cry, "Akashi Nun! Akashi Nun!"

His Cloistered Eminence[39] devoted himself wholly to pious practice and ignored events at court. The spring and autumn progresses[40] were what brought him memories

---

36. One of Murasaki's women.

37. *Matsu no chitose*, one of the stock congratulatory phrases with which such poems bristle.

38. These meals would have been brought by men of the fourth rank or below, depending on the standing of the recipients.

39. Suzaku.

40. Every spring and autumn the Emperor formally visited his mother and the Retired Emperor(s).

of the past. The only care he had not yet renounced was his concern for Her Highness his daughter. For her general welfare he counted on Genji, but he also asked His Majesty quietly to do what he could. She rose to the second rank and her emoluments increased, which gave her a more commanding brilliance than ever.

Seeing her prestige rise in time so high above that of everyone else at Rokujō, the mistress of Genji's east wing continually reflected that although the personal favor she enjoyed was equal to anyone's, age by and by would dull her in his eyes, and that she preferred to leave the world on her own before that should happen; but she found it impossible to say so clearly, because she feared that he might condemn her for being too forward. Even His Majesty was especially fond of Her Highness, and Genji, who did not want to be called remiss, came after all to divide his nights equally between them. The lady in his east wing understood and accepted this, but it confirmed her fears, although she never allowed them to show. She had undertaken to look after the First Princess, His Majesty's second child, and this responsibility was a comfort on the lonely nights when Genji was away. In fact, she gave equally tender affection to all His Highness's children.

The lady of summer envied her having all these grandchildren to look after, and she insisted on taking on the Commander's daughter by the Dame of Staff.[41] The girl was extremely pretty, and very lively and grown-up for her age. Genji was fond of her as well. He had always felt that he had too few children, but his descendants had multiplied, and now there were so many on one hand and on the other that minding them and playing with them relieved the monotony of his days.

The Minister of the Right visited more often and more familiarly than in the past, and now that his wife[42] was a matron, she, too, came calling on suitable occasions—no doubt especially because Genji had given up his wanton fancies. She and the mistress of the east wing would then meet and talk very nicely. Only Her Highness continued to be as girlishly complacent as before. As for the Consort, Genji now left her entirely to His Majesty; it was Her Highness who aroused his sympathy, and he took care of her like a young daughter of his own.

His Cloistered Eminence was apprehensive now that he felt his end so near, and he had resolved to turn away from the things of this world, but he wanted to see his daughter a last time, and lest profane desires arise in him once more, he asked Genji to have her come to him without pomp or ceremony.

"Yes, you must do that," Genji told her. "You should have already without prompting from him. I am very sorry that you have made him wait." He considered how the visit should proceed. She cannot just go, he decided; there must be some sort of reason. What can one do to provide an occasion for her to visit him? Ah! he thought, he will soon begin his fiftieth year: she might offer him the new spring shoots. The different vestments required, the fasting meal, and many other things made this event unusual, and he sought his ladies' advice to plan it.

He was particularly careful to choose only the best dancers and musicians, for

---

41. Koremitsu's daughter. This child has not been mentioned before. She appears later as Yūgiri's Sixth Daughter (Roku no Kimi).
42. Higekuro and Tamakazura.

His Eminence had always loved music. In order to prepare for a large number of dances he sent to the privy chamber two sons of His Excellency of the Right and three of the Commander's, including one by the Dame of Staff—in other words, all the little ones over the age of seven[43]—and he also chose the sons of His Highness of War, those of all the Princes who mattered, and those of the highest nobles, to whom he further added any good-looking sons of privy gentlemen who were likely to dance well. This was to be an outstanding event, you see, and everyone involved did his very best. The music and dancing masters never had a moment's rest.

Her Highness had begun learning the *kin* long ago, but His Eminence was concerned because she had been parted from him at a very young age. "I hope that I shall hear her play when she comes," he said privately. "I am sure she has at least mastered the *kin*."[44]

"Quite so," said His Majesty; "her playing will have a particular quality at any rate. I should like to be there to hear her when she shows Your Eminence what she can do."

These remarks reached Genji, who had been giving her lessons for years whenever he had a chance to do so, and she had indeed improved. However, he reflected, she does not yet know anything worthy of his ears, and it would be extremely embarrassing if she turned up quite unprepared and he then insisted that she play. He was worried enough now to begin teaching her in earnest.

He saw to it that she should learn two or three striking melodies and the most beautiful major pieces,[45] including all the noble devices to convey in music the changes of the four seasons or of warm or cold weather, and although she lacked confidence at first, she gradually gained it and did very well indeed. "There are too many people about in the daytime, and every time you think you might after all try putting a quaver to a note, something comes up," he said. "I shall teach you what you need to know in the evening." He excused himself from the east wing and gave her lessons day and night.

He had never taught the *kin* either to the Consort or to the mistress of his east wing, and the Consort, who longed to hear the rare pieces she gathered he had been playing lately, therefore managed to beg rare leave to withdraw to her home. She had two children already,[46] and since she was into her fifth month with the third, she cited the rites for the gods as the reason for her to go.[47] Once the eleventh month was over, she received frequent letters from His Majesty asking her to return, but she envied the delightful music that went on every evening and wondered resentfully why Genji had never taught all this to *her*.

Genji, unlike other people, greatly admired the winter moon, and by snow-light on lovely nights he would therefore play music in tune with the season and give each gentlewoman present, if she felt at all inclined, her own moment on an in-

---

43. Presumably they are to learn deportment as privy pages.

44. Suzaku, her first teacher, hopes that Genji has continued her lessons, but he rather doubts it.

45. The repertoire of the *kin* seems to have been divided into major, medium, and minor pieces (*taikyoku, chūkyoku, shōkyoku*), although it is no longer clear what these were.

46. A son (the Heir Apparent) and a daughter, the First Princess.

47. Being pregnant, she might conceivably have polluted the rites in honor of the *kami* (gods) that were done in the palace in the eleventh month.

strument. The end of the year was approaching, and the mistress of his east wing was kept very busy looking in here and there to see that all was well. She often spoke of hoping that on some fine spring evening she, too, might be able to hear Her Highness play. Meanwhile the New Year came.

The events for His Cloistered Eminence's fiftieth jubilee were to begin magnificently with His Majesty's own, and Genji slightly delayed the one he was planning so as to avoid a clash between them. He had decided on a day or two past the tenth of the second month. All the musicians and dancers had assembled, and there were endless rehearsals.

"I should like to arrange a women's concert, in order to bring your *kin*, which the lady here in my wing is always so eager to hear, together with the *sō no koto* and *biwa* of the others," he said to Her Highness. "None of our master musicians these days can compare with the women here at Rokujō. I really learned very little properly, but when I was young, I was sufficiently anxious to miss nothing that I got what there was to be had from all the best masters and the greatest lords, and none of them struck me as too intimidatingly profound. Anyway, things have changed since then, and young people's affectations these days tend to make their music shallow. The *kin* especially—why, no one seems to study it anymore. There can hardly be anyone who has learned to play it even as well as you!"

He must think I am quite good by now! she reflected with a smile of innocent pleasure. At twenty-one or -two she still looked extremely immature; a frail sweetness was really all she had. "It has been many years now since His Cloistered Eminence last had a look at you," Genji would often remind her. "Please make sure when you are in his presence that he sees what a fine young lady you have grown up to be!" In truth, none of her women doubted that without his help her childishness would be even more difficult to conceal.

By the twentieth of the first month balmy breezes blew under lovely skies, and the plum tree before Genji's residence was in glorious bloom. Buds on the other flowering trees swelled with promise, and spring mists swathed them all. "All these preparations mean that there will be a lot to do once next month begins," Genji said to the mistress of his east wing, "and people will assume that any music you make with Her Highness is a rehearsal. We might as well try it now, while things are still quiet." He sent her over to the main house.[48] Her women all longed to go, too, but Genji had the unmusical ones stay behind, and even from among the more senior ones he picked to go with her only those with some particular quality.

He summoned four particularly pretty page girls, stylish and graceful in cherry blossom jackets over pale gray-violet and red figured outer trousers in scarlet beaten silk. The Consort's residence had lately been redone very gaily indeed, and the women vied to dress brilliantly. Her page girls similarly had on sappan jackets over leaf green, golden yellow Chinese silk twill gowns, and outer trousers of Chinese damask. Those belonging to the lady from Akashi were more discreet, all four

48. Where Onna San no Miya lives.

wearing light or dark purple jackets beaten to the most
exquisite gloss over ash green, with, for two, red
plum, and for the two others, cherry blossom.
Her Highness had her page girls dressed
with special care when she learned that
these ladies would be gathering in her
company. Their grape-colored jackets over
willow and earth green were neither novel nor
strikingly appropriate, but they managed on the
whole to look quite dignified and imposing.

Cushion

The sliding-panel partition was removed from the
aisle room, so that the room was divided only by standing
curtains, and Genji's seat was prepared in the space in the middle.[49] He appointed
pages and sat them on the veranda to provide the rhythmic ground for the occasion: the third son of the Minister of the Right—the Mistress of Staff's eldest—on
the *shō* and the Left Commander's[50] eldest on the flute. Cushions were placed inside
the blinds and an instrument laid before each lady.[51] Genji brought out the ones he
valued most in elegant, indigo-dyed bags: a *biwa* for Akashi, a *wagon* for Lady
Murasaki, and a *sō no koto* for the Consort. He was concerned that Her Highness
might never have played on grand instruments like these, and for her he therefore
tuned the *kin* on which she usually practiced.

"The strings of a *sō no koto* do not exactly go slack," he said, "but the bridges
sometimes slip when you tune one to play in concert like this. That needs to be
taken into account. I doubt that a woman could actually stretch the strings tightly
enough, though. I must have the Commander do it. These two with their flute and
shō are so young, and I am not sure they will really manage to support the rhythm."
He smiled. "Have the Commander come here, please."

The embarrassed ladies prepared themselves for his arrival. All except Akashi
were Genji's favorite students, and he hoped, as they did, that the Commander
would hear nothing unworthy. The Consort felt quite at ease because she was accustomed to playing for His Majesty, but the *wagon*, while limited in range, also
lacks set performance patterns, and that makes it if anything trickier for a woman to
play. Stringed instruments are played together in spring, and Genji was a little worried about false notes.[52]

The Commander came exquisitely groomed in a colorful dress cloak and
scented gowns, his sleeves suffused with the fragrance of incense. He was all keyed
up and much more nervous than for a formal rehearsal before His Majesty. The sun
had just set. Beneath a haunting twilight sky a rich profusion of blossoms weighed
down the branches, evoking the snows of the old year. Ineffable perfumes wafted

49. Genji is in the middle of the long, narrow aisle room. On either side of him are two standing curtains, one behind the other; and behind each standing curtain is one of the participants in the concert.
50. Yūgiri.
51. The cushions are to put the instruments on.
52. The meaning of this sentence is unclear.

toward him on a gentle breeze from within the blinds and filled the air all around this exquisite dwelling with such odors as to entice any warbler.[53]

The end of the *sō no koto* protruded a little from under the blinds.[54] "Forgive me for asking, but I wonder whether you would mind stretching the strings properly and tuning them," Genji said. "I cannot ask just anyone, you know." The Commander respectfully assented and took the instrument. After tuning the tonic string to the dominant note of the *ichikotsu* mode,[55] he sat a moment without testing it.

"Do at least play a modal prelude, and put yourself into it a little."

"But I am not nearly good enough to join such company!" the Commander modestly protested.

"Perhaps not, but it would be too bad if everyone knew you had fled from a women's concert without getting in a single note of your own!" Genji laughed.

The Commander finished tuning, went through the prelude very nicely, and returned the instrument. Meanwhile, the pages, looking ever so sweet in their dress cloaks, played away in a manner still boyish but filled with future promise.

Once the instruments were tuned and the ladies were playing in concert, the *biwa* rang out with a marvelous skill, superb in touch and limpid in tone, that lifted its music above the rest. The Commander listened especially to the *wagon*. Her sweetly enchanting touch on the strings[56] had a wonderful freshness; in fact, she matched in the brilliance of her music the most loudly celebrated masters of the time, and he was amazed that it should be possible to play the *wagon* that way. Her profoundly sensitive tact was clear, to Genji's delight, and he felt relieved and very grateful. The *sō no koto*, often heard so tentatively through the other instruments, had the most charming grace. There was still something immature about the *kin*, but all that practice had given her confidence, and her music blended very nicely with that of the others. The Commander thought how lovely they all sounded together, and he sang the notes, marking the beat.[57] Now and again Genji did so, too, in a voice more beautiful than ever and endowed with a new, slightly throaty richness. The Commander's voice was exceptional as well, and in the growing hush of the night the concert became lovely beyond words.

The moon was rising very late then, and Genji had had suitably bright lanterns hung here and there. He peered past the curtain at Her Highness and saw an unusually small, pretty figure who seemed to be all clothes. She still lacked any womanly appeal, but she offered instead the charming grace of new willow fronds halfway through the second month, frail enough to tangle in the breeze from a warbler's wing. Her hair spilled left and right over her cherry blossom long dress, and it, too, recalled willow fronds. *This* is how an exalted lady looks, one would have said, yet the equally elegant Consort had a somewhat fuller appeal and such exquisite

---

53. *Kokinshū* 13, by Ki no Tomonori: "The scent of blossoms rides upon the breeze and sends an invitation for the warbler to come."

54. Yūgiri is on the veranda.

55. One of the six *gagaku* modes. The "tonic string" (*hachi no o*) is the one tuned to the *kyū*, or ground note of the mode; in this mode it is the instrument's second string.

56. The original praises the touch both of her left hand (*tsumaoto*) and of her right (*kakikaeshitaru ne*).

57. He marks the beat with his fan and sings the names of the notes (solfège).

distinction of figure and manner that she resembled a rich cluster of wisteria blossoms in an early-summer dawn, when wisteria has no rival.[58] She was rather big by
now,[59] though, and she pushed her instrument away and leaned on her armrest because she did not feel quite well. Slight as she was, in this languid pose the armrest
looked too large for her, although it was the usual size, and one wanted in sympathy
to give her a smaller one. She wore a red plum blossom layering, and the slender,
graceful sweep of her hair in the lamplight lent her an unearthly charm. Meanwhile,
over a dark dress gown—perhaps grape—Lady Murasaki wore a light sappan long
dress smothered in the rich profusion of her hair. She made a figure so beautiful and
so perfect in size that she seemed to perfume all the air around her and, to express it
in terms of flowers, to put even cherry blossoms to shame.

Akashi could easily have suffered in such company, but not at all, for she had
a daunting nobility of manner, and through her undefinable grace and distinction
one divined profound depth of heart. She wore her willow long dress over what
may have been a grass green dress gown with a slight, intentionally modest[60] silk
gauze train, but nothing about her figure or demeanor encouraged one to look
down on her. Seated partly off a cushion bordered in ash green Koma brocade,[61]
with her *biwa* before her, she had only to touch her plectrum gracefully to the
strings to call forth a warm and tender sound evoking an orange branch plucked in
the fifth month and fragrant with both flowers and fruit.[62]

The music that the Commander heard from all these exquisitely elegant ladies
made him very eager to see deeper into the shadows within. He particularly longed
for a view of the lady from the east wing, whom he imagined even richer in beauty
than when he had actually seen her. As for Her Highness, he thought, if destiny had
favored me just a little, I could easily have had her for myself instead. I only wish I
had had the courage! His Eminence dropped repeated hints and talked about it privately, too, but no . . . He was very put out, but while a hardly forbidding glimpse
had given him no reason to think less well of her, it had not particularly stirred him
either. It was that other one who had always been far away, beyond his reach; and
he sighed with yearning to make her at least understand the strength of his perfectly respectable feeling for her. He controlled himself very well, though, and he
did nothing rash or ill considered.

The air turned chilly as the night wore on. The moon one awaits reclining[63]
rose, thin and pale. "How dim it is, a spring night with a misty moon!" Genji remarked. "To my mind, autumn with its touching beauty weaves the instruments together with cricket songs to make the music truly sublime."

"Bright moonlight on an autumn night leaves nothing unrevealed," the Com-

58. Wisteria blossoms from late spring into early summer, at a time when no other poetically sanctioned
flower is in bloom.

59. In her seventh month of pregnancy.

60. By wearing a train, however small, she acknowledges her humble standing and adopts the posture of
a gentlewoman in a great lady's service.

61. She modestly avoids sitting squarely on so fine a cushion.

62. The original includes a phrase from *Kokinshū* 139: "The perfume of orange blossoms awaiting the fifth
month recalls the sleeves of someone long ago."

63. *Fushimachi no tsuki*, the moon of the nineteenth night, which rises very late.

mander replied, "and one feels that flutes and strings sound equally brilliant, but a sky that seems conceived for just that effect and dew gleaming in every color on the flowers distract the eye, seduce the heart, and so limit the pleasures of music after all. How could that surpass a quiet concert under a veiled moon just peeping through the vague mists of a spring sky? A flute's enchantment cannot really fill the heavens, you know. The ancients observed that a woman is more touched by spring,[64] and I imagine that that is true. It is on a spring evening that all things fuse most sweetly and harmoniously together."

"Oh, no, there goes *that* debate again! No one has ever been able to decide it, and I cannot imagine that we poor denizens of this latter age can contribute anything more to it either! As far as modes and musical pieces go, it is true, *richi* always comes second, so I suppose you have a point."[65] He went on, "I wonder, though. These days His Majesty often has this or that gentleman famed for his skill perform for him, but few of them are that good—perhaps the great masters they look up to did not really know that much either. I doubt that their playing would particularly distinguish them even if they were to join these women, who are hardly expert. It is a shame; I must have lost my ear a little from living so long in retirement! How extraordinary that everyone here should make such a success of every amusement! I wonder how they really compare with all those people chosen as expert musicians to play at the palace!"

"I had been meaning to come to that," the Commander answered, "but I thought that it might be presumptuous of me to speak my mind when I know so little. I really have no opinion of the masters of the past, which may be why the *wagon* of the Intendant of the Gate Watch and the *biwa* of His Highness of War[66] have always struck me as wonders of our time. They *are* incomparable, certainly, but the music I have heard tonight is just as remarkable. Perhaps it is just that I was nervous because I assumed that this would be a casual concert and so was hardly prepared for it, but I found it a challenge to sing the notes. Talk about the *wagon*, His Excellency is a marvel because only he can modulate the notes as he pleases, in tune with the moment, but although the instrument seldom really stands out, this evening it was very impressive indeed."

"Oh, come, it was not *that* good. I am sure you are only being polite." Genji smiled complacently. "They are not bad students, though, I agree. I cannot comment very well on the *biwa*, of course, but even there I am sure that I made a difference. Her playing surprised me a good deal when I first heard it in that unlikely spot, but she has improved enormously since then." The way he *would* take the credit had the gentlewomen exchanging secret glances and tugging at each other's sleeves.

"Once you begin studying an art, no matter which one, there turns out to be no limit to what there is to learn, and you hardly ever master it well enough really to please yourself. Never mind, though—after all, so few people these days ever go

64. A canonical commentary on the Chinese *Book of Songs* observes, "A woman feels the yang spirit of spring and longs for a man; a man feels the yin spirit of autumn and longs for a woman."
65. *Richi*, a Japanese mode, was generally associated with autumn. The *ryo* mode, from China, was associated with spring. *Ryo* predominates in the *saibara* repertoire.
66. Kashiwagi and Hotaru.

very deep or far that anyone who has actually got anywhere at all may indeed feel proud to have done that well, and the *kin* is especially tricky. Those in the past who could really play it as it should be played subdued Heaven and Earth and soothed gods and demons,[67] and their music drew that of everyone else with it until those who were lost in sorrow rejoiced, and the poor and lowly were lifted up, laden with treasures, and honored by all the world. It often happened. Until it began to be taught in our country, those who pursued it spent many years in foreign lands without a thought for themselves, and even then, despite all their trouble, they still found it difficult to master.[68] Yes, it clearly does move the moon and stars in the sky, bring down frost and snow out of season, and stir a tumult of clouds and lightning, as many examples from early times attest. Anyone who learns it well is a treasure; but I suppose that it must be this latter age, because where is there any trace of those old days now? Perhaps the way it caught the ear of gods and demons and made them long to hear it is just the reason why, once people began learning it only halfway and getting almost nowhere, it gained the reputation of doing those who play it no good and of being generally a bore. I gather that hardly anyone studies it any longer. That is too bad. What other instrument helps one so well to learn and to tune the scales? Yes, in this world of ours, where everything seems to be going from bad to worse, one is no doubt merely eccentric to leave one's family and sally forth alone to roam Koma and Cathay.[69] Why not at least acquire a general acquaintance with the instrument? There is no end to the challenge of even a single mode. In the days when I was so keen to learn all the modes and all the most difficult pieces, I looked over every score that has reached this country, until there was no one left from whom I could learn, but even so, I am sure that I do not play as well as people used to, and it is a particularly great shame that there is no one to carry on after me." The Commander felt thoroughly inadequate and remiss.

"If any of His Majesty's Princes grows up as I hope, I look forward to giving him whatever poor knowledge I have, once he is old enough and provided I myself manage to live that long. The Second Prince is already showing promise." At this Akashi wept with pride.

The Consort gave her *sō no koto* to the mistress of the east wing and lay down, and that lady put her *wagon* before Genji. The music then became less formal, and their performance of "Kazuraki" was delightfully spirited. Genji's voice conveyed an inexpressibly happy charm as he sang the words over again. By and by the moon rose, and one could enjoy the sight as well as the fragrance of the blossoms. It was all quite lovely.

The Consort's touch on the *sō no koto* had been entrancingly sweet, with a deep quaver and a marvelous clarity of tone that reminded one of her mother, but her successor's playing left a different impression, for its calm elegance had entrancing charm, and her every ornament gave her music a touch of sheer mastery.

---

67. These powers, accorded to poetry (*uta*, "song") in the Japanese preface to the *Kokinshū*, were already generally attributed to poetry and music in China.

68. In the tenth-century *Tale of the Hollow Tree*, Toshikage went all the way to Persia in order to learn the secrets of the *kin*.

69. Like Toshikage in *The Tale of the Hollow Tree.* "Cathay" (*morokoshi*) includes here not only China but Central Asia and even the Near East.

The *richi* prelude that followed the mode change[70] sounded engagingly fresh, and there was nothing at all approximate about the voice of Her Highness's *kin*, which rang out very clearly.[71] The mode was now one suited to spring, autumn, or any other season, and the way she took care to adapt it, just as he had taught her to do, showed how well she had understood him. It was very pretty, and he was proud of her.

Genji thought the two boys sweet because they had played very nicely and put their hearts into it, too. "You must be sleepy," he said. "I thought we would have just a little music this evening—I never meant it to go on so long, but it would have been a shame to stop it, and while I tried with my dull ears to tell which instrument I liked best, it has become very late. I am sorry." He offered the boy who had played the *shō* a cup of wine and laid a robe of his own across his shoulders. The one who had played the flute got a figured long dress and trousers—a discreet, token gift[72]— from the mistress of the house,[73] while Her Highness sent a wine cup to the Commander and presented him with a full set of women's gowns.

"What is this? You are to honor your teacher first! I am shocked!" Genji protested, whereupon he was offered a flute from behind Her Highness's standing curtain. He took it with a grin. It was a very beautiful Koma flute.[74] He played it a little, and everyone began to leave, but the Commander then stopped, picked up the flute his son had played, and drew from it such exquisite notes that Genji saw how superbly his own teaching had succeeded with each, and he congratulated himself on the magnificence of his accomplishment.

The Commander got the boys into his carriage and set out under a clear moon. On the way he still heard, after that lady's *wagon*, her marvelous *sō no koto*, and he thought of her with longing. His own wife had received instruction from Her Highness her grandmother,[75] but she had been taken away before it really bore fruit, so that she could not play with confidence and was too embarrassed to do so at all in his presence. Instead she forever maintained an air of artless innocence, left herself no time for anything but minding one child after another, and seemed to him to lack any interest at all. She was at her most beguiling when jealous or angry.

Genji went to the east wing, while his lady stayed behind talking to Her Highness. She did not return until daybreak, and they slept until the sun was high in the sky. "It is remarkable how well Her Highness does at the *kin*, isn't it!" Genji remarked. "How did it strike you?"

"I wondered about her when I first heard her play a little, over there, but she has become very good. How could she fail to, when you have been giving all your time to her lessons?"

"You are quite right. For step-by-step progress I suppose I am not a bad teacher. I have not taught it to the others because it is so demanding and tricky and

70. A shift from *ryo* to *richi*, a common transition in *gagaku*.
71. The original describes the virtues of Onna San no Miya's playing in more technical detail, but the meaning of the terms used is poorly understood.
72. Yūgiri's son is probably younger than Higekuro's and so gets a lesser gift.
73. Presumably Murasaki.
74. A six-holed flute a little shorter and thinner than the Japanese *yokobue*.
75. Ōmiya, Kumoi no Kari's paternal grandmother.

takes so much time, but I was troubled to hear His Cloistered Eminence and His Majesty both assume that I must at least be teaching her the *kin*, so I resolved to do that much at any rate, since His Eminence had done me the honor of entrusting her to me in the first place."

He went on in this connection, "I never gave you any quiet lessons in the old days, when you were young and I was looking after you, because I hardly ever had the leisure for it, and one thing after another has kept me distracted more recently as well; I have never even paused to hear you play, which you did so beautifully in company that I was proud of you. The look on the Commander's face, as though he could hardly get over it, made me very pleased and happy, too."

With such accomplishments as these, and the authority with which she looked after His Majesty's children, she was a success in every way, so much so that Genji even feared for her, remembering the example of others, equally perfect, whose lives had not been long, for she was that rarity: someone who in every single thing she did remained beyond cavil or reproach. His wide experience of women convinced him that all her qualities made her incomparable. She was thirty-seven this year.[76]

He looked back fondly over the years they had spent together. "Do be especially careful this year and have more of the necessary prayers done than usual," he said. "I have so much on my mind that I may sometimes forget things, but please think about it yourself, and if you plan anything large, I shall of course look after it. What a pity that His Reverence[77] is no longer with us. He was someone to trust in matters of this nature."

He went on, "As for me, I grew up from my earliest youth amid grandeur that others never know, and by now I enjoy such honor as has seldom been known before. At the same time, though, I have also seen more tragedy than most. First, I lost the people I loved, and then all these years later, after surviving them, I still have many reasons for sorrow and regret. My own worst transgressions have brought me extremes of misery, and I have also suffered many disappointments, which suggests that my reward may well be precisely having remained alive until today, so much longer than I ever expected. For you, though, it seems to me that apart from that time when we were separated there has been little either before or after it really to cause you serious unhappiness. The greatest lady in the land, all the way up to the Empress herself, is certain to have reason to be anxious. One is never at ease in exalted company, where the spirit of rivalry is a constant torment, but *you* have always lived with your father, as it were, and you have had less of that than anyone, ever. Do you see how in that sense you have been more fortunate than others? I am sure that it was difficult for you to have Her Highness turn up here suddenly, but since it directly affects you, you cannot have failed to notice how much more devoted I am to you since she came. You who understand so many things must have grasped that."

"As you say," she replied, "I expect that to others I seem to enjoy favor beyond

---

76. Fujitsubo died in her thirty-seventh year, which was thought to be especially dangerous for a woman.

77. Murasaki's great-uncle.

what I deserve, but by now more sorrow than I can bear has entered my life, and that is what has inspired all my prayers."[78] She seemed to have much more to say but to be too shy to do so. "Seriously, though, I feel as if I have little time left, and the thought of spending this year, too, pretending otherwise worries me very much. If you would kindly permit what I once asked . . ."[79]

"That is out of the question, I tell you. What would my life mean without you? My greatest joy over all these years has always been simply to be with you day and night. What I feel for you is extraordinary. Please see my devotion through to the end!" That was all he said, which hurt her, since she had heard that much before; meanwhile he was moved to see her eyes fill with tears, and he talked on so as to turn her mind to other things.

"I do not know that many women, but the more I have learned that each has *something* to say for herself, the more I have had to conclude that a woman genuinely quiet and mild through and through is exceedingly rare. I took up with the Commander's mother when I was still very young, but things never went well between us, although she always meant a great deal to me, and now I am sorry both for her sake and for mine that it should have ended when she and I were estranged—not that I personally believe it was all my fault. She was just too unassailably correct—admirable from a distance, one might say, but really quite difficult in intimacy.

"Her Majesty's mother the Haven comes to mind as someone of unusual grace and depth, but she made painfully trying company. I agree that she had reason to be angry with me, but the way she brooded so interminably over the matter, and with such bitter rancor, made things very unpleasant. There was something so daunting about her that I could never enjoy with her the daily intimacies of life; I could never drop my guard, lest informality invite her contempt, and so she and I soon drifted apart. I regretted her distress when scandal touched her and her good name suffered, and in fact, considering who she was, I felt in the end that I was to blame; but to make it up to her I ensured that her daughter, who of course was so destined anyway, rose to be Empress, ignoring by the way a good deal of slander and resentment, and I expect that by now, in the afterworld, she has come to think better of me. Casual amusements always risk grave and painful consequences."

Little by little he went over the women in his past. "I looked down at first on our Consort's mother as being unworthy of me, and I assumed that she was a passing amusement, but her heart is an abyss beyond sounding. She has immeasurable depth. On the surface she yields and seems mild, but within she has such imposing dignity that she can be quite forbidding."

"I do not know the others because I have not met them, but of course I have seen *her* now and again, though never for long, and there is clearly something remarkably austere and intimidating about her; I hate to imagine what a simpleton like me must look like to her, and I only hope that the Consort is good enough to overlook my shortcomings after all."

Genji was greatly moved to reflect that she who had once sharply resented

---

78. The last clause of this sentence is unsatisfactory in the original and may be corrupt.
79. To become a nun.

this lady now, out of pure devotion to the Consort, admitted her indulgently to her presence. "You are not without your dark recesses,"[80] he said, "but it is a wonder how well you adapt your feelings to person and circumstance. I have known a good many women, but never anyone else like you. There is just that one thing about you, though." He smiled.

Toward evening he went to Her Highness's. "I must let her know how pleased I was with her playing," he said.

It had never occurred to Her Highness that anyone might dislike her, and she was giving her heart like a child to playing the *kin*. "I hope that you will now allow me some time away from our lessons," he said. "You must give your teacher a rest. All your work has had its reward, and I need no longer worry about you." He pushed their instruments away and retired to bed.

As usual on the nights when he was away, the lady in his wing sat up late and had her women read her tales. These old stories are all about what happens in life, she thought, and they are full of women involved with fickle, wanton, or treacherous men, and so on, but each one seems to find her own in the end. How strange it is, the insecure life I have led! Yes, it is true, as he said, that I have enjoyed better fortune than most, but am I to end my days burdened with these miseries that other women, too, find hateful and unendurable? Oh, it is too hard! She went to bed very late, and as dawn came on, she began to suffer chest pains. Her women did what they could for her. "Shall we inform His Grace?" they asked, but she would not have it, and she bore her agony until it was light. She became feverish and felt extremely ill, but no one told Genji as long as he failed to come on his own.

A messenger from the Consort got the answer that the lady was unwell, and she then informed Genji, who hastened home in shock to find her clearly very ill. "How do you feel?" he asked, putting his hand to her forehead. She was burning with fever, and he remembered with terror warning her just the day before about all the precautions she needed to take. Breakfast was served, but he never even glanced at it. He stayed with her all day, tending her and sighing. For days she refused the slightest nourishment, until she no longer even sat up. Desperately anxious about what the matter might be, he ordered countless prayers begun and summoned priests to perform healing rites. Her suffering seemed to be unbearable, for she hurt everywhere, and sometimes she felt agonizing chest spasms. Countless penances did no good at all. The gravest illness may still leave room for hope as long as some possibility of recovery remains, but as far as Genji could see, she felt only fear and despair. He was far too preoccupied to think of anything else, and there was no more talk of His Eminence Suzaku's jubilee. The news of her illness elicited many expressions of concern from His Eminence, who sent her repeated messages.

The second month passed, and her condition remained as before. In unspeakable distress Genji decided that a change might do her good, and he moved her to Nijō. His Rokujō estate was in turmoil, and great numbers of people mourned. The news saddened His Eminence Reizei as well. The Commander devoted himself to her care, knowing that if she were to die, his father would certainly act on his long-

80. "Dark recesses" (*kuma*) refers to Murasaki's jealous streak.

standing desire to leave the world. Quite apart from the Great Rite already under way, he commissioned another of his own.

In lucid moments she spoke only to reproach him, saying, "You are so cruel not to grant what I ask!"; but for Genji the sorrow and pain of seeing her a single instant, with his very eyes, wearing by her own wish the habit of renunciation, instead of parting from her at the end of life itself, would be more than he could ever bear. "It is exactly what *I* have always longed to do," he said, "but anxiety about how you would feel once you were left alone has always detained me. Do you mean to say that you would now abandon *me?*" This was his only response, and meanwhile, she weakened so alarmingly that it often seemed as though she would soon be gone. In his confusion he had no idea what to do, and he no longer took even a moment to visit Her Highness. His musical instruments, which meant nothing to him anymore, were all put away, while his whole staff gathered at Nijō, leaving Rokujō as empty as though its light were gone. Only the ladies who lived there stayed on, but it felt as though she alone had made the place what it was.

The Consort came, and she and Genji nursed her together. "You are in an unusual condition, and spirits are so dangerous!" she managed to say through her pain. "Please go straight back to His Majesty!" She wept bitterly when she saw the dear little Princess[81] beside her, and she said, "To think I shall never see you grow up! I know you will forget all about me." The Consort's tears of grief overflowed.

"Mind what you say!" Genji warned her. "Please do not think such things. Besides, I am sure you are not that ill. The heart decides what is to become of us. The great-hearted have great good fortune, and likewise the pusillanimous. Those who rise high have little peace, the reckless do not last, and those whose hearts are meek and mild are most likely to endure." He declared before the buddhas and gods that she had rare quality and that her sins were light.

The Adepts performing the Great Rite, the priests in night attendance, and all the other holy monks there to serve her were deeply affected by this evidence of his anguish, and they prayed for her mightily. Sometimes she was a little better for five or six days, only to lapse again into torment, and this went on month after month. What is to become of her? Genji groaned. Perhaps she will never get better! No spirit came forth to speak. No particular part of her was in pain; she simply weakened visibly day by day until he was at his wits' end with sorrow and despair.

Oh, yes, the Intendant of the Gate Watch was now also a Counselor.[82] He was in fact the man of the hour, for in this reign he enjoyed His Majesty's fullest trust. His failure to obtain what he desired still weighed upon him, however, despite his rising reputation, and he had therefore secured Her Highness's elder sister, the Second Princess. He took her somewhat lightly, since her mother had been a junior Intimate. In her person she had far more to commend her than some others, but his old infatuation still ran deep, and his was the desolation of Mount Obasute,[83] although he made sure never to betray it in his behavior.

---

81. *Wakamiya*, presumably the girl who has been under Murasaki's care.
82. He now holds this office in parallel with that of Intendant of the Right Gate Watch.
83. *Kokinshū* 878: "My heart is desolate at Sarashina when I see the moon shining down on Mount Obasute."

No, he had not yet forgotten his secret longing, and the woman he turned to for help was Kojijū, the daughter of Jijū, Her Highness's nurse.[84] Since Jijū's elder sister was *his* nurse, he had been hearing about Her Highness for a long time in a quite familiar way. Ever since her childhood he had had his ears filled with stories about how pretty she was and how much her father loved her, and that was how the thought of her had come to him in the first place. Guessing that the house would be quiet and half-deserted now that Genji was away, he had Kojijū come to see him now and then, and he worked with might and main to bring her round.

"I have long thought that I may die of love for her," he would say, "and I am extremely hurt that nothing whatever has come of the access you give me, except that I have news of her and can trust that she hears of my eternal devotion. Even His Cloistered Eminence seems to have been somewhat disappointed to learn that as far as one can tell His Grace's other attachments have meant that she has been overshadowed, so that she sleeps alone night after night and has little to fill her days. I gather he says that as long as he meant to settle on a commoner capable of looking after her properly, he might as well have picked one who would have done a good job of it. 'Judging from what I hear, the Second Princess is actually better off and has a more secure future'—so he remarked, and you can imagine how distressed I was when I heard it. Yes, they have the same father, those two, but what a difference there is between them!" He heaved a great sigh.

"Come now, my lord, you are going too far!" Kojijū smiled. "You have his Second Princess—what more do you want?"

He smiled, too. "That is just it. When I took the liberty of expressing an interest in her, His Eminence and His Majesty both found me acceptable. 'Why not have *him* serve her?' His Eminence was once pleased to remark. Why, if only he had been just a *little* more generous with me . . ."

"But that is impossible, my lord! Your karma, or whatever they call it, is what it is. Did you actually imagine that you had the stature to challenge and thwart His Grace, once His Grace himself had approached His Eminence so eagerly on the subject? You have only just begun lately to carry a little more weight and to wear a more imposing color."[85]

She spoke so curtly and severely that he cut short what he had to say. "Enough, enough! I will not talk about the past! Just make sure that while this rare opportunity lasts, you find me a way to tell her in person a little of how I feel. Do you think I would misbehave? Just look at me! The idea is too frightening to contemplate."

"What worse misbehavior could one imagine?" she retorted. "What you want is terrifying! Why did I ever come?

"Now, now, that is too much! You exaggerate. One never knows what to expect next between men and women. Why, has no Consort or Empress ever taken advantage of such an opportunity? Then just think of Her Highness! There she is, as

84. Jijū means "Adviser" (presumably the woman's husband was one), and Kojijū means "Little Jijū."
85. Kashiwagi has been promoted. As a Counselor he now has the third rank, junior grade, and should wear a light purple formal cloak.

well off as anyone could be, but no doubt with many secret griefs. His Eminence brought her up more affectionately than any of his other children, yet she must associate with people who are not her equals, and I am sure that she must suffer affronts to her dignity. Oh, I hear all about it! No, life is uncertain, and I wish you would just accept that once and for all and stop scolding me this way.

"So she is overshadowed—does that mean she is supposed to find someone more promising? I hardly think that she could do much better. His Eminence gave her to His Grace as though to a father, to save her from being left unprotected, and I assume that that is the sort of feeling they have for each other. Your complaints are unfair."

She was genuinely angry by now, and he did all he could to calm her. "Well, yes, since she is so accustomed to the company of a man unlike any other in the world, I can hardly imagine her pleased to be intimate with an unprepossessing boor like me. But what harm would it do her to listen to a word or two from me through her blinds? It is no sin to unburden oneself to the gods and buddhas, after all."

He swore great oaths, and despite her continued protests that she would have none of it, this not especially deep young woman could not resist his headlong zeal. "I will do what I can if an opportunity arises," she said. "There are many women around her curtained bed on the nights when His Grace is away, and the responsible ones are always in attendance nearby. I have no idea when I might find a chance like that." She returned to her mistress sorely perplexed.

Day after day he hounded her, until she let him know that she had found the moment. Overjoyed though he was, he arrived in deep disguise.[86] In truth, he himself knew all too well how outrageously he was behaving, and it never occurred to him that being near Her Highness might only drive him further out of his senses; he just hoped that he might catch a somewhat closer look at the figure he had never forgotten since that spring evening when he first glimpsed the skirts of her robe, and that once he had opened his heart to her, she might vouchsafe him a line in reply and pity him.

The tenth of the fourth month had just passed. The Purification was the next day, and the twelve gentlewomen who were to attend the Priestess, as well as the more junior women and page girls, were all busy sewing and making themselves up for their outing. There were few women about, and Her Highness's rooms were quiet. Azechi, who served her intimately, had been called away urgently by a frequent visitor, the Minamoto Captain,[87] and in her absence Her Highness had only Kojijū with her. Kojijū saw her chance and quietly seated the Intendant just inside the curtained bed, on the east side. Did she really have to let him in that far?[88]

Her Highness had innocently retired to sleep when she detected a man nearby and assumed that it was Genji, but then the man lifted her deferentially down from the bed, and she felt oppressed as though by a bad dream. At last she peered up at him and saw that he was someone else; and he was talking to her, telling her things

86. His dress and carriage are far below his normal standard.

87. Does not figure otherwise in the tale.

88. She has brought Kashiwagi closer than he asked. She may be more anxious to keep him out of sight than to protect her mistress. The curtained bed being fairly spacious, there is probably a standing curtain between him and Onna San no Miya.

that made no sense! She called out in shock and fright, but nobody came because there was no one nearby to hear. Shaking and distraught, and with perspiration running from her like water, she seemed to him very sweet and dear.

"I know that I do not matter," he said, "but surely *this* is not what I deserve from you. Years ago I began to entertain an impudent wish that I might have smothered once and for all if I had confined it in my heart, but I gave it voice, and His Eminence heard of it and did not strongly disapprove, which at last gave me hope. Alas, my particular insignificance then frustrated a devotion deeper than any man's, and while I know that it is now too late, that thought must have truly possessed me, for as the months and years go by, I burst with more regret, bitterness, fear, and love than I can possibly contain; which is why I have now presumed to come before you, despite the shame my unkindness brings upon me. I would never dream of further compounding my crime."

As he talked, she realized who he must be, and she was too shocked and afraid to answer a word.

"I quite understand, of course," he went on, trying every means to persuade her, "but it is not as though this sort of thing has never happened before, and if it is your wish to be so astonishingly cruel, then I shall be very deeply hurt, and blind passion may master me after all. Just tell me you pity me, and I shall obey you and leave."

Having imagined her haughty from a distance and forbidding in intimacy, he had resolved merely to hint at his torment and to try nothing more daring, but when he discovered less lofty pride than a sweet, nobly yielding and captivating charm, he took her to be unique among women. Every thought of wise self-restraint vanished, and he longed in confusion only to carry her off into hiding somewhere, anywhere, so as to vanish forever from life in the world.

Upon dozing off a moment he dreamed that the cat he had made into such a pet came to him, mewing sweetly, and that he brought it to Her Highness as a gift. He awoke wondering why and perplexed about what his dream meant.

For Her Highness the shock had banished all sense of reality, and she remained stricken and mute. "You must simply accept this as your destiny," he said, "one you could not evade. I do not feel as though it can be real either." He told her about that evening when, unknown to her, the cat had lifted a corner of the blind with its cord. She understood with bitter regret that it must really have happened, and she lamented her awful fate. How could she ever appear again before His Grace? She wept like a girl in misery and dread, and while he watched her, both guilty and fond, his already dewy sleeves grew wetter still from wiping away her tears as well.

Dawn was breaking, but he could not yet summon the will to leave. "What am I to do? Your rejection leaves me wondering how I shall ever be able to address you again. Please give me just a word in your own voice!" He tormented her with his pleading, but she was too repelled and distressed to speak at all.

"Very well, my only sentiment now is consternation. Surely no one has ever been treated this way before!" He was quivering with resentment. "It is useless, then, is it not? I might as well just die. This was all I had lived for. To think that tonight will have been my last! Just grant me a word of forgiveness, and I shall at least meet my end in peace!" He took her in his arms and carried her out. She was terrified to imagine what he was doing.

He opened out a screen in the aisle corner,[89] opened the double doors, and found that the door on the south side of the bridgeway (the one through which he had stolen the evening before) was still open. He therefore lifted the lattice shutter gently in the hope of catching a faint look at her, for it must still have been only first light. "Your extraordinary cruelty is driving me out of my senses! If you have any wish to calm me, tell me at least that you pity me!" he railed; and she did want to speak, for she was outraged, except that she was trembling like a little girl.

Daylight grew, and his anxiety with it. "I had a moving dream, and I would tell you about it if you did not hate me so. You may soon know what I mean, though." He set forth apprehensively into the half-light of dawn, beneath a sky more poignant than any in autumn.

> "I rise and go forth by the first, dim light of dawn, under unknown skies,
> and I find my sleeves are wet with dews from I know not where,"

he said, holding forth a sleeve to confirm his complaint.

Now that he was going, she felt sufficiently better to reply,

> "In my misery, O that I might melt away into the dawn sky
> and believe forever more that it was only a dream!"

He went away feeling as though she were still speaking in that sweet voice of hers, so young and frail, and that his spirit had left his body and stayed behind to listen.

Instead of returning to the Princess his wife, he went to his father's residence, where he lay down; but his eyelids would not close. He reflected how unlikely it was that his dream should be true, and he dwelled fondly in memory on the image of the cat. I have done a terrible thing! he told himself in fear and shame. I can no longer face the world. In this spirit he ceased going out at all. What his abominable conduct might mean for himself seriously alarmed him, quite apart from the possible consequences for Her Highness, and he simply could not mingle with other people as he might otherwise have wished to do. He would have faced death willingly enough if he had violated an Emperor's woman and the thing had then come to light and cost him such agony as this, and even if his present crime was not quite that grave, dread and shame overcame him at the thought that His Grace might look at him askance.

There *are* great ladies with some experience of life, flawless on the surface yet childishly bent underneath on having their way, who yield to one blandishment or another and indulge in intimacy with other men; but there were no such depths to Her Highness. Desperately timid by nature, she felt the same burning shame as if

---

89. The southwest corner of the main house, next to the double doors leading onto the bridgeway.

the news were already abroad, and she could not bear to go out into the light of day. She certainly grasped the bitterness of her fate.

Word that she was not well reached Genji, who came to her wondering what new misfortune might have joined the one that already absorbed him. It was hard to tell what was the matter, but she was extremely reticent and downcast, and she refused properly to meet his gaze, which he sadly attributed to pique over his long absence.

He told her how that other lady was. "This may well be the end. I simply cannot neglect her now, you know—it is too difficult for me to leave her, when I have looked after her ever since she was a girl. That is why these past months I have ignored everything else. I hope that once all this is over, you will look at me with other eyes." Secretly Her Highness could have wept with sorrow and pain when she understood that he knew nothing about what had happened.

The Intendant felt more and more convinced that he had erred, and he lapsed into a despair that pervaded his whole life, day and night. On the day of the Festival, senior nobles eager to see it came to try to persuade him to join them, but he said that he was not feeling well and lay down in a dark mood. He seldom spent any intimate time with the Princess,[90] although he continued to treat her with respect; instead he withdrew to his own room, where he gave himself up to tedium, despondency, and gloom. The sight of heart-to-heart in a page girl's hand inspired this thought:

> *"Ah, how bitterly I now rue my wickedness, picking heart-to-heart*
> *when the gods gave me no leave to sport such an ornament."*[91]

Yes, he regretted his folly. The noise of all the carriages outside meant nothing to him, and the endless day dragged on through a monotony of his own creation.

The Princess was hurt and ashamed when she noted his dreary behavior, and she, too, became downcast. Quiet reigned around her, since her gentlewomen had all gone off to watch the Festival. In an abstracted mood she toyed gently with her *sō no koto*, displaying as she did so a worthily noble grace, but her husband still lamented that as long as he was to have a Princess, he had been destined to fall short of getting the one he desired.

> *"O wreath of twinned green, what possessed me to pick up just the fallen leaf,*
> *though in name it seemed to be as welcome as the other?"*[92]

he idly wrote, and a thoroughly discourteous remark it was.

Genji, who now visited Her Highness so rarely, could hardly leave again

90. His wife, Princess Ochiba.
91. "I wish I had not taken Onna San no Miya, when Genji never allowed me to do so." The poem plays on *aoi* (the plant "heart-to-heart" and "day of meeting") as well as on *tsumi* ("pluck" and "sin").
92. "When both are Suzaku's daughters, so that both should be equally desirable, why did I get the inferior one?" The first word of the poem, *morokazura* ("twinned green"), refers to the combination of *aoi* and *katsura* leaves in the headdress for the Festival. Because of this poem Kashiwagi's wife, the Second Princess, is known to readers as Ochiba ("fallen leaf").

Healer

straightaway, and he was already anxious when a messenger came to announce that the lady at Nijō had breathed her last. Stunned, he went to her with darkness in his heart. The journey was maddeningly slow, and he found that there was indeed an agitated crowd all around the residence and out to the nearby avenue. The weeping and wailing within were repellent in the extreme. He entered, distraught. "My lady seemed a little better lately," they told him, "and then, my lord, suddenly, here she is like this!" Every woman attending her was crying out in a frenzy of grief that she would go with her. The altars for the Great Rite had been taken down, and when he saw the priests busily clattering about—although the ones still needed[93] remained—he realized with a horror beyond words that this must really be the end.

"But surely there is a spirit at work here," he said to calm them. "Please make less noise!" To these words he added more and more ardent prayers and then summoned all the most successful healers. "Her life may well have reached its term, but I still ask you to lengthen it a little," he told them. "There is the vow of Lord Fudō.[94] You must keep her in this world at least that long."

They prayed with mighty courage until black smoke really did rise above their heads.[95] Oh, just look at me one more time! he silently begged. It is too sad, too awful that I was not even with you at the end! One easily imagines the feelings of those watching, for they doubted that he would survive her. Perhaps the Buddha responded to his intense grief, because the spirit, which had refused for months to declare itself, now moved into a little girl in whom it screamed and raged, while his love began at last to breathe again. He was overcome with happiness and dread.

Once severely confined, the spirit spoke. "Leave, all of you. I wish to speak to His Grace alone," it said.

"For months you have cruelly chastised me and caused me such pain that I had thought I might teach you a proper lesson, but even now, when I have assumed this shocking form, the sight of you broken by a grief that may cost you your life has quickened feelings from long ago and brought me to you here. No, I could not ignore your suffering, and that is why I have appeared to you. I never meant you actually to know me."

The weeping figure with her hair over her face looked like the spirit he had seen that other time.[96] Shuddering with the same fear and amazement, he took the girl's hands and held her down lest she embarrass him. "Is it really you? They say evil foxes and so on, bent on mischief, sometimes blurt out things to bring shame on the dead. Say clearly who you are, or else tell me something to make it obvious, something no one else could know! Then I will believe you, at least a little."

93. To perform prayer rites for the deceased.

94. The Buddhist deity Fudō, whose spiritual power was vital to healing rites, was believed to have promised to add half a year to the devotee's natural life.

95. They look like Fudō, who is visualized surrounded by smoke and flames.

96. When Rokujō's living spirit possessed Aoi.

The spirit sobbed loudly.

"Yes, as I am now, my form is one new and strange, but plainly the while
you are still just the same you, who always refuse to know.

I hate you, oh, I hate you!" Her air of proud reserve had not changed at all, despite
her weeping and wailing, and it filled him with such fear and loathing that he
wanted only to silence her.

"I kept my eye on you from on high, and what you did for Her Majesty made
me pleased and grateful, but perhaps I do not care that much about my daughter
now that she and I inhabit different realms, because that bitterness of mine, which
made you hateful to me, remains. What I find particularly offensive, more so even
than your spurning me for others when I was among the living, is that in conversation with one for whom you do care you callously made me out to be a disagreeable
woman. I had hoped, as I did then, that you might at least be forgiving toward the
dead and come to my defense when others maligned me; and that is why, since I
have this shocking appearance, things have come to this at last. I have little enough
against this woman, but *you* are strongly guarded. I feel far away and cannot approach you, and even your voice reaches me only faintly. Very well, do now what
must be done to ensure that my sins are lifted. These rites and these noisy scripture
readings only surround me with searing flame, and I hear nothing holy in them.
That is my torment. Please let Her Majesty know what I have told you. As long as
she serves His Majesty, may she never indulge in jealous rivalry with other women.
Make sure that she acquires the merit to lighten the sin of the time she spent as Ise
Priestess.[97] I so wish that she had never done it!" She went on at length, but Genji,
who detested conversing with a spirit, shut her away[98] and quietly moved his love
elsewhere.

So it was that the news of her death filled all the world, and he was repelled to
find people arriving to offer their condolences. One senior noble who had gone to
watch the Kamo Priestess's return[99] immediately remarked on his way back, upon
learning what had happened, "This is a very great loss! No wonder a gentle rain is
falling today, when a most happy and fortunate lady has seen the light of day for the
last time!"

"No one as perfect in all ways as she was ever lives long," another whispered.
"There is that old poem after all, 'Why prefer cherry blossoms?'[100] The longer someone like that lives, enjoying all the pleasures that life has to offer, the more other
people find existence a burden. *Now* Her Highness the Third Princess can regain
the honor she deserves."

Getting through the day before had been too painful, and today the Intendant

---

97. The sin of neglecting the Buddhist faith, since at Ise all things Buddhist were shunned.
98. He shut the girl (the medium) into another room. There is no distinction between the spirit and the
possessed medium.
99. From the Kamo Shrine, after the Festival.
100. *Kokinshū* 70: "Were they, when one called 'Stay!' to linger on and never fall, why would one ever
prefer cherry blossoms?"

put his younger brothers, the Left Grand Controller and the Fujiwara Consultant, in the back of his carriage and went to see the Priestess's return. His heart stopped when he heard what they were talking about. "What in this sad world ever lasts long?"[101] he hummed to himself, accompanying the others to call on His Grace. Preferring caution, since the news was no more than a rumor, he went only to inquire after the lady's health, but he knew that it was true when he found everyone weeping and wailing, and he mourned her in his turn.

His Highness of Ceremonial arrived as well and entered, utterly distraught; he could not possibly have conveyed messages from other people. The Commander then emerged, wiping his eyes, and the Intendant begged him to tell him what had happened. "People are talking about a great misfortune, but it is so difficult to believe!" he said. "I really came only to offer sympathy that her ladyship has been ill so long."

"Her condition has been serious for months, and this morning at dawn her breathing stopped," the Commander replied. "A spirit has been at work, you see. I gather that she has at last begun breathing again, and they are all feeling better now, but there is no reason yet to be optimistic. I feel so sorry for her!" He had clearly been weeping copiously, and his eyes were a little swollen. The Intendant noted with surprise, perhaps because of his own heart's strange vagaries, how taken his friend seemed to be with this stepmother to whom he had never even been close.

Genji heard that the Intendant and the others had arrived. "She was very, very ill," he said, "and it seemed as though the end had come. The distraught women were carrying on so loudly that I myself was caught up in the confusion and despair. I shall find a suitable occasion later on to thank you all for your kind visit." The Intendant's heart failed him, for he would never have come if the occasion had not obliged him to do so, and his guilty conscience made him feel acutely ashamed.

Genji remained sufficiently fearful, even after her breathing resumed, to redouble his commissions for the most solemn rites. To think that someone frightening enough already when she was alive had now assumed so appalling a guise in another world! For the time being he shrank in revulsion from tending Her Majesty and concluded, in short, that all women are a source of dire sin; every dealing with them was hateful. Why, the spirit spoke of things I said in an intimate conversation no one else could hear! He remembered that with horror. Yes, it was she!

Since his love longed to take the tonsure, he cut a token lock of her hair to give her the strength to observe the Five Precepts, and he allowed her to receive them.[102] The officiating priest enlarged so nobly on the merit of abstaining from these things that Genji, seated closer to her than was really becoming, wiped the tears from his eyes again and again, and they both called with all their heart upon the Buddha. In this way he demonstrated how little even the wisest in this world can remain composed when overwhelmed by sorrow. Through days and nights of anguish he thought only of how to save her and keep her from leaving him, his face acquiring as he did so something of the gaunt look of the obsessed.

101. *Ise monogatari* 145 (section 82): "It is because cherry blossoms fall that they are so precious; what in this sad world ever lasts long?"

102. He allows her to receive (vow formally to uphold) only the Five Precepts administered to laymen: to abstain from killing, stealing, wanton conduct, slander, and wine.

She never felt quite herself during the fifth month, when the skies are so seldom clear, but she was a little better than before; even so, though, she was constantly unwell. Genji had a complete copy of the Lotus Sutra made and dedicated for the spirit each day, to expunge its sin, and he daily commissioned other holy works as well. He arranged a perpetual reading of the scriptures at her pillow, too, though only by priests with inspiring voices. Having once appeared, the spirit declared its complaint again from time to time, but it never left her. With the onset of warmer weather her breathing became irregular, and to his unspeakable anxiety she became even weaker. Even in her semiconscious condition she observed the state he was in with pity. For herself the thought of dying called forth no regrets, but it would be too selfish of her to make him look on her lifeless body when he was plainly in such distress already, and she therefore summoned the courage to sip medicinal infusions; and perhaps that is why by the sixth month she could sometimes even lift her head. He watched her with wonder, but he still felt a great dread, and he never once called at Rokujō.

Immediately after suffering that most painful intrusion, Her Highness changed and began to feel unwell. Her condition gave no cause for alarm, but the next month she started refusing all food, and she looked very pale and ill. The culprit would come to her as though in a dream, whenever he was mastered by an excess of desire, but she found his visits infinitely repellent. She lived in terror of His Grace, and this young man was very far from being His Grace's equal, either in his person or in the weight of his rank. No doubt he was thoroughly stylish and elegant, and to any ordinary eyes clearly superior to the common run of men, but she had been accustomed ever since she was a girl to a gentleman quite unlike any other, and his presence only offended her. It was unhappy karma indeed that she should now continually feel ill. Her nurses noted her condition and whispered bitter complaints that His Grace came to see her so seldom.

The news that she was indisposed brought Genji to her. His love, whom the heat troubled, had had her hair washed and was feeling somewhat refreshed. It was slow to dry, since she lay with it spread out all around her, but not a strand was tangled or out of place, and it had a beautifully supple richness; meanwhile, despite her pallor, her skin was so exquisitely white as to seem almost transparent, and she made an utterly enchanting sight. She still looked as frail as a cicada shell. It had been a long time since she last lived in the house, and the place needed work and felt quite cramped. She looked out with new pleasure on the stream and garden, which had been carefully redone now that lately her mind was clear again, and she found herself surprised to be still alive.

The beautifully cool-looking lake was covered with flowering lotuses, and dewdrops shone like jewels on the deep green leaves. "Look at that!" Genji said. "*They* look nice and cool anyway!" She sat up and followed his gaze, which was a wonder so rare that he went on with tears in his eyes, "It is almost a dream to see you like this! You know, I often felt as though I, too, would soon be gone."

She responded with equal feeling,

"*Will I last as long as those swiftly vanished drops? The time I have still*
can hardly outlast the life dew has on a lotus leaf."

He replied,

> *"Let us promise, then, that not in this life alone but beyond it, too,*
> *we both shall still share as one the lotus leaves' pearls of dew."*[103]

His next destination was a place where he did not wish to go, but His Majesty and His Cloistered Eminence would both learn of his doings, and it had been several days since he heard that Her Highness was unwell, so he went after all. His distress over the lady before him meant that he had hardly seen her, and he knew that he could not remain absent even during this break in the clouds.

Her Highness, tormented by conscience, was ashamed to appear in his presence. She answered nothing he said, which he took with a pang of sympathy for a hidden reproach over how long it had been, and he strove to lighten her mood. He also summoned a senior gentlewoman to inquire after her health. "My lady is in a delicate condition, my lord," the woman replied and went on to describe the symptoms.

"Strange! How extraordinary, after all this time!" He said no more, but he reflected silently that this had not happened with the others he had known so much longer, and he found the news all but impossible to believe. For that reason he therefore said nothing about it to Her Highness and only considered tenderly how sweet she looked when unwell.

It had taken him so long to make up his mind to come that he did not go straight back again but instead stayed for two or three days, which he spent constantly worrying and writing letters. "What a lot he has to say!" remarked those who did not know of their mistress's slip. "This does not bode well!" The one who felt truly alarmed was Kojijū.

The news of Genji's presence there provoked the gentleman in question to an insolent misapprehension, and he sent Her Highness a long letter full of strong expressions of feeling. Kojijū secretly showed it to her when Genji was off for a moment in the east wing and no one else was about.

"I wish you would not show me these horrid things!" Her Highness lay down. "They only make me feel worse."

"Do read it, though, my lady! The beginning here makes one feel so sorry for him!" Kojijū had just spread out the letter when she heard Genji coming back and got a fright; she drew up the standing curtain and fled. In he came, to Her Highness's consternation, and since she could not hide the letter properly, she slipped it under her cushion.

He took leave of her in preparation for returning that night to Nijō. "Here at Rokujō you do not seem really to be very ill," he said, "whereas at Nijō I felt when I left her that she was extremely weak, and I am very anxious about her. Do not for a moment believe the unpleasant things people may tell you. You will soon have reason to think better of me." She usually prattled merrily to him, but this time she was thoroughly gloomy and would not meet his eyes properly, which he took for mere

---

103. "Let us promise each other to be reborn on the same lotus throne in paradise."

pique. He lay down in her day sitting room and chatted with her until the sun finally set.

He had dropped off to sleep for a moment when a cicada broke into loud song and woke him up. "Very well, then," he said, putting his cloak back on, "I might as well be on my way before the path becomes too shadowy."[104]

"It says, 'Await the moon,' though, doesn't it?" she replied in a youthful tone that was really quite nice. I suppose she means, "I shall have you that much longer," he thought guiltily while preparing to leave.

> *"You whose ears ring, too, with the cicadas' shrilling, will you leave me now*
> *as though to say, 'Soak your sleeves in the cruel evening dew'?"*

Her words conveyed the naive quality of her feelings so sweetly that he sat down again and heaved a frustrated sigh.

> *"How, then, may it sound in that village over there, where another waits?*
> *Alas, the cicada's song brings torment on either hand!"*

he answered, now irresolute. It was too painful to be that cruel to her, and he decided to stay. Still, he remained anxious and abstracted, and he took no more than fruit and so on before going to bed.

He arose early, meaning to set off while the morning was still cool. "I dropped that fan I had yesterday," he said. "This one does not give as nice a breeze." He put it down and looked around the room where he had taken that nap the day before. There, protruding from beneath Her Highness's slightly disturbed cushion, was the end of a rolled-up letter on thin, light green paper. Thinking no harm, he slipped it out and had a look. The hand was a man's. The paper had a delicious fragrance, and the letter seemed to have been prepared with great care. He noticed that there were two sheets, both completely covered with writing. Yes, he saw, the writing was *his*, there was no doubt about it. The woman who put up the mirror for him assumed that the letter was his own and thought nothing of it, but Kojijū felt her heart pound thunderously when she saw him and recognized the color of the letter that had come the day before. No! she cried to herself without looking at Genji, who was eating his breakfast. No, no, it cannot be! This is a catastrophe! But is it possible? She *must* have hidden it! Meanwhile Her Highness innocently slept on. What a baby she is, Genji thought, to leave something like that lying about where someone might find it! His respect for her sank. I was right after all. I always worried that she seemed to have no sense.

Kojijū went to Her Highness once he was gone and the women had drifted away a little. "My lady, what did you do with that letter yesterday? This morning His Grace was looking at one almost the same color."

Her Highness wept and wept from the shock. Kojijū commiserated with her,

---

104. *Kokin rokujō* 371: "The path is shadowy in the evening dusk: await the moon, love, to go, and I shall have you that much longer!" Onna San no Miya picks up the allusion in her answer.

but she also could not help thinking how hopeless she was. "Where did you put it, my lady? People were coming, and I had rather a bad conscience, so I withdrew because I did not want it to look as though we were up to something. His Grace came in a little after that. I was sure that you must have hidden it."

"Why, no. He came in while I was reading it. I could not put it away that fast, so I slipped it under where I was sitting. Then I forgot all about it."

Kojijū was speechless. She went to her mistress and looked around her, but of course it was not there. Then she gave her a piece of her mind. "Oh, my lady, how awful! The gentleman was absolutely terrified, and he dreaded the very idea that His Grace might ever hear of it! It is all so recent, and look what has already happened! You allowed him to see you, in that childish way you have, and far from forgetting it, he has pursued me ever since with his complaints; but did I ever imagine it would come to *this*? This means disaster for you both!" She must have spoken this way because Her Highness was so young and meek. Her Highness just went on crying and never answered a word.

She now looked distinctly ill and refused to eat. "To think that he has abandoned her, when she is so unwell, to tend someone else who is all better by now!" the women complained.

The letter still puzzled Genji, and he read it over and over again where no one could see him. He even wondered whether it had been written by a gentlewoman of hers whose hand resembled the Counselor's, but its language was too accomplished for that. No, it could only be his. His account of how he had at last satisfied his long-cherished desire, and of his sufferings thereafter, was beautiful and moving, but was it really necessary for him to spell it all out that way? What a letter for such a man to write! he said to himself. Even years ago, when I myself might easily have written with this degree of passion, I knew perfectly well that a letter could go astray, and I was brief and indirect. That degree of caution is not easy. Genji found it impossible to have much respect for him.

What am I to do with her now, though? *This* is why she is in this delicate condition of hers! Ah, what a disaster! Shall I to go on with her as before, now that I have seen the awful truth with my own eyes? He wanted to give her the benefit of the doubt but found that he could not. It is bad enough when a woman one never much liked, a passing amusement, turns out to be involved with somebody else, and one then loses interest in her; but in this case, to think of the insolence of the man! In early times as well there were those who might violate an Emperor's wife, but that was different. No wonder liaisons like that may occur, when there are so many people in palace service waiting on the Sovereign. What with one thing and another it must happen quite often. Even a Consort or an Intimate may err for this reason or that. They are not all as serious as they might be, and strange things happen, but as long as no obvious lapse comes to light the man can carry on as before, and it may be ages before anyone finds out. I honor her above anyone else and sacrifice my personal feelings to treat her with the highest respect, and she just sets me aside? Why, I have never heard of such a thing! He snapped his fingers in anger.

When a woman wearies of giving her service meekly and all too respectably, even to the Emperor himself, she may yield after all to urgent pleas, love where she is loved, respond when she feels she must, and so embark on an affair that might well be as culpable as this one, but at least it would make some sense! Look at who I am! I cannot imagine how she could share her affections with a man like that! He realized bitterly that despite his fury he could not afford to show it, and he thought of his father, His Late Eminence. Did *he* really know all the time and just pretend not to? *That*, yes, that *was* a fearful and a heinous crime! Reflection on his own example suggested that he was in no position to criticize someone else lost in the mountains of love.[105]

Despite his pretense that all was well, he was obviously upset. His love, who took it that he had come to her despairing that she was gone, assumed that this time he could not help feeling sorry for Her Highness instead. "I am quite well now," she said, "but I am sure that Her Highness is not, and I wish you had not come back so soon."

"You are right. Her condition is somewhat unusual, but it is hard to say just what the matter is, so I felt that I need not really worry. There have been several messengers from His Majesty. I gather another letter came from him today. His Eminence has been imploring him to do all he can for her, and that is probably why he is so concerned. I am afraid the slightest neglect on my part could earn me the disapproval of both." He sighed.

"The idea that she herself may be angry with you bothers me more than anything His Majesty may feel. It might never occur to her on her own, but there are certainly people who put the worst light on things to her, and I do not like that at all."

"Ah, yes, you have no relatives to hound me—you mean quite enough to me already—but look how deeply you understand things! You even consider how her women may feel, while all I do is fear to displease our exalted Sovereign. How shallow can one be?" He smiled and turned their conversation elsewhere. "I will go when you can go with me," he said on the subject of returning to Her Highness. "Let us just make ourselves comfortable here."

"I should like to be quiet here a little longer. Go on ahead, and I shall follow once she feels better about you." Days went by while they continued their debate.

In the past Her Highness had resented it when Genji stayed away for days on end, but this time she knew that the fault was partly her own, and she recoiled from the thought of how His Eminence would feel if he were to learn the truth.

The gentleman in question kept up a stream of impassioned messages until Kojijū, at her wits' end, explained what had happened. He was aghast. When can it have been? I always assumed that a thing like this might get out in time, which is humiliating enough—I feel the eye of Heaven upon me. But that His Grace should have seen such damning proof! Shame, dread, remorse—morning or evening there was no relief then from the heat, but he felt frozen, and his thoughts were beyond words. All these years His Grace has been calling me to him on every occasion, serious or merry, and I have always gone. How good and kind he has been to single me out that way for

---

105. *Kokin rokujō* 1980: "How vast must the mountains of love be, that all those who enter them still lose their way!"

such unusual attention! How can I ever look him in the eye again, when he now abhors me for my heinous misdeed? It will look strange, though, if I simply vanish and never go there anymore, and just imagine the conclusions he himself may draw! Sick with anguish, he gave up going to court. There would be no formal punishment for what he had done, but it seemed to him that his life was ruined, for which he hated himself, since he had always known this might happen. It is not as though she has any dignity or depth, after all! What business did she have letting herself be seen that way in the first place, past that blind? He could tell that the Commander had thought her careless. No doubt he wanted to dwell on the worst things about her so as to put her out of his mind. It may look very nice for her to be so excessively mild and ladylike, but she knows nothing of life, and she never gives a thought to keeping an eye on her women, which just invites disaster, not only for herself, poor thing, but for other people as well. He could not rid himself of his tender sympathy for her.

Her Highness's suffering was sweetly touching, and although Genji was fed up, he still felt tenderly enough to go and see her. What he found whenever he did so caused him sharp pangs of pity, and he commissioned all sorts of prayers on her behalf. He did not change in his overt treatment of her—in fact, he redoubled his attentions and his marks of respect—but this was only to keep up appearances, because in private he remained excruciatingly aloof. His conflicting feelings meant anguish for her as well. He never even told her what he had read, which left her as crushed as a little girl. I suppose that is just what she is like, he told himself. It is all very well for her to be ladylike, but she is too agonizingly slow to be trusted. Yes, the world is a perilous place. Our Consort is so meek and mild that she would probably be confused, too, if anyone were that desperate to have her. Men look down on women for being pliant and moody, and I suppose that is why they lose control of themselves when they suddenly take an outrageous fancy to one. The Minister of the Right's wife[106] grew up wandering dim and distant regions without any real support at all, but she is quick and intelligent. I was a father to her for the most part, but there were also times when I had quite different thoughts, and she still managed to pretend not to notice and to let it pass. When His Excellency prevailed on an unthinking gentlewoman to help him make his way in to her, she made sure everyone understood clearly that she had had nothing to do with it, that what was happening had full authorization, and that for her own part she was completely blameless. Looking back on it now, I can appreciate how very shrewd she was. It was their destiny to be together, and never mind how it began, as long as it lasts; but people would think a little less well of her if they retained the impression that she had willingly acquiesced. She really did it very, very well.

He still thought often of the Nijō Mistress of Staff,[107] but by now he had learned for himself what grief this sort of hazardous affair can cause, and her susceptibility made him think somewhat less well of her than before. The news that she had finally done what she had long wished to do[108] moved him to deep pity and re-

---

106. Tamakazura.
107. Oborozukiyo.
108. Become a nun.

gret, and he immediately sent her a letter. He was extremely put out to have had no word from her to suggest that she meant to act.

"Am I not to care that your life is now a nun's? For you, after all,
for you alone I dripped brine far away on Suma Shore.

You have left me to lament that you have gone before me, when my heart is already so full with life's many treacheries, but I trust that you will put me first among those to whom I am certain you will dedicate the merit of your prayers." He wrote a great deal else besides.

She had decided on this step long ago, but his opposition in the past had detained her, and she had therefore said nothing to anyone about actually taking it. Still, doing so meant a secret wrench, for the old and painful bond between them was no trifle to her even now, and she remembered the good as well as the bad. She wrote an intent, heartfelt reply, knowing as she did that this sort of letter hardly became her any longer and that there would be no more. Her writing was very beautiful. "I thought that life's vagaries might

Nun

have touched me alone, but your talk of my going before you makes me wonder,

Why is it you failed in your time to sail away on a pious craft,
you who were a fisherman along the Akashi coast?[109]

As to my prayers, which are for all beings, how could they fail to include you?"

The letter, on dark blue-gray paper and tied to a branch of star anise,[110] offered nothing unusual beside the supreme elegance of the writer's brush, of which he felt that he would never tire. He showed it to his love, too, while he was at Nijō, since all that was really over now. "I feel quite ashamed of myself," he said. "No, I do not like it at all. I have seen a good many troubles in my time, although, happily, I have survived them, and she and the former Kamo Priestess[111] were the only women left with whom I could still freely discuss the little things of life and exchange an uncompli-

109. The familiar play on *ama*, present in Genji's poem as well, is prominent here. The poem's import is not especially clear, except for Oborozukiyo's appeal to a distant past that both share.
110. *Shikimi* (*Illicium religiosum*), a broadleaf evergreen normally offered on a Buddhist altar in Japan. It is strongly associated with Buddhist practice.
111. Asagao.

cated friendship—the only ones who understood the mood of every season and who never missed the point. Now they have both renounced the world, and the Priestess has become particularly caught up in her devotions. Among all the women I have known, I have never otherwise seen her like, because she was profoundly thoughtful and yet at the same time warm and kind. It must be so difficult to bring up a girl! It is not only up to her parents to have her turn out as they wish, since she has the destiny her karma gives her, which remains unseen; but even so, it takes a great effort to rear her properly. Happily, it was my good fortune to escape having too many to worry about. That was a disappointment to me in my younger days, and I often sighed to myself that I wanted more. Please give the greatest care to bringing up our Princess! There are many things the Consort does not understand yet, and she probably worries a great deal, since she is never away from His Majesty. Princesses need to be instilled with the proper disposition to escape tedious criticism and make their way smoothly through life. A commoner woman of limited rank, of course, has a husband to look after her, so she gets help with that sort of thing."

"My assistance may not do her much good, but I will not neglect her as long as I draw breath," she replied. "I wonder, though . . ." She was still unhappy, and she envied those who could give themselves without hindrance to their devotions.

"I should do something for the Nijō Mistress of Staff in the way of the clothing she needs now, as long as she is not yet used to making it herself. How *do* you sew a stole anyway? Do have one made. I shall ask the lady of the northeast at Rokujō to look after a set of robes. She cannot very well feel comfortable with proper vestments, but whatever you do for her should still have an ecclesiastical feel to it." He asked her for a set of blue-gray robes. Then he summoned people from the Crafts Workshop and quietly ordered first a set of the implements that a nun might need and then cushions, sleeping mats, screens, standing curtains, and so on; and with the greatest discretion he saw to the execution of all these things.

The jubilee event for His Cloistered Eminence on his mountain thus continued to be put off. Autumn came, but for the Commander the eighth month was one of mourning[112] and therefore unsuitable, since he was to supervise the musicians, while the ninth was the one in which the Empress Mother had passed away. Genji therefore considered the tenth, but Her Highness by then felt so unwell that the event was postponed again. In that month the Intendant's Princess went to visit her father. His Retired Excellency saw to it that the accompanying ceremonies should be as solemnly perfect and splendid as possible, and the Intendant roused himself to be present for the occasion. He was still in quite uncharacteristic ill health.

Her Highness remained as stricken as ever with shame and remorse, which is perhaps why her condition only worsened as the months went by, until she was in such a state that Genji, who wanted nothing to do with her, still grieved at the same time to see anyone so sweet and frail endure such suffering, and he sighed many a time over what was to become of her. He spent the year preoccupied by healing prayers.

His Eminence, cloistered on his mountain, heard about her condition and

112. Yūgiri's grandmother, Ōmiya, had died in this month.

thought of her with tender longing. People told him that Genji had been away for months and hardly visited her at all, at which he wondered despairingly what had happened and resented more than ever the vagaries of conjugal life. He felt uneasy when that other was seriously ill and Genji, so he heard, spent all his time looking after her. Moreover, he reflected, His Grace seems not to have changed his ways since then. *Did* something unfortunate occur while he was elsewhere? Did those hopeless women of hers take some sort of initiative without her knowledge or consent? I hear that even the elegant banter two people may naturally exchange at court can give rise to scurrilous rumor. This line of thought made it impossible for him to give up his fatherly concern, despite his having renounced engagement with the things of this world, and he sent his daughter a long, earnest letter. She read it while Genji was with her.

"I have seldom written to you, having had little reason to do so, and I can hardly bear to recall how long it has been since we were last in touch. News of your poor health has reached me, and I regret to say[113] that you are always in my prayers. You must bear up, whatever loneliness or sorrow life may bring. It would not become you to show resentment in your expression or to betray any knowledge that you have reason to be displeased." Such were his admonitions to her.

Genji, pained and sorry, assumed that His Eminence could hardly know of the secret disaster and that his displeasure must therefore have to do with news of Genji's neglect. "How do you mean to answer him?" he asked. "This distressing letter troubles me very much. Despite the shock of what has happened, I do not want anyone to think I am failing you. Who can have been talking to him? I wonder." She looked very sweet, turned away from Genji in shame, and the melancholy of her drawn features gave her a new distinction.

"I quite understand that His Eminence should be disappointed to find you so childish and that he should worry so much about you, and I hope that in a great many ways you will be more cautious in the future. I had not meant to say this, but I do not at all like His Eminence gaining from other people the impression that my conduct is not what he would wish, and I think that I should at least mention this to you now. To you I may seem no more than shallow and indifferent, since you grasp so little on your own and are swayed only by what others tell you, and perhaps in your eyes I am merely a tiresome and contemptible old man; either thought is cruel and bitter. Do at least contain yourself while His Eminence is still alive, though, since this appears to be what he wanted. Resign yourself to humoring an old man and spare me the worst of your scorn. I am forever irresolute, and even on the path I have long yearned to take I now lag behind women who properly speaking should understand little of these things, when in reality I have no reason to hesitate. It touched and pleased me, though, you know, that he should turn to me to look after you, and I have not wanted to disillusion him by then leaving you in my turn, as though all I had in mind was to keep up with others. The women I have loved hardly stand in my way any longer. One never knows how the Consort may get on

113. Because one who has renounced the world should not be so concerned about it.

Writing a letter

in the end, but she seems to be having lots of children, and I think I can trust that she will manage at least as long as I am alive. As for the others, I feel less burdened by them now, since at their age nothing need keep them from giving up worldly life with me. I doubt that His Eminence has much longer to live; his health continues to decline, and his spirits are very low. You must not allow unfortunate rumors about yourself to disturb him. This world is dross. It is nothing. It would be a terrible sin to stand in his way on the path toward the life to come."

He said nothing pointed, but she wept as he spoke, and was so undone that he, too, shed tears. "Look what an old busybody I am," he said self-deprecatingly, "talking about people in just the way that once so annoyed me in others! Why, you must be more than ever fed up with me for being such a mean old fool!"

He drew her inkstone to him, ground ink himself, put the paper before her, and set her to writing, but her hand shook, and she could not do it. She cannot have been this slow to answer that ardent letter I read, he thought bitterly, feeling no sympathy for her; but he nonetheless told her what to write.

So it was that the month when she had been supposed to go to her father passed on by. The Second Princess's visit had been magnificent, but Her Highness had lost the freshness of youth and was reluctant now to invite any comparisons.

"The eleventh month is one of mourning for me,"[114] Genji remarked, "and the end of the year is always frantically busy. It also worries me that he should be so eager to see you when you are becoming less and less presentable. Can we really put it off that long, though? Please cheer up, be more lively, and do something about those haggard looks of yours!" He found her very appealing even so.

He had always made sure that the Intendant of the Gate Watch was beside him whenever an occasion promised particularly well, but that was all over now, and contact between them ceased. He imagined people wondering why, but the shame of looking like a decrepit old fool to the Intendant when they met, and of losing his own composure at the same time, dissuaded him from doing anything about it, and soon months had passed without a murmur of protest from him. As far as most people were concerned, the Intendant was merely in poor health, and in any case there had been no concerts at Rokujō this year, but the Commander suspected that there

114. The Kiritsubo Emperor, the father of Genji and Suzaku, died in the eleventh month.

was more to it than that. That glimpse we both had of her must have been too much for so impressionable a man, the Commander reflected, but it never occurred to him that Genji already knew everything.

The twelfth month came. The date was set for just after the tenth, and the entire estate rang with music and dances. The lady at Nijō was not back yet, but she returned when the prospect of the grand rehearsal proved to be too tempting. Her ladyship the Consort was at home as well. Her most recent child was another boy. Her children were all so dear that Genji played with them day and night, delighted by the blessing that the years had brought him. The wife of His Excellency of the Right came for the rehearsal, too. The Commander spent morning and evening holding so many preparatory rehearsals in the northeast quarter that the lady there never even attended the main one in Genji's presence.

Genji felt that it would cast a pall over the occasion if he issued no invitation even now to the Intendant of the Gate Watch, and that moreover people would wonder at the omission. He therefore let the Intendant know that he was expected, but the gentleman pleaded grave illness and failed to appear. Still, there was nothing in particular actually wrong with him. Genji wondered sympathetically whether he might not just be feeling guilty, and he sent him a message to press him further. The gentleman's father, too, was meanwhile urging him to accept. "Why did you decline?" he asked. "Your refusal must sound quite strange to His Grace, and you really are not so very ill. Do pull yourself together and go!" Genji's second invitation then arrived, and the Intendant went after all, over his own inner protests.

The senior nobles had not yet assembled. Genji seated the Intendant near him as always, inside the blinds,[115] with the lowered blinds of the chamber between them. Yes, he really was very thin and wan, and in bold pride of manner his brothers overshadowed him as usual. What singled him out instead was his thoughtful poise. His present exceptionally quiet demeanor commended him to Genji as a highly suitable match for a Princess, were it not that those two had been too unforgivably tactless.

"Things have been quiet lately, and it has been a long time since we last saw each other," Genji began warmly, as though nothing were wrong. "Spending these last months tending the sick has given me little time to myself. Her Highness here was to have arranged the events for His Eminence's jubilee, but it has had to be put off again and again, and now that the end of the year is coming, I can after all offer only a token meal of fasting fare. A proper jubilee is of course a much greater occasion, but with all the children there are here, I thought that I might at least have them learn some dances and so on to show them off; and then, you see, I could think of no one but you to set the rhythm, so I decided to give up blaming you for your months of silence."

He spoke affably enough, but the Intendant felt his face change color, and he was too acutely ashamed to find an immediate reply. "I was very sorry to learn that certain ladies have been unwell all these months, but this spring I myself began suffering from an old complaint of mine that affects my legs and makes me unsteady on my feet, and this condition has continued in so disturbing a manner that I no longer

115. The blinds between the aisle room and the veranda. Kashiwagi is in the aisle, Genji in the chamber.

go to court. I prefer instead to remain at home as though the world had ceased to exist for me. His Retired Excellency observed to me that this is His Eminence's jubilee year and that he feels it behooves him more than anyone else to acknowledge it properly. 'It would be awkward for me to put myself forward, though,' he said, 'now that I have hung up my hat and put away my carriage. You are still junior, I know, but you understand things as well as I do, and you should make that clear to His Grace.' His encouragement was what roused me sufficiently from my grave condition to come. If I may venture to express my humble opinion, now that His Eminence has settled into so quiet and pious a mode of life, he may well prefer to forgo any grandly ceremonial event, and I believe that your proposal to keep things simple and to satisfy his longing for a quiet talk with Her Highness is greatly preferable."

Genji silently commended him for not mentioning the jubilee event the Second Princess had given her father, considering his relationship to her, for he gathered that it had been splendid. "Quite so," he replied. "Most people would take this simplicity for mere indifference, but you understand, and you have reassured me that I am right. The Commander is fully competent by now to serve the realm, but he seems not to have much of a gift for the finer things of life, few of which are foreign to His Eminence. His Eminence is particularly fond of music, at which he is expert, and I expect that despite his appearance of renunciation he is looking forward to enjoying it in peace. Do take care of things, you and the Commander, and make sure that the children who will dance know what to do and how to behave. Their teachers may be very good at what they know, but they are hopeless otherwise."

The Intendant found the warmth of Genji's manner encouraging, but he also felt painfully constrained and had little to say, and he wanted to get away as quickly as possible. He left at last without ever engaging in his usual intent conversation.

In the northeast quarter the Intendant added further touches to the musicians and dancers, for whom the Commander had provided the costumes. The Commander had dressed them magnificently, but the Intendant's finer discernment showed him indeed to be a master in these matters.

Today was the day for the rehearsal, and Genji wanted to be sure that it was worth watching, since all the ladies of Rokujō were to see it. For the jubilee proper the children would wear red over a grape layering, but today they had on leaf green over sappan. The thirty musicians, in white layerings for the occasion, performed in the gallery leading out to the southeast fishing pavilion. They came round the garden hill to appear before Genji playing "Immortal in the Mist,"[116] while a sprinkling of snow fell to confirm that spring was not far away and plum buds swelled on the bough. Genji sat inside the blinds of the aisle, attended only by His Highness of Ceremonial and His Excellency of the Right. The lesser senior nobles occupied the veranda and served them their meal without ado, for the day's event was purely informal.

---

116. "Senyūka," a *gagaku* piece said to have no accompanying dance. It alludes by its title to Genji's status as an Honorary Retired Emperor, because a Retired Emperor was imagined as a Taoist Immortal and inhabited a Sentō Gosho ("Palace of the Cave of the Immortal"). Immortals (*sennin*) were supposed to sport among the mists of mountain peaks and to need no other food.

The fourth son of His Excellency of the Right, the Commander's third son, and two grandsons of His Highness of War danced "Ten Thousand Years," and they looked very attractive indeed despite still being so small. None of these sons of the great houses stood out above the others; all were handsome and beautifully turned out, and each had the distinction one expected of him. The Commander's second son from the Dame of Staff, and the son of the Minamoto Counselor—himself His Highness of Ceremonial's son and formerly the Intendant of the Watch—danced "The Royal Deer," while His Excellency of the Right's third son did "The Warrior King"

The dance "The Royal Deer"

and the Commander's eldest, "Twin Dragons." "Great Peace" and "The Return of Spring" were performed by the men and boys of the same families. When twilight came on, Genji had his blinds raised, and the pleasures of the moment mounted. His grandsons were so dear and so handsome, their dancing offered such novel delights, and their teachers had taught them so fully all they knew that their own native talent added to all the rest made their dancing a wonder. Genji looked on each with delight, and the older senior nobles shed tears. His Highness of Ceremonial, whose thoughts were on his own grandsons, wept till his nose was red.

"The older you are, the harder it gets to stop drunken tears," Genji said. "Look at the Intendant of the Right Gate Watch, smiling away to himself—it is so embarrassing! Never mind, though, his time will come. The sun and moon never turn back. No one escapes old age." He peered at the Intendant, who seemed far less cheerful than the others and really did look so unwell that the wonders of the day were lost on him. The way Genji singled him out in mock drunkenness appeared to be simple teasing, but it deepened his despair, and by the time the wine cup came round, he had such a headache that he took no more than a token sip, which Genji did not fail to miss. Genji had him keep the cup and made him drink again and again, to his discomfort and embarrassment, even though in that state he still cut a finer figure than most.

Too miserable to bear up any longer, he withdrew before the evening was over, feeling perfectly awful. I am not that drunk, though, he said to himself. What is the matter with me? Have anxiety and fright made me light-headed? There is no reason to feel completely destroyed, just because he talked to me that way. Why, this is ridiculous!

No, he was not suffering from any passing intoxication. Soon his condition was grave. His dismayed parents moved him to their own residence on the grounds that they would worry too much as long as he remained elsewhere, which was a cruel blow to the Princess, his wife. All through their uneventful life together he had entertained no more than a wan hope that he might eventually warm to her, but sorrow filled him now that he was going, perhaps forever, and he felt keenly the affront of leaving her to her grief.

Her mother the Haven was distraught. "A son certainly owes his parents their due," she said, "but as a rule a tie such as the one you have with my daughter does not permit you to leave her under any ordinary circumstances. It can only be very painful to her that you should propose to do so until you recover. Please stay here longer and see whether that will not be good enough." She spoke to him through a mere curtain that stood beside where he lay.

"I understand," he answered. "Having been permitted the undeserved honor of intimacy with your daughter, unworthy as I am, I had hoped to acknowledge my debt by living long and allowing you to watch me rise from my present insignificance to a somewhat more honorable station, but under the circumstances I am afraid that I may never be able to make all my devotion to her clear, and even now, when I feel myself called away, I doubt that the regret I feel will leave me free to go."[117] By now both were in tears.

His failure to move to his father's house immediately provoked an indignant appeal from his mother. "Why do you not hasten here so that I may see you? Whenever my spirits are a little low, you are the one among all the others whom I most long to see and who brings me the greatest comfort. As things are, I worry so!"

He well understood her feelings, too. "I mean something special to them," he told his wife, "perhaps because I am their eldest, and they still feel strongly about me and miss me very much when they do not see me for some time, so that I would feel deeply remiss if I were not to go to them now, when I feel that my end is near. Please come with all discretion and visit me there if you hear that the time has come to despair of my life. I promise you that we shall then meet again. I am a strangely dull and feckless man, and I regret having sometimes given you reason to feel that I neglected you. To think that I never knew my life might soon be over, and that I assumed I still had many, many years before me!" He left bathed in tears, and the Princess remained behind, missing him beyond words.

His Excellency's household was expecting him, and his arrival caused a great stir. It is not as though his condition there rapidly became alarming, however. Rather, he had eaten nothing for some months, and now he would no longer touch even a tangerine or anything else of the kind, so that he simply wasted away as though absorbed by an unseen power. All the world grieved to see one of the most gifted men of his time laid low, and no one failed to visit him. His Majesty and His Cloistered Eminence both inquired after him often, and their great affliction only added to the wretchedness of his parents. His Grace at Rokujō thought with surprise what a shame it was, and he sent His Excellency warm and frequent inquiries. The Commander, who was such an old friend, was of course far closer to him than that, and he went about in a state of profound grief.

His Eminence's jubilee celebration took place on the twenty-fifth of the month. There was little enthusiasm for it at a time when the most highly esteemed

117. To rebirth in Amida's paradise.

senior noble of the day was gravely ill, and his parents, brothers, sisters, and many other distinguished persons connected to him were lost in sorrow, but the event had already been postponed repeatedly, and Genji felt that it simply could not at last be canceled. He sadly imagined how Her Highness must feel. He had scriptures read, properly enough, in fifty temples, and more at His Cloistered Eminence's own in order to dedicate an image of Mahavairochana.[118]

118. The Sanskrit name (transliterated in the original as Makabirusana) of the supreme deity of the Eso-teric Buddhist (Shingon) pantheon, whose name appears more often in Japan in its translated form of Dainichi (Great Sun). Ninnaji, the historical temple traditionally associated with Suzaku's in the tale, is dedicated to this deity. In the original this sentence is incomplete.

36

KASHIWAGI
The Oak Tree

Kashiwagi means "oak tree." After Kashiwagi's death, his widow's mother uses the word in an answer to Yūgiri:

"He indeed is gone, the god who stood watchful guard over this oak tree, but may such familiar boughs start a new intimacy?"

This oak tree is less Kashiwagi than his widow, but the poem gave Kashiwagi and the chapter their name.

RELATIONSHIP TO EARLIER CHAPTERS

"The Oak Tree" continues from "Spring Shoots II" without a break.

PERSONS

His Grace, the Honorary Retired Emperor, Genji, age 48

The Intendant of the Right Gate Watch,
then Acting Grand Counselor, 32 or 33 (Kashiwagi)

Her Highness, the Third Princess, then Her Cloistered Highness,
22 or 23 (Onna San no Miya)

Kojijū, Onna San no Miya's gentlewoman

His Retired Excellency (Tō no Chūjō)

Her Majesty, the Empress, 40 (Akikonomu)

His Majesty, the Emperor, 22

His Cloistered Eminence, the Retired Emperor, 51 (Suzaku In)

His Retired Excellency's wife, Kashiwagi's mother (Shi no Kimi)

The Right Commander, Genji's son, 27 (Yūgiri)

Her Highness, the Second Princess (Ochiba no Miya)

The Right Grand Controller, son of Tō no Chūjō

The son of Onna San no Miya and Kashiwagi, born (Kaoru)

The Consort, Genji's daughter, 20 (Akashi no Nyōgo)

The Haven, mother of Ochiba no Miya (Ichijō no Miyasudokoro)

The Intendant of the Right Gate Watch remained as ill as before, and meanwhile the New Year came. He saw his parents' grief and knew that willing himself to go would not help, since that would be a grave sin;[1] but where was he to find the wish to cling to life? Even as a boy, he reflected, I nursed high ambition and strove in all things to stand above my peers, and I therefore approached every matter, public or private, with particular pride; but then a failure or two taught the likes of me how little to expect success, and all of life turned to disappointment. I longed more and more to prepare for the life to come,[2] except that my parents' distress would then seriously hinder me from wandering moor and mountain, and I managed one way or another to put the idea aside. Whom but myself have I to blame, if knowing I can never show my face in the world again has brought me in the end to the last pitch of despair? Yes, the error was mine alone. I have no one else to accuse, nor do I have any complaint to lay before the gods and buddhas, because all this must have been destiny. No one in this world is a thousand-year pine,[3] no one lingers forever, and as long as there is someone to remember me a little, someone to give me some slight, pitying thought, let that be my reward for having burned with a single flame.[4] If I were to live, my name would be dishonored, and she and I would both be held up to scandal, while this way I may even find forgiveness where now I am only condemned! All is well that ends well. Perhaps the warmth that moved His Grace to desire my company so often through the years will restore his feeling for me, as long I do nothing else to offend him. So the Intendant's idle thoughts ran on and on—and yet, he felt, it was just too cruel.

He wondered in anguish why he had trapped himself this way. His pillow might have floated away,[5] so endlessly did he weep over his own lapse, until a slight respite gave his family a moment to be away, and he sent *her* a letter. "You must have

1. The sin of preceding one's parents in death.
2. To take religious vows.
3. *Kokin rokujō* 2096: "How little this world answers my desires, when no one in it is a thousand-year pine!"
4. *Kokin rokujō* 3984: "The summer fly comes in the end to grief because it burns with a single flame." The "summer fly" (*natsumushi*) is the firefly, whose light in poetry is the flame of love.
5. *Kokin rokujō* 3241: "With all the tears that fall upon the bed of one who sleeps alone, even a pillow of stone might well float away."

had occasion to hear that everything may well be over for me soon. The news means so little to you that you do not even ask how I am, and I understand that, but still, your silence is bitterly unkind!" he wrote, but his hand was trembling badly, and he gave up trying to say all he wished.

"When the end has come, and from my smoldering pyre smoke rises at last,
I know this undying flame even then will burn for you.

Oh, tell me at least that you pity me! Your comforting words will light my way on the dark road I have chosen to follow."

He also sent an unrepentantly passionate appeal to Kojijū. "I *must* speak to her one last time in person," he wrote; and despite her shock at his presumption, Kojijū was overcome with sorrow to gather that he would soon be no more, for she had run errands between his household and Her Highness's ever since she was a child, and she knew both well. "Oh, please answer him, my lady!" she pleaded in tears. "I am afraid that it may be for the very last time."

"I sympathize with him in a general sort of way, because I, too, suffer from the feeling that each day may be my last, but what happened was too awful, and I want no more of it. No, I just cannot risk it." Her Highness absolutely refused. Although neither sensible nor sober by nature, she was probably frightened of the displeasure betrayed at times by the gentleman who so overawed her. Kojijū placed the inkstone before her nonetheless, and she begged and pleaded until Her Highness grudgingly wrote after all. She took the letter to its destination secretly, under cover of darkness.

His Retired Excellency had called in a powerful ascetic from the Kazuraki Mountains, and now he received the man and set him to working his prayers. The Great Rite and the chanting of scriptures went forward amid a tremendous din. He also sent his younger sons to look for others as well, wherever people said they might be found—more or less holy men of every kind, hidden deep in the hills and hardly known to the world at all—and he summoned these, too, until odious, repellent mountain ascetics began gathering to his residence in large numbers. The patient just suffered from vague fears and at times only sobbed. Most of the yin-yang masters reported after divination that the cause was a woman's spirit, which His Excellency found easy enough to believe. The spirit's refusal to declare itself was baffling, though, and that was why he searched every corner of the hills.

The tall, fierce ascetic from Kazuraki chanted the *darani*[6] with wild and fearful power. "Oh, I cannot bear it!" the Intendant cried. "Surely my sins are very great, because the *darani* chanted so loud is terrifying, and I feel certain that I must die!" He stole away to talk to Kojijū. His Excellency did not know this, however, and he believed it when he was told the Intendant was asleep.

He therefore had a discreet talk with the ascetic. Lively and merry though he still was, despite his advancing age, he now received such people as this face-to-face, describing how his son's illness had first declared itself and how in a meander-

---

6. A spell transliterated from Sanskrit via Chinese and unintelligible as language.

ing way it had then grown worse and worse. It was a sad thing to hear him beg, "Do something, please, to make this spirit appear!"

"Listen to him!" the Intendant said. "Why, he has no idea what I have done! I would value myself a lot more than I do if this woman's spirit their divination is supposed to have hit on really *were* she, clinging to me. There is no point, though, in arguing that this is hardly the first time a man has had the face to blunder as I did, hold up someone else's name to scandal, and destroy himself as well, because I still feel guilty toward him, and now that he knows what I did, I shrink from the prospect of living—which I should say only confirms what a special light he has. My crime is not really that serious,[7] but as soon as I met his gaze that evening, my soul fled in anguish, and it has never come back. Please, if it is haunting Rokujō, please bind it for me!" He wept and laughed feebly as he spoke, like an empty shell.

Kojijū described how guilt and shame continually overwhelmed Her Highness, too. He felt as though he could actually see her, with her despondent air and her wasted face. Then his wandering soul must really be going to her! The idea made him more wretched than ever. "No," he said, "I shall never speak of her again. The little she and I shared is over now, and it is awful to think that it may detain me forever. I just want to know that the event that concerns me so has gone smoothly for her. I have told no one else about that dream of mine, but I have thought about it on my own, and I am extremely anxious." The depth of his despair was too much for Kojijū, despite the awful folly of what he had done, and she, too, wept bitterly.

The Intendant called for a hand torch and read Her Highness's reply. She had written it quite nicely, although her writing was still uncertain. "I am very sorry to hear how you are, but what can I really say? I know that you will understand. 'Even then will burn for you,' you wrote:

> I would rise with you, yes, and vanish forever, that your smoke and mine
> might decide which one of us burns with the greater sorrows.

Do you suppose that I could survive you?"

That was all, but he was moved and grateful. "Very well," he said, "her smoke will be all I retain of this life. How fragile it was!" His tears flowed faster now, and he wrote his reply lying down, between bouts of weeping. The words made no sense and resembled the tracks of strange birds.

> "Though I turn to smoke and forever melt away into the wide sky,
> I shall never leave your side, who remain all my desire.

Gaze upward, then, especially in the evening. Never mind that he may see you and understand: only let me always have your unavailing pity."

He felt even worse after this confused effort at writing. "Very well, go back to Her Highness before too much of the night is over and tell her that I am all but

---

7. Onna San no Miya is not an Empress or a Consort.

gone. It hurts to look even past my own death to people's shock when they understand. What old tie between her and me can have so enslaved my heart?" He slipped away in tears to retire. Usually he kept Kojijū with him interminably to chat on and on about nothing at all, and seeing him so silent now upset her until she felt unable to leave.

The Intendant's nurse described his condition to her, too, weeping profusely. The grief of His Excellency and the others was heartrending. "But you were feeling a little better yesterday and today!" His Excellency protested. "Why do you seem so much weaker now?"

"What can I say?" His son was in tears as well. "It is just that I seem to have no more time left."

Double trays

That evening Her Highness felt a discomfort that her excited women recognized as meaning that the moment was at hand, and the startled Genji came immediately when they let him know. It is too bad! he reflected. How very glad I would be if I could assist her without dwelling on my doubts! He wished to keep his thoughts to himself, however, and he therefore summoned healers and commissioned a perpetual Great Rite. Every monk with healing powers came to offer up noisy prayers.

She gave birth at sunrise, after a long and painful night. The secret is still safe, Genji thought when he heard the news that it was a boy, but things could be very difficult if he looks too much like his father. A girl would be much safer, since one could always divert attention from her and since few people would see her in any case. On the other hand, considering this painful suspicion, it is just as well the child is one who needs less care rather than more. But how strange! This must be retribution for what has terrified me so long. Perhaps my sins will be lighter in the next life, now that I have reaped so surprising a reward in this one. The women, who knew nothing of all this, assumed that a child born late in his life to so special a mother would mean a great deal to him, and they busied themselves dutifully in his service.

The rites attending the birth[8] were done with great pomp and splendor. At the birth celebrations offered by his ladies the usual trays, double trays,[9] and tall stands[10] showed how keenly each vied with the others. On the fifth evening it was Her Majesty's turn magnificently to provide, as a government gesture, the meal for the new mother and suitably graded gifts for each of her gentlewomen. She saw to it that each detail was perfect, from the gruel to the fifty sets of rice dumplings and the meals for the different estate officials, servants, and grooms. The Commissioner

---

8. The cutting of the umbilical cord, the ritual bathing, the first suckling, and so on.

9. *Tsuigasane*, a tray (*oshiki*) combined with a simple rectangular stand.

10. *Takatsuki*, a tall stand for food or drink, resting on a single foot.

and the rest of her household gentlemen were all there, and so were His Eminence Reizei's privy gentlemen.

The seventh evening was provided by His Majesty, also as a government gesture. His Excellency should have been eager to attend, but he now had only one thing on his mind, and he sent no more than the customary congratulations. A great many Princes and senior nobles were present. Appearances conveyed the impression that Genji held mother and child in the highest regard, but he had reason to be bitter at heart, and he did not greatly put himself out for the guests. There was no music.

Her Highness, already so frail, had found the unfamiliar experience quite terrifying, and she refused all medicinal infusions; instead, she brooded anew upon her misfortune and thought how much she would rather die. Despite his fine show, Genji paid no particular attention to the little boy, who seemed still to be restless. "Just look how little His Grace seems to care!" a brazen old gentlewoman remarked commiseratingly. "It is not as though he had many, and this one is frighteningly pretty!" Her Highness, listening with half an ear, reflected bitterly that the distance between them would only grow, and she was sufficiently distressed to decide that she wanted to become a nun.

Genji did not spend the night there, and he only looked in during the day. He peered round her standing curtain. "The sad conviction that I have little time left has turned me to my devotions, life being as treacherous as it is, and all the commotion lately has discouraged me from coming. How are you? Are you feeling better? I worry about you."

She lifted her head. "I still doubt that I will live, and they say that that sort of sin is very grave.[11] I think I shall become a nun, because that might help me live longer, or at least it might lighten this burden of sin if I am to die after all." She spoke in a much more grown-up manner than usual.

"You will do nothing of the kind. It is out of the question. What you have been through has frightened you, I imagine, but it hardly threatens your life." Privately, though, his thoughts ran differently. It might be rather moving to help her do it, if that is really what she wants. The poor thing is all too likely to come under a cloud again if she goes on with me this way. I doubt that with the best will in the world I can change my opinion of her anymore, and there will be some difficult times; people will note my indifference, and that will be unfortunate, because when His Cloistered Eminence hears of it, the fault will appear to be entirely mine. Her present indisposition makes a good excuse to let her do it—I might as well.

At the same time the idea repelled him. It hurt to imagine her so sadly renouncing her long, long hair and with it the long life that still lay before her. "Do pluck up your courage," he said. "You will come to no harm. You have at hand the example of someone who seemed to be at death's door and who recovered nonetheless. Life does not always play us false, you know." She drank her medicine. Lying there all pale and thin and troublingly frail, she had such a quiet sweetness about her that he felt he must indulgently forgive her after all, despite the gravity of her fault.

11. The sin of dying in consequence of childbirth.

His Eminence at his mountain temple was relieved to hear that his daughter's great moment had passed smoothly, and he was eager to see her; but then he heard nothing but talk of how ill she was, and anxiety disturbed his devotions.

She was weak already, and by now she had not eaten for some days, which made her condition very worrying indeed. She missed her father far more than she had during all those years when she had not seen him at all. "I may never see him again!" she cried, weeping bitterly. Genji had a suitable messenger convey her words to His Eminence, who was so devastated that he set forth under cover of night, despite knowing full well that he should not.

His sudden, completely unannounced arrival took Genji by surprise and covered him with confusion. "I understood that it was wrong of me to succumb again to worldly affections," he said, "but the hardest delusion of all to renounce is the darkness in a father's heart. I was neglecting my practice, and fear that lasting ill feeling might arise between her and me if we were to lose each other in so untimely a manner decided me to ignore censure and come after all." His unfamiliar guise was nonetheless appealingly and gracefully discreet, since he was not in formal religious robes, and he made so fine a figure in gray that Genji envied him.

Genji began as usual by shedding tears. "There is nothing in *particular* wrong with her," he explained. "It is probably just that she has been growing weaker for months and that she has gone so long now without eating properly.

"I can only apologize for receiving you in such a room," he went on, and led His Eminence to a cushion before his daughter's curtained bed. Her women tidied up their mistress as well as they could and brought her down to the floor.[12]

His Eminence brushed the curtain slightly aside. "I feel rather like a monk on night prayer duty, although unfortunately I have done little yet to acquire any healing power; all I can offer you is my own person, which I gather you have been anxious to see." He wiped his eyes, and Her Highness wept feebly as well.

"I do not think I shall live," she said. "Oh, please, now that you are here, make me a nun!"

"That is an admirable request if you really mean it, but you cannot actually be sure how much longer you have, and you know, someone like you, with a long future before her, could easily regret it later on. People could well criticize you for it, too. You would do better to refrain." He turned to Genji. "I *would* do it if she seemed to be dying, since she herself wants it. I believe that any time at all as a nun would help her."

"She has been talking that way for days, but an evil spirit may trick a person into entertaining that wish, and I have therefore ignored her."

"It would be one thing if there were anything wrong in this case with giving in to an evil spirit, even if it had put the idea into her head, but in fact I would bitterly regret it later on if I failed to listen to her when she is so weak already and almost gone." His Eminence silently reflected that after accepting the daughter offered him with such boundless trust, Genji had failed in his devotion to her, as His Eminence

12. Down from the raised platform of the bed.

himself had been greatly disappointed to learn over the years, although he had never been able to voice his reproaches and so had been reduced merely to deploring what other people thought and said. Why not take this opportunity to remove her from His Grace, he thought, without exposing her to ridicule by leaving the impression that she had merely despaired of him? He can still be counted on to look after her in the ways that matter most, and for that, at least, I did well to entrust her to him. She need not pointedly reject him; instead I might do up the large, pleasant house I have from our father and invite her to move there. As long as I am alive, I want to see her secure, and say what one will, His Grace is hardly likely to abandon her completely. Yes, His Eminence decided, that is what I shall do; and he continued aloud, "Well, then, I might take this opportunity to let her acquire a link with enlightenment by receiving the Precepts."

What does this mean? Genji silently protested, forgetting in his pity and dismay everything that he had against her. It was too much. He went straight in to her. "How can you consider abandoning me this way, when I have so few years left? Do calm down for a moment, drink your medicine, and have something to eat! I am sure that you mean well, but how can you possibly perform your devotions in your weakened condition? You must look after yourself first!" But she shook her head and thought how hatefully he spoke. He saw with sorrow and regret that despite her composure she must indeed feel she had reason to be angry with him.

Daybreak came while he continued his wavering efforts to dissuade her. His Eminence wished to avoid being caught by daylight on the way back, and he summoned the worthiest of the monks present to pray and to cut off his daughter's hair. The ceremony during which she cast aside her rich and beautiful tresses and received the Precepts was simply too pathetic. Genji, who could not bear it, wept copiously.

Having always felt so strongly and wanted the very best for her, His Eminence was deeply saddened to see all his hopes for her reduced to naught, and he wept, too. "There," he said, "you must get well now, and it would be a good idea for you also to call the Name and chant the scriptures." It was full day, and he hastened away. Her Highness was still all but fainting with weakness, and she had been unable to enjoy his visit properly or even to talk to him.

"All this has been like a dream, and in the turmoil of my mind I have boorishly failed to show my gratitude for the visit I remember you paying me long ago.[13] I shall call upon you later to that end." Genji ordered an escort for His Eminence's journey back.

"As long as I felt that every day might be my last," His Eminence replied, "I could not bear imagining her lost and deprived of anyone else to give her his protection. That is why I approached you, although you might have preferred me not to, and after that I felt at peace for years; but if she survives now, it may not suit her to go on living among many people in so thoroughly unfamiliar a guise, and at the

13. Nine years ago, in "New Wisteria Leaves."

same time it could be extremely lonely for her off in some mountain village or other. I hope that you will remain concerned about her, in consonance with her new circumstances."

"I am only embarrassed that you should feel the need to say so. My confusion has been such that I hardly know what is happening." His Grace did indeed seem extremely agitated.

The spirit afflicting Her Highness came forth[14] during the late-night prayers. "Take *that*, then!" it ranted. "You thought you were ever so clever getting the last one[15] back, which was so annoying that I just kept lying in wait. Now I can go." It laughed aloud. Genji was horrified. Why, has that spirit been here, too, all the time? He felt pity and dismay. Her Highness seemed to have revived a little, but she did not yet look out of danger. Her women kept their feelings to themselves, despite their shock, because they recognized that their mistress might be better off this way. Meanwhile, Genji had the Great Rite continued without a break and did everything he could for her.

The Intendant lapsed close to unconsciousness when Her Highness's news reached him, until very little hope remained. He thought of having the Princess his wife come to him, because he was deeply concerned about her, but that might injure her dignity, and besides, his mother and father were with him all the time, and he felt that it would be disastrous if by some misfortune they were to see her. He told them that he would like to visit her one last time, but they would not hear of it.

He begged them both to look after her. Her mother the Haven had never favored this alliance, but His Excellency had urged it on her with such enthusiasm that she allowed herself to be persuaded, and His Eminence had agreed as well, hardly knowing what else to do. His Eminence's anxiety over Her Highness moved him to observe in the end that *she* was the one after all who had found a promising, reliable protector, and the Intendant, who heard of his remark, now recalled it with despair. "I feel very sorry for many reasons whenever I reflect that I must soon leave her behind," he said to his mother, "but it is not up to me whether I live or die, and what troubles me most is the idea that she may bitterly resent the broken tie between us. Do be kind to her and see to her needs."

"Please do not talk like that!" she replied. "How long do you suppose I will live, once you are gone, that you should speak to me this way about what lies in the future?" She was weeping too profusely for him to continue, and so he entrusted the rest of what he had to say to the Right Grand Controller.[16]

The Intendant was so poised and capable that his younger brothers, especially the very youngest, looked up to him as to a father, and all were saddened that he should talk so bleakly. Every member of the household grieved. His Majesty, too, was extremely sorry. Upon learning that the Intendant was dying, His Majesty appointed him an Acting Grand Counselor on the spot, and he wondered whether the Intendant's gratitude might not give him the strength for a last visit to the palace;

---

14. To speak through a medium. Genji seems to assume it is Rokujō, though she has never spoken like this before.

15. Murasaki.

16. A younger brother, possibly Kōbai.

but the Intendant felt no such respite, and it was from his sickbed that he expressed his thanks for His Majesty's generosity. His Excellency was more stricken than ever by this evidence of His Majesty's high regard.

The Commander deeply lamented his friend's condition and inquired after him often, and he came straight to congratulate him on his appointment. A noisy throng of people had gathered with their press of horses and carriages around the gate near the Intendant's wing. The Intendant had hardly risen at all since the year began, and he hesitated to receive so great a lord casually; but he also regretted having wasted away like this without ever doing so. "Never mind, then, come in," he said. "I know that you will forgive me for receiving you amid such disorder." He dismissed the monks a moment from around his pillow and had the Commander shown in.

They had long been so close that nothing could come between them, and no parent, brother, or sister could have felt greater pain at the prospect of parting. The Commander hoped that today's happy occasion might have put the Intendant in a more cheerful mood, but alas, it had not. "Why is your health failing this way? I thought that the congratulations due you today would make you feel a little better." He lifted a corner of the standing curtain.

"Unfortunately, I am no longer the man I was." The Intendant had his hat on,[17] and he tried to sit up, but the effort seemed too much for him; instead he lay with the covers over him, wearing layers of comfortably soft white gowns. The room was clean and tidy, there was incense in the air, and his graceful mode of life showed that he remained alert despite his infirmity. Many a man when gravely ill becomes unkempt in beard and hair and makes a painful sight, but the Intendant in his wasted condition only looked paler and more distinguished than before. One saw how very weak he was when he raised his pillow and spoke, and one noted the pitiful faintness of his breath.

"You have deteriorated very little, considering how long you have been unwell. Actually, you look even better now than before." The Commander wiped his eyes nonetheless. "We promised ourselves that neither of us would go before the other. This is a terrible thing! I cannot even make out why you are so ill. We are so close, and yet I still do not know!"

"I myself cannot say just when my condition became this serious. Nothing definable is wrong, and so I did not immediately realize what was happening to me, but I was soon so weak that by now I am hardly myself at all. Perhaps these prayers and vows are holding me back. I would gladly go, though, because it is actually a great trial to linger on like this, and if it were up to me, I would be quickly on my way. Still, there are many things I shall be sorry to leave. My parents will grieve even more when I am no longer there to serve them, and my service to my Sovereign will remain incomplete as well. As to my own fortunes, alas, there is something else besides the sorrow of leaving so many commonplace regrets, something that is my secret agony, and I wonder why I should confess it now, as my end approaches. Still, I feel as though I must speak after all, and to whom if not to you? I have all

---

17. It was proper for a gentleman to wear his hat (*eboshi*) even indoors.

Two monks

those brothers, I know, but for various reasons I cannot imagine bringing it up with them. There is a little matter on which I wronged His Grace of Rokujō, and for months I begged his pardon in my heart, until I became so miserable that I despaired of life and found that I was ill. Then I received his invitation to the music rehearsal for His Eminence's jubilee. I gathered from the way he looked at me while I was there that I was not yet forgiven, and that left me more than ever convinced that I dared live no longer. The horror I felt stirred a tempest in my heart, and as you see, I never knew peace again. I probably never counted that much for him, but he has meant a great deal to me since I was a boy, and since the question of what evil report reached him will remain my most bitter preoccupation in this life, it may easily stand in my way in the next as well. Please get his ear for a moment and explain my feelings properly to him, if you can manage to do so. If he ever pardons me, even after I am gone, you will deserve the credit for it." The longer he spoke, the more the effort seemed to cost him. The Commander was powerfully moved. He had his own idea what the matter might be, but he could not be certain.

"What could possibly prick your conscience this way? His Grace has never betrayed any such feelings. It has surprised and pained him to learn how ill you are, and he seems to be very sorry indeed about it. Why have you said nothing about this, when it worries you so much? I should have been speaking for each of you to the other. By now I suppose it is too late." He sadly wished that he could turn back time.

"Yes, I should really have talked to you in one of those moments when I felt a little better. Still, it never occurred to me that my hour might come so soon, and I foolishly went on telling myself that one cannot possibly know how long one has yet to live. Please never mention this to anyone else. I have told you, you know, only in order to ask you to speak for me when a suitable occasion arises. Please keep in touch with Her Highness at Ichijō[18] whenever it seems proper to do so. His Eminence is certain to learn of her plight, and I hope that you will do what you can to reassure him."

He must have had much more to say, but he no longer had the strength to speak; instead he gestured with his hand that the Commander should leave him. The monks who were there to pray returned to his side, his parents and the others gathered around him, a great commotion arose, and the weeping Commander withdrew.

18. His wife, the Second Princess. The location of her residence ("First Avenue") has not been mentioned before.

The Commander's wife[19] was grief-stricken, to say nothing of the Kokiden Consort. So generous was the Intendant's spirit, and so brotherly were his affections, that the wife of His Excellency of the Right[20] felt close to him as well, and she therefore mourned him with all her heart and had prayer rites commissioned on his behalf; but no such remedy could heal his affliction,[21] and it made no difference. He died as foam melts from the water, without ever managing to see the Princess again.

His feeling for the Princess had never been deep or heartfelt, but he had treated her correctly in all ordinary matters, and since he had always been thoughtful and kind, without undue familiarity, she had never had cause to complain. She reflected on looking back that it must have been the very brevity of his life that had made him so strangely indifferent to the commonplace things of this world, and the thought was so painful that she sank into a pathetic melancholy. Her mother bitterly lamented the cruel ridicule that would be visited on her daughter.[22] His Excellency and his wife naturally wished only that they had preceded their son, and they vainly burned with the pain of this break in the proper order of life.

Her Cloistered Highness,[23] to whom the Intendant's audacity had never been other than hateful and who did not wish him to live long, pitied him nonetheless when she heard the news. The way he had foreseen the birth of her son seemed to her to confirm that that dreadful incident had indeed been foreordained, and such were her many fears and sorrows that she, too, burst into tears.

The skies were mild since it was the third month, and the time had come to celebrate the little boy's fiftieth day. Very fair and pretty, he was advanced for his age and babbled already. Genji came. "Are you feeling better now?" he asked. "What you did was such a waste! How gladly I would have seen you like this when you were as you used to be! It was cruel of you to leave me that way." There were tears in his eyes, and his tone was bitter. He came daily, and now at last he began to treat her with the highest consideration.

The fiftieth-day celebration of Kaoru's birth

19. Kumoi no Kari, Kashiwagi's sister.
20. Tamakazura.
21. *Shūishū* 665: "I am sick from the absence of my beloved; no medicine but heart-to-heart [*aoi*] will heal me."
22. For having been driven by need to marry below her, only to have her husband leave her a widow.
23. Onna San no Miya, now a nun.

On the fiftieth day the baby's own parents were supposed to feed him *mochii*,[24] and because of her unusual guise Her Highness's women were wondering what to do when Genji arrived. "Where is the difficulty?" he said. "His mother's habit might mean bad luck only if he were a girl." He had a little room beautifully done up on the front, south side. The little boy's nurses were splendidly dressed, the things before him—fruit baskets and cypress partitioned boxes—were nicely done in all sorts of lovely colors, and the women inside and outside his blinds fussed over him with innocent pleasure, having no idea of the truth; and Genji watched it all and thought, What a dismally shameful business!

Her Highness arose and turned away from Genji, acutely embarrassed that he had set aside the curtain that stood between them, to brush from her forehead the troublesome, thickly spreading ends of her hair. She was smaller and slighter than ever, and from the back one could hardly tell that there was anything different about her, since her hair had been left quite long, since it had seemed a pity to cut it.[25] In her layer after layer of gray under a plum red veering to yellow, and with her profile that still hardly seemed a nun's, she more resembled a pretty child. Her figure conveyed an impression of charm and grace. "You are a sight!" Genji said. "It is a dull and depressing color, gray. I am glad I shall go on seeing you, even as you are now, but for various reasons I am extremely sorry to gather that my own stubbornly helpless and foolish tears are what made you forsake me like this. I only wish you could take it back." He sighed. "If you leave me now, sorrow and shame will convince me that you yourself really did reject me. Please still have pity on me!"

"I hear that someone like me, now, knows little of human feelings. What can I possibly say, then, since I have never known them anyway?"

"Oh, what is the use? You certainly *have* had occasion to learn something about them!" Genji said no more and watched the little boy instead.

The many nurses in waiting on him were both noble and handsome. Genji summoned them and instructed them on how to look after him. "Alas, to think that he has come into the world when I myself have so little time left!" he said. The baby was deliciously fair and plump, and he smiled winningly when Genji took him in his arms. He did not look much like what Genji remembered of the Commander at this age. The Consort's[26] children favored His Majesty their father, and they had a properly imperial distinction, although they were not otherwise strikingly attractive. He was touched to find this little boy not only noble but charming, with lovely eyes and a ready smile. Perhaps it is just my imagination, he thought, but he really does look very much like him. Those eyes of his will have an extraordinarily lofty serenity, and what a delightful face! Her Cloistered Highness saw little of what he did, and her women knew nothing at all; it was therefore only in the secrecy of his own heart that he sighed and thought, Ah, how short a while he was destined to live!

His tears threatened to fall like rain while he pondered the fragility of life, but

24. Glutinous rice, to be fed to the baby with chopsticks. Onna San no Miya's women are unsure how to arrange the ceremony now that she is a nun.

25. The hair at her forehead has been cut, and the ends are bothering her, but at the back her hair is still much longer than the normal "nun's cut" (*ama sogi*).

26. Genji's daughter's.

he stealthily wiped them away because the character of the day forbade them,[27] and he hummed to himself, "I have long known the sorrows of silent thought."[28] He felt as though his life were over, even though he was ten years younger than the poet, and melancholy absorbed him. He must have felt like adding the warning "Do not take after your father!"[29]

One or two of her women must know what happened. How I wish she would understand me! But no, to her I probably look like a fool. Never mind my own part in this, though—I feel sorrier for her than for me. Genji's face betrayed none of these thoughts. How do that innocent babbling, those sweet eyes, and that dear mouth look to someone who does not know? The resemblance is very close, though. And to think that he left no more than this pitiful and completely unknown legacy—a child he could never have shown his parents, even though they were no doubt weeping for him to have one. Proud and accomplished as he was, he brought about his own destruction! Pity and regret drove the affront from Genji's heart, and he burst into tears.

He approached Her Highness while all the women were elsewhere. "What does he mean to you? Are you really glad to have given up a child like this to turn your back on the world? What a thing to do!" She sat there, blushing.

"Should anyone ask who it is who, in his time, cast that seed abroad,
what reply will he then give, the pine planted on the rock?[30]

I pity him," he whispered; but she lay down without answering. He understood and did not press her further. What can she be thinking? She may lack depth, but even so, this cannot mean *nothing* to her! The effort to divine her feelings was very painful.

The Commander longed to know what that hint the Intendant had felt impelled to give him could possibly mean. He would have let me know enough to work it out, since he had gone that far anyway, if only his mind had remained clear a little longer. What a sad end, and at how unfortunate a time, leaving his story unfinished that way! The Commander could not forget how his friend had looked then, and he was far more affected than the Intendant's brothers. Her Cloistered Highness was not that seriously ill when she renounced the world, he reflected, and she certainly had no difficulty making up her mind! And anyway, would His Grace have allowed it? I hear that when his lady was dying at Nijō, she begged him in tears to grant her the same thing, and the idea upset him so much that in the end he refused. The Commander pondered every clue. Yes, there must have been times when the Intendant failed to master that obvious leaning of his. He managed to maintain an unruffled surface, and he remained far more circumspect than most men, so much so that his composure made it hard to tell what he was thinking and even troubled those who knew him, but he had rather a weak side to him as well,

---

27. Kaoru's fiftieth day is in principle a happy occasion at which tears are taboo (*kotoimi*).
28. A collapsed line from a poem by Bai Juyi (*Hakushi monjū* 2821), composed when the poet had his first son at the age of fifty-eight. The full line mentions joys as well as sorrows.
29. Another phrase from Bai Juyi's poem.
30. The "pine" is Kaoru. Genji's poem varies on *Kokinshū* 907.

and he was too emotional—that must be why. Passion or not, how could he have allowed a forbidden desire to overwhelm him at the cost of his own life? What a terrible thing for her! What business did he have to go and destroy himself? Perhaps that was his destiny after all—who knows?—but it was a foolish, monstrous thing to do! Such were the Commander's private reflections, but he said nothing about them even to his wife, and he could not broach the subject to Genji either, without sufficient reason. Still, he looked forward to seeing the expression on Genji's face when he told Genji that the Intendant had brought it up.

The Intendant's mother and father remained lost in tears and knew nothing even of the sad passage of the days, and so they left arranging the vestments for the funeral, fitting out the room, and making all the other preparations to their sons and daughters. The Right Grand Controller was charged with looking after the scripture texts and the sacred images. Whenever anyone drew his attention to the seventh-day scripture readings, His Excellency would only say vacantly, like one no longer among the living, "Please do not speak to me about it. My anguish might only detain him on his way."

The Princess at Ichijō was naturally hurt that she had not seen the Intendant before he died, and although his most trusted retainers still came to offer her their services, her large residence seemed lonelier and more deserted with every passing day. The sight of the grooms and falconers wandering aimlessly and disconsolately in and out with his favorite hawks or horses often reminded her how endlessly sorrow can be renewed. There were the furnishings he had favored, and the *biwa* and *wagon* he had liked to play, now unstrung and mute: how painful her solitude was now!

One forlorn and dreary day she was gazing sadly at the garden's budding trees and at the flowers that always return in their time, surrounded meanwhile by women in mourning gray, when an escort's loud warning shouts were heard outside, and someone stopped before her house. "Oh, I thought it was my late lord!" one of the women exclaimed, weeping. "I had forgotten!" It was the Commander, who sent in word that he had arrived. The Princess had assumed that it must be the Controller, the Consultant, or one of the others as usual, but then in he came, as dauntingly elegant in his person as he could possibly be.

A seat was prepared for him in the aisle outside the chamber. He was far too grand to be treated like any other guest, and the Haven herself received him.

"This tragedy affected me even more than those who were naturally bound to feel it," he began, "but the constraints of custom prevented me from offering my condolences earlier, and by now I mourn him more as another might. He entrusted me at the end with certain instructions that could not leave me indifferent. No one escapes life's sorrows, but now that he is gone, I mean for as long as I live to show you in every way within my power that I remain devoted to you. It might not have been proper for me to confine myself long in your company at a time when there were so many rites addressed to the gods,[31] and I delayed calling on you for that

31. The second month (it is now the third) was particularly busy, with events such as the Kasuga Shrine festival, the Ōharano Shrine festival, and others.

reason, because I would only have been disappointed to have to remain standing in your presence.[32] The darkness in any parent's heart is one thing, but what I have seen and heard of His Excellency's suffering suggests vividly how deeply your daughter must feel about all that she and the Intendant shared, and I confess that I am overcome." He often wiped his eyes and blew his nose as he spoke. Despite his dazzling distinction he was very warm and kind.

The Haven answered him with tears in her voice. "Sorrows are the way of this fickle world. No pain they cause us can ever be new, and in that spirit I try to be brave, burdened though I am by the years, but I fear for her in her despair, because she seems unlikely to survive him long, and after all I have endured, I tremble that I may have lived on only to see the end of everyone dear to me. I did not welcome him at first, as he may have told you, since you both were so close, but I found His Excellency's enthusiasm difficult to deny, and since His Cloistered Eminence, too, seemed quite satisfied, I gathered that my feelings would not prevail. I therefore accepted him, although to my great regret I conclude from this nightmare that I would have done well to insist more on my own opinion. I never imagined things turning out as they did. I am old-fashioned enough to believe that as a rule it ill becomes a Princess to marry, regardless of the outcome, but I doubt that it would do her reputation any harm if she were now to mingle her smoke with his, since it has in any case been her destiny to be caught betwixt and between. I most certainly cannot resign myself to the idea, however, and I still give her my tenderest care. Your warm and repeated expressions of concern, which I doubtless owe to your friendship with him, have been a great comfort, and I wish you to know how grateful I am. He was not as attentive to her as I could have hoped, but those touching last words he spoke to you are a ray of light in the darkness." He gathered that she was weeping bitterly.

He could not immediately stop his own tears. "Perhaps this was indeed the way so remarkably accomplished a man was destined to meet his end," he replied, "because two or three years ago he began looking very downcast and melancholy, and I often warned him, despite my own want of sense, that a man who sees too far into life and thinks about things too deeply becomes too detached from them to be attractive and only loses whatever luster he may have had; but he seemed merely to find my opinion shallow. My heart goes out above all to Her Highness, if I may say so, in the quite natural intensity of her grief." After speaking very warmly and kindly, and staying a little longer than he might have done, he took his leave.

Although five or six years older than the Commander, the Intendant had retained all the grace and charm of youth. The Commander himself surpassed everyone else, thanks to his robust dignity and to a figure so manly that his face alone conveyed youth's true beauty. It gave the young gentlewomen a little relief from their sorrows to watch him go. Near the house stood a magnificent cherry tree that

32. If Yūgiri had visited Ochiba and her mother during the second month, he would have had to remain standing and refrain from actually entering the house, because service to the gods prohibited any contact with the pollution of death.

reminded him of the poem "I beg you, just this year!"[33] but that one had an unlucky ring, and instead he hummed, "I shall see you no more."[34]

> "When that season comes, it still blossoms as before with beauty unchanged,
>   this familiar cherry tree that has yet lost a great branch."[35]

He voiced the poem casually, and while he stood there, the Haven promptly replied,

> "Now that spring is here, the fresh-budding willow fronds gleam with dewdrop pearls,
>   for they know not what awaits blossoms scattered from the bough."[36]

Although not as deep as some, she had been known as an Intimate for her stylishness and wit. It seemed to the Commander that she indeed deserved her reputation.

He went on to His Excellency's, where he found many of His Excellency's sons. Upon being invited in, he entered the reception room, where His Excellency composed himself sufficiently to receive him. His Excellency's still handsome figure was more sadly wasted than any filial son's, and his beard was more ragged with neglect.[37] The sight was too painful to endure, but the Commander shrank from any unbridled display of tears and strove to conceal them. His Excellency wept and wept to think how particularly close the Commander had been to his son. They talked at length.

His Excellency wet his sleeves more thoroughly still, as though with drops from the eaves in heavy spring rain, when the Commander described his visit to Ichijō. The Commander had written the Haven's "budding willow fronds" down on a piece of folding paper that he now gave to His Excellency. "I cannot see!" His Excellency lamented, wiping his eyes. The tearful expression with which he read it bore embarrassingly little resemblance to his usual look of stalwart pride. The poem was not actually remarkable, but "gleam with dewdrop pearls" so touched him that for some time his own tears overflowed. "That autumn when your mother passed away, I felt as though there could be no greater sorrow, but this restriction and that mean that a woman is seldom seen and most of the time never appears at all, so that my grief for her remained invisible as well. The Intendant's ability left much to be desired, but His Majesty always thought well of him, and when at last he became a man, a large number of people naturally began to look to him for appointment and promotion. Each of them in his own way must feel shock and sorrow. My own grief, though, has nothing to do with promotion and all that, or with what the world

---

33. *Kokinshū* 832, by Kamutsuke no Mineo, lamenting the death of Fujiwara no Mototsune: "O cherry trees upon Fukakusa Moor, if you are kind, I beg you, just this year, blossom in gray!" The allusion may be unlucky because of the gray robes now worn by Onna San no Miya.

34. *Kokinshū* 97: "The blossoms' glory returns every spring, yet in this life I shall see them no more."

35. A compliment to Ochiba in her bereavement: like the cherry tree that always blossoms in season, she retains her beauty despite having lost her husband (the "great branch").

36. "I weep, not knowing what my daughter's fate will be."

37. Not even a truly filial son, mourning his father, would have so neglected his beard. The thought is Chinese.

thought of him. I simply miss him unbearably, just as he was. I wonder how I shall ever recover." His Excellency gazed up into the sky.

The evening clouds were a misty gray, and he noticed only now that the branches were bare of flowers. He wrote on the same folding paper,

> "Wet with falling drops that rain from the trees above, it is upside down
> that this spring has clothed me in a cheerless garment of mist!"[38]

The Commander replied,

> "He whom we have lost surely never imagined leaving you behind
> as though to say you should wear a garment of evening mist."

And the Right Grand Controller,

> "Ah, it is too cruel! When that blossom fluttered down before his own spring,
> who is it he meant to wear such garments of misty gray?"

The funerary observances were unusually impressive. Naturally, the Commander's wife, but especially the Commander himself, added to the scripture readings deeply fond touches of their own.

The Commander called often at the Princess's Ichijō residence. The skies of the fourth month somehow lifted the heart, and the color of the budding trees was lovely everywhere, but for that house, plunged in mourning, all things fed a life of quiet woe, and he therefore set off there as he did so often. The grounds were filling with new green, and here and there in shadowed places, where the sand was thin, wormwood had made itself at home. The near garden, once so carefully tended, now grew as it pleased. A spreading clump of pampas grass grew bravely there, and he made his way through it moist with dew, mindful of the insect cries that autumn would bring.[39] The outside of the house was hung with Iyo blinds,[40] through which he caught cooling glimpses of the new season's gray standing curtains and of pretty page girls' hair and dark gray skirts—all of which was very pleasant were it not that the color was so sad.

This time he sat on the veranda, where he was provided with a cushion. The women felt that it was rude to leave him there, and they tried to persuade the Haven to receive him as usual, but she had been feeling unwell lately and was half reclining. While they did what they could to divert him, he looked out sorrowfully on the trees that grew in the grounds, indifferent to human cares. There stood an oak and a maple,

---

38. "Wet with tears shed for my son, I wear this spring the mourning gray that, properly, he was to wear for me." Ko ("tree" or "trees") in the expression ko no shita no shizuku ("drops that rain from the trees") is homophonous with "child"; and the "garment of mist" (kasumi no koromo, an image associated with spring) refers here as in the poems that follow to the gray of mourning. "Upside down" (sakasama) refers to the reversal of the natural order, according to which a father dies before his son.

39. Kokinshū 853, by Miharu no Arisuke: "The clump of pampas grass that you once planted is now a wilderness filled with insect cries."

40. A humble sort of blind, suitable for a household in mourning.

Veranda and blinds

fresher in color than the rest and with their branches intertwined. "I wonder what bond they share, that their mingling branches should promise them both so happy a future?" he said, and he quietly went to them.

> *"If that were to be, I would gladly share these boughs' close friendship with you,*
> *for the god who guards their leaves has declared that it is meet!*[41]

It is galling to be left this way outside your blinds!" he said, leaning on the lintel.

The women nudged each other. "What a graceful, languishing figure he makes!"

The Haven replied through Koshōshō,[42] who was entertaining him,

> *"He indeed is gone, the god who stood watchful guard over this oak tree,*
> *but may such familiar boughs start a new intimacy?*

I think that you speak rashly and that you may be shallow."

The Commander took her point with a smile, and he straightened himself discreetly when he gathered that she had slipped out to receive him. "I have not been

41. "I want to know you [Ochiba] better, and Kashiwagi gave me leave to do so." Ochiba is a silent (and invisible) presence in this scene.

42. One of the gentlewomen.

myself," she began, "perhaps because sorrow has weighed upon me so long, and I have hardly been aware of life around me. However, deep gratitude for the kindness of your visits has moved me to rouse myself after all." She really did seem unwell.

"It is only natural that you should mourn, but surely not so much," he said soothingly. "Whatever happens seems to happen in its time. All things in this life have their proper term."

He had sensed depth in the Princess herself ever since first hearing of her, but he also imagined anxiously how much unhappier, alas, it must indeed make her to have people laughing at her, and keen interest led him to try to find out what she was like. I suppose she is no great beauty, he said to himself, but assuming that she is not horribly deformed, why did he have to reject her just because of her looks and torment himself with feelings that he should never have entertained? What a thing to do! Character is all that really matters in the end.

"I hope that you will give me the same place in your thoughts that you gave him and not keep me at too great a distance." He carefully avoided any hint of suggestiveness, but he certainly was strikingly attentive. In a dress cloak he looked very fine indeed, and his height gave him an imposing dignity.

"The late Intendant always had a sweeter grace and a nobler charm than anyone else," the women whispered, "but this lord is a magnificent figure of a man, and you cannot help being struck by how handsome he is—there is no one like him!"

"Actually, it would be quite nice if he were to come calling this way regularly."

"The grass grows green on the Right Commander's grave,"[43] the Commander hummed. That death, too,[44] was recent. High and low united in lamenting the departed, in this world where tragedy has always struck so often, for apart from the more obvious qualities that made him admirable, he was a man of such extraordinary warmth that even old officials or gentlewomen, people who hardly mattered, mourned him and regretted his passing. No wonder, then, that His Majesty thought of him each time there was music and dwelled on him in memory. "Ah, the poor Intendant!" people would say on every occasion. As the months and days slipped by, Genji, at Rokujō, recalled him more and more often with emotion. The little boy kept his memory alive for him, although that did not help, since no one else knew. By the time autumn came, the baby was crawling.

---

43. An early commentary attributes this line (originally in Chinese) to Ki no Arimasa, in a now lost lament on the death of Fujiwara no Yasutada.

44. Yasutada's death in 937.

37

YOKOBUE

The Flute

The *yokobue* was the most common kind of transverse bamboo flute at the Heian court. It was originally Chinese, unlike the somewhat lighter *komabue* (Koma, or Korean, flute) and *yamatobue* (Japanese flute). In this chapter Ochiba no Miya's mother gives Yūgiri a flute that Kashiwagi often played, and Yūgiri uses the word in his poem of thanks:

"Nothing much has changed in the music of the flute, but that perfect tone missing ever since he died will live on forevermore."

"The Flute" begins about a year after the end of "The Oak Tree" and covers spring through autumn.

PERSONS

His Grace, the Honorary Retired Emperor, Genji, age 49

The little boy, son of Onna San no Miya and Kashiwagi, 2 (Kaoru)

His Retired Excellency (Tō no Chūjō)

The Commander, Genji's son, 28 (Yūgiri)

Her Highness, the Second Princess (Ochiba no Miya)

His Cloistered Eminence, the Retired Emperor, 52 (Suzaku In)

Her Cloistered Highness, the Third Princess, 23 or 24 (Onna San no Miya)

The Haven, mother of Ochiba no Miya (Ichijō no Miyasudokoro)

The Commander's wife, 30 (Kumoi no Kari)

The Consort, Genji's daughter, 21 (Akashi no Nyōgo)

His Highness, the Third Prince, 3 (Niou)

His Highness, the Second Prince (Ni no Miya)

Many people continued bitterly mourning the late Acting Grand Counselor's[1] passing. His Grace of Rokujō, who regretted the death of anyone pleasant, even if he hardly knew him, was extremely sorry and often felt moved to dwell on his memory, for despite that one outraged recollection the gentleman had been a constant companion whom he had particularly liked. He made a point of having scriptures read for the anniversary. The little boy's utterly childlike innocence made a sight so touching that Genji felt for him keenly after all, and he privately decided to offer an extra hundred ounces of gold[2] on his behalf. His Excellency, who did not know why, expressed his humble gratitude.

The Commander did a great deal, too, and he took it upon himself to sponsor many observances. At the same time he redoubled his attentions to the Princess at Ichijō.[3] His Excellency and his wife, who had never expected to find him more devoted than their son's own brothers, were very pleased. Evidence of just how high the Intendant still stood in the world's esteem, even after his death, impressed them more painfully than ever with the magnitude of their loss.

His Cloistered Eminence on his mountain was saddened to gather that his Second Princess was causing amusement, and since Her Cloistered Highness had joined him in renouncing the world's commonplace concerns, he felt disappointment for both, although he bore it, having resolved that nothing profane should trouble him. He reflected during his devotions that Her Cloistered Highness must be occupied with following the same path, and now that she had taken it up, he took advantage of the least occasion to keep in touch with her.

The bamboo shoots growing in the forest beside the temple and the taro roots dug from the mountains nearby evoked life in the hills so movingly that he sent her some of each, and with them a long letter to which he added, at the end, "Though spring mists veil moor and mountain, I have had these dug for you with deep affection, only to let you know how much you mean to me.

---

1. Kashiwagi, who was promoted on his deathbed. This is his proper title, but people continued to remember him as the Intendant of the Gate Watch, and he will remain "the Intendant" below.

2. For further memorial services. The gold is probably gold dust.

3. Princess Ochiba, Kashiwagi's widow.

You come after me in leaving the world behind to follow this path,
yet seek that same root of peace as I do with all my heart!"[4]

She read his words with tears in her eyes. Genji arrived just then and was surprised to see the tall lacquered stands[5] before her. "How strange!" he said. "What are
those?" There was His Eminence's letter. He read it and found it very moving. "To
think that I cannot see you as I wish, even when I feel as though every day could be
my last!" he had written, and a great deal else besides. The part about them both
reaching "the same root of peace" was pious talk of little interest, but he still sympathized. *I am very sorry indeed to have given him such anxiety over my treatment of
her,* he said to himself.

She wrote her reply shyly and presented the messenger with a set of blue-gray
robes in silk twill. Genji saw a bit of paper she had discarded peeping out beside her
standing curtain and picked it up. In a tenuous hand she had written,

"Longing for the peace of a place beyond this world and all its sorrows,
I dwell on the mountain where you have renounced it all."

"He seems worried about you, you know," he said. "This wish of yours to be
elsewhere is very hurtful and unkind."

Her Highness no longer received him directly, but the hair at her forehead
was very sweet and pretty, and her face seemed to him just like a girl's; he could not
look at her charming figure without wondering guiltily why all this had had to happen, and with only a standing curtain between them he was therefore careful not to
be too distant.

The little boy had been asleep with his nurse, but he now came crawling in
and tugged very fetchingly at Genji's sleeve. The skirts of his plum-pink robe, worn
over white silk gauze, trailed long and loose behind him, leaving much of him bare,
which is common enough for little children but still extremely appealing; he looked
as though he had been carved from supple white willow. His head might have been
dyed with dayflower,[6] and while his delightful mouth and his look of wide-eyed innocence certainly recalled someone else, *he* had not had anything like this beauty.
Where does he get it from? Genji wondered as he watched. *He does not resemble
Her Highness. The extraordinary nobility and distinction of his face would not
look out of place in my own mirror.*

The child was just beginning to walk. He toddled up to the lacquered stands
without knowing what was on them and began merrily gobbling bamboo shoots
and throwing them about. "You naughty boy!" Genji laughed. "What a way to be-

---

4. Literally, "seek the same *tokoro* as I." In the sense of "place," *tokoro* refers to paradise, but the same syllables also mean "taro root."

5. *Raishi,* a tall stand shaped rather like a *takatsuki* ("footed stand") but with a deep lip, lacquered black
outside and red within, customarily used for such things as fruit and nuts. These hold Suzaku's gifts.

6. The sky blue flowers of *tsuyukusa* ("dayflower," "spiderwort"), a common weed, yield a blue dye. A very
young child's head was shaven.

have! Here, someone, take them away from him! Gossipy gentlewomen will be saying he cannot resist food!" He picked him up. "There is something special about his
eyes, isn't there? I know that I have not seen that many children this young, but I
thought that at this age they all just looked like babies, whereas he has a remarkable
quality even now. That is a worry. Our First Princess[7] is here already, and it could
mean trouble for them both now that he is, too. But alas, will I even see them all
grow up? 'Though the blossoms flower in glory . . . ' "[8] He gazed at the boy.

"What a frightening thing to say, my lord!" the women protested.

Eager to test his new teeth, the boy clutched a bamboo shoot and mouthed it,
drooling. "He certainly has an odd idea of gallantry!" Genji remarked.

> *"I do not forget that passage of bitterness, but this little shoot*
> *is much too dear after all to reject only for that!"*[9]

He got the bamboo shoot away from him and took him back to where he was sitting, but the boy only smiled and registered nothing; instead, he crawled off again
at great speed.

As the months and days went by, the boy grew so alarmingly pretty that Genji
might easily have forgotten all about "that bitter incident." Perhaps the inadmissible
occurred only because destiny required him be born, he mused, in which case little
could have been done to avoid it. *My own karma is disappointing, too, in many
ways. Among all the women I have brought together, Her Highness is the one who
should have been the most perfectly satisfactory and whose person should have left
the least to be desired, and yet every time I reflect how extraordinary it is to see her
as she is now, I find that lapse of hers impossible to forgive.* His regrets were still
fully alive.

The Commander continued to ponder what the Intendant's parting words
might mean, and he wanted very much to question Genji about them and watch his
face as he did so, but he could not actually bring himself to mention them, since he
had an idea what the matter must be. Still, he kept hoping for a chance to find out
what had really happened and to tell Genji what had preoccupied the Intendant so.

One melancholy autumn evening his thoughts went to the Princess at Ichijō,
and he set off there. She seemed just then to have been quietly playing a *wagon*, and
without putting it fully away again, she had him brought straight into the southern
aisle. He clearly glimpsed the women who had been near the aisle as they slipped
off deeper into the room; their rustling silks and the sweet fragrance that hung in
the air left him with an elegant impression. The Haven received him as usual, and
they talked over the past. He found the house very quiet and sad, being used to one
bustling and crowded day and night, as well as to a noisy throng of his own children. The place itself seemed neglected, but their mode of life there had great dis-

---

7. The Akashi Empress's eldest daughter.
8. *Kokinshū* 97: "The blossoms' glory returns every spring, yet in this life I shall see them no more."
9. This poem (Genji presumably says it only to himself) plays on words associated with bamboo. The
most important is *fushi* ("that *passage* of bitterness"); *fushi* also means a "joint" of bamboo.

tinction. He looked out at the flowers in the near garden and at the twilight glow over the "wilderness filled with insect cries."[10]

He drew the *wagon* to him. It was tuned to the *richi* mode and clearly much played, and the scent that clung to it aroused tender feelings. While playing it himself, he dreamed on about how in a place like this a man with a weakness for gallantry might forget himself and behave unworthily, to his public shame. The *wagon* was the one his friend had favored. He played a little of a pretty piece and said, "Alas, what a beautiful tone he used to draw from this instrument! Surely his touch is still present in Her Highness's. I would be so pleased if she were to permit me to hear it!"

"She has forgotten all about her old childish amusements since the thread of his life broke,"[11] the Haven replied. "When His Eminence's Princesses practiced in his presence, he judged that she did very well at such things, but she is so abstracted now that she is hardly the same person. She seems to spend all her time in sorrow, and as far as I can tell, this instrument only awakens painful memories."

"I do not wonder that it should. 'If only there were an end in this world . . . '"[12] he mused as he pushed it from him.

"Do play, then, so that I may listen for his touch in the music! It will do these ears of mine such good, when I have been sad so long!"

"It is the middle string that would convey his touch and yield a truly remarkable tone,"[13] he answered. "That is what I myself was hoping to hear." He pushed the *wagon* up to the blinds, but he did not insist when she gave no sign of consenting to play.

The moon shone in a cloudless sky while lines of geese passed aloft, wing to wing. With what envy the Princess must have heard them, from whose ranks none ever strayed: for with a chill breeze blowing and a heart full of care, she lightly touched the strings of a *sō no koto*, giving its voice such depth that the Commander's fascination with her grew. Wishing that she would give him more, he himself picked up a *biwa*, very softly to play "I Love Him So." "I do not wish to seem to divine your thoughts, but I hope that this piece may draw a word from you." He addressed her eagerly, there within her blinds, but his music had only deepened her reticence, and she remained lost in her sad thoughts.

> "I see in you now depths of bashful reticence that only confirm
> silence to be far more wise than a vain attempt at words,"

he said.

She played a little of the end and replied,

---

10. *Kokinshū* 853, by Miharu no Arisuke: "The clump of pampas grass that you once planted is now a wilderness filled with insect cries."

11. Literally, "ever since the koto string broke." *Kagerō nikki* 93 (also *Goshūishū* 894), by Michitsuna no Haha: "The departed does not come back again, and the time when the koto string broke has returned once more."

12. *Genji monogatari kochūshakusho in'yō waka* 275: "If only there were an end in this world to longing, one would live carefree year after year."

13. "It is your daughter whose playing would truly convey his touch." As in "Akashi," the image evokes the loyalty of lover to lover.

"I hear very well all the sadness of midnight in what you have played,
but I have no words myself, save a music of my own."

It was lovely but all too short. Her touch had the graceful simplicity that the late Intendant had devotedly taught her, and the mode was the one he had favored, but she had played only a small part of a very moving piece, and he was disappointed. "My music has no doubt betrayed the gallant cast of my feelings," he said nonetheless. "I should be going now, I think; the late Intendant might well reprove me for staying so long with you on an autumn night. I shall return and wait on you again. Will you be good enough to leave the tuning of these instruments unchanged? I shall worry otherwise, for there is so little one can count on in this world." Without expressing himself plainly he managed after all to suggest his meaning before he left.

"He would surely have forgiven you the pleasures of this evening," the Haven said. "You spent so much time in desultory talk about the past that I am sorry to say I feel no younger for it." She gave him a flute as a parting gift. "This flute, you see, always seemed to me to convey the quality of its noble past, and I have been sorry to see it buried in this wormwood waste. I look forward to hearing its voice rise above the cries of your escort."

The Commander examined it. "I am unworthy of such an attendant," he replied. Yes, this instrument, too, was one that the Intendant had always had with him; he remembered him often saying that he did not get from it the very finest sound it could give and that he wanted it to go to someone able to appreciate it. He put it to his lips, feeling if anything sadder than ever. "I could be forgiven for playing the *wagon* as I did in his memory," he said, stopping halfway through the *banshiki* modal prelude, "but this is beyond me."

The Haven sent out to him as he was leaving,

"Here beside a home sadly overgrown with weeds a cricket now sings
in that voice I knew so well in those autumns long ago."

He replied,

"Nothing much has changed in the music of the flute, but that perfect tone
missing ever since he died will live on forevermore."

He could hardly bring himself to go, but it was extremely late.

When he got home, he found all the lattice shutters down and everyone asleep. Having heard that his heart was set on the Princess and that he was courting her, she[14] must have objected to his being out late and pretended to be asleep as soon as she heard him come in.

"My love and I on Irusa Mountain,"[15] he sang very prettily to himself, but

14. Yūgiri's wife, Kumoi no Kari.
15. The opening words of a *saibara* song.

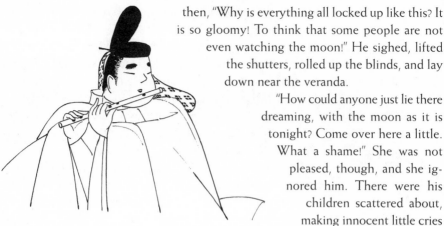

Playing the flute

then, "Why is everything all locked up like this? It is so gloomy! To think that some people are not even watching the moon!" He sighed, lifted the shutters, rolled up the blinds, and lay down near the veranda.

"How could anyone just lie there dreaming, with the moon as it is tonight? Come over here a little. What a shame!" She was not pleased, though, and she ignored him. There were his children scattered about, making innocent little cries in their sleep, and gentle-women were lying among them; they all made a scene very different from the one he had just left.

He played the flute and imagined her still absorbed in her sorrow long after his departure. I *know* she will play without changing the tuning! And her mother is so good on the *wagon*, too! Things like this ran through his mind as he lay there. The late Intendant had given her all the consideration that was her due, but he seemed to have felt no deep attachment to her, which puzzled the Commander greatly. What a pity it would be if she turned out to have no looks! That could easily be the case with any woman reputed to be a beauty. He counted the years since he and his wife had given themselves to each other without any of these elaborate hints and mysteries. No wonder she had settled into being so proud and overbearing!

He dozed off a little and dreamed that the late Intendant of the Gate Watch, dressed exactly as he had been then, sat beside him and that he picked up the flute and examined it. He wished even in his dream that the departed had not come to its sound.

> *"I would have the wind, if I may indulge that hope, blow upon this flute*
> *a music for generations to pass on down in my own line.*

I had someone else in mind," the figure said.

The Commander was about to ask a question when he woke up to the crying of a baby boy, frightened in his sleep. The boy was crying very loudly and retching up milk. His nurse arose in haste while the lady of the house had the lamp brought near, tucked her hair behind her ears, wiped and tidied the baby, and held him in her arms. She bared a beautifully full, rounded breast for him to suck. He was a very sweet baby, ever so white and pretty, and she enjoyed comforting him this way even though she had no milk.

"What is the matter?" he asked, going to her. The commotion of the women scattering rice[16] must have completely dispelled the mood of his dream.

"He seems upset. I suppose that a spirit has got in as usual, what with you

---

16. To purify the room and drive away any evil spirits that may have been tormenting the baby.

wandering around like a young man and then coming back to raise the shutters and admire the moon."

This reproach from a face so young and pretty made him smile. "I let in a spirit? It could not have got in if I had not raised that shutter, though, I agree. The more children you have, the more wisely you talk."

Minding a baby

The way he looked at her made her shy, and she fell silent after all. "Now, stop that. I am not fit to be seen," she said. Her bashful figure in the bright lamplight made quite a nice picture. The baby took up the rest of the night with his fussing.

What *am* I to do with this flute, then? the Commander wondered, remembering his dream. It means a great deal to him, and it is not for me. Having it from a woman means nothing.[17] What can he have been thinking? They say someone caught up at the end in single-minded love or hate must wander the darkness of eternal night. That is exactly why I do not want to leave any attachment behind when I go. In this mood he had scriptures read at Otagi and at other temples the late Intendant had favored, and he decided that while it certainly would be a good deed to offer the flute directly to the Buddha, since it had come to him as a treasured gift, that would be too easy. Accordingly, he set out for Rokujō.

Genji was then with the Consort. He had chosen her Third Prince, now three and the most attractive of her children, to live with him, and the little boy came running up to the visitor.[18] "Commander, Commander," he cried with mischievous self-deference, "pick up His Highness and take him with you!"[19]

The Commander smiled. "Come, then. But I cannot very well walk straight past her ladyship's[20] blinds with you! That would be very rude." He sat down and took the boy in his arms.

"Nobody is looking! I'll hide! Do it! Do it!" The enchanting little fellow put his sleeve over his face, and the Commander took him along. He found Genji there, fussing over the Second Prince and his own little boy,[21] who were playing together.

"The Commander has to carry *me*, too!" the Second Prince announced when he saw the Commander put his younger brother down in the corner.[22]

"But the Commander is mine!" the Third Prince protested, holding tightly to him.

17. A flute was properly passed from father to son. Since women did not play the flute, receiving it from a woman could be seen as a break in the line of proper transmission.

18. Yūgiri has gone first to the east wing, where Genji is most likely to be. The little boy is Niou.

19. He uses for himself the same honorific language that he hears others use toward him.

20. Murasaki's, presumably. For some reason Murasaki must have earlier stopped Niou from going to his mother's, and Yūgiri now hesitates to give in to the little boy and take him anyway.

21. Kaoru.

22. The veranda at the southeast corner of the main house.

"You are naughty boys!" Genji scolded them when he noticed. "There you are, fighting over His Majesty's guardsman and wanting him all for yourselves! You, the Third Prince, are a proper rascal. You are always trying to do your brother in!"

The Commander laughed. "The Second Prince is such a good fellow, giving in that way just as an elder brother should. To my mind he is almost frightening for his age."

The smiling Genji thought them both quite delightful. "That is no place for a senior noble like you to sit," he said. "Let us go back." However, the Princes clung to him when he moved to set off, and they would not let him go. At heart he did not believe that he should treat Her Cloistered Highness's child as their equal, but the boy's mother, with her bad conscience, might mistake his reason for not doing so, and he was kind enough by nature to give him all the care that he would have lavished on a treasure.

Acutely aware that he had not yet had a good look at the boy, the Commander picked up a fallen branch from a flowering tree and beckoned to him with it when he appeared in the gap between two blinds. The boy came running. He had on only a violet dress cloak, and his plump figure was very pleasing indeed, with his beautifully white, glowing skin and his features that outshone the Princes'. Perhaps it was the Commander's imagination, but while the boy's glance had somewhat more force and intelligence than that of the gentleman he had in mind, the strikingly graceful outline of his eyes was almost the same. That mouth, with its peculiarly brilliant smile—perhaps his eyes were deceiving him, but Genji must surely have noticed. He wanted more and more to see how his father would take the subject he meant to bring up. The Princes of course displayed becoming pride, but otherwise they were quite ordinarily attractive children, while *this* boy's great distinction made him unusually appealing. How awful! The Commander compared them in his mind. If my suspicion is correct, then my father is quite wrong not to inform His Excellency, who weeps and grieves that no one should come forward to call himself the Intendant's son and who so wishes that the Intendant had left a child to be remembered by. But no, he caught himself, it cannot be. He could make no sense of it. The little boy was sweet and dear, and he found him a pleasure to play with.

They went to the east wing, and the sun began to set while they talked quietly. Genji smiled at the Commander's account of how he had been to the Princess's at Ichijō the day before and of how he had found her. They were going over various memories of the late, lamented Intendant when Genji observed, "Yes, her idea of playing 'I Love Him So' certainly deserves to be cited as an example hereafter, but it all goes to remind one that a woman should never make the slightest gesture that might arouse a man's interest. As long as you have given her to understand that you have not forgotten his kindness in the past and that you remain devoted to his memory, I believe you are better off, both for your sake and for hers, to keep everything with her perfectly proper and to let no common temptation lead you astray."

Right you are! the Commander said to himself. You are expert enough at giving other people advice, but what about when the gallantry is *yours?* "In what way would I go astray?" he asked aloud. "Obviously, now that I have begun to show sym-

pathy for her loss, I would only come under the usual kind of suspicion if I were suddenly to stop. As for 'I Love Him So,' it would be one thing if she had been forward
enough to start it herself, but the little she played in response to me was entirely appropriate and, I thought, very nice. Everything depends on the person and the circumstances. She is not that young anymore, nor am I myself much given to light or
gallant behavior, and I suppose she must have felt at ease with me, because her
whole manner was warm and pleasant."

He had contrived the perfect moment, and he now moved a little closer to
Genji to bring up his dream. Genji listened but did not immediately reply. He saw
that the dream made sense.

"The flute is for me to look after," he said. "There is a reason for that. It once
belonged to Emperor Yōzei.[23] His Late Highness of Ceremonial,[24] who valued it extremely, felt that even as a boy the Intendant had drawn a particularly beautiful tone
from it, and so one day at a party he gave to celebrate *hagi*, he made him a present of
it. The Haven probably did not quite understand what she was doing." How could
one possibly mistake "to pass down in my own line"? he wondered. That *must* be
what he had in mind. The Commander is extremely quick, and he has undoubtedly
got it.

The Commander kept his eyes on his father's face and felt increasingly constrained. For a moment he found nothing to say, but being determined to press the
matter, he remarked vaguely, as though only now reminded of the moment, "I went
to see him at the very end, and one of the things he asked me again and again to do
after he was gone was to convey to you the profound apology that he felt he owed
you. I wonder what he meant. So far I have not been able to make any sense of it."
He spoke as though quite mystified.

I knew it! Still, Genji saw no reason to acknowledge what had happened, and
for a moment he feigned incomprehension. "I am afraid that I cannot remember ever
giving him reason to feel bitterly toward me. At any rate, I shall think over the
dream you describe and let you know. Women often warn against discussing a
dream at night."

It was hardly an answer, and they say that it left the Commander anxious
about what his father might think of him for having brought up the matter at all.

23. Lived 868–949, reigned 877–84.
24. In the tale perhaps the father of Asagao, and in history perhaps Prince Sadayasu, a younger brother
of Emperor Yōzei.

38

SUZUMUSHI

The Bell Cricket

The *suzumushi* ("bell cricket") sings
in autumn. On the great full-
moon night of the eighth month,
Genji and Onna San no Miya
exchange poems in praise of its
song. To Onna San no Miya's

*"I have long since learned how very cruel a time autumn often brings,
yet I would not wish to lose the bell cricket's lovely song,"*

Genji answers,

*"You may, for yourself, have no wish but to be free of this poor abode,
yet your sweet bell cricket song for me never will grow old."*

RELATIONSHIP TO EARLIER CHAPTERS

"The Bell Cricket" takes place in the summer and early autumn of the year following "The Flute."

PERSONS

His Grace, the Honorary Retired Emperor, Genji, age 50

Her Cloistered Highness, 24 or 25 (Onna San no Miya)

The Lecturer (Kōji)

His Highness of War, Genji's brother (Hotaru Hyōbukyō no Miya)

The Commander, Genji's son, 29 (Yūgiri)

His Eminence, Retired Emperor Reizei, 31

Her Majesty, the Empress, 42 (Akikonomu)

Genji arranged to have Her Cloistered Highness's sacred images[1] made and dedicated that summer, when the lotuses were in full bloom. For the occasion he took advantage of all the things that he had had assembled for her personal chapel. He had the banners[2] made from a particularly lovely and intriguing Chinese brocade; Lady Murasaki had them sewn. The flower-stand covers, with their pretty tie-dyed pattern, were especially attractive, and the dyeing had been done in a most unusual way. The night curtains were rolled up on all four sides,[3] and a Lotus Mandala[4] hung at the back. Offerings of flowers in magnificent colors stood before it in tall silver vases. The incense burning on the altar was Chinese and of "hundred paces" quality, and the Amida and his two attendant bodhisattvas[5] were very finely and beautifully made from white sandalwood. The holy-water vessel was notably small, as usual, and adorned with blue, white, and purple lotuses. The incense, compounded according to the "lotus petal" method with the addition of only a sprinkling of honey,[6] diffused a fragrance that blended perfectly with that of the lotuses on the altar. Genji had provided six copies of the sutra, one for sentient beings in each of the six realms,[7] and he himself had made her own. The prayer he had written to accompany it expressed the wish that this scripture, at least, should preserve the bond between them and that they should assist one another on the path. As for the Amida Sutra,[8] he doubted that Chinese paper was strong enough for a scripture that she would handle day and night, and he had called in men from the paper workshop to make paper for the purpose. In the

1. *Jibutsu,* the images that she will always have with her and that will be the object of her daily devotions.
2. *Hata,* hangings that surround the altar and decorate the pillars of the hall.
3. Onna San no Miya's curtained bed is serving provisionally as her chapel.
4. A painting either of the Buddha preaching the Lotus Sutra on Vulture Peak or of scenes illustrating key passages of the text.
5. The Buddha Amida is flanked by the bodhisattvas Kannon and Seishi.
6. "Lotus petal" (*kayō*) is a summer incense. Honey, the binding material, has been reduced in order to avoid making the incense too sweet.
7. Heaven, the human realm, the realm of the *ashuras* (warring demons), and the realms of beasts, hungry ghosts, and hell.
8. The Shōmuryōju-kyō (Lesser Sutra of Eternal Life), a short text considered the most sacred of the three sutras devoted to Amida.

spring he had applied himself with all his heart to copying out the text, and the least glimpse of the scroll dazzled the viewer. The luminous quality of the writing itself was even more extraordinary than the lines ruled in gold. There is no need to describe the scroll's roller, mounting paper, or box. It rested on an aloeswood stand that stood on the dais with the sacred images.

The Lecturer[9] arrived once the chapel was finished, and the gentlemen gathered to distribute the incense.[10] On his way there, Genji looked into the west aisle, where Her Highness was, and found her installed in rather hot and cramped surroundings among fifty or sixty elaborately dressed gentlewomen. Page girls were wandering about all the way to the north aisle, and the air was heavy with smoke fanned from several incense burners. He went to the women. "When you want to perfume the air, you should arrange it so that no one knows where the smoke is coming from," he said. "More smoke than ever rose from Mount Fuji is not a good idea. You must make no noise while the preaching is going on, and you should also avoid any unrestrained, casual rustling or movement, since one is supposed to listen quietly and with full attention." It was just like him to have a few words of advice even for the inexperienced young women. Her Highness lay there oppressed by all the people and looking very pretty and small. "Your little boy may get in the way," he said. "You should send him somewhere out of sight."

The sliding panels on the north had been replaced by blinds through which the women entered. It was touching to see how Genji made sure they were settled and then carefully explained to Her Highness the progress of the rite.

The sight of this beautiful altar where she had once slept stirred many thoughts. "I never imagined us arranging any ceremony like this together," he said. "Very well, imagine us both lodged in one flower at least in the life to come!" He burst into tears, then moistened a brush on her inkstone to write on her clove-dyed fan,

> "In our future life we will share one lotus throne, that I promise you;
>   yet how sad it is today that we part as dewdrops do."

She wrote in reply,

> "Promise as you please a single throne for us both on one lotus flower,
>   surely you do not at heart wish to be with me at all."

"How you dash my hopes!" He smiled, but one easily saw how sad he felt.

The Princes all came, as usual, and the ladies of Rokujō had eagerly provided generous offerings of their own. Everything else, including the vestments for the seven priests,[11] had been prepared by Lady Murasaki. The vestments were silk twill, and even the way the stoles were sewn must have impressed the discerning eye, but

---

9. Kōji, the officiating priest, whose function was to expound the sutra.

10. During a rite in honor of the Lotus Sutra incense was distributed to the participating priests, in this case probably by privy gentlemen.

11. Each of whom performed a distinct function in the rite. Only a major ceremony used all seven.

these little things are all too much to describe. The Lecturer gave an inspiring explanation of the rite, and with a flood of the learned eloquence that had justly earned him his fame, he acknowledged the holy resolve with which Her Cloistered Highness was now putting behind her all thought of worldly glory to entrust herself for all future lives to the Lotus Sutra. It was a solemn moment, and the assembly wept.

Genji had hoped to keep this inauguration of Her Cloistered Highness's private chapel a secret, but His Majesty and His Cloistered Eminence on his mountain had both heard of it, and both sent envoys. Offerings for the scripture readings poured in on an impressive scale. An event arranged by Genji was always out of the ordinary, even when he had originally meant to keep it simple, and the splendid touches added to this one naturally meant that the monks returned to their temple that evening laden with such wealth that they hardly knew where to put it all.

Genji now felt worse about Her Cloistered Highness than ever, and he pampered her without reserve. Her father let him know that appearances would be served if she were to move to the residence that he intended for her, but Genji would not have it. "I would worry about her if she were that far away," he said, "and I would greatly miss being able to see her and talk to her day or night. It is true that I now have little time left, but at least for as long as I live, I prefer not to be deprived of the opportunity to make it clear how much she means to me." Meanwhile, he had the Sanjō residence in question done up very beautifully indeed, and he had its storehouses filled with the best of the products derived from her emoluments or sent in offering from her estates and pastures in the provinces. Indeed, he built new ones as well and placed in them, with scrupulous care, every treasure that was hers or that had been given to her in such vast abundance by her father. The attentions he continually lavished on her and his kindness toward her many women, high or low, all proceeded entirely from his own generosity.

That autumn he turned the garden before the western bridgeway, up to the east side of the median fence,[12] into a wild moor, and he decorated that part of the house most becomingly with a holy-water shelf and so on. He also chose and assigned to her service not only those who had become nuns for love of her—her nurses and senior women and so on—but also the younger ones, still in the flower of their youth, whom it had suited to spend the rest of their lives in this manner.

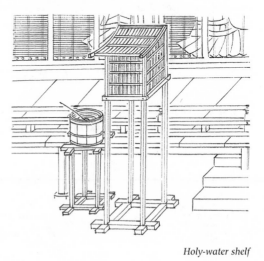

Holy-water shelf

12. The bridgeway connects the main house to the west wing. The fence (*naka no hei*) appears to stand between the house and the wing and to screen the two from each other.

Many vied to join them, but when Genji heard how eager they were, he declared that he would not allow it. "The presence among them of a single one who lacks the heart for it would disturb the others around her and would risk giving them all an invidious name," he warned. Hardly more than ten now served Her Cloistered Highness in their new guise.

He had crickets[13] released on the garden moor, and on evenings when the breeze was a little cooler, he would come there as though to listen to their song. This caused Her Highness very great distress, because he still made it plain to her that he had not given her up, and she saw that what he had in mind could not be allowed. To all appearances he treated her exactly as before, but it was obvious that his anger lived on and that he had in fact completely changed toward her. Her wish at all costs to avoid him in this mood was what had decided her to become a nun, and he should have left her in peace by now, but instead she suffered so much from his continued pursuit that she longed to move elsewhere, far away. However, she lacked the courage to insist.

At dusk on the fifteenth night Her Highness sat before her altar, near the veranda, abstractedly calling the Name. Two or three young nuns were offering flowers. The holy-water vessel rang, there were water sounds, and all this bustle over such unfamiliar tasks put her in a very melancholy mood. Just then, as so often, Genji entered. "The crickets are singing everywhere this evening!" he remarked and quietly joined her, in low but inspiring tones, to chant the great *darani* of the Buddha Amida. There were indeed many crickets singing, and among them the bell crickets' voices rose bravely and beautifully above the rest. "All the autumn crickets' songs are lovely," he said, "but Her Majesty[14] especially preferred pine crickets, and those are the ones she gathered from distant moors to release in her garden. I hear very few went on singing there, though. Pine crickets probably do not live long, despite what their name suggests.[15] They really and truly sing only in the mountains, where no one can hear them, or among the pine forests below, which suggests that they prefer solitude. The bell cricket's gentle freshness is what makes it so appealing."

> "I have long since learned how very cruel a time autumn often brings,
>   yet I would not wish to lose the bell cricket's lovely song,"

she said very low, and with a wonderful air of grace and artless distinction.

"What do you mean?" Genji replied. "I never thought to hear you say that!

> You may, for yourself, have no wish but to be free of this poor abode,
>   yet your sweet bell cricket song for me never will grow old."[16]

He called for a *kin* and played, as he had not done for so long. She forgot to tell her beads and listened intently after all. The moon was out in moving glory. Genji

---

13. Especially *matsumushi* ("pine crickets") and *suzumushi* ("bell crickets"), which sing prettily in autumn.
14. Akikonomu.
15. Since the pine is an emblem of longevity.
16. "You may want to leave, but for me you remain as charming and desirable as ever."

gazed into the sky and lost himself in reflections on life's shifting ways, playing more beautifully than ever as he did so.

His Highness of War arrived on the assumption that there would be the customary music tonight; then the Commander appeared, too, accompanied by suitable privy gentlemen. Genji's *kin* announced where he was, and they all went straight to join him. "I have so little to do that I wanted to hear again that rare sound I have missed so long," he said, "although my playing alone hardly makes a proper concert. I am glad you have come." He had a seat prepared and His Highness shown in. A moon-viewing party had been planned for tonight in His Majesty's presence, but then it had been disappointingly canceled, and the news that people were gathering at Rokujō brought several senior nobles there. They discussed which of the crickets sang best.

Several instruments were playing to delightful effect when Genji remarked, "Every moonlit night has its own mood, but the moon's brilliance tonight sends one's thoughts soaring far beyond this world. I think of the late Intendant more and more now he is gone, and it seems to me that events both public and private have lost their savor without him. He perfectly appreciated the colors of flowers and the songs of birds, and his great intelligence always made him worth talking to." The music he himself was playing moistened his sleeves with tears. He remained partly aware that Her Highness must be listening from within her blinds, but it was on musical occasions of this kind that he missed the gentleman the most, and His Majesty remembered him fondly, too.

"Let us spend tonight honoring the bell cricket," he said. The wine cup had gone round twice when a message came from Retired Emperor Reizei. The Left Grand Controller[17] and the Commissioner of Ceremonial,[18] disappointed by the sudden cancellation of the music at the palace, had arrived with a group of like-minded companions, and His Eminence had just learned that the Commander and several others were at Rokujō.

> *"Even where I live, far removed from that realm high above the clouds,*
> *the moon still remembers me on a lovely autumn night.*[19]

'Oh, that I might only show . . . ' "[20] His Eminence had written.

"As I am, I have few claims on my time, but I hardly call on him anymore now that he has taken up a life of quiet retirement, and I am afraid he wishes to remind me that he finds me remiss," Genji explained, preparing to set off despite the appearance of acting precipitately.

> *"Your moon as before shines aloft for all to see, high above the clouds,*
> *while such is this home of mine that for me autumn has changed."*[21]

---

17. A younger brother of Kashiwagi.
18. Otherwise unknown.
19. "Moonlight comes to visit me, but you do not."
20. *Gosenshū* 103, by Minamoto no Saneakira: "Alas for the moon tonight, and the blossoms—Oh, that I might only show them to someone who would appreciate them!"
21. "Your glory remains undimmed, but not so mine, and that is why I have not come."

The poem could have been better—it had probably just come to him while his thoughts dwelled on memories of His Eminence, old and new. He offered the messenger wine and rewarded him handsomely.

The carriages were rearranged in order of rank, a large escort gathered, the quiet concert came to an end, and the party set forth. His Highness rode in Genji's carriage, and the Commander, the Intendant of the Left Gate Watch, the Fujiwara Consultant,[22] and the others followed behind. They added train-robes to their costumes, since they had been wearing only dress cloaks, and under a moon risen higher yet in a lovely, late-night sky the discreet procession moved on while at Genji's request the young gentlemen casually played their flutes. Genji and His Eminence had seen each other on formal occasions amid imposing pomp and ceremony, but Genji remembered, too, the days when he had been a mere commoner, and tonight he arrived in that spirit so very simply that His Eminence was greatly surprised and delighted. In his mature years he looked more than ever like Genji. All on his own he had renounced a glorious reign, and Genji was moved to note the tranquillity of his present life. Their Chinese and Japanese poems that night were all touching and deeply felt, and I cannot bring myself to record, as usual, only a few.[23] The Chinese poems were read out as dawn came on, and then everyone withdrew.

Before going home, Genji went to Her Majesty's, and the two of them talked. "I should really visit him often now," he said, "considering the quiet life he leads, because even in the absence of any particular occasion to do so, I would like to talk over all sorts of things from a past that at my age I never forget. However, since I am really neither one thing nor the other, I am afraid of either presuming or imposing.[24] So many younger people seem to have gone on before me[25] that life's shifting ways have left me almost without comfort, and I find myself longing for a peaceful place to live at last, far removed from the world; except that those who remained behind would then be left forlorn. Please see to keeping them from harm, as I have already begged you to do in the past." He spoke very gravely.

Her Majesty replied with all her customary youth and composure. "After years spent confined in the palace, I deplore more and more frequently that my present state makes any meeting with you so difficult to arrange, and while the world that so many are leaving now is hateful to me as well, I have not yet mentioned these feelings to you because it has always been my practice to turn to you first in all things, and I have hesitated to do so."

"Indeed, when you were at court, I could count on certain times when you were obliged to withdraw to your home and could look forward to greeting you then, but as things are now, what excuse could you cite to move about as you wish? Life is treacherous, I know, but no one rejects the world just like that, without some

---

22. The last two are probably both younger brothers of Kashiwagi.
23. The woman narrator could not decently record the Chinese ones anyway.
24. Although nominally an Honorary Retired Emperor, Genji has never reigned, and yet he is not exactly a commoner either. His standing is ambiguous. If he visited Reizei as a Retired Emperor, he might be thought to impose, while as a commoner he might seem to presume.
25. Either to death (Kashiwagi) or to the religious life (Asagao, Oborozukiyo, Onna San no Miya).

grievance against it, and there are always ties to detain even someone in a position to please himself. What makes you talk this way? To some people a religious aspiration like yours, one that seeks to emulate the example of others, could only seem strange. You must give up the idea once and for all."

She gathered bitterly from his response that he had understood very little of what moved her. Through what hellish fumes might her mother, the Rokujō Haven, now be wandering in her agony? His Grace had done all he could to conceal the way her mother had announced her by now detested presence even after death, but gossip about it had of course reached her, and the intense shock had made life hateful. She longed to know exactly what her mother had said in the course of these visitations,[26] but she could not bring herself to speak plainly and instead touched only obliquely on the matter. "I have vaguely gathered that the departed's present state suggests a heavy burden of sin, which is easy enough to assume even in the absence of proof, but I myself will never forget the sorrow of losing her, and it is very distressing to me not to be more considerate of her in the beyond. I long more and more to accept the guidance of those who speak comfort[27] and to quench those flames, all on my own if need be, and that is the reason I now feel as I do."

Genji quite understood her mood, and he was moved. "Those are flames that no one evades, as we all know, yet we who go with the morning dew still cling to what we have. The holy man Mokuren was close to the Buddha, and they say that he saved his mother immediately, but I doubt that you are up to following his example,[28] and even if you renounced the jade in your hair, you might still regret this world bitterly. Cultivate the resolve you mentioned and do what must be done to free her from the smoke. I share your wish, and yet what with one thing and another, I spend my days and nights in a manner far removed from the peace I desire; all I can do now is quietly to add prayers for her to my own devotions, which, as you say, is indeed all too little." Thus they confessed to each other their distaste for this world and their wish to renounce it, but it was not yet time for them, as they still were, to put off their finery.

Genji's discreet, lighthearted excursion of the evening before was well known by morning, and all the senior nobles and others gathered at His Eminence's attended him on his return. He derived great satisfaction from the success with which he had reared the Heir Apparent's Consort, since it was evident in her present glory and from the Commander's clear superiority over all others, but his deepest affection still went to His Eminence Reizei, who meant so much to him. His Eminence, too, had always longed to be closer to Genji, and the unfortunate rarity of their meetings was what had spurred him to take up his present, quieter life.

In contrast, Her Majesty could now leave him even less than before, for they were constantly together like any commoner couple, and they enjoyed music more

---

26. English requires a choice between singular and plural. The plural acknowledges the possession involving Onna San no Miya in "The Oak Tree."

27. Clerics, who speak the Buddha's word.

28. Mokuren learned, thanks to his supernormal powers, that his mother was suffering in the realm of hungry ghosts or of hell (versions differ), but he was able to save her, thanks to the Buddha's teaching.

brilliant and stylish than any heard during his reign. No aspect of her circumstances could fail to please her, were it not that concern for her mother confirmed her desire to devote herself to pious practice. She would never have leave to do so, however, and she therefore busied herself with good works, realizing meanwhile ever more profoundly the true character of this world.

39

Evening Mist

One misty evening Yūgiri (the
word means "evening mist") visits
the villa in the hills to which
Ochiba no Miya has retired with
her mother, and there he sends
her the poem that gave both him
and the chapter their name:

*"While such evening mists as bring a mountain village new melancholy
veil the sky, I cannot wish to leave and set out for home."*

"Evening Mist" begins at about the same time as the end of "The Bell Cricket" (the two chapters overlap slightly) and lasts into the winter of the same year.

PERSONS

His Grace, the Honorary Retired Emperor, Genji, age 50

Her Highness of Ichijō, the Second Princess (Ochiba no Miya)

The Commander, Genji's son, 29 (Yūgiri)

The Haven, mother of Ochiba no Miya (Ichijō no Miyasudokoro)

His Reverence, the Master of Discipline

The Commander's wife, 31 (Kumoi no Kari)

Koshōshō, a gentlewoman in Ochiba no Miya's household and also her cousin

The Governor of Yamato, Ochiba no Miya's cousin and Koshōshō's brother

Lady Murasaki, 42

His Excellency (Tō no Chūjō)

His Cloistered Eminence, 53 (Suzaku In)

The lady of the northeast quarter (Hanachirusato)

The Chamberlain Lieutenant, one of Tō no Chūjō 's sons

The Dame of Staff, Koremitsu's daughter

The Commander, ever the stalwart gentleman he was reputed to be, had decided that Her Highness at Ichijō was exactly what he wanted, and he cultivated her goodwill assiduously, maintaining meanwhile before the world an appearance of respect for the memory of the departed. Secretly, he became more and more convinced as the months and days went by that things could not end as they were now. Amid the growing loneliness and monotony of her life the Haven was touched and grateful for his attentions, because his constant visits were often a great comfort to her.

He had never ventured the slightest hint to Her Highness, for, he thought, I would only give offense if all at once I were to start putting on suggestive airs and graces, but I will show her the depth of my devotion, and I know that she will yield in time. He seized every chance for a glimpse of her. She herself never said a word. He was watching for an opportunity to express himself plainly and to gauge her response when the Haven became gravely afflicted by a spirit and moved to a mountain villa of hers at Ono.[1] She did so because her preferred healer, a Master of Discipline[2] who had always banished spirits for her, had retired into the mountains and sworn never to go out among men again; and since the place was among the foothills, it was one to which she could have him come. The Commander provided her escort and even her carriage, while all the young gentlemen[3] who really had once been close to her were too busy with their own lives to give her a moment's thought. The Controller[4] had let it be known that he was not uninterested, but he had met such a rebuff that he never insisted on calling again.

The Commander went about his approach very discreetly and cautiously. He was thoughtful enough even to send offerings of pure raiment[5] for the monks and so on when he learned that the Haven was commissioning prayer services. Since she

1. In the hills northeast of Kyoto, probably the general area of the present Shugakuin imperial villa.
2. Rishi (Risshi), the lowest on the ladder of ecclesiastical ranks accessible to elite, fully ordained clerics; "discipline" refers to the body of Buddhist monastic discipline.
3. Kashiwagi's brothers.
4. Kōbai.
5. Jōe, robes to be worn by the monks during the rite. They could be blue-black, yellow, red, white, gray, or brown, depending on the deity to whom the rite was addressed.

Brushwood fence

was unable to thank him, Her Highness was the one who replied when her gentlewomen observed to her that a note written by them would offend so grand a gentleman. The unassumingly pleasing writing of her single line,[6] and the warmth of her accompanying words, made him more eager than ever to be with her, and he began to send her frequent letters. Things became difficult when his wife noticed that there seemed to be something going on between them, and he could not call on her immediately, as he would have so much liked to do.

It was the middle of the eighth month, and the countryside was lovely; he longed to see what it was like at her villa in the hills. "The Master of Discipline is down there for once, I hear," he blandly explained, "and there is something I simply must discuss with him. I am off, then, since this will also give me an opportunity to inquire after the Haven's health." His discreet escort consisted of no more than five or six men in hunting cloaks. The destination was far into the mountains, but the hills above Matsugasaki, if not exactly noble crags, nonetheless wore their autumn colors, and their beauty absorbed him more than did that superb garden in the City.[7]

The light, brushwood fence had genuine style and distinction, although the Haven planned only a short stay. A fire altar[8] had been built in an extension on the east side of what he took to be the main house, and since she occupied the north, Her Highness was at the front of the chamber, to the west. The Haven would have preferred her daughter not to come at all, for fear of the afflicting spirit, but Her Highness had not wanted to leave her mother, who had therefore had a light partition put up between them. She would not allow her any nearer, lest the spirit move to her.

There being nowhere to receive a guest, he was brought in to sit before Her Highness's blinds,[9] whence the older gentlewomen conveyed his greetings. "I am extremely grateful for all your kind letters and for this thoughtful visit from you," the Haven replied. "The fear of being unable to thank you properly, should anything happen to me, has inspired me to wish to live a little longer."

"I had hoped to escort you here, but alas, I was detained at Rokujō and therefore could not do so. So many things preoccupy me from day to day that I regret having been far less attentive to you than I would wish."

Her Highness sat very quietly far back in the room, but among such simple

6. Perhaps a poem written in a single line rather than in a freer, more ornamental manner.
7. Probably Akikonomu's autumn garden at Rokujō.
8. *Dan*, an altar that included an earthen hearth for the sacred *goma* fire.
9. Yūgiri seems to be seated in the west aisle.

furnishings and in so plain a setting it naturally was clear that she was there. The rustle of her slightest movement made it obvious. The agitated Commander talked as usual with Koshōshō[10] and the other women, while messages passed between him and the rather distant Haven. "I have been calling for some years now," he remarked, "and it is very disappointing that Her Highness still receives me so coolly. To think that even now, before her very blinds, I send her my distant greetings through somebody else! I have never seen the like! My old-fashioned ways must be making her and the rest of you smile—it is so embarrassing! I would feel less awkward now if only I had practiced gallantry a little more when I was young and hardly mattered. No, no one else at my age could possibly be so fussy and dull!"

Indeed, nothing about him encouraged cavalier treatment, and his words confirmed the women in what they had long assumed. "My lady, it would not become you to fail to reply as he deserves," they said, nudging one another. "It is as though his complaint meant nothing to you."

This is the message that reached him: "I should properly remedy my mother's unfortunate inability to reply to you in person, but it has tested me greatly to nurse her through such a time of danger, and I am afraid that I simply cannot do so."

"Is this from Her Highness?" He sat up straight. "Why is it that I feel your mother's suffering as though it were my own?" he answered. "What has brought me here, if I may say so, is my conviction that it is vital for you both, when you yourself have had such occasion to mourn, that she should remain in good health to see you into happier times. I am very sorry that you should take my goodwill to be directed to her alone and fail to perceive my long-standing concern for you as well."

The gentlewomen assured Her Highness that what he said was quite right.

Sunset was approaching, mist beautifully veiled the sky, and the mountain's shadow seemed to dim, while everywhere cicadas sang[11] and pinks gracefully nodded their pretty colors along the fence.[12] The flowers in the near garden bloomed in bright profusion to cooling water sounds, while the pines sighed like a forest in the mournful mountain wind; and when the bell rang in new monks to take up the perpetual scripture reading for the old, the voices of both blended a moment to awesome effect. The melancholy of the place gave a sad cast to all his thoughts. He did not wish to leave. The Master of Discipline could be heard at his prayers, chanting the *darani* in inspiring tones.

The women gathered to the Haven, who apparently felt extremely ill. Not many had followed their mistress to the country, and Her Highness was therefore left all but alone with her thoughts. The moment struck the Commander as perfect for a quiet declaration. Mist now shrouded the house itself, and he said, "I shall not be able to see my way back. What am I to do?

---

10. A gentlewoman already encountered in "The Oak Tree." A later passage suggests that she is a niece of Princess Ochiba's mother and a cousin of Ochiba herself.

11. *Kokinshū* 204: "A cicada sang, and I thought the sun had set; but I had just come under the shadow of the mountain." Thanks to a wordplay, *higurashi*, the name of this species of cicada, suggests the image of sunset.

12. *Kokinshū* 685 evokes a similar mood: "Ah, I miss them so, and how I long to see them, the pinks abloom in that rustic fence!"

*While such evening mists as bring a mountain village new melancholy
veil the sky, I cannot wish to leave and set out for home."*

*"Even mists that rise and muffle a mountain rustic's humble garden fence
surely need never detain one who hastens to be gone."*

Sliding panel

The faint murmur of her answer consoled him, and he really did forget all thought of leaving. "I hardly know what to do. I could not see the path home, yet you tell me that your mist-shrouded fence need not keep me. That is what I get for being so poor at this sort of thing." Still reluctant to go, he began to touch on what threatened to burst from him, and she, who had always ignored his feelings even though she had not failed to note them through the years, wished bitterly that he would keep them to himself. He was very upset when she was troubled enough to lapse into almost complete silence, but he reflected that no such chance would ever come again. Never mind if she thinks me cruel and shallow, he said to himself; I *must* tell her what has been on my mind all this time.

He called, and an intimate retainer—one of his own guardsmen, recently promoted from Aide[13]—presented himself. Quietly, he had the man approach. "I have something to discuss with the Master of Discipline. I know that his rites keep him busy, but just now he seems to be resting. I shall stay tonight and go to see him once the evening service is over. See that the right men remain on duty here. As for the rest, I believe that my Kurusuno estate is nearby. They are to go there and feed the horses. I do not want too many of them here, talking. People might feel that I have no business spending the night." The man, who gathered that the Commander must have his reasons, assented and set off.

"The way back will be too difficult. I shall find somewhere to stay nearby," he then remarked with apparent unconcern. "I should appreciate your allowing me to remain here in front of your blinds just until His Reverence is finished."

Oh, no! He does not usually stay this late or act the gallant as he is doing now! Still, she did not think that it would look right for her to move too quickly or too obviously to join her mother, and she therefore sat in silence until he began to engage her in conversation; then he stole in behind the woman who took her his

13. The man has apparently been promoted from Aide (Zō, sixth rank) to Commissioner (Taifu, fifth).

words. Night was falling, the mist was still thick, and all was dark inside the blinds. The woman glanced back in dismay, and Her Highness slipped in horror through the panel on the north side of the room while the Commander, in successful pursuit, seized her robe to stop her. She got through herself, but her skirts trailed behind her, and since the panel did not lock from that side, she gave up trying to shut it and simply sat there shaking, bathed in perspiration. Her shocked gentlewomen had no idea what to do. His side had a lock catch, but that hardly helped, and he was not a man whom they could drag roughly away.

"This is awful! My lord, I would never have thought it of you!" The woman was almost in tears.

"Why should Her Highness find it shocking or especially distasteful of me to wait upon her this way? No doubt I am unworthy, but she has been acquainted with me for years." With unruffled composure he began to speak of what so burdened his heart. Her Highness was in no mood to listen; instead, she only rued her folly and shuddered at the idea that *that* was what he thought of her. The very notion of a reply was beyond her.

"You have all the cruelty of a little girl," he complained. "Yes, I confess to the wanton crime of secret longings that my heart can no longer contain, but as for permitting myself any greater liberty, I would never do so without your leave. In what unbearable turmoil I find myself! I have had every right to expect you to understand my feelings in time, and yet you have so willfully ignored them and remained so cold that I am at my wits' end for any way to approach you. You may find my sentiments alien and repellent, but I assure you that my only wish is to tell you clearly what they are, for it would be very bitter to allow them to languish and die. I respect you too highly to do otherwise, despite your unspeakable treatment of me." He spoke with exaggerated consideration.

He did not open the panel, even though she had it only very approximately closed. "To think that you insist on keeping no more than this between us!" He laughed. "It is touching!" Still, he indulged in no worse outrage. He had not been prepared for such sweet nobility and grace. She seemed to him very thin and frail, perhaps because she had been in mourning so long, and the elegantly casual sleeves of her at-home dress, which she had not been able to change, as well as their inviting fragrance, together made her so appealing that his mood softened.

The night had grown late, and a mournful wind was blowing. Cricket songs, a stag's belling, the noise of the waterfall—all blended to such wild and stirring effect that the dullest simpleton would have lain sleepless under these skies, for the shutters were still up, and the setting moon that hung above the rim of the mountains gave the scene a quality too poignant not to call forth tears. "Your complete failure to understand my feelings has at least taught me how sadly your own heart lacks depth," he went on. "I cannot imagine another man sharing my degree of foolish, reassuring innocence; anyone able to do as he wished would laugh at an idiot like me and then, as I understand it, would act to please himself. I cannot promise to control myself indefinitely, considering how deeply you despise me. You cannot possibly be this ignorant of life."

He tried every kind of argument and threat, which left her miserable and at an utter loss how to respond. Shocked by his repeated intimations that her experience of life should have prepared her to yield, she reflected that her position was indeed a very great misfortune, and she wanted to die. "Unhappy as I am, I acknowledge my own shortcomings, but I hardly know what to think of your extraordinary behavior," she replied very low, weeping piteously.

> *"Must I be the one, just because life has taught me all love's cruelty,*
> *to have my name soiled again by the sorrows of wet sleeves?"*[14]

she added under her breath; whereupon to her consternation he pieced the poem together[15] and repeated it softly to himself. She wished that she had never said it.

"Indeed, I was wrong to say what I did." He added with a smile,

> *"I am not the kind who would ever willingly clothe you in wet robes,*
> *but sleeves soaking even now can hardly protect your name.*[16]

You might as well resign yourself to it." To her consternation he invited her out into the moonlight, and he drew her to him easily, despite her brave resistance. "Please acknowledge my singular devotion and feel at ease with me," he pleaded. "Without your leave I would never, never . . ." He made himself painfully clear. Meanwhile dawn came on.

A brilliant moon shone in from on high, undimmed by mist. To Her Highness the aisle's light eaves seemed very narrow indeed. In her dismay and embarrassment she felt as though she and the moon were face-to-face, and her efforts to evade its light revealed an inexpressible grace. The Commander began to speak quietly and decorously of the late Intendant, but still he expressed resentment that she should think himself the lesser man.

She recalled silently how all concerned had approved the match, although the Intendant had not yet risen as high as he might, and how he had taken a very distressing attitude toward her when in the natural course of things she came to know him fully. It is not as though *this* outrage concerns no one else close to me, she reflected—what will His Excellency think when he hears about it? Quite apart from the world's commonplace censure, how will the news affect His Cloistered Eminence? The more she imagined the way those near her would feel, the more she despaired. *I* may remain adamant, but people will talk nonetheless, and although it would be wrong for my mother not to know, she will certainly condemn my thoughtlessness when she finds out. The very idea was distressing. "Do at least leave before dawn," she said. She could think of nothing else.

---

14. "Must I who have lost my husband now have my reputation ruined as well by rumors of a new affair?" "Wet sleeves," or the "wet robes" of Yūgiri's answer, have to do with betraying a love affair and making it a subject of gossip.

15. The unclear original may suggest that Yūgiri caught only the gist of her poem and made up a similar one from what he overheard.

16. "Though I have no wish to hold you up to scandal because of any involvement with me, you are already the subject of gossip because of your unfortunate marriage to Kashiwagi, and there is nothing you can do about that. So would yielding to me really make that much difference?"

"You are too cruel! Imagine what the morning dew will think of me when I leave you as though something had really happened! I warn you, then: if you believe that you have me outwitted, and you will have no more to do with me now that I have shown myself to be a fool, I shall no longer be able to contain myself, and since I have never felt like this before, I cannot answer for what I may do." He was worried, too. He did not want to go yet, but he knew that in truth he had never before been in such a passion. Concern for her and fear that he might come to despise himself moved him for both their sakes to leave while the mist would still hide him.

He was desperate.

"I must leave you now to make my way through many veils of thick morning mists
through fields of reeds, soaking wet with dew dripping from the eaves,"

he said. "You will not get that wet robe of yours dry either.[17] It is your fault for insisting that I go."

Yes, she thought, her name would be bandied about shamefully enough, but she meant to answer her own heart's questions with honor, and she therefore gave him a very distant answer indeed:

"Is this your excuse, that you must now make your way through such dewy fields,
to oblige me after all to wear culpably wet robes?

What a thing to say!" Her severity gave her an air at once daunting and delightful. He had long been more loyal to her than anyone else might have been and had been kind to her in countless ways, and now all that was gone. He had erred, and his wanton behavior filled him with such shame and compunction that he bitterly rued what he had done, and yet he feared that meek acquiescence might only make him look a fool again. He set off with his mind in turmoil. Heavy dews attended him all along the way.

Unaccustomed as he was to such expeditions, he found this one both intriguing and despairing. If he went home, his wife would wonder suspiciously how he had got himself so wet, so he went instead to the northeast quarter of Rokujō. The morning mist was not yet gone, and his thoughts went to *her* house, where it must be thicker still. The women whispered among themselves about this unusual outing of his. He rested and changed his clothes. The lady there always had beautiful things ready for him, summer or winter, and he took them from a fragrant chest.[18] After breakfast he went to see Genji.

She never glanced at the letter he sent her. His suddenly outrageous behavior had shocked and embarrassed her. It was reprehensible. She burned with shame to think that her mother might learn what had happened, because even if her mother could hardly imagine anything of the kind, she might still notice something amiss, and

---

17. "You will not escape notoriety for this either."

18. *Kō no ōn karabitsu,* a chest either containing incense wood, to perfume its contents, or actually made of incense wood.

besides, gossip always got out in the end; she could easily put one clue and another to-gether and decide that her daughter had been keeping the truth from her—the very idea was so painful that she wished the women would tell her the whole story now, and never mind how hateful she thought it. Even for mother and daughter the two were un-usually close. In the old tales, yes, a daughter might sometimes hide from her mother things that outsiders knew, but for Her Highness that was out of the question.

"No, no," the gentlewomen decided, "my lady would only be upset to hear a rumor that makes it seem as though something happened when really it did not, and that would be too bad." The ones who longed to find out what came next were curi-ous about the letter and impatient when Her Highness made no move to open it. "He will wonder about you, my lady, and he will think you quite childish if you do not answer him at all." They opened it themselves.

"I know it is my own fault that I had such extraordinary behavior inflicted on me when I least expected it, but I simply cannot get over his offensive lack of con-sideration," Her Highness replied. "Answer him that I will not read it." She lay back with a look of stern displeasure.

However, there was nothing objectionable about the letter, because he had written it with great goodwill.

> "I have helplessly left my soul all entangled in your cruel sleeves,
>   and through no fault but my own I remain vacant and lost.[19]

My heart is elsewhere, as others have said before, I know, but it is true: I find my love everywhere."[20]

There seemed to be a great deal more, but they could not see it properly. Al-though it did not resemble an ordinary morning letter, they could not make out just what the matter was. Her Highness's mood aroused their pity, and they watched her sadly. What could it possibly be? He had been so kind to her in so many ways, and for so long—was it possible that this new kind of dependence on him had given her reason to think less well of him? It was very worrying, and the ones who served her intimately were quite upset.

Meanwhile, the Haven knew nothing at all. The spirit's attacks were serious, but at times she was still perfectly lucid. At midday, when the noon prayers were over, the Master of Discipline remained alone with her, reading the *darani*. "The Buddha Dainichi[21] never lies," he said, pleased to find her so well. "How could such prayers as mine, offered wholeheartedly, fail to have their effect? The evil spirit is indeed stub-born, but it is only a poor phantom caught in its own karmic impediments."[22] His

---

19. *Kokinshū* 992, by Michinoku: "Perhaps my soul went in among the sleeves I still desire, for I feel as though it is gone from me."

20. *Kokinshū* 977, by Ōshikōchi no Mitsune: "It must have left me and gone away, for since I first loved you, my heart has been elsewhere." *Kokinshū* 488: "My love must have filled the boundless heavens, for though I would escape it, I find it everywhere."

21. Dainichi Nyorai, the cosmic buddha of the Esoteric Buddhist (Shingon) pantheon.

22. *Gōshō*, the Buddhist term for all karmic factors that impede progress toward enlightenment. Chief among them are greed, anger, and stupidity.

hoarse voice was vehement, and his manner awesomely holy and severe.

"Oh, yes!" he said abruptly. "The Commander: how long has he been a regular caller here?"[23]

"But he is not. He and the late Intendant were close friends, and he has visited us now and again for a long time so as to keep the promise he made then. He has certainly become a familiar presence, but he came this time purposely to inquire after my health, for which I am very grateful."

"Now, now, that will not do. You must not keep it from me. This morning, on the way to the late-night service, I saw a very imposing gentleman come out through the double doors to the west, and my monks told me it was the

Double doors

Commander, although the mist was too thick for me to recognize him myself; they all said that he sent his carriage back yesterday evening and spent the night. The intense fragrance that lingered behind him on the air—it practically gave me a headache—convinced me that it must indeed have been he, since he is always perfumed that way. This is not good at all. He is highly accomplished, and at Her Late Highness's[24] request I have performed rites for him ever since he was a boy, so I would gladly do anything proper for him, but this is unfortunate, to say the least. His wife is a woman to reckon with. Her family is extremely distinguished and has great influence, and she has given him seven or eight children. Her Highness cannot possibly stand beside her. This is exactly the sort of sin that leads to birth in an evil female body and endless wandering in the darkness of eternal night: that is the terrible retribution it calls down. She will suffer for it if his wife is ever angry with her. No, no, I cannot accept it." He shook his head.

"I do not know what you are talking about," the Haven replied to this rush of plain speech. "Why, he has never shown any sign of such intentions. I was not feeling at all well, and he therefore waited here quietly for me to be able to receive him—that is what my women say, so I suppose that must be why he stayed on. He is always ever so serious and correct." However, in her heart of hearts she wondered despite these assurances whether it might not be true. He *has* sometimes seemed a bit excited, she thought, but his manner is so intelligent and he is so obviously eager to avoid doing anything to provoke criticism that I have trusted him not to take any liberties. Perhaps he went straight in when he saw that there was practically nobody with her.

23. "How long is it since he married your daughter?"
24. Ōmiya, Yūgiri's grandmother.

Once the Master of Discipline had gone, she summoned Koshōshō and told her what she had just heard. "What happened? And why has she not told me? Not that I can believe it is true."

With great regret Koshōshō described to her exactly what had happened, including the letter this morning and the veiled statements made by Her Highness. "I suppose that all he meant to do was to let her know what he had kept shut up in his heart over the years," she said. "Fortunately, he was disposed to restrain himself, and he left before it was day. Who can have told you, my lady?" The Master of Discipline had never occurred to her; she assumed that it must have been one of the women.

The Haven said nothing, but she was shocked, and tears began streaming down her cheeks. Koshōshō was deeply sorry to see them. She wondered why she had ever told the plain truth and feared that her mistress's health would be more than ever affected. "The panel *was* locked, though," she insisted soothingly.

"Whether it was or not, it is disastrous that she should so imprudently have let him see her. Never mind how pure she may know herself to be: do you suppose that after talking so much already, the monks and the rascals who serve them will really say no more about it? What will gossip make of it? What lies will people invent? You are such innocents, the lot of you!" She could not go on, because this new crisis, added to her already painful condition, had put her in a thoroughly pathetic state. She who had always aspired to uphold her daughter's pride suffered profoundly to think that her daughter would now be known for her light and wanton ways. "Please ask her to come to me while my mind is more or less clear. I know that I should go to her, but I am afraid that I cannot move. I feel as though it is so long since I last saw her!" There were tears in her eyes.

Koshōshō did as bidden. Her Highness tidied up the wet, tangled hair at her forehead and changed out of her torn shift in preparation for going, but she could not immediately find the strength to do so. What did the women think of her? How cruel my mother will feel I have been if she does not know yet, and she hears only some of the story later on! The thought filled her with shame, and she lay down again. "I feel extremely ill," she said, "and it might just be for the better if it turns out that I do not recover. The vapors seem to have come up from my feet."[25] She had them massaged down again. The vapors had risen because of her intense distress.

"Someone has already spoken to my lady," Koshōshō explained, "and when she asked me what it was all about, I told her exactly what happened, except that I added a bit about the sliding panel having been locked. Please tell her the same thing, my lady, if you tell her about it yourself." She said nothing about how hard the Haven had taken the news.

Then that *was* it! Her Highness was miserable, and drops spilled from the pillow where she lay in silence. And this is not all, since I have done nothing but cause her grief ever since that first, unforeseen change in my fortunes.[26] I cannot now feel

---

25. These "vapors" (*ke*) are baneful influences that because of cold, heat, damp, and so on may rise from the earth into the feet and thence, in serious cases, to the upper part of the body.
26. Her marriage to Kashiwagi.

that my life is worth living. It will end painfully and badly if this gentleman refuses to give up and continues to insist on pursuing me. And just imagine what damage my reputation might have suffered if I had weakly given him his will! That thought, at least, was a comfort, but she despaired of the detestable fate that had led so great a lady as herself carelessly to expose herself to a man's gaze.

Toward evening Her Highness received another appeal from her mother to come and see her, and so she had the retreat between them opened and stepped through.[27] The Haven greeted her despite her suffering with great affection and respect, sitting up and observing every customary mark of politeness. "I am so sorry that my poor health should oblige you to come to me," she said. "It feels like ages since we last met, although it is really only two or three days. I know that it is foolish of me, but you know, this may be the last time you and I are together, and what good will it do us to meet again only in a future life?[28] How I now wish that I had never allowed affection to bind me to this one, when I must leave it so soon!" She was weeping.

Her Highness was too weighed down by her sorrows to do more than watch in silence. Too profoundly reserved by nature ever to speak up in her own defense, she merely sat there in shame, and her mother refrained out of pity from questioning her. She quickly had a lamp lit and meal trays brought in. Having heard that her daughter was not eating, she did what she could to encourage her, but Her Highness would not touch anything. The only ray of comfort for her was that her mother seemed a little better.

Another letter arrived. Someone unfamiliar with the circumstances received it and announced a letter from the Commander for Koshōshō. Her Highness's heart sank. Koshōshō took it. "What does it say?" the Haven allowed herself to ask. Privately, she had begun to accept the idea after all and had been expecting the Commander's visit, and she was troubled by his apparent failure to appear. "You *must* answer it, you know," she said. "You have no choice. No one speaks up to redress a reputation. You yourself may know that you are pure, but hardly anyone will ever believe it. The best thing would be to correspond nicely with him and to go on with him as before. Not to answer would only seem like provocation on your part." She asked for the letter, and most unwillingly Koshōshō gave it to her.

"Experiencing the full force of your cruelty has only confirmed me in the conviction that I shall soon be in no mood to tolerate further delay.

> *Your damming the stream only betrays your shallows, for the mountain brook*
> *even now runs babbling on, till nothing can hide your name.*"[29]

It was a long letter, but she did not read it all. It, too,[30] failed to make his intentions clear, and his insufferable self-satisfaction, together with his indifference this

---

27. Perhaps because she wished to avoid being seen. A partition has been put up between the north and west aisles, and she cannot go round on the veranda.

28. People brought together again in another life by karma do not recognize each other.

29. "It is useless to thwart me, as you should know, because everyone already knows what happened."

30. Like his treatment of the Princess the previous evening.

evening,[31] struck her as extremely offensive. It is thoroughly disappointing, she reflected, when the late Intendant's devotion fell short of what one might have hoped, and despite the reassurance of knowing that she did not actually have any rival, her position was never a pleasant one. This is dreadful, though. I wonder what they can be saying at His Excellency's.

She resolved to press the Commander further. Wiping eyes dimmed by illness, she wrote as though in the strange tracks of a bird, "Her Highness is with me now, since the state of my health gives reason for concern, and I have urged her to send you an answer; but she is so downcast that the sight is more than I can bear.

> *What is it to you, this meadow where a forlorn maidenflower weeps,*
> *that you should have wished to spend no more than a single night?*"[32]

That was all she could manage; she twisted the ends[33] and sent it off. Just then, as she lay there, she had a very severe attack. Her women cried out that the spirit must have purposely put them off their guard. All the tested healers again raised their clamor. The women urged Her Highness to leave, but she had no wish to survive her mother, and she refused.

The Commander, who had returned to Sanjō[34] at about midday, had refrained from going back that very evening because it would start premature and unfortunate gossip to leave the impression that something had really happened. His distress was

great enough to be a thousand times worse than anything he had been through in the last few years. His wife had heard a little about his stealthy expedition and did not like the news at all, but she feigned ignorance and lay down in her day sitting room, where she distracted herself by playing with her children.

The Haven's answer came in the evening. The writing was so

Kumoi no Kari steals a letter

---

31. His failure to come in person. If he really meant to marry her, he should have come for three nights in a row.

32. The "meadow" (*nobe*) is her villa and the "maidenflower" (*ominaeshi*) her daughter. *Ominaeshi* contains the word *omina* (more commonly *onna*), "woman"; and *shioruru* ("weeps") also means "wilts." The poem is based on *Kokin rokujō* 1201, by Ki no Tsurayuki: "Maidenflower I find after a day hunting on the autumn moors, will you have me to stay just tonight?"

33. The letter is rolled, and the ends are then twisted to seal it.

34. His home.

unusual that he could not immediately make it out and drew up a lamp for a better look. His wife had seemed to be safely behind a curtain, but she now slipped up to him and seized it from behind.

"Oh, no! What are you doing? You should be ashamed of yourself! It is from the lady in the northeast at Rokujō. She was suffering from a cold this morning. I was worried about her because I came straight home from seeing His Grace, so I sent to ask how she is. Read it if you like! Does it look like a love letter? What a way to behave! It is infuriating, the way you treat me more like an idiot with every passing year! *My* feelings mean nothing to you, do they!"

He showed no visible alarm and did not try to snatch it back, so even though she kept it, she did not read it immediately after all. "If anyone is treating anyone more and more like an idiot, I should say it is you!" she retorted, dampened by his composure, in such a delightfully youthful manner that he laughed.

"Either way, then! Quarrels like this happen all the time anyway. What *must* be unique is a husband who seeks no diversion elsewhere, even after he reaches a certain level of prominence, but remains as tremulously faithful to his one and only wife as a hawk to his mate.[35] People must be laughing their heads off at me. It is hardly to your credit, either, that you command such loyalty from anyone so dull. What really sets off a woman is to stand out among a range of others and be honored above them all. It keeps her young at heart, too, and it prolongs all the pleasures and tender moments of life. I am very sorry that you have an old fool like me hanging on to you, the way that one did in the story![36] What pleasure is there in that?" The only object of this speech was somehow to get the letter out of her after all, without seeming to care whether he did or not.

"It is a bit hard on your old woman if you are out for pleasure," she said with a dazzling smile. "This new gaiety of yours is strange to me. I am not used to it, and it upsets me. You should have accustomed me to it sooner." It was rather a fetching complaint.

"Where on earth did you get the idea I have suddenly changed? You are so quick to nurse a grudge! Somebody must have been telling you unpleasant rumors— no doubt someone who for some reason never approved of me in the first place. I expect that she invokes those miserable light blue sleeves of mine[37] even now to convince you. She must whisper all sorts of awful things. There is someone else, though, who has nothing to do with any of this, and I feel sorry for her, too."[38] He talked on this way, but he was too certain of eventual success really to argue the matter. Her nurse, Taifu, listened in pained silence.[39]

The Commander made no effort to look for the letter, since his wife had hidden it after their little spat, and he went to bed as though it made no difference to him. His heart was racing. It had seemed to be from the Haven; he simply had to get it back. What could the matter possibly be? He lay there wide-eyed. Once his wife was asleep,

35. A female hawk is larger and more aggressive than her mate.
36. The allusion has not been identified.
37. The light blue of the sixth rank, of which Yūgiri was so ashamed in "The Maidens."
38. Ochiba no Miya.
39. Taifu is presumably the culprit. In "The Maidens" she is not named.

he felt casually around where she had sat during the evening, but it was not there. This was extremely annoying, because she could not have hidden it anywhere else. He did not get up immediately when daybreak came, and only started hunting everywhere, as though he had just woken up, after the children woke her and she slipped out.[40] He could not find it. She had decided that it was not a love letter and so had dismissed it, since he seemed so little interested in searching for it himself, and what with all the children's commotion—their busy games dressing and playing with their dolls, their reading and writing practice, and so on, as well as the baby crawling around tugging at her skirts—the letter she had taken had slipped her mind completely. Her husband meanwhile could think of nothing else. He considered replying immediately but then hesitated, because his answer would probably show that he had not read yesterday's properly, and she might assume that he had lost it.

It was near midday, after their meal, when his anxiety got the better of him. "What did you do with that letter yesterday evening? You never let me read it at all, you know. I should get in touch with her today, too. I do not feel up to visiting Rokujō, though—well, I shall send a note. I wonder what it was about."

He spoke with such apparent lack of interest that she said nothing, since by now she felt foolish for having taken it at all. "Why not give her an amusing excuse about not feeling quite well because you let the mountain wind get at you the other night?" she suggested.

"*Please* do not always talk such nonsense. What is so amusing about that? It is embarrassing, the way you make me out to be just like anyone else. For all I know, these women can hardly hear you without a rueful smile, talking as you do about someone so hopelessly dull."

After this banter he returned to the subject. "That letter, though—where is it?" When she still made no move to produce it, he continued chatting and then lay down a little[41] until sunset.

He awoke to the singing of cicadas and thought how thick the mist must be below the hills. What a miserable business! Impatient to reply at least today, he casually ground some ink and then sat wondering vacantly how to explain what had happened to the letter. Then he noticed a slight bulge near the back of his cushion and decided that he might as well have a look. When he turned up the cushion, there it was: she must have slipped it in *there!* Feeling both pleased and silly, he read it with a smile, only to discover how disturbing it was. His heart sank. It really hurt to see that she had pointedly brought up that single night. How she must have watched and waited for me yesterday evening! And today again I have not even managed to get a letter to her! His dismay was indescribable. The letter, which was pitifully difficult to decipher, had clearly cost her a great effort. She must have written this in terrible anguish, and now I have failed her for a second night! He was at a loss for words and very angry indeed with his wife. This nonsense of hers, hiding it that way—why, I must not have trained her properly! He blamed himself bitterly for many things and all in all felt very close to tears.

40. From their curtained bed.
41. They may lie down together.

He made ready to set off straightaway, but he knew that despite what her mother had written she would not willingly receive him. What to do? Besides, he reminded himself, today is a pitfall day,[42] and it might not be a good idea even if she *did* give in. I must think of something better. His punctiliousness was showing.

He hastened to compose his reply. "Your rare letter has pleased me greatly for many reasons, but I do not understand your reproach, and I wonder what you may have heard.

> *Yes, I went to her through the dense and tangled growth of autumn meadows,*
> *but I made no pillow there to rest on in fleeting sleep.*[43]

It may make little sense for me to seek to excuse myself, but I hope that I may explain my delinquency of yesterday." After writing to Her Highness at great length, he had a swift horse from his stables saddled and dispatched the Commissioner of the other night. "Tell them I have been at Rokujō since yesterday evening and have only just come home," he whispered to the man.

When that day, too, ended in the hills without any answer to the letter that the Haven, angrily careless of rumor, had felt compelled to write by the Commander's failure to appear the evening before, she despaired of him. With every hope dashed, she lapsed from her recent respite back into acute suffering. Privately, Her Highness was neither surprised nor particularly upset, and although she regretted having exposed herself so unexpectedly under intimate circumstances, she did not take the outcome that hard; instead, the agony she had caused her mother filled her with such shame that she could not offer a word in her own defense. Her mother found her unusually bashful, guilty manner very painful, and she grieved with all her heart to see care piled for her this way upon care.

"I have no wish to dwell on an unhappy subject," she said, "but I must say that although your destiny has undoubtedly played its part in all this, your surprising naiveté is likely to earn you considerable disapproval. There is no help for it now, but please be more careful in the future. Of course I myself hardly matter, but having done for you what I could, I trusted that by now you must know what you need to know and that you must have made your own sense of the vagaries to which life subjects us, whereas to my dismay I find you still a girl and so lacking in the firmness you require that I only wish I had a little longer to live. It is unfortunately true that no woman of respectable standing can decently give herself to two men, even as a commoner, and you can still less afford to allow one to approach you this way. It was your destiny, I suppose, but it saddened me to see what those years were like for you. His Eminence himself had consented, the gentleman's father was plainly disposed to agree, and I yielded because I did not see how I could very well hold out alone. I could only complain before Heaven when I saw you caught after that, through no fault of your own, in so distressing a position. Now I am afraid that there will be new rumors damaging to both sides. Well, as long as you ignore the gossip and keep up perfectly ordinary appearances, I expect that

42. *Kannichi,* a day defined by the yin-yang (*onmyōdō*) almanac as one on which all enterprises were destined to fail. There was one per month.

43. "I visited your daughter, but I did not sleep with her."

time will do the rest—though I must say, he seems to be most extraordinarily callous!" Her tears flowed freely.

She had not allowed Her Highness a single word, nor did Her Highness have any with which to defend herself; she merely wept, looking as she did so the picture of innocence and sweetness. Her mother gazed at her. "Alas," she said, "what is it that makes you worth less than anyone else? What destiny requires you to suffer so?"

She talked on like this until she became acutely ill. The spirit had seized upon her weakness: suddenly, she fainted away and began to grow cold. The Master of Discipline arose in agitation and prayed noisily. He did so with all his heart, because after swearing to confine himself for life to the Mountain, he surely dreaded the shame of breaking up his altar[44] and returning there, now that he had bravely left, and he must have been angry with the Buddha, too. Her Highness wept in utter misery.

The Commander's letter arrived in the midst of this confusion, and the Haven knew when she heard of it that they could not expect him that evening either. How cruelly people will be talking about her! Why did I ever write as I did?[45] Amid such thoughts as these, she breathed her last that very moment. "Undeserved" and "cruel" are pale words for such a passing. She had suffered from this spirit off and on in the past, and since this was not the first time she had seemed lost, the monks redoubled their prayers on the assumption that it had taken her as before. However, there could be no doubt that now she really was gone.

Her Highness's only thought was to go, too, and she lay close beside her. Her women came. "It is too late, my lady," they protested tritely. "This is her last journey, and she cannot come back from it. How could you possibly follow her as you wish?"

"No, my lady, you must not![46] It is a grave offense for you both! Oh, please leave her!" They tried dragging her away, but she was as though rigid and unconscious. The priests broke up their altar and drifted off, leaving behind the few still needed.[47] It was all over, and only grief and desolation remained.

Messages of condolence soon began to arrive. The Commander was astonished by the news and wrote immediately. Many other expressions of sorrow came from Rokujō, His Excellency, and elsewhere. His Eminence on his mountain learned of the event as well, and he wrote his daughter a very touching letter. Not until it came did she raise her head at last. "I was told often enough during the past days that your mother was gravely ill," he had written, "but I regret to say that I assumed it to be her usual complaint, and I gave the matter little thought. Quite apart from our mutual loss, it pains me deeply to imagine how you must be grieving. Please take comfort from the thought that such misfortunes visit us all." Through the tears that blinded her, she wrote him a reply.

The Haven had often spoken of what she wanted done, and her nephew, the Governor of Yamato,[48] now arrived to see to all the arrangements for the funeral,

---

44. As a monk did when healing rites had failed. The altar, or hearth, is built of earth.
45. Her poem let Yūgiri know that she would not oppose his marrying her daughter.
46. Cling to the body.
47. To conduct funeral rites and call the name of Amida.
48. The post of Governor of Yamato commanded only the fifth rank, junior grade. The Haven's origins were quite modest.

which was to take place without delay, that very day. Her Highness wished to contemplate the remains a little longer, but there would be no comfort in that, and the
preparations therefore went forward in haste. At the most upsetting moment[49] the
Commander arrived.

He vividly realized how deeply Her Highness must be grieving. "The next
several days are all wrong,[50] you see," he had declared for everyone to hear.

"But, my lord, there is no need for you to go there in such haste!" his women
had protested.

Nevertheless, he went.

It was a long way, and he was overwhelmed, as soon as he entered, by the immediacy of the tragedy. The ceremony itself was discreetly hidden behind curtains.
They admitted him to the west side of the house, and the Governor of Yamato
emerged in tears to thank him for coming. He sat on the veranda beside the double
doors, leaned against the railing, and called for a gentlewoman, but they were too
upset just then to know what was going on. Koshōshō came at last, somewhat comforted by his arrival. He could not speak. He was not usually given to tears, but the
character of the setting and the atmosphere of mourning so powerfully conveyed by
those around him sadly reminded him that the passing away of all things touched
him as well.

"I had had the impression that she was better," he said after regaining something of his composure, "and the idea lulled me into complacency. A dream is over
soon enough, but this a terrible thing!"

This is the man who destroyed my mother's peace of mind, Her Highness said
to herself. Perhaps her mother's time had come, but this tie with him was so bitter
that she did not even answer.

"But we must let him know your reply, my lady!" her women protested.

"He is a very great lord, and it would be too much if you failed to acknowledge the kindness that has brought him here in such haste."

"Sort it out yourselves, then. I can think of nothing to say." Her Highness lay
down, as well she might.

"My lord, my lady is hardly among the living just now," Koshōshō informed
him, "but I have let her know that you are here."

"I have no help to offer. I shall be back when I myself am a little less agitated,
and when she is feeling more composed. However, I should like to know how it
came to happen so suddenly."

Little by little, Koshōshō told him some, although not all, of what had so
troubled her late mistress. "I am afraid that I may seem to be criticizing you, my
lord," she said apologetically. "I am more and more muddled today, and I have probably got some things wrong. My lady will not always be in such a state, and I hope
that you will inquire again when she is a little calmer."

She really did not seem to be herself, and the Commander withheld what
came to his lips. "Yes, I, too, feel lost in darkness. I hope that you may yet console
her well enough for me to have a token answer from her." With those words he

---

49. Presumably, the placing of the body in the coffin.
50. According to the almanac.

started back, because it would not become him to linger, and there were after all a great many people present.

He had never imagined that everything would be finished tonight, and he disapproved of the summary character of the arrangements; summoning people from his nearby estates, he left them orders for the services they were to perform. He saw to it that wherever haste had encouraged excessive simplicity, there was a sufficient crowd to convey grandeur. The Governor of Yamato was very pleased and thanked him earnestly. Her Highness lay prostrate with vain misery that nothing of her mother remained. No one should be that close to anyone, not even to her mother. The sight saddened and disturbed her women.

"You cannot just go on being so unhappy, and there is nothing here to distract you," the Governor said once he had had everything tidied up; but she meant to end her days in this mountain village, since here at least she felt near the hill where her mother had turned to smoke. The monks who had come for the mourning confinement had arranged flimsy rooms for themselves on the east side, on the bridgeway nearby, in the servants' hall, and so on, and one hardly knew they were there. In the western aisle, now stripped of all decoration, Her Highness hardly recognized the passage of day or night, but the months went by nonetheless, and soon the ninth had come.

Strong winds swept down the Mountain, the trees were bare of leaves, and all things weighed so on her heart that the skies drew from her endless sighs and tears. She bitterly resented it that her very life was not hers to command. The women in her service were despondent and distraught. The Commander called often. He provided whatever might cheer up the lonely monks chanting the Name and meanwhile poured forth countless, heartfelt assurances and reproaches to Her Highness, showering her with endless letters. She would not even pick them up to read them, though, because she remembered how her already weakened mother had died convinced that that unspeakably wicked moment had ruined her daughter, and she knew with awful certainty that the thought would harm her mother even in the life to come. The mere mention of the Commander brought on ever more bitter, anguished tears. Her women hardly knew what to say.

When the Commander got not a single line in answer, he assumed at first that she was just too upset, but soon far too much time had passed for that. Surely grieving has an end, he reflected angrily. How can she so completely fail to understand me? She is hopelessly immature! It would be all very well if I were pursuing her with talk of flowers and butterflies, but someone who actually shares one's feelings and asks after one's sorrows deserves a warm, sympathetic response. I felt my grandmother's death deeply, but His Excellency hardly seemed affected—for him it was just a matter of course, and it hurt and upset me that he did her no more honor than what public decency required. It was actually His Grace who saw to everything, and that especially pleased me, even from my father. That was when I became particularly fond of the Intendant. He was so quiet and thoughtful, and it seemed to me that he felt things more deeply and warmly than other people. Such reflections as these filled the Commander's leisure day and night.

His wife continued meanwhile to wonder what was going on between him and Her Highness. She could not make out why he had corresponded so freely with Her Highness's mother, and she therefore had their little son take a note to him, where he lay gazing out at the twilight sky. She had written on a slip of paper,

> *"How am I to take the sorrow I see you feel, that I may soothe you:*
> *is it the living you love, or is it the dead you mourn?"*

He smiled ruefully. How thoroughly disingenuous of her, after all she has been imagining and saying, to pretend she thinks I may be mourning that lady! He wrote straight back, quite casually,

> *"Why should either one rouse me to a partial grief, when the fleeting dew,*
> *so swiftly gone, speaks of more than the lives of fragile leaves?*

My melancholy is all-embracing."

Yes, he was still keeping something from her, she knew it, and bother the dew on the fragile leaf; she was angry and hurt.

The Commander set forth again, anxious to know how Her Highness was getting on. He often told himself that he must move gently once her mourning retreat had passed, but that degree of restraint was beyond him. Why was he still so intent on upholding the lost cause of her honor? He might as well do as others did and have his way with her at last. He would

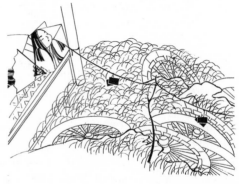

Bird clappers

no longer argue the matter with his wife. He would appeal to the authority of the reproachful letter that single night had earned him, even if Her Highness hated him for it. No, she would *not* succeed in presenting herself as unblemished.

It was a little past the tenth of the ninth month, and no one, however dull, could have failed to be stirred by the prospect of the moors and hills. Down a mountain wind that stripped the trees and swept a rushing storm of leaves from the kudzu vines on high came faint scripture chanting and the calling of the Name. The place was all but deserted beneath the gales; a stag stood by the garden fence, untroubled by clappers in the fields,[51] while others belled plaintively amid the deep green rice, and the waterfall[52] roared as though to rouse the stricken from their sorrows. Crickets among the grasses sang forlornly, in failing voices, while tall, dewy gentians sprang from beneath withered weeds as though autumn were theirs alone. These were no more than the sights of the season, but perhaps the place and the

---

51. Wooden clappers, moved by cords, strung across rice fields to frighten away birds, deer, and so on.
52. The Otowa waterfall, often mentioned in poetry.

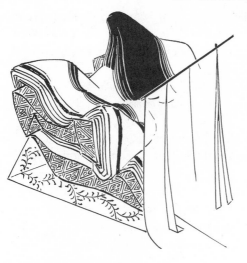

Woman in a kouchiki *dress gown*

moment made them unbearably poignant.

He walked up to the double doors as usual and stood looking about him. The deep scarlet gown beneath his soft dress cloak, beaten beautifully transparent, glowed in the waning sunlight that lay guilelessly upon him, and with an enchantingly casual gesture he lifted his fan to cover his face, looking, so it seemed to the watching women, exactly as a woman should look, although none ever quite succeeds. He smiled as though to charm away their cares and expressly summoned Koshōshō. The veranda was narrow, but he worried that there might be others farther back in the room, and he still did not go straight to the point.

"Come closer," he said. "Do not fail me now. I have not come all the way into these hills to have you ignore me. Besides, there is a thick mist." He pointedly avoided looking in and gazed off toward the mountains. "Closer, closer," he urged, until she finally pushed a gray standing curtain partially out through the blinds and sat behind it, rearranging her skirts. Being the Governor's sister, she was a close relative of the late Haven,[53] who had brought her up since childhood, and her costume was therefore very dark. She wore her dress gown over a dark gray layering.

"Quite apart from the enduring sorrow of our loss, Her Highness's unspeakable coldness has so added to my cares that the heart and soul have left my body, as all those who know me attest, until I can no longer bear it." He enlarged at length on his complaint and wept copiously when he spoke of the Haven's last letter.

Koshōshō wept even more than he. "When no answer came from you that evening, my lady, who knew she was dying, sank straightaway into herself, and after nightfall her mind wandered. The spirit seemed to seize that moment of weakness to take her. She nearly lost consciousness that way several times when his lordship[54] was so ill, and it was her resolve to comfort Her Highness, who was in equal despair, that returned her at last to herself. After this most recent loss Her Highness seems hardly to be aware of her surroundings, and most of the time she has been oblivious to the world." She spoke haltingly, amid many tears and sighs.

"That is just it. She is much too removed and distant. If I may say so, I do not see who else she can turn to now, except me. His Eminence lives off on the mountain among clouds that cut him off from the world, and she will not find it easy to keep in touch with him. Please tell her how much her treatment of me leaves to be desired. All things turn out as they must. She may be weary of life, but life does not

53. She is the Haven's niece and the Princess's cousin.
54. Kashiwagi.

heed our wishes. After all, would she have suffered this loss if it did?" He talked on at length, but she had nothing to say in answer and only sat there sighing.

Just then a stag belled loudly. "Shall I do less?"[55] he said, and he went on,

> "Having made my way through broad wastes of bamboo grass to far-off Ono,
> I would gladly join the stag in lifting my loud complaint."[56]

> "In our mourning weeds all too often wet with dew, we of autumn hills
> add our voices to the stag's, to cry aloud our complaint,"

she replied. It was not very good, but spoken just at that moment, in her hushed voice, it pleased him well enough.

He managed to have Her Highness given his regards. "I shall acknowledge the kindness of your many visits when life ceases to be so cruel a dream," she answered curtly. That was all. He went away again, sighing over her extraordinary obduracy.

All the way he gazed up to the boundless heavens, where a thirteenth-night[57] moon shone in such glory as to illumine even the road past Dark Mountain.[58] Her Highness's Ichijō residence was on his way, and it was more ruinous than he had known it. Through a gap in the crumbling boundary wall, near the southwest corner, he glimpsed rows of lowered shutters. There was no trace of human presence. Moonlight alone gave life to the garden brook, and he remembered the many occasions on which the late Intendant had made music here.

> "That beloved form has now vanished from a lake whose waters detain,
> to watch a deserted house, only a late-autumn moon,"

he murmured to himself. Even when he was home again, his eyes remained on the moon, and his heart wandered off into the skies. The annoyed old women muttered, "What a spectacle he is making of himself! He never used to do things like this!"

To put it plainly, his wife was furious. He seems to have lost his mind! I suppose he is thinking of those paragons at Rokujō, who have long taken this sort of thing for granted, and making me out to be brash and forward—well, I cannot help it! I would not mind so much either, if I had been used to it as long as they; in fact, things might have been a lot easier that way. Everyone, including my family, thought I had the most perfect luck, what with his being such a model of devotion, but now it looks as though all these years may only end in humiliation! She was deeply wounded.

---

55. *Kokinshū* 582: "Autumn has come, and the mountains ring with the belling of the stag: shall I do less, on nights I spend alone?"

56. The poem plays on *shika* ("stag" and "thus" [like the stag]). The "wastes of bamboo grass" are *shinohara*, expanses of *sasa*, a low, ground-cover bamboo.

57. Two nights before full.

58. A literary flourish. "Dark Mountain" is Ogura no Yama, the name of which (*ogura*) can be read to mean "dim." However, Mount Ogura is far away on the other (the west) side of northern Kyoto from where Yūgiri is now, and he could not possibly have passed it. It appears here only for the sake of the wordplay.

Dawn approached while they sighed their separate sighs in mutual silence, until the night was over and the Commander hastened as always to write *her* a letter; he could not wait for the morning mists to lift. She was extremely put out, but she did not snatch it from him as before.

He wrote intently, then put the paper down and hummed his poem, keeping his voice low; but she still heard it.

> *"And when will it be, that you would have me rouse you—for that word of yours*
> *asks me to refrain until you wake from the long night's dream.*

'What am I to do?' "[59] That, she gathered, was what he had written. He wrapped it up and still went on humming "O what am I to do?" and so on. Then he called for a messenger and sent it off. I should like to see her answer, she thought, consumed by curiosity. What on earth is going on?

The sun was high when the reply arrived. It was on dark purple paper, short, and from Koshōshō as usual. What she had to report was the same as always: nothing. "I felt so sorry, my lord, that I made off with your letter—my lady had done some writing practice on it." She had torn off those parts and enclosed them.

She actually looked at my letter! He felt a ridiculous rush of joy. By piecing together a word here and a word there he managed to read,

> *"In these Ono hills, where in sore lamentation I cry night and day,*
> *are the ceaseless tears I weep to be the Silent Cascade?"*

That seemed to be right. The old poems she had written out dejectedly here and there were in a fine hand. Others who burned with this sort of desire had always seemed to him laughably mad, and now that he was doing it, too, he understood how unbearable it could be. How strange! He kept wondering why he should have to suffer this way, but there was nothing he could do about it.

At Rokujō, Genji heard what was going on. He had always taken the Commander's thoroughly mature, deliberate manner and his blameless mode of life as a credit to himself, one that redeemed the unfortunate reputation his own somewhat gallant ways of the past had earned him. How sad this is for them both,[60] he thought, and what a very difficult time they are going to have! What can His Excellency think of all this, when they are so close to him? Surely the young man understands that much. Destiny drives us in the end, though. No, it is not for me to speak up or to intervene. At this distance the news moved him to lament particularly the pain this would cause the women.

---

59. In the original, "Spilling from on high." *Genji monogatari kochūshakusho in'yō waka* 1481: "What am I to do, and how, O silent cascade spilling from the heights of the hills of Ono?" The "silent cascade" (*otonashi no taki*) is presumably Ochiba, who never responds; but it is also the Otonashi Cascade, famous in poetry and situated near Ono. The water slips soundlessly over a smooth rockface.

60. Probably Ochiba and Kumoi no Kari, although perhaps Ochiba and Yūgiri.

While musing to Lady Murasaki on things past and future, he remarked how this sort of thing reminded him to worry about what would happen to her once he was gone, at which she blushed and wondered unhappily just how long he expected to leave her on her own. Ah, she reflected, there is nothing so pitifully confined and constricted as a woman. What will reward her passage through the world if she remains sunk in herself, blind to life's joys and sorrows and to every delight? What will brighten the monotony of her fleeting days? And will she not bitterly disappoint the parents who reared her if she turns out hopelessly dull and insensitive to anything around her? What a waste for her to shut herself up in her thoughts, like that Silent Prince the monks cite as the patron of their own trials,[61] and when she knows the good from the bad to say nothing at all! How to strike the proper balance? These questions absorbed her now only for the sake of the First Princess.

Genji was curious to know how the Commander felt about all this, and he remarked once when that gentleman was at Rokujō, "The mourning for the Haven must be over. Why, thirty years are gone before you know it![62] How sad and cruel it is, the way we cling to what lasts like evening dew! I long to shave my head and give it all up, but here I still am, enjoying my comforts. No, it is no good, no good at all."

"How true!" the Commander replied. "Even the man without regrets must have trouble taking that step." He continued, "The Governor of Yamato is looking after the memorial services for the forty-nine days all on his own. What a pity! Someone with that little support may prosper in life only to come to a sad end after all."

"I imagine that His Cloistered Eminence sent his condolences. How Her Highness his daughter must mourn her! The Haven had more to be said for her than most, judging from what I gather lately—more than I knew. It is a great loss for us all. The people who deserve most to live are always the ones to go. It has been a great shock for His Eminence. He was particularly attached to this Princess, after Her Cloistered Highness here. I am sure she has much to recommend her."

"I wonder what she is like. The Haven was beyond reproach in manner and disposition—not that I was ever particularly close to her, but even little things can reveal a great deal about character." On the subject of her daughter he gave away nothing at all.

If he is that set on her, nothing I can say will make any difference, Genji decided; there is no point in my offering unwanted advice—he will just ignore it anyway. He gave up.

So it was that the Commander took the memorial rites in hand. Word of this naturally got about, and His Excellency therefore heard it, too. He was outraged, and unfortunately he blamed it on the lightness of the Princess's ways.[63] His sons

61. According to a sutra known in Japan as Taishi Bohaku-kyō, Prince Bohaku of the kingdom of Harana (in India) so feared the karmic perils of speech that for the first thirteen years of his life he remained mute. His father, the King, then ordered that he be buried alive. The order was about to be executed when the Prince spoke at last and succeeded to the throne. The monks' "trials" are presumably the times when they are required to observe a vow of silence.

62. A proverbial expression. Some manuscripts have "three years," to make this a reference to Kashiwagi's death.

63. Yūgiri is pointedly and publicly claiming to have married Ochiba already.

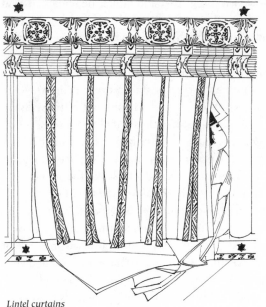

Lintel curtains

took part as well because of that old tie, and he provided generously for the scripture readings and so on. Everyone was eager to excel, and things were done as though for a very great lady.

Her Highness wanted to spend the rest of her life where she was, but when His Eminence learned of her desire, he declared that out of the question. "It is perfectly true that you should not properly pass from one such involvement to another, but someone without a protector can easily assume the guise you have in mind only to err and to provoke a scandal that leaves her caught between this world and the next, and guilty in the eyes of all. Now that I have left the world and Her Cloistered Highness has, too, people are saying that I have no posterity. That need not distress someone who has renounced the world, but it certainly would not become you to be too eager to follow her example and mine. It actually leaves a poor impression to reject the world merely because of some bitter experience. Do what you like, but not until you have collected your thoughts and considered the matter more calmly."

He conveyed her this message repeatedly; the gossip about her must have already reached him. It upset him to find it being said of her that she had acted from pique and disappointment, but while on the other hand it would do her no good to acknowledge her new state openly, he felt that it was no business of his to say so, since he did not wish to embarrass her, and he therefore never touched on the matter at all.

The Commander meanwhile saw no point in making any further vain attempt to persuade her. She will never give me her consent. I shall let it be known that I had the Haven's approval. What else can I do? I shall imply a mild lapse on her part and make sure that no one can tell exactly when it all began. It would be impossibly awkward to go back to plying her with a lover's tearful appeals. In this spirit he chose a suitable day for her return to Ichijō, summoned the Governor of Yamato to instruct him on the procedure he wanted followed, and had the house cleaned and done up. The ladies had been accustomed to living there among thickets of weeds, despite the best they could do, but he had the place made immaculate and personally saw to it that the Governor of Yamato should have all the required lintel curtains, screens, standing curtains, and mats made at his own house.

On the day, he went in person to offer her a carriage and an escort. Her women sought vigorously to change her mind when she insisted that she had no intention of going. "I cannot agree, Your Highness," the Governor said. "I have served you so far as well as I could, out of compassion for your bereavement, but now I must go down to my province. I have business there. There is no one else to entrust with looking after your residence, and I have been feeling remiss at the thought of leaving things as they are. Now that the Commander has taken it all on, however, it seems to me that although you are not for that matter, strictly speaking, obliged to agree, this is by no means the first time a lady like you has had to put up with circumstances she disliked, and I see no reason why you should be singled out for any particular criticism. You are being quite childish. Whatever your pride may tell you, it is just not possible for a woman to manage entirely on her own. You might as well accept the help of a commoner who will respect and cherish you; *that* is the way for you to enjoy the sort of life that you quite properly desire. The trouble is that neither of you reminds your mistress of these things. No, instead you have taken it into your own hands to do just what you should not." His last reproaches were addressed to Sakon and Koshōshō.[64]

The women gathered around their mistress to persuade her, and she helplessly allowed them to change her into brighter colors. Absently, she swept aside[65] the hair that she yearned only to cut, and it turned out to be six feet long. They felt that she could be proud of it, though it had thinned a little, but to her it was ruined; she could not possibly show herself to anyone like this, and her cares so overwhelmed her that she lay down again. "It is late, my lady," they cried. "The night is advancing!"

Gusting wind and rain compounded her misery.

> "O to join her smoke that rose high above the hills and into the sky,
> and never follow the wind where I have no wish to go!"

she murmured. She had the resolve, but her women had lately been keeping anything like scissors carefully hidden from her; and anyway, she wondered, what makes my fate so important that I am entitled to act in secret like a silly child or to shock those to whom I still matter with the news of what I have done? She therefore never carried out what she had planned.

Her women had already packed their combs, accessory boxes, clothing chests, and whatnot, however flimsily, in bags that had been sent on ahead, and she could hardly stay on alone. In tears she therefore entered her carriage, all too aware of the vacant place beside her, and mist clouded her eyes when she remembered how her mother, already ill, had tidied her hair for her when they arrived, and had helped her down. With her dagger[66] she kept a scripture case from which she was never parted.

> "O dear, pretty case, clouded though you are with tears!—for you still recall
> someone whom I miss too much ever to forget her loss,"

---

64. He is accusing them of passing on objectionable letters to their mistress.
65. So as to be able to change robes.
66. A highborn girl received a dagger (*mihakashi*) at birth, and it remained a highly personal possession.

she murmured. It was the one inlaid with mother-of-pearl that her mother had favored, for she had not yet managed to procure a black case[67] of her own. She had retained it as a memento of her mother, even though her mother herself had wanted it to go for scripture readings. She felt like Master Urashima.[68]

There was nothing gloomy about the place when she reached it. She had never seen it so fully populated. The carriage was drawn up, and she prepared to alight, but then she hesitated because the house felt so upsettingly unlike home. Her gentlewomen thought it very childish of her and hardly knew what to do.

The Commander had had the south side of the east wing done up for himself for the time being, and he was now installed there with a proprietary air. Astonished people at Sanjō were muttering, "He is impossible all of a sudden! How long has he been this way?" He who had never countenanced anything languorous or suggestive now turned out to have an unfamiliar side, but they assumed nonetheless that this had been going on for years without his betraying it; no one imagined that Her Highness was still refusing him. Her position was detestable either way.

The unusual welcome meal was not exactly propitious for a new beginning,[69] but once it was over and everyone had settled down for the night, he came and demanded satisfaction from Koshōshō. "My lord, if you really are devoted to my lady for all the years to come, *please* let a day or two pass before you approach her! It has only depressed her to come home, and she is lying there as though she were no longer among the living. She resents every effort to cheer her up, and that makes things very difficult for me. I can hardly talk to her at all."

"I just do not understand her. She seems beyond reach, like a girl, which is not what I expected." He protested at length that his intentions were such as to discredit neither himself nor her.

"Oh, no, my lord, what so worries me now, until I can hardly think straight, is the fear of losing her, too. Please, my dear lord, please do nothing too willful or assertive!" She rubbed her hands together.

"I have never known anything like this! What about me, then, whom she apparently despises as the most vulgar and odious of men? I should just like to see what someone else might have to say about that!" He so obviously thought Her Highness's treatment of him unconscionable that Koshōshō pitied him, too.

"You have never known anything like it, you say, my lord—perhaps that is because you have never really known that much of life. As to who is right and who is wrong," she added, smiling, "I wonder what someone else *would* say."

He had no intention of allowing any resistance, however concerted, to thwart him, and he therefore went straight off, ahead of Koshōshō, toward where he judged Her Highness to be. Shocked and horrified by his callous boorishness, Her

---

67. Suitable for mourning.

68. Master Urashima, a fisherman, drifted to the island of the immortals and married a beautiful maiden there. Three years later he became homesick and returned to his village carrying a box that his wife had given him with the warning never to open it. He found that three hundred years had passed and that everything had changed. When he opened the box in despair, his wife's wraith floated out of it and into the sky, and he instantly aged three hundred years. The earliest occurrence of the story is among the surviving fragments of the early-eighth-century *Tango fudoki*.

69. Ochiba's mourning restricted the meal and made it disappointing for the start of a marriage.

Highness decided he could complain all he liked that she was acting childishly; she had a mat spread in the retreat, locked the door from the inside, and went to bed. How long would *that* save her, though? She bitterly deplored her women's mad indiscretion. As for the gentleman, despite his anger and outrage he quietly resolved that he would not let this deter him, and he spent the rest of the night considering what might follow. He felt like a mountain pheasant.[70] At last dawn came, and he prepared to go, since it would soon be light enough for people to recognize him. "Please, at least open the door a crack!" he begged, but she ignored him.

> "On this winter night, when my heart feels forever locked in agony,
> ah, what new chains bar my way through your adamantine door!

Your attitude leaves me speechless." He left in tears and went to rest at Rokujō.

"They are saying at His Excellency's that you have brought Her Highness back to Ichijō. What are you up to?" the lady of the northeast quarter inquired innocently. She had a standing curtain in front of her, too, but he could still see something of her past it.

"Yes, I imagine that they are talking about it. The late Haven strongly opposed the idea at first, but she relented near the end—I suppose she was worried that she might not find anyone else—and she let me know that she hoped I would look after her daughter once she was gone; so for the sake of my old friend I decided that I would. I wonder how people are taking it. It is no great event, but they so love to gossip." He smiled and went on, "She herself is determined to have no more to do with this world, and she seems to be in such despair, she wants to become a nun. What would she have me do, though? Yes, there may be unpleasant talk, but I do not intend to disappoint her mother, not even if she has decided to put herself above suspicion that way, and that is the simple reason I am doing all I can for her. Please explain that to His Grace the next time he comes, if you can find a moment to do so. I have not wanted to give him any reason to accuse me of folly at my age, but it is true that on this sort of matter one all too easily ignores not only the remonstrances of others but the warnings of one's own heart."

"Then there really is something to it! I thought that people were making it all up. This sort of thing is certainly commonplace enough, but I am sorry to imagine what this must be doing to your young lady at Sanjō. She is used to feeling so secure."

"You are too kind to refer to her as a young lady. A fiendish shrew, that is what she is. But anyway, why should I neglect her? Consider, if I may be so bold, the case of all of you who live here. People value peace above all. Ill temper and querulous ways may harry one into temporary retreat, but they cannot be allowed to rule one's life, and there is certain to be trouble between a couple when some sort of incident crops up. As far as that goes, the disposition of the lady in the southeast quarter[71] is rare in many ways, and to my mind you are admirable as well."

She smiled at his praise. "If you mean to cite *me* as a model, I am afraid that

70. Literary tradition had it that the male and female of the mountain pheasant (or copper pheasant, *ya-madori*) roosted in separate valleys.
71. Murasaki.

everyone will soon find out just how deficient I am. What is curious, you know, is the way His Grace makes so much of the least slip on your part so as to screen his own errant ways, and either lectures you or censures you in your absence. To my mind he is like someone who fancies himself wise and yet remains unaware of what he himself is doing."

"True enough. He is always lecturing me about such things. I manage to look out for myself, though, even without his sage advice." Yes, he thought, that *was* an amusing comment.

He next called on Genji, who saw no reason to let on that he knew, even though he had already heard all about it. Instead he complacently studied his son and said to himself, Handsome as he is, he seems lately to have acquired a new dignity and presence. Who could blame him for occasionally indulging himself a little? With that bright aura of youth and beauty, the very gods would forgive him. It is all quite natural, considering that he is no callow boy but a mature man in his best years! Why should a woman not be pleased with him? He may well take pride in what he sees in the mirror!

The sun was high when the Commander got home. His children were all over him as soon as he came in, each one more winning than the last. Their mother lay in the curtained bed. She did not meet his eyes when he entered. He understood that she might be angry with him, but his face showed no contrition when he pulled the bedclothes off her.

"Where do you think you are?" she said. "I'm dead. I thought I might as well be a demon, since you're always calling me one."

"You may be a demon and worse at heart, but you're too pretty to dislike!"

His flippancy galled her. "You won't find *me* clinging forever to a handsome charmer like you! I'm going away somewhere, anywhere! I don't want you just happening to remember me now and again! Look at all these years! They've been nothing but a waste of time!" She was sitting up now, looking extremely alluring. Her flushed face had an enchanting glow.

"*Now* I feel at home—it must be this childish tantrum of yours. No, this is one demon I am not afraid of. In fact," he joked, "I would like a little more of the real thing."

"What are you talking about? Just oblige me and die! *I'm* going to! I can't stand to see you, and I don't want to hear about you. Who knows what you would be up to once I was gone?"

He chortled merrily, better and better pleased. "Perhaps you won't look at me while I am here, but why would you not want to hear about me when I am elsewhere? Anyway, you seem to want me to understand how close we are. And talk about us suddenly following each other off to the underworld, I have already promised you I would." He refused to take her seriously, and he did so well at winning her over that she began to come round even though she knew perfectly well that he was joking, which he thought very dear of her. Still, he remained intensely uneasy. And *she*, he thought—I can hardly believe that she is capable of resisting me forever, but I will look a perfect idiot if she manages to become a nun after all. He felt that for the time being he could not afford to miss a single night, and he realized as evening came on that today, too, had passed without an answer from her, which made him thoroughly morose.

At last, after eating nothing that day or the one before, she took a light meal. "His Excellency did not at all approve of my always being so keen on you," he said, "but I bore the unbearable, although everyone just thought I was being silly, and I ignored the approaches that I got from here and there. 'Not even a woman would be *that* faithful!' they used to laugh. When I think about it now, I wonder how I ever did it, and I realize how steady I was even then, though I say so myself. You may hate me, but we have a houseful of children by now, and you would never give them up; and so I trust that in your heart of hearts you do not really mean to leave me. And besides, look at me—it is life that is treacherous, not me!" He wept at times as he spoke. Thinking back, she, too, felt despite everything the wonderfully rare strength of the tie between them. He changed from his soft, rumpled clothes into particularly beautiful, perfumed new ones and set off, elegantly attired and made up. By the light of the lamp she watched him go, and when bitter tears started from her eyes, she caught the sleeve of the shift he had just removed, and murmured to herself,

> "Rather than lament that for him my charm is lost, I might just as well
> change into a quite new guise—a nun's at Matsushima.

I just cannot go on this way!"

He stopped. "You are so cruel!" he exclaimed.

> "Is that what you think? That you may before the world wear the briny robe,
> now you are fed up with me, they wear at Matsushima?"[72]

It was a hurried poem, and very trite.

At Ichijō, Her Highness was still shut up in her retreat. "Do you think that you can stay this way forever, my lady? Everyone will know you as impossibly childish. You *must* come out and talk to him properly." Her women did all they could to persuade her, and she knew that they were perfectly right, but to her he was the hateful man to whom she owed both her future reputation and her suffering in the past, and she refused to receive him that night either.

"This is no joke!" he insisted repeatedly. "It is preposterous!"

Koshōshō pitied him. "My lord, I know that my lady will feel a little more herself in time, and if you have not forgotten her by then, I will talk to her again. She says that her greatest wish is to live without other distractions as long as she is in mourning, and she is still furious that by now everyone in the world unfortunately knows her situation."

"But my intentions are not what she imagines! She need not be afraid!" He sighed and went on at great length, in an appeal to Her Highness. "If you will only

---

72. "Do you think it is right to have me known as a man whose wife had enough of him and went off to become a nun?"

come out to sit where you usually do, I shall explain my feelings to you, through blinds and so on if you wish, and disturb you no further. I am quite willing to be patient for years."

"Your relentless pursuit is very painful," she replied, "coming as it does after the blow that I have already suffered. Your attitude is thoroughly offensive, quite apart from my distress over the extraordinary things that people must be thinking and saying about me." With such repeated expressions of her displeasure she continued to keep him as far from her as possible.

This cannot go on, he said to himself. He felt trapped. People are obviously going to hear about it, and then there are these women, too. "I want to keep up a pretense for a time, even if nothing actually happens contrary to her wishes," he insisted to Koshōshō. "The foolish position she has put me in is cruel, but at the same time, if I suddenly stop coming, her own reputation will suffer for it. It is pitiful, the way she indulges her own feelings and insists on being such a child."

Koshōshō agreed. By now the very sight of him distressed her, and she deeply regretted what he was going through. She therefore introduced him into the retreat through its north door, the one that Her Highness had her women use. Her Highness was aghast to discover that even her gentlewomen were as worldly-minded as anyone else and that she might expect still worse from them henceforth; and she bewailed her misfortune now that she could no longer trust a single one.

At great length, and with endless moving or pleasant touches, he reminded her of what she should already know, but she remained as bitterly hostile as before. "That you find me unspeakable covers me with such shame that I regret the folly of ever having aspired to please you, but it is too late now, and your proud name will not come through this unscathed. It is no use. Give in. They say people sometimes drown themselves in disappointment: well, resign yourself to having leaped into the abyss of my devotion!"

She had pulled a shift over her head, and the best she could do was weep. He pitied her from the bottom of his heart. This is really awful! But *why* does she feel so strongly? Anyone would show some sign of yielding by the time things had got this far, no matter how stubborn she was, but no, a rock or a tree would be more easily moved. I suppose she has hardly any karmic tie with me—that must be why she dislikes me so. It was just too much. Bitter speculation about *her* feelings, at Sanjō, and memories of how they had once innocently loved each other or of how she had sweetly and trustingly yielded to him more recently so tormented him that he did not insist on coaxing her further, and he spent the rest of the night sighing.

It would have been too silly to keep coming and going to her under these circumstances, and he therefore allowed himself today to remain where he was. Her Highness was aghast that he should go that far, and her resistance only stiffened. This struck him as at once ludicrous, detestable, and sad.

The retreat had little in it apart from some fragrant chests and a cabinet tidily ranged against the walls; she had actually made it quite comfortable. It seemed dark, but enough light got in to show that the morning sun was up. He removed the garment under which she was hiding, brushed her badly disordered hair aside, and briefly knew her.[73]

She had a thoroughly noble, feminine grace, while he himself was a pleasure, and incomparably more so in casual intimacy than when disposed to be formal. She remembered how the late Intendant, whose pride made up for his lack of any particular looks, had sometimes made it clear that he thought her no beauty, and she wondered in shame how he could tolerate the sight of her, now that she had lost what little attractiveness she had once had. One way or another she strove to reconcile herself to

Bringing washing water

her situation. Alas, she knew that she would not escape censure when the news spread, and even the timing was unfortunate.[74] She remained unconsoled.

Washing water and breakfast were brought to her usual sitting room.[75] The color in which the room was done up clashed unpleasantly with the occasion,[76] and screens had therefore been placed along the east side,[77] while along the edge of the chamber itself stood clove-dyed curtains[78] and other, tastefully discreet items such as an aloeswood tiered cabinet. All this was thanks to the Governor of Yamato. He had changed the gentlewomen into quiet colors like kerria rose and scarlet layerings, or dark purple, or blue-gray, with a scattering of pale gray-violet trains and autumn green.[79] They brought in the meals on their stands. Her Highness's household of women had become a little lax in some ways, but when the Governor noticed this, he put order among the few servants who remained, and saw to everything all on his own. The news of so unexpected and distinguished a visitor brought long-dispersed retainers to the house, and they busied themselves in the household office with whatever needed to be done.

With her husband lording it at Ichijō, the lady at Sanjō decided that this must be the end. Why, he would never! she had once told herself, but now she felt as though she had personally tested the adage that the truehearted man who falters is lost for good, and she wanted to see no more of this outrageous behavior. She therefore went to her father's on the pretext of a directional taboo. The company of

73. Literally, "had a look at her," but the expression is unambiguous. The next sentence corresponds to the one that follows Genji's first, between-the-lines intercourse in "Akashi."
74. Because she is still in mourning.
75. Presumably the chamber proper.
76. The curtains and so on were all mourning gray.
77. In the aisle, probably to hide paraphernalia related to mourning.
78. Cloves yield a buff dye. The color was suitable for any occasion, happy or sad.
79. A layering of cloth woven of leaf green warp and yellow weft threads over leaf green cloth.

the Consort,[80] who was then at home, gave her some relief from her cares, and she did not hurry back as she usually did.

I knew it! The Commander was startled. She has such a temper! So does His Excellency. Neither of them shows a trace of measure or calm. Considering how vehement they are, and how quick to anger, they are perfectly capable of reaching the preposterous decision that I am obnoxious and that they want never to see me or hear of me again. He hurried back to Sanjō to find that she had left him their sons and taken their daughters and the littlest baby with her. The boys were very happy to see him, although to his chagrin some were also crying for their mother.

He sent repeated messages and also an envoy to bring her back, but he had no reply. Despite his disgust over her stubbornly willful behavior there were His Excellency's feelings to consider in the matter, and he therefore set out there himself, after dark. He assumed that she would be in the main house[81] and went there as usual, but he found only her women. The children were with their nurse.

"Look at you, amusing yourself like a girl with her friends!" he bitterly reproached her.[82] "You scatter all these children about and now there you are—what do you mean by it? I have always known that there are things about you I do not care for, but for some reason—destiny, I suppose—I have never wanted to leave you, and now we have so many children to look after, and such dear ones, too, I have never even imagined that we might go our separate ways. Are you going to do this to me over a little thing like *that*?"

"Why not? You have had enough of me as I am, and I am certainly not going to change anymore. If you want to keep those hopeless children of mine, so much the better!"

"A magnificent answer! And which of us will come off the worse for it, I should like to know?" He did not insist on having her come to him, and that night he slept alone. How strangely these days I am caught betwixt and between! he thought, putting the children to bed beside him. He wondered what anguish *she* must be suffering, at Ichijō. Who could possibly enjoy this sort of thing? He felt miserably that he had learned his lesson.

At daybreak he sent her another threat. "People will think that you are behaving like a headstrong girl. If you must have it that everything is over between us, very well, let us see. I suppose you had your reasons for leaving some of the children at home, although the poor things seemed to miss you badly, but *I* cannot just walk out on them, and I mean to do everything for them that I can."

She was dismayed in her uncomplicated way to gather that he might take even the ones she had with her away somewhere beyond her reach.

"Now, come along," he said to one of his daughters. "Things are too difficult, and I shall not be able to come and see you here all the time. Your brothers are still at home, and they are very nice, too, and I want to have you all together." Still very

---

80. Kumoi no Kari's elder sister and the Kokiden Consort of Retired Emperor Reizei.
81. In the room customarily reserved for her when she was at her father's.
82. He presumably sends someone to Kumoi no Kari with this message.

little and sweet, she considered him gravely. "You must not listen to your mother," he admonished her. "I am sorry to say that there is a great deal she does not understand."

When His Excellency heard what was going on, he sighed to imagine how the world would laugh. "To think that you never even gave him a chance!" he said to his daughter. "I know that he would have apologized in time. A woman is foolish to be so quick-tempered. But very well, now that you have said it, you cannot very well give in and go straight home. No doubt you will soon discover his real disposition."

He sent the Chamberlain Lieutenant[83] with a message to Her Highness.

> *"We must share a bond, for you are present to me always in my heart,*
> *while I think of you fondly and hear hateful things of you.*

Surely you have not yet forgotten us," he had written. The Lieutenant brought the letter straight in.

A round mat was put out for him on the southern veranda. The women hardly knew what to say to him, and Her Highness felt even more painfully awkward. The young man, the best-looking of all the brothers, gazed calmly around him as though thinking back to times past. "It all seems so familiar. You might prefer me not to feel comfortable here, though," he briefly remarked.

Her Highness did not know what to answer. "I simply cannot write it!" she said.

Her women gathered around her. "But, my lady, he will never know then how you feel, and besides, it will look childish of you. You cannot have us write it for you!"

She began to weep. If only Mother were here, she would have managed to cover up all my

Monk seated on a round mat

shortcomings, however little she might have liked doing it! Feeling as though her tears would outrun her brush, she failed to write anything except

> *"Ah, how can it be that there should be one of me, and of no account,*
> *yet you think angrily of me, and you hear of me with love?"*

She set it down just as it came to her, without even finishing it properly, then wrapped it up and sent it off.

Meanwhile the Lieutenant was talking to her women. "I do come here from time to time, you know," he hinted before setting off, "and I feel out of place sitting in front of the blinds. Now I have a proper reason to visit, though, I shall do so

83. One of his sons.

often. You must let me inside, too. I trust that my years of loyal service will be rewarded."

Her Highness's worsening mood drove the Commander to distraction, and meanwhile His Excellency's daughter mourned more bitterly with every passing day. The Dame of Staff[84] had heard the news, which to her meant that a lady who had always objected to her must now contend with someone whom she could not despise. From time to time she wrote her a note.

> "If I were someone, I would know all on my own of life's cruelty,
>   but I can still wet my sleeves to lament another's woe."

His Excellency's daughter thought this a bit much, but during the tedium of these trying days it occurred to her indulgently that the sender, too, had reason to be upset with Her Highness. She replied simply, as the words came to her,

> "I had pitied, too, others for all the sorrows life forever brings,
>   yet never thought to arouse someone else's sympathy."

The Dame of Staff was touched.

Long ago, when His Excellency was keeping his daughter and Genji's son apart, the young man had secretly given this Dame of Staff all his affection, and he had remained in touch with her once the marriage resumed, though only rarely and with diminishing enthusiasm. Still, she had given him a good many children. By His Excellency's daughter he had his first, third, fifth, and sixth sons and his second, fourth, and fifth daughters; while by the Dame of Staff he had his first, third, and sixth daughters and his second and fourth sons. There was nothing wrong with any of these twelve children, and they all grew up to be a pleasure, but the Dame of Staff's stood out in looks and cleverness. The third daughter and second son were being carefully brought up in the northeast quarter of Rokujō. Genji himself kept an eye on them and treated them fondly. The relationships between these people are all too complicated to explain, though.

---

84. The daughter of Koremitsu, Genji's confidant in earlier days, whom Yūgiri first met in "The Maidens."

40

MINORI

The Law

Minori means, above all, "the Law" (Dharma)—that is, the truth the Buddha taught, that all things pass—and in this sense it refers to Murasaki's death. However, it can also mean the "rites" that proclaim and honor the Law: in particular, the ceremony at which Murasaki solemnly dedicates a thousand copies of the Lotus Sutra. It owes its role as the chapter title to its presence in an exchange between Murasaki and Hanachirusato after the ceremony. Murasaki:

"This is the last time rites of mine will serve the Law, yet I have great faith
they shall be to you and me a bond that lasts many lives."

Hanachirusato:

"They shall be a tie that endures for ages yet, though it is too true
few will ever see again such pious magnificence."

RELATIONSHIP TO EARLIER CHAPTERS

"The Law" begins a few months after the end of "Evening Mist" and covers from spring to autumn of Genji's fifty-first year.

PERSONS

His Grace, the Honorary Retired Emperor, Genji, age 51

Lady Murasaki, 43

The lady of Falling Flowers (Hanachirusato)

The lady from Akashi, 42 (Akashi no Kimi)

The Third Prince, 5 (Niou Miya)

Her Majesty, the Empress, 23 (Akashi no Chūgū)

The Commander, Genji's son, 30 (Yūgiri)

His Excellency (Tō no Chūjō)

His Eminence Reizei's Empress, 42 (Akikonomu)

L ady Murasaki's health remained very poor after her serious illness, and she had suffered ever since from a vague, lingering malaise. It was not especially threatening, but all those months and years did not bode well, and by now she was so frail that Genji felt very anxious indeed. The thought of outliving her even briefly appalled him. She herself asked nothing more of this life and had no particular wish to stay, for she had no fond ties[1] to detain her; at heart she regretted only what he would suffer when the bond between them failed. She commissioned many holy services for her own good in her next life, and she often asked to become what she still wished to be, so that she could give the little time she had left entirely to her devotions; but he refused. Actually, he had conceived the same desire, and her yearning had fostered it until he would gladly have taken that path with her, except that he meant never to look back on this world once he had left it, and while he knew that he could trust their promise to share one lotus throne in the life to come, he understood that as long as they pursued their practice in this one, even at the same temple, they would live on different sides of the mountain and never see each other at all. Her peril and suffering were too painful, and leaving her would be so hard when the time came that his feelings then would only taint his refuge among the mountains and waters. Such reluctance on his part meant that he fell far behind others whose aspiration hardly amounted to more than personal whim. She resented his refusal because it would obviously be too unkind and contrary of her to act on her own, without his permission, but she also feared that she might owe it to her own burden of sins.

She hastened to dedicate the thousand copies of the Lotus Sutra that she herself had had made over the years. The event took place at Nijō, which she considered her home. She gave the seven monks vestments proper to their ranks, all extremely beautiful in color and finish. The event was very grand in every way. She had never told him that it was to be so solemn, and so he had offered her no particular advice. The excellence of her judgment and even her knowledge of Buddhist things impressed him profoundly, and his only role was to look after quite ordinary

1. Children.

matters of altar adornment and so on. The Commander undertook to provide the musicians and dancers.

The Emperor, the Heir Apparent, the Empresses, and the ladies of Rokujō contributed a wealth of scripture readings and altar offerings, and the whole court busied itself similarly until the result was astonishing abundance. When could she have managed to plan it all? It was as though she had made a holy vow venerable ages ago.[2] The lady of Falling Flowers went, and so did Akashi. Murasaki sat within the open, southeast doors—those of the west retreat in the main house. Only sliding panels separated the ladies in the northern aisle.

It was the tenth of the third month. No deep faith was needed then to be relieved of sin, for the blossoms were perfect and the sky so mildly lovely that the land where they say the Buddha dwells might have looked just the same. The voices of the great assembly resounded impressively in the cutting-firewood hymn,[3] and she felt sad even in the silence that followed it, because lately anything at all could put her in a desolate mood.

She had the Third Prince[4] take this to the lady from Akashi:

> *"As I am, by now I care little for my life, yet withal I grieve*
> *that the firewood runs low and will very soon be gone."*

The reply was oblique; perhaps the lady feared that people might talk if she adopted the same poignant tone:

> *"Burning as you do with zeal to cut firewood, you have just begun*
> *in this life to seek the Law and will yet for years to come."*

All night long, ceaseless drums pleasantly accompanied the holy services. The growing light of early dawn revealed flowers in many colors peeping out from between banks of mist and still wholly beguiling, while a hundred birds sang as sweetly as the flutes. Beauty and delight were at their peak when the rapid closing music of "The Warrior King" rang out brilliantly, and the colors of the garments doffed then by all present[5] turned the moment into an enchanting spectacle. Every Prince or senior noble accomplished at music showed off all his skill. It stirred many feelings in her to see everyone so pleased and so merry, high or low, because privately she knew how little time remained.

Now she lay prostrate and in pain, perhaps because she had for once been up the day before. For years she had wondered on every such occasion whether she would ever again see the faces and figures of those assembled, ever again enjoy their skill on flutes and strings, and she looked with emotion even on some who barely

2. Literally "Isonokami ages ago." Isonokami (south of Nara) is the site of the venerable shrine to the Furu deity, and the name therefore implies a play on *furu*, "old."

3. The "Devadatta" chapter of the Lotus Sutra describes how the Buddha served his teacher by picking fruit, drawing water, and gathering firewood until he was taught the sutra. The assembly sang the hymn "I have the Lotus Sutra, thanks to humbly cutting firewood, picking fruit, and drawing water, and in this way I obtained it."

4. The future Niou, grandson of Genji and Akashi.

5. To reward the dancers.

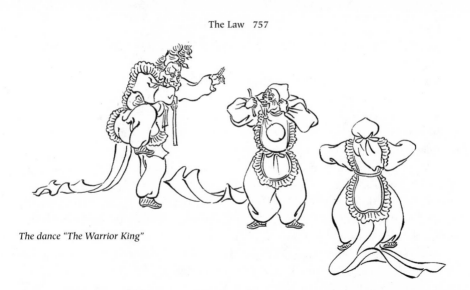

The dance "The Warrior King"

deserved notice. None of the ladies present at the summer or winter concerts and games—not without a sense of mutual rivalry, though they got on so well—would live forever, but it struck her vividly that she would go before them, alone, into the unknown, and the thought filled her with great sorrow.

Once the event was over and they all prepared to go, she mourned what to her was an eternal farewell. She sent the lady of Falling Flowers,

> *"This is the last time rites of mine will serve the Law, yet I have great faith*
> *they shall be to you and me a bond that lasts many lives."*

The lady responded,

> *"They shall be a tie that endures for ages yet, though it is too true*
> *few will ever see again such pious magnificence."*

At Genji's behest the dedication ceremony continued without a break into other holy services like perpetual scripture readings and the Rite of Confession.[6] He had the Great Rite performed continuously, as a matter of daily practice, at several worthy temples, because otherwise it had for some time done her no visible good.

That summer she felt increasingly faint in no more than the usual heat. She did not suffer in any particular or alarming way; she simply went on growing weaker and weaker. Nothing about her illness was distressing or demanding. To her women it was darkness to imagine what would follow, and they looked on her with deep pity and regret.

When her condition failed to improve, Her Majesty withdrew from the palace to Nijō. She managed to receive Her Majesty in the east wing, where Her Majesty was to stay. The ceremony was the usual one, but she knew that she would never see

6. (Hokke) Senbō, a rite that combined chanting the Lotus Sutra with confession of sins, for the purpose of erasing the sins of the beneficiary.

it again, and that made it very moving. She carefully heeded each name announced by the gentlemen in Her Majesty's escort.[7] Many senior nobles had come to serve the Empress.

Their rare meeting was the first for a long time, and they talked intently together. Then Genji came in. "I feel like a bird banished from the nest! I am useless! I might as well be off to bed!" he said and went away again. His great pleasure at seeing her up was a fragile consolation.

"You are to be lodged separately," she told Her Majesty, "and I apologize that you will have to come to me; you see, it simply is not possible for me to go to you." She stayed a little longer. The lady from Akashi then arrived, and they all quietly pursued their intimate conversation. Lady Murasaki had many things on her mind, but wisely she never spoke about when she would be gone. She confined herself to a few, quiet remarks about the fleeting character of life, but the conviction in her voice conveyed her desolation better than any words.

She saw the little Princes and Princesses, too. "I wanted so much to know how each of you would turn out—do you suppose that means something in me still wishes I had longer?" she said. There were tears in her eyes, and her face shone with extraordinary beauty.

Oh, why is she so sure? Her Majesty thought, and she wept.

When the conversation took such a turn that her remarks need not sound ill omened, she mentioned those who had served her well through the years and who invited pity because they had nowhere else to go. "Do give them a thought after I am gone," she said. That was all. Then she returned to her own rooms, for Her Majesty's scripture reading[8] was soon to begin.

The Third Prince was the most attractive of the children, and when she felt a little better for a moment, she had him come and sit beside her. "Would you remember me if I were not here anymore?" she asked him while no one else was listening.

"I would miss you very, very much! I love *you*, Grandma, much more than Their Majesties! I would be so unhappy without you!" He rubbed the tears so sweetly from his eyes that she wept through her smiles.

"You must live here when you grow up, and you must be sure to enjoy the red plum and the cherry here, in front of this wing, when they are in bloom. You must offer their flowers to the Buddha, too, when those times come."[9]

He gazed at her face, nodded solemnly, then rose and went away just as he seemed about to cry. She had reared him and her Princess herself, and she felt very, very sad that she would not see them anymore.

She seemed to revive somewhat when autumn came at last and the weather turned a little cooler, but even so, she was far from well. The autumn wind was not yet such as to pierce her through and through,[10] but she spent many a day amid gathering dews.

---

7. The nobles who had accompanied the Empress called out their names (*nadaimen*).

8. Perhaps the formal reading of the Daihannya-kyō that the Empress sponsored at set moments of the year.

9. Particularly on the anniversary of her own death.

10. *Izumi Shikibu shū* 132 (also *Shikashū* 109): "What kind of wind is the one that blows in autumn, that it should pierce me through and through with sorrow?"

Her Majesty would soon return to the palace, and she wanted to ask her to stay a little longer, but she thought that that might be forward of her, and besides, an awkward stream of messengers kept coming from the Emperor; so in the end she never asked it at all. Since she could not go to the east wing, Her Majesty came to her. This was thoroughly embarrassing, but it would have been very sad for them not to meet, and she had her rooms done up specially for the occasion.

She was extremely thin, but her infinitely noble grace gained from precisely that a wonderful new quality, because where once the overflowing richness and brilliance of her looks had evoked the magnificence of worldly blossoms, her beauty now really was sublime, and her pensive air—for she knew that her time was nearly over—was more sorrowful and more profoundly moving than anything in the world.

At dusk a dreary wind had just begun to blow, and she was leaning on an armrest looking out into the garden, when Genji came in. "You managed to stay up very nicely today!" he said. "Her Majesty's visit seems to have done you so much good!"

With a pang she saw how happy her little reprieve had made him, and she grieved to imagine him soon in despair.

> "Alas, not for long will you see what you do now: any breath of wind
> may spill from a hagi frond the last trembling drop of dew."[11]

It was true, her image fitted all too well: no dew could linger on such tossing fronds. The thought was unbearable. He answered while he gazed out into the garden,

> "When all life is dew and at any touch may go, one drop then the next,
> how I pray that you and I may leave nearly together!"

He wiped the tears from his eyes.

Her Majesty added,

> "In this fleeting world where no dewdrop can linger in the autumn wind,
> why imagine us to be unlike the bending grasses?"

They made a perfect picture as they talked, one well worth seeing, but the moment could not last, as Genji well knew, though he wished it might endure a thousand years. He mourned that nothing could detain someone destined to go.

"Please leave me. I feel very, very ill. Oh, forgive me for being so rude, however reduced I may be!"[12] She drew her standing curtain closer and lay down, obviously in greater danger than ever before.

"What is the matter?" Her Majesty took her hand and watched her, weeping. She really did look like a dewdrop that would vanish soon. Countless messengers

11. "I will not be up for long; soon I will be gone like dew." The poem plays on two verbs pronounced *oku*: "be up" or "get up," and "settle," speaking of dew.

12. She addresses the Empress.

clattered off to order more scripture readings. She had been like this before and still revived, and Genji, who suspected the spirit, spent the night ordering every measure against it; but in vain. She died with the coming of day.

Her Majesty took it as a very great blessing that she had not returned to the palace and had been there at the end. Neither she nor His Grace could accept this parting as being the kind one expects in life, for it was too strange and too bitter; no wonder they felt lost in a waking dream. Both were distraught, and all the women too were overcome.

The Commander had come closer, and His Grace, who of course had lost every trace of composure, invited him to approach her curtain. "I think it is all over," he said. "I cannot refuse her now in this extremity what she wanted so much for all those years. I hear no worthy monks and healers chanting scriptures anymore, but they cannot all have gone yet. I know it is too late for her in this life, but please tell them they are to cut her hair, so that she may at least have the Buddha's mercy on the dark road before her.[13] Is any monk who can do that still here?" He struggled to speak bravely, but his face belied his manner, and the sorrowing Commander understood all too well his helplessly streaming tears.

"A spirit can apparently do this sort of thing, especially at a time like this, if it intends to make someone suffer. Perhaps that is what the matter is," the Commander suggested. "At any rate, it might be just as well to do as she wished. They say that one day and night of abstinence will have their reward.[14] It would not light her way to the world beyond just to cut her hair, though, if she is gone, and she would only be more painful to look at, so I am not sure that I recommend it." He summoned this monk and that from among those who had gone to prepare for the mourning confinement, and he arranged whatever else was needed as well.

He had not once during those years thought of her in any culpable way, but he asked himself, When *will* I ever see her again as I saw her then? I have always been aware that I never heard her voice, and I know that that voice is now one I will never hear, but this is the moment, if there is ever to be one, for me to satisfy this longing for another look at her, or at least at her mortal shell. At the thought he wept without shame. Meanwhile the women were sobbing and wailing. "Do be quiet!" he cried as though to reprove them, and at the same time he lifted the curtain.

The glimmer of dawn was not bright enough to see by, and his father had put the lamp beside her with its wick raised high. He was gazing at a face of perfect sweetness and beauty, so absorbed that when his son looked in, he seemed not even to think of screening her. "There she is, just as she always was, but you can tell that it is all over," he said. He pressed a sleeve to his face while the Commander, his eyes dim with tears, blinked hard so as to look longer, though his overwhelming sorrow

---

13. "Dark road," an expression from the Lotus Sutra, occurs in *Izumi Shikibu shū* 150 (*Shūishū* 1342), by Izumi Shikibu: "From darkness a dark road is now mine to follow: shine on me from afar, O moon at the mountains' rim!"

14. According to the Kanmuryōju-kyō, an essential sutra on Amida, a single day and night spent observing the Precepts proper to one's station (those proper to a layman if one is a layman, etc.) can lead to birth in paradise.

must have made that difficult. Her exquisitely lovely hair lay simply beside her, each strand in place and gleaming with the kindliest of lights. In the lamp's bright glow her face shone very white. Stretched out this way in all the innocence of her state, she looked even more flawless than she had in life, when she had so studiously kept out of sight. Contemplating her perfection, the Commander longed for her soul to come back from death into her body, but there was no hope of that.

The gentlewomen who had served her so long were beyond making themselves useful, and His Grace was therefore obliged to rally his wits and see to all the final arrangements. None of the many sorrows he had known in the past had ever so wholly engulfed him; he thought that there could never have been one like this before and that there never would be again.

The funeral was somehow done that very day; stern custom in this cruel world forbade him to contemplate her cast-off husk forever.[15] The mourners crowded the broad field into the distance, and the last rites went forward with the greatest magnificence, but her frail wisp of smoke pitifully rising to the heavens, athough not an uncommon sight, was still cruelly disappointing. The lowliest and most ignorant of those who watched His Grace wept to see so very great a lord lean on others as though he thought he trod on empty air. The gentlewomen present felt lost in a nightmare, and their attendants worried that as they writhed about, they might even fall from their carriages. Genji recollected that dawn all those years ago when the Commander's mother died, and he realized that he must still have been himself then, since he clearly remembered a bright moon, whereas this evening he was engulfed in darkness.

She had died on the fourteenth, and now the fifteenth day was dawning. A dazzling sun rose over the dewy fields, and life to Genji now seemed more hateful than ever. He had survived her, but for how long? He considered allowing this tragedy to persuade him to act on his cherished desire, but people would then speak ill of him for being so fainthearted, and that convinced him to bear up a little longer, even though he could hardly endure the suffocating pain.

The Commander, who went into mourning confinement with him, stayed with him day and night and never went home at all. Compassion for his father's obvious and natural despair made him wish to do everything he could to console him.

Early one evening, when a stormy wind was blowing, the Commander thought back to the past and longingly recalled that brief glimpse of her. He secretly pondered her last, dreamlike moments, too, and so as not too clearly to betray his grief, he disguised the beads of his tears by counting on his rosary the call to Amida.

> "Yearning too fondly for a twilight one autumn many years ago,
> I saw the end come at last in a cruel dream at dawn,"

a dream that lingered on in bitter memory. He engaged worthy monks to call the Name, of course, but also to chant the Lotus Sutra, and both moved him profoundly.

15. *Kokinshū* 831, by Shōen (a lament on the death of Fujiwara no Mototsune): "As to the cicada, one finds consolation in gazing on its cast-off shell, but O that smoke at least might rise from Mount Fukakusa!"

Waking or sleeping, Genji's tears never dried, and he spent his days and nights swathed in fog. He reflected, looking back over his life: Everything, beginning with my face in the mirror, assured me that I resembled no one else, and yet the Buddha encouraged me even in my childhood to understand the sorrow and treachery of life, and I bore these bravely, until now at last I suffer a grief unknown before or ever again. Nothing in this world need concern me anymore, and there is nothing to deter me from devoted practice, but this despair could make my chosen path difficult to follow. In his trouble he prayed to Amida, "I beg you, allow me to forget something of my pain!"

Messages of condolence arrived from many places, especially from the palace, and not just for form's sake, because they came thick and fast. Genji firmly declined to read or listen to them, lest anything in them tug too strongly at his heart. He did not wish to appear weak, however, and he refused to have it said of him that he had left the world at last in a fit of feebleminded misery; and so he added to his burden of sorrow the anguish of not following the prompting of his heart.

His Excellency sent many messages, quick as he always was to offer sympathy, for he greatly mourned the loss of a lady unlike any other in the world. In the quiet of an autumn twilight he remembered that this season was the one when the Commander's mother had died, and he reflected sadly that most of those who mourned her then had now passed on themselves. No, one never knew in this life who would go and who would stay. The sky's moving quality prompted him to have the Chamberlain Lieutenant, his son, take Genji a very touching letter, in the margin of which he had written,

> "That autumn for me retains the living presence it had long ago,
> and the sleeves I moistened then are wet again with fresh dew."

Genji answered,

> "Dews of long ago and dews that settle lately to me are all one,
> for alas each autumn night brings the same bitter sorrow."

To keep up appearances he added thanks for many kind messages of sympathy, because if he had freely expressed his grief, His Excellency, being the man he was, would have seen from his letter how little courage he had left.

He wore a rather darker shade than when he had spoken of "light gray."[16] Some who are blessed with good fortune and success unfortunately arouse envy, and the arrogance of the great may cause much suffering, but she had had a wonderful capacity to attract even those who were distant from her, and her smallest deed had inspired widespread praise. Quite ordinary people with no real reason to mourn her wept in those days to hear the wind sigh or crickets sing, and all who had known her slightly were beyond consolation. The women long in her intimate

---

16. In a poem in "Heart-to-Heart." His now-darker shade means deeper mourning.

service mourned bitterly that they survived her at all. They resolved to become nuns and live in the mountains, far away from the troubles of this world.

Moving messages came also from His Eminence Reizei's Empress,[17] who expressed her infinite sorrow.

> "Had she no love then for sere wastes of withered moors, that the departed
> never wished to set her heart on all that commends autumn?"

she wrote. "Now at last I understand."

Even Genji, to whom all was dim, found himself unable again and again to put her letter down. She alone, he reflected, has the wit and discernment to be any comfort. He went on thinking about her, feeling a little better, while streaming tears kept his sleeve pressed to his eyes. He could not write for some time.

> "You who have risen far aloft into the sky, look down upon me,
> caught here by a fleeting life hateful to my autumn years."

Even after wrapping it, he gazed for a time absently before him.

His thoughts were unsteady, and even he knew that he was quite confused about many things. For this reason he sought distraction among the women. He kept just a few before the altar with him while he quietly pursued his devotions. A thousand years with her: that was what he had wanted, and the parting that none evades had been a crushing blow. There now arose in him a pure and lasting aspiration to look only toward the life to come, so that nothing should distract him from the lotus dew of paradise; but unfortunately, he also still dreaded what people might feel like saying about him.

He had said nothing very clear about the memorial rites, and the Commander therefore took responsibility for all that. Time and again he wondered whether he would live out the day, but the days and months somehow passed anyway, and he felt as though he was dreaming them all.

Her Majesty, like others, never once forgot her, because she had loved her, too.

17. Akikonomu.

41

The Seer

Maboroshi means a seer or sorcerer who travels between this world and the afterworld. The word is the chapter title because of its presence in Genji's poem:

"O seer who roams the vastness of the heavens, go and find for me a soul I now seek in vain even when I chance to dream."

"The Seer" begins in the first month of the year after "The Law" ends and reaches the twelfth month of that year.

PERSONS

His Grace, the Honorary Retired Emperor, Genji, age 52

His Highness of War, Genji's brother (Hotaru Hyōbukyō no Miya)

Chūjō, a gentlewoman in Genji's service

Chūnagon, a gentlewoman in Genji's service

His Highness, the Third Prince, 6 (Niou)

Her Cloistered Highness, 26 to 27 (Onna San no Miya)

The lady from Akashi, 43 (Akashi no Kimi)

The lady of summer (Hanachirusato)

The Commander, 31 (Yūgiri)

The officiant at the Assembly of the Holy Names

The light of spring plunged him only further into darkness, and he felt at heart as though he would never have relief from his sorrow. Outside, people gathered to his residence as usual,[1] but he pleaded illness to remain behind his blinds. When His Highness of War arrived, he at last sent out a message that he would receive his visitor privately.

> "This house is my home, and yet there is no one here to love the blossoms: what can have drawn spring again to come round as it did then?"

Tears sprang to His Highness's eyes.

> "I came for their scent: that alone—was it in vain? And do you suggest nothing more drew me this way than common taste for blossoms?"[2]

Genji watched his graceful figure beneath the red plum blossoms and doubted that anyone else would enjoy them properly. They were only just beginning to open and were as pretty as they could be. There was no music this year, and many other things were different, too.

The gentlewomen long in her service wore dark gray, and they mourned her too intensely ever to be consoled. Their only comfort was Genji's constant presence, since he never even went to call on the other ladies, and their own familiar attendance upon him. Those who had sometimes caught his eye, although without any great feeling of attachment on his part, he now merely treated like the rest, for he spent his dreary nights alone. When those on duty gathered around him, he had them keep well away from where he lay.

To pass the time he would often discuss the past with them. Remembering from the depths of his present detachment how affairs he never thought would last,

---

1. For their formal New Year visits. Genji is at Rokujō.
2. "Spring" in Genji's poem suggests Hotaru, and "scent" (the essence) in Hotaru's suggests Genji. Hotaru takes Genji's poem as a rebuff.

some amusing and others genuinely painful, had sometimes put her in a temper, he wondered why he had been so unkind, and he felt his heart burst with sorrow and regret at ever having upset her. In her wisdom she had seen through him perfectly well, but even so, she had never turned against him, although she worried each time about what might become of her. Sometimes the women who knew how things had been and who were still close to him touched lightly on the subject.

She had betrayed no hint of her feelings even when Her Cloistered Highness first came, although he gathered sadly at certain moments how much she was hurt. The most vivid was that snowy dawn when he stood waiting, frozen, until the sky became threatening and she sweetly and warmly took him in, meanwhile hiding sleeves wet with tears and tactfully disguising the state she was in. He spent the night wondering, even while he dreamed, in what future life he would ever see her again. He felt as though he were reliving that moment when dawn came and he heard a gentlewoman on her way back to her room say, "Why, look at all the snow!" Her absence from beside him gave him unspeakable pain.

> *"When I only long to melt from this sorry world as this snow will soon,*
> *how strange still to linger on once again to watch it fall!"*

He called for washing water and absorbed himself in his devotions, as he did so often to dispel such thoughts. The women revived the embers and offered him the brazier. Chūnagon and Chūjō[3] stayed with him to talk.

"Last night was lonelier than ever!" he said. "I should have seen through it all by now, but no, this life still holds me captive." He stared absently into space, then glanced at them and imagined sadly how much more forlorn they would be if he abandoned them, too. His voice at his devotions, quietly chanting a sutra, could move anyone to weep, and those who were with him day and night and whose sleeves could not stay the flood of their tears[4] of course felt boundless sorrow.

"Very little in this life has really satisfied me, and despite my high birth I always think how much less fortunate my destiny has been than other people's. The Buddha must have wanted me to know that the world slips away from us and plays us false. I who long set myself to ignore this truth have suffered in the twilight of my life so awful and so final a blow that I have at last seen the extent of my failings, but while no attachment binds me any longer, it will be a fresh sorrow to leave you both behind, when I now know you so much better than before. Ties like ours are fragile. Oh, I know that I should not feel this way!" He wiped his eyes to hide his tears, but he failed, and they quickly spilled over; and of course the women watching him were still less able to keep themselves from weeping. Each wanted to tell

---

3. Both have appeared before (assuming they are the same women) as particular favorites of Genji; they are probably "those who had sometimes caught his eye, although without any great feeling of attachment on his part."

4. Literally, "the weir of their sleeves could not contain [their tears]"; probably from *Shūishū* 876, by Ki no Tsurayuki: "O river of tears, your waters flow so swiftly from their source that the weir of my sleeves cannot contain them."

him how much she hoped that he would never leave them, but speech failed them, and they could only sob.

So it was that in the silence of dawn, after a night spent wakeful and sighing, or the quiet of dusk after a vacant day, he would often spend time in intimate conversation with these women, who seemed to him to be more than usually worthwhile. The one called Chūjō had been so close to him since girlhood that he cannot have failed secretly to enjoy her, and that is probably why she had kept warily away from him; but after Lady Murasaki died, he remembered how particularly she had liked her and so became fond of her himself, although not like *that*, but only because she reminded him of her. Chūjō's looks and disposition recalled a young pine,[5] and under the circumstances he thought her cleverer than he might have otherwise.

He met no one to whom he was not already close. Senior nobles he knew well, or the Princes his brothers, came calling often, but he seldom received them; for he said to himself, I may do my best to maintain some composure while I am with other people, but I have been confused for months, and I must be eccentric in some ways. They would make too much of it later on, and I do not want that. I suppose that it comes to the same thing if people are saying I am too distraught to see anyone, but it would still be much worse to show off my peculiarities than to have them merely gossiped about and imagined. He spoke even to the Commander only through blinds. Nevertheless, he contained himself; he would not hurry even now, when people might well be telling each other that he was no longer the man he had been. He could not yet turn his back on the sorrows of this world. A brief, rare visit to one of his ladies would call forth a rain of tears too copious for him to bear, and he let days go by without sending either[6] a word.

Her Majesty returned to the palace, leaving the Third Prince to give Genji what consolation he could. The little boy looked very carefully after the red plum that stood before the wing.[7] "Grandma told me to," he said. Genji thought it extremely touching. In the second month, when mist prettily veiled the trees in flower and others yet to bloom, a warbler appeared in that favorite red plum tree, singing splendidly, and Genji went to watch it.

> "How the warbler sings, just as though nothing had changed, there among the flowers,
> in the tree she planted then, even when she is no more,"

he repeated as he went.

The further the season advanced into spring, the more her garden looked just as it had then,[8] but this gave him no pleasure; on the contrary, it was troubling, and so many things tugged painfully at his heart that he longed only for mountains as

5. This may mean that she reminded him of Murasaki. The meaning of the original expression (*unai matsu*) is uncertain. Since *unai* means the short hair worn by a child, an *unai matsu* may be a young, growing pine; but an early commentary refers to a line of Chinese verse to suggest that an *unai matsu* grows on a grave mound—presumably Murasaki's in this case.

6. Akashi or Hanachirusato.

7. At Murasaki's Nijō residence.

8. The scene seems now to be Rokujō.

remote as another world, where no bird would ever sing.[9] The kerria roses blooming in merry profusion only called to his eyes a sudden rush of dew.

Elsewhere the single-petaled cherry blossoms fell, the doubles faded, mountain cherries bloomed, and the wisteria colored, but *she* had known precisely which flowers blossom early and which late, and she had planted them accordingly for their many colors, so that in her garden they all yielded their richest beauty in their time.

"There are flowers on my cherry tree! I will not let them fall, ever! We must put up a curtain all round them—that way the wind will not get at them!" the little Prince announced very proudly.

The sweet look on his face made Genji smile. "That is a *much* better idea than trying to find someone with sleeves wide enough to cover the sky,"[10] he said. His Highness was really his only pleasure.

"I do not have much longer with you," he said, and, as so often, tears came to his eyes. "Life may go on for me a little after that, but I shall not be able to see you anymore."

His Highness did not like this at all. "Grandma said things like that. It is bad luck to talk that way." He looked down and toyed with his sleeves to hide his tears.

Genji leaned against the railing outside the corner room[11] and gazed sadly now out into the garden, now back through the blinds. Some of the women still wore a gray that acknowledged their loss, while others had on common colors, although their damasks had nothing bright about them. Genji himself wore a dress cloak ordinary in color but intentionally plain and discreet. The room was furnished very simply indeed, and it felt sadly quiet and empty.

> "Now the time has come, must I consign to ruin what she who is gone
> specially loved with all her heart, her hedge bright with spring flowers?"

His own decision filled him with sorrow.

To pass the time he went to call on Her Cloistered Highness. A nurse carried the Third Prince there with him, and he ran about with Her Highness's little boy just like the child he was; his fear for the blossoms had not run very deep. Her Highness was chanting a scripture before the altar. There was nothing profound about her spiritual aspiration, but bitterness toward the world never troubled her, and she pursued her devotions in undistracted peace. Genji envied her her steadfast detachment and deplored his own failure to match the piety of so shallow a woman.

The flowers on the holy-water shelf handsomely caught the light of the setting sun. "Flowers hardly move me anymore, now that she who so loved spring is no longer here, but they look pleasant when offered to the Buddha," he remarked. And

9. *Kokinshū* 535: "Would that she understood the depth of my love, deep as a mountain fastness where no birds sing."
10. *Gosenshū* 64: "O for sleeves wide enough to cover the sky, that I might keep from the wind the flowers that bloom in spring!"
11. Probably the southwest corner of the east wing of the southeast quarter at Rokujō, where he had lived with Murasaki; however, some commentators take the scene to be at Nijō.

he went on, "Still, I have never seen anything like the kerria roses before her wing—the flower clusters are so big! They obviously do not pretend to good manners, but their richness and exuberance are simply delightful! It is sad, though, how they seem not to know that this spring the lady who planted them is no more—they are only flowering more magnificently than ever."

" 'A valley far removed from spring,' "[12] she replied, meaning nothing in particular by it.

Genji was annoyed. She could have thought of something else! Nothing *she* ever said or did made me wish it otherwise, even in little things like this! He thought back over what she had been like since childhood: no, he could think of nothing, nothing at all. Instead he found himself dwelling on countless moments that confirmed her wit, wisdom, and charm, and on all sorts of things that she had said and done, until his weakness for tears overcame him, and he suddenly wept.

The twilight was so pretty, through the mists that veiled the distances, that he went straight to visit the lady from Akashi. She was not expecting him, since he had hardly looked in on her for ages, and his arrival was therefore a surprise, but when she received him with perfect composure and grace, he saw how remarkable she still was. No, he thought (the comparison made itself for him), *she* was different, she had another range of gifts and accomplishments; and longing for her made him so sad that he hardly knew how to seek consolation.

He lingered there quietly to talk over the past. "I grasped long ago that it is not at all a good idea to set one's heart too fondly on anyone," he said, "and on the whole I have done what I could to avoid attachment to anything in this world; in fact, thinking things over during those years when people assumed that I was destined for oblivion made me realize that nothing really prevented me from giving my life to wander the farthest mountains and plains. In the end, though, even now when my own time is coming, I am still caught up in ties that I should properly shun. It is maddening to be so fainthearted!"

He did not complain that all his sorrow had a single cause, but she understood with a pang how he felt, and she sympathized. "I have the impression that even someone whom one easily imagines regretting nothing is still restrained at heart by many, many ties," she said, "and I certainly do not see how you of all people could renounce the world that quickly. A step taken that way, on impulse, will only provoke blame for being ill considered and turn out to be a mistake after all, so that your slowness to make up your mind seems to me to promise deeper peace in the end. Past example suggests that it is not a good idea to act on disenchantment due merely to disappointment or shock. You will be happier and feel easier in your mind if you continue as you are now until you have seen Their Highnesses grow up and reach a position beyond any challenge."[13] She looked very handsome as she offered her sage advice.

---

12. *Kokinshū* 967, by Kiyowara no Fukayabu: "In a lightless valley far removed from spring, there is no grief for flowers that bloom only to fall." Onna San no Miya seems to mean "lightless valley" to allude modestly to herself. However, she has not taken the rest of the poem into account, and Genji is annoyed because it implies that Murasaki's death leaves her indifferent.

13. Above all, until the present Heir Apparent, their grandson, becomes Emperor in his turn.

"But such an abyss of circumspection would be even less commendable than shallow haste," he replied, and he went on to talk of things that had long been on his mind. "That spring when Her Cloistered Eminence passed away, I really did wish the blossoms would be kind.[14] She was so admirable, you know, as everyone acknowledged, and having known her since I was a boy, I felt her loss more keenly than most; not that I mourned her for anything more than quite general reasons. If *she*, too, still means more to me than I can forget after so many years, it is not just that I miss what she was to me later on. I brought her up from childhood, after all, and we aged together, and now that she has left me, I can hardly bear the sorrow of remembering it all and of endlessly recalling what she and I were to each other. Everything about her that moved me, or impressed me, or gave me pleasure, comes back in an overwhelming flood of memories." After talking over things old and new with her late into the night, he felt as though he should stay on until morning, but he went back anyway to the southeast quarter, which must have moved and saddened her. Even he was astonished to find himself so disposed.

He returned to his devotions, and it was only in the middle of the night that he lay down to rest a little in his day sitting room. Early the next morning he sent her a letter, and with it,

> "Crying as geese cry, I made my way home again in a fleeting world
> where no creature ever finds a last haven beyond time."[15]

He had hurt her the evening before, but she felt sorry for him, too, for she had never seen him looking so lost. She therefore set her own feelings aside, and tears came to her eyes.

> "The geese once haunted waters around seedling rice that now are all gone,
> and ever since, the flower reflected there comes no more."[16]

The unfailing excellence of her writing made him think of the way the two had come in the end, despite *her* initial objections, to respect each another and to acknowledge a mutual trust—not that that meant they had ever been close, since she always treated the lady from Akashi with a fine formality hardly noticed by anyone else. Sometimes, when he was feeling particularly lonely, he would look in on her this way just to talk. Nothing of what he had once been to her remained.

From the lady of summer there came clothes for the new season, with a poem:

> "Summer clothes today: and with the new season's change there will come, I know,
> a tide of old memories to sweep all else from your thoughts."

14. And blossom in mourning gray. From *Kokinshū* 832, by Kamitsuke no Mineo.

15. Wordplays in this poem evoke both Genji's mourning for Murasaki and the return of the wild geese to the north in spring. *Nakunaku* ("crying") refers both to weeping and to the cries of the geese; *kari* ("fleeting," "nothing lasts") also means "wild goose"; and the *toko* of *toko no yo* ("haven beyond time," the distant, eternal home of the geese) also means "sleeping place," "marriage bed."

16. "Now that Murasaki [the "water"], who so attracted you [the "geese"] is gone, you [the "flower"] never take the occasion to visit me ["reflected there"] either anymore."

He answered,

> *"Today, with the change to clothing gossamer thin and feathery light,*
> *I lament this life the more, this flimsy cicada shell."*

"I expect that everyone is looking forward to enjoying the sights today," he remarked on the day of the Festival,[17] imagining the shrine. "You women must hate the thought of missing it all. Go home quietly, then, and see what there is to see."

Chūjō had fallen asleep a moment on the east side of the house, and Genji went to look at her. She got straight up, very dainty and pretty, and the way her slightly disordered hair fell over her bright, flushed face was quite enchanting. She had on trousers of a scarlet veering toward yellow and a leaf gold shift under dark, dark gray and black,[18] all of which lay untidily one layer over another; and she had slipped off a train and Chinese jacket that she now attempted to put back on again. Beside her she had laid a sprig of heart-to-heart.

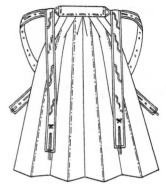

Woman's train

Genji picked it up. "What is this called?" he asked. "Why, I have forgotten its name!"[19]

> *"So it may well be that waterweeds choke a bank once nobly favored,*
> *but the leaf I sport today—you forget even its name!"*[20]

she answered bashfully.

He took her point and was sorry.

> *"In most things by now I have given up the world and its temptations,*
> *but I shall perhaps today wickedly pick heart-to-heart!"*[21]

He seemed not to have rejected *her*, at least.

The long rains of the fifth month left him with less and less to do all day, save for vacant dreaming, but the Commander came to wait upon him a few days past the tenth, when the moon at last shone brilliantly from among the clouds. Entranced by the scent of an orange tree that stood out sharply in the moonlight, Genji was just waiting for the cuckoo to sing his song of a thousand

---

17. The Kamo Festival, in the middle of the fourth month.
18. All colors associated with mourning.
19. *Aoi* (in Heian spellng *afuhi*, "day of meeting"). Genji has not made love for so long that he claims to have forgotten what it is like.
20. "I know it is a long time since we last made love, but still . . ."
21. "I would gladly commit enough of a sin [*tsumi*] to pick [*tsumi*] this leaf [make love with you]."

years[22] when startling clouds appeared, accompanied by a violent shower and howling wind that blew the lanterns about. The sky seemed to go black. Genji hummed "The pattering of rain on the window" and other well-worn lines[23] in a voice that his visitor would gladly have had ring out "at my darling's hedge."[24]

"There is nothing all that strange about living by yourself, except that you get so lonely," Genji remarked. "If you mean to live far off in the mountains, I am sure you really can find peace there if you accustom yourself to it as I am doing."

"Here, you women, bring us some refreshments!" he called. "I suppose it would be making too much of a fuss to send for the men."[25]

The Commander could see perfectly well that at heart his father was only gazing aloft to the heavens,[26] and he felt extremely sorry for him. How can his devotions possibly bring him peace if he can think of nothing else? he wondered. I can hardly blame him, though—even I can never forget that glimpse of her. "It feels as though it was only yesterday, but I suppose the mourning will be over soon," he said. "May I ask what you have decided to do?"

"Nothing unusual—what good would it do? There is the Paradise Mandala[27] she had made, and it is time now to dedicate it. There are lots of scriptures, too; she told His Reverence all about what they are for.[28] As for anything else that may need to be added, I plan to do as His Reverence suggests."

"I am very glad for her sake that she always took such an interest in these things, but she seems to me to have been destined for only a brief passage through this life, and it is a great pity that she did not even have any children."

"But others who have lived longer are still, in that respect, almost the same. For that I blame myself. I trust that you are the one who will bring increase to our line." Genji was too wary of his own feeble susceptibility to touch very much on the past. Just then the cuckoo he had been expecting gave a single, distant cry, at which he murmured with deep feeling, " 'How did you know?'[29]

> Have you come hither with your wings wet with showers, O mountain cuckoo,
> from so many memories this evening of one now gone?"

His gaze was more than ever on the heavens.

---

22. *Gosenshū* 186: "Upon the orange tree, unchanging in hue, the cuckoo sings his song of a thousand years." The cuckoo (*hototogisu*), like orange blossoms (*tachibana*), was associated with fond recollections of the past.

23. From Bai Juyi (*Hakushi monjū* 0131).

24. "Would have liked Murasaki to hear." Early commentaries attribute the quotation to an otherwise unknown poem (*Genji monogatari kochūshakusho in'yō waka* 300): "It is sad to listen to you alone, O cuckoo; I would have your song ring out at my darling's hedge."

25. Genji's personal retainers.

26. That Genji was thinking only of Murasaki. *Kokinshū* 743, by Sakai no Hitozane: "The heavens are no memento of the one I love, yet whenever I miss her, I gaze aloft."

27. A painting of Amida in the midst of his paradise.

28. Murasaki had scriptures copied for the posthumous benefit of particular people. "His Reverence" was presumably Murasaki's spiritual adviser.

29. *Kokin rokujō* 2804: "I talk about the past, and, cuckoo, how did you know, that you should sing in the voice I heard long ago?"

"Hear me, O cuckoo, and take this message to her: You have gone away,
     but at home your orange tree now blooms in perfect glory,"

the Commander replied.

The gentlewomen added many more of their own, but I have left them out. The Commander stayed on to keep his father company for the night, as he had done at other times in the past, out of pity for all the nights that his father spent alone; and it brought back many memories to be so often like this in a room always forbidden to him while she was alive.

At the height of the summer heat Genji gazed out from a somewhat cooler spot and noticed that the lotuses on the lake were all in flower. "There are so many!"[30]—that was his first thought, and he remained absorbed in melancholy contemplation until at last the sun sank low. The cicadas were singing shrilly, but yes, it was sad to be all alone, admiring the garden pinks aglow in the light of the setting sun.[31]

     "How their voices cry, as though all reproaching me on a summer's day
          for spending my idleness on sighs and on ceaseless tears."

Countless fireflies were crisscrossing before him, and he murmured as so often an old line that matched his mood, "Fireflies roam before the evening pavilion."[32] Then he went on,

     "Fireflies rule the night, and it is sad to see them when at every hour
          one burns with the searing flame of love now forever lost."[33]

On the seventh night of the seventh month[34] very little resembled earlier years, for Genji had no music and spent the day in blank monotony. No one watched the meeting of the stars. Very late that night he got up by himself and opened the double doors. The near garden was thick with dew. He glanced through the door and along the bridgeway[35] and then went out.

     "Far above the clouds the Tanabata stars meet in another world,
          while below, gathering dews water the garden she left."

30. "There are so many dewdrops [tears] on their leaves!" *Kokin rokujō* 2479 (also *Ise shū* 176), by Ise: "There are so many, the tears of one who suffers a mounting burden of sorrow."
31. *Kokinshū* 244, by Sosei: "Am I to admire them all alone, the pinks in the sun's last rays, while crickets sing?"
32. From a passage of Bai Juyi's "Song of Unending Sorrow," in which the Emperor remembers his lost love: "Fireflies roam before the evening pavilion, and I mourn."
33. The idea that "fireflies rule the night" is from *Wakan rōei shū* 187, by the Tang poet Xu Hun (Japanese Kyokon, 791–854).
34. The Tanabata Festival, when the celestial lovers on either side of the Milky Way were said to come together for their one night a year.
35. Probably the bridgeway from the east wing to the main house.

The sound of the wind was growing more mournful day by day, but the memorial services early in the month[36] provided him with some distraction. He could hardly believe how many months had passed. On the anniversary the whole household fasted, high and low, and he had the Paradise Mandala dedicated.

Chūjō, who brought him washing water before his regular evening devotions, had written on her fan,

> "When there is no end to the tears I shed for you after all this time,
> who could ever call today the day when we cease to mourn?"[37]

He read her words and wrote beside them,

> "I, who mourn her so, soon enough will find my life reaching its own term,
> but I still have even now many tears as yet unshed."

The ninth month came, and on the ninth day he contemplated chrysanthemums wrapped in cotton.[38]

> "Chrysanthemum dew from the mornings we both knew in life together
> moistens for me this autumn sleeves that I must wear alone."

In the tenth month, with its cold rains, his melancholy grew, and he murmured in the unspeakable anguish of dusk, "Yes, they always fall."[39] Gazing up at the wild geese passing aloft, he envied them their wings.

> "O seer who roams the vastness of the heavens, go and find for me
> a soul I now seek in vain even when I chance to dream."[40]

The months and days continued to slip by, and soon nothing could distract him from his grief.

When the time came for everyone gaily to prepare the Gosechi Festival,[41] the Commander's sons went to serve as privy pages and came to call on His Grace. They were close in age and very attractive. Their uncles—the Secretary Captain, the Chamberlain Lieutenant, and the others—were all festival officials, and they came, too, to mind them, looking very handsome in their green printed

---

36. The eighth.

37. The day is apparently the one that marks the formal close of mourning.

38. To absorb dew from the flowers. Chrysanthemum dew was an elixir, and rubbing the dew-soaked cotton on oneself kept old age at bay. The ninth of the ninth month was Chōyō no Sechie, the Chrysanthemum Festival.

39. An early commentary attributes this expression to the otherwise unknown poem (*Genji monogatari kochūshaku in'yō waka* 304), "The cold rains of the tenth month, yes, they always fall, but never before have they so soaked my sleeves."

40. Genji alludes to "The Song of Unending Sorrow," in which the Emperor has a seer search the afterworld for the soul of his beloved Yang Gueifei.

41. In the eleventh month.

robes.[42] The sight of their carefree figures must have brought back to him after all his mischief that day with the sunshade band.[43]

"Those of the palace hasten there today to join in the Warmth of Wine
while I let the day drift by, now a stranger to the sun."[44]

Having suffered patiently through the year, Genji knew that he would leave the world before long, even though his sorrow remained unassuaged. At last he gave thought to all that needed doing and bestowed a gift, according to rank, on each member of his household. He did not do so ostentatiously, as though to suggest that they would not see him again, but his manner showed that he would soon be taking the step he had considered so long, and for them the year closed in boundless loneliness and sorrow.

There were many letters that he could not decently leave behind, but he did after all spare a few from each writer, perhaps feeling that "I cannot destroy them,"[45] and while examining them for disposal he found some in *her* writing, in a neat packet among those from his Suma years. He had made the packet himself, but it seemed so long ago; yet the writing looked perfectly fresh. Yes, he reflected, with these I could keep her memory alive a thousand years, but *I* would no longer be there to read them. There was only one thing to do. He had two or three gentlewomen he knew well destroy them in his presence.

One always feels a pang upon recognizing the handwriting of someone who has died, even someone of less moment than she, and Genji's sight therefore naturally went dark. Blinding tears might have streamed down to flow away with the brushstrokes on the page, were it not that he recoiled in shame from betraying his weakness to the women. He pushed the letters away.

"Swept on by longing to follow her now she has crossed the Mountain of Death,
I looked on the signs she left, and still I strayed from the path."[46]

The women waiting on him were never able actually to open them and read them, but they caught glimpses here and there, and these were quite upsetting enough. The words describing the depth of her despair over their separation—not that he had really been that far away—called forth sorrow sharper than it had ever been,

---

42. Printed with patterns of flowers, butterflies, and so on in the blue or light leaf green of *yamaai* (wild indigo) and characteristic of the Gosechi Festival.

43. With the Gosechi Dancer, who wore it. The moment alluded to is not actually told in the tale.

44. The "Warmth of Wine" is Toyo no Akari, a court banquet that took place after the First Fruits Festival (Niinamesai) or the Enthronement Festival (Daijōsai), and that was accompanied by the Gosechi dance; the name means literally "ruddy faces" (from drink). "Sun" alludes to the *hikage* (literally, either "sunshade" or "sunlight") worn by the dancers; hence "stranger to the sun" implies "stranger to the pleasures of dalliance."

45. *Gosenshū* 1143, by Prince Motoyoshi, composed when asked to return some letters: "I cannot destroy them, yet they will come to light if I do not; how bitterly I weep therefore to return them to you."

46. The "Mountain of Death" (*shide no yama*) looms before those newly arrived in the land of the dead, who must cross it on the way to the palace of the King of the afterworld. "Signs" (*ato*) refers both to footprints and to writing in a letter.

and tears, too, in a stream not to be stemmed. He knew with dismay that any greater shock would reveal an unseemly, womanish weakness, so he did not go over them carefully; he only wrote in the margin of a long one,

> *"I shall have no joy from gathering sea-tangle traces of her brush:*
> *let them rise above the clouds as she also rose, in smoke."*

He had them all burned.

He knew that this year's Assembly of the Holy Names[47] would be his last, and perhaps that is what made the ringing of the monks' staffs[48] so especially moving. He wondered apprehensively how the buddhas would receive these prayers that he live long. It was snowing hard, and a good deal already lay on the ground. He summoned the officiant when he withdrew, treated him to more wine and so on than custom required, and gave him a markedly generous gift. The monk had been coming to Rokujō for a long time and had also served at the palace, and Genji therefore knew him well. Genji was touched to note that his hair was now white. As always a great many Princes and senior nobles were present. The plum blossoms were just beginning to open, and there should have been music, but Genji felt that at least this year it would still unman him, and he only had poems sung in consonance with the occasion.

Monk with his staff

Oh, yes, he said when he gave the officiant the cup,

> *"We who may not live until spring comes round again: here amid our snows*
> *let us sport for all to see the hue of new-budding plum!"*

The officiant replied,

> *"My own prayer shall be that you may watch these blossoms for a thousand springs,*
> *for I am the one, not you, crowned with all the snows of age."*

Many others added theirs, but I have left them out.

On that day Genji at last appeared in company. The light of his face far surpassed even his radiance of long ago; he was such a marvel to behold that for no reason the old monk wept on and on.

He was feeling desolate because the year was over when the young Prince ran

---

47. The Butsumyō-e began on the nineteenth day of the twelfth month, in the palace and in other great houses, and lasted three days. The ceremony invoked the names of the buddhas of past, present, and future in a spirit of repentance and atonement.

48. The chanting monks mark the rhythm with their *shakujō*, staffs topped with jangling metal rings.

in, crying, "What makes the most noise when you want to chase out devils?"[49] Genji could hardly bear the thought of losing the delightful little boy.

"Lost in my sorrows I never knew months and days were still passing by—
is the year really over, and my time, too, in the world?"

He decreed that everything on the first day of the year should be done exceptionally well. They say that he prepared superb gifts for the Princes and Ministers and equally generous rewards, according to rank, for those below them.

49. For the devil-expelling rite (*tsuina no gi*) held on the last night of the year.

Vanished into the Clouds

This chapter is blank. The title
evokes Genji's death.

42

NIOU MIYA

The Perfumed Prince

"The Perfumed Prince" refers to
the young Prince known as Niou.
This chapter introduces as a pair
the two gentlemen who will dom-
inate the tale hereafter: Niou and
Kaoru, "the Fragrant Captain."

RELATIONSHIP TO EARLIER CHAPTERS

An eight-year gap separates "The Perfumed Prince" from "The Seer." One gathers (in "The Ivy") that Genji died after two or three years spent in seclusion at his Saga temple. Retired Emperor Suzaku, Hotaru, Tō no Chūjō, and Higekuro all have died.

PERSONS

The Consultant Captain, age 14 to 20 (Kaoru)

Her Majesty, the Empress, 33 to 39 (Akashi no Chūgū)

His Majesty, the Emperor, 35 to 41

The Third Prince, His Highness of War, 15 to 21 (Niou)

The First Prince, the Heir Apparent, married to Yūgiri's first daughter

The First Princess

The Second Prince, married to Yūgiri's second daughter

His Excellency, the Minister of the Right,
Commander of the Left Palace Guards, 40 to 46 (Yūgiri)

The Empress Mother, the former Shōkyōden Consort

His Excellency's Sixth Daughter, 10 or 11 to midteens (Roku no Kimi)

Her Cloistered Highness, mid-30s to early 40s (Onna San no Miya)

Her Highness of Ichijō (Ochiba no Miya)

His Eminence Reizei, son of Genji and Fujitsubo, 43 to 49

His First Princess, daughter of the Kokiden Consort

His Empress, 52 to 58 (Akikonomu)

His light was gone, and none among his many descendants could compare to what he had been. To cite His Eminence Reizei would be impertinent. His Majesty's Third Prince and Her Cloistered Highness's son, who had grown up with him,[1] were both known to be handsome in their way, and they certainly stood out, but they seem not to have been especially dazzling. For quite ordinary young men they were graceful and distinguished, and the honor and esteem they owed to their connection to him gave them fame somewhat beyond his own in his early years; and they were indeed extremely attractive. The Third Prince lived at Nijō, thanks to Lady Murasaki's special fondness for him.[2] Their Majesties, who loved and cherished him, installed him in the palace once they had seen the Heir Apparent[3] safely appointed, but he still preferred his more comfortable life at home. When of age, he was known as His Highness of the Bureau of War.

The First Princess lived in the east wing of the southeast quarter at Rokujō. She had kept its furnishings as her predecessor had left them, and she remembered her fondly both day and night. The Second Prince had the main house when away from the palace, where he occupied the Umetsubo. He had married the second daughter of His Excellency of the Right,[4] and he carried great weight as the next candidate for Heir Apparent. His manner displayed a commensurate gravity.

His Excellency had a large number of daughters.[5] The eldest had gone to the Heir Apparent, in whose service she had no rival. The Empress Mother said plainly that, as everyone assumed, the others would all go in a like manner when their turn came, but His Highness of War had no wish to vindicate this prediction, and he seems to have made it perfectly clear that he would frown on anyone not chosen by himself.

Why should it matter? It is all one to me, His Excellency assured himself.

1. Niou and Kaoru, who both grew up at Rokujō.
2. She had left the house to him.
3. The Empress's first son.
4. Yūgiri.
5. Six: three from Kumoi no Kari and three from Koremitsu's daughter, "the Dame of Staff."

Bother these proprieties![6] However, he let it be known that he would not refuse an eventual approach, and he continued meanwhile to groom his daughters with great care. At the time his sixth daughter was the one to whose hand every self-respecting Prince or senior noble ardently aspired.

The ladies gathered around His Grace had dispersed, weeping, to what thenceforth were to be their homes, and the one known as the lady of Falling Flowers had moved to the east pavilion at Nijō, which now was hers. Her Cloistered Highness resided at Sanjō. Rokujō was lonely and all but deserted, for Her Majesty spent her time in waiting at the palace. His Excellency of the Right observed, "Other examples I have noted from the past show how the house that a man may build with care during his life is then left to crumble away, as though to demonstrate that nothing lasts, and this makes too sad a lesson on the passing of all things. While I live, I will not have his estate go to rack and ruin or allow those who people the avenue nearby to move away."[7] He moved Her Highness of Ichijō to the northeast quarter and then punctiliously divided his nights, fifteen each every month, between her house and Sanjō.[8]

The Nijō residence that Genji had made so splendid, and the spring quarter of Rokujō so widely and extravagantly praised, seemed destined for the descendants of a single lady: the one from Akashi, who looked after all the young Princes and Princesses and kept them company. His Excellency did nothing to change the lives of those whom His Grace had favored away from what His Grace himself had wished them to be, and he reflected with filial zeal how eagerly he would have served the mistress of the east wing if she had lived. He always remembered with regret that she had passed on before he had found the moment to let her know how much she was in his thoughts.

Everyone in the realm mourned His Grace, lamenting on every occasion that there was no life in anything anymore, as though the flame of it all had burned out. His household staff, his ladies, and Their Majesties and Highnesses[9] were of course even more deeply affected, and they also cherished at heart the image of Murasaki, whose memory remained ever present to them. It is true, as they say, that the blossoms of spring are all the more precious because they bloom so briefly.

His Eminence Reizei gave Her Cloistered Highness's young son special attention, as His Grace had asked him to do, and his Empress, who regretted having no children of her own, was pleased to see to all his needs. His coming-of-age was held at the Reizei Palace, and in the second month of his fourteenth year he became an Adviser. That autumn he was appointed a Right Palace Guards Captain. So it was that His Eminence, moved by who knows what anxiety, used the promotions he had in his special gift to make him quickly a man. He saw personally to furnishing a room for him in the wing near his own residence; selected for him only the best

6. In principle, a gentleman's daughters married in order of age.
7. When Genji built Rokujō, few other great nobles lived nearby, and Yūgiri is afraid that the ones his father attracted there may move away again.
8. Yūgiri moves Ochiba to where Hanachirusato used to live, but his main residence remains at Sanjō, with Kumoi no Kari.
9. Akikonomu (Reizei's Empress), Akashi no Chūgū, Onna San no Miya, and perhaps Akashi no Chūgū's children as well.

young gentlewomen, page girls, and even servants; and arranged everything even more brilliantly than for a girl. Both Their Majesties moved the prettiest, noblest, and most pleasing of their women to the young lord's household and did all they could to make him feel welcome, for they dearly wanted him to be happy and comfortable there. His Eminence cherished him no less than his First Princess, his beloved only daughter by the late Chancellor's Consort.[10] This may have been because he valued his Empress more with every passing year, but even so, one still wonders why.

Her Cloistered Highness, the young gentleman's mother, now confined herself to quiet devotions, monthly callings of the Name, twice-a-year Rites of the Eight Discourses, and other such holy offices as the calendar brought round. Otherwise she had so little to do that she looked up to him in his comings and goings as though to a father, which affected him considerably. On top of that, His Majesty and His Eminence were always calling for him, and the Heir Apparent and the other Princes loved to include him in their amusements, so that he unfortunately had no time at all and wished that there were more than one of him.

He often fretted and worried boyishly over rumors that chanced to come his way, but he had no one to question about them. The matter was always on his mind, although his mother would have been horrified to know that he suspected anything at all. What *did* happen? he often wondered. Why was I born to such constant anxiety? If only I were enlightened like Prince Zengyō, when he asked himself the same sort of thing![11]

> *"What can it all mean, and whom have I to question? What is my secret,*
> *when I myself do not know whence I come or where I go?"*

But there was no one to give him an answer.

Sometimes he felt as though there must be something wrong with him, and that thought, too, started anguished reflections. What pious resolve could have suddenly made Her Highness renounce her finery at the height of her youth? Yes, she must have had a shock. How could no one else have known? I suppose no one will tell me because it is all supposed still to be a secret. She does her devotions day and night, as far as I can tell, but I do not see how a woman's vague, weak grasp of things will ever enable her to polish lotus dew into a jewel.[12] Those five—whatever you call them[13]—are a worry, and I want at least to help her toward the life to come. And that gentleman they talk about, the one who died: did he die in torment? The idea made him long to speak to the man, in the next life if not in this one, until he lost all interest in his coming-of-age, although he did not actually decline to go

---

10. A daughter of Tō no Chūjō, also known as the Kokiden Consort.

11. This Buddhist allusion remains unclear. Perhaps the author conflated more than one source, or perhaps the text is faulty.

12. "Turning worldly feelings into enlightenment." Apparently, a synthetic allusion to a range of Buddhist writings.

13. This evasive expression (*itsutsu no nanigashi*) suggests that out of respect for Onna San no Miya, Kaoru cannot bring himself to name the "five hindrances" (*goshō*) that prevent a woman from attaining enlightenment.

through with it. The world of course made much of him, and he went about in daz-zling finery, but he remained meanwhile calm and aloof from it all.

Deep affection for the young gentleman's mother encouraged His Majesty's strong interest in him,[14] and Her Majesty treated him almost as she had done when he was growing up with her children and they all played together. "I had him so late, poor boy," His Grace had said, "and I am so sorry that I shall not see him be-come a man." She remembered that and remained attached to him. His Excellency of the Right honored him above his own sons.

Long ago the Shining Lord, as he was called, had enjoyed similarly lofty favor, but many envied him, and he lacked support on his mother's side. After pon-dering the matter in his deeply thoughtful way, he therefore dimmed his peerless light, lest it dazzle others, safely survived when turmoil all but engulfed the world, and for all that never neglected to pray for his next life, because without seeming ever to do so, he looked far ahead before reaching any decision. In contrast, this young gentleman had soared in favor prematurely and had extraordinary pride, in which destiny in fact confirmed him, since something about him suggested a holy being briefly resident in a world that he seemed to inhabit only provisionally. One could hardly say of his features just what distinguished them or made them espe-cially worthy of admiration; he simply had superb grace and was at heart unlike what appears to be the common run of men.

He gave off a delicious smell, an otherworldly fragrance, and it was a wonder how no matter where he went, the breeze that eddied behind him seemed really to perfume the air to a hundred paces. No one else born like that would dream of being modest in costume or behavior. No, he would purposely dress to be noticed, but not this young man, who objected to being unable even to steal behind a screen without revealing his presence and who hardly ever perfumed what he wore. Nonetheless, his fragrance added an ineffable touch to the scents slumbering in his clothing chests, until even the flowering plum trees in his garden mingled their per-fume with his when brushed by his sleeves, yielding scented spring raindrops that left many enchanted; while thoroughwort, flowering forgotten in the autumn fields, would when he plucked it lend its fragrance to the delicious breeze that always fol-lowed him.

This most unusually personal fragrance roused His Highness of War to special rivalry. He purposely suffused his clothes with the finest incenses and spent day and night blending more. In spring he contemplated his garden's plum blossoms, while in autumn he spurned the much-praised maidenflower, as well as the *hagi* so favored by the stag, to prefer instead chrysanthemums that banish old age,[15] fading thorough-wort, and humble burnet that he ostentatiously preserved until it was dismally with-ered by frost. In this way he proclaimed an elegant passion for perfumes. All this left the impression that he was somewhat soft and languid and addicted to fastidious tastes. Certainly, the Genji of long ago had indulged in no such eccentricities.

---

14. The reigning Emperor and Onna San no Miya are both Suzaku's children.

15. *Hagi*, which flowers in autumn, was accorded a feminine grace and so considered rhetorically the "wife" of the stag, who seeks his mate also in autumn. Chrysanthemums, which flower so late and last so long, were associated with longevity.

The Consultant Captain[16] called often at His Highness's, where the two vied with each other to make music on their flutes, for in their rivalry they were the best of friends. Of course, people in their tiresome way *would* call one the Perfumed Prince of War and the other the Fragrant Captain. When any great lord with a presentable daughter proudly aspired to win over His Highness, His Highness responded to each hint of promise and found out all he could about the young lady's quality and looks. However, he found none to be particularly attractive. *She* is still the one I want, he said to himself of His Eminence Reizei's First Princess; *she* would be worth it. Her mother, a Consort, had great dignity and elegance, she herself was widely credited with rare distinction, and the more circumstantial reports he had from the women who served her must have made him want her even more.

The Captain meanwhile believed deeply that this world is dross, and he knew that he might never free himself from lingering affection if he gave his heart nonetheless. He therefore renounced any wish to engage his feelings where doing so might entail troublesome regrets. Of course, he may just have been playing the sage because he had no one in mind at the time. One certainly could not imagine him dispensing with obtaining a father's permission.

At nineteen he became a Third Rank Consultant and retained at the same time his Captain's post. Being close to Their Majesties gained him such honor as a commoner that he had no need to defer to anyone, but he well knew in his heart what he was, and the knowledge sufficiently affected him that he had no taste for rash adventures and never allowed himself to lose his composure. In time everyone came to understand how serious he was.

He caught occasional glimpses and rumors of His Eminence's daughter, for whom His Highness had been pining for years, because she lived in the palace he frequented, and these encouraged him to believe her indeed exceptional. What endlessly marvelous grace and depth she has! he said to himself. Yes, it *might* make life worth living after all to have such a woman for my own! However, despite generally welcoming his presence, His Eminence had always kept him strictly apart from his daughter, and the young man quite understood. Considering the risk involved, he did not insist on attempting to approach her. He realized that if he ever became attached to her, against his own wishes, the consequences might prove unfortunate for both.[17] He made no move to court her.

Now that he seemed certain to be widely admired, no word from him, however light, provoked stern rejection but instead met only assent, and in the natural course of things he therefore began calling casually at a good number of houses. However, he always extricated himself adeptly without committing himself anywhere. Tepid, noncommittal attentions of this kind can be particularly annoying, but many women with a weakness for him were drawn to gather around Her Cloistered Highness at Sanjō. His aloofness there was certainly painful, but some whose rank really excused them from service still looked forward to a passing encounter with him and preferred disappointment to the loss of all hope. After all, he was so kind and such a pleasure to be

16. Kaoru.
17. Reizei thinks Kaoru is his half brother.

The New Year's archery contest

with that those so privileged could not really keep themselves from forgiving him.

"I certainly mean to stay with Her Cloistered Highness as long as she lives," he would say, "so that she may have my company." His Excellency of the Right said nothing, but this made him want to offer the young man one of his daughters. It was not that he found the marriage particularly attractive,[18] but apart from those two young gentlemen he had no idea where in the present world to find anyone else worthy. His Sixth Daughter, as she was called—one he had from the Dame of Staff—was much prettier than his better-born girls and also more gifted, and he thought it a great shame to have the world look down on her. He therefore took her in and entrusted her to Her Highness of Ichijō, who missed having children of her own. When I give those two a look at her, she will certainly please them, he assured himself; no one who knows women could fail to be especially attracted. Rather than keep her strictly sheltered, he instilled in her a taste for stylish, pleasing accomplishments and so gave her many charms to capture a young man's heart.

The banquet that followed the New Year's archery contest was to take place at Rokujō, and His Excellency prepared it especially carefully because he wanted His Highness to come, too. All the adult Princes attended on the day. Those born to Her Majesty were handsome and distinguished, but His Highness of War did indeed stand well above them. The Fourth Prince, known as His Highness of Hitachi, was an Intimate's son, which perhaps explained why he seemed so much less prepossessing than the others.

As always, the Left won decisively. The contest ended sooner than usual, and the victorious Commander,[19] His Excellency himself, then withdrew. Before going, he invited His Highness of War, His Highness of Hitachi, and Her Majesty's Fifth Prince to join him in his carriage. The Consultant Captain, who belonged to the losing side, was leaving quietly when His Excellency detained him. "Will you not join us to see Their Highnesses on their way?" he said; and the Captain, yielding to his insistence, followed him together with such of His Excellency's sons as the Intendant of the Gate Watch, the Acting Counselor, and the Right Grand Controller, as well as with other senior nobles. All accompanied His Excellency to Rokujō.[20] A

---

18. All other things being equal, Kaoru is (or is supposed to be) too close a relative to make an attractive marriage partner for one of Yūgiri's daughters. Such a marriage would gain neither side any particular advantage.

19. Yūgiri in his military capacity.

20. Kaoru and the others all appear to be riding in their own carriages.

sprinkling of snow fell during their journey, which was quite long, and the twilight was lovely. They were making music when they arrived, at the very hour when a flute rings out most beautifully, and one could only wonder where else, indeed in what buddha-land, such a moment could give richer pleasure.

The Captains and Lieutenants sat facing south as usual, in the south aisle of the main house, while their attendants, the Princes and senior nobles,[21] sat across from them facing north. The wine cup began its rounds, and once the party had become lively, breezes from whirling sleeves dancing "Motomego"[22] ushered in gusts of scent from nearby plum blossoms just then opening exquisitely in the garden; and to these the Captain's own perfume added an ineffably delicious touch. "Alas, it is too dark to see," said the wondering gentlewomen as they peered in at the scene, "but how true it is that nothing matches that scent!"[23] His Excellency was delighted as well. "Come, you Right Captain, you must sing, too!" he cried, noting the young man's glowing looks and flawless manner. "You should not so much play the guest!" The Captain sang "There Dwells the God" and so on with exactly the right degree of animation.

21. The ostensible purpose of the banquet was to honor the winning archers, who for the occasion were given the seat of honor (facing south) and extravagantly noble attendants.

22. A piece from the group known as Eastern Dances (Azuma Asobi); the song is said to have been given new words each time it was sung. The meaning of the title is unclear.

23. On the subject of plum blossoms in darkness, the women allude to Kokinshū 41, by Ōshikōchi no Mitsune.

43

Red Plum Blossoms

Kōbai means "red plum [blossoms]." The chapter derives its title from a poetic exchange between the Inspector Grand Counselor (Kōbai) and Niou.

RELATIONSHIP TO EARLIER CHAPTERS

While "The Perfumed Prince" ends early in Kaoru's twentieth year, "Red Plum Blossoms" begins early in his twenty-fourth, so that there is a four-year gap between the two. Chronologically, these intervening years are covered by the three chapters that follow.

PERSONS

The Minamoto Counselor, age 24 (Kaoru)

The Inspector Grand Counselor,
Tō no Chūjō 's second son, 54 or 55 (Kōbai)

His wife, Higekuro's daughter, 46 or 47 (Makibashira)

Her Highness, Makibashira's daughter by Hotaru

A boy, the son of Makibashira and Kōbai

Kōbai's elder daughter, Consort to the Heir Apparent

Kōbai's younger daughter

His Highness of War, 25 (Niou)

His Excellency, the Minister of the Right, 50 (Yūgiri)

There was in those days a gentleman known as the Inspector Grand Counselor, the late Chancellor's second son, hence the younger brother of the Intendant of the Watch.[1] The promise he had shown even as a boy, and his native liveliness of character, had encouraged a gratifyingly swift rise over the years to a standing that did him great credit and to a very high degree of favor. His first wife had died, and he was therefore in his second marriage. His present wife, the daughter of his father's successor as Chancellor,[2] was the lady who had so regretted leaving the "handsome pillar";[3] that is, the one His Highness of Ceremonial had married to His Late Highness of War.[4] The Grand Counselor had begun paying her secret visits after the Prince's death and with the passage of time had apparently come openly to acknowledge the tie between them. By his first wife he had only two children, which he thought too few, and he therefore prayed to the gods and buddhas until his present wife bore him a son. There was also a daughter from his wife's marriage to the late Prince. He rejected none and was equally fond of them all, although some of their women took a less commendable attitude, one that caused a degree of friction now and then; but his wife, who was bright and forthcoming, took it all in good part, let pass whatever she heard that might sound dismissive toward her own daughter, and managed to think no ill of anyone. The result was a well-ordered, well-considered household.

As each daughter in turn grew up, the Grand Counselor gave her her donning of the train. He enlarged the main house to seven bays and installed himself and his elder daughter at the front, on the south; his younger daughter on the west; and Her Highness[5] on the east. One would have thought Her Highness would suffer from no longer having her father, but not at all, for a great deal of valuable property

1. Kashiwagi.
2. Higekuro, who seems to have become Chancellor between "The Seer" and "The Perfumed Prince." The beginning of "Bamboo River" makes it clear that he is no longer alive.
3. In "The Handsome Pillar." She is known as Makibashira.
4. Makibashira's grandfather (Murasaki's father) married her to Prince Hotaru (His Late Highness of War), Genji's younger half brother who once courted Tamakazura. His Highness of Ceremonial was earlier His Highness of War.
5. Makibashira's daughter by Hotaru.

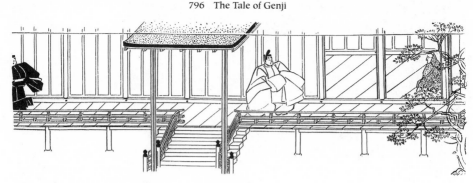

The south side of a main house

had come to her both from his side and from her mother's, and she led at home a life distinguished by great courtesy and elegance. She lacked nothing at all.

Talk of the way the Grand Counselor prized his daughters spread, as talk will, until many gentlemen came forward to court each in turn, and intimations of interest arrived from His Majesty and the Heir Apparent. However, the Grand Counselor reflected: His Majesty has an Empress[6] whom no other lady, whatever her quality, could possibly match, although at the same time it would be too bad not to think well enough of one's daughter to wish to try. As for the Heir Apparent, it would be difficult to challenge the favor that His Excellency of the Right's daughter already enjoys. Still, there *must* be more to be said on the matter than that. What satisfaction could there be in giving up the idea of sending a daughter into service at court, when all the while one genuinely believes her to be especially deserving? His mind was made up, and he offered the Heir Apparent his elder daughter, who at seventeen or eighteen was pretty and delightful in every way.

His younger daughter had her own noble grace, and a quieter poise than her sister's gave her such charm that he could not bear to imagine her wasted on a commoner. A word from His Highness of War, he decided, would be welcome.

Whenever His Highness came across the Grand Counselor's little son at court,[7] he would call him over to make friends and pass the time. The boy had character, and his eyes and forehead suggested real depth. "Tell the Grand Counselor that I am not satisfied to know only the little brother," he said.

The Grand Counselor smiled at this and felt well pleased. "I should much rather give a deserving daughter to His Highness than send her to rank below others in service at court. His Highness is a gentleman whom one could indulge with pleasure to one's heart's content." Meanwhile he urged forward the preparations affecting the Heir Apparent, praying in his heart as he did so, If the Kasuga God's decree is to be fulfilled in my time, may that serve to redress His Late Excellency's bitter chagrin over His Eminence's Consort![8]

6. This is the first time the text actually calls Genji's daughter Empress (Chūgū).
7. The boy is presumably a privy page.
8. He is dreaming of his elder daughter becoming Empress. The Kasuga God, the patron deity of the Fujiwara, decreed (at least so he believes) that only a Fujiwara should become Empress, but the last three Empresses (Fujitsubo, Akikonomu, and Akashi no Chūgū) have been non-Fujiwaras. One of the daughters of Tō no Chūjō ("His Late Excellency"), hence one of the Grand Counselor's sisters, was a Consort to Reizei and could have become Empress, but Tō no Chūjō was outmaneuvered by Genji, and the honor went to Akikonomu instead.

His daughter went to the Heir Apparent, and he gathered from what people told him that she stood high in his favor. In a gesture of selfless devotion his wife waited on her there, out of concern that as long as this life remained new to her, she might not get on without sound support. With both of them gone, the Grand Counselor languished, and his younger daughter, who was accustomed to spending all her time with her sister, was listless and gloomy.

Her Highness had never insisted on keeping her distance from the others, for they slept together every night and practiced together whatever they were learning, and in the least of their amusements the other two had always deferred to her as though to a teacher. She was unusually modest and seldom allowed even her mother to see her plainly face-to-face, which was no doubt a failing on her part; still, she was not at all diffident in personality or manner, being in fact more attractive than most.

This business of sending his daughter to the palace and so on made the Grand Counselor feel guilty to be so exclusively preoccupied with his own children. "Please let me know if you have any reasonable suggestion about what we should do for her," he said to his wife. "I intend to treat her just the same as the others."

However, his wife replied, "I see no sign that she is prepared to make so worldly a choice, and I expect that we will only make her unhappy if we insist. I will look after her as long as I live. What will happen after that is a matter of great concern, but she might become a nun—at any rate, I do hope that she manages to get through life without arousing mockery or scandal!" She wept and went on to tell him how admirable the young lady really was.

The Grand Counselor felt equally fatherly toward all the children, but he nonetheless found that he wanted to know what this one looked like. "It is unkind of you to hide from me this way," he complained, and he secretly went peering about on the chance of catching sight of her; but he got no glimpse at all. "I should be calling on you while your mother is away, but the way you single me out for rejection makes that very difficult," he said, stationing himself before her blinds. She answered him in a faint voice, one sufficiently pleasing in its distinction to give him an idea of her looks, and he was stirred by what he gathered of her. Being proudly convinced that his own daughters outshone anyone else, he was more and more inclined to suspect that they might not surpass *her*. It all goes to show what tricks life in this wide world can play, he thought. You may believe a girl is the best, but no doubt there is always one better.

"I have not heard your music for ages," he began; "things have been so busy here lately. The young lady on the west[9] is keen on the *biwa*, but alas, I doubt that she will ever really learn it properly. It is a trial to listen to her halting efforts. It would be kind of you to give her lessons. I myself never particularly mastered any instrument, but I suppose that the concerts I used to join long ago, when I was young, taught me enough to know how to appreciate them all. I no longer play even for pleasure, but it brings back the old days to hear your *biwa* now and then. His Excellency of the Right is the one who now carries on the style of His Grace of Rokujō. The Minamoto

9. His younger daughter.

Counselor[10] and His Highness of War are sufficiently favored by destiny to equal their forebears in every way, and they particularly like to make music, but it seems to me that their somewhat languid touch with the plectrum ranks them below His Excellency, and your playing reminds me of his. They say that one must depress the strings lightly to play the *biwa* well, but the change in the way a string held to the fret rings under the plectrum is characteristic of a woman's playing, and in truth it is very pleasing. Come, will you not play? Here, bring my lady a *biwa*!"

The women seldom took the trouble with him to stay out of sight, but a very young one, to all appearances nobly born, sat as far off as she felt she must to keep him from seeing her. "I hardly know what to think," he muttered irritably, "when even your gentlewomen treat me this way!"

His young son, on his way to the palace, now came by in service dress and looking to his father's fond eye even better than he did with his hair carefully bound in twin tresses.[11] He gave the boy a message to take to the Reikeiden.[12] "Tell her that I leave everything to her, and that I shall not come this evening either—I do not feel well," he said.

"Let us hear your flute a little." He smiled. "You never know when His Majesty may ask you to join in a concert, and *then* you will be sorry. You still sound awfully childish." He had him play in the *sō* mode, which he did very nicely. "Well, soon you will not be bad at all! Why, you must have been accompanying Her Highness! Please, both of you, play me the modal prelude!" His enthusiasm clearly embarrassed her, but she briefly complied, plucking the strings very prettily with her fingers.[13] The Counselor whistled ostentatiously along with them.

A deliciously fragrant red plum grew near the eaves on the east side of the house. "These plum blossoms seem to have a message," he remarked to his son. "I gather that His Highness of War is at the palace. Pick a branch and present it to him. He who knows will know.[14]

"Ah," he went on, "when the Shining Genji, as they called him, was a Commander and I was a boy, I was just as close to him as this, and I loved him forever after. People nowadays think very highly of those two young gentlemen, who certainly deserve all the praise they get, but they are nothing compared to him. No, there could never be one like him, or so at least it seems to me, though perhaps I am only imagining things. And if someone perfectly ordinary like me cannot recall him without a pang of sorrow, I imagine that those who were really close to him and who survived him must find life very long indeed."

This melancholy turn in his speech had brought tears to his eyes, and perhaps

---

10. Kaoru, though he has not been mentioned as a Counselor before. In "Bamboo River" he is an Adviser.

11. When in full civil dress (*sokutai*) a privy page wore his hair in twin tresses (*mizura*), but in service dress (*tonoi sugata*) he wore his hair loose.

12. To take to Makibashira at the Reikeiden, where his elder daughter is now living as a Consort to the Heir Apparent.

13. Rather than with a plectrum.

14. *Kokinshū* 38, by Ki no Tomonori: "To whom shall I show off these plum blossoms, if not to you; for he who knows their hue and scent will know."

he really was overcome, for he had his son break off a spray and hurry away. "What else can I do," he said, "when His Highness is the only remaining token of the lord to whom I look back so fondly? They say that Ananda carried on after the Buddha was gone and that in his wisdom he shone with such light that the Buddha seemed to have come again. Perhaps I may presume to address His Highness, when to someone lost in darkness he is the light:

> *When invitingly the plum tree in my garden perfumes every breeze,*
> *O warbler, will you not come to sport among those blossoms?"*

He wrote this in a youthful hand on scarlet paper discreetly wrapped in folding paper that his son happened to have in his robe, then sent the boy off. The boy hurried away, childishly eager to know His Highness better.

Folding paper

His Highness was just then leaving Her Majesty's private room near the Emperor's, accompanied by a crowd of privy gentlemen. "Why did you leave so early yesterday?" he said when he saw the boy. "And when did you get back?"

"I was sorry to have done it, and I hurried back when I heard that you were still here," the boy replied in a youthful but nonetheless practiced manner.

"You must come and enjoy yourself somewhere more comfortable now and then, somewhere not at the palace.[15] There are lots of young people there." He took the boy aside, and the others dropped back. Once they were gone and it was quiet, His Highness went on, "I gather that you have leave from the Heir Apparent to be away for a while. I thought he would never let you go, but it appears that someone else[16] may have taken your place."

"It was so hard, Your Highness, the way he kept me all to himself. I wish I had been with you." The boy said no more.

"She would have none of *me*, would she,"[17] His Highness went on. "Not that I really blame her, but still, I am not pleased about it. Try quietly finding out whether that young lady there on the east side of the house might be kinder. After all, she and I are of the same old stock."[18]

This was the moment to give His Highness the flowers. He smiled. "Now, if these followed reproaches . . ."[19] he said, gazing at them without putting them

15. Niou's residence at Nijō.
16. Kōbai's elder daughter.
17. The elder daughter, now the Heir Apparent's Consort.
18. Imperial.
19. The implication of this remark is uncertain. If he had received these flowers after making some sort of reproach to the sender, would they be more welcome or less?

down. The shape of the spray, the abundance of the blossoms, and their color and scent were all superb. "They say the red plum that sets off a garden is all color but lacks the scent of the white, but these flowers are magnificent in both ways!" He was very fond of plum blossoms, and he granted these gratifying praise.

"I believe that you are on duty tonight. Just stay with me, then." He would not dismiss the boy, who thus failed to go to the Heir Apparent's at all. Instead he took supreme and childlike pleasure in lying beside His Highness, by His Highness's own wish, enveloped in a marvelous fragrance that all but put the blossoms' scent to shame.

"Why did the lady to whom these flowers belong not go to the Heir Apparent?"

"I do not know. I was told only that they were for someone who would appreciate them." His Highness took it that the Grand Counselor must have his *own* daughter in mind, and he therefore gave no clear answer, his affections being already engaged elsewhere.

The next morning, when the boy was leaving, His Highness casually wrote,

> "If I were a man easily enticed to come by fragrant flowers,
>   would I have allowed their call to pass by me on the breeze?"

"Now, then," he said repeatedly, "after this you must keep that old man and his people from bothering me and follow my secret instructions," at which the boy liked and respected the lady on the east even better. The two others let him see them more often, as though they were his full sisters, but she was the one who really impressed the child in him and who struck him as the most worthy. The sister at the Heir Apparent's was getting on extremely well, which he thought very nice, too, but he felt bad about Her Highness and wanted particularly to help her. The plum blossoms had given him a happy occasion to do so.

He showed the Grand Counselor the reply to yesterday's message. "How tiresome of him!" the Grand Counselor complained. "It is curious that he should act so prim and proper whenever His Excellency of the Right and I are watching, just because he gathers that we disapprove of his taking gallantry too far. Everything about him suggests the ladies' man, and this trumped-up seriousness only risks making him look a bore." Grumbling, the Grand Counselor sent his son off to the palace that day again with yet another note:

> "Once touched by your sleeves, always so deliciously fragrant on their own,
>   these flowers will scent the breeze with a most exquisite fame.

I hope that you will forgive me the liberty," he added gravely.

He really seems to be trying to convince me, His Highness reflected, finding his interest piqued after all.

> "Were I to set forth for a house that spreads abroad the scent of blossoms,
>   people here and there might note my weakness for tempting hues."

The Grand Counselor was annoyed that his answer still conceded nothing.

His wife, now home again, was talking about what had been going on at court when she remarked, "Our son was there for a night on duty, and he smelled so good when he left that the Heir Apparent knew straight off he had been with His Highness of War, although most people thought nothing of it. 'No wonder he no longer cares about me!' he complained. It was quite amusing. Did you send His Highness a letter? It did not seem as though you had."

"I did, though. His Highness likes plum blossoms, and I could not refrain from picking him a branch of the red plum over there by the eaves, since it is so beautiful now. The perfume he leaves behind him is really quite delicious. Not even a woman preparing for a great occasion could scent herself like that. The Minamoto Counselor makes no effort to perfume himself at all—oddly enough, he is that way naturally. It is quite extraordinary. I cannot help wondering what fortunate karma from past lives could have produced that reward. Plum blossoms are plum blossoms, but what counts is the root from which the plum tree grows. That is why His Highness liked ours so much, I am sure." Even on the subject of flowers, His Highness was all he could talk about.

It is not as though Her Highness failed to grasp what went on around her, since she was quite old enough to understand a thing or two, but she had decisively rejected any thought of giving herself to a man as others did. A gentleman makes heroic efforts on behalf of the daughters he has by his wife, no doubt because he knows where his advantage lies, and he sets them off in many stylish ways, but rumor suggested to His Highness that *she*, always so quiet and withdrawn, was the one he wanted and whom he meant by all means to have. He kept the Grand Counselor's son with him constantly and sent off secret notes, but the gentleman's wife was sorry to see her husband so set on him and, if he ever showed that he had made up his mind to seek the younger daughter, so eager to agree. "What a shame," she remarked, "that His Highness is courting instead, however lightheartedly, a girl he can have no hope of winning. What a waste!"

His Highness took his failure to get a word in reply as a challenge, and he seemed to have no intention of giving up. What could be wrong with that, the Grand Counselor's wife reflected sometimes, considering who he is? Why not? He would be a pleasure to look after, and he certainly has a bright future. Still, he *was* hopelessly given to gallantry. He was secretly visiting many houses, and he seemed very keen on the Eighth Prince's daughters, considering how often he went there.[20] His gallant, frivolous ways gave her pause, until in the end she renounced the idea. Still, he was a very great lord, and it was therefore she who now and again took it upon herself stealthily to send him a note.

20. This story is told in "The Maiden of the Bridge" and subsequent chapters.

44

TAKEKAWA

Bamboo River

"Takekawa" ("Bamboo River") is a *saibara* folk song. It is first sung in this chapter by the Fujiwara Adviser (Tamakazura's youngest son) and apparently also by Kaoru, and the two then exchange poems alluding to it. Later it is sung again by the Chamberlain Lieutenant (Yūgiri's son), a disappointed suitor of Tamakazura's elder daughter.

RELATIONSHIP TO EARLIER CHAPTERS

Chronologically, "Bamboo River" overlaps "The Perfumed Prince," "The Maiden of the Bridge," and the first part of "Beneath the Oak," but the story it tells has little to do with these chapters.

PERSONS

The Minamoto Adviser, then Consultant Captain,
then Counselor, age 14 to 23 (Kaoru)

The Mistress of Staff, Higekuro's wife, 47 to 56 (Tamakazura)

The Left Palace Guards Captain, Tamakazura's son,
27 or 28 when Kaoru is 15 (Sakon no Chūjō)

The Right Controller, Tamakazura's son (Uchūben)

The Fujiwara Adviser, Tamakazura's youngest son (Tō Jijū)

The Haven, Tamakazura's elder daughter, 18 or 19 when Kaoru is 15

Tamakazura's younger daughter, becomes Mistress of Staff,
18 or 19 when Kaoru is 15

His Excellency, the Minister of the Right, then of the Left, 40 to 49 (Yūgiri)

His Majesty, the Emperor, 35 to 44

His Eminence, Retired Emperor Reizei, 43 to 52

The Chamberlain Lieutenant, then Third Rank Captain, then Consultant,
son of Yūgiri, late teens to late 20s

His mother, wife of Yūgiri, 42 to 51 (Kumoi no Kari)

The Grand Counselor, then Minister of the Right, late 40s to early 50s (Kōbai)

His wife, daughter of Higekuro and his first wife (Makibashira)

Her full brother, the Fujiwara Counselor

The Consort of His Eminence Reizei, daughter of Tō no Chūjō,
44 to 53 (Kokiden no Nyōgo)

Saishō, a gentlewoman in Tamakazura's household

Taifu, a gentlewoman of Tamakazura's younger daughter

A page girl of Tamakazura's younger daughter

Nareki and Chūjō, gentlewomen of Tamakazura's elder daughter

This is gossip volunteered by certain sharp-tongued old women, once of the successor Chancellor's[1] household, who lingered on after him. It is nothing like the stories about Lady Murasaki, but they held that some things told of Genji's descendants were wrong, and hinted that this might be because women older and more muddled than they had been spreading lies. One wonders which side to believe.

By the Mistress of Staff that late Chancellor had three sons and two daughters, whom he set out to endow with every advantage and whose future preoccupied him more with every passing month and year; but then, alas, he died, and the palace service he had anticipated so eagerly for his daughters melted away like a dream. While this great and powerful lord's private wealth and estates survived him undiminished, men's feelings shift with the times, and his profoundly changed residence fell silent and still. The Mistress of Staff had close relatives everywhere, but relations with the mighty are never easy, and it may be that His Late Excellency's arbitrary manner and lack of real warmth had aroused their dislike, for she was not in proper touch with any of them. His Grace of Rokujō had continued as before to treat her as a daughter, and he mentioned her immediately after Her Majesty in the testament he left to indicate his posthumous wishes. His Excellency of the Right therefore called on her in that spirit whenever the occasion encouraged him to do so.

Her sons suffered a good deal of worry and grief because of the loss of their father, since by then they were of age and adult, but they seem all in the natural course of things to have done well enough. There remained the question of what to do with her daughters. The late Chancellor had let His Majesty know how earnestly he hoped that the elder would serve him, and His Majesty, counting the years, often remarked that she must now be a woman; but by then the Empress enjoyed such supreme favor that all others seemed an afterthought in comparison, and the Mistress of Staff therefore hesitated, for she did not want any daughter of hers reduced to catching His Majesty's eye from afar, and it pained her to imagine her less esteemed than others.

Retired Emperor Reizei pressed an avid suit, speaking reproachfully of wish-

1. Higekuro's.

ing at least to make up for the bitter disappointment she had inflicted on him long ago.[2] "Now that I am old and useless, you may think even less of me than you did then," he said gravely, "but please give her to me as you would to a good father." She hardly knew what to do. What *would* be best? she wondered. I feel with my miserable destiny so ashamed and so wrong to have angered him, though I never meant to—perhaps he might then think better of me at last. However, she could not make up her mind.

Both daughters were said to be very pretty, and they had many suitors. The young gentleman called the Chamberlain Lieutenant, His Excellency of the Right's son by his wife at Sanjō[3]—a delightful young man and a particular favorite among all his brothers—was especially keen. The Mistress of Staff welcomed visits from all the brothers, since they were related on both sides.[4] This one managed to convey his intentions very effectively by cultivating her gentlewomen as well, and she found the insistence with which he constantly did so both tedious and touching. His mother sent her frequent notes, and His Excellency, too, implored her to "find a way to look favorably on him, despite his tender age." She was reluctant to accept so common a match for her elder daughter, but she felt that he might do for the younger once he carried just a little more weight in the world. He meanwhile had his heart so fiercely set on the elder that he was prepared to abduct her if her mother withheld her permission. To the Mistress of Staff such a marriage might not have been a complete disaster, but anything of the kind before the girl had consented would start a scandal, and she therefore warned the woman who spoke for him, as strenuously as she knew how, to look out and to avoid any blunder. The woman hardly knew which way to turn.

The Minamoto Adviser, whom His Cloistered Eminence Suzaku's daughter had given so late to His Grace of Rokujō and whom His Eminence Reizei now treated as his son, was then fourteen or fifteen. Far from being the child one expects at that age, he behaved so well and had such manners that his bright future was plain to see, and the Mistress of Staff wanted him for a son-in-law. She lived very near his mother's Sanjō residence, and he would turn up at her house whenever her sons brought him home to join in their amusements. The presence of such noble young ladies there put every youth on his mettle, and among those who went about preening themselves, it was this clinging Chamberlain Lieutenant who excelled in looks, while in sweet grace and distinction of manner none matched the Minamoto Adviser. The world at large could hardly help favoring him, perhaps because of the difference it made that they thought him so like His Grace. The young gentlewomen were especially captivated. Their mistress agreed that he really was very nice, and she allowed him intimate conversations with her.

"When I look back on all His Grace's kindness, I feel that I shall always miss him," she said. "Who else is left now to remind me of him? His Excellency of the Right is so grand that I can only meet him when circumstances allow it." To her the

2. When Tamakazura married Higekuro instead of serving Reizei as Mistress of Staff.

3. Kumoi no Kari.

4. Yūgiri's sons by Kumoi no Kari are related to Tamakazura through their mother (a half sister of Tamakazura) and through Yūgiri (a cousin of Tamakazura).

young man was a brother, and he himself thought of her house as one where he was fully entitled to call. He showed no taste at all for commonplace gallantry, and his remarkable seriousness so disappointed the young women of both households[5] that they teased him about it.

In the first days of the New Year the Mistress of Staff had a visit from her brother the Grand Counselor (the one who sang "Takasago," you know),[6] as well as the Fujiwara Counselor (the later Chancellor's eldest and Makibashira's full brother), and so on. His Excellency of the Right came, too, with his six sons. In looks and in every other aspect of his person he left nothing to be desired, and his reputation was correspondingly high. His sons, each handsome, too, in his way, enjoyed rank and office beyond their years and must have seemed quite free of care. Nevertheless, the Chamberlain Lieutenant, always so visibly the favorite, looked somber and downcast.

His Excellency and the Mistress of Staff conversed as always with a standing curtain between them. "I can seldom call on you without good reason," he began. "As the years go by, I feel more and more constrained from going anywhere at all except to the palace, and so, you see, I ignore many moments when I would like to talk to you about the old days. Please call on the services of my sons whenever you need to do so. I am always telling them to show you how much you mean to them."

"The kindness with which you continue to honor me, when after all this time I really no longer matter, makes it increasingly difficult for me ever to forget the gentleman who has preceded us," she replied; and she took advantage of this opportunity to tell him discreetly about His Eminence's approaches. "I find it difficult to make up my mind," she went on, "because in such company someone without adequate backing may only be worse off than before."

"I gather that His Majesty has expressed interest as well, and I wonder which of the two you mean to prefer. One does feel that His Eminence has had the best of his years, now that he has abdicated, but he seems to have lost so little of his rare looks that it has occurred to me to wish I had a suitably promising daughter; but alas, to my great regret I have none worthy to join such daunting company. The question is, would the Consort,[7] his First Princess's mother, really allow it? Others before have refrained for precisely that reason."

"Actually, His Eminence suggests that by now the Consort has little to occupy her time and that she would welcome the opportunity to cherish her with him. I wonder, though, what really to think of it all."

All sorts of people were gathering at her residence and then going on to Sanjō. Those who had been close to Retired Emperor Suzaku, and those more associated with His Grace of Rokujō, seemed not yet to wish to neglect Her Cloistered Highness. The Mistress of Staff's sons, the Left Palace Guards Captain, the Right Controller, and the Fujiwara Adviser, went off with His Excellency, whose entourage was strikingly imposing.

The Minamoto Adviser came that evening. Among the many young men

5. Tamakazura's and Onna San no Miya's.
6. Kōbai, the Inspector Grand Counselor prominent in "Red Plum Blossoms."
7. Reizei's Kokiden Consort, a daughter of Tō no Chūjō and thus a half sister of Tamakazura.

present—very handsome young men, each flawless in his way—this latecomer seemed to draw all eyes when he arrived, and a susceptible young woman remarked, "Yes, he really is different!"

"I would like to match him up with the elder of our young mistresses here!" another added naughtily. He certainly had youth's perfect grace, and the scent he gave off was simply not of this world. One could not imagine anyone with any appreciation, not even a great lord's sheltered daughter, failing to recognize that he stood out.

When the Mistress of Staff started for her private chapel, inviting him to "please come this way," he mounted the eastern steps and sat by the blinds over the doorway.[8] The buds on the young plum tree nearby were promising blossoms at last, a warbler was singing its first tremulous song, and the young man's sober figure so called for an added touch of romance that the women tried bantering with him, until his laconic replies provoked an older one, known as Saishō, to say,

> "If someone picked you, you might smell even sweeter—why not try it, then?
> Show your colors a little, early flowers of the plum!"[9]

She is quick! he thought and teased back,

> "You may think you see a tree stripped of leaf and branch, barren forever,
> but what sweet perfume within boasts the early flowering plum!

Just try brushing sleeves with me!"

"That is right: 'Rather than the color . . .' "[10] they all murmured, coming near enough almost to tug in earnest at his sleeves.

The Mistress of Staff slipped toward them from farther back in the room. "You wicked girls!" she whispered. "Must you tease even so fine and stalwart a young man? You have no shame!"

Stalwart, they call me! he thought. What a tiresome word!

Her own son, the Fujiwara Adviser, was there, too, since he did not yet have the privilege of the privy chamber and so was not going round on New Year's calls. He offered the company two aloeswood trays, one of fruit and nuts and the other bearing wine.

With age His Excellency looks more and more like His Grace, the Mistress of Staff reflected, but while this young lord does not resemble His Grace at all, in quiet charm of looks and bearing he does remind one of His Grace in his early years. That is just what he must have been like. The memories brought tears to her eyes. Her women extravagantly praised even the fragrance that lingered on after the young gentleman had gone.

---

8. The double doors are open and blinds hang in the entrance. Kaoru seems to have avoided coming up the southern, front steps. Tamakazura's chapel is inside her house, probably on the west side.

9. *Kokinshū* 37, by Sosei: "Plum blossoms I thought so lovely from afar—I only knew once I had picked them how marvelous they were in scent and hue!"

10. "Just try me, and you will see!" *Kokinshū* 33: "Rather than the color, the scent is what moves me: whose sleeves have brushed past you, plum tree at my door?"

The young gentleman himself resented the tag "stalwart," and after the twentieth of the month, when the plum trees were in full bloom, he went to see the Fujiwara Adviser. He had decided that he would no longer be thought of as lacking in savor and that he would learn the ways of gallantry. When he came in through the middle gate, he found someone else stationed there, also in a dress cloak. Detaining the man as he moved to hide, he discovered him to be the Chamberlain Lieutenant, who was always lurking around the house. The Lieutenant seemed rooted to the spot by the music of a *biwa* and a *sō no koto* coming from the west side of the main house. The poor fellow! the Minamoto Adviser said to himself. It can only be a great sin to indulge a desire that others condemn.

The music stopped. "Come, then, show me the way," he said, drawing the Lieutenant with him. "I do not know the house at all." They stood under the red plum before the western bridgeway, humming "The Plum Tree Branch," and the Adviser's fragrance signaled his presence even more plainly than the flowers' scent did the tree's. The double doors opened, and someone inside joined them very nicely on a *wagon*. Remarkable! the Adviser thought, since no woman normally accompanied a song in the *ryo* mode this well. They sang the song again. The *biwa* sounded wonderfully stylish, too. The ladies here were certainly accomplished! He liked the place and spent the evening chatting a little more casually than he usually did.

Someone slid a *wagon* out under the blinds. The two young men ceded each other the honor until the Mistress of Staff, through her son, begged the Minamoto Adviser, "They say that you have His Excellency the late Chancellor's[11] touch. I should love to hear you. Do let the warbler this evening entice you to play!" He knew that he could not seek refuge in bashful protestations, and so he played a little, without undue emphasis. His tone was very rich and full.

"I spent hardly any time with my father," the Mistress of Staff remarked, "but I miss him very much now that he is gone, and I find the least memory of him quite moving. It is extraordinary how this young man reminds me of the late Intendant,[12] and his touch on the instrument is just the same." Perhaps age inclined her to tears, for she wept.

The Lieutenant then sang "Sakikusa"[13] in a very pleasant voice. The absence from the gathering of anyone elderly and quick to criticize naturally encouraged each gentleman to elicit more music from the other, but the Fujiwara Adviser was a little slow at such things, being in this no doubt his father's son, and he really preferred simply drinking. At last, challenged by calls to "give us at least a merry song, won't you?" he sang "Bamboo River"[14] with them very nicely, despite being so young.

11. Tō no Chūjō's. He is Tamakazura's father and also Kaoru's grandfather, although ostensibly no one knows that, and the resemblance between his touch and Kaoru's on the *wagon* is a token of their blood tie. Meanwhile, the Lieutenant is a grandson of Tō no Chūjō.

12. Kashiwagi. The original actually calls him "Grand Counselor," the office awarded him on his deathbed.

13. A congratulatory passage from the *saibara* song "This Gentleman." The plant *sakikusa*, no longer identifiable with certainty, was thought felicitous in ancient times.

14. The words of the *saibara* song "Bamboo River" go something like "Let me go, go, go, hand in hand with a fair maiden, to the bed of flowers, oh, to that bed of flowers by the bridge, the bridge over Bamboo River." The song is felicitous because it suggests praise for the ladies of the household.

Gift robe

A wine cup appeared from under the blinds. "They say that once drink gets the better of a man, he can no longer keep a secret and courts disgrace. Is that your intention, my lady?" the Minamoto Adviser asked, declining it.[15] The Mistress of Staff picked up a gown and long dress and laid them, still sweetly redolent of their wearer, one on the other across his shoulders. "What could these be for?" he protested, placing them over his host's in preparation for leaving. Then he fled, despite his host's attempts to stop him, saying, "I came only for light refreshments, and now look how late it is!"[16]

The Lieutenant gathered that this Adviser's frequent visits to the house must have won him the allegiance of everyone there. More than ever dispirited and sorry for himself, he murmured bitterly,

> *"Every one of them seems to have given her heart to the blossoms here,*
> *and I wander all alone through the dark of a spring night."*[17]

His complaint roused someone within to reply,

> *"You will be welcome, even you, in your season: a blossoming plum*
> *offers far more than its scent to beguile the willing heart."*

The next morning the Minamoto Adviser wrote to his host, using many *kana* as though he meant others[18] to see it, too, "I was rather rowdy yesterday evening—I wonder what everyone thought of me." Along the edge he added,

> *"That measure of song I made bold to give you all on Bamboo River,*
> *did you gather from its depths the true bottom of my heart?"*

The Fujiwara Adviser took this message to the main house, where the ladies read it. "What lovely handwriting!" the Mistress of Staff exclaimed. "How could

15. The text has the Fujiwara Adviser (Tamakazura's son) singing "Bamboo River," but Kaoru seems to have sung it, too.

16. Kaoru pretends that he is taking part in the New Year's mumming and that he has simply stopped at the house for light refreshments (*mizumumaya*), as the mummers did in their rounds.

17. The "blossoms" are Kaoru. "The dark of a spring night" (*haru no yo no yami*) also alludes to Kaoru's personal scent because of *Kokinshū* 41 by Ōshikōchi no Mitsune: "The dark of a spring night is unavailing, for though the plum blossoms remain unseen, what could hide their perfume?"

18. Especially Tamakazura and her elder daughter.

anyone so young be so accomplished? He was just a boy when he lost His Grace, and Her Highness his mother did hardly anything for him, and yet he seems to do better than anyone else!" She reproved her daughters for writing so poorly themselves.

Her son replied in a manner that did indeed betray his youth, "Your 'light refreshments' yesterday evening was a rude surprise.

> You hastened away lest the night advance too far on Bamboo River:
> what, then, were those depths you raise to be gathered from your song?"

Actually, that visit was the first of many by the young gentleman to his fellow Adviser, as well as the beginning of a courtship. Everyone preferred him—the Lieutenant had been quite right. The Fujiwara Adviser in his youthful way was delighted to spend so much time day and night with his relation.

The third month came. Once the cherries were in bloom, falling petals clouded the sky,[19] and the leisure of blossom time left the Mistress of Staff with little enough to do; there could be nothing wrong even with sitting near the veranda.

Her daughters must then have been eighteen or nineteen. Both were delightful in person and looks. The elder was so vivid, stylish, and proud that one felt she would indeed be wasted on a commoner. She fairly exuded charm in her timely choice of a cherry blossom long dress and a kerria rose layering, and her deportment suggested dignity and intelligence as well. The younger sister, in light plum pink, her hair glinting with a beautiful sheen, had all the grace of spring willow fronds. Yet despite the tall, slender poise of her figure and her air of graver depth, many felt it was the elder who conveyed the most exquisite appeal.

The forehead line and sweep of their hair presented a lovely picture as they faced each other at Go, and the Fujiwara Adviser sat beside them to referee. Just then his elder brothers[20] peered in. "You do think a lot of him!" they cried. "You even have him refereeing your game!" Both knelt on one knee in a manly fashion, and the women in attendance straightened themselves as well as they could.

"I have been too busy at the palace and have fallen behind!" the Captain complained. "It is so disappointing!"

"How could you forget all about a poor Controller, when his duties leave him still less free to wait on his sisters!"

The young ladies stopped playing and put on a very pretty show of bashfulness.

"I so often wish that His Late Excellency were still here!" the Captain said, watching them with tears in his eyes. At twenty-seven or -eight he made an admirable figure of a man, and he longed only to give his sisters the future his father had wished for them.

The sisters sent someone to pick a branch from a particularly lovely cherry

---

19. An awkward allusion to *Kokinshū* 349 by Ariwara no Narihira: "O cherry blossoms, cover me with clouds of falling petals, that no one may know how age is coming for me."
20. The Left Palace Guards Captain and the Right Controller.

tree that grew among the others in the garden nearby. "There has never been one like it!" they exclaimed, toying with the spray.

"When you were young," the Captain said, "you quarreled over these flowers, each of you crying that they were hers, and His Late Excellency awarded them to the elder of you; at which our mother decided that the tree itself belonged to the younger. I myself did not make so loud a fuss about it, but it meant a great deal to me, too." He went on, "The thought that this cherry tree is old now brings to mind all the years that have passed, and the sorrow of having outlived so many people is almost too much for me." He lingered there longer than usual, amid laughter and tears. Now that he was married, he no longer came on leisurely visits, but he had stayed on this time for love of the flowers.

The Mistress of Staff, who still had all her looks, seemed much too young to have such grown-up sons. What made Retired Emperor Reizei so keen was above all his fond memory of the time when he had wanted her, and he insisted on seeking her daughter only to keep that old fancy alive. Her sons said of the prospect that their sister might go to him, "There is no reason at all to be eager. The timely choice seems always to be the one that gains broad approval. He is a great pleasure to behold, it is true, for there is no one like him, but one has the impression that he is no longer what he was. The harmonies of flutes and strings, the pleasures of blossoms or birdsong, charm the eye or the ear only in their time. What about the Heir Apparent?"

"I wonder," she replied. "A very powerful lady,[21] you see, has always claimed him so much as her own. I worry that the poor thing might just be laughed at if she went. If only His Excellency were still alive, he could have managed something for the time being, at least, whatever her future may be in the end." The thought saddened them all.

Once the Captain and the others were gone, the sisters returned to their game, wagering the cherry tree that each had always claimed. "Two out of three wins the flowers," they teased each other.

It was getting dark, and they finished their game near the veranda. The women rolled up the blinds, and each cheered on her own mistress. Just then, as so often, the Lieutenant turned up at the Fujiwara Adviser's room. Finding the brothers gone and no one about, he stole up to peer through the open door.

The foolish young man felt as though happy fortune had brought him a vision of living buddhas. Twilight mists somewhat veiled the scene, but his ardent gaze discerned nonetheless that the one in cherry blossom could only be she. She did indeed make a most lovely "token of blossoms soon to be gone,"[22] and he lamented more bitterly than ever that she would soon go to someone else. The casually disposed young women looked very pretty in the evening light.

The Right[23] won. "Where is the Koma victory music?"[24] excited voices cried.

---

21. Yūgiri's daughter.
22. *Kokinshū* 66: "I shall wear robes deeply dyed in cherry hues, in token of blossoms soon to be gone."
23. The younger sister.
24. The women are joking. "Koma" (Korean) *rajō* music was played to mark a victory by the "Right" in a contest.

"His Excellency awarded the Left a tree that leaned west, which means that he favored the Right[25]—that is where all the trouble began!" someone on the Right cheerfully declared.

The Lieutenant did not know what they were talking about, but still, it all sounded like fun, and he felt like joining in. He decided that that would be tactless of him, though, when they were all in such a casual mood, and instead he went away. After that he went about spying in case a similar chance should come again.

The sisters spent day and night contesting each other's claim to the blossoming tree, but one stormy evening they were horrified to see the petals flying in all directions. The loser said,

> "Ah, cherry blossoms! How one's heart trembles for them when stormy winds blow,
> although anyone can see they themselves care not at all."

Saishō added,

> "Such flowers as these blossom there before our eyes only to scatter:
> never mind that we have lost: I shall not long hold the grudge."

The sister on the Right:

> "It is the world's way, that the wind should scatter them, but how sad it is
> to see blossoms fade away even while still on the bough."

And her Taifu:

> "Come, wayward petals, who because it pleases you fall beside the lake,
> when you are foam on the waves, even so, do come my way!"

A page girl from the winning side went down into the garden, gathered lots of fallen petals from under the tree, and brought them to her mistress:

> "You may well scatter on the winds through the wide sky, O cherry blossoms,
> yet I shall gather you in and enjoy you as my own."

Then the Left's Nareki:

> "Are those sleeves of yours broad enough to overspread all cherry petals
> and retain their full beauty just for you and no one else?

You must be so stingy!"

---

25. The younger sister, being junior, lives on the right (west) side of the house from the standpoint of someone facing south.

The days and months continued to slip by, and the Mistress of Staff meanwhile worried more and more about the future. Every day brought a new message from His Eminence, whose Consort reassured her gravely in such terms as these: "Do you mean to keep your distance from me, then? His Eminence assumes that I am turning you against him, and he is not at all pleased about it. I am not joking, I assure you. Please, if you can, make your mind up soon."

This must be her destiny, then, the Mistress of Staff reflected. I hardly dare refuse such urgent pleas. She had an ample trousseau prepared for her daughter, and clothing and everything else needed made up for her women.

The Lieutenant thought that he would die when he heard the news, and his bitter reproaches upset his mother. "It is the foolish darkness in a parent's heart, you see, that emboldens me to touch upon so delicate a matter," she wrote urgently. "I implore you to understand me if you possibly can and even now to grant me the comfort I beg."

How very difficult all this is! the Mistress of Staff sighed; and she answered, "I myself remain uncertain what course I should choose, but alas, His Eminence's insistence is very troubling. Please be patient a little, if you are truly in earnest, for I believe that it may be possible to give you satisfaction after all, and in such a way as to displease no one." She presumably meant that she might suggest her younger daughter once her elder had gone.

It would be too presumptuous to marry off both at the same time! she reflected, and besides, his rank is still so low.[26] However, the young man showed no sign of wishing to shift his affection elsewhere. That glimpse of her had so impressed him that he only longed for another like it, and now he was plunged in misery upon finding all his hopes dashed.

When he reached the Fujiwara Adviser's room to voice his vain complaint, he found him reading a letter from his Minamoto colleague. The Adviser moved to hide it. I knew it! the Lieutenant thought and snatched it from him. The Adviser made no great effort to retain it, since his visitor might then only suspect the matter to be more serious than it was.

The Minamoto Adviser's letter conveyed merely general dissatisfaction with the way things had gone.

> "One by one, alas, the indifferent months and days pass serenely by,
>   leaving a vague bitterness to darken the close of spring."

How calm, how dignified some people are! The Lieutenant was annoyed. All that my ridiculous agitation earns me is dismissal or contempt. It was too much. He said nothing at all; instead he set off for the room occupied by Chūjō, the gentlewoman he normally saw, sighing meanwhile that he would get nowhere this time either. It enraged him to see the Minamoto Adviser go to show his answer to his mother, and he was overcome by youthful despair.

---

26. It would slight Reizei to do so, since the house would then have to divide its efforts between two marriages instead of giving all its attention to the one with him, and since Yūgiri's son is too junior to merit being paired openly with Reizei as a son-in-law.

His feelings were so violent that his intercessor found it all but impossible to carry on any banter with him; she hardly even ventured any replies. He brought up the evening he had watched the game of Go. "If only I could at least dream that dream again! Ah," he cried portentously, "what do I now have to live for? I shall not even be in touch with you this way much longer. How true it is that bitter experience yields fond memories!"

Chūjō was sympathetic, but she had nothing to say. It seemed unlikely that he would ever derive any pleasure from the sister who might console him. Yes, she noted without surprise, catching the elder exposed that evening had made him still madder for her. "My lady would despise you if she ever found out, and she would reject you even more firmly," she retorted. "I am all but fed up with you. Your attitude is extremely unfortunate."

"So be it, then. I fear nothing anymore; my life is over now anyway. I am sorry she lost, though. Could she not just have called me in? She would have done very well if only I could have signaled to her with my eyes.

Only tell me why I who am no one in life may not have the pride
to honor within myself the will not to be outdone?"

Chūjō smiled.

"You ask for too much! Victory or loss depends on the strength you have:
what could lead you to believe your own heart counts above all?"

she answered, and he took offense even at that.

"Then just have pity, leave me to do as I please, for such as I am,
it is for you to decide whether I live or I die."

They spent their night together between tears and laughter.

The next day was the first of the fourth month, and the Lieutenant's brothers went to the palace, but the Lieutenant himself stayed gloomily behind. This brought tears to his mother's eyes. "His Eminence must know about him," His Excellency said. "I doubted that if I raised the matter the Mistress of Staff would simply agree, and I regret having said nothing about it when I met her. She could not very well have refused if I had made myself clear on the subject in person."

Yet another complaint arrived from the Lieutenant:

"I spent all my spring gazing out at the blossoms, but after today
I may be condemned to roam a thick forest of sorrows."[27]

The Mistress of Staff's senior gentlewomen appealed to her one way or another on the poor suitor's behalf, and Chūjō in particular insisted, "My lady, I am

27. The poem plays on *shigeki* ("many" or "many trees") and *nageki* ("sorrows" or "rejected trees").

very much afraid that he means what he says when he talks of 'whether I live or I die.'"

Their mistress was sorry for him, too. She already knew how His Excellency and his wife felt on the subject and how angry the Lieutenant would be, and she was therefore prepared to offer something in return, but his attempt to thwart her elder daughter's marriage struck her as outrageous. Her husband had long ago decreed that this daughter should under no circumstances go to a commoner, however well-born, but it was not as though going to His Eminence assured her a brilliant future. Her head was full of these thoughts when her women brought her that note and enlarged on its author's plight. She replied,

"Now at last I know: you who feign such innocence with your skyward gaze
all the time had lost your heart hopelessly to the blossoms."

"The poor man! Why, she is making a joke of it!" Chūjō complained, but she did not bother to redo the poem.[28]

Their mistress's elder daughter went to His Eminence on the ninth. His Excellency of the Right gave her a carriage and a large escort. Despite her annoyance his wife did not want her correspondence with the Mistress of Staff now to lapse again over this affair, when it had been so scanty for years and had picked up only lately, and she accordingly contributed gifts[29] of fine women's clothing. "It was unkind of you not to let me know," she wrote, "because I was preoccupied with a son who seems strangely to have taken leave of his senses, and I never had a word about it." The hint she dropped was mild enough, but the Mistress of Staff felt a pang of sympathy for her.

His Excellency sent a letter, too. "It seemed to me that I should call on you, but there were certain penances, you see. I shall send my sons to wait upon you. Please do not hesitate to employ them." He dispatched the Minamoto Lieutenant and the Second of the Watch. The Mistress of Staff thanked him warmly for his kindness.

The Grand Counselor contributed carriages for the women. His wife, His Late Excellency's daughter Makibashira, should have been on close terms with both parties,[30] but in reality she was not. The Fujiwara Counselor[31] was the one who actually came and did everything, with the help of the Captain and the Right Controller. It was all too obviously a shame that His Late Excellency was no longer alive.

Through his usual representative the Lieutenant sent a new, desperate plea. "This is the end for me today, and I have given up all thought of living, but I am still sad. Just one word from you, that you pity me, might after all give me the courage to linger on a little longer," and so on. Chūjō delivered it. She found the two sisters talking very sadly to each other. They were used to being together day and night,

28. Instead of toning down Tamakazura's reply, she passed it on to the Lieutenant exactly as written.
29. *Kazukemono,* gifts to be distributed on the occasion of the wedding.
30. Tamakazura and Kōbai (the Grand Counselor) are half brother and sister, while Tamakazura is Makibashira's stepmother.
31. Higekuro's eldest son by his first wife, hence Makibashira's brother.

and it so upset them to occupy separate rooms, east and west, with a single door between them, that they were going back and forth to each other constantly; and now they knew they were soon really to be parted. The elder, whom her mother had dressed and adorned with great care, looked perfectly lovely. The sorrow with which she recalled all that her father had wanted for her may explain why she picked up the Lieutenant's note and read it. It was a mystery to her how he could say such extraordinary things when he still enjoyed the security of having both his parents, and she wondered whether he could really mean his talk of "the end." She immediately wrote in the margin:

> "To what sort of man would I then address myself, with that little word
> 'pity' people always use of this ever-changing world?[32]

If sorrow and disappointment are what you mean, I know something about them."

"That is what you are to give him," she said, and the woman passed her words straight to him.

He was amazed, especially considering the day, and his tears flowed on and on. His reproachful reply mentioned "They will talk of no one else,"[33] and so on.

> "In this life we live, death may all too easily come at any time,
> so that I may never hear that one word I ask of you.

I would gladly hasten to my grave, if only I knew that you would speak it over me."

What an awful answer I sent! She must have given it to him without redoing a word! She thoroughly regretted it and said no more.

Only the worthy were admitted to her company of page girls and grown-up gentlewomen, and the event entailed the same ceremony as if she had been going to the palace. She went first to call on the Consort, and her mother and the Consort talked. Night had fallen when she came to His Eminence. His Empress and his Consort were both older now, so that her captivating beauty could hardly fail to stir him, and she won his favor brilliantly. The ease and kindness of his manner, so like a commoner's,[34] were indeed as pleasant as anyone could wish. He had hoped that the Mistress of Staff might wait on him a little while as well, but to his chagrin she quickly and discreetly slipped away.

The Minamoto Adviser stood just as high in favor as the Shining Genji had done long ago, and His Eminence desired his presence day and night. The young gentleman had good relations with all His Eminence's ladies. He, too, welcomed the new arrival warmly, although it occurred to him to wonder secretly what His Eminence might make of these attentions.

32. In his note the Lieutenant asked her to "feel *aware* for me," and this *aware* corresponds to the "pity" that desperate lovers beg from their heartless ladies in many literatures. However, *aware* (as in *mono no aware*) is also the "pity of things," an expression associated with thoughts of evanescence.

33. "They will blame no one but you." *Kokinshū* 603, by Kiyowara no Fukayabu: "They will talk of no one else if I die for love, however you may wish to claim that all things in this world pass."

34. In retirement he is no longer a prisoner of ceremony and protocol, and he can therefore behave like an ordinary householder.

One quiet evening at twilight he and the Fujiwara Adviser were out for a stroll together when they sat on mossy stones at the water's edge, gazing off toward a five-needled pine, entwined by beautifully blossoming wisteria, that stood near the new arrival's dwelling. The Minamoto Adviser's talk conveyed a veiled bitterness.

> *"If it had been mine to reach out my hand to you, wisteria flowers,*
> *would I look on from afar while your hues surpass the pine's?"*[35]

he said, gazing up at the flowers.

His friend found his figure touchingly pathetic, and he hinted that this outcome was not one he had encouraged:

> *"Your* murasaki *is a hue I myself share, wisteria flowers,*
> *and yet you never embraced what I would have wished for you."*[36]

Being an earnest young man, he felt extremely sorry for his friend. For the Minamoto Adviser the blow was not really that severe, but he was certainly disappointed.

Meanwhile the Lieutenant was frantic to the point of seriously considering drastic action. The suitors now shifted their aspiration to the younger daughter. The Mistress of Staff let the Lieutenant's mother know that in view of the vehemence with which she had expressed herself on the subject, her son might well receive favorable consideration, but the young man himself was no longer calling. He and all his brothers had often haunted His Eminence's palace, but he hardly went there anymore after the new arrival came, and on the rare occasions when he showed his face there in the privy chamber, he soon fled in obvious distress.

His Majesty was surprised that the elder daughter should have gone into service elsewhere, despite His Late Excellency's express wishes, and he therefore summoned the Captain to demand an explanation.

"He is not pleased," the Captain told the Mistress of Staff. "I knew that this would happen. I *told* you that people would have private reservations, but no, you had another idea, and your decision to proceed made it impossible for me to question it further, and considering what His Majesty now has to say on the matter, I am very much afraid that we will both suffer for it." He was furious.

"Now, now," his mother replied. "I can assure you that I decided nothing in haste, but His Eminence insisted so pathetically, you see, and I thought that it might be risky for her to appear at the palace without assistance. That is why I made up my mind in favor of His Eminence's now-easier circumstances. I am afraid that I am in a very difficult position, because not one of you clearly warned me of the consequences, and now even His Excellency of the Right is letting it be known that he considers me to have acted wrongly. It is all just her destiny, I suppose." She spoke calmly and without agitation.

---

35. The wisteria is the elder daughter and the pine Reizei.
36. "You and I, both Fujiwaras, are also brother and sister. . . ." *Murasaki*, purple, is the color of romantic or fraternal love and also the color of the Fujiwara clan. (*Fuji* means "wisteria.")

"No eye can see the destiny her past karma gives her, whatever it may be, and now that His Majesty is talking this way, how can I blandly submit to him that her fate meant her for someone else? Very well, you felt apprehensive about his Empress, but what, then, do you have to say about His Eminence's? For all I know, she may already have agreed to offer her 'assistance,' or whatever you prefer to call it, but I cannot imagine that such feelings go very far. Well, we shall have to wait and see. *Other* young ladies go to court, do they not, Empress or no Empress? Devoted service to our Sovereign is what makes life worthwhile; *that* is what has always been a genuine pleasure. As for His Eminence's Consort, once the slightest misstep offends her, everyone will say that she should never have gone to him in the first place."

With both brothers saying the same thing, the Mistress of Staff felt very uncomfortable indeed, but His Eminence nonetheless treasured her daughter more and more as time went by.

In the seventh month she conceived. It is certainly no surprise that her indisposition prompted many gentlemen to send her expressions of sympathy. How could they possibly have remained indifferent to the plight of so lovely a lady? His Eminence called day and night for music, for which he had the Minamoto Adviser join him, and the Adviser therefore heard her play. To play the *wagon* His Eminence regularly summoned also the Chūjō to whose accompaniment the Adviser had once sung "The Plum Tree Branch." The Adviser found all of this distinctly troubling.

The New Year came, and with it the mumming. Many of the privy gentlemen then were very accomplished. His Majesty selected the best and named the Minamoto Adviser one of the song leaders of the Right. The Chamberlain Lieutenant was among the musicians. They all set out from the palace to appear before His Eminence under a brilliant, unclouded fourteenth-night moon. The Consort and the new Haven each had her screened-off space, and all the senior nobles and Princes came. There seemed to be no one in all the world but the late Chancellor's sons and those of the Minister of the Right who stood out in polish and looks. His Eminence's presence, as everyone agreed, commanded greater awe than any known at the palace, and people minded themselves very carefully indeed. The most agitated among them was the Lieutenant, since he felt *her* eyes on him. The tedious and unsightly white cotton flowers they all wore in their headdresses looked better on some than on others, and he was certainly commendable in looks and voice. When the dance took them to the foot of the stairway to perform "Bamboo River," he nearly forgot the steps, and his eyes filled with tears as he recalled the same moment the year before. Then they moved on to appear before the Empress, and His Eminence followed them to watch. The moon rose high as the night wore on, and it shone untrammeled, brighter than day, while he wondered with what eyes *she* might have watched him. He felt drunk, as though treading on air, and the way they called on him alone, again and again, to accept the wine cup covered him with embarrassment.

They roamed hither and thither all night long, and the exhausted Minamoto Adviser had just lain down at last when a call came from His Eminence. "Bother!" he grumbled as he went. "I just wanted to rest!"

His Eminence asked how the mumming had gone at the palace. "Past song leaders have generally been men who are already getting on. You did very well to be chosen!" he said. He seemed quite delighted. Then he set off for the Haven's rooms, humming "Ten Thousand Springs."[37] The Adviser went with him. Many people from the women's homes were there to see the mumming, and the atmosphere was livelier and more stylish than usual.

The Adviser sat awhile by the door onto a bridgeway, talking to a gentle-woman whose voice he knew. "The moon has been awfully bright all night," he re-marked, "but I doubt that the way the Chamberlain Lieutenant's face shone in its light had much to do with feeling picked out by the moon. That is not the way he looked at the palace."

Some of the listening women pitied the poor fellow. "No doubt the darkness is unavailing,[38] but we all decided that the moonlight sets you off beautifully," one said coyly; and another, from inside the door:

> *"Do you remember that night, the one when you sang of Bamboo River?*
> *Not that any special passage really returns to mind."*[39]

It was hardly a poem at all, but he knew by the tears that sprang again to his eyes how deeply he had been affected.

> *"Ever flowing on, Bamboo River gave me hopes then dashed all too soon,*
> *whence I learned the lesson of the treachery of life,"*

he replied.

The women were enchanted by his melancholy air. Actually, he was not one to grieve as fully as another might, but there was still something very touching about him.

"Alas, I have said too much!" As he rose to go, he received an invitation to "please come this way," and with some embarrassment he did so.[40]

"Once," His Eminence remarked, "His Grace of Rokujō had his ladies make music for him on the morning after the mumming,[41] and according to His Excellency of the Right it was lovely. One can hardly imagine anyone in our own time really carrying on after him. There were so many fine musicians then, even among the women around him, that the least concert must have been a delight." This example inspired him to have the instruments tuned. The *sō no koto* went to the Haven and the *biwa* to the Adviser, while His Eminence himself took the *wagon*. They played "This Gentle-man" and so on. The Haven's playing was still immature in some ways, but still, he had

---

37. *Bansuraku,* the refrain of a song always sung during the mumming.
38. Another allusion to *Kokinshū* 41: "The dark of a spring night is unavailing, for though the plum blossoms remain unseen, what could hide their perfume?"
39. The speaker means the singing of "Bamboo River" at the mumming a year ago, when Kaoru, too, was beginning to court Tamakazura's elder daughter. "Passage" (*fushi*) conveys a conventional play on "passage [of music]" or "moment [of time]" and "joint [of bamboo]."
40. He has received an invitation to join Reizei.
41. The event is mentioned briefly at the end of "The Warbler's First Song."

taught her successfully. She had a nicely fresh touch and did very well both at accompaniments and at instrumental pieces. One gathered that there was never any need to worry about her being a little slow. The Adviser of course knew very well that she was likely to be beautiful. There were many similar moments, but he managed a natural ease with her, was never tempted to misbehave, and never presumed on their closeness to express any complaint. Now and again, however, he lightly conveyed his disappointment. I have no idea what she thought about it.

The fiftieth-day celebration of a birth

A Princess was born in the fourth month. The event was not strikingly brilliant, but His Excellency of the Right and everyone else joined in the birth celebrations, in deference to His Eminence's feelings. The Mistress of Staff loved to fondle the baby and hold her,[42] but His Eminence often reminded her that he wanted his daughter brought to him, and on the newborn's fiftieth day she complied. She was exceptionally attractive, and His Eminence, who became extremely attached to her despite already having his First Princess, spent all his time at her mother's. The Consort's women complained to each other that they could have done very well without *that*.

The Haven and the Consort were not at all inclined to behave pettishly toward each other, but unpleasant incidents that occurred between their women confirmed the fears wisely voiced by the Counselor, the Haven's elder brother. Where will these quarrels end? the Mistress of Staff wondered. Will she be held up to shame and ridicule? She means a great deal to His Eminence, but it will be a disaster if the ladies who have already served him so long turn against her. Meanwhile she received reports that His Majesty was thoroughly annoyed and making no secret of it, and this so upset her that she decided to send her younger daughter to court and to cede her her own title of Mistress of Staff. Her resignation was by no means easy for an Emperor to accept, but she declared that it was a step she had long hoped in vain to take, cited His Late Excellency's wishes, and put forward such precedents, though old ones by now, that she obtained what she wished. One gathered that she had previously encountered repeated refusals only because her younger daughter's destiny required them.

If only palace life smiles on her! she thought, her thoughts turning unhappily at the same time to the Lieutenant and his mother's entreaties. I did give her to understand that I would consider him favorably—what *will* she think of me?

42. The child had been born at Tamakazura's house.

She approached His Excellency on the subject through her son the Controller, putting the best face on it that she could. "This, then, is what I have been hearing from His Majesty," she said, "and it upsets me very much, you know, to imagine some people in the world perhaps accusing me of having aimed too high for my daughter."

"I quite understand His Majesty's expressions of displeasure," His Excellency replied. "It would be unfortunate if she did not fulfill her obligation to serve him, and I believe that you should resolve to have her do so immediately."

Once more she sought an Empress's goodwill before sending off a daughter. They could never even consider dismissing her if only His Late Excellency were still alive! she said to herself. His Majesty was not particularly pleased, since he had heard that the elder sister was famed for her beauty, but this one, too, had a great deal to commend her, and she served him with distinction.

The former Mistress of Staff was now resolved to enter religion, but she put off doing so when her sons pointed out that she would never have peace in her prayers as long as she remained so concerned about her daughters. They urged her first to see both of them through to a more settled life, after which she could give herself fully and wholeheartedly to her devotions. Now and again she visited the palace discreetly. However, she refrained from calling on His Eminence even when she might well have done so, for his importunities had never ceased. She thought back to how with feigned innocence she had allowed a marriage condemned by everyone else in order to make up after all for having once dared to disappoint him, and she reflected that if any such foolishness on *her* part were now to be noised abroad, however lightly it might be meant, the result for her would be complete disgrace; and yet she could reveal nothing of this to her daughter, who therefore assumed resentfully that despite all she had meant to her father, her mother had always favored her sister, as in their rivalry over the cherry tree, and that she simply dismissed her. "Look how she has just abandoned you to an old man like me!" His Eminence would say. "Not that I am surprised she thinks so little of me." He felt more and more sorry for her.

A few years later she gave His Eminence a son, something that none of his many other women had ever managed to do, and the world was startled by this evidence of her remarkable destiny. His Eminence was even more deeply astonished, and he loved his little boy very much. What an event this would be if I had not already abdicated! he thought, lamenting that nothing in life had the old savor anymore. His First Princess had always been his greatest treasure, but these enchanting new arrivals struck him as all but miraculous, and his Consort came to feel that things simply could not go on this way. Unfortunate, spiteful incidents began to occur, inevitably straining relations between the two ladies. When women of no importance come into conflict, then, too, bystanders as a rule favor the one with the earlier claim, and staff high and low throughout His Eminence's palace therefore took the part of the lady who had reigned there so long, and condemned the newcomer for the tiniest lapse.

"We told you so!" her brothers said, ever more accusingly. "Were we wrong?"

"But so many people lead quiet, respectable lives, and nothing like that ever happens to *them!*" their unhappy mother replied. "No, I should never have sent her into such service unless she could aspire there to the greatest good fortune of all."[43]

Those who had courted her elder daughter rose nicely in rank and office, and a good many of them would have done her credit enough. One, the Minamoto Adviser, once seemingly so slight and young, was now a Consultant Captain, and people praised him until one wearied of hearing "His suave perfume, ah, his fragrance!" Indeed, he had acquired so noble a dignity that one gathers the greatest Princes and Ministers would approach him on behalf of their daughters, although he ignored them. The former Mistress of Staff was moved to observe, "Years ago he seemed such a young man, and so insubstantial, but look how fine he is now!"

The former Lieutenant was now well regarded as a Third Rank Captain. "And he is handsome, too!" her officious women cried, adding in low voices, "Better at any rate than that oh-so-difficult gentleman . . ." She was in a sad plight. The Captain in question still felt all the ardor of his first love, and while bitterness and sorrow had led him to accept the daughter of His Excellency of the Left, he cared very little about her; instead he was constantly scribbling or humming "Hitachi sash far down the road . . ."[44] until one wondered what on earth he meant by it.

All the unpleasantness that the Haven had to suffer meant that she spent more and more time at home, and her mother lamented an outcome so different from the one she had imagined. In contrast, the younger daughter was getting on admirably at the palace, where she was respected by the world at large and pleasingly favored by His Majesty.

His Excellency of the Right took over the Left[45] after that Minister's death, and the Fujiwara Grand Counselor[46] assumed the Right, with a concurrent appointment as Left Commander. Their juniors all rose in turn. The Fragrant Captain became a Counselor and the Third Rank Captain a Consultant. No one seemed to matter then but those two gentlemen's sons.[47]

The new Counselor called on the former Mistress of Staff to express his pleasure and made his obeisance from the garden before her residence. She then received him in person.[48] "It is very good of you not to shun a gate by now so sadly overgrown," she said, "and your kindness brings straight to mind the gentleman whose loss we still mourn." Her voice had distinction, charm, and perfect immediacy of presence. She never ages! he thought. That is why His Eminence is still angry about her. He could make trouble over her at any time.

"This success does not mean that much to me personally," he answered, "but I wanted to come and present myself to you.[49] I am sure that when you spoke of my

<hr />

43. To bear an imperial heir.

44. "If only I could spend a moment with her!" The words begin *Kokin rokujō* 3360: "Hitachi sash far down the road to the East—might I just see her long enough to voice my complaint!"

45. Yūgiri. This appointment is problematical because in the subsequent chapters most manuscripts (hence this translation) still have him as Minister of the Right.

46. Kōbai.

47. Yūgiri's and Tō no Chūjō's.

48. She spoke to him herself, through blinds.

49. As a Counselor he now holds the third rank, junior grade, rather than the fourth rank he held before. This critical promotion makes him a senior noble.

not shunning your gate, you meant only to remind me how seldom I actually come."

"I should refrain from burdening you with my troubles, because I am an old woman, and today is not the day for that, but your visits here are indeed rare, and some things, you know, unless said face-to-face . . . I am so upset! I always thought that my daughter who serves His Eminence could talk to his Consort when things became too much for her, or that his Empress would not really mind her coming to *her*, whereas in fact both have turned against her. It is too hard! She has her little Prince and Princess, but life there is so difficult now that she has come home at my invitation at least to regain some peace of mind, and look at all the talk *that* has started! I understand that His Eminence disapproves as well. Please tell him something of how I feel, if you can find the moment to do so. I sent her to him because I thought that I could count on them both, and I believed the assurances they both gave me, but it has all turned out so badly that I hate myself for being so childishly credulous." He gathered that she was weeping.

"You should not allow the matter to upset you so," he replied discouragingly. "It has always been well understood that joining such company presents certain risks. His Eminence's ladies may seem willing to live and let live, now that His Eminence is in quiet retirement and no longer commands attention for what he does, but each must feel at heart the same need to be preferred. I expect that the Consort and the Empress both easily take as affronts to their dignity things to which no one else would object at all. Did you really believe when you originally made your decision that no friction of this kind would ever arise? You should simply ignore it all and let it pass. I am afraid that it is not something a man can bring up with His Eminence."

"I had looked forward to our next talk so that I might confide my sorrows to you, but alas"—she smiled—"you have given me little hope."

Her youth and innocence struck him far more than all her earnestly maternal concern. The Haven must be like that, too, he reflected, and I suppose what attracts me to the elder daughter in Uji is that she has this wonderful quality as well. The Mistress of Staff,[50] too, was then at home from the palace, and the two sisters made a lovely presence, installed there each on her own side of the main house. The awed Counselor knew that behind their blinds they were wholly at leisure, and he minded himself so perfectly that their mother wished he were her son-in-law.

His Excellency of the Right's[51] residence stood immediately to the east, and his sons and the other attendants for the celebratory banquet all gathered there. As guest of honor he had invited His Highness of War,[52] remembering how His Highness had been to the Minister of the Left's New Year archery banquet, to the wrestling meet,[53] and so on; but His Highness did not come. His Excellency was

50. Tamakazura's younger daughter.
51. Kōbai, although only for the rest of this chapter.
52. Niou.
53. A banquet (*noriyumi no kaeri aruji*) given by the Commander of the winning side after the regular New Year archery contest (*noriyumi*), held on the eighteenth of the first month; and a wrestling meet (*sumai no sechi*), which also involved a banquet, held in the seventh month. Niou's attendance at these events is not mentioned elsewhere.

particularly eager to win His Highness's favor on behalf of the daughters of whom he thought so highly, but for some reason His Highness did not respond. The Minamoto Counselor meanwhile had grown into a gentleman so fine and so well endowed with every quality that His Excellency's wife now cast her eye upon him.

The commotion next door, the noise of carriages coming and going, and the escorts' cries turned the former Mistress of Staff's thoughts back to old memories, and there in her residence she yielded to sorrowful dreaming. "His Excellency began calling on her almost as soon as His Late Highness was gone," she said, "and I gather that many people dismissed her then as all too easy, but their affection lasted, and by now they on the contrary make a very fine couple. One never knows how things will turn out. Which of them has really done better, she or my elder daughter?"

The Consultant Captain, His Excellency of the Left's son, came to call the evening of the day after the banquet. The thought that the Haven was there made him especially eager. "It means nothing to me that His Majesty has deigned to acknowledge my merit," he said, "for I suffer more with each passing year from the sorrow of having lost what I so desired." The way he dried his tears had something self-conscious about it. At twenty-seven or -eight he had all a fine young gentleman's glow and brilliant good looks.

"Look at him, the way he thinks the world is his!" the former Mistress of Staff exclaimed and burst into tears. "Why, rank and office mean nothing to *him*! If only His Late Excellency were alive, my sons, too, could indulge in these frivolous cares!" She resented it that the Intendant of the Right Watch and the Right Grand Controller were still only "qualified" for Consultant. The one earlier called the Adviser seems by then to have become the Secretary Captain. The appointment was not out of keeping with his age, but his mother lamented that he was falling behind. The Consultant Captain kept up his smooth talk.

45

The Maiden of the Bridge

Hashihime ("the Maiden of the Bridge") is a shadowy figure from early Japanese folkore. She appears to be a jealous goddess of bridges, and she has a close poetic association with the bridge over the Uji River at Uji, south of Kyoto. This chapter, which is set at Uji, introduces two sisters who live there. It is entitled "Hashihime" because Kaoru uses the word in a poem to the elder, Ōigimi:

"What drops wet these sleeves, when the river boatman's oar, skimming the shallows, sounds out the most secret heart of the Maiden of the Bridge!"

RELATIONSHIP TO EARLIER CHAPTERS

"The Maiden of the Bridge" begins by describing the earlier life of the Eighth Prince (Hachi no Miya). Kaoru enters when he is already a Consultant Captain. After the passage of some time the story resumes late in the autumn, apparently when Kaoru is twenty-two. The main story seems to begin where "The Perfumed Prince" leaves off, and ends before the end of "Bamboo River."

PERSONS

The Consultant Captain, age 20 to 22 (Kaoru)

His Highness, the Eighth Prince (Hachi no Miya)

His wife

His older daughter, 22 to 24 (Ōigimi)

His younger daughter, 20 to 22 (Naka no Kimi)

The Adept (Uji no Ajari)

His Eminence Reizei, 49 to 51

The watchman at Uji

Ben, a gentlewoman of Hachi no Miya's daughters, nearly 60

The Third Prince, His Highness of War, 21 to 23 (Niou)

Her Cloistered Highness, Kaoru's mother, early to mid-40s (Onna San no Miya)

There was in those days an aged Prince who no longer mattered to the world. Of extremely distinguished birth on his mother's side as well, he had seemed destined for great things, but then times changed, and disgrace brought him a downfall so thorough that for one reason and another everyone who upheld his interests renounced the world, leaving him completely alone in both public and private. His wife, a former Minister's daughter, suffered sadly from this outcome, the many and extremely painful circumstances of which little resembled what she remembered her parents wishing for her; but the unequaled affection she shared with her husband comforted her in her sorrow, for they were as devoted to each other as a couple can be.

It troubled them more and more over the years to have no children, and His Highness often longed desperately for a pretty child to relieve the loneliness and tedium of their lives until, wonder of wonders, a beautiful little girl was born. They loved and cherished her exceedingly, and meanwhile it soon became clear that the lady was expecting again. They rather hoped for a boy this time, but it was a girl as before. The birth itself went well, but she became gravely ill afterward and died. His Highness was distraught.

Life has tried me sorely and often, he reflected, but I loved her too well to leave it, and her looks and ways bound me to it after all. Things will be even worse now that I am alone! What a spectacle I shall make, constrained as I am,[1] bringing up my daughters all by myself! He longed to act on his deepest desire,[2] but there was no one else to look after them. His agonizing hesitations continued until in time both grew up into perfectly lovely girls who were an unfailing comfort to him after all.

The women who served the last born whispered of her, "Look what misfortune she brought!" and gave her only halfhearted attention. However, her mother in her final moments, when no longer aware of her surroundings, had still been sufficiently concerned about her to repeat again and again to His Highness, "Please be

1. As a Prince, he cannot decently do many things natural to a lesser man.
2. To leave the world.

good to her, in memory of me!" and despite bitterness that their tie from past lives had failed, the thought that his loss was destiny and that she had to the last spoken tenderly of their new child inspired him to treat the girl with great affection. She was extremely pretty, indeed, alarmingly so. The elder, with her quiet poise, was wonderfully distinguished in looks and manner, but the younger displayed a nobler charm, and he therefore treasured them both. Still, there were many things that he could not do for them, and loneliness pervaded his residence more and more as the years went by. This was too much for the people in his service, who felt bereft of hope, and one by one they all drifted away. In the confusion His Highness had never managed to find his new daughter a reliable nurse, and the one chosen abandoned her charge with the nonchalance typical of her class, leaving His Highness to look after everything on his own.

His Highness's residence was large and handsome nonetheless, and the lake and knolls of the park, although now sadly neglected, remained as they had always been. He spent his days gazing vacantly out at the scenery they offered. There was no one to tidy it all up because he no longer had any capable retainers. Weeds grew everywhere, thick and green, and green ferns[3] along the eaves seemed to claim his dwelling as their own. The colors and scents of each season's leaves and flowers consoled him many a time simply because she, too, had once enjoyed them, but his growing loneliness and sense of helplessness prompted him to adorn his chapel and spend day and night there at his devotions. It was a bitter disappointment still to be detained by such ties, and the thought of thus being prevented from acting on his desire decided him ever more firmly that nothing obliged him any longer to behave like other people; no, the world was no concern of his. A thoroughgoing hermit at heart, he never again after his wife's death shared even casually the more common-place feelings.

"But Your Highness, why must you do this?" people would say. "You seemed to grieve more deeply than anyone has ever done when my lady died, but what is the point of going on and on that way? You might surely manage still to live as others do;[4] it would do this miserably neglected place a world of good!" But he ignored every one of the many attempts made through his relations to change his mind.

Between periods of prayer he spent his time with his daughters, and since they were growing up now, he taught them music and games like Go and character guessing. To his eye the elder showed greater thoughtfulness and depth, while the younger, more artlessly winning, had a delightfully bashful appeal. Each was different in her way.

One fine spring day the waterbirds were all chattering away, wing to wing, on the lake—a sight he seldom deigned to notice—and while he watched, he envied them for never leaving their mates. Meanwhile he gave his daughters their music lesson. They were so small and sweet, and the way they each played was so touchingly pretty that tears began to come.

3. *Shinobu*, a fern that grows readily in neglected bark or thatch roofs. As a verb, *shinobu* also means "to dwell in memory on the past," and the wordplay is intended here.
4. Marry again.

"Now that waterbird has left her mate forsaken and gone far away,
how can her nestlings linger in this cruel, shifting world?[5]

It is so sad!" he said, wiping his eyes. He was a very handsome Prince. Gaunt from his years of pious devotion, he only looked the nobler for it, and in his dress cloak, negligently worn and rumpled from tending his daughters, he made an imposing figure.

His elder softly drew the inkstone to her and traced words on it, as though for casual practice. "Write on this," he said, and gave her some paper. "They say that one should never write on an inkstone."

Embarrassed, she wrote,

"I only wonder how this nestling can have grown, and such reflections
tell this little waterbird her uncertain destiny."

It was not very good, but under the circumstances it was extremely affecting. Her hand showed promise, even if she did not yet connect her letters very well.

"Now *you* write something!" His Highness said to the younger, who was more of a child and so took a good deal longer about it.

"Why, without those wings you spread wide to shelter me, tenderly weeping,
I would have remained behind ever unhatched in the nest."

How could he not have looked with pity on such lovable daughters when their clothes were all rumpled and limp and they spent their lonely days with nothing to do because they had no one else to mind them? Sutra text in one hand, he now chanted the scriptures and now sang them their solfège.[6] The elder had a *biwa* and the younger a *sō no koto*, and they were so used to playing together that they did not sound bad at all; in fact, they did very nicely.

He had never acquired much learning because he had lost his father the Emperor and his mother the Consort at an early age and so had been deprived of any real support. How could he possibly have been prepared for life in this world? Even for someone so exalted, he was nobly innocent to an astonishing degree, like a woman. The treasures of past generations and his inheritance from his grandfather the Minister all vanished without a trace, although he had assumed that they would somehow last forever, leaving him nothing but a lot of ostentatiously imposing household furnishings. No one came to call, no one offered him assistance. With little else to do, he summoned first-class musicians from the Office of Music and so on and became very good indeed at that sort of thing, having already devoted his youth to similarly trifling amusements.

His Highness was His Grace Genji's younger brother. In the days when His

---

5. This poem plays on the syllables *mizutori no kari no ko* ("the children of the goose, the waterbird") and *kari no kono yo* ("this fleeting world").
6. *Sōga.* Here, singing out the notes of the score the girls are to play.

The weir at Uji

Eminence Reizei was Heir Apparent, His Eminence Suzaku's mother[7] had plotted to have the imperial dignity pass to *him* instead, but the turmoil she caused by championing him while in power unfortunately led to the other side severing all relations with him, and since after that the world belonged entirely to His Grace's descendants, he had been unable to appear in society at all. He had therefore become a sort of holy man years ago and given up any other hope.

Meanwhile his residence burned down. This on top of everything else was a crushing blow, and since he really had nowhere else to go, he moved to an attractive villa he owned at Uji. The immediate prospect of leaving upset him, despite his thoughts of renunciation. The place was near the weir, and the loud noise of the river ill suited his longing for peace, but there was nothing else to do. Blossoms, autumn leaves, and the flowing river: these were his solace in the gloomy reverie that now more than ever was his only refuge. Even after vanishing into this wilderness, he constantly missed the lady he had lost.

> "My old companion and the house where I once lived both have turned to smoke;
> why is it that only I linger on just as before?"

So it was that he burned on with nothing left to live for.

Fewer and fewer people came to visit this dwelling of his across the intervening range on range of hills. Only rare, uncouth peasants or mountain rustics saw to his needs. For him the morning fog on the hills never lifted, day or night.[8]

There lived meanwhile among the Uji hills an Adept and something of a holy man, deeply learned and possessed of no light reputation in the world at large, who yet remained in retreat and seldom went to serve at court. His Highness, who lived nearby in dismal solitude, impressed him with his good works and his study of the scriptures, and he therefore called often at His Highness's house, where he enlarged on the profound meaning of all that His Highness had learned through the years, until he convinced His Highness more thoroughly than ever that this fleeting world is dross. "My heart aspires to the lotus throne and would inhabit the clear lake of

---

7. The Kokiden Consort of the early chapters.

8. "Range on range of hills" just above and "morning fog on the hills" are from *Kokin rokujō* 2841 and *Kokinshū* 935, respectively. Fog is indeed common at Uji.

Paradise, but you see," His Highness confessed, "I worry too much about the fate of my young daughters after I have left them; I cannot possibly assume that new guise."

This Adept served His Eminence Reizei intimately, teaching him the scriptures and so on. Once, when he was in the City and His Eminence was going over worthy texts as usual and questioning him on them, he happened to remark, "His Highness the Eighth Prince knows a great deal, and he has acquired a profound understanding of the Inner Teaching.[9] I suppose that he must have been born to it because of his karma. He is so completely devoted to his practice that he has the appearance of a true holy man."

"Does he not wear the habit yet?" His Eminence inquired. "My young people call him the holy layman, or something like that. It is rather sad."

The Consultant Captain was in attendance, too, and he took note of what he had heard. *I know very well how disappointing this world is,* he told himself, *but I do not practice to an extent that anyone might actually notice, and so far in this life I have just wasted my time.* He wondered about the state of mind of someone who had become a holy man while still a layman.

"He seems to have aspired for a long time to leave the world," the Adept went on, "but a trifling matter caused him to hesitate, and by now he laments that it is impossible for him to give up his beloved daughters."

Monk though he was, the Adept loved music. "Yes, Your Eminence, when his daughters play together against the noise of the rushing river, one cannot help thinking of Paradise," he remarked in somewhat old-fashioned praise.

His Eminence smiled. "How nice! You would hardly think that they knew much of such worldly pursuits after growing up with a holy man. His reluctance to abandon them seems to have put him in a difficult position—I wonder whether he might be willing to give them to *me,* if I survive him for any length of time." His Eminence was his father's tenth child. He definitely wanted them, for he remembered how His Eminence Suzaku had entrusted Her Cloistered Highness to His Grace of Rokujō, and it occurred to him that they might relieve the tedium of his life.

What caught the Captain's interest, on the other hand, was this Prince's spirit of quiet devotion. He very much wanted to meet him, and he discussed the matter with the Adept before the Adept began his journey back. "Please sound him out discreetly so that I may go and study with him," he said. "My mind is made up to it."

His Eminence sent off a messenger to say, "Having learned indirectly of the sad circumstances under which you are living . . ." and so on, together with the poem

"My heart scorns the world and goes to you in your hills—are you then the one
who conceals yourself from me yonder beyond eightfold clouds?"

The Adept let the messenger reach His Highness first, and His Highness received the man with surprise and delight. Practically nobody ever came to him here

9. Buddhism as distinguished from the "Outer Teaching" of Confucianism.

below these hills, even from anyone far less exalted, and he entertained his guest with such delicacies as the place afforded. He replied,

> "It is not, alas, that I am lost forever in enlightenment;
> I only deplore this world from here in the Uji hills."[10]

To His Eminence's regret, his modesty about his accomplishment as a holy man betrayed a lingering bitterness against the world.

The Adept described the Captain's apparently profound religious aspiration. "He told me that he has longed since youth to grasp the meaning of the scriptures," he explained, "but that, like it or not, he has had to accept life in the world and to remain caught up day and night in concerns public and private. He says, 'It is not that someone like myself, since after all I hardly matter, need really be that shy of shutting himself away to study the scriptures or of showing an interest in renouncing the world, but as things are, I cannot help being neglectful and distracted, and the news of your thoroughly admirable example has so inspired me that I wish to learn from you.' That is what he said, Your Highness, and very earnestly, too."

"The insight that the world is dross, hence the first thoughts of hatred for it, generally follows from personal unhappiness, for it is at such times that one rejects the world and conceives the aspiration to higher things; and it is remarkable to hear of so fortunate a young man, who presumably lacks nothing that he might desire, being so preoccupied by the life to come. I suppose that I myself was destined to take this path, since it was as though the Buddha himself urged me to shun the world, and in due course I had my wish for peace and quiet. Still, I doubt that I have much time left now, and considering how approximate my mode of life really is and how little likely I am ever fully to understand the past or the future, he will be a friend in the Teaching before whom I should properly feel deficient." He talked on like this for some time, and after an exchange of letters the young man himself arrived.

It was a sadder place than he had been led to imagine, and considering who His Highness was, everything about his life there suggested the drastic simplicity of the grass hut built to last little more than a day. There are other quiet mountain villages with an appeal all their own, but here amid the roar of waters and the clamor of waves one seemed unlikely ever to forget one's cares or, at night amid the wind's dreary moan, to dream a consoling dream.

Surroundings like these undoubtedly stir thoughts of renunciation in His Highness, the Captain reflected, inclined as he is to seek a holy life, but how must they affect his daughters? He easily imagined them as having few of the common feminine graces. Only a sliding panel separated the chapel from what he took to be their room. A man given to gallantry would have approached them all aquiver to discover what they were like, for there *was* something about them that made one want to know more; but the Captain thought better of it, since any venture of the

---

10. The main wordplay in this poem recurs in the succeeding chapters: *yo o uji* ("find the world hateful") leads into *ujiyama* ("the Uji hills"). Its canonical source is the famous but practically untranslatable *Kokinshū* 983, by Kisen Hōshi: "My hut is southeast of the City: I live with the deer in the Uji hills, where, they say, I reject the world."

"Grass hut"

kind would frustrate the wish to renounce all such things that had first led him to seek out His Highness among these hills. Under the circumstances it might be out of place for him to indulge in suggestive pleasantries. He instead plied His Highness with questions touching on His Highness's melancholy plight, and he returned to visit him again and again because, layman or not, His Highness had a deep understanding gained from practice among these hills, and he enlightened the Captain wonderfully on the scriptures, just as the Captain had hoped that he would.

There are many saintly men and many learned monks in this world, but it seemed to the Captain that the high and mighty prelate, with his lofty title and his air of impatience with trifles, was too forbidding to question on the deep meaning of things, while the more humble disciple of the Buddha, despite meritorious observance of the Precepts, was crude in looks, rough in speech, offensively familiar in manner, and sufficiently repellent that when he called a man like that to his bedside to talk, on a quiet evening after a day spent on nothing but official business, the outcome was certain to be unpleasantly disappointing; whereas His Highness was superbly distinguished, and he mingled with his every word and with all his talk of that same Buddha's teaching such familiar similes that although by no means profoundly enlightened, he certainly had a wonderful gift for making a listener of good birth understand. After each such intimate visit the Captain wished to stay with His Highness always, and the welter of duties that kept him away only made him miss His Highness more.

The Captain's reverence for him led His Eminence Reizei to write to him frequently, too, so that callers again appeared sometimes at the lonely residence of a Prince whom hardly anyone had even mentioned for years. A message from His Eminence, when the moment prompted one, was always delivered magnificently, and our young gentleman, too, took every opportunity to cultivate His Highness's goodwill with attentions both pleasant and practical. Meanwhile, three years passed.[11]

---

11. Not three twelve-month years but perhaps, in this way of counting, as little as eighteen months or so, starting in one year and ending in the second calendar year after it.

Late one autumn, when the time had come for his season-by-season calling of the Name, and when the noise of waves against the weir was too loud to give one a moment's peace, His Highness moved to the main hall of the Adept's temple to spend seven days at his devotions. His daughters were suffering more than ever from the dreariness and tedium of their life when the young Captain remembered how long it had been since he last visited His Highness and set straight off, in disguise and so discreetly as to be almost alone, under a moon that still hung in the predawn sky. He rode, since the place was on the near side of the river and there was no need to bother with a boat.

The farther he went, the thicker the fog before him, and while he struggled through brush dense enough to hide the path, a blustering wind showered him with heavy dew from the leaves until he was thoroughly cold and wet, although he had no one but himself to blame. Caught between misery and excitement, he felt as though he had never been on such an adventure before.

"More fragile than dew that the winds down mountain slopes sweep from off the leaves,
my tears, though I know not why, fall in an unending stream."

He enjoined silence on his attendants lest a peasant waken and wonder, and the splash of their horses' hooves in rivulets here and there, skirting brushwood fences, made him more cautious still. Even so, in some houses startled sleepers caught on the wind a perfume they did not know[12]—the scent he could never hide.

A forlorn music greeted him as he approached, although from what instrument he could not tell. They say His Highness often plays this way, he thought, and I have never yet had a chance to hear his famous music! I have come at a good time! He found it when he entered to be a *biwa* tuned to the *ōshiki* mode. The quite ordinary playing sounded unfamiliar in this setting, and the notes struck on the return of the plectrum were beautifully clean. The *sō no koto*, which came in now and again, had a touching, graceful tone.

Wishing to listen awhile, he kept out of sight, but a kind of watchman who had clearly heard him arrive, a gruff sort of man, now appeared. "His Highness is off on retreat, my lord," he said. "I shall inform him that you are here."

"But why? It would be wrong of me to disturb him while he has a set number of days of practice to accomplish. I will be quite satisfied if you will kindly tell his daughters how disappointed I would be, after arriving here soaking wet, to return with nothing to show for my journey."

The unlovely face broke into a smile. "I shall do so, my lord," the man said and started off.

"Just a moment!" The Captain called him back. "For years I have been hearing such reports of their music that I have been eager to hear it, and this is the perfect moment to do so. Is there no nook or cranny where I might hide for a little while to listen? It would be a shame if my unforeseen arrival obliged them to stop."

The Captain's manner and looks could only deeply impress anyone so hope-

12. "A perfume they did not know" (*nushi shiranu ka*) is from *Kokinshū* 241, by Sosei.

lessly common. "They play that way day and night when no one else can hear them, but they make not a sound when anyone from the City, even an underling, is here. Most of the time His Highness keeps the presence of women here hidden, and his instructions are that we are not to let anyone know."

The Captain smiled. "That is not very nice of him, is it! There he is, keeping secrets, and meanwhile everyone seems to be citing him as a model for all the world! Anyway," he insisted, "I want you to help me. *I* have no gallant intentions! Their life here intrigues me, and I can hardly imagine them to be like other young ladies."

"Very well, my lord. It might be thought rather silly of me to refuse." He led the Captain to a bamboo screening fence that set the garden before their rooms entirely apart. Then he invited the Captain's attendants into the gallery to the west, where he seated them and looked after them himself.

The Captain cracked open the door that seemed to lead through the fence and peered in through prettily moonlit mist to where the women sat, beyond the rolled-up blinds. A single page girl was on the veranda, thin and looking awfully cold in her rumpled costume. One of the women within, partially hidden behind a pillar, had a *biwa* before her and was toying with the plectrum. Just then the moon, which had been clouded, burst forth brilliantly. "You can call out the moon with this, too," she said, "though it is not a fan."[13] Her face as she peered outside was wonderfully fresh and appealing.

The one reclining beside her was leaning over her instrument. "There is a plectrum that calls back the setting *sun*," she said, "but what odd ideas you have!"[14] Her smiling figure suggested somewhat greater dignity and depth.

"Very well, I am wrong, but this *does* have something to do with the moon!"[15] her sister answered, and their casual, bantering exchange struck him as more engagingly attractive than anything he had imagined. When he heard young gentlewomen read old tales with scenes like this, he always assumed disappointedly that nothing of the kind could actually happen, but there were after all such corners in real life! He was already losing his heart to them.

The mist was too thick for him to see them very well. If only the moon would come out again! But then someone must have announced from within that a visitor had arrived, because the blinds were lowered and they all went inside. The unhurried way they slipped from sight without a sign of alarm or so much as a rustle of silks entranced him with its grace, and their wonderfully noble elegance touched his heart.

He stole away and with all haste sent a man to the City for a carriage. To the

13. The speaker is Naka no Kimi, the younger sister; or so scholars now believe. Older readings of the tale identify her as Ōigimi, the elder. A line of Chinese verse (*Wakan rōei shū* 587) suggests the idea that one can call the moon out from behind clouds with a fan.

14. A variant of the *bugaku* dance "Ryōō" ("The Warrior King") is said to have included a passage in which the dancer lifts his baton toward the sun. The baton in "Ryōō" and the plectrum of a *biwa* are both *bachi*, although in each case the word is written with a different character.

15. Because the *biwa* plectrum when not in use may be slipped between the upper face of the instrument and the *fukuju*, the wooden piece to which the strings are secured. In the face of *biwa*, under the *fukuju*, there is an elliptical sound hole called the *ingetsu* ("hidden moon").

watchman he said, "Although I came at the wrong time, it has given me joy and some relief from my cares to do so. Please inform His Highness that I was here to wait upon him. I should like him to know how very wet I got on the way." The man went to give His Highness the message.

His Highness's daughters, whom his arrival had so surprised, burned with embarrassment that he might have overheard their casual remarks to each other. In shame and dismay they bewailed their dullness—the hour was so improbable—in having failed to notice anything even when a strangely delicious perfume reached them on the wind. The woman charged with taking them his message seemed hopelessly inexperienced, and he decided that there was a time for all things. Under cover of the mist he sallied forth to go down on one knee before those very blinds. The rustic young women had no idea what to answer and hardly managed even to offer him a cushion.

"It is awkward for me here, outside the blinds," he declared earnestly. "I would hardly have come all the way here along those impossible mountain trails on a frivolous whim, and this is not how I expect to be greeted. I trust that repeated visits from me, through these dews, will nonetheless gain your understanding."

The younger women, incapable of mustering a proper reply and apparently fainting with shyness, did so painfully badly that someone was sent to rouse the older, wiser ones now asleep in an inner room, but this took some time, and the young ladies did not wish to leave the impression that they were toying with him. "How are we to address you as though we understood, when we know nothing of these things?" the elder replied with barely audible reticence, though in a most elegant and distinguished tone.

"It is the way of the world, I know, to feign ignorance of sorrows one sees all too well, but I regret that you in particular should insist on remaining aloof. It seems to me that you who enjoy the company of a gentleman of rare understanding should have a fine insight into all things, and that it would therefore become you to judge fairly how deep or shallow are the sentiments that I cannot disguise. Must you reject me on the assumption that I have nothing better in mind than common gallantry? Should anyone wish to urge me in that direction, I assure you that I am far too stubborn to yield. You are undoubtedly acquainted with my reputation. How happy I would be if I might trust you with confidences on the tedious life I lead, and if you would accept me well enough to call on me to distract you from the melancholy of your lonely existence." He spoke at considerable length, but she was too reserved to respond. Instead she ceded her place to an older gentlewoman who had been woken up and who now came forth.[16]

The woman expressed herself excessively freely. "Goodness, we cannot have this!" she cried. "Look how poorly my lord is seated! He belongs *inside* the blinds. You young things seem to have no idea who he is!" This sharp rebuke in an aged voice pained the two young ladies.

"When the world so strangely ignores His Highness that very few who by

16. This older woman refers to herself a few paragraphs later as Ben. The appellation suggests a connection (perhaps brother or husband) with a man who had been a Controller.

rights should keep up with him ever actually do so, your devotion to him, my lord, is a wonder for which even I, who hardly matter, am very grateful indeed, and my young mistresses undoubtedly appreciate it; it is just that they find their sentiments a little difficult to express."

What he gathered of her presence suggested genuine distinction, despite her disconcertingly voluble familiarity, and there was quality in her voice. "Your presence is very welcome," he replied; "I hardly knew what to say next. I am delighted to know that the young ladies really did understand me." The women peering round their standing curtains in the gathering light of dawn noted that his hunting cloak, indeed a discreet one, was thoroughly damp and that meanwhile a fragrance not of this world strangely filled all the air around him.

The older one to whom he was talking began to weep. "I might restrain myself for fear of appearing too forward," she said, "but for many years I have added to my prayers the hope one day to take up with you the sad story of your past and to tell you at least some of it, and a moment that seems to answer that prayer is therefore a joy to me—if it were not that importunate tears blind me until I can no longer speak!" Her trembling made plain the emotion she really felt.

He had both heard and seen for himself how much more easily old people cry, but he still wondered that she should be so deeply affected. "I have visited this house many times," he replied, "but there was no one to commiserate with me, as you do now, when I followed the path here alone and arrived soaked with dew. If this is as you say a happy occasion, please, tell me all!"

"A chance like this may never come again, my lord, and even if it were to do so, I myself may not live from one day to the next. I only want you to know that there was once an old woman like me. The news that Kojijū, once of Sanjō,[17] had passed away managed dimly to reach me, and in my declining years, when most of the women her age whom I knew then were gone, I therefore came up from a distant province, and for the last five or six years I have been in service here. You probably never knew the present Fujiwara Grand Counselor's elder brother, my lord, the one who when he died was the Intendant of the Right Gate Watch. Perhaps you have sometimes heard people talk about him. I can never help feeling as though he passed away only a little while ago. It seems to me that my sleeves are still wet from the sorrow I felt then, and I think that I must be dreaming when I count the years to see how old you are now. I am Ben, and my mother was his nurse. I waited intimately on him day and night, and although I hardly mattered, he occasionally confided to me glimpses of things that he had told no one else but could not keep to himself. Near the end of his illness, when he lay dying, he called me to his side and told me a certain number of things, one of which, my lord, I should tell you in my turn; but, having said that much, I leave it to you to hear the rest at your leisure, if you wish. The shocked young women seem to be nudging each other as though they feel I have gone too far already, and I cannot blame them." She managed to stop talking after all.

---

17. The residence of Kaoru's mother, Onna San no Miya. Kojijū is the gentlewoman through whom Kashiwagi gained access to her.

The astonished young gentleman felt as though he had dreamed her speech or else heard it blurted out by a medium, but it concerned things that had always stirred and puzzled him, and it therefore aroused his intense curiosity. It was true, though, that they were being observed, and besides, it would also be impolite of him so quickly to spend the night caught up in talk of the past. "I can make nothing of what you say," he replied, "but it is moving to listen to talk of times gone by. Yes, you must tell me the rest. For the present, however, I would not wish to be seen dressed as I am once the mist lifts, and it would be embarrassing to have your mistresses catch sight of me; not that I would not much rather stay." As he rose, he caught the faint sound of the bell at the temple where His Highness was. Everything was muffled in the mist.

Already regretting that banks of cloud clinging to the peaks should so come between himself and His Highness, he sympathized more keenly than ever with the mood of His Highness's daughters. What sorrow would spare them here? he wondered. No wonder they are so withdrawn!

> "Day now is breaking, but the path I must take home is invisible,
> and the wooded hills I crossed lie thickly shrouded in mist.

I feel so forlorn!" he wrote, still reluctant to leave. He who caught even the jaded eye of people in the City must have looked a marvel here.

The elder sister, anxious to skirt any indiscretion, replied cautiously as before,

> "Yes, this is the time when clouds sit upon the peaks and the autumn mists
> shroud all the paths up the heights, to remove them from our world."

Her little sighs were extremely touching.

Nothing about the surroundings especially appealed to him, although much elicited his sympathy, but day was coming on, and he felt uncomfortably visible. "I regret that we cannot talk any longer," he answered, "because there is so much more that I would like to know, but I should no doubt forgo any complaint until we know one another a little better. As long as you insist on treating me as you would anyone, I shall with great surprise take it amiss that you fail to understand me at all." He moved to the west end of the front side of the house, which the watchman had made ready for him, and there he gave himself up to gloomy musings.

"There is a great commotion at the weir," one of his men observed. "The spirit seems not really to be in it, though—I suppose the fish are not actually coming." They seemed to know all about it. Curious boats piled with cut brushwood were passing up and down, each man aboard intent on his poor labors, and the way they glided by at the mercy of the waters reminded him that life holds similar dangers for all. Am I to imagine that their peril in this world is not mine, and that I live secure in a jeweled palace? he asked himself time and again.

He called for an inkstone and sent her,

"What drops wet these sleeves, when the river boatman's oar, skimming the shallows,
sounds out the most secret heart of the Maiden of the Bridge![18]

You are in a sad reverie, I know." He gave it to the watchman, who took it there, blue with cold.

Although embarrassed over her paper's rather common scent, she felt that what mattered most was a swift reply:

"These drops day and night while the Uji ferryman plies the running river
soak these ever-moistened sleeves till they may soon rot away.

I am all but floating."[19]

It was very prettily written. How absolutely lovely! he thought and longed for more; but his men were crying, "His lordship's carriage has arrived!" and pressing him urgently. He therefore only summoned the watchman to say that he would be back when His Highness had returned. Then he changed from his wet robes, which he presented to the man, into the dress cloak he had sent for.

His thoughts still dwelled on what the old woman had told him, and there also lingered in his mind the image of figures more enchanting than he had ever expected: no, he saw with chagrin, it was more than he could do yet to give up this world.

He sent off a letter, one not in the style of a love note but set down instead on thick white paper. He chose his brush with care and gave his strokes a distinctive charm. "I am afraid that excessive reticence, lest perhaps I say too much, led me in the end to leave unsaid more than I wished. I hope that henceforth, as I briefly suggested, you will allow me a more comfortable place before your blinds. I have noted how long His Highness's retreat is to last, and I look forward to canceling then the disappointment of having been kept from him by the mist"; and so on. It was all very proper. His messenger was the Aide of the Left Palace Guards. "Find that old woman and give the letter to her," he said. With the letter he sent several large partitioned boxes, remembering how cold the watchman had looked on his rounds.

The next day he sent a letter also to His Highness's temple, and it occurred to him to accompany it with silk, cotton wadding, and other such things, so that His Highness might offer them while he was there, since he did not doubt that the resident monks had been extremely uncomfortable during the recent storms. His Highness was to leave this morning, his retreat over, and he therefore included cotton, silk, stoles, and a set of robes for each of the holy practitioner monks.[20]

The watchman immediately put on the exquisitely beautiful hunting cloak and the soft gown of lovely white figured silk, indescribably perfumed, that the

---

18. Kaoru likens Ōigimi to the mysterious Maiden of Uji Bridge (*Uji no Hashihime*), mentioned canonically in *Kokinshū* 689: "Lonely sleeves spread on her narrow mat, tonight again does she await me, the Maiden of Uji Bridge?"

19. *Genji monogatari kochūshakusho in'yō waka* 321: "I am so wet with drops from the boatman's oar that I am all but floating." The sleeves of the ferryman are Ōigimi's own.

20. Practitioner monks and scholar monks belonged to different categories and played different roles in a temple community. On his retreat Hachi no Miya would have had more to do with the practitioner side.

Captain had left him, but he could not put on a new body as well. Even while praising the clothes, everyone noticed how poorly the fragrance suited him, and in the
end it was all rather embarrassing. Ill at ease in such finery, the watchman decided to
rid it of the perfume that always caused such an unpleasant stir, but alas, the Captain's scent permeated it, and no amount of washing would make it go away.

The Captain was delighted to see such artless accomplishment in the elder
sister's reply. As for His Highness, they told him about the Captain's letter and gave
it to him to read.

"What is the matter with it?" His Highness said. "It would be thoughtless of
him to write as a suitor. His sentiments seem quite unlike other young men's, and I
imagine his reason for showing her these attentions is that I have already hinted to
him what I expect from him once I am gone." He expressed thanks for the gifts that
had more than filled his mountain cave,[21] and this put the Captain in the mood to
visit him.

Now, the Third Prince[22] had been talking about a fantasy of his, that it would
be a particular pleasure to be involved with someone who lived far away from it all,
and the Captain therefore decided to encourage his friend in these thoughts and to
urge him on. One quiet dusk he went to see him.

They were chatting about this and that when the Captain brought up the
Prince who lived at Uji and, to His Highness's delight, gave a full description of
what he had seen that dawn. I knew it! the Captain said to himself, noting his
friend's excitement; and he continued in a manner calculated to enhance the effect.

"You mentioned an answering note from her, though," His Highness objected.
"Why have you not let me see it? I would have shown it to you!"

"But that is just it!" the Captain replied. "I am sure you get all sorts of letters
like that, and you never let me see a single one. No one leading my sheltered life
could possibly keep those young women, as they are, all to himself, and I am eager
for you to know them, although I cannot imagine how you are actually to visit
them. As far as gallantry goes, the world belongs to those less burdened with rank.
Hidden treasures surely exist in plenty. There must obviously be other women with
that sort of appeal, secretly inhabiting the gloomy nooks and crannies of mountain
villages and so on. For years I despised the two I have been describing on the assumption that life with so unworldly a holy man must have made them utter boors,
and I ignored everything I heard about them; but if they measure up to what I saw
of them by faint moonlight, then they are without a doubt the real thing. Their
looks, their bearing—women like *that*, one has to agree, are exactly what a woman
should be."

His Highness came in the end to feel seriously jealous and also frantic to discover more about these wonders who had deeply affected a man impervious to any
common appeal. "Keep a good eye on them, then," he admonished the Captain, intensely frustrated and annoyed by the pompous rank that imposed such restrictions
on him.

21. A figurative expression.
22. Niou.

The Captain was amused. "Now, now," he said, "this is nonsense. I am resolved never to set my heart on anything in this world, and I am therefore wary of any frivolity. I would be thoroughly disappointed if despite myself I were ever to entertain such stubborn desires."

"A noble speech!" His Highness laughed. "I just hope that you can carry through on all your loftily pious talk!"

At heart the Captain was ever more deeply absorbed by what the old woman's talk had suggested, and he cared relatively little that a young woman should be seen as delightful or called a pleasure to look at.

The tenth month came, and on the fifth or sixth he started for Uji. "You must have a look at the weir this time, my lord," his people told him, but he retorted, "What? Am I to approach the weir, when I feel my life to be as precarious as the mayfly's?"[23] Abandoning any such thought, he set out as usual with the greatest discretion. He traveled lightly in a basketwork carriage, wearing a dress cloak and gathered trousers that he had had especially sewn for such occasions from plain, stiff silk.

His Highness was pleased to receive him and entertained him handsomely with what the place offered. After dark he drew up the lamp and called the Adept down to explain the profundities of the scripture that he had left off reading earlier. They never closed their eyes, for a strong wind was blowing on the river, and the clattering of leaves torn from the trees and the noise of the water were all too affecting. It was a frightening, lonely place.

When the Captain judged that daybreak was near, he could not help looking back to that other dawn and purposely began to talk of the spell of music. "The last time I came," he said, "that dawn when the mist led me astray, I heard a passage of music so wonderful that I only long to hear more."

"After renouncing color and fragrance, I have forgotten all the music I had once learned," His Highness replied; but he had someone bring him a *kin*. "No," he said, "this really will not do. Perhaps it will come back to me after I have heard *you* play." He called for a *biwa* that he pressed on his guest.

The Captain took it and tuned it. "I cannot believe that this is the instrument I heard briefly then," he said. "I had supposed that the magic lay in the instrument's tone." He was reluctant to play at all.

"Come, you are being unkind. How could any music so pleasing to you have reached your ears here? It is quite impossible." His Highness began plucking the *kin*, to profoundly moving effect; no doubt the wind through the mountain pines sustained his music.[24] With a show of much faltering and hesitation he played a single, beautiful piece.

"Now and again, to my surprise, I catch such faint sounds from a *sō no koto* as to

23. Kaoru plays on *hio*, the fish that the weir is built to catch, and *hiomushi*, a kind of mayfly that lives only a day. Since the *hio* are caught when they "approach" the weir, Kaoru suggests that approaching the weir could mean the end of his life as well. *Hio* are the nearly transparent juveniles, about an inch long, of the *ayu* (sweetfish), a delicacy of Japan's rivers and lakes.

24. *Shūishū* 451 (also *Wakan rōei shū* 469), by Saigū no Nyōgo, established the poetic link between the music of the *kin* and the sound of wind in the pines: "The sound of the pines on the mountain wind mingles with the music of the *kin*; and, for this concert, which string was tuned to which?"

suggest that they have learned to play," he said, "but it has been a long time since I actually listened. They both seem to toy with the instrument as they please, but I expect that their only accompaniment is the waves on the river; I certainly cannot imagine them providing a competent rhythm themselves."

He sent to his daughters to ask them to play, but they shrank from the idea, for the Captain had overheard them making music for themselves, and they knew that they would do badly. Both declined, and they responded to His Highness's repeated encouragement only with excuses. The Captain was very disappointed.

His Highness then felt ashamed of their strangely unworldly and, to him, most unfortunate mode of life. "I brought them up hoping that no one would ever know they were here," he said, "but now that each day may be my last, I am afraid the only tie to keep me from leaving the world is the thought of how they, who have all their lives before them, may face abandonment and destitution."

The Captain was pained to witness his predicament. "I am in no position to offer them properly reliable assistance," he replied, "but I would be very grateful if you were not to consider me a stranger. I assure you that for as long as I live I will not go back on the undertaking I give you now, however briefly I may express it." His Highness was very pleased and said so.

The Captain called for that old woman to come while His Highness went about his morning devotions. She was known as Mistress Ben, and her role was to look after the daughters. Her manner of addressing him retained its elegance and distinction, although she was nearly sixty years old. She wept endlessly as she told him how the Acting Grand Counselor[25] had lapsed deeper and deeper into melancholy and of how he had then sickened and died. Yes, her talk of times gone by would touch anyone, the Captain reflected, but for me, after wondering for years what happened and how it began, and after begging the Buddha to clear up the matter, it is extraordinary to have this prayer unexpectedly answered—so it seems—in an account as disturbing as any dream! He could not stop his tears.

"So," he said, "there is still someone living who knows what happened! Is it possible that this astonishing and shameful knowledge has passed on in the same way to anyone else? All this time I myself have heard nothing of the kind."

"No, my lord, no one but Kojijū and I can have known. I have never breathed a word to anyone. I myself am nothing and no one, but I was beside him day and night, and once I began inevitably to grasp the truth, it was through us two, and only through us, that he sent her the occasional letter whenever the anguish was more than he could bear. I cannot tell you everything because I would not dare. At the end he entrusted me with a few words that have been a painful burden for someone like me, and also an anxiety so great that my longing to convey them to you led me to include the hope of doing so in all my poor prayers. Now at last I know that there really is a Buddha in this world. I have some things to show you. I used to tell

---

25. Kashiwagi, who was awarded this promotion shortly before his death. I have retained the title here and below, rather than substitute the more familiar "Intendant," because Kashiwagi's last promotion clearly means a great deal to Ben.

myself that it was hopeless and that I might as well burn them, because I was afraid they might get out after all if I who may go at any moment were ever to leave them behind. Then you began calling now and then on His Highness, and I regained the courage to pray for this moment after all. That it has actually come must be a matter of destiny from past lives." In tears she told him everything about how he came to be born.

"In the commotion surrounding the Acting Grand Counselor's death my mother immediately fell ill and soon passed away, which was another heavy blow. In my double mourning I knew only sorrow. Then a nobody who had been pursuing me for years persuaded me to accompany him to the most distant reaches of the western sea,[26] so that I fell completely out of touch with the City. He died there, and I returned ten years later with the feeling that everything in the City had changed. I had been in and out of His Highness's residence ever since I was small, thanks to a connection on my father's side, and by then I certainly was not the sort of person any longer to go out among people. I should properly have appealed to her ladyship, the Consort of His Cloistered Eminence Reizei, since I had been an intimate of her household for so long, except that in truth I shrank from doing so and in the end never went there at all. Instead I have turned into a tree withering away deep in the mountains.[27] When was it, I wonder, that Kojijū died? By now very few of those whom I knew then, in their youth, are left, and I cannot help lamenting a life during which so many have been taken from me. Still, here I am." She talked on as before until it was day.

"Very well, then," the Captain said, "I am sure that there is no end to all you could tell me about the past. I must speak to you again another time, in some quiet place where we cannot be overheard. I have a dim memory of the woman they called Kojijū; I must have been five or six at the time. I gather that she suddenly caught a chest ailment and died. If it were not for our conversation, I would have spent the rest of my life deep in sin."[28]

She gave him a collection of papers, tightly rolled and smelling of mold, sewn into a bag. "Please, my lord, have these burned in your presence. The Acting Grand Counselor collected them and gave them to me, assuring me that he could live no longer, and I thought then that the very next time I saw Kojijū, I would have her take them to where they should properly have gone,[29] but she and I never met again, and I was left after all with the sad burden of this secret."

The Captain's face betrayed nothing as he hid what he had just received. He wondered unhappily whether the old woman, like others, had simply indulged the urge to recount a piece of sensational gossip, but that seemed unlikely, considering the way she had promised over and over again never to tell anyone else.

He had some gruel and steamed rice. Offices had been closed yesterday, but

26. Kyushu.
27. From *Kokinshū* 875, by Kengei: "In form I am a withered tree, hidden in the mountains, but my heart will blossom if you wish."
28. The sin resulting from not honoring his real father.
29. To Onna San no Miya.

today the seclusion at the palace would be over, and besides, he had to present his wishes for the recovery of His Eminence's First Princess,[30] who was ill, and for both reasons he would be fully occupied. He assured his host that he would be back before the autumn leaves were gone from the hills.[31] Pleased, His Highness replied, "For me, you know, your frequent visits bring a little light into the shadows of these mountains."

The first thing he did when he got home again was to inspect the bag. It was sewn from Chinese brocade and had "For Her Highness" written on it. The knot of slender, braided cord that tied it shut bore *his* signature seal. To open it was terrifying. Inside, he found sheets of paper in various colors, including five or six replies from his mother. In *his* hand there were five or six sheets of Michinokuni paper that evoked at length, in letters like the tracks of some strange bird, how extremely ill he was; how he could no longer get the slightest message to her, which only made him yearn for her the more; how he supposed that by now she must have assumed the guise of a nun; and other such sorrowful topics.

> "Still more than for you, who before my very eyes have renounced this world,
> I grieve for this soul of mine, soon to leave you forever,"

he had written, and in the margin, "I have no reason to worry about the little shoot[32] of whom I have had such marvelous news, and yet,

> If I were to live, I would know that he was mine and watch from afar
> how tall the pine tree will grow my secret leaves among the rocks."

It was all quite untidy, and it just seemed to stop. On it was written "To Kojijū." The paper was now inhabited by silverfish and smelled of age and mold, but the writing was still there, as fresh as though just set down, and the words stood out with perfect clarity. Yes, he thought, if this had ever gone astray . . . ; and he trembled and ached for them both.

Could anything like this ever happen again? What he knew now so weighed on him that he renounced his intention of going to the palace. Instead he went to visit Her Cloistered Highness, whom he found, all youth and innocence, reading a scripture that she bashfully hid. What would be the point of telling her I know? No, he kept it to himself, to reflect on in every way.

---

30. Reizei's daughter by his Kokiden Consort.
31. In other words, soon. The day is roughly the sixth of the tenth lunar month, and the leaves will not be on the trees much longer.
32. Kaoru, here referred to as a *futaba* ("seedling").

46

Beneath the Oak

Shiigamoto ("beneath the oak")
serves as the chapter title because of its presence in a poem
by Kaoru, lamenting the death of
Hachi no Miya:

"The oak tree I sought to give me happy refuge under spreading shade
is no more, and where he lived emptiness and silence reign."

"Beneath the Oak" continues "The Maiden of the Bridge" and appears to overlap chronologically with the end of "Bamboo River."

PERSONS

The Consultant Captain, then Counselor, age 23 to 24 (Kaoru)

His Highness of War, 24 to 25 (Niou)

His Highness, the Eighth Prince, around 60 (Hachi no Miya)

His elder daughter, 25 to 26 (Ōigimi)

His younger daughter, 23 to 24 (Naka no Kimi)

Ben, a gentlewoman of Hachi no Miya's daughters, around 60

The Adept (Uji no Ajari)

Niou's messenger

The watchman at Uji

On about the twentieth of the second month His Highness of the Bureau of War made a pilgrimage to Hatsuse. His vow to do so was already old, but years had passed while he failed to make up his mind to honor it, and no doubt the main reason why he did so now was the attraction of breaking his journey at Uji. It was hardly serious of him to feel so drawn to a place that others have called "detestable."[1] A great many senior nobles accompanied him, and needless to say the privy gentlemen did, too, so that practically no one remained behind.

Across the river there was a large and handsome property that His Excellency of the Right had inherited from His Grace of Rokujō, and His Excellency had arranged to have the party received there. He had even meant to go and greet the Prince there himself, on His Highness's way back, but, unfortunately, he received advice to confine himself in strict seclusion and so was unable to do so. His Highness was somewhat disappointed; but then, on that very day, the Consultant Captain arrived to meet him. This was an altogether more agreeable prospect, and he looked forward also to hearing from him about things on the other bank. He felt that His Excellency was much too grand and made rather demanding company. This gentleman's sons—the Right Grand Controller, the Adviser Consultant, the Acting Captain, the Secretary Lieutenant, the Chamberlain Second of the Watch— were there to attend him. His Highness was very highly regarded by all, for he was Their Majesties' favorite, and of course His Excellency and everyone else at Rokujō accorded him their personal allegiance.

The place was done up just right for what it was. They took out Go, backgammon, and *tagi* boards and spent the day enjoying themselves as they pleased. Worn out by the unfamiliar experience of travel, His Highness had other reasons as well to want very much to stay on there, and so toward evening, after a little rest, he called for instruments and music.

---

1. *Kokinshū* 983, by Kisen Hōshi ("My hut is southeast of the city: I live with the deer in the Uji hills, where they say, I reject the world"), plays so effectively on the place name of Uji and on *ushi* ("vexing," "hateful") that "Uji" was associated forever after with sentiments such as *ushi* or, as here, *urameshi* ("detestable").

It seemed to him that in so remote a spot the noise of the water only helped the instruments to ring out more beautifully; while yonder, just across the river at the hermit Prince's house, the music carried there on the breeze reminded His Highness of days gone by.

"What a delightful tone the player gives that flute!" he murmured to himself. "Who can it be? Long ago I heard His Grace of Rokujō play the flute like that, and he gave the music great sweetness and charm. Whoever this is, though, he makes the heavens ring and gives the music a touch of grandeur; it sounds like the way His Excellency the late Chancellor[2] and his sons play." And he continued, "Ah, it has been so long, so long! All these years, half living and half dead, with never a moment of music like this—no, it would be meaningless to count them all!" While talking on this way, he thought what a shame it was for his daughters, and he longed that they might not forever be trapped in these hills. An eventual alliance with the Consultant Captain would be welcome, he sighed, but I see no likely prospect of it, and I cannot for a moment imagine accepting any of the light-minded young men so common nowadays. The sorrows besetting his house therefore made the spring night all too long,[3] while for the travelers in their lodging across the river the giddiness of drink brought dawn surprisingly soon, and His Highness of War regretted having already to leave.

Beneath a sky veiled far and wide by the mists of spring, some cherry trees were shedding their petals while others were just coming into bloom, and one admired along the river a lovely prospect of wind-tossed willows reflected in the stream.[4] His Highness of War, unaccustomed to such sights, was struck with wonder and found the scene very hard to leave.

The Captain did not wish to miss this opportunity to visit the residence across the river, but he hesitated to act because he felt that it might look frivolous of him to disappear from among all these people and row off by himself. Meanwhile a letter arrived from there.

> "Winds from off the hills sweep away lingering mists with strains of music,
>   yet there still stretch between us distances of tossing waves,"

the gentleman had written. It was beautifully done in the running style.

His Highness was delighted when he understood that it came from the place already on his mind. "I shall answer it!" he declared:

> "A great reach of waves stretches in truth between us, from this bank to yours,
>   yet blow greetings there from me, O wind across the river!"

The Captain went to deliver it and invited several young gentlemen keen on music to come with him. On the way across they played "Magic of Wine," after

---

2. Tō no Chūjō. Hachi no Miya hears the musical heritage of Tō no Chūjō and Kashiwagi in Kaoru's playing, even though he does not know that Kaoru is Kashiwagi's son.

3. Whereas a spring night is conventionally described as short.

4. An image from *Kokin rokujō* 4155, attributed in *Nihon shoki* to Emperor Kenzō.

which they all respectfully disembarked, pleased to find the steps down to the water from the riverside gallery so perfectly suitable in style. The place was different again from the one they had just left. Its basketwork screens, which were as utterly plain as any one might find in a mountain village, lent their own touch to the furnishings' particular charm, although His Highness had had them carefully cleared away in preparation for receiving his guests. He had most discreetly laid out venerable instruments, each with a magnificent tone, on which they played "Cherry Blossom Man" in the *ichikotsu* mode. Everyone had hoped that on such an occasion their host would play the *kin*, but instead he only

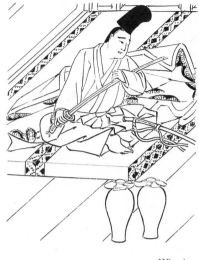

Wine jars

touched now and again, quite casually, the strings of a *sō no koto*. The sound deeply impressed the younger gentlemen, perhaps because they so seldom heard anything like it. A very pleasant meal of local fare followed, served by attendants far more closely resembling imperial descendants than they had ever imagined, or by old, unrecognized princes of the fourth rank who with the prospect of these guests arriving had all come forward, no doubt eager to provide His Highness with much-needed help; and those charged with bearing the wine jars were so thoroughly presentable, too, that the Prince's welcome acquired from them all a wonderfully antique elegance. Meanwhile the guests strove to imagine how His Highness's daughters got on here, and some of them no doubt felt eager to try their luck.

His Highness of War, whose rank gave him much less than their freedom, now felt the constraint keenly and could not contain himself. He ordered a beautifully flowering branch picked and had it presented by a handsome privy page in his service. The note said,

> *"I have come to you seeking in all their beauty mountain cherry flowers,*
> *and I myself have plucked a spray to set in my hair.*[5]

In fondness for the meadow, . . ."[6] or something of the sort.

His Highness's daughters had great difficulty contriving an answer. "People have always felt that at such a moment it does *not* do to take one's time and delay the reply," their more experienced gentlewomen warned, and His Highness had the younger sister write,

---

5. "I come seeking your friendship as a fellow member of the imperial lineage." *Gosenshū* 809, by Ise: "If you come to Yoshino, where I make my home, do so with a spray of the same flowers in your hair."

6. Varied from *Man'yōshū* 1428 (also *Kokin rokujō* 3916), by Yamabe no Akahito: "I, who came to pick violets in a springtime meadow, for love of the meadow slept there that night." Niou hints that he wants to stay.

"Those flowers you plucked for your hair have led you here to the rustic's hedge,
and you will pass swiftly by, O you who travel with spring.

What charm has the meadow?" Her hand was very pretty and accomplished.

The impartial river breeze did indeed carry back and forth the sound of music. The Fujiwara Grand Counselor[7] arrived to give His Highness His Majesty's greetings. His large retinue joined His Highness's party, and it was a lively, contentious throng that returned from there to the City. The younger lords, who longed to stay, looked back again and again, while His Highness anticipated the next occasion of the kind. The blossoms were at their height, and the spring haze made a lovely view in all directions, inspiring them to compose verse after verse in Chinese and Japanese; but I did not bother to inquire about them.

His Highness remained displeased that in the confusion he had never managed to convey what he really had in mind, but his letters kept coming, even in the absence of anyone to present them for him.[8] "You must answer him," the young ladies' father explained, "although you should avoid any hint of courtship. That would just incite him more. He is a Prince much given to gallantry, and no doubt he has little intention of letting the matter rest now that he knows you are here." His younger daughter was the one who wrote each time, at his urging; the elder was too prudent to engage in any such banter.

Their father, always so given to melancholy, found the empty calm of spring more and more difficult to endure and passed his time in vacant musing. It only made it worse that their looks had matured with the years into such flawlessly winning beauty, and he lamented day and night that his pain and regret might well have been less if they had been unsightly. The elder by now was twenty-five and the younger twenty-three.

For His Highness this year required great caution, and in his despondency he absorbed himself more than ever in his devotions. Since the world meant nothing to him, and his every thought was of preparing for the great departure, he seemed certain to set out along the serene path;[9] and yet this single matter of his daughters was a growing worry, and it seemed to those who knew him that despite his staunch resolve he would waver when the time to leave them actually came. How gladly he would have winked at courtship from anyone, even if not ideal, who genuinely wished to take one in hand, provided only that he was acceptable enough not to cause unfavorable gossip! It would be such a comfort to approve any refuge that might afford each a place in the world; but alas, no one wanted them anything like that seriously. The rare approaches they received amounted to mere gallantry from young men intent only on passing the time on the way out and back from a pilgrimage, and His Highness, who recoiled from the thought that these might imagine his daughters' dreary life and despise them for it, never permitted the most perfunctory answer. It was His Highness of War who was absolutely determined to have them. Perhaps that was his destiny.

7. Kōbai, Kashiwagi's younger brother.
8. Without Kaoru's help.
9. To Amida's paradise.

That autumn the Consultant Captain became a Counselor, but despite increased prestige and greater responsibility he still had many cares. After wanting to know the truth for so many years, he now pondered the gentleman who had died so tragic a death and longed by pious devotions to lighten his sin. He also took pity on the old woman from whom he had had the story, and did what he could for her as quietly and as invisibly as possible.

He remembered that he had not been to Uji for a long time and went straight there. It was the seventh month. Autumn had not yet come to the City, but near Mount Otowa one felt a sharp chill in the sound of the wind, and the wooded hills farther on were slightly tinged with color. The landscape when he arrived filled him with wonder and delight, but His Highness, still more delighted to greet him, now poured out at length the tale of his sorrows.

"I hope," he ventured, "that after I am gone you will see your way to providing for my daughters' needs when they arise, and to count them as before among those who matter to you."

"You were good enough to mention this matter earlier, and I have no intention of failing in the promise that I made you then," the Counselor replied. "I who wish to reduce my attachment to the world have little time before me to be of service to them, but I hope to show you clearly that my feelings have not changed, as long as I have the capacity to do so." His Highness was pleased.

Late that night the moon shone forth brilliantly, but one knew that it would soon be gone behind the crest of the hills. His Highness movingly chanted the Name and began to talk about the past. "What is the world like by now? I wonder," he said. "When I joined in music making at the palace, under this sort of autumn moon, the recognized experts would do their best, and the effect in concert was certainly grand; but what generally caught one's interest more was the plaintive sound of a single instrument late at night, after everyone had retired, faintly heard here and there from the apartments of a Consort or an Intimate, those highly respected ladies so intent on their rivalry even while they maintain a surface regard for one another. Women are trifling creatures on the whole, good only for passing pleasures, but they arouse strong feelings. I suppose that that is why their sin is so profound. Parents feel deep concern for all their children, but a son is much less trouble. A daughter is a daughter,[10] and she is likely to be a great worry even when one must acknowledge how little she is worth." He put his own anxiety in general terms, and his visitor agreed sympathetically at heart that he had every reason to feel as he did.

"I have truly given up all those things, as you know, and, to speak of myself, that is no doubt why I know very little indeed about them," the Counselor replied, "but however inconsequential music may be, the taste for it is indeed very difficult to renounce. That is why even the saintly Kashō rose to dance."[11] He seemed still to long for the sound of the koto he had once heard so briefly, and His Highness therefore went in person to his daughters to urge them to play, hoping perhaps to

10. Constrained by all the strictures that make her so different from a son, one being her subjection to her eventual husband.

11. Kashō, a prominent disciple of the Buddha, could not help dancing when the divinities of music played.

bring them and his visitor closer together. There came a very faint, brief passage on the *sō no koto*. In such a place, under a sky that increasingly evoked sorrow and desolation, this impromptu music pleased the Counselor well, but the sisters would certainly not agree to play freely together.

"Very well, now that I have managed this much, I leave the rest to you, who have your lives ahead of you." His Highness disappeared into his altar room, saying,

> *"After I am gone, this grass hermitage of mine may well fall to ruin,*
>   *yet I know that you will be true as ever to your word.*[12]

This meeting of ours may be the last, and sorrow has kept me from containing myself; I have talked too much nonsense." He was weeping.

His guest:

> *"In what age to come will that solemn promise fail, when I gave my word*
>   *for all time not to forsake this, the hermitage you made?*[13]

I shall wait upon you once the wrestling tournament[14] and other such distractions are over."

Left to his own devices, the Counselor summoned the old woman who had so surprised him with her story and questioned him on many matters that remained to be told. The setting moon shone in brightly, lending his figure a wonderful grace,[15] while the sisters kept to the inner recesses of the room. He addressed them so quietly and sincerely, in a tone free of any hint of common gallantry, that they answered him as the

moment prompted them to do. Silently recalling how eager His Highness of War was to know them, he reflected that he *was* still unlike other men. Look how willingly His Highness encouraged me, he said to himself, and I still feel in no particular hurry! Not that it is really out of the question, as far as I can see. It will be very pleasant to talk to them this way and to exchange praise of the beauty of blossoms and autumn leaves, and yes, it *will* be a shame if they go to others. He felt as though they were his already.

He returned to the City late at night. The figure of his host, who seemed so sadly convinced that he had not long to live, lingered in his mind, and he planned to return once the busy season was over. His Highness of War, too, was considering the right moment to go there that autumn on a trip to enjoy the leaves. He sent constant letters. The sister who answered them[16] did

Kashō

12. The poem plays on *hitokoto*, "one passage of koto music" and "your single word" (your promise to look after my daughters); and on *kare*, "neglect" (to come) and "die" (speaking of grass).

13. The poem plays on *musuberu*, "make" (a promise) and "bundle" (together the grass for a simple hut).

14. The wrestling tournament (*sumai no sechi*) was held toward the end of the seventh month. Wrestlers gathered from all the provinces to compete in the Emperor's presence, and a banquet followed.

15. Those in the room can apparently see him through the blinds, picked out in the moonlight.

16. Naka no Kimi, the younger.

not believe him for a moment to be serious, and she therefore took little trouble with her replies, but she kept up the exchange, however lightly.

As autumn advanced, His Highness's thoughts became still gloomier, until he decided as before to devote himself in peace to calling the Name, and with this in mind he spoke the inevitable words to his daughters. "Such is this life that no one escapes the final parting, but it helps to look forward to finding comfort. It is tragic that I should now have to leave you alone when you have no one else to look after you, and yet it will not help for me to wander for that reason the darkness of the eternal night. I cannot say what may happen after I am gone, in a world that I renounced even while I was still with you, but I warn you, do nothing ill considered that might bring shame not only on me but on your late mother. Never let yourselves be persuaded to leave this mountain village unless by someone worthy of you. Simply accept that your destiny is not that of others and decide to remain here all your lives. As long as you persist in that resolve, you will find that the months and years pass smoothly. What matters above all, particularly for a woman, is to remain unseen and never to arouse such criticism as to bring her to others' unfriendly attention."

His daughters could picture no future at all for themselves, and they only wondered how they would survive his loss. Merely to imagine this dismal prospect troubled them beyond words. At heart he had indeed no doubt given them up, but he still had them with him day and night, and they could hardly help holding this abrupt separation against him, even though it had nothing to do with cruelty on his part.

The day before he was to go, he wandered about in his usual manner, having a last look at his house. It was a flimsy, insubstantial place that had been his home so long, and he wondered with tears in his eyes, meanwhile calling the Name, how his young daughters could possibly remain shut up here once he had left them. He was the picture of distinction and grace as he did so. Then he called the older gentlewomen together. "Give your mistresses faithful service," he said. "It is the way of things that those not born to come to the world's notice should in time decline unseen, but for such as they it is a sad offense against gentle birth to lapse into ignoble degradation. Most people lead unhappy, lonely lives. Loyalty to the dignity and customs of their house will make them blameless in their own and in others' eyes. Respectable prosperity may tempt them, but never, never urge any thoughtless imprudence on them if circumstances turn out not to promise it."

He went once more to his daughters at dawn, when he was about to leave. "Do not be downcast while I am gone," he said. "Be merry in spirit at least, and play music. This world is always so contrary—do not take it too seriously." He looked back again and again as he left.

The sisters remained more disconsolate than ever, and they talked these things over day and night. "How would life be possible at all if one of us were no longer to be here?" they asked each other. "There is no telling what awaits us now, and if by any chance we came to be parted . . ." Weeping and laughing, playful and serious, they sought with one mind each other's consolation.

A messenger arrived on the evening of the day when his retreat was over and

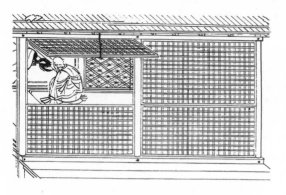

Shutter

they were expecting him home at any moment. "This morning I began to feel unwell, and I am afraid that I cannot come," he said, repeating His Highness's words. "I am having myself looked after, you see, on the assumption that it is a cold, but I long more than ever to be with you again."

Dismayed and anxious about what the matter could be, they had thick, padded robes made up and sent to him. Two or three days passed, and he never came down from the mountain. They sent again and again to find out how he was. "There is nothing that badly wrong with me," he told the messenger, "but I just do not feel well. I promise to come as soon as I am a little better."

The Adept remained in close attendance on him. "You appear only to be slightly indisposed, but I believe that you may be setting out on your final journey," he cautioned. "There is no reason you should mourn for your daughters. We each have our own distinct destiny, and you need not be concerned about them." He urged His Highness more and more to give up every tie, and he warned, "Your Highness, you must not leave this temple."

It was about the twentieth of the eighth month, and the sky was assuming a melancholy cast. The mists never cleared from morning to night, and the sisters mourned and sighed. Near dawn the moon came out, brightly illuminating the surface of the river, and they raised the shutters on that side to look out at the scene. The distant sound of the temple bell announced the coming of dawn. Several men arrived just then to inform them, weeping, that His Highness had died in the middle of the night.

They had never stopped thinking of him or wondering how he was, but the shock of this news deprived them of their senses, leaving them unable—for even their tears had vanished—to do anything but lie prostrate on the ground. When the greatest loss of all occurs, one is normally present and therefore in no doubt of what has transpired, but ignorance of how it had happened only added to their grief, and it is no wonder that they mourned. They who could hardly imagine living on after him wept with desperate longing to join him, but his time had come, and all their lamentations were in vain.

The Adept took in hand all that needed to be done, as he had always promised to do. "We would gladly see his face and form one last time, now that we gather he is gone," his daughters said, but the Adept replied, "What good would that accomplish? His Highness himself had already cautioned you that you might not see him again, and for his sake you must now dispose yourselves no longer to cling to him." That was all. When the sisters learned how their father had been accommodated, they bitterly condemned the Adept's excessively ascetic zeal.

His Highness had wanted for many, many years to take the vows of a Novice, but reluctance to abandon his daughters when there was no one else to look after them had prompted him to remain with them all his life, and they were such a comfort to him in his sad circumstances that he never really wished to leave them. Both he on his last journey and they who mourned his loss were therefore left unconsoled.

The news was a great blow to the Counselor, who felt as though he had still had many things to discuss a last time with His Highness, and he wept bitterly at this new reminder of what life brings. "I doubt that we shall meet again," His Highness had said, but such remarks from him were all too common, since he always remained acutely aware that in this life each day or night may be one's last, and the Counselor had never imagined that what he foretold might come yesterday or today.[17] Overcome with grief, he addressed long letters of condolence to His Highness's daughters through the Adept, and since they had had no word from anyone else, they understood even in their distraught condition the depth of his devotion through the years. The most ordinary parting of this kind affects everyone at the time as an unheard-of tragedy, and he could well imagine what their feelings might be when they had no other comfort at all. He therefore foresaw everything required for the necessary rites and sent suitable offerings also to the Adept. Through the older gentlewomen he provided what was needed for the scripture readings at His Highness's residence.

It felt as though the night would never dawn, but even so, the ninth month came. The cold rains of the season, so apt to start tears, lowered over meadow and mountain, and now and then the sound of falling leaves or the noise of the river seem to mingle with the flood of their weeping, until those who served them wondered miserably how their mistresses would ever live out their allotted years and strove in vain to comfort them. Priests were there, too,[18] to call the Name, and those who visited the house to confine themselves in prayer before His Highness's altar, in the room where His Highness had done so himself, absorbed themselves in the rites of mourning.

Repeated messages came as well from His Highness of War. The sisters did not have the heart to answer them. Their silence, when as far as he could tell they responded quite differently to the Counselor, left him offended that they should seem to have forgotten him. He had meant to go there when the autumn leaves were in their glory and to have his party compose Chinese verses, but this was no time for such an excursion, and in disappointment he gave up the idea.

The period of mourning came to an end, and he sent them a long, long letter, for he guessed that since tears cannot flow forever, even theirs might now dry from time to time. It came one evening when rain was threatening:

> "*What can your life be, where the stag cries in autumn round your mountain village*
> *and at dusk the dewdrops hang on the drooping* hagi *fronds?*"[19]

17. *Kokinshū* 861, by Ariwara no Narihira, said to be Narihira's death poem: "This is a path, so I had heard, that all must walk, but never thought yesterday or today."
18. As well as at the temple.
19. "When I myself am in tears."

It would be too unkind of you to pretend that you do not share the mood of the sky this evening. This is after all just the season to contemplate the withering moors,"[20] he wrote, and so on.

"It is true, we have ignored him repeatedly," the elder said. "Do answer him." She appealed as usual to her younger sister to write a reply.

How could I have imagined that I would live long enough ever to draw an inkstone to me again? the younger one asked herself. How bitter a time we have been through! Her eyes clouded once more, and it seemed to her that she could see nothing. She pushed the inkstone away. "I cannot write to him, not yet," she said. "Here I am, beginning to stir myself again—yes, clearly, there *is* an end to mourning, but how hateful it is, and how distressing!" Her sweetly weeping figure made a very touching sight.

The messenger had set out from the City at dusk, and he arrived some way into the evening. "How can you possibly go straight back?" they had him asked. "You must spend the night." However, he insisted that he must return immediately; at which the elder, who certainly did not yet feel herself, still felt sorry enough for her sister to write,

> *"Mists of endless tears shut this mountain village in, and there at the fence*
> *the stag comes to cry aloud in concert with our sorrow."*

It was on gray paper, and in the dark her writing was uncertain, but nothing required her to make it clean and neat. She let her brush move as it would, then wrapped the letter and sent it out.

The messenger was alarmed by the prospect of passing Kohata in the rain,[21] but His Highness had chosen no coward, and the man urged his horse so swiftly along narrow trails overgrown by dwarf bamboo that he arrived in no time at all. He appeared before his lord so soaking wet that His Highness gave him a reward. The letter was in a hand that His Highness had not seen before, one that suggested a somewhat greater maturity and distinction. Unable to put it down, he gazed at it, wondering which sister was which, and did not go to bed for some time. "He stayed up waiting and waiting, and now look at how long he has been staring at it!" his gentlewomen grumbled in whispers to each other. "Whatever it is must mean a lot to him!" They were probably complaining because they were sleepy.

He rose early the next morning while the mists were still thick to write his reply:

> *"Shall these ears then hear without heartfelt sympathy the stag's doleful cry*
> *for a companion vanished into the mists of morning?*[22]

'In concert,' you say—but I, too, and just as loudly!"

20. *Shinsenzaishū* 526, by Prince Tomohira: "Sadder to me than the withering of the lower *hagi* fronds, on the hilltop haunted by the stag, is the withering of the moors."

21. Kohata was reputed to be a wild and deserted area, and possibly the haunt of bandits.

22. *Gosenshū* 372, by Ki no Tomonori: "I might well lift my voice to cry aloud into the autumn mists, though I am no stag who has lost his mate."

There will be trouble if I show him too great a warmth, she said to herself. We always managed well enough when we were safe beneath Father's shelter, but now that we unwillingly survive him, the slightest misstep, however little intended, could easily injure the spirit of a father whose only concern was to avoid precisely that. A comprehensive wariness and fear discouraged her from replying. It is not that she dismissed the Prince or thought him dull, for his slightest word or stroke of the brush testified to his wit and grace, and while she had not read many such letters, it struck her that this one was very pleasing; all the same, though, it would not do for either of them to enter into any such elegantly suggestive exchange. No, she decided, I shall simply continue on as the rustic I am.

She answered the Counselor, though, because he addressed her so soberly that she gave him back not-unfriendly replies. Once the mourning was over, he came himself. He approached the east aisle, where the sisters in their subdued dress occupied a lowered section,[23] and called out the old woman.[24] To those lost in the darkness of grief the fragrance that filled all the air around him was too much to bear, and neither could manage a reply.

"Such a conversation can be worthwhile only if you will be good enough to leave off treating me this way and assent to the wishes expressed by His Late Highness," he said. "I am not accustomed to putting on airs and graces, and it is impossible to talk sensibly through someone else."

"Alas," the elder replied, "we may appear to live on, and yet, wandering as we do through a dream from which there is no waking, we shrink from allowing ourselves to look upon the light of day. I cannot approach the veranda."

"I can only commend the depth of your boundless devotion, while as to the sun and moon, I agree that it might indeed be wrong of you to go forth blithely beneath their light; but I nonetheless find myself at a loss what to do. I long, you see, to relieve for a moment the sorrows that weigh upon you."

"It really is awfully good of him, my lady, to wish to console you in the midst of your unspeakable misfortune," her women assured her.

She herself, despite everything, slowly recovered her calm, and since her mind was perfectly clear, she must have understood the feelings that had brought him so far across moor and meadow, if only to honor the past. She slipped forward a little toward him. He spoke at length of their loss and of his promises to their father, and nothing about his presence repelled her, since his manner did not at all suggest a man's peremptory ways; yet it was painful, too, to allow someone wholly other to hear her and to reflect that these last days she had had no choice but to lean on him, and she kept her reserve. Her faint answers, each hardly more than a word, conveyed her sadness, and he felt extremely sorry. It was a thoroughly pathetic figure that he glimpsed through her gray curtains, and to imagine her more clearly he thought back to what he had once dimly seen in the dawn. As though to himself he said,

23. When in mourning for a close relative, one occupied in principle a room from which the floorboards had been removed, making it a *tsuchidono* ("earth house").

24. To relay his messages to the sisters.

"I need only see the changed color of the reeds to know all too well
the sad color of your sleeves, deeply dyed in mourning gray."[25]

She replied,

"Sleeves so changed in hue give a capacious welcome to abundant dews,
yet I myself, as I am, have no refuge in the world.

On the tangled threads . . ."[26] But her voice broke, and she retired within, plainly overcome.

He could hardly detain her at such a moment, and he was therefore both moved and sorry. The old woman came forward assertively in her stead and told him a series of poignant stories about the old days and the recent past. She had witnessed many extraordinary things, and he could not simply dismiss her as ancient and unsightly; instead he engaged her in intent conversation.

"His Grace passed away when I was young," he said, "and it was then that I understood life to be suffering; so that when in time I became a man, the rank and office prized by the world held no attraction for me. Now that I have seen His Highness go, too, when he was pleased enough just to live here in peace, I am more alive than ever to the truth that the world is dross; but while it might seem forward of me to describe those who sadly survive him as ties capable of detaining me, I am resolved for as long as I live to uphold the promise I made him and to remain in close touch. Even so, though, your astonishing story has made me want still less to leave my mark on the world." He was in tears, and she was weeping too much to be able to answer. He so resembled *him* in manner that the quality of *his* presence, which she had long forgotten, now came back to her vividly and deprived her of speech.

She was a daughter of the Intendant's nurse. Her father, a Left Controller when he died, was the son of a maternal uncle of their mistresses' mother. After years of wandering distant provinces she had lost touch with the Grand Counselor's house once this lady died, and she had been taken in by His Highness. Although of no remarkable distinction in her own person and quite accustomed to such service, she understood things well enough that His Highness himself recognized her merit and put her in charge of his daughters. Concerning that incident long ago, she had kept the secret and breathed no word of it even to the young ladies with whom she had lived day and night for years, and from whom she kept nothing. The Counselor, however, assumed that since old women are always such gossips, she must at least have told the tale to her bashful mistresses, even if she had not simply blurted it out to everyone, and this was no doubt so galling and embarrassing that he considered it reason enough to make sure that neither sister went to anyone else.

He prepared to start back, since it no longer seemed right to spend the night.

25. The "reeds" are *asaji* (*chigaya*), a reedlike plant common on fields and moors and often mentioned in poetry for the way it changes color in autumn.
26. *Kokinshū* 841, by Mibu no Tadamine, on mourning his father's death: "On the tangled threads of my robe of mourning I thread my tears for the life of him I have lost."

Why, when His Highness had said that this might be the last time, had he blithely believed there was really no reason to worry and so in the end never seen him again? Just this autumn it had been, not that many days earlier, and now His Highness was gone, he knew not where. Oh, the pity of it! His Highness had lived so simply, with none of the amenities most took for granted, but his residence nonetheless was always clean, swept, and perfectly kept. Now those going in and out were holy monks, and while in His Highness's part of the house, divided off from that of his daughters, the implements for his devotions remained as they had always been, the monks had informed his daughters that they would move all the images on the altar to their temple. At this news the Counselor well understood how the sisters would feel once they alone remained behind and even the monks were gone, and the thought was very painful indeed. "The sun set long ago!" his men warned him, and so he collected himself and set out. Just then a wild goose cried overhead.

> "Geese passing aloft where unbroken autumn mists cover the heavens
> bring it back to me again, that in this world nothing lasts."[27]

The sisters were the first subject he mentioned when he met His Highness of War. Gathering that things would be easier now, His Highness wrote to them often. They shrank from giving such a correspondent the slightest reply. He was well known to be a gallant, and despite his apparently languishing thoughts about them, they knew with gloomy certainty that any letter from their remote and weedy fastness would look to him clumsy and out of date.

"Ah, how cruelly the months and days pass by!" they said to each other. "I never imagined that his life, fragile as it naturally was, might end yesterday or today, and while all I ever heard reminded me that nothing endures, I took it for granted that little time would separate his passing from mine. Looking back on the past now, I see how misplaced that trust was, yet I simply lived on vacantly from day to day, without fear or apprehension; whereas now a gust of wind, the sight of unknown visitors, or the sound of people clearing their throats sets my heart pounding and indeed fills me with helpless terror. Oh, it is too much to bear!" Their sleeves were never, never dry. Meanwhile the year drew to a close.

In the season of snow and hail, the sound of the wind, which blows just as mournfully everywhere, made them feel nonetheless as though they had only just withdrawn from the world into these hills. "Ah, the New Year is coming!" their women would sometimes exclaim bravely. "This one has been so lonely and sad. I can hardly wait for spring to make everything new!" They themselves, however, expected nothing of the kind. It was only because their father had gone into retreat from time to time on the mountain nearby that there had been any comings or goings at all from the house, apart from the Adept's occasional visits to inquire after His Highness's health; but what could bring *anyone* there now? This saddened them very much, even though they quite understood that visitors should be fewer than

27. The poem plays on *kari*, "goose" and "impermanent."

ever. It was a rare occasion for them, now that their father was gone, when a mountain rustic once beneath their notice arrived to look in on them. The people from the hills sometimes brought them nuts and firewood, the season being what it was, and the Adept sent them charcoal and so on. "I would be very sorry indeed to give up serving His Highness in this manner, after having become accustomed to doing so over the years," he wrote. They remembered how their father had always sent padded garments to the temple, to help those on retreat there ward off the mountain wind, and they therefore did so now; and with tears in their eyes they came forth to watch the priests and acolytes carry them away up the slope, in and out of view, through the deep snow.

"Even if Father had taken the tonsure, there would still have been lots of people calling here like that as long as he was alive," they assured each other. "We might have been sad and lonely, but we would certainly have continued to see him." The elder asked,

> *"Now that he is gone and no one treads anymore the rough hillside path,*
> *what is it that your eyes see in the snow upon the pines?"*

And the younger replied,

> *"How glad I would be to know at least that the snow on those mountain pines*
> *is none other than the man whose loss leaves us desolate.*

I envy the way new snow keeps falling!"

The Counselor now arrived, knowing that he would have no time to do so once the New Year came. The sisters fully understood what it meant for him to come casually calling then, incomparable as always, when the humblest gentlemen would no longer venture out into such snow, and they had a seat prepared for him with more than their usual care. The women found and dusted off a brazier that was not mourning gray, and they, too, recalled the pleasure with which His Highness had looked forward to these visits. The elder still hesitated to receive him, but she yielded to necessity, since she did not wish him to think her unkind. She did not drop her reserve, but she gave him somewhat fuller answers than before, conveying as she did so an imposing elegance. No, he thought, we cannot go on like *this* forever—but look what my mind is suddenly up to! How easily this sort of thing can change it!

"His Highness of War is extraordinarily annoyed with me," he said. "I must once have happened to mention to him those most moving words that your late father left me, or perhaps his searching insight has guessed them, for he constantly complains that whereas he trusts me to speak to you for him, your cool response suggests that I do it very poorly. To my mind this is quite unfair, but I cannot very well just refuse to serve as his 'village guide,'[28] and I wonder *why* you

---

28. *Kokinshū* 727, by Ono no Komachi: "I am no guide to the village where the seafolk dwell, that he should always be saying how displeased he is with me." The poem depends on a wordplay on *uramin*, "be angry (with someone)" and "wish to see the shore."

must treat him this way. People seem often to talk about what a rake he is, but he really has remarkable depth of heart. I hear also that he is inclined to think little of anyone he gathers might give herself too easily. The yielding woman, quiet and unassuming, who sensibly winks at one thing and another and resigns herself if she feels a little hurt, is the one who actually inspires truly lasting devotion. Once a couple's mutual loyalty begins to crumble, mud soils the clear waters of her Tatsuta River,[29] and all that she shared with him is lost. It happens all too often. His Highness is a man of deep feeling, you know, one who would never lightly waver in his devotion to someone who responded in kind and who seldom appeared to oppose his wishes. I am sufficiently close to him to know him as others do not, and if the idea strikes you as worth pursuing, I will do everything in my power to bring it to fruition. I shall wear myself out dashing back and forth!"

She did not see how so long and grave a speech could possibly refer to herself, and she considered replying as a mother might. However, no words came. "What can I say?" she answered. "So suggestive an appeal from you only leaves me at a loss how to respond." Her light laugh sounded at once artless and delightful.

"I do not mean you to take what I say as being addressed necessarily only to yourself. I would be grateful if you would accept the goodwill that has brought me here through the snow in the spirit of an elder sister. It is someone else, I believe, who has particularly aroused His Highness's interest. He seems to have intimated as much to her, although unfortunately an outsider cannot easily judge these things. May I ask which one of you answered him?"

What a blessing that *I* never did, not even in a light moment! she said to herself. Not that it makes that much difference, but I would be mortified if he had said things like that! Not knowing what to say, she wrote,

> "No brush but your own has marked the steep mountain trails buried deep in snow
> with footprints, while back and forth letters go across the hills,"[30]

and slipped the note out to him.

"Your denial might only raise further doubts," he said and replied,

> "Then let it be I who first ride across these hills, though on his mission,
> where ice under my horse's hooves crackles along frozen streams.

Then mine will be no shallow reward for the reflection in the water."[31]

This unexpected turn to the conversation upset her, and she left the matter unanswered. Although she did not appear strikingly inaccessible or reserved, she affected none of the airs and graces so favored by modern young women, and what he

---

29. *Kokinshū* 389, by Takamuka no Kusaharu: "Surely the bank below the sacred mountain is beginning to crumble, for the Tatsuta River is running turbid."

30. The poem plays on *fumikayou*, "tread back and forth" and "letters go back and forth."

31. *Man'yōshū* 3289 (also in the Japanese preface to the *Kokinshū*), spoken in ancient times by a young palace lady to a visiting lord whose ill humor instantly vanished: "Mount Asaka! Reflecting you, the rocky pool is shallow, but not this heart of mine in desire."

Bushy beard

gathered of her presence left an impression of admirably quiet poise. It seemed to him that she was indeed exactly what he wanted in a woman. She met his every hint with such well-feigned incomprehension that he turned in embarrassment to talking gravely of the past.

His men cleared their throats and warned, "The snow will only be worse after sunset, my lord!" He therefore made ready to go back. "What I see of your house around me is distressing," he said. "How happy I would be if you were inclined to favor another place I know, as quiet as any mountain village and just as deserted!"[32]

"What a lovely idea!" some of the women remarked, smiling, as they listened with half an ear; but the thought horrified their younger mistress nearby, and she resolved that such a thing should never be.

At the sisters' request their visitor was offered fruit and nuts, and his men, too, were served wine accompanied by handsomely arranged refreshments. There was the watchman with the unpleasantly bushy beard, whom a certain gentleman's scent had rendered notorious. The Counselor, who thought him a thoroughly dubious character, summoned him nonetheless. "How are you?" he asked. "You must miss His Highness now that he is gone."

The man's face puckered up, and he shed feeble tears. "My lord, I who have nowhere else in all the world to go spent more than thirty years here, under His Highness's protection, and now that he has left me to wander moor and mountain, I can only wonder what tree will ever give me shelter again."[33] He made a more and more painful impression.

The Counselor had the rooms once occupied by His Highness opened for him. Dust lay thick everywhere; only the altar was adorned as before, and the low dais on which His Highness must have performed his devotions was swept clean. Remembering what he had promised to do once he had acted on his desire,[34] he murmured,

> *"The oak tree I sought to give me happy refuge under spreading shade*
> *is no more, and where he lived emptiness and silence reign."*[35]

32. The house at Sanjō where he lives with his mother.

33. *Kokinshū* 292, by Henjō: "The tree one turned to in distress for shelter offered none, for its leaves changed color with autumn."

34. He had presumably promised Hachi no Miya that if he acted on his desire to enter religion, he would come to Uji and live with Hachi no Miya as his disciple.

35. *Utsuho monogatari* 212, which includes the words *shii ga moto* ("beneath the oak") and *toko* ("eternal" in the *Utsuho* poem but "floor" [of a room] in Kaoru's), speaks also of a "mountain where a lay devotee performs his practices" (*ubasoku ga okonau yama*).

He was leaning against a pillar, and the young women peeping in at him praised him to the skies.

By now the sun had set. He did not know that the stewards of his nearby estates had been summoned to bring fodder for the horses, and he was therefore unpleasantly surprised and embarrassed when a horde of rustic people noisily burst in on the place, but he disguised his presence there as having been intended as a visit to the old woman. Before he left, he ordered them to continue making themselves similarly useful.

The weather turned mild in the New Year, and the wondering sisters watched the ice melt from the edge of the river. "These were picked in patches free of snow," said a message from the temple, accompanied by bracken shoots and also parsley from the low places. The women served them on stands for fasting fare, remarking to each other as they did so, "How pleasant it is in a place like this to follow the passage of the months and days in the plants and trees!" The sisters could not imagine what they meant.

> "If only I saw the bracken shoots he brought down from the upper slopes,
> then I, too, might know that spring really has come round again,"

the elder said; and the younger,

> "For whose pleasure now shall I gather by the river, from banks deep in snow,
> the first parsley shoots of spring, now that our father is gone?"

So it was that they passed their days and nights, exchanging trifles like these.

There were constant messages from both the Counselor and His Highness of War. So little of what they said was worth retaining that it seems as usual not to have been passed on.

At the height of the cherry blossoms His Highness remembered that exchange about them, and all the young gentlemen who had been with him then expressed their regrets. "What a pity that we shall never again see the residence of so noble a Prince!" they said, and His Highness felt a keen wish to go back there.

> "Those cherry blossoms I once spied, passing your home, now at last this spring
> will be mine to pluck and wear; no mist will hide them from me,"

he wrote, with complete abandon.

They found the sentiment unacceptable, but the days were passing very slowly for them then, and it was such a pretty letter that they did not wish to ignore it completely. The younger replied,

> "Where, then, will you go to pluck and claim such flowers, when it is in gray
> that mist swathes every blossom on the trees around my home?"

His Highness was profoundly annoyed to note that she still refused to encourage him in any way.

The Counselor, the only one to whom he could vent his complaint, found the situation amusing, although he took care to answer him with all the gravity of a staunch guardian, and he would mutter whenever His Highness's giddy hopes became too obvious, "Now, now, this will never do"; at which His Highness, perhaps feeling chastened, would protest, "It is just that I have not yet found anyone who really suits me!"

It was a matter of considerable disappointment to His Excellency that His Highness had no interest in his Sixth Daughter,[36] but His Highness was in no mood to yield. As he privately observed, "There is nothing attractive about the proposal, and besides, His Excellency's pompous ways are such a nuisance—I could never get away with the smallest indiscretion."

That year Her Cloistered Highness's[37] Sanjō residence burned down, and she moved to Rokujō. In the confusion the Counselor failed for a long time to visit Uji. With his exceptionally stalwart disposition he remained calmly persuaded that the elder sister[38] was his, but he meant to do nothing brusque or offensive as long as she failed to soften toward him, and he wanted to make sure that she knew he had not forgotten what her father had asked of him.

The unusual heat that summer was very trying, and when it occurred to him that the air beside the river might be cool, he set off straightaway. Dazzling sunlight was pouring in when he arrived, for he had started out in the cool of the morning. He rested in the western aisle, which had been His Highness's, and called for the watchman. The sisters, who were before the altar in the chamber, slipped off to their own rooms because they did not wish to be so close to him, but despite their attempt to evade notice, he of course detected their movement nearby and could not sit still. He found a small hole beside the lock at one edge of the sliding panel into the aisle where he was, moved the screen that stood there aside, and peered through. There was a standing curtain on the other side, which was very disappointing, and he was just about to withdraw again when a gust of wind lifted the blinds. "Why, anyone could see us!" a woman exclaimed. "Slide that curtain out here!" Her blunder delighted him, and he peered through again. Standing screens tall and short had been placed inside the blinds, and the sisters were just then passing into the room beyond, through the open panel opposite his own.

The first[39] stepped into view to look round a standing curtain and watch his men roaming about in the cool. The bright, unusual effect of leaf gold trousers with a dark gray shift no doubt suggested what she was like. Her shoulder cords[40] were casually tied, and she carried a half-hidden rosary. Her slender height gave her a lovely carriage, and he admired the lustrous, perfectly ordered sweep of her abundant hair, which appeared to him nearly to reach the hem of her gown. Her en-

36. Yūgiri's daughter, Roku no Kimi, whose mother is the daughter of Koremitsu.
37. Onna San no Miya.
38. As so often elsewhere, the text specifies neither elder nor younger, singular nor plural.
39. The younger sister, Naka no Kimi.
40. *Obi*, more properly *kakeobi*: red silk cords that passed over each shoulder and were tied together in the back, worn by a woman on pilgrimage or when performing religious devotions.

chanting profile, all fresh and yielding innocence, recalled the First Princess,[41] whom he had glimpsed in passing and whom he imagined with a sigh to look very similar.

The second now slipped into view. "There is nothing in front of that sliding panel!" she said, glancing toward it with wary vigilance, and her manner seemed to him to promise real distinction. In felicitous poise and line, her head and hair conveyed a somewhat nobler grace than her sister's.

"There is a screen on the other side," the thoughtless young woman replied. "He could not peek through so soon!"

Girl in a shift and trousers

"It would be awful if he did, though," she said, slipping out of sight again with a worried look, and her proud elegance struck him vividly. The colors she wore were dominated by mourning gray and very like her sister's, but she had a more winning loveliness, and his heart went to her in sympathy. She seemed to have lost just enough hair to give what she had a clean sobriety, and while the ends were a little thin, it fell as perfectly as combed thread, showing those prized glints of kingfisher blue that he particularly liked. The hand that held her sutra text, written on purple paper, was less plump than the other's, for she seemed to have become very thin. The one who had been standing before was now seated in front of the opening of the far sliding panel, and for some reason she looked around, straight at him, smiling. She was extremely attractive.

41. Niou's elder sister, the daughter of the present Emperor and of Akashi no Chūgū.

47

AGEMAKI

Trefoil Knots

Agemaki ("trefoil knots," used to decorate a gift) is the chapter title because of the word's oc- curence in a poem by Kaoru:

"In these trefoil knots may you secure forever our eternal bond,
that our threads may always merge in that one place where they meet."

The poem is based in turn on a *saibara* song also known as "Tre- foil Knots."

"Trefoil Knots," which continues "Beneath the Oak" without a break, overlaps with parts of "The Ivy" and "Red Plum Blossoms."

PERSONS

The Counselor, age 24 (Kaoru)

The Adept (Uji no Ajari)

Her Highness, the elder daughter of Hachi no Miya, 26 (Ōigimi)

The Princess, the younger daughter of Hachi no Miya, 24 (Naka no Kimi)

Ben, a gentlewoman of Hachi no Miya's daughters, around 60

His Highness of War, 25 (Niou)

Her Majesty, the Empress, 43 (Akashi no Chūgū)

His Excellency, the Minister of the Right, 50 (Yūgiri)

The Consultant Captain, earlier the Chamberlain Lieutenant,
son of Yūgiri

His elder brother, the Intendant of the Gate Watch

Her Majesty's Commissioner

His Majesty, the Emperor, 45

That autumn the wind along the river, a sound so familiar for years, troubled and saddened them while they prepared for the first anniversary of their father's death. The Counselor and the Adept looked after most of the arrangements. Frail and sorrowing, the sisters pursued the fine work of making the vestments and the adornments for the scripture texts, under the guidance of their gentlewomen, and one imagined all too easily their plight without this help. The Counselor himself arrived and presented heartfelt greetings on an occasion that marked for them the end of mourning. The Adept came as well.

The sisters were just then arranging the threads for presenting the incense[1] and saying to each other, "I follow even in this guise the thread of the days."[2] The Counselor understood them, because past the edge of the blind he spied a full winding frame, just visible through a gap in a standing curtain. "O that I might thread on it the gleaming beads of my own tears,"[3] he said, struck to imagine Lady Ise feeling the same way. The elder sister within the blinds, too shy to show by her reply that she knew the poem, answered, "No, it is nothing";[4] for Tsurayuki had evoked his misery on losing someone he loved in terms of courage as slender as a thread, and the memory reminded her how well an old poem may speak for oneself.

The Counselor was already engaged in composing the dedicatory prayer, and to explain his intention in offering these images and scriptures he wrote,

> "In these trefoil knots may you secure forever our eternal bond,
> that our threads may always merge in that one place where they meet."[5]

1. Ornamental, five-colored threads adorned both a wrapped package of incense and the stand on which the incense rested.

2. *Kokinshū* 806: "Though my life is a burden to me I still linger, and I follow even in this guise the thread of the days." The poem plays on *henuru*, "pass (time)" and "comb (thread)."

3. *Ise shū* 483: "O that, twisting thread together, I might upon these weeping voices thread the gleaming beads of my own tears." The poem was composed while the poetess Ise (died circa 939) was making thread to be used in the funeral observances for an Empress.

4. Varied from *Kokinshū* 415 (also *Tsurayuki shū* 764): "No, it is nothing one might twist into thread, yet how slender is my courage as the road leads me away!" Ki no Tsurayuki lived 868–945.

5. "Trefoil knots" are *agemaki*, three-lobed knots used to decorate an object for formal presentation; these no doubt have to do with the packages of incense that the sisters have been preparing. However, *agemaki* is

He gave it to her, and despite dismay over his renewed appeal she replied,

"What thin thread of life, too weak for long to sustain gleaming beads of tears,
could bear the steady weight of an everlasting bond?"

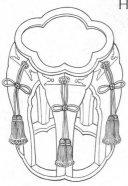

Her disheartened and resentful visitor rejoined, "Then 'on what, if they do not meet'?"[6]

Now that she had removed herself so forbiddingly as a topic from their exchange, he gave up approaching her directly and instead spoke earnestly of His Highness of War. "Observing him in various ways, I can hardly doubt that as he is, perhaps a little more given to certain pursuits than you would wish, he is bent on success with the correspondence that I gather he has begun. Why must you always be so distant, when there seems really to be nothing that need alarm you? I do not see how you could fail to understand the way of the world, and I am afraid that your stubborn insistence on removing yourself from him is very disappointing to me, who address you in good faith. I hope that you will let me know clearly what you intend, one way or another."[7]

Trefoil knots

"A wish not to disappoint you is precisely what has led me to receive you this informally, at the risk of starting a good deal of talk. Your failure to understand that also suggests a certain shallowness on your part. It is quite true that no one with feelings, living in a place like this, could fail to know every variety of melancholy, but we have never been very clever, and besides, on the issue you mention, my father never said a word about anything of the kind when he discussed what we were to do in this future case or that. I gather therefore that he wished us to remain as we are and to renounce any thought of marrying; and alas, for that reason I have no answer to give you, one way or the other. Still, I regret that my sister, who is a little younger, should be hidden away among these hills, and I would much rather not have her languish here forever. Personally, that worries me very much, but I have no idea what to do for her." She sighed, and her troubled manner touched him extremely.

It was perfectly natural, he felt, that she should not be up to deciding the matter, despite being so grown-up, and, as often before, he summoned the old woman. "For years all that brought me here was the desire to prepare for the life to come," he began, "but toward the end, when His Highness seemed very discouraged, he enjoined me to make whatever dispositions I wished with respect to his

---

also a hairstyle (hair parted down the middle and done up in two round masses on either side) typical of boys and girls in ancient times, and the word in this sense occurs in a *saibara* song ("Trefoil Knots") to which Kaoru no doubt also alludes. The song is quite suggestive: "Ah, *agemaki,* tra-la tra-la, a mere arm's length, tra-la tra-la, the gap between us as we lie, and see how we roll together, tra-la tra-la, how we've come together!"

6. *Kokinshū* 483: "So we twist together your strand and mine, and on what, if they do not meet, am I to thread my life?"

7. Grammatically, this speech appears to be addressed to Ōigimi alone, but Niou's correspondence was with Naka no Kimi. Kaoru must therefore want Ōigimi to agree to accept him and to have Naka no Kimi accept Niou.

daughters, and I promised to do so; and yet they themselves contravene what His Highness decided for them by remaining so stubbornly intractable that I even find myself wondering whether he might have settled on other alliances for them. You would of course know about it if he had. Being as peculiar as I am, I have never before been much interested in the things of this world, and I suppose it must be karma that has brought me so close to them. Considering that others, too, seem now to be talking about it, I would just as soon honor His Highness's wishes and share a respectable intimacy with his elder daughter. I concede the mismatch,[8] but it is not as though such a thing were unheard of." And he continued somberly, "I speak on behalf also of His Highness of War, and the elder's refusal to accept my reassurances suggests to me that privately she may have other plans for her sister. Does she? Please tell me!"

Many a deplorable gentlewoman might have answered him with a mixture of flattery and impertinent advice, but not she, because although at heart she desired nothing else, she only said, "It has always been their way to be contrary in these matters, my lord, and perhaps that is why they have never shown any sign of the sort of leanings one would expect. We who serve them, such as we are, have for years lacked any sturdy tree to shelter us. All those with a mind to look after themselves have gone elsewhere, wherever they could, and even those with an old tie to His Highness have in the main abandoned the house as well, until the ones left complain more bitterly than ever that they cannot bear to stay one moment longer. 'It was all very well when His Highness was alive,' they say; 'then he had your dignity to uphold, and he might insist on an old-fashioned standard for fear of demeaning you. Now, though, you have no one else, and anyone who blamed you for giving the world its due in whatever way you can would understand nothing and deserve no respect. Who would want to spend her life *this* way? Even mountain ascetics, who live off pine needles, are so keen to look after themselves that they divide practice of the Buddha's teaching into different paths.' This is the sort of unkind speech they keep making to my mistresses, who, young as they are, have every reason to be troubled. The elder concedes nothing, but she seems to long to give her sister a proper place in the world. Your kindness in coming here, so far into the hills, has made you a familiar figure for her over the years, and she feels so little removed from you that, since you are now talking seriously with her, I believe she would welcome any hint of interest in my younger mistress. As to all the notes and messages from His Highness of War, she cannot believe that he really means what he says."

"I heeded His Highness's last, moving injunction and mean to remain in touch as long as I draw breath, and I would therefore gladly give myself to either, since they are equally deserving; and I am delighted that your elder mistress should think so well of me. Nonetheless, my heart will continue to draw me in a certain direction, despite my wish to renounce the world, and I know that I can do nothing to change that. The attraction I feel is no ordinary one. It would please me best of all, you know, if she no longer kept blinds and so on between us, as she does now, so

---

8. Because the sisters are Princesses (granddaughters of an Emperor in the male line), whereas Kaoru (whether as Genji's son or as Kashiwagi's) is a commoner's son.

that a great deal remains unsaid, but received me face-to-face so that I might tell her whatever I please about this treacherous world and she in turn open to me the heart that at present she withholds. I greatly miss having brothers or sisters to be close to in that way, and since, as I am, I can only keep to myself the things that crop up in life to move, amuse, or pain me, I feel sufficiently alone to hope that she will admit me to her confidence. I can hardly confide everything that comes into my head that way to Her Majesty.[9] Her Cloistered Highness at Sanjō is still so youthful that I can hardly think of her as my mother, but still, she is who she is,[10] and I cannot very well speak freely to her either. As to other women, I am so distant, reserved, and timid with them all that in truth I feel extremely lonely. I am hopelessly awkward, to the point that the most casual flirtation repels and disconcerts me; I am tongue-tied with anyone I genuinely like; and I am sorry to say that as far as I am concerned, your elder mistress's failure even to notice how she upsets and frustrates me is extremely unfortunate. With respect to His Highness of War, I wonder whether she might not leave the matter to me, with the understanding that he means no harm."

The old woman longed to satisfy both, considering how admirably they would fill the void of the household's present life, but they were too daunting, and she could not approach her mistresses adequately on the subject.

The Counselor let the day drift by, for he wished to spend the night and engage the elder in quiet conversation. This troubled her, since the vague irritation she detected in his manner was becoming obvious, and she disliked more and more the idea of conversing with him privately; yet in most respects he was so wonderfully kind that she found she could not turn him away and received him after all.

She had the panel between the altar room and the aisle slid open and the altar lamps raised high, and she doubled the blinds she sat behind with a screen. A lamp was lit outside as well, in the aisle, at which he protested that he was unwell and in no state to be seen. "Why, I am in full view!" he said. He stretched out on his side. She had him discreetly brought refreshments, and she sent out very nice garnishes to the men with him as well, for their wine. The men were together in a gallery of some sort, while her gentlewomen kept their distance, and the two therefore talked undisturbed. He detected no sign of softening toward him, but he found her so sweet and charming that he liked her very much indeed and soon began after all to burn for her.

He kept thinking how silly it was of him, with no more than a screen and a blind between them, to remain so slow to act on his ardent desire, but he betrayed nothing and went on talking instead about one thing after another, touching or amusing, that had caught his attention in the world. Inside the room she called her women nearer, but they had no wish to intrude and made no real move to obey; on the contrary, they retreated still farther and lay down. Not one even raised the wicks of the altar lamps. She called to them again in some distress but got no response.

9. Who is supposed to be Kaoru's half sister.
10. Not only his mother but a nun.

"I am not feeling very well," she said, "and so I shall retire for now. I shall talk to you again closer to dawn." He heard her preparing to withdraw.

Lamp

"Such conversation as we have been having is a great comfort for one who has come here over mountain paths and who is less well even than you, and you will therefore leave me disconsolate." Silently, he swept the screen aside and entered. She, already halfway into the next room, was aghast to feel herself being drawn back again. She was furious and extremely put out.

"Is this what you meant by 'keeping nothing between us'? What an appalling way to behave!" she cried, her scorn only adding to her appeal.

"You will not understand that to me nothing *does* come between us, and I only want to convince you of that! What do you mean by calling my behavior appalling? I shall gladly swear otherwise before the Buddha. Now, now, *please* do not be afraid of me! I have never had the least intention of violating your wishes, and I remain the strange fool I have always been, though I am sure that no one would ever believe it!" By the intriguingly dim lamplight he swept her streaming hair aside and looked at her face. She was as deliciously beautiful as anyone could wish.

In so horribly lonely a house a lustful man would find nothing to stand in his way, he reflected, and he certainly would not stop here! How awful! Even his own past wavering could obviously have gone just as easily another way, but the spectacle of her weeping with outrage was too pathetic, and he did nothing of the kind; no, he kept up his hope that in time she would yield to him on her own. It would be too painful to force her, and he did his best to soothe her instead.

"I allowed you near enough even to court scandal because I never even imagined such a thing of you," she said accusingly, "and now the churlishness that has shown you the unfortunate color of my sleeves has taught me how little I myself am worth.[11] Nothing can console me for that." The thought of her innocently worn mourning gray, caught in the lamplight, was misery to her.

"I quite understand that you should feel as you do, and I am too ashamed of myself to know what to say. Nothing could be more natural than your appeal to the color of your sleeves, yet the goodwill that let you see me so often through the years might dispense you from rejecting me so and from treating me as though you had never met me before. I am afraid that you have the matter quite wrong." He told her about many, many times when the thought of her had inspired unbearable longing, including the one when that music had reached him beneath the moon at dawn. All this embarrassed and repelled her. She kept saying to herself, To think that he was acting so serious and detached and all the while actually felt *that* way!

He placed a short curtain standing nearby between them and the altar and for a time lay down beside her. The strong fragrance of incense and the highly distinc-

11. Although embarrassed to have been seen in mourning gray, she may be even more so that he saw her face—a humiliation perhaps too great to mention directly.

tive scent of star anise troubled him, for the Buddha meant far more to him than to most people. Especially now when she is still in mourning, he thought, struggling to regain his composure, any thoughtless concession to my impatience would be an offense against what I aspired to first; surely when her mourning is over she will soften toward me at least a little. An autumn night stirs many feelings, even somewhere less lonely, and no wonder that here gales on the peaks and crickets crying in the hedge spoke to them only of desolation. Her occasional responses to his talk of the fleeting world left an admirable impression. The women, so difficult to waken before, gathered that it was done now, and they all withdrew. She recalled what His Highness her father had said, and reflected how true it is that the longer one lives, the more unforeseen trials one must bear. In her despair she felt as though her tears would flow to join the noise of the brawling river.[12]

Daybreak came at last. The Counselor's men arose and cleared their throats to rouse him, and the neighing of the horses reminded him pleasantly of what he had heard of nights spent on the road. He opened the panel toward the light of dawn, and they looked out together at the poignant sky. She, too, slipped forward slightly, while, little by little, light caught the dewdrops on the ferns fringing the shallow eaves. Their figures side by side lent each other a sweet grace. "How I should love just to be with you always like this, enjoying with one heart the moon or the blossoms and sharing observations on this passing world."

He spoke so kindly that by and by she forgot her fear. "If only I could talk to you not all exposed like this, but with something between us, I am sure that at heart nothing *would* part us," she replied.

The light grew, and they heard a rush of wings nearby as flocks of birds took to the air. A distant bell rang to mark the last of the night and the new morning. "Go *now*," she said, desperately ashamed. "You must not stay."

"I cannot make my way straight home through the morning dew as though something really happened. What would people think?[13] Please grant me the latitude you would if it had, and do the same hereafter as well, even if we are not to each other what the world assumes. Be sure that I will do nothing to offend you. Ah, you are cruel not to pity me for all the intensity of my devotion!" He made not the slightest move to leave.

"Very well," she said, foreseeing disaster, "it shall be as you wish hereafter, but this morning please do as I say!" She was desperate.

"It is too hard! I know nothing of partings at dawn, and I am quite certain that I shall lose my way!" He sighed again and again.

Somewhere a cock crowed faintly, and his thoughts went to the City.

> "Ah, the break of day, when many cockcrow voices gather into dawn
> all a mountain village's throng of wandering sorrows!"

She replied,

---

12. An allusion to *Wakan rōei shū* 701 (in Chinese), by Ōe no Asatsuna.

13. An ordinary lover would go straight home, but since all the observers (her gentlewomen, his men) assume he has married her, they might think something was wrong if he did so.

"I believed this place, far away among these hills, had no cocks to crow,
and yet life with all its grief has found me out even here."

After accompanying her to the sliding panel,[14] he left by the way he had entered the evening before and lay down, but he could not sleep. Still longing for her presence, he realized that he could not possibly have taken the matter so calmly all these months if he had felt *this* way about her. The prospect of returning to the City seemed very bleak.

The elder Princess did not go straight to lie down because she worried about what her people might be thinking. What misery it is to get through life with no one to lean on, she reflected, and what unfortunate surprises life may easily bring, when some *will* go on and on plying me with unsound advice! I cannot really object to this gentleman's looks or manner, and my father himself suggested often enough that if he were so inclined . . . But no, for myself I will continue as I am. It is my far prettier and far more deserving sister whom I would gladly see live as others do. Once I have done that for her, I shall look after her with all my heart. But who, then, will look out for *me*? If this gentleman were anyone ordinary, I might well after all these years feel like accepting him, but he is so overwhelming, so daunting in his glory, that he only makes me hopelessly shy. No, I will live out my life just like this. Sleepless and often in tears, she awaited day, feeling so unwell after what she had been through that she went into the inner room to lie beside her sister.

The younger Princess had been lying there wondering what the women could be whispering about, and she was glad that her sister had come, but when she drew the covers over her, she felt enveloped by his penetrating fragrance and remembered what trouble it had given the watchman. Well, then, it must be true. Feeling very sorry, she said nothing and pretended to be asleep.

Their visitor called out the old woman Ben, talked to her intently, and, before he left, gave her a thoroughly proper note[15] for her mistress, who reflected, Even after I took his "trefoil knots" so lightly, my sister must assume that I have ended up with him, whatever "mere arm's length" I may have meant to keep between him and me. She was deeply ashamed and spent the day quite indisposed, claiming to be ill.

"It[16] will be soon, my lady!" a gentlewoman reminded her. "There is no one else to look after all the little things that need doing, and your indisposition comes at a very bad time!"

The younger Princess finished wrapping the packets.[17] "I have no idea how to do the gift knots," she insisted; and so in the sheltering darkness her sister got up, and they did the tying together. A letter came from the Counselor, but in her reply she spoke only of how unwell she had been all day. "What a thing to do!" the women whispered. "She is such a little girl!"

Their time of mourning ended, and when changing out of their old robes they reflected how swiftly the months and days had passed, even though they had never

14. Between the room where they are and the part of the house where the sisters live.
15. Instead of a "morning after" (*kinuginu*) poem full of love and the sorrow of parting.
16. The anniversary of Hachi no Miya's death.
17. Of incense, presumably.

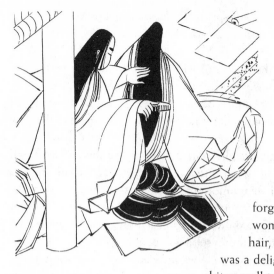

Combing a lady's hair

actually thought to survive him at all. They had made a pathetic sight, prostrate with despair over their unexpected and tragic misfortune. After going about for so long in darkest gray, they looked quite lovely now in a far lighter shade, and the younger, who was indeed in full flower, surpassed her sister in winsome grace. The elder all but forgot her sorrows as she watched the women wash and comb her sister's hair, for she was such a pleasure that it was a delight to imagine her looking every bit as well to *him*. There was now no one else she could have look after her, and she therefore did so herself with all a mother's tenderness.

The Counselor, too eager to await the ninth month when she would no longer wear the mourning he had felt obliged to respect, now came again.[18] "I should like to talk to you as I did before," he reminded her, but she declined to receive him on the pretext that, unfortunately, she did not feel herself.

"You are extraordinarily harsh!" he protested in an answering note. "What can your women be thinking?"

"I am too overcome to speak to you—it has been too upsetting to face changing out of mourning," she replied. Outraged, he called the same woman as always and poured out his complaint.

The gentlewomen, who looked to him alone for relief from dire misery, felt that it would be wonderful if he were to have his desire and their mistress were then to move somewhere far more respectable; and they had all agreed simply to let him in. The elder Princess knew little enough of this but noted her peril nonetheless, for, she reflected, He does seem to make rather a lot of that old woman, and she might cause trouble if she were to fall in with him. When something happens in an old tale, there, too, it is not the lady who starts it. No, one must always beware of what people may be up to.

As long as he is so angry with me, I must put my sister forward, she continued. He may be disappointed, but I cannot imagine him treating her lightly once he has made her his, and besides, the slightest acquaintance with her will please him very well. Who, though, would just accept the idea straight off, if I were to mention it? Not he, surely—that is not what he had in mind, he would say, and in any case he would refrain for fear of being thought fickle.

She felt that it would be wrong of her to breathe no word of her plan to her

---

18. Kaoru arrives in the eighth month because the almanac discouraged consummating a marriage in the fifth or ninth month.

sister, for whom her own experience encouraged sympathy, and accordingly she told her all. "Our father said we must never take it into our heads to act lightly or provoke laughter, even if that were to mean remaining alone like this all our lives, and considering how sinfully we kept him tied to the world while he lived, and troubled his pious devotions, I am resolved to honor his every word, which is why I myself hardly feel lonely at all. These women, though, seem to resent this strange obstinacy on my part, and that places me in a painful position. And yes, as far as that goes, the prospect of having you living on and on this way strikes me with every passing month and day as a sadder and greater shame. I long to give you, at least, a life such as others lead and so to assure myself, as I am, some comfort and dignity."

What could she be thinking? her sister wondered indignantly. "Do you suppose he meant just *one* of us to spend the rest of her life this way? Hopeless as I am, I am sure that I worried him far more than you! What comfort could I be to you unless I were here with you day and night?" She really was quite angry, and the elder, who could only agree, thought her very sweet.

"But to all of *them* I am impossibly obstinate—it makes me so upset!" She said no more.

The sun began to go down, but still their visitor did not leave. Her Highness was at her wits' end. Ben came with a message from him and went on at some length about how rightly he was annoyed. She just sighed in answer and wondered what on earth to do. If only we still had just *one* of them,[19] she thought, there would at least be someone able to look after all this for me, and since the vagaries of destiny make it so difficult ever to please oneself,[20] failure then would look decent enough and provoke no smiles. They are all growing old, every one, and each thinks herself wise. They carry on as they please about what would be right for me, but am I to believe *them*? No, they do not deserve it, and they have only one thing in mind! The way the women all kept at her, as though they would drag her off by main force, annoyed her extremely, and she remained completely unmoved. On this topic her sister, with whom she discussed everything in perfect accord, was somewhat more naive even than she, so much so that she hardly understood the issue at all. What a hopeless situation this is! the elder cried to herself, resolutely turning away from them.

"Will you not change into other colors, my lady?" they kept insisting, each apparently intent on the same thing, and in dismay she realized that there was indeed nothing here to stand in a man's way. The house was so small that it offered no hope; there was nowhere for a *yamanashi* blossom to hide.[21]

The visitor himself made no distinct approach to any of them, having decided long ago to remain as perfectly discreet as though this bond had never had any marked beginning. "I shall be patient in exactly this way for as long as it takes her to

19. Of her parents.
20. *Gosenshū* 938, by Ise: "I can say neither yes nor no, for alas, in this world one can never please oneself."
21. *Kokin rokujō* 4268: "Though you reject the world, where will you go to hide, *yamanashi* blossom?" *Yamanashi* ("mountain *nashi*") is a wild relative of the cultivated fruit, and *yama nashi* means "there is no mountain (for you to hide behind)."

give me her consent": that was the resolve of which he spoke. That old woman of his talked it over with the others, all of them whispering openly together, but they were foolish and, at their age, stubborn, and that is probably why Her Highness remained in so sad a plight.

Being at a loss, she talked to Ben when Ben approached her. "I remember how His Highness used to speak of this gentleman's rare devotion," she said, "and by now I rely on him in all things. Indeed, I am more casual with him than it is proper for me to be. Yet his temperament betrays something else as well, something I had not thought to find, and he seems to be angry with me, which I find quite disturbing. If it were sensible for me, as I am, to wish to live in the world as others do, I would have no reason to refuse him. However, I gave up that sort of idea long ago, and all this is very painful. What I do regret is that my sister and the beauty of her youth should go to waste. For her needs, yes, a house like this one here is far too constricting, and if he really aspires to honor His Highness's wishes, I would have him accept her as myself. I feel as though I should then be with both, and our two hearts, hers and mine, would be one in her. Please let him know that, and put it as persuasively as you can." Despite her shyness she said very well what she wanted to say, and Ben was deeply moved.

"My lady, I had already gathered that much from you, and I have explained the matter to him perfectly clearly, but he says that he cannot possibly shift his affections that way, and that since His Highness of War is more and more seriously displeased with him, he means to be of all the assistance he can in that direction as well. That would be excellent for you both, my lady. Your mother and father could not arrange two more advantageous alliances, even if they were both alive and intent on doing their best for you. If I may say so, I wonder sadly what is to become of you when I consider the perilous circumstances of your present life, and although I cannot vouch for these gentlemen's feelings in the future, I do think that they represent a wonderful stroke of good fortune for you both. I quite understand that you should not wish to disobey His Highness's last words, but surely he meant only to leave you a warning, lest no party worthy of you appear and you be tempted to consider one insufficiently distinguished. He said often enough that should this gentleman be so inclined, he would very gladly see you that well settled. High or low, someone who loses those who uphold her best interests may easily find herself caught in circumstances to which she should never have assented, and that, I believe, is what often happens. It is all too common, and no one will blame her for it. In this case, though, my lady, when a gentleman whose standing so honors you that he might have been born for just that purpose assures you of deep and rare devotion, very well, you may insist on fending him off to carry through your own pious resolve, but will you then subsist on nothing but clouds and mist?"[22]

Her Highness, who found this lengthy speech repellent and offensive, lay facedown on the floor. At the sight her younger sister felt extremely sorry for her. They went to bed together as usual. The elder was worried and anxious about what

---

22. Like the immortal sages alleged to inhabit high and distant peaks.

to do next, but the house offered no nook or cranny where she could hide. She therefore simply drew a nice soft robe over her sister and lay down a little distance from her, since it was still quite warm.

Ben told their visitor what Her Highness had said. Why, he wondered, did she so reject the world and its ways? Perhaps she had learned from her saintly father that all things pass. She seemed to him at heart more than ever like himself, and he felt no aversion or any wish to make himself out to be wiser than she. "I see," he said. "At present she will not consider receiving me, not even with something between us. Tonight, then, you must find me a way to steal in to where she is sleeping." Ben had the others go off to bed early and arranged things with those who knew.

The evening was hardly over before a roaring wind set in, rattling the flimsy shutters and, he realized, providing a perfect opportunity to slip in unheard. Ben softly led him in. It bothered her that the sisters were sleeping together, but they always did that, and she could not very well have asked them just this once to sleep apart; in any case, she assumed that he would manage well enough to recognize the one he had in mind. Her Highness, however, was still awake. On detecting a sudden sound she silently rose and slipped off quickly to hide. What are they up to? Her heart went out in anguish to her still peacefully sleeping sister. How I wish we could both hide together! But she could not go back. Shaking, she watched a gentleman in a gown[23] enter by the lamp's dim glow, as though the room were his own, and lift the cloth of the standing curtain. With sharp pity she wondered, What can she be feeling? Meanwhile she sat cramped between the screen that stood there and the shabby wall. It so hurt to imagine her sister's utter repugnance, when the mere prospect was apparently hateful to her. And all this, she kept thinking, is our misfortune for having been left alone in the world without any real protector! She seemed to see her father before her, just as he had been that evening when he set off up the mountain, and she longed for him desperately.

That single figure set the Counselor's heart beating with pleasure, for he thought that she must be expecting him; but no, he saw all too soon that it was not she. This one seemed a little prettier, a little more sweetly appealing. Her horror and dismay told him plainly enough that she really did not know what he was doing there, and he felt very sorry for her, although at the same time the cruelty of her sister, who must at present be hidden somewhere, genuinely infuriated him. He did not like the thought of this one either belonging to anyone else, but he bitterly rued being so thwarted in what he truly desired, and he had no wish to seem capricious in her eyes. Very well, he assured himself, I shall let this pass, and if destiny then really will have it that this one is to be mine, why should she, just for that, have to go to somebody else? On this resolve he spent the night, as before, in sweet and amusing conversation.

The old women, who thought it was done, asked each other, "Where can our younger mistress possibly be? It is very strange!"

"She must be somewhere!"

---

23. Kaoru has his dress cloak and his trousers off. He is in his dressing gown or pajamas, so to speak.

"Quite apart from all this, you know, the very sight of him is enough to smooth your wrinkles away, and I can't imagine why Her Highness should want nothing to do with anyone so wonderfully handsome and kind!"

"I suppose that terrifying god they talk about must have possessed her,"[24] ventured a gap-toothed old woman with an evil tongue.

"Oh, no, you'll bring bad luck! What could have got into her head? She just grew up a long way from anyone else, that's all—she doesn't know what to do with herself because she has no one to advise her properly on something like this. She'll like him well enough once they're actually together."

"Well, I wish she'd give him his way," said a last sleepy voice, "and be what we hope she'll be!" Distressing snores came from here and there.

This was no autumn night for "the one you spend it with" to shorten,[25] but he felt even so that dawn came all too soon, and it occurred quite naturally to him that he was very sorry to leave her, for both were equally lovely. "Love me, too!" he said. "Please do not pattern yourself on someone else, who is very cruel!" He promised that they would meet once more. Despite himself he felt as though it had been strangely like a dream, but he was reassuring himself when he left to lie down, as he had done before, that another time he would try again with the one who spurned him.

Ben came in, saying, "This is so strange! Where can my young mistress be?" And there she was, lying there, baffled and mortified, wondering what it could all possibly mean. She was angry with her sister, remembering what she had said the previous day.

Only the coming light of day brought the cricket out from the wall.[26] She could hardly bear to imagine how her younger sister was feeling, and they said not a word to each other. This is dreadful: now we have both lost our mystery! she lamented. After this we can never relax our vigilance for a moment!

Ben went to their visitor, from whom she learned all about Her Highness's extraordinary obduracy. The account left her seated before him dumbfounded and filled with pity, for she felt that this was simply too much and deserved no sympathy. "Until now I had felt that there might still be some remedy for her harshness," he said bitterly, "and I did what I could to reassure her, but last night was thoroughly humiliating, and I wish I could die. All that dissuades me from doing so is the thought of how reluctant His Highness himself was to abandon them, loving them as dearly as he did. I shall not approach either of them, ever again, with courtship in mind. No, I shall not forget the anger and bitterness they have caused me. I gather that His Highness of War is unashamedly pursuing the younger, and I suppose she feels that she might as well reach as high as she can. That much I understand, and to my shame I can so little blame her that I would much rather never come here again for you all to see. At any rate, please say nothing to anyone about what a fool I am." He left much sooner than usual.

24. Popular belief had it that a woman past the normal marriage age might be possessed by a "god" (*kami*), or power, that made her behave strangely.

25. *Kokinshū* 636, by Ōshikōchi no Mitsune: "To me no autumn night is long, for that always depends on the one you spend it with."

26. Ōigimi, from where she had been cowering between the screen and the wall.

"This is a disaster for them both," the women whispered to one another.

Where will this lead? the elder wondered, despairing that he might now turn against them, and she condemned her women's hopelessly muddled officiousness. She was pondering these things when a letter came, and to her own surprise she was more pleased than usual to receive it. As though disdaining to notice the colors of autumn, he had tied it to a green bough of which just one twig sported deep red leaves.

> "Goddess of the hills, who dyed one and the same branch in two different ways,
> I would gladly ask of you: which has the deeper color?"[27]

Her heart beat when she understood that he had said little of his great indignation, concealing it[28] so well that he seemed to wish to let the matter pass. Her women loudly insisted that she must answer it, and she knew that it would be quite wrong of her to leave the task to her sister, but she still found the reply a painful challenge to compose.[29]

> "What the goddess means by the way she dyes the hills I could never guess,
> but it seems to me perhaps the true color is the new."[30]

She dashed it off rapidly, and he found it sufficiently handsome to doubt that he could remain angry with her forever.

This is not the first time I have gathered that she wants me to have herself in her sister, he reflected, and she must have planned this when I thwarted her by not acquiescing. I suppose that if her effort fails, my indifference will make her pity her sister, she will hate me for being cruel, and I will be less likely than ever to get what I have always actually wanted. That old woman who passes our messages back and forth must think me a bit frivolous, too. All in all, I wish I had never fallen in love with her—everyone will see far too clearly how I, who so longed to renounce the world, could not in the end bring it off, and I will resemble the little boat people laugh at so—the one that, like any common gallant, keeps rowing back and back to the same woman."[31] Such thoughts as these occupied him all night, and the sky was still lovely with dawn when he set off to call on His Highness of War.

He had not far to go, since to His Highness's great pleasure he had moved to Rokujō after his mother's Sanjō residence burned. His Highness, wholly at leisure, occupied an exquisite house where the near garden resembled no other, where the

27. The branch is the two sisters; the twig with the red leaves is Kaoru's attachment to Ōigimi; and the "Goddess of the hills" (*yamahime*) is Ōigimi. "Which one of you do I love more? Judge for yourself: it is you."

28. *Tsutsumi* ("concealed") also suggests that Kaoru has sent a *tsutsumi-bumi*, or "wrapped letter," rather than a knotted *musubi-bumi*, or love note.

29. A reply from either might suggest that Kaoru has indeed consummated a marriage with her, but this risk is obviously most acute in the case of Naka no Kimi.

30. "You now prefer Naka no Kimi."

31. *Kokinshū* 732: "Like the little boat that rows out Horie Channel but turns back, I return every time to loving the same woman."

shapes even of familiar flowers or the swaying of trees and grasses seemed unique, and where the very moon, clean and bright in the garden brook, would have done for a painting. He was still up, as the Counselor assumed he would be. His Highness suddenly noted that unmistakable scent on the breeze, hastily donned a dress cloak, and came forward perfectly arrayed. The Counselor knelt halfway up the steps, and His Highness did not even invite him to come higher; he simply sat leaning against the railing while they chatted of this and that. Something recalled *that* place to His Highness, who then, to his visitor's consternation, proceeded to voice a bitter complaint. But even *I* am getting nowhere! the Counselor thought to himself. Nonetheless, he had reason to wish His Highness success, and he told him more carefully than usual what dispositions would be required.

Alas, fog arose as dawn came on, a chill spread across the sky, and, under a veiled moon, darkness lingered provocatively beneath the trees. "We must go there soon," His Highness said, perhaps recalling the mountain village's melancholy charm; "I want you to take me with you." And when his friend seemed to demur, he added lightly,

> "When maidenflowers bloom on so broad a meadow, why need you keep watch
> and stretch a rope around them to claim they are all your own?"

> "These maidenflowers abloom among all the dews of the morning fields:
> they are only for the eyes of the one whose heart is theirs—

not just anyone's, you know!" his visitor replied provokingly.

"Come, that is enough out of *you!*" His Highness exclaimed, properly annoyed at last.

His Highness had long been talking this way, but it had worried the Counselor that the looks of the lady in question might not please him. Now, however, he could hardly imagine his friend despising her beauty, and while he had always preferred caution, lest her wit not be found to improve on closer acquaintance, he now knew that there was no need for concern on that score either. He therefore decided silently that although it might be unkind of him to thwart what the elder herself was secretly plotting, he simply could not shift his affections that way from one to the other; no, he would cede the younger to His Highness, which would spare him the censure of both.[32] His friend did not know this, however, and it amused the Counselor to be accused of wanting to keep the sisters for himself. "I should hate to see the habitual lightness of your ways cause her any distress," he retorted in an avuncular tone.

"Very well, you will see. I have never been so keen on anyone in my life," His Highness replied gravely.

"I see no indication that either has any thought of satisfying you. You have set me a very difficult task." He described to His Highness exactly what he was to do when they were there.

---

32. Niou and Ōigimi.

The twenty-eighth, the last day of the equinox, was a lucky one, and with invisible precautions the Counselor took His Highness on a clandestine visit to Uji. He went to extraordinary lengths to make it appear that nothing in particular was afoot, for His Highness had his heart set on going, and it would be a catastrophe if Her Majesty were to learn of the expedition, since she was then certain to put a stop to it. They sought no imposing lodging[33] because the boat crossing was too risky; instead the Counselor secretly left His Highness on an estate he owned nearby, at the house of his man there, and he went ahead by himself. No one was likely to notice His Highness in any case, but the Counselor presumably wished to avoid any possibility of detection even by the occasional watchman who might look round the house. He was greeted as always by cries of "Here is his lordship!" The sisters heard the news with little pleasure; but, the elder reflected, she had at least given him to understand that he must now aspire elsewhere, while the younger resigned herself to his presence in the knowledge that *she* could hardly be the one he had in mind. Still, that dreadful experience had left her angry with her sister, and she no longer thought of her as she had before. When her elder sister had something to say to the Counselor or a reply to receive, she insisted on having the message passed by one of the women, who wondered unhappily where it would all end.

The Counselor had His Highness ride to the house under cover of darkness and then summoned Ben. "There is just a word I would like to have with Her Highness," he explained. "I am still extremely ashamed because she seemed not to want anything to do with me, but I simply must speak to her. Will you please take me to her as you did before, a little later on?" His speech was all innocence. One or another, then, thought Ben—it is all the same! She went to her mistress.

There! Her Highness said to herself when she heard the old woman. His affections *have* shifted! Pleased and reassured, she received him after firmly locking all the sliding panels onto the aisle except the one through which he would enter.

"I have something to tell you, and I would much rather not need to talk so loudly that others may hear me!" he began. "Please open the panel a little! I feel so awkward."

"I am certain that I shall hear you quite well," she replied, leaving it shut. I suppose he feels that he must at least acknowledge me, she mused, now that his feelings really *are* moving to her. Besides, it is not as though I have never met him before, or that I mean unkindly to let the night pass while he waits for my replies. She had come so far forward that he seized her sleeve through a crack between the panels and tugged at it, filling her ears with bitter reproaches. Oh, no! What can have induced me to listen to him? Bewildered and sorry, she nonetheless persisted gallantly in trying to bring him round to seeing her sister as herself and to get him to go to *her*.

Meanwhile His Highness of War, as instructed, went to the door the Counselor had passed through that other night and rustled his fan. Ben came and ushered him in, and he smiled to think that she had done the same more than once before.[34] The elder Princess, still intent on redirecting her visitor, knew nothing of his coming;

33. Yūgiri's villa, across the river.
34. For Kaoru.

and the Counselor, touched and amused, saw that he would have no defense if she ever blamed him for having failed to give her any hint of the plot. "His Highness of War insisted on coming with me, and I could not refuse," he therefore confessed. "He is here now, and he has got in without a sound. I imagine he has persuaded that officious old woman to help him. He has left me looking like a bumbling fool!"

Her Highness was speechless. "Well," she said, "not for a moment did I ever expect anything so utterly extraordinary from you, and you are now free to despise me for a lapse that has betrayed the full extent of my deplorable innocence."

"Alas, it is too late now. Pinch and scratch me if you like, if my repeated apologies will not suffice. It appears that you aspired higher than me, and yet the destiny ordained by karma never seems to match one's desires, and *he* turned out to have someone else in mind, for which you have my sympathy, although I am the one worse caught out and more bitterly disappointed. You might as well resign yourself to what must be. No one will really believe that you and I are immaculate, however admirably this panel may protect you. Do you suppose the gentleman who asked me to bring him here imagines the two of us spending the whole night like this, with nothing but anguish in our hearts?"

She strove to calm him, despite her inexpressible outrage, because he seemed ready at any moment to break the panel down. "The destiny you are pleased to mention is something no one can see, and I have no idea what it might be; I only feel tears of ignorance of what lies ahead[35] envelop me like a mist. The thought of what you may do next disturbs me like a bad dream, and if in times yet to come people still talk about all this, I do not doubt they will cite the story as a model of how ridiculous someone can be. What do you suppose His Highness will make of all your scheming? Please, do not add more miseries to the ones you have already heaped upon me. If I survive this, as I hope I shall not, I may perhaps speak to you again after recovering some semblance of calm. I feel a darkness coming over me, and a great weakness, and I must rest. Let go of me."

Her distress was so acute that he felt both shamed and charmed when he recognized despite himself the justice of her complaint. "Oh, my darling, respecting your wishes as no one else would have done is precisely what has made such a fool of me!" he said. "I have no reply, since you seem to find me unspeakably hateful and offensive. I know quite clearly now that the world will soon see no more of me." And he continued, "Very well, I shall address you this way, from a distance. I beg you not to leave me!" He let go of her sleeve, and she slipped toward the inner room—and yet, he was deeply moved to find, not all the way. "Until day dawns, I shall take comfort from having you just that near," he assured her. "I will do nothing more, I promise!" Sleep would not come, and he listened wide-eyed while the river roared ever louder. Midnight gales left him feeling like a solitary pheasant[36] while the night dragged on.

---

35. *Gosenshū* 1333, by Minamoto no Wataru, when leaving his province to return to the City: "What is so sad about tears of ignorance of what lies ahead is that they keep falling straight before one's eyes."
36. The male and female of a pheasant pair were said to spend the night on separate slopes.

Dawn came, and with it as always the sound of temple bells. His Highness seemed to be sleeping on and on, since there was no sign of him, and the annoyed Counselor cleared his throat. Yes, it was very strange.

"I who brought him here, am I now to be the one who must lose his way
in the dim twilight of dawn, on a road that I would shun?[37]

Has the like ever been seen before?"
In a low voice she replied,

"Give a thought to one whose heart so burdened with care is all in darkness,
on the road you must wander through no one's fault but your own."

He just could not bear it. *"Must you do this to me?"* he complained bitterly. "You keep yourself so impossibly removed—it is too much, it really is!" Meanwhile day was slowly coming on, and they heard His Highness leave as he had entered the evening before. His soft, stealthy movements diffused the perfume that he had so beautifully burned, with fond anticipation, into his clothes. The astonished old women were all confused, for they could not make out how this could have happened, but they felt comforted to reflect that his lordship could never have meant any harm.

Both hastened back to the City while it was still dark. The return journey seemed very long indeed, especially to His Highness, who had lamented from the start that he could by no means go there whenever he wished, and who seemed to suffer from the thought of missing a single night.[38] They arrived in the early morning, before people were up and about. His Highness had the carriage drawn up to the gallery[39] before alighting. Both young gentlemen laughed to think how they had stolen in so strangely, in what looked like a woman's carriage.[40] "I gather you are keen to be assiduous in your attentions," the Counselor remarked. He said nothing of his own mishap, since he still rued the foolish part the guide had played. His Highness hastened to dispatch his letter.

The sisters yonder in the mountain village were so upset that they could hardly believe it had really happened. The younger now detested the elder—Why, she never gave me the slightest hint of what she was planning!—and would not even look her in the eye. The elder, who could not convince her that she had known nothing at all, sympathized with her completely. What can possibly have happened? the women wondered. They kept watching their mistresses for clues, but the one they looked to most was as though dazed, and they remained none the wiser.

37. *Shūishū* 736, by Minamoto no Shitagō, "on returning in the dark from being with a lady": "Lost among the shadows of dawn, my heart that loves you would not leave you at all."
38. *Kokin rokujō* 2749: "Now my new wife and I have shared a single pillow, shall I miss a single night with her, when I love her so?"
39. Adjoining the middle gate of Niou's residence.
40. Because they had had the carriage blinds lowered.

The elder opened His Highness's letter and showed it to her sister, but she refused to get up at all. It seemed to the unfortunate messenger that it was taking a very long time indeed.

> *"Do I love you, then, only as might anyone? See how through thick dew*
> *I came so far to find you, over wastes of sasa[41] moors!"*

His elegantly practiced hand had a marked allure that, all things being equal, Her Highness had once found quite pleasing, but now it upset and worried her, and she shrank from taking it upon herself to compose the reply. Instead she told her sister gravely what to write and sternly made sure that she actually did so. She presented the messenger with an aster layered long dress and triple-layered trousers,[42] and since the gift seemed to embarrass him, she had it wrapped and then borne by one of the others with him.[43] There was nothing imposing about him; he was simply the privy page His Highness usually sent. His Highness, who wished to avoid betraying his secret to anyone, heard of the messenger's reward with annoyance and assumed it had to do with that officious old woman of the evening before.

His Highness wanted his guide with him that evening, too, but the Counselor declined. "His Eminence Reizei has summoned me to wait upon him," he explained, and stayed behind. His Highness was put out. There he goes again, he thought, treating this world as though it hardly mattered!

There is no help for it: this is not what we wanted, but that does not authorize us to ignore him, Her Highness assured herself in resignation. Their house was not one that lent itself to being decorated, but she did what she could to make it pretty in anticipation of his arrival. He had a long way to come, and she was startled to find herself pleased that he should be in such haste.

The younger Princess, the one affected, was in no condition to do more than allow herself to be dressed, and the sleeves of her deep pink robe were soaked with tears, until even her older and wiser sister began to weep. "I doubt that I will be with you much longer," she said, "and while my whole concern is for you, day and night, these women keep dinning it into my ears that your new state will turn out for the best; and I expect they are right after all, since no doubt they have lived long enough to know what is what. Even I, who have so little sense, never imagined that I could insist on your always remaining the same, but it certainly did not occur to me that you might suffer at any moment, as now, so disturbing a shock. I suppose that this must be what they like to call destiny. It is so hard, you know. When you are feeling a little better, I will make you understand that I knew nothing about it. Please, please, do not hate me! It would be bad karma for you!" She was stroking and combing her sister's hair. Her sister, who did not reply, reflected nonetheless that

---

41. A general word for several species of ground-cover plants related to bamboo. *Sasa* is very common in Japan.

42. The messenger's reward is especially elaborate, in keeping with the felicitous character of the occasion: a marriage.

43. Normally, the clothes would have been laid across his shoulders, and he would have displayed them proudly.

what she had heard suggested only a wish to spare her distress and harm. Alas, she thought, the ridicule and contempt I now face mean misery for her, and all the while I have her looking after me!

His Highness derived particular pleasure from the very dismay her unsuspecting innocence aroused in her, and, needless to say, he liked her still better with a somewhat greater measure of womanly sweetness. Distressed then to the point of pain that those endless mountain trails should put her almost beyond his reach, he assured her with deep feeling that she would always command his devotion, but she made nothing of any of it, whether for good or ill. A girl, however carefully sheltered, is likely to feel only moderate shyness or fear if she has been among more or less normally peopled surroundings and has had parents and brothers from whom to learn what men are like; but although the younger Princess had never been forbidden the company of others, she had always lived far off among the hills, and habitual isolation and reserve had made this new, unsought presence in her life very daunting indeed. She knew that she could only be an impossible rustic in every way, and her courage failed her at every attempt to pronounce the most trivial answer. Nevertheless, she was the one whose manner suggested the livelier intelligence and wit.

"On the third night people have rice cakes," the women reminded Her Highness, upon whom it then dawned that these would have to be made for the occasion. She hardly knew what orders to give while the work went on before her, and the way she blushed with embarrassment at being seen grandly directing things was utterly charming. Being the elder gave her the greater dignity and poise, but she really was very fond of her sister, and very kind.

A letter came from the Counselor: "I would have come yesterday evening, were it not for chagrin that my devotion should have gone unrewarded. I know that I might make myself useful tonight, but that ignominious guard duty has left me feeling unwell, and in the end I have not been able to make up my mind to it." Written with punctilious formality on Michinokuni paper, it arrived thoughtfully accompanied by cloth for the occasion, still unsewn, in many-colored rolls packed in several chests that he had sent to Ben and marked "For the Women." It was all simply what had been available at Her Cloistered Highness's, and he seemed not to have managed to collect a great deal, for hidden underneath there were damasks and plain silk, while on top, apparently for the sisters, lay two very beautiful sets of robes. On a sleeve of one of the shifts she found, trite though it was,

> "Nightclothes you may need: no indeed, I cannot say we ever shared them,
> but I might ask you to wear at least this reproach from me."

To her this intensified the shame of both, whose mystery was now gone, and she struggled for words to answer him; meanwhile, one of the messengers ran off and disappeared. She detained a miserable servant to give him her reply:

> "At heart you and I may well be so much at one that nothing parts us,
> yet I would not wear from you any hint that we are joined."

It was a very ordinary effort, what with her agitation and the thoughts that troubled her so, but he who received it at last was pleased to be touched that she had expressed her feelings plainly.

His Highness had gone to the palace, and that night he privately despaired at seeing no chance to get away. "There you are, still single," Her Majesty admonished him, disliking that he lived so often at home, "and I gather that everyone is talking about what a gallant you are. One simply cannot approve. You would do well not to insist on acting just as you please. His Majesty is concerned about you as well." Shattered, His Highness withdrew to his palace apartment, where he wrote and sent off a letter.

He was still sunk in gloom when the Counselor arrived, and he received him with greater pleasure than usual; for, he thought, here at least is an ally. "What am I to do?" he lamented. "It seems to be getting dark, and I am at my wits' end."

The Counselor decided to probe his feelings. "It has been days since you were last at the palace," he said, "and I expect that Her Majesty will be even more upset with you if you fail to stay and run off again. I was in the gentlewomen's sitting room, and I heard what she said. Secretly, I paled to imagine that troublesome service I did you earning me Their Majesties' undeserved censure."

"I would much rather not hear what she has to say on the subject!" His Highness replied. "Someone has been spreading rumors, I suppose. What have I done to deserve this sort of reproach? I tell you, I could do without being a man who has to mind his manners this way!" He really did seem to hate it.

The Counselor pitied him. "You seem to be in trouble either way. For tonight, then, let me take the blame and risk my own good name. What about *riding* over the Kohata hills?[44] I expect that will start more talk,[45] but never mind."

It was quite dark by now, and His Highness could think of nothing else to do. He set out on horseback. "Unfortunately, I cannot accompany you," the Counselor informed him, "but I shall do what I can for you here." He was therefore the one who stayed on in attendance at the palace.

He went to wait upon the Empress. "I heard His Highness go out," she said. "He is completely impossible! What *will* people think? It is so awkward for me when His Majesty hears about this sort of thing, because he scolds me for not being strict enough with him."

Despite all her grown-up children, the quality of her presence suggested ever more delightful youth. Her Highness the First Princess must be very like her, he reflected, longing sometime at least to hear her voice this close. This sort of ease between people is what starts a gallant thinking forbidden thoughts, I suppose—when she is so near and familiar and yet inaccessible. Could any heart in all the world be as peculiar as mine? Still, once anyone *has* touched it, I am hers forever. Every one of the gentlewomen in Her Majesty's service had something in looks or wit to commend her, and some among their handsome company were very striking indeed, but he had resolved that none should disturb him, and he behaved perfectly correctly

---

44. *Man'yōshū* 2429 or *Shūishū* 1243 (a later variant): "For love of you I have crossed on foot the hills of Kohata in Yamashina, even though I have a horse!"

45. Niou should not ride. His dignity requires him to travel by carriage.

with them all. Certain of them purposely tempted him. Her Majesty set a tone of such calm and dignity that they were serene on the surface, but people are all different, and some still betrayed romantic leanings. Now pleased, now moved, he took it all as evidence of the world's fleeting ways.

At Uji the night was growing late, and despite the Counselor's solemn assurances His Highness had still not arrived. Instead there was a letter from him. I knew it! Her Highness thought, and she was nursing her bitter hurt when he came after all, near midnight, as though racing the wild wind, the very picture of sweetly perfumed grace. How could she not think well of him? Surely even the bride understood that the time had come to yield a little. She looked quite lovely, and it seemed to him that, so perfectly dressed, she was truly without equal. That she should please even his eye, when he knew so many great ladies, and that in looks as in all other aspects of her person she should charm him so much *more* in intimacy—this brought broad, unabashed smiles to the rustic old women's faces. "*What* a shame it would have been to see so ravishing a young lady go to someone of no interest at all! He is perfect for her!" they all exclaimed to each other, meanwhile clucking with disapproval over their elder mistress's strange obstinacy.

Her Highness looked them over without indulgence, old and faded as they were, in all the bright colors they had prepared and now wore so gracelessly. My own best years will soon be behind me, she reflected. In the mirror I see myself wasting away. It must never occur to these old women that they are unsightly. Their hair is thinning at the back, but that is nothing to them; they dress up their front locks instead and put on a lot of bright makeup. I am not *that* bad yet, but perhaps I am only imagining that my eyes and nose will still do. These anxious thoughts ran through her mind while she lay looking out into the garden. The idea that she might be with anyone so dauntingly magnificent left her more and more aghast. Why, she said to herself, in a year or two I will have deteriorated even further! Look how little there is left of me! She held up a pitifully thin, weak hand and pondered again the sorrows of life.

His Highness reflected on how difficult it had been to get away and realized with a sharp pang that coming here would never be easy; and he told his Princess what Her Majesty had said. "Sometimes I will want to come and still not be able to," he said, "but you must not worry. I would not have come all the way here tonight if I had the slightest thought of neglecting you. I threw caution to the winds because I was so worried that you might be upset and doubt my feeling for you. I shall not always be able to go about like this, though. I must make proper arrangements to bring you somewhere closer." But despite these earnest assurances, his prediction that he would have to stay away sometimes led her to assume that what she had heard about him was true, and her plight filled her with sadness.

When the sky began to lighten, he opened the double doors and invited her to come and look out with him. Banks of mist lent a particular poignancy to the scene, and his passionate heart responded with wonder and delight to this unusual dwelling, whence one looked out as always over white waves from the wake of dim passing boats piled high with brushwood. By the brightness spreading from the rim of the mountains, he saw now how truly lovely she was. She might have been the

The Uji Bridge

most treasured Princess in the land, although, being naturally partial, he did not doubt that his own sister was very attractive, too; and the longing to contemplate her beauty more at his ease was almost more than he could bear. He had a full view of the ancient Uji Bridge, with the river roaring by forbiddingly, and the clearing mist revealed more and more of the wild banks. How *can* you have lived so long in such a place? he murmured with tears in his eyes, and she felt thoroughly ashamed.

All grace and elegance, he promised her his heart not just for this life but for all their lives to come, and despite the abruptness of what had happened, she found that she actually preferred him to the dauntingly serious Counselor whom she knew so much better. *That* gentleman had remained extraordinarily composed, his affections being engaged elsewhere, and this had made him rather awkward company; whereas after imagining His Highness with far greater awe, so much so that she shrank from answering a single line from him, she now found herself expecting to miss him if he was gone too long, and she could not help condemning her own inconstancy.

His Highness's men were clearing their throats loudly to rouse him, and he was extremely anxious to return to the City before he should be caught out in full daylight. Again and again he reassured her about the nights he would have to spend far from her, much against his will.

> *"The span will not fail, noble Maiden of the Bridge, that brings me to you,*
> *though tears many a long night moisten your lonely sleeves,"*[46]

he said, returning to linger with her when he found that he could not yet leave.

> *"Must I wait and wait, always trusting your promise that the span will last,*
> *while an Uji River Bridge of distances divides us?"*[47]

She said no more, but the sorrow in her manner affected him unbearably.

---

46. *Kokinshū* 689: "Will she again tonight spread lonely sleeves on her narrow mat and await my coming, the Maiden of Uji Bridge?"

47. The bridge over the Uji River, first built in 646, was famous for being so long (roughly 160 yards).

She watched him recede into the light of dawn, a figure to impress any young woman's heart, and the perfume that still lingered with her called forth many a secret stirring—yes, now she knew exactly what was what! The dawn was light enough to reveal things clearly, and the gentlewomen peeped out at him, too. "The Counselor is very kind," they said, "but there is also something so unapproachable about him. Perhaps it is just knowing that His Highness is a step above him, but he really does have something quite special."

All the way there he kept remembering her sweetly sorrowing air, until his longing to go back risked compromising his dignity; but he was returning in secret so as not to start talk, and if he did that, he could not escape notice. He wrote to her at least daily. It seemed to Her Highness that he really was in earnest, yet day after day went by while he never came, and she who had decided not to court any such misery now pitied her sister still more than she did herself, though she feigned equanimity lest her sister lapse further into melancholy. Meanwhile she strengthened her resolve never, never to add *this* to the sum of her own griefs.

The Counselor well knew how they must long for His Highness to come, and he felt his own fault in the matter keenly. While urging His Highness to action, he constantly sought to read his feelings from his face. He seemed so thoroughly dejected that the Counselor felt satisfied at least of his good intentions.

It was the tenth of the ninth month, and the dreariness of moor and mountain came easily to mind. At dusk one day, with cold rain threatening and the sky all heavy, menacing cloud, His Highness fell prey to growing despair, for in the end he could not make up his mind what to do.[48] Then the Counselor arrived, divining His Highness's mood. " 'What must it be like for them at Furu, in that mountain village'?"[49] he said to rouse him. Very pleased, His Highness invited him to come, too, and as before they set out in a single carriage.

The farther they went, the more easily they imagined what melancholy must prevail where they were going. They talked of nothing else all the way there. Damp from the cold rain that fell through the twilight gloom, they diffused into the dreary late-fall landscape as they passed an inexpressibly alluring fragrance that must have troubled many a mountain rustic's heart.

All the women's whisperings of the past days were gone, and, wreathed in smiles, they prepared a room to welcome the Prince. They had got in touch with a few daughters, nieces, and so on, who had drifted off to respectable places in the City and had brought them back; and these foolish creatures, long contemptuous of the household, now marveled at so astonishing a caller. His arrival pleased Her Highness, but that other, trying presence with him troubled and constrained her, although she recognized when she compared them the rare depth and patience that made the Counselor so wholly unlike the Prince.

His Highness was admitted and entertained with all the hospitality that the

48. *Kokinshū* 509: "Am I the float on the fisherman's line, on the sea of Ise, that I should not be able to make up my mind?"

49. *Shinsenzaishū* 599: "What must it be like for them at Furu, in that mountain village, in the first, cold rains; surely even she who lives there has wet sleeves." The mention of Furu, a place in the hills a good way south of Uji, plays on *furu* ("fall," speaking of rain).

place afforded, while his companion, comfortably treated more as one of the household, raged nonetheless at having been relegated to a distant room suitable for a guest.[50] Her Highness was sensitive after all to his displeasure, and she spoke to him through the sliding panel. "It is no joke,"[51] he complained bitterly. "Is this the best you mean to do?" She understood and sympathized, but her sister's plight greatly depressed her, and she could only conclude that her new state was a very sad one. No, she told herself, I will *not* give in to his wishes! The man whose heart promises happiness will, I am sure, all too soon seem cruel enough. I shall not let such differences come between him and me, until each thinks less well of the other. He inquired about how His Highness was behaving, and she gave him such hints as to allow him to guess the truth. He explained with regret how much His Highness really did care, and how he himself constantly had his eye on him.

After conversing more warmly than usual, she concluded, "Let us talk again once these new worries have passed and I am more at peace." She was neither unpleasant nor distant, but the panel was securely shut. Very well, he decided, she would be horrified if I were to break it down, and besides, she must have something in mind—I cannot imagine her lightly giving herself to anyone else. His patience therefore won out in the end over his agitation.

"It is just that I feel so uncomfortable," he insisted. "With something between us like this I simply cannot say all I long to say. Do let me speak to you as I did once!"

"My looks distress me more than they used to, and I would not wish you to find me unsightly. Why? I wonder." He thought he heard a little laugh, which he found extremely appealing.

"What will become of me once I allow you to give me hope?" he asked, amid many sighs. Dawn came for them, as always, as it comes for mountain pheasants.

"I envy the Counselor apparently feeling so at home, as though he were lord and master here," His Highness remarked, never imagining that his friend might still be spending his nights alone. The younger Princess was shocked.

He had taken rather a risk to come, and he was extremely sorry and disappointed to have to go back so soon. The sisters, who did not understand this, wondered again in dismay what they had to look forward to and whether the younger one faced only mockery. Hers was indeed a sad and distressing plight. There was nowhere at all in the City where she might move and remain undiscovered. As to Rokujō itself, His Excellency of the Right occupied one quarter of it, and he was so eager to give His Highness his Sixth Daughter—a prospect His Highness himself did not relish—that he would undoubtedly take a dim view of her. He made a practice of denouncing His Highness mercilessly as a profligate and voiced such complaints even to Their Majesties, and His Highness therefore had every reason to be cautious about bringing forward someone otherwise completely unknown. A common affair would actually have been easier to manage, since she could have become

---

50. As Naka no Kimi's husband, Niou has probably been admitted to the chamber, while Kaoru languishes in the aisle.

51. *Kokinshū* 1025: "I test myself to see whether I can bear it, and her absence makes me miss her so much, it is no joke at all."

one of his gentlewomen. However, that was *not* the way he thought of her, for when the new reign came and things then went as Their Majesties hoped, he meant to raise her above all others;[52] but alas, for the present, he could do nothing at all, despite the honor in which he held her.

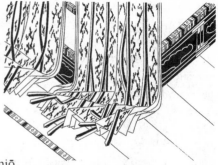

Curtains of a curtained bed

The Counselor meant to receive the elder Princess with all due ceremony at Sanjō, once the work on the place was done. How true it is that many things are easier for a commoner! He felt very sorry for His Highness, who despite his unhappy passion could only steal off to Uji in secret, to the great distress of both. An unfortunate flurry of reproaches might ensue, he reflected, if word of His Highness's clandestine visits were to reach Her Majesty's ears, but that would do *her* no harm, and it really is too bad that, as it is, His Highness cannot even spend the whole night with her! How I should like to do something that really makes a difference for her! In that spirit he did not try very hard to conceal the truth.

It occurred to him that if he did not look after the new season's change of clothes[53] at Uji properly, no one else would; and so after explaining discreetly to his mother that they were needed now, he sent off the bed curtains, lintel curtains, and so on that he had had made for when Sanjō was finished and *his* Princess moved there. He asked his nurse and others also to make clothes specially for the women.

In the tenth month he began insinuating to His Highness that this was a good time to see the weir and suggesting a trip to view the autumn leaves. His Highness preferred to go very quietly, accompanied by his intimate retainers and by the privy gentlemen he particularly favored, but he was too great a lord for that, and the party grew until it was joined by the Consultant Captain, His Excellency of the Right's son.[54] The Counselor was the only other senior noble, though. Most of the party were common gentlemen.

The Counselor kept the elder sister fully informed. "Bear in mind that His Highness will naturally need to break his journey," he wrote. "Everyone who came with him in the spring of last year to see the blossoms will take advantage of the rain to try to get a glimpse of you." The blinds were changed, corners swept here and there, a few dead leaves cleared from around the rocks, and the garden brook freed of its waterweeds. He sent refreshments, too, as well as the staff needed to prepare them. Caught between gratitude and exasperation, she resigned herself to the inevitable and prepared herself for what was to come.

From the house they could hear His Highness's party rowing up and down the

---

52. The Emperor intends to make Niou Heir Apparent when the current one (his eldest son) accedes to the throne.

53. The change to winter clothing and drapery on the first day of the tenth month.

54. In "Bamboo River" this son of Yūgiri was a Chamberlain Lieutenant who courted Tamakazura's elder daughter.

river and making very nice music. They could see a little of them, too, and the younger women went to that side of the house to look. His Highness was too far away to recognize, but the boats, roofed with colored leaves, looked as though they were spread with brocade, and on the wind all the instruments playing together sounded almost loud. Even on so discreet an excursion this great Prince, honored and cherished by all the world, appeared especially glorious to the sisters, and it seemed to their gentlewomen that his light would be well worth awaiting if he were the Herd Boy Star himself.[55]

His Highness had Doctors in attendance, too, since he planned to have the gathering compose Chinese verse. At dusk he drew his boat up to the bank[56] and, to music, set about doing so. Everyone seemed to be in high spirits as with light and dark leaves adorning their hair they played "Immortal of the Deep"; only His Highness was downcast[57] and distraught from imagining that there across the river she must be angry with him. All were presented[58] with topics that suited the season and hummed their lines of verse.

The Counselor planned that His Highness should go to her once the general exhilaration had subsided somewhat, and he was just telling His Highness what to do when the Intendant of the Gate Watch, the Consultant Captain's elder brother, arrived with a sternly formal escort to deliver a message from Her Majesty. Word of His Highness's excursion had of course spread, despite his desire to keep it quiet, and the excursion would no doubt be cited in time as a precedent; however, Her Majesty had been surprised to learn that he had set off in an impromptu manner, without a suitably large and dignified retinue. The Intendant had therefore come accompanied by numerous senior nobles, whose presence crippled any further plans. Prince and Counselor alike felt too wretched to take any further interest in the proceedings, but the others, who had no idea what was at stake, drank, roistered, and played music till dawn.

His Highness had hoped to spend the day where he was, but Her Majesty sent a further, large deputation of her Commissioner[59] and other privy gentlemen. Upset and bitterly disappointed, he still had no desire to leave. He wrote to the house across the river. There was nothing artful about the letter, for he had put down quite seriously everything on his mind, but she knew that there was a noisy crowd around him, and she did not answer. It is *hopeless* for someone as inconsequential as I am to associate with anyone as exalted as he! That was more and more clear to her. It was one thing to resign herself to having him elsewhere, far away, for days and months on end, but for him to carry on this way right in front of her and then to pass on as though she meant nothing to him—that was too cruel and bitter a blow.

55. Who once a year at Tanabata (the seventh night of the seventh month) crosses the River of Heaven (the Milky Way) to spend one night with the Weaver Maid.

56. The opposite bank from the sisters' house.

57. Literally, "Only His Highness felt like the Lake of Ōmi" (Lake Biwa, in Ōmi Province). The name Ōmi plays on *au mi*, "one who meets (his love)." Niou feels like that because despite the good fortune the name suggests, the lake water is fresh and so has no *mirume* (a kind of seaweed) in it; and *miru me* means "lovers' meeting."

58. By the Doctors.

59. The senior officer of the Empress's household.

By this time His Highness was beside himself with anxiety and frustration. The very sweetfish of the weir favored him, for they offered themselves to be caught in large numbers and were served on many-colored leaves, to the delight even of the servants. Everyone else, too, felt thoroughly pleased with the excursion. Only His Highness gazed up at the skies in despair and contemplated the fine trees around the old house yonder or the deep hues of the vines twined around the evergreens. Their surroundings look forbidding even from a distance, the Counselor said to himself; and think what assurances he had given them! It was a disaster.

The gentlemen who had been with His Highness the previous spring remembered the beauty of the blossoms and talked of how lonely the bereaved sisters must be. Some of them must already have caught wind of his secret visits. Others, who knew nothing, chatted on about the sisters anyway, since talk of them had got about despite their isolation among these hills. "I hear they are very pretty," one remarked; and another, "They are very good on the *sō no koto*—His Late Highness had them practice day and night."

The Consultant Captain said,

> *"When can it have been, I caught a glimpse of those trees all in glorious bloom,*
> *and now autumn has set in, their branches are left forlorn."*

The Counselor, who felt called on to speak for them, replied,

> *"Yes, the cherry trees put this truth very plainly: none of the glory*
> *of blossoms and autumn leaves lasts long in this fleeting world."*

And the Intendant:

> *"What could be the path autumn took to move elsewhere, when among these hills*
> *the bright hues of the fall leaves make it so painful to go?"*

Her Majesty's Commissioner:

> *"The man I once knew forsook his mountain village, yet the loyal vines*
> *still clamber among the stones along his old garden wall!"*

He was an old, old man, and he began to weep. He must have been thinking back to when the late Prince was young.

His Highness:

> *"Now autumn is over, loneliness grows and gathers there beneath the trees:*
> *O do not blow unkindly, wind from pines that clothe the hills!"*

He was very close to tears, and those who knew something of his feelings understood perfectly. Some thought it a great shame that he should let this opportunity pass, but the grandeur of his train made it impossible for him to do otherwise.

There was much humming of the best parts of their Chinese poems, and they had made up lots of poems in Japanese, too; but how many could really have been worth anything, drunk as they all were? It would be embarrassing to set down any of them.

Across the river they listened in anguish while the escort's warning cries rang out from farther and farther away. The women had eagerly looked forward to his coming, and they were extremely disappointed, too. No wonder Her Highness was moved to bitter reflections. Why, his heart is just like the dayflower they tell of![60] The little I hear people say suggests that men lie all the time. These worthless women talk when they reminisce about how a man with his endless words can make someone believe he loves her when he does not, and I always assumed people that common were the only ones who could be so perfectly awful—those of a quite different quality would care too much what others might hear of them or think of them, and they would restrain themselves; but no, I was wrong. His Late Highness often heard that this Prince was not to be trusted, and he never even considered allowing him this close. It is just too cruel that after all those impossibly passionate letters and the completely unforeseen moment that joined my sister to him, her misery and mine should only have grown! How is the Counselor taking this despicable behavior? There is no special need to worry about the opinion of anyone *here*, but whatever they may think, he has made fools of us and held us up to mockery! She was so upset that her mood turned, and she felt very ill.

As for her younger sister, the one most affected, when His Highness did come, he reassured her with such profound sincerity that she derived some comfort from thinking that he would never really and truly reject her and that his absences were due only to obstacles he could not surmount. It bothered her, though, that he stayed away so long, and the way he had gone straight past was too bitterly cruel. She became increasingly melancholy, which her elder sister found very hard to bear. He could never treat her this way if I could do all I should for her and we had a house like other people's. Amid such reflections as these she sank into deepening despair.

And this is the sort of thing that will happen to me, too, if I go on living. The Counselor goes around promising this and that, but I know he only does it to try me. I cannot put him off forever, though for myself I want none of him. These women here will never learn; all they can think about is bringing this off, too, and I am sure they will get their way in the end, whether I like it or not. This is exactly what *he* meant when he told us always to be watchful; he was warning us against precisely this. I have no doubt that with our miserable luck we would both outlive *anyone* who mattered that much to us. There I would be, with people laughing that I had gone just the same way,[61] and what cruel suffering I would then have inflicted even on my parents! No, no, I, at least, shall not languish in any such misery. I shall die before I am too deep in sin.[62]

---

60. The dayflower (*tsukikusa*, in modern Japanese *tsuyukusa*) yields a blue dye that fades quickly.
61. Abandoned by my husband, like my sister.
62. Sin (*tsumi*) because this sort of misery, however little deserved, creates bad karma.

In her anguish she refused all food and instead spent day and night pondering nothing but what might lie ahead once she was gone. Her distress made it painful for her merely to look at her sister. How bereft of comfort she will be once she has lost me as well! She is so lovely and so deserving, and she is my pleasure morning and night. I tried to give her a life worthy of her, and secretly that was all I ever wanted, but it would be very bitter indeed for anyone so held up to mockery, however exalted she might be, to go out into the world and make a show of living as others do. No, she concluded miserably, we are hopeless, and it cannot be for the likes of us ever to find comfort in this life!

His Highness nearly went straight back on one of his usual, clandestine visits, but the Intendant of the Gate Watch had already told His Majesty. "The reason why His Highness suddenly rushed off to that mountain village is that he has a secret affair going on there," he explained. "I gather that people are privately censuring his reckless behavior."

The news troubled Her Majesty, too, when she heard it, and His Majesty was no longer in any mood to allow the young man such freedom. "It is not right for him in any case to spend all the time he wishes at home," he observed. Strict orders went out, and His Majesty required His Highness immediately to place himself at his disposal at the palace. The young gentleman had resolved that His Excellency of the Right's Sixth Daughter was *not* for him, but everyone else decreed that he should have her forthwith.

The Counselor could only deplore this when he heard of it. I am just too odd, he thought. Perhaps it was simply destiny, but I felt for the sisters whose future so worried His Late Highness, and I could never forget them. With all their qualities it seemed such a shame that they should merely waste away, and my zeal to give them a proper life surprised even me. In the end I did what I did, what with His Highness hounding me as well and the unfortunate way the one I want insisted on yielding to her sister, but now that I think it over, I wish I had not. No one could possibly have blamed me for claiming them both for myself. He suffered many foolish torments, but alas, it was too late.

The matter weighed on His Highness even more. He longed for his Princess at Uji and worried about her. Her Majesty kept telling him, "If there is someone you like especially, give her to me and treat her with normal discretion.[63] His Majesty has particular plans for you, and I am extremely sorry to hear that people are calling you reckless."

One dull day of hard winter rain he went to call on the First Princess.[64] She and the few women with her were looking at pictures together. They talked from either side of a standing curtain. Her infinitely noble distinction, tempered by sweetly yielding grace, had always seemed peerless to him, and he wished there were another like her in all the world. He gathered that His Eminence Reizei's daughter enjoyed her father's high regard and cultivated most elegant ways, but he had never

---

63. "Let me have her as one of my gentlewomen; then you can see her whenever you want without making trouble."

64. His elder sister.

been able to tell her of his enduring admiration. But, ah, *she* in that mountain village—*she* in sweetness and nobility yielded nothing to anyone, and the thought of her filled him with intense yearning. By way of distraction he had a look at Her Highness's pictures, which were scattered here and there. They were amusing "ladies' paintings,"[65] and they included pictures from the life of a lover. There was a charming house in a mountain village, as well as all sorts of other scenes that had appealed to those who had done them, and many caught his attention especially because they brought his own experience to mind. He thought of asking Her Highness for a few and sending them to Uji. They were illustrations of *Tales of Ise*,[66] and one showed a man teaching his sister the *kin* and saying, "Alas, that it should go to another."[67]

The sight prompted him for some reason to draw a little closer to her and to whisper, "People in the old days used to see each other face-to-face, when it was proper for them to do so, but *you* always put such a distance between us!" She could not tell which picture he had in mind, and so he rolled it up and slid it under the curtain to her, and the little of her hair that he glimpsed when she leaned over to look, spilling forth in billowing waves, seemed such a marvel that he longed to think of her as he would have done of someone less closely related. He said,

> "Not that I would dare to lie down in such a place on such tender grasses,
> but still, it is very sad that I have to feel that way!"

Her women, who were in awe of His Highness, had hidden behind curtains and screens. What a thing to say! He is shocking! she thought and remained silent, which he accepted, because it seemed to him that the lady in the story, "her thoughts all innocence,"[68] caught on rather too quickly. Among all the brothers and sisters these two were especially close, since Lady Murasaki had been particularly fond of them. Her Majesty so pampered them that any gentlewomen of theirs with the slightest defect felt very uncomfortable indeed. Most were the daughters of very great lords. His Highness, with his easily shifting feelings, made sure that he had a playful moment or two with every new arrival, and while he never actually forgot Uji, a great many days went by while he failed to undertake any journey there.

To those awaiting him it was a very long time indeed, and they were sighing that all their fears were confirmed when the Counselor arrived. He had come at the

---

65. *Onna e*, colored paintings with a generally romantic, narrative content.

66. *Ise monogatari*, a tenth-century set of short tales built around poems and centered in theme on the varieties of love. It is almost impossible to exaggerate the importance of this work in the literary tradition.

67. Section 49 of *Ise monogatari* tells of a young man so taken with his sister that he gives her this poem: "This regret will not leave me, that such grass, so fresh and young, and so sweet to rest upon, alas, should go to another." The "grass" is the sister, and the poem plays on *ne*: "root"; "lie down"; "sleep (with)"; and also "sound" of an instrument—hence probably the *kin* shown in the painting but not present in the text.

68. From the sister's reply in *Ise monogatari* 49, which means something like "What strange words, as rare as new grass in spring! And here I was, my thoughts all innocence!" The exchange has been interpreted variously, and the sister's reply can be taken either as innocent or as complicitly erotic. Niou favors the latter.

news that the elder was unwell. Although her illness was not grave enough to confuse her wits, she cited it as a pretext for not receiving him.

"But I have come all this way, and in great anxiety!" he protested. "You *must* take me to where she is lying"; and so he was led to the blinds behind which she had made herself as comfortable as she could. His presence upset her, but she lifted her head politely enough and answered him as required.

He told her how His Highness had come so unwillingly to pass by. "Please do not worry," he said. "You must not hastily condemn him."

"She seems not to have said anything about it to him one way or another," she replied. "As far as I can see, this is the sort of thing our father warned us against. I feel so sorry for her!" He gathered that she was weeping.

He was deeply pained on her behalf, and even he felt ashamed of himself. "Life seldom remains the same for long one way or another. You may well be angry with him now, knowing as little of these things as you both do, but please make an effort to be patient. For myself, I do not believe that you have any reason to be anxious." He found himself surprised to be pleading someone else's cause.

She felt worse at night, and her sister was very worried to have an outsider so near her. "Please, my lord, if you would, there is your usual room . . ." the women suggested; but he complained to the old woman Ben, "The news that your mistress was ill troubled me very greatly, and I came as soon as I possibly could, and now I am asked to leave her! Why, it is intolerable! Who is to look after her properly at a time like this, if I do not?" He ordered healing rites for her, which dismayed her because she herself had no wish to live, but she could not very well tell him so plainly, and despite everything she was touched that he should wish her to.

"Are you feeling a little better now?" he inquired the next morning. "I should like to talk to you, if only as I did yesterday."

She sent him out the message, "Perhaps I am getting worse day by day, but today, at any rate, I feel very ill. Do come in, then."[69] He was greatly moved and wondered what her condition could be, because this unaccustomed warmth was alarming. He approached and began to talk of this and that. "I feel too unwell to answer you," she said; "perhaps when I am a little better." Her voice was pathetically faint, and he sat there in sorrow, overcome by pity. Still, he could not stay on there forever with nothing to do, and despite his concern he returned to the City. "It only makes her worse to be living in a place like this," he told the old woman," and I plan to move her somewhere more suitable." He left word for the Adept to pray earnestly as well.

One of the Counselor's men had ingratiated himself with a young woman of the household, and the two were chatting when he happened to remark, "His Highness of War will be making no more secret trips here: he has been confined to the palace. I hear they mean to marry him to the daughter of His Excellency of the Right. Since that has been the idea all along on *her* side, His Excellency will hardly object, and they say it is to happen before the end of the year. His Highness is not at all pleased; he spends all his time in gallant pastimes at the palace and seems to show

---

69. Ōigimi herself, this time, invites Kaoru to come and talk from where he sat yesterday.

Taking a nap

little sign of behaving himself as Their Majesties would like him to do. *My* master, on the other hand, continues to distinguish himself by being so awfully serious that people hardly know what to do with him. The way he keeps coming here surprises them a good deal, and they say that he must be rather deeply involved."

The woman repeated this to the others, and Her Highness, who overheard her, was devastated. This is the end! she thought. I suppose that he was pleased enough to amuse himself here as long as he was not yet settled with a great lady, and that he carried on about deep devotion only out of deference to the Counselor. However, she had not the strength to dwell on how hateful His Highness was, because she lay there overwhelmed by the growing conviction that she herself had failed completely, and in her weakness she felt more than ever certain that she could not go on living.

Her sister lay as though asleep and oblivious to their talk, since their thoughts were painful to imagine, even if in fact they hardly mattered. She had heard that people sometimes doze off like that when profoundly troubled, and her sleeping form was very dear. Her head rested on her arm, and the nearby mass of her hair was enchanting. While she gazed at her, the instructions their father had left them passed again and again through her mind. Surely he cannot have sunk to the depths they say await those who are immersed in sin![70] Gather me to you, wherever you are! You have abandoned us to despair and no longer come to us even in dreams!

The dreary twilight sky was heavy with rain, and the sound of the wind sweeping through the trees beggared description. Her recumbent figure, pondering what had been and what was to be, conveyed immeasurable distinction. She was in white,[71] and her hair, long uncombed, nevertheless streamed over her shoulders with not a strand out of place. The slight pallor she had lately acquired only enhanced her delicate grace, and one would have loved to show someone who cared the perfect line of her forehead as she gazed out into the dusk.

A violent gust startled the sleeping sister awake. Her pale gray-violet and golden yellow looked bright and lively together, and her face, as beautifully rosy as though dyed, showed no trace of care. "I just dreamed of our father," she said. "I just saw him, *there,* looking terribly sad." Her elder sister felt a renewed weight of sorrow. "I have longed to dream of him ever since he died, but I never have," she said. Both wept bit-

---

70. A parent too preoccupied at death with the fate of a child risked being dragged by this attachment into hell.

71. Because of being ill.

terly. He had been in their thoughts day and night lately, and it had occurred to them that they might have such a dream. Oh, to go to him! But how could we, when we are so deep in sin?[72] They knew that their grief would last into the life to come. How they yearned for the smoke of that incense they are said to have across the sea![73]

It was quite dark when a messenger arrived from His Highness, which under the circumstances was a slight comfort. The lady addressed did not read it immediately. "Please answer him nicely and thoughtfully, though," her sister urged her. "If it happened that I were no longer here, you see, someone might turn up who would treat you far worse than he does. I know that nothing like that could happen as long as His Highness remembers you now and again, and it seems to me that he is still good for that, however hateful you may think him."

"What *is* awful is the very idea that you might leave me!" She buried her face even deeper in her sleeves.

"That time will come when it comes; I did not want to live on a moment longer, then, but here I still am after all. Who do you think even now makes my life worthwhile,[74] when I know that I may never see tomorrow?"[75] She had the lamp brought up, and they looked at the letter.

As usual it was a long one.

> *"When my eyes behold every day the selfsame skies, why now should it be*
> *that as the rains of winter fall, so my longing for you grows?"*

he had written, and no doubt with it "these sleeves have never been so wet!"[76] or something of the sort, because it was all rather trite, and Her Highness detested him more than ever when she saw how little he meant it; but he showed off his wonderfully rare good looks to such winning advantage that it was no wonder the younger sister should still feel drawn to him nonetheless. The longer he stayed away, the more she missed him, and what with all the promises he had made her, she could not believe that there would really never be any more to it than this.

When the messenger let it be known that he planned to return that night, they all pressed her to write a reply. She gave him just this:

> *"Deep in these mountains, in a village lashed by hail, the heavens themselves*
> *before my eyes dawn and dusk are darkness and lowering cloud."*[77]

---

72. Because they are women.

73. "Incense for the return of the soul" (*hangonkō*). Bai Juyi described in a long poem (*Hakushi monjū* 0160) how Emperor Wu of the Early Han called back the soul of Lady Li, thanks to a special incense that a wizard compounded for him.

74. *Ise shū* 424: "Dipping water from the rippling mountain spring, I realize who even now makes my life worthwhile."

75. *Kokinshū* 838, by Ki no Tsurayuki: "I who know I may never see tomorrow grieve for him who did not live out today."

76. *Genji monogatari kochūshakusho in'yō waka* 514: "Winter rains always fall in the month when the gods are gone [*kaminazuki*, the tenth month], but these sleeves have never been so wet!"

77. *Gosenshū* 468: "Deep in these mountains, in a village lashed by hail, such is the loneliness that surely no one else will ever come."

This was on the last day of the tenth month. When it dawned on His Highness that another month had gone by, he became anxious enough every night to want to go to Uji, but many obstacles rose before him,[78] and besides, the Gosechi Festival was early this year,[79] and he could not help letting more days slip by when the court was constantly distracted by the brilliant preparations. Her wait became dreadfully long. He never for a moment forgot her through all his passing encounters.

Her Majesty said to him on the matter that concerned His Excellency of the Right,[80] "Once you have achieved so sound an alliance, then behave yourself and bring anyone else you may be keen on to *you*."[81]

"Please be patient. I still need to think," he replied discouragingly. To the sisters, who had no idea that he wanted at all costs to spare the younger this disaster, the months and days brought only further gloom.

He is less trustworthy than he looks! the Counselor reflected, regretting having given him the benefit of the doubt, and he all but stopped calling on him. Again and again he sent to the mountain village for news. He learned that she was a little better this month, but then for five or six days he was so taken up in public and private that he sent nobody there, until he wondered again with a start how she was and dropped all other urgent affairs to hurry to Uji himself.

He had ordered the healing rites continued until she was wholly recovered, but she had sent the Adept back to his temple on the grounds that she was much improved, and few people were about. The old woman appeared as usual and gave him a report. "My lady feels no particular pain anywhere," she said, "and her illness is not alarming; it is just that she will not eat. She has always been unusually frail, and now, ever since this began with His Highness, her spirits have sunk lower and lower, till she will not look at the smallest bit of fruit—I am sure that that is why she is so very weak and seems unlikely to live. It has been my misfortune to survive long enough to see this, and my only wish now is to go before she does." She was weeping before she could finish, and no wonder.

"This is very bad news. Why did you not let me know? This is an extremely busy time at His Eminence's as well as at the palace, and I was so worried when day after day I could not send her any message at all!"

He went in to her as before and spoke from close to her pillow, but she could not answer him; it was as though she had no voice at all. "I am outraged that no one should have told me anything until you were as ill as this. It is enough to make a mockery of all my concern for you!" he said reproachfully, and as always he sent for the Adept, as well as for all others known to the world for their healing power. His retainers gathered in large numbers, since the rites and scripture readings were to

78. *Shūishū* 853, attributed to Hitomaro: "This is a time when, like a boat pushing into port through the reeds and facing many obstacles, I cannot meet my love."

79. In most years the tenth month had three days of the Ox, and the Gosechi Festival began on the second of them, around the middle of the month; but in some years there were only two, and in that case the festival began on the first, near the beginning of the month.

80. Niou's marriage to Roku no Kimi.

81. As a gentlewoman.

begin the next day, and with so many people of all degrees rushing busily about, the desolate mood of the place yielded to one of confidence.

After sundown they sought to take him to his usual room, offering him hot watered rice[82] and so on, but he declared that he would stay with her, and since the southern aisle was occupied by the priests, he went in to sit a little nearer to her, on the east side, behind a screen. This upset her younger sister, but the women all agreed that he and their elder mistress were too close to each other to be parted now. He had a perpetual reading of the Lotus Sutra begun at the evening service. The chanters were twelve monks with particularly fine voices, and the effect was awe-inspiring.

The lamp was lit near him, in the space to the south, while all remained dark farther in.[83] He lifted her standing curtain and slipped inside it a little to look at her, at which two or three of the older women moved to attend her. Their younger mistress meanwhile moved swiftly to hide and lay all alone with almost no one beside her.

"Will you not let me at least hear your voice?" he pleaded, taking her hand to rouse her.

"I would, but it is difficult to talk," she murmured under her breath. "You have not come for so long. I thought I might go in the end without seeing you again, and I was very sorry."

"To think that I kept you waiting so long!" He was sobbing now. Her forehead felt a little warm. "What wrong did you do to bring this on?" he whispered in her ear. "They say that this is what happens when you make someone unhappy!" She covered her face in embarrassment and annoyance when he went on talking. He wondered as he watched her lying there, ever more frail and weak, with what feelings he would look on her if she were gone, and a sharp pang oppressed him.

"It must have been so difficult for you, looking after her all this time. Do at least get a good rest tonight," he said to her sister. "I shall be on duty." She did not like the idea, but she supposed that he must have his reasons and withdrew a little.

He was not really supposed to be with her face-to-face, but when he crept nearer to look at her, she felt despite her repugnance and shame that what they were to each other was fated, for his wonderfully loyal patience, compared to that other gentleman's ways, told her well enough how worthy he was. She could not abruptly send him away, no; she would not have him remember her after her death as obstinate or unkind. All night he kept the women at work bringing her medicines and so on, but she seemed to take nothing at all. He sat confounded and despairing. This was too cruel a blow. What *could* he do to keep her from leaving him?

Just before dawn new monks took up the perpetual scripture chanting, and at this most holy sound the Adept, dozing on night attendance, woke up and chanted a *darani*. His voice, although hoarse with age, inspired trust and awe.

"How did she get on during the night?" he asked, and then began to talk of His Late Highness, meanwhile frequently blowing his nose. "I wonder what sort of

82. *Mi-yuzuke*, brown rice in hot water, a winter food; in summer one ate *suiban*, rice in cold water.

83. He appears to be in the chamber with her, in the southern half, while she lies in the northern half behind a curtain. The lamp is as far from her as possible.

place he is in now," he said. "I had been sure it was a serene one after all,[84] but a little while ago I dreamed about him. He was dressed as a layman, and he said, 'I never set my heart on this world, for I loathed it and all its works, and yet little affections have confused me, and I shall remain for some time far removed from where I long to go. It is a bitter thought. Do what you must to help me move on!' He spoke very distinctly, and since I did not immediately know what to do, I had as many monks as I could, five or six, begin calling the Name. Then I had another idea and set some to saluting all people everywhere as imminent buddhas."[85] The Counselor wept copiously as well. To Her Highness, already in profound despair, it seemed that she must now breathe her last for the sin of having hindered him even in the life to come. As she lay there listening, she wanted only to find him before his destination was certain and to go there with him.

The Adept finished his brief account and left. Having gone round the neighboring villages and even as far as the City, those sent to salute all people as buddhas now found the dawn gales too much for them, and they gathered where the Adept had been previously called, to sit by the middle gate and continue bowing in a most holy manner. The way they ended their prayer[86] was very moving. The Counselor, who deeply shared their faith, was intensely affected. He heard the desperately anxious younger sister approach the curtain that stood far back in the room and sat up straight. "How did the monks' chanting impress you?" he asked. "That is not the most weighty of practices, but it can leave one struck with awe." He added as though in simple speech,

"Plovers all forlorn, caught here at the water's edge thick with early frost:
how sorrowfully their cries ring out in the coming dawn!"

In what she gathered of his presence he resembled that other gentleman whom she found so cruel, and she silently compared the two; but a direct answer was beyond her, and she had it conveyed to him by Ben:

"Do they know so well, those plovers who from their wings brush the frosts of dawn,
all that weighs upon the heart of one in thrall to sorrow?"

The messenger is unworthy, he reflected, but certainly not the message. And she—what warmth she gives the slightest exchange! Ah, his troubled thoughts ran on, what would my feelings be if she were to be taken from me!

Considering the way His Highness had appeared in that dream, he could well imagine how this pathetic spectacle must look to him, gazing down from on high, and he had scriptures read also at the temple where His Highness had stayed. He sent men

84. Paradise, despite Hachi no Miya's worry over his daughters when he died.
85. Literally "I sent some to [do] Never-Despise." In the chapter on the Bodhisattva Never-Despise (Jōfukyō Bosatsu bon), the Lotus Sutra describes how a follower of the Buddha prostrated himself in homage before all monks, nuns, laymen, and laywomen as future buddhas. The Adept sent priests out in all directions to do this.
86. The end of the Lotus Sutra passage, chanted as a prayer for the benefit of all sentient beings (ekō). The passage concludes, ". . . because they are all to be buddhas."

to order prayers in other temples, too, excused himself from all engagements public or private, and neglected no rite of celebration or purification.[87] However, these things did no good, because the illness did not proceed from any wrong she had done.

It would have been one thing if Her Highness had prayed to the buddhas for her own recovery, but instead her mind was made up to die. I cannot possibly keep him away, now that he is close beside me and knows everything about me,[88] she reflected, but even so, what seems to be strong affection would fade on both sides with familiarity and end in misery and grief. If I live after all, I must appeal to this illness to become a nun. That is the only way for him and me to remain to each other what we are now. She could not give such complexities open expression, however, despite having decided to act on her decision. Instead she said to her sister, "I feel less and less that I shall survive, and, you know, they say that the Precepts really can help one live longer. Please tell the Adept."

They all wept and cried out. "My lady, that is impossible! Here is my lord the Counselor, beside himself with anxiety for you—just think what a blow it would be to him!" They vigorously disapproved and would not pass it on even to the gentleman on whom they all depended. She was acutely disappointed.

Word of the way he had secluded himself got about, and some gentlemen took the trouble to come and visit him. His close retainers and household officials commissioned prayers on their own when they saw how affected he was, and all of them shared his grief.

His thoughts went to the City, and he realized that the Warmth of Wine banquet was today. A fierce wind was blowing, and falling snow swirled madly by. It would be different if I were there, he reflected, yielding to loneliness. Then are she and I never to be together? It is a hard fate for us both, but I shall not complain. She was so dear and sweet to me—oh, I must make her well awhile and tell her all these thoughts of mine! Meanwhile night came without a gleam of light.

> "Deep in these mountains where thick clouds cover the sky, shutting out the sun,
> how through all these long, long days darkness comes to fill the heart!"

The women found no strength but in his presence. He sat near her as usual, and the wind blew the curtains about so much that her sister retired farther back into the room. When the disreputable-looking creatures went to hide from him in embarrassment, he moved closer still. "How do you feel?" he asked through his tears. "I have prayed for you in every way I know, but none of it has done any good, and you will not even let me hear your voice. It is so painful! I shall never forgive you for leaving me this way."

Although apparently unaware of what went on around her, she still had her face well hidden. "There are things I should like to tell you if I felt a little better, but

---

87. "Celebration" (*matsuri*), a rite to summon, honor, and influence a non-Buddhist deity; "purification" (*harae*), a rite to remove evil influences by infusing them into dolls or other objects. Both were characteristic of yin-yang (*onmyōdō*) practice.

88. Kaoru has seen her face, felt her forehead, etc. He has physical knowledge of her and so is close to being her husband after all.

I am afraid that I may go at any moment." Her manner conveyed great sadness. His tears flowed faster and faster now, as his well-meant effort to conceal his grief failed, and he sobbed aloud.

What has destiny made her to me, he wondered, contemplating her, that despite my endless love I should now be close to losing her, after so many sorrows? She might mean less to me if she could only betray the slightest blemish! But she seemed only dearer and more precious, and lovelier as well. Her thin arms, as weak as shadows, still had all their pale, slender grace, and in soft white robes, with the covers off her, she lay like a bodiless doll. Her hair, not excessively long, gleamed most beautifully where it streamed away from the pillow. Oh, what is to become of her? he asked himself in desperate anguish, for she did not look as though she could last. Ungroomed throughout her long illness, she nevertheless retained a dignity inaccessible to those who go about making so much of themselves, and it seemed to him as he watched her that his very spirit might wander away.

"If you leave me, I shall not linger on long either," he said; "or if the term of my life is more distant, I shall wander the depths of the mountains. I shall regret only the plight of the one I leave behind." He mentioned her sister in the hope of eliciting an answer from her.

She drew away a little of the sleeve that concealed her face. "My life is over," she said, "and since there is no help for it now that you have thought me cruel, I would have peace if only you had not ignored what I ventured to ask of you, that you should regard my sister, who will survive me, as myself; that is the one bitter thought that may detain me."

"I was certainly born to great sorrow," he replied, "because I have never been able to love anyone but you, and that is the reason why I did not obey you. Now I regret it, and for your sake wish that I had done otherwise. I assure you, though, that you need not worry." He sought to comfort her, but she seemed to be suffering so much that he called in the Adepts performing the healing rites and had them work the most powerful of their spells. He himself prayed to the Buddha with all his heart.

He wondered whether the Buddha gives us despair at such times purposely to make us reject this world, for she faded before his eyes, and then, O sorrow, she was gone. He all but stamped his feet in frenzy at being helpless to detain her, and never mind those who might think him mad. It was all over; her sister had seen that and was clearly desperate to follow. Who could blame her? She was beside herself, and the ever-so-sensible women pulled her away because that sort of thing was now of very ill omen.[89]

No, no, it cannot be! I must be dreaming! He brought the lamp close and raised the wick to see her. The face she had hidden seemed only asleep, for nothing about it had changed, and in anguish he wished that he could see her as no more than a cicada shell.[90] During their last ministrations to her the women tidied her hair, which gave forth a breath of the same dear fragrance it had had when she was

---

89. Because of the pollution of death.
90. *Kokinshū* 831, by the priest Shōen, lamenting the cremation of Fujiwara no Mototsune at Fukakusa in 891: "It was some consolation to see the cicada shell he left behind; but now, O Mount Fukakusa, at least put forth smoke [to remember him by]!"

alive, and he prayed to the buddhas, Oh, please allow me as a rare boon to find some taint of the common in her, that I may mourn her less! If it is you who truly show the way to renunciation, let me at least find in her some horror that will relieve me of this grief! But he was beyond comfort, and now that she was no more, he resolved at least to look after her until she was smoke. It was in a sad, sad state that he assured the usual rites. He wavered as though walking on air, and she remained frail to the last, for there rose from her in the end only a very little smoke. He went away numb with sorrow.

Many people joined the mourning confinement,[91] which should have lightened the loneliness a little, but the young Princess was despondent with shame over what they must think of her plight, and she herself seemed scarcely alive. A great many messages came from His Highness. She recalled how her sister had maintained her condemnation of him to the end, and her bond with him seemed very bitter indeed.

Disgusted now with the world, the Counselor considered doing what he had so long wished to do, but he feared the disapproval of Her Cloistered Highness at Sanjō,[92] and pity for the younger Princess troubled his thoughts as well; because his task after all, once *she* was gone, was, as she had said, to accept her sister as herself. I knew that even if she *had* become her sister, I could not really have loved anyone else, but still, I should never have caused her such sorrow; I should have courted her sister instead and accepted her in consolation for my infinite loss. He never went to the City. People there understood from his silence and from his retreat there, unconsoled, that he had cared for her very much indeed, and many messages reached him from the palace and elsewhere.

Meanwhile the days slipped by. He had the service each seventh day done very solemnly, and he honored her memory with great devotion, but there was a limit to what he could do, and he who still wore the same colors as always[93] sighed to see the women to whom she had meant so much now dressed in dark gray:

> "They are all in vain, these my endless tears that fall blood red with sorrow,
> for I may wear nothing dyed the color of remembrance."

Mournful in a sanctioned rose gleaming like ice with his tears of sorrow, he was the picture of grace and beauty. The women peered at him. "Granted the tragedy of what has happened," they said, "it is a very harsh blow that we must soon become strangers to this lord whom we know so well!"

"What an extraordinary fate theirs has been!"

"To think that they both refused him, when he has been so kind!" They all wept.

He addressed the young Princess to say, "I hope that I may now talk freely with you, in memory of our loss. Please do not remain distant from me!" But she

---

91. *On-imi*, a ritual seclusion of thirty days to avoid spreading the pollution due to contact with death. "Many people" took part because of Kaoru's presence.

92. His mother, Onna San no Miya. He is thinking of taking religious vows, too.

93. He was not entitled to wear mourning because he had no formal connection with Ōigimi.

knew the depth of her misfortune too well to be anything other than desperately shy, and she would not yet meet him or talk to him. Now and again it seemed to him that although more vivid in character, and a little more childlike and proud, she did not match her sister in warmth or depth of charm.

It had snowed all day while he gazed and dreamed, until at last a twelfth-month moon, the one they always call so dreary, shone forth in cloudless splendor, and he rolled up the blinds to look out. A temple bell yonder rang out faintly, as when one lay with pillow raised and heard it announce the close of day.[94]

> "Lest I linger on, oh, I would follow the moon coursing through the sky,
>   for when all is said and done, this world cannot be my home."

He lowered the shutters against the strong wind, and there at the water's edge was the moon, shining up from the ice that mirrored the mountains. No touch he might add to his house in the City, he thought, could give him *this*. If she could live again for a while, I would talk of this beauty with her! His endless longing was more than his heart could contain.

> "I would so make mine, suffering these pangs of love, the draft that brings death,
>   that I may quite soon be gone into the Snowy Mountains."

Oh, for a demon to teach me the last half of the verse, that I might follow that great example and cast myself from the heights! he said to himself, which made him rather a tainted holy man![95]

The women saw wholly admirable gentleness and depth of heart in the way he called them out to chat, and the younger ones were especially captivated. The older women were more and more stricken with regret. "The shock of what happened with His Highness, and her apparent certainty of suffering ridicule: those are the things that made our mistress so very ill," they said, "but she did not want her sister to know and kept all her anger to herself, and meanwhile she ate nothing at all until in the end she just wasted away. On the surface she never made the slightest show of being wise, but underneath she had vast depth and pondered all things, so that her sister's fate pained her greatly, because to her it meant that His Late Highness's command to them had been set at naught." They went on to tell each other what the elder Princess had said on this or that occasion, and soon they were all weeping bitterly.

The Counselor saw himself as responsible for the disasters they had suffered and wished that he could undo what he had done, and he came so to detest all the

---

94. The rolling up of the blinds and parts of the sentence that follows come from a poem by Bai Juyi (*Hakushi monjū* 0978).

95. The Snowy Mountains (*yuki no yama, sessen*) are the Himalayas. Once Sessen Dōji ("Snowy Mountain Youth," the Buddha in a former life) learned from a demon the first half of a verse in praise of enlightenment. The demon then required his flesh and blood in exchange for the second half. Sessen Dōji agreed, received the verse, and engraved it on the wall of his cave. Then he leaped from a cliff, whereupon the demon changed into the god Indra and saved him. The story is told in the Nehan-gyō and elsewhere.

world that he gave himself to fervent prayer. He was so engaged one night, sleepless, when long before dawn, amid the snow and the bitter cold he heard the shouting of many men and the sound of horses. The worthy monks woke with a start, wondering who could have arrived in the dead of night through the snow: it was His Highness, who entered, wet through, in a miserable hunting cloak. His way of knocking at the gate made it clear who he was, and the Counselor stole away to hide in an inner room. The mourning retreat was not yet over, but His Highness had been so anxious to come that he had spent all night on the way, thwarted by the snow.

His arrival might have promised her some relief from her days of sorrow, but she was in no mood to receive him; she shrank from the man who had caused her sister such grief and was profoundly angry that it was too late now for him to change, since her sister was no longer there to improve her opinion of him. Her attitude prompted the women to reason urgently with her, until at last she sat and heard him present at voluble length, through the blinds, his apologies for his long absence. Judging from what he gathered of her presence, she herself seemed so pathetically near expiring that she might soon join her elder sister, and he found this truly alarming.

He took the risk of staying on into the day. To his pleas that she receive him face-to-face she only replied with cruel indifference, "If I ever feel a little more myself . . ."

The Counselor, who could hear them, summoned a likely one of the women to give her a secret and somewhat officious message: "You may well condemn his crimes against you in the course of these recent months, for his casual treatment of you offends your dignity, but please give some thought to receiving him nicely after all. He has never encountered such feelings before, and he must be very unhappy." Its effect was to confirm the young Princess in her shy reserve, and she did not reply.

"You are extremely unkind," His Highness protested. "You seem to have completely forgotten every assurance I gave you!" He spent the day lamenting his fate.

That night, while the wind howled louder than ever, he lay there sighing over the misery he had brought on himself, until she began to pity him and received him through the blinds, as before. The way he swore eternal fidelity by every god in the land[96] made her wonder in dismay where he had learned such glib eloquence, but as she listened, she found that she could not reject him wholly, for now sympathy tempered her anger over his slights when he was away, and his looks were enough to charm anyone. Softly, she said,

> "The way we have come calls no memory to mind but of treachery;
> what, then, might the future bring, that you should deserve my trust?"

This did nothing whatever to reassure him.

---

96. *Genji monogatari kochūshakusho in'yō waka* 927: "I have sworn so many times to be true that you must know the name of every god in the land."

"If the way ahead appears destined in your mind very soon to end,
now at least, in the present, O do not turn me away!

We have so little time to be together anyway! Please do not be too severe with me!"
He did all he could to bring her round, but she answered that she felt unwell and retired, and he spent the rest of a miserable night smarting to think how he must look
to her women. He did not blame her for being angry with him, but she really was too
cruel! From his own bitter tears he learned to understand her greater unhappiness.

He was moved and amused to note the Counselor's proprietary manner when
he called on the women's services or had several of them wait on him at meals. Saddened to see him so thin and pale and so apparently distracted, His Highness let
him know how sorry he was. As for the Counselor, he longed to talk to His Highness about his loss, although he knew how little good that would do him, but he
also feared that it would seem weak and foolish of him, and so he refrained, which
left him little to say. After many days of tears his features had changed, although
not for the worse, for they now had so fine a beauty and grace that His Highness,
who deplored his own waywardness, saw that *he* would certainly lose his heart to
him, if he himself were a woman. That was a worry. He decided to move her to the
City while somehow evading at the same time the censure and anger he could otherwise expect.

Despite her rebuff he started back in the morning, for he knew that he would
rue the day if Their Majesties ever learned where he had been. Again he tried all his
eloquence on her, but she wanted him to taste for himself the bitterness of his own
indifference, and she refused to yield.

As the year draws to a close, even in happier places, something new comes
into the sky, and every tempestuous day it snows and snows; meanwhile the Counselor grieved on and on as though it were all a dream. His Highness sent great
quantities of offerings for scripture readings. Some in the City wondered whether
the Counselor might really mourn into the New Year, and they sufficiently deplored
the way he had shut himself off from the world that the time came at last for him to
return. His feelings as he prepared to do so passed all description. None of the
callers his presence had brought to the house would be seen again once he was
gone, that the sorrowing women knew, and they feared the ensuing quiet more than
the busier grief of the tragedy itself. "A bantering word or two with him was all very
well now and again, over the years, whenever he happened to come," they assured
one another, "but he has been so good and kind all through this unbroken stay, so
attentive to little things and so thoughtful in every way—and to think that we shall
not see him again!" They were distraught.

A message came from His Highness. "It has become exceedingly difficult for
me to go to you," he said, "and not knowing what else to do, I am seeking a way to
bring you closer." Her Majesty felt for him when she learned this, reflecting that if
even the Counselor's feelings were as strongly engaged as they seemed to be, then
everyone would surely agree that the lady deserved special consideration; and she
discreetly suggested that he bring her to the west wing at Nijō, where he could visit

her at any time. She must want to have it appear that she will go to the First Princess! His Highness, when he grasped this, was delighted by the prospect of having her so nearby, and he let her know.

I see, the Counselor reflected when he heard. I meant to bring her sister to Sanjō once the building was finished, and I certainly should have managed to move *her* there instead! He felt his loss afresh, and His Highness's apparent suspicions seemed to him utterly unfounded. Who but me will provide her with everything she needs? they say he demanded to know.

48

Bracken Shoots

Sawarabi ("bracken shoots") were gathered and eaten in early spring. The chapter derives its title from a poem by Naka no Kimi, acknowledging a gift of *sawarabi* from the Adept:

"As I am this spring, who will enjoy them with me, now that he is gone: these bracken shoots from the hills, picked in memory of him?"

RELATIONSHIP TO EARLIER CHAPTERS

"Bracken Shoots" continues "Trefoil Knots." It takes place in the spring of Kaoru's twenty-fifth year.

PERSONS

The Counselor, age 25 (Kaoru)

The younger daughter of Hachi no Miya, 25 (Naka no Kimi)

His Highness of War, 26 (Niou Miya)

The Adept (Uji no Ajari)

Ben, a gentlewoman, then a nun (Ben no Ama)

Taifu, a gentlewoman

His Excellency, the Minister of the Right, 51 (Yūgiri)

The mere sight of spring sunlight, which shines even in the wilds,[1] convinced her that she must be dreaming, and she would then wonder how she had lived through those months and days. Ever at one before the flowers and birdsong of the passing seasons, they had combined their little half verses[2] on each and talked over every shock or sorrow their lonely life brought them, which had comforted them both; but now, with no one to understand the things that moved or amused her, her mood was all darkness, torment, and a desolation still more complete than when her father had died. In the confusion of her mind she barely knew dusk from dawn, but we each have our allotted time in the world, and alas, life would not leave her.

A note came from the Adept: "How is your mistress getting on in the New Year? I perform rites for her constantly, and now that she is alone, she is always in my anxious prayers." He had sent a pretty basket of bracken and horsetail shoots.[3] "These are from among the very first the acolytes have picked for the altar," he said. His poem, in a very poor hand, was purposely written all in quite separate letters:

> "Then, it was for him that I would spring after spring gather this same gift,
> and in honor of those days these first bracken shoots are yours.[4]

Please read this to her."

He had obviously taken great trouble over it, and she liked it much better than any she had ever received from that gentleman whose facile eloquence seemed only to show how little he really cared. She wept and had her women write down her reply:

---

1. *Kokinshū* 870, by Furu no Imamichi: "Since the light of the sun shines even in the wilds, flowers bloom here at Isonokami, in this ancient village."
2. One makes the first half of a poem (five-seven-five syllables), and the other adds the rest (seven-seven).
3. *Sawarabi* and *tsukuzukushi* (modern Japanese *tsukushi*), the early shoots of *Pteridium aquilinum* and *Equisetum arvense*.
4. The poem plays on *tsumi*, "pick" and "grow in number" (speaking of the years).

"As I am this spring, who will enjoy them with me, now that he is gone:
these bracken shoots from the hills, picked in memory of him?"

She had the messenger given a reward.

Lovely as she already was in the full bloom of youth, her cares had drawn her features a little, giving her a nobler grace that made her resemble the sister she had lost. Side by side they had seemed quite different, but now the resemblance was so striking that if one forgot for a moment, one could imagine that she was her sister. The sight moved the women to lament, "His lordship the Counselor mourned our lady night and day, until he longed to be able to contemplate at least her empty shell—what a shame *her* destiny was not to be his, when she would have done just as well!" The arrival of one of his men gave each an occasion to inquire after the other. The news that despite the New Year he was always lost in thought and often in tears convinced her that his attachment had been no passing whim, and she felt for him now more than ever.

His Highness, whose life hardly ever allowed him a moment to go to her, now resolved that he would bring her to the City.

Once the privy banquet and other such distractions were over, his lordship the Counselor went to call on His Highness of War, since he could not unburden himself of his despair to anyone else. It was a quiet evening, and His Highness sat near the veranda, lost in thought. He was enjoying the scent of the plum blossoms he loved, toying meanwhile with a *sō no koto*, when the Counselor broke off one of the tree's lower branches and approached him with it. The sweetly delicious, mingled fragrance struck His Highness as just right.

"Are they so attuned to your least shade of feeling, you who have picked them,
that, their color all unseen, these blossoms yet scent the air?"[5]

he said, and the Counselor returned the pleasantry:

"Let him then beware, before he picks as his own the bough in full bloom
that to its admirer brings taunts and accusations!"

They were the best of friends.

They settled down to talk, and His Highness hastened to inquire about the mountain village. The Counselor then spoke in his turn of how deeply he felt his loss and of how his heart had been hers from the start until this very day. Amid tears and smiles, as they say, he enlarged on his memories, sad or amusing, through the round of the years, until His Highness himself, always quick both to love and to weep, was wringing the tears from his sleeves even over someone else's misfortune and giving his friend every reason to be pleased with him. Meanwhile the sky veiled itself in mist as though it, too, understood.

That night a howling wind brought with it a still-wintry chill, and the lamp

5. "Your expression shows nothing, but you seem still to love her."

kept blowing out. They could not bring themselves to break off their conversation despite such gloom as when darkness covers all,[6] and they talked on until very late without yet finishing what they had to say. "Come now, that cannot be all!" His Highness exclaimed, for his friend had described a tender bond unexampled in all the world, and His Highness's own willful ways led him to press the matter on the assumption that there must be more. Still, he was a man of understanding, and he so skillfully offered now words of consolation and now appeals to deep feeling that his charm swept the Counselor on little by little to tell him all of the pent-up sorrows in his heart; and he felt much better for having done so.

His Highness, for his part, described his plan to bring *her* closer. "That is very good news!" the Counselor replied. "Alas, I cannot help thinking that it is all my fault. She is now my only link to someone I will always miss, and I feel it is generally up to me to do for her whatever I possibly can—I hope you do not mind." He touched a little on the elder sister's wish that he should accept the younger as herself, but he left out that night of, so to speak, birdcalls in Iwase Wood.[7] At heart he increasingly regretted not having done with this token of his dear lost love exactly what she had said he should, but it was too late now, and he would only encourage inadmissible desires if he were to continue feeling this way. No, he rejected the thought as a foolish and reprehensible betrayal of both. There was her move to consider, though, and who else was there to take it in hand? He had the preparations for it begun.

At Uji they brought in pretty young women and page girls, and the gentlewomen merrily got themselves ready while their mistress, in despair that her Fushimi should go to ruin,[8] spent her every moment grieving; not that she really could defiantly shut herself up there forever. Time and again he reproached her, "How can you even think of staying, when the precious bond we share must then fail?" and she could not wholly disagree. In sad confusion she wondered what to do.

The day agreed was the first of the second month, and the closer it came, the more the budding trees' promise called out to her to linger for the blossoms; besides, it seemed to her that to give up watching the mists rise over the hills in order to travel to no eternal home would only invite shame and cruel laughter, until she shrank from the thought and spent day and night absorbed only in her cares. When the time came to put off her mourning, the purification seemed to her very shallow.[9] Not having known her mother, she had never missed her, and to make up for it she had wanted this time to dye her clothes a very dark shade;[10] but no, to her unending disappointment and sorrow that was not reason enough.

6. From *Kokinshū* 41, by Ōshikōchi no Mitsune: "On a night in spring, darkness covers all; plum blossoms remain unseen, but their scent cannot be hidden."

7. The night he spent with Naka no Kimi. *Genji monogatari kochūshakusho in'yō waka* 367: "If you love me, come to be with me, that we may speak in person, as birds call to each other in Iwase Wood."

8. *Kokinshū* 981: "Come, here I shall spend my life, for here at Sugawara I would not have Fushimi village go to rack and ruin." The locality mentioned is near the present town of Nara.

9. The prescribed mourning for a brother or sister lasted three months, and when that period was over the mourner underwent purificatory ablutions on the bank of a stream. "Shallow" (*asaki*) is conventionally associated with "purification" (*misogi*), perhaps because of the shallowness of a shrine's sacred brook.

10. She had wanted to mourn her sister as she would have her mother.

The Counselor sent her carriage, her escort, the Doctor,[11] and so on. He wrote,

> "Ah, how nothing lasts! Hardly have you cut yourself a garment of mist
> than the time comes round again for flowers to burst into bloom."[12]

And indeed, he had sent her also all sorts of bright and pretty clothes. The gifts for everyone who accompanied her, though never ostentatious, were plentiful and carefully gauged to the proper standing of each. "My lord's kindness is such a wonder, and the way he never forgets us—why, no brother would do as much!" the women reminded her. The older ones, who cared nothing for show, treasured his more practical help, while the younger, who saw him so often, were sorry that now he would be a stranger. "Ah, my lady," they said, "you will miss him!"

The Counselor himself arrived early in the morning on the day before she was to leave. He was installed in the guest room as usual, and there he gave himself over to bitter reflections. By now she and I would have been close after all, he said to himself, and I would have been the first to bring off this sort of move. He recalled the way she had looked, the things she had told him about herself. After all, he thought with a pang, she never rejected me outright or embarrassed me acutely; it was I who remained all too strangely aloof from her. He remembered the sliding panel through which he had peered and went for another look, but alas, the blinds on the other side were down and blocked his view.

There, too, within, they were recalling her in great sorrow, and the young Princess especially lay with streaming eyes, absorbed in grief and lost to all thought of her journey tomorrow. A message then reached her from the Counselor: "It is not that I have anything in particular to say after my months away, but it would be a comfort to tell you a little of what has been on my mind. Please be less forbiddingly distant with me than you have been before. This house now seems more and more to me to be a different world."

"I would not wish you to think me forbidding," she replied, "but I do not feel at all myself, and in my present troubled state, I am afraid that I cannot be certain what I might say." She looked distressed, but her women insisted that he deserved better, and she received him at the sliding panel between the rooms.

Such was the charm of his presence that she could hardly believe her eyes, for he was dauntingly elegant and by now seemed more fully a man. Yes, he had supreme poise, and how fine he looked! Seeing him this way brought most vividly to mind the image that in any case never left her, and she was deeply stirred.

"Perhaps today I should refrain from going on and on about her,"[13] he kept saying, and he remarked instead, "I myself shall soon be moving to near where you are going, and as good friends say, midnight or dawn, whenever you need anything,

---

11. An expert in yin-yang lore, whose services were required at the end of any period of mourning as well as for any occasion as momentous as Naka no Kimi's departure.

12. The "garment of mist" (*kasumi no koromo*) is at once Naka no Kimi's mourning robes and the mists that rise among the hills in early spring.

13. Ōigimi, a subject too sad to be appropriate on the happy occasion of a move to the City.

please do not hesitate to let me know, for as long as I live, I will always be at your disposal. I hope that that will be agreeable. People in this world feel very different about things, and the matter is not for me alone to decide, since I know that you may object."

"I would much, much rather never leave," she replied, "and now that you say you will be nearby, I find myself very troubled and cannot answer." At times her voice was inaudible, and in her mood of desperate sorrow she was so very like her sister that he rued the folly of letting her go, of his own will, to someone else. Still, it was now too late for regret, and he said nothing of that night, maintaining instead a manner so forthright that he seemed almost to have forgotten it.

The red plum in the garden was so lovely in color and scent that even the warblers seemed unable to pass by without a song, and the moment especially touched those troubled, as they talked, by the thought that this spring was not at all the spring of old.[14] A gust of the flowers' perfume mingled on the breeze with the visitor's own to recall the past more vividly than any fragrance of orange blossom. This tree meant so much to her, for the way it relieved monotony or gave comfort in sorrow! The thought was more than she could contain:

> *"Soon all will be gone, who loved them, and leave to storms this mountain village*
> *where the plum tree in full bloom with its scent calls back the past."*[15]

Her voice was so low, so faltering, that he could hardly tell whether or not she spoke, and he replied warmly,

> *"Once these sleeves of mine brushed the blossoms of a plum that, sweet as before,*
> *must move away root and branch to a home no more my own!"*

Discreetly and decorously he dried his streaming tears and pursued their conversation no further. "I hope that we may meet like this again—you are so easy to talk to," he said before he left.

He gave out instructions for her journey and entrusted the men on his nearby estates with providing what the bearded watchman would need, since he was to stay on in charge of the house. Nothing, not even the most practical matters, escaped his attention.

The old woman Ben had said to her mistress, "People might take it amiss if I were now to accompany you, my lady, because I have lived longer than I ever wished to do, and my life is a burden to me." She had made herself a nun. The Counselor insisted that she come forth, and the sight of her moved him very much.

As so often before, he had her talk about the past. "I shall still be back from time to time," he said, "and the place will seem very empty and lonely. It will be such a pleasure to find you here after all!" Tears kept him from saying more.

---

14. *Kokinshū* 747, by Ariwara no Narihira: "Is this not the moon, is this spring not the spring of old, while only I remain just as I was then?"

15. The poem plays on *arashi* ("storm wind") and *araji* ("will not be there").

"The more I wish to be rid of my life, the longer I seem to live," she answered. "I reproach my lady for leaving me—what would she have me do, once she is gone? I suppose my way of condemning all the world[16] means that I am very sinful indeed." It was rather selfish of her to pour out her complaint as she did, but he comforted her nicely.

She was very old, but now that she had cut off what recalled her former beauty, her forehead looked younger than before,[17] and to that extent she had gained a new refinement. He wondered desperately, Why did I not provide for *her* to do the same? After all, she might have lived longer that way, and just think how she and I could then have talked heart-to-heart! This absorbing fancy made him envy even the woman before him, and he set her standing curtain aside so that they might talk more easily. She seemed disconsolate, it was true, but her speech and her sense still had a good deal to commend them, and she had clearly had considerable distinction.

> *"If I had instead drowned in the great stream of tears age so quickly sheds,*
> *I would never have lived on, once she whom I loved was gone,"*

she said and began to weep.

"But *that* would have been a very great sin!" he protested. "How, then, could you ever have reached the other shore? It would be terrible to sink into the pit for such a dreadful deed. No, nothing matters but to see that all is vanity."

> *"Cast yourself away into that sad stream of tears where you wish to drown,*
> *and each shoal or shallow reach would undo your forgetting.[18]*

Ah, what life will ever bring consolation?" He felt as though his love could have no end.[19] Lacking the courage to leave, he stayed on, sorrowing, until after sunset; but then he set off back to the City after all, since he disliked the thought that someone might note his casual overnight absence with disapproval.

Ben reported to her mistress everything that he had said, and she felt still further removed from any possibility of comfort. The others were all sewing merrily away and getting themselves dressed up without a thought for their crabbed looks, while she felt more and more a nun.

> *"Where on the long sweep of Sleeve Beach all busily cut themselves new clothes,*
> *one, a woman of the sea, weeps an old nun's bitter brine,"[20]*

---

16. *Shūishū* 953, by Ki no Tsurayuki: "So encompassing are the sorrows that afflict me alone, that I have come to condemn all the world."

17. She has cut her hair to a nun's shoulder length (*ama sogi*).

18. The shallows or rapids (*seze*) of a river are an image for the vicissitudes of life.

19. *Kokinshū* 611, by Ōshikōchi no Mitsune: "My love knows no destination and has no end; the only boundary, to me, is the next time we meet."

20. The poem plays on *ama* ("nun" and "woman of the sea") as well as on a set of words associated with the sea. In this spirit the place-name Sode no Ura ("Sleeve Beach," in northern Japan) adds poetic luster to the *sode* ("sleeves," the new clothes) that the women are making for the next day.

she said to voice her complaint, and her mistress replied,

> *"Are these sleeves of mine not a woman of the sea's, weeping drops of brine,*
> *when I toss upon the waves, wet with tears of bitter care?*[21]

I cannot imagine ever feeling at home where I am going," she went on very kindly, "and you see, depending on how things turn out, I have in mind not to let this house go to rack and ruin after all, in which case you and I will meet again; but the thought of leaving you here like this, alone and forlorn, troubles me more and more. Those who lead this new life of yours need not simply shut themselves away. No, you must take the matter as anyone else would and come and see me often. She left the old woman all the furnishings she might need from among those that had once been her elder sister's. "When I see you like this, so much more downcast than the others," she said, "it actually seems to me that you and I must share a tie from past lives, and I feel so much for you!" The old woman dissolved in tears like a little girl crying for her mother.

Once everything was clean and tidy, the carriages were drawn up. The escort included many gentlemen of the fourth and fifth ranks. His Highness had wanted badly to come himself, but that would have meant an awkward degree of pomp and circumstance. He therefore arranged a discreet arrival that he awaited anxiously. The Counselor, too, sent many men to join her retinue, and although the main decisions seem to have been His Highness's, it was he who, with admirable thoroughness, saw to all the more modest details.

She was flustered to hear voices within and without the house warning that the sun was setting, and the thought that she did not know where she was going made her feel pathetically vulnerable. A gentlewoman called Taifu, who was with her in her carriage, said with a smile,

> *"Living after all has brought us at last today to a happy shoal—*
> *ah, but had I drowned myself, despairing, in the Uji!"*[22]

Her mistress did not like that at all, and she thought, How different she is from the nun Ben!

Another added,

> *"Not that one forgets the sadness of missing her, whom we all have lost,*
> *and yet today, even so, happy prospects lie ahead!"*

Both old women had been very fond of their elder mistress, but their resolute effort now to avoid dwelling on her memory struck the younger as very painful, and she found nothing further to say.

---

21. "Is not my sorrow just as bitter as yours, when I must set out tomorrow to a new home, on a journey I have never made before?"
22. "Shoal" is an image for one of life's vicissitudes.

Seeing for herself how far it was and how steep the pathways through the hills, she who had condemned him for his absences understood a little better why he had come so seldom. She gazed out at mists prettily illumined by a bright seventh-night moon, and the fatigue of the long, unfamiliar journey lulled her into troubled reverie:

> "Looking out, I see how the wandering moon as well rises from the hills,
>   finds no solace in the world, and then to the hills returns."[23]

Filled with forebodings about what might await her once she entered her new state, she longed to cancel all that had happened, for it seemed to her that her cares all those years were nothing to what they might be soon.

She arrived very late in the evening. They led her carriage in among the three- or fourfold pavilions[24] of a dazzling residence unlike anything her party had ever seen, and His Highness, who had awaited her impatiently, came himself to help her alight. Her rooms were done up to perfection, and the care lavished even on those for her women made it clear that he had given everything his personal attention. Seeing him all at once settled with her, when it had never been clear what treatment she might expect from him, decided people that he must be very keen on her indeed, and they were astonished by her evident quality.

Carriage with escort

The Counselor, who planned to move to his Sanjō residence after the twentieth of the month, was going daily to look the place over, and since it was near Nijō, he got there well before midnight to find out how things had gone. The men he had sent to escort her from Uji then returned and reported to him. The news that His Highness had received her with every mark of attention naturally pleased him, but despite himself he also felt a keen but foolish pang of disappointment. "Ah, were there but a way," he murmured again and again.[25]

> "Ah, glimmering waters! As across the Lake of Grebes one spies a shimmering sail,
>   she and I though yet apart did once lie down together!"[26]

23. She expects disappointment and a return to Uji.
24. Words used in the *saibara* song "This Gentleman" to describe an imposing residence.
25. *Genji monogatari kochūshakusho in'yō waka* 1933: "Were there but a way to turn present into past, for I would have the world be as I knew it then!"
26. The poem begins with *shinateru ya,* a conventional epithet (*makura kotoba*) for Nio no Umi ("Lake of Grebes," Lake Biwa); but since the meaning of the expression is unknown, "Ah, glimmering waters!" is less a guess than simply a replacement for it. The poem also plays on *maho,* "fine sail" and "truly" (I was with her, but not truly).

he said to himself, to spoil their happiness.

His Excellency of the Right, who planned to present His Highness with his Sixth Daughter that very same month, was outraged that as though to forestall the event His Highness should welcome someone wholly undeserving to his house and should now be avoiding him. His Highness was sorry to hear this, and now and again he sent the young lady a note. The preparations for her donning of the train had set all the world talking, and since he could no longer delay the event without courting ridicule, he performed the ceremony near the end of the month.

The idea of letting the Counselor go to a complete outsider struck him as a great shame. So close a marriage might well be dull, but even so he thought, Well, then, perhaps that is what I should do! He seems so despondent after all, now that he has lost an old and secret love. He had someone sound out the young gentleman.

"Having seen with my own eyes the fragility of life and suffered so greatly from it, I feel that my own existence is blighted, and for that reason I could not under any circumstances consider taking such a step": that, he gathered, was the Counselor's thoroughly discouraging reply.

"What? Even *he* turns up his nose at a perfectly straightforward proposal from me?" he exclaimed bitterly; but the young man, although a near relation, had such daunting dignity that he could not seek to persuade him further.

In the season of blossoms the Counselor looked across to the cherry trees at Nijō, and his thoughts went straight to the ones now abandoned at Uji. Do they scatter more blithely?[27] he wondered; and he set off to see His Highness. His Highness now spent most of his time at home, where he had settled down so nicely that the prospect was gratifying to a dutiful eye, except that as usual it was now also strangely upsetting. Nonetheless, in sober truth he was both touched and pleased.

They chatted about this and that until evening, when a large retinue gathered and His Highness's carriage was prepared to take him to the palace. The Counselor saw him to it and then went to her wing. No trace of the mountain village remained, for behind her blinds she lived amid elegant luxury. Noting through them the dim form of a pretty page girl, he asked her to let her mistress know that he was there, at which a cushion emerged, and someone who must have known him from before came out to give him the reply.

"I should have been coming regularly all this time to call," he began, "but no particular matter prompted me to do so, and I hesitated to presume on our acquaintance. How different things are now! The sight of your blossoming boughs through the mist stirs many poignant thoughts."

His pensive air aroused her sympathy, and she reflected that yes, if *she* had lived, they would now be visiting each other at will, and her life would offer the joy of exchanging with her, in season, tributes to the beauty of flowers or the songs of birds. She felt the present bitter sorrow of her loss far more keenly than their desolation during all the years they had lived shut away from the world.

"My lady," her women said, "please do not keep yourself from him as you

27. *Shūishū* 62, by Egyō Hōshi: "Could it be that the cherry blossoms abandoned by an empty house scatter more blithely on the wind?"

would from any other guest! Especially now, you really must let him know how much you appreciate everything he has done for you!" But she hesitated, for she could not yet bring herself to speak to him in person. Meanwhile His Highness came to say good-bye before setting off. Beautifully dressed and made up as he was, he made a very fine sight.

"Why are you keeping him all the way out there?" he asked when he noticed the Counselor. "Just think of the quite extraordinary amount he has done for you! I know I may have cause to regret it, but even so, it is wrong of you always to be this distant with him. Do have him come in and talk over your memories." But then in a changed mood he added, "Do not be *too* free with him, though. You never know what might happen. That man has his murky depths!" This left her at a loss toward both, but she had every reason now to humor someone whose great kindness to her she herself fully acknowledged, and she would have welcomed a chance to show him her gratitude, considering that, as he had said, he was now to be to her as her sister had once been. Still, with His Highness sometimes betraying anxiety of that kind, she could not help finding her position rather difficult.

49

YADORIGI

The Ivy

Yadorigi, or *yadoriki*, refers in this chapter to vines that "lodge" (*yadori*) on other trees. The chapter derives its title from a poetic exchange between Kaoru and Ben, in which both poems play on the two meanings of the syllables *yadoriki*: "climbing vine" (perhaps ivy, but not necessarily) and "I lodged [here]." Kaoru says,

"Did not memory tell me I have lodged before beneath these ivied trees, ah, then, how forlorn this night, spent lonely and far from home";

and Ben replies,

"You have lodged before here beneath the withered boughs of this ivied tree—how sad, then, it is to think that you keep that memory!"

The beginning of "The Ivy" takes place at the same time as "Red Plum Blossoms," the end of "Beneath the Oak," and the beginning of "Trefoil Knots," when Kaoru is twenty-four; it then continues during the time of "Bracken Shoots" and "The Eastern Cottage," when Kaoru is twenty-five and twenty-six.

PERSONS

The Counselor, then the Commander, age 24 to 26 (Kaoru)

The Fujitsubo Consort, daughter of the late Minister of the Left

His Majesty, the Emperor, 45 to 47

The Second Princess, daughter of the Fujitsubo Consort,
14 to 16 (Onna Ni no Miya)

His Highness of War, 25 to 27 (Niou)

His Excellency, the Minister of the Right, 50 to 52 (Yūgiri)

His Sixth Daughter, early 20s (Roku no Kimi)

Her Majesty, the Empress, 43 to 45 (Akashi no Chūgū)

The lady in the wing at Nijō, younger daughter of Hachi no Miya, 24 to 26
(Naka no Kimi)

The Right City Commissioner

Her Cloistered Highness, Kaoru's mother, mid- to late 40s (Onna San no Miya)

The Secretary Captain, brother of Roku no Kimi

Her Highness, the Second Princess, Roku no Kimi's stepmother
(Ochiba no Miya)

Azechi, a gentlewoman at Sanjō

Taifu, a gentlewoman of Naka no Kimi

Shōshō, a gentlewoman of Naka no Kimi

Ben, a nun at Uji (Ben no Ama)

The Adept (Uji no Ajari)

A young woman, the unrecognized third daughter of Hachi no Miya,
around 19 to 21 (Ukifune)

Chūjō, now wife of the Governor of Hitachi, Ukifune's mother

The Inspector Grand Counselor, mid-50s (Kōbai)

There was in those days a Consort known as Fujitsubo, a daughter of the late Minister of the Left.[1] His Majesty was distinctly fond of her because she had been the first to go to him when he was still Heir Apparent, but he had done nothing further for her over the years, and while it was his Empress's happy fortune also to have many growing children, *her* pleasures of that sort were few, since she had only a single daughter. It rankled that her bitter fate had been to be swept aside by another, and she brought up her daughter with great care so as to have the comfort of seeing her, at least, succeed. The Princess, who was extremely pretty, delighted His Majesty. She commanded less widespread regard than the First Princess, whom he cherished as peerless, but she was equally worthy in her own person, and she certainly was secure, since her father's great wealth had hardly declined. In dress and style those who served her lacked nothing, and her mode of life displayed on every occasion an admirable flair for tasteful fashion.

In the spring of Her Highness's fourteenth year[2] her mother gave up all else to prepare her donning of the train, which she planned to make exceptional in every way. She brought out each treasure that had come down to her from the past— After all, she thought, this is what they are for!—and was thus busily engaged when, that summer, she began to suffer from the workings of a baneful spirit and very soon was gone. His Majesty mourned her passing as a grievous loss. She had had such warmth and kindness that the senior nobles, too, knew they would miss her greatly. Even palace women[3] whose rank discouraged personal sentiment remembered her with sorrow.

Of course the young Princess grieved more pathetically than any for her mother, which moved His Majesty to pity when he learned of her condition, and as

1. "Those days" (*sono koro*) lie in a vague past. (The same expression, one suitable for starting a new tale, also begins "Red Plum Blossoms," "The Maiden of the Bridge," and "Writing Practice.") This Minister of the Left is probably the one mentioned briefly in "The Imperial Progress" and "Spring Shoots I." In "The Plum Tree Branch" his third daughter is described as having gone to the Heir Apparent before the future Akashi no Chūgū, and the chapter specifies that "she was known as Reikeiden." She must have moved to the Fujitsubo later on.
2. The spring of Kaoru's twenty-fourth year.
3. *Nyōkan*, lower-ranking women appointed to tend the baths, the kitchen, and so on.

Playing Go

soon as the forty-nine days were over, he had her return discreetly to the palace.[4] He went to visit her daily. Her modest robes of dark, mourning gray gave her a still more sweetly noble appeal. She was quite grown-up in manner, too, and she had if anything a somewhat greater poise and dignity than her mother, which His Majesty found gratifying; however, the truth of it was that her mother's side could not offer a single uncle properly able to look after her interests—nothing but two half brothers, a Lord of the Treasury and a Director of Upkeep. Neither enjoyed any great reputation, and for herself the consequences of having to lean on men of insufficient distinction were often unfortunate. The matter was His Majesty's, and his alone, to decide, and he dwelled on it constantly.

One day, when the chrysanthemums in the garden were most beautifully touched by frost and a cold rain was setting in to fall from a lowering sky, he went straight to the Princess's, where he spoke to her of her mother, and he found himself very pleased by her artless yet by no means childish answers. There must be someone, he said to himself, who would recognize her qualities and honor her properly for them. He recalled all His Eminence Suzaku's deliberations at the time when he gave his daughter to His Grace of Rokujō. Yes, for a time I disapproved, and I let His Majesty know that I wished he would desist; but still, the Minamoto Counselor is a very fine young man, and he looks after her so well that she continues to command all the respect she did then, whereas without him some sort of unpleasantness could easily have discredited her. Reflections like these convinced him that he might as well resolve the issue while he still reigned, and there really was nothing for it but to take the same course, since no one except the Counselor would do. He is worthy in every way to stand beside a Princess, he continued, and while for a very long time he had his heart set on someone else, there is no reason to think that he would ever do anything to injure her good name. He cannot possibly remain unattached forever, and I had better drop him a hint before anything happens to remove him from consideration.

He and she played a game of Go. Toward sundown, amid a pleasantly melancholy rain, he noticed how the sun's last light colored the chrysanthemums, and he summoned an attendant. "Who is in the privy chamber just now?" he asked.

"His Highness of Central Affairs, His Highness of Kanzuke, and the Minamoto Counselor are present in waiting, Your Majesty."

"Have his lordship the Counselor come to me." The Counselor soon arrived. His Majesty's reward for singling him out this way was the delicious fragrance that announced from afar how little he resembled other men.

---

4. To the Fujitsubo, where her mother had lived. She had been at home during the forty-nine days.

"The rain this evening is very soothing," His Majesty began, "but music would be out of place,[5] and nothing helps more to while away the day when there is little else to do."[6] He called for a Go board and invited the Counselor to play. The Counselor, who was often called into such intimate service, assumed that this time would be no different from the rest.

"I have something of value to wager," His Majesty declared, "but I could not let you have it too easily. What else would do? I wonder." Noting His Majesty's self-conscious air, the Counselor adopted a manner more circumspect than before.

They played, and His Majesty lost two out of three. "What a bore!" he exclaimed. Then he continued, "In any case, today you may have a flower."[7]

Without a word the Counselor went down into the garden, picked a beautiful flower, and brought it back inside.

> "Were this a flower blossoming very sweetly in a common hedge,
> I would have followed my heart and picked it for my pleasure,"

he said, with an air of grave respect.

> "This chrysanthemum comes, alas, from a garden withered by the frost,
> yet what color lingers on glows as ever fresh and new!"[8]

His Majesty replied.

Despite repeated intimations of this kind from His Majesty himself, the Counselor remained true to his penchant for indecision. Come now, he reflected, this is not what I want. Over the years I have let pass more than one opportunity to accept someone whose fortunes deeply concerned me, and now I feel like a holy man contemplating a return to the world. It *is* odd of me, though, when some would be only too pleased. Still, he knew at heart that he might well feel otherwise if she were Her Majesty's daughter, which was most impudent of him.

This unexpected development annoyed His Excellency of the Right when he caught wind of it, since he had been telling himself, Well, I shall at least be able to give *him* my Sixth Daughter, and bother him if he does not like the idea; he will have to concede in the end, as long as I insist loudly enough. His mind therefore turned again to His Highness of War, who now and again was still casually sending her perfectly nice notes. Very well, he thought, never mind if he is only amusing himself. Why should he not take a fancy to her, if that is his destiny? It would be all very well to choose for the sake of her happiness, but in the end it would be an embarrassment, and a great disappointment as well, to have her stoop too tediously low.

5. Because the Second Princess is in mourning.
6. On the value of Go to while away an idle day, the Emperor is alluding to a line by Bai Juyi (*Hakushi monjū* 0920).
7. The conceit and the wording are based on a Chinese couplet, *Wakan rōei shū* 783, by Ki no Tadana: "I hear that you have beautiful flowers in your garden: Sir, I ask your leave to pluck a branch of these spring blossoms." These flowers are autumn chrysanthemums.
8. The "withered" garden refers to the young lady's mother and the still-fresh color to herself.

"Any girl in these latter days is worry enough, and when the Emperor himself must hunt for a son-in-law, it certainly is a crying shame that the best years of a commoner's daughter should have to go to waste!" In this evident mood of complaint he broached the subject with bitter insistence several times to Her Majesty,[9] who was then sufficiently troubled to make His Highness an uncharacteristically long speech.

"Unfortunately," she said, "he has had this matter quite openly on his mind for years, and it has been unkind of you to go on evading him. How well a Prince gets on depends on his backing.[10] His Majesty says often enough that he does not expect to reign much longer, and while a commoner can no longer really share his heart with many, once he is settled with one, His Excellency, however staid he may be, still manages to get on without jealousy on either side.[11] Is that not so? Well, then, if what His Majesty plans for you comes to pass, why should you not keep as many as you like?"

Her remarks made perfect sense, and he saw no excuse for insisting on dismissing the prospect outright, since he himself had never entirely rejected it. What did bother him, unfortunately, was the thought of being caught in surroundings so excessively proper that he would no longer be able to do as he pleased; at the same time, though, yes, he certainly might regret turning His Excellency against him. Such reflections as these are no doubt what led him at last to yield. His roving fancy had not yet renounced the Inspector Grand Counselor's daughter—she of the red plum blossoms—and he continued sending notes to both, tied to spring blossoms or autumn leaves, for both retained his interest.

Meanwhile the New Year came. Now that the Second Princess's mourning was over, there was less reason than ever to hesitate. When one person after another suggested to the Counselor that His Majesty seemed reluctant to proceed without a word from him, the Counselor made up his mind that it would be strange and rude of him to pretend not to have heard, and he let it be known to His Majesty several times that he aspired to the favor in question. The response was hardly likely to embarrass him. He gathered that His Majesty himself had decided the day, and he received his approval in person. At heart, though, he knew that he would never forget a loss he still felt keenly, and he simply could not understand why, when they had clearly been meant for each other, they had nonetheless remained strangers to the end. Oh, how I could love someone whose looks recalled hers a little, even if she was unworthy in rank! If only I might see her again, just once, at least in the incense smoke of that old story![12] He was in no hurry to consummate this exalted alliance.

His Excellency of the Right hastened to inform His Highness that *that* event would take place in the eighth month, and she who inhabited His Highness's wing at Nijō cried to herself when she heard the news, Oh, I knew this would happen!

9. His half sister.

10. In other words, a Prince's fortunes depend on support from a father-in-law with wealth and political power—a commoner.

11. Yūgiri, a commoner, shares his time equally between Kumoi no Kari and Ochiba no Miya.

12. Bai Juyi's poem "Lady Li" (*Hakushi monjū* 0160) tells how Emperor Wu of Han, after losing his beloved Lady Li, saw her face in the smoke of incense burned by a magician.

How could it not? What had the miserable likes of me to expect, ever since this began, but mockery and humiliation? I had always heard what a rascal he was, and no, I never trusted him, but in person I never saw in him anything strikingly reprehensible, and he made me such heartfelt promises! How am I ever to know peace again, now that he has suddenly changed? This may not mean a final break, as it would between commoners, but there will often be unpleasantness like this! I am sure one as wedded as I to misfortune should go straight back to her hills, but if I were simply to disappear that way, I know the mountain folk there would only laugh at me! In anger and shame she knew the folly of having wandered away, against her father's advice, from the home that had always been her own.

What my sister voiced of her thoughts was always so slight, so tentative—but deep in her heart she had a superb strength. His lordship the Counselor seems to be mourning her even now as though he will never forget her, but I do not doubt that if she were alive, she would have cares just like mine. She decided at all costs to avoid giving what he wanted of her, even to the point of proposing to leave the world, because she was convinced that it could not be otherwise. And she would have done so! At last I understand how farsighted she was. Now that they are gone, they must both be watching me and thinking me an unmitigated fool! These were her thoughts, but despite her hurt and shame she kept them well hidden—For am I to betray how I feel, when I can do nothing at all about it?—and ignored the news as though she had not heard a word.

His Highness was now more attentive and affectionate than he had been, and he assured her that he was hers not only for this life but for all lives to come. Meanwhile it came to pass that in the fifth month she began to feel not herself and quite unwell; not that she was in any great pain, but she ate less and less, and she spent all her time lying down, which he, who had never really known anyone in her condition, attributed simply to the heat. Still, he noticed certain things that puzzled him. "Could it be?" he would sometimes say. "Is there something new with you? I hear that people feel then just as you do." She was acutely embarrassed and passed it off as nothing, and since no one came forward to tell him, he never actually found out.

The eighth month came, and she learned the day from someone else. His Highness had never wanted to keep it from her, but sorrow and pity undid him whenever he actually meant to tell her, so that in the end he never did, and she resented that as well. There was nothing secret about it—the whole world knew—and he had not even let her know when it would be! How could she not be angry with him? Nothing much had happened since she came. He made a point of not staying the night even when he went to the palace, and he had never gone off for a night elsewhere. Now, to dull his unhappiness over what she might think of this sudden change, he began going to the palace now and then for night duty, so as to inure her to his absences in advance; but she only took this badly as well.

His lordship the Counselor was greatly saddened to hear all this. His Highness enjoys diversion, he said to himself, and even if he feels guilty toward her, his affections can hardly help shifting to someone new. He is marrying into a very powerful house, too, and if they leave him in no doubt that they expect him *there*, then alas, she will spend many lonely nights waiting, which she has never had to do over these last few months. How wrong I was! Ah, why did I come forward to let him have her? I wanted *her*, the one I loved, to be mine, and ever since, my heart has been clouded, although it once ran clear toward renouncing the world, and one way or another she is all I think of; and yet I held back because it seemed to me from the beginning that I wanted no consummation without her consent, and meanwhile I only looked to the future, gauging her mood and hoping that she would somehow have pity and yield at last. But no, she felt otherwise, and to make up for it, since she did not really wish just to send me away, she assured me that she and her sister were one and the same and urged me in a direction for which I had no heart. That baffled and angered me, and I hastened to thwart her plan once and for all. He thought back over how in a mad fit of womanish scheming he had taken His Highness down to Uji, and he bitterly regretted doing so, because yes, that had been despicable! At any rate, he reflected with rancor, what I hear now should affect His Highness a little if he remembers all that; but no, he will never say a word to me about it. So impossibly frivolous a man, with so fickle a heart, may betray more than women—no folly of his would surprise me. His way of nursing an all too single-minded obsession must be what made him so furious with His Highness.

He had truly lost his love, and he thought, It is no pleasure to have His Majesty offer me his daughter—ah, if only I had accepted *this* one! Every month, every day, his regrets multiplied, and knowing that they were sisters made giving her up impossible, since as far as that went, the two had been almost as one and since, besides, *she* had told him near the end that her sister, who would survive her, must be to him as she was herself; for she had said, "There is nothing now that I would wish otherwise, save that you never did as I asked, and that is a hurt and a sorrow that may yet detain me in the world"; and now that this had happened, she must be looking down from on high and hating him more and more. These reflections ran through his head while night after night, through no fault but his own, he lay wakeful at every breath of a breeze, pondering the past and the future and also the cruel trials that life might well impose on someone else as well.[13]

He must of course have been fond of some whom he had flattered in passing and admitted to his intimacy, but no, not one of them truly had his heart. Actually, a great many women no less distinguished than the sisters, women whom fortune had abandoned to misery, had been found and called into service at Sanjō, but he was resolved that when the time came for him to turn his back on the world, *she* would remain the sole passionate tie that detained him. "Come now, this will not do! I simply do not understand myself!" he would murmur as he lay sleepless into dawn. Among the lovely many-colored flowers along the misty fence, his eye lighted especially on the fragile morning glories that, they say, "bloom at daybreak"[14] to suggest that nothing lasts; and he must have felt for them, because after lying comfortless

---

13. Naka no Kimi.
14. From an otherwise unknown poem cited in an early commentary: "Perhaps the morning glory is the flower of transience, for it blooms at daybreak and afterward dies."

into the new day, with his shutters raised, he watched them unfold alone while the light came on.

He summoned one of his men. "I wish to visit the residence to the north,"[15] he said. "Have a simple carriage brought forward."

"My lord, His Highness went to the palace yesterday. They brought his carriage back yesterday evening."

"Never mind. I shall call on the lady in his wing; they say that she is not well. I must go to the palace today, so have the carriage ready before the sun is high."

He dressed, and on his way out he stepped down among the flowers. He did nothing to convey languor or allure, but at a glance one saw in him such grace and dignity that the most self-conscious gallant could not hope to imitate him. The picture he made was delightful, and the morning glory he drew to him shed copious dew.

"Shall I prize these hues, gone sooner than the morning, when before my eyes
the dew gleaming on the leaf outlasts the fragile flower?

How soon it will be gone!" he murmured, picking it to take with him. He did not give the maidenflowers a glance.

The loveliest mist swathed the sky as dawn brightened into day. The women must be indulging in sleeping late! he thought; I can hardly go about clearing my throat or rapping on shutters and doors. Ah, I am here too early, much too early!

He called one of his men and had him peer in through the open middle gate. "The shutters seem to be up, my lord. I just glimpsed a gentlewoman," the man reported.

He alighted and went in, veiled by morning mists and looking so charming that the women took him for His Highness returning from a secret assignation, until they caught as always the delicious scent of his dewy robes. "He *is* such a wonder!" the young women exclaimed gratuitously to one other. "What a shame he is so serious!"

Undismayed, and with pleasantly rustling skirts, they very nicely put out a cushion for him. "It is an honor to be seated here," he said, "but I cannot very well call more often, considering how painful it is still to be kept so far away on the other side of your blinds."

"What would you prefer, then, my lord?" the women asked.

"A quiet room like the one to the north:[16] that is the proper sort of place for an old friend like me. It all depends on you, though; I do not mean to complain further." He was leaning against the lintel.

"You might perhaps go to him, my lady," they continued to urge her.

Never having been known to behave with masculine impetuousness, he had seemed so quiet lately that she felt less reluctant than before to converse with him

15. Niou's Nijō residence, just north of Kaoru's.
16. The gentlewomen's sitting room.

directly and did so willingly enough. "May I inquire what is the matter?" he asked. She gave him no distinct answer, but he was moved and saddened by her unusually subdued manner, and he enlarged to her as a brother might on how to make her peace with the world as she found it.

Her voice had not struck him before as especially like her sister's, but now he was startled to find them almost the same, and if decency had not forbidden it, he would have lifted her blinds to talk to her face-to-face, for he longed to see how she looked now that she was unwell. All this only served to remind him that there can hardly be anyone in the world who does not suffer the sorrows of the heart. "I do not seek to distinguish myself or to impress others," he said, "but I had thought that one could manage in life without any great burden of anxiety or care. Unfortunately, however, through no fault but my own I suffer at once from the grief of loss and the pain of bitter regret. In that respect my sin is no doubt graver than that of the man who values rank and office above all and who suffers perfectly understandably from that sort of disappointment." He put the flower he had picked on his fan and sat gazing at it. The red it was turning[17] actually struck him as even prettier, and he gently slid it through to her under the blind.

> "This should all the while have looked to me just the same as the silver dew
>   that promised me long ago a morning glory flower."[18]

The gesture was casual, but it was pleasant that he had brought the flower without spilling its dew, and since the flower would clearly wither before the dew was gone, she replied,

> "Frail, yes, the flower that withered so soon and died ere the dew was gone,
>   yet still less so than the dew that now lingers on behind.[19]

What other refuge does it have?" she said, very low and in a faltering voice, as though too shy to wish to be heard; and to his sorrow he thought again how alike they were.

"One feels a little more sadly pensive under an autumn sky," he remarked. "The other day I sought distraction by going down to Uji, and I found the fence and garden[20] in a pitiful state—there was so much that was hard to bear! The sight was overwhelming for those who looked in at Rokujō after His Grace's death, or at the Saga temple where he withdrew those last two or three years. Every one of them came back moved to tears by the look of the plants and trees. No one close to him, high or low, was ever shallow of feeling, but even so, everyone who had gathered around him in the several quarters of the estate seemed to have drifted away to live removed from the world. The lowest of the gentlewomen were of course incon-

---

17. As it withered.
18. "In my eyes you should have been the same as your sister, who wished me to have you."
19. "My fate is still more fragile than my sister's."
20. *Kokinshū* 248, by Henjō: "It is a poor village, and those who inhabit my home are old: the fence and garden have turned to an autumn moor."

solable, and for the most part the poor things scattered into the mountains and forests, hardly knowing what they were doing, until in the end they became mere country women.[21] Rokujō became a waste overgrown by the grasses of forgetting,[22] but then the present Minister of the Right moved in, the Prince and Princess[23] began to reside there, too, and the place came again to resemble what it had once been. There seemed to me to be no words for the grief one felt at the time, but I see now that the years do bring consolation and that it is true, there is an end to mourning. I say that, of course, but perhaps I was too young then to feel his loss as deeply as I might have done otherwise. Certainly, I do not think I will ever recover from this more recent one, and while both are the sorrows one expects of this life in which nothing lasts, I am afraid that for me, alas, this one entails the graver sin."[24] His weeping figure conveyed profound emotion.

No woman seeing him like this could have failed to be moved in turn, even one far less attached than this lady was to her sister, and so, naturally, the lady herself, already sadly troubled and more than ever disposed to miss her sister most painfully, found herself too moved to answer at all. Instead she lost her composure, and each felt the other's emotion all too keenly.

" 'Happier than this troubled world'[25]—so someone once said, but for all those years I could not make the comparison. Now, though, I should be happy to have that peace again, because in fact it suits me so little to be here that I envy Ben. How I long after all to hear the temple bell nearby, after the twentieth of this month![26] It has even occurred to me to ask you to take me there in secret."

"Alas, there is nothing you can do to save the place from ruin. The mountain path is very rough, even for a man who can go as he pleases, and I myself take it far less often than I would like. I have given the Adept all the instructions he needs for His Late Highness's memorial service. Please consider devoting the place to holy works. What I find there when I go unfortunately upsets me very much, and I have thought of dedicating it to canceling my own sins. I wonder what you think. I will do nothing, you know, that you yourself do not intend. You need only let me know your wishes. I simply ask that you take me into your confidence on everything." He continued addressing her in this way about quite serious matters. Apparently, he also meant to dedicate scripture texts and sacred images on his own. When she gave him to understand that she now wished to steal off there on retreat, he replied, "No, no, that is impossible. You must always be accepting and patient."

The sun rose high, and her women gathered around her. He was preparing to go, since too long a stay might leave the impression that there was something going on, when he said, "It is not my custom to be left outside the blinds anywhere, and I feel quite uncomfortable when I am. That is up to you, however. I shall be back." Then he went away. He knew that His Highness would wonder why he had come

---

21. This probably means that they married provincial officials.

22. The literal meaning of *wasuregusa* (modern Japanese *yabukanzō*), an orange daylily.

23. The Empress's First Princess and Second Prince, according to "The Perfumed Prince."

24. That of attachment to the things of this world.

25. *Kokinshū* 944: "A mountain village makes a lonely home indeed, yet it is a happier place than this troubled world."

26. The bell for the third anniversary of her father's death, in the eighth month.

in his absence, and that was enough of a concern that he summoned the Right City Commissioner, His Highness's Master of the Household. "I came when I heard that His Highness withdrew from the palace yesterday evening," he said. "I am sorry to have missed him. Perhaps I should look for him there."

"He will be leaving there today, my lord."

"Very well, I shall return this evening."

It was still true: each time he caught her voice and the sounds of her presence, he wondered with keener regret why he had been foolish enough not to do as her sister had wished, and the matter weighed very heavily on his mind, for as he asked himself time and again, Why must I make myself suffer this way?

He had begun to fast[27] the moment *she* died, and day and night he gave himself so wholly to his devotions that Her Highness his mother, as girlish, naive, and careless as ever, came to worry a great deal and to fear for him. "I have little enough time left,"[28] she said; "please look after yourself while I am still with you! I can hardly object to your wishing to leave the world, considering what I am, but I am afraid that I would then feel I had no reason to go on living, and the pain of that might only deepen my sins." Troubled and sorry, he did what he could to forget and to affect in her presence a carefree nonchalance.

His Excellency of the Right did up the northeast quarter at Rokujō,[29] made everything there perfect, and then awaited His Highness anxiously until the moon of the sixteenth night rose into the sky. He was concerned about the way things might go, since His Highness was not that eager. The man he sent to inquire brought back the report, "His Highness withdrew from the palace this evening, my lord, and I gather that he is now at Nijō." It was galling to reflect that this was no doubt because he kept his lady love there, and he knew that he would be a laughingstock if the whole evening went by without a groom. He therefore sent off his son the Secretary Captain[30] with a message:

> "While this house of mine welcomes even the bright moon aloft in the sky,
> the evening is passing by, and I see nothing of you!"[31]

The poor thing, I cannot let her see that this is the night! His Highness had said to himself when he set off for the palace, and he had sent her a note; but her answer, whatever it said, had made him feel sufficiently guilty to steal home again. She was too dear, and he could not bear to leave her. He was tenderly renewing all his promises instead, and the two were gazing at the moon. Resolved as she was,

---

27. Abstention from meat and fish.

28. *Kokinshū* 934: "I who have little enough time left, why am I so troubled by a nun's abundant sorrows?" The poem plays on *karumo*, the seaweed the *ama* gathers, which is likened to tangled cares.

29. Where Hanachirusato had lived. It was now occupied by Ochiba no Miya and her adopted daughter, Roku no Kimi.

30. Presumably the Secretary Lieutenant mentioned in "Beneath the Oak," a full brother of Roku no Kimi.

31. *Motoyoshi Shinnō shū* 150: "While this house of mine welcomes even the moon aloft in the sky, you yourself pass by beyond the clouds!"

even after days of despair, to betray nothing, she remained aloof and pretended not to hear.[32] The mildness of her manner touched him very much.

Nonetheless, he felt for the other side, too, when he learned that the Captain had arrived. While preparing to leave he said, "I am going now, but only for a little while. Please do not watch the moon alone. One's thoughts wander so painfully." Still feeling guilty, he set off to the main house by a hidden way. Nothing in particular passed through her mind as she watched him go, save the feeling that her pillow would float away,[33] and she understood all too well how treacherous another's heart can be.

Ever since my sister and I were small, she reflected, our only refuge was a gentleman who seemed to have so little taste for the world that we lived year after year in that mountain village; but although it was always dull and lonely there, I never had reason as now really to detest the world. Then came those terrible losses, one after the other, and it seemed while I was mourning them that I could not possibly survive them for long, because the blow was too great and those two had meant so much to me. Now that I have survived them after all, though, I doubt that I shall enjoy this honored state much longer, even if he is so good to me when we are together that I had begun to feel less apprehensive. This new misery is beyond all words, and I do not think I can bear any more. I might at least have expected to see him more often than I do those who are now gone forever, but tonight he has abandoned me with such cruelty that nothing, past or future, any longer makes sense, and I see nowhere to turn for comfort from this desolation. Ah, it is too unkind! But perhaps if I live long enough . . . Groping for consolation, she suffered on into the night while a brilliant moon climbed the sky as it did over the Mountain of the Abandoned Crone.[34] The wind in the pines sighed very gently, compared to the roar of the gales off the Uji hills, and this house she had to live in was very quiet and nice, but she would have preferred tonight the noise of the great oaks.

> "No such autumn wind at my home in the mountains, sheltered under pines,
> blew as bitterly as this or so pierced one to the bone."

Perhaps she had forgotten what had happened there.

"Oh, do come in, my lady!" the old women urged her. "It is not right for you to watch the moon! What is to become of you, when you will not look at the smallest bit of fruit? Oh, dear, and such fearful memories come to mind! What are we to do?"

"Yes, but look what His Highness is doing!" others sighed. "Still, he cannot mean simply to discard her. It is all very well, but a first love never really dies."

She did not wish to hear their talk and longed only for them to be silent. *I*

---

32. Presumably, the news of the arrival of Yūgiri's messenger.

33. From copious weeping. *Kokin rokujō* 3241, by Hitomaro: "Upon the tears I weep as I lie alone, even a pillow of stone could well float away."

34. Legend had it that a man once left his aged and useless mother to die on Obasute-yama, a mountain in Shinano (Nagano Prefecture). *Kokinshū* 878: "My heart has no comfort at Sarashina, watching the moon shine down on the Mountain of the Abandoned Crone."

shall watch and wait, she thought; for perhaps she did not want anyone to speak for her, so that she might nurse her anger alone.

"And look what a good, kind gentleman the Counselor is!" the talk went on among the women who had known her before. "How strange destiny can be!"

His Highness felt extremely sorry, but he was too high-spirited not to be eager to make a good impression, and his exquisitely perfumed figure beggared description. The house where they received him was very pretty indeed. She herself was neither slight nor frail but instead, in his opinion, nicely grown out. What could she be like, though? Would she turn out to be tiresomely assertive, with no gentleness in her, only pride? *That* would be a disaster! But she must not have been like that after all, because he felt not the slightest inclination to dismiss her. Perhaps it was just that he had got there so late, but even if it was autumn, the night was over all too soon.[35]

He did not go straight to the wing when he got home. Instead he slept a little and then wrote his letter when he got up.

"He looks quite pleased," the women attending him remarked to each other.

"I feel so sorry for my lady in the wing. She really cannot help being overshadowed, however admirably fair-minded he may be." They were upset, since all of them waited intimately on her, and some even voiced bitter words. It was a sad blow to each.

He had hoped to read the reply to his note in his own rooms, but it pained him to think that his absence that night must have troubled her more than at other such times, and he hurried to her. He looked splendid as he came in, his face fresh from sleep. She was embarrassed to be caught lying down and sat up a little, her face prettily flushed and, to his mind, this morning lovelier than ever. Abruptly his eyes clouded with tears, and he gazed at her until she turned bashfully away and lay facedown, displaying a beauty rare indeed in the line of her forehead and the sweep of her hair.

Perhaps to break the silence when the awkwardness of the moment suggested nothing more tender to say, he took up an earnest subject. "Why is it that you always seem so unwell?" he asked. "You said that it was because of the heat, so I looked forward to cooler weather, but I am very sorry to see that you are not better yet. It is odd—nothing I have had done for you seems to have worked. Still, I suppose I should have the prayers continued. What I need is a priest with real power. I should have had His Reverence ———— come and attend you at night."

She did not care for his glibness on this sort of topic either, but she knew it would have been unlike her not to answer at all. "I have always been a little different," she said. "I have been like this before, but it goes away quite well by itself."

"How lighthearted you are!" he said, smiling. It seemed to him that no one else could ever have so seductive a sweetness, but he was also still eager to go back where he had just been, since he seems to have been quite keen on *her* as well. But as long as she was before him, she seemed to him exactly the same, which must be why he made her countless promises even for the next life. However, she reflected

35. Autumn nights were supposed to be long.

as she listened to his protestations that yes, it was true, her time would be soon[36] and that he was so certain to cause her more grief that those vows for the next life were probably the ones he would keep. The thought taught her that she had not learned her lesson,[37] since even now she was inclined to trust him, and that may have been too much for her, for despite no doubt valiant efforts, today at last she wept. She had been disguising her feelings all this time, lest she betray them to him, but by now she had too many cares to hide them any longer—or so at least it seemed, since once the tears started, she could not easily stop them, and she turned sharply away from him in shame and misery.

He drew her by force to face him again. "I was sure that you were kind and that you believed everything I have told you, yet you have been keeping yourself from me, have you not? Or have your feelings toward me changed in a single night?" He dried her tears with his own sleeve.

"You talk of feelings changing in a night, but I know all too well whose feelings those are!" she retorted with a little smile.

"But, my darling, you are talking like a child! Really, though, my conscience is clear: I am hiding nothing at all. If I were, I could defend myself as much as I liked, and the truth would still be perfectly plain. You understand nothing of the world, which is at once one of your charms and a great difficulty. Very well, think it over from my point of view. One can never do as one pleases:[38] that is my own situation. If what I hope for comes to pass, I will then have it within my power to convince you that you mean more to me than anyone else.[39] This is not something I could ever say lightly. As long as I have breath . . ."[40]

Meanwhile, his messenger to His Excellency's forgot all shame and came barging straight into the southern front of their wing, very drunk indeed. He carried heaped across his shoulders so marvelous a burden of gifts[41] that the women saw why he was there, and they must have wondered anxiously when His Highness could have written *his* letter. His Highness, who did not mean to conceal what the man had brought him, still had no desire to show it off, and he wished angrily that he would behave himself. It was too late, though, and he had a gentlewoman bring the letter to him. Resolved to have no secrets on the matter, he opened the message, to find it written apparently in the hand of Her Highness the lady's stepmother.[42] That made him feel a little better, and he put it down—a risky thing to do, whether

---

36. *Kokinshū* 965, by Taira no Sadafumi: "I, whose time will be soon, only wish that, that short while, I might have few sorrows."

37. *Kokinshū* 631: "I have not learned my lesson, for soon they will be bandying my name about again; but after all he and I do get on together."

38. *Gosenshū* 938, by Ise: "I can say neither yes nor no, for alas, in this world one can never do as one pleases."

39. "If I become Heir Apparent and then Emperor, I will make you my Empress."

40. Apparently a fragment of a poem, intended to suggest either "If I live long enough, I will do this for you" or "You must see to it that you live long enough for me to do this for you."

41. The messenger bringing the answer to Niou's letter has been plied with wine and showered with gifts (robes), in keeping with the happy character of the occasion. The original plays on *kazuki* ("dive" and "receive across one's shoulders") to say, more literally, "He was buried under the marvelous, gleaming seaweeds that the seafolk dive down to harvest."

42. Ochiba.

or not someone else had written it for her! It said, "Please forgive my presumption, but I am afraid that despite all I did to encourage her, she felt too unwell.

> *This maidenflower seems only to wilt and wilt in the morning dew—*
> *what, in settling and leaving, can the dew have ever done?*"[43]

Her writing had charm and distinction.

"She might spare me her complaints!" he said. "All I really wanted was to be left in peace with you, and now *this* had to happen!" Actually, though, anyone could certainly have shared her resentment if he had been a commoner,[44] who properly has one wife, not two, but in his case it was not really so. This had been bound to happen. The world knew that his destiny differed from that of the other Princes, and it would have raised no objection no matter how many women he had. It is unlikely that anyone pitied her. People apparently spoke of her good fortune because of the way he had taken her in so grandly and continued to honor and love her. The tragedy for her seems to have been that she found her position compromised suddenly, after he had let her become too accustomed to his intimacy. Why, she had always wondered, reading an old tale or listening to talk about somebody else, why does this aspect of life upset people so? But now that these difficulties touched *her*, she knew quite clearly that they were no joke.

His Highness, who felt particularly sorry for her, was more than usually tender and attentive. "It is not right for you to eat nothing at all," he said. He pressed her to take something, calling for the most pleasing refreshments and summoning an expert to make things specially for her, but they failed to appeal to her at all. "Ah," he sighed, "it is too bad!"

The sun was setting by now, and at dusk he went off to the main house. The chilly winds and splendid skies of the season stirred him to languorous thoughts, fond as he was of novelty; while to her, with all her cares, things were too painful to bear. A cicada's singing only made her miss the shadow of the hills.[45]

> "Nothing of that song, there, would have struck me at all, yet this autumn dusk,
> how a cicada's singing calls forth bitter, bitter thoughts!"

This evening he set out before it was late. Seafolk might well have fished below her pillow[46] while the cries of his escort receded into the distance, and she reproached herself as she lay there even for this. She remembered the sorrows he had caused her from the start and wished that it had never happened. And this con-

43. Thanks to a play on *oki* ("arise" in the morning, "leave," as well as "settle," speaking of dew), the poem seems to ask not only what the dew (Niou) did to the maidenflower (Roku no Kimi) during the night, but what he did when he took his leave of her to upset her so.

44. Or "someone ordinary." It is not clear that the meaning here is intended to be specifically "nonimperial."

45. *Kokinshū* 204: "A cicada sang, and I thought the sun had set, but it was just that I had come under the shadow of the hills."

46. *Genji monogatari kochūshakusho in'yō waka* 381: "While I weep aloud for the sorrows of love, seafolk are fishing below my pillow."

dition that makes me so uncomfortable—how will it end? People in my family are so short-lived—perhaps I will not live after all! She did not regret the prospect, but it saddened her, and besides, it would be a very great sin. Such thoughts as these ran through her mind while she lay sleepless through the night.

The next day Her Majesty felt unwell, and the whole court gathered to attend her, but it was only a slight indisposition and not serious at all. His Excellency withdrew from the palace at midday and invited the Counselor to accompany him; they drove away in the same carriage. He wondered about the ceremony tonight,[47] which he seemed to want to be as magnificent as possible, although he could obviously do only so much and no more.[48] He felt somewhat constrained in the Counselor's presence, but the Counselor was after all a very close relative, and having no one else of the kind to turn to, he no doubt felt that he would do perfectly to lend a special touch to the event. The Counselor came more quickly than usual[49] and was a great help in all sorts of ways, since in his estimation the matter did not concern him and he felt no regret. His Excellency secretly found his attitude quite annoying.

His Highness arrived some way into the evening. A seat had been prepared for him at the east end of the southern aisle in the main house. Eight tall stands were set out there in formally handsome array, bearing the usual dishes,[50] and beside them two smaller stands, bearing in stylish fashion blossom-footed dishes containing rice cakes—but it is tiresome of me to record anything that ordinary. Upon noting how late it was, His Excellency went to have the gentlewomen remind His Highness that it was time,[51] but His Highness was absorbed in dalliance and did not immediately go. The others present included two brothers of His Excellency's wife, the Intendant of the Left Gate Watch, and the Fujiwara Consultant.

When at last His Highness appeared, he was a wonder to behold. His host, the Secretary Captain, offered him a wine cup and presented him with his meal. Others offered him their cups, turn by turn, and he drank two or three. The way the Counselor pressed wine on him rather made him smile. The Counselor must have been remembering how His Highness, who did not feel at home in this house, had once remarked what a tiresome place it was, but his grave expression betrayed nothing of the kind. He then proceeded to the east wing to entertain His Highness's retinue, among whom he knew a great many of the privy gentlemen. The six gentlemen of the fourth rank each received a set of women's robes and a long dress; the ten of the fifth got a triple-layered Chinese jacket and a train that acknowledged their station;[52] and the four of the sixth got trousers and a damask long dress. Impatient at not being allowed to do better, His Excellency had made sure that these things were all exceptionally beautiful in color and finish. The gifts for

47. For the second night of Niou's marriage to Roku no Kimi.
48. Because as a subject he was forbidden to emulate certain aspects of imperial splendor.
49. Although he and Yūgiri left the palace together, he seems to have returned home briefly before going to Rokujō.
50. The dishes would have been silver.
51. To leave Roku no Kimi, with whom he has been up to now, and to go and enjoy the festive meal prepared for him.
52. Presumably by color or pattern.

His Highness's household staff and grooms were so grand as to border on the outrageous. Yes, crowded, brilliant scenes are well worth seeing, which is no doubt why tales always feature them, but unfortunately it seems to have been impossible to note everything.

One of the Counselor's retainers had enjoyed little of all this opulence (perhaps he had been standing somewhere lost in shadows), and he whispered as they passed through the middle gate at Sanjō, on their way back, "Why will his lordship not act sensibly and marry into His Excellency's house? This solitary life of his is a bore!" The Counselor caught what he said and was quite amused. The man was probably envious because it was late and they were all tired, and because after their lavish welcome His Highness's people must still be lying about here and there, pleasantly drunk.

The Counselor went in and lay down. How awkward these things are! he thought. In came the father, looking ever so grand, and everyone raised the lamp wicks and kept pressing wine on His Highness, even though we are all related. They certainly looked after him nicely! He remembered His Highness's figure with pleasure. Yes indeed, if I had a daughter of whom I thought highly, I would rather give her to *him* than send her to the palace; which reminded him, I hear everyone with a daughter he wants His Highness to have also talks of offering her to the Minamoto Counselor—why, there seems to be nothing wrong with *my* reputation either! I am too unworldly and too old-fashioned, though. These prideful thoughts were followed by others. His Majesty is dropping hints, but what will I do when he makes up his mind, if I am still as reluctant as I am now? It would be a great honor, of course, but how would it actually turn out? I wonder. How happy I would be if by any chance she looked just like the Princess I lost! No, he did not really feel like refusing her.

As so often, he slept poorly, and to relieve the boredom of lying awake he went to the room of Azechi,[53] whom he preferred somewhat to the others, and spent the night there. It is not as though anyone would have taken any particular notice even if morning had come, but he arose in such haste and with such a preoccupied air that she was offended.

"*When neither of us has the leave of anyone to cross Barrier Brook,*
I regret to have my name known thanks to your attentions!"[54]

He was touched and said,

"*At first glance indeed it may seem shallow enough, yet this Barrier Brook*
underneath runs on and on, its depths beyond all sounding."[55]

---

53. Presumably one of his mother's gentlewomen.
54. "Barrier Brook" (Sekigawa) alludes to the brook at Ōsaka pass, between Kyoto and Lake Biwa. Ōsaka means literally "slope of meeting," and it is associated in poetry with the motifs of meeting (of lovers) and separation.
55. *Yamato monogatari* 161 (episode 106): "You may well think it shallow, but I know that at heart Barrier Brook will never run dry."

His mention of "depths" must only have confirmed her doubts, and she can hardly have liked this business of "shallow at first glance."

He opened the double doors. "Really, though," he said, "come and see this sky! I wonder how you can just lie there and ignore it. I do not mean to put on airs, but seem to be sleeping less and less well, and when I lie awake night after night into a dawn like this, you know, I cannot help thinking over this life and the one to come." Before leaving he thus turned her mind to other things. No doubt the grace of his looks made up for his lack of winning eloquence, for no one ever thought him unkind. Any woman to whom he had once addressed a playful word aspired to know him better, which may explain why among those who had gathered so eagerly to serve Her Highness his mother, many, in keeping with their station, nursed variously wounded feelings.

His Highness was still better pleased when he saw his new lady by daylight.[56] Her height was perfect, and the length of her sidelocks and the set of her head struck him as exceptionally lovely. Her skin had an exquisite tone, her face an imposing dignity, and her glance a quickness so daunting that he was completely satisfied. She lacked nothing worthy of a beauty. At twenty-one or -two she was no longer a girl, and nothing about her conveyed immaturity; she resembled a flower in brilliant bloom. The studied care of her upbringing had rounded her perfectly. Her father must have worried endlessly on her behalf. For sweet, yielding charm, though, he thought first of the other one in the wing of his own residence. This one answered bashfully enough when spoken to, but she was not excessively reserved, and she was both handsome and intelligent. Her thirty young gentlewomen and six page girls were all flawless, and as far as their dress was concerned, His Highness's distaste for commonplace formality had prompted her father instead to encourage an almost baffling chic. The favor enjoyed by His Highness, as well as his personal quality, had apparently made His Excellency even keener on this daughter than on his eldest, by his wife at Sanjō,[57] who had gone to the Heir Apparent.

His Highness could not go easily to Nijō after that. Such restrictions affected him at his rank that he could not go out as he pleased during the day, so that he quickly settled into the southeast quarter,[58] where he lived as he had done years before; and since he could not then after dark escape the house that claimed him to set off to Nijō, she awaited him there in vain many and many a time, until it seemed to her that although she had expected nothing else, the reality of it was very cruel indeed. How true it is, she reflected, that this is no world for anyone with any sense to join in ignorance of her own worthlessness. Her regrets were so bitter that time after time she found it all but impossible to believe that she had actually come here over those mountain paths. She wanted desperately to go back—not so much that she wanted no more of him, since it would be wrong of her to treat him unkindly, but simply to seek a little peace and quiet. So her thoughts ran, and, not knowing what else to do, she overcame her modesty to write to the Counselor.

56. On the morning after their third night together.
57. Kumoi no Kari.
58. Roku no Kimi is in the northeast.

"The Adept has let me know about the ceremony the other day, and I am therefore well informed," she had written. "I owe you the deepest gratitude, since without your enduring kindness I should have been in great distress on behalf of those whom I have lost. I hope that you will allow me to thank you in person, if I may."

It was a serious letter on Michinokuni paper, and nothing about it sought to impress, but precisely that delighted him. Her gratitude for the solemnity given the customary memorial rites for His Highness was not at all exaggerated, but she certainly was sensitive to what he had done. She who normally shrank even from answering his notes had written neither explicitly nor fully, but her use of "in person" was a wonder and a joy, and it must have quite excited him. He deduced sadly that His Highness was neglecting her lately in favor of the pleasures of novelty, and although her note offered no touch of charm, he felt so sorry for her that he could not put it down. Instead he read and reread it.

In his reply he wrote, "Thank you for your letter. I went there the other day with intentional discretion, feeling rather like a holy man myself. At the time I thought that the best thing to do. Your mention of my 'enduring kindness' suggests that you suspect me of feeling less by now, and I must protest. I shall do nothing without consulting you. Your obedient servant." It was on white paper, thoroughly businesslike and formal.

He went to call on her late the next day. Being also secretly in love, he was more attentive than necessary to his dress, giving each layer of his soft robes an extra, exquisite scent; and as if that were not enough, he fanned himself with a clove-dyed fan so that he wafted an indescribably delicious fragrance toward her.

She herself now and again remembered their strange night together, and having seen how much more truly kind he was than other men, she must only have wished that things had turned out otherwise. She was no longer an innocent girl, and comparing him to the man who caused her such suffering must have made the difference between them all too plain, for she spared him the distance she usually put between them and, lest he think her unkind, admitted him this time within the blinds.[59] She received him sitting some way back from a curtain placed against the blinds of the chamber.[60]

"You have not actually invited me to visit you before," he said, "but this unaccustomed gesture has given me great pleasure, and I would have come immediately if I had not gathered that His Highness might be here, so that I feared I might be unwanted. That is why I decided to come today. Perhaps my devotion over the years has found its reward, though, because I see that you have relaxed a little the space between us and that I am *inside* the blinds!"

Still extremely shy, she felt at a loss for words. "After the pleasure of hearing about the other day," she replied very circumspectly, "I thought how much I would regret it if as usual I kept my feelings to myself and never even tried to tell you how

59. The blinds between the veranda and the aisle.
60. The blinds between the aisle and the chamber. Kaoru is in the aisle.

grateful I am." She spoke from very far back, and her voice reached him only uncertainly, which aroused him further.

"You are such a long way off!" he said. "To tell the truth, there is something that I should like to discuss with you."

She granted him that, and his heart pounded when he heard her move just a little closer, but he let none of it show and mastered himself better than ever. He hinted that to his mind His Highness's attitude, alas, left much to be desired, and he ventured to chide him for that and to console her as well. For some time he talked quietly on such topics as these.

She could not very well voice her resentment, and she only gave him to understand that she blamed no one but herself,[61] skirting the matter in a mere few words and begging him meanwhile to take her back for a visit to her mountain village.

"*That* is not a service that is up to me alone to render you," he said. "The best thing would be for you to bring the matter up honestly with His Highness and to do as he prefers. Otherwise the least misunderstanding might lead him to suspect some sort of foolishness, and that would be a disaster. Were it not for that, I would not hesitate a moment to devote my efforts to accompanying you there and back. His Highness knows quite well that he can trust me more readily than anyone else." Nevertheless, he never really forgot how much he regretted what was past, and he went on to intimate that he would gladly take back what he had done, until by and by it began to grow dark, and she wished desperately that he would go.

"I am afraid that I am unwell," she said. "We must of course talk again when I feel a little better." To his great chagrin he gathered that she was about to retire.

"But when would you like to go?" he asked, to distract her. "The path there is very overgrown, and I should want to have it cleared a little."

She paused. "Early next month, I think—this month is nearly over. The best would be to keep it a secret. Why ask for leave and make an issue of it?"

What a perfectly dear voice! he thought, and the memory of her sister came back to him so vividly that he could bear it no longer. From where he was sitting, leaning against a pillar, he softly reached under the blind and caught her sleeve.

Oh, no! Not that! How awful! That was what she thought. What could she possibly have said? In silence she slipped farther from him, at which he came halfway under the blind himself, as though quite at home, and lay down beside her. "You do not understand!" he protested. "I am so delighted to know that you prefer secrecy; I just want to ask you whether I heard you rightly! How unfriendly you are! After all, it is not as though you had any need to treat me coldly!"

She was in no mood to answer. The shock was too great, and she now thought him hateful, but she controlled herself well enough to upbraid him, "Your attitude is astonishing! Think what this will look like to other people! I am appalled!"

---

61. *Genji monogatari kochūshakusho in'yō waka* 940: "Is it the world that is harsh or he who is cruel? No, I blame none but myself." The poem includes a long, conventional play on *warekara*, "of my own will," as well as the name of a creature said to live in "seaweed gathered by the seafolk."

Seeing her nearly in tears, he felt for her, and he could not entirely blame her. Still, he answered, "Why should anyone mind? Very well, here we are together, but just remember that other time! Your sister approved, after all! *I* am the one whom your outrage might well offend! Rest assured that I have nothing rash or indecent in mind." He spoke quite calmly, but his months of bitter regret now tortured him so much that he went on and on about it without ever making a move to release her sleeve. She could do nothing, and, to put it mildly, she was aghast.

"What is *this* now? Why, you might be a little girl!" he said when she wept, more intensely ashamed and repelled than if she had hardly known him. She was indescribably sweet and pathetic, but he also found in her a daunting gravity far beyond the younger sister of *those* days. At last, tormented by having had to suffer this way for intentionally letting her go to someone else, he burst into tears.

The two gentlewomen in waiting nearby would certainly have gone to defend their mistress from an unwanted intruder, but this gentleman was in a position to carry on a familiar conversation with her, and they assumed that if he was doing so, there must be a reason for it. They therefore pretended to notice nothing, despite their dismay, and unfortunately withdrew in silence. He himself must have struggled to contain his burning regret for what he had done *then*, but the rare tact that was always his, even long ago, restrained him now from acting on his desire. The scene was not of the kind one may dwell on at length. Although disappointed, he knew that he must avoid attracting attention, and he therefore took his leave, ruing what he had done.

He had not thought the early night over yet, but dawn was near. If he feared that someone might see him, no doubt it was for her sake. No wonder she feels unwell, he reflected, as I keep hearing she does. Yes, what kept me back was mainly feeling sorry for her over that hip band[62] she was so embarrassed about. What a fool I have made of myself yet again! Still, he would certainly have shrunk from any cruelty toward her. Besides, he would have suffered torments later if a moment of ardor had led him to force her; arranging impossible, clandestine meetings would have tested him sorely, and just think of the misery of contesting her with His Highness! At this very moment,[63] though, none of these sage reflections could save him from desperate yearning. He could not imagine not having her, which was really and truly hopeless of him. The quality of her presence, a little more slender than before and nobly captivating, seemed to him never to have left him at all but to be with him even now, and he knew nothing else. She wants so much to go to Uji, and I would gladly take her there, but would His Highness ever agree? Assuming that he would not, it could mean disaster to do so in secret. How can I possibly have my desire without causing a scandal? He lay there sleepless, his thoughts in turmoil.

It was still dark when his letter arrived. As before, it had the appearance of a straight-folded, formal one.

---

62. *Koshi,* a band worn by a pregnant woman around her lower belly.
63. *Gosenshū* 563: "What can those times when we never met have been, when I so long for you because at this very moment I do not see you?"

"So heavy a dew lay along that painful path I followed in vain,
the autumn sky called to mind those sad skies of long ago.

Your unkind reception was incomprehensibly cruel.[64] What else can I say?"

Her women would notice something unusual if she failed to answer, and she wrote most unhappily, "Thank you for your note. I am too unwell to give you a reply." That was all, and it struck him as disappointingly brief. Instead he yearningly recalled her entrancing presence.

Despite her extreme distress and alarm, she had not refused him in grim silence, perhaps because she now knew a little more of the world. She had instead shown great discernment and dignity and had actually sent him on his way with kind and comforting words, so that in memory her manner stirred keen regret and filled his mind until he felt only despair. She seemed to him wonderfully improved in every way. Well, then, he reflected, if His Highness were to abandon her, she would simply

Messenger with a straight-fold letter

have to rely on me. It could never be easy or open even so, but she would be my only love, although no one else would know, and I would set her above all others. Reprehensibly enough, he never thought about anything else. How treacherous men are, for all their airs of deep thought and wise understanding! So much for his desolation over the sister he had lost—no, he was not after all suffering *that* much. Such reflections went round and round in his mind. He forgot about being her trusty support when he heard someone say, "His Highness has gone to Nijō today"; his heart pounded, and jealousy consumed him.

His Highness had not been home for so long that even he deplored it, and at last he went there on the spur of the moment. Oh, no, she told herself, I will not let him see that I am displeased with him! She wanted to visit her mountain village, but the only man she could look to for that had turned out to have obnoxious intentions, and knowing that now, she saw how very cramped her world was and how unfortunate her place in it, and she made up her mind to accept things patiently for as long as she lived. She therefore received him so sweetly and prettily that she pleased him better than ever, and he excused himself endlessly for his neglect over the past days. Her belly had swelled a little, and he was filled with sympathy to find her wearing the telltale hip band that had so embarrassed her, for he had never before been close to a woman in her condition. He was actually quite taken with the novelty of it. After having had to get used to minding his manners, he felt very comfortably at home, and he assured her in various ways of his deep affection. She wondered as she listened whether all men were such good talkers, and the memory of that importunate presence returned to mind. All these years she had thought him so good and kind, but if that was what his kindness meant, she wanted no more of

64. *Genji monogatari kochūshakusho in'yō waka* 382: "I who know how little I am worth will not complain; and yet whence this incomprehensible cruelty?"

it; and as for all *this* one's promises of lasting devotion, We shall see, We shall see! was the silent thought with which she greeted each one, although she did at the same time believe them a little.

To think, though, how cruelly he took advantage of me and came straight in! she reflected. He assured me that he and my sister were never close in that way, which is certainly remarkable, but I should not have allowed that to make me careless. So it was that she resolved to multiply her precautions. Understanding the terrible danger that any prolonged absence by His Highness might pose, she said nothing about it but instead did rather more than before to make him want to be with her. This utterly enchanted him, until the expert that he was noted with surprise, behind the perfectly commonplace fragrance she had given her clothes, another one, distinct and utterly different; for *his* scent had suffused them. He then sought to discover what had been going on, and his not wholly unexpected questions left her desperately at a loss for a reply. I knew it! he thought with beating heart. This was sure to happen! I always assumed he would yield to temptation! Actually, she had changed her shift and so on, but remarkably enough, the scent had permeated even her person.

"He must have taken the last liberties if his scent is this strong on you," he kept saying, hatefully enough to reduce her to utter misery and confusion. "Here I have been telling you all you mean to me, and *you* meanwhile have decided to be the first to forget![65] No one of your rank may stoop to such betrayal! Have I really been gone *that* long? I can hardly believe this of you!" He said a great deal more, although it would all be too painful to repeat, but to his intense annoyance she answered not a word. He added,

> "The scent that passes sleeve to sleeve in close embrace, one to another,
> has suffused my mood as well and made me very angry!"

To that outrageous speech of his she had no reply, but *this* was another matter.

> "When so trustingly I believed this middle robe always would be ours,
> would you for a touch of scent abandon me forever?"[66]

She wept as she spoke. The sight affected him deeply; but then he thought, *This* is exactly why it happened![67] and felt such a wave of revulsion that he, too, always the tenderhearted gallant, burst into tears. Never mind if she had erred gravely, he could never, never reject her, she was just too sweet and too dear; and so it was that his anger left him, and he said no more. Instead he turned to consoling her.

---

65. *Kokin rokujō* 2122: "I, not he, shall be the first to forget; why should I trust him when he has been so cold toward me?"

66. "When I trusted that you and I would always be as close to one another as we have been . . ." "Middle robe" (*naka no koromo*), an expression proper to poetry, alludes to the bond between lovers. The poem also repeats words (*kabakari nite*) just used by Niou and translated a few lines above as "if his scent is *this strong* on you"; to which it adds a double meaning on *ka*, "this (much)" and "scent."

67. Because she is so irresistible.

The next morning he arose from a pleasant night, washed up, and took his breakfast there as well. The style of her rooms made a striking change from the glittering layers yonder of brocade or damask from Koma and Cathay. It all felt so plain and familiar, and her women, too, some in softly rumpled clothes, gave him a feeling of peace. She herself had on pale gray-violet over a pink layered long dress, all quite casually worn, and the comparison with the other one, always so perfect in every detail and almost oppressively beautiful, put her at no disadvantage. She was too gentle and too lovely that he need feel in the least embarrassed by his fondness for her. Once prettily round-faced and plump, she was a little thinner now, and her much paler skin gave her a pleasingly noble air. Even before that scent betrayed her, he had found her enchanting appeal so far beyond any ordinary woman's that he worried constantly, since knowing the world as well as he did, he felt certain that any man but a brother who visited and talked with her, and who for any reason grew accustomed to hearing her voice or glimpsing her presence, would sooner or later be stirred and come to feel about her just as he did himself. He searched cabinets, chests, and so on for compromising letters, as though looking for something else, but he found none. There were only prim, terse notes on commonplace topics, mixed in among other things without any particular care. Strange! he thought. There *must* be others! Now he was more suspicious than ever, and no wonder. Any discerning woman should fancy the Counselor, he reflected, considering what he is like, and why should he then sternly reject her? They would make such a fine couple. I suppose they must be in love. By the time he had got this far, he was miserable, resentful, and angry, and he remained sufficiently agitated not to leave that day either. Of the two or three notes he sent to Rokujō, some old women there whispered, "How quickly one message from him piles on another, like fallen leaves!"

The Counselor was not pleased to learn that His Highness had stayed on and on. But, he told himself, I can do nothing about it. I am an idiot, that is the trouble. What business do I have feeling this way about someone I only wanted to see happily settled? Having managed to bring himself round, he was glad that His Highness had at least not abandoned her, and the thought of her women in their comfortably rumpled clothes prompted him to call on his mother.

"I wonder whether you have anything decent to wear already made up," he said. "You see, I have in mind a use for it."

"I suppose there must be some plain white ones, as usual, for the services next month,"[68] she replied. "I doubt that there are any dyed ones, but I could have that done without delay."

"No, no, it is not that important. Whatever you happen to have now will do." He had her wardrobe inspected and sent off several sets of women's robes and long dresses—whatever there was—together with bolts of undyed plain silk and silk damask. For the lady herself he included, from among his own things, scarlet silk beaten to an especially beautiful luster, white silk damask, and so on in generous

---

68. The ninth, when there were several important Buddhist rites. The clothes Onna San no Miya mentions are probably intended as offerings.

quantities; and since it turned out that there were no trousers, he also put in for some reason a trouser cord, to which he tied,

> *"You whose single tie binds you elsewhere forever, as this cord is one,*
> *I shall not run on and on, charging you with cruelty."*

He addressed it to Taifu, an experienced gentlewoman who seemed to be close to her mistress. "I apologize for these; they are no more than what was ready to hand. Please dispose of them as you think best," his message said; but discreetly or not, he had wrapped up *her* portion separately in a box. Taifu showed her mistress none of it, but experience had made such instances of his thoughtfulness quite familiar by now, and it never occurred to her to make an issue of the matter and return them. Instead she passed them out to the women of the household, and they all busied themselves sewing. The younger ones, who waited most closely on her, undoubtedly deserved the best. The lower servants, who had been going about looking terribly untidy, now made a fine sight in white clothes all the more pleasant for being so discreet.

Who else would have been so attentive to her needs? His Highness, who was devoted to her, certainly saw that she should lack nothing, but he could hardly keep his eye on every familiar detail. Having always been thoroughly pampered, he of course did not know what it was to languish in penury. To him life meant shivering with delicious pleasure before the dew on a flower, and when he went so far as quite naturally to provide the woman he loved with the practical necessities of life, as time or season required, the response was astonishment and, from someone like her sharp-tongued nurse, cries of "Oh, but he *shouldn't* have!" She had had occasion to feel acutely, if silently, ashamed to note among her page girls some whose costume did her no credit, and to wonder what right she really had to live in so fine a house; and lately, what with the celebrated brilliance of that other woman's life at Rokujō, she had been quite mortified to imagine what His Highness's own people must think of her. This the Counselor understood perfectly, and she by no means despised a solicitude that might have been merely officious had he been less close to her, but she also feared that any too-obvious generosity on his part might attract unwanted attention. And now he had yet again sent Taifu some very nice clothing he had had made, with an outer gown that he had had specially woven for Taifu's mistress, and thread for damask as well. He, too, had enjoyed privilege, just as much as His Highness. He was absurdly proud, held the world in disdain, and boasted superb loftiness of mind, yet ever since first witnessing His Late Highness's life among the hills, he had painfully grasped what special sorrow such isolation could bring, and with deep sympathy he had extended these reflections to the world at large. Such, they say, was the bitter lesson that Uji had taught him.

What he still wanted was therefore always to be her trusted and courteous friend, but instead she painfully absorbed his every thought, so that his letters to her became longer and longer and at times betrayed feelings he wished to conceal. She would sigh then over the misfortune that seemed to cling to her. If he were a complete stranger, I could easily dismiss him ignominiously as a madman, she reflected, but I have so long relied on him as a somewhat unusual benefactor that it would only look strange if things were to sour between us now. Besides, I am not ungrateful for all his kindness and consideration. However, that does not mean I can possibly treat him as though he and I were really close. What am I to do? It was a very troubling dilemma. The younger women in her service, the ones who might have been worth talking to, were all new, and the ones she actually knew were the old women from her hills. In the absence of anyone with whom to discuss her feelings heart-to-heart, she thought constantly of her sister. Would he have these notions now, if she were alive? It was all very sad, and it tried her even more sorely than her anxiety that His Highness might betray her.

The Counselor, who could bear it no longer, came one quiet evening to call. She had a cushion put out for him on the veranda and let him know that just at the moment she was feeling too unwell to be able to talk. Stung nearly to tears, he nonetheless forced himself in the women's presence to disguise what he felt. "But when you are not well, you have priests you do not know at all very near you! Will you not have me within your blinds even as you might a physician? Passing messages back and forth through other people this way seems to me perfectly pointless!" He was so plainly angry that the witnesses to the other night agreed that she was indeed taking it too far. They lowered the blinds of the chamber and admitted him to where the priest sat on night duty. This was truly excruciating for her, but with her women talking that way she did not wish to be too obvious about it, and so she slipped forward a little, most unwillingly, to receive him.

Her faint voice and her halting responses brought straight to mind the memory of her sister when she was first unwell, which was so sad and frightening that he felt a darkness within him and was unable for some time to continue speaking. Deeply offended by the distance she was keeping between them, he reached under the blind to slide the standing curtain back a little and leaned in toward her as before, as though quite at home. This was too much, and she summoned one Shōshō. "My chest hurts," she said. "I should like you to press on it for me."

"But that will only make it worse!" he said with a sigh when he heard her, and sat up straight again, for underneath he was indeed quite uneasy. "Why are you always so unwell? I asked about that and was told that one does feel ill at first, but that most of the time later on one feels perfectly well. You seem to be taking this much too much like a child."

"I often have this pain in my chest," she replied, acutely embarrassed. "My sister did, too. They say that is the way people are when they are not meant to live long."

No, he thought with a sharp pang of sorrow, no one lives the life of the thousand-year pine![69] Never mind that the woman she had called to her side might hear him; he passed over in silence anything that could possibly be compromising, but he still managed to tell her everything that he had felt for her for so long, in words that only she, and no one else listening, could understand. The charm with

---

69. *Kokin rokujō* 2096: "Alas that in this life we should not have what we wish, when neither of us is a thousand-year pine!"

which he spoke was so engaging that Shōshō thought, Oh, yes, he is *such* a kind gentleman!

Everything reminded him endlessly of the love he had lost. "The only thing I have ever really wanted since childhood is to give up the world for good," he said, "but perhaps that is not my destiny, because even though she was never mine, I felt such passion for her that that alone seems to have thwarted my hope of leading a holy life. I have looked elsewhere for consolation, but although someone may have seemed now and then, when I came to know her, to promise distraction, I have never felt my heart turn toward anyone else. The failure of all my attempts, when no one else really attracted me, has left me ashamed that you might think me capricious, but while I should certainly deserve your rebuke if I were most strangely to entertain culpable desires, I do not see who could possibly blame me for wishing to share my thoughts with you from time to time, just as we are now, and to talk things over in friendship. My feelings are not those of other men, and I will never give anyone cause for disapproval. Please, please give me your trust." He spoke between reproach and tears.

"Would I talk to you at all, in a manner that others might question, if I distrusted you? I have often had occasion over the years to discern your feelings, and that is precisely why I turn to you, although you are unusual in that role, and why I continue to ask so much of you."

"I do not remember your ever asking anything of me. You are making much too much of this. Your wish to visit your mountain village marks your first request for my help. How could I not indeed appreciate your confidence in the matter?" He still seemed quite resentful, but he could hardly go on as he pleased with others listening.

He glanced mournfully outside. It was dark by now, and insect cries were the only sound that reached him. Shadows shrouded the garden knoll. There he remained, leaning quite at his ease against a pillar and arousing only consternation within. "If love ever had an end,"[70] he murmured, and so on; then he said, "I give up. The village of Not-a-Sound:[71] that is where I long to go, and never mind if your hills offer no proper temple, because I would make a doll in her likeness there, and paint her picture, too, and pursue my devotions before them."[72]

"It is a very touching desire," she said, "but disturbing, too, because alas, it brings to mind a doll in a lustration stream.[73] And I worry, too, that the painter might only want gold."[74]

---

70. *Kokin rokujō* 2571, by Sakanoue no Korenori: "If love ever had an end in this world, with the years my cares would melt away."

71. *Otonashi no sato*, mentioned in *Kokin rokujō* 1296: "Ah, to bewail my unhappiness in love! Where is it, that I may cry aloud, the village of Not-a-Sound?"

72. Kaoru's wish may recall that of Emperor Wu, who had a painting made of his beloved Lady Li.

73. *Mitarashigawa*, a stream near a shrine, used for purification. Kaoru's wish to make a *hitokata* ("doll") of Ōigimi reminds Naka no Kimi of the *hitokata* used in a purification rite (*misogi*): the evil influences to be purged were ritually infused into *hitokata* that were then sent floating away down the stream.

74. From the sad story of Wang Zhaojun, whom a Chinese Emperor sent as a concubine to a Tartar King. When the Huns threatened the Han capital, the Emperor decided to send their King a woman from the harem, to appease him, and he made his choice from portraits the women had painted for the purpose. All the women except Wang Zhaojun bribed the painters to improve their looks, so that the Emperor would not wish to give them up. As a result, Zhaojun's portrait showed her to be the least favored of them all, hence the most expendable, although in reality she was the great beauty among them. The Emperor discovered the truth when Zhaojun was gone, and he condemned the venal painters to death.

"You are right," he replied. "In my eyes no sculptor or painter could do her justice. It is not that long since a sculptor's work brought petals fluttering down from the heavens:[75] that is the sort of genius I need."

The way he talked on about how little he could ever forget her, and the deep sorrow conveyed by his dolorous air, so affected her that she slipped a little nearer to say, "Speaking of a doll image of her, I now remember a very strange thing, something quite incredible."

"What do you mean?" he asked, elated by the new warmth in her manner, and he reached beneath the standing curtain to take her hand. Despite her intense annoyance she resolved at all costs to check his ardor and to make him behave, and she therefore ignored his gesture lest the woman nearby draw any false conclusion.

"This summer someone whose very existence was long unknown to me came here from very far away, and although it would have been wrong of me not to be friendly to her, I also saw no reason why I should receive her too quickly into my intimacy. She has just been here, and I was moved to find her extraordinarily like my sister. You keep saying that for you she lives on in me, but those who knew us both say we looked quite different, so that it is difficult to imagine how my visitor, for whom the resemblance is so much less plausible, should have it to so astonishing a degree."

He thought that he must be dreaming. "But that tie between you must be just the reason why she wished to approach you," he said. "Why have you never told me anything about this?"

"No, no, I do not know exactly how the tie you speak of came to be. My father always feared that we might both become destitute and fall into aimless wandering, and now that I, the only one left, reflect on the matter, I find it very painful to imagine burdening his memory with anything that gossip might wish to pass on." He understood from her words that His Highness must have known someone in secret and therefore left ferns of memory to be plucked.[76]

Her talk of that close resemblance struck him particularly, and he was intensely curious. "Is that all? You might as well tell me the whole story." It was a distressing one, though, and she could not bring herself to do so.

"I will tell you where she is, if you wish to go to her," she said, "but I actually know very little. And if I told you too much, you know, you might only be disappointed."

"I would gladly give my all to travel out onto the ocean to seek the place where her spirit dwells, if you told me to do so, but in this case I doubt that I shall feel that strongly. Still, I know that I would prefer a doll to remaining comfortless, and in that spirit I might well accept her as my buddha[77] of the mountain village." His tone was urgent.

"Ah, I ought not to have told you so much, since my father never recognized

---

75. This story has not been traced. It probably concerned a Buddha image so alive that lotus petals fell on it from the skies in homage.

76. "Had a child by that woman." *Kokin rokujō* 3133 (or *Gosenshū* 1187), by Kanetada no Ason no Haha no Menoto: "Were it not for the child she left behind, where would we pluck the ferns of memory?"

77. *Honzon*, the image (sculpted or painted) representing the deity to which a Buddhist rite is addressed.

her; it is just that I felt so sorry for you when you spoke of wanting a sculptor of genius." And she went on, "She has been living very, very far away, which her mother thought such a shame that she took the trouble to bring her all the way here. They actually came to call on me—I could not very well turn them away. I saw too little of her to be certain, but it seemed to me that she was less uncouth than she might have been. Considering how worried her mother is about what to do with her, it might be just the thing for her to become your buddha. But surely you will not really do that."

He saw that for all her innocent airs she longed to say something that would deflect his unwanted attentions, and he resented it. Still, he was moved as well. Despite her resolve to refuse his approaches, she was sympathetic enough not to wish to humiliate him openly, and his heart beat at the thought. Meanwhile the night was well advanced, and she, within, was appalled to think what this scene must look like. She allowed their talk to lapse and retired, which he quite understood, but she still left him angry and chagrined to the degree that he felt self-control elude him, and tears sprang to his eyes. This did not become him, though, he knew that. With a great effort he therefore resisted the tumult of his feelings, for any rashness now would be not only barbarous toward her but damaging to himself. He went his way more than usually burdened with sighs.

What am I to do about this obsession with her? he wondered. It means nothing but suffering. How can I possibly manage to avoid widespread censure and have at the same time what I so desire? He spent the rest of the night despairing that his lack of true experience in these matters no doubt put them both at risk. He *must* see for himself whether the resemblance she had mentioned was real. That would be easy enough to do if he chose, considering the young woman's station in life, but what a nuisance if she turned out *not* to be what he had in mind! He still felt no urge to do anything in that direction.

It seemed to him when he went too long without seeing the house at Uji that the past slipped further and further from him, which somehow felt so sad that after the twentieth of the ninth month he made the journey there. The place was more windblown than ever, and he was greeted only by the river's desolate noise. There was no one about. What he saw pierced his heart, and sorrow overwhelmed him. He called out the nun Ben, and she came to the opening of the sliding panel, thrusting a blue-gray standing curtain before her.

"Please forgive me, my lord," she said, "but your presence is very daunting, and I could not presume . . ." She did not come all the way out.

"I imagined how melancholy your life here must be, and I thought that I might come to talk to you, now that I have no one else with whom to share my heart. How quickly the months and years pass by!" His eyes filled with tears, and the old woman could not refrain from weeping freely.

"This is just the time of year when my lady was in such useless torment over her sister, and that always painful memory makes the autumn wind feel especially biting and cruel. Alas, I gather vaguely that the prospect that worried her so has turned out to be real enough, which is sadly distressing news."

"All things may well come out right in the fullness of time, but I am painfully convinced that my own error caused her anguish. Her sister's current circumstances are, well, just what one might expect, but I see nothing worrying in them. It must come to us all at last, as to her, to rise in smoke to the sky, but whatever anyone may say, the going and staying[78] are very painful for the one who remains!" He wept anew.

As was his custom, he had the Adept come to discuss the scriptures and images for the elder sister's memorial service. "Every time I am here, I feel how pointless it is to lament what cannot be undone," he said, "and I think of dismantling the main house to build a temple near yours. I should just as soon begin immediately." He sketched or described the number of halls, galleries, and monks' lodges that he had in mind, and the Adept enlarged to him on the merit of such holy works.

"It might seem cruel to take down the house that once meant so much to His Highness, but he, too, aspired to progress on the path of merit, although it appears that consideration for those who would survive him kept him from doing so. Now the land belongs to the wife of His Highness of War, which amounts to saying that it is at His Highness's disposal. Therefore it would not be right to turn it into a temple just as it is. One may not follow one's own wishes in such a matter. Besides, the spot is too near the river and too exposed. That is why I propose to remove the main house and rebuild it elsewhere."

"Your intentions are wholly laudable either way, my lord. Once someone who mourned a great loss wrapped up the bones and carried them in a bag around her neck for many years, after which she cast that bag from her, thanks to the Buddha's skill, and took up the path of the holy life.[79] I have no doubt that the sight of this house troubles you deeply, and that is something to look out for. At the same time what you propose will further your happiness in the life to come. I hasten to place myself at your service. I shall have a Doctor of the Almanac indicate the right day to begin and then set two or three carpenters, men familiar with these things, to work according to the Buddha's teaching."

After confirming his wishes the Counselor sent for men from his estates and instructed them to place themselves under the Adept's orders. All too soon it was dark, and he disposed himself to spend the night.

I may not see the place again, he thought, wandering about to look at it. All the holy images had gone to the temple, and nothing remained but the implements the nun needed for her devotions. He gazed at them, wondering how she managed to get through her pitiful life.

"For various reasons the main house is to be redone," he said. "You must move to the gallery while the work is going on. If there is anything to send to His Highness's in the City, call in men from my estates and let them know what to do with

---

78. *Kokin rokujō* 593 (also *Shinkokinshū* 757), by Henjō: "The dew on the leaf tip, the drop on the stalk, show how in this world some go and some stay."

79. The precise source of this story is unknown. A related one, from a commentary on the Dainichi-kyō identifies the deceased as a beloved wife, while an early *Genji* commentary cites a Buddhist tale about a child killed by a jealous stepmother.

it." He gave her all sorts of practical instructions. Elsewhere he would never have seen fit to admit so old a woman to his company, but he had her lie beside him for the night and got her talking about the old days.

No one else was listening nearby, and she was therefore able to speak freely about the late Acting Grand Counselor.[80] "Whenever I remember how he still clearly longed at the last to see what you looked like, since you had just been born, I feel happy and sad all at once to think that my reward for intimate service to him[81] while he lived is to have you now before my eyes when my own improbable life is nearly over. My unfortunately long life has shown and taught me many things that fill me with revulsion and shame. From my lady I now and again have a letter urging me to come and see her, because, she says, it is not nice of me to shut myself up here forever this way; but I am unfit for her company, and there is no one I wish to see save Amida Buddha himself." She went on to talk at great length about the mistress she had lost—what she had been like over the years, what she had said at this moment or that, how she had made some little poem on the beauty of blossoms or autumn leaves; and while listening to that quavering voice he silently added reflections on how childlike she had been, how reluctant to speak, and yet, for all that, how wonderful to know. The sister who had gone to His Highness, although somewhat brighter and livelier, seemed quite prepared to embarrass anyone whose attentions she declined to honor; but, he said to himself, she seems warmly disposed toward me, and she wants it to continue in one way or another. So in his thoughts he compared the two.

Then came the moment for him to bring up the double of whom he had heard. "I cannot say whether or not she is now in the City," the old woman replied; "but I believe that I have heard of her. Soon after his wife died, and before he moved to these hills, His Late Highness took up in passing, very secretly, with a rather nice senior gentlewoman called Chūjō. No one knew anything about it. When she had a girl who, as he well knew, was presumably his, he was shocked, dismayed, and outraged, and he never looked at her again. Remarkably enough, he learned his lesson from that and became more or less a holy man, which made her position so awkward that she left his service. She married the Governor of Michinokuni. One year she came back up to the City and let His Highness's household know that his daughter was safe and well, but when His Highness heard that, he flatly forbade any more such messages, which was a bitter disappointment to her. She next accompanied her husband to Hitachi,[82] where he had been posted, and for years there was no more news of her. Then, so I hear, she came up to the City this spring and went to call at His Highness's. Her daughter must be twenty by now. Some years ago she actually wrote to me about how pretty her girl was growing up to be, how she longed to do better for her, and so on."

He decided after questioning her further that it must really be true, and he

---

80. Kashiwagi.
81. She is the daughter of Kashiwagi's nurse and was therefore brought up with him.
82. Where he had presumably been sent as Deputy Governor, since the post of Governor of Hitachi was a sinecure held by a Prince.

began to want to see this young woman. "Why, I would go gladly to lands unknown in order to meet anyone in the least like what *she* used to be!" he said. "No doubt His Highness rejected her, but still, she was very, very closely related to him. Please, if she ever has occasion to come here, do just mention to her what I have said."

"Her mother is a relation of mine, since she is a niece of His Highness's wife, but she and I were separated at the time,[83] and we saw very little of each other. Lately I had word from Taifu, in the City, that the daughter says she wishes at least to visit His Highness's grave and that Taifu has encouraged her to do so, but I have not yet heard anything from her. Very well, then, my lord, I shall pass on your remarks when she comes."

Before starting back at daybreak, he had the Adept presented with silks and cottons that he had had brought late the evening before. He gave the nun some, too. He had also ordered other cloth[84] that he distributed to the monks and to the nun's servants. It was a desolate place for her to live, but his continuing generosity allowed her to pursue her devotions in peace, in a manner quite presentable for her station. He paused as he was leaving, detained by the prospect of autumn leaves thickly strewn, untrodden, beneath boughs stripped bare by the merciless savagery of autumn gales. Color lingered only in the vines clinging to the picturesque mountain trees. He had someone pick him a sprig of *kodani*,[85] thinking to give it to the lady at His Highness's.

> "Did not memory tell me I have lodged before beneath these ivied trees,
> ah, then, how forlorn this night, spent lonely and far from home,"

he murmured to himself, and the nun replied,

> "You have lodged before here beneath the withered boughs of this ivied tree—
> how sad, then, it is to think that you keep that memory!"

The poem had its own distinction, despite being thoroughly old-fashioned, and it helped to console him.

His Highness was with her when the sprig of colored leaves came. Oh, no, not again! she fretted when the messenger innocently delivered them with the mention that they were from Sanjō; but she could hardly try to hide them.

"What pretty ivy!" His Highness remarked sarcastically. He had it brought to him for a better look.

The letter said, "How have you been lately? I wonder. I shall tell you in person about my trip to your mountain village and about how the morning fog on the hills led me more than ever astray. I asked the Adept to turn the main house into a temple. Once I have your permission, I shall have it moved elsewhere. Please send the nun Ben your instructions to that effect"; and so on.

---

83. Ben was probably in Kyushu when Hachi no Miya had his affair with Chūjō and Ukifune was born.
84. *Nuno*, cloth made of hemp, kudzu, or other fibers.
85. An unidentified vine, apparently one of several species that supply the color still lingering on the trees.

"He did well to keep what he wrote sober. He must have heard I am here," said His Highness, and to some extent he was doubtless right. Greatly relieved, she thought him awful to insist on talking like that, and her angry looks were charming enough to make him forgive everything.

"Answer him, then. I promise not to look." He turned away. And so she did, since it would have seemed odd of her to flatter him and refrain.

"I envy your going there," she wrote. "I myself had decided that what you suggest is just what needs to be done. Rather than seek another refuge among the rocks,[86] I should much prefer to keep this one from going to rack and ruin, and I shall be much obliged to you if you will kindly see to whatever there is to do."

His Highness saw in this no sign of anything wrong in their friendship, but, given his own proclivities, he must have suspected that there was more to it than that.

The plume grass stood out prettily in the already wintry garden nearby, for the plumes seemed to beckon like hands, while the stems not yet in head made strings of perilously swaying dewdrop pearls—a common sight, of course, but there was something especially affecting then about the evening breeze.

> "I feel a sadness from a stem not yet in plume among these grasses,
> beckoning like waving sleeves moistened already with dew,"[87]

he murmured as he sat there playing a *biwa*, wearing only a dress cloak over his pleasantly soft garments.[88] It was a piece in the *ōshiki* mode, one so moving that she, who played the *biwa*, too, could not long remain angry; instead she leaned on her armrest to peer at him for a moment around her low curtain, in a manner so appealing that one longed to see more.

> "Ah, the plume grass stem by the sighing of the wind knows now all too well
> how the fall has come at last to blight once-happy meadows.[89]

Such things afflict me alone . . ."[90] To her chagrin there were tears in her eyes, and she covered her face with her fan. He well understood how she felt and thought her very dear; but this, he could see, was exactly why *he* could not give her up either, and he felt acutely suspicious and angry.

The chrysanthemums had not yet properly turned color, being slow to do so despite all the care he had them given, but it happened that one after all was

---

86. *Kokinshū* 952: "Where could I live, among what rocks, that I should hear no more of the world and its troubles?"

87. "You seem sad because of something that you are not telling me." In poetry the seed plumes of *susuki* ("plume grass") are often evoked as beckoning like waving hands, and "to come into plume" (*ho ni izu*) is a common image for "to say what had been unspoken." *Kokinshū* 243, by Ariwara no Muneyana: "Are they the sleeves of the grasses in the autumn fields? For the plume grasses, once in plume, look like beckoning sleeves." Muneyana's poem suggests the image of someone who, having declared love, beckons to the lover.

88. He is not wearing gathered trousers, which makes his costume very casual.

89. "You who no longer care for me, now I know what your feelings are." The poem relies on a play on *aki*, "autumn" and "want no more [of something or someone]."

90. *Shūishū* 953, by Ki no Tsurayuki: "So encompassing are the sorrows that afflict me alone, I have come to condemn all the world."

beautifully transformed, and he had it picked. "Not alone among all flowers,"[91] he hummed, and then went on to say, "One evening, you know, a long time ago, an Emperor's son was enjoying flowers like this one, and an angel came down and taught him some *biwa* music.[92] Ah, it is a sad world, now that everything is so shallow!"

"Hearts are shallow, yes," she rejoined, "but surely not what has come down to us from the past!" She longed to hear music she did not know.

"But there is nothing amusing about playing alone. Do accompany me!"

He had brought her a *sō no koto*.

"Once I had someone to give me lessons, but I never learned to play anything properly," she protested modestly. She would not touch it.

"Will you not humor me even in this? You are too cruel! The lady with whom I spend so much time these days has not completely given herself to me yet, but even so, *she* does not hide things that she has not quite mastered. A woman should be sweet and yielding, or so I hear that Counselor of yours has declared. No doubt you are less shy with *him*. You two seem just as friendly as you could be."

With a sigh at this blunt rebuke she played a little. Once she had retuned the slack strings to the *banshiki* mode, her touch in the modal prelude was very nice indeed. His voice singing "Sea of Ise" had a noble grace, and the women who moved closer to hear him behind their curtains and screens sat listening with broad smiles.

"One so wishes that his affections were not divided, but it is only to be expected, and I still think my lady is fortunate," one said.

"I feel awfully sorry for her, though—she talks as though she wants to go home to that place where she could never normally have met His Highness at all." They kept chatting until the younger ones asked them to be quiet.

He spent three or four days there teaching her music and so on, and excusing himself elsewhere on the grounds of seclusion. At His Excellency's they were so little pleased that His Excellency himself soon appeared on his way home from the palace.

"What is *he* doing here, all pomp and circumstance?" His Highness grumbled, but he went to the main house anyway to receive him.

"It is such a shame that for so long nothing has brought me back to see this house again!" His Excellency remarked, and he talked for some time about his memories of the place until, soon enough, he swept His Highness off with him. The sight of the vast throng following in his train, including his sons and many other senior nobles, made it depressingly clear to her women how little their mistress could ever hope to stand beside his daughter.

"His Excellency is such a fine-looking gentleman!"

"And just look how young and handsome his sons are, every one—there is simply no one else like them! Yes indeed, he is a wonder!"

Still, there were also unhappy sighs. "One could do without his coming so grandly to fetch His Highness, though. My lady had better look out."

---

91. From a Chinese couplet by Yuan Zhen (778–831), *Wakan rōei shū* 267: "It is not that I love the chrysanthemum alone among all flowers, but there are no more blossoms after it has bloomed."

92. This was said to have happened to Minamoto no Takaakira (914–82), a son of Emperor Daigo. The angel first explained to Takaakira the true meaning of Yuan Zhen's couplet.

She herself remembered what her life had once been and felt more than ever sadly convinced that she counted too little to belong in such brilliant company. It seemed to her that the right course would indeed be to go into peaceful seclusion among her hills.

By and by the year came to a close.

From the end of the first month on, she began to feel unusual discomfort, and His Highness, to whom such things were still quite unfamiliar, became sufficiently concerned about her to commission healing rites in temple after temple and then, time and again, to add still more. She was so unwell that Her Majesty sent inquiries after her health. This was her third year with His Highness, but while he himself remained devoted, the world at large had never accorded her much respect. Now, however, the news startled all and sundry, and messages reached her from far and wide.

The Counselor was just as apprehensive as His Highness, and he sighed and fretted over what the outcome might be, but he kept the expressions of his concern within the bounds of propriety and did not call on her too often; instead he commissioned secret prayers on her behalf. Meanwhile the world busied itself preparing for the Second Princess's donning of the train, which was to take place soon. His Majesty took such interest in the preparations that he might as well have been directing them all himself, with the result that her lack of other support actually came to seem a blessing. Quite apart from the provisions already made for her by the Consort her mother, the Crafts Workshop and the provincial Governors concerned all offered her what she needed in great abundance. It was high time for the Counselor to give some thought to the matter, too, since he was to begin visiting her immediately afterward, but, being the man he was, he never thought about it, since he cared only about the lady at Nijō.

At the Rectification,[93] as it is apparently called, on the first day of the second month, the Counselor was named Acting Grand Counselor and concurrently Right Commander. The vacancy was due to the Minister of the Right's resignation as Left Commander.[94] On his rounds of thanks he called also at Nijō, where he hastened to go because she was extremely unwell and His Highness was there with her. His Highness was surprised by his visit, since it was an awkward place for him to be with all these priests about. He donned a striking dress cloak over a train-robe, tidied himself up, and went down the steps to answer his caller's formal salutation with his own; and very fine indeed they both looked as they did it. The Commander then invited His Highness to the banquet he was to give that evening for his guardsmen, but His Highness hesitated to accept because of the concern that kept him at home.

The event was held at Rokujō, following an example set by His Excellency of the Right. The attendants—Princes and senior nobles—were all there, as at the grandest banquets, in such numbers as to make the event very lively indeed. His Highness came, too, although his anxiety prompted him to leave early and hurry

93. Naoshimono, a supplement to the regular announcement of official appointments (meshina) made at the appointments list (jimoku) ceremony twice a year.
94. When Yūgiri, who had served concurrently as Left Commander, resigned that post, it was taken up by the then–Right Commander; hence the vacancy filled by Kaoru.

home. "I must say!" His Excellency exclaimed. "What nerve!" In principle, she was worth no less than His Excellency's own daughter, but the adulation accorded that young lady seems to have turned his head and flattered his vanity.

His Highness was delighted and highly gratified when at dawn his son at last was born. This gave the Commander an added reason to rejoice. He went straight to His Highness's to express, standing,[95] both his thanks for coming the evening before and his congratulations. Now that His Highness was sequestered at home, the whole court came to call on him there. The third night's birth celebration was done as usual privately, at home. For the fifth night the Commander supplied, according to custom, fifty sets of rice dumplings, coins to wager at Go, bowls of garnished rice, and so on, as well as thirty meals on double trays for the new mother and her gentlewomen and a five-layered costume and bedding for the infant. This was all quite discreet and unassertive, but he seems on reflection to have purposely avoided appearing too familiar. For His Highness he provided five-colored cakes[96] on tall stands that rested on a tray of fragrant wood. The gentlewomen got their double trays, of course, but also thirty partitioned boxes filled with particularly good things. He did nothing to make them especially eye-catching. The birth celebration on the seventh night was Her Majesty's, and a great many people came. The Commissioner of the Empress's household was among them, as well as countless privy gentlemen and senior nobles. "I must do *something*, now that His Highness has at last grown up," His Majesty had said when he heard about the preparations, and he presented the child with a dagger.

His Excellency looked after the ninth day. He did not much like the occasion, but he did not wish to offend His Highness, and all his distinguished sons were present. Everything went so well that even she, whose gloom and ill health had made the future look dark to her for months, must have felt somewhat better amid these lively and magnificent rejoicings. Now that she was so fully a woman, the Commander feared she would keep farther away from him than ever and also, alas, that His Highness would be extremely attached to her. On the other hand, from the standpoint of what he had originally wished for her, he was delighted.

The Second Princess's donning of the train was held after the twentieth of the same month. The Commander went to her the following day, and the event that night was kept private. It was a sad disappointment to see a Princess so ostentatiously favored by His Majesty paired after all with a commoner. "Even if he was not against it, he should never have been in such a hurry to get it over with *now!*" Such was the uncomplimentary opinion heard from certain distinguished quarters; but His Majesty was one to act swiftly once his mind was made up, and he seems to have decided that there was no reason why he should not accord the Commander unprecedented honor. Many men, past and present, have become the son-in-law of an Emperor, but there may be no other example of a reigning Emperor hastening to accept a commoner almost as though he had been one, too.

---

95. In order to avoid the pollution of childbirth.

96. *Fuzuku*, cakes in the five colors, made of five different grains pounded to a paste with *amazuru* (sweet-vine) syrup.

His Excellency of the Right ventured to remark, "What an extraordinary destiny that young gentleman has! Even His Grace did not get Her Cloistered Highness, his mother, until late in His Eminence Suzaku's life, when he was on the point of leaving the world. And look at me: I simply scooped you up without leave from anyone at all." His own Second Princess[97] had to agree, but she was too embarrassed to reply.

For the third night His Majesty instructed the Lord of the Treasury and all others responsible for Her Highness, as well as their retainers, discreetly to provide gifts for the Commander's escort, retinue, grooms, and guards. The thing was done all but privately.

Thereafter he visited her more or less secretly. His heart held only the thought of *her*, whom he could never forget. After spending his melancholy time at home during the day, he hastened at dark most unwillingly to Her Highness, and this mode of life became such a burden that he considered bringing her to Sanjō instead. The idea pleased his mother, who declared that she would give up the main house. He protested that that would be too much and had an extension built onto the gallery between the main house and the chapel, presumably so that she could move to the west side of the house. The east wing and so on had been rebuilt to the most exacting standards after the fire, but he now had it all refined and done up even more beautifully.

When His Majesty heard of this plan, he wondered whether it was not rather soon for his daughter to take so compliant a step. Emperor or not, his concern for her was that of any other father. A messenger brought Her Cloistered Highness a letter in which he spoke of nothing else. His Eminence Suzaku had commended Her Cloistered Highness particularly to his protection, and despite her renouncing the world, he remained as devoted to her as before, and as inclined to grant her any wish she cared to express. The honor of stirring such fond concern in two most exalted personages somehow gave the Commander no particular pleasure, for he was still given to many sighs. Meanwhile he pursued the work on the temple at Uji.

His Highness's little son would soon be fifty days old, and the Commander took care to have the rice cakes done nicely, personally inspecting the fruit baskets and partitioned boxes and calling a large number of craftsmen to work in aloeswood, sandalwood, silver, and gold. They all strove to outdo one another in originality.

He continued to call at Nijō as before, when His Highness was away, and he felt that unless he was imagining things, she had grown somewhat in noble dignity. She received him willingly enough, on the assumption that those old importunate ways of his would now be gone; but no, he had not changed at all, and his eyes straightaway filled with tears.

"This marriage, which I never desired, is a sad and most unexpected trial, and I am more than ever heartily sick of the world," he unabashedly complained.

"I am extremely sorry to hear that," she replied. "Do be careful, though, be-

97. Ochiba.

cause someone might hear you." Still, she was moved by a depth of heart that left him unconsoled despite his good fortune and made it impossible for him ever to forget; and she understood how deep his feelings ran. If only *she* were still alive! she said to herself with bitter regret; but if she were, she would only be lamenting her lot like me, and neither of us would have any reason to envy the other. No, without proper recognition it is impossible ever to be anyone in this world! She found herself more than ever impressed by her sister's decision never to yield her person to anyone.

It seemed to her despite her reserve that she might as well allow the Commander to see the child when he begged to do so. Otherwise, she thought, I might seem cold. It may be all very well for me to be angry with him over that one painful incident, but I would much rather not offend him. Without answering him one way or the other, she therefore had a nurse bring the little boy out. Needless to say, he was a delight to behold. Almost eerily sweet and fair, he was all laughter and childish noises, and the watching Commander wished enviously that he were his own. Apparently he had not quite managed to renounce the things of this world. Ah, he kept thinking, if only *she* had been able after all to lead with me the life that others lead and to give me a child like this! How like him it was, since he was so impossible, never even to wonder whether the very great lady he had just married might not soon do the same for him! But it would be unkind to go on making petty complaints about him, for His Majesty would hardly have brought him into his intimacy that way if he had really been that hopeless, and one easily imagines that in serious matters he had thoroughly sound judgment.

Touched that she had shown him her son while he was still so small, he talked on at greater than usual length until the light began to fail. Then he took his leave amid many sighs, for he knew that he could not stay on as he pleased into the night.

"What a lovely fragrance he has!"

" 'Now that I have plucked them,'[98] as they say, I am sure the warbler will be round in no time." Some young women can say very naughty things.

That summer the Sanjō residence would be in a taboo direction, or so the almanac said, and he therefore brought her there early in the fourth month, before summer began. The day before, His Majesty went to the Fujitsubo and held a party to celebrate the wisteria blossoms. His throne stood in the south aisle, before raised blinds. Since the event was an official court function, Her Highness, the resident of the pavilion, did not preside. The banquet for the senior nobles and privy gentlemen was provided by the Chamberlains' Office. In attendance were His Excellency of the Right, the Inspector Grand Counselor,[99] the Fujiwara Counselor, the Intendant of the Left Watch,[100] His Highness of War, and His Highness of Hitachi. The privy gentlemen were seated beneath the wisteria blossoms in the southern garden.

---

98. *Kokinshū* 32: "Now that I have plucked them, my very sleeves are perfumed; ah, plum blossoms— perhaps their presence has brought the warbler here to sing!"

99. Kōbai.

100. Two sons of Higekuro.

The palace musicians, called to their places east of the Kōrōden, played in the *sō* mode while the sun went down. The music for His Majesty himself was to be on flutes and strings provided by Her Highness, and His Excellency led other distinguished guests to place the instruments before him. His Excellency presented him with two scrolls of music for the *kin* that His Grace of Rokujō had written out and given to Her Cloistered Highness; they were attached to a branch of five-needled pine. Next came a *sō no koto*, a *biwa*, and a *wagon* that had once belonged to His Eminence Suzaku. The flute was the one bestowed in that dream.[101] His Majesty had once praised the tone of this token from the past as unequaled, and the Commander had therefore chosen it to grace the occasion—for when, he wondered, would there ever come a finer one? His Majesty had His Excellency take the *wagon* and His Highness of War the *biwa*. The Commander himself played the flute with magnificent skill. His Majesty summoned privy gentlemen disposed to sing the solfège, and the result was pleasant indeed.

The five-color cakes came from Her Highness. Their tall stands of red sandalwood rested on cloths dappled in wisteria purple and embroidered with wisteria flowers, and these were spread on four fragrant aloeswood trays. The vessels were silver, the wine cups glass, and the wine jars glass of a deep lapis lazuli blue. The Intendant of the Watch waited upon His Majesty. His Excellency, disconcerted by the idea of receiving the cup too often from His Majesty, ceded it to the Commander; none of the Princes present would do. The Commander modestly declined, but His Majesty must have had the same thought, for the cup came to him after all; and if the very way he called out, "Sire, your health!" seemed to set him apart, even at so conventionally formal a moment, perhaps it was because everyone on this occasion was so prepared to see something unique in him. He looked incomparable when, after returning the cup, he descended the steps to perform his obeisance of thanks.[102] It was a great privilege even for a senior Prince or a Minister to receive the cup, and that His Majesty should so honor his son-in-law made plain the astonishing regard in which he held him. It was almost painful to see the Commander resume the humble seat to which his nominal rank assigned him.

The Inspector Grand Counselor, who had aspired to this honor himself, was extremely put out. Long ago he had set his heart on the Consort herself, the Princess's mother, and he had kept in touch with her even after she went to the palace. In the end he let the Consort know that he would gladly accept her daughter instead, but to his intense chagrin she never conveyed this wish to His Majesty. "The Commander is undoubtedly blessed with good fortune," he whispered bitterly, "but I cannot imagine why a reigning Emperor should make such a thing of taking him as a son-in-law. Surely nothing like this has ever been seen before. It is a bit

<hr />

101. In 'The Flute,' Kashiwagi came to Yūgiri in a dream and hinted to him that he wished the flute to go to his son.

102. On receiving the Emperor's cup, a courtier poured the wine it contained into another cup and returned the Emperor's before drinking it. He then went down the steps into the garden to dance his obeisance (*butō*), after which he returned to his seat.

much that a commoner should install himself almost next to His Majesty, at the very heart of the palace, and then to top it all be showered with banquets and what-not." Nonetheless, he had wanted to be there; and there he sat, secretly seething.

Hand torches were lit, and the company presented His Majesty with poems. Each gentleman seemed pleased enough with himself as he approached the desk,[103] but one easily imagines what crabbed, trite efforts they were, and I made no effort to hear them all and write them down. I just got one or two from the greatest lords present—not that these seemed likely to be any better than the others. This, I gather, is the Commander's, when he stepped down to pick a cluster of blossoms for His Majesty's headdress:

> *"When I went to pluck for our august Sovereign's hair wisteria blossoms,*
> *ah, how far above my head was the branch that caught my sleeve!"*[104]

He was quite full of himself, the rascal.

His Majesty replied,

> *"Flowers such as these will grace the world with their scent for ten thousand years,*
> *and to us their hue today shall ever be a pleasure."*

> *"Blossoms such as these, plucked to grace our Sovereign's hair, to the wondering eye*
> *offer in present vision beauty of the purple clouds."*[105]

> *"Nothing in their hue calls to mind the common world, for unto the skies*
> *in a mighty surge they rise, these wisteria blossom waves!"*

This last one seems to have been that angry Grand Counselor's. I may have got some of them wrong. Obviously, none of them had anything in particular to say for itself.

The music got better and better as the night wore on. The Commander's voice was quite lovely as he sang "Ah, Wondrous Day!" The Grand Counselor sang with him, and most impressively, because his voice retained its great beauty of long ago. His Excellency of the Right's seventh son, still a boy, accompanied them on the *shō.* He was so sweet that His Majesty bestowed a robe on him, and His Excellency descended the steps to dance his obeisance. It was nearly dawn when His Majesty took his leave. The gifts for the senior nobles and Princes were from him, while those for the privy gentlemen and the palace musicians, graduated according to rank, came from Her Highness.

---

103. *Bundai,* a low writing table, placed below the steps on a formal occasion such as this one, on which poetry was presented to the host. Each participant went in turn to place his composition on it.

104. "How great a prize [the Princess] I have won in my zeal to please His Majesty!"

105. This poem, probably Yūgiri's, seems to be based on *Shūishū* 1068, by Fujiwara no Kuniaki: "Wisteria blossoms within the palace could easily be mistaken for the purple clouds." These clouds are the ones seen when a soul is welcomed into Amida's paradise.

Display carriage

The following night the Commander took Her Highness out of the palace, and she went amid exceptional splendor. His Majesty sent all his gentlewomen to see her to her new home. Her carriage with its broad eaves was accompanied by three gaily colored ones without eaves and by six trimmed with gold, as well as by twenty palm-leaf and two basketwork carriages, with eight pages and servants attending each; and twelve display carriages filled with gentlewomen came forward from Sanjō to greet her train. Her escort of senior nobles, privy gentlemen, gentlemen of the sixth rank, and so on was indescribably magnificent.

Now that he could look at her at his ease, he found her thoroughly pleasing. She was slight but quietly poised and noble in her bearing, and he could find no fault at all with her, at which he congratulated himself on his really quite good fortune. And yet, he told himself, if only I *could* forget my loss; but I cannot, for nothing ever distracts me from my longing, and it appears that in this life I will never be consoled. Enlightenment alone will give me the insight to know what retribution caused this strangely painful bond, so that I can let it go. Absorbed in such thoughts as these, he gave all his attention to building the temple.

After the twentieth of the month, once the commotion of the Kamo Festival was past, he set off to Uji as so often before. He looked over the temple then under construction and issued orders about the work to done, and he was on his way to visit the old nun—for it would be unkind to pass straight on by those withered boughs[106]—when he spied a quite modest woman's carriage just now crossing the bridge, securely accompanied by a band of rough warriors from the East with quivers at their backs and a throng of servants. How provincial! he thought and went in. His own escort was still standing about, making a good deal of noise, and meanwhile he saw the carriage start toward the house. Suppressing his escort's chatter, he sent to find out who it was. "The daughter of my lord the former Governor of Hitachi is back from a pilgrimage to the temple at Hatsuse," the answer came in a rich brogue. "She stayed here on the way there, too."

Astonishing! It was the young woman of whom he had heard! He asked his men to disappear and sent the party the message "Bring the carriage straight in! There is someone else staying here, too, but only on the north."[107] His men had

---

106. An allusion to an exchange of poems between Kaoru and Ben, earlier in the chapter.
107. The north aisle of the main house, rebuilt after the old one was moved to the temple. "Please make your mistress at home on the south side," which was the proper place for a guest.

nothing imposing about them, since they were all in hunting cloaks, but the new arrivals felt awkward and remained discreet, leading their horses round a good distance from the house.

They brought the carriage in and drew it up to the west end of the gallery. No blinds yet hung in the main house, so that it was open to all eyes. He peered at the party through a hole in the sliding panel that closed off that part of the south aisle, which was otherwise protected by lowered shutters. When his outer robes rustled, he took them off and stayed on in only dress cloak and trousers.

She did not alight immediately; instead she sent someone to the nun, no doubt to ask who the other, apparently exalted visitor might be. However, the moment he learned whose carriage it was, he let it be known that no one under any circumstances was to reveal his identity, and the women understood him well enough. The reply came back, "Please alight. There is another guest, but he is in another part of the house."

The first to get out was a young woman who lifted the carriage blind. She was far more polished and presentable than the escort of guards. Then another appeared, a little older. "Quickly, my lady!" she said.

"But I feel strangely exposed." The voice was low but certainly distinguished.

"You keep saying that! The shutters were all down last time, too, though. From where else could anyone be watching?" The speaker felt quite at ease. Her mistress cautiously alighted from the carriage, and his first glimpse of her head and her slender, noble figure must have brought back vivid memories. It was a bitter disappointment when she immediately hid behind her fan, for he could not then see her face. She had to step down from the carriage, which the first two women had done with ease, but she herself could not work out how to follow them, and she took a very long time about it. Once she was down, she slipped inside. Over a deep scarlet gown she had on, as far as he could tell, a pink long dress and over that a spring green dress gown. A four-foot folding screen stood against the panel, but he had a full view of her nonetheless, since his hole was higher than that. Apparently worried about the direction from which he was looking, she lay down facing the other way.

"What a time you had, my lady! The ferry across the Izumi River[108] was just terrifying today!"

"It was a lot easier in the second month, when the river was lower. Talk about travel, though, what is there anywhere here to be frightened about, compared to the East?" The two women sat chatting with no sign of fatigue while their mistress lay there in silence. Her extended arm was too plump and pretty to belong to any daughter of a Hitachi Governor. She had true distinction.

His back was beginning to hurt from standing so still, but he stayed that way lest they notice his presence.

"What a lovely smell!" the young one exclaimed. "There's some delicious incense in the air. It must be something the nun is burning, I suppose."

"Yes, it's wonderful, it certainly is," the older one rejoined enthusiastically.

---

108. The present Kizu River, between Uji and the Yamato Plain. One crossed it on the road between Kyoto or Uji and Hatsuse.

"People from the City are so stylish and elegant! Her ladyship[109] is ever so proud of what she can do, but out in the East she never managed to blend anything like this. This nun may have vanished from the world, and she dresses as she should in her gray and blue-gray, but she lives very well!"

A page girl came from the opposite direction along the veranda. "Please give your mistress some hot water," she said; and in came a series of trays.

They brought their mistress some fruit. "Excuse me, my lady—will you not have some?" They tried to rouse her, but when she failed to stir, they both gobbled up chestnuts and such.

He at first recoiled, never having heard the like before, but then curiosity got the better of him, and he crept up for another look. Here and there, in Her Majesty's household or elsewhere, he had seen any number of bright and pretty women who outranked this one, and ordinarily they meant nothing to him. How strange he was, when he who struck many people as far too serious should now be unable to tear his eyes from anyone so wholly unremarkable!

A message came from the nun, but his alert men answered that he was feeling unwell and was resting. She never imagined that he might be spying; instead she assumed that he was waiting for evening to approach the new arrival, since he had already made it clear that he wanted to meet her. Men from his estates had as usual brought partitioned boxes and so on, and they had left some with her. She fed the Easterners from them, looked after this and that, then tidied herself up and went to call on her guest. The costume the gentlewomen had praised was indeed very fresh and neat, and she still had some of her looks.

"I was expecting you yesterday," he heard her say. "How did you come to arrive today, when the sun is already high?"

"For some strange reason my lady was so exhausted that we stopped by the Izumi River yesterday, and this morning it was ages before she felt able to go on," an elderly gentlewoman explained. This time the young lady sat up when roused, and when she looked shyly away from the nun, *he* got a perfect view. Her beautiful eyes and the line of the hair at her forehead irresistibly recalled that face that he had never actually seen very well, and he wept as so often before. Her voice when she answered the nun was very like her half sister's at Nijō.

What a dear, dear girl! he exclaimed to himself. To think that I have gone so long without even knowing about her! I could not be indifferent to any relative, even one still lower in station, whose looks were so similar, and this one, although unrecognized, is most certainly His Late Highness's daughter! He was filled with boundless love and happiness now that his own eyes had told him so. He wanted to go to her, right now, to taste the joy of saying, "But there you are! You are alive!" No wonder that Emperor was disappointed, the one who sent the wizard to Hōrai and got back only a hairpin;[110] but he knew that this girl, even if not the same, promised real consolation. He and she must have shared a bond of destiny from the past. The

109. Ukifune's mother.
110. In "The Song of Unending Sorrow," the Emperor sends a Taoist wizard to Hōrai to find his beloved Yang Guifei. The wizard finds her, but he brings back from her only an ornamental hairpin and one or two other things.

nun soon left, after a short chat. She had apparently decided against sharing any confidences, having grasped from the scent the women had noticed that he must be peering in from nearby.

When the sun was low, he stole away, dressed again, called the nun to her usual doorway, and asked for news of the visitor. "I am very fortunate indeed to have come when I did," he said. "Tell me—have you done as I asked?"

"I waited all last year to pass on the message you gave me, my lord, after you asked me to, and in the second month of this year I finally met her and her mother when they were on their way to Hatsuse. Her mother was shocked when I gave her some intimation of what you wish—the resemblance in question did her daughter far too much honor, she said—so I preferred not to mention it, since I gathered that you were then rather preoccupied. Then, this month, the young lady made the same pilgrimage, and today she is here on her way back. I suppose that she breaks her journey here in memory of her father. Something detained her mother, and I cannot very well say anything to her when she is here like this by herself."

"I asked everyone to keep her people from knowing that I am here, because on a private trip like this I do not wish to be recognized, but I wonder—servants can never keep a secret. What should I do, though? Surely her being alone makes it easier to talk to her. Do assure her that the strong tie between us is what has brought us together here."

"That tie certainly took you little enough time to discover!" she said with a smile. "Very well, I shall tell her." She slipped inside.

> "Does that lovely bird sing, too, in the lovely voice I heard long ago?
> Wondering, I came today to seek her through the grasses,"[111]

he hummed casually, as though to himself. She heard him and went off to pass it on.

---

111. Kaoru's poem plays on *kaodori*, a bird (*tori*) probably named originally for its cry or song (*ka-o*). By Heian times, however, its name was understood as meaning "face [*kao*] bird," that is, "lovely bird." *Kaodori* appears first in *Man'yōshū* 1902 and, with the wordplay visible here, in *Kokin rokujō* 4488.

50

AZUMAYA

The Eastern Cottage

Azumaya ("eastern cottage") refers to a modest sort of thatched dwelling mentioned in the *saibara* song by that name. As the chapter title, it comes from a poem by Kaoru:

"Are the weeds so thick that they wholly bar your gate, O eastern cottage—
too long, too long I waited while the pouring rain came down!"

"The Eastern Cottage" roughly overlaps with the end of "The Ivy" and extends slightly beyond it, into Kaoru's twenty-sixth year.

PERSONS

The Commander, age 26 (Kaoru)

Ben, a nun at Uji (Ben no Ama)

The wife of the Governor of Hitachi (Chūjō no Kimi)

A young woman, her favorite daughter, half sister
of Naka no Kimi, about 21 (Ukifune)

The Governor of Hitachi

The young lady, his favorite daughter, 15 or 16

A Lieutenant of the Left Palace Guards, 22 or 23 (Sakon no Shōshō)

His intermediary

Ukifune's nurse

The wife of His Highness of War, 26 (Naka no Kimi)

Her gentlewoman, Taifu

His Highness of War, 27 (Niou)

Ukon, Taifu's daughter, Naka no Kimi's gentlewoman

Shōshō, Naka no Kimi's gentlewoman

Jijū, Ukifune's gentlewoman

He refrained from exploring the fastnesses of Mount Tsukuba, despite his desire to do so, because considering what she was, he would make himself perfectly ridiculous by insisting on sallying forth come what may into the thickets of her foothills.[1] He did not even write. The old nun sent her mother more than one hint of what he had told her, but that lady could not imagine him to be seriously interested, and she was merely intrigued that he should take such trouble to seek out her daughter. His distinction, so rare in this day and age, set her dreaming of what might have been if her daughter had been more worthy of him.

The Governor[2] had a good many children by the wife he had lost, a daughter he specially favored by his present one, and five or six younger children of varying ages, all of whose care so preoccupied him that his stepdaughter was almost a stranger. The young woman's mother, who resented this frequently and bitterly, longed day and night to marry her to particularly striking advantage. She would have had less reason to take it so hard if this daughter had belonged with the others in looks, in which case she could have let people assume that they were all one and the same, but the girl did *not* belong in the same company, having grown up to be impossibly superior, and it struck her that it would be a very great shame to do so.

The news of all these daughters brought courting letters from a great many scions of more or less reputable families, and the Governor managed well enough to settle the two or three from his first wife. Now his second spent every moment on watch for an opportunity to do as *she* hoped for *hers*, and she looked after her very tenderly indeed.

The Governor was no churl. Descended from the senior nobility, he had thoroughly respectable relatives and great wealth as well. He also had pride to match, and he lived a life of ostentatious refinement, but for all his fastidious ways, he remained at heart strangely crude and countrified. No doubt because he had been

1. The literary conceit of this beginning exploits that of *Shinkokinshū* 1013, a love poem by Minamoto no Shigeyuki: "Mount Tsukuba, foothills and thickly grown hills, thickets everywhere: none of that will stop me from going in to you" ("I love you so much that no obstacle can stop me from going to be with you"). Mount Tsukuba is in Hitachi, the province of which Ukifune's stepfather is the (Deputy) Governor.
2. Ukifune's stepfather.

buried so long, ever since his youth, in the distant wilds of the East, peculiar sounds crept into his voice, and he spoke with something of an accent; and for this reason he feared and shunned the company of the mighty. In all things he was quick to assure his own advantage. As to pretty accomplishments, he knew nothing of flutes or strings, being instead very good with a bow. His wealth attracted nice young women to his household, common though it might be, to dress in the height of fashion, to vie with one another over broken-backed poems, to amuse themselves with tales and Kōshin vigils,[3] and generally to immerse themselves in deplorably vain tastes and amusements.

"She's clever, I'm sure, and they say she's a real beauty": so the suitors maintained with optimistic ardor. Particularly assiduous in his courtship was a certain Lieutenant of the Left Palace Guards, a quiet young man of twenty-two or -three who, although known to be good at his books, could never manage much sparkle or animation; which may explain why whatever women he had once been accustomed to visit no longer received him.

The young woman's mother told herself of him especially, among all those from whom she had such approaches: I hear that he is of good family, he seems to be settled in his ways and to know what is what, and he has some distinction of his own. All things considered, I cannot imagine anyone grander than he taking much interest in her. She passed his notes to her daughter and made sure as necessary that he got attractive answers. All on her own she decided that however little the girl might mean to the Governor, *she* would give her life to doing her best for her, and she felt certain that no one who had actually seen how perfectly lovely the girl was could then possibly neglect her. She set the date for the eighth month and began collecting the trousseau of furnishings and accessories. After having the least little trinket she ordered given a fresh, amusing touch and done in an intricate, tasteful design of painted lacquer or mother-of-pearl, she would put it away for her daughter and show the Governor something less good, remarking, "This should do very well." The Governor, who hardly knew one thing from another, collected it all, worthless or not, as long as it might fill out a trousseau, and laid it out until *his* daughters were fairly buried in it. He brought in teachers of koto and *biwa* from the Women's Music Pavilion to give them lessons, and whenever one actually mastered a piece, he would all but fall at the teacher's feet; after which, with much fuss and bluster, he would deluge him with gifts. When one was learning some lively piece and sat there in the lovely half-light of dusk playing it with her teacher, he would weep without shame and heap her with grotesque praise. To his wife, who had some discrimination, this was all quite painful, and she avoided chiming in. "You do not think much of my little girl, do you!" he would complain.

Meanwhile the Lieutenant could not wait for the agreed day. He insisted that they might as well go ahead now until she, who had been so keen to press forward

---

3. A popular belief derived from Chinese religion required people to avoid falling asleep on a *kōshin* night, which recurred in a sixty-day cycle. They amused themselves instead with poetry, music, and so on. The belief held that everyone's body was inhabited by three "worms," which on a *kōshin* night would rise from anyone who slept to report on that person's misdeeds to the Emperor of Heaven. This Emperor would then require the offender's life.

all on her own, began gingerly to reflect how hard it was to be certain of his intentions. When the man who represented him came round, she called him into a private conversation to voice her misgivings.

"He has been urging his cause for months now this way, over my many reasons for caution," she said, "and since he is not just anyone, I decided to agree; I felt that it would be wrong of me not to. But my daughter has no father, you see, and I am afraid now that it might seem forward of me, and somewhat thoughtless as well, if I were actually to proceed on my own. The Governor has several young daughters, but I trust they will all do well with him to look after them, whereas this one is a very great worry, considering how fickle life can be. I am sure that I need not feel anxious, since I gather that the Lieutenant is a man of understanding, but you know, it would be so hard if by chance he should ever turn out to feel otherwise about her and she were then exposed to ridicule."

The intermediary went to the Lieutenant and explained the situation. The Lieutenant looked dark. "If she is not the Governor's daughter, then this is the first I have heard of it!" he said. "It is all very well, but I doubt that this will do me any good if anyone hears about it, and visiting her there is hardly an attractive prospect either. Look what you got me into, without even checking properly!"

"But this is all new to me!" his embarrassed friend replied. "I only began passing your notes because I know one of their women, and when I learned that that daughter was the favorite, I of course assumed she must be the Governor's. I certainly never inquired whether one of them was somebody else's. All I heard was that she is exceptionally bright and pretty, and that her mother adores her and has her heart set on doing her particular credit. You said you wanted someone to represent you there, and I simply let you know that I was able to do so. You have no reason at all to accuse me of being remiss."

To this heated and voluble speech the Lieutenant replied without tact or measure, "For me to take up with a house like that is not something *anyone* could approve of, but they are all doing it these days, and no one could blame me; why, some with awestruck fathers-in-law only too eager to please them do very well indeed at disguising their lapse. For all I know, the Governor may cherish her as though she were his own, but other people will just assume that I am currying favor with him. With men like the Minamoto Junior Counselor and the Governor of Sanuki strutting in and out there the way they do, I would look perfectly hopeless if I were to join them in a way that suggests he does not respect me!"

The intermediary, who was excessively anxious to please and in some ways quite unpleasant, thoroughly regretted what both sides were likely to feel. "The Governor's own daughters are young," he said, "but if you really want one, I will pass the message on. The next one down is the one they call 'our young lady,'[4] and he is extremely fond of her."

"Hmm—it would be one thing if I had been after her from the beginning, but it would not be very nice to ask for another one now. Still, what started me off in

---

4. The daughter of Ukifune's mother by the Governor of Hitachi. The household calls her *himegimi*, which means roughly "eldest daughter."

the first place was the happy prospect of his support, since he is a man of such weight and substance. A pretty face makes no difference to me. If grace and distinction were what I wanted in a woman, I could have them easily enough. Look at what happens, though, to people with elegant tastes who fall behind and fail to make ends meet—they can do nothing right, and people simply ignore them. No, never mind a little carping. What I want is to live in comfort. Just let the Governor know that, and why worry if he then seems disposed to agree?"

The man had begun taking the Lieutenant's letters to the house because his younger sister was in service there in the west wing,[5] but he hardly knew the Governor at all. Off he went to him at once and had it announced that he had something to discuss. "I understand that he sometimes calls here," the Governor said, "but he has never been introduced to me. What can he possibly want?" He did not look at all pleased.

"I have come to wait on you on behalf of his lordship, the Lieutenant of the Left Palace Guards," the man had him told.

The Governor received him. The man seated himself nearby, looking as though he hardly knew how to begin. "For some months, sir," he ventured, "his lordship has been in touch with your esteemed wife, and she has granted his wish; they have agreed that the event is to take place during the course of this month. He has been considering the day and has been eager that it should be soon. However, sir, he recently learned that although the young lady in question is indeed your wife's daughter, she is not actually yours, and he fears that if a gentleman such as himself were to accept her, the world might take it that he was fawning upon you. A young nobleman who becomes the son-in-law of a provincial governor counts on full honor within the family and also on devoted support as though he were, so to speak, a prized jewel; and that really is often what happens. As many people have urgently warned him, however, it would do him no credit at all to be received so scantily here that any such hope was plainly deluded and to frequent the house as the last among others. He is therefore now in a quandary. What he chose from the very start was the great renown that you, sir, enjoy, one that inspires the utmost trust in the brilliant prospects you offer; that is why he undertook to press his suit. Not for a moment did he imagine that the young lady might not be yours, and he would therefore be most grateful if you were kind enough to grant him what he originally desired, even though he understands that some of your daughters are still very young. It is in that spirit that he asked me to come and sound you out on the matter."

"I myself know hardly anything about such an approach," the Governor replied. "She is just like one of my own to me, but I have quite a few foolish girls, and while I do my poor best for them all, her mother accuses me of treating her like a foreigner and gives me no say in anything touching her, so that although I heard a distant rumor of this gentleman's approach, I had no idea that I was the one who had particularly attracted his interest. In fact, I may say that I am delighted by what you have told me. There is one of my daughters whom I love very much, one for

5. Where Ukifune lives.

whom I would give my life gladly. She has her suitors, but men these days are not to be trusted, judging from what I hear, and I have been too worried that any decision might only mean disaster ever really to make up my mind. Day and night I wonder fondly what I can do to secure her future. As to his lordship the Lieutenant, though, in my youth I served his father, the late Commander.[6] I knew the Lieutenant as one of his father's retainers. He is a very fine gentleman, and I would have been pleased to serve him, too, but I felt that all those years I spent in one far-flung post after another rendered me unfit to appear before him, and I never presented myself to him again. It would be the easiest thing in the world to offer him my daughter, since that is what he himself wishes, but I cannot help being wary of what my wife may feel about it, since for months now she has had quite different intentions." He kept back nothing of what he had to say.

This is promising nicely, his delighted visitor told himself. "Surely you have no reason to worry," he said. "*Your* permission, sir, is all the Lieutenant desires, and even if the young lady is not actually quite old enough yet, he will be fully satisfied with a daughter who means that much to *you*. As he said himself, this is not a decision that anyone else can properly make for you. He is a very distinguished gentleman and very highly regarded. He may be young, but he does not put on airs, and he well understands the ways of the world. Moreover, he has a large number of estates. These do not seem to yield a great deal at present, but when all is said and done, the scion of so noble a lineage confers luster worth far more than the might of any common gentleman's boundless wealth. He will have the fourth rank next year, and, as His Majesty himself says, he is certain to be the next Secretary. 'There you are,' His Majesty tells him, 'a handsome young lord with every advantage, and you do not yet have a wife! Then waste no more time: pick out someone worthy and get yourself some proper backing! As for your rising to senior noble, well, here I am—I shall be making you one any day!' That, I gather, is the sort of thing His Majesty says. The Lieutenant is the only one who always serves him so intimately. He has such quality, you see, and such imposing dignity. Now that you know how eager he is, you really should make up your mind immediately in favor of so perfect a son-in-law. People everywhere seem to be after him with just that in mind, and if you are slow, you may lose him. I say this, sir, only because I have your best interests at heart." His flattering speech went on and on, and the horribly countrified Governor just sat there smiling, taking it in.

"If he is strapped for revenue lately, I do not want to know about it," he replied. "He will have it from me, with the greatest respect, while I have life and breath. I promise he will lack nothing. Even if something happens to me and I can no longer provide for him, no one else will be able to claim one jot or tittle of what I leave behind in property and estates. No doubt I have a good many other children, but she is the one who has always really mattered to me. All he need do is put his heart into looking after her, and say he has his eye on appointment as Minister and for that must lay out a vast fortune: he will have it, every bit. If His

6. Commander (Taishō) of the Palace Guards was a third-rank post. The Lieutenant's father belonged to the senior nobility.

Majesty is that eager to do things for him, he certainly need not worry about being provided for. For all I know, this may be the very best thing both for him and for my girl."

Although thoroughly satisfied by this favorable reception the intermediary said not a word about it to his sister, nor did he call on the ladies concerned; he went intead, bursting with glee, to report the Governor's words to the Lieutenant. The Lieutenant thought the man rather a bumpkin, but he was not ill pleased and sat listening with a smile. The business about meeting the cost of becoming a Minister particularly struck him as a bit much. "Have you let his wife know?" he asked. "She seems to have been keen on me from the start, and some people may think me a strange sort of cad if I switch now. I don't know." He was wavering.

"But why? I hear she is absolutely *devoted* to this other daughter, the Governor's. It is just that she directed you to the first one because she is the eldest, and she felt sorry for her."

It occurred to the Lieutenant that this story was suddenly quite different from the one he had been hearing for months, about how the eldest was by far her mother's favorite, and this gave him pause; but he was a sensible young man, and he decided that it was worth suffering a moment's hatred and a little criticism in exchange for long years of secure comfort. He did not even change the day. Off he went on the evening agreed for his first night with his bride.

The Governor's wife secretly continued her preparations. She had her women dressed and everything done up just right. She also had her daughter's hair washed and got her all ready. Ah, what a miserable shame it is to let her go to the likes of that Lieutenant! she reflected, contemplating her. If she had only had her father's recognition while she grew up, then even now when he is gone there would be no reason not to presume just a little and to accept the Commander's proposal. I may think highly of her, but to everyone else she is just another of the Governor's daughters, and, poor thing, anyone who found out the truth would only despise her for it. What else can I do? I cannot just let the flower of her beauty go to waste, especially when there *is* a perfectly decent, respectable man who is eager to have her." As far as her deciding the matter all on her own was concerned, the intermediary had been wonderfully persuasive, and in any case, it may well be that a woman is just there to be fooled.

While she was rushing hither and yon to see to this or that, all aflutter because the great day was almost upon her, the Governor came in and made her an interminable speech. "Who do you think you are, trying to steal my girl's suitor like that behind my back?" he demanded to know. "No gentleman will have any use for that fancy daughter of yours. I may be low and thick in the head, but I gather the one this fellow wants is *mine*. You planned it all very nicely, but no, he was not interested, and it seems that he was about to go elsewhere, so I thought I might as well get him back, and I let him know he can have the one he actually wants." He blurted all this out with astonishing bluntness and never a thought for her feelings. Speechless with shock, she remained for a moment lost in thought. Then the bitterness of it brought tears to her eyes, and she stole away.

She went to her daughter, and when she saw again how sweet and lovely she was, she took comfort from the thought that she was still every bit as worthy as anyone else. "Other people can be so cruel!" she said, weeping, when she was alone with her daughter's nurse. "Of course I wish to treat all my sons-in-law the same, but I know that I would give my life for *her* husband. I suppose he must look down on her because she has no father; that must be why he prefers a girl who is still hardly more than a child. I want no sight or sound of this horrible business anywhere near me, but the Governor takes it as a great honor, and he is making such a fuss that I suppose he and the Lieutenant deserve each other. I shall not say a word. I only wish I could go elsewhere for a while."

The nurse was furious, and she decided that it was just as well her young mistress had been insulted this way. "Oh, no, my lady," she exclaimed, "I expect that she is fortunate to have had this go wrong! No one as dreary as that could possibly appreciate her anyway. I would like to see my dear young mistress go to someone good and kind, someone who really understands things. I felt as though the little glimpse I caught of the Commander had added years to my life, and just look, he is actually interested in her! Why not simply accept him and let her destiny take its course?"

"What a thing to say! I hear he said for years that he would never marry any ordinary woman. What kind *would* it take really to attract him, considering that His Excellency of the Right, the Inspector Grand Counselor, and His Highness of Ceremonial all let him know they were serious about him and that he ignored them and got His Majesty's own cherished daughter instead? He probably just wants to have her serve Her Highness, his mother, and to see her from time to time; and there might be a lot to be said for that, except that it would be so painful. They call her sister at His Highness of War's extraordinarily fortunate, but I realized when I saw how unhappy *she* is that the only really worthy, reliable husband is the one who does not divide his affections. In fact, my own experience has taught me that. His Late Highness was a very fine and handsome gentleman and very kind, but I meant nothing at all to him, and you can imagine how that hurt. The Governor is a difficult man, inconsiderate and uncouth, but *his* affections have never been divided, and that has always been a great comfort to me. Sometimes his abruptness and his discourtesy are a great trial, as they are now, but he has never made me suffer from jealousy, and even when we have quarreled, we have made it clear where we disagreed. Insignificant as I am, I could never get on with a senior noble or a Prince, however elegant or distinguished. The poor thing, I feel so sorry for her when I think that it is all because of me! I must do something to make sure no one ever feels like laughing at her!"

The Governor got to work. "Lend me some women," he said. "I hear you have lots of pretty ones. And the bed curtains, the new ones you just had done—this has all happened so fast, I shall take them. They will do just as they are." He came to the west wing and charged about giving orders. Into the nice, cleanly furnished room his wife had designed so carefully, he busily stuffed a strange profusion of screens, cabinets, and two-tiered shelves, with results that she found deplorable. Having de-

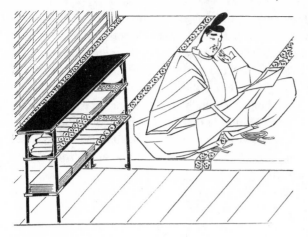

Two-tiered shelves

clared that she would not say a word, however, she only watched. Her beloved daughter was to the north.[7]

"*Now* I know how you feel!" he said. "I never thought you would just turn your back on my girl. She is yours, too, you know. All right, there are other girls in this world who get on without their mothers!" At midday he and her nurse started dressing her, and the result was not bad at all. At fifteen or sixteen she was very small and plump, with beautiful hair the length of her dress gown and rich and thick at the ends. Her father, who thought it a treasure, stroked it smooth. "Well, now, I really shouldn't have made off this way with a gentleman your mother meant for someone else," he said, "but in rank he is a prize, and in personal quality he is so outstanding that many people are desperate to have him as a son-in-law, and I hated the thought of losing him." The fool! He was repeating exactly what the intermediary had put into his head.

The Lieutenant gathered from such evidence of the Governor's headlong enthusiasm that he could do no wrong. He turned up for the first night without even changing the date. The Governor's wife was horrified, as was her favorite daughter's nurse. Not wishing to lend herself further to anything so crass, she addressed an appeal to the wife of His Highness of War.

"In the absence of any particular reason to get in touch with you, the fear of seeming to presume has hitherto restrained me from acting on my wish to do so," she wrote. "Now, however, I find that my daughter has come under a directional taboo and that I must take her elsewhere for a time. I would therefore be extremely grateful if she might avail herself of a hidden corner in which briefly to remain unnoticed. Alas, it is more than I can do alone to provide her with the shelter she needs, and what with all the troubles there are in this world, I have no choice but to turn to you."

The letter, written in tears, certainly moved His Highness's wife, but now that she was the only sister left, she hesitated to admit her acquaintance with someone whom her late father had never recognized, although she also recoiled from the thought of merely ignoring someone who had fallen into such sad difficulties. It would not honor her father's memory either, unnecessarily to estrange herself from her half sister. At a loss what to do, she sent Taifu an urgent message.

"There must be a reason for this," Taifu replied. "You should not put her off

7. Presumably the north side of the chamber in the west wing, the room having apparently been divided into two sections, north and south.

too readily or embarrass her. There is nothing unusual about a lesser daughter mingling with her betters. The position His Late Highness took was really too unkind."

"Very well, then, you shall have a discreet room on the west side," Taifu sent in reply to the letter. "It is not very comfortable, but if you do not mind too much, you are welcome there for a little while." The young woman looked forward to knowing her half sister, and she felt more pleased than anything else that things had worked out this way.

The Governor was eager to treat his new son-in-law magnificently, but he did not actually know how to convey any brilliance; he just rolled some coarse Azuma silks into a ball and tossed them in.[8] The food was brought in with much noise and in vast abundance, which so impressed the Lieutenant's servants that the Lieutenant, too, congratulated himself on his admirable success. The Governor's wife, who knew how ill tempered it would be to ignore the proceedings, bore it all and just sat and watched. It was a big house, but what with the space now done up with so much fuss for the new son-in-law and his men, and the east wing where the Minamoto Junior Counselor lived, and rooms for all the Governor's sons, it was full. The Lieutenant now occupied what had once been her favorite daughter's room, and she could hardly bear the thought of the poor girl being obliged to make do with some odd corner along a gallery, for example. That was what had set her mind working and made her think of His Highness's. No one here seems to have any respect for her at all, she reflected; and so it was that she whisked her off, with blind hope, to a place where the young woman's father would not have wished to find her. Only her daughter's nurse and two or three young gentlewomen accompanied them. They were lodged at the north end of the west aisle, a spot far away from anyone else.

The lady at His Highness's had not seen her guest for many years, but she did not feel that she was a stranger and maintained no reserve in her presence, welcoming her instead most graciously. Her unhappy guest was filled with envy as she watched her play with her little son. Have I, then, *nothing* to do with His Late Highness's wife?[9] she asked herself. He despised me just because I was in service, and everyone else is cruel enough to do the same. It is so hard to have to go about begging this way! No one came to them, since she had said her daughter was under a taboo. She stayed for two or three days, which gave her time to become familiar with the house.

When His Highness visited the wing, she peered curiously at him through a crack. He was as perfectly beautiful as a plucked spray of cherry blossoms, and household retainers of the fourth or fifth rank, far finer in looks and manner than her Governor, whom despite her anger she had no wish to offend, knelt before him to report on one matter or another. Most of the young gentlemen of the fifth rank were ones she did not recognize. Her own stepson, an Aide in the Bureau of Cere-

8. Lengths of coarse-woven Azuma silk (from the Governor's province of Hitachi), tossed in to the Lieutenant under the blinds. They are for the Lieutenant's retainers.
9. She is a niece of Hachi no Miya's wife.

monial and also a Chamberlain, appeared with a message from His Majesty, but it was not for such as he actually to approach a Prince. Ah, she said to herself, what a wonder he is to behold, and how fortunate she is to be near him! From a distance one may entertain all sorts of dark thoughts about the terrible things he might do to her, however splendid a man like him may be, but that is foolishness! Just look at him! What an extraordinary privilege it would be to be with him that way just once a year, like Tanabata! And there he was, holding and caressing his little boy. His wife was sitting behind a low standing curtain, but he pushed it aside to talk to her, and the two made a most beautiful couple. His Late Highness was a Prince, too, but how utterly different in his dismal solitude!

His Highness went into the curtained bed, leaving the young gentlewomen and the nurse to look after his little son. All sorts of people came to him, but he claimed not to be feeling well and rested until sunset. They brought him his meal right there. In the presence of such elegance and grandeur she saw that her own household, which she had thought very splendid indeed, was really deplorably common. My own daughter, though, would not look out of place beside him, she told herself. Those girls may be mine, too, the ones their father, with all his pride in his wealth, boasts he will make great ladies, but I know that I must continue hoping for better when I think how far *this* one outshines them! She spent the night in fantasies of the future.

The sun was high when His Highness arose. "Her Majesty is unwell, as she is so often, and I must go to her," he said, and got dressed. The Governor's wife peeped through, eager to know what he looked like now. Incomparable in formal dress, and glowing with noble beauty, he was playing with his son, whom he found it difficult to leave. He set out directly from the wing after partaking of gruel and steamed rice.

Now was the time for the gentlemen who had gathered to his residence at dawn, and who had been waiting patiently in his household office ever since, to come forward and report to him whatever they had to say. One of them, a man with pretensions to looks but with a drearily unremarkable face, wore a dress cloak and a sword.

"That's that Lieutenant, Hitachi's son-in-law," the women told each other. "He was first going to marry our visitor, but he said he preferred to enjoy the advantages of having the Governor's own daughter instead, so they say that little chit of a girl is what he got."

"Our guest's women won't talk about it, though. I got it all from one of his."

They had no idea that their guest's mother was listening, and she was aghast at what she heard. How could I have ever imagined him to be worth anything? He seems to have nothing at all. She now despised him more than ever.

The little boy came crawling out and peeked under the blinds, and His Highness turned back at the sight and went to him. "I shall withdraw immediately if Her Majesty seems well," he said. "If she is as indisposed as ever, I shall spend the night attending her. I hate to spend a single night away from you lately." He played with him a little while to humor him and then set out once more, a figure too marvelous ever to tire of watching, and so perfectly pleasing that his departure left rather a void.

She went to visit the lady who had given her refuge, and praised His Highness to the skies, till the lady smiled at her country ways. "You were still an infant when your mother passed away," she said. "We who looked after you felt deep regret on your behalf, as did His Late Highness himself. Still, great good fortune was yours after all, and you managed to grow up very well even in the depths of those hills. It is so sad that you lost your sister, though." She had tears in her eyes.

The lady was weeping, too. "My life has its bitter moments," she replied, "and then others as well when it seems to me that I may still hope for some consolation. As for those who brought me into the world, I am resigned to their loss, since such things are only to be expected. There it is—after all, I never even knew my mother. But I shall always miss my sister very much. I feel so sorry whenever I see how loyal the Commander is to her, even now, because he often laments that his heart is still drawn to nothing and no one but her."

"The Commander must be proud to stand so extraordinarily high in His Majesty's esteem, though. Might all that not have turned out to be an obstacle if your sister had lived?"

"Ah, *that* certainly would have been cruel, if both of us had felt ourselves mocked for having suffered just the same fate. I suppose that what keeps her memory so fresh for him is that he never actually made her his; but even so, it is extraordinary how for some reason he simply cannot forget her. He even went to immense trouble to look after the memorial services for my father." She spoke with gentle warmth.

"He actually talked to the nun Ben in the hope of having my unworthy daughter take your sister's place. I could not possibly consider such a thing, of course, but it is a great honor all the same that that 'single stem'[10] should mean so much to him, and I cannot help admiring his depth of feeling." Fresh tears sprang to her eyes as she spoke, at the thought of the daughter whose prospects so concerned her.

She went on to convey in a general way the Lieutenant's contempt for her daughter, on the assumption that the gentlewomen around her already knew. "She will be a comfort to me as long as I live," she said, "whatever happens. It would be so sad, though, for her to be reduced to homeless misery after I am gone that I believe in the end I may have no choice but to make her a nun and send her somewhere, perhaps far off in the mountains, where she may learn to give up all hope in the world."

"Hers is a very distressing plight, but you know, the contempt that she has suffered is the common lot of anyone in her position. What you propose would be too hard for her. Even I, who by my father's solemn choice lived rather that way, and who now find myself in circumstances quite unlike anything I had imagined, could not possibly manage what you suggest. Besides, it would be such a pity for her to adopt the drab habit of a nun." Her deliberate manner of speaking gave her visitor great pleasure.

The young woman's mother showed her age, but she was handsome enough,

10. *Kokinshū* 867: "Because of a single stem of *murasaki*, I love all the grasses on Musashi Plain."

and she did not lack distinction. She certainly was remarkably heavy, but in that she matched the Governor of Hitachi very well.

"As far as I can see, His Late Highness's most unkind rejection has meant that people are more and more inclined to look down on her as though she were not one of them, but meeting you and talking to you this way consoles me for those past griefs." She went on to tell of the life they had led, and of how melancholy Ukishima[11] had been. "Now that I have told you all about Mount Tsukuba and about how the world there seemed to have turned hateful just for me,[12] since I had no one to talk to, I should like to continue presuming on your kindness, but those hopeless scamps of mine at home must be calling for me and making a nuisance of themselves. These worries give me no peace. Knowing as I do all too well how sadly I have lowered myself by assuming my present guise, I shall leave it to you to do as you think best for my daughter and say no more about it." Her urgent appeal left His Highness's wife hoping that her half sister really deserved all this.

In looks as in temperament the young woman was distinctly attractive. Not excessively reticent, she was pleasingly artless yet never willful, and she did very well at keeping out of sight of the women in her intimate service. How like my sister she is when she speaks! His Highness's wife thought. The Commander wants an image of her so badly—I do wish I could have him see her!

Just then the Commander's arrival was announced. Her women arranged a standing curtain and prepared to receive him as usual. "Oh, I *do* want a look at him!" the Governor's wife exclaimed. "People who have seen him say the most wonderful things about him, but surely he does not compare with His Highness!"

"You may find that he does!" the women all answered.

"But how could any gentleman possibly outshine His Highness?"

The Commander must have alighted from his carriage, judging from his escort's boisterous cries, but he did not immediately appear. To those awaiting him with bated breath, his figure as he entered evoked less wonder and delight than elegance and noble grace. One felt one's hand move to tidy a wayward lock of hair, for his presence conveyed a daunting refinement, and his manner was one of the very highest distinction. He must have just come from the palace, since his escort was so large.

"I went to call on Her Majesty yesterday evening, having heard that she was unwell," he said, "and I was sorry to find none of the Princes with her. I have been there all this time in place of His Highness. He got there very late this morning. It occurred to me, if I may say so, that you might have sufficiently forgotten yourself to detain him!"

"You have been most kind." That was her only reply. He seemed to have ar-

---

11. Ukishima ("floating island") is an *utamakura* (a poetically recognized place) in the far northern province of Mutsu, where the husband of Ukifune's mother was once posted as Governor. Its name suggests the common wordplay on *uki* (or *ushi*, "hateful"). *Kokin rokujō* 1796 (also *Shinkokinshū* 1379) plays on the name this way in a particularly elaborate fashion.

12. *Kokinshū* 948: "Can the world have always been so hateful a place, or did it become this way just for me?"

rived in a rather excited mood, knowing that His Highness would be staying on at court.

He spoke to her most affectionately, as always. Whatever the subject, he turned it not bluntly but with the lightest of touches to sad musings on how he could never forget the past and how the world now was ever more hateful to him. How was it possible that the memory of her sister should always so absorb him? Since he had already dwelled on the subject to her with great feeling, she could only suppose that he wished her to know that he could say even more. Still, manner betrays sentiment, and since she was neither stock nor stone, the more she watched him, the more she acknowledged his pathetically genuine depth of feeling.

He spoke at such length of the disappointments he had suffered that she sighed bitterly. Perhaps it was a wish to cleanse him of this passion that prompted her to speak of the "doll" he had mentioned. "She is here in hiding," she said—just a word, no more.

This was another stirring topic, and he looked forward to meeting her, but he preferred not to make too sudden a shift. "Ah, that would be a boon indeed, if my buddha[13] were to answer my prayers; but then any occasional wish of mine that things might still be otherwise[14] would only muddy the waters of my mountain stream."

"You and your thoughts of a holy life—you are impossible!" she said at last, with a little laugh that he found delightful.

"Very well, then, please tell her. It occurs to me that that evasion of yours does not seem to bode well." Tears again came to his eyes.

> *"If she is truly the double of her I knew, I shall keep her close:*
> *she shall be my cleansing charm through the cruel shoals of love,"*

he said, as so often turning his tears to levity.[15]

> *"No one would believe a charm you send down the shoals of a cleansing stream*
> *to be the cherished double you keep close to you always.*

'So many hands are tugging,' the poem goes[16]—why, I would feel very sorry for her."

"I need hardly say that she is the last shoal my love would catch upon. Yes, I

---

13. As Kaoru called his desired "doll" of Ōigimi in "The Ivy."

14. That I had you instead of Ukifune.

15. "Double" (*katashiro*) suggests a doll, and "cleansing charm" is *nademono*. Although in this poem *nademono* also suggests an object to "stroke" (*nade*) for pleasure, it principally means a paper doll used for purification. One stroked oneself with the *nademono* so as to infuse into it the impurities in one's own person; then one dropped it into a stream so that the stream should carry it away. "Shoals" is *seze*, a word "related" (*engo*) to *nademono* because it means the "rapids and shallows" of a stream, although figuratively it means "vicissitudes."

16. *Kokinshū* 706, sent by a woman to Ariwara no Narihira after she had learned that he was visiting many women: "So many hands are tugging at the great purification wand, I who love you can no longer trust you." The "great purification wand" (*ōnusa*) is a Shintō ritual object that one passed over one's body in roughly the same manner as one did a *nademono*.

am just like that sad foam on the water.[17] A cleansing doll sent floating down the stream: that is what I am!"

Meanwhile it was getting dark, and she did not wish her visitors to wonder what might be going on. "Please do not stay too long, at least this evening," she said, and she talked him round so nicely that she managed to get him to go.

"Very well," he conceded, "but do let your visitor know that she should not imagine me to be following a passing whim, since I have desired this for years. And please ask her to be thoroughly discreet. I am completely unaccustomed to this sort of thing, and I am likely to proceed awkwardly enough." He left after making this final request.

"What an absolutely perfect gentleman he is!" The Governor's wife gave voice to her praise and went on again to ponder the idea first brought up and then often repeated by her daughter's nurse. I told her it was out of the question, but now that I have actually seen him, I would gladly have her await the light of that Herdboy Star, even if he has to cross the River of Heaven to reach her. She is just too pretty to give to anyone common. To think that I, who have spent all my time with people who are practically barbarians, once thought that Lieutenant a prize! She regretted having ever had such an idea. The fine pillar on which he had leaned, the cushion on which he had sat, the delicious perfume that lingered behind him—all seemed to her rare and wonderful.

Even those who saw him quite often praised him every time. "You read in the scriptures about certain things that have especially great merit, and according to the Buddha himself, giving off a fragrance like that is certainly one of them. In the Medicine King chapter[18] especially he talks about Oxhead sandalwood[19] or something."

"What a ghastly name! But when that gentleman is nearby, you realize how right the Buddha was."

"It is because he has been absorbed in pious devotions ever since he was a boy."

The women talked on, and another added, "I would just like to know what *he* was in his past lives!" The Governor's wife sat listening to all this with a happy smile.

His Highness's wife quietly passed on to her something of what the Commander had said. "Once he has conceived an affection, he never wavers; he pursues it almost to the point of obsession, which is why I believe that you might as well give him a chance, even though his present situation certainly seems to invite great caution. You were thinking of having her leave the world in any case."

"I thought that she should live where no birds sing[20] only because I want to spare her pain and contempt. Yes, now that I have seen for myself what he is like, I think that anyone might wish to be close to such a gentleman, if only as one of his servants, and certainly a young woman could hardly help being keen on him; but

---

17. *Kokinshū* 792, by Ki no Tomonori: "Although I am like foam on the water that somehow lingers on, as long as the stream bears me, she may trust in me."

18. The twenty-third chapter of the Lotus Sutra.

19. Sandalwood from Oxhead Mountain (Japanese Gozu-san) in India.

20. Deep in the mountains, as a nun. *Kokinshū* 535: "Would that she understood the depth of my love, deep as a mountain fastness where one hears no song from the birds of the air."

for one so unworthy that might only sow the seeds of further sorrow. It seems to me that for any woman, high or low, this sort of thing is all too likely to mean suffering in this life and the next, and that is why I feel so sorry for her. However, I leave the matter entirely to you. I only ask that whatever you do, you do not abandon her."

It was a troubling responsibility. "Ah," the lady sighed, "so far I have always had faith in his depth of heart, but it is not easy to foresee the future." She said no more.

At dawn a carriage came from the Governor's residence, together with an angry and threatening message. "Forgive me, but I must go now," his wife said. "I look to you for everything. Please give her refuge a little longer; and while I continue to ponder whether she should live among the rocks[21] or elsewhere, please do not reject her, unworthy though she may be, and teach her whatever she needs to know." This first separation was a sad trial for her daughter, but the prospect of spending time in such pretty and fashionable surroundings pleased her nonetheless.

The carriage was just driving away under a barely lightening sky when His Highness withdrew from the palace. Eager to see his little boy again, he set out discreetly with an unusually modest escort. He met the departing guest head-on. She stopped her carriage, and His Highness drew his up to the gallery. "What carriage is that, hurrying off while it is still dark?" he asked, intrigued. He was terrifyingly quick to note from his own experience that this is exactly the way a man leaves after a secret visit.

"My lady of Hitachi is going home," came the report from the Hitachi party.

"*My lady?*" The young men in His Highness's escort all burst into laughter. The Governor's wife sadly recognized that it *was* rather an overstatement. She dearly wished to be as good as anyone else, though, for her daughter's sake, and of course by now the thought of her daughter lowering herself to a level as common as her own simply horrified her.

His Highness came in. "Are you receiving visits from someone associated with Hitachi?" he asked, still suspicious. "There seems to be something going on, with that carriage and all its attendants hurrying away like that in this beautiful dawn."

This offended his wife, who objected. "It was a friend of Taifu's, from when Taifu was a girl," she said. "There seemed to be nothing very interesting about her, but she talked as though she had something particular in mind. You are always insinuating that this or that will start unpleasant gossip. Please do not accuse me falsely."[22] The way she turned away from him was perfectly delightful.

He slept on, oblivious of the dawn,[23] until people began gathering to wait upon him, and he went over to the main house. There he found the sons of His Excellency of the Right merrily playing Go or guessing rhymes. Her Majesty was not seriously ill, and she was feeling better.

---

21. *Kokinshū* 952: "Where should I choose to live, among what rocks, so as to hear no more of the miseries of the world?"

22. *Shūishū* 662, by a woman responding to a lover who had accused her of seeing someone else: "You who assured me you would always love me, do not accuse me falsely: just forget me."

23. *Ise shū* 55: "Behind jeweled blinds I slept on, oblivious of the dawn, yet never thought I would never see you even in my dreams."

When he returned late in the day, his wife was having her hair washed, and her women were all resting. There was practically no one with her. He sent her a little page girl with the remark, "You picked a fine time to wash your hair! Am I simply to languish here all by myself?"

"It is true, my lady usually does it while he is away," Taifu replied. "For some reason, though, she has not felt like it lately, and I advised her that if she did not do it today, there would be no more days this month, and the ninth and tenth months are out of the question."[24] She felt very unhappy about it.

The little boy was in bed, and the women were all with him. His Highness went wandering aimlessly about until, toward the west,[25] he glimpsed a page girl he did not know. She must be new, he thought, peering in at her. Between the sliding panels there was a narrow gap through which, a foot or so away, he saw a screen. At one end, against the blinds, stood a curtain with a single width of its material up over the crosspiece, and through this opening there spilled sleeves in bright aster and maidenflower layerings. The single folded-back panel of the screen thus offered a surprising view. For a newly arrived gentlewoman she looked thoroughly respectable.

He quietly opened the panel into the aisle and stole closer, but she did not hear him. She was leaning on an armrest near the veranda, gazing out at the lovely little garden before her, enclosed by the gallery, with its profusion of flowers in many colors and its tall rocks all along the brook. Then he slid the panel open a little wider and peered at her round the end of the screen, but it never occurred to her that it might be His Highness; she assumed that it must be someone else[26] who often came that way. When she sat up, she made a picture so lovely that his usual proclivity kept him from allowing the moment to pass. He caught her skirts, slid the panel shut, and sat down in the space between two screens. In surprise she glanced back at him entrancingly from behind her fan.

He took the hand that held the fan. "Who are you? I long to know your name!" Now she was frightened. Preferring to be thoroughly cautious, he turned his face away from her to hide it behind a screen, and she wondered whether he was that Commander who had apparently expressed such an interest in her—his perfume suggested that he might be. Embarrassment overcame her.

This unexpected presence aroused her nurse's suspicion, and she opened a screen on the far side of the room and came in. "What is this?" she demanded to know. "These are strange goings-on!" However, it would have taken more than that to put him off. All this was no more than a whim, but his innate ease of speech gave him such eloquence that the sun soon set while he still insisted, "I shall not let you go till you tell me who you are!" and lay down quite naturally beside her. It was His Highness! Her nurse, speechless with horror, grasped that at last.

Lanterns were lit, and voices announced her ladyship's return. There were

---

24. A woman could wash her hair only on a lucky day as defined by the almanac, and the ninth month was one of abstinence. The tenth month, the *kaminashi* month, is usually written and understood to be the one "without gods," but *kami* (with a different character) also means "hair," hence the prohibition referred to.
25. The aisle space on the west side of the wing. Ukifune occupies the north end of it.
26. Presumably one of Naka no Kimi's women.

sounds of shutters being lowered everywhere but in her room. The visitor's, a space used for other purposes, was abandoned to considerable disorder, containing as it did a pair of tall cabinets with shelves and a scattering of screens stored in bags. One sliding panel's width had been cleared as a passageway when it turned out that someone would be staying there, and through this opening now came Ukon, Taifu's daughter, who also served in the house, to lower the shutters there as well. "It is so dark!" she exclaimed. "Why, the lamps are not yet lit! Dear me, your women were in such a hurry to get the shutters down—I know they are hard to manage—that now one cannot see a thing!" She raised one again, somewhat to His Highness's embarrassment.

That was too much for the nurse, an impatient and assertive woman. "I beg your pardon!" she said. "Something outrageous is going on here, and I am all worn out with keeping my eye on things. I simply cannot move."

"What is it?" Ukon felt around until she touched a man without a dress cloak but deliciously perfumed lying next to a woman, and she understood that His Highness was back to his bad old habits. She took it for granted that the woman herself had nothing to do with it. "Oh. This *is* unfortunate, isn't it. What am I going to say to my lady? I suppose I must go straight to her and tell her privately all about it!" She started off.

Their shock and consternation left His Highness unfazed. What extraordinary distinction she has! But who *is* she? He was baffled. She can hardly be just any new gentlewoman, the way Ukon was talking. He reproached her in all sorts of ways. Nothing in her manner betrayed her revulsion; she simply seemed almost to be expiring, which made him so sorry for her that he kindly did his best to make her feel better.

Ukon reported to her mistress what His Highness was up to. "The poor dear!" she said. "She must be feeling awful!"

"Oh, no, there he goes again! Her mother will think the worst of me for having failed so dismally to look out for her daughter. She told me again and again that she knew she need not worry." What can I say to him, though? she wondered to herself in dismay. He misses not a single woman in service here, as long as she has any youth or looks at all—he is just like that, unfortunately. How did he manage to come across her? The shock was too great. She had no words at all.

"His Highness amuses himself with the senior nobles on days when a lot of them come calling, and normally he gets back here quite late, so you see, all the women were resting," Ukon explained unhappily to Shōshō.[27] "What can you do, though? That nurse is a bold one! She stayed right with her—I thought she was going to *drag* him away from her!"

Just then a messenger came from the palace to announce that Her Majesty, who had begun feeling unwell at dusk, was now extremely ill. "She could have picked a better moment!" Ukon whispered. "I must tell him." She moved to go.

"Now, now," Shōshō answered, "don't reprimand him too severely—I imagine it's too late by now, and you would only waste your breath."

27. Another of Naka no Kimi's gentlewomen.

"Oh, no, I'm sure she's still all right."

Look at what horrid talk this quirk of his can start! their mistress said to herself. Anyone with any sense would despise *me* for it, too!

Ukon went to His Highness and conveyed the message to him somewhat more urgently than she had received it. "Who brought it?" he asked in a tone that suggested no intention of moving. "You are just trying to alarm me."

"A retainer of Her Majesty's, Your Highness. He said his name is Taira no Shigetsune."

He would have to go, like it or not, and since he cared nothing about being seen, Ukon went and got the messenger to come around to the west side so that he could question him further. The retainer[28] who had first passed the message in came round as well. "Prince Nakatsukasa[29] is with Her Majesty now," he reported, "and the Commissioner has just gone. I saw his carriage setting out on the way here."

True enough, His Highness reflected, she does have these sudden attacks sometimes. Suddenly embarrassed to imagine what other people might think of him, he left amid a flurry of reproaches and promises to return.

The visitor lay bathed in perspiration, feeling as though she had just awakened from a terrifying dream. Her nurse fanned her. "You cannot stay here," she said; "it is too risky and too confining. Nothing good can happen now that he has come after you this way. The prospect is too frightening! I am sure that he is a very great lord, but such behavior is not acceptable. Someone unconnected with you could think whatever he liked, for good or ill, but I realized that the gossip could be devastating, and I glared at him like the Demon Queller.[30] He thought I was some sort of frightening menial and pinched my hand hard—it really was very funny, as though he were making advances to the likes of me! At home today they had a big fight. He reprimanded her for paying no attention to anyone but you and forgetting all about his own children, and for being off somewhere just when a new bridegroom was coming to the house. It was a disgrace, he said. The whole staff heard it, and they all felt sorry for you. This Lieutenant of his is a loss, as far as I am concerned. If it were not for this marriage, they might have had their differences and disagreements sometimes, but they could have gone on perfectly well as they have always done so far." She spoke in tears.

For the present her charge was in no condition to think about such things. She lay facedown, acutely mortified and weeping with despair not only at the strange experience she had just been through but at the thought of what His Highness's wife must think of her.

The sight alarmed her worried nurse. "But why are you so upset?" she asked. "A girl who has no mother, yes, she really *is* lost. It certainly does one no good in the wider world to have no father, but that is a lot easier to put up with than being hated by a spiteful stepmother. Your mother will do something for you. Please do not be so sad. The Kannon of Hatsuse is there, after all, and I am sure that he will take pity on you. You have made the pilgrimage over and over again by now, when you really are

---

28. Of Niou's.

29. Probably a younger brother of Niou.

30. Gōma: one of the eight stages of the life of the Buddha Shakyamuni, when he sat beneath the Bodhi Tree and quelled the demonic forces that would have prevented him from reaching enlightenment.

not used to such journeys, and I pray
that you will have such fortune
as to amaze everyone who has
been looking down on you.
Do you really think that
you are going to have
everyone laughing
at you in the end?"
Hers was an opti-
mistic view of life.

Driving a horse

They heard His
Highness hurrying away. He
went out the gate on their side, presumably because
it was closer to the palace, and his voice reached them. It had a superbly noble quality, but they found themselves wishing to stop their ears when he passed by humming some fine old poem. A ten-man escort went with him, mounted on horses
from distant provinces.

The mistress of His Highness's wing at Nijō pitied her visitor and easily imagined how upset she must be, but she sent her a message as though she knew nothing
about it. "Her Majesty is ill, and His Highness has gone to her," she said. "He will
not be back this evening. I am not feeling quite right—perhaps it was washing my
hair—and I am still up. Do come and see me. You must be rather bored."

"I am feeling very unwell just now. Perhaps later, when I feel better." The nurse
brought her the answer.

"What is the matter?" she immediately inquired.

"I do not know exactly. I just feel very ill."

Ukon and Shōshō exchanged glances. "She must be feeling absolutely miserable."

It was worse than if the young woman had been no concern of hers. The
Commander is talking as though he had some interest in her, she reflected, but how
shameless he will think her now! That man has no self-control whatever, and he
loves to pour out false and offensive accusations, but he seems to take a wonderfully
indulgent view of his own somewhat strange carryings-on. On the other hand, *he*,
who is always so dauntingly judicious about declaring himself at all, seems now to
be faced with yet another undeserved disappointment. I knew nothing about her for
all those years, but she is so pretty and has so much character that I cannot abandon
her now—she is too sweet and dear, and life is just too difficult and too full of trials.
I know my own position leaves much to be desired as well, but although I might
have had the same sort of trouble, I quite agree that I am indeed fortunate never to
have fallen so far. I myself would have nothing to worry about if the Commander
could only now safely give up his tiresome advances. Her abundant hair took a long
time to dry, and she grew weary of having to stay up. In her plain white shift and
gown[31] she looked perfectly charming.

---

31. She cannot wear more layers or colors because her hair is still wet.

Her visitor really was not feeling well, but the nurse insisted on having her be-stir herself. "This will not do! You *must* be sensible and go to see her, or she will think something actually happened. Let me tell Ukon and the others the whole story."

She went to the sliding panel. "I should like to speak to Ukon," she said. Ukon came. "There has been a most unpleasant incident here, and my mistress has a fever. The poor thing is seriously unwell. She says that she would be grateful for some words of comfort from Her Highness. She has done nothing wrong, but she still feels extremely bad. It would be one thing if she already knew a little of the world, but she does not, and I think that she is much to be pitied." She got her mistress up and made her go.

Propelled by her nurse, she came to sit before Her Highness, hardly knowing where she was and ashamed of what everyone must be thinking of her, yet at the same time all too innocently docile. With her back to the lamp and hiding the soak-ing hair at her forehead, she had no less to commend her than did her half sister, whom the women thought peerless. In fact, she was quite lovely. Something dread-ful will happen, Ukon and Shōshō realized, if he decides that he simply must have her. He is so quick to admire anyone new, even if she has nothing like these looks! They could see the young woman quite well, since in Her Highness's presence she could not always keep her face turned the other way.

Her Highness talked to her very kindly. "Please do not feel as though you are a stranger here," she said. "I have so little forgotten my sister during all the time that has passed since she died that I wish I myself had never survived her; but it is a great comfort to see you, who look so like her. I have no one else who cares for me, you see, and I should be very happy if you were to think of me as fondly as she did."

She was too overcome with shyness and too much from the country. The only reply she could manage was "All these years you seemed so far away, and seeing you now makes me feel much better." Her voice was very youthful.

Her Highness had her women bring out pictures and looked at them while Ukon read the words. Her visitor could not remain shy forever, even when sitting straight across from her, and she gazed at them, too, her face flawlessly lovely in the lamplight. Her forehead and her eyes seemed fragrant with a sweet beauty, and her unaffected nobility of manner so precisely recalled the sister whom Her Highness had lost that Her Highness barely had eyes for the pictures at all. What a dear face! she thought. How can she possibly be so like her? She must take after our father. My sister took after our father and I after our mother, or so I gather the old women used to say. How extraordinary that someone else should so resemble her! Tears came to her eyes while she contemplated her visitor and recalled the image of those whom she had lost. *She* was sweetly pliant, too, despite her infinitely lofty distinc-tion of manner; in fact, she was gentle and yielding to a fault. This young woman seems still to be shy and ill at ease about everything—perhaps that is why she seems on the whole to lack grace in comparison. With a little more polish she will not be at all unworthy of the Commander. She weighed the matter like an elder sister.

It was nearly dawn when they lay down to sleep after a long talk. Her High-ness had her half sister lie next to her and touched a little on their father's life over-the years. The young woman wished that she had known him and bitterly regretted never having seen him at all.

The women who knew about the evening before went on whispering commiseratingly about it. "I wonder what happened. She's awfully pretty. No good will come of this for her, no matter how fond of her Her Highness may be. The poor thing!"

"No, no, that cannot be right!" Ukon broke in. "Her nurse caught me and poured out the whole sad story, and, judging from what she said, nothing happened at all. His Highness went off humming and whistling in the mood of 'together yet not together.' "[32]

"Oh, come. He probably did that on purpose. I just don't know."

"She was quite cool and collected last night in the lamplight—she didn't *look* as though anything had happened."

The nurse ordered a carriage and returned to the Hitachi residence, where she reported the incident to her charge's mother. The Governor's wife was devastated. People will make the worst of this, she said to herself, leaping to her own conclusions. And what can Her Highness be thinking? In a case like this, jealousy knows no rank.

She went there that same evening. Fortunately, His Highness was not at home. "I know that I brought you my impossibly childish daughter in the belief that she would be safe here, but I am afraid that I have a weasel-like turn of mind[33]—my household, such as it is, hates me for it."

"She does not seem nearly as childish as you say." Her Highness smiled. "What worries me, though, is that you should seem so anxious about her!" The superb look in her eyes pricked the woman's conscience. What is she thinking? she wondered. She could not broach what she really had to say.

"I take it as a great honor to have my daughter here with you," she began; "I feel as though an old prayer of mine has been answered, and as far as others are concerned—those who may hear of it—it is all to her credit. Nonetheless, I can see that I should have refrained. I should have sent her off to the mountains, as I had first meant to do." She was weeping piteously.

"Why need you worry so about her being here? I do not intend to reject her, whatever happens, and even if a certain gentleman misbehaves sometimes, everyone here knows about it and is on the lookout for it. I am sure that she will come to no harm. May I ask what it is that you fear?"

"I do not believe for a moment that you would withdraw your goodwill from her, and as to His Late Highness's having preferred not to recognize her, I would not dream of even mentioning it. No, it is not because of that that I look to you, but rather because of another tie, one that I know you will honor."[34] After this earnest appeal she went on, "Tomorrow and the next day she has strict seclusion to observe, and she ought to be somewhere where she can do it properly. I shall bring her

---

32. *Genji monogatari kochūshakusho in'yō waka* 394 includes the same expression (*aitemo awanu*, "together yet not together"), but the poem does not seem to fit, since it suggests that the lovers were in fact "together" (made love), however briefly.

33. A suspicious, anxious disposition.

34. She is a niece of Naka no Kimi's mother.

back." She took her daughter away with her. This was a sad disappointment for Her Highness, but she did not try to stop her. The calamity had so upset the young woman's mother that she left without even a proper good-bye.

She had a little house for the times when she might need to respect a directional taboo. It was in the Sanjō district and very pretty, but it was not fully furnished yet because it was not quite finished. "Oh, dear, what a time I am having with you!" she said. "What is the point of living at all when absolutely nothing goes right? If I had only myself to look after, I would just disappear somewhere and be a nobody. As for this connection with Her Highness, people will think us perfectly ridiculous if we get too close to her, when her father used to make me so angry, and then something really dreadful happens. Oh, it is awful! This place is not very nice, I know, but please stay here, and do not let *anyone* know where you are. I will manage something for you somehow." She prepared to go.

Her daughter burst into tears and made a very sad sight as she reflected despondently on her dwindling prospects in life. The mother was of course even sorrier to imagine her going to waste and longed to see her safely settled after all, but after that dismal incident she worried that the whole world might now call her daughter shameless. Despite understanding a good deal, she tended still to be irritable and to act on her own whim. She might manage to keep her out of sight at the Hitachi residence, but she hated to hide her that way and had chosen this course instead. Still, they had never been apart for all those years, and both were now disconsolate. They had always been together day and night.

"The house is not really safe yet in this state," she said. "Remember that. Have all the things brought out and use them. I have left orders for guards to be on duty at night, but I am quite worried even so. It is just that it is so unpleasant at home, with the Governor furious and fed up with me as he is." She left in tears.

The Governor took the Lieutenant for a priceless jewel, and as he prepared to receive him in that spirit, he was angry with his wife for failing most deplorably to join in the effort. To her, however, the Lieutenant was the detestable cause of all her troubles. She reviled the man, considering the present plight of *her* priceless jewel, and she was very little help indeed. He had looked like nothing beside His Highness, and that had so lowered him in her esteem that despite having once meant to treat him as a treasure, she was now quite finished with that idea.

I wonder what he looks like in *my* house, she thought; I have never seen him at his ease. She therefore went to peer in at him in the middle of the day, when he was quietly there with his new wife. He was near the veranda, looking into the garden and wearing plum red over soft white silk twill. He looked quite handsome. What was wrong with him?

Her daughter, not yet fully grown, lay innocently beside him. They made a disappointing pair beside her memory of Their Highnesses side by side. He was joking with the women nearby. Relaxed like this, he was not the insipid embarrassment that she had seen, and she had just decided that that Lieutenant must have been someone else when he said, "His Highness of War of course has especially beautiful *hagi*. I wonder where he got the seeds. The fronds are just like these, but they have exceptional charm. I was there the other day, but I never managed to pick any because he was just on his way out. He was humming 'when one mourns just to see them fade';[35] I wish I could have let you young women see him! Then he made a poem of his own."

Well, well, she found herself whispering, so *that* is what he has to say for himself! Why, he is worthless, and yes, he does make a pathetic spectacle. How dare he spout poems? Still, he seemed not to be completely illiterate, and she thought that she might try him. She sent him,

> *"You claimed for your own a little* hagi *plant whose fronds, above, keep their grace;*
> *tell me, then, what sort of dew has wilted the ones below?"*[36]

This gave him a pang of guilt.

> *"Alas, had I known the young* hagi *plant to spring from Miyagi Moor,*
> *not for anything at all would I have aspired elsewhere.*[37]

I should like very much to explain myself to you in person," he replied.

He must have heard about His Highness, she said to herself; and she could think of nothing but making her beloved daughter the equal of her half sister. Somehow the figure of the Commander kept returning fondly to mind. She had thought him as splendid as His Highness, for whom she no longer had any use at all; it infuriated her to think how contemptuously the man had imposed himself on her daughter. The Commander, on the other hand, had refrained from making any hasty approaches, even though in truth he was keen on her. What remarkable discretion! She was impressed, and now that he was always on her mind, she reflected, A young woman would, then, obviously think of him even more. I should be ashamed of myself for ever having wanted that horrid fellow! Nothing mattered to her but her daughter, and she lapsed easily into reverie, during which she imagined everything turning out well after all—a thoroughly unlikely prospect, for, she reminded herself, he is of lofty birth and of very great personal distinction, and the lady he has accepted is no more commonplace than he. What could possibly attract him to my daughter? Judging from what I gather of the way people are, worth or lack of it, distinction or vulgarity, all depends on birth, and likewise looks and wit. Look at my own children! Are they anything like this one? Everyone in this house thinks the Lieutenant a wonder, but now that I have seen him after His Highness, I know all too well how dreary he is. And she—what could she do but feel awe and shame in the sight of someone who now has the Emperor's cherished daughter? Her mind was wandering.

The unfinished house offered little to do, the greenery in the garden was depressing, the only people going in and out had uncouth, Eastern accents, and there

---

35. *Shūishū* 183, by Ise, written to go on a painted screen: "Ah, dew that might well break the autumn *hagi* fronds, when one mourns just to see them fade!"

36. The "little *hagi* plant" (*kohagi*) is Ukifune and the dew the Lieutenant.

37. "If I had known she was a Prince's daughter . . ." Miyagi Moor (Miyagino), a place-name associated with *hagi* in poetry, contains the syllables *miya*, "Prince."

was not a single flower to look at anywhere. The days and nights followed one another amid these untidy, cheerless surroundings, and meanwhile the young woman dwelled on the memory of Her Highness, whom she missed in her youthful way. Impressions of that most importunate presence came back to her, too. What were all those things he was saying? He had talked on so long and so sweetly! And the delicious smell he left behind him—she felt as though it was with her still. The frightening memory came back as well.

Her mother wrote her a most touching letter. She seemed extremely anxious about her and very sorry, but her daughter could hardly believe that anything would come of it. She began to cry. "You must feel so bored there and so out of place!" her mother had written. "Please put up with it a little longer, though"; in answer to which she wrote, "Why should I be bored? It is very nice here.

> A pure joy to me it would be, and nothing else, if I only knew
> that the place where I am now was not in the world at all."[38]

At these lines, so like a young girl's, she burst into tears. It was hard, having to send her away like this and make her so unhappy! She replied,

> "Seek out if you will somewhere very far away from this sorry world,
> yet I would still wish to see honor for you and just praise."

This exchange of quite commonplace sentiments gave comfort to both.

The Commander often lay awake at night, as was usual for him when late autumn approached, filled with sad thoughts of one whom he could never forget, and the news that the temple was finished therefore prompted him to go to Uji in person. He had not been there for so long that the colored leaves on the hills were a wonder to him. The main house, at first dismantled, had been magnificently rebuilt. He remembered how frugally His Late Highness had lived there, and he missed him enough to wish that he had changed nothing. This left him in a more than usually thoughtful mood. The original, thoroughly sober furnishings as well as the daintier, more feminine ones, all quite unusual, from the sisters' part of the house had gone to serve in the monks' lodges together with such larger, more practical items as palm-leaf screens. He had had new furnishings nicely made, in a style suitable for a mountain villa, and now that they were in place, the house looked very handsome and elegant.

He sat on a rock beside the garden brook and sighed.

> "Why should this clear stream, running on so forever, not even retain
> the insubstantial image of dear faces long since gone?"

He brushed away his tears and went to talk to the nun Ben. At the sight of his visible distress she, too, looked as though she would weep. He sat for a while leaning

---

38. *Shūishū* 506: "How I long for somewhere not in the world at all to hide the many years that burden me!"

on the lintel, and they talked with the edge of the blind between them raised. Ben remained out of sight behind a standing screen.

"I gather that a young woman you know has been at His Highness's recently," he said when their conversation gave him an opening to do so. "I felt too awkward to go and visit her there, though. Please continue to convey my messages."

"I had a letter from her mother the other day," Ben replied. "Apparently she has been moving here and there because of a directional taboo. Lately the poor thing has been in hiding in a curious little house. She would bring her here, where she feels that she would be quite safe, if only the place were a little closer; but the steep mountain trails on the way give her pause. That is what she wrote."

"People are always afraid of those mountain trails, but *I* never tire of coming here! I am overcome when I think what sort of tie from past lives may explain it." As so often, there were tears in his eyes. "Very well, then," he went on, "please get in touch with her at her refuge. You do not plan to go there yourself, by any chance?"

"I can easily send her a message from you there, but I am quite reluctant to see the City; I never even go to call at His Highness's."

"But why? It would be all very well if your trip were likely to start people talking, but surely even the holy men of Mount Atago[39] leave the mountain now and again. What *is* holy is to break a great vow to assist a layman in need."

"Saving someone else is too much for me, and besides, there would certainly be unpleasant talk." She was clearly troubled.

"But this is the perfect time!" He was unusually insistent. "I shall send you a carriage the day after tomorrow. You must find out exactly where she is. I promise not to misbehave." He smiled.

I do not like this, she thought. What does he intend? Still, he was not a man to do anything rash or ill considered, and she knew that he would be discreet for her sake, too. "Very well, then, I will do it. She is apparently not far from where you live. She must have a letter from you first. Otherwise, if she gets the impression that I started all this, she may think me an officious old Iga matchmaker,[40] and I would not want that."

"A letter is easy; the trouble is the way people talk. For all I know, they may decide that the Right Commander now aspires to marry the daughter of the Governor of Hitachi. I gather that the man likes to assert himself." Ben sympathized with a bitter smile.

He left at dark. On the way he had autumn leaves and woodland flowers picked so that he could give them to Her Highness his wife. He was quite good about such things, but he treated her with formal constraint, and it does not appear that he and she were very close. He granted her the highest respect, however, since His Majesty had spoken to Her Cloistered Highness about the matter, as any father might have done. It made things difficult for him to have so many tricky private concerns on top of all that he had to do to satisfy these two.

---

39. A mountain (3,049 feet) just northwest of Kyoto. It is unclear whether "holy men" is meant to be singular or plural.

40. Iga is a province in central Japan, but it is not really clear what *Iga tōme* means. An old woman matchmaker is the interpretation of the eighteenth-century scholar Motoori Norinaga.

Very early on the appointed day, he sent off a favorite junior retainer and an ox driver chosen because no one knew him. "Get some country people from my estates to fill out the escort," he said.

The nun got ready and boarded the carriage, despite her very great reluctance, since he had told her that she simply must go. Seeing the hills and moors brought all sorts of old memories to mind, and she arrived at the end of a day spent lost in thought. Her carriage was drawn in to a thoroughly deserted spot, and she announced her arrival through the man who had guided her to the house. A young person who had been on the pilgrimage to Hatsuse came out and helped her to alight.

After dreary days and nights in this distressing place, the young woman she had come to see was delighted by the arrival of someone with whom she could talk over the past, and she readily invited her in; after all, the nun had served her father, and she had no doubt that they would soon be close. "I have treasured the memory of our first meeting, and you have never been out of my mind," the nun began, "but since I have renounced the world, I do not even call on Her Highness. Nevertheless, the Commander insisted so strenuously that I made up my mind to come after all." The young woman and her nurse, whom he had so impressed, were grateful for this evidence that he had not forgotten, but they were startled nonetheless by his swiftness to act.

The evening was all but over when a discreet rapping at the gate announced the arrival of a messenger from Uji. Ben suspected who it was, but she nevertheless had the gate opened. To everyone's surprise a carriage was led in.

"I should like to speak to my lady the nun." The man had been instructed to announce himself as the steward of one of the Commander's nearby estates. Ben slipped out to the doorway. A light rain was falling, and an icy wind blew in raindrops accompanied by an indescribably delicious fragrance. Ah, so it was he! He was a figure to make a girl's heart beat fast, and they felt caught out not to be ready for him; in fact, his arrival was so unexpected that they were quite upset. "What is going on?" they asked each other.

"I have come to tell you, undisturbed, all the feelings that have so filled my heart for months now." Such was the message he gave the nun for her.

What can I possibly say to him? The young woman was plainly at a loss, and her nurse took pity on her. "Now that he is here, you cannot possibly send him away again just like that," she said. "I shall secretly inform your mother. It is no distance, you know."

"That is silly!" Ben interjected. "Why do that? Just because two young people want to talk, that hardly means that all of a sudden they are going to be everything to each other! His lordship is an extraordinarily patient, circumspect man, and he would never take any liberties that had not been granted him."

Meanwhile it was raining somewhat harder, and the sky was very dark. The guards were making their rounds, calling to each other in their strange accents.

"The wall there to the southeast has collapsed—it's a spot to watch."

"If we're going to get that carriage in, let's do it and shut the gate."

"The men in the visitor's escort are so slow!"

To the Commander all this sounded quite strange and rather alarming. He sat at the edge of the rustic veranda, humming "there is not one house at Sano ford!"[41]

"Are the weeds so thick that they wholly bar your gate, O eastern cottage—
too long, too long I waited while the pouring rain came down!"[42]

Sliding door

The little breezes he made as he brushed off the raindrops carried a striking scent that must have astonished the country folk from the East.

He could not possibly be put off with excuses, and they therefore admitted him after preparing a seat in the southern aisle. When their mistress turned out to be reluctant to receive him, they made her move forward toward him and then slightly opened the locked sliding door. "I deplore the Hida carpenter who made this door. Never before have I been on the wrong side of one like this,"[43] he complained; and then, somehow, in he came. He never mentioned seeking the doll image of someone else. He only said, "I have wanted you, you know, ever since to my surprise I glimpsed you through a crack. This must be destiny at work. It is extraordinary how much you mean to me!" This seems to be the sort of thing he told her. She was so very sweet and gentle that he was deeply touched and found her thoroughly worthy.

In no time it felt as though day must have broken, but no cock crowed, and all sorts of drawling voices passed in the nearby avenue, hawking things that meant nothing to him. They looked to him like demons, bearing their wares on their heads that way in the first light of dawn, but the novelty of a night spent among these weeds was delightful as well.

There came sounds of guards opening the gate and leaving. When he heard the other men come in and lie down, he called for his carriage to be brought to the double doors. Then he picked her up and put her in it. Her women were aghast. It

---

41. *Man'yōshū* 267, by Naganoimiki Okimaro: "Alas that it should now be raining, when on Miwa Cape there is not one house at Sano ford!"

42. Kaoru's poem incorporates words and phrases from the *saibara* song "The Eastern Cottage."

43. The best carpenters were thought to come from the province of Hida, in the mountains of central Japan. There was not normally a wooden sliding door (*yarido*) between the chamber and the aisle.

was all so sudden! "But, my lord," they protested, "it is the ninth month![44] This is not right! What are you doing?"

The nun Ben had not foreseen this, and she felt very upset, but she did what she could to calm them. "Obviously his lordship has his own plans," she said. "Please set your minds at rest. Ninth month or not, tomorrow, I hear, is the equinox."[45] It was the thirteenth of the month.

"I cannot come with you now," she told him. "Her Highness might learn that I have been in the City, and it would then be extremely tactless of me to go back again without telling her."

"I would prefer you to make your apologies later," the Commander insisted, embarrassed to think of anyone telling Her Highness quite yet. "Besides, I will need your help when we get there."

"Would someone else please come, too?" he added. The nun got in with Jijū, who was particularly close to her mistress. The nurse, the page girl who had come with Ben, and the others remained behind, feeling quite stunned.

Ben assumed that they had not far to go, but it turned out that they were off to Uji. The Commander had provided for a change of oxen. By daybreak they had left the bank of the Kamo River and reached Hōshōji.[46] Now that Jijū could see him a little, she forgot every demand of decent manners and gave in to rapt and longing wonder.

The young woman herself lay facedown, dazed by the shock. "The rocky places are very difficult," he said, taking her in his arms. The silk gauze long dress hung to divide the carriage[47] glowed in the light of the newly risen sun, and the nun felt excruciatingly out of place. Ah, she reflected sadly, it is His Late Highness's eldest daughter I should have seen like this with the Commander! What strange surprises old age can bring! Her face puckered up, and despite her best efforts she wept. The heartless Jijū thought her perfectly horrid. Why, she thought, she doesn't belong here anyway at the happy start of a marriage! What business does she have blubbering away like that? She just took it for granted that old people are all too given to tears.

The young woman was his now, and the Commander certainly found her very nice, but under such skies his sense of loss only mounted, and the farther they went into the hills, the more thickly the mists seemed to rise around him. His sleeves as he leaned on an armrest, lost in thought, trailed away out of the carriage, one on the other, wet with the mists of the river. The scarlet of the gown looked wrong against the petal blue of the dress cloak:[48] he noticed it at the top of a steep slope and drew them both in.

---

44. An inauspicious month for a marriage.

45. In other words, the first day of winter. If true (it is possible in the lunar calendar), this might make the moment less inauspicious.

46. A temple built by Fujiwara no Tadahira in 925 on the site of present Tōfukuji, east of the Kamo River and a little way south of the City.

47. Into a front compartment for Kaoru and Ukifune and a rear one for Ben and Jijū.

48. The two colors together suggest futaai (a violet or blue-gray), which reminds Kaoru of mourning.

"Now that she is mine, to keep fresh that memory, how the morning dew
settles in fast-falling drops on these sadly moistened sleeves!"

he murmured unconsciously. At this the nun only drenched her sleeves the more, to
young Jijū's disgust and dismay, for it seemed to her that their happy trip had taken
on a thoroughly dismal character. Ben's stifled sniffling started the Commander quietly blowing his nose as well.

Concern for the feelings of the young woman beside him prompted him to
observe, "It saddens me, somehow, to think how often I have taken this path over
the years. Do sit up a little and look at the colors on the hills. You are so silent!" He
made her sit up, and the way she looked out shyly, her face prettily hidden behind
her fan, struck him as remarkably similar, except that she seemed all too worryingly
meek and mild. His lost love had had a childlike quality, too, but also what depth of
reflection! His sorrow, which still had nowhere to go, seemed capable of filling the
vast, empty heavens.[49]

He thought when they arrived, Ah, perhaps her spirit is still lingering here,
watching me! And whose fault is it, then, if I myself am still wandering back and
forth this way? After alighting he made sure that she was comfortable before going
off elsewhere. He was so kind, and he spoke to her so gently, that despite bitter
sighs over what her mother might be thinking, she plucked up the courage to get
down as well. The nun took care not to alight at the same spot but had the carriage
brought round to her gallery, which the Commander thought excessive in a setting
that really required no such punctiliousness. From his estates he summoned as usual
a bustling throng of men. The nun provided the young woman's meal. The journey
had taken them through dense and gloomy woods, but here all was bright and
open. After those days spent in dreary isolation, she enjoyed seeing how the design
of house and grounds took advantage of the riverside setting and of the colors of
the hills, but she still wondered nervously what he meant to do with her.

He sent letters to the City. "I had left the altar decorations unfinished, so I
hurried down here today, since the day is propitious. Now, however, I am feeling
unwell, and I have also remembered that I should be in seclusion. I shall take care to
stay here today and tomorrow." So he wrote, more or less, both to his mother and to
Her Highness his wife.

She was shy when he came in looking even better in casual dress, but she sat
there without feeling any need to hide her face. The layered colors she had on were
ones that she thought became her, but they had a touch of the country about them,
and all he could think of was *her* noble grace then, in those comfortably soft clothes
she wore. However, he could appreciate the lovely sweep and neatly trimmed end
line of her hair. Her Highness had had particularly beautiful hair, but this was just as
good. What am I to do with her, though? he wondered. I do not like to imagine
how people will talk if I make much of her and take her into Sanjō,[50] but at the same

49. *Kokinshū* 488: "My love seems to fill all the vast, empty heavens; though I seek to dispel it, it has
nowhere else to go."
50. As a wife.

time I do *not* want just to treat her as one more gentlewoman. No, I must keep her hidden here awhile. Out of sympathy with her loneliness in his absence, he spent the rest of the day with her in intimate talk. He touched on the subject of His Late Highness and told her all sorts of amusing things about those days, but she remained so desperately shy and so bashfully unresponsive that he felt disappointed. Never mind, he thought, reconsidering, it is better to have her unfinished this way. I must teach her things. She would be no double of *her* if she liked to show off as rustics do, and if she were coarse and talked too fast.

He called for the *kin* and the *sō no koto* that were in the house. Alas, he did not for a moment suppose that she could play them, and he therefore tuned them himself. He himself was surprised to touch such instruments here, not having done so for ages—not since His Late Highness had died. The moon rose while he toyed nostalgically with the strings. His Late Highness's music on the *kin*, although never powerful, was always so beautiful and so profoundly moving! That came back to him now, and he went on to say, "You would have a little more depth if you, too, had grown up here while they were both alive. Even I, who am no relation, remember His Highness with great affection. Why did you have to spend so many years in a place like that?"

Her profile as she lay beside him, deeply embarrassed and fingering her white fan, was itself perfectly white, and the graceful lines of her hair brought *her* most poignantly to mind. Yes, he thought, I *must* cultivate in her a taste for such music. "Have you ever played an instrument like this, just a little?" he asked. " 'Ah, my darling!'—*that* koto[51] is one you *must* have learned."

"How could I, when I never even learned Yamato speech properly?"[52] she replied. She was not slow, he could see that. It would be painful for him, too, now, he knew, to have to leave her here and not to be able to come as he pleased. Yes, he certainly must have felt unusually strongly about her.

He pushed his instrument away. "On the terrace of the King of So, music of an evening *kin*,"[53] he sang; and the listening Jijū, who had known only men who draw the bow, was profoundly impressed. Actually, her admiration was somewhat misplaced because the color of the fan meant nothing to her—she did not know the story.[54] It is all very well, the Commander thought, but why did I sing *those* lines?

Refreshments arrived from the nun. Colored leaves, sprigs of ivy, and so on had been quite prettily disposed in the lid of a box, and the bright moonlight re-

---

51. The *wagon*, also known as *azuma-goto* ("Eastern koto"). "Ah, my darling!" (*aware waga tsuma*) seems to be a nickname for it, derived from the closing words of the *saibara* song "The Eastern Cottage."

52. A wordplay: "How should I know how to play the Eastern koto, when I never even learned Yamato *kotoba* ["Yamato speech"] properly?" Yamato speech is the language of the court: proper Japanese, so to speak, not a dialect like the language of the East.

53. From a couplet in Chinese, *Wakan rōei shū* 380, by Minamoto no Shitagō: "In Lady Ban's chamber, whiteness of an autumn fan; on the terrace of the King of So, music of an evening *kin*."

54. The couplet evokes the sad story of Lady Han (Chinese Ban), who was abandoned by the King of So (Chinese Chu) like a summer fan in autumn. To cool the flames of hurt and jealousy she had herself fanned with a large white fan, and Ukifune's fan, too, is white. It is not a good omen, hence Kaoru's dismay in the next sentence.

vealed that the paper on which they rested bore sturdy brush strokes.[55] His haste to read them when he noticed them made him look unusually hungry.

> *"A change of color has come over the ivy, now that it is fall,*
> *and yet how the past lives on in the brilliance of the moon!"*[56]

she had written in an old-fashioned hand. Moved and somewhat ashamed, he replied,

> *"The name of this place means what it has always meant, yet the love I knew*
> *has assumed another face in the moonlight of our room."*[57]

It was not really meant to be an answer, but they say Jijū took it to the nun.

55. Thick writing, presumably characteristic of an old woman like Ben.

56. The "change of color" alludes to Kaoru's shift of feeling from Ōigimi to Ukifune, and the moon to Kaoru himself. There is a wordplay on *sumeru* ("shine brightly" and "live").

57. "The name of this place" is Uji, which according to a conventional wordplay means also "hateful" to one bent on renunciation. In other words, "The profane world is still as hateful to me as it has always been . . ."

51

UKIFUNE

A Drifting Boat

Ukifune ("drifting boat," "boat adrift") is Ukifune's simile for herself in her poem of reply to Niou as they cross the Uji River together in this chapter:

"The enduring hue of the Isle of Orange Trees may well never change,
yet there is no knowing now where this drifting boat is bound."

RELATIONSHIP TO EARLIER CHAPTERS

"A Drifting Boat" begins where "The Eastern Cottage" and "The Ivy" end, and covers the beginning of Kaoru's twenty-seventh year.

PERSONS

The Commander, age 27 (Kaoru)

His Highness of War, 28 (Niou)

Her Highness, the wife of His Highness of War, 27 (Naka no Kimi)

A young woman, her half sister, around 22 (Ukifune)

A page girl of Naka no Kimi

Shōshō, Naka no Kimi's gentlewoman

The Chief Clerk and Deputy Commissioner of Ceremonial, Lord Michisada, Niou's retainer

Nakanobu, the Chief Clerk's father-in-law and Kaoru's retainer

Tokikata, the Deputy Governor of Izumo and Niou's retainer

Ukon, Ukifune's gentlewoman

Jijū, Ukifune's gentlewoman

Ukifune's nurse, Nanny

Ukifune's mother, the wife of the Governor of Hitachi (Chūjō no Kimi)

Ben, a nun at Uji (Ben no Ama)

Kaoru's messenger, a member of his escort

Niou's messenger

His Excellency, the Minister of the Right, 53 (Yūgiri)

A Constable

His Highness never forgot that all too approximate twilight encounter. She seems not to have been anyone of any great moment, he reflected, but in herself she was certainly *very* nice; and he chafed, ever the incorrigible gallant, at that frustration of his desire.

"What a fuss you *will* make over a little thing like that! I would never have thought it of you!" he complained scornfully. Her Highness considered in her dismay telling him the whole story but then thought better of it. No doubt *he* has not given her the most elevated reception,[1] she reflected, but he is sufficiently attached to her to keep her hidden away for himself, and if I were to tell His Highness about her, I cannot imagine him letting the matter pass. He is impossible. He has done each of the women here—every one who has at all caught his fancy—the injury of pursuing her even to her own home, and in *her* case he is quite certain to do something awful sooner or later, considering how long he has been smitten. If he gets news of her from somebody else, there it is—the result could be disaster for both, but there is simply no stopping him, and her being a relation would just make it worse. No, I will not have anything go wrong through any fault of mine. She therefore reluctantly told him nothing, and since she was not one to dissemble, she lived her life as might any other silently jealous woman.

The Commander meanwhile maintained a most remarkably leisurely attitude. It always pained him to imagine her looking forward to his coming, but his situation gave him little latitude, and in the absence of any plausible reason for making the journey, it was harder for him to do so than if the gods themselves had forbidden it.[2] I am going to look after her properly, he assured himself nevertheless. She will be my consolation in that mountain village, that much I have decided, and I must devise errands that will allow me to spend several quiet days with her there. Yes, now that I have her living where no one else can find her, I need only bring her round to seeing that it is all for the best; that way no one will have anything to say against me. Discretion is what matters. I would hate to have people thinking that it happened

---

1. Kaoru has not recognized Ukifune as a wife.
2. *Ise monogatari* 131 (section 71): "If you love me, then come to me—the journey is not one the gods forbid you."

Fringed basket

suddenly and wondering who she is and when it all began; that would not be what I have in mind. Besides, I do not like to imagine how the lady at His Highness's would feel when she found out; I would seem to have abandoned forever the place where I knew *her* and to have forgotten the past completely. Perhaps he was as usual being altogether too nonchalant. Still, he laid plans for bringing the young woman to the City and secretly had the necessary building work done.

To the considerable surprise of Her Highness's women, he continued to wait on Her Highness as faithfully as before, although he seemed quite taken up otherwise by a great many things. She had come to know the world rather better, and the more she saw and heard of him, the more she admired a steadfast loyalty to the past that struck her by now as the very model of enduring homage to a cherished memory. But while age conferred growing personal merit and public esteem on *him*, her husband's waywardness often made her wonder at destiny's strange ways. Why had she ended up not at all as her sister had wished, but given over instead to these anxieties and cares?

Still, she could not receive the Commander often. Too many months and years had come between what was now and what had once been, and to someone who did not know what he meant to her, she might look like an utter commoner for keeping up an old friendship that way, and considering who she was, she would do better to avoid flouting convention; besides, increasingly painful sensitivity to His Highness's endless suspicion made her so wary that she could not help distancing herself from him. Nevertheless, he continued to feel exactly the same regard for her as before. Meanwhile, quite apart from the strange unpleasantness provoked by his wanton nature, His Highness treasured his little son more and more as the irresistible child continued to grow, for he doubted that he would have another like him from anyone else, and his especially warm affection for his son's mother, with whom he felt so much more at home, allowed her to feel a little more secure than before.

He came to her once the early days of the first month were past, and he was playing with his son, now a year older, when toward midday a little page girl came tripping in carelessly to Her Highness with a wrapped letter done up in thin, deep green paper, a fringed basket attached to a seedling pine, and a formal, straight-folded letter.

"Where is all that from?" His Highness asked.

" 'From Uji, for Mistress Taifu,' the messenger said, but he did not quite know what to do with it, so I took it—I thought it should go to my lady as usual," the girl replied. She seemed quite excited.

"The basket is all colored metal,[3] and the pine is so well done it looks almost real!" the girl explained brightly, wreathed in smiles.

"Come, I want a look, too!" His Highness laughed, motioning for the things.

"Take the letters to Taifu," she said in dismay. She was blushing, which suggested to His Highness that they might be nicely disguised messages from the Commander; the fact that they were supposed to come from Uji certainly suggested as much. He took them himself. Still, he realized, it would be very awkward indeed if they *were*. "I shall open them, then," he said. "Will you be angry with me?"

"It is wrong, though! What business is it of yours to read casual letters between gentlewomen?" She spoke with affected calm.

"In that case I *shall* read them! Now, what could a woman's letter be like?" He opened one. The writing was very youthful.

"The year is over, and I have been out of touch so long," it read. "This mountain village is a dreary place. There is always mist clinging to the hills." And along one edge the sender had written, "Please give these to your little Prince—not that they are worth much, I am afraid." Nothing about it showed any particular character, but he could not imagine who it was from, and he therefore read the straight-folded letter with particularly eager interest. It, too, was indeed in a woman's hand.

"How are you getting on in the New Year? There must be all sorts of things happening to keep you amused. Here, the house is really very nice, but I do not think that it suits my lady well. I wish she would call on Her Highness now and then, instead of moping all the time as she does. It would do her good, but the idea seems to make her too timid and nervous. She sends a hare mallet for the little Prince and says please to give it to him when His Highness is away." It was a talkative letter, and the writer insisted on her dreary circumstances regardless of words out of keeping with the season.[4] He read it over and over, wondering.

"Now, tell me," he said. "Who wrote this?"

"They say that the daughter of one of the women who used to live in the mountain village has gone back there again lately for some reason," she replied. However, he noted that "she" seemed not to be just another woman in common service, and he thought back to that unfortunate incident.

The delightful hare mallet was obviously the work of someone with a great deal of time on her hands. He found, tied to a branch of the forked seedling pine threaded with made-up spearflower berries,[5]

> *"While no breath of age has yet touched this little pine, I would have you know*
> *it carries every heartfelt wish for the health of my young lord."*[6]

3. Probably copper green with verdigris.

4. She does not observe *kotoimi*, the avoidance of words like "unsuitable" ("I do not think it suits my lady very well"), "nervous," "fearful," and so on.

5. The red berries of the *yamatachibana* (modern Japanese *yabukōji*), which grows wild in the hills.

6. Ukifune's poem plays on *mataburi* ("fork") and *madafuri[nu]* ("not yet old"); and on *matsu* ("pine" and "await [a bright future]").

The poem had nothing unusual about it, but it caught his attention when he saw that it must be from the young woman who was so often on his mind.

"Answer it. You really must. I see no reason why you should have kept it from me. Why are you looking so unhappy? Anyway, I shall be off," he said, and left.

She had a quiet word with Shōshō. "This means trouble, you know. How could that little girl have taken in letters that none of you even managed to notice?"

"If we *had* noticed them, my lady, we would *never* have given them to you. That girl is a scatterbrain and much too forward. She does not promise well—the nice ones are the quiet ones."

"Now, now, you must not be angry with her. She is so little." She had been given the girl as a page in the winter of the year before, and His Highness was extremely fond of her because she was so sweet and pretty.

Hare mallet

His Highness went off to his own rooms in the main house. How odd! he reflected. I hear the Commander has gone on making trips to Uji over the years, and someone was saying that now and again he secretly even stays the night. I thought at the time that it was going rather far for him to be spending nights off in a place where he should not be anyway, just to honor old memories, but now I see he must have someone hidden there! At last it all seemed to make sense.

He summoned a Chief Clerk whom he employed as an authority on Chinese learning and who, he now remembered, had a close connection with the Commander's household. The man came. He asked him to take out some poetry collections for guessing rhymes and put them in a nearby cabinet. "By the way," he said, "is the Right Commander still going to Uji? He has done the new temple beautifully, I hear. I should very much like to see it."

"He has made the temple very large and handsome, they tell me, and the hall for the Perpetual Calling of the Name is particularly impressive. Last autumn he seems to have begun going there more often than before. Some of his servants were saying in confidence that he has a woman hidden there—someone he must certainly be quite keen on. All the men on his estates thereabouts have orders to place themselves at her disposal, act as guards, and so on, and he secretly sends her whatever she may need from the City as well. Just this twelfth month past they were wondering who the lucky woman could be and talking about how lonely it must be for her there even so, or so I was told."

Well, thought His Highness, I am glad I asked! "You have not heard clearly who she is, have you? There has always been a nun living there, and I gather that he visits her."

"No, Your Highness, the nun lives in the gallery. The person they mean has the new main house, where she is quite respectably installed with a number of rather nice gentlewomen."

"This is fascinating. But why does he have her there, and who can she be?

There really is something quite curious about him—he is just not like other people. I hear His Excellency of the Right complains how frivolous it is of him to be caught up in religion to the point even of spending the occasional night in a mountain temple, and indeed, I myself have wondered why he must be so devoted in private to following the path of the Buddha. His heart is still there in that village, they say, but then *this* is what it was all about! Well, well! The man who makes himself out to be worthier than anyone else turns out to be just the one with the completely unsuspected secret!" He was absolutely delighted. The Chief Clerk was the son-in-law of one of the Commander's closest retainers, and he presumably heard even things that the Commander wished to hide.

How am I to go about seeing for myself whether or not she is the one I happened on that time? His Highness wondered. She must have a good deal more to offer than just any attractive girl, if he is keeping her there that carefully. And how does she come to be close to my wife? It particularly annoyed him that his wife and the Commander had obviously conspired to hide her from him.

For the moment that was all he could think about. Once the New Year archery contest and the privy banquet were over and he had more leisure—since the announcement of the appointments list,[7] vital to the interests of so many, did not concern him—he spent all his time devising a secret trip to Uji. The Chief Clerk, who had certain hopes of his own, was then eager to do anything to please His Highness, day or night, and His Highness made more intimate use of him than usual.

"Are you prepared to carry out any task that I may set you, no matter how difficult?" The Chief Clerk respectfully signified that he was at His Highness's disposal. "It pains me very much to say this," His Highness went on, "but I have reason to believe that that woman now living in Uji is one who disappeared after I myself had come to know her a little, and that it is the Commander who made off with her. I cannot be certain, though, and I should therefore like to get a look at her so as to be able to tell whether or not it is really she. How can I be quite sure of evading discovery?"

That *is* difficult! the Chief Clerk said to himself. "The way there involves a very difficult passage through the hills, my lord," he nonetheless replied, "but the journey is not especially long. You could leave at nightfall and be there by the hour of the Boar or the Rat.[8] You should then be able to return just before dawn. Only the men who actually accompany you need know, and there is no reason why even they should have any real idea what you are doing."

"Exactly. I have been there myself once or twice. Anyone as likely to be criticized for thoughtless behavior as I am, though, is bound to feel nervous about what people may make of it." In fact he knew all too well that he most certainly should not do it, but now that he had already said that much, he could not give up the idea.

He chose his most intimate retainers to accompany him, including two or

---

7. In the middle or toward the end of the first month.
8. The hour of the Boar was roughly 9:00 to 11:00 P.M., that of the Rat between 11:00 P.M. and 1:00 A.M.

three men who had taken him there of old, the Chief Clerk, and, in addition, his own young foster brother, a Chamberlain who had been given a promotion to the fifth rank. Upon setting out this way, after ascertaining through the Chief Clerk that there was no chance of the Commander going there himself that day or the next, he thought back to times gone by. What a thing to do to the man who had then always taken him there in a spirit of extraordinarily close friendship! His every movement even within the City was of course likely to be noted, and he knew that the journey was not for such as he to make, but he still set out, despite fear and guilt, on horseback and in disguise.[9] The farther they advanced into the hills, the more his heart beat as he wondered, Will I *ever* get there? How will it go? And what a miserable disappointment if I have to go back again without really meeting her! A carriage took him to the vicinity of Hōshōji, but after that he rode.

He hastened on and arrived late in the evening. The Chief Clerk had found out all he needed to know from people at the Commander's residence who were familiar with the Uji house, so that he was able to evade the guards. He slipped in through the reed fence that screened off the west side, damaging it very little in the process. He did not quite know how to go farther, since he had never been there before, but he found that there were few people about, and on the south side of the main house he noted the glow of a lamp and heard the rustling of silks.

He went back to His Highness. "They seem still to be up, my lord," he reported. "You need only enter through here."[10] He led His Highness in.

His Highness stepped up silently and found a lattice shutter with a crack, though the Iyo blind rattled alarmingly when he went up to it. The house was certainly new and handsome, but it was not after all perfectly finished, for there were gaps here and there that they had done nothing to fill; no doubt they assumed that no one would ever approach and wish to peer in. The cloth panel of the standing curtain was draped over the crosspiece. Three or four women sat sewing by the lamp's brightest light, and a pretty page girl was spinning. He recognized the girl's face: yes, he had seen it before at home, also by lamplight. Not that a first glance may not be deceptive; but there was the young woman they had called Ukon. The girl herself was lying with her head on her arm, gazing at the lamp. Her eyes and forehead, with her hair spilling over them, had a wonderfully elegant beauty. She looked very like the lady in his wing at Nijō.

Ukon was preparing to sew a hem. "If you do go, though, my lady," she said, "it will be some time before you return. His lordship is supposed definitely to come on the first, after the business of the appointments list is over. A messenger told us yesterday. What did he say in his letter?"

The girl seemed thoroughly dispirited and did not answer.

"Just think how bad it would look if you appeared just to have gone off to hide!" Ukon continued.

"You should at least write to him, to let him know you have gone," the woman sitting across from Ukon added. "How could you allow yourself to disappear with-

9. He is probably in a hunting cloak, a level of dress far below the one proper for him.
10. Through the break in the reed fence.

out a word? And you must come straight back when you are done with your pilgrimage. I know that you are not happy here, but you are used to being as quiet and comfortable as you could wish, and I expect it will soon be at your mother's that you feel away from home."

"It would look better and be much easier if you were to wait a little longer for his lordship to come," another ventured. "You can see your mother as much as you like once he has taken you to the City. Your nurse, with all due respect, is awfully hasty, and she was much too quick to persuade your mother that this was a good idea. It has always been true, and it still is, that patience and caution prevail in the end."

"I wonder why you do not keep Nanny[11] here. Old people can make so much trouble!" Ukon seemed to have it in for anyone like the nurse. His Highness heartily agreed when he looked back on that evening, and he felt as though he must have dreamed it all.

After more talk of the same painfully private nature, one of the women remarked, "Her Highness at Nijō has been remarkably fortunate, though. His Excellency of the Right may be ever so impressive, but despite all that grand fuss of his, *she* is the one who has done extraordinarily well ever since the young Prince was born. *She* has no one pestering her with bright ideas. Apparently she can live in peace and give due thought to whatever she does."

"You will do just as well, though, if his lordship goes on being this attentive!"

The girl sat up a little. "I will not listen to such talk! You are welcome to compare me to complete strangers in whatever way you like, but I would appreciate it if you did not discuss Her Highness that way. It would be mortifying if she were to hear of it."

How *are* the two of them related? he wondered. She looks so like her. Still, the lady at Nijō far outdid the girl before him in distinction and noble grace. This one was certainly attractive in all sorts of ways, but no more. In any case, now that he had recognized her as the one who had been so continually on his mind, he was in no mood to give up even if he noted a discordant trait or two and a touch of the commonplace; in fact, after getting so full a view of her, he just went on staring, frantic to find a way to possess her.

"I am so sleepy!" said Ukon. "For some reason I slept badly last night. I shall finish this sewing first thing in the morning. Even if your mother comes as fast as she can, her carriage will not get here until the sun is high." She gathered up all the things she had been working on, hung them over the crosspiece of the standing curtain, and lay down in a corner as though for a nap. Her mistress moved to lie down farther back in the room. Ukon went briefly to the north aisle, came back again, and stretched out at her mistress's feet.

The sleepy Ukon dropped off immediately—that much His Highness could tell. Not knowing what else to do, he rapped softly on the shutter. Ukon heard him. "Who is it?" she asked. She gathered from the dignity of his voice when he

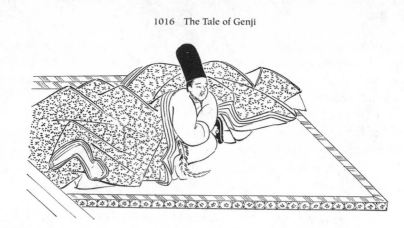

Bedclothes

cleared his throat that the Commander must have arrived, and she rose and came toward him.

"Please open this," he said.

"But this is strange! We were not expecting you at all! And it must be so late!"

"Nakanobu said your mistress is going on a pilgrimage, and the shock brought me here straightaway. I had an awful journey. Anyhow, open up!" He spoke so low and mimicked the Commander's voice so expertly that the truth never occurred to her. She unlocked the shutter and swung it open.

"I had a very frightening experience on the way—that is why I am dressed like this. Dim the lamp."

"Oh, how dreadful!" Ukon removed it, all aflutter.

"Do not let anyone see me. And do not get people up just because I am here." He cleverly managed to make his voice, which slightly resembled the Commander's anyway, sound exactly like it. In he came. Something awful had happened to him, he said. Ukon wondered with sympathy how he was dressed, and she peered at him discreetly. His costume was very soft and fine, and his fragrance was as delicious as always.

He went straight to the girl, undressed, and lay down beside her as though it were the most natural thing in the world. "Surely you would prefer your usual room, my lord," Ukon offered, but he did not reply, so she drew the covers over him and got the women to move off a little before going back to sleep. They were not accustomed to entertaining his escort in any case.

"How remarkable of him to come like this in the middle of the night!" the women murmured. "She has no idea how strongly he feels about her!"

"Hush! Be quiet! Whispering is especially tiresome at night!" Ukon silenced them before she lay down, too.

The young woman beside him realized with utter horror that he was not who he claimed to be, but he stopped her crying out. The outrage was worthy of someone capable of almost anything, even in a place that required him to be on his best behavior. She might have been able to resist him if she had known from the start that he was someone else, but by now she felt she was dreaming, and meanwhile, little by little, he told her how painful it had been for him that time and how he had continued to think of her ever since, until she soon understood that it was His Highness.

Transfixed with shame, she thought of his wife and wept copiously, being quite unable to do anything else. His Highness himself was more upset than elated, and he, too, wept to think how impossible it might be for him ever to be with her again.

Daybreak came, and the light grew. His men came around, clearing their throats. Ukon heard them and prepared to wait upon her mistress. His Highness, who had not the slightest wish to go, longed only for more time with her, and he was so afraid of being unable ever to return that he decided instead to spend the day exactly where he was. Bother them if they are rushing about in the City looking for me, he thought, I might as well enjoy life while it lasts! The very idea of going back now made him feel as though he really *was* going to die.

He therefore summoned Ukon. "You may think me mad, but I do not plan to leave today. Have my men disappear somewhere nearby. Tokikata is to go to the City and give out some plausible story that I am on secret retreat at a mountain temple."

Ukon, aghast, fought to master the panic that threatened to engulf her as she contemplated her error of the evening before. There is no point in making a great thing of it now, she assured herself, and besides, that would only give offense. If she came to mean this much to him during that strange encounter, it was obviously a matter of inevitable destiny for both. Nobody in particular had anything to do with it.

"It appears that her mother is to come for her today, Your Highness," she said. "May I ask what you propose to do? It is too late to inform her of the destiny that has overtaken her daughter. This is the wrong moment, to say the least. Perhaps I might suggest that you leave today and return at your leisure if you still wish to do so."

Well spoken! he thought, and he continued aloud, "I have been thinking about her lately until I hardly know what I am doing, and people's gossip and complaints mean nothing to me anymore. I am a desperate man. Would anyone like me undertake such a journey if he had any concern for himself? Answer her mother that, for example, she has to remain in seclusion today. Just think up *something* to spare her and me having anyone else find out about this. You may save yourself making any other suggestion." His enchantment seemed almost to have obliterated any concern for criticism.

Ukon went out and spoke to the men who had been hoping to rouse His Highness. "Those are His Highness's wishes," she said, "but please remind him how very bad this looks. Surely his escort can discourage completely outrageous behavior, even if he himself means to pursue it. How can you possibly have brought him here like children? What if a peasant were to insult him?" The Chief Clerk stood there thinking how thoroughly unfortunate it indeed was.

"And which of you is Tokikata? Well, then, this is what you are to do." She passed on His Highness's orders.

"I shall be off, then, in fear of your wrath, whether he himself wishes it or not!" Tokikata laughed. "Seriously, though, we risked a good deal to accompany him when we saw how set he was on her. But enough—I hear the guards getting up." He hurried away.

Ukon had not the faintest idea how to prevent everyone from finding out what was going on. "For certain reasons his lordship wishes to remain completely unseen," she told the women when they arose. "What I gather of his appearance suggests that he had a serious misadventure on the way here. He has ordered new clothes to be brought from the City tonight."

"How awful!" the older ones exclaimed. "They say the Kohata hills are quite terrifying! I suppose he came in disguise, as usual, without anyone to clear his path. Oh, dear, oh, dear!"

"Quiet, quiet! It will be a calamity if the servants and so on ever catch wind of this." She trembled at the very thought. And what would she say if, horror of horrors, a messenger were to arrive from his lordship himself? "O Kannon of Hatsuse," she prayed from the bottom of her heart, "get me safely through this day!"

The mother of Ukon's mistress was to come and fetch her daughter that day for a pilgrimage to Ishiyama,[12] and all the gentlewomen, too, had fasted and gone through purification. "Well, then," they said, "she will not be able to go today. That *is* a shame!"

The sun was up, the shutters were raised, and Ukon waited intimately on the couple. She had the blinds of the chamber lowered and the words IN SECLUSION posted on them. She also devised a story about threatening dreams in case her mistress's mother should come in person. As for the washing water, she presented it to His Highness as she always did to the Commander, but he was shocked when her mistress moved to assist her.

"*You* might wash first, darling," he said; and she, accustomed by now to someone so nice and so gentlemanly, supposed that a man sufficiently ardent to believe he would die if torn an instant from her must be what people called "deeply in love." She could hardly believe what had happened. Oh, what will people think when they hear about this? Her thoughts went first to Her Highness at Nijō; but he, who knew nothing of what was passing through her mind, insisted, "You are so cruel—please, *please* just tell me who you are! Never mind if you are a complete nobody—I shall only love you better for it!" She did not answer that, but on other matters she gave the most delightfully affectionate replies, and he found her perfectly enchanting.

The sun was high when the party arrived to fetch her. There were two carriages, seven or eight rough men on horseback as usual, and a large number of attendants, all chattering away in their uncouth jargon; and in they came, to the women's dismay. "Go and tell his lordship to keep out of sight!" they warned. Ukon hardly knew what to do. I could say his lordship is here, she reflected, but if someone that important were absent from the City, the news would certainly have got about, and everyone would know.

Without a word to the other women she wrote to her mistress's mother: "Last evening my lady got her defilement, to her great disappointment, and during the night she had such frightening dreams that I advised great caution all day today. She is therefore in seclusion. I am extremely sorry to say that something appears to be causing her trouble." After writing this, she gave the party something to eat. She also let the nun know that her mistress would be in seclusion today and so would not go.

For the young woman so prized by His Highness most days dragged by in vacant gazing at the misty hills, but not this one, which passed quickly, sped on by an

---

12. The temple at the southern end of Lake Biwa where, according to legend, Murasaki Shikibu conceived *The Tale of Genji*. Like Hatsuse (Hasedera), it is dedicated to Kannon.

ardor that could not abide the sinking of the sun. It was a
serene and perfectly peaceful spring day. He could not
get his fill of looking at her,[13] for she struck him as
flawless, and she had a deliciously warm and winning appeal. Not that she equaled the lady in his
wing at Nijō. The daughter of His Excellency of
the Right, as lovely as at her age she could possibly be, could certainly claim also to be distinctly superior, but to His Highness just
now the one before him was incomparable,
and his eyes saw charms that he had
never known before. As for herself, she
had thought the Commander so handsome that there could surely be no one
else like him, but she found His Highness far
more intensely beautiful and fascinating.

Attendants

His Highness drew up an inkstone and tried some
writing practice. The things he dashed off were so pretty and the pictures he
painted were all so delightful that he undoubtedly won her girlish heart. "You must
look at this whenever, alas, I am unable to be with you," he said; and he did a very
amusing picture of a man and woman lying side by side. "This is how I wish we
could always be," he added, and tears spilled from his eyes.

> *"What I promise you might be my love forever, yet it is so sad*
> *that life keeps from you and me whether we have tomorrow.*

But no, it is very wrong of me to have such thoughts. I can so seldom do as I please,
and all the plotting and scheming just makes me want to die. How did I ever manage to find you, after you were so cruel to me that time?"

She picked up the brush he had wetted and wrote,

> *"Never would my heart give me any wish to mourn, could I just believe*
> *life in this world we two share to be all that may soon change."*

She was obviously reproaching him for future infidelities. He thought her
very sweet. "Whose fickle ways could have prompted *that*?" he said with a smile and
then, to her great embarrassment, went on to press her for an account of how the
Commander had first come to bring her here.

"I do wish you would not ask me questions that I may not answer!" she
protested girlishly.

Oh, well, it will all come out in the end, he said to himself; but it was not very
nice of him to want so much to hear it from *her*.

---

13. *Kokinshū* 684, by Ki no Tomonori: "Like cherry blossoms on the hills, seen through trailing spring
mists, dear, I will never have my fill of looking at you."

Night came, and Tokikata returned from his mission to the City. He sought out Ukon. "There was a messenger from Her Majesty, you know," he reported, "and His Excellency of the Right complained bitterly that for His Highness to go off like that without a word to anyone was extremely improper and could result in a serious affront to his dignity, and that, furthermore, the consequences could be disastrous for himself as well if His Majesty were to hear of it. I managed to insist that His Highness had gone to see a holy man in the Eastern Hills. It is all *her* fault, though!" he added. "Women have a lot to answer for! Look what trouble she got even a simple retainer into, making him tell lies and everything!"

"That was a fine idea, to call my mistress a holy man! For that I am sure your lie will be forgiven. Seriously, though, I wonder where His Highness got these strange ways of his. We could certainly have managed something for him, considering who he is, if only we had known beforehand that he was coming. What an extraordinary way to arrive!" Such were Ukon's remarks on the subject.

She went to His Highness and reported what she had heard. He could well imagine what was going on. "It is such a nuisance, never being able to do anything!" he complained to the young woman beside him. "How I wish I could be one of those footloose and fancy-free privy gentlemen for a while! What am I to do? I cannot *always* satisfy those people I am supposed to please! And how will the Commander take it? He and I are likely to be on decent terms anyway,[14] but actually, we have always been remarkably close, and I will hardly be able to look him in the eye if he ever finds out what I have done to him. Another thing that worries me is that I can indeed imagine him forgetting that he has neglected you and blaming *you* for this! I must take you away somewhere else to make sure *no one* ever finds out." He prepared to go, since he could not possibly spend yet another such day with her, but even so, he seemed to have lost his soul among her sleeves.[15]

His men cleared their throats to warn him that he must be on his way before daybreak. They came together out to the double doors, but he could go no farther.

> *"I shall lose my way as no one has ever done, for before me goes,*
> *all along the endless road, the blinding veil of my tears."*

She herself was profoundly moved.

> *"When these sleeves of mine can never be broad enough to contain my tears,*
> *how can I, such as I am, ever hope to keep you here?"*

He mounted his horse while the wind whistled in the frosty dawn, feeling as though his clothes and hers had been taken by the cold,[16] and such was the pain of parting

---

14. Being (as far as Niou knows) close relatives.

15. *Kokinshū* 992, by Michinoku: "Perhaps my soul went in among the sleeves I still desire, for I feel as though it is gone from me."

16. As though the warm clothes they had spread over each other as they lay together were all cold, now that they were apart. The expression *ono ga kinuginu* ("his clothes and hers") appears in *Kokinshū* 637, though it is difficult to translate it the same way: "When the light of dawn begins slowly to fill the sky, there is such sorrow in the parting of our clothes!"

that he might have turned back if his escort, in no mood to dawdle, had not set off in very great haste, and he therefore with them, although he hardly knew what he was doing. The two gentlemen of the fifth rank, the Chief Clerk and Tokikata, took his bridle, and neither mounted his own horse until after the steep passage through the hills. The very crackle of ice beneath the horses' hooves along the river evoked solitude and desolation. He had never followed any other mountain road like this, not even in years past. How strange it is, he thought, to have such a tie to that one village!

When he reached Nijō, he went to bed in his own room, where he felt at home; the cruel way the lady in his wing had kept the girl hidden from him made him too angry to do otherwise. He could not sleep, however, and in time he yielded to loneliness and misery and went over to the wing after all. There she was, unsuspecting and very beautiful, but while he granted her a rare quality beyond anything in the girl who had so entranced him, he saw also a striking resemblance, and it was with a heavy heart and a thoroughly downcast air that he went into the curtained bed to lie down. She followed him.

"I am not at all well," he said. "I feel apprehensive, as though something is going to happen to me. Your life would change very quickly then, no matter how much I may love you. He would have his desire in the end, I know he would."

He is talking the worst nonsense, and quite seriously, too, she thought. "If he ever heard the awful things you say, he would wonder what on earth I have been telling you. It is too painful. The most casual joke can be very hard to bear for one as familiar with misfortune as I am." She turned away.

His Highness began to speak in earnest. "How would you feel if I really did have reason to be angry with you? Have I not treated you well? Some people even complain that few would have done as much for you as I have, and yet you seem to think nothing of me, compared with him. It is destiny, no doubt, I understand that, but even so, it is very hard to have you hide things from me the way you do." And what a remarkable destiny it was that led me to find her at last at Uji! he reflected meanwhile, the memory bringing tears to his eyes.

His obvious emotion left her at a loss. What sort of talk can he have been hearing? She was dismayed and found no reply. First he took me on a whim of his own, and now he seems to misinterpret unflatteringly everything I do. That is what has earned me his contempt: the mistake I made when I relied too greatly on someone whom nothing obliged to assist me, and when I began to feel grateful for everything he had done. The sadness attending these melancholy reflections made her look very dear indeed. He did not wish to let her know quite yet what he had discovered and had therefore disguised the cause of his annoyance, so that she took him seriously as referring to the Commander and assumed that he believed some nonsense or other that someone had told him. She felt too ashamed to face him until she had found out for certain whether or not this was so.

He was surprised by the arrival of a note from Her Majesty and returned to the main house with his frown intact. "Yesterday you were absent, and now it appears that you are unwell. Please come if you are feeling at all better. It has been too long," she had written. He did not wish to upset her further, but it was quite true, he was not feeling himself, and he did not go to the palace that day. Many senior nobles came to call on him, but he spent the day behind his blinds.

The Commander came toward evening. His Highness invited him in and received him in a very casual state of dress.

"Her Majesty has been extremely worried to learn that you are ill," the Commander began. "What is the matter?"

With the Commander there before him, His Highness felt more agitated than ever and had little to say. Talk about acting the holy man, he said to himself, *you* make a fine mountain ascetic, leaving a lovely girl like that down there, sweetly expecting you for days and months on end! He could never stand the way the Commander missed no opportunity great or small to show himself off as a pillar of virtue, and he regularly did his best to cut him down to size; but what might he have said *this* time, after being found out on such a matter! He ventured no taunts on the subject, however, and instead looked genuinely ill.

"This will not do!" the Commander expostulated gravely as he left. "A quite mild indisposition may still be very serious when it continues for days on end. Please look after yourself!"

He makes one feel so small! I wonder how I looked to *her* in comparison. Such were His Highness's thoughts, since she was so constantly on his mind that everything reminded him of her.

Life at Uji was very dull now that the trip to Ishiyama was off. He wrote her a letter full of the most earnest assurances, but it was a worry just to send it. He had it delivered by a retainer of Tokikata, one who did not know what the issue was. "A gentleman I used to know came here among his lordship's escort and rediscovered me, and now he is courting me again," Ukon explained to the other women. Yes, by now she had a lie for every occasion.

The next month came.[17] His Highness simply could not go, despite his intense longing to do so. I doubt I will live much longer if I go on like this, he groaned miserably to himself.

The Commander went there discreetly, as usual, after the busiest time at court was over. At the temple he worshipped the Buddha, and then, after distributing largesse to the monks he had chanting the scriptures, he went on quietly toward evening to call at the house. *He* did not go in heavy disguise, and in his hat and dress cloak he looked dauntingly splendid from the moment he walked in.

She could hardly imagine being with him—the very idea filled her with terror and shame—and moreover the memory of that most impetuous lord made the thought of receiving this one cruelly distasteful. "I can feel myself losing interest in every one of the women I have been with all this time," His Highness had assured her, and it was true: she gathered that he had been quite ill ever since, so that he was no longer going to any of the places he commonly frequented and loud prayers were being said for him. What would he think of her if he heard? It was an appalling idea. In contrast, this visitor had marvelous distinction, grace, and depth of heart, and when he apologized for his long absence, he did so not in glowing

17. The second.

speeches about longing and regret but in a few words more eloquent than any burning soliloquy, for he had the gift of appealing directly to anyone's deepest sympathy. Languid elegance he had, of course, but also, and to extraordinary degree, a quality that inspired trust in his enduring loyalty. How absolutely awful it would be if anyone were to breathe a word to him about how different I feel now, she said to herself. It would be such a shock! How wrong it is of me, and how giddy, to prefer instead the one who insists on pursuing me with such mad abandon! The misery of contemplating the possibility that the Commander might condemn and then forget her had given her such a troubled, melancholy air that he noted a far greater maturity and understanding in her since his last visit. He reflected with a pang that she must feel the burden of every sort of care, living here like this with so little to do, and he devoted himself to her more attentively than usual.

Hat and dress cloak

"The house I am having built is finally taking shape," he said. "I had a look at it the other day. The brook there is much less forbidding than this river, and you will have lots of flowers to look at. Also, Sanjō, where I live, is not far away. We will no longer be so far apart that I must always worry about you. If all goes well, I shall move you there this spring."

His talk of his plan reminded her that just the day before *he*, too, had written about finding somewhere for them to meet comfortably. I suppose he does not know about this new house, she thought sadly; oh, but no, I *must* not give myself to him! Yet remembering him as he had been then obliged her despite herself to mourn her cruel fate, and she wept.

"I was much happier before, when you seemed so much more at peace," he said. "Has anyone been filling your ears with worthless insinuations? Considering who I am, I would hardly come all the way here to see you if I had the slightest intention of neglecting you, and certainly not over that road!" It was the first day of the month, and they lay near the veranda looking out at the evening moon. He dwelled silently on old and moving memories, while she sighed over the fresh cares that had come to afflict her. Both were absorbed in their troubles.

The hills were veiled in mist, and crested herons stood on a sandspit, giving the scene a perfect touch, while the full span of the Uji Bridge stretched away into the distance and boats passed up and down laden with brushwood: a scene so picturesque that it always made the past very vivid for him. The presence of this young woman beside him would have had a rich and marvelous poignancy even if she had not been who she was, and her extraordinary resemblance to the lady he had loved, as well as her new awareness in intimate matters and her increasingly courtly ways, made it all the more plain how greatly the pleasure of her company had grown since he had first come to know her. Just the same, the many cares gathered in her heart now and again started tears from her eyes. When he saw that he had failed to console her, he said,

"No, it will not fail, that enduring promise made by the Uji Bridge:
never fear, for you may cross, sure it will uphold your trust.

Just wait and see!"
    She replied,

"When the Uji Bridge seems so perilous to cross, with its many gaps,[18]
do you mean me to believe it will never, never fail?"

He considered staying longer, since it was now so much more difficult to leave her, but then he thought better of it. Rumors started all too readily, and besides, there was no need to, since things would soon be so much easier. He returned to the City at dawn. She certainly is a woman now! he reflected as he left, more fondly than ever before.

On the tenth of the second month His Majesty convened a Chinese poetry gathering at the palace. His Highness and the Commander were both there. His Highness's voice sounded quite lovely, singing "The Plum Tree Branch" in the mode proper to the moment. Considering how far he stood above all his contemporaries, it was very wrong of him to burn for anyone so unworthy.

All at once a snowstorm set in, with a high wind, and the music ceased immediately. Everyone repaired to His Highness's palace apartments, where they rested and enjoyed refreshments. The Commander, who had a message to send, moved a little closer to the veranda, where by dim starlight he glimpsed the deepening snow and hummed "Lonely sleeves spread on her narrow mat, tonight again,"[19] as though "Darkness covers all"[20] had come to life; for it was his profound genius to give the most extraordinary charm to the least passage of verse that he might wish to voice.

Of all the poems he might have chosen! His Highness lay there with a beating heart, pretending to be asleep. *He* seems to feel strongly about her, too, he complained to himself. I thought I was the only one who cared about her lonely sleeves, but the poor fellow feels the same way. It is a bit hard! With a first lover like that, how could she possibly come to prefer me?

The next morning, with snow deep on the ground, His Highness, glowing with all the beauty of youth, came before His Majesty to present his poem. The Commander was close to him in age, but his two or three more years[21] seemed to give him such added maturity and poise that he might have been expressly devised as a model for every courtier. All the world agreed that he was perfect as an imperial son-in-law. In learning and in ability at public affairs he certainly was second to none. Once the poems had been read out, everyone withdrew, humming His High-

18. Kaoru's long absences from Uji.
19. *Kokinshū* 689: "Lonely sleeves spread on her narrow mat, tonight again does she await me, the maiden of Uji Bridge?"
20. *Kokinshū* 41, by Ōshikōchi no Mitsune: "On a night in spring, darkness covers all; plum blossoms remain unseen, but their scent cannot be hidden." The reference is to Kaoru's personal scent.
21. "Two or three more years" is puzzling. As far as one can tell from "Spring Shoots II" and "The Oak Tree," Niou is roughly a half year older than Kaoru.

ness's, which they agreed was the best of the lot; but this meant nothing to His Highness himself, since he could not even recall what he had had in mind when he composed it.

What he gathered of the Commander's feelings enjoined still greater vigilance than before, and it was therefore with infinite caution that he set out for Uji once more. The snow, which in the City seemed to linger only to await a friend,[22] became much deeper once he entered the hills. The deserted track was now nearly impossible to follow, and his companions all but wept with fear of the disasters they might suffer. The Chief Clerk, his guide, was concurrently Deputy Commissioner of Ceremonial, both of which were thoroughly dignified posts, and it was therefore amusing to see him dressed for yet another role, with his trousers hitched up high.

At Uji they had had notice that His Highness was coming, but it never occurred to them that he would brave this snow, and they were wholly unprepared when, late in the night, a message reached Ukon. Ukon's mistress was as surprised and touched as Ukon herself. Ukon had been wondering what was to become of her young lady, and she certainly was also disturbed, but tonight she must have thrown caution to the winds. It was out of the question to send him back, and she therefore had a talk with Jijū, another young woman with whom her mistress was friendly and who did not lack sense. "This is a very tricky business," she said. "I want you to help me keep him out of sight." Together they admitted him to the house. His perfume was especially penetrating, since he was wet from his journey, and that could easily have caused trouble, but they successfully passed him off as the Commander, whom he so closely resembled in build.

It would have been too disappointing to have to start back again before the night was even quite over, and all the women in the house were a worry. For these reasons he had sent Tokikata ahead with instructions to arrange it so that he could take her to another house across the river.

Tokikata returned very late that night to report that all was ready. What *is* he going to do with her? The question agitated even Ukon, who, freshly roused from sleep, trembled in a frenzy of apprehension; she shook just the way a page girl does after playing in the snow. His Highness had carried her mistress off before she could get out a word of protest. She sent Jijū with them and stayed behind to look after the house.

They got into a little boat just like the ones that from the house always looked so frail, and while they rowed across the river, the young woman felt as forlorn as though both banks were receding behind her. There in his arms she clung to him tightly, and he thought her utterly enchanting. The moon rode aloft in the dawn sky,[23] and the river's limpid expanse stretched away. "This is the Isle of Orange

❀

22. To linger on only so as to greet the next fall of snow. The conceit is derived from two poems. (1) *Yakamochi shū* 284, by Ōtomo no Yakamochi: "Upon the plum tree's boughs white snow, indistinguishable from the blossoms, lingers as though awaiting a friend." (2) *Kokin rokujō* 4131 (also *Tsurayuki shū* 60), by Ki no Tsurayuki: "In the Yoshino hills, where they know nothing of plum trees in bloom, they must be watching the snow that only awaits a friend."

23. The moon shines in the dawn sky around the twentieth of the lunar month, and Niou's expedition to Uji therefore seems to be about ten days after the Chinese poetry party.

Trees," the boatman told them, and drew the boat up a moment to the bank. Shaped like a great rock, it was covered with striking evergreens.[24]

"Look at them! They are little enough in themselves, but green like theirs will last a thousand years!" His Highness said, and he added,

> *"Many years may pass, yet one thing will never change: that my heart is yours,*
> *for that I now promise you by the Isle of Orange Trees."*

She, too, wondered at their journey:

> *"The enduring hue of the Isle of Orange Trees may well never change,*
> *yet there is no knowing now where this drifting boat is bound."*

Such was the moment and so lovely the woman that her poem, too, struck him as a delight.

They reached the far bank and disembarked. It seemed too cruel to have one of his men carry her; assisted by his escort, he therefore walked on with her in his arms, to the dismay of those looking on, for they could not think what woman might have stirred him to that degree. The house was a modest one built by Tokikata's uncle, the Governor of Inaba, on one of his estates. It was not quite finished yet, and the basketwork screens—something His Highness had never seen before—hardly slowed the wind. Snow still lay in patches along the fence, and more was falling from a lowering sky.

The rising sun gleamed from the icicles at the eaves, and by its light she looked even lovelier than before. He had come dressed simply for so risky a journey, and now, after slipping off her outer robe, he could delight in his view of her slender form. She herself was acutely embarrassed to be seen this way, hardly dressed at all—and to think she was here before so dazzling a lord!—but there was nowhere for her to hide. Her gowns, in five comfortably soft layers, looked very pretty at hem and sleeve and set her off to better advantage than layered colors. He was not used to seeing a woman dressed so informally, not even the one with whom he normally spent his time, and he found even that a wonder and a delight.

Jijū was a very pretty young woman, too. To think that even *she* is seeing me like this! her mistress lamented. "Who is she?" His Highness asked. "You must not tell her who I am!" Jijū was thoroughly impressed. Meanwhile the resident caretaker honored Tokikata as the senior member of the party, and Tokikata was therefore resplendently installed on the other side of the sliding door from His Highness. In a voice quivering with respect the caretaker asked Tokikata questions that Tokikata was amused to be unable to answer. He claimed to have come because a yin-yang master's terrifying prediction required him not merely to go into seclusion but to do so outside the City. "Do not let any outsider anywhere near this house," he warned.

---

24. *Tachibana* ("orange") trees, a broadleaf evergreen. The island no longer exists.

Alone with his love at last, His Highness spent the day in undisturbed intimacy. The idea that she must have received the Commander very similarly when *he* came to see her threw him into a fit of jealousy, and he described the Commander's profound respect for his wife, the Second Princess. Unfortunately, he did not mention the line of poetry he had overheard that time. Then Tokikata came with washing water and refreshments. "The honored guest had better not let himself be seen doing *this!*" His Highness jokingly cautioned him. As for Jijū, passionate young thing that she was, she thought it all a great lark and spent the day closeted with Tokikata.

Snow now blanketed the ground, and His Highness, looking out toward where she lived, saw only treetops through gaps in the mist. The hills glittered in the setting sun as though hung with mirrors. He began to tell her, with many dramatic touches, about the perilous journey he had made the previous night.

> *"Snow upon the hills, ice along frozen rivers: these for you I trod,*
> *yet for all that never lost the way to be lost in you;*

though there was a horse at Kohata village,"[25] he wrote with careless ease, after calling for a poor inkstone that happened to be at hand.

> *"Quicker than the snow, swirling down at last to lie by the frozen stream,*
> *I think I shall melt away while aloft yet in mid-sky,"*

she wrote, as though to refute his. He faulted her "while aloft yet in mid-sky,"[26] and she was embarrassed to recognize that it had not been nice of her to write it. She tore it up. This touched him even more keenly, delighted with her as he already was, and his eloquence and sweetness of manner rose to new heights of captivating charm.

They had two quiet days together during which to deepen their tender feelings for each other, for he had arranged that his "seclusion" was to last that long. Ukon went on putting out plausible excuses and meanwhile sent over fresh clothes. Today her mistress had her tangled hair combed and changed into a lovely combination of plum pink over deep red-violet. Jijū gave up the rude apron she had been wearing, whereupon His Highness picked it up and had his darling wear it to bring him his washing water. Ah, he thought, if I were to let my elder sister have her, she would treat her as a real prize! She has a good many very wellborn women, but I doubt that she has any beauty like this! He spent the day with her absorbed in the most trifling of pastimes.

Over and over again he assured her that he planned to hide her away somewhere, and he tried to extract from her the most solemn promises in case *he* should

---

25. *Shūishū* 1243, by Hitomaro: "Though there was a horse at Kohata village in Yamashina, I came on foot for love of you."

26. Her phrase suggests a fear that he will abandon her.

turn up in the meantime. This was so painful that she could not answer him at all, and her tears filled him with the bitter conviction that even in his own presence, *he* was the one who still had her heart. All day he poured out his tears and reproaches, and the night was late when he took her home. He carried her himself, as before. "*He* would never do this much for you, you know," he said, "that man who means so much to you." No, she thought, he probably would not, and she nodded in enchanting agreement. Ukon opened the double doors to let her in. So they parted, and he started back again in an agony of unappeased longing.

He returned to Nijō, as he usually did under such circumstances. Feeling extremely unwell, he ate nothing at all and grew paler and thinner by the day, until at the palace and elsewhere there was only distress over his changed appearance; so much so that amid the mounting commotion he did not even send her a proper letter. At Uji, meanwhile, she could hardly read what he did send in peace, because that officious nurse of hers was now back again from where her daughter had given birth to a child.

Her mother had taken comfort from knowing that although her daughter's accommodation was hardly inadequate, the Commander would certainly do better by her than that; and now, rejoicing to imagine the advantageous consequences of his plan to move her daughter closer, she began gathering gentlewomen and handsome page girls and sending them down to her. Her daughter herself had always looked forward to the move eagerly, but whenever she thought of that other, most insistent suitor, his accusing manner and his many reproaches rose all too vividly before her, and she had only to drop off to sleep to dream of him. All this left her very troubled indeed.

It had been raining and raining for days on end, and His Highness had reached the unbearable conclusion that he simply could not cross those hills now. Ah, he was sufficiently ungrateful to reflect, pity the poor silkworm in his parents' cocoon![27] While setting down for her some of his endless thoughts, he wrote,

> "O sadness of days when the very skies grow dark, and I cannot see
> the clouds above where you are through the endless veil of rain."

The things he wrote most casually were the ones that afforded the greatest pleasure and delight. Not being especially given to weighty pondering, she felt the tug of his ardent feelings, and yet the gentleman who had claimed her earlier, yes, *he* was the one with the greater depth and nobility, and also the first whom she had really known; and no doubt that is why she wondered, What would happen if he heard about this unfortunate business and came because of it to reject me? What a blow that would be for my mother, too, when she so longs for him to come for me! And that man with his burning ardor—people keep telling me he is a hopeless gallant, which he may well be, yet he still might hide me somewhere in the City and

---

27. *Shūishū* 895, by Hitomaro: "Caught in a cocoon like one of my parents' silkworms, O how I miss you, darling, when we cannot meet!"

go on caring enough not to forget me; but then there are Her Highness's feelings to consider, since nothing in this world remains hidden for long—after all, all it took him was that single strange evening, and sure enough, he found me again, so obviously his lordship could not possibly fail to find out what had happened to me either. Her mind ran on in this vein, and she was just reflecting how terrible it would be if her lapse should cause his lordship to turn against her when a messenger arrived with a letter from him.

The idea of reading both letters together repelled her, but she lay down to read the longer one. Jijū and Ukon exchanged glances. "Yes, he is the one she wants" was the message that passed between them.

"And I can understand that," Jijū added. "I myself had thought his lordship as handsome as any man alive, but His Highness is really extraordinary. The charm he has, when he is being amusing! It would be too much for me, if I were she and I knew he cared that much about me. I would go straight to Her Majesty's so as to be with him all the time."

"You worry me, you really do. Anyway, I do not see who could possibly be an improvement on his lordship. Looks are all very well, but just think of character and behavior! No, His Highness leaves a great deal to be desired. Oh, what is to become of our mistress!" So the two of them talked. Ukon was glad no longer to be alone devising her lies; it was good to have a confederate.

His lordship's letter said, "Please forgive my silence, but I have been thinking of you. If you were to write to me from time to time, I could not ask for more. Can you possibly imagine that you do not matter to me?" and so on. In the margin he had added,

> "How is it with her, she of that far-off village where the waters rise,
> while these days the endless rains here shroud the skies in darkness?

My thoughts are with you more than ever." It was a straight-folded letter, on white paper. The writing, which had little flair or charm, nonetheless displayed a marked distinction.

His Highness's, very long and knotted very tight, gave equal pleasure. "This is the one you ought to answer first, before anyone sees you," Jijū suggested.

"Oh, no, I could not possibly, not today!" she answered bashfully and then wrote for herself,

> "This village's name I know now for my own fate, and Uji to me,
> in this land, Yamashiro, means only more misery."[28]

Now and again she looked at the painting His Highness had left her and wept. The thought of going away somewhere and never seeing him again must have

---

28. Uji, "this village's name," plays on *ushi,* "hateful." The double meaning was made famous by *Kokinshū* 983, by Kisen Hōshi: "My hut is southeast of the City: I live with the deer in the Uji hills, where they say, I reject the world."

hurt very much, although she often reminded herself of all the reasons why it could
not last.

> *"A cloud dark with rain, shrouding in melancholy ever-brooding hills:*
> *that is what I wish to be and drift all my life away.*

O to join the clouds!"[29] Such was her answer, and from His Highness it drew helpless sobs. Still, he told himself, she *does* seem to want me! All he could see now was a
vision of her lost in gloom.

His lordship, that stalwart gentleman, tranquilly read her reply and imagined
with great sympathy how downcast she must be. He missed her very much.

> *"No break in the rains brings relief from this lonely brooding on my lot,*
> *and the waters rise and rise, till they flood these sleeves of mine,"*[30]

she had written. He stared at it and could not put it down.

He was talking to his wife, the Second Princess. "I have hesitated to mention
this for fear that you might take offense," he said, "but actually, there is someone I
have known for many years, someone I left in a dreary, distant place, who is miserable there, and she concerns me so much that I am thinking of bringing her to live
nearby. I have always seen things differently from other people, and I had meant not
to live my life as everyone else does,[31] but I cannot give up everything now that I
have you; and so, you see, I feel sympathy and guilt even toward someone whom I
have never mentioned to anyone before."

"I do not understand why I should be displeased," Her Highness replied.

"Someone might give His Majesty the wrong idea, though. People can express
themselves very cruelly—not that I think she need command that much interest."

He was resolved to move her to the house he had built, but he hated to imagine starting scurrilous rumors and have people saying, "Ah, so *that's* what that new
place of his is for!" For the work of putting up the sliding panels and so on he therefore addressed himself very discreetly to Nakanobu, of all people, that Chief Clerk's
father-in-law: a Treasury Commissioner whom he felt he could take into his confidence. Everything he said therefore went straight to His Highness.

"He has chosen only intimates from his Palace Guards escort to do the paintings,[32] but even so, he certainly seems keen on the place," the Chief Clerk explained.

---

29. Probably a phrase from a poem, although no convincing source has been identified. Ukifune's poem
suggests to some that she wishes never to have to decide between Kaoru and Niou, and to others that she
wishes to rise into the sky as a cloud of smoke from her own funeral pyre.

30. Ukifune's poem draws on *Kokinshū* 617, by Fujiwara no Toshiyuki, for the image of lonely tears
swelling into a river that wets the speaker's sleeves (*namidagawa*); and on *Kokinshū* 705, by Ariwara no Narihira, for that of a rain of tears shed by the speaker in acknowledgment of an unhappy lot (*mi o shiru ame*).
Both poems also appear in *Ise monogatari*, section 107.

31. "I have always been interested in religion, and I had not meant to marry."

32. The paintings will go on the sliding panels. The men officially assigned to guard such ranking nobles
as Kaoru were often skilled in the arts.

His Highness, almost beside himself, remembered an old nurse of his, a woman who was about to go down with her husband to a distant province where her husband was to be the new Governor. "I am secretly involved with someone, and I need to hide her for a while," he pleaded. Her husband wondered who she could possibly be, but he nonetheless decided that His Highness's wish was his command. "As you please, my lord," he replied. His consent brought some relief.

The Governor's party was to leave at the end of the month, and he decided to move his darling there that very day. "That is my plan. Say not a word about it!" So said his repeated messages to Uji. It was quite impossible then for him to go himself, though, and moreover he got back warnings about how difficult that know-it-all nurse of hers might make things.

His lordship the Commander, meanwhile, had settled on the tenth of the fourth month. "Should a current call, O I would go"[33]—such was *not* the mood of the young woman he had in mind, for she was instead stricken with horror and close to panic, wondering what on earth she was to do; until she decided that a stay at her mother's might after all give her some time to think. Unfortunately, the Lieutenant's wife[34] was due soon to have a baby, and the house was so perpetually loud with litanies and scripture chanting that a trip to Ishiyama together seemed out of the question. Instead her mother came to her.

Out came the nurse. "His lordship keeps us all beautifully supplied with clothes! I should like so much to look after us this nicely myself, but I am sure I would only spoil everything if I tried!" she rattled on, but her excitement only made her mistress wonder how everyone would feel if the whole dreadful secret came to light and she were to have the whole world laughing at her. That man who insists he wants me at all costs, she thought, *he* would find me even if I were to vanish far into the mountains where eightfold clouds rise,[35] and both of us would then come to grief. Why, just today he sent word that I should be ready to slip off into hiding! What am I to do? It was all too much for her, and she lay down feeling ill.

"What is the matter with you?" her worried mother asked. "You are awfully thin and pale."

"She has not been at all herself lately," her nurse added. "She will not eat, and she often feels unwell."

What can it be? A spirit perhaps? What is actually the matter with her? they all wondered.

"She gave up the trip to Ishiyama, but I now wonder just why she felt she had to," her mother remarked.

It was too awful. She stared at the floor.

The sun set, and a bright moon rose. She remembered the moon that had

---

33. *Kokinshū* 938, by Ono no Komachi: "I am forlorn, a drifting waterweed cut off at the root: should a current call, O I would go."

34. Ukifune's half sister by Hitachi.

35. *Genji monogatari kochūshakusho in'yō waka* 983: "Though you hide in the mountains where eightfold clouds rise, once my mind was made up, would I not come to find you?"

hung in the sky that dawn, and she could not keep from crying. Oh, she thought, I mustn't, I mustn't!

Her mother began talking about the old days and called out the nun Ben, who described what His Late Highness's elder daughter had been like, how unfailingly responsible she had been, and how she had simply wasted away before one's eyes. "She would be like His Highness's dear lady, if only she were still alive!" Ben said. "They would be in touch with each other, and they who were once so sad and lonely would now both enjoy all the blessings of good fortune!"

Is my daughter, then, different from them? her mother reflected. Yes, she will be every bit as worthy, once the destiny she merits is hers! To Ben she went on aloud, "At heart I have always worried so much about my girl, but I feel a little better now that it seems she is to move to the City, although that may mean I will not be able to come here anymore. It is always such a pleasure when we meet to talk quietly with you about the past."

"The misfortune that seems to cling to me has always discouraged me from seeking out your daughter's company too often or too long, but even so, it will be very lonely here once she is gone. I will be very happy for *her*, though, because I do not at all like seeing her obliged to live in a place like this. I hope I did not presume too much when I reminded her that it obviously means a great deal when a lord of such unrivaled stature wishes to seek her out as he is doing."

"What the future will bring one cannot tell, of course, but for the present I know that she owes his continuing interest entirely to your kind intervention. It was extremely good of His Highness's lady, too, to receive her so amiably, and I was very sorry indeed when that unfortunate incident reminded me how vulnerable she really is."

The nun smiled. "I gather His Highness's gallantry causes such trouble that nice young women prefer not to go into service there at all. He is a very fine gentleman in every other respect, but according to Taifu's daughter, things can become extremely difficult on that score because of the offense to Her Highness."

I can well imagine! the young woman reflected as she lay there. Then just think how *I* feel!

"How very distressing! His lordship, now, enjoys the privilege of being married to His Majesty's daughter, but the two are not close, and I have taken the liberty of deciding that for better or worse there is little I can do about it. If she were to misbehave *that* way, though, I would want nothing more to do with her, however excruciatingly painful that might be."

For her daughter this was a devastating blow. I want to die! she thought. The awful secret will get out sooner or later!

Outside, the river roared menacingly past. "Not all rivers sound like that. No wonder he has taken pity on her, when she has had to spend so long in a place so dismally wild!" her mother remarked with satisfaction.

One of the women described how fast and frightening the river had always been. "The other day, you know, the ferryman's grandson missed his stroke on the oar and fell in. That river has taken so many people!" With that, everyone agreed.

I see. If I disappeared they would all be very upset for a while, but if I live to be laughed at in the end, when something awful happens, this misery will go on forever. There was nothing to stop her, as far as she could see, and it would certainly put an end to her cares, but the thought was very sad nonetheless. Lying there in feigned sleep, listening to her mother talk, she sank deeper and deeper into despair.

Her mother spoke to the nurse about how thin and ill her daughter seemed, and she instructed her on what prayers and purifications to have done.[36] She went on anxiously, never knowing how much her daughter longed to be purified in a lustration stream,[37] "She will need more women, I think. Find some reliable ones, properly brought up, and leave the new girls here. Her Highness, his lordship's wife, will probably take it all well, but there could be unpleasantness if anything were to come between them. Always remember to be discreet." She left nothing to chance. "But I am worried about my other daughter, who is having such a difficult time at home," she said at last, and prepared to set off. *This* daughter was very downcast indeed, though, because she believed that she would never see her mother again.

"I feel so ill, and I am so unhappy away from you!" she pleaded. "Oh, please let me come with you and stay a little while!"

"I wish I could, but everything there is in a complete uproar. The women are hopeless at doing the least thing on their own, you see, and the house is really so small. I would steal off to see you even if you moved all the way to Takefu,[38] but, my poor dear, I am not nearly important enough to be able to do anything for you now!" She wept as she spoke.

A letter came that day from his lordship: "How are you? I gather that you have not been well." He went on, "I wish that I could come and find out in person, but for one reason and another that is impossible. It is so much harder lately to be patient!"[39]

Meanwhile her failure to reply the day before had elicited this from His Highness, "Why do you waver? I worry so much about the way the wind is blowing![40] By now I can think of nothing but you." His letter, all in this vein, was the longer by far.

The two messengers who had met that rainy day at Uji both arrived there again today. One, a member of his lordship's escort, recognized the other as a man he often saw at the Chief Clerk's house. "What brings *you* here all the time?" he asked.

"There just happens to be someone I am visiting."

"Someone *you* are visiting? Then what are you doing delivering these elaborate letters? It looks to me as though there is something going on. What are you hiding?"

---

36. The "prayers" are Buddhist and the "purifications" what is now called Shinto.

37. How her daughter longed to rid herself of her unwanted passion for Niou. *Kokinshū* 501: "I purified myself in a lustration stream, that I might love no more; but the gods, it seems, did not accept my prayer."

38. An allusion to the *saibara* song "Where the Road Begins" ("Michi no kuchi"). Takefu was the capital of the province of Echizen, on the Japan Sea. Murasaki Shikibu had lived there for two years with her father. A passage in the song could be translated, "Go and tell my mother I am here in Takefu . . ."

39. Now that you will soon be here yourself.

40. *Ise monogatari* 193 (section 112; also *Kokinshū* 708): "The wind is so strong, the smoke from the fire of the saltmaker girl at Suma is blowing in a surprising direction" ("The girl is in love with someone unexpected").

"Actually, the letter is my Governor's to one of the women here."

The way he contradicted himself made his lordship's man suspicious, but he could not very well pursue the matter on the spot, and each therefore went his way. His lordship's man was alert, though, and he said to the page with him, "Keep your eye on that man, but stay out of sight. See whether he goes into the house of Lord Tokikata, the Deputy Governor of Izumo."

"He went to His Highness's and delivered the letter to the Chief Clerk," the page reported in due course. The dismal menial had never imagined that he might actually be followed, and besides, he knew very little about the real purpose of his errand. As a result he unfortunately betrayed the whole affair.

The Commander's messenger delivered *his* letter just as his lordship was setting off in a dress cloak to Rokujō, where Her Majesty was at the time, so that he had no great retinue with him. "I have made a discovery," the messenger told the woman who actually passed his lordship the letter. "It took me this long to make quite sure."

The Commander caught what he said and walked straight up to him. "What did you discover?" he asked. The messenger, who did not want anyone else to hear what he had to say, maintained an attitude of silent deference. The Commander understood and continued on his way.

Her Majesty was indisposed, and all the Princes, her sons, therefore came to visit her. A great many senior nobles were there, too, so that there was constant coming and going, but she was not in fact seriously unwell. The Chief Clerk, an official of the Council of State, arrived late, and when he went to deliver his letter, His Highness was in the gentlewomen's sitting room; His Highness called him to the door to receive it from him. The Commander happened to glance that way just as he was leaving Her Majesty's presence and saw him take it. That letter certainly seems to mean a lot to him! he thought, and stopped, amused, to watch.

His Highness opened the letter, visibly a long one on thin plum pink paper. Absorbed in his reading, he took some time to turn the Commander's way, and before he could do so, His Excellency of the Right swept through on his way out. The Commander, who was about to leave through the sliding panel, cleared his throat in warning, and His Highness put the letter away just as His Excellency looked in. His Highness readjusted the cords of his cloak.

His Excellency knelt on one knee. "I shall excuse myself, Your Highness, if I may. It is quite frightening that Her Majesty's indisposition should persist in this manner. I shall send immediately for the Abbot of the Mountain." He hurried off.

The night wore on, and everyone withdrew. His Excellency and his sons, the senior nobles, and the others followed His Highness in a single party to His Excellency's residence.[41] Then the Commander left. Strange! he thought—that man of his had seemed to have something to say. Once his retinue had gone to light the torches,[42] he called the fellow to his side. "What was it you had to tell me?"

41. The northeast quarter of Rokujō, formerly occupied by Hanachirusato.
42. To light his way back to his Sanjō residence.

"This morning, my lord, at Uji, I saw a man who serves Lord Tokikata, the Deputy Governor of Izumo, give a letter to a woman at the west double doors of the house there. It was on thin purple paper and tied to a cherry branch. When I asked him about it, he contradicted himself in a way that suggested he was lying, and to find out why, I had my page follow him. He went to the residence of His Highness of the Bureau of War, where he passed the reply from Uji to Lord Michisada, the Chief Clerk."

"In what way did the man receive the letter in the first place?"

"I did not see that, my lord. It happened on the other side of the house. According to my page, it was a beautiful letter on red paper."

Delivering a letter

All things considered, the truth was not in doubt. The man had done extremely well to find out that much, but now there were people nearby, and the Commander could not pursue the matter.

On the way home he thought it over. Why, he reflected, it is absolutely terrifying, the way that Prince gets into everything! How can he possibly have come to learn of her existence? How did he manage to approach her? What an idiot I was to imagine that nothing like this could happen while she was in the country! He could at least carry on with someone who isn't *mine*, though! How can he do this to me, when he and I have always been so close, and after all the extraordinary help I gave him, taking him there in the first place and introducing him into the house! He was furious.

Look how careful *I* have been, all these years I have spent desperately wanting his wife! And besides, *that* is no sudden, disgraceful flight of fancy—there is an old and excellent reason for it, and I restrained myself only because I knew how painful it would be to have so dark and guilty a cranny in my heart. I was a fool, though. And there he is, not feeling well lately, and yet right in the middle of that unusually large crowd of people he manages to send off a letter all the way to Uji. How does he do it? I suppose he must be visiting her there already. It certainly is a long way for love to take him! Yes, they say there have been days when he had people looking for him everywhere. That must be why he is not feeling himself—he is all in a dither about *this*! He thought back to the old days and remembered what a pitiful state His Highness had been in when he could not manage to get down to Uji, and he also began to understand why the young woman there now had been so dispirited last time. These were extremely painful conclusions. Ah, he thought, how difficult the heart can be! She seems so sweet and mild, but she obviously has a passionate side to her as well. She and her Prince make a perfect pair. He felt like withdrawing and allowing His Highness to have her; but no, that might have been all right if she had been someone he meant truly to honor,[43] but he would just let her go on being whatever she was to him. I will only miss her if I break it off with her now, he said to himself. Such were his unbecomingly troubled reflections.

He would certainly take her away somewhere if I decided I had had enough and abandoned her, but I cannot imagine him giving much thought to what might become of her later on. They say that he has already given two or three girls to his sister the First Princess after similar affairs. I would be very sorry if that were to happen to *her.*

No, he still could not give her up. Instead he sent her a letter to see whether he could find out a little more. Summoning the man who had just served him so well, he called him in to talk to him personally when no one else happened to be about. "Is Lord Michisada still received at Nakanobu's house?"[44] he asked.

"Yes, my lord, he is."

"Perhaps he sends that fellow you met down to Uji quite often. The lady there lives very quietly—I suppose Michisada must be courting her." He spoke with obvious distress. "Go down there, then, but keep out of sight. I do not want to look ridiculous."

The man respectfully assented. It occurred to him that the Chief Clerk was always informing himself about his lordship's affairs and that he had made inquiries about Uji as well, but he did not indulge in saying so. Meanwhile the Commander, who had no wish to betray the truth to an underling, refrained from questioning him further.

More messengers were arriving at Uji than ever, and the young woman there had many cares. The Commander had written just this:

> "That these days great waves wash across the Sue pines I would not have guessed,
> who only trusted faithfully that you pined alone for me.[45]

Please do not make me any more ridiculous than I am already."

The shock of this strange note made her heart pound. She could not possibly bring herself to show by her answer that she knew what he meant, and besides, it would look very odd if by any chance there had been a mistake. Instead she folded the letter back up again and added before returning it, "I believe that this letter may have been intended for someone else. Unfortunately, I am not feeling well enough to write more."

Well, he thought with a smile when he read it, she got out of that very nicely after all! I had no idea she had it in her! He seems to have been unable in the end to hold it against her.

The broad hint he had given her, though certainly not yet explicit, made her

---

43. A future wife.
44. As a husband to Nakanobu's daughter.
45. *Kokinshū* 1093: "If I ever leave you and love another, waves will wash over the pine-clad hill of Sue!" The image of waves washing over Sue no Matsuyama (a hill near the coast in present Miyagi Prefecture) appears in many an accusing poem like Kaoru's.

feel a great deal worse, and she was just reflecting in despair that she was destined for some ignominious end when Ukon came in. "Why are you returning his lordship's letter?" she asked. "You must not do such a thing; it invites misfortune."

"It seemed to be a mistake. I thought it must have been for someone else."

The puzzled Ukon opened it on the way out. Wicked Ukon! "Dear me!" she said to her mistress, without telling her that she had read it. "This promises to be very difficult for you both! His lordship seems to have caught wind of what is going on."

Her mistress flushed scarlet and fell silent. Not suspecting Ukon of having read the letter, she assumed instead that she had heard this from someone who had actually seen his lordship. She could not even ask who it was, and she was desperately ashamed to imagine what these women might think of her now. It is too hard! she lamented to herself, lying sunk in gloom. I never asked for this to happen!

Ukon began talking to her, with Jijū beside her. "In Hitachi my sister had two lovers—this can happen to little people, too, you know. Both were equally keen on her, and she could not decide between them, but she favored the more recent one just a little. That made the first one jealous, and in the end he killed the other! The man never visited my sister again either. The upshot was that the provincial government lost a fine warrior and that the murderer himself was expelled from the province, even though he was a fine warrior, too—the government could hardly go on employing him. As for my sister, she was told to get out of the residence on the grounds that it was all her fault, so she had to stay on in the East. Nanny still cries for her, which I am afraid will not do her any good for the life to come. I know that this is no time to be telling such a terrible story, but no one, high or low, should ever allow herself to remain entangled in this sort of predicament. Perhaps no one's life is at stake in this case, but there are other risks, too, in keeping with these great lords' rank. For people like them, you know, shame can sometimes actually be worse than death. You *must* decide on one or the other. If His Highness is the more eager of the two and sounds more sincere, why, then, my lady, choose him and stop making yourself so miserable! There is simply no point in your wasting away like this. It really is too bad, when your mother cares so much about you and Nanny is putting herself out in all sorts of ways to prepare for his lordship coming to fetch you, that His Highness is telling you he means to do so first!"

"Goodness, don't frighten her like that!" Jijū protested. "What matters is your own destiny, my lady, whatever it may be. Understand in your heart that the one to choose is the one you yourself slightly prefer. No, considering how ardent His Highness is, and what honor that does you, I am not impressed by all these plans his lordship is making. Take the one who wants you more, if you ask me, even if that means going into hiding for a time." To Jijū, who was so taken with His Highness, there could be no possible doubt.

"Never mind. Either way, I just pray to Hatsuse and Ishiyama that you will be happy. The men of his lordship the Commander's estates are a fine lot of ruffians, and this village is full of their confederates. In fact, I hear all the men on his estates in Yamashiro and Yamato are connected with that Constable[46]—the one who gets

---

46. Udoneri, one of about a hundred men affiliated with the Bureau of Central Affairs and selected from the families of men of the fourth and fifth ranks. Assigned to guard the highest nobles, they could be arrogant and rough.

his son-in-law, the Right Guards Commissioner,[47] to do everything his lordship wants done here. One great lord is unlikely to order any harsh action against another, but those who actually take guard duty are unthinking country people whose only care is to make sure that nothing goes wrong on their watch. I was terrified to see His Highness arrive as he did the other night. He is so anxious not to be seen that he did not even bring an escort. If he ever came to a guard's attention, disguised like that, the result could be disaster."

Their mistress gathered with shame from all this that they both assumed she preferred His Highness, when she herself was not aware of leaning either way; she simply felt lost in a nightmare. Why, why is His Highness so desperate for me? she wondered, knowing full well at the same time that it was precisely her reluctance to leave the Commander, to whom she had long owed everything, that was making things so horribly difficult for her. What if something unfortunate *did* happen? She could not leave off being anxious.

"I wish I were dead!" she said, still lying facedown. "Look what an awful fate is mine! Surely even menials seldom suffer misfortune like this!"

"No, no, you must not be so upset! I keep telling you there is no need! Before, things that might well have troubled you seemed never to bother you at all, but now, ever since this started with His Highness, you are in such a state that I have never seen anything like it!" The women who knew what was going on were beside themselves with worry.

Meanwhile the nurse was working away to her heart's content at dyeing. She called over a pretty page girl who had just come into the household. "Now," she said to her mistress, "I want you two to amuse yourselves together. The way you keep lying about for some reason, there must be some spirit trying to spoil everything!" She sighed.

Days went by without an answer from the Commander. That menacing Constable arrived. He was a rough, uncouth old man with a hoarse voice, but still, there was something about him. "I want to talk to one of the women," he said. Ukon went out to him.

"His lordship summoned me, and I went there this morning. I only just got back. While conveying his wishes on this and that, he told me that he has not sent any guards of his own while the young lady is here because he knows my men are on watch through the night and on into dawn, but that recently he had a report of an unidentified man visiting one of the women here; and that, he said, is inexcusable. He maintained that those on guard must know all about it, since he did not see how they could have failed to notice. When he questioned me about it, I told him that I had not heard, since I have been ill and have not stood guard duty myself for months, so that I knew nothing. I have assigned good men to do the job properly there, I said,[48] and if anything like that happened, I cannot imagine not being told. He answered that I had better be careful, because if there is

---

47. Ukon no Taifu, an Aide of the Right Guards (Ukon no Zō, a sixth-rank post), exceptionally promoted to the fifth rank. Kaoru himself is Commander of the Right Guards.
48. The verb form indicates that the Constable is talking to Kaoru through an intermediary.

any incident, I will feel the full weight of his anger. I shudder to think what he may mean."

Ukon got a worse fright than from the hoot of an owl. She answered not a word but went straight to her mistress. "I knew it!" she cried. "Listen to me: this is exactly what I told you must have happened! His lordship has obviously found out. You have not even heard from him, and that is why!"

"I am very glad to hear of his lordship's new orders," remarked the nurse, who had caught a little of this. "There are supposed to be a lot of bandits around here, and the guards are not working the way they used to. They are all just filling in for someone else—he sends nothing but menials so useless that they cannot even manage their rounds at night!"

This is the end, then, the young woman said to herself; whereupon a message most unfortunately arrived from His Highness, burning with impatience and filled with protestations about ravaged moss.[49] One way or the other, then, something awful is going to happen to one of them! The only decent way out is for me to die. Women have drowned themselves before, when they could not choose between suitors.[50] If I live, I will have cause to regret it, so why should I not wish to die? My mother will be upset and will mourn me awhile, but she has many other children to think about, and she will of course come to pluck the grasses of forgetting. It will be worse for her if my fall comes while I am still alive and I am lost for good after being roundly mocked. So her thoughts ran. Her upbringing had given her little true pride or knowledge of the ways of the world, and perhaps that is why she had been able, despite her air of girlishly mild innocence, to conceive of taking this almost brutal step.

She tore up any compromising papers, and rather than dispose of them grandly, all at once, she burned them little by little in the flame of the lamp or had them taken to be thrown in the river until they were all gone. The women, who did not know what she was up to, assumed that she was destroying a casual collection of bits of practice calligraphy, accumulated over the months, in preparation for her move to the City.

"What are you doing *that* for?" Jijū asked when she found her at it. "Of course you do not want anyone to see letters lovingly exchanged between you and someone else, but it is a moving pleasure for anybody, high or low, to look now and then at old letters safely kept in the bottom of a box. What a terrible thing to do, to tear up his letters, when he has written you so many beautiful things, and on such beautiful paper!"

"It is just that I do not feel well, you see, and I doubt that I shall live much longer. They would embarrass him, too, if anyone found them later on. I would be so ashamed if anyone were to tell him that I willfully insisted on keeping them." It was also that the more she contemplated the dismal act she planned, the more she wondered whether she really had the courage for it. She reflected, too, on what even she had heard, that it is a very grave sin to precede one's parents in death.

---

49. *Kokin rokujō* 3962: "I who, like a pine tree, pine for our next meeting to come soon, find the moss around my base these days all ravaged with longing." The poem plays on *matsu*, "pine tree" and "await."

50. A particularly famous legend on this theme is found in *Man'yōshū* 1813ff., *Yamato monogatari* 147, and elsewhere.

The twentieth of the month had come and gone. The owner of the house to which His Highness meant to take her was due to go down from the City on the twenty-eighth.

"I will come for you that night," he wrote. "Make sure your women and servants guess nothing. I promise not to betray our secret from my side. Never doubt me!" But ah, she lamented, I will never be able to speak to him again, even if he tempts fate and comes! I shall have to send him back without even seeing him! Why, I cannot even invite him here for a little rest! She imagined him going back again, disappointed and angry, and as so often she seemed to see him before her, until sorrow overwhelmed her. She pressed his letter to her face, and after a brief attempt to control herself she burst into bitter weeping.

"Oh, my dear!" Ukon cried, "people will see what is happening if you go on like this! Some of them must be wondering already. *Please* make up your mind and give him whatever answer you wish! I am here, and as long as I devise some mad scheme, I am sure I can have him come down from the sky—you are such a slip of a thing anyway—to fetch you!"

Her mistress stopped her tears a moment. "I wish that you would not keep talking that way! It would be easy enough if I thought that *was* the thing to do, but I know quite well it is not, and meanwhile he makes things impossible by writing as though *I* were the one whose only thought was that he should come for me, until I hardly know what to expect of him next, and I myself am in despair!" She never answered His Highness at all.

Detecting no sign of assent from her, and noting that she now seldom answered his letters, His Highness took it that the Commander's well-considered arguments had swayed her and that she had made the somewhat safer choice. He did not blame her for that, but all the same he felt extremely put out; and, he told himself, I *know* she loved me! Obviously, she must have given in to all those women of hers, preaching at her while I was away! The gloom he felt seemed to him to fill all the vast, empty heavens,[51] until he again forgot all caution and set off for Uji.

The first approach to the reed fence drew, as never before, a chorus of alert voices, shouting, "Who goes there?" His Highness's man retreated and sent in someone who knew the house well. They challenged him, too. Things were different this time. "I have an urgent letter from the City!" he said, hardly knowing what else to do, and he called out the name of Ukon's servant. At last he was admitted. The situation was more difficult than ever.

"I cannot apologize enough to His Highness," Ukon said, "but this evening is out of the question."

To His Highness, who could not understand their turning against him in such a way, this was not an acceptable answer. "Tokikata, go in there, talk to Jijū, and do whatever needs to be done," he said, and sent the man off.

The clever Tokikata talked his way handily past the guards and found Jijū. "For some reason his lordship has issued orders that have made the men on guard

---

51. *Kokinshū* 488: "My love seems to fill all the vast, empty heavens; though I seek to dispel it, it has nowhere else to go."

duty here very assertive lately," she explained, "and we are at our wits' end. My mistress herself seems to be in great distress, and it is very painful to see her so upset over this affront to His Highness. No, no, there is no hope for tonight. Things will only get worse, much worse, if they ever catch sight of His Highness, so please tell him that we, too, are preparing for the night that I believe he has mentioned to my mistress." She also told him how sharp-eyed her mistress's nurse was.

"It is no joke, you know, his coming all the way here," Tokikata replied, "and considering the risk he is taking, I would merely look incompetent if I brought him a useless answer like that. All right, come with me. We can explain it to him together!"

Saddle blanket

"But I cannot do that!" Jijū protested, and the night wore on while they argued about it.

His Highness was waiting some distance away, still mounted, when dogs with barbarous voices came barking terrifyingly around him, until everyone with him—and on a mad escapade like this there were very few—was beside himself with worry over what might happen if ruffians of some sort were to rush him.

"Very well, you are going to come with me *now*," Tokikata brusquely announced, and dragged Jijū off. She looked charming, with her hair tucked that way under her arm. He tried to get her on a horse, and when she would have none of it, he picked up her skirts and walked beside her, giving her his own good shoes to wear while he wore an underling's. It became clear when they reached His Highness, and Tokikata began his report, that conversation would be impossible as long as His Highness remained on horseback. Tokikata therefore spread what they called a saddle blanket beneath a peasant's weedy hedge, so that His Highness might dismount. Even His Highness was shocked by his situation. I doubt that I can count on an assured future if I get hurt on an errand like this, he reflected, and at the thought he could only weep. This made the susceptible Jijū particularly sad. She could not have ignored anyone so beautiful, even if he had been her worst enemy in demon form.

He dried his tears a moment. "Can I not have *one* word with her? Why does it have to be this way now? It must be you women who put her up to this!"

Jijū explained to him exactly what was going on. "Please, Your Highness, you must make absolutely certain not to let anyone know the day you have fixed upon. I am ready to do everything I possibly can for you, at whatever cost to myself, when I see you so generously risk everything for her this way." His Highness greatly feared discovery, too, and he could not insist on being angry with her.

It was very late by now, but the watchdogs were still barking, and when His Highness's men chased them off, there came sounds of twanging bowstrings and uncouth men's voices, crying, "Look out for fire!" It was all extremely disconcerting, and His Highness's state as he prepared to return to the City was beyond description.

> "Where I may go now to cast this life of mine away, I know not: white clouds
> hang upon every mountain and my way is dark with tears.[52]

Go now, quickly!" He sent Jijū back. His figure was all charm and grace, and no words can convey the richness of his fragrance, drenched as he was in the dews of the night.

Ukon was just telling her mistress, who lay prostrate and despairing, how she had curtly refused to admit His Highness, when Jijū came in and told her own story. Their mistress did not answer, but she wished that they could not see her like this, with her pillow all but floating away. The next morning she lay long in bed, for shame that they might notice her swollen eyes; then to uphold the barest decency she donned shoulder cords and read the scriptures, praying only to be forgiven the sin of dying before her mother. She took out the picture he had made, and she felt as she gazed at it that he was there before her, enchanting as always, painting it afresh. It was so especially cruel that she had not been able to say a word to him the night before! And how, then, will *he* feel, when he so often promised me long and peaceful years together? She could well imagine, to her shame, that some might speak ill of her, but better that than that he should have to hear people mock her despicable folly! These thoughts brought a poem to mind:

> "Though in black despair I give up this life of mine, an abhorrent name,
> as alas I know full well, will mark me when I am gone."

She missed her mother, too, and even her ill-favored brothers and sisters, of whom she thought so seldom otherwise. Then she remembered Her Highness at Nijō, for there were so many whom she longed to see just one more time. Her women were all chatting away, busy with their dyeing, but she paid them no heed. Once it was night again, she lay sleepless, planning a way to get out of the house without being seen. When dawn came, she looked toward the river and felt death even nearer than for the reluctant sheep.[53]

His Highness sent a bitterly accusing letter, but even now the fear that someone might be watching kept her from writing the answer she wished. She only wrote,

> "If I left no trace, not even an empty husk, behind in this world,
> where, love, would you seek my grave, to accuse me of my wrongs?"[54]

---

52. *Shūishū* 1217: "There can, I know, be no mountain not overspread by wandering, white clouds." The poem plays on *shira[zu]* ("know not") and *shirakumo* ("white clouds"); and on *naku* ("is / are not" and "weep").
53. A sheep walking slowly to be slaughtered; the figure of speech is from the Nehan-gyō.
54. *Gosenshū* 640, by Chūjō no Kōi: "I would die after today, but then, even in dream, where, love, would you go to seek my grave?"

and sent it out to the messenger. She wanted to give his lordship a last word as well, but she could not bear the idea that if she did so, these two fast friends might in time compare what she had sent to each. No, she thought, I shall just leave both wondering what happened to me.

A letter from her mother arrived from the City: "I had an extremely upsetting dream about you last night, and I asked that scriptures be read for you in several temples. I suppose it is because I never got back to sleep, but today I dozed off and dreamed of you again, in the way that they say announces misfortune.[55] That is why I am writing to you, now that I am awake again. Please, please be careful. I greatly fear someone connected with that distinguished lord who calls on you sometimes at that lonely house of yours,[56] and it is especially worrying to dream of you this way when you are already in poor health. I want to go to you, but the Lieutenant's wife is still causing us serious concern because she is ill in a way that suggests the work of a spirit, and I have been forbidden to leave the house at all. You must have scriptures read also in the temple near you." She had included a letter to the temple, as well as a suitable donation. Her daughter was deeply saddened to read the things she had written without ever knowing that, for *her*, her life was now over.

She composed her reply while someone went off to the temple. She had a great deal to say, but she confined herself after all to this:

> "I would have you pray that we two may meet again, in the life to come,
> unconfused by any dream of this present, hapless world."

The wind brought her the sound of the temple bell, announcing the beginning of the scripture reading, and she lay there listening to it intently.

> "To your dying tones add, O temple bell, my voice, lifted in weeping:
> take it to my mother there, to tell her I am no more."

She wrote this on the list of scriptures read,[57] only to be told that the messenger would not return to the City that night; so she left it instead tied to the branch of a tree.

"My heart is racing strangely, and our mistress's mother mentioned frightening dreams," her nurse remarked to the women. "Go and tell the guards to be watchful tonight!"

Oh, no! she thought as she lay nearby.

"I cannot see why you will not eat anything," Nanny went on. "Some gruel, perhaps?" Ever so busily solicitous, she nonetheless was very old now and quite unsightly.

What will she do when I am gone? she wondered touchingly. If only I might hint to her that I can no longer remain in this world! But for fear of instant alarm and tears, she said nothing at all.

55. According to a treatise on dream reading cited in an early commentary, to dream of someone being ill announces that the person is going to die.
56. She fears the jealousy of Kaoru's wife.
57. A paper sent back by the temple, listing the titles of sutras read and the number of scrolls.

Ukon lay down beside her. "They say that the soul of someone with cares like yours may go wandering far away," she said. "Perhaps that is why your mother had those dreams. I implore you to make up your mind and accept the consequences, whatever they may be." She sighed.

Her mistress only lay with her face buried in her soft sleeves.

52

KAGERŌ

The Mayfly

The *kagerō* ("mayfly") hatches in summer and dies only a few hours later. The chapter title comes from the chapter's closing poem, by Kaoru:

"There it is, just there, yet ever beyond my reach, till I look once more, and it is gone, the mayfly, never to be seen again."

The story in "The Mayfly" takes up where it left off in "A Drifting Boat," in Kaoru's twenty-seventh year.

PERSONS

The Commander, age 27 (Kaoru)

Ukifune's mother, the wife of the Governor of Hitachi (Chūjō no Kimi)

Ukon, a gentlewoman at Uji, daughter of Ukifune's nurse

His Highness of War, 28 (Niou)

Tokikata, Niou's retainer

Ukifune's nurse

Jijū, Ukifune's gentlewoman, then enters the service of the Empress

The Treasury Commissioner, Nakanobu, Kaoru's retainer

Her Highness, a wife of His Highness of War, 27 (Naka no Kimi)

The Master of Discipline, formerly the Adept (Uji no Ajari)

Ben, the nun at Uji (Ben no Ama)

The Governor of Hitachi, Ukifune's stepfather

Kozaishō, a gentlewoman in the service of the First Princess

Her Majesty, the Empress, 46 (Akashi no Chūgū)

Her daughter, the First Princess (Onna Ichi no Miya)

Her Highness, the Second Princess, Kaoru's wife, 17 (Onna Ni no Miya)

Dainagon, a gentlewoman in the service of the First Princess

Miya no Kimi, daughter of His Late Highness of Ceremonial, in the service of the Empress

Ben, a gentlewoman in the service of the Empress

Chūjō , a gentlewoman in the service of the First Princess

Down there at Uji the women had discovered that their mistress was gone and were looking for her frantically, but in vain. I shall not describe the scene further, since it resembled the morning after a maiden's abduction in a tale.

The young woman's mother had been worried when her messenger from the City the previous day failed to return, and she dispatched another. "The cocks were still crowing when she sent me off," the man explained. Neither the nurse nor anyone else knew what answer to give him; they were too desperately upset and confused. But although some could only mill about in distress, those who knew what the trouble was remembered how severely despondent she had been and understood that she might well have drowned herself.

They wept as they opened her mother's letter: "I worry about you until I can hardly sleep, which I suppose is why last night I did not even dream of you properly. I had only nightmares, which have left me feeling so strange and so frightened that I want you here for whatever time remains, although I know that you are soon to move to the City. Unfortunately, it will probably rain today."

Ukon wept bitterly when she opened her mistress's note to her mother, written the evening before. There it is, then! She told her mother that she felt she had no hope! Why did she say nothing to *me*? She was never displeased with me, not once, since we were children, and I never kept anything from her, but she has gone off on her last journey without a hint to me of what she meant to do! It is too cruel! Ukon stamped her feet and wept like a little child. She had certainly seen her mistress despondent day after day, but nothing about her had ever suggested that she could conceive anything so utterly horrible. What *had* happened to her, though? Ukon was desperate to know. Meanwhile the shock had left her mistress's nurse unable to do more than mutter, "What are we to do? What are we to do?"

That last reply's most unusual character had seriously alarmed His Highness as well. What can she possibly mean? Has she gone off to hide somewhere, even though she seems to love me, because she is too afraid of just being an amusement of mine? His messenger arrived to find everyone in the household wailing and distraught, and he could not even deliver his letter. "What has happened?" he asked a maid. "Our mistress suddenly died last night," she replied, "and her women are all beside themselves. We have no one here now to look to, and for the moment no one in her service knows quite what to do." The man knew little about His Highness's interest in the matter, and he returned to the City without inquiring further.

His Highness felt that he must be dreaming when the man brought him the news. How very strange! I never heard that she was seriously ill, and although I keep being told that she has been unwell lately, that answer I had from her yesterday showed no sign of it; in fact, it was even prettier than usual. At a loss what to think, he ordered Tokikata to go there and find out exactly what was going on.

"But, Your Highness, his lordship the Commander seems to have heard something, because I gather that he has sternly reprimanded the guards for being lax, and they now challenge anyone who turns up there, even an underling. If I were to go there without a proper excuse, and his lordship were then to hear of it, he might well understand everything. Besides, any house where someone has died suddenly like that is bound to be in an uproar and full of people."

"No doubt, but do you really expect me to bear the uncertainty? Just do whatever you must to talk to Jijū or to someone else who knows, and find out exactly what that story my man brought back means. Servants sometimes talk complete nonsense."

Tokikata pitied him in his obvious distress and set off that evening. Being unencumbered, he traveled swiftly. For the moment it was not raining, but he had dressed for a difficult journey, and he arrived in very humble guise to hear many voices loudly lamenting that the funeral was to be that very night. This was a great shock. He sent in a message to Ukon but was unable to talk to her. "I am afraid that I am too dazed to be able to see you," she sent back. "I am sorry that I cannot meet you, though, because I do not suppose you will be back after this evening."

"Yes, but how can I return to His Highness without learning what happened? May I not at least talk to someone else, then?"

His insistence won him a meeting with Jijū. "It is too awful!" she said. "Surely she herself never imagined going so suddenly, and there are just no words to describe the horror of it. It is like a nightmare. Tell His Highness that we are all stunned. I will tell you about her despair, and about how sorry she felt that night for His Highness, but not until I have composed myself a little. Please come again once the normal mourning confinement is over." She was weeping bitterly.

Inside the house, too, he heard nothing but weeping voices, among which he thought he recognized the nurse's. "Oh, my darling," she was crying, "where have you gone? Oh, come back, come back! It is too hard not even to have your body! I never tired of seeing you, morning or evening, and I always looked forward so much to your being well settled! That is what I have lived for all this time! To think that you have now left me, and that you never even told me where you were going! No god or demon could take you, my darling! Why, they say Taishaku himself sends back those who are too sorely missed![1] Whoever you are who took my darling,

---

1. A scripture tells how Taishaku (Indra) brought a man (a previous incarnation of the Buddha) back to life in answer to the prayers of the man's mother. The tale was known in Japan particularly, thanks to the Buddhist tale collection *Sanbōe*.

human or demon, oh, give her back! Let me at least see her body!" She went on like this, sometimes not even making sense.

"Please tell me more. Can someone have made off with her? His Highness sent me here to represent him in an effort to find out exactly what happened. There is no help for it now, whatever the truth may be, and he will only blame me, his messenger, if later on he hears anything that suggests I misinformed him. I am sure that you understand how much it means to him to know, since he sent me here to talk to you in full faith that you would tell me. There are old instances in the other realm,[2] too, of men lost because of love for a woman, but I doubt that any man has ever been as much in love as he."

Yes, Jijū thought, it *is* remarkable to see his messenger here, and anything this unusual will certainly come out in the end, whatever one may do to hide it. "Do you think that the whole household would be this upset if there were the slightest reason to believe someone made off with her? She was suffering a great deal lately, and then, as luck would have it, his lordship dropped her a very troubling hint as well. Her mother and her nurse—the one you hear wailing that way—were getting her ready to go to the gentleman who knew her first, but in the secret of her own thoughts she felt a more tender leaning toward His Highness, and I expect that that is what made her so unhappy. I am afraid that she does seem to have purposely done away with herself, and I am sure that that is why her nurse is babbling all sorts of things that hardly make sense."

In this circuitous manner she conveyed some of what had happened, but Tokikata found that he did not yet quite understand. "Very well, then, I shall be back in due course. It is so frustrating to remain standing this way.[3] I expect that next time His Highness will come himself."

"Oh, no, that would be too good of him! As things are now, it would only honor her memory if people were to learn what she meant to him, but it was a secret after all, and I am sure he would agree that it should remain one." She cautioned him this way before he left because the household was doing everything to avoid revealing that its mistress had died so strangely, and he had of course gathered what the real situation was.

Their mistress's mother now arrived, too, in pouring rain. Lacking words to express her feelings, she murmured confusedly, "It is a great sorrow actually to see someone die, but at least such things are common enough. What *can* have happened, though, in her case?" The idea that her daughter might have drowned herself had not occurred to her, since she knew nothing about her anguish over what had been going on, and she could only suppose that a demon had devoured her or that some foxlike creature had made off with her—she remembered strange things just like that turning up in old tales;[4] or perhaps an evil-minded nurse, for example,

---

2. China.

3. To avoid the pollution of death.

4. *Ise monogatari* 6 tells a particularly famous story about a demon who ate a hapless young woman "in one gulp." Tales of magic foxes who take the form of a beautiful young woman to lead men astray are common in the folklore of the period, although there are no obvious surviving examples of a fox abducting a young woman.

someone close to the great lady who frightened her so much,[5] had learned that his lordship planned to bring her daughter to the City and had felt sufficiently offended to enlist someone's help in plotting her abduction.

"Is there anyone new here?" she asked, suspecting a servant, but the women said, "No, this place is so isolated that no one unused to it ever manages to stay on. They always go home again to the City, saying they will come straight back and taking with them everything they need to remain away." Half even of those who had long served her daughter were now gone, and in fact the household had very few people in it.

Jijū, remembering those last days, thought how often her mistress had wept bitterly and said that she only wanted to die. She found beneath her mistress's ink-stone a piece of paper bearing the scribbled words "mark me when I am gone," and this turned her gaze toward the river, whose loud roar was now dreary and hateful. "It is so difficult," she said, "having everyone imagining this and that about what happened, doubting all we say, and wondering what has really become of her."

"It was a secret, of course," Ukon replied, "but it is not as though she started it, and considering who His Highness is, there is really no reason now that she is gone why her mother should be ashamed to hear of it. I think we might just tell her what happened and relieve some of the agony she is going through, including these particular little fears of hers that worry her so. The usual thing when someone has died is to lay out the body and proceed with what follows, and there will be no hiding the truth if the strange situation we have now continues day after day. Yes, we should tell her and at least keep up appearances for the world at large."

They agreed to do so and privately told their mistress's mother everything, although as they spoke, the terrible words died on their lips. She thought as she listened in consternation, Why, then, my daughter drowned in the current of that fearsome river! and she wanted only to throw herself in after her. "But we must go and look for her and at least dispose of her body properly!"

"No," Ukon answered, "it would be useless to try. She must be out to sea by now. Besides, that would just start even worse talk."

This sort of idea just made the poor lady feel sick, and she asked the two women to have her carriage brought up, since she had not the faintest idea what else to do. They placed in it the mats and bedding from their mistress's room,[6] as well as all the accessories she had used daily and the bedclothes that still lay there as though she had just thrown them off. Then they sent the carriage on its way exactly as when someone has died, accompanied by the reverend monk their mistress's foster brother, by her uncle the Adept, and by his close disciples as well as by the other monks with whom she had long been acquainted—in short, by all those who would be present during the mourning confinement. Meanwhile their mistress's mother and nurse writhed in paroxysms of disturbing grief.

The Commissioner,[7] the Constable, and other such menacing characters ar-

5. Kaoru's wife, the Second Princess.
6. The corpse would normally be laid on these for cremation.
7. The Right Guards Commissioner, a son-in-law of the Constable who appeared in the last chapter.

rived. "You should inform his lordship about the funeral, set a date for it, and do the thing properly," they said, but Ukon told them that the household wanted particularly to have it over with tonight. "We have reasons for keeping it extremely discreet," she explained. She directed the carriage to the meadow below the hill opposite, kept everyone at a distance, and had the monks called in to proceed with the cremation. The smoke died out distressingly soon.

The country people, who take such things particularly seriously and who carefully observe the injunction against ill-omened speech, were shocked. "How very strange!" they complained. "They are not doing it right at all! They are just rushing through it as though she were a worthless menial!"

"I hear people from the City do it this way on purpose when there are surviving brothers or sisters." Such were the dubious comments exchanged on the subject.

Even *these* people's talk is a worry, Jijū and Ukon said to themselves, and if out there in the wider world his lordship the Commander learns that she left no corpse when she died, he will certainly have grave doubts about the whole thing. For a while he may wonder whether she is with His Highness, who is at least a relative of his, but in the end he will discover the truth about that. And he may not suspect only His Highness; he will start wondering who else could have stolen her from him. Dreadful suspicions may well indeed mark her when she is gone, despite the good fortune she enjoyed while she lived. They took care to seal the lips of all the household servants who had witnessed this morning's commotion and to make sure that they did not discuss it with outsiders. "All in good time we will quietly tell everyone concerned what really happened," they assured each other, "but for the moment it would be too awful if people were suddenly to learn anything that distracted them from mourning her." Guilt made them both eager to keep the secret.

It was a busy time for his lordship the Commander, because Her Cloistered Highness his mother was ill, and he had therefore gone on retreat to Ishiyama. Being away only heightened his concern about Uji, but no one actually told him what had happened, and as a result the household there felt shamed before everyone that even so great a misfortune had failed to elicit a messenger from him. A man from one of his estates brought him the news at last. He was shocked, and a messenger from him reached Uji early the next morning.

"Word of this tragedy should have brought me straight to you in person," his message went, "but my mother is unwell, and for that reason I have undertaken to remain on retreat here for a certain number of days. Why did you proceed with the ceremony in haste yesterday evening, when you could perfectly well have got in touch with me and postponed it for some time? It is all over now, of course, but it is also very painful for me to have the rustics of your hills criticizing the way the last rites were done."

This was delivered by his intimate retainer the Treasury Commissioner,[8] whose arrival provoked a fresh outburst of grief. They could not possibly tell him what had actually happened, though, and they avoided giving any proper answer by taking refuge in a flood of tears.

8. The Nakanobu mentioned in the previous chapter.

What a pathetic end! the Commander thought when he heard his messenger's report. And what an awful place it is! There must be a demon living there. What can have possessed me, to leave her so long in a place like that? As to that most unfortunate business of His Highness, no doubt my complacent way of all but abandoning her there is what gave him the chance to impose himself on her in the first place! He felt a sharp pang of regret over his own strangely nonchalant manner. It was too deplorable of him to be preoccupied by an affair of this kind when his mother was ill, and he returned to the City.

He did not go to see Her Highness when he arrived; instead he sent her a message that he had just had some disastrous news about someone close to him, though of no great rank, and that for the moment he was too upset to present himself. Then he gave himself up to lamenting his tragic loves. Why, when I now desperately miss those looks of hers, and her sweet charm, and all the delight of her presence, why did I not wholeheartedly love her while she lived, and instead let time slip carelessly by? Countless regrets tormented him now that he could no longer assuage them. Ah, how thoroughly in such things I am destined for the blackest sorrow! I whose aspiration always lay in another direction have ended up to my own surprise living as all men do, until the very Buddha must have had enough of me! He must have smothered his compassion and devised just this sort of trial as an expedient means to lead people's hearts toward higher things. So his thoughts ran on, while he gave himself over entirely to holy devotions.

His Highness meanwhile was still more deeply affected. For two or three days he seemed completely to have lost his senses, causing frenzied anxiety that some sort of spirit might have possessed him, until at last his tears ceased to flow and he regained a measure of calm, although even then he dwelled on her memory with desperate longing. For the benefit of those around him he skillfully pretended to suffer only from a grave illness, lest they note his inexplicably tear-swollen eyes, but the nature of his trouble was nonetheless plain to see, and some of his people wondered aloud what woman could possibly have reduced him to such an extremity of distress that his very life seemed in danger.

The Commander of course had reports of all this. I was right, then, he said to himself. They were *not* just exchanging letters. Once he had seen her, he would certainly have wanted her—that is just what she was like. I would not have gone unscathed if she had lived; something would undoubtedly have happened to make me look a fool. Reflections of this kind seemed to him to quell somewhat the flames that burned in his breast.

Day after day the whole court came calling to inquire after His Highness's health, and the Commander therefore decided to do so, too, since with all the world in such an uproar it might have seemed strange if mourning for someone inconsequential were to detain him. He was wearing blue-gray anyway in mourning for an uncle, His Highness of Ceremonial, who had recently died, and this suited him perfectly, for in the depths of his heart he felt as though he were wearing it for *her.* He was a little thinner than he had been, which only enhanced his elegant looks.

It was a quiet dusk, after all the other visitors had gone. His Highness, who did not really feel like keeping entirely to his bed, received personally only those close to him, and he could not very well turn away someone who was accustomed to coming straight in through his blinds. He shrank from the thought of seeing him, since he did not doubt that doing so would bring on fresh tears, but he nonetheless composed himself sufficiently to say, "There is really nothing seriously wrong with me, but everyone is talking as though I were in serious danger, and I am sorry that Their Majesties should be so alarmed. It is true, though, that life is very uncertain, and I wonder what is to become of me." He wiped away tears meant only to divert his visitor's attention, but to his acute embarrassment they flowed on and on. Still, he said to himself, he can hardly know why; he probably just thinks me weak and unmanly.

Sure enough! thought the Commander. All this misery of his is over *her*! When can it have begun? He must have been laughing at me for months!

The grief vanished so visibly from his expression that His Highness exclaimed to himself how cold the fellow was. When something is seriously troubling *me*, even something far short of this, the mere cry of a bird passing overhead can overwhelm me.[9] Here I am, obviously very upset, and if he knows what the matter is, which he must, he cannot be *that* impervious to human feelings! How detached a man can be when he really knows that all things pass! He both envied and admired his visitor's composure, but he was touched as well to remember the stalwart support he had been to the Uji house.[10] He is a token of her, after all! he thought, gazing at the Commander and imagining the two of them together.

After some time spent chatting about this and that, the Commander decided that he could no longer remain silent. "In the old days," he began, "I never felt at ease with myself as long as I kept anything from you, however briefly, although by now, what with the rank to which I have risen and the many preoccupations that leave you so little leisure, I am unable to wait upon you at night, say, as I used to, in the absence of any particular pressing need, so that I cannot keep in touch with you as well as I would like. Some time ago I happened to hear that a relative of the young woman who passed away in that mountain village—the one where you used to call—lived where I would not have expected to find her, and it occurred to me that I might see her now and again, if it had not been that at the time I might unfortunately have risked a degree of criticism by doing so. I therefore installed her there, in that distant and lonely place, and I managed to visit her all too rarely. Meanwhile I gathered that *she* was not especially eager to rely solely on me. However, that would have mattered only if I had meant to treat her with high honor, which I did not, and it was of little consequence as long as my main wish was simply to provide for her welfare; and now it has come to pass that this young person, whose sweetness and charm I found engaging, has tragically died. It is very sad in-

---

9. A common motif in poetry; the bird would probably be a cuckoo (*hototogisu*) in spring or a wild goose (*kari*) in autumn.

10. The entire second half of the sentence ("he was touched as well . . .") is in the original simply *maki-bashira aware nari*, more literally, "the pillar of fine wood was touching."

deed to have to contemplate in her example all the treachery of life. I expect that you may have had word of this yourself." Now, at last, he wept. These were not tears that he had wished His Highness to see, but once they began to flow, he was powerless to stop them.

His Highness was surprised to see his visitor somewhat undone, and he felt at once pained and troubled, but he maintained his composure. "I am very, very sorry to hear it," he said. "I heard a rumor to that effect only yesterday, and I wanted to ask you more about it, but I gathered that you did not wish it to be widely known." The great difficulty of sustaining his air of detachment prevented him from saying more.

"I had thought that I might offer you the pleasure of knowing her, you see—or perhaps you yourself knew her already, since she had reason to call on Her Highness." Little by little he was showing his colors. "But I must apologize for troubling you with idle and tedious talk during a time when you yourself are so unwell," he concluded, and took his leave.

It really has affected him deeply! he said to himself. How high her destiny was, even though she lived so briefly! He is a Prince, Their Majesties' favorite, and he enjoys looks and every other advantage beyond anyone else of our time. The great ladies whom he honors with his allegiance are both of the very highest distinction, and yet it is she who moved him to folly, she for whom he indulged in such madness that all the world rang with litanies, scripture chanting, purifications, and prayers to the gods! Even I, such as I am, who am privileged to claim His Majesty's daughter as my own, seem to have been as entranced with her as he, and now that she is gone, I, too, am inconsolable! No, I will have no more of this foolishness! Alas, his effort to be reasonable failed in every way, and he lay humming to himself, "Every man is subject to passion, for he is neither stock nor stone."[11]

He wondered with pain and disappointment how His Highness[12] might have taken the news of the poor way things had been done afterward—he supposed that it had all been kept very plain because her mother was common and because she had surviving brothers and sisters, as he gathered someone had remarked, and the very idea offended him. There were a great many things that he did not quite understand, and he longed to ask for himself exactly what had happened, but he could not work out how to go about it because he simply could not join the long mourning confinement, and it would hurt too much to go there only to come straight back again.

The new month began,[13] and nightfall on the day when he remembered she was to have moved to the City was very sad indeed. The orange tree in his garden brought back with its scent poignant memories, and a cuckoo called twice as it flew by. "Should you visit her where she has gone,"[14] he murmured in anguish; and since

---

11. Derived from a poem by Bai Juyi (*Hakushi monjū* 0160).
12. Or Her Highness, Naka no Kimi.
13. The fourth.
14. *Kokinshū* 855: "Should you visit her where she has gone, O cuckoo, tell her that I ever lift my voice in lamentation."

His Highness was just then due to go to Nijō, he sent him there, with a spray that he had had picked,

> *"You, too, I suppose, softly cry your secret grief, as long as your heart*
> *goes to where she oversees the fields on the road of death."*[15]

His Highness and his wife were just then musing together in sad silence, while her resemblance to the love he had lost sharpened his sorrow. Seeing that the note was fraught with meaning, he wrote,

> *"Take heed, O cuckoo, when you think to lift your cry there where such fragrance*
> *wafts from the orange blossoms, bringing back dear memories!*

It is too much!"

The lady beside him knew very well what the matter was. Alas! she sadly reflected. How tragically short a while they[16] lived, with all their cares! I who have so few have now outlived them both, though for how long? His Highness could no longer bear to keep from her something that had ceased to be a secret, and he gave her a somewhat doctored account of all that had happened. "I hated you for hiding her from me!" he added, amid laughter and tears, because the two had been sisters, which made him feel especially close to her. At that other house, so grand and proper, there was no end to the vexations visited on him when he was indisposed by *that* lady's importunately solicitous father, the Minister, and by her many brothers; but he knew that here he could always feel comfortably at home.

He still kept wondering, though, whether he had dreamed it all, because he did not see how it could really have been that sudden. He therefore summoned his usual band of men and sent them off to fetch Ukon. Her late mistress's mother had returned to the City because the roar of the river called to her too urgently to follow her daughter, and she doubted that at Uji she would ever have relief from her sorrow. The place was almost deserted when they arrived, apart from a few priests chanting the Name. The guards who had appeared so suddenly and so ostentatiously never challenged them at all, and they thought bitterly how cruel it was that those same guards had refused to admit His Highness even on that last journey to her. Yes, they, too, had silently condemned him for yielding to such unbecoming folly, but now the memory of those nights when he had gone to her, and of the noble grace with which he had carried her that time into the boat, left the bravest of them unmanned.

Ukon received Tokikata, naturally enough amid a flood of tears. "That is what

---

15. As suggested by the poem in the previous note, the cuckoo was held in poetry to pass back and forth between the world of the living and the land of the dead, crying its low cry, *shinobine:* the word used also for stifled sobs of secret grief. It could therefore also be assimilated to *shide no taosa* ("master of the paddy fields in the realm of the dead"), a shadowy figure widely encountered in Japanese folklore. Kaoru supposes that, like the cuckoo he has just heard, Niou is crying his *shinobine,* and that Niou's heart, like the cuckoo, goes to Ukifune among the dead.

16. Ōigimi and Ukifune.

His Highness wished me to tell you," Tokikata explained, "and I have come to fetch you for him."

"I am afraid that some here might find it strange if I were to go just now," she replied, "and besides, even if I did, I doubt that in my present state I would be up to making anything very clear to him. It will look a bit better if I wait till later, after our confinement is over, to give them an excuse for a trip to the City, and I promise that I will, although for myself I hardly wish to live that long. By then I shall be feeling a little more composed. I should like to call upon him then—he need not repeat his invitation—and tell him the whole story, which I quite agree is just like a dream." For today there was no sign that she was to be moved.

Tokikata wept. "I myself was never privy to what passed between those two," he said, "and it is not for such as I to pretend to understand them, but my own eyes witnessed his extraordinary devotion, and I saw no reason to seek your friendship too quickly, since it seemed obvious that in time I would have the pleasure of serving you myself. This dreadful thing that has happened has only confirmed me in my feeling for you." He concluded his speech by saying, "It would be a great shame to have to bring the carriage back empty, when His Highness has been kind enough to send it for you. Perhaps someone else would agree to go."

Ukon called out Jijū. "Please go yourself, then," she said.

"But what could I possibly tell him?" Jijū protested. "No, no, I must not, not as long we remain confined. Does His Highness have no fear of defilement?"

"What with the commotion caused by his illness, there are all sorts of penances being done for him, but he does not look to me as though he himself has the patience to wait that long. In fact, he might well prefer to go into retreat for someone who meant so much to him. There are not many days left anyway. Do come, one of you."

His insistence convinced Jijū to comply after all, for she remembered His Highness very fondly indeed, and, as she said to herself, When will I ever again have such a chance to see him? Dressed all in dark gray and handsomely groomed, she really was very pretty. Since she no longer had a mistress, she had neglected to dye herself a train in the same color, and she had a page girl bring a pale gray-violet one instead. It saddened her very much to think that this was the path her mistress would have quietly taken, if she had lived, since her own secret inclination lay that way.

His Highness felt a pang when they announced her arrival, but he said nothing about it to his wife; that would have been too unkind. He went to the main house and had Jijū alight in the gallery. In response to his pressing questions about her mistress's last days, Jijū described her state of despair and told him how she had wept that night. "She usually had extraordinarily little to say, Your Highness," she explained. "She was never one to express herself clearly, and it was rare for her to tell anyone else even about things that affected her deeply. I expect that this reticence of hers is the reason why she left no last words either. We never dreamed that she could be planning such a thing."

Her circumstantial account troubled His Highness still further. What can have impelled her to drown herself in such a river, he wondered, rather than entrust her days to the destiny prepared for her by karma? He wished desperately, though in vain, that he had found her and stopped her.

"Oh, why did this never occur to us when she burned and disposed of her letters?" Jijū cried. They talked the night through, and she told him about her mistress's reply to her mother, left written on the list of scriptures.

His Highness had never paid any particular attention to Jijū before, but the intimacy of their shared grief moved him to say, "Come into service here! It is not as though you were nothing to Her Highness."

"I should be honored to do so, Your Highness, but for the time being I think it would make me too sad. Perhaps after the mourning is over."

"You·must come again, then." He could not bear to part even with her. She started back at dawn, and he sent a set of comb boxes and one of clothing chests with her, gifts meant originally for her mistress. He had actually had many, many things made for her, but for Jijū he confined himself to these, since he did not wish to overdo his generosity.

What will they think of me, after my innocent visit to him, when I come back with all *this*? she wondered. This is a surprising embarrassment! She could hardly refuse them, though, despite her dismay. She and Ukon examined them privately together, having so little else to do, and they wept copiously when they saw how utterly exquisite and stylish they were. The clothes in the chests, too, were perfectly beautiful. "We had better keep these out of sight during mourning," they said to each other, not really knowing what to do with them.

His lordship the Commander now arrived, for he could no longer contain his desire to know more. All the way there he pondered the past and wondered what bond from lives gone by had first led him to seek out His Late Highness. And ever since then, he reflected, I have looked after his daughters, even to the strange end of this last and least expected of them, and suffered constantly over them! He was such a saintly man, and our tie was always our hope for the life to come, under the Buddha's guidance, but for me it led only to error and sin—which I suppose must have been the Buddha's way of bringing me to the truth after all.

He summoned Ukon. "I never heard properly just what happened," he said, "and what I was told so shocked me that I had meant to come after your mourning confinement was over, since that will be soon; but then I could bear it no longer, and I came anyway. What was your mistress's condition when she died?"

The nun Ben knows what the matter was, Ukon reflected, and since he is likely to have the story from her in any case, any attempt on my part to conceal it from him will only fail when she tells him something quite different. She had armed herself with lies to cover up the distressing affair, but in the presence of such sincere concern she forgot the tall tales she had meant to tell and, not knowing what else to do, simply told him the truth.

Her unexpected revelation stunned him, and he found himself at a loss for words. That is beyond belief! he thought. She who had so little to say, even on matters that others discuss easily, and who was always so mild—how *could* she have made up her mind to do such a terrible thing? What were these women trying to hide? The thought only increased his dismay; and yet His Highness's grief had been perfectly plain. And the scene here at the house in Uji: if they had been merely feigning calm, he would certainly have been able to tell, whereas he could hear that in fact his arrival had plunged them all again, high or low, into loud lamentation.

"Did anyone else disappear with her? Tell me more about precisely what happened. I doubt that she wanted to leave me because she was disappointed in me. What unspeakable anguish can suddenly made her do such a thing? I simply cannot believe it."

So here we are, thought Ukon, at once sorry and troubled. "You probably know the whole story already, my lord," she said. "Having been brought up in the first place under unfortunate circumstances, my mistress slipped into unbroken melancholy after she came to live here, so far away from anywhere else; but rare as your visits were, she always looked forward to them, and I know, although she never said so, that whenever her mind was off her old troubles, she eagerly anticipated being able to see you often and at your leisure. We who served her were happy to learn that this hope of hers was to be realized, and we set about preparing for the day, as her mother did very gladly when it seemed that what she had wanted for her daughter was to come true and that she was to move to the City. But then there was that mystifying note from you, and your stern reprimand to the guards about some trouble caused by one of her women, which the rough country people here, who understand nothing, took in the worst way they could. After that there was nothing more from you for a long time, and she who had known all too well since childhood what misfortune she was born to became convinced that her mother's efforts to see her respectably settled would in the end yield nothing but ridicule. She knew how cruel a blow that would be to her mother, and it caused her constant agony. Apart from that, I cannot imagine what might have put such a thought into her head. They say that if a demon had made off with her, it would at least have left *something* of her behind!" She was weeping so much that his suspicions melted away, and he could not stop his tears either.

"Being who I am, I am not free to do as I please," he replied, "for my every move may be scrutinized; and that is why, when your mistress's welfare here concerned me most, I at least felt confident of assuring her a future close by and in a style that no one could fault; and if that made her feel I was treating her coldly, then I can only assume that some part of her affections was engaged elsewhere. I had not meant to bring up the subject now, nor would I if anyone else could hear me, but there *is* the matter of His Highness. I wonder when it began. When it comes to this sort of thing, he is unfortunately a master at turning a young woman's head, and I am therefore inclined to believe that she took her life because she could not have him all the time. You must tell me more about that. Please keep nothing from me."

So he *does* know! she thought in profound dismay. "I gather that you have heard some extremely cruel talk, my lord. And yet I myself was always with her, I assure you." She paused a moment. "Well, I expect that you have heard what happened. That time when my mistress sought quiet refuge with Her Highness at Nijō, he came straight into her room, to our horror, although we spoke to him so sharply that he went away again. That fright decided her to move to the curious little house you know. She was determined that he should hear no more of her after that, but he still managed somehow to find out where she was, and this past second month she had a letter from him. Many more came after that, but she would never read them. We told her that she should feel honored and that it was actually rude of her not to reply, and so I believe that she did answer him once or twice. That is all I know."

What else could he expect her to say? It would be cruel to question her further. Instead he lapsed into thought. Even if she was swept away by His Highness, she did not just for that think less well of *me*, and being as vague as she was, and as easily swayed, she must have got the idea for what she did simply from having the river nearby. She would never, never have sought out the abyss,[17] whatever suffering life brought her, if I had not left her here in the first place. How he detested that river and all the dire grief it meant to him! For many years affection had drawn him here, back and forth over those rough mountain roads, but he hated the place now; he did not want even to hear the sound of its name. He shivered just to remember when Her Highness at Nijō had first mentioned her half sister and he had first talked of a "doll" of the love he had lost. He kept telling himself, It is my fault that she died. He had assumed with disapproval that her mother had arranged the last rites badly and meanly because she herself was of low birth, but he could only sympathize with her now that he knew the whole story. It seemed to him that her daughter was thoroughly deserving, having the father she did, but that she herself, who could not know her daughter's secret, must wonder what could have happened between her daughter and people close to himself. The whole thing was very painful. No defilement was involved, that much he now knew, but to keep up appearances before his men he did not actually enter the house; instead he called for a carriage shaft bench and sat on it before the double doors. However, that did not become a man in his position, and he therefore moved to sit on the moss in the dense grove of trees. From there he looked about him, doubting that he would ever want to see this place again.

> "If now even I leave this old and hateful place to go to ruin,
> who will keep in memory the shade of these ivied trees?"

The Adept by now was a Master of Discipline. The Commander summoned him and let him know what rites he was to perform. He also added to the number of monks calling the Name. With the gravity of the sin in mind, he gave detailed instructions on the scriptures and images to be dedicated on each seventh day, in order to lighten the burden it imposed. It was quite dark by the time he left, reflecting as he did so that he would certainly not have gone back that evening if she had been alive. He sent the nun a message, but she did not appear. "Alas," she replied, "I shall continue to lie here, for I am by now a horror even to myself, and I retain too little of my wits to understand anything at all." He did not insist on approaching her in person. All the way home he nursed bitter regret that he had not called her to the City earlier, when she was so dear to him, and turmoil overwhelmed him as long as

---

17. *Kokinshū* 1061: "If we all drowned ourselves when life tries us too sorely, the abyss would all too soon be filled."

he still heard the river. Ah, he thought, sighing helplessly, she met such a terrible end, and they never even found her body! What watery gulf has claimed her now?

Vehemently expressed fears of defilement that might affect her pregnant daughter in the City had prevented the grieving mother from going home, and she had had to make do with temporary lodgings, where she worried about the fate of this child, too. However, the birth went smoothly after all. She could not go to her yet, though, because the threat of pollution remained, and she was lamenting her unhappy circumstances, oblivious to any thought of her other children, when a messenger quietly arrived from the Commander. She was deliriously pleased and touched.

"I had wished straightaway to convey to you my deep sympathy over the tragedy that has touched us both," he had written, "but I myself was too distraught to do so, and I seemed to see only darkness before my eyes, even while I knew that you were lost in sorrow blacker still. And yet how quickly the days have passed! The fleeting character of life is more intolerable than ever, but having somehow managed to survive this long, I look forward to hearing from you at your convenience, in memory of her."

It was a long letter, and his messenger was the Treasury Commissioner, who now added this spoken message from him: "While I patiently allowed the months to pass and the New Year to arrive, you yourself may have come to doubt the sincerity of my intentions. Please know, however, that after this I shall never forget you. You may be privately certain of that. Moreover, I gather that you have several other children, and you may count on my support when they come to serve His Majesty."

"My contact with defilement was actually rather slight," she said, since there was indeed no great need for caution, and she insisted on inviting the Commissioner in. Then in tears she wrote her reply.

"I have lamented ever since the tragedy that I am still all too cruelly alive, but your kind words are what I have after all lived on to receive. Hitherto the spectacle of my daughter's unhappiness gave me cause to reflect that the fault was mine, considering how insignificant I am, but the wish you then expressed, to do her the honor of bringing her to the City, inspired great confidence in the future. That village means only misery and sorrow, now that all that has come to naught. Your most welcome communications have lightened the burden of my years, and the idea that I may continue to look to you, provided that my life is to last a little longer, brings such tears to my eyes that I can write no more."

The sort of reward usually given a messenger might have seemed out of place at such a time, but she did not want to send him away empty-handed. Accordingly, she placed in a bag a handsome sword and a fine belt of mottled rhinoceros horn[18] that she had meant to give her daughter, and she sent them out to him as he was boarding his carriage, with the message that her late daughter would have wished it.

"She should not have done it," the Commander remarked when he examined them.

---

18. A "stone belt" adorned with rhinoceros horn was worn by a gentleman of the fourth or fifth rank.

"She was kind enough to receive me in person, my lord," the Commissioner reported, "and she wept a great deal as she spoke. She said that your words about her children did them far too much honor and that their lack of any merit could only discourage her from acting on your offer, but that she will send them all, such as they are, to serve you without revealing the reason why. That was her message to you."

Yes, the Commander thought, relations like these certainly confer no luster on one, but have not even Emperors accepted the daughters of such people? And who would criticize their bestowing such favor, when in any case it was meant to be? As to commoners, many have accepted women low in rank or previously married. Never mind if the world at large assumes her to have been that Governor's daughter—it is not as though my own courtship of her was sullied at the start by any such understanding. What I want is to let her mother know that despite the sorrow of losing a daughter, her tie with me will honor her yet.

The Governor of Hitachi, her husband, turned up briefly, although he remained standing. "Look at you, off by yourself here at a time like this!" he exclaimed angrily. She had never told him where her daughter was or let him know anything about her circumstances, and he had therefore always assumed that the girl had come to grief, while she on her side had been planning to tell him in triumph once the Commander had brought her to the City. Now, though, it was pointless to remain silent any longer, and through her tears she told him everything. His provincial awe of the true nobility moved him to wonder and fear when she took out the Commander's letter and showed it to him, and he read it over and over again. "What grand good fortune she lost when she died!" he said at last. "I myself serve among his distant retainers, but he has never called me into his presence, for he is a very great and proud lord indeed. It means so much, you know, that he should have spoken that way of the children!"

Before the spectacle of his pleasure she could only writhe, weeping, on the floor, aching for her daughter still to be alive. Now the Governor shed a tear himself. Nonetheless, he doubted that a man like the Commander would really have taken much interest in her if she had lived. He probably feels guilty because it is his fault that she died, he told himself, and he just wants to make her mother feel better. That is why he does not too much mind putting up with a little disapproval.

What *did* happen to her, though? the Commander wondered when the time came to hold the forty-ninth-day rites. They could do her no harm either way, however, so he had them done quietly at the Master of Discipline's temple. He had arranged generous offerings for the sixty monks. The Governor's wife, who was present as well, added others of her own. Through Ukon, His Highness sent a silver jar filled with gold. Since he could not make his offering grandly, in a manner that might draw attention to himself, Ukon made it for him as though it were her own, at which those who did not know the truth wondered to each other how she could possibly afford it. His lordship sent all his closest retainers to assist. Many who had not known of the deceased before remarked how extraordinary it all was. "See how he honors the memory of somebody of whom no one has ever heard!" they said. "Who can she have been?" The Governor of Hitachi came, too, boorishly lording it about the place to general shock and dismay. Having seen the Lieutenant's[19] child into the world, he was keen to celebrate the birth magnificently, and his house lacked very little in the way of adornments from Koma and Cathay; but there was only so much the likes of him could manage, and it made a poor show after all. These rites, he knew, were meant to be discreet, but when he saw with his own eyes their utter grandeur, he understood that if his wife's first daughter had lived, she would have been destined to heights far loftier than his own. His Highness's wife provided for the scripture readings and for the meals served the seven officiants. By now His Majesty himself had heard of this love of the Commander's, and he regretted that the Commander should have kept her concealed in deference to the Second Princess, his wife.

The sorrow of mourning remained ever fresh both for His Highness and for the Commander, and His Highness suffered especially from the pain of suddenly losing so perilous a passion, but his roving heart soon began to seek consolation elsewhere. As for the Commander, he continued as before his loyal solicitude toward all those left to claim his attention, though he did not for a moment forget what his loss meant to him.

Her Majesty remained at Rokujō during her light mourning,[20] and meanwhile the Second Prince became Lord of the Bureau of Ceremonial. His now weighty position gave him little leisure to visit her. That other son of hers, His Highness of War, often sought refuge from loneliness and sorrow at the residence of his sister, the First Princess, where, to his regret, he had not yet quite managed to possess all of her beauties. One among them, a certain Kozaishō, with whom his lordship the Commander had succeeded at last in establishing secret relations, was particularly lovely and, to the Commander's mind, strikingly accomplished as well. Any stringed instrument in her hands yielded a superior tone. The letters she wrote, the little things she said, always had something memorable about them. His Highness had long been impressed with her, too, and he typically did his best to talk her into thinking less well of the Commander, but she saw no reason to give in like all the others, and her maddening obstinacy convinced her more stalwart admirer that she was indeed a rather exceptional woman.

Knowing full well how deeply the Commander felt his loss, she wrote to him in a rush of emotion:

> "*Quick to sympathy: that my heart has always been, more than anyone's,*
> *but I matter not at all, and silence must be my rule.*

Had it been I, not she . . ."[21]

Her choice of paper was just right, and in the quiet of so melancholy a twilight he was touched by the precision with which she had gauged his mood.

---

19. His son-in-law's.

20. She is in mourning for her adoptive mother Murasaki's father, the late Lord of the Bureau of Ceremonial. Mourning for an uncle (the period lasted three months) was defined as "light," in contrast to that for a parent.

21. "If I had died, rather than Ukifune, [you would not feel it so much]." Kozaishō's phrase (*kaetaraba*) may be from the second half of *Gosenshū* 1364, by Teiji no In (Emperor Uda).

"Schooled by misfortune, many and many a time, to learn nothing lasts,
I yet never meant to sigh so loudly that all might know."

He went straight to thank her by telling her how particularly that word from her had pleased him at such a time. Dauntingly dignified as he was, he rarely called on a gentlewoman this way, and her room was unworthy of so great a lord, since it was really very small and had such a narrow door. This greatly embarrassed her; but she did not overdo her apologies, and she spoke to him very nicely indeed. She has a good deal more to her than *she* did, he thought—I wonder why she went into service like this. I would gladly have her all to myself! However, his manner betrayed nothing of these secret feelings.

In lotus blossom season Her Majesty held a Rite of the Eight Discourses. Each day was dedicated to His Grace of Rokujō, to Lady Murasaki, and so on, and the scriptures and images she had prepared for the occasion were extremely impressive. The day for the fifth scroll promised such a spectacle that people everywhere took advantage of their connection with one gentlewoman or another to come and see it.[22]

Once the rite was over, after the morning session on the fifth day, the household staff came straight in—the sliding panels between the chamber and the north aisle having been removed for the occasion—to take down the chapel adornments and change the room's furnishings. The First Princess repaired to the west bridgeway, and her gentlewomen retired to their own rooms, exhausted from listening to so much preaching. Very few were actually with her in the gathering dusk. Meanwhile the Commander had changed into a dress cloak and gone to the fishing pavilion to discuss something urgently with the monks, only to find them already gone; he was out over the lake, enjoying the cool. So few people were about that Kozaishō and the others had put up only standing curtains and so on to give themselves a place to rest. Ah, she must be *there!* he thought when he heard the rustling of silks, and he peeped in through a slender gap between the sliding panels off toward the passageway. So great a lady seldom sat in a place like that, and they had given her so much room that he could actually see straight in past the staggered curtains. Three women and a page girl were chipping with great animation at a block of ice that rested before them on a tray.[23] Their attire was so casual, since they wore neither Chinese jackets nor dress gowns, that he did not see how they really could be with Her Highness, and yet there she was, in white silk gauze,[24] holding a bit of ice and watching the fray with a slight smile on her enchantingly beautiful face. Her rich hair must have oppressed her on such an intolerably hot day, for she had swept it forward a little, toward him, and he felt as though he had never seen its like before. He had certainly known many beautiful women, but never one of this order. Her women seemed to him dirt before her, until he collected himself and noted one

---

22. The expounding of the fifth scroll of the Lotus Sutra provided the occasion for the assembly to process around the garden lake (assimilating it to the lake in paradise) while bearing bundles of firewood, buckets of water, and offerings attached to artificial gold or silver branches. The scene is briefly evoked in "The Green Branch."

23. Ice cut in the winter was kept though the summer in specially insulated rooms or caves (*himuro*).

24. From the waist up, at least; the material is all but transparent.

who was fanning herself in a gossamer shift of yellow raw silk and a pale gray-violet train. Ah, he thought, she has taste, that one!

"I should say all that work is just making you hotter!" she remarked. "Why not leave it for us to look at as it is?" Her laughing eyes were charming, and by her voice he recognized his friend Kozaishō.

At last they managed bravely to split it. Each took a piece that she put to her forehead or applied to her chest, and some no doubt got into a degree of mischief as they did so. Kozaishō wrapped a bit in paper to present to her mistress, but Her Highness just put out her lovely hands for Kozaishō to dry them. "No, thank you," she said, "not for me. One gets so wet!" She spoke very low, but the sound of her voice gave him incomparable pleasure. Once, he said to himself, when she was just a little girl and I was equally young and innocent, I saw her and thought how very pretty she was, but I never again heard so much as the rustling of her sleeves. What god or buddha can have shown me this sight? That power, whatever it may be, must only have meant to throw my feelings into turmoil as usual!

While he stood there staring, troubled at heart, a junior gentlewoman who lived on the north side of the wing remembered withdrawing to her room in such haste that she had forgotten to close a sliding panel, and she now came hurrying toward him in fear of being scolded for having left them all in full view. Her heart beat fast when she spied his dress cloak, and she wondered who he was, but she was sufficiently anxious to keep coming, having forgotten that she herself ought not to be seen. He quickly slipped away and disappeared, for he did not want to be recognized in so compromising a posture.

Oh, no! she exclaimed to herself. Even the standing curtain is drawn aside, and anyone could see in! It must have been one of the sons of His Excellency of the Right. No one without any right to be here could possibly come in this far. If anyone ever hears of this, there will be questions about who left that panel open. His shift and trousers both looked like gossamer silk—it is quite possible that no one ever heard him. She hardly knew what to do.

The culprit meanwhile reflected ruefully, There was a time when I aspired to the holy life, but once I stumbled, I came to have so many, many cares! If I had left the world then, long ago, I would now be living in the depths of the mountains and would not be tormenting my heart this way! He was thoroughly upset. Why have I always wanted to see her again? It has only meant pain and can do me no good.

Her Highness his wife arose the next morning looking very handsome indeed—to his eye perhaps no less so than the Princess on whom he had spied the day before. Still, he reflected, they do not look in the least alike, and *she* is the one who conveys the most extraordinarily noble grace, unless I only imagined it or just got that impression because of the setting.

"It is so hot!" he said. "Do put on something thinner! It can be pleasant to see a woman wear something new for a change." To a gentlewoman he added, "Go and ask Daini to make up a shift in silk gauze." Her women were delighted to see him appreciate her so, for she was then at the very height of her looks.

He returned toward midday, after going back to his own rooms for his customary devotions, and there was the shift he had ordered, hanging over the cross-

bar of her standing curtain. "Why do you not have it on?" he asked. "I can understand your preferring not to wear anything transparent when many people can see
you, but it is surely all right now!" He put the shift on her himself. Her trousers were
crimson, as *hers* had been yesterday, and her abundant hair was as superbly long, but
alas, the effect was not at all the same; perhaps they were really too unlike each
other. He called for a block of ice that he had the women split, and he felt secretly
amused with himself when he gave her a piece. Come, he thought, has no one ever
painted his love so as to be able to contemplate her portrait? Surely the lady before
me is worthy to afford me this consolation! Still, he only wished that he had been
able to join Her Highness yesterday and to feast his eyes on her to his heart's content, and he could not help heaving a sigh.

"Do you ever write to Her Highness the First Princess?" he inquired.

"I did sometimes when I lived in the palace, because His Majesty asked me to,
but I have not done so for a long time."

"I suppose that she no longer writes to you because you are a commoner now.
That is unkind of her. I shall tell Her Majesty that you say you are hurt."

"But why should I be? No, please do not!"

"Yes, and that the reason why she never sends you a line is that she despises
you for being too far beneath her!"

He spent the day at home and went to talk to Her Majesty the next morning.
His Highness was there, too, as so often, looking very fine in a dark dress cloak
worn over deeply clove-dyed silk gauze. He was just as captivating as his elder sister
had been, and his exquisitely white skin, together with his new slenderness of feature, made him a particular pleasure to see. His resemblance to her aroused fresh
longing, and the effort to quell these outrageous feelings was more painful than ever
before. His Highness had brought a large number of pictures with him, and he had
the women take some to Her Highness's room before going there himself.

The Commander approached Her Majesty, told her how much her Eight Discourses had moved him, and talked a little with her about times gone by, glancing
meanwhile at the pictures His Highness had left behind. "I am very sorry to see the
Princess who resides with me so dispirited now that she is away from the palace," he
remarked. "She never has a word from Her Highness your daughter, and it saddens
her to assume that Her Highness does not wish to be in touch with her because of
the character of her marriage. It would be kind of you to allow her a look now and
again at pictures like these."

"I cannot imagine why she should feel that way," Her Majesty replied, "although
it seems quite understandable that their correspondence should have lapsed once they
were apart, even if they were in touch when they were neighbors in the palace. I shall
ask her to write, although I do not see why your wife should not do so herself."

"Write first? No, no, she could never do that. It would please me very much,
though, if the tie that allows me to wait upon you as I do[25] were to encourage you to
grant her some consideration, even if you have not particularly done so before. In
any case, the two of them once wrote to each other very nicely, and it would be a

25. Kaoru is supposed to be the Empress's younger half brother.

great pity if Her Highness were to prefer not to do so again." It never occurred to Her Majesty that his own gallant designs moved him to speak as he did.

When he withdrew from Her Majesty's presence, he thought that he might seek out the gentlewoman whose company he had enjoyed the other night, and to that end he set off westward toward that very gallery the sight of which might, he hoped, afford him another sort of consolation. The women behind the blinds of the wing drew themselves up when they saw him coming, for the dignity of his gait was truly superb. Noticing the sons of His Excellency of the Right seated in the gallery talking, he stopped and sat down before the double doors. "I come here quite often," he said,[26] "but I encounter you ladies here so seldom that I feel as though I have grown old since the last time; and so, you see, I have decided henceforth to mend my ways. No doubt those young gentlemen over there do not feel that I belong here at all." He glanced toward his nephews.

"If that is your wish, my lord, you must be growing young again!" Their light wit reminded him of their own mistress's extraordinary elegance. He stayed on chatting idly with them, although nothing really called him to do so, a good deal longer than he had meant.

The First Princess was meanwhile with Her Majesty. "But the Commander went off to your wing!" Her Majesty remarked inquiringly.

"I am sure a word or two with Kozaishō was what he had in mind," said Dainagon, who had accompanied Her Highness.

"When a man that utterly serious takes up with a woman anyway, she had better not be slow—he will soon see straight through her. There is no need to worry about Kozaishō, though." It was true that she and the Commander were brother and sister, but she was still somewhat in awe of him, and she hoped that any gentlewoman he favored would mind herself properly.

"He is particularly fond of her, my lady," Dainagon explained; "he has probably even gone to her room. He often stays on talking with her until late at night—she obviously means more to him than most. To her His Highness is the one whose sweet words are not to be trusted, and she will not even answer him. It certainly takes a lot to please her!" Dainagon laughed, and so did Her Majesty.

"I congratulate her for having seen what a reprobate he is. What can I possibly do to stop him, though?" Her Majesty said. "I am ashamed for him, even before all of you."

"I have heard something really extraordinary," Dainagon went on. "That lady the Commander lost was actually the younger sister of His Highness's wife at Nijō—a half sister, I imagine. The former Governor of Hitachi's wife is supposed to be either her aunt or her mother, I cannot say which. And in the greatest secrecy His Highness was visiting her, too! His lordship the Commander must have heard about it, because all of a sudden he made a great show of putting her house under guard, in preparation for bringing her to the City, and the next time His Highness stole off down there, in deep disguise, he could not get in; he waited most ingloriously for ages, just as he was, still on horseback, and then he had to go home again.

26. To the First Princess's gentlewomen, behind the blinds.

Perhaps the lady preferred him, though, because the next thing you know she disappeared, and people like her nurse have been crying and frantic because, they say, she must have drowned herself."

Her Majesty was thoroughly shocked. "Where on earth did you hear that? What an absolutely dreadful business! But surely everyone would know by now about anything that sensational! The Commander has never mentioned it, although he *did* talk ever so sadly about how nothing lasts and about how no one in the family of that Prince at Uji ever lives long."

"No, no, my lady, I quite agree that servants are not to be believed, but a page girl who was in service down there just lately joined Kozaishō's own household, and she told the whole story as though there could be no possible doubt about it. She says everyone down there was desperate to hush it up because of the awful way the lady died and the unpleasant scandal that would follow if it were known. They may not even have told the Commander himself everything."

"Tell that girl she is not to say one more word about it. This sort of thing could well be disastrous for His Highness. People might easily lose all respect for him." Her Majesty was profoundly shaken.

Some time later a letter from the First Princess arrived for the Second. The sight of her simply delightful handwriting pleased the Commander very much indeed. I wish I had seen this long ago! he thought. Many amusing pictures came from Her Majesty, too. The Commander added some even nicer ones and sent them on to Her Highness the First Princess. He must have seen himself particularly in a lovely one of Tōgimi, the Serikawa Commander's son, setting out all forlorn into the autumn twilight for love of *his* First Princess.[27] The poor gentleman, if only his had been as kind!

"How the autumn wind, adorning with drops of dew the bending rushes,
brings at evening above all a chill to the longing heart!"

He wanted to write it on the picture itself, but such is life that even so slight a hint could have grave consequences, and he knew that he could give her none at all. After such a succession of sorrows he thought, Ah, if only the lady I lost long ago had lived, I should never, never have loved anyone else! I could not have accepted His Majesty's daughter even if he had bestowed her on me, and he would not have wished to do so in any case if he had known that I had so great a love. How cruel she was, though, that Maiden of the Bridge, and how sorely she tried my heart! His anguished reflections swept him on to consider the sister His Highness had married, and such impossibly conflicting bitterness and longing ran through him that he condemned himself for foolishly nursing these regrets. And there remained, even after that, the one who had died that terrible death—a child at heart, he felt, and guilty of willful folly, and yet the thought of how she must have suffered from her fears and of how sharply his changed manner must have pricked her conscience confirmed nonetheless how sweet she had been and how rightly he had wanted her,

27. This tale has not survived.

if not truly as a wife, then at least as an always charming companion. No, he assured himself, I shall give no more thought to His Highness or hold what she did against *her*, because the cause of it all was my own naive failure. Reflections like these absorbed him many and many a time.

When even a man as calm, collected, and dignified as the Commander may suffer so from these miseries, His Highness understandably remained wholly inconsolable, for he had no one whose presence brought the thought of her nearer or to whom he could confide the sorrow of his unslaked longing. Her Highness his wife might well have given him a few words of sympathy, but she had never known her half sister very well, nor after their sudden and brief acquaintance could she really mourn her very deeply. Besides, he shrank from requiring her to commiserate with him as much as he wished someone would, and he therefore sent to Uji for Jijū.

The women of the household there had all gone their separate ways, leaving behind the nurse, Ukon, and Jijū, who were reluctant to forget their mistress's favor. Jijū had not been as close to her mistress as the others, but after the long time they had spent together, she had come to take occasional comfort from the hope that in the river's frightful roar one still caught the purling of happier shoals ahead.[28] Just recently, however, fear and hatred of the sound had driven her to a poor little house in the City. His Highness found her there and invited her into his service, but it seemed to her despite her gratitude that under the circumstances the others might not speak kindly of her if she did, and she therefore declined, although she hinted at the same time that she would gladly serve Her Majesty. "That is an excellent idea," His Highness replied. "You can still be mine there, and no one will know." Jijū, to whom the prospect offered relief from anxiety and loneliness, found a suitable avenue of approach to the household.[29] No one already there complained, for she was thoroughly presentable even if she had no rank. His lordship the Commander visited often, but it always made her unhappy to see him. Everyone said that Her Majesty had gathered together only the daughters of the very greatest houses, but when she began to look around her at last, she saw no one there like the mistress she had lost.

A daughter of His Highness of Ceremonial, who had passed away that spring, inspired no great affection in her stepmother, the gentleman's wife, and she was moreover being sought by this lady's brother, a most unpromising Chief Equerry. The lady, who was quite indifferent to her plight, made up her mind that he should have her. "What a shame to let her go to waste like that!" Her Majesty said when she heard about it. "Her father was so fond of her!"

The young lady herself remained despondent about this outcome until her brother, an Adviser, expressed his gratitude for Her Majesty's kind concern. It had therefore recently come to pass that she was taken into Her Majesty's service. Her birth made her the perfect companion for Her Highness the First Princess, and she

---

28. *Se* (the rapids, shoals, or shallow places of a stream) is commonly used, figuratively, to mean "moment," "occasion," "passage of time," and so on.

29. Niou could not just place her there; she had to appeal to someone already on the Empress's staff, someone with whom she could claim a connection, to introduce her.

enjoyed special consideration. Still, she was nonetheless a gentlewoman, and so she was known as Miya no Kimi.[30] It was so touching to see her wearing only a train![31]

Now *she* (so it occurred to His Highness of War) may well deserve to be likened to my poor darling! After all, the Princes their fathers were brothers! Being the sort of man he was, he still had that peculiar way of thirsting for the new even as he mourned the old, and he could not wait to meet her.

The Commander found her fate difficult to accept. To the very end His Highness her father considered offering her to the Heir Apparent, he reflected, and he even betrayed an interest in *me!* The spectacle of such dishonor makes it all too plain that anyone who casts herself into the waters escapes many a misery by doing so. He sympathized more with her than with anyone else.

Her Majesty's residence at Rokujō was larger and more handsome than at the palace, and all her gentlewomen, even those not always present in waiting on her, came from far away to enjoy the comfort there, until every wing, gallery, or bridge-way was full. His Excellency of the Right looked after the estate as magnificently as his father had done. Indeed, his family was so large and prosperous that Rokujō in the present actually surpassed in brilliance what it had been then. His Highness, who for months could have been up to who knows what amorous mischief if he had truly been himself, was extraordinarily subdued and seemed in fact to have matured a little. However, Miya no Kimi now brought out his true nature once more, and he went about scheming to win her.

Her Majesty was planning to return to the palace now that the weather was cooler, but her younger gentlewomen objected. "It would be such a shame not to see the best of autumn here," they said, "and the beautiful leaves." All of them had gathered around her to enjoy the lake and delight in the moon, and they often made music so particularly fresh and stylish that His Highness took great pleasure in joining them. He was like the first flower of the season, even to eyes that saw him day and night. They all found the Commander's presence somewhat daunting, though, because he did not join so readily in their amusements. Once when they were both there with Her Majesty, Jijū peeped out at them from behind a curtain, meanwhile reflecting, If only my dear mistress had taken one of them, since either promised her a splendid future, and if only she were still alive! What a mad, ghastly, and hateful thing she chose to do instead! But Jijū kept the sharp pain of it to herself, and she never said a word to anyone there to suggest that she knew anything about Uji. Meanwhile His Highness was telling Her Majesty at length about things at the palace, and the Commander left. Jijū did not want him to see her, and she hid. She was afraid that he might think her heartless for leaving before the mourning was over.

The Commander went to where several women were chatting in low voices in a doorway along the bridgeway to the east. "You women should feel comfortable

30. Being a gentlewoman after all, she has to be given a *meshina*, a "service name," like all the others. Miya no Kimi means something like "His Highness's girl."

31. A gentlewoman on duty would properly wear both a train and a Chinese jacket, but Miya no Kimi, who is not really like the other gentlewomen, wears only the train.

Woman without her Chinese jacket

with me," he said. "You could not get on better even with another woman! Besides, I have some worthwhile things to teach you. I am glad to say that you will understand that in time."

The women were wondering what to reply when an older and more experienced one called Ben answered, "My lord, is it not the woman past desiring your intimacy who can actually be comfortable with you? That is how things really are. I did not particularly aspire to talk to you so intimately, but, shameless as I am by now, I felt that it was at least my duty to do so."

"Then I am very sorry that you feel you need not be shy with me!" he answered. She had slipped off her Chinese jacket and swept it aside, apparently to engage in writing practice, and he gathered, too, that she was enjoying the few autumn flowers that she had picked and placed in the lid of her writing box. Many of the women had disappeared behind curtains, while others had simply turned away so that they could not be recognized from the open door. He surveyed the backs of their heads with amusement. Then he drew the inkstone to him and wrote,

> *"Ah, maidenflowers, here I am in a meadow where so many bloom,*
> *and still not a drop of dew gleams on me to harm my name!*[32]

Yet you will not smile on me!" He showed the poem to one who sat with her back to him by the sliding panel. Without a quiver she calmly wrote straight back,

> *"They of all blossoms sport a compromising name, yet maidenflowers*
> *never bend to the fancy of just any passing dew."*

---

32. *Kokinshū* 229, by Ono no Yoshiki: "Were I to linger in a meadow filled with maidenflowers in bloom, I would quite unjustly harm my name."

This little sample of her writing had such impeccable distinction that he wondered who she could be. She must have been on her way to Her Majesty when she found her path obstructed by his presence.

"You talk like an old man, I am afraid," Ben said.

"Rest on your journey, try yourself again, and see whether maidenflowers
in all their blooming beauty do or do not tempt your heart.

Then I, too, will make up my mind."

"If you will have me, then I will lie here a night, though this heart of mine
never lets itself be drawn to any common flower,"

he answered.

"Why insult me so? I was only joking about your 'meadow' in a general way!"

The least word from him made the women long to hear more. "I beg your pardon," he said. "Then I shall clear out. I am sure that at any moment you will have reason to feel shy again!"[33] He arose and went away. Some of the others hoped unkindly enough that he did not take them all to be as blunt as Ben.

He leaned against the railing to the east, watching the sun go down and looking out over the garden with all its flowers. "The most poignant of all is the autumn sky,"[34] he murmured very low to himself, feeling unaccountably sad. A familiar rustle of silks signaled that the wearer was passing through the sliding panel from the near side of the chamber into the far one.

Then His Highness came up to him. "Who went in there just now?" he asked.

"That was Chūjō, who serves Her Highness the First Princess," he heard a gentlewoman reply.

What a thing to do! To think she identified Chūjō, just like that, to a man suddenly keen to know who she was! He felt sorry for Chūjō and regretted that the women here should so willingly let that man have his way. Apparently they all let him get away with his forward, willful conduct! Alas, I have reason only to be angry with them both, brother and sister alike.[35] Ah, how gladly I would seduce one of the women here away from him, some beauty he is after with all his usual passion, and make him as miserable as he made me! Surely anyone worth anything should prefer *me* to him! But no, women's hearts seem not to work that way. His wife at Nijō does not condone his behavior, and she worries about what people will think of her growing and unfortunate preference for me, but I am touched and grateful that she, at least, has not yet rejected me. Is there a single woman here with her good taste? I do not know, since I have never really tried to find out. I would not at all mind a little fling, considering how poorly I am sleeping lately! But no, he still did not feel like it.

33. "No doubt your lover will be here soon."
34. From a poem by Bai Juyi (*Hakushi monjū* 0790).
35. Niou for obvious reasons, and the First Princess because of his unrequited infatuation.

What had happened on that west bridgeway drew him, curiously enough, to seek out the place again. The gentlewomen were there chatting comfortably with one another on the pretext of admiring the moon, since their mistress the First Princess was with her mother for the night. He heard with pleasure casual notes on a *sō no koto*. "What do you mean by leading people on this way with your music?"[36] he asked, coming up to them unexpectedly, but despite their surprise they did not lower the blinds, which were raised a little.

One sat up. "Is there an elder brother here to look like me?" she said—she must have been the one they were calling Chūjō.

"No, but *I* am the maternal uncle!" he bantered. "I suppose Her Highness is with Her Majesty as usual. What has she been doing with herself during all this time at home?" It was a question he could have refrained from asking.

"Why, nothing in particular, here or at the palace. This is just the way she lives, as far as I know."

What elegance her rank allows her! he reflected with an involuntary sigh that he instantly regretted enough to seek to divert attention from it, lest anyone notice it and wonder, by toying with a *wagon* that protruded toward him from beneath the blinds. It was tuned to the *richi* mode, one remarkably well suited to the season, and his playing sounded quite nice. Those among the listeners who fancied music were acutely disappointed when he left the piece unfinished.

Is my own mother less than she? Her Highness is an Empress's daughter—that is the only difference between them.[37] Her Highness is the favorite of His Majesty, her father, but my mother was her father's favorite, too! How strange it is that one should have greater distinction than the other! Akashi must be a remarkable place! Reflections like these led him to ponder his own destiny. I myself have been extremely fortunate, he thought, but how much more so if I had been given *her*, too! On that score, however, he was asking too much.

Miya no Kimi's room was in this same west wing where there seemed to be so many young women admiring the moon. The poor thing! he thought when he remembered her: she herself is no different from those two! Why, His Highness her father once considered me! This was excuse enough. He set off to find her. Two or three page girls came along, prettily dressed to wait on their mistress that night. Obviously shy, they disappeared when they saw him, and he reflected that that was what girls were like.

He came up to the southeast corner of the wing and cleared his throat, at which a somewhat older gentlewoman emerged to receive him. "If I said that I am secretly drawn to your mistress, that would amount only to repeating awkwardly the words used by everyone else. I cannot help wanting 'some other word.' "[38]

---

36. Kaoru alludes, as does Chūjō just below, to a passage in the Tang Chinese story *You xian ku* (*Cavern of the Disporting Fairies*). The hero is drawn by koto music to a fairy maiden said to resemble her maternal uncle and her elder brother, both famously handsome men.

37. Kaoru's mother, Onna San no Miya, is the daughter of Emperor Suzaku and a Consort, not his Empress.

38. *Kokin rokujō* 2640: "How I wish to find some other word than *omou*, that I might use it only for my love for you!" *Omou*, which means "dwell fondly on someone in one's thoughts," is a very common verb that in proper context can correspond to "love."

The woman did not pass his remarks on to her mistress; instead she officiously replied, "Now that my lady is in such unforeseen circumstances, my lord, I cannot help remembering the thoughts entertained toward you by His Late Highness her father. I have no doubt that my lady is grateful for any such intimations of warm feeling toward her as I gather you are moved at times to express."

She has nerve, treating me as though I were just anyone! Annoyed, he continued aloud, "Quite apart from a tie between her and me that should make it difficult for her wholly to reject me,[39] I would be very pleased if as things now stand she were to call upon me whenever she may feel so inclined. I shall hardly be able to respond, however, if she must talk to me only through someone else."

In some agitation the woman took his point and urged Miya no Kimi to do better.

"When my present melancholy situation recalls 'The very Takasago Pine, of old,'[40] I assure you that your appeal to that tie inspires me to hope and trust." She spoke directly to him in a charmingly gentle, youthful voice. Such a response from any ordinary woman in a household of this kind would have delighted him, but in her case it upset him a little that such as she, even as she was now, need not shrink from allowing a man to hear her own voice. What he gathered of her presence made him eager to see her as well, since she was probably just as appealing in looks. He assumed with some interest that to His Highness she must be yet another occasion for folly, but the thought also reminded him to reflect on how rare constancy is. There she is, a young lady lovingly brought up by a father of the very highest distinction, but I suppose that there are a good many others like her. What *is* extraordinary is that two such flawless sisters should have grown up among those hills in the care of a veritable holy man. And she, who seemed so light-minded, so rash—the brief time I had with her was simply wonderful after all. So it was that his every thought turned at last to memories of one family, always the same. While he pondered that strangely painful tie on into the twilight, mayflies flitted before him in the air.

> "There it is, just there, yet ever beyond my reach, till I look once more,
> and it is gone, the mayfly, never to be seen again.

It might not be there at all,"[41] they say he murmured to himself.

---

39. Miya no Kimi and Kaoru are supposed to be cousins.

40. *Kokinshū* 909, by Fujiwara no Okikaze: "In all the world, whom am I to call a friend? Alas, the very Takasago Pine, of old, stood me no company." Lamenting the loneliness of old age, the poet evokes himself rhetorically as even older than the Takasago Pine, famed for its immemorial age.

41. *Gosenshū* 1264: "That which they call this world lasts just the little while a mayfly lives, so briefly it might not be there at all."

53

TENARAI

Writing Practice

Tenarai ("writing practice") means not just practicing calligraphy by copying out model examples but also writing out poems, including new ones of one's own, for pleasure or consolation. In the second part of this chapter Ukifune consoles herself in this way.

RELATIONSHIP TO EARLIER CHAPTERS

"Writing Practice" covers the same time as does "The Mayfly" and extends somewhat beyond it, into Kaoru's twenty-eighth year.

PERSONS

The Commander, age 27 to 28 (Kaoru)

His Reverence, the Prelate of Yokawa, over 60 (Yokawa no Sōzu)

His mother, an old nun, over 80

His younger sister, a nun, around 50

His disciple, an Adept

The caretaker of the Uji Villa

A young woman, around 22 to 23 (Ukifune)

The Captain, son-in-law of the Prelate's sister, late 20s

Shōshō, a nun

Komoki, a page girl serving Ukifune

Saemon, a nun

Her Majesty, the Empress, 46 to 47 (Akashi no Chūgū)

Kozaishō, a gentlewoman in the service of the First Princess

The Governor of Kii, grandson of the old nun, 29 to 30

There lived in those days at Yokawa[1] a reverend Prelate, a thoroughly saintly man with a mother in her eighties and a sister of fifty. These two women made a pilgrimage to Hatsuse in connection with an old vow, accompanied by an Adept, His Reverence's closest and most respected disciple, who performed the dedications for their images and scriptures. After these observances they started back. They were crossing the Nara Heights[2] when His Reverence's mother, now a nun, began to feel so unwell that the party was thrown into a quandary, for they did not see how she was to get all the way home. They therefore stopped at a friend's house near Uji, where they decided to have her rest for the day; but when her condition remained poor, they sent word to Yokawa. His Reverence, who wished only to remain on the Mountain, had not planned this year to leave it at all, but the dramatic news that his mother was gravely ill and might conceivably die on her journey brought him swiftly to her.

He and his disciples with the greatest healing powers were loudly engaged in their rites, although she had certainly lived a full life already, when their host heard what they were doing and expressed his dismay at lodging someone very old and very ill when he was now purifying himself for a pilgrimage to the Holy Mountain.[3] His Reverence sadly recognized that the man had reason to be upset, and since the house was in any case hopelessly cramped, he prepared slowly and cautiously to move his mother elsewhere. Unfortunately, the Mid-God was obstructing her direction home and had to be avoided. He then remembered that the so-called Uji Villa,[4] once the property of His Late Eminence Suzaku, must be nearby. Since he knew the steward there, he sent word that he wished to stay a day or two.

"The steward and his party left for Hatsuse yesterday," reported the messenger, who had brought with him instead a thoroughly shabby old man, the caretaker.

1. One of the three major sectors of the great monastic complex on Mount Hiei.
2. A stretch of low hills north of Nara, between Nara and the Kizu River.
3. The pollution of death will taint him if the old nun dies in his house, and he will be unable to make his pilgrimage to Mitake, a sacred mountain south of Nara.
4. There is evidence that the historical Suzaku actually visited such a place at Uji. The precise location of this one is a matter of conjecture, but it was probably near the north bank of the Uji River, the side toward the City.

"Please come now if you like," the caretaker said. "The main house is only going to waste. Pilgrims often stop there."

"Excellent! It is an imperial villa, but we will not be disturbed as long as no one is there." His Reverence sent his messenger to look the place over. The old caretaker, who was quite used to visitors, had made rudimentary preparations to receive them.

His Reverence went first. The badly run-down house struck him as thoroughly frightening, and he had the monks with him chant scriptures. The Adept who had gone to Hatsuse and another monk of similar rank had a lesser colleague familiar with such things light them a torch, after which they set off to look around the deserted back of the house for anything unusual.[5] They seemed to be in a wood. Peering through the eerie gloom beneath the trees, they made out some sort of white expanse and stopped short, wondering what it could be. The one with the torch lifted it high: something was there.

"It must be some shape-changed fox.[6] The rascal! I'll make it show itself!" He stepped forward a little.

"Look out! It's probably nasty!" The other formed the mudra for quelling such creatures and meanwhile glared at it. He felt as though his hair would have stood on end if he had had any. The one with the torch went straight up to it, quite calmly, for a better look. It had long, glossy hair, and it was leaning against the great gnarled root of a tree, weeping bitterly.

"Extraordinary! We must have His Reverence look at it!" The speaker went back to his master and told him what they had found.

"I have always heard that a fox may take human form, but I have never seen one that has actually done it!" His Reverence stepped straight down from the house and went for a look.

His mother would soon be arriving, and the more able domestics were fully occupied in the kitchen and elsewhere. All was quiet in the wood as four or five monks kept watch over whatever it was. Nothing special happened. Mystified, they continued watching. Why, it will soon be dawn! We must see whether it is human or what! Silently, they intoned the proper mantra and formed the proper mudra, but to His Reverence the answer was apparently obvious already.

"She is human," he said. "There is nothing unusual or evil about her. Go and ask her who she is. I see no reason to believe she is dead. If she was left here for dead, then she has apparently revived."

"But why would anyone leave a dead body here at this villa? Perhaps she *is* human, but a fox, a tree spirit, or something like that must then have addled her wits and brought her here. This is serious. I am sure the place is now polluted."

They shouted for the old caretaker, and the answering echoes were terrifying. He arrived, a shabby figure with one hand to his hat to prevent it from sliding down over his face.

---

5. Troublesome creatures or spirits.
6. Foxes were seen as shape-changers in both China and Japan. They particularly favored the shape of a beautiful young woman.

"Does any young woman live nearby?" They showed him what they were talking about.

"Foxes do this," he replied. "Strange things can happen under this tree. One autumn, the year before last, they made off with a little boy just a year or so old, the son of someone in service here, and this is where they brought him. It is hardly surprising."

"Did the boy die?"

"No, he is still alive. Foxes love to give people a fright, but they never actually do anything much." He had seen it all before, and the arrival of a party of people in the middle of the night seemed to preoccupy him a good deal more.

"I see. *That*, then, is the sort of thing we are dealing with. But please look again." His Reverence had his fearless disciple step forward.

"Are you a demon? A god? Are you a fox or a tree spirit? You can't hide, you know, not with all these great wonder-workers around you! Tell me who you are, tell me!" He tugged at her clothing, at which she covered her face and wept the more.

"Why, you have your nerve, you tree spirit, you demon, you! Do you think you can hide from me?" He wanted a look at her face, but he was terrified that she might be one of those demonesses he had heard there used to be, the ones without eyes or nose, and to show off his stalwart bravery he therefore tried to strip off her clothes. She turned to lie facedown and sobbed aloud.

The disciple was sure that nothing this strange could belong to the everyday world, whatever it might be, and he wanted to see what she really was; but unfortunately, a downpour was threatening. "She will die if we just leave her like this," he said. "We must get her outside the wall."[7]

"She is shaped like a real human," His Reverence objected, "and it would be a terrible thing just to leave her to die before our eyes. No, it would be grievous indeed not to save the fish that swims in the lake or the stag that bells in the hills when it has been captured and is about to die. Human life is short enough as it is, and we must respect what remains of hers, even if it is no more than a day or two. Perhaps she was ravished by some god or demon, or driven from home, or cruelly deceived, and she may well be destined for an unnatural death, but the Buddha's grace is for just such as she, and it is up to us to give her medicine and so on and to try to save her. If she then dies anyway, we will at least have done our best."

Over protests from some of the rest he had his favorite disciple carry her into the house. "Oh, no, Your Reverence, please do not! Your mother is very ill, and bringing in an evil creature like that can only lead to defilement!" Others retorted, "Shape-changer or not, it would be very, very wrong of us just to watch a living being die in this rain!" Because of the fuss servants make over everything and the awful way they talk, they laid her down in an out-of-the-way corner of the house.

There was a great commotion when the carriage bringing His Reverence's mother was drawn up and she alighted, because she was just then feeling very ill in-

---

7. Get her outside the wall surrounding the grounds so that her death should not pollute the house and all in it.

deed. "How is that young woman we found getting on?" His Reverence inquired when a degree of calm had returned.

"She is still all limp, and she has not spoken. She is hardly breathing. A spirit seems to have stolen her wits."

"What are you talking about?" the nun, His Reverence's younger sister, asked.

His Reverence explained the circumstances. "I have never seen anything like this in all my sixty years and more," he said.

His sister had no sooner heard the story than she replied in tears, "I had a dream at the temple where we were. What is she like? I must see her!"

"Do. She is just there by the sliding door to the east."

The nun hurried to her and found that she had been left lying there all alone. She saw before her a very pretty young woman in a white damask layering and scarlet trousers. Her clothing was beautifully perfumed, and her appearance suggested very great distinction. "Why, it must be the daughter I miss so much, come back to me!" Weeping, she called in her senior women and had them move the young woman to the inner room. They did so without fear, since they knew nothing of what had happened.

The young woman seemed only barely alive, but still, she opened her eyes a little. "Speak to me!" the nun begged. "Who are you, and how did this happen?" She got no answer, however; the young woman was apparently unconscious. She put some medicine to her lips herself, but she seemed to be fading fast.

"This is too much!" she implored the Adept. "She is dying! Pray for her, please, pray!"

"I knew it! His Reverence should never have been so generous with his help!" The Adept prayed nonetheless and chanted the scripture for the gods.[8]

His Reverence looked in. "How is she? Find out exactly what has done this to her and drive it away." But the young woman was very weak indeed, and her breathing might stop at any time.

"She cannot possibly live," a woman remarked.

"We could all do without having to shut ourselves up for a defilement we could perfectly well have avoided."

"But she *does* seem to be a lady. We cannot just abandon her, even if she is actually going to die. What an awful bother!"

"Hush!" The nun silenced them. "You must tell no one else about this. It could cause trouble." The young woman's condition disturbed her more than her own mother's, and she was so anxious to make sure she lived that she now never left her side. Not that she knew who she was, but she could not bear to let anyone so marvelously pretty die; and the women she had looking after her tended her eagerly in the same spirit.

The young woman opened her eyes from time to time, and then she wept endlessly. "Oh, dear, oh, dear!" the nun cried, "I believe that the Buddha has brought you to me in place of the daughter I still mourn, but I will only be more heartbroken

---

8. The Heart Sutra, which was recited before a healing ritual (*kitō*) proper in order to repel evil influences and attract good ones.

than I was before if I lose you, too! Surely a tie from past lives has brought us together. Please say something to me, please!"

She kept pleading until at last the young woman said under her breath, "I suppose that I am alive again, but I do not deserve it. I am too despicable. Do not let
anyone see me, please, but throw me tonight into the river!"

"These rare words from you are a joy, but how terrible they are! Why do you
talk this way? How did you come to be in such a place?" But the young woman said
no more. The nun looked for anything that might be wrong with her,[9] but she
found nothing, and in the presence of such loveliness she was overcome by sorrow
and dismay. Could she really, then, be an apparition come only to trouble a too-
fond heart?

His Reverence's party remained secluded for two days, while ceaseless chanting called down divine assistance for the two afflicted women. The strange event
that had occurred caused general consternation. The humble folk from nearby who
had served His Reverence in the past came to present their respects when they
learned that he was there, and one remarked as they talked, "There is a great commotion going on because the daughter of His Late Highness the Eighth Prince—
the one his lordship the Right Commander was visiting—suddenly died when there
was nothing really wrong with her. I helped with the funeral, and that is why I could
not come yesterday."

Perhaps a demon seized her soul and brought it here, His Reverence reflected.
She never looked at all real to me—there was something disturbingly insubstantial
about her.

"The fire we saw last night did not really seem big enough for that."

"It was kept small on purpose. The funeral was not at all grand." The speaker
stood outside because of the pollution he had incurred, and he was soon dismissed.

"His lordship the Commander did have one of His Late Highness's daughters,
but she died years ago. Which daughter can he have meant? His lordship would
never leave Her Highness to take up with someone else."[10]

The party now prepared to leave. His Reverence's mother had recovered, the
direction home was open for her, too, by now, and there was nothing attractive
about the idea of lingering in so forbidding a place. Some nonetheless wondered
about the young woman. "She is still very weak, and the journey could be too much
for her," they said. "It is very worrying."

They went in two carriages. The old nun rode in the first, with two nuns to
look after her, and they laid the young woman in the second,[11] attended by an
added gentlewoman. Progress along the way was slow because they often stopped
to give the young woman medicine. The nuns lived at Ono, below Mount Hiei, and
it was a long way. They arrived late at night, wishing that they had arranged to stop
somewhere in between. His Reverence helped his mother to alight, and his sister
tended the young woman while they all lifted her down together. The fatigue of the

---

9. She looks for *kizu*: in part physical "wounds," but perhaps, even more, defects that would show that
the girl is not really human.

10. The speaker cannot be identified.

11. The one occupied also by the Prelate's sister.

long journey had no doubt given the old nun reason to lament the endless miseries of age, but she recovered soon enough, and His Reverence returned to the Mountain. He did not mention the young woman to anyone who had not actually been there, for it hardly became a monk to travel in company like hers. His sister, too, made her women promise silence, because the idea that someone might come looking for the young woman troubled her very much.

How could such a girl come to that pass in a place inhabited otherwise only by country people? she wondered. Perhaps her stepmother or someone like that took her on a pilgrimage and then deceitfully left her behind when she became ill. After that one request to "throw me in the river" she had not said a word more, which baffled the younger nun and made her long to restore the poor thing to health. Alas, the young woman never sat up at all but lay so strangely absorbed that she seemed unlikely to live, although the idea of abandoning her was too painful to contemplate. His Reverence's sister spoke of that dream she had had, and secretly she had the Adept to whom she had first appealed for prayers burn poppy seeds.[12]

So the fourth and fifth months went by. In despair over her failure to bring about any improvement, she wrote to His Reverence: "Come back down from the Mountain! Please save her! That she is still alive at all suggests that she is not meant to die, but whatever it is that has possessed her apparently refuses to leave. My dearest and most saintly brother, you may well wish to avoid the City, but surely it can do you no harm to come here!"

She implored him in such terms as these, and he reflected how strange it all was. What if I had abandoned her at the start? That I discovered her in the first place surely means that a tie already links me to her. Yes, I must do all I can to save her, and if I fail, I shall simply take it that her allotted span of life was over. He came down from the Mountain.

His sister thanked him reverently and described the young woman's condition during the past months. "Anyone who remains ill this long could naturally be expected to suffer a good deal," she said, "but her condition is no worse now than it was at the start. She has kept all her lovely looks, nothing about her is in the least distressing, and while she appears to be dying, she is, as you see, nonetheless still alive." She wept bitterly.

"She astonished me from the very moment I first saw her," he replied. "Come, then." He peeped in at her. "Yes, she is remarkably beautiful! It must be her reward for good deeds in the past to have been born with such looks! I wonder what slip of hers can have brought her so low. Have you not heard anything to suggest an answer?"

"No, nothing at all. Well, actually, she is a gift from the Kannon of Hatsuse."

"Surely not! The Buddha vouchsafes such guidance in accordance with karmic ties, and in the absence of any such tie I do not see how it is possible!" With such wondering words as these he began his rites.

Considering that His Reverence turned away requests even from the palace, it seemed to his sister that it might not redound to his credit if it were to be noised

---

12. Perform the purificatory fire ritual (*goma*), during which poppy seeds were thrown onto the sacred fire.

about that he had left deep retreat on the Mountain to pray earnestly for a woman who really meant nothing to him at all, and since his disciples agreed, she urged them to silence.

"No, no, my worthies," he said, "I will have no more of this from you. As a monk I am hopeless enough already, and I am sure that I violate this precept or that all the time, but I have never suffered reproach over a woman, nor have I ever erred in that direction. If I do so now, when I am over sixty years old, it will only have been my destiny."

"But, Your Reverence, the Buddha's teaching will suffer if evil-tongued people spread malicious rumors," his disciples protested. They were not pleased.

His Reverence made a mighty vow that the rite he was about to undertake would succeed, whatever it cost him, and he went at it the entire night. At dawn he successfully got the spirit to flee into the medium,[13] whereupon he and the Adept, his disciple, redoubled their efforts to make it say what sort of power it was and why it was tormenting its victim this way.

After months of refusal to declare itself, the conquered spirit now began to rant, "I am not someone you may force here and subdue. Once I was a practicing monk,[14] and a little grudge against this world kept me wandering until I settled in a house full of pretty women. I killed one of them, and then this one chose to turn against life and kept saying day and night that she wanted only to die. That gave me my chance, and I seized her one dark night when she was alone. Somehow, however, Kannon managed to protect her after all, and now I have lost to this Prelate. I shall go."

"What is speaking?" But perhaps the possessed medium was weak by then, because there was no useful answer.

The young woman's mind now cleared, and she returned somewhat to her senses and looked around. She did not see a single face she knew, and surrounded this way by decrepit old monks, she felt the loneliness of one who has come to an unknown land. She could not clearly recall where she had lived or who she was. I threw myself into the water (didn't I?) because I could bear no more. But where am I now? She tried and tried to remember, and at last it came to her that she had been in dark despair. They were all asleep, and I opened the double doors and went out. There was a strong wind blowing, and I could hear the river's roar. Out there all alone I was frightened, too frightened to think clearly about what had happened or what was to come next, and when I stepped down onto the veranda, I became confused about where I was going; I only knew that going back in would not help and that all I wanted was to disappear bravely from life. Come and eat me, demons or whatever things are out there, do not leave me to be found foolishly cowering here! I was saying that, sitting rooted to the spot, when a very beautiful man approached me and said, "Come with me to where I live!" and it seemed to me that he took me in his arms. I assumed that he was the gentleman they addressed as "Your Highness," but after that my mind must have wandered, until he put me down in a place I did not know.

13. Probably a woman he employed for the purpose.
14. Not a scholar monk (gakusō), but one whose principal occupation was religious practice.

Double doors

Then he vanished. When it was over, I realized that I had not done what I had meant to do, and I cried and cried. She could get no further, for, she thought, After that I remember nothing. They say many, many days have passed, and here I am, a miserable foundling, now being tended by people I do not even recognize! Acutely ashamed, she regretted ever coming back to life. Despite being unconscious during her long illness, she had still taken a little food sometimes, but now she was upset enough to refuse everything, even the tiniest drop of medicine.

"Why must you still be so frail?" His Reverence's sister asked in tears. "You used always to have a fever, and I am so happy that it is gone and that your mind seems to have cleared!" She never left her side and tended her devotedly; and her women looked after her equally lovingly, not wishing such beauty to be lost.

At heart the young woman still wanted only to die, but life remained stubborn in her even after everything she had been through, and by and by she lifted her head and began once more to take nourishment, although her face continued to grow thinner and thinner. She said to His Reverence's sister, who was happily anticipating her full recovery, "Make me a nun, please! That is the only way I can go on living!"

"How could I do that? It would be such a shame!" She had just a little hair cut from the top of her head and had her given the Five Precepts. Her young charge was not satisfied, but she was too vague and wavering to insist on better.

"That will do, then. Just look after her now," His Reverence said, and went back up the Mountain.

For His Reverence's sister it was like a dream to devote herself to caring for such a young woman, and she was so happy that she made her sit up and combed her hair herself. It was not seriously tangled, despite having been neglected and left just lying, bound, beside her, and once properly combed, it proved to be beautifully lustrous. She made a dazzling sight here, where so many grizzled heads were only a year short of a hundred.[15] It was as though the most exquisite angel had come down from the heavens.[16] The thought disturbed His Reverence's sister a good deal.

"Why do you seem to have so cruelly closed yourself against me, when I love you so much? Who are you? Where did you live, and how did you come to be where you were?"

15. *Ise monogatari* 63 (section 30): "I seem to be in love with grizzled locks a year short of one hundred, for their image lingers in my mind."

16. As did Kaguya-hime, the heroine of *The Old Bamboo Cutter*. This allusion becomes explicit below.

"I must have forgotten all that while I was in that strange state, because I remember nothing about what my life may have been before. My only dim memory is of sitting evening after evening staring out into the night and not wanting to live, until someone appeared from under a great tree in front of me and, as it seemed to me, took me away. Otherwise I cannot even remember who I am." She spoke with sweet innocence and added, weeping, "I do not want anyone to know that I am still alive. It would be too awful if anyone were to come looking for me."

The nun asked no further questions; they were obviously too painful. She was as wonder-struck as the old bamboo cutter must have been when he found Kaguya-hime, and she waited apprehensively to see through what crack she might vanish forever.

His Reverence's mother, also a nun, had been a considerable lady. Her daughter, who had married a senior noble, had continued after his death to lavish care on their daughter and had married her advantageously to a cherished son-in-law; but then her daughter had died. The blow was so cruel that she turned inward, became a nun, and took up life in this mountain village, where, lonely and with little to do, she went on longing for someone to remind her of the daughter she so desperately missed, and she could hardly believe her good fortune now that so unexpected a treasure had come her way, one perhaps even lovelier than her own daughter had been. Astonished she was indeed, but also glad. Although now getting on in years, she retained her fine looks and an air of great distinction.

The river ran more quietly here than at Uji, and the house had a certain charm. It stood in a handsome grove, and the near garden was prettily laid out and nicely tended. With autumn coming on, the sky had a moving quality, and young women sang their rustic songs while harvesting the rice fields nearby. There was something pleasing, too, about the sound of the bird clappers. It all reminded her of the East she had once known. The place was somewhat farther into the hills than that house of evening mists once inhabited by the mother of Her Highness, the wife of His Excellency of the Right, and it was built against a steep slope, so that the shadows were dark there beneath the pines, and the wind sighed mournfully. Quiet reigned while the nuns occupied themselves with their devotions. They had little else to do.

On moonlit nights His Reverence's sister often played the *kin*, accompanied on the *biwa* by the nun known as Shōshō. "Do you play?" she asked her guest. "You have so little to occupy you!"

Whenever these old women indulged in their pastimes, she recalled her unfortunate upbringing and the way she had never had the time for such things. Why, she thought, I grew up without acquiring a single accomplishment! It was very bitter to be so hopeless, and she wrote casually, as though for practice,

> "Oh, who built that weir across the river of tears, when in its swift stream
> I had cast myself to drown, and detained me in this life?"[17]

---

17. *Ōkagami* 14 (the "Tokihira-den" section), by Sugawara no Michizane: "I am now the unwanted plaything of the waters: make yourself a weir, I beg you, and detain me!"

She resented it deeply, and in fear of the future she recalled the moment with hatred.

Every night when the moon was bright, the old women composed elegant poems and talked over their memories. Since she could not join in, she would gaze out absently at the sky.

> "It has been my lot to inhabit once again this world of sorrows,
>   yet in the moonlit City nobody will ever know."

There had been many people whom she missed when she resolved to die, but she hardly remembered them now, apart from imagining her mother's anguish and the bitter disappointment of her nurse, who had always so longed to see her honorably settled. Where are they now? she wondered. How could they know that I am still alive? Sometimes there also came to her the memory of the Ukon with whom she had talked over everything, for she had had no one else with whom to share her feelings.

A young woman cannot easily resign herself to giving up all other hope and shut herself away like this in the hills, and the only people in service here were seven or eight other nuns, all very old. Their daughters and granddaughters, some in service in the City and some not, came visiting from time to time. Any of them might be serving one of the gentlemen she herself had known, and she foresaw the acute shame she would feel if either chanced to learn that she was alive after all, since he would then imagine her reduced to the most demeaning circumstances. For that reason she kept completely out of sight.

The nun who looked after her had given her two of her own women, Jijū and Komoki,[18] but neither resembled in looks or wit the "city birds"[19] she had known. She resigned herself to the thought that this must be just what the poem meant by "a place not in the world at all."[20] Her insistence on remaining hidden convinced the nun that she must have a compelling reason, and she told no one else in the household anything about her.

The nun's former son-in-law was a Captain by now. His younger brother, a monk, had become His Reverence's disciple and was on retreat with him on the Mountain, where his brothers often went to visit him. The path to Yokawa took the Captain past the nun's house, and his escort's cries announced the arrival of a considerable gentleman. The young woman looked out at him, and what she saw recalled vividly the image of that lord who had come to her secretly at Uji. It was just as drearily quiet and lonely where she was now, but the nuns long resident here had made the place very pretty. The hedge was full of charming pinks and of maiden-flowers and bluebells just coming into bloom, and there among them now were young men in hunting cloaks of many colors. Meanwhile their master, similarly

---

18. One (Jijū) is a gentlewoman and the other a page girl.

19. "City people." *Miyako-dori,* a kind of gull, appears in *Ise monogatari* 13 (section 9; *Kokinshū* 411), by Ariwara no Narihira: "Are you true to your name? Then, city birds, I put you this question: the one I love—does she live or does she die?"

20. *Shūishū* 506: "How I long for somewhere not in the world at all to hide the many years that burden me!"

dressed, sat gazing out sadly from the south aisle where he had been received. He was a fine-looking man of twenty-seven or -eight, visibly cultivated in manner.

The nun spoke to him from behind a curtain placed in the sliding panel doorway. "The old days seem to recede farther and farther as the years go by," she said, "and it is a wonder to me that I need not forget you even now but may still look forward to the light of your presence in this mountain village."

"My heart is as moved as ever by the memory of the past, which is always with me, but I regret that I frequently neglect you, now that you have so thoroughly removed yourself from the world. I often visit my brother on the Mountain, envying him his retreat there as I do, but so many people wish to come with me that I usually prefer to avoid inflicting them on you. Today, however, I have managed to reduce their number."

"It seems to me that when you say you envy your brother's retreat on the Mountain, you are only repeating sentiments that are in fashion these days, but there are nonetheless many times when I am grateful to you for not bowing sufficiently to the world's ways to forget everything that is over now."

She had her visitors served rice and so on, and for the Captain she brought out as well such delicacies as lotus seeds. Knowing her as he did, he felt no constraint, and when a shower discouraged him from continuing on his way, he stayed for a quiet talk. Why, she thought, he is even more admirable in character than my daughter, and it is very sad indeed to think of his becoming a stranger again. I wonder why my daughter never even left a child for me to remember her by. She missed her daughter so badly that even the Captain's rare visits seem to have set her off on interminable speeches about how much they touched and pleased her.

The young woman, who by now was so like the nun's own daughter, looked utterly charming gazing out at the scene, filled with memories of when she had been properly herself. In her pitilessly plain white shift and the drab, dark trousers they gave her to wear, no doubt because everyone here wore ones the color of cypress bark, she suffered from the sad contrast between her present state and the one she had once enjoyed, although she looked quite lovely even in this stiff, rough cloth.

"My lady," the old nuns said as they attended their mistress, "it feels just as though your daughter were with us once more, and how wonderful it would be if his lordship the Captain were to agree! It would be so nice to have him coming again as he did then! They would make such a fine couple!"

Oh, dear, no! the young woman thought. I will never marry, not for as long as I live! It would only remind me of what is past. No, I will never again have anything to do with that sort of thing!

The nun went back into the house for a moment, and the Captain was anxiously watching the rain when he recognized the voice of the nun known as Shōshō. He called her to him. "I expect that all of you whom I knew then are still here," he said, "but it is so difficult for me to make these visits that I am afraid you must think me very fickle." Shōshō had once served him intimately, and her presence brought back the days when he and his wife were happily married. "When I came in past the end of that gallery, a puff of air opened the blind a moment, and I spied some long, long hair," he said. "It seemed to me that she must be beautiful. It was a surprise, since all of you here have renounced the world, and I wondered who she could be."

Shōshō realized that he must have glimpsed her mistress's young lady from behind, just as she was leaving, and she wanted to give him a much *better* look; she knew that he would be impressed. Why, he seems not yet to have forgotten his wife, and she was not nearly as pretty! She replied, "My lady, whom nothing could ever comfort after her loss, has to her great surprise found a young lady who delights her eyes day and night. I wonder how you managed to see her in so unguarded a moment."

What extraordinary things can happen! the Captain reflected with growing interest. Who can she be? The very brevity of that delightful glimpse had graven it vividly in his memory. However, Shōshō gave him no real answer when he sought to discover more. "You will know all in good time": that was all she would say, and he could hardly insist on questioning her further. Besides, his men were announcing, "The rain has stopped, and it is almost sunset!" At their urging he therefore prepared to go.

He picked some maidenflowers that grew nearby and stood humming to himself, "How come the maidenflowers to bloom so beautifully?"[21]

"Look how cautious he is being, lest we gossip about him!" the old women said to each other admiringly. "What a fine, handsome gentleman he has turned out to be! How nice if we could welcome him into the household again!"

"They say that he often goes to the Fujiwara Counselor's, but that he is not really that eager and spends most of his time at his father's house," their mistress observed; and to her new daughter she went on, "It is very unkind of you, you know, to keep us at such a distance. I hope you will agree that this was meant to be and treat him with favor. For five or six years I never for a moment left off mourning my daughter, but I have forgotten all about her now that I have you. I have no doubt that those who loved you are alive, but by now they must assume that you yourself are no longer in this world. The deepest griefs fade in time."

Tears sprang to the young woman's eyes. "I do not wish to keep anything from you, but coming so strangely back to life again has made everything seem a confusing dream. This must be the way one feels when reborn in an unknown world. There may still be people who knew me, but I do not remember them. The only person who means anything to me now is you." How sweet and innocent she was! The nun sat gazing at her, smiling.

The Captain arrived on the Mountain, to His Reverence's surprise, and the two spent some time in conversation. After deciding to stay the night, he had monks with fine voices chant the scriptures and spent the rest of the night making music. He mentioned during a long talk with his brother that he had stopped at Ono. "It was really very touching," he said. "I know she has given up the world and

---

21. *Shūishū* 1098, by Sōjō Henjō (a priest), written when he saw young women visiting his temple garden: "How come the maidenflowers to bloom so beautifully here, when in this world people have such evil tongues?"

all that, but even so, few women have her wit and taste." And he went on, "A breeze lifted a blind a moment, and through the gap I caught a glimpse of a pretty girl with very long hair. I just got a look at her back as she was leaving—I suppose that she knew she might be seen—but there certainly was something remarkable about her. It seems to me that a girl of good family does not belong in a place like that. Nuns are all she ever sees, day in and day out. She probably thinks nothing of it by now, but it is a great pity."

"It must be the young woman whom I gather she found this spring under un-usual circumstances, while she was on her pilgrimage to Hatsuse," his brother replied, although he said no more because he had not seen her himself.

"How extraordinary! Who can she be? I suppose that she must have decided to hide there because she wants no more of the world. It sounds like an old ro-mance, doesn't it!"

He could not resist calling at Ono again the next day, on his way back. The nun was prepared for him this time, and Shōshō's warm welcome, so reminiscent of bygone days, delighted him despite the color of her sleeves. The nun kept him company, too, and she was more than usually prone to tears. In the course of their conversation he ventured to ask, "Who is it that you have so discreetly living here?"

His question troubled the nun, but he had clearly caught a glimpse of her, and it would only seem strange of her to deny it. "I could never forget my daughter, you know," she replied, "and that seemed to me a very grave sin, but for the past several months she has consoled me for that loss. She seems to have many cares, although I do not know what they are, and she seems acutely distressed to think that anyone might find out she is alive. I cannot imagine anyone looking for her in the depths of this valley, though, and I wonder how you found out about her."

"I confess that a mere whim has brought me to you, but I hope that a traveler in these mountains may put his plea to you. I do not believe that you can remain in-sensitive to it, if she really is to you what another once was. Who is she, and what has led her to reject the world? I should so like to comfort her!" He was eager to know more.

Before leaving again, he wrote on a sheet of folding paper:

> *"Bend not to the breeze that flatters Adashino, O maidenflower,*
> *for my garden you shall be, though you are so far away."*[22]

He had Shōshō take it to her.

"Do answer him," the nun urged her when she read it. "He is such a fine man—you need not mistrust him."

"But my writing is so poor! How could I?" She would not do it, which the nun thought very awkward.

"As I told you," she wrote back in her note, "she is more unworldly than any-one I have ever known.

---

22. "Do not yield to anyone else's blandishments, because I want you for my own." The name Adashino (actually, a burning ground northwest of the City) suggests *ada*, erotic frivolity.

What I am to do I know not, who have planted a maidenflower
here at the hut of grasses where I have renounced the world."

He understood that the young woman should feel that way, this first time, and on his way home he did not hold it against her.

He hesitated to insist on sending her letters, but still, he could not forget that glimpse, and even though he knew nothing of her sorrows, the thought of her so absorbed him that a little after the tenth of the eighth month he took advantage of a hunt with small falcons[23] to visit Ono again.

As usual he called for Shōshō. "My heart, you see, has been troubled ever since I first saw her," he explained; but the nun's new daughter gave no sign of replying to him on her own, and the nun herself sent out to him, "I think of 'Mount Matsuchi' when I see her."[24]

At last the nun received him. "Concerning the young lady who, I gather, now finds herself in such painful circumstances," he said, "I hope that you will tell me more. My life goes so little as I would wish that I, too, should like to retire into the hills if I were not prevented from doing so by those whose opinion I am bound to respect. I am afraid that my gloomy character makes me a poor match for a person without a care in the world.[25] I should prefer to confide my feelings to someone who has sorrows of her own." Judging from the way he spoke, he was serious about her.

"As to your desire for someone with her own cares, I believe that her conversation would please you, but the strength of her bitterness against this life makes her very unusual indeed. Even I, who have so few years left me, found it very painful when I actually came to turn my back on the world, and it is difficult for me to believe that she, whose youth promises her a fine future, will really persist in her present resolve." She spoke as though she were indeed the young woman's mother.

"You are not being kind," the nun reproached her when she went back in. "Please answer him at least a word. It would only be right for someone living in a place like this to respond feelingly to the lightest remark."

Every attempt at persuasion failed, however. "I do not know how to talk to people, and as I am, there is no point in my trying." She lay there, ignoring the nun completely.

"What? That is too hard! Your talk of 'plighted to a lover this autumn'[26] was meant only to put me off!" He was angry enough to add,

---

23. *Kotakagari*, done in autumn for small birds such as quail. *Tsurayuki shū* 15 (*Kokin rokujō* 1201), by Ki no Tsurayuki, associates *kotakagari* with the hunter's request to a "maidenflower" to give him lodging for the night.

24. "I think she may be in love with someone else." *Komachi shū* 98 (*Shinkokinshū* 336), by Ono no Komachi: "Whom do you await, O maidenflower, on Mount Matsuchi? For you seem plighted to a lover this autumn."

25. His present wife, the daughter of the Fujiwara Counselor.

26. Another phrase from the "Mount Matsuchi" poem, above.

> *"I came from afar, drawn by the pine cricket's call and promised welcome,*
> *only to wander again through dew-laden fields of reeds."*[27]

"The poor man! Surely you can at least answer this!" the nun pressed her; but she could not bear the thought of engaging in such banter, and besides, once she started, he would be after her again and again, and she did not like that idea at all. Her complete failure to respond disappointed everyone. The nun must have called on memories of a livelier past to answer,

> *"You whose hunting cloak is wet with the many dews of the autumn moors,*
> *never seek to blame a house lost among these wastes of weeds!*

I gather that she finds this sort of thing distasteful."

The other nuns, within, could not conceive how painful it would be for their mistress's new daughter if against her wishes word were to begin to spread that she was still alive, and they remembered the gentleman with such fond pleasure that they did all they possibly could to move her. "But an obliging reply from you on so trifling an occasion does not mean that he would ever dream of doing anything to upset you!" they protested. "Perhaps you have no taste for such worldly ways, but do at least respond well enough not to be uncivil!"

But no, she did not trust these ancient nuns with their distressingly youthful airs and their fashionable pretensions to broken-backed verse. She reflected as she lay there, How cruelly I survived after all, when I had wished to put an end to my dire misfortune! What dismal wanderings lie before me now? If only they might all be sure that I am dead and then forget me! Meanwhile the Captain sighed deeply over her undoubted suffering. He quietly played a little on his flute and hummed to himself "the belling of the stag,"[28] thus showing himself clearly to be a man of feeling.

"Not only am I beset by sad memories of the past," he said as he prepared unhappily to leave, "but my hope for a new, tender love now seems to be dashed. No, I can hardly believe any longer in mountains untouched by worldly cares!"[29]

"But why will you have no more of this beautiful night?"[30] the nun protested, slipping out toward him.

"Why, I have tested the feelings of yonder village,"[31] he lightly replied. He had no wish to insist on pursuing his gallantry. That little glimpse I had of her

27. The word *matsumushi* ("pine cricket") allows a familiar play on *matsu* ("pine" and "await"); moreover, a Chinese story known in Japan tells of a man drawn deep into the forest by the pine cricket's beckoning call, only to lose his way and never come out again. The "dew" refers to tears.

28. *Kokinshū* 214, by Mibu no Tadamine: "In a mountain village autumn is the loneliest time, when one is awoken by the belling of the stag."

29. *Kokinshū* 955, by Mononobe no Yoshina: "When I seek to escape into mountains untouched by worldly cares, the one I love holds me back still!"

30. *Gosenshū* 103, by Minamoto no Saneakira: "On this beautiful night of moon and blossoms, how I should like to show it to someone able to appreciate it!"

31. "I have discovered that Ukifune does not want me." His words probably allude to *Kokin rokujō* 174.

struck me, and during my leisure moments I have recalled it with pleasure, but she is simply too distant and too reserved for a place like this! he said to himself, preparing to go. The nun, however, knew that she would miss even the music of his flute, and she said,

> *"Does a glorious moon shining from the depths of night mean nothing to you,*
> *that you should not wish to stay, here beside the mountains' rim?"*

She remarked of this somewhat ill-formed verse, "That is what the young lady wishes to say to you."

That caught his interest:

> *"Then I shall watch on, till behind the mountains' rim the bright moon goes down,*
> *and be blessed perhaps like rays slipping through your chamber roof."*

Meanwhile the old nun, His Reverence's mother, had caught the distant music of the Captain's flute, and she now came forth after all. Voice quavering and speech broken by coughing, she never even mentioned the past because she probably did not recognize him. "Come," she said to her daughter, "you must play your *kin!* How lovely a flute sounds in the moonlight! Here, you women, bring her the *kin!*"

Why, it is *she!* The Captain knew her voice. But what is she doing hidden away in a place like this? Ah, the treachery of life! Moved, he played very prettily in the *banshiki* mode.

"Now it is your turn," he encouraged the old lady's daughter.

"I should say that you play much better than you used to," she remarked, for she knew something about music herself; "or perhaps it is just that all I ever hear is

Playing the flute

wind down the mountain. But I shall, I shall, though I know my instrument is out of tune." To the Captain her music was a rare pleasure, for the *kin* is no longer favored these days, and fewer and fewer people play it. The wind in the pines gave it a specially beautiful quality, and the accompanying voice of the flute seemed to elicit new brilliance from the moon. More and more delighted, the old lady sat on and on and never felt sleepy at all.

"Once upon a time I played the *wagon* very nicely," she said, "but I suppose tastes have changed by now, because His Reverence says my playing grates on his ears; and besides, he tells me, I should only call the Name, since everything else is folly. He makes me feel so guilty about it that I no longer play at all. My *wagon* has a lovely tone, though."

She was clearly longing to play, and the Captain answered with a smile, "Surely His Reverence does wrong to discourage you! After all, in the place they call Paradise the bodhisattvas play instruments like these, and the angels dance, and *that*, they say, is very holy. What sin could there be in your doing the same when you are not at your devotions? I should love to hear you tonight!"

His winning words pleased her. "Come, then, my Dame of the Chamber,[32] fetch me my *wagon*!" she cried, and was racked by a fit of coughing. Her embarrassed women were too pained to reprove her for her tearful complaint against His Reverence. She drew the instrument to her and began playing just as she pleased, without a thought for the Captain's flute music of a moment ago, in the *azuma* mode and in a very sprightly style. The other instruments fell silent, which she took for a tribute to her own performance. *"Takefu chichiri chichiri taritana,"*[33] she went as she swept through her flourishes. It was all terribly old-fashioned.

"How delightful! One never hears that song anymore!" The Captain's praise escaped her, however, because she was deaf, and she had to ask someone beside her what he had said.

"Young people nowadays seem not to appreciate that sort of thing," she complained. "Look at that young woman we have had with us all this time—she is very pretty and all that, I know, but she refuses to join in any of these amusements. She seems to do absolutely nothing at all!" She gave a raucous, self-satisfied laugh, to her daughter's consternation. The life went out of the party, and the Captain started back. The lovely music of his flute, carried to them on the mountain wind, kept them all up till dawn.

A note came from him early the next morning: "I apologize for having hurried away so soon. I had many things on my mind.

> *Alas, how I wept for days never forgotten, and for the music*
> *of a bitter, bitter night spent so cruelly ignored!*

Please teach her to understand others' feelings a little! Why should I go on courting her affection if she really cannot bear it?"

The old nun's daughter, more and more at a loss what to do, could not help weeping as she wrote,

> *"The notes of your flute brought so vividly to mind days forever gone,*
> *and then, when you went away, once again tears wet my sleeves.*

I expect you heard my mother talking in her heedless way of how little this young lady of mine appears to understand life's sorrows." It was a tedious reply, he

---

32. Tonomori, a court title that does not appear elsewhere in the tale and that is certainly unrelated to the old nun's present circumstances.

33. Presumably solfège syllables.

thought, with nothing to commend it, and he undoubtedly put it down immediately.

Letters kept coming from him, as often as autumn winds rustle the reeds, which to her was an endless trial. She was remembering now all those moments that had taught her how impossibly single-minded men are. "Please, please allow me now to assume that guise before which he must give up all such intentions!" she begged, and she set herself to learning to chant the scriptures. She also prayed to the Buddha in her heart. So thoroughly did she reject the things of this world that the nun missed in her all the pretty ways of youth and concluded that melancholy was in her nature. She forgave her these shortcomings, however, because of her enchanting looks, and she took pleasure in gazing at her morning and night. Each of her rare smiles was a wonder and a delight.

The ninth month came, and the nun made a pilgrimage to Hatsuse. During all these years of feeling so sadly alone, her every thought had gone to the daughter she had lost, and now that she had the comfort of another very like her, she wanted to thank Kannon for so great a blessing.

"Do come with me!" she urged her new daughter. "No one need ever know. Of course one may pray to Kannon here as well, but many examples show what blessings may come from doing so at so holy a temple." Alas, the young woman's mother, nurse, and others had been fond of saying just the same thing, and she had been to Hatsuse several times. But it never did me any good at all! she said to herself. I could not dispose of my life as I wished, and I have suffered terrible misfortune! Besides, she was afraid to take a journey like that with someone she did not know.

"I do not feel well," she said, "and I hesitate to travel that way; I am afraid that it might not be good for me." The nun quite understood her anxiety and did not insist further.

Among the sheets of paper on which her new daughter had been practicing writing, the nun found this:

> "Lingering this way in a life so hateful now, no, I shall not go
> where the Furu River flows, to any twin-trunked cedar!"[34]

"That twin-trunked cedar must mean that there is someone you still want to see again," the nun ventured lightly; at which the stricken young woman blushed, looking particularly entrancing.

> "Of that twin cedar along the Furu River I can say nothing,
> save that now you are to me the very daughter I lost!"

---

34. Perhaps "I never want another lover!" The poem varies on *Kokinshū* 1009 (a *sedōka*): "Beside the Hatsuse River, beside the Furu River, year after year a twin-trunked cedar stands, and O to be again together, twin-trunked cedar!" Furu River appears to be an alternate name of the river at Hatsuse. Twin-trunked evergreens at temples and shrines still evoke the image of a loving couple. Ukifune's poem plays on *se* ("shallow place in a stream," "passage in life") and *furu* ("live on," and the name of the river).

There was nothing noteworthy about the nun's rapidly spoken reply.

The nun had said that she wanted to travel discreetly, but the whole household was eager to go with her, and it consequently troubled her to leave so few people at home. She therefore had two sensible women, the nuns Shōshō and Saemon, stay behind with a page girl.

The young woman watched the party go, lamenting her cruel fate as before. There is no help for it now, she thought, but how hard it is to have no one in the world!

The tedium of her days was interrupted by a letter from the Captain. "Please read it!" Shōshō urged her, but she refused.

With so few people in the house, the lack of anything to do left her at full leisure to contemplate gloomily what was past and what might come. "It hurts to see you so melancholy," Shōshō said. "Do let us play Go!"

"I was never any good at it," she said, but she decided to play anyway, and Shōshō sent for the board. Shōshō let her go first, assuming that she herself was the better player, but she found herself outclassed, and *she* went first next time.

She was quite excited. "I wish my mistress would come back soon!" she said. "I look forward to showing her how you play. She used to be very good at it, too. His Reverence has loved the game all his life, and he thought he was not bad at it—not that he ever went about challenging people as though he were the Holy Master of Go.[35] He assured her that she could not outplay him, but in the end *he* was the one who lost, twice. *You* are better than the Holy Master, though. I am amazed!"

The young woman regretted her indiscretion, for she did not relish the prospect of playing Go with an unbecomingly eager, shaven-headed old nun. She said that she felt unwell and lay down.

"You really should enjoy yourself a little more sometimes!" Shōshō remarked. You are so young and pretty, and it is a shame for you to be so gloomy and pensive all the time! Perhaps the jewel has a flaw in it after all."

As night came on, the sound of the wind stirred many poignant memories.

> *"To this heart of mine the end of an autumn day speaks of nothing new,*
> *yet, gazing into the dusk, I find dew has soaked my sleeves."*

A lovely moon was up when the Captain, whose note had come during the day, arrived himself. She was horrified and fled into the depths of the house.

"This is really too much!" Shōshō exclaimed. "Particularly at a time like this you should respond to his devoted attentions. You must heed at least a little of what he has to say! You seem to believe that just listening to him will commit you to him forever!"

Nonetheless, the young woman was profoundly alarmed. They told the Captain that she was away, but his daytime messenger must have informed him that she

---

35. Kisei Daitoku, as the great master Kanren (lay name Tachibana no Yoshitoshi) was known in the early tenth century.

was there alone, because he then proceeded to pour out a long and bitter complaint. "I do not even ask to hear her answer me!" he said. "I just want her to decide for herself whether what I have to say to her, in person, is that painful to listen to!" When every effort at persuasion failed, he added accusingly, "How astonishingly cruel! Surely she should be capable of some sympathy, living in a place like this! It is just too much!

> All the sweet sadness depths of night in autumn bring a mountain village:
> that anyone ought to feel who has learned to feel at all.

Obviously, her heart should share these things with mine!"

"Your behavior is quite extraordinary, considering that my mistress is away and that you have no one else to keep you amused!" Shōshō insisted.

> "I who pass my days never aware of feeling misfortune is mine:
> in me you think to have found one who knows what feelings are!"

The young woman had not said the poem for anyone to hear, but Shōshō told it to the Captain anyway, and he was moved. "Do convince her to come for just a moment!" he said, unreasoningly annoyed with the two women.

"She is quite extraordinarily unresponsive, my lord," Shōshō warned him, going back inside only to find that the young woman had disappeared into the old nun's room, which normally she never entered at all. At her wits' end, she informed the Captain.

"My heart goes out to her for all the sorrows that must weigh on her while she spends her empty days in a place like this," he said, "and I have the impression that in principle she is not without feeling at all. Behavior like hers goes far beyond that of someone merely unacquainted with life. Has life taught her a bitter lesson? I wonder. Why is her heart so set against the world, and how long do you expect her to stay?" He wanted to know all about her, but what was there that she could tell him?

"She is someone my mistress should have been looking after all along," she said, "but for some years they had not been on good terms. My mistress met her again on her pilgrimage to Hatsuse, and then she succeeded in having her come here." That was the best she could do.

The young woman lay facedown, wide awake, near the old nun, who from all she had heard was very difficult indeed. The old lady was sound asleep by now and snoring thunderously, and two nuns just like her were valiantly holding their own in a chorus of snores. The terrified young woman wondered whether tonight was the night when they would eat her; not that she much valued her life, but, as timid as ever, she felt as forlorn as the one who was too afraid to cross the log bridge and had to turn back.[36] She had brought Komoki with her, but Komoki, who was begin-

---

36. This story has not been identified. However, the motif of a demon swallowing a hapless girl is well known.

ning to have coquettish thoughts, had been too fascinated by the rare and handsome visitor to stay. If only she would come back! Komoki was hardly likely to be much help, though.

The Captain left, since he hardly knew what else to say, and the women lay down together to sleep. "She is so willfully withdrawn and aloof!" they complained to each other. "To think how she is wasting those looks of hers!"

It must have been the very middle of the night when the old nun sat up with a fit of coughing. Her head in the lamplight was all white, and over it she had something black. Startled to see the young woman lying nearby, she put her hand to her forehead the way a weasel is said to do, glared at her, and demanded in an imperious tone to know who she was and what she was doing there.

Now she is going to eat me! she thought. That time when the demon made off with me, I was unconscious—it was so much easier! What am I to do? She felt trapped. I came back to life in that shocking guise,[37] I became human, and now those awful things that happened are tormenting me again! Bewilderment, terror— oh, yes, I have feelings! And if I had died, I would now be surrounded by beings more terrifying still!

She lay there sleepless, and her thoughts meanwhile ranged as never before over the whole course of her life. How cruel it is that I never even saw the man they used to call my father! Back and forth we went for years to the East, and when at last I came across a sister who gave me both joy and hope, I abruptly lost touch with her, only to find the prospect of consolation now held out by a gentleman who had decided to accept me as deserving. What a fool I was then—for now I see my ghastly mistake—to entertain the slightest feeling of love for that Prince! He is the one who ruined my life! *Why* did I listen so gladly to those promises he made me by the green trees on the islet? She was heartily sick of him, and it was that gentleman, never really passionate yet always so patient, whom she now remembered sometimes with very great pleasure. I would feel most ashamed before him if he were ever to learn what my life is now—but oh, she suddenly thought, will I ever see him again in this world, as he was then, even from afar? No, no, I *must* not feel that way! I will not have it! So she reproved herself in her heart.

She was very glad indeed at last to hear cocks crowing. How much happier my mother's voice would make me, though! she reflected while dawn came on. She was in very low spirits indeed. The girl with whom she should have returned to her own room did not appear, and she lay there waiting. Meanwhile the snoring old women got up immediately to busy themselves preparing the depressing morning meal of gruel and so on. "Eat up your breakfast, now!" said the one who brought it, but she did not at all appreciate such service, and what she had before her did not even look to her like food. "I do not feel well," she said to excuse herself from eating, though they went on discourteously pressing her anyway.

A group of religious menials arrived. "His Reverence will be coming down

---

37. That of the spirit who had possessed her. *Imijiki sama* ("shocking guise") is similar to *imijiki mi* ("shocking form") and *imijiki mi no kehai* ("shocking appearance"), two self-descriptive expressions used by the spirit of Rokujō in "Spring Shoots II."

from the Mountain today," they announced, and she heard someone ask, "But why, so suddenly?"

"A spirit has been afflicting Her Highness the First Princess, and the Abbot of the Mountain has been doing the Great Rite for her, but he says that it can have no effect without His Reverence," they explained proudly. "Twice yesterday His Reverence received an invitation to go, and then late in the evening the Fourth Rank Lieutenant, the son of His Excellency of the Right, came with an appeal from Her Majesty. That decided him."

Oh, I know it would be very forward of me, but I hope that I can meet him and ask him to make me a nun! This is the perfect moment, now that there are so few people here to interfere! She sat up and said aloud to the old nun, "Please tell His Reverence that I keep feeling very ill and that if he comes down here today, I should be grateful to receive the full Precepts." The old nun nodded blankly.

At last she returned to her own room. She only loosened her hair a little, since His Reverence's sister always combed it for her; she hated letting anyone else touch it, and she certainly could not comb it herself. Meanwhile she sadly reflected that her mother would never see her like this again. She assumed that her long illness must have caused some of it to fall out, but no, it was just as lovely as ever: very thick, six feet long, and beautifully even at the ends. Each fine hair seemed to have a luster of its own. "Wishing me to be what I am now,"[38] she murmured.

His Reverence came toward evening. The south aisle had been swept and tidied, and she found all the shaven heads bustling about unusually frightening. His Reverence called on his mother to inquire after her health. "I gather that my sister is on a pilgrimage," he continued. "Is that young woman still here?"

"Yes, she is," the old nun replied. "She says that she is ill and that she wishes to receive the full Precepts."

His Reverence went to talk to her himself. "Are you there?" he asked, seating himself before her standing curtain. She overcame her shyness to slip out toward him and speak to him in person.

"It has always seemed to me, ever since that astonishing moment when I first saw you, that some ancient tie had brought you and me together, and I have been praying for you with all my heart. However, a monk like me may not keep up a profane correspondence without sufficient reason, and that is why you have heard so little from me. I wonder how you have been getting on among these nuns whose company so little suits you."

"It is a great burden to me, when I had resolved to quit this life, that I should still be inexplicably alive," she replied, "but however hopeless I may be, I deeply appreciate all your kindness, and since I no longer believe that I can live in the world, I ask you please to make me a nun. Such as I am, I cannot go on as other women do, not even if I remain in lay life."

"But you have so many years before you! What can possibly have led you to wish this for yourself? For you, such a step would only be a sin. A woman may

---

38. *Gosenshū* 1240, by Sōjō Henjō, when he became a priest: "Surely my mother never stroked my black hair wishing me to be what I am now."

well feel brave in her resolve when she first conceives an aspiration like yours, but, being what she is, she is all too likely as time goes by to regret it."

Comb box

"I have suffered misfortune ever since I was a child, and my mother told me that she considered making me a nun even then, so that when I came to understand a little on my own, I longed to live not as others do but ever absorbed in prayer to be granted that better life to come. Now, however, when I feel my end approaching—for that is the reason, I suppose—I feel all my strength draining away from me. Oh, please, I beg you . . ." She was speaking through her tears.

His Reverence could not understand it. What could have caused her, with all her beauty, so profoundly to detest what she was? The spirit possessing her had talked about that, he remembered. Yes, no doubt she has good reason! Why, it is a wonder that she even survived! She is in fearful danger, now that that evil thing has noticed her.

"At any rate," he said aloud, "the Three Treasures can only praise your resolve. It is not for me, a monk, to oppose you. Nothing could be easier than to give you the Precepts, but an urgent matter has brought me down from the Mountain in the first place, and I must go to the palace tonight. I am to begin the Great Rite tomorrow. It will take seven days, and when it is over, I shall come back and do as you ask."

This was a bitter disappointment, because by then his sister might easily be back, and she would certainly object. "My state now is just as bad as it was last time,"[39] she said, "and I feel so ill already that if I get much worse, the Precepts will no longer do me any good. I thought that today was such a perfect chance!"

Her sobbing tugged at his saintly heart. "The night must be getting on by now. In the old days I thought nothing of coming down the Mountain, but the older I get, the more of a trial it becomes, and I suppose that I had better rest before I go on to the palace. Very well, since you are in such haste, I shall do it for you now."

In glad relief she picked up her scissors and slid her comb-box lid out toward him. "Come, worthy monks! Come here!" he called. The two who had first found her were with him now, and he had them enter. "I want you to cut off her hair," he said. The Adept, who agreed that no one in her apparently grave condition should be required to remain in lay life, hesitated nonetheless to wield the scissors, because he felt that the hair she gave him through the gap in her curtain was really far too beautiful to cut.

Meanwhile Shōshō was in her own room with her elder brother, an Adept who had also come with His Reverence, while Saemon was entertaining another monk whom she happened to know. In such a place any friendly visitor was particularly welcome and elicited at least a modest reception, one with which both were

39. When she received the Five Precepts given to laymen.

A woman becomes a nun

occupied when Komoki, the only one left with her mistress, came to tell Shōshō what was going on.

The dismayed Shōshō rushed to see for herself and found her now wearing, for form's sake, His Reverence's own outer robe and stole, while His Reverence said, "Now, bow toward where your parents are."[40] Alas, she had no idea where that might be, and the thought called forth fresh tears.

"But this is a calamity! How could you possibly do anything so foolish! What will my mistress say when she gets back?" But His Reverence had gone too far to consider Shōshō's protests anything but misplaced, and he silenced her so effectively that she came no nearer and did not interfere.

"Turning and turning among the Three Realms,"[41] His Reverence intoned, and she thought, But I cut off obligation and affection *then*! Even so, she felt a pang of sadness. The Adept was having trouble actually cutting her hair. "Later on will do," His Reverence said. "Just leave it to the nuns." He himself cut the hair at her forehead. "You must not regret looking this way now," he reminded her, adding many pious admonishments besides.[42] To her it was a joy to have done what they all had protested must be long delayed, and she felt as though for this it had been worth living after all.

His Reverence's party left, and all was quiet. Through the sound of the night wind the women chided her, "We were so looking forward to your lonely stay here being quickly followed by a brilliant marriage, but *now* how will you spend the long life you have ahead of you, after what you have done? Even people decrepit with age are miserable when they see that life as they have known it is over for them!" Nonetheless, she felt only peace and happiness, because to her, who could not imagine living much longer, her new state was something wonderful, and she was filled with joy.

However, the next morning she was ashamed of this appearance for which she had no one else's approval. The ends of her hair all at once felt rough and even sloppily cut, and she longed for someone to come and trim them properly without going on at her. Shy and reserved as always, she stayed in her darkened room. She had never been good at telling other people her feelings, and since in any case she now had no one close to talk to, she could only sit before her inkstone and bravely set down her emotions, when they overflowed, as writing practice.

40. This moment in the ordination rite immediately precedes the ordination itself.
41. From a verse (in Chinese) that is a part of the rite: "Turning and turning among the Three Realms, [sentient beings] can never cut off obligation and affection, but in renouncing obligation and entering nondoing, they truly requite all obligation."
42. Her head is not to be shaven. Her hair will be cut below her shoulders, and she will not have a young woman's attractive sidelocks.

"This world that to me—myself and all others, too—meant nothing at all
until I cast it from me, I have now renounced again.

It is over at last," she wrote; but, still and all, she could only reread it with sorrow.

"That world I knew well, a world I had come to feel was mine no longer,
I put sternly from me then, and now have done so again."

She was setting down such thoughts as these when a letter came from the Captain. They had written to let him know how dismayed and upset they were, and he, acutely disappointed, understood that her resolve to take this step explained her refusal ever to answer him. What a shame, though! Just the other night he had been trying to persuade them to give him a proper look at that lovely hair, and he had been told, Yes, when the moment comes. He wrote back with bitter regret, "There is nothing I can say to you.

How this heart of mine, when the sea maiden's boat rows far off from this shore,
longs to share that same journey, lest I not embark at all!"

Surprisingly, she accepted the note and read it. This was a moving time for her, and despite the relief of feeling that it was over now, for reasons best known to herself she wrote along the edge of a scrap of paper,

"Yes, this heart of mine rides away now from this shore and all the sad world,
yet the sea maiden knows not where her floating craft is bound."

She treated it simply as writing practice, as before, but Shōshō wrapped it up and prepared to send it to him.

"You could at least have made a fair copy," she protested.

"But I would only have got something wrong." Shōshō sent it anyway. There are no words to describe how sorry the astonished Captain was.

His Reverence's sister returned from her pilgrimage, and she was extremely upset. "I agree that a nun like me should be pleased to approve, but how will you get through all the years you have left? And I who never know whether I will even see tomorrow prayed so hard to Kannon because I worry about you and want so much to see you secure!" She collapsed, weeping and to all appearances completely overcome, and the young woman's stricken thoughts went to her own mother, for she could easily imagine her despair even in the absence of a body to mourn. She sat with her back turned, silent as usual, looking very young and pretty indeed.

"You have been very, very foolish!" the nun said, tearfully arranging for her to have a habit. They made her an outer robe and stole in their customary gray.

"It is too hard," the women lamented as they clothed her, "when to us in this mountain village you had so unexpectedly brought so glad a light!" They thought it all a terrible waste and blamed His Reverence bitterly.

The First Princess recovered, thanks to an intervention as dramatic and effective as His Reverence's disciples had said it would be, and all praised their master loudly as a mighty healer. His Reverence did not go straight back to the Mountain, however. Instead he stayed on in attendance, since fear of the spirit had prompted Her Majesty to have the Great Rite prolonged, and one quiet, rainy evening she summoned him to remain on duty through the night. The gentlewomen had gone to bed, exhausted as they were after the past few days, and there were very few still nearby in waiting. Her Majesty and her daughter shared the same curtained bed.

"Among those in whom His Majesty has long placed his trust," she said, "it is now, I think, to you above all that he looks for sure guidance toward the life to come."

"I have little time left me, and I know from what the Buddha has kindly told me that I may well not live past this year or the next; and for that reason I have been on strict retreat, invoking the Buddha without interruption. Only this summons from you, Your Majesty, could have brought me down from the Mountain."

He went on to speak of the spirit's stubbornness and of the terrifying things it had said, and in this connection he went on, "I recently witnessed the strangest thing. This third month past my aged mother made a pilgrimage to Hatsuse because of a vow, and on her way back she lodged at the place they call the Uji Villa. It is a large house, long uninhabited, and I was afraid that evil creatures might have taken it over and perhaps harm anyone gravely ill, and that fear proved to be well founded." He described the discovery of the young woman.

"That is indeed extraordinary!" Her Majesty said. She was so frightened that she woke up her waiting women, who by now were asleep. Only Kozaishō, the one the Commander had been courting, had heard His Reverence's story; the others, whom she wakened, had heard nothing at all. His Reverence was disturbed that his account should have so alarmed Her Majesty, and he remained silent about what he had not yet told.

"On my way down this time I thought that I might call on the nuns at Ono, and when I did so, the young woman begged me in tears to satisfy her desire to leave the world; so I did as she asked. My younger sister, a nun once married to a late Intendant of the Gate Watch, has been happy to have her in place of the daughter she lost and has been looking after her extremely well. I gather that this has made her furious with me. For that matter, the young woman really is exceptionally beautiful, and it is certainly a shame to have her dressed as a nun. I wonder who she is." He was a fluent talker, and he had gone on at some length.

"But why did the spirit take a wellborn girl to a place like that?" Kozaishō asked. "Anyway, you *must* know who she is by now."

"No, I do not. Perhaps she has said something to my sister. If she really was of good birth, surely everyone would know. I do not doubt that even a peasant girl may have looks like hers. It is not as though no buddha is ever born among the dragons.[43] She is just a common young woman with a particularly light burden of karmic sin."

---

43. In the Buddhist cosmos, dragons inhabit the depths of the waters and are the lowest of beings, but in a celebrated passage of the Lotus Sutra a young dragon girl becomes a buddha.

Her Majesty then remembered the young woman said to have died some time ago near there. Kozaishō, too, had heard from her sister about a young woman who had died under mysterious circumstances. That must be the one! she reflected, although she was not sure.

"I only mentioned the matter to you, Your Majesty, because I am so struck by the way she has been hiding in order to avoid letting anyone know that she is even alive, as though she felt pursued by a deadly enemy." His Reverence seemed reluctant to pursue the matter, and Kozaishō therefore said no more.

"She *must* be the one!" Her Majesty said to Kozaishō. "I must tell the Commander about this." She left it at that, though, because she did not wish to raise with so daunting a gentleman a matter of which she had no certain knowledge and which, moreover, he and His Reverence had no doubt both wished to conceal.

Once the First Princess was well, His Reverence returned to the Mountain. On the way he called at Ono, where his sister sternly reproved him. "I cannot understand why you never said a word to me about this, when her present state only invites worse sin!" But her complaint was too late.

"You need now only pursue your devotions," His Reverence assured the young woman. "Life is as uncertain for the young as for the old. Your understanding that all is fleeting is entirely proper to your present state." She felt abashed.

"Please have a new habit made," he said, and he gave her damask, silk gauze, and plain silk.[44] "I shall look after you as long as I live. You need not worry. No one born into this common life and still entangled in thoughts of worldly glory can help finding renunciation nearly impossible; but why should you, pursuing your devotions here in the forest, feel either bitterness or shame? After all, this life is as tenuous as a leaf." And he added, " 'The moon roams till dawn over the gate among the pines' ";[45] for although a monk, he was also a man of impressive elegance.

That is just the advice I wanted, she told herself.

The wind howled mournfully all day long, and she heard His Reverence murmur, "Ah, on a day like this the mountain ascetic can only weep!" I am a mountain ascetic, too, now, she thought. No wonder my tears flow on and on. She went out near the veranda and saw men in many-colored hunting cloaks at the distant mouth of the valley. They seemed to be going up the Mountain, although people very rarely went that way. One usually saw no more than the occasional monk coming from Kurodani,[46] and this party in civil dress made a rather surprising sight.

It was the Captain who had been so angry with her. He was coming with yet another vain complaint, but the autumn leaves were so lovely here, and so much more richly red than elsewhere, that their beauty had captivated him as soon as he entered the valley. How extraordinary it would be to come across an especially attractive girl here!

"I was not on duty, and so I decided to have a look at the autumn leaves, since little else required my attention," he explained. "These trees fairly invite one to spend a night beneath their spreading boughs!" He gazed at the view.

---

44. Gifts to him from the Empress.
45. Two lines from a poem by Bai Juyi (*Hakushi monjū* 0161).
46. A place on the way down from Mount Hiei in the direction of Ono.

His Reverence's sister, as always ready with her tears, said,

> *"Alas, this mountain, swept by the withering winds that blow in autumn,*
> *offers you upon its slopes no kind refuge from the storm,"*

and he replied,

> *"Your mountain village, where as I know all too well no one awaits me,*
> *called to me not to pass by when I saw these lovely trees."*

He talked on after all about the young woman who was now beyond his reach. "Please give me a glimpse of her as she is now," he begged the nun Shōshō. "You can at least do that for me, after the promise you made me."

Shōshō went inside, and what she saw convinced her that she did indeed want to show off that slight, graceful figure in refreshingly clear colors, light gray over leaf gold, with her rich hair spread out over her shoulders like a many-ribbed fan. Her exquisitely fine features glowed as though perfectly and tenderly powdered. Shōshō would have liked to paint her like that, caught up in her devotions, with her rosary hung on the nearby curtain crossbar, conscientiously reading the scriptures. The sight of her always makes *me* weep, she thought—what will she look like to the man who had his heart set on her? The moment was clearly at hand, for she was able to show him a little hole below a sliding-panel latch and to remove the standing curtain that might have blocked his view. Never had he imagined what he saw. Why, what an extraordinary beauty! He was so overcome by regret and sorrow, as though it had been all his fault, that he could not stop his tears, and he drew back for fear that the sound of his mad weeping might reach her.

Is it possible that whoever lost such a girl should not be trying to find her again? And surely everyone would know if this or that lord's daughter had disappeared or had renounced the world in a fit of jealousy. It was a complete mystery to him. A girl with her looks could not possibly put me off even as a nun, he reflected; in fact, she is all the prettier for it, and I am only going to find her more irresistible. Yes, I must secretly make sure I have her.

He therefore ventured a serious approach. "She was perhaps reluctant to permit a common courtship," he said, "but surely I may address her without constraint now that she has entered her present state. Please be good enough to remind her of that. I can never forget the past that brought me to you, and she will give me one more reason to continue to come."

His Reverence's sister replied, "The thought of what may await her in the future is a matter of painful concern, and I shall be very pleased indeed if you will continue your interest and your visits in that loyal spirit. Her plight will be a very sad one once I am gone."

He guessed from the way she wept that the two must be related, but he could not imagine who the young woman might be. "Regarding my attention to her future needs, I naturally cannot know how long a life awaits me, but once I have undertaken to provide for her, you may be sure that I will not change my mind. Does no one really come here for her? Not that that sort of uncertainty need deter me, but I wonder whether you are not keeping something back."

"If her life were such as to encourage ordinary associations, I am sure that people would indeed be coming for her, but as she is now, you see, she has put all that behind her. That is all I can gather of her intentions."

He sent the young woman a message:

> *"It is all the world you have turned your back upon, that I know full well,*
> *yet that you should hate it so makes me hateful to myself."*

The woman who brought it to her also conveyed a long and earnest speech from him. "Please consider me your brother," he had added. "It will be a great comfort to be able to talk to you about the little things that crop up in life."

"Unfortunately, the deep significance of your conversation would be beyond me," she answered. She did not even reply to his poem.

She wanted none of it, after the terrible things that had happened to her. As far as she was concerned, she preferred to be left as solitary as a stump. That was why for months she had been so gloomy and withdrawn. She cheered up a little now that she had at last done what she wished to do, exchanging pleasantries with His Reverence's sister and also playing Go. She was attentive to her devotions and quite apart from the Lotus Sutra read a great many other scriptures as well. Still, in the season of deep snows, when no one came to the house at all, she found very little to lighten her mood.

The New Year came, though with no sign of spring, and the very silence of the frozen streams inspired melancholy; until despite all she had against the man who said he had "never lost the way to be lost in you,"[47] she found that she still could not forget that time.

> *"Gaze on though I may at snowy fields and mountains under a dark sky,*
> *all those things of long ago sadden me again today,"*

she wrote, as so often between her devotions seeking consolation in writing practice. She wondered whether anyone remembered her, now that a New Year had come since she vanished from the world.

Someone brought them new spring shoots in a rough basket, and the nun had them taken to her with,

> *"Spring shoots picked with joy between wastes of lingering snow among the mountains*
> *in their own way give me hope for all your years yet ahead";*

to which she replied,

47. Niou's poem to her in "A Drifting Boat," in the house across the river.

*"From this very day, spring shoots from mountain meadows that lie deep in snow
are for you, that you yourself may yet enjoy long, long years."*

Why, I believe she really means it! the nun thought, very touched; but if only
her state were such as to reward my care! She shed heartfelt tears.

In color and fragrance the red plum blossoms near her room were as they had
always been. She had loved this flower more than any other, for the way it told her
that spring was still spring,[48] and perhaps she was still intoxicated by its beloved
scent, for when she offered up the late-night holy water, she called a lesser nun, one
a little younger than the rest, to pick her a branch,[49] from which petals then scattered as though in complaint, broadcasting their delicious perfume.

*"Him I do not see, whose sleeves long ago brushed mine, yet the blossoms' scent
calls his presence back again as the spring night yields to dawn."*

The Governor of Kii, the old nun's grandson, came up for a visit. He was a
proud and handsome man of thirty. "Were you well last year and the year before?"
he asked; but his grandmother appeared to be quite vague, and he therefore went to
call on her daughter.

"The poor thing seems not to understand anything anymore," he said. "I have
been so far away, for so long, that I have not been able to visit her during these last
years of her life. She was mother and father to me after my parents died. Is the Governor of Hitachi's wife ever in touch with you?" He presumably meant his younger
sister.

"Year by year we are abandoned more and more to our solitude. No, we
have not heard from Hitachi for ages. I doubt that my mother will last until her
return."

The young woman was surprised to hear the title that she knew as her mother's.

"I have been back in the City for some days now, but official matters have kept
me all too busy, and I am afraid that I have neglected you. I had wanted to wait upon
you yesterday, but I had to go to Uji instead with his lordship the Right Commander.
He spent the whole day at the house where His Late Highness the Eighth Prince
once lived. He used to visit His Late Highness's daughters there, but then some years
ago one of them died. He had installed a younger sister of hers there in secret, but in
the spring of last year she died, too, and so he had instructions for the Master of Discipline at the temple there about what he wants done for the anniversary. I need a set
of women's clothes made.[50] Could you possibly have that done for me? I shall have
the necessary weaving done as quickly as possible."

How could *this* not disturb the young woman? She sat bashfully facing the
inner room, lest anyone suspect that something was wrong.

---

48. *Kokinshū* 747, by Ariwara no Narihira: "Is this not the moon, is this spring not the spring of old, while
only I remain just as I was then?"

49. *Shūishū* 1005, by Tomohira Shinnō: "Out of longing for your scent, with which I am still intoxicated,
I picked this morning a branch of flowering plum."

50. As an offering at the ceremony.

"I heard that the Eighth Prince had two daughters," the nun replied. "Which one married His Highness of War?"

"The second one favored by his lordship the Commander was the daughter of a lesser mother, I believe. He did not honor her openly, but he was devastated when she died. The first was the one who really broke his heart, though. He very nearly renounced the world."

He must be among his lordship's intimates! Grasping that gave her a fright.

"It is strange that both should have died there at Uji. It was so sad

Making a robe

to watch him again yesterday. He went to the river and stared at the water, and he wept and wept. Then he returned to her room in the house and wrote a poem that he attached to a pillar:

> *'Upon these waters, where the image of my love lingers on no more,*
> *the tears I shed in mourning fall in an unending stream.'*

He actually said very little, but he seemed to me sadly downcast. Women must think the world of him. He has made a deep impression on me ever since I was young, so much so that I would rather entrust myself to him than to the most powerful lord in the land."

He has no great depth to him, she thought, but even he is discerning enough to do his lordship justice!

"I doubt that he could stand beside His Grace of Rokujō, whom people called the Shining Lord," the nun observed; "I gather that his descendants are doing very well indeed in our own time. And compared to His Excellency of the Right?"

"His Excellency is the more magnificently handsome, and he has a particularly grave dignity. His Highness of War is the one of really striking beauty, though. I would gladly be a woman in his intimate service."

He talked as though discoursing on the subject, and it all seemed to her to concern another world. When his lecture was over, he went away.

She was moved that his lordship had not forgotten her, and she understood better how her mother must feel, but she still shrank from the thought of ever allowing her to see what she had become. It felt extremely strange to see the women dyeing the clothes the Governor had asked for, but she studiously avoided saying anything.

"Would you be kind enough to look after this?" the nun asked when they got to the sewing. "You are so good at doing a hem!" She held out a dress gown. That was too much, though. The young woman did not touch it. Instead she lay down, saying she was unwell.

The nun put her work down. "What is the matter?" she asked anxiously. A woman laid a scarlet shift over a gown in a cherry blossom layering. "This is the sort of thing you should be wearing," she said. "What a shame you are in gray!"

> "O nun's robes of gray: now that you are all I wear, how my former life
> comes again to memory in the colors of these sleeves!"

she wrote, saddened that, the world being what it is, the nun would no doubt learn the truth if she should die and that she might well be hurt by the way her new daughter had kept her secret from her.

"I have forgotten everything about my past, but now that you are making these things I feel a few sad memories beginning to come back," she said innocently.

"But you must remember *lots* of things!" the nun answered. "It is cruel of you never to tell me any of them. I myself had long forgotten these colors that people wear in the world, but dreary as I am, I cannot help wishing that my daughter were alive. Is there not still someone to whom you were as she was to me? Even I, whose daughter really did die, still wonder where she has gone and long to go and find her. There must be people who still think of you—after all, you only disappeared."

"Yes, there actually was someone, but I am afraid that she may have died in the last few months." She was crying, and to cover her tears she went on, "I can tell you nothing about all that, though; it hurts too much to try to remember it. I promise that I am not keeping anything from you." Silent as ever, she said no more.

Now that the Commander had seen to the anniversary, he reflected how very fragile that bond had been. He had done all he could for the two Hitachi sons who were now of age, having made one a Chamberlain and the other an Aide in his own Palace Guards. He had decided to take the best-looking of them, still a boy, into his own intimate service.

One quiet, rainy evening he went to call on Her Majesty, who had few women with her at the time. During their conversation he remarked, "I was once criticized for going off year after year to a remote mountain village, but I continued to do so because I liked to think that some things are fated and that one needs sometimes to follow one's heart; but I came to dislike the place in the end, probably because of the particular quality it has, and the journey there then seemed very long. For a good while I stopped going altogether, but recently I went again and found renewed occasion to reflect on the brevity of life. The house there struck me as a hermit's dwelling, purposely built to arouse sacred aspiration."

Her Majesty remembered what she had heard from His Reverence, and she pitied the Commander. "Some terrifying spirit must live there," she said. "How did you come to lose her?"

Ah, he thought, she must have noticed that this was not the first time. "Perhaps it does. There are always evil things lurking in isolated places like that. It was strange, you know, the way she died." He told her no more. It pained Her Majesty to imagine him guessing that she already knew what he had hoped to conceal. She thought of how preoccupied His Highness had been and of how he had even been ill at the time, and she felt for him after all. She decided that for the sake of them both the subject was too delicate to pursue.

She said quietly to Kozaishō, "The Commander spoke of that young woman with very great feeling, and I was so sorry for him that I almost talked to him about her, but then I thought better of it, in case she might not really be the same one. You are the one who actually heard the story. The next time you talk to him, tell him what His Reverence said, but keep the difficult parts to yourself."

"But, Your Majesty, how could I bring up with him something of which even you hesitate to speak?"

"No, no, everything in its place. Besides, I have a particular reason to be discreet."

Kozaishō understood and admired Her Majesty's tact.

Kozaishō told the Commander the next time he saw her. How could he not have been speechless with amazement? That question Her Majesty asked me must mean that she has heard something of what happened, but why did she not tell me? he wondered bitterly. Of course, I never said anything to her at the time; in fact, I assumed that I would look a worse fool once people knew, and I never told anyone at all. No doubt people have heard anyway, though. The way the world is, secrets that people want to keep always get out in the end.

Still, he could not yet bring himself to confess everything to Kozaishō. "The person you describe sounds very like one whose fate has puzzled me," he said. "Do you think that she is still there?"

"His Reverence made her a nun the day he came down from the Mountain. The people looking after her would not allow it even when she was extremely ill, because it seemed such a shame. I gather that she herself is the one who told His Reverence that it was her ardent wish."

It was the same place, and all the details matched. How strange it will feel if this young woman really turns out to be she! How can I make sure? People may well think me an idiot if I start making inquiries in person, and if His Highness were to hear of it, he would certainly do everything in his power to prevent her from following the path she has chosen. Perhaps Her Majesty said nothing, despite her knowledge of this extraordinary matter, because he asked her not to. If he is involved, I shall have to consider her well and truly dead, however strongly I may feel about her. If she is among the living again, then in the fullness of time she and I will no doubt have occasion to talk together about the Yellow Springs.[51] I shall not wish to have her for myself again. These anguished reflections led him to doubt that Her Majesty would ever tell him, and he therefore decided to contrive a moment to raise the matter with her himself.

"I was recently surprised to learn that someone whose loss distressed me very much is still alive under painful circumstances," he said. "I found the report difficult to believe, but I had never imagined her acting so drastically to leave me, and I

51. The land of the dead.

therefore took it as quite possibly true, since it sounded rather like her after all." He told Her Majesty a little more, refraining with admirable dignity from speaking angrily of the role His Highness had played in the story. "His Highness is sure to think me ridiculously obsessed if he hears that I am looking for her again, so I mean to pretend that I know nothing."

"His Reverence described a night so terrifying that I retained little of what he said. I doubt that His Highness has heard any of this. What I gather of his attitude is shocking, and I would be very sorry indeed if he were ever to learn of *this*. I regret it extremely that he should be known for his deplorable frivolity." She was thoroughly deliberate, and he knew that even in intimate conversation she would never betray anything told her in confidence.

He pondered the matter day and night. What mountain village can she be living in? How am I to go quietly about finding her? I suppose the best thing would be to go and see His Reverence and hear from him what actually happened.

He regularly visited the Main Hall[52] on the Mountain in connection with solemn rites he had performed there monthly, on the eighth day, in honor of the Buddha Yakushi,[53] and he therefore decided to go on from there to Yokawa. He took her young brother with him. I shall not tell her mother immediately—I had better see first how things stand, he decided, perhaps to heighten the dreamlike character of their eventual reunion. Still, he dwelled apprehensively all the way there on how painful it would be, even if he recognized her, to find her in pathetic guise among strange-looking women and with a distressing tale to tell.

52. Chūdō (Konpon chūdō), the central temple building on Mount Hiei. It is some distance south of Yokawa.

53. The Medicine Buddha, whose cult flourished in Heian times. The eighth of the month was one of his feast days.

54

YUME NO UKIHASHI

The Floating Bridge of Dreams

The expression *yume no ukihashi* ("the floating bridge of dreams") does not appear in this chapter, and its significance as the chapter title is a matter of debate.

RELATIONSHIP TO EARLIER CHAPTERS

"The Floating Bridge of Dreams" continues the story of "Writing Practice" without any break, during Kaoru's twenty-eighth year.

PERSONS

The Commander, age 28 (Kaoru)

His Reverence, the Prelate of Yokawa, over 60 (Yokawa no Sōzu)

Ukifune's younger half brother (Kogimi)

A young woman, around 22 to 23 (Ukifune)

The Prelate's sister, a nun

The Commander went to the Mountain and had images and copies of the scriptures dedicated there, according to his custom. The next day he continued on to Yokawa, where His Reverence received him with awe and surprise. The two had never been particularly close, although the Commander had commissioned prayers from him over the years, but now, after witnessing the remarkable wonders that His Reverence had worked for the ailing First Princess, he presumably felt new respect for him and somewhat greater faith than before; surely, His Reverence said to himself as he hastened to greet him, that must explain this visit from so weighty a lord. The Commander spoke at length, and His Reverence offered him rice and so on.

"Do you by any chance have a house at Ono?" the Commander asked once his men had settled down a little.

"Yes, I do. It is not much of a place, you know. My mother is a nun, and very old by now, and I thought that it might do for her while I am on retreat on the Mountain, since I have no proper house in the City. I can visit her there at any time, day or night."

"I gather that a good many people lived at the place until recently, but that now it is almost deserted." He moved closer to His Reverence and went on, very low, "You could hardly approve, I am afraid, and I hesitate to bring the matter up in any case, but you see, I have heard that someone for whom I feel responsible is in hiding there. I had meant to speak to you once I was certain about her, but I am told that you have given her the Precepts and that she is now your disciple. Is that true? The thing is, she is still young, and she has a mother, and I am being accused of having caused her death."

I see, His Reverence said to himself. I *knew* that she did not look like any common girl, and judging from the way he talks about her, she meant a great deal to him. Monk though he was, he rued having clothed her so thoughtlessly and so abruptly in the habit of a nun, and it took him some effort to devise an answer. He obviously has good information, his thoughts went on, and it would be pointless to keep anything from him if he knows that much and now wants more. Any attempt to do so would only make more trouble.

After a moment's reflection His Reverence therefore replied, "I wonder whom you mean. Perhaps you have in mind the young woman who has privately baffled me a good deal over the past few months." He continued, "The nuns there went on pilgrimage to pray at Hatsuse, and on the way back they stayed at the place called the Uji Villa. While they were there, I had word that my mother was suddenly very ill, and I went to her. I made that strange discovery as soon as I arrived." He went on in a whisper, "My sister abandoned her dying mother to care very tenderly for *her* instead. The young woman appeared to be dead, but she was still breathing, and I was reminded in my astonishment of that old tale about someone's coming back to life after being put in the soul sanctuary.[1] I summoned disciples with healing powers and had them perform rites for her turn by turn. As for myself, my mother is of course old enough that one need not regret her passing, but I prayed to the Buddha to spare her such suffering while she was away from home and to allow her to call the Name without distraction, and meanwhile I saw very little of the young woman. I assumed on reflection that a goblin[2] or tree spirit must have taken her to the spot by deceit. She remained as though dead for three months, even after she had been saved and taken to the City.[3] My sister, the widow of a late Intendant of the Gate Watch and now a nun herself, lost her only daughter quite a long time ago, and she has mourned her deeply ever since. To her it was simply a marvelous gift from Kannon to come across a girl of the same age, and a remarkable beauty besides. She did everything she possibly could to keep her alive, and she begged me with such tears to come down myself that I eventually did. I performed a protective rite, after which the young woman at last revived and became human; but she told me sadly that she felt as though the thing that had possessed her was still with her after all, and that she wanted to escape its evil influence and devote herself to praying for the life to come. I found her wish praiseworthy, since I am a monk myself, and I allowed her to become a nun. Of course it never occurred to me that you yourself had a claim to responsibility for her. I have said nothing for all these months because my old nuns insisted that there would be trouble if people heard about her—the circumstances are so extraordinary that they would certainly talk if they did."

Having already come this far to verify a distant rumor, the Commander nonetheless felt as though he must be dreaming when he realized that the young woman he had been sure was dead was in point of fact alive, and he could not keep tears from springing to his eyes. He did not wish to betray any such weakness in His Reverence's daunting presence, however, and he therefore managed to maintain his composure.

Meanwhile His Reverence felt as though he had committed a grave error in turning a young woman so important to the Commander into someone who might as well be dead. "No doubt she was possessed by an evil spirit, but it must have been her destiny from past lives that led her to it. I assume that she was born into a noble family. What possible slip of hers can have earned her this fate?"

---

1. *Tamadono*, where the body was laid out before the cremation. The tale the speaker refers to is unknown.
2. *Tengu*, a shape-changing trickster often mentioned in Japanese folklore.
3. An odd way to refer to Ono, even seen from the distance of Uji.

"I believe that one can say she is more or less of imperial descent. I myself did not intend to honor her particularly, but although it was hardly more than chance that brought her to me, I never felt that she deserved to fall this far. After her extraordinary disappearance I considered among many other things the possibility that she might have drowned herself, but you see, I had no credible information to go on. As far as I am concerned, I am just as glad that she is what she is now, since that will lighten her sins, but I gather that her mother is distraught. I would like to tell her mother what I have learned, but I am afraid that my doing so would cancel out the care you have taken to hide her all this time and that it might only cause trouble. A still-lively affection for her daughter would certainly make her want to go and visit her."

The Commander then came to the heart of the matter. "I apologize for requesting a favor so beneath your dignity," he said, "but please be good enough to take me to Ono. She is not someone whom I can now merely set aside, after what I have heard, and I should like to discuss with her all these things that sound so much like a dream."

He spoke as though he loved her very much, and His Reverence felt most unpleasantly caught. She thinks that she is a nun now and has renounced the world, but even a shaven-headed monk still has unworthy desires, and what then of her, a woman? Alas, the poor girl's present state only invites her to sin! "I cannot go down there in the next few days," he said. "I shall be in touch with you early next month."

The Commander was not in a position to insist too impatiently, whatever the degree of his frustration, and he therefore resigned himself and prepared to leave. He had brought her little brother—a better-looking boy than her other half brothers—with him, and he now called him in. "He is the young woman's close relative, and I mean to send him there straightaway," he explained. "Please give him a note to take with him. Do not mention me directly; just let her know that someone is looking for her."

"It would be a sin for me to play any such part in bringing you to her. I have already told you everything. It is up to you now to go to her yourself and then to act according to your judgment. I see nothing wrong with your doing so."

The Commander smiled. "I am mortified that my request should seem to you to carry the danger of sin. I myself hardly understand how I can have lived this long as a layman. My deepest desire ever since my youth has been to leave the world, but unfortunately, Her Cloistered Highness of Sanjō has no one but me, not that I am worthy, and she is a tie that I have never been able to ignore. While looking after her I have continued to rise in rank, and by now I am no longer really my own master. The matter preoccupies me as always, but new concerns keep arising to dissuade me from acting, until there is little I can do to evade them, in either my private or my official life. For the rest, however, I take care never to do what the Buddha forbids, to the extent that I understand these things, and at heart I am no less than a holy man myself. How could I possibly place myself at risk of sin in so trivial a matter? No, that cannot be! You must not doubt me. I shall be perfectly happy if only I am able to discover her circumstances for myself and to set her mother's heart at rest."

His Reverence nodded his assent. "Your intentions are most praiseworthy," he said. The sun was going down. Ono would have been a good place to spend the night on the way back, but the Commander did not feel prepared to go there himself while still as confused as he felt, and he prepared to return directly to the City.

Meanwhile the boy had caught His Reverence's eye. "You might just have him let her know what to expect," the Commander remarked. His Reverence therefore wrote the note and gave it to the boy. "You must come and see me sometimes on the Mountain," he said. "You may feel that I am not really a stranger." The boy did not understand him, but he took the note and set off with the Commander. The Commander had his escort spread out a little when they reached Ono. "I do not want to attract attention," he said.

At Ono the view was all of green and leafy mountains, and there was little otherwise to distract the eye. The young woman was seeking the comfort of old memories in the fireflies along the garden brook and gazing as usual out toward the mouth of the valley when she noticed there a large escort with bright torches ceremoniously making their way past.

His Reverence's sister came out to the veranda. "I wonder who it is," said one of her women. "It seems to be a very large escort indeed."

"Today when His Reverence thanked me for that dried seaweed I sent him, he said that it had come at just the right time, because he was entertaining his lordship the Commander," the nun replied.

"Do you mean the Commander who married Her Highness the Second Princess?"

How remote the place was, and how dismally rustic! Yes, it must be he. She clearly recognized the voices of retainers who had come with him sometimes on his journeys to Uji. Time had not effaced those memories, but what good were they to her now? Repelled, she sought refuge in the thought of Amida and sat in more than usually profound silence. The only people who went that way were those traveling to or from Yokawa.

The Commander wanted to send the boy straight to her, but there were too many people with him for that to be advisable. Instead he returned home and discreetly sent him off the next day, with two or three particularly close retainers and the attendant he used to dispatch to Uji.

He called in the boy while no one else was listening. "Do you remember what your sister looked like—the one who died? I had concluded that she was no longer in this world, but now it seems that she is quite definitely alive. Go and see her, then. I want to avoid letting anyone not close to her know. Do not tell your mother yet. It is too soon. She would only start a commotion, and people who ought not to know would find out. I am pursuing this matter only because I feel so sorry for her." He swore the boy again to silence.

The boy had many brothers and sisters, but this one's exceptional beauty had always deeply impressed him in his childish way, and the news of her death had made him very sad. The Commander's words started tears of joy, and his embarrassed attempt to hide them produced a rather brusque "As you wish!"

A note from His Reverence reached Ono early that morning. He had written,

"Did a boy, a messenger from his lordship the Commander, come to you yesterday evening? Please tell the young lady that I am dismayed, now that I have heard what happened, and that I actually have some regrets. I myself have a great deal to tell her, and I shall wait upon you in a few days."

What could this mean? The astonished nun took the young woman the letter and had her read it. The young woman sat there in silence, blushing scarlet, for the painful thought that her secret was out and that the nun would resent her having withheld it left her at a loss to reply.

"You *must* tell me!" the nun pressed her angrily. "You have been very cruel to treat me this way!" She had worked herself into a frenzy, ignorant as she was of the circumstances, when a voice announced, "Someone is here from the Mountain with a letter from His Reverence."

This was a new surprise, but she assumed that this letter must be the real one and asked to have the messenger approach. A very nice-looking, well-mannered boy then came forward, beautifully dressed. A cushion was put out for him, and he knelt before the blinds. "His Reverence told me that I would not be received quite this way," he said, and the nun therefore spoke to him in person. She took the letter and read, "To the young lady nun, from the Mountain." His Reverence had signed it with his name.

The young woman could not claim that it was not for her. She shrank back farther into the room, acutely embarrassed, and would not meet anyone's eyes. "You certainly are always very quiet, but this is just too much." The nun read His Reverence's letter.

"His lordship the Commander came here this morning to inquire about you, and I told him everything I know. You have turned your back on his deep devotion to renounce the world among uncouth mountain rustics, and judging from what I am now startled to learn, this could to the contrary earn you the Buddha's condemnation. There is no help for it. I wish you to know that you must not further compromise your tie with him and that you must dispel instead the sin of his attachment to you, trusting meanwhile that a day of renunciation does indeed confer immeasurable merit. I shall discuss the matter with you further in person. The young boy who brings you this will no doubt tell you more." He had made himself perfectly clear, and yet no one but she could have fully understood what he had written.

"Who is this boy?" the nun demanded to know. "Is there no end to your cruelty? You are keeping everything from me even now!"

The young woman turned a little and looked outside. It was the brother she had missed so much on that evening she had thought was her last. He had been an arrogant little mischief when they all lived together, but their mother was very fond of him, and now and then she had even brought him to Uji. He and she had come to like each other as he grew older, and the memory of his childish ways now seemed to her like a dream. What she wanted above all was to ask him how their mother was, because although she had heard some news of the others, not a word about her mother had ever reached her. The sight of her brother therefore overwhelmed her with sorrow, and she burst into tears.

He was a very attractive boy, and the nun thought that she noted a slight resemblance. "He is your brother, is he not? I am sure that he has a great deal to tell you. I shall have him come in."

Oh, no! I would be too ashamed to have him see me suddenly so horribly changed, when now he does not even believe I am alive! She stopped crying for a moment. "You see, the reason I told you nothing is that I hated to imagine you then knowing how much I had kept from you. The distressing spectacle I undoubtedly made must have offended you, but I could not remember anything of my past then, I suppose because I was not in my right mind and because my soul, if that is the word, was no longer what it had been. But then I heard the gentleman they told me was the Governor of Kii talking to you about people whom I felt that I had once known, and it seemed to me that I was beginning to remember things. I went on thinking about it all after that, but I still could not grasp anything clearly. There was one lady, though, who longed only for me to be happy, and I kept wondering whether she might still be alive. In the midst of my sorrows the thought of her never left me. The face of the boy here now gives me the feeling that I knew him when I was little, but the memory is too painful, and I do not want anyone like him to know that I am still alive. The lady I mentioned is the only one I want to see, if she is still living. I do not want that gentleman whom His Reverence mentioned to know anything about me. Please, please tell him that there has been a mistake and continue to hide me."

"That is not possible," the nun answered in great agitation. "His Reverence is unusually open even for a holy man, and I am sure he told that gentleman everything. He will soon know all about you, and so great a lord is not someone to trifle with."

"Who ever heard of anyone so brazenly stubborn?" the women said to each other. They stood a curtain at the edge of the chamber and invited the boy in.[4]

The boy had been told that his sister was there, but being so young, he was too shy to address her on his own. "I have another letter I am supposed to give her," he said, his eyes to the floor. "His Reverence was quite sure that she is here, but I am afraid I just cannot tell!"

"Why, the dear thing!" the nun exclaimed. "Yes, I believe the lady the letter is for is here. We others do not quite understand what the matter is, so you must talk to her yourself. You are very young, but I am sure that his lordship is right to have confidence in you."

"What can I possibly say to her, when she will not even acknowledge that she knows me? If she wants nothing to do with me, then I have nothing to say to her. He told me to give her this letter in person, though, so I must do that."

"Of course he does," the nun pressed the young woman. "Please do not be so obstinate. Your attitude is really quite frightening." She made her move up to the standing curtain, where she sat as though not actually present at all—a quality that gave the boy the feeling that he did indeed recognize her. He placed the letter beside the curtain.

---

4. Having been on the veranda, outside the blinds between the veranda and the aisle, he is now brought in to sit in the aisle, outside the blinds between the aisle and the chamber. The standing curtain is just inside the chamber, next to those same blinds.

"I should like to ask for a quick reply so that I can then be on my way." After this cruelly cold reception he was eager to go.

The nun opened the letter and gave it to her. His handwriting was as it had always been, and the fragrance suffused into the paper had an almost eerie intensity. The women, always far too quick with their praise, were no doubt transported with delight when they glimpsed it.

He had written, "For the sake of His Reverence I forgive your heart your unspeakably many and weighty sins; and my own, which now yearns at least to talk over those terrible days, days that seem a dream, leaves me despite myself prey to great anxiety. What, then, will people think of me?" He had not managed to put his feelings into words.

> *"Following the path I trusted would take me to a teacher of the Law,*
> *I lost my way and wandered a mountain I never sought.*[5]

Have you forgotten this boy? I keep him beside me in memory of someone who vanished without a trace."

The letter was deeply felt and sufficiently precise to discourage any thought of pretending that it was not for her, but even so, the shame of letting him see her in her present, distressingly changed guise threw her into such confusion that she sank into deeper gloom and found nothing to say; instead she lay there weeping. The women could not imagine what to do with her and thought her extremely odd.

"How shall I answer him?" the nun insisted.

"I am not well, I think, not well at all. I will answer later on, when I feel better. I am trying to remember, but nothing will come back, and I cannot make out what it was that I dreamed. Perhaps I will recognize this letter when I have regained a little calm. For today, please, just take it back to him. It would be awful if it were for someone else." She slid the open letter toward the nun.

"Your attitude is unspeakable! If you must be so excessively rude, you will implicate us, too, who are looking after you!" The young woman, who did not wish to listen to these sharp reproaches, lay with her face buried in her clothes.

The nun had a word with the boy. "There may be a spirit afflicting her," she said. "She never seems to be in a normal frame of mind and is constantly unwell, and ever since she assumed this unusual guise, I have worried that there might be serious trouble if anyone did come for her. I was right, too, because now, when his lordship has made it touchingly plain how much she means to him, I can only make abject apologies. She has been quite ill lately, and I suppose all this may just have confused her more, because at the moment she seems even less lucid than usual."

She provided him with a very pleasant meal of delicacies from the mountains nearby, but he was very young, and he remained thoroughly ill at ease. "What can I possibly tell him now, after all the trouble he has gone to?" he asked. "If only she would just give me a word!"

---

5. The mountain of love.

"Of course," the nun replied, and she repeated what he had said to the young woman, but to no avail. The young woman said nothing.

"I suppose that you can only describe to his lordship the reduced state she is in. Not that vast an expanse of cloud separates us from the City, and whatever mountain winds may blow, I hope very much that you will come again."

For him to stay on until evening would only have been a foolish imposition, and he prepared to leave. Bitterly disappointed not even to have seen her, when secretly he had longed to meet her again, he returned to the Commander with a heavy heart.

The Commander, who had awaited him eagerly, was confounded by this inconclusive outcome. He reflected that he would have done better to refrain and went on to ponder, among other things, the thought that someone else might be hiding her there, just as he himself had once, after full deliberation, consigned her to invisibility.

That appears to be what is in the book.[6]

---

6. Either the closing note of a copyist, certifying that the copy is correct, or a standard concluding formula for a tale. *The Tale of the Hollow Tree*, a somewhat earlier work than *The Tale of Genji* and roughly two-thirds its length, ends with the same words.

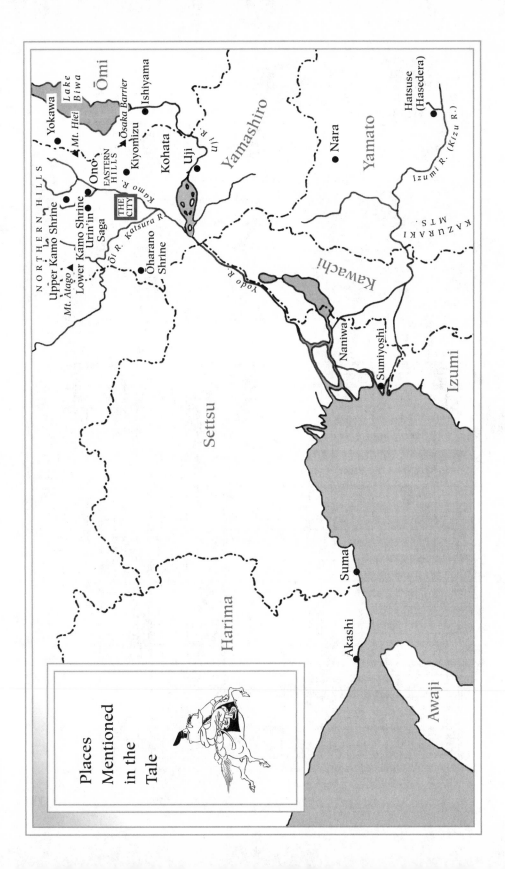

Places
Mentioned
in the
Tale

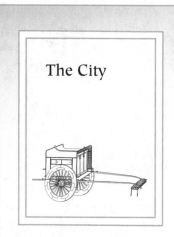

The City

1. Inner Palace
2. Eight Bureaus and Great Hall of State
3. Academy
4. Suzaku Palace
5. Reizei Palace
6. Kawara no In
7. Kōrokan

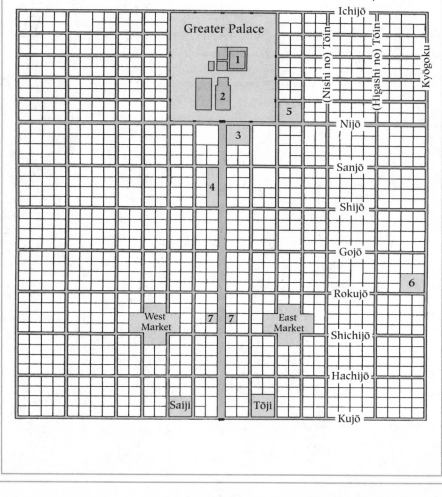

Right City

Left City

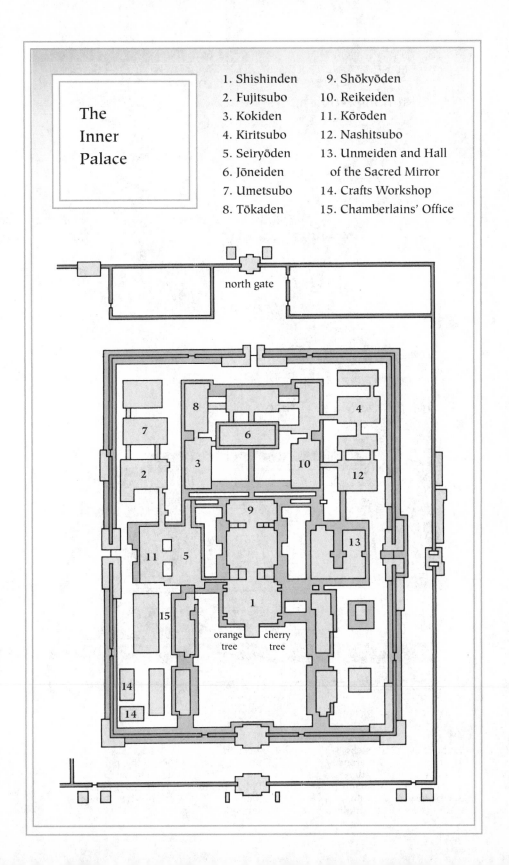

The
Inner
Palace

1. Shishinden
2. Fujitsubo
3. Kokiden
4. Kiritsubo
5. Seiryōden
6. Jōneiden
7. Umetsubo
8. Tōkaden
9. Shōkyōden
10. Reikeiden
11. Kōrōden
12. Nashitsubo
13. Unmeiden and Hall
    of the Sacred Mirror
14. Crafts Workshop
15. Chamberlains' Office

north gate

orange tree   cherry tree

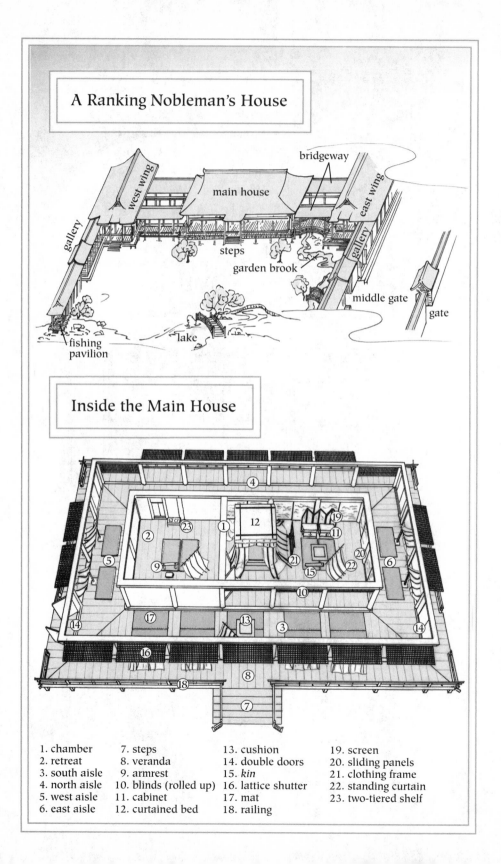

A Ranking Nobleman's House

bridgeway

west wing

main house

east wing

gallery

gallery

steps

garden brook

middle gate

gate

fishing pavilion

lake

Inside the Main House

1. chamber	7. steps	13. cushion	19. screen
2. retreat	8. veranda	14. double doors	20. sliding panels
3. south aisle	9. armrest	15. *kin*	21. clothing frame
4. north aisle	10. blinds (rolled up)	16. lattice shutter	22. standing curtain
5. west aisle	11. cabinet	17. mat	23. two-tiered shelf
6. east aisle	12. curtained bed	18. railing	

Chronology

CHAP.	AGE	EVENT
	Genji	
1	Birth	• Genji is born.
	3	• Genji's mother dies and is posthumously awarded the third rank.
	4	• The Emperor names his eldest son (age 7) Heir Apparent. The boy's mother is the Kokiden Consort, the daughter of the Minister of the Right.
	6	• Genji's maternal grandmother dies.
	7	• Genji gives his first reading.
	8–11	• A Korean physiognomist foretells Genji's future. The Emperor excludes Genji from the imperial lineage and gives him the surname Minamoto (Genji). Fujitsubo (16), an earlier Emperor's fourth daughter, becomes the Emperor's Consort.
	12	• Genji comes of age and marries Aoi (16), the daughter of the Minister of the Left.
		• Tō no Chūjō, Aoi's elder brother, marries the fourth daughter of the Minister of the Right.
		• The house that belonged to Genji's mother is rebuilt and becomes Genji's Nijō ("Second Avenue") residence.
2	17	• 5th month: Genji, Tō no Chūjō, and other young men discuss women in the "rainy night conversation."
		• The next evening Genji first discovers Utsusemi.
		• Genji returns to Utsusemi's house. She evades him.
3		• A third visit to Utsusemi's house. By mistake, Genji sleeps with Nokiba no Ogi instead.
4		• Summer: Genji discovers Yūgao (19).
		• 16th of 8th month: a spirit kills Yūgao. Genji remains ill until the 20th of the 9th month.
		• Genji observes the forty-ninth day after Yūgao's death.
		• 10th month: Utsusemi accompanies her husband to the province of Iyo.
6	18	• Early spring: Genji first hears Suetsumuhana's *kin*.

CHAP.	AGE	EVENT
	Genji	
5		• Late 3rd month: Genji seeks relief from malarial fever at a mountain temple and first sees Murasaki.
		• Fujitsubo goes home from the palace. Genji makes love to her there.
		• 6th month: Fujitsubo is three months pregnant.
		• 7th month: Fujitsubo returns to the palace.
6		• Circa 20th of 8th month: Genji's first meeting with Suetsumuhana.
5		• Late 9th month: death of Murasaki's grandmother.
		• Genji whisks Murasaki away to Nijō.
7		• Circa 10th of 10th month: imperial progress to Suzaku Palace. Genji dances "Blue Sea Waves."
		• Genji rises to third rank, Tō no Chūjō to fourth rank.
	19	• Circa 20th of 2nd month: Fujitsubo gives birth to Genji's secret son, the future Emperor Reizei.
		• 4th month: the little boy's first visit to the palace.
		• 7th month: Fujitsubo becomes Empress. Genji is appointed Consultant.
8	20	• Circa 20th of 2nd month: the party under the cherry blossoms. Genji first makes love with Oborozukiyo.
		• Circa 20th of 3rd month: the wisteria blossom party at the Minister of the Right's. Genji finds Oborozukiyo again.
Bet. 8 and 9	21	• Genji is promoted to Commander. The Emperor, Genji's father, abdicates. Suzaku (25) succeeds him. The future Reizei (4) becomes Heir Apparent. The Minister of the Right and the Kokiden Consort now dominate the court.
9	22	• Spring: the Rokujō Haven's daughter Akikonomu (13) becomes Ise Priestess. Aoi becomes pregnant.
		• Genji's father's third daughter from the Kokiden Consort becomes Kamo Priestess.
		• 4th month: the Rokujō Haven is humiliated by Aoi in the carriage quarrel at Kamo.
		• Day of the Kamo Festival: Genji cuts Murasaki's hair and takes her to see the festival.
		• 8th month: Aoi gives birth to Yūgiri.
		• Circa 20th of 8th month: Aoi suddenly dies. Genji goes into mourning at his father-in-law's.
		• 9th month: Akikonomu moves to the Shrine on the Moor.
		• 10th month: Genji returns to his Nijō residence, where he consummates his marriage with Murasaki.
	23	• 1st of 1st month: Genji calls on his father and the Heir Apparent, then visits Aoi's parents.
10		• Circa 7th of 9th month: Genji visits the Rokujō Haven at the Shrine on the Moor.
		• 16th of 9th month: Rokujō and her daughter Akikonomu leave for Ise.
		• 1st of 11th month: Genji's father dies.
		• 20th of 12th month: end of the forty-nine days of memorial services. Fujitsubo withdraws to her own home.
	24	• 2nd month: Oborozukiyo becomes Mistress of Staff.
		• The Kamo Priestess resigns and is succeeded by Asagao.
		• Autumn: Genji goes on retreat at Urin'in.
		• 1st of 11th month: anniversary of Genji's father's death.
		• 10th or so of 12th month: Fujitsubo holds the Rite of the Eight Discourses and becomes a nun.
	25	• 1st month: Genji visits Fujitsubo, now a nun.
		• The Minister of the Left (Aoi's father) resigns.
		• Summer: Oborozukiyo retires from the palace to her home because of illness. Genji visits her repeatedly and is found with her by her father, the Minister of the Right.

CHAP.	AGE	EVENT
	Genji	
11		• After 20th of 5th month: Genji visits Hanachirusato.
12	26	• Genji decides to exile himself to Suma. He visits Aoi's father, Fujitsubo, and the tomb of his father.
		• After 20th of 3rd month: Genji leaves for Suma.
		• 7th month: Oborozukiyo returns to the palace.
		• 8th month: the Dazaifu Deputy passes Suma. Genji exchanges poems with his daughter, the Gosechi Dancer.
	27	• After 20th of 2nd month: Tō no Chūjō (now Consultant Captain) visits Genji at Suma.
		• 1st of 3rd month (day of the Serpent): Genji goes for purification on the shore and a great storm begins.
13		• Several days later Murasaki's messenger arrives from the City.
		• Genji dreams of his father, who tells him to leave Suma.
		• 13th of 3rd month: the Akashi Novice takes Genji to Akashi.
		• 1st of 4th month: the Akashi Novice gives Genji new clothes for the change of season.
		• Emperor Suzaku and the Kokiden Consort both become seriously ill.
		• The Chancellor (the former Minister of the Right, Kokiden's father) dies.
		• 13th of 8th month: Genji spends his first night with the Akashi lady.
	28	• Circa 6th month: the lady becomes pregnant.
		• After 20th of 7th month: Genji is called back to the City.
		• 8th month: Genji returns to the City and is named Acting Grand Counselor.
		• 15th of 8th month: Genji first calls on Emperor Suzaku.
14, 15		• 10th month: Genji has the Rite of the Eight Discourses done for his father.
14	29	• 2nd month: the Heir Apparent (Reizei, 11) comes of age.
		• After 20th of 2nd month: Suzaku abdicates, Reizei becomes Emperor.
		• Suzaku's son by the Shōkyōden Consort becomes Heir Apparent.
		• Genji is appointed Palace Minister; Aoi's father, Regent and Chancellor; Tō no Chūjō, Acting Counselor.
		• Genji begins building the east pavilion of his Nijō residence.
15		• 16th of 3rd month: the Akashi lady gives birth to a daughter.
		• 4th month: Genji goes to visit Hanachirusato and discovers Suetsumuhana's ruinous house on the way there.
14		• 5th of 5th month: Genji sends a messenger to the celebration for his new daughter's fiftieth day.
		• Fujitsubo receives the rank of a Retired Emperor.
		• 8th month: Tō no Chūjō's daughter becomes a Consort.
		• Autumn: Genji goes on pilgrimage to Sumiyoshi. On the same day the Akashi lady arrives on her own pilgrimage, but they do not meet. Rokujō and Akikonomu return to the City from Ise. Rokujō entrusts her daughter to Genji and dies.
16		• 28th of 9th month: Utsusemi and her husband return to the City. Utsusemi meets Genji, who is on his way out of the City to Ishiyama.
—	30	——————
17	31	• Akikonomu becomes a Consort.
		• 10th or so of 3rd month: the picture contest before Fujitsubo.
		• After 20th of 3rd month: the picture contest before Emperor Reizei.
		• Genji begins building a temple outside the City.
18		• Autumn: Genji's east pavilion is finished. Hanachirusato moves into its east wing.
		• The Akashi lady moves to Ōi, where Genji visits her.
19		• 12th month: the Akashi lady cedes her daughter to Murasaki.
	32	• Aoi's father dies.
		• 3rd month: Fujitsubo becomes gravely ill, then dies.

CHAP.	AGE	EVENT
	Genji	

- On the forty-ninth day after Fujitsubo's death, an old monk tells Emperor Reizei the secret of his birth.
- On the same day Asagao's father dies.
- Emperor Reizei hints at abdicating in Genji's favor. Genji refuses and refuses also appointment as Chancellor.

20
- 9th month: Asagao resigns as Kamo Priestess because of her father's death and returns to her residence.
- Genji calls on the Fifth Princess and on Asagao.
- 11th month: Genji calls again on the Fifth Princess and especially on Asagao. He has a dream of Fujitsubo.

21   33
- 3rd month: the first anniversary of Fujitsubo's death.
- 4th month: Asagao changes out of mourning, and Genji visits her.
- Yūgiri comes of age, is given the sixth rank, and enters the Academy.
- The Lord of Ceremonial's daughter (Murasaki's younger half sister) becomes a Consort.
- Akikonomu becomes Empress.
- Genji becomes Chancellor.
- Tō no Chūjō is promoted to Palace Minister. He separates Kumoi no Kari (his daughter) and Yūgiri (Genji's son).
- 11th month: Genji presents Koremitsu's daughter as a Gosechi dancer.
- Yūgiri notices Koremitsu's daughter and gives her a note.
- Genji entrusts Yūgiri to Hanachirusato's care.

34
- After 20th of 2nd month: Emperor Reizei visits Retired Emperor Suzaku.
- Yūgiri passes his examination. In the autumn he is awarded the fifth rank and appointed Adviser.
- Genji builds his Rokujō estate.

35
- Genji prepares to celebrate the fiftieth year of Murasaki's father.

22
- Yūgao's daughter Tamakazura, who has grown up in Kyushu, is courted by a local strongman, the Audit Commissioner.

21
- 4th month: Tamakazura's nurse takes her up to the City.
- 8th month: Genji's Rokujō estate is finished, and his principal ladies move in.

22
- Tamakazura, on pilgrimage to Hasedera, at last encounters Ukon. She moves to Ukon's house on Gojō.
- Yūgiri is appointed Captain.

21
- 10th month: Genji takes Tamakazura into Rokujō and entrusts her to Hanachirusato.

22
- The Akashi lady moves to Rokujō.
- At the end of the year Genji sends gifts of clothes to his various ladies.

23   36
- 1st of 1st month: Genji visits each of the Rokujō ladies.
- 2nd of 1st month: Genji entertains New Year guests.
- 14th of 1st month: the men's mumming.
- 15th of 1st month: Genji entertains the mummers.

24
- After 20th of 3rd month: a concert in Murasaki's spring garden.
- The next day: the spring scripture reading at Akikonomu's.
- 4th month: Tamakazura receives letters from Hotaru, Higekuro, and Kashiwagi. Genji pursues her as well.

25
- 5th month, on a rainy evening: Hotaru calls on Tamakazura and sees her by the light of fireflies released by Genji.
- 5th of 5th month: a riding contest at the Rokujō riding ground.
- The Rokujō ladies become absorbed in tales. Genji discourses to Tamakazura on the value of tales.

26
- 6th month: Genji hears about Tō no Chūjō's acceptance of his Ōmi daughter.
- Genji wonders what to do with Tamakazura, and Tō no Chūjō wonders what to do with his Ōmi daughter.

CHAP.	AGE	EVENT
	Genji	
27		• Early autumn: Genji and Tamakazura talk by the light of cressets.
		• Genji holds a concert with Yūgiri and Kashiwagi.
28		• 8th month: a typhoon. In the aftermath Yūgiri glimpses Murasaki and also sees Genji with Tamakazura.
		• Yūgiri visits Ōmiya, his grandmother. Tō no Chūjō calls on Ōmiya for the first time in ages.
29		• 12th month: the Emperor makes a progress to Ōharano.
	37	• 1st of 2nd month: Genji calls on Ōmiya, who is ill. He meets Tō no Chūjō and finally tells him about Tamakazura.
		• 26th of 2nd month: Tamakazura's donning of the train, under the sponsorship of her father, Tō no Chūjō.
30		• 20th of 3rd month: Ōmiya dies.
		• 13th of 8th month: Tamakazura's mourning for Ōmiya, her grandmother, ends. It is decided that she will go to the palace in the 10th month or so.
		• Tamakazura is courted by Hotaru, Higekuro, and others.
31		• Circa 10th month: Higekuro marries Tamakazura.
		• Uproar in Higekuro's house. His wife (Murasaki's elder half sister) empties ashes over him. She returns to her father's residence.
	38	• 1st month: the men's mumming. Tamakazura goes to the palace as Mistress of Staff. Higekuro takes her home.
		• 11th month: Tamakazura has a son.
32	39	• Last day of 1st month: Genji asks various ladies to blend incense for his daughter's donning of the train.
		• 10th of 2nd month: Hotaru (His Highness of War) judges the incense. A concert follows.
		• Preparations for Genji's daughter's 4th-month entry into the palace. Yūgiri longs for Kumoi no Kari.
33		• 20th of 3rd month: the anniversary of Ōmiya's death. Tō no Chūjō speaks with Yūgiri.
		• 7th of 4th month: Tō no Chūjō invites Yūgiri to a wisteria blossom party and that evening gives him Kumoi no Kari.
		• 8th of 4th month: the rite of lustration of the Buddha.
		• Murasaki goes to the Divine Birth (Miare) at Kamo.
		• Murasaki attends the Kamo Festival.
		• After 20th of 4th month: Genji's daughter enters the palace. Murasaki accompanies her.
		• Three days later: Murasaki leaves the palace. The Akashi lady replaces her, and the two meet for the first time.
		• Preparations to celebrate Genji's fortieth year begin.
		• Autumn: Genji becomes Honorary Retired Emperor.
		• Tō no Chūjō becomes Chancellor. Yūgiri is appointed Counselor.
		• After 20th of 10th month: Emperor Reizei and Retired Emperor Suzaku visit Genji's Rokujō estate. Genji is at the summit of his glory.
		• Retired Emperor Suzaku falls ill after his visit to Rokujō.
34		• Near the end of the year Suzaku's Third Princess (Onna San no Miya, 13 or 14) has her donning of the train.
		• Three days later, Suzaku enters religion and entrusts Onna San no Miya to Genji.
	40	• 23rd of 1st month: Tamakazura offers Genji spring shoots for his fortieth year.
		• 10th or so of 2nd month: Onna San no Miya moves to Rokujō. Genji has married her.
		• End of 2nd month: Suzaku moves to a mountain temple.
		• Genji and Oborozukiyo meet.
		• Summer: the Consort (Genji's daughter) is pregnant. She withdraws from the palace to Rokujō.

CHAP.	AGE	EVENT
	Genji	

- 10th month: Murasaki dedicates an image of Yakushi for Genji's fortieth year.
- 23rd of 10th month: a banquet at Nijō.
- After 20th of 12th month: Akikonomu has sutras read at the Seven Great Temples of Nara for Genji's fortieth year.
- Emperor Reizei celebrates Genji's fortieth year. Yūgiri is appointed Right Commander.

41
- 1st month: a continuous Great Rite begins for the safe delivery of the Consort's child.
- 10th or so of 3rd month: the Consort (Genji's daughter) gives birth to a son, the future Heir Apparent.
- The Akashi Novice sends the Akashi lady, his daughter, a letter and vanishes into the mountains.
- 3rd month: a kickball party at Rokujō. Kashiwagi (25 or 26, Tō no Chūjō's eldest son) glimpses Onna San no Miya and desires her.

35
- End of 3rd month: an archery competition at Rokujō.
- Hotaru begins his affair with Makibashira.

42–45   A four-year gap.

46
- Emperor Reizei abdicates after eighteen years. The Heir Apparent (Suzaku's son) becomes Emperor. The son of the Consort (Genji's daughter) becomes Heir Apparent. Tō no Chūjō resigns as Chancellor. Higekuro, the Left Commander, becomes Minister of the Right and Regent. Yūgiri becomes Grand Counselor and Left Commander.
- 20th of 10th month: Genji goes on a pilgrimage of thanks to Sumiyoshi with Murasaki, the Consort, and the Akashi lady and her mother.
- Onna San no Miya is promoted in rank.

47
- Preparations to celebrate Retired Emperor Suzaku's fiftieth year.
- 19th of 1st month: Genji's ladies play together in concert at Rokujō.
- Murasaki becomes ill. Suzaku's jubilee event is postponed.
- 3rd month: Genji moves Murasaki to Nijō.
- Kashiwagi marries Ochiba, Suzaku's Second Princess.
- 10th or so of 4th month: Kashiwagi succeeds in meeting Onna San no Miya.
- 6th month: Murasaki's condition improves a little. Genji permits her to receive the Buddhist precepts for laymen. Onna San no Miya is pregnant with Kashiwagi's child.
- Oborozukiyo becomes a nun.
- The Consort (Genji's daughter) gives birth to Niou.
- 10th or so of 12th month: the rehearsal for Suzaku's jubilee. Genji invites Kashiwagi. Kashiwagi then becomes ill.
- 25th of 12th month: Suzaku's jubilee event is held.

36   **48**
- Spring: Onna San no Miya gives birth to Kaoru, Kashiwagi's son.
- Onna San no Miya becomes a nun.
- Kashiwagi is promoted on his deathbed to Acting Grand Counselor. He then dies.
- 3rd month: the celebrations for Kaoru's fiftieth day.
- 4th month: Yūgiri visits Ochiba, Kashiwagi's widow.

37   **49**
- Spring: Genji and Yūgiri observe the first anniversary of Kashiwagi's death.
- Autumn: Yūgiri visits Ochiba and receives from her mother the flute that Kashiwagi had prized.
- Yūgiri dreams of Kashiwagi.

38   **50**
- Summer: Dedication of the sacred image for Onna San no Miya's private chapel. Genji personally copies out her sutras.
- Autumn: Bell crickets are released in Onna San no Miya's Rokujō garden.
- 15th of 8th month: a full-moon banquet.

CHAP.	AGE	EVENT
	Genji	
		• Akikonomu holds a Rite of the Eight Discourses for her late mother, the Rokujō Haven.
39		• Ochiba's mother moves to Ono, in the hills, because she is ill.
		• Mid-8th month: Yūgiri visits Ono and declares his interest in Ochiba.
		• Ochiba's mother (the Ichijō Haven) dies.
		• Yūgiri brings Ochiba, who wants to become a nun, back to her Ichijō residence instead as his wife. Kumoi no Kari, his first wife, is jealous and returns to her father's home.
40	51	• Murasaki, who remains weak after her major illness, wishes to become a nun. Genji will not allow it.
		• 10th of 3rd month: Murasaki, at Nijō, dedicates one thousand copies of the Lotus Sutra.
		• Summer: the Empress (Genji's daughter) visits Murasaki.
		• 14th of 8th month: Murasaki dies.
		• 15th of 8th month: Murasaki's funeral. Genji resolves to leave the world.
41	52	• Spring: Genji remains in seclusion, mourning Murasaki.
		• 14th of 8th month: the first anniversary of Murasaki's death.
		• 12th month: Genji prepares to take religious vows.

An eight-year gap. Genji seems to have spent two or three years in seclusion in his Saga temple before his death. Retired Emperor Suzaku, Hotaru, Tō no Chūjō, and Higekuro die.

CHAP.	AGE	EVENT
	Kaoru	
42	14	• 2nd month: Kaoru comes of age. He is appointed Adviser and awarded the fourth rank.
44		• Autumn: Kaoru is appointed Right Captain.
	15	• 1st of 1st month: Yūgiri (41) and his children visit Tamakazura (48).
		• The same evening: Kaoru visits Tamakazura.
		• After 20th of 1st month: Kaoru visits Tamakazura's third son. A red plum blossom party ensues.
		• 3rd month: Tamakazura's daughters play Go together, secretly watched by the Chamberlain Lieutenant (Yūgiri's sixth son).
		• 9th of 4th month: Tamakazura's elder daughter marries Retired Emperor Reizei. The Chamberlain Lieutenant laments his fortunes in love.
		• 7th month: Tamakazura's elder daughter becomes pregnant.
	16	• 14th of 1st month: the men's mumming and a concert in the presence of Retired Emperor Reizei.
		• 4th month: Tamakazura's elder daughter gives birth to a girl.
		• Tamakazura's second daughter goes into palace service.
42		• Niou and Kaoru, often rivals, are presented as a pair.
	19	• Kaoru is promoted to the third rank and Consultant Captain.
	20	• 1st month: Yūgiri holds a banquet at Rokujō.
—	21	————
45	22	• Late autumn: Hachi no Miya (the Eighth Prince), who lives at Uji, goes on religious retreat. Kaoru visits his residence during his absence and glimpses Hachi no Miya's two daughters, Ōigimi (24) and Naka no Kimi (22).
		• That night Kaoru hears from Ben, an old gentlewoman in Hachi no Miya's service, hints concerning his own birth.
		• Back in the City, Kaoru tells Niou (23) about Uji.
		• 5th or 6th of 10th month: Kaoru goes to Uji and plays music with Hachi no Miya. He then hears from Ben the full story of his birth.
46	23	• After 20th of 2nd month: Niou goes to Hasedera and visits Uji on his way back.
		• Kaoru visits Hachi no Miya.
		• Niou sends repeated letters to Uji. Naka no Kimi responds.

CHAP.	AGE	EVENT
	Kaoru	

- Autumn: Kaoru is promoted to Counselor; Yūgiri, to Minister of the Left (a possible symptom of a textual problem); Kōbai, to Minister of the Right and Left Commander; and the Chamberlain Lieutenant, to Consultant Captain.
- Mid-autumn: Hachi no Miya goes on retreat.
- After 20th of 8th month: Hachi no Miya dies.
- Winter: Niou writes frequently to Uji.
- End of the year: Kaoru visits Uji and confesses his feelings to Ōigimi.

43 **24**
- Spring: Kōbai's elder daughter goes to the Heir Apparent.

46
- Onna San no Miya's Sanjō residence burns down, and she moves to Rokujō.

49
- Summer: death of the mother of the reigning Emperor's Second Princess, whose donning of the train is postponed.
- The Emperor moves to have Kaoru marry his Second Princess.

47
- Autumn: first anniversary of Hachi no Miya's death. Kaoru again presses Ōigimi, but she rebuffs him.
- 28th of 8th month: Kaoru accompanies Niou to Uji. Kaoru gets nowhere with Ōigimi. Meanwhile Niou makes love to Naka no Kimi.
- Circa 10th of 9th month: Niou and Kaoru go to Uji. Ōigimi again rebuffs Kaoru.
- 1st of 10th month: Niou and Kaoru go autumn-leaf viewing in Uji. Niou is unable to meet Naka no Kimi.
- Negotiations begin to bring about the marriage of Niou to Roku no Kimi (Yūgiri's Sixth Daughter). The Empress reproves Niou's wanton ways. Niou moves to the palace.
- Ōigimi, at Uji, falls ill. Kaoru visits her.
- 11th month: The Uji sisters lament Niou's neglect.
- Kaoru again visits Ōigimi. Her condition becomes grave, and he remains at Uji.
- Ōigimi dies. The funeral. Kaoru remains at Uji to absorb himself in Buddhist rites.
- 12th month: Niou visits Uji. He prepares to bring Naka no Kimi to Nijō.

48 **25**
- 7th of 2nd month: Naka no Kimi moves to Niou's residence at Nijō.
- After 20th of 2nd month: Roku no Kimi has her donning of the train.
- Kaoru moves to the rebuilt Sanjō residence of his mother.

49
- 5th month: Naka no Kimi is pregnant.
- 16th of 8th month: Niou marries Roku no Kimi at Rokujō.
- Naka no Kimi begs Kaoru to take her back to Uji. Niou suspects them of being involved with each other.
- Kaoru visits Naka no Kimi. Naka no Kimi first mentions her half sister, Ukifune.
- After 20th of 9th month: Kaoru goes to Uji and decides to turn Hachi no Miya's residence there into a temple. He asks Ben about Ukifune.
- Kaoru sends Naka no Kimi red leaves from Uji. Niou is increasingly suspicious.

26
- 1st of 2nd month: Kaoru becomes Acting Grand Counselor and Right Commander. Naka no Kimi gives Niou a son.
- After 20th of 2nd month: the Second Princess's donning of the train. She is married to Kaoru the next day.
- Last day of 3rd month: The Second Princess gives a wisteria party at the Fujitsubo. That night she moves to Kaoru's Sanjō residence.
- After 20th of 4th month: Kaoru goes to Uji to inspect the new temple. Ukifune arrives at Uji on her way back from a pilgrimage to Hasedera, and Kaoru spies on her.

50
- A plan to marry Ukifune to a certain Lieutenant breaks down.
- Ukifune's mother asks Naka no Kimi to protect Ukifune. Naka no

CHAP.	AGE	EVENT
	Kaoru	

Kimi commends Ukifune to Kaoru. Niou discovers Ukifune and begins pursuing her.
- Autumn: the new temple at Uji is finished. Kaoru goes there and asks Ben to mediate between him and Ukifune.
- 13th of 9th month: Kaoru moves Ukifune to Uji.

| 51 | 27 | |

- Late 1st month: Niou pursues Ukifune to Uji and sleeps with her under the pretense of being Kaoru.
- Kaoru prepares to bring Ukifune to the City in the 4th month.
- Circa 10th of 2nd month: a Chinese-poetry gathering at the palace. The next day Niou goes to Uji and spends two days with Ukifune in a house on the other side of the river. He plans to take her to the City before Kaoru can do so. Kaoru discovers the affair between the two and posts guards at Uji. Caught between Kaoru and Niou, Ukifune decides to drown herself in the Uji River.
- Niou goes to Uji but is prevented by Kaoru's guards from meeting Ukifune.

| 52 | | |

- Ukifune has disappeared. A funeral is held without a body.

| 53 | | |

- The Prelate of Yokawa, who is visiting Uji, finds a young woman (Ukifune) lying under a tree. He takes her back to his mother's house at Ono, below Mount Hiei.

| 52 | | |

- Kaoru and Niou learn of Ukifune's suicide and mourn her.
- Kaoru conducts forty-ninth-day memorial services for Ukifune.
- The Empress holds a Rite of the Eight Discourses at Rokujō.

| 53 | | |

- 4th or 5th month: Ukifune is exorcised and recovers her senses.
- Autumn: a Captain, once married to the daughter of the Prelate's sister (now a nun), visits Ono and glimpses Ukifune. He pursues her, but she avoids him.
- 9th month: Ukifune becomes a nun.
- The Prelate of Yokawa tells the Empress about Ukifune.

| | 28 | |

- Kaoru observes the first anniversary of Ukifune's supposed death.

| 54 | | |

- Kaoru visits the Empress, who lets him know that Ukifune is alive. He then visits Yokawa, where the Prelate tells him about Ukifune.
- Kaoru seeks to meet Ukifune and sends her a note. He returns to the City but the next day sends her young half brother as his messenger to her. Ukifune refuses to meet her half brother and refuses to answer Kaoru's note. The boy returns to Kaoru empty-handed. Kaoru grieves.

General Glossary

academic style *azana*—A two-character, Chinese-style name conferred on a degree candidate at the Academy.

Academy Daigaku—An institution to train sons of the aristocracy, especially those below the highest level, in the fields of Chinese-based knowledge required for a career as an official. Staffed by Doctors and more junior scholars, it came under the Bureau of Ceremonial. It accepted any boy between his thirteenth and sixteenth years whose father held the fifth rank or above, as well as selected boys from an eighth-rank background.

"Ah, Wondrous Day!" "Anatōto"—A congratulatory *saibara* song summed up by its first line and with little narrative content.

aisle *hisashi*—The space in a house that surrounded the chamber (*moya*), between the chamber and the veranda (*sunoko*). It was normally divided into sections, or rooms. The aisle was lower than the chamber by the depth of the lintel (*nageshi*). Exceptionally, there could be a second aisle width beyond the first, again a lintel-depth lower.

aloeswood *jin*—A wood prized for incense and also for making various small items of furniture.

Amida—The Buddha of infinite light, who presides over a paradise located immeasurably far away toward the west. According to his great vow, all who call his name (in the formula "Namu Amida Butsu," known as the Nenbutsu) will achieve rebirth into this paradise, and this invocation was therefore the single most common Buddhist practice in the author's time. Usually voiced, it was recited silently for a funeral.

anteroom *on yasumi dokoro*—A south-facing room attached to the privy chamber.

appointments list *jimoku, tsukasameshi*—The appointments and promotions announced twice a year, in spring and autumn. The Minister of the Left presided over the event.

arched bridge *soribashi*—A bridge over a garden stream.

armrest *kyōsoku*—A common item of furniture, to lean on when seated on the floor.

Assembly of the Holy Names Butsumyō-e—A religious event held for three days in the palace and in other aristocratic houses, starting on the nineteenth day of the twelfth month. The ceremony involved invoking the names of the Buddhas of past, present, and future, in a spirit of repentance and atonement.

Atago, Mount—A sacred mountain (3,049 feet) just northwest of Kyoto.

"At Kawaguchi" *"Kawaguchi no"*—A *saibara* song in the voice of a girl who boasts of having escaped through "the rough fence of the Kawaguchi Barrier," despite her father's watchful eye, to lie with her lover.

"Autumn Wind" *"Shūfūraku"*—A "Chinese" *bugaku* piece that dates in its present form from the reign of Emperor Saga (reigned 809–23).

Azuma—"The East": roughly, the modern Kanto region in which Tokyo is situated. It was then seen as remote and uncouth.

azuma **mode**—A musical mode associated with eastern Japan and with the *wagon*. Its character is unknown.

backgammon *sugoroku*—A board game related to backgammon and popular in the world of the tale.

banshiki **mode**—A musical mode particularly suitable for winter.

bark shingles *hiwada*—Slats of cypress (*hinoki*) bark used, many layers deep, for roofing.

basketwork carriage *ajiro guruma*—A carriage whose cabin was woven from strips of cypress (*hinoki*) and bamboo. Adequate for formal use by a privy gentleman, it was informal for a senior noble.

basketwork screen *ajiro byōbu*—A screen made of woven slats of cypress (*hinoki*) or cryptomeria (*sugi*) wood.

baton *shaku*—A flat length of wood about a foot long, slightly tapering and with rounded ends, that a court official held vertically before him when in formal posture.

bay *ma*—The unit of length between two structural pillars. Most houses were five bays long: three for the chamber (*moya*) and two (one on each side) for the aisle (*hisashi*).

beardgrass *karukaya*—A type of tall grass with long awns, distantly related to rice.

beaten silk *uchimono*—Silk beaten on a fulling block (*kinuta*) to bring out its luster.

bell cricket *suzumushi*—A species of cricket with a particularly melodious call.

benefice *kōburi*—Income similar to "sinecure," although from a slightly different source.

Benevolent King, Rite of the *Ninnō-e*—A solemn Buddhist rite performed in the palace for the protection of the realm.

bird clappers *hita*—Slats of wood or bamboo attached to a string, so that they could be clapped together to frighten birds off the fields.

birth celebration *ubuyashinai*—A series of celebratory gatherings on the third, fifth, seventh, and ninth evenings after a birth. The guests brought gifts of food and clothing for the child.

biwa—A four-stringed musical instrument of the lute family, from China.

biwa **minstrel** *biwa hōshi*—A strolling musician who wore Buddhist robes and sang to his own *biwa* accompaniment.

blinds *sudare, misu*—Fine, roll-up bamboo blinds that hung from the upper lintel between the chamber and the aisle, and between the aisle and the veranda.

bluebell *asagao*—Literally "morning face." This is now the name of the morning glory, but many scholars doubt that the *asagao* of the earlier chapters, especially the one directly associated with Princess Asagao, is that flower. The leading possibility otherwise is the *kikyō* (*Platycodon grandiflorum*), the "Chinese bellflower," a sort of bluebell. In "The Bluebell" the beauty of the *asagao* is described in terms of *nioi*, a word associated with red, purple, violet, or yellow but not with pure blue or white, the only colors known for the morning glory in Heian times. (Red, purple, and so on did not appear until four or five centuries later.) "Bluebell" therefore appears in this translation in the chapters covering Genji's life. However, the *asagao* of "The Ivy" seems indeed to be the morning glory, since the passage so insists on the very transience for which the morning glory is known; moreover the *kikyō* is mentioned by name in "Writing Practice."

Blue Roans, Festival of the *Aouma (no Sechie)*—Twenty-one horses, in principle rare blue roans, led before the Emperor, the Retired Emperor, the senior imperial ladies, and the Heir Apparent on the seventh day of the first month. The sight of them was held to be auspicious. The horses really were blue roans up to Murakami's reign (946–67), through the time covered in the tale, but thereafter they were white. This was the only New Year observance retained when an Emperor was in mourning. The custom was originally Chinese.

"Blue Sea Waves" *"Seigaiha"*—A "Chinese" *bugaku* piece for two dancers. The tossing of the dancers' sleeves is said to evoke the waves of the sea.

board fence *kirikake*—A cheap fence made of overlapping, diagonally placed boards.

board-roofed dwelling *itaya*—A dwelling simply and cheaply roofed with thin, overlapped planks held down by branches and stones.

brazier *hioke*—A portable tub generally made of wood and designed to hold charcoal burning in insulating ashes.

breakfast *ōnkayu*—Rice gruel or cooked rice (*katagayu*).

breakfast room *asagarei*—Adjoined the gentlewomen's sitting room to the north in the Emperor's residence in the palace.

bridgeway *watadono*—A short, raised passageway that connected the main house to one of the wings. It could be enclosed, with doors, and even with rooms, or could be an open, roofed bridge.

broom tree *hahakigi*—In modern Japanese *hōkigusa*. An annual plant about three feet high, from the stems of which brooms could indeed be made.

bugaku—A repertoire of dances from the continent, accompanied by *gagaku* music and a large drum. The dances are separated into two subrepertoires: Tōgaku ("music from Tang [China]"), defined as the Left, and Komagaku ("music from Koma [Korea]"), defined as the Right.

Bureau (of Central Affairs, Ceremonial, Civil Affairs, Treasury, War)—See glossary of "Offices and Titles."

burnet *waremokō*—A perennial plant two to three feet high, with compound pinnate leaves. In late summer each twig tip puts forth a small, elongated ball made up of tiny dark red flowers.

Butokuden—A pavilion in the greater palace compound from which the Emperor watched archery contests, horse races, and so on.

cabinet *mizushi*—A cabinet with doors, often surmounted by a tier of open shelves.

censer *hitori*—A vessel of silver or gilt bronze in which to burn incense. In use, it was placed inside a larger container of lacquered wood (*hitorimo*) and covered with a lid of metal mesh.

censer frame *ko* or *fusego*—A cagelike structure placed over a censer. Clothes could be draped over it to be warmed and scented.

Ceremonial Bureau examination *Shikibu no Tsukasa no kokoromi*—The second-level examination for students at the Academy. It allowed the student to pass from *gimonjō* (provisional candidate) status to *monjōshō* (regular candidate). See **foundation examination.**

chamber *moya*—The central structural and residential space within a house, sometimes divided into a smaller and larger room. The living space extended from the chamber into the aisle (*hisashi*), which could be partitioned into distinct rooms, and further into a veranda (*sunoko*) covered by eaves (*noki*). The smaller room of the chamber (*nurigome*, "retreat"), if present, could serve for sleeping or as a storeroom.

change of clothes for the new season *koromogae*—The prescribed change to summer clothes (including a change of interior decoration) on the first of the fourth month, and to winter ones on the first of the tenth month.

character-guessing games *hen-tsugi*—Games that involved guessing partly hidden characters or making up new ones by adding elements to given parts.

"Cherry Blossom Man" "Sakurabito"—A *saibara* song in dialogue form: "[The husband] Stay your boat, O cherry blossom man, I've to see to my fields on the island, and I'll be back tomorrow, yes, I'll be back tomorrow! [The wife] Tomorrow, you say, but he who has a woman there won't really be back tomorrow, no, not really back tomorrow."

chest *karabitsu*—A long chest on legs, mainly for storing clothes. There also existed a somewhat longer "narrow chest" (*hosobitsu*).

Chrysanthemum Festival Chōyō no Sechie—A festival held on the ninth day of the ninth month, though it had lapsed by the author's time. In a setting decorated with chrysanthemums (associated with long life and good fortune), the Emperor offered chrysanthemum wine to his courtiers, and the gathering composed poems in Chinese.

clappers *hyōshi*—Two lengths of wood clapped together for the rhythm in music.

cloth panel *zejō* or *zenjō*—A panel of cloth hung to protect someone from being seen. It might have a scene painted on the inner side, toward the person concealed.

coming-of-age *genbuku*—The coming-of-age ceremony for a boy, at which he first had his hair bound up, donned the costume and headdress of an adult, and assumed an adult name.

common gentleman *naobito*—A man of the fourth or fifth rank.

commoner *tadabito*—A gentleman who is not a member of the imperial family.

concluding banquet *goen*—The banquet given by the Emperor, normally in the second or third month, to those who had taken part in the New Year mumming.

concubine *meshiudo*—A gentlewomen (*nyōbō*) taken by her master as a sort of lesser mistress.

Confession (Rite of) (Hokke) Senbō—A ritual that combined chanting of the Lotus Sutra with confession of sins, to erase all sin for the beneficiary of the rite.

court—No word in the text distinguishes "palace" (see entry) from "court," which appears in the translation when the emphasis seems to be particularly on the company present at the palace.

Court Repository Kurazukasa—A palace office charged with the care of various treasures and gifts to the court.

cover *hyōshi*—A cover for a rolled scroll, one that might also serve as a label. It could be made of paper or silk.

Crafts Workshop Tsukumodokoro—A palace office responsible for making accessories and furnishings. It came under the Chamberlains' Office.

cresset *kagaribi*—A wood fire contained in an iron cage, used for illuminating a garden at night or by cormorant fishermen to attract fish.

curtained bed *michōdai*—A curtained-off dais, like a small room within a room, that served as a sleeping chamber.

cushion *shitone*—A square, quilted mat four feet or so on a side, made of cloth filled with cotton padding and bordered with brocade. It was used for sitting or sleeping.

cypress box *hiwarigo*—A square, round, or fan-shaped tiered box made of finely split cypress wood.

dagger *mihakashi*—A dagger given a wellborn child at birth.

Dainichi Nyorai—The cosmic buddha of the Shingon Buddhist pantheon.

darani—A spell transliterated from Sanskrit via Chinese, hence unintelligible as language, and used to ward off sickness or disaster.

day of the (Rat, Ox, etc.)—See **hour**.

dayflower *tsukikusa*—Modern Japanese *tsuyukusa* (*Commelina communis*), a common plant with sky blue flowers that yield a quickly fading blue dye.

dedicatory prayer *ganmon*—A text composed by the sponsor of a rite, in order to communicate the rite's intent to the deity or deities addressed.

demon *oni*—A supernatural creature variously imagined, but typically a terrifying red or blue-black variant on the human form.

desk *bundai*—A low writing table used on a formal occasion when poetry was presented to the host. The desk was placed below the steps leading up to the center of the south side of the residence, and each participant went in turn to place his composition on it.

directional taboo *futagari, kataimi, katatagae*—See **Mid-God**.

display carriage *idashiguruma*—A carriage under the blinds of which gentlewomen allowed their sleeves to hang in a brilliant display of color.

diver—See **seafolk**.

Divine Birth at Kamo *Kamo no Miare*—A nighttime rite that reenacted the appearance on earth of Wakeikazuchi, the deity of the Upper Kamo Shrine. It took place on the middle Monkey day in the fourth month and was followed the next day by the Kamo Festival.

doll *hitogata*—A simulacrum of a human being, three-dimensional or cut out of paper, used in purification rites. Evil influences were ritually infused into the doll (or dolls), which was then sent floating down a river or out to sea.

donning of the train *mogi*—The coming-of-age ceremony for a girl, at which she first put on a train (*mo*). It was often done in preparation for the girl's marriage.

donning of the trousers *hakama gi*—A rite of passage during which a little boy or girl, typically three or five years old, was first dressed in trousers.

double doors *tsumado*—hinged doors, opening outward, near the corners of the main house (*shinden*), placed so that one could walk through them and across a bridgeway (*watadono*) to the wing (*tai*) on either side.

double tray *tsuigasane*—A tray (*oshiki*) combined with a simple rectangular stand.

East, the *Azuma*—The eastern region of Japan's main island, seen from the City. It was centered on the present Kanto area.

"Eastern Cottage, The" **"Azumaya"**—A *saibara* song in which a man arrives at a woman's door in the pouring rain and demands to be admitted. The woman, inside, answers that the door is unlocked and urges him to come in. The "eastern cottage" was a form of thatched house characteristic of eastern Japan.

Eastern Dances *Azuma Asobi*—A set of dances based on folk songs from Azuma. They were prominent in the dance repertoire of the Heian court.

Eastern Hills *Higashi Yama*—The hills on the eastern side of the City.

east pavilion *higashi no in*—The new house that Genji built on the Nijō property he had inherited from his mother, in order to accommodate some of his women.

Eight Bureaus *Hasshō*—The eight major government bureaus: Central Affairs, Ceremonial, Civil Affairs, Popular Affairs, Punishments, Treasury, War, and Palace Affairs. These were located in a compound that was continuous with the Great Hall of State (Daigokuden), the major ceremonial building in the palace precincts.

Eight Discourses, Rite of the *Mi-hakō*—A four-day rite celebrating the Lotus Sutra. Each day a formal debate, held in morning and afternoon sessions, developed the content of two of the sutra's eight scrolls.

emolument *mifu*—Income attached to court rank and derived from the labor of a set number of households.

equinox *higan*—A seven-day period in the second (spring) and eighth (autumn) months, surrounding the day of the equinox itself. The first and last days of *higan* were particularly lucky.

escort *saki*—Men who preceded a great lord and gave cries to warn others from their master's path.

evening service *soya (no tsutome)*—A Buddhist service that started at about 6:00 P.M. and ended at about 10:00.

extension *hanachiide*—An enlargement to the living space of a house, though its precise nature is a little unclear. It seems to have been made by removing the partitions (blinds, sliding panels) between the chamber and the aisle, but the word may sometimes also refer to an extension to the existing structure.

fasting *sōjin*—Abstinence from wine and meat, and chanting of Buddhist scriptures.

"Fence of Rushes" "Ashigaki"—A *saibara* song about a lover who comes to steal his bride from her father's house and gets caught.

ferns (of memory) *shinobu*—See **grasses of remembering.**

Festival, the—See **Kamo Festival.**

fire altar *dan*—An altar that included an earthen hearth for the sacred *goma* fire.

first reading *fumi-hajime*—A ceremony in which a Prince, Heir Apparent, or young Emperor gave a first, formal reading from the Chinese classics.

fishing pavilion *tsuridono*—A pavilion built on stilts over the garden lake of a Heian dwelling and joined to one of the wings (*tai*) by an open gallery. It was used for relaxing pastimes.

Five Altar Rite Godan Mizuhō—See **Great Rite.**

Five Classics—*The Book of Changes* (*Yiching*), *The Book of Songs* (*Shijing*), *The Book of Documents* (*Shujing*), *The Spring and Autumn Annals* (*Chunqiu*), and *The Book of Rites* (*Liji*).

five-color cakes *fuzuku*—Cakes in the five recognized Buddhist colors (red, white, black, yellow, and blue or green), made of five different grains pounded to a paste with sweetvine (*amazuru*) syrup.

Five Precepts, the Itsutsu no Imashime, Gokai—The Buddhist prohibitions against killing, stealing, fornication, deceit, and drunkenness. These simple rules of conduct could be upheld by a layman or a novice (*nyūdō*), but for fully ordained monks and nuns there were many more.

floating bridge *ukihashi*—A temporary bridge (boards laid across boats or rafts) over a river.

floral circles *kemonryō*—Circles containing a floral motif on a plain, light ground.

flute *yokobue*—A transverse, seven-holed flute.

folding paper *tatōgami, futokorogami*—A kind of general-purpose paper often kept, folded up, in the front fold of one's robe. It could be used when necessary instead of letter paper.

forty-nine days—A period after death during which rites were performed every seven days, in order to guide the deceased through various intermediate states to a fortunate rebirth. See also **memorial rites.**

foundation examination *ryōshi*—The entry-level Academy examination in the letters (*kiden*) line of study. It covered Chinese history as contained in the *Shiji* (see **Records of the Historian, The**) and the *Hanshu*. Passing three of its five parts gave the student "provisional candidate" (*gimonjō*) status; that is, qualified him to become (after a further Ceremonial Bureau examination [*Shikibu no Tsukasa no kokoromi*]) a regular candidate (*monjōshō*) for the Academy's first full degree.

fox *kitsune*—A supernatural creature associated with the image of the commonplace fox. In Japan as in China the magic fox was believed to be a shape-changer that particularly favored the shape of a beautiful young woman.

fragrant chest *kō no ōn karabitsu*—Either a chest containing incense wood to perfume its contents or a chest actually made of incense wood.

fringed basket *higeko*—A basket or box woven of bamboo, with the edges left untrimmed. It was used for fruit or flowers.

fruit basket *komono*—A basket lined with thin paper and containing five kinds of fruit and nuts (tangerines [*kōji*], oranges [*tachibana*], chestnuts, persimmons, and *nashi* or Japanese pear), together with decorative sprigs of pine.

Fudō—A Buddhist deity whose name means "the Unmoving." Fudō sits or stands on a rock, surrounded by flames. Usually blue-black in color, he holds an upraised sword in his right hand to cut down the demons of craving and a noose in his left to bind them. The principal deity of mountain ascetic rites, he was also the central deity of the Great Rite.

Fugen—A bodhisattva representing the teaching and practice of the Buddha and closely associated with the Lotus Sutra. Fugen's canonical mount is a white elephant.

Fujitsubo—One of the pavilions in the palace compound that was reserved for a Consort or an Empress, north of the Emperor's residence (Seiryōden) and west of the Kokiden. It had wisteria (*fuji*) growing in its garden.

Fujiwara—The surname of the dominant nonimperial clan in the author's time and for centuries on either side of it. The author herself was a minor Fujiwara. In the tale the Minister of the Left (Genji's father-in-law), hence Aoi and her brother Tō no Chūjō, belong to this clan, and so do the Minister of the Right and his family, as well as many other figures.

gagaku—The repertoire of music known and performed at the Heian court, including not only the music of the *bugaku* (dance) repertoire but also *saibara* and *rōei* songs.

gallery *rō*—Of various forms, these covered passageways provided access to the different structures of a large dwelling complex, extending from the main house (*shinden*) or wings (*tai*) to and beyond gates, to supplementary buildings and subsidiary residences. There could be rooms opening off them.

garden court *tsubo senzai*—The garden space between the Emperor's residence (Seiryōden) and the Kōrōden, immediately to the west.

"Garden of Flowers and Willows" "Ryūkaen"—A "Chinese" *bugaku* piece last known to have been performed in 960.

Gate Watch—See glossary of "Offices and Titles."

Genji—"A member of the Minamoto (*gen*) clan (*ji*)." A first-generation Genji, or Minamoto, was a man who, like the Genji of the tale, had been excluded from the imperial family by having been given a surname and so made a commoner; and, by extension in the tale's usage, a non-Fujiwara (especially an imperial) aspirant to a position normally considered the prerogative of the Fujiwara. The surname Minamoto was first conferred by the Emperor in 814, and many surplus imperial brothers, sons, and grandsons received it thereafter.

gentian *ryūtan*—*Gentiaea scabra*, in modern Japanese *rindō*.

gentlewoman *nyōbō*—A woman of good family who serves a higher-ranking lord or lady. Murasaki Shikibu was a gentlewoman in an Empress's service. In some cases the woman could be of considerable rank; for example, in "The Mayfly" a Princess becomes a gentlewoman to the Empress.

gentlewomen's sitting room *daibandokoro, saburai*—The room at the northwest of a great personage's residence where the gentlewomen waited.

gift knot *kokoroba*—A kind of decorative knot, a paper flower, or a cluster of paper leaves or pine needles, attached to a gift.

gillyflower *tokonatsu*—A flower of the dianthus family, the same one as the "pink" (*nadeshiko*). The two terms are distinguished by their use in the tale. Partly because of an established pun on the lovers' "sleeping place" (*toko*), *tokonatsu* refers to lovers and *nadeshiko* to a child.

Go—A board game of great complexity and sophistication, played on a board with small black and white stones.

godchild *amagatsu*—A doll that for a child served a purpose similar to that of a purification doll. Up to about his or her third year the child was to transfer any harmful influences into the godchild.

Gokurakuji—A funerary temple for the senior Fujiwara nobility.

Gosechi (Festival, dancer)—A festival that accompanied the Enthronement Festival (Daijōsai) in the year of a new Emperor's accession, or the First Fruits Festival (Niinamesai) in other years; it took place on the middle days of the Ox, Tiger, Rabbit, and Dragon in the eleventh month. In the former case there were five dancers and in the latter four; of these, in a Niinamesai year, two came from among the senior nobles and two (three in a Daijōsai year) from among the privy gentlemen or provincial Governors. On the day of the Ox the dancers and their escort of gentlewomen entered the Gosechi chamber in the Jōneiden. On the last day (that of the Dragon) there was the great court banquet known as Warmth of Wine (Toyo no Akari), and on this occasion the Gosechi dancers danced the dance of the heavenly maidens. On the day of the Rabbit the page girls (warawa) were viewed by the Emperor.

grasses of forgetting *wasuregusa*—The flower called *yabukanzō* in modern Japanese, an orange daylily.

grasses of remembering *shinobu*—A kind of fern that grows readily in roofs of bark or thatch. The word is homophonous with one that means "to dwell fondly in memory on the past."

Great Hall of State Daigokuden—The hall used for the enthronement ceremony and for other major functions presided over by the Emperor.

"Great Peace" "Taiheiraku"—A "Chinese" *bugaku* piece, martial in spirit, for four dancers.

Great Rite Mizuhō—A protective rite to ward off misfortune and promote vital force, and often intended to encourage safe childbirth. More formally known as Godan Mizuhō, the "Five Altar Rite," it was performed by five Officiants before altars to the deity Fudō and his four directional protector deities. In grave cases it could be performed in the palace.

grebe *nio, niodori*—A diving bird that was reputed to pair for life and that gave Nio no Umi (Lake of Grebes), the modern Lake Biwa, its name.

"Green Willow" "Aoyagi"—A *saibara* song that evokes a warbler (*uguisu*) weaving a garland of spring flowers with weeping willow fronds.

guessing rhymes *in futagi*—A game that involved guessing the rhyme words in a Chinese poem unknown to the contestant.

hagi—An autumn plant with long, graceful fronds and deep pink, violet, or white flowers. Although *hagi* is often translated "bush clover," no such plant actually exists.

hairdressing chest *kakage no hako*—A chest of implements for dressing the hair.

hairpin *kōgai*—A hairdressing implement shaped something like a chopstick and made of silver or some other precious material.

half-panel shutter *hajitomi*—See **lattice shutter**.

Hall of the Sacred Mirror Naishidokoro—A room in the Unmeiden where the sacred mirror (*yata no kagami*, one of the three imperial regalia) was kept.

hand carriage *teguruma*—A sort of palanquin on two wheels for use within the palace grounds. Its use required imperial permission and was normally restricted to personages of the highest dignity. A new Consort always arrived at the palace in one.

hand torch *shisoku*—A slip of pinewood with one end dipped in oil; the other end, held by the bearer, was wrapped in paper.

hare mallet *uzuchi*—A rectangular block of peachwood roughly four inches long, with a tassel of five-colored threads hanging from it, used in the palace and in the great houses to drive out demons on the first day of the Hare in the first month.

Harima—A province corresponding to a part of modern Hyōgo Prefecture, on the Inland Sea.

Hatsuse—The place-name associated with Hasedera, a temple in the mountains roughly east of Nara. Hasedera is dedicated to Eleven-Headed Kannon (Jūichimen Kannon), and its sacred image is particularly revered. It was a major pilgrimage center.

healing rites *kaji*—Rites performed for healing by Buddhist monks. They involved calling on the power of specific deities.

heart-to-heart *aoi*—A small plant (*Asarum caulescens*), known more precisely as *futaba aoi* ("twin-leaf *aoi*") and sacred to the Kamo Shrine. A forest plant, it consists of a symmetrically opposed pair of broad, heart-shaped leaves, with which people decorated their headdresses and carriages for the Kamo Festival (as they did also with laurel [*katsura*]). *Aoi* in its Heian spelling (*afuhi*) can be read to mean "day of (lovers') meeting" and this double meaning is often exploited in poetry.

Heichū—A stock comic hero of Heian court folklore.

herbal balls *kusudama*—See **Sweet Flag Festival**.

Herdboy Star Hikoboshi—See **Tanabata**.

hichiriki—A small but loud reed pipe made of bamboo. The "greater *hichiriki*" mentioned in "The Safflower," a larger version of the standard instrument, was not normally played by ranking nobles, and its use had died out by the author's time.

Hiei, Mount—A mountain (2,799 feet) just northeast of the City, the site of a large temple complex that was the center of Tendai Buddhism.

Higo—Roughly the present Kumamoto Prefecture in southwest Kyushu.

Hitachi—A province in the Azuma region (now the Kanto), corresponding to the northern part of Ibaraki Prefecture.

Hizen—A province in Kyushu, now divided between the modern prefectures of Saga and Naga.

holy man *hijiri*—A common word for a Buddhist monk who lives removed from the world and whose practice is conducive to the accumulation of spiritual power.

Holy Mountain Mitake (now Sanjō-ga-take, 5,676 feet)—A mountain in the Ōmine range, south of Nara. The Mitake cult was addressed to Miroku, the Buddha of the Future.

holy-water shelf *akadana*—A shelf for offerings of holy water and flowers, set up just outside the veranda of a house.

Hōrai—A fabulous mountain in the middle of the sea, inhabited by immortal beings. In "The Song of Unending Sorrow," by Bai Juyi, the grieving Emperor sends a wizard there to find his beloved Yang Guifei.

"Hosoroguseri"—One section of the music for a *bugaku* dance called "Chōhōraku". The syllable sequence in the name sounds strange in Japanese.

Hosshōji—A temple built by Fujiwara no Tadahira in 925 on the site of the present Tōfukuji, east of the Kamo River and a little south of the City. It was on the way from Kyoto to Uji.

hour of the (Rat, Ox, etc.)—The hours of the day-night cycle and the days of the month were named according to the succession of the twelve zodiacal signs: Rat, Ox, Tiger, Rabbit, Dragon, Snake, Horse, Sheep, Monkey, Bird, Dog, and Boar. The daily cycle began with the hour of the Rat (starting roughly at midnight) and ended with the hour of the Boar (starting roughly at 10 P.M.). Since the number of zodiacal signs and the number of days in a month (twenty-eight) did not match, the zodiacal designations for the days shifted from month to month.

household office *mandokoro, saburai*—The office out of which household affairs were run, including in some cases estates and other, larger interests.

humulus *mugura*—*Humulus japonicus*, a member of the hemp family and related to the hop (*Humulus lupulus*); a plant with fairly large, five- or seven-lobed leaves. It appears in the tale as a typical weed.

hyōjō mode—One of the six *gagaku* modes.

ichikotsu mode—One of the *gakaku* modes.

"I Love Him So" "Sōfuren"—A *gagaku* piece. The characters properly used to write its title mean something like "The Lotus in the Minister's Garden," but the Japanese preferred to use others (homophones) that suggest this romantic meaning.

"Immortal in the Mist" "Senyūka"—A *gagaku* piece. Its title as used in the tale alludes to Genji's status as the Honorary Retired Emperor, since a Retired Emperor was commonly imagined as a Taoist Immortal and inhabited a Sentō Gosho ("Palace of the Cave of the Immortal"). Immortals (*sennin*) were supposed to sport among the mists of mountain peaks and to need no other food.

"Immortal of the Deep" "Kaisenraku"—A *gagaku* piece in the ōshiki mode.

Imperial Granary Kokusōin—The storehouse for rice and cash collected from the Inner Provinces (Kinai).

Imperial Kitchen Mizushidokoro—Responsible for preparing the Emperor's meals.

Imperial Stores Osamedono—An office of the Emperor's household responsible for his personal treasure.

Ishiyama—A temple at the southern end of Lake Biwa, and a popular pilgrimage goal for residents of the City. Legend has it that Murasaki Shikibu conceived her tale there. The temple is dedicated to Kannon.

ivy *yadorigi*—A word that now means "mistletoe," but that in the tale clearly means "ivy" and perhaps other kinds of tree-climbing vines.

Iyo—A province on the island of Shikoku, corresponding to the present Ehime Prefecture.

Iyo blind *Iyo su*—A rough sort of blind, suitable for the country, made of woven bamboo (*shinotake*).

Jōneiden—A residential pavilion in the palace compound, suitable for an Empress or a Consort. It also contained a room used by the Gosechi dancers.

"Joy of Spring" "Kishunraku"—A *bugaku* piece for which neither the music nor the dance survives.

jubilee—A great personage's fortieth or fiftieth year, for which a celebration or series of celebrations (*ga*) could be held.

kagura—Music and dance offered at a shrine to a Shinto divinity.

Kaguya-hime—The heroine of *The Old Bamboo Cutter* (see entry), a radiant baby discovered by an old bamboo cutter in a joint of bamboo. Her name means something like "Lady Light." Kaguya-hime grows up to be dazzlingly beautiful; is courted by many suitors, culminating in the Emperor himself; and at the end of the tale returns to her real home, the moon.

Kamo Festival Kamo no Matsuri—The annual festival of the two Kamo Shrines (Upper Kamo and Lower Kamo) along the Kamo River, to the north of the City. It was held on the middle day of the Bird in the fourth month. On that day a grand procession went from the palace to call at both shrines, providing a brilliant spectacle for the people at large. It was also known as the Aoi Festival because for the occasion people decked their headdresses, carriages, and so on with *aoi* leaves, sacred to Kamo. There was in addition a Special Kamo Festival (Kamo no Rinji Matsuri) on the last day of the Bird in the eleventh month; some of the Eastern Dances were performed for the deity by the palace musicians, and the rehearsal was held in the palace.

kana—The letters of the phonetic syllabary, as opposed to Chinese characters.

Kannon—The bodhisattva of compassion, particularly prominent in the tale in connection with Hatsuse and Ishiyama.

karmic impediments *gōshō*—The Buddhist term for all karmic factors that impede progress toward enlightenment; chief among them are greed, anger, and stupidity.

Kasuga Shrine—In Nara, the ancestral shrine of the Fujiwara.

Katano Lieutenant Katano no Shōshō—An amorous hero whose story has not survived.

"Kazuraki"—A *saibara* song.

Kazuraki Mountains—A range of mountains south of present Osaka. Kazuraki was known for wizards and wonder-workers, since En no Gyōja (late seventh century), the half-legendary founder of the mountain ascetic tradition in Japan, came from there. In modern Japanese the name is read Katsuragi.

kickball *kemari*—A game in which the players stood in a circle and kicked a ball (*mari*) high in the air. The point of the game was to keep the ball in the air so that it never fell to the ground.

Kii—An ancient province corresponding roughly to Wakayama Prefecture.

kin—A seven-stringed, unfretted koto (see entry) from China. It was popular during the first half of the ninth century and was played as part of an aristocrat's normal accomplishments up to the mid-tenth (the present of the tale). By the end of the century it had been all but abandoned.

Kiritsubo—A residence with a paulownia tree (*kiri*) in its garden in the far northeast corner of the inner palace compound. It was assigned to a lower-ranking imperial wife. To reach the Emperor's residence from it meant walking through areas immediately adjacent to the living quarters of other imperial wives. Shigeisha or Shigeisa was another, Chinese, name of the same residence.

knotted letter *musubi-bumi*—A love letter, written on a piece of thin paper, then folded up very tightly and knotted.

Kokiden—A residential pavilion in the palace compound, normally occupied by an Empress, an Empress Mother, or a Consort.

Koma—Koguryo, an ancient Korean kingdom.

Koma flute *komabue*—A six-hole flute, shorter and thinner than the plain "flute" (*yokobue*).

Kōrōden—A residential pavilion in the palace compound, just west of the Seiryōden. It was normally occupied by a Consort or another imperial lady.

"Kōryō"—A musical piece traditionally identified as the "secret" Chinese piece "Kōryōsan."

koto—A term that in the tale may refer to any stringed instrument, including the *biwa* (see entry). More usually it designates one of a class of long, zitherlike instruments that rest on the floor before the player. These include the *kin*, the *sō no koto*, and the *wagon* (see entries for each).

ladies' paintings *onna e*—Colored paintings with a generally romantic, narrative content.

lanterns *tōrō*—Lanterns of wood, bamboo, or metal that hung from the eaves of the house and held oil lamps.

late-night devotions, prayers *goya*—Regular devotions that lasted roughly from midnight to dawn.

lattice shutter *kōshi*, also *shitomido*, *hajitomi*—Shutters or half-panel shutters made of square latticework backed by thin wood or paper; when down they acted as walls, particularly on the outside of buildings, but also sometimes between the chamber (*moya*) and the aisle (*hisashi*). They were hung horizontally from the upper lintel beam (*nageshi*) and were lifted open and hooked up; or they could be removed entirely. In some cases they folded in, as along the south side of the Emperor's residence (Seiryōden), and in some cases they folded out, as they usually did when they bordered the veranda (*sunoko*). Originally a single, hinged shutter panel filled the entire expanse between posts; later the half-panel shutter (*hajitomi*) filled the upper part, and a removable lattice panel (also *kōshi*) filled the lower part.

laurel *katsura*—Cercidiphyllum japonicum, a kind of tree with heart-shaped leaves, resembling a laurel and believed in East Asia to grow in the moon. Its leaves, with those of heart-to-heart (*aoi*), were used as decorations for the Kamo Festival.

Leech Child Hiru no Ko—The first offspring of Izanagi and Izanami, the primordial pair in the creation myth. It was defective, since it had no bones, and in its third year it was sent drifting out to sea.

Library Funnotsukasa—An office of the Emperor's personal household that looked after books, paper and brushes, and musical instruments.

light refreshments *mizumumaya*—See **water stop.**

lintel *nageshi*—Structural timbers set horizontally over and between posts in the framework of a building at floor level and overhead. In post-and-lintel construction, light and movable partitions may be used between spaces instead of walls.

lintel curtains *kabeshiro*—Curtains hung from the lintels of a building, often inside blinds (*misu, sudare*). They normally had simple decorations, but they could be gray or black for mourning or pure white for a birth.

lodge *bō, sōbō*—The buildings inhabited by the monks of a temple community.

long bridge *nagahashi*—The bridge between the Emperor's residence (Seiryōden) and the Shishinden.

Lotus Sutra Hoke-Kyō—The central text of Tendai Buddhism and one of the most important in Japanese Buddhism. It is rich in parables that became almost part of the language.

Lustration Buddha Kanbutsu—A statue of the Buddha as a baby that figured in the Lustration Rite (Kanbutsu-e) held on the eighth day of the fourth month to honor the Buddha's birthday. The rite involved lustrating (pouring water or sweet tea) over the statue.

lustration stream *mitarashigawa, misogigawa*—A stream near a shrine, used for purification.

"Magic of Wine" "Kansuiraku"—A "Korean" *bugaku* piece that seems not to have survived beyond the mid-fourteenth century.

maid *miuchiki no hito*—A woman charged with helping the Emperor to change clothes; or *shimotsukae*—simply a young female servant.

maidenflower *ominaeshi*—Patrinia, a plant of the valerian family that puts forth clusters of small, muted yellow flowers.

main house *shinden*—The central structure of a Heian house, normally linked by bridgeways (*watadono*) on either side to more or less symmetrical wings (*tai*).

mantra *shingon*—A series of syllables, sometimes meaningful in the original Sanskrit and sometimes not, that encapsulates in sound the nature of a Buddhist deity.

mat *tatami*—A mat woven of rice straw.

mayfly *kagerō*—A long-winged fly that hatches in swarms, generally near water, in summer. It dies only a few hours later, after mating and laying its eggs.

meal stand *dai, kakeban*—The modern *o-zen*, a sort of small, individual meal table.

memorial rites—Rites to guide the soul toward a happy rebirth or, ultimately, toward rebirth in paradise. They were held every seven days during the first forty-nine days after death and at widening intervals thereafter. New paintings of the principal Buddhist divinities involved were made for each service during the initial forty-nine-day period. During this period the spirit wandered in a "transitional state" (*chūu*), then went to its future rebirth, according to its karma, in one of the six realms of transmigration: celestial beings, humans, warring demons, beasts, starving ghosts, or hell.

Michinokuni paper *Michinokuni-gami*—A white paper made especially in northern Japan (Michinokuni, Michinoku) from tree bark and used for practical, businesslike purposes.

middle gate *chūmon*—One of the two symmetrically placed gates in the galleries that extended south from the wings of a residence. They afforded access to the area between the main house and the garden lake.

Mid-God Nakagami—A yin-yang (*onmyōdō*) deity who moved in a regular sixty-day cycle. After sixteen days in the heavens the deity descended to earth and circled the compass, spending five or six days in each of the eight compass directions. One shunned (*imu*) travel in a direction thus "blocked" or "closed" (*futagaru*). In "The Broom Tree," Genji's intention of spending the night at his father-in-law's violates this taboo, and he must "evade" (*tagau*) the closed direction by taking refuge elsewhere, in some other direction from his point of departure, the palace.

Minamoto—See **Genji**.

Miroku—The future Buddha who is to descend into a transfigured world many eons from now. The site of his descent was believed to be the Holy Mountain (Mitake).

modal prelude *kaki-awase, chōshi*—A short piece played on a stringed instrument (*kaki-awase*) or by an orchestra (*chōshi*) to verify the tuning and establish the musical mode.

moorhen *kuina*—A kind of moorhen or water rail, the cry of which, in summer, sounds like someone knocking lightly on a gate. In poetry the hearer thinks of a young man on a secret visit to his love.

morning glory *asagao*—See **bluebell**.

morning salutation *chōhai*—A ceremony in which the assembled courtiers saluted the Emperor on the morning of the first day of the New Year.

"Motomego"—One of the pieces from the Eastern Dances. The words of its song appear not to have been stable.

Mountain, the—See **Hiei**.

mountain ascetic *yamabushi*—A low-ranking Buddhist practitioner, often a healer, who might not be fully ordained and whose practice took him to sacred mountains.

mountain rustic *yamagatsu*—The general term for an uncouth inhabitant of a "mountain village" (see entry), as seen from the City.

mountain village *yamazato*—A country locality, which because of Japan's topography was bound to be either in hills or mountains or below them along a river or on the sea. Examples in the tale include Suma, Akashi, Ōi, Uji, and Ono.

mourning, close of *ōn-hate*—The end of a period of formal mourning. The length of such a period varied according to the relationship between the mourner and the deceased.

mourning confinement *ōn-imi*—A ritual seclusion, generally of thirty days, to avoid spreading the pollution due to contact with death.

mourning retreat *imi*—The period of the first forty-nine days (see entry) after death.

mudra *in*—A set posture of the hands and fingers that invokes the presence of a Buddhist deity in a ritual.

mulberry-cloth streamer *yū*—A streamer cut in a zigzag pattern from mulberry-bark cloth or from paper and used in yin-yang or Shinto rites.

mumming *otoko tōka*—A regular New Year observance at the palace. On the fourteenth day of the first month, six song leaders (*katō*, of Left and Right), as well as dancers and musicians chosen from among the privy gentlemen (*tenjōbito*) and the lesser ranks (*jige*), would appear before the residence of the Emperor, the Empress, the Retired Emperor, and so on, dancing and singing *saibara* songs. The practice lapsed in 983. Women performed mumming, too, but not in the tale.

murasaki—A plant (*Lithospermum erythrorhizon*) the roots of which yield a purple dye; also, the dye and its color. The color stands for relationship and lasting passion.

musical ground *hyōshi awase*—A ground against which the rhythm was played.

Nakagawa—Said to be the Kyōgoku River north of Nijō.

Name (of Amida), the—The invocation to the Buddha Amida. See **Amida**.

Nara Heights *Narazaka*—A stretch of low hills north of Nara, between Nara and the Kizu River.

narrow chest *hosobitsu*—A somewhat long and narrow form of the legged chest (*hitsu*).

Nashitsubo—Also Shōyōsha. A pavilion in the palace compound. It had a nashi, or Japanese pear tree, in its garden.

near garden *senzai*—The part of the garden near a house, as distinguished from the park, farther away.

New Year archery contest *noriyumi*—A contest held on the eighteenth of the first month by the archers of the Gate Watch and the Palace Guards. (A month or two later the privy gentleman held a similar one.) A banquet (*noriyumi no kaeri aruji*) was given by the Commander of the winning side. By the author's time this event seems to have lapsed.

night attendance, night prayer duty *yai*—An important duty of a lord or lady's chaplain. The chaplain remained in attendance through the night, in a room close to where his patron slept, so that the patron should enjoy while sleeping the beneficent influence of his prayers. For the Emperor, priests performed this function in a small room (*futama*) separated from his pillow by a partition.

Ninefold Palace Kokonoe—One of the ornamental names for the Emperor's palace.

north gate *kita no jin*—Also referred to as *sakuheimon*, the north gate to the inner palace compound. This was the gate normally used by women for entering or leaving the palace.

Northern Hills Kita Yama—The mountains to the north of Kyoto.

"Nuki River" "Nukigawa"—A *saibara* song, the complaint of a lover who is barred by his girl's parents from seeing her.

nurse *menoto*—In principle, a woman who nursed a highborn infant in place of its mother, since such a mother did not normally nurse her child; although perhaps not all *menoto* nursed, since a child could have more than one. A highborn child's relationship with his or her nurse was lasting and intimate, and so was that with her own children.

obeisance (of thanks) *butō*—A dancelike gesture of formal thanks, performed on ceremonial occasions by the recipient of the favor of the Emperor or a great lord.

Office of Artisans Takumizukasa—An office under the Bureau of Central Affairs, responsible for making and maintaining the furniture and furnishings in the palace.

Office of Medicine Ten'yaku Ryō—A palace office in charge of medicine, medicinal products, and healing spells.

Office of Music Utazukasa—The palace office responsible for music and dance.

Office of Painting Edokoro—The palace's painting workshop.

Office of Staff Naishizukasa—A palace office staffed by women who were responsible to the Emperor for a variety of matters, especially those pertaining to the imperial ladies.

Office of Upkeep Suri Shiki—The office responsible for palace construction and repairs.

Ōharano Shrine—The Kyoto counterpart of the Kasuga Shrine in Nara; it enshrines the same deities. Built at the end of the eighth century, just west of the City below Mount Oshio, it enabled the Fujiwara nobles to honor their family deities without going all the way to Nara.

Old Bamboo Cutter, The Taketori monogatari—Generally agreed to be the oldest surviving Japanese tale, dating perhaps to the eighth century. See **Kaguya-hime**.

orange *tachibana*—Citrus tachibana, a kind of ornamental citrus tree prized especially for its fragrant blossoms. Their scent recalled past loves.

Ōsaka Barrier, Pass Ōsaka no Seki—A low pass east of Kyoto, between the City and Lake Biwa. The road to the eastern provinces went that way, and to cross Ōsaka meant really to leave the City. The Ō of the name was often used to play on *au* (pronounced the same way), "meet."

ōshiki mode—A musical mode said to be close to the key of A.

Ōshōkun—Wang Zhaojun, beloved of Emperor Yuan of Han, who was tricked into sending her as a gift to a barbarian chieftain.

Otagi—A burning ground, with its associated temple, probably northwest of the City as it was then, in the general area of present Kyoto University.

"Our Sovereign's Grace" "Gaōn"—A "Chinese" *bugaku* piece.

outer blinds *hashi no sudare*—The blinds between the aisle (*hisashi*) and the veranda (*sunoko*).

outside mother *sotobara*—A mother other than the father's formal wife.

padded mat *uwamushiro*—A thinly padded mat laid out for the occupant of a curtained bed (*michōdai*) to sleep on.

palace *uchi, dairi*—Not a single imposing building, but a large complex of smaller buildings, some residential, some administrative, and some ceremonial, linked by passages and galleries. The text often makes no distinction between the palace and its great resident, the Emperor. The *dairi* can also be called the "inner palace," as distinguished from the "greater palace" (*daidairi*), a far larger compound containing such major buildings as the Great Hall of State (Daigokuden) and the Eight Bureaus (Hasshōin).

Palace Guards—See "Offices and Titles."

Palace Mountain *Ōuchi Yama*—A literary term for the palace of a reigning or retired Emperor.

palanquin *mikoshi*—A conveyance consisting of a small cabin mounted on parallel poles and borne by porters.

palm-leaf carriage *birōge*—A kind of ox carriage covered with woven palm leaves and used by high-ranking personages.

Paper Workshop *Kamuya*—A palace workshop that made paper for the use of court.

parsley *seri*—*Oenanthe javanica* (dropwort or Japanese parsley), an edible plant that flourishes in low, damp places.

partitioned box *warigo*—A partitioned box of plain wood, used for carrying food.

passageway *medō*—A corridor built through the center of certain palace buildings.

penance *tsutsushimi*—Ritual abstinences performed to keep someone else safe from harm.

petition *miakashi-bumi*—A written prayer formally offered up by suitably commissioned priests.

physician *kusushi*—A specialist in medicines and physical treatments, as distinguished from a healer (a practitioner of healing rites).

pine cricket *matsumushi*—A kind of cricket with a melodious cry; perhaps the same as the **bell cricket**.

pink *nadeshiko*—See **gillyflower** and also the "Clothing and Color" glossary.

pitfall day *kannichi*—A day defined by the yin-yang (*onmyōdō*) almanac, on which all enterprises were destined to fail. There was one per month.

plume grass *obana, susuki*—*Miscanthus sinensis*, a grass that puts forth a tall, nodding seed plume.

"Plum Tree Branch, The" *"Umegae"*—A *saibara* song: "To the plum tree branch the warbler comes, to sing all spring long, all spring long, yet snow is still falling, Look, how lovely! snow is falling."

poem pictures *utae*—Illustrations in which a poem was written over a painting derived from the poem's meaning and done in fainter ink.

Precepts *Imu Koto, Kai*—The Buddhist rules of conduct. Especially the Five Precepts that prohibited killing, stealing, fornication, deceit, and drunkenness. These simple rules of conduct could be upheld by a layman or a novice (*nyūdō*), but for fully ordained monks and nuns there were many more.

privy banquet *naien*—A banquet given personally by the Emperor on the day of the Rat that fell on the twenty-first, twenty-second, or twenty-third of the first month. The guests composed poetry in Chinese.

privy chamber *tenjō no ma*—The room frequented by courtiers on duty to wait upon the Emperor, at the palace, or upon the Retired Emperor in his own palace. The Emperor's was in the Seiryōden, his private residence.

Purification *Misogi*—A preparatory rite for the Kamo Festival. The Festival took place on the middle day of the Bird in the fourth month, while the Purification took place on the preceding day of the Horse or day of the Sheep.

railing *kōran*—The railing along the outside of the veranda (*sunoko*) of a house.

Records of the Historian, The *Shiji* (Japanese *Shiki*)—The official history of China from the beginning up to the reign of Emperor Wu of the Early Han dynasty, completed by Sima Qian (Japanese Shiba Sen) in 91 B.C. It covers up to the Early Han dynasty and is the model for all later dynastic histories. A basic text at the Academy (together with the *Hanshu*), and essential reading for Heian officials, it left traces in the tale itself.

reception room *idei*—A room in the south aisle of the main house, used especially for receiving guests.

Rectification *Naoshimono*—A supplement to the regular announcement of official appointments (*meshina*) made at the appointments list (*jimoku*) ceremony twice a year.

red sandalwood *shitan*—The prized dark red heartwood of the sandalwood tree.

reed fence *ashigaki*—A screening fence made of woven reeds, typical of a waterside dwelling.

reed writing *ashide*—A manner of painting a waterside scene (with reeds, water swirls, rocks, and so on) in such a way that the lines of the painting formed the *kana* letters of a poem.

Reikeiden—A pavilion within the inner palace compound, occupied by a Consort or an Empress. Its prestigious location, on the east, was symmetrical with that of the Kokiden on the west.

retreat *nurigome*—A walled space normally two bays square and located at one end of the chamber (*moya*). It could be used as both a storeroom and a sleeping room, and it might contain a curtained bed (*michōdai*). There were small double doors (*tsumado*) between it and the chamber, and perhaps also between it and the northern aisle.

"Return of Spring, The" *"Kishunraku"*—A "Chinese" *bugaku* piece for four dancers.

rice *mi-yuzuke*—Brown rice in hot water, a winter food; or, for summer, *suihan*, rice chilled in cold water.

rice dumplings *tonjiki*—Egg-shaped balls of rice that were given out to lower servants as gifts after a festive event.

richi mode—A scale with a "minor" feel to it, commonly used at the time of the tale for songs and particularly favored in autumn.

roller *jiku*—The spindle around which a scroll was rolled.

rouge *beni*—The dye essence extracted from safflower blossoms.

round mat *warafuda*—A round sitting mat made of rice straw.

"Royal Deer, The" *"Ōjō"*—A festive *bugaku* piece for which only the music now survives.

ryo mode—In "Bamboo River," possibly an error for "*richi* mode."

sacred rope *shimenawa*—The rice-straw rope drawn around a sacred object or space.

saibara—A body of Nara-period (eighth-century) folk songs that were taken up by the Heian aristocracy and incorporated into the Heian musical repertoire (*gagaku*).

sakaki—A broadleaf evergreen shrub or small tree that was and remains sacred in Shinto.

sakuhachi—An end-blown flute related to the *shakuhachi* of later times. Its use had died out by the author's time.

sasa—A general word for several ground-cover plant species related to bamboo.

screen *byōbu*—Between two and eight decorated panels joined at their vertical edges to form when open a temporary, movable partition.

screening fence *suigai*—A fence of woven wood or bamboo strips that stood between buildings as a sort of screen.

scripture—A sutra, a sacred Buddhist text.

scripture case *kyōbako*—A case to contain Buddhist sacred texts.

scripture reading *mi-dokyō*—A four-day event held twice a year, in the second and eighth or third and ninth months, in the palace as well as the homes of the highest nobles. The sutra ceremonially read was the Daihannya-kyō (Greater Sutra on the Perfection of Wisdom).

scrubby reeds *asaji*—A low, grassy plant, sometimes described as a reed and commonly associated with moors or neglected gardens; a low-growing form of *chigaya* (*Imperata cylindrica*).

seafolk, sea girl *ama*—People who inhabit the shore and live from the sea, whether men or women, fishermen, divers for shellfish and seaweed, or saltmakers. In poetry, an *ama* is often a particularly young and attractive girl, and the seashore imagery associated with the word could easily have erotic overtones. Since *ama* is homophonous with the word for "nun," a good many poems exploit this double meaning.

"Sea of Ise" *"Ise no umi"*—A *saibara* song.

seclusion *monoimi*—A time during which one confined oneself indoors in order to avoid evil influences. Periodic seclusions were mandated according to the teachings of yin-yang divination (*onmyōdō*).

sedōka—A poetic form slightly larger than the *tanka* mentioned in the Introduction. A *sedōka* consists of thirty-eight syllables, in the pattern 5-7-7-5-7-7.

Seiryōden—The Emperor's private residence in the inner palace compound.

servants' hall *shimoya*—A separate building, to the rear of a house, where various servants lived.

serving table *daiban*—A rectangular table on which meal stands were placed.

shaft bench *shiji*—A small bench on which to rest the shafts of a carriage when the oxen were unyoked.

Shaka—Shakyamuni, the historical Buddha.

Shiji—See *Records of the Historian, The.*

Shishinden—The main ceremonial hall of the inner palace compound.

shō—A wind instrument consisting of seven slender bamboo pipes rising from a central wind chest.

Shōkyōden—A centrally located palace pavilion not far from the Emperor's residence, the Seiryōden.

shutter *shitomido, hajitomi, kōshi*—See **lattice shutter.**

Silent Cascade Otonashi no Taki—Otonashi Cascade, famous in poetry and situated near Ono, just east of the City. The water slips soundlessly over a smooth rockface.

sin *tsumi*—A religiously defined offense. The standards governing the definition of *tsumi* vary according to a complex religious and quasi-religious tradition.

sinecure *tsukasa*—Income to the court derived from fees paid by persons appointed to sinecures; this income was redistributed to high-ranking officeholders, including women.

sliding door *yarido*—A sliding wooden door.

sliding panel *shōji, sōji*—The equivalent of the modern *fusuma*, a lightweight, usually paper-covered panel in a frame held in runners at top and bottom and used to partition a room.

slip (out, backward, etc.) *izari*—To slide on the shins, without rising: the way a lady moved within a room.

small bow *koyumi*—The small bow, used only for contests, was drawn in a half-kneeling position.

solfège *sōga* or *shōga*—Voicing the names of the notes of a musical score.

sō **mode** *sōjō*—One of the six *gagaku* modes, associated with spring.

sō no koto—A thirteen-stringed koto (see entry).

song leader *katō*—See **mumming.**

"Song of the Spring Warbler" "Shun'ōden"—A "Chinese" *bugaku* piece said to have been commissioned by the founding Emperor of the Tang dynasty.

"Song of Unending Sorrow, The" Chinese "Changhenge," Japanese "Chōgonka"—A narrative poem by Bai Juyi (772–846), extremely popular in Heian Japan. It tells the story of the love of the Tang Chinese Emperor Xuanzong for Yang Gueifei (Japanese Yōkihi). His passion for her led him to neglect the state and invite a dangerous rebellion, for which he was forced by his own army to have her executed.

soul sanctuary *tamadono*—A place at the burning ground where the body was laid out before the cremation.

spearflower berries *yamatachibana*—The red berries of a plant (in modern Japanese *yabukōji*) that grows wild in the hills.

spells *majinai*—Healing magic performed by Masters of Spells from the Office of Medicine.

spindle tree *mayumi no ki*—A deciduous tree that bears small blue-green flowers and reddens nicely in autumn.

spirit *mononoke*—Illnesses and derangements were easily attributed to the actions of a spirit tormenting the affected person. Exorcism could draw the spirit out to speak and express its grievance, usually through a medium, and then to be pacified or dismissed.

spring and autumn progresses *haruaki no gyōgō*—Formal visits that the Emperor made every spring and autumn to his mother and to living Retired Emperors.

staff office *kurōdodokoro*—The gathering place for lower-level household staff.

standing archery *kachiyumi*—Archery with the longbow, done standing; as distinguished from *umayumi*, longbow archery from horseback.

standing curtain *kichō*—A trailing curtain on a movable stand, suitable for placing so as to shield someone seated from view. They came in several different heights, taller or shorter. The standing curtain was a basic item of domestic furniture.

standing panel *kosōji*—A low, stiff panel mounted on a stand so that it could be moved about.

standing shutter *tatejitomi*—A lattice shutter backed by boards that was stood between house and garden as a screen.

star anise *shikimi*—*Illicium religiosum*, a broadleaf evergreen normally placed as an offering on a Japanese Buddhist altar and therefore strongly associated with Buddhist practice.

steamed rice *kowaii*—Rice cooked in a steamer, as opposed to rice boiled in a pot.

steward *azukari, inmori*—The resident keeper of a house or estate.

straight-folded letter *tate-bumi*—A letter folded long and straight, hence visibly a formal or business note, not a love letter, which would be knotted.

"Strike the Ball" "Dagyūraku" or "Tagyūraku"—A "Chinese" *bugaku* dance for four dancers, often performed at archery meets, horse races, wrestling contests, and so on. It evokes a game played on horseback and very close to polo.

Suzaku Palace *Suzaku-in*—The Retired Emperor's palace, first mentioned in connection with a Retired Emperor who is probably Genji's grandfather. For much of the tale it is occupied by Retired Emperor Suzaku. It stood on a large tract not far south of the imperial palace compound.

sweetfish *hio*—The nearly transparent juveniles, about an inch long, of *ayu*, a delicacy offered by Japan's river and lakes.

Sweet Flag Festival *Tango no Sechie*—A festival held on the fifth day of the fifth month. The Emperor went to the Butokuden and bestowed herbal balls (*kusudama*) on the assembled courtiers, who were crowned with sweet flag (*ayame*, calamus, a fragrant medicinal plant). Horse races (*kurabeuma*, races between pairs of horses) were held as well. The event was abolished in 968, but the custom of adorning the roof of one's house or one's own person with sweet flag roots persisted long afterward.

Taishaku *Sanskrit Indra*—The lord of the Tōri heaven, on the summit of Shumisen (Mount Sumeru), the central mountain of the Buddhist cosmos.

tall stand *takatsuki, dai*—A tall stand for food or drink, resting on a single foot.

Tanabata—The Tanabata Festival, on the seventh night of the seventh month. This was when, according to an originally Chinese legend, the celestial lovers (the Weaver Star and the Herdboy Star, on either side of the Milky Way) came together for their one night a year. The festival celebrated particularly poetry, calligraphy, and sewing.

Tatsuta Lady *Tatsuta-hime*—The goddess of autumn and patron of the art of dyeing, whose presence is conveyed by the "brocade" of autumn leaves.

tent *hirabari*—A curtained-off space with flat panels of cloth stretched over it to form a roof.

"Ten Thousand Years" "Manzairaku"—A felicitous *bugaku* piece performed on particularly grand occasions.

"That Horse of Mine" "Sono Koma"—A *saibara* song.

"There Dwells the God" "Kami no masu"—A folk song that mentions "the High Plain of Heaven" (Takama ga Hara) and, over and over, "eight divine maidens" (*yaotome*).

"This Gentleman" "Kono Tono wa"—A felicitous *saibara* song.

thoroughwort *fujibakama*—*Eupatorium fortunei*, a wildflower closely related to the North American boneset (*E. perfoliatum*). It puts forth clusters of tiny, light mauve flowers in autumn.

three-foot cabinet *sanshaku no mizushi*—A cabinet three feet tall, with doors.

Three Histories—The three basic Chinese dynastic histories: *The Records of the Historian* (*Shiji*), *The History of the Han Dynasty* (*Hanshu*), and *The History of the Later Han Dynasty* (*Hou Hanshu*).

Three Realms *Sangai*—A term that in Buddhist discourse sums up the universe inhabited by sentient beings. The Three Realms are canonically defined as those of desire, form, and no-form.

Three Treasures *Sanbō*—The Buddha, the Dharma (teaching), and the Sangha (community of monks and lay believers).

throne *ishi*—A chairlike piece of furniture on which the Emperor or another exalted personage sat during a solemn ceremony.

Tōkaden—A residential pavilion in the palace compound, north of the Kokiden. It was normally occupied by an Empress or a Consort.

torch *taimatsu*—A bundle of resin-rich slivers of pine.

Toribeno—A burning ground just east of the City.

torii—The characteristic gate of a Shinto shrine.

transformed presence *henge*—The temporary, limited, "transformed" manifestation of a divine being.

tray *oshiki*—A plain, square wooden tray.

trefoil knot *agemaki*—Three-lobed knots used to decorate an object for formal presentation. There is also a *saibara* song known by this name.

Tsukuba, Mount *Tsukuba Yama*—A poetically famous mountain in Hitachi, the province to which Ukifune's stepfather was once posted.

Tsukushi—The old name for Kyushu.

twilight beauty *yūgao*—"Evening face," a gourd flower.

"Twin Dragons" "Rakuson," also known as "Sōryū"—A "Korean" *bugaku* dance performed on the same sort of occasions as "Strike the Ball." It involved one or two masked dancers.

twin tresses *mizura*—Hair bunches that divided the hair evenly on either side of the head. Boys wore twin tresses until they came of age.

two-tiered shelf *nikai(dana)*—A piece of furniture resembling an open-back bookcase, with two useful shelves.

Uji—A locality on the Uji River, south of the City. The site of many country villas of the nobility, Uji nonetheless had a doleful literary reputation thanks to a celebrated poem (*Kokinshū* 983) by Kisen Hōshi, in which the poet played on the place-name and on *ushi*, "hateful."

Uji Villa *Uji no In*—A country villa that had apparently belonged to the tale's Emperor Suzaku. There is evidence that the historical Emperor Suzaku actually visited such a place. This one was probably near the north bank of the Uji River, toward the City.

Umetsubo—The Umetsubo ("plum pavilion") was a relatively long and narrow (east-west) pavilion near the center of the inner palace compound. A passageway (*medō*, north-south) divided it into two apartments, each of which consisted of a chamber and of aisle spaces on three sides. Red and white blossoming plum trees grew beside it.

Unmeiden—The palace building that housed the Hall of the Sacred Mirror (Naishidokoro).

Urashima, Master *Urashima no Ko*—A fisherman who wandered in his boat to the island of the Immortals and married a beautiful maiden there. Three years later he returned, homesick, to his village, carrying a box that his wife had given him with the warning never to open it. Three hundred years had passed, and everything had changed. In despair he opened the box. His wife's wraith floated out of it and into the sky, and in that instant he aged three hundred years. The earliest occurrence of the story is among the surviving fragments of an early-eighth-century work (*Tango fudoki*).

utility paper *kamuya-gami* or *kōya-gami*—"Paper from the government paper workshop," generally gray and made of recycled materials, for government office use.

veranda *sunoko*—The open space, floored with wood or bamboo and covered by the eaves (*noki*), that edged a house.

victory music *rajō*—Music on flute, *shō*, and *hichiriki* played to mark the winning side's victory in a "Left" and "Right" contest. The "Korean" *rajō* was played for a victory by the "Right" and the "Chinese" one for the "Left."

wagon—The six-stringed "Japanese koto" (see **koto**), also known as *azumagoto* ("koto of the East").

warbler *uguisu*—A small warbler that sings in spring, prominent in poetry.

Warmth of Wine Toyo no Akari—A gathering that took place in the eleventh month, after the First Fruits Festival (Niinamesai) or the Enthronement Festival (Daijōsai). The Emperor invited his courtiers to partake of "light" and "dark" wine. One of the major events of the court calendar, it was accompanied by the Gosechi dance (see entry).

"Warrior King, The" "Ryōō"—A "Chinese" solo *bugaku* dance that evokes a mighty warrior.

Watch—See "Offices and Titles."

watered rice *yuzuke*—Steamed brown rice in hot water; a winter food.

water stop *mizumumaya*—Literally "water and stabling for the horses," but actually wine and hot rice gruel offered participants in the New Year's mumming (see entry). Certain stops along the route were designated as *mizumumaya*, while at others, called *iimumaya*, the mummers could expect a meal.

weeds *yomogi, mugura*—Plants that in the tale are the sign of a neglected residence or an abandoned field. See **humulus, wormwood**.

weir *ajiro*—A barrier of wood or bamboo slats built across a river to trap fish.

"Where the Road Begins" "Michi no kuchi"—A *saibara* song.

winding frame *tatari*—Three pegs set in a base, on which spun thread was wound to make a skein.

wing *tai*—A residential structure linked to the main house (*shinden*) of a Heian dwelling by one or more bridgeways (*watadono*). A normal dwelling, which faced south, had east and west wings.

Women's Music Pavilion Naikyōbō—The place where the women musicians and dancers of the palace were trained.

wormwood *yomogi*—*Artemisia vulgaris*, also known in English as mugwort. A plant typical of a weed-infested garden.

wrapped letter *tsutsumi-bumi*—A knotted letter (*musubi-bumi*) wrapped in thin paper (*usuyō*) and suitable for a morning parting letter (*kinuginu no fumi*), sent by the man to the woman with whom he had just spent the night.

Wrestling Tournament Sumai no Sechi—Held near the end of the seventh month, when wrestlers gathered from all the provinces to compete in the Emperor's presence. A banquet followed.

Yakushi—The Medicine Buddha, whose cult flourished in Heian times. The eighth of the month was one of his feast days.

Yamashiro—The province in which Uji was located.

Yamato—The province south of Uji, roughly surrounding Nara.

yin-yang lore *onmyōdō*—A complex body of geomantic, divination, calendration, and other lore learned from China and practiced by professionals known as diviners or yin-yang masters (*onmyōji*).

Yokawa—One of the three major sectors of the great monastic complex on Mount Hiei.

Clothing and Color

Words for clothing are impossible to translate except in general terms that convey at best only vague impressions. The colors and color combinations ("layerings") listed here are more evocative, but they are not necessarily more precise. The range of colors current in the time of the tale was too wide to permit usefully precise translation, and in any case much about their names remains uncertain. Moreover, a good many terms for single colors refer more to the dye source (safflower, cloves, sappanwood, dayflower, gardenia seeds, and so on) than to the resulting hue, which in practice could vary widely. Therefore these color terms, too, are no more than distant approximations.

apron *shibira, uwamo*—Worn by a gentlewoman when serving her mistress.

ash green *aoji*.

aster layering *shion (kasane)*—A layering of colors (perhaps pale gray-violet [*usuiro*] over blue or green [*ao*]) that gave an impression of violet-blue, like this flower.

autumn green layering *aokuchiba*—Fabric woven of leaf green (*ao*) warp and yellow weft threads, over leaf green.

azure *hanada*—A medium, morning glory blue from indigo.

bead tree layering *ōchi*—Possibly purple lined with a lighter shade of the same color. *Ōchi* is the old name for the Japanese bead tree (*sendan, Melia azedarach*, var. *subtripinnata*), which reaches about twenty-six feet in height and in spring bears light purple, five-petaled flowers.

beaten silk *uchimono*—Silk beaten on a fulling block (*kinuta*) to bring out its luster.

blue *koki hanada*.

blue-gray *aonibi*—May also be visualized in the green range (gray-green), since *ao* in practice covers both ranges.

Cathay tendril pattern *karakusa*—A family of textile patterns consisting of arabesque-like leafy tendrils and sometimes flowers.

cherry blossom layering *sakura gasane*—White over scarlet (*kurenai*) or, if worn by a young man, violet (*futaai*).

Chinese jacket *karaginu*—A short jacket, longer in front than in back, that formed the outermost layer of a woman's formal dress.

clove-dyed *chōjizome, kōzome*—A warm tan.

court dress *nōshi sugata*—The ordinary costume worn by a nobleman at the palace or when dressed up at home. The level of formality could be varied: with a formal cap (*kanmuri*) it was more formal than with a hat (*eboshi*). The dress cloak (*nōshi*) was tied on and worn over a gown (*uchiki, akome, onzo, kinu*) and shift (*hitoe*), with gathered trousers (*sashinuki*).

cover *kinu*—A gown used for cover at night.

cypress bark *hiwada iro*—The color of the bark of the Japanese cypress (*hinoki*), a dark red-brown.

damask *aya*—More properly figured twill. Twill weaving was originally Chinese.

dark blue *kon*—A color associated in the tale with *ruri* (lapis lazuli or glass).

dark gray *tsurubami*.

dayflower *tsuyukusa, tsukikusa*—A fugitive blue dye from the sky blue flowers of the dayflower, a common wild plant in Japan.

deep blue *komayaka naru*—A deep shade (*komayaka*) of azure (*hanada*).

deep blue-gray *koki aonibi*—See **blue-gray**.

deep green *midori*—A color range that actually extends from gray to blue-green and deep blue.

deep hat *tsubo sōzoku*—The attire for a respectable woman outdoors. She draped an unlined gown over her head and hair, then put on a deep, broad-brimmed hat. She also hitched up her skirts a little for walking.

deep red-violet *koki iro*.

deep scarlet layering *koki hitokasane*—Two very dark scarlet shifts, one over the other.

deutzia layering *unohana*—White over grass green (*moegi*). The deutzia flowers in the fourth lunar month, in long clusters of small white blossoms.

dress cloak *nōshi*—The outer garment ordinarily worn by a courtier at court or fully dressed at home. The dress cloak and the formal cloak (*hō*) were ample, straight garments tied at the neck and with the front and back joined at the hem by a circular band of cloth (*ran*), pressed flat. However, the color of a dress cloak was not determined by the wearer's rank. It could be made of a single layer of sheer, dark cloth in summer and of light-colored, lined cloth in winter. It was generally worn with gathered trousers (*sashinuki*).

dress gown *kouchiki*—A gown of fancy stuff of the same shape as a gown (*uchiki*) but somewhat shorter, worn by a woman at home when some formality was desired. Also *kazami*—A long garment worn on top, especially by page girls in formal dress.

earth green *aoni*.

fallen chestnut *ochiguri*—Thought to be a deep, reddish brown.

formal cap *kanmuri*—A small cap with various attachments worn with full civil dress and with more formal court dress.

formal cloak *hō*—The outer garment worn by men on official business and when participating in court ceremonies. The formal cloak was not a layering (*kasane*) but was made either of an opaque cloth with a figure worked into it in the same or nearly the same color, or of a single layer of sheer cloth. Its color matched the wearer's rank in the time of the tale.

formal dress—The full-dress costume worn by women at court or by gentlewomen in an aristocratic household. The Chinese jacket (*karaginu*) was worn over a train (*mo*) tied at the waist over an outer gown (*uwagi*) that was the most elaborate of a layer of gowns of identical shape (*uchiki, kinu, onzo*) worn over a shift (*hitoe*) and long, ample trousers (*hakama*) tied at the waist with a sash. The layers of gowns were cut smaller as they reached the outside so that the edges of the underlayers could be seen.

full civil dress *sokutai*—The costume worn by noblemen on official business and when participating in court ceremonies. The formal cloak (*hō*), in the color appropriate to the wearer's
rank, was worn with a sword and a stone belt (*sekitai*) likewise matched to the wearer's rank.
It was worn over a train-robe (*shitagasane*), which was a midthigh-length garment with a train
(*kyo*), worn in turn over gowns (*akome, onzo, kinu, uchiki*) and a shift (*hitoe*), with two pair of
wide, open-legged trousers (*hakama*). The costume was completed by the formal cap (*kanmuri*) and baton (*shaku*). At least in later times, for somewhat less formal occasions, including ceremonies at home, the formality of this costume could be lowered by wearing
gathered trousers (*sashinuki*) instead of trousers (*hakama*) and lowered still further (*ikan*) by
omitting the belt and sword and using a narrow sash instead, and by carrying a fan instead
of a baton.

gathered trousers *sashinuki*—Ample trousers gathered around the ankles and worn with a
dress cloak (*nōshi*) or a hunting cloak (*kariginu*).

golden yellow *yamabuki*—The color of kerria rose flowers.

gossamer silk *suzushi*—A thin, raw silk for an unlined garment.

gown (1) *uchiki, onzo, kinu*—Any woman's gown worn, often in several layers, between dress
gown (*uwagi*) and shift (*hitoe*). (2) *akome, onzo, kinu, uchiki*—A man's robe worn over the shift
(*hitoe*) but under the train-robe (*shitagasane*) or the dress cloak. (3) *akome*—A garment worn
by young girls between dress gown and shift. However, *akome* is sometimes translated
"jacket" because page girls could wear their *akome* on top.

grape (colored) *ebi, ebizome*—Grape purple to reddish brown.

grape layering *ebizome kasane*—A winter layering of sappan (*suō*) over azure (*hanada*).

grass green *moegi*.

gray *nibiiro* (light gray, *usunibi*; dark gray, *tsurubami*).

green *asamidori*.

hail pattern *arare-ji*—A check pattern of dark and light squares. Also called *ishidatami*, "paving
stones."

hat *eboshi*—A tall hat worn with court dress (*nōshi sugata*) and with informal dress (*kariginu
sugata*).

hunting cloak *kari no onzo, kariginu*—An outer garment originally worn for hunting and then
adopted by the nobles as everyday informal wear. The hunting cloak had cords laced
through the sleeves to allow them to be gathered at the wrist, and it had sleeves semide-
tached from the body of the garment, for ease of movement. It was worn with gathered
trousers (*sashinuki*) or hunting trousers (*karibakama*) and a hat (*eboshi*). A gentleman normally wore a hunting cloak while traveling, and his attendants would wear it even when
he was in court dress (*nōshi sugata*). He also might wear it as a disguise.

indigo *ai*—A plant that yields a blue dye.

jacket *akome*—A type of gown worn as an outer garment by page girls.

kerria rose *yamabuki*—The color, also listed as "golden yellow," obtained from gardenia-
seed dye.

kerria rose layering *yamabuki kasane*—Ocher (*kuchiba*) over yellow (*kuchinashi*).

layering *kasane*—Usually a combination of two garments of different colors, or of garment
and lining, so that one color could be seen through the other. Layerings had names, but
the colors in them changed over time, and they are often uncertain. The name often refers
to the overall effect. For example, "cherry blossom," white over scarlet, produced a pale
cherry blossom pink. Many layerings were seasonal and were also affected by the wearer's
age and rank.

leaf gold *kanzō iro*.

leaf green *ao, ao-iro*—A light leaf green veering toward yellow. The color also known as *kiku-
jin* (although the word does not appear in the tale) and favored by the Emperor for daily
wear.

light blue *asagi.*

light gray *usunibi, usuki nibi.*

light russet *akakuchiba.*

light silk twill *ki.*

long dress *hosonaga*—A lady's outer garment, divided in front and with long panels that trailed behind on either side.

madder red *hiiro*—The color dyed with *akane.*

maidenflower layering *ominaeshi (kasane)*—A layering that recalls the valerian family flower of that name. The outer layer has a leaf green (*ao*) warp and a yellow (*ki*) weft, and the underlayer is leaf green.

mauve-gray (paper) *murasaki no nibameru (kami).*

mourning weeds *fujigoromo*—Mourning robes figuratively made (as perhaps they really were in ancient times) from the bark of wild *fuji* (wisteria) vines.

murasaki—A plant (*Lithospermum erythrorhizon*) the roots of which yield a purple dye; also, the dye and its color. The color stands for relationship and lasting passion.

night service wear *tonoi sugata*—A simple costume, perhaps just a white gown, worn by a page girl on night attendance.

ocher *kuchiba*—The Japanese word means "dead leaves."

pale gray-violet *usuiro.*

petal blue *hana (iro)*—A pale indigo.

pink layering *nadeshiko (kasane)*—A layering that suggests the pink, or gillyflower. According to some authorities, dark pink over light purple; others cite plum pink (*kōbai*) over leaf green (*ao*).

plum pink *kōbai*—A pink veering toward violet, reminiscent of plum blossoms.

plum red *imayō.*

pure raiment *jōe*—Robes worn by priests during a rite; blue-black, yellow, red, white, gray, or brown, depending on the deity to whom the rite was addressed.

purple *murasaki*—The color from the roots of the *murasaki* plant, a common field plant with white flowers. In poetry *murasaki* stands for close relationship. The color figures prominently in the tale as the color of enduring love.

red *aka.*

red plum blossom layering *kōbai kasane*—Scarlet (*kurenai*) over purple (*murasaki*) or sappan (*suō*).

rouge red *beniiro*—A scarlet color produced with safflower (*benibana*) dye, the source of scarlet (*kurenai*).

sanctioned rose *yurushiiro*—A pale scarlet (*kurenai*). The counterpart "forbidden color" (*kinjiki*), not mentioned in the tale, was a deep shade of dark red or purple allowed only to the Emperor and the senior nobles.

sappan layering *suō gasane*—A winter layering of sappan over dark sappan (a dull reddish purple).

sappan (wood) *suō*—A red from the wood of the sappan tree, imported from Southeast Asia.

sash *obi.*

scarlet *kurenai*—The color from the carthame dye, a fugitive red lake made from safflowers (*Carthamus tinctorius*). The dye has both red and yellow components, but with some difficulty the yellow can be eliminated. The pigment from the flowers can also be used to produce a makeup rouge.

scarlet layering *kaineri kasane*—Scarlet (*kurenai*) over scarlet.

seaside *kaifu*—A textile pattern showing waves, beachside pines, seaweed, shells, and so on.

service dress *tonoi sugata*—The costume worn by men in regular service at the palace, characterized especially by the dress cloak (*nōshi*).

shift *hitoe*—An unlined garment worn by men or women under the outer layers of clothing and cut larger. Like all other garments listed in this glossary, it was open in front, like a jacket, so that "shift" is only an expedient approximation.

shoulder cords *obi*, or, more properly, *kakeobi*—Red silk cords passed over each shoulder and tied together in the back, worn by a woman on pilgrimage or when performing religious devotions.

silk gauze *usumono*—Very thinly woven silk, used especially for summer wear.

sky blue *asahanada*.

softened silk *kaineri*—Silk boiled with lye to soften it.

spring green layering *wakanae kasane*—Light grass green (*moegi*) over light grass green.

stone belt *sekitai, shakutai*—A broad black leather belt worn with the formal cloak (*hō*), with a row of squares or circles made of stone, jade, or horn set in it so as to show at the wearer's back. (A fold of the *hō* covered the front.) The "stone" varied according to the wearer's rank.

sunshade band *hikage*—A band of dangling white or blue-green braided threads (originally club moss fronds) worn by a Gosechi dancer as well as by other women, such as the Kamo Priestess, engaged in certain sacred functions.

sweet-flag layering *ayame gasane*—Probably green over plum pink.

tail *ei*—A long, narrow, springy appendage to a man's court cap, made of lacquered cloth. Usually straight, but rolled as a sign of mourning.

tan *kurumi iro, kō-iro*—A yellowish tan from cloves.

train *kyo, mo*—The man's train (*kyo*) was a long, rectangular piece of cloth extending from the train-robe (*shitagasane*) worn with full civil dress (*sokutai*). The woman's train (*mo*) was a long, sheer, decorated piece of cloth pleated into a sash tied at the front, at the waist, over the gown (*uchiki, uwagi*), and under the Chinese jacket (*karaginu*). A woman wore a train in service or on formal occasions to indicate a subservient position.

train-robe *shitagasane*—The man's garment worn in full civil dress (*sokutai*) over the mid-robe and under the formal cloak (*hō*); it was of midthigh length and had a train (*kyo*).

trousers *hakama, nagabakama*—Men wore two pair of wide-legged, ankle-length trousers (an inner one and an outer *ue no hakama*) with full civil dress, and a different sort of under-trousers under gathered trousers (*sashinuki*) in less formal costume. Women wore long trousers (*nagabakama*), with legs that extended well beyond their feet.

twill *aya*—See damask.

violet *futaai*—A "double-dyed" (*futaai*) color produced by dyeing cloth in safflower (the source of scarlet, *kurenai*) dye and then in indigo (*ai*). The actual hue varied. Brighter, deeper shades with little blue were worn by young men, while duller, paler tints with little red were worn by older men.

violet-blue *shion*—A color reminiscent of the aster (*shion*).

white layering *shiragasane*—White over white.

wild indigo *yamaai*—The green color derived from the wild indigo plant.

willow *yanagi*—White weft and pale green warp threads.

willow layering *yanagi kasane*—White over green.

wisteria layering *fuji gasane*—Violet over green.

yellow *ki*, a general term; or *kuchinashi*—A yellow from gardenia-seed dye. The color is that of kerria rose (*yamabuki*) flowers. (The color specified in the text as *yamabuki* is translated "golden yellow.")

young pink leaves *nadeshiko no wakaba no iro*—A light yellow-green (*usumoegi*).

Offices and Titles

This glossary lists all the official or customary titles that appear in *The Tale of Genji*, explains their meaning, and in most cases indicates the numbered rank corresponding to the office in question. Each office had an officially defined and numbered rank. The ranks descended from the first to the ninth. All were divided into two levels, full (indicated below by the number alone) and junior; and below the third rank each of these two levels was likewise subdivided into upper and lower grades. However, the Emperor was outside this numbered system. The text sometimes describes the imperial dignity as being "without rank," or words to that effect, and this was literally true. For more information on Heian government offices and organization, one may consult such sources as Appendix A ("Some Notes on Rank and Office") in volume two of William H. and Helen Craig McCullough's *A Tale of Flowering Fortunes*. (The translations adopted here are not always those of the McCulloughs.) Still more information is of course available in Japanese.

Even translated this way, most of the terms adopted will not at first mean much to the reader. However, they are at least made up of English words, so that they should be easier in the long run to make sense of and to remember. They are a significant aspect of the translation as a whole because the people in the tale themselves are so acutely conscious of rank and office. Rank and office and, more generally, degrees of power and prestige defined the structure of their social world.

Two features of the nomenclature of official appointments are especially striking. The first is that many government organs were divided into Left and Right components. For example, the two senior Ministers were the Ministers of the Left and of the Right. This pattern is Chinese: when seated in state, the Emperor faced south, with his two Ministers symmetrically stationed to his left (east) and right (west). Since the east took precedence in principle, the Minister of the Left normally took precedence over his colleague of the Right, and this distinction held—again, in principle—down through the lower levels. In fact, this symmetry extended beyond matters of government. All contests, from wrestling (*sumai*) to poetry, were divided into "east" and "west" sides, and so were the repertories of court music and dance. The City itself was administratively divided into Left and Right.

The second striking feature of this nomenclature is that the titles of many men mentioned in the tale, especially young ones of high birth, indicate a dual appointment. That is to say, these men hold two positions in different official organs, of which one is often "civil" and the other "military." For instance, Tō no Chūjō, the great friend of Genji's youth, spends some time as both a Secretary (Tō) in the Chamberlains' Office and a Captain (Chūjō) in the Palace Guards. I have translated this dual title as Secretary Captain. Other examples are Consultant Captain, Controller Chamberlain, Controller Lieutenant, and Inspector Grand Counselor.

Many official titles, even ones that do not indicate a dual appointment, can become quite long in translation if one is to get in all their major elements. I have therefore made them as compact as I could. An example is the nomenclature of the "Counselor" range, which has three levels. The highest of these, Dainagon, is usually translated "Major Counselor," but I have chosen Grand Counselor instead because it is a syllable shorter. For the same reasons of economy I have adopted simply Counselor for Chūnagon, over the more familiar and literal "Middle Counselor." (Shōnagon, Minor Counselor, occurs once or twice as a man's title.)

Finally, I have not necessarily adopted every title as it occurs in the original. It happens that a single figure is referred to on adjacent pages by two quite different titles that he or she holds simultaneously, and in such cases I have usually repeated the title that occurs first, in the interests of intelligibility. My most consistent "homogenization" of titles or honorific appellations has to do with Fujitsubo, after she ceases to be Empress, and above all with Genji himself. After his return from exile, Genji is often referred to as His Grace, an appellation I chose originally to correspond to his appointment much later as Honorary Retired Emperor. This retrospective use of it acknowledges the distinctive prestige that gathers to him immediately after his return from Akashi and serves to make him immediately identifiable throughout.

Abbot (of the Mountain) (Yama no) Zasu—The superior of the entire Mount Hiei temple complex.

Acting . . . Gon . . . —A prefix to the title of certain male officials, indicating that the appointment is in excess of the normal number of incumbents in that post.

Acting Captain Gon Chūjō.

Acting Grand Counselor Gon Dainagon.

Adept Azari, Ajari—An imperially conferred title held by a distinguished practitioner monk, one expert in healing and other rituals to avert illness and disaster and summon good fortune.

Adviser Jijū—A junior official (junior fifth rank, lower grade) under the Bureau of Central Affairs, who acted as an assistant to the Emperor. There were generally eight of them.

Adviser Consultant Jijū no Saishō—A dual appointment as Adviser and Consultant.

Aide Zō, Jō—A third-level appointee in the bureaus and in some guards units (Gate Watch, Watch), but a fourth-level officer in the Palace Guards.

Aide of Ceremonial Shikibu no Jō—A third-level post in the Bureau of Ceremonial (sixth-rank range).

Aide of the Gate Watch Yugei no Jō (junior sixth rank).

Aide of the Right Palace Guards Ukon no Zō (sixth rank, lower grade).

Aide of the Watch Hyōe no Zō (seventh rank).

Audit Commissioner Taifu no Gen—Auditor (Gen) was a post in a provincial administration, responsible for discovering and correcting various irregularities. The most senior incumbent could attain the fifth rank, lower grade, in which case "Commissioner" (Taifu) was added to the title.

Bath Nurse Mukaeyu—The "assistant" role in the bathing of a newborn child of high birth.

Bungo Deputy Bungo no Suke—In principle, Deputy Governor of Bungo (now Ōita Prefecture), a post in the sixth-rank range. However, it is unclear just what weight this title has where it occurs in the tale ("The Tendril Wreath").

Bureau of Central Affairs Nakatsukasa Shō—The bureau that administered the palace. The senior among the eight major government bureaus, it was always headed by a Prince.

Bureau of Ceremonial Shikibu Shō—One of the eight major government bureaus, in charge of ceremonies, appointments, and awards.

Bureau of Civil Affairs Minbu Shō—One of the eight major government bureaus, in charge of population registers, corvée, and taxation.

Bureau of the Treasury Ōkura Shō—One of the eight major government bureaus, in charge of managing the tax goods collected from the provinces.

Bureau of War Hyōbu Shō—One of the eight major government bureaus, in charge of military affairs and equipment.

Captain Chūjō—The second-level officer in the Palace Guards of Left or Right (junior fourth rank, lower grade).

Captain of the Left Palace Guards Sakon no Chūjō.

Chamberlain Kurōdo—An official of fifth or sixth rank, responsible to the Chamberlains' Office (Kurōdodokoro) and under the supervision of two Secretaries (Kurōdo no Tō) of somewhat higher rank. A Chamberlain was admitted to the privy chamber and had direct access to the Emperor; he was also allowed to wear colors and fabrics normally forbidden to a man of his rank.

Chamberlain Aide of the Left Gate Watch Kurōdo no Saemon no Jō—A dual appointment as a Chamberlain and either a third-level (Daijō) or fourth-level (Shōjō) officer in the Left Gate Watch.

Chamberlain Aide of the Right Palace Guards Ukon no Zō no Kurōdo—A dual appointment as a Chamberlain and a fourth-level officer (sixth rank, upper grade) in the Right Palace Guards.

Chamberlain Controller Kurōdo no Ben—A dual appointment as a Chamberlain and a Controller.

Chamberlain Lieutenant Kurōdo no Shōshō—A dual appointment as a Chamberlain and a Lieutenant in the Palace Guards.

Chamberlain Second of the Watch Kurōdo Hyōe no Suke—A dual appointment as a Chamberlain and a Second of the Watch.

Chamberlains' Office Kurōdodokoro—An office that functioned as an imperial secretariat, serving the Emperor and carrying messages and imperial orders. It was staffed by two higher-ranking Secretaries (Kurōdo no Tō), by Chamberlains (Kurōdo) of the fifth and sixth ranks, and by a number of lesser figures. A Chamberlain moved in circles above his official rank, served the Emperor directly, and held privileges such as the right to wear colors normally not allowed a man of his rank. The Chamberlains' Office also looked after the Emperor's falcons and took care of musical instruments, books, coins (metal currency), and clothing.

Chancellor Ōkiotodo, Daijōdaijin—The highest possible civil post (first rank or junior first rank), one not provided for in the government's nominal table of organization. In theory it was filled only by a candidate able to serve as an example of virtue, and the incumbent was to be above actual administration.

chaplain *inori no shi*—The monk who regularly performed prayer rituals for great a lord or lady.

Chief Clerk Dainaiki—A functionary (sixth rank, upper grade) in the Bureau of Central Affairs, charged with composing imperial rescripts, maintaining court records, and so on.

Chief Equerry Kami—The senior officer (junior fifth rank, upper grade) in charge of the Left (Sama no Kami) or Right (Uma no Kami) Imperial Stables (Meryō, Uma no Tsukasa). The incumbent held the junior fifth rank, upper grade. In "The Broom Tree" also **Chief Left Equerry.**

Chief Lady in Waiting Naishi—A translation devised to suit the context in "The Pilgrimage to Sumiyoshi." The precise nature of the office is unclear.

Cloistered Eminence—See **Eminence**.

Commander Taishō—The commanding officer (third rank, lower grade) of the Right (Udaishō) or Left (Sadaishō) Palace Guards.

Commissioner Taifu or Daibu—A title held by the head of some government or quasi-government organs, such as the Office of Upkeep or the Empress's Household; and by the second-level official in others, such as the Bureau of War. The title properly carried the fifth rank, upper or lower grade.

Commissioner of Ceremonial Shikibu no Taifu—The second-ranking officer (fifth rank, lower grade) in the Bureau of Ceremonial.

Commissioner of Civil Affairs Minbu no Taifu—The second-ranking officer (fifth rank, lower grade) in the Bureau of Civil Affairs.

Commissioner of the Household Daibu (Chūgū no Daibu)—The chief administrator of the Empress's household.

Commissioner of War Hyōbu no Taifu—The second-ranking officer (fifth rank, lower grade) in the Bureau of War.

Consort Nyōgo—An imperial wife whose father was at least a Minister or a Prince. An Empress was normally chosen from among the Consorts.

Constable Udoneri—One of about a hundred men affiliated with the Bureau of Central Affairs and selected from the families of men of the fourth and fifth ranks. Assigned to guard the highest nobles, Constables could be arrogant and rough.

Consultant Sangi, Saishō—The junior post (fourth rank, lower grade) in the Council of State, below Counselor and Minister. There were normally eight.

Consultant Captain Saishō no Chūjō—A dual appointment as Consultant and as Captain in the Palace Guards.

Controller Ben—One of a body of officials under the Council of State. The Controllers were attached to the eight major government bureaus and were divided into Left and Right (four bureaus each). There were three grades: Grand Controller (Daiben, junior fourth rank, upper grade), Controller (Chūben, fifth rank, upper grade), and Minor Controller (Shōben, fifth rank, lower grade).

Controller Chamberlain Kurōdo no Ben—A dual appointment as a Controller and as a fifth-rank Chamberlain.

Controller Lieutenant Ben no Shōshō—A dual appointment as a Controller and as a Lieutenant in the Palace Guards.

Council of State Daijōkan—Stood above the eight major bureaus as the highest organ of government. Its members were the three Ministers (Left, Right, and Palace); the Counselors (Counselor, Grand Counselor); and the Consultants. The executive office of the Council of State employed Junior Counselors and Controllers, among other lesser officials.

Counselor Chūnagon—A middle-level post (junior third rank) in the Council of State.

Court Ritualists Gishikikan—Officers of various ranks charged with conducting court ceremonials. In their formal stance they held their elbows stiffly out to either side as they held their batons.

Dame of Staff Naishi no Suke—One of four women officials (junior fourth rank, upper or lower grade) under the Mistress of Staff, in the Office of Staff.

(Dazaifu) Assistant (Dazai no) Shōni—The assistant (fifth rank, upper grade) to the (Dazaifu) Deputy.

(Dazaifu) Deputy (Dazai no) Daini—The Deputy (junior fourth rank, lower grade) who represented the court at Dazaifu, in Kyushu. His senior was the Viceroy, whose post was a sinecure; the incumbent, a Prince, did not leave the City.

Deputy Commissioner of Ceremonial Shikibu no Shō—A third-level official (junior fifth rank, lower grade) in the Bureau of Ceremonial.

Deputy (Governor) Suke—The deputy to a provincial Governor. In the case of Hitachi, Kazusa, and Shimōsa, the titular Governor was a Prince, but since the post was a sinecure, only the Deputy Governor actually went to the province. (The Governor of Hitachi who figures in "The Ivy" and succeeding chapters is actually such a Deputy.) The rank of a Deputy Governor, like that of a Governor, depended on the standing of his province, but it was in the sixth-rank range.

Director of Reckoning Kazoe no Kami—The director (junior fifth rank, upper grade) of an office within the Bureau of Civil Affairs, charged with calculating and allocating certain types of tax revenue.

Director of Upkeep Suri no Kami—The head (junior fourth rank, lower grade) of the Office of Upkeep.

Doctor Hakase—A senior scholar engaged to teach in the Academy, typically Chinese language (written), literature, history, law, and so on. The appointment was in the junior fifth-rank range. Also Doctor of Letters (Monjō Hakase).

Doctor of the Almanac Koyomi no Hakase—A calendar or almanac specialist from the Yin-Yang Office.

Eminence (His, His Cloistered, Her Cloistered)—An honorific term, devised for the purposes of translation, for a former Empress or a Retired Emperor (In). If the figure has taken the vows of a monk or a nun, he or she is also called Cloistered, although this term is omitted where possible. The only "Her Cloistered Eminence" (Nyūdō Kisai no Miya) in the tale is Fujitsubo; there is no "Her Eminence."

Empress Chūgū, Kisaki—The Emperor's highest-ranking wife. There could be only one. She was normally appointed from among the Consorts.

Empress Mother Ōkisai no Miya, Ōkisaki—The mother of an Emperor. She had not necessarily held the title of Empress under the previous reign.

Excellency—See **His Excellency.**

Fourth Rank Lieutenant Shii no Shōshō—A Lieutenant (normally in the fifth-rank range) who exceptionally holds the fourth rank.

Fujiwara Aide of Ceremonial Tō Shikibu no Jō.

Fujiwara Consultant Tō Saishō.

Fujiwara Grand Counselor Tō Dainagon.

Fujiwara Lieutenant Tō Shōshō.

Gate Watch Emonfu, Yugei—The corps of guards who guarded the gates of the palace compound. They were divided into Left Gate Watch (Saemon) and Right Gate Watch (Uemon). The chief officer on each side was the Intendant (junior fourth rank, lower grade), followed by Deputy (junior fifth rank, upper grade) and Aide (junior sixth rank, upper grade).

Governor Kami—The official appointed by the Emperor to govern a province. His rank, which depended on the standing of his province (the provinces were classified as great, major, medium, or minor) could vary from junior fifth rank, upper grade, down to junior sixth rank, lower grade. The term was sometimes used not only for a Governor proper but also for a Deputy Governor, in cases where only the Deputy actually went to the province. Governors in general were also referred to as Zuryō ("Grant Holder").

Grace—See **His Grace**.

Grand Counselor Dainagon—The office (third rank) below Minister in the Council of State.

Haven Miyasudokoro—In the tale an unofficial title for a woman (especially an Intimate or a Consort) who had borne a child to an Heir Apparent, an Emperor, or a Retired Emperor. The Japanese term suggests either "place (person) in whom the august affection found rest" or "place (person) in whom the august seed found rest." Examples in the tale include Genji's mother after Genji's birth; the Rokujō Haven, whose daughter is by a deceased Heir Apparent; Genji's daughter after she bears the Heir Apparent a son; the mother of Ochiba, Emperor Suzaku's daughter; and Tamakazura's elder daughter, who bears a child to Retired Emperor Reizei.

Heir Apparent Bō, Tōgū—The formally designated successor to the reigning Emperor. He was not necessarily the Emperor's firstborn son.

Highness (His, Her)—An honorific term of address, used in translation for a Prince or Princess.

High Priestess (of Ise)—See **Ise Priestess**.

High Priestess of the Kamo Shrine—See **Kamo Priestess**.

His Eminence—See **Eminence**.

His Excellency Ōitono, Otodo—Refers to a Minister or a Chancellor. The use of "the Minister" rather than "His Excellency" implies a greater distance between that figure and the narrator (or the side with which her sympathies and those of her audience lie). An example is the Minister of the Right, as distinguished from His Excellency (of the Left) in the chapters leading up to Genji's exile.

His Grace—An honorific term, devised for the purposes of translation, for Genji in "The Pilgrimage to Sumiyoshi" and after, following his return from exile.

His Highness of Central Affairs Nakatsukasa no Miko—The Prince who headed the Bureau of Central Affairs.

His Highness of Ceremonial Shikibukyō no Miya—The Prince who was the titular head (fourth rank, lower grade) of the Bureau of Ceremonial.

His Highness of Kanzuke Kanzuke no Miko—The Governor of the province of Kanzuke (also Kamutsuke or Kōzuke, roughly present Gumma Prefecture), like that of Hitachi and Kazusa, was a Prince, but the post was a sinecure, and the province was actually administered by a deputy.

His Highness of War Hyōbukyō no Miya—The Prince who was the titular head (fourth rank, lower grade) of the Bureau of War.

His Reverence—See **Prelate**.

Honorary Deputy Governor Yōmei no Suke—A sinecure post bought from a high-ranking nobleman.

Honorary Retired Emperor Jundaijōtennō—An extraordinary title awarded Genji (in "New Wisteria Leaves ") by his secret son, Emperor Reizei.

Household Deputy Suke—The second-level officer (junior fifth rank, lower grade) in charge of the Empress's household.

Inspector Azechi—A high-level Inspector appointed to review the administration of the provinces. By Heian times the post survived only for the northernmost provinces, and it was mainly honorary.

Inspector Grand Counselor Azechi no Dainagon—A dual appointment as Inspector and Grand Counselor.

Intendant of the (Left, Right) Gate Watch Emon (Saemon, Uemon) no Kami—The senior officer of the Gate Watch (junior fourth rank, lower grade).

Intendant of the (Left, Right) Watch Hyōe (Sahyōe, Uhyōe) no Kami—The senior officer of the Watch.

Intimate Kōi—An imperial wife of lower standing than a Consort; her father was at most a Grand Counselor. The word *kōi* refers literally to someone who dresses the Emperor.

Ise Consort Saikū no Nyōgo—Literally "(Ise) Priestess Consort." Akikonomu's appellation as Consort, since she had been the High Priestess of Ise.

Ise Priestess Saikū—An unmarried Princess who represented the Emperor as the chief priestess of the Ise Shrine, where the ancestral deity of the imperial line was enshrined.

Junior Counselor Shōnagon—A junior official (junior fifth rank, upper grade) attached to the Council of State.

Kamo Priestess Saiin—The chief priestess of the Upper and Lower Kamo Shrines, just north of the City. Like the Ise Priestess, she was a Princess.

Lecturer Kōji—The officiating priest at certain major Buddhist rituals.

Left City Commissioner Sakyō no Daibu—The chief officer (junior fourth rank, lower grade) charged with population registration, tax collection, legal appeals, security, and so on in the left (east) sector of the City.

Left Controller Sachūben.

Left Gate Watch—See **Gate Watch.**

Left Grand Controller Sadaiben—See **Controller.**

Left Lieutenant Sashōshō—A Lieutenant in the Left Palace Guards (fifth rank, lower grade).

Left Palace Guards Captain Sakon no Chūjō.

Lieutenant Shōshō—A third-level officer (fifth rank, lower grade) in the Palace Guards, below Commander and Captain.

Lord of Ceremonial Shikibukyō—The head (fourth rank, lower grade) of the Bureau of Ceremonial. The holder of this title was a Prince.

Lord of Civil Affairs Minbukyō—The head (fourth rank, lower grade) of the Bureau of Civil Affairs.

Lord of the Palace Bureau Kunaikyō—The head (fourth rank, lower grade) of the one among the eight major government bureaus that was concerned with all matters affecting the Emperor's household.

Lord of the Treasury Ōkurakyō—The head (fourth rank, lower grade) of the Bureau of the Treasury.

Majesty (His, Her)—Used for the Emperor and Empress.

Master of Discipline Risshi, Rishi—The lowest on the ladder of ecclesiastical ranks accessible to elite, fully ordained priests. In the time of the tale it is still a distinguished appointment—more so than in later times. "Discipline" means the body of Buddhist monastic discipline.

Master (of the Household) (Saburai no) Betō—The chief administrator of the household of an imperial family member, such as a Prince or a Retired Emperor.

Master of Spells Jugonshi—A specialist in performing spells (*majinai*) as healing magic, employed by the Office of Medicine (Ten'yaku Ryō).

Minister Otodo—The highest nonimperial office (second rank) provided for in the government's formal table of organization, as the office of Chancellor was not; however, the post of Palace Minister (Naidaijin, Uchi no Otodo) was also a later addition. The Minister of the Left (Sadaijin, Hidari no Otodo) was normally but not necessarily senior to the Minister of the Right (Udaijin, Migi no Otodo), and the Palace Minister was somewhat junior in standing.

Mistress of Staff Naishi no Kami—The senior woman official (third rank) in the Office of Staff. In principle, the incumbent supervised female palace staff, palace ceremonies, and the transmission of petitions and decrees. In practice, she was a junior wife to the Emperor.

Mistress of the Household Nyobettō—The ranking female official in a great lady's household.

Mistress of the Wardrobe Mikushigedono—The woman official in charge of the palace office that made the Emperor's clothing.

Mother of the Realm Kuni no Haha—An expression or title used to refer to an Empress or an Empress Mother.

Myōbu—A title borne in palace service by middle-ranking gentlewomen (fifth rank or above) or by the wives of gentlemen of those ranks. Since a number of gentlewomen bore this title at the same time, people distinguished one from another by attaching to her title the name of the major office associated with her husband, father, or brother.

Novice Nyūdō—A man or woman of noble birth who had taken preliminary vows as a monk or nun. A Novice did not join a monastic community but pursued Buddhist practice at home.

Ōmyōbu—A Myōbu (palace gentlewoman) of imperial birth.

page, page girl *warawa*—A boy or girl of good family, in service in a noble household. Particularly on the male side there were *warawa* of mature years as well, as a kind of long-term servant, but these hardly figure in the tale. See also **privy page**.

Palace Guards Konoefu—The double (Left and Right, Sakon and Ukon) corps of guards assigned to protect the palace proper and stationed in its innermost areas. The Palace Guards had precedence over the Watch and the Gate Watch. Their two Commanders (third rank, lower grade) outranked the Intendants of those units (fourth rank, lower grade). A second-level officer was a Captain (Chūjō; fourth rank, lower grade), a third-level officer a Lieutenant (Shōshō; fifth rank, lower grade), and a fourth-level officer an Aide (Zō; sixth rank, upper grade).

Palace Minister Naidaijin, Uchi no Otodo—Normally the junior among the three Ministers who constituted the senior level of the Council of State.

Prelate (His Reverence) Sōzu—The highest ecclesiastical rank mentioned in the tale. Two higher ranks existed, but at the time of the tale (unlike later) they were rarely filled.

Prince (His Highness) Miya—An imperial son appointed to this title by his father. (Genji is therefore not a Prince.) Historically, most Princes were ranked in four grades and received an imperial stipend accordingly, but some were "unranked" (*muhon*). The tale says nothing about according this kind of status to an imperial grandson.

Princess (Her Highness) Miya—An imperial daughter appointed to this title by her father, or the recognized granddaughter of an Emperor in the male line. Suetsumuhana, whose father was a Prince, is therefore a Princess. In contrast, Aoi, whose mother is a Princess, is not one herself; the narration treats her purely as a commoner. Ukifune, the daughter of a Prince, is not a Princess because her father did not recognize her.

privy gentleman *uebito, tenjōbito*—A gentleman individually authorized by the Emperor to enter the privy chamber. The term referred more specifically to those gentlemen of the fourth and fifth ranks, together with Chamberlains (Kurōdo) of the sixth rank, who would not otherwise have enjoyed the privilege automatically granted the top three ranks. The number of privy gentlemen varied but usually fell below one hundred and was sometimes less than a third of that.

privy page *tenjō warawa*—A boy of good family, not yet of age, who served in the privy chamber in order to learn court customs and manners.

Reader Kōji—The official charged with reading out the Chinese poems composed at a festive gathering.

Regent Sesshō—A high-ranking, nonimperial nobleman appointed to act for the Emperor while the Emperor was a minor. (The title "Kanpaku," also translated "Regent" and held by someone who acted similarly for an adult Emperor, does not appear in the tale.)

Retired Emperor (His [Cloistered] Eminence) In—An Emperor who has abdicated and who now resides in a separate palace. Such a figure appears most often in this translation as His Eminence or, if he has taken Buddhist vows, as His Cloistered Eminence.

Right Captain Uchūjō—See **Captain.**

Right City Commissoner Ukyō no Kami (Daibu)—The chief officer (junor fourth rank, lower grade) charged with population registration, tax collection, legal appeals, security, and so on in the right (west) sector of the City.

Right Controller Uchūben.

Right Deputy Migi no Suke—A second-level officer in the Right Gate Watch (fifth rank, lower grade).

Right Gate Watch—See **Gate Watch.**

Right Grand Controller Udaiben—See **Controller.**

Right Guards Commissioner Ukon no Taifu—An Aide of the Right Palace Guards, exceptionally promoted to the fifth rank, so that he bears the fifth-rank title of Commissioner.

Second Equerry Uma no Suke—A second-level officer (sixth rank, lower grade) of the imperial stables Left or Right.

Second of the Left Gate Watch Saemon no Taifu—The second-ranking officer (junior fifth rank, upper grade) in the Left Gate Watch. (The title "Taifu" acknowledges the fifth-rank appointment.)

Second of the Watch Hyōe no Suke—A second-level officer in the Watch (junior fifth rank, upper grade).

Secretary Kurōdo no Tō—A senior appointee in the Chamberlains' Office. Of the two Secretaries, one was concurrently a Controller (fifth rank, upper grade) and the other normally a Captain (junior fourth rank, lower grade).

Secretary Captain Tō no Chūjō—A dual appointment as a Secretary and as a Captain in the Palace Guards.

Secretary Controller Tō no Ben—A dual appointment as a Secretary and as a Controller.

Secretary Lieutenant Tō no Shōshō—A dual appointment as a Secretary and as a Lieutenant (fifth rank, lower grade) in the Palace Guards.

senior noble *kandachime*—A noble of at least the third rank (*sanmi*) and holding a post at least at the level of Consultant (Sangi).

Treasury Commissioner Ōkura no Taifu—The second level (fifth rank, lower grade) in the Office of the Treasury.

Upkeep Consultant Suri no Saishō—A dual appointment as Director of Upkeep and Consultant.

Viceroy Dazai no Sochi—The senior appointee to Dazaifu, the government outpost in Kyushu that was particularly responsible for such foreign relations as Japan had at the time. The post (junior third rank) was held by a Prince. Since it was a sinecure and the incumbent never actually went to Kyushu, the real government representative there was the Dazaifu Deputy.

Watch Hyōefu—The corps (divided into Left [Sahyōefu] and Right [Uhyōefu]) of guards charged with maintaining general security in the palace compound and in the City at large. The senior officer was the Intendant (junior fourth rank, lower grade), followed by the Second (junior fifth rank, upper grade).

yin-yang master—An expert in yin-yang lore, connected with the Yin-Yang Office (Onmyō Ryō), an organ of the Bureau of Central Affairs in charge of matters pertaining to astrology, weather, the calendar, timekeeping, and divination.

Summary of Poetic Allusions
Identified in the Notes

Introduction

The world of *The Tale of Genji* considered poetry (*uta*, literally "song") the highest form of art and, in principle, the most perfect mode of human communication. Cultivated people knew a great many poems by heart, and these naturally crept into their speech, their writing, and their own poems. When moved or troubled, they might well write out old poems brought to mind by their mood, mingled with new ones of their own. The text of the tale therefore contains a very large number of poetic allusions, of which a small but significant minority consists of allusions to Chinese poetry, especially that of Bai Juyi (772–846).

Many of these allusions are pointed and obvious, but in other cases it may be unclear whether the allusion is to a specific poem or whether that image or turn of phrase had simply become current in the literary language. For this sort of reason, different authorities may disagree on the allusions they recognize or exclude. The ones identified in the notes and summarized below therefore are neither exhaustive nor particularly authoritative.

The corpus of classical Japanese poetry is available in the printed and CD-ROM editions of *Shinpen kokka taikan* (Tokyo: Kadokawa). The identifying numbers given here were taken from the CD-ROM edition, released in 1996. The numbers for the poems of Bai Juyi are from Hanabusa Hideki, ed., *Hakushi monjū no kisoteki kenkyū* (Tokyo: Hōyū Shoten, 1974).

The identifications in the notes and below attribute each poem to a specific collection, of which the corpus contains a great many. However, this is often only a matter of convenience. Any cultivated person in the author's time should have known the *Kokinshū* (*Collection of Poems Ancient and Modern*, 905) by heart and been thoroughly familiar with *Ise monogatari* (*Tales of Ise*, tenth century), but otherwise it is not always easy to be sure in what context a particular poem reached the author. The expedient character of some of these identifications is obvious from the fact that they refer to collections that postdate *The Tale of Genji* itself.

The tale alludes to some poems more than once. Numbers in parentheses following poem numbers indicate the number of such recurrences. Some poem numbers are also followed by a particularly significant alternative source for the same poem.

Poems Listed by Collection

Fukuro no sōshi

A treatise on the art of poetry written by Fujiwara no Kiyosuke (1104–72?).
140

Genji monogatari kochūshakusho in'yō waka

This is not a poetry collection but a compilation peculiar to the *Shinpen kokka taikan*. Its title means "Poems quoted in old commentaries on *The Tale of Genji*." A good many allusions in the tale are to poems known only from commentaries of roughly the twelfth to fourteenth centuries.
1, 76, 126, 148, 157, 160, 165, 177, 186, 199, 205, 244, 275, 300, 304, 367, 381, 382, 392, 394, 448, 464, 475, 514 (2), 639, 745, 927, 983, 1394, 1481(2), 1933

Gosenshū

An imperially commissioned collection completed in 951.
64 (3), 100, 103 (3), 199, 372, 468, 479, 481, 563, 608, 640, 683, 705, 718, 719, 731, 809, 899, 900, 938 (2), 960, 1036, 1089, 1093 (2), 1102 (*Kokin rokujō* 1412), 1107, 1143, 1173, 1187 (2, *Kokin rokujō* 3133), 1188, 1224, 1240, 1260, 1264, 1333 (2), 1364

Goshūishū

An imperially commissioned collection completed in 1086.
82, 216 (*Shigeyuki shū* 264), 894 (*Kagerō nikki* 93), 1041

Hakushi monjū

The complete poetic works of the Chinese poet Bai Juyi (772–846), as cataloged in Hanabusa Hideki, ed., *Hakushi monjū no kisoteki kenkyū*. Allusions to themes from Bai Juyi abound in the tale, and the examples listed are only the most obvious ones.
0004, 0075, 0076, 0131, 0144, 0160 (3), 0161, 0498, 0596 (3), 0603, 0631 (*Wakan rōei shū* 52), 0695, 0724, 0790, 0850, 0911, 0920, 0975, 0978, 1055, 1107, 1280, 1287, 2392, 2565, 2821, 3564

Ichijō no Sesshō go-shū

The personal collection of Fujiwara no Koremasa (924–72).
132

Ise monogatari

An immensely influential tenth-century collection of short tales built around poems, especially those by Ariwara no Narihira (825–80). The number cited first is that of the individual poem, followed by the number of times it is alluded to (if more then one), followed by the number of the section, or episode, in which that poem occurs.
1 (section 1), 6 (2, section 5; *Kokinshū* 632), 8 (2, section 7), 13 (section 9; *Kokinshū* 411), 63 (section 30), 90 (section 49), 119 (2, section 65; *Kokinshū* 501), 131 (section 71), 145 (section 82), 154 (section 84; *Kokinshū* 901), 174 (section 99; *Kokinshū* 476), 193 (section 112; *Kokinshū* 708)

Ise shū

The personal collection of a woman poet known as Ise. Mid-tenth century.
55 (2), 176 (*Kokin rokujō* 2479), 424, 483

Izumi Shikibu shū

The personal collection of a major woman poet contemporary with the author.
132 (also *Shikashū* 109), 150 (*Shūishū* 1342)

Kagerō nikki

The poetic diary of a woman known as "The Mother of Michitsuna." Late tenth century.
93 (also *Goshūishū* 894)

Kokin rokujō

A large compendium of poetry from the mid- or late tenth century.
174, 371 (2), 423, 593 (*Shinkokinshū* 757), 987 (2), 1049, 1201 (*Tsurayuki shū* 15), 1296, 1412 (*Gosenshū* 1102), 1796 (2, *Shinkokinshū* 1379), 1888 (2), 1980, 1986, 2096 (2), 2122, 2233, 2345, 2479 (*Ise shū* 176), 2571, 2640, 2749, 2804 (2), 2841, 3019, 3057, 3133 (2, *Gosenshū* 1187), 3241 (3), 3333, 3360, 3507, 3508, 3874, 3916 (2, *Man'yōshū* 1428), 3962, 3984, 4131 (*Tsurayuki shū* 60), 4155, 4268, 4385, 4417 (*Man'yōshū* 1477), 4488 (2)

Kokinshū

The first imperially commissioned collection, completed in 905. A cultivated person needed to know it by heart (roughly a thousand poems).
13, 28, 31, 32 (2), 33, 37, 38 (2), 41 (5), 44, 66, 68, 70, 97 (2), 139 (2), 153, 167 (2), 171, 200, 204 (2), 214, 223, 229, 241, 243, 244, 248, 262, 279, 292, 297, 349, 356, 389, 405, 409 (2), 411 (*Ise monogatari* 13), 415 (*Tsurayuki shū* 764), 476 (*Ise monogatari* 174), 488 (3), 498, 500, 501 (2, *Ise monogatari* 119), 503, 506, 508, 509 (2), 535 (3), 546, 582, 603, 611, 617, 631, 632 (2, *Ise monogatari* 6), 636, 637, 647, 683, 684, 685, 689 (3), 694 (2), 695, 699, 701, 705, 706, 708 (*Ise monogatari* 193), 713, 727, 732 (3), 743, 747, 756, 792, 806, 831 (2), 832 (3), 838, 839, 841, 853 (2), 855, 861, 867 (4), 868, 870, 875, 878, 892 (2), 901 (*Ise monogatari* 154), 907, 909 (2), 934, 935, 938, 944, 948 (2), 951 (2), 952 (3), 955 (2), 961 (3), 962, 965, 967, 968, 970, 977, 981, 982 (3), 983 (3), 987, 992 (2), 1007, 1008, 1009 (2), 1025 (2), 1037, 1041, 1061, 1080, 1086, 1091, 1093 (2), 1098, 1108, 1110 (2)

Komachi shū

The personal collection of a major tenth-century woman poet.
98 (*Shinkokinshū* 336)

Man'yōshū

A large and immensely important collection compiled in the eighth century. It was not widely read in the author's time because its language was too archaic and its script too difficult to read.
267, 1234, 1398 (*Shūishū* 967), 1428 (2, *Kokin rokujō* 3916), 1477 (*Kokin rokujō* 4417), 2325, 2429 (2, *Shūishū* 1243, a later variant), 3829, 4482

Motoyoshi Shinnō shū

The personal collection of Prince Motoyoshi (890–943).
150

Nakatsukasa shū

The personal collection of the woman poet Nakatsukasa (tenth century).
249

Nihon shoki

A court-sponsored history of Japan written in Chinese and completed in 720.
66 (2)

Ōkagami

A historical work in Japanese. Roughly 1100.
14 (the "Tokihira-den" section)

Saneakira shū

The personal collection of Minamoto no Saneakira (910–70).
28, 50

Shigeyuki shū

The personal collection of Minamoto no Shigeyuki (tenth century).
264 (*Goshūishū* 216)

Shikashū

An imperially commissioned collection of the mid-twelfth century.
109 (*Izumi Shikibu shū* 132)

Shinkokinshū

A particularly important, imperially commissioned collection completed in 1205.
55, 336 (*Komachi shū* 98), 757 (*Kokin rokujō* 593), 1013, 1052, 1379 (2, *Kokin rokujō* 1796), 1494, 1515 (2), 1599, 1703 (*Wakan rōei shū* 722)

Shinsenzaishū

An imperially commissioned collection completed in 1359.
526, 599

Shūishū

An imperially commissioned collection of the late tenth century.
5, 29, 62, 183, 351, 451 (2, *Wakan rōei shū* 469), 477, 506 (2), 511, 545, 577, 579, 662, 665, 668, 685, 727, 735, 736, 844, 853, 870, 876, 894, 895, 953 (2), 967 (*Man'yōshū* 1398), 985, 1005, 1063, 1068, 1098, 1210 (2), 1217, 1243 (2, *Man'yōshū* 2429), 1342 (*Izumi Shikibu shū* 150), 1350

Tsurayuki shū

The personal collection of Ki no Tsurayuki (868–945), the compiler of the *Kokinshū*.
15 (*Kokin rokujō* 1201), 60 (*Kokin rokujō* 4131), 764 (*Kokinshū* 415)

Utsubo monogatari

A long tale datable to the tenth century.
212

Wakan rōei shū

An influential collection of poems in both Chinese and Japanese, roughly contemporary with the author. Circa 1012.
25, 52 (*Hakushi monjū* 0631), 187, 267, 380, 469 (2, *Shūishū* 451), 536, 587, 701, 703, 722 (*Shinkokinshū* 1703), 783

Yakamochi shū

The personal collection of Ōtomo no Yakamochi (716–85).
284 (2)

Yamato monogatari

A mid-tenth-century collection of tales built around poems.
161 (section 106)

Characters in *The Tale of Genji*

Characters are listed wherever possible by Japanese designation and identified, with their English appellations and the chapters in which they appear.

Chūjō no Kimi, Ukifune's mother, Hitachi no Kami's wife
49, 50, 51, 52

Dazai no Shōni, husband of Yūgao's nurse
The Dazaifu Assistant, 22

Fujitsubo, Kiritsubo no Mikado's Empress, Reizei's mother
Daughter of an earlier Emperor, 1; Her Highness, 5; Her Highness, then Her Majesty, 7; Her Majesty, 8, 9; Her Majesty, then Her Cloistered Eminence, 10, 12, 13, 14, 17, 19; a dream phantom, 20

Genji
(Birth through 12), 1; a Captain in the Palace Guards, 2, 3, 4, 5, 6; a Captain in the Palace Guards, then a Consultant, 7; a Consultant, 8; the Commander of the Right, 9, 10, 11; no rank, 12; no rank, then promoted to Acting Grand Counselor, 13; becomes Palace Minister, 14; the Commander, then the Acting Grand Counselor, 15; the Palace Minister, 16, 17; His Grace, the Palace Minister, 18, 19, 20; His Grace, the Chancellor, 21, 22, 23, 24, 25, 26, 27, 28, 29, 30, 31, 32; His Grace, the Chancellor, then the Honorary Retired Emperor, 33; His Grace, the Honorary Retired Emperor, 34, 35, 36, 37, 38, 39, 40, 41

Gen no Naishi, a randy old woman
The Dame of Staff, 7, 9; the former Dame of Staff, 20

Gentlewomen, nurses, page girls
Ateki (serves Aoi), 9; Ateki, later called Hyōbu (daughter of Dazai no Daini; serves Tamakazura), 22, 24; Azechi (serves Onna San no Miya), 49; Ben (Shōnagon's daughter; serves Murasaki), 9; Ben (serves Fujitsubo), 10; Ben (serves Ōigimi and Naka no Kimi, then a nun), 45, 46, 47, (as a nun) 48, 49, 50, 51, 52; Ben (serves Empress), 52; Chūjō (serves Utsusemi), 2; Chūjō (serves Rokujō no Miyasudokoro), 4; Chūjō (serves Asagao), 10; Chūjō (serves Genji, then Murasaki, then Genji), 12, 19, 23, 41; Chūjō (serves Higekuro's first wife), 31; Chūjō (serves Tamakazura's elder daughter), 44; Chūjō (serves Onna Ichi no Miya), 52; Chūnagon (serves Sadaijin), 2, 9, 12; Chūnagon (serves Oborozukiyo), 10, 12, 34; Chūnagon (serves Kokiden no Nyōgo II), 26; Dainagon (serves Onna Ichi no Miya), 52; Gosechi (serves Ōmi no Kimi), 26; Inuki (serves Murasaki), 5; Jijū (serves Suetsumuhana, also her foster sister), 6, 15; Jijū (serves Ukifune), 50, 51, 52; Kojijū (serves Onna San no Miya, also her foster sister), 34, 35, 36; Komoki (serves Ukifune), 53; Koshōshō (serves Ochiba no Miya), 39; Kozaishō (Kaoru's lover, serves Onna Ichi no Miya), 52, 53; Miruko (serves Tamakazura), 24; Miya no Kimi (serves Empress), 52; Moku (serves Higekuro), 31; Nakatsukasa (serves Sadaijin), 2, 6; Nakatsukasa (serves Genji), 12, 35; Nareki (serves Tamakazura's elder daughter), 44; Nurse (Akashi no Himegimi's), 14, 18, 19; Nurse (Yūgao's), 22; Nurse (Onna San no Miya's), 34; Nurse (Ukifune's), 50, 51, 52, 53; Ōmyōbu (serves Fujitsubo), 5, 7, 10, 12; Saemon (serves Yokawa no Sōzu's sister, as a nun), 53; Saishō (Yūgiri's nurse), 12, 21, 33; Saishō (serves Tamakazura), 24, 30, 44; Sanjō (serves Tamakazura), 22; Senji (serves Asagao), 20, 21; Shōnagon (serves Murasaki), 4, 7, 9, 10, 12; Shōshō (serves Suetsumuhana), 15; Shōshō (serves Naka no Kimi), 49, 50, 51; Shōshō (serves Yokawa no Sōzu's sister, as a nun), 53; Taifu (serves Suetsumuhana), 6; Taifu

(Kumoi no Kari's nurse), 33; Taifu (serves Tamakazura's younger daughter), 44; Taifu (serves Naka no Kimi), 48, 49, 50; Ukon (Yūgao's nurse, then serves Murasaki), 4, 22; Ukon (serves Naka no Kimi, also Taifu's daughter), 50, 51; Ukon (serves Ukifune at Uji, a daughter of Ukifune's nurse), 52; Yugei no Myōbu (serves Kiritsubo no Mikado), 1

Gosechi, a young woman favored by Genji
    The Gosechi Dancer, 12, 13, 14

Hachi no Miya, Genji and Suzaku's half brother
    His Highness, the Eighth Prince, 45, 46

Hanachirusato
    Younger sister of the Reikeiden Consort, 11; the lady of the falling flowers, 12, 14; the lady of the village of falling flowers, 13; the lady of Falling Flowers, 18, 40; the lady in Genji's east pavilion, 19; the lady of the northeast quarter of Rokujō, the lady of summer, 22; the lady in/of the northeast quarter, 23, 25, 28, 39; the lady of summer, mistress of the northeast quarter, 35; the lady of summer, 41

Higekuro, Tamakazura's husband
    The Commander (of the Right), 24, 29, 30, 31; the Left Commander, then Minister of the Right, 35

Hitachi no Kami, Chūjō no Kimi's husband, Ukifune's stepfather
    The Governor of Hitachi, 50, 52

Hotaru, Genji's half brother
    His Highness, the Viceroy Prince (Sochi no Miya), 12, 17; His Highness of War (Hyōbukyō no Miya), 21, 24, 25, 29, 30, 31, 32, 34, 35, 38, 41

Hyōbukyō no Miya, Fujitsubo's elder brother, Murasaki's father; becomes Shikibukyō no Miya
    His Highness of War, His Highness, 1, 5, 7, 10, 12, 14, 17; the Lord of Ceremonial, 21; His Highness of Ceremonial, 31, 34, 35

Hyōtōda, Dazai no Shōni's eldest son
    The Bungo Deputy, 22

Ichijō no Miyasudokoro, Ochiba no Miya's mother
    The Haven, 35, 36, 37, 39

Iyo no Suke, father of Ki no Kami I, Utsusemi's husband, later Hitachi no Suke
    The Iyo Deputy, 2, 4; the Deputy Governor of Hitachi, 16

Kaoru, son of Onna San no Miya and Kashiwagi
    (Born), 36; the little boy, 37; the Consultant Captain, 42; the Minamoto Counselor, 43; the Minamoto Adviser, then Consultant Captain, then Counselor, 44; the Consultant Captain, 45; the Consultant Captain, then Counselor, 46; the Counselor, 47, 48; the Counselor, then the Commander, 49; the Commander, 50, 51, 52, 53, 54

Kashiwagi, Tō no Chūjō's eldest son
    The Captain, 24, 29; the Right Captain, 25, 26; the Secretary Captain, 27, 30, 31, 32, 33; the Intendant of the Right Gate Watch, 34; the Intendant of the Right Gate Watch, then also Counselor, 35; the Intendant of the Right Gate Watch, then Acting Grand Counselor, 36 (as a phantom), 37

Naishi no Suke, Koremitsu's daughter
  A Gosechi dancer, 21; the Fujiwara Dame of Staff, 33; the Dame of Staff, 39
Nakanobu, Kaoru's retainer, Michisada's father-in-law
  Nakanobu, the Treasury Commissioner, 51, 52
Naka no Kimi, second daughter of Hachi no Miya, eventually wife of Niou
  45, 46, 47, 48; the lady in the wing at Nijō, 49; the wife of His Highness of War,
  50; Her Highness, the wife of His Highness of War, 51, 52
Niou, Akashi no Himegimi's son, Murasaki's favorite, Naka no Kimi's husband, Uki-
  fune's lover
  His Highness, the Third Prince, 37, 40, 41; His Highness of the Bureau of War,
  His Highness of War, 42, 43, 45, 46, 47, 48, 49, 50, 51, 52
Nokiba no Ogi, Ki no Kami's sister, Iyo no Suke's daughter
  The lady from the west wing, 3; the daughter of the Iyo Deputy, 4
Oborozukiyo, Udaijin's sixth daughter, sister of Kokiden no Nyōgo I
  The lady of the misty moon, 8; the Mistress of the Wardrobe, 9; the Mistress of the
  Wardrobe, then the Mistress of Staff, 10; the Mistress of Staff, 12, 14, 21, 34; the
  Nijō Mistress of Staff, 35
Ochiba no Miya, Suzaku's second daughter, Roku no Kimi's adoptive mother
  Her Highness, the Second Princess, 35, 36, 37; Her Highness at/of Ichijō, 39, 42;
  Her Highness, 49
Ōigimi, Hachi no Miya's elder daughter
  45, 46; Her Highness, 47
Ōmi no Kimi, Tō no Chūjō's lost daughter
  26; the girl from Ōmi, 29, 31
Ōmiya, Kiritsubo no Mikado's sister, Sadaijin's wife, Aoi and Tō no Chūjō's mother,
  Yūgiri and Kumoi no Kari's grandmother
  The Princess, 1; Her Highness, 9, 12, 28, 29; Her Highness, the Third Princess, 21
Onna Go no Miya, Asagao's aunt
  Her Highness, the Fifth Princess, 20, 21
Onna Ichi no Miya, daughter of Reizei and the Kokiden Consort II
  His Eminence's daughter, 42; the First Princess, 52
Onna Ni no Miya, Kaoru's wife, daughter of Kinjō and the Fujitsubo Consort
  Her Highness, the Second Princess, 49, 52
Onna San no Miya, Suzaku's favorite daughter, Genji's wife, Kaoru's mother
  Her Highness, the Third Princess, 34, 35; Her Highness, the Third Princess, Her
  Cloisered Highness, 36; Her Cloistered Highness, the Third Princess, 37, 38, 41,
  42, 45, 49
Reizei, Emperor, son of Genji and Fujitsubo
  (Born), 7; the Heir Apparent, 9, 10, 12, 13; His Highness, the Heir Apparent,
  then His Majesty, 14; His Majesty, 17, 18, 19, 21, 29, 31, 33, 34; His Majesty,
  then His Eminence, Retired Emperor, 35; His Eminence, 38, 44, 45
Risshi
  His Reverence, the Master of Discipline, 39
Rokujō no Miyasudokoro, widow of a former Heir Apparent
  The Rokujō Haven, 4, 9, 10, 12, 14; (as a spirit), 35, 36

Roku no Kimi, Yūgiri's sixth daughter (by Koremitsu's daughter), later Niou's wife
His Excellency's sixth daughter, 42, 49

Sachūben, Onna San no Miya's retainer, also serves Genji
The Left Controller, 34

Sadaijin, the Minister of the Left (resigns), then Chancellor; Aoi's father
His Excellency, 1, 2, 5, 6, 7, 8, 9, 10; (resigns), 12, 14; becomes Chancellor, 19

Sakon no Shōshō, marries Hitachi no Kami's favorite daughter
The Lieutenant of the Left Palace Guards, 50

Shikibukyō no Miya, Asagao's father
His Highness of Ceremonial, 9, 19

Shi no Kimi, Tō no Chūjō's wife, Kashiwagi's mother
4, 35, 36

Suetsumuhana, daughter of the Hitachi Prince
Her Highness, daughter of His Highness of Hitachi, 6, 15; the safflower, 22; Her
Highness of Hitachi, 23

Suetsumuhana's aunt
15

Suzaku, Emperor, then Retired Emperor; Kiritsubo no Mikado's eldest son
Appointed Heir Apparent, 1; the Heir Apparent, 7, 8; His Majesty, 10, 12, 13;
His Majesty, the Emperor, then His Eminence, 14; His Eminence, 17, 21, 33, 34;
His Cloistered Eminence, 35, 36, 37, 39

Taifu no Gen, pursues Tamakazura in Tsukushi
The Audit Commissioner, 22

Tamakazura, Yūgao and Tō no Chūjō's daughter, later Higekuro's wife
The pink, 4; the young lady, 22; the (young) lady in the west wing, 23, 24, 25,
26, 27, 28, 29; the lady, 30; the Mistress of Staff, 31, 34, 35, 44

Tamakazura's daughters
The Haven (the elder), the Mistress of Staff (the younger), 44

Tamakazura's sons
The Left Palace Guards Captain, the Right Controller, the Fujiwara Adviser, 44

Tokikata, Niou's retainer
The Deputy Governor of Izumo, 51, 52

Tō no Chūjō, the Minister of the Left's eldest son, Aoi's brother
The Chamberlain Lieutenant, 1; the Secretary Captain, 2, 4, 5, 6, 7, 8; the Third
Rank Captain, 9; the Captain, 9, 10; the Captain, also appointed a Consultant,
12; the Consultant Captain, then the Acting Counselor, 14; the Acting Counselor, 17; the Acting Counselor, then Grand Counselor and Commander of the
Right, 19; the Commander, then His Excellency, the Palace Minister, 21; His Excellency, the Palace Minister, 25, 26, 28, 29, 30, 31, 32; His Excellency, the
Palace Minister, then Chancellor, 33; His Excellency, the Chancellor, 34; His Excellency, the Chancellor, then His Retired Excellency, 35; His Retired Excellency, 36, 37; His Excellency, 39, 40

Udaijin, the Minister of the Right, then Chancellor; father of Kokiden no Nyōgo I,
Suzaku's grandfather

The Minister of the Right, 1, 9, 10; the Minister of the Right, His Excellency, 8, 12; the Chancellor, 13

Uji no Ajari, Hachi no Miya's spiritual adviser

The Adept, 45, 46, 47, 48, 49; the Master of Discipline, 52

Ukifune, Hachi no Miya's unrecognized daughter

A young woman, 49, 50, 51, 53, 54

Utsusemi, stepmother of Ki no Kami I, the Iyo Deputy's wife

2, 3; the lady of the cicada shell, 4, 16; the cicada shell, 23

Yamato no Kami, Ochiba no Miya's cousin and Koshōshō's brother

The Governor of Yamato, 39

Yoshikiyo, Genji's retainer, son of the Governor of Harima

5; Yoshikiyo, 8, 12; the Minamoto Junior Counselor, 13; the Governor of Ōmi, 21

Yokawa no Sōzu

His Reverence, the Prelate of Yokawa, 53, 54

Yokawa no Sōzu's mother

An old nun, 51, 53, 54

Yokawa no Sōzu's sister

A nun, 51, 53

Yūgao, mother of Tamakazura

4

Yūgiri, son of Genji and Aoi

(Born), 9, 12, 14; a student at the Academy, the Adviser, 21; the Captain, 22, 23, 24, 25, 26, 27, 28, 29; the Consultant Captain, 30, 31, 32; the Consultant Captain, then Counselor, 33; the Counselor, then Right Commander, 34; the Right Commander, then also Grand Counselor, 35; the Right Commander, 36; the Commander, 37, 38, 39, 40, 41; His Excellency, the Minister of the Right, the Commander of the Left Palace Guards, 42; His Excellency, the Minister of the Right, 43; His Excellency, the Minister of the Right, then of the Left, 44; His Excellency, the Minister of the Right, 47, 48, 49, 51

Further Reading

Bargen, Doris. *A Woman's Weapon: Spirit Possession in "The Tale of Genji."* Honolulu: University of Hawaii Press, 1997.

Bowring, Richard. *Murasaki Shikibu: "The Tale of Genji."* Landmarks of World Literature. Cambridge: Cambridge University Press, 1988.

———, trans. *The Diary of Lady Murasaki.* New York: Penguin, 1999.

Childs, Margaret H. "The Value of Vulnerability: Sexual Coercion and the Nature of Love in Japanese Court Literature." *Journal of Asian Studies* 58:4 (November 1999).

Dalby, Liza. "The Cultured Nature of Heian Colors." *Transactions of the Asiatic Society of Japan,* 4th series, vol. 3 (1988).

Field, Norma. *The Splendor of Longing in "The Tale of Genji."* Princeton: Princeton University Press, 1987.

Gatten, Aileen. "The Order of the Early Chapters in the *Genji monogatari.*" *Harvard Journal of Asiatic Studies* 41:1 (June 1981).

Kamens, Edward, ed. *Approaches to Teaching Murasaki Shikibu's "The Tale of Genji."* New York: Modern Language Association, 1993.

Keene, Donald. *Seeds in the Heart: Japanese Literature from Earliest Times to the Late Sixteenth Century.* New York: Henry Holt and Co., 1993.

Konishi, Jin'ichi. *A History of Japanese Literature, Vol. 2, The Early Middle Ages.* Translated by Aileen Gatten. Princeton: Princeton University Press, 1984.

McCullough, William H. "Japanese Marriage Institutions in the Heian Period." *Harvard Journal of Asiatic Studies* 27 (1967).

McCullough, William H., and Helen Craig McCullough, trans. *A Tale of Flowering Fortunes: Annals of Japanese Aristocratic Life in the Heian Period.* 2 vols. Stanford: Stanford University Press, 1980.

Miner, Earl. "Some Thematic and Structural Features of the *Genji Monogatari.*" *Monumenta Nipponica* 24:1 (1969).

Morris, Ivan. *The World of the Shining Prince: Court Life in Ancient Japan.* Various editions.

Nickerson, Peter. "The Meaning of Matrilocality: Kinship, Property, and Politics in Mid-Heian." *Monumenta Nipponica* 48:4 (1993).

Okada, Richard H. *Figures of Resistance: Language, Poetry, and Narrating in "The Tale of Genji" and Other Mid-Heian Texts.* Durham, N.C.: Duke University Press, 1992.

Pekarik, Andrew, ed. *Ukifune: Love in "The Tale of Genji."* New York: Columbia University Press, 1982.

Pollack, David. "The Informing Image: 'China' in *Genji monogatari.*" *Monumenta Nipponica* 38:4 (1983).

Rowley, G. G. *Yosano Akiko and "The Tale of Genji."* Ann Arbor: Center for Japanese Studies, University of Michigan, 2000.

Seidensticker, Edward, trans. *The Tale of Genji.* New York: Alfred A. Knopf, 1976.

Shirane, Haruo. *The Bridge of Dreams: A Poetics of "The Tale of Genji."* Stanford: Stanford University Press, 1987.

Stinchecum, Amanda Mayer. "Who Tells the Tale? 'Ukifune': A Study in Narrative Voice." *Monumenta Nipponica* 35:4 (1980).

Tyler, Royall. " 'I Am I': Genji and Murasaki." *Monumenta Nipponica* 54:4 (1999).

Waley, Arthur, trans. *The Tale of Genji.* Various editions.

Yoda, Tomiko. "Fractured Dialogues: *Mono no aware* and Poetic Communication in *The Tale of Genji.*" *Harvard Journal of Asiatic Studies* 59:2 (1999).